THE STAND

'[*The Stand*] has everything – adventure, romance, prophecy, allegory, satire, fantasy, realism, apocalypse . . . Great!' – *New York Times Book Review*

'A masterpiece . . . King says in the novel's introduction that he "wanted to write a fantasy epic like *The Lord of the Rings*, only with an American setting", and that's absolutely what he did . . . *The Stand* is dense and rich. Every character is full and alive' – *Guardian*

'A fabulous teller of stories who can create an entire new world and make the reader live in it' – *Express*

ABOUT THE AUTHOR

There is a reason why Stephen King is one of the bestselling writers in the world, *ever*. Described by John Connolly as 'utterly compelling', Stephen King writes books that draw you in and are *impossible to put down*.

King is the author of more than sixty books, all of them worldwide bestsellers, including the epic thrillers *Cell*, *It*, *Under the Dome*, *11.22.63* and *The Institute*.

Many of his novels and short stories have been turned into celebrated films, TV series and streamed events including *Misery*, *The Outsider* and *The Shawshank Redemption*.

King was the recipient of America's prestigious 2014 National Medal of Arts and the 2003 National Book Foundation Medal for Distinguished Contribution to American Letters. He lives with his wife Tabitha King in Maine.

By Stephen King and published by Hodder & Stoughton

NOVELS:

Carrie
'Salem's Lot
The Shining
The Stand
The Dead Zone
Firestarter
Cujo
Cycle of the Werewolf
Christine
Pet Sematary
IT
The Eyes of the Dragon
Misery
The Tommyknockers
The Dark Half
Needful Things
Gerald's Game
Dolores Claiborne
Insomnia
Rose Madder
Desperation
Bag of Bones
The Girl Who Loved Tom Gordon
Dreamcatcher
From a Buick 8
Cell
Lisey's Story
Duma Key
Under the Dome
11.22.63
Doctor Sleep
Mr Mercedes
Revival
Finders Keepers
End of Watch
Sleeping Beauties (with Owen King)
The Outsider
Elevation
The Institute

The Dark Tower I: The Gunslinger
The Dark Tower II:
The Drawing of the Three
The Dark Tower III: The Waste Lands
The Dark Tower IV: Wizard and Glass
The Dark Tower V: Wolves of the Calla
The Dark Tower VI: Song of Susannah
The Dark Tower VII: The Dark Tower
The Wind through the Keyhole:
A Dark Tower Novel

As Richard Bachman

Thinner
The Running Man
The Bachman Books
The Regulators
Blaze

STORY COLLECTIONS:

Night Shift
Different Seasons
Skeleton Crew
Four Past Midnight
Nightmares and Dreamscapes
Hearts in Atlantis
Everything's Eventual
Just After Sunset
Stephen King Goes to the Movies
Full Dark, No Stars
The Bazaar of Bad Dreams
If It Bleeds

NON-FICTION:

Danse Macabre
On Writing (A Memoir of the Craft)

STEPHEN KING
KING
THE STAND

HODDER

British Library Cataloguing in Publication Data

King, Stephen, *1947* –
The Stand. – New ed.
I. Title
813'.54[54]

B Format ISBN 978 1 5293 7051 5
eBook ISBN 978 1 8489 4083 3

Typeset in Bembo by Palimpsest Book Production Ltd, Falkirk, Stirlingshire

Printed and bound in Great Britain by
by Clays Ltd, Elcograf S.p.A.

Hodder & Stoughton Ltd
Carmelite House
50 Victoria Embankment
London EC4Y 0DZ

www.hodder.co.uk

For Tabby:
This dark chest of wonders

AUTHOR'S NOTE

The Stand is a work of fiction, as its subject matter makes perfectly clear. Many of the events occur in real places – such as Ogunquit, Maine; Las Vegas, Nevada; and Boulder, Colorado – and with these places I have taken the liberty of changing them to whatever degree best suited the course of my fiction. I hope that those readers who live in these and the other real places that are mentioned in this novel will not be too upset by my 'monstrous impertinence,' to quote Dorothy Sayers, who indulged freely in the same sort of thing.

Other places, such as Arnette, Texas, and Shoyo, Arkansas, are as fictional as the plot itself.

S.K.

A PREFACE IN TWO PARTS

Part 1: To Be Read Before Purchase

There are a couple of things you need to know about this version of *The Stand* right away, even before you leave the bookstore. For that reason I hope I've caught you early – hopefully standing there by the *K* section of new fiction, with your other purchases tucked under your arm and the book open in front of you. In other words, I hope I've caught you while your wallet is still safely in your pocket. Ready? Okay; thanks. I promise to be brief.

First, this is not a new novel. If you hold misapprehensions on that score, let them be dispelled right here and now, while you are still a safe distance from the cash register which will take money out of your pocket and put it in mine. *The Stand* was originally published over ten years ago.

Second, this is not a brand-new, entirely different version of *The Stand*. You will not discover old characters behaving in new ways, nor will the course of the tale branch off at some point from the old narrative, taking you, Constant Reader, in an entirely different direction.

This version of *The Stand* is an *expansion* of the novel which has been in print since 1979 or so. As I've said, you won't find old characters behaving in strange new ways, but you will discover that almost all of the characters were, in the book's original form, doing *more* things, and if I didn't think some of those things were interesting – perhaps even enlightening – I would never have agreed to this project.

If this is not what you want, don't buy this book. If you have bought it already, I hope you saved your sales receipt. The bookshop where you made your purchase will want it before granting you credit or a cash refund.

If this expansion *is* something you want, I invite you to come along with me just a little farther. I have lots to tell you, and I think we can talk better around the corner.

In the dark.

Part 2: To Be Read After Purchase

This is not so much a Preface, actually, as it is an explanation of why this new version of *The Stand* exists at all. It was a long novel to begin with, and this expanded version will be regarded by some – perhaps many – as an act of indulgence by an author whose works have been successful enough to allow it. I hope not, but I'd have to be pretty stupid not to realize that such criticism is in the offing. After all, many critics of the novel regarded it bloated and overlong to begin with.

Whether the book *was* too long to begin with, or has become so in this edition, is a matter I leave to the individual reader. I only wanted to take this little space to say that I am republishing *The Stand* as it was originally written not to serve myself or any individual reader, but to serve a body of readers who have asked to have it. I would not offer it if I myself didn't think those portions which were dropped from the original manuscript made the story a richer one, and I'd be a liar if I didn't admit I am curious as to what its reception will be.

I'll spare you the story of how *The Stand* came to be written – the chain of thought which produces a novel rarely interests anyone but aspiring novelists. They tend to believe there is a 'secret formula' to writing a commercially successful novel, but there isn't. You get an idea; at some point another idea kicks in; you make a connection or a series of them between ideas; a few characters (usually little more than shadows at first) suggest themselves; a possible ending occurs to the writer's mind (although when the ending comes, it's rarely much like the one the writer envisioned); and at some point, the novelist sits down with a paper and pen, a typewriter, or a word cruncher. When asked, 'How do you write?' I invariably answer, 'One word at a time,' and the answer is invariably dismissed. But that is all it is. It sounds too simple to be true, but consider the Great Wall of China, if you will: one stone at a time, man. That's all. One stone at a time. But I've read you can see that motherfucker from space without a telescope.

For readers who *are* interested, the story is told in the final chapter of *Danse Macabre*, a rambling but user-friendly overview of the horror genre I published in 1982. This is not a commercial for that book; I'm just saying the tale is there if you want it, although it's told not because it is interesting in itself but to illustrate an entirely different point.

For the purposes of this book, what's important is that approximately four hundred pages of manuscript were deleted from the final draft. The reason was not an editorial one; if that had been the case, I would be content to let the book live its life and die its eventual death as it was originally published.

The cuts were made at the behest of the accounting department. They toted up production costs, laid these next to the hardcover sales of my previous four books, and decided that a cover price of £6.95 was about what the market would bear (compare that price to this one, friends and neighbors!). I was asked if I would like to make the cuts, or if I would prefer someone in the editorial department to do it. I reluctantly agreed to do the surgery myself. I think I did a fairly good job, for a writer who has been accused over and over again of having diarrhea of the word processor. There is only one place – Trashcan Man's trip across the country from Indiana to Las Vegas – that seems noticeably scarred in the original version.

If all of the story is there, one might ask, then why bother? Isn't it indulgence after all? It better not be; if it is, then I have spent a large portion of my life wasting my time. As it happens, I think that in really good stories, the whole is always greater than the sum of the parts. If that were not so, the following would be a perfectly acceptable version of 'Hansel and Gretel':

Hansel and Gretel were two children with a nice father and a nice mother. The nice mother died, and the father married a bitch. The bitch wanted the kids out of the way so she'd have more money to spend on herself. She bullied her spineless, soft-headed hubby into taking Hansel and Gretel into the woods and killing them. The kids' father relented at the last moment, allowing them to live so they could starve to death in the woods instead of dying quickly and mercifully at the blade of his knife. While they were wandering around, they found a house made out of candy. It was owned by a witch who was into cannibalism. She locked them up and told them that when they were good and fat, she was going to eat them. But the kids got the best of her. Hansel shoved her into her own oven. They found the witch's treasure, and they must have found a map, too, because they eventually arrived home again. When they got there, Dad gave the bitch the boot and they lived happily ever after. The End.

I don't know what you think, but for me, that version's a loser. The story is there, but it's not elegant. It's like a Cadillac with the chrome stripped off and the paint sanded down to dull metal. It goes somewhere, but it ain't, you know, *boss*.

I haven't restored all four hundred of the missing pages; there is a difference between doing it up right and just being downright vulgar. Some of what was left on the cutting room floor when I turned in the truncated version deserved to be left there, and there it remains. Other things, such as Frannie's confrontation with her mother early in the book, seem to add that richness and dimension which I, as a reader, enjoy deeply. Returning to 'Hansel and Gretel' for just a moment, you may remember that the wicked stepmother demands that her husband bring her the hearts of the children as proof that the hapless woodcutter has done as she has ordered. The woodcutter demonstrates one dim vestige of intelligence by bringing her the hearts of two rabbits. Or take the famous trail of breadcrumbs Hansel leaves behind, so he and his sister can find their way back. Thinking dude! But when he attempts to follow the backtrail, he finds that the birds have eaten it. Neither of these bits are strictly essential to the plot, but in another way they *make* the plot – they are great and magical bits of storytelling. They change what could have been a dull piece of work into a tale which has charmed and terrified readers for over a hundred years.

I suspect nothing added here is as good as Hansel's trail of breadcrumbs, but I have always regretted the fact that no one but me and a few in-house readers at Doubleday ever met that maniac who simply calls himself The Kid . . . or witnessed what happens to him outside a tunnel which counterpoints another tunnel half a continent away – the Lincoln Tunnel in New York, which two of the characters negotiate earlier in the story.

So here is *The Stand*, Constant Reader, as its author originally intended for it to roll out of the showroom. All its chrome is now intact, for better or for worse. And the final reason for presenting this version is the simplest. Although it has never been my favorite novel, it is the one people who like my books seem to like the most. When I speak (which is as rarely as possible), people always speak to me about *The Stand*. They discuss the characters as though they were living people, and ask frequently, 'What happened to so-and-so,' . . . as if I got letters from them every now and again.

I am inevitably asked if it is ever going to be a movie. The answer, by the way, is probably yes. Will it be a good one? I don't know. Bad or good, movies nearly always have a strange diminishing effect on works of fantasy (of course there are exceptions; *The Wizard of Oz* is an example which springs immediately to mind). In discussions, people are willing to cast various parts endlessly. I've always thought Robert Duvall would make a splendid Randall Flagg, but I've heard people suggest such people as Clint Eastwood, Bruce Dern, and Christopher Walken. They all *sound* good, just as Bruce Springsteen would seem to make an interesting Larry Underwood, if he ever chose to try acting (and, based on his videos, I think he would do very well . . . although my personal choice would be Marshall Crenshaw). But in the end, I think it's perhaps best for Stu, Larry, Glen, Frannie, Ralph, Tom Cullen, Lloyd, and that dark fellow to belong to the reader, who will visualize them through the lens of imagination in a vivid and constantly changing way no camera can duplicate. Movies, after all, are only an illusion of motion comprised of thousands of still photographs. The imagination, however, moves with its own tidal flow. Films, even the best of them, freeze fiction – anyone who has ever seen *One Flew Over the Cuckoo's Nest* and then reads Ken Kesey's novel will find it hard or impossible not to see Jack Nicholson's face on Randle Patrick McMurphy. That is not necessarily bad . . . but it *is* limiting. The glory of a good tale is that it is limitless and fluid; a good tale belongs to each reader in its own particular way.

Finally, I write for only two reasons: to please myself and to please others. In returning to this long tale of dark Christianity, I hope I have done both.

Stephen King

October 24, 1989

THE STAND

Outside the street's on fire
In a real death waltz
Between what's flesh and fantasy
And the poets down here
Don't write nothin at all
They just stand back and let it all be
And in the quick of the night
They reach for their moment
And try to make an honest stand
But they wind up wounded
Not even dead
Tonight in Jungle Land.

                                    Bruce Springsteen

And it was clear she couldn't go on!
The door was opened and the wind appeared,
The candles blew and then disappeared,
The curtains flew and then he appeared,
Said, 'Don't be afraid,
Come on, Mary,'
And she had no fear
And she ran to him
And they started to fly . . .
She had taken his hand . . .
'Come on, Mary;
Don't fear the Reaper!'

                                    Blue Öyster Cult

WHAT'S THAT SPELL?
WHAT'S THAT SPELL?
WHAT'S THAT SPELL?

                                    Country Joe and the Fish

THE CIRCLE OPENS

We need help, the Poet reckoned.
Edward Dorn

'Sally.'

A mutter.

'Wake up now, Sally.'

A louder mutter: *leeme lone.*

He shook her harder.

'Wake up. You got to wake up!'

Charlie.

Charlie's voice. Calling her. For how long?

Sally swam up out of sleep.

First she glanced at the clock on the night table and saw it was quarter past two in the morning. Charlie shouldn't even be here; he should be on shift. Then she got her first good look at him and something leaped up inside her, some deadly intuition.

Her husband was deathly pale. His eyes started and bulged from their sockets. The car keys were in one hand. He was still using the other to shake her, although her eyes were open. It was as if he hadn't been able to register the fact that she was awake.

'Charlie, what is it? What's wrong?'

He didn't seem to know what to say. His adam's apple bobbed futilely but there was no sound in the small service bungalow but the ticking of the clock.

'Is it a fire?' she asked stupidly. It was the only thing she could think of which might have put him in such a state. She knew his parents had perished in a housefire.

'In a way,' he said. 'In a way it's worse. You got to get dressed, honey. Get Baby LaVon. We got to get out of here.'

'Why?' she asked, getting out of bed. Dark fear had seized her. Nothing seemed right. This was like a dream. 'Where? You mean the back yard?' But she knew it wasn't the back yard. She had never seen Charlie look afraid like this. She drew a deep breath and could smell no smoke or burning.

'Sally, honey, don't ask questions. We have to get away. Far away. You just go get Baby LaVon and get her dressed.'

'But should I . . . is there time to pack?'

This seemed to stop him. To derail him somehow. She thought she was as afraid as she could be, but apparently she wasn't. She recognized that what she had taken for fright on his part was closer to raw panic. He ran a distracted hand through his hair and replied, 'I don't know. I'll have to test the wind.'

And he left her with this bizarre statement which meant nothing to her, left her standing cold and afraid and disoriented in her bare feet and babydoll nightie. It was as if he had gone mad. What did testing the wind have to do with whether or not she had time to pack? And where was far away? Reno? Vegas? Salt Lake City? And . . .

She put her hand against her throat as a new idea struck her.

AWOL. Leaving in the middle of the night meant Charlie was planning to go AWOL.

She went into the small room which served as Baby LaVon's nursery and stood for a moment, indecisive, looking at the sleeping infant in her pink blanket suit. She held to the faint hope that this might be no more than an extraordinarily vivid dream. It would pass, she would wake up at seven in the morning just like usual, feed Baby LaVon and herself while she watched the first hour of the 'Today' show, and be cooking Charlie's eggs when he came off-shift at 8 AM, his nightly tour in the Reservation's north tower over for another night. And in two weeks he would be back on days and not so cranky and if he was sleeping with her at night she wouldn't have crazy dreams like this one and –

'Hurry it *up!*' he hissed at her, breaking her faint hope. 'We got just time to throw a few things together . . . but for Christ's sake, woman, if you love her' – he pointed at the crib – 'you get her dressed!' He coughed nervously into his hand and began to yank things out of their bureau drawers and pile them helter-skelter into a couple of old suitcases.

She woke up Baby LaVon, soothing the little one as best she could; the three-year-old was cranky and bewildered at being awakened in the middle of the night, and she began to cry as Sally got her into underpants, a blouse, and a romper. The sound of the child's crying made her more afraid than ever. She associated it with the other times LaVon, usually the most angelic of babies, had cried in the night: diaper rash, teething, croup, colic. Fear slowly changed to anger as she saw Charlie almost run past the door with a double handful of her own underwear. Bra straps trailed out behind him like the streamers from New Year's Eve noisemakers. He flung them into one of the suitcases and slammed it shut. The hem of her best slip hung out, and she just bet it was torn.

'What *is* it?' she cried, and the distraught tone of her voice caused Baby LaVon to burst into fresh tears just as she was winding down to sniffles. 'Have you gone crazy? They'll send soldiers after us, Charlie! *Soldiers!*'

'Not tonight they won't,' he said, and there was something so sure in his voice that it was horrible. 'Point is, sugar-babe, if we don't get our asses in gear, we ain't never gonna make it off'n the base. I don't even know how in hell I got out of the tower. Malfunction somewhere, I guess. Why not? Everything else sure-God malfunctioned.' And he uttered a high, loonlike laugh that frightened her more than anything else had done. 'The baby dressed? Good. Put some of her clothes in that other suitcase. Use the blue tote-bag in the closet for the rest. Then we're going to get the hell out. I think we're all right. Wind's blowing east to west. Thank God for that.'

He coughed into his hand again.

'Daddy!' Baby LaVon demanded, holding her arms up. 'Want Daddy! Sure! Horsey-ride, Daddy! Horsey-ride! Sure!'

'Not now,' Charlie said, and disappeared into the kitchen. A moment later, Sally heard the rattle of crockery. He was getting her pin-money out of the blue soup dish on the top shelf. Some thirty or forty dollars she had put away – a dollar, sometimes fifty cents, at a time. Her *house* money. It was real, then. Whatever it was, it was really real.

Baby LaVon, denied her horsey-ride by her daddy, who rarely if ever denied her anything, began to weep again. Sally struggled to get her into her light jacket and then threw most of her clothes into the tote, cramming them in helter-skelter. The idea of putting anything else into the other suitcase was ridiculous. It would burst. She had to kneel on it to snap the catches. She found herself thanking God Baby LaVon was trained, and there was no need to bother with diapers.

Charlie came back into the bedroom, and now he *was* running. He was still stuffing the crumpled ones and fives from the soup dish into the front pocket of his suntans. Sally scooped Baby LaVon up.

She was fully awake now and could walk perfectly well, but Sally wanted her in her arms. She bent and snagged the tote-bag.

'Where we going, Daddy?' Baby LaVon asked. 'I was aseepin.'

'Baby can be aseepin in the car,' Charlie said, grabbing the two suitcases. The hem of Sally's slip flapped. His eyes still had that white, starey look. An idea, a growing certainty, began to dawn in Sally's mind.

'Was there an accident?' she whispered. 'Oh Jesus Mary and Joseph, there was, wasn't there? An accident. Out *there*.'

'I was playing solitaire,' he said. 'I looked up and saw the clock had gone from green to red. I turned on the monitor. Sally, they're all −'

He paused, looked at Baby LaVon's eyes, wide and, although still rimmed with tears, curious.

'They're all D-E-A-D down there,' he said. 'All but one or two, and they're probably gone now.'

'What's D-E-D, Daddy?' Baby LaVon asked.

'Never mind, honey,' Sally said. Her voice seemed to come to her from down a very long canyon.

Charlie swallowed. Something clicked in his throat. 'Everything's supposed to mag-lock if the clock goes red. They got a Chubb computer that runs the whole place and it's supposed to be fail-safe. I saw what was on the monitor, and I jumped out the door. I thought the goddamn thing would cut me in half. It should have shut the second the clock went red, and I don't know how long it *was* red before I looked up and noticed it. But I was almost to the parking lot before I heard it thump shut behind me. Still, if I'd looked up even thirty seconds later, I'd be shut up in that tower control room right now, like a bug in a bottle.'

'What is it? What −'

'I dunno. I don't *want* to know. All I know is that it ki − that it K-I-L-L-E-D them quick. If they want me, they'll have to catch me. I was gettin hazard pay, but they ain't payin me enough to hang around here. Wind's blowing west. We're driving east. Come on, now.'

Still feeling half-asleep, caught in some awful grinding dream, she followed him out to the driveway where their fifteen-year-old Chevy stood, quietly rusting in the fragrant desert darkness of the California night.

Charlie dumped the suitcases in the trunk and the tote-bag in the back seat. Sally stood for a moment by the passenger door with the baby in her arms, looking at the bungalow where they had spent the last four years. When they had moved in, she reflected, Baby LaVon was still growing inside her body, all her horsey-rides ahead of her.

'Come on!' he said. 'Get in, woman!'

She did. He backed out, the Chevy's headlights momentarily splashing across the house. Their reflection in the windows looked like the eyes of some hunted beast.

He was hunched tensely over the steering wheel, his face drawn in the dim glow of the dashboard instruments. 'If the base gates are closed, I'm gonna try to crash through.' And he meant it. She could tell. Suddenly her knees felt watery.

But there was no need for such desperate measures. The base gates were standing open. One guard was nodding over a magazine. She couldn't see the other; perhaps he was in the head. This was the outer part of the base, a conventional army vehicle depot. What went on at the hub of the base was of no concern to these fellows.

I looked up and saw the clock had gone red.

She shivered and put her hand on his leg. Baby LaVon was sleeping again. Charlie patted her hand briefly and said: 'It's going to be all right, hon.'

By dawn they were running east across Nevada and Charlie was coughing steadily.

BOOK I
CAPTAIN TRIPS

JUNE 16, 1990 – JULY 4, 1990

I called the doctor on the telephone,
Said doctor, doctor, please,
I got this feeling, rocking and reeling,
Tell me, what can it be?
Is it some new disease?

The Sylvers

Baby, can you dig your man?
He's a righteous man,
Baby, can you dig your man?

Larry Underwood

CHAPTER 1

Hapscomb's Texaco sat on Number 93 just north of Arnette, a pissant four-street burg about 110 miles from Houston. Tonight the regulars were there, sitting by the cash register, drinking beer, talking idly, watching the bugs fly into the big lighted sign.

It was Bill Hapscomb's station, so the others deferred to him even though he was a pure fool. They would have expected the same deferral if they had been gathered together in one of their business establishments. Except they had none. In Arnette, it was hard times. In 1980 the town had had two industries, a factory that made paper products (for picnics and barbecues, mostly) and a plant that made electronic calculators. Now the paper factory was shut down and the calculator plant was ailing – they could make them a lot cheaper in Taiwan, it turned out, just like those portable TVs and transistor radios.

Norman Bruett and Tommy Wannamaker, who had both worked in the paper factory, were on relief, having run out of unemployment some time ago. Henry Carmichael and Stu Redman both worked at the calculator plant but rarely got more than thirty hours a week. Victor Palfrey was retired and smoked stinking home-rolled cigarettes, which were all he could afford.

'Now what I say is this,' Hap told them, putting his hands on his knees and leaning forward. 'They just gotta say screw this inflation shit. Screw this national debt shit. We got the presses and we got the paper. We're gonna run off fifty million thousand-dollar bills and hump them right the Christ into circulation.'

Palfrey, who had been a machinist until 1984, was the only one present with sufficient self-respect to point out Hap's most obvious damfool statements. Now, rolling another of his shitty-smelling cigarettes, he said, 'That wouldn't get us nowhere. If they do that, it'll be just like Richmond in the last two years of the States War. In those days, when you wanted a piece of gingerbread, you gave the baker a Confederate dollar, he'd put it on the gingerbread, and cut out a piece just that size. Money's just paper, you know.'

'I know some people don't agree with you,' Hap said sourly. He picked up a greasy red plastic paper-holder from his desk. 'I owe these people. And they're starting to get pretty itchy about it.'

Stuart Redman, who was perhaps the quietest man in Arnette, was sitting in one of the cracked plastic Woolco chairs, a can of Pabst in his hand, looking out the big service station window at Number 93. Stu knew about poor. He had grown up that way right here in town, the son of a dentist who had died when Stu was seven, leaving his wife and two other children besides Stu.

His mother had gotten work at the Red Ball Truck Stop just outside of Arnette – Stu could have seen it from where he sat right now if it hadn't burned down in 1979. It had been enough to keep the four of them eating, but that was all. At the age of nine, Stu had gone to work, first for Rog Tucker, who owned the Red Ball, helping to unload trucks after school for thirty-five cents an hour, and then at the stockyards in the neighboring town of Braintree, lying about his age to get twenty backbreaking hours of labor a week at the minimum wage.

Now, listening to Hap and Vic Palfrey argue on about money and the mysterious way it had of drying up, he thought about the way his hands had bled at first from pulling the endless handtrucks of hides and guts. He had tried to keep that from his mother, but she had seen, less than a week after he started. She wept over them a little, and she hadn't been a woman who wept easily. But she hadn't asked him to quit the job. She knew what the situation was. She was a realist.

Some of the silence in him came from the fact that he had never had friends, or the time for them. There was school, and there was work. His youngest brother, Dev, had died of pneumonia the year he began at the yards, and Stu had never quite gotten over that. Guilt, he supposed. He had loved Dev the best . . . but his passing had also meant there was one less mouth to feed.

In high school he had found football, and that was something his mother had encouraged even though it cut into his work hours. 'You play,' she said. 'If you got a ticket out of here, it's football, Stuart. You play. Remember Eddie Warfield.' Eddie Warfield was a local hero. He had come from a family even poorer than Stu's own, had covered himself with glory as quarterback of the regional high school team, had gone on to Texas A&M with an athletic scholarship, and had played for ten years with the Green Bay Packers, mostly as a second-string quarterback but on several memorable occasions as the starter. Eddie now owned a string of fast-food restaurants across the West and Southwest, and in Arnette he was an enduring figure of myth. In Arnette, when you said 'success,' you meant Eddie Warfield.

Stu was no quarterback, and he was no Eddie Warfield. But it did seem to him as he began his junior year in high school that there was at least a fighting chance for him to get a small athletic scholarship . . . and then there were work-study programs, and the school's guidance counselor had told him about the NDEA loan program.

Then his mother had gotten sick, had become unable to work. It was cancer. Two months before he graduated from high school, she had died, leaving Stu with his brother Bryce to support. Stu had turned down the athletic scholarship and had gone to work in the calculator factory. And finally it was Bryce, three years' Stu's junior, who had made it out. He was now in Minnesota, a systems analyst for IBM. He didn't write often, and the last time he had seen Bryce was at the funeral, after Stu's wife had died – died of exactly the same sort of cancer that had killed his mother. He thought that Bryce might have his own guilt to carry . . . and that Bryce might be a little ashamed of the fact that his brother had turned into just another good old boy in a dying Texas town, spending his days doing time in the calculator plant, and his nights either down at Hap's or over at the Indian Head drinking Lone Star beer.

The marriage had been the best time, and it had only lasted eighteen months. The womb of his young wife had borne a single dark and malignant child. That had been four years ago. Since, he had thought of leaving Arnette, searching for something better, but small-town inertia held him – the low siren song of familiar places and familiar faces. He was well liked in Arnette, and Vic Palfrey had once paid him the ultimate compliment of calling him 'Old Time Tough.'

As Vic and Hap chewed it out, there was still a little dusk left in the sky, but the land was in shadow. Cars didn't go by on 93 much now, which was one reason that Hap had so many unpaid bills. But there was a car coming now, Stu saw.

It was still a quarter of a mile distant, the day's last light putting a dusty shine on what little chrome was left to it. Stu's eyes were sharp, and he made it as a very old Chevrolet, maybe a '75. A Chevy, no lights on, doing no more than fifteen miles an hour, weaving all over the road. No one had seen it yet but him.

'Now let's say you got a mortgage payment on this station,' Vic was saying, 'and let's say it's fifty dollars a month.'

'It's a hell of a lot more than that.'

'Well, for the sake of the argument, let's say fifty. And let's say the Federals went ahead and printed you a whole carload of money. Well then, those bank people would turn round and want a *hundred* and fifty. You'd be just as poorly off.'

'That's right,' Henry Carmichael added. Hap looked at him, irritated. He happened to know that Hank had gotten in the habit of taking Cokes out of the machine without paying the deposit, and furthermore, Hank *knew* he knew, and if Hank wanted to come in on any side it ought to be his.

'That ain't necessarily how it would be,' Hap said weightily from the depths of his ninth-grade education. He went on to explain why.

Stu, who only understood that they were in a hell of a pinch, tuned Hap's voice down to a meaningless drone and watched the Chevy pitch and yaw its way on up the road. The way it was going Stu didn't think it was going to make it much farther. It crossed the white line and its lefthand tires spumed up dust from the left shoulder. Now it lurched back, held its own lane briefly, then nearly pitched off into the ditch. Then, as if the driver had picked out the big lighted Texaco station sign as a beacon, it arrowed toward the tarmac like a projectile whose velocity is very nearly spent. Stu could hear the worn-out thump of its engine now, the steady gurgle-and-wheeze of a dying carb and a loose set of valves. It missed the lower entrance and bumped up over the curb. The fluorescent bars over the pumps were reflecting off the Chevy's dirt-streaked windshield so it was hard to see what was inside, but Stu saw the vague shape of the driver roll loosely with the bump. The car showed no sign of slowing from its relentless fifteen.

'So I say with more money in circulation you'd be –'

'Better turn off your pumps, Hap,' Stu said mildly.

'The pumps? What?'

Norm Bruett had turned to look out the window. 'Christ on a pony,' he said.

Stu got out of his chair, leaned over Tommy Wannamaker and

Hank Carmichael, and flicked off all eight switches at once, four with each hand. So he was the only one who didn't see the Chevy as it hit the gas pumps on the upper island and sheared them off.

It plowed into them with a slowness that seemed implacable and somehow grand. Tommy Wannamaker swore in the Indian Head the next day that the taillights never flashed once. The Chevy just kept coming at a steady fifteen or so, like the pace car in the Tournament of Roses parade. The undercarriage screeched over the concrete island, and when the wheels hit it everyone but Stu saw the driver's head swing limply and strike the windshield, starring the glass.

The Chevy jumped like an old dog that had been kicked and plowed away the hi-test pump. It snapped off and rolled away, spilling a few dribbles of gas. The nozzle came unhooked and lay glittering under the fluorescents.

They all saw the sparks produced by the Chevy's exhaust pipe grating across the cement, and Hap, who had seen a gas station explosion in Mexico, instinctively shielded his eyes against the fireball he expected. Instead, the Chevy's rear end flirted around and fell off the pump island on the station side. The front end smashed into the low-lead pump, knocking it off with a hollow *bang*.

Almost deliberately, the Chevrolet finished its 360-degree turn, hitting the island again, broadside this time. The rear end popped up on the island and knocked the regular gas pump asprawl. And there the Chevy came to rest, trailing its rusty exhaust pipe behind it. It had destroyed all three of the gas pumps on that island nearest the highway. The motor continued to run choppily for a few seconds and then quit. The silence was so loud it was alarming.

'Holy moly,' Tommy Wannamaker said breathlessly. 'Will she blow, Hap?'

'If it was gonna, it already woulda,' Hap said, getting up. His shoulder bumped the map case, scattering Texas, New Mexico, and Arizona every whichway. Hap felt a cautious sort of jubilation. His pumps were insured, and the insurance was paid up. Mary had harped on the insurance ahead of everything.

'Guy must have been pretty drunk,' Norm said.

'I seen his taillights,' Tommy said, his voice high with excitement. 'They never flashed once. Holy moly! If he'd a been doing sixty we'd all be dead now.'

They hurried out of the office, Hap first and Stu bringing up the rear. Hap, Tommy, and Norm reached the car together. They could smell gas and hear the slow, clocklike tick of the Chevy's cooling engine. Hap opened the driver's side door and the man behind the wheel spilled out like an old laundry sack.

'God-*damn*,' Norm Bruett shouted, almost screamed. He turned away, clutched his ample belly, and was sick. It wasn't the man who had fallen out (Hap had caught him neatly before he could thump to the pavement) but the smell that was issuing from the car, a sick stench compounded of blood, fecal matter, vomit, and human decay. It was a ghastly rich sick-dead smell.

A moment later Hap turned away, dragging the driver by the armpits. Tommy hastily grabbed the dragging feet and he and Hap carried him into the office. In the glow of the overhead fluorescents their faces were cheesy-looking and revolted. Hap had forgotten about his insurance money.

The others looked into the car and then Hank turned away, one hand over his mouth, little finger sticking off like a man who has just raised his wineglass to make a toast. He trotted to the north end of the station's lot and let his supper come up.

Vic and Stu looked into the car for some time, looked at each other, and then looked back in. On the passenger side was a young woman, her shift dress hiked up high on her thighs. Leaning against her was a boy or girl, about three years old. They were both dead. Their necks had swelled up like inner tubes and the flesh there was a purple-black color, like a bruise. The flesh was puffed up under their eyes, too. They looked, Vic later said, like those baseball players who put lampblack under their eyes to cut the glare. Their eyes bulged sightlessly. The woman was holding the child's hand. Thick mucus had run from their noses and was now clotted there. Flies buzzed around them, lighting in the mucus, crawling in and out of their open mouths. Stu had been in the war, but he had never seen anything so terribly pitiful as this. His eyes were constantly drawn back to those linked hands.

He and Vic backed away together and looked blankly at each other. Then they turned to the station. They could see Hap, jawing frantically into the pay phone. Norm was walking toward the station behind them, throwing glances at the wreck over his shoulder. The Chevy's driver's side door stood sadly open. There was a pair of baby shoes dangling from the rear-view mirror.

Hank was standing by the door, rubbing his mouth with a dirty handkerchief. 'Jesus, Stu,' he said unhappily, and Stu nodded.

Hap hung up the phone. The Chevy's driver was lying on the floor. 'Ambulance will be here in ten minutes. Do you figure they're —?' He jerked his thumb at the Chevy.

'They're dead, okay.' Vic nodded. His lined face was yellow-pale, and he was sprinkling tobacco all over the floor as he tried to make one of his shitty-smelling cigarettes. 'They're the two deadest people I've ever seen.' He looked at Stu and Stu nodded, putting his hands in his pockets. He had the butterflies.

The man on the floor moaned thickly in his throat and they all looked down at him. After a moment, when it became obvious that the man was speaking or trying very hard to speak, Hap knelt beside him. It was, after all, his station.

Whatever had been wrong with the woman and child in the car was also wrong with this man. His nose was running freely, and his respiration had a peculiar undersea sound, a churning from somewhere in his chest. The flesh beneath his eyes was puffing, not black yet, but a bruised purple. His neck looked too thick, and the flesh had pushed up in a column to give him two extra chins. He was running a high fever; being close to him was like squatting on the edge of an open barbecue pit where good coals have been laid.

'The dog,' he muttered. 'Did you put him out?'

'Mister,' Hap said, shaking him gently. 'I called the ambulance. You're going to be all right.'

'Clock went red,' the man on the floor grunted, and then began to cough, racking chainlike explosions that sent heavy mucus spraying from his mouth in long and ropy splatters. Hap leaned backward, grimacing desperately.

'Better roll him over,' Vic said. 'He's goan choke on it.'

But before they could, the coughing tapered off into bellowsed, uneven breathing again. His eyes blinked slowly and he looked at the men gathered above him.

'Where's . . . this?'

'Arnette,' Hap said. 'Bill Hapscomb's Texaco. You crashed out some of my pumps.' And then, hastily, he added: 'That's okay. They was insured.'

The man on the floor tried to sit up and was unable. He had to settle for putting a hand on Hap's arm.

'My wife . . . my little girl . . .'

'They're fine,' Hap said, grinning a foolish dog grin.

'Seems like I'm awful sick,' the man said. Breath came in and out of him in a thick, soft roar. 'They were sick, too. Since we got up two days ago. Salt Lake City . . .' His eyes flickered slowly closed. 'Sick . . . guess we didn't move quick enough after all . . .'

Far off but getting closer, they could hear the whoop of the Arnette Volunteer Ambulance.

'Man,' Tommy Wannamaker said. 'Oh man.'

The sick man's eyes fluttered open again, and now they were filled with an intense, sharp concern. He struggled again to sit up. Sweat ran down his face. He grabbed Hap.

'Are Sally and Baby LaVon all right?' he demanded. Spittle flew from his lips and Hap could feel the man's burning heat radiating outward. The man was sick, half crazy, he stank. Hap was reminded of the smell an old dog blanket gets sometimes.

'They're all right,' he insisted, a little frantically. 'You just . . . lay down and take it easy, okay?'

The man lay back down. His breathing was rougher now. Hap and Hank helped roll him over on his side, and his respiration seemed to ease a trifle. 'I felt pretty good until last night,' he said. 'Coughing, but all right. Woke up with it in the night. Didn't get away quick enough. Is Baby LaVon okay?'

The last trailed off into something none of them could make out. The ambulance siren warbled closer and closer. Stu went over to the window to watch for it. The others remained in a circle around the man on the floor.

'What's he got, Vic, any idea?' Hap asked.

Vic shook his head. 'Dunno.'

'Might have been something they ate,' Norm Bruett said. 'That car's got a California plate. They was probably eatin at a lot of road-side stands, you know. Maybe they got a poison hamburger. It happens.'

The ambulance pulled in and skirted the wrecked Chevy to stop between it and the station door. The red light on top made crazy sweeping circles. It was full dark now.

'Gimme your hand and I'll pull you up outta there!' the man on the floor cried suddenly, and then was silent.

'Food poisoning,' Vic said. 'Yeah, that could be. I hope so, because –'

'Because what?' Hank asked.

'Because otherwise it might be something catching.' Vic looked at them with troubled eyes. 'I seen cholera back in 1958, down near Nogales, and it looked something like this.'

Three men came in, wheeling a stretcher. 'Hap,' one of them said. 'You're lucky you didn't get your scraggy ass blown to kingdom come. This guy, huh?'

They broke apart to let them through – Billy Verecker, Monty Sullivan, Carlos Ortega, men they all knew.

'There's two folks in that car,' Hap said, drawing Monty aside. 'Woman and a little girl. Both dead.'

'Holy crow! You sure?'

'Yeah. This guy, he don't know. You going to take him to Braintree?'

'I guess.' Monty looked at him, bewildered. 'What do I do with the two in the car? I don't know how to handle this, Hap.'

'Stu can call the State Patrol. You mind if I ride in with you?'

'Hell no.'

They got the man onto the stretcher, and while they ran him out, Hap went over to Stu. 'I'm gonna ride into Braintree with that guy. Would you call the State Patrol?'

'Sure.'

'And Mary, too. Call and tell her what happened.'

'Okay.'

Hap trotted out to the ambulance and climbed in. Billy Verecker shut the doors behind him and then called the other two. They had been staring into the wrecked Chevy with dread fascination.

A few moments later the ambulance pulled out, siren warbling, red domelight pulsing blood-shadows across the gas station's tarmac. Stu went to the phone and put a quarter in.

The man from the Chevy died twenty miles from the hospital. He drew one final bubbling gasp, let it out, hitched in a smaller one, and just quit.

Hap got the man's wallet out of his hip pocket and looked at it. There were seventeen dollars in cash. A California driver's license identified him as Charles D. Campion. There was an army card, and pictures of his wife and daughter encased in plastic. Hap didn't want to look at the pictures.

He stuffed the wallet back into the dead man's pocket and told Carlos to turn off the siren. It was ten after nine.

CHAPTER 2

There was a long rock pier running out into the Atlantic Ocean from the Ogunquit, Maine, town beach. Today it reminded her of an accusatory gray finger, and when Frannie Goldsmith parked her car in the public lot, she could see Jess sitting out at the end of it, just a silhouette in the afternoon sunlight. Gulls wheeled and cried above him, a New England portrait drawn in real life, and she doubted if any gull would dare spoil it by dropping a splat of white doodoo on Jess Rider's immaculate blue chambray workshirt. After all, he was a practicing poet.

She knew it was Jess because his ten-speed was bolted to the iron railing that ran behind the parking attendant's building! Gus, a balding, paunchy town fixture, was coming out to meet her. The fee for visitors was a dollar a car, but he knew Frannie lived in town without bothering to look at the RESIDENT sticker on the corner of her Volvo's windshield. Fran came here a lot.

Sure I do, Fran thought. In fact, I got pregnant right down there on the beach, just about twelve feet above the high tide line. Dear Lump: You were conceived on the scenic coast of Maine, twelve feet above the high tide line and twenty yards east of the seawall. X marks the spot.

Gus raised his hand toward her, making a peace sign.

'Your fella's out on the end of the pier, Miss Goldsmith.'

'Thanks, Gus. How's business?'

He waved smilingly at the parking lot. There were maybe two dozen cars in all, and she could see blue and white RESIDENT stickers on most of them.

'Not much trade this early,' he said. It was June 17. 'Wait two weeks and we'll make the town some money.'

'I'll bet. If you don't embezzle it all.'

Gus laughed and went back inside.

Frannie leaned one hand against the warm metal of her car, took off her sneakers, and put on a pair of rubber thongs. She was a tall girl with chestnut hair that fell halfway down the back of the buff-colored shift she was wearing. Good figure. Long legs that got appreciative glances. *Prime stuff* was the correct frathouse term, she believed. Looky-looky-looky-here-comes-nooky. Miss College Girl, 1990.

Then she had to laugh at herself, and the laugh was a trifle bitter. You are carrying on, she told herself, as if this was the news of the world. Chapter Six: Hester Prynne Brings the News of Pearl's Impending Arrival to Rev. Dimmesdale. Dimmesdale he wasn't. He was Jess Rider, age twenty, one year younger than Our Heroine, Little Fran. He was a practicing college-student-undergraduate-poet. You could tell by his immaculate blue chambray workshirt.

She paused at the edge of the sand, feeling the good heat baking the soles of her feet even through the rubber thongs. The silhouette at the far end of the pier was still tossing small rocks into the water. Her thought was partly amusing but mostly dismaying. He knows what he looks like out there, she thought. Lord Byron, lonely but unafraid. Sitting in lonely solitude and surveying the sea which leads back, back to where England lies. But I, an exile, may never –

Oh balls!

It wasn't so much the thought that disturbed her as what it indicated about her own state of mind. The young man she assumed she loved was sitting out there, and she was standing here caricaturing him behind his back.

She began to walk out along the pier, picking her way with careful grace over the rocks and crevices. It was an old pier, once part of a breakwater. Now most of the boats tied up on the southern end of town, where there were three marinas and seven honky-tonk motels that boomed all summer long.

She walked slowly, trying her best to cope with the thought that she might have fallen out of love with him in the space of the eleven days that she had known she was 'a little bit preggers,' in the words of Amy Lauder. Well, he had gotten her into that condition, hadn't he?

But not alone, that was for sure. And she had been on the pill. That had been the simplest thing in the world. She'd gone to the campus infirmary, told the doctor she was having painful menstruation and all sorts of embarrassing eructations on her skin, and the doctor had written her a prescription. In fact, he had given her a month of freebies.

She stopped again, out over the water now, the waves beginning to break toward the beach on her right and left. It occurred to her that the infirmary doctors probably heard about painful menstruation and too many pimples about as often as druggists heard about how I gotta buy these condoms for my brother – even more often in this day and age. She could just as easily have gone to him and said: 'Gimme the pill. I'm gonna fuck.' She was of age. Why be coy? She looked at Jesse's back and sighed. Because coyness gets to be a way of life. She began to walk again.

Anyway, the pill hadn't worked. Somebody in the quality control department at the jolly old Ovril factory had been asleep at the switch. Either that or she had forgotten a pill and then had forgotten she'd forgotten.

She walked softly up behind him and laid both hands on his shoulders.

Jess, who had been holding his rocks in his left hand and plunking them into Mother Atlantic with his right, let out a scream and lurched to his feet. Pebbles scattered everywhere, and he almost knocked Frannie off the side and into the water. He almost went in himself, head first.

She started to giggle helplessly and backed away with her hands over her mouth as he turned furiously around, a well-built young man with black hair, gold-rimmed glasses, and regular features which, to Jess's eternal discomfort, would never quite reflect the sensitivity inside him.

'You scared the *hell* out of me!' he roared.

'Oh Jess,' she giggled, 'oh Jess, I'm sorry, but that was funny, it really was.'

'We almost fell in the water,' he said, taking a resentful step toward her.

She took a step backward to compensate, tripped over a rock, and sat down hard. Her jaws clicked together hard with her tongue between them – exquisite pain! – and she stopped giggling as if the sound had been cut off with a knife. The very fact of her sudden silence – you turn me off, I'm a radio – seemed funniest of all and she began to giggle again, in spite of the fact that her tongue was bleeding and tears of pain were streaming from her eyes.

'Are you okay, Frannie?' He knelt beside her, concerned.

I *do* love him, she thought with some relief. Good thing for me. 'Did you hurt yourself, Fran?'

'Only my pride,' she said, letting him help her up. 'And I bit my tongue. See?' She ran it out for him, expecting to get a smile as a reward, but he frowned.

'Jesus, Fran, you're really bleeding.' He pulled a handkerchief out of his back pocket and looked at it doubtfully. Then he put it back.

The image of the two of them walking hand in hand back to the parking lot came to her, young lovers under a summer sun, her with his handkerchief stuffed in her mouth. She raises her hand to the smiling, benevolent attendant and says: Hung-huh-Guth.

She began to giggle again, even though her tongue did hurt and there was a bloody taste in her mouth that was a little nauseating.

'Look the other way,' she said primly. 'I'm going to be unladylike.'

Smiling a little, he theatrically covered his eyes. Propped on one arm, she stuck her head off the side of the pier and spat – bright red. Uck. Again. And again. At last her mouth seemed to clear and she looked around to see him peeking through his fingers.

'I'm sorry,' she said. 'I'm such an asshole.'

'No,' Jesse said, obviously meaning yes.

'Could we go get ice cream?' she asked. 'You drive. I'll buy.'

'That's a deal.' He got to his feet and helped her up. She spat over the side again. Bright red.

Apprehensively, Fran asked him: 'I didn't bite any of it off, did I?'

'I don't know,' Jess answered pleasantly. 'Did you swallow a lump?'

She put a revolted hand to her mouth. 'That's not funny.'

'No. I'm sorry. You just bit it, Frannie.'

'Are there any arteries in a person's tongue?'

They were walking back along the pier now, hand in hand. She paused every now and then to spit over the side. Bright red. She wasn't going to swallow any of that stuff, uh-uh, no way.

'Nope.'

'Good.' She squeezed his hand and smiled at him reassuringly. 'I'm pregnant.'

'Really? That's good. Do you know who I saw in Port –'

He stopped and looked at her, his face suddenly inflexible and very, very careful. It broke her heart a little to see the wariness there.

'What did you say?'

'I'm pregnant.' She smiled at him brightly and then spat over the side of the pier. Bright red.

'Big joke, Frannie,' he said uncertainly.

'No joke.'

He kept looking at her. After a while they started walking again. As they crossed the parking lot, Gus came out and waved to them. Frannie waved back. So did Jess.

They stopped at the Dairy Queen on US 1. Jess got a Coke and sat sipping it thoughtfully behind the Volvo's wheel. Fran made him get her a Banana Boat Supreme and she sat against her door, two feet of seat between them, spooning up nuts and pineapple sauce and ersatz Dairy Queen ice cream.

'You know,' she said, 'D. Q. ice cream is mostly bubbles. Did you know that? Lots of people don't.'

Jess looked at her and said nothing.

'Truth,' she said. 'Those ice cream machines are really nothing but giant bubble machines. That's how Dairy Queen can sell their ice cream so cheap. We had an offprint about it in Business Theory. There are many ways to defur a feline.'

Jess looked at her and said nothing.

'Now if you want real ice cream, you have to go to some place like a Deering Ice Cream Shop, and that's –'

She burst into tears.

He slid across the seat to her and put his arms around her neck. 'Frannie, don't do that. Please.'

'My Banana Boat is dripping on me,' she said, still weeping.

His handkerchief came out again and he mopped her off. By then her tears had trailed off to sniffles.

'Banana Boat Supreme with Blood Sauce,' she said, looking at him with red eyes. 'I guess I can't eat any more. I'm sorry, Jess. Would you throw it away?'

'Sure,' he said stiffly.

He took it from her, got out, and tossed it in the waste can. He was walking funny, Fran thought, as if he had been hit hard down low where it hurts boys. In a way she supposed that was just where he had been hit. But if you wanted to look at it another way, well, that was just about the way she had walked after he had taken her virginity on the beach. She had felt like she had a bad case of diaper rash. Only diaper rash didn't make you preggers.

He came back and got in.

'Are you really, Fran?' he asked abruptly.

'I am really.'

'How did it happen? I thought you were on the pill.'

'Well, what I figure is one, somebody in the quality control department of the jolly old Ovril factory was asleep at the switch when my batch of pills went by on the conveyor belt, or two, they are feeding you boys something in the UNH messhall that builds up sperm, or three, I forgot to take a pill and have since forgotten that I forgot.'

She offered him a hard, thin, sunny smile that he recoiled from just a bit.

'What are you mad about, Fran? I just asked.'

'Well, to answer your question in a different way, on a warm night in April, it must have been the twelfth, thirteenth, or fourteenth, you put your penis into my vagina and had an orgasm, thus ejaculating sperm by the millions –'

'Stop it,' he said sharply. 'You don't have to –'

'To what?' Outwardly stony, she was dismayed inside. In all her imaginings of how the scene might play, she had never seen it quite like this.

'To be so mad,' he said lamely. 'I'm not going to run out on you.'

'No,' she said more softly. At this point she could have plucked one of his hands off the wheel, held it, and healed the breach entirely. But she couldn't make herself do it. He had no business wanting to be comforted, no matter how tacit or unconscious his wanting was. She suddenly realized that one way or another, the laughs and the good times were over for a while. That made her want to cry again and she staved the tears off grimly. She was Frannie Goldsmith, Peter Goldsmith's daughter, and she wasn't going to sit in the parking lot of the Ogunquit Dairy Queen crying her damn stupid eyes out.

'What do you want to do?' Jess asked, getting out his cigarettes.

'What do *you* want to do?'

He struck a light and for just a moment as cigarette smoke raftered up she clearly saw a man and a boy fighting for control of the same face.

'Oh hell,' he said.

'The choices as I see them,' she said. 'We can get married and keep the baby. We can get married and give the baby up. Or we don't get married and I keep the baby. Or –'

'*Frannie* –'

'*Or* we don't get married and I don't keep the baby. Or I could get an abortion. Does that cover everything? Have I left anything out?'

'Frannie, can't we just talk –'

'We *are* talking!' she flashed at him. 'You had your chance and you said "Oh hell." Your exact words. I have just outlined all of the possible choices. Of course I've had a little more time to work up an agenda.'

'You want a cigarette?'

'No. They're bad for the baby.'

'Frannie, goddammit!'

'Why are you shouting?' she asked softly.

'Because you seem determined to aggravate me as much as you can,' Jess said hotly. He controlled himself. 'I'm sorry. I just can't think of this as my fault.'

'You can't?' She looked at him with a cocked eyebrow. 'And behold, a virgin shall conceive.'

'Do you have to be so goddam flip? You had the pill, you said. I took you at your word. Was I so wrong?'

'No. You weren't so wrong. But that doesn't change the fact.'

'I guess not,' he said gloomily, and pitched his cigarette out half-smoked. 'So what do we do?'

'You keep asking me, Jesse. I just outlined the choices as I see them. I thought you might have some ideas. There's suicide, but I'm not considering it at this point. So pick the other choice you like and we'll talk about it.'

'Let's get married,' he said in a sudden strong voice. He had the air of a man who has decided that the best way to solve the Gordian knot problem would be to hack right down through the middle of it. Full speed ahead and get the whiners belowdecks.

'No,' she said. 'I don't want to marry you.'

It was as if his face was held together by a number of unseen bolts and each of them had suddenly been loosened a turn and a half. Everything sagged at once. The image was so cruelly comical that she had to rub her wounded tongue against the rough top of her mouth to keep from getting the giggles again. She didn't want to laugh at Jess.

'Why not?' he asked. 'Fran —'

'I have to think of my reasons why not. I'm not going to let you draw me into a discussion of my reasons why not, because right now I don't know.'

'You don't love me,' he said sulkily.

'In most cases, love and marriage are mutually exclusive states. Pick another choice.'

He was silent for a long time. He fiddled with a fresh cigarette but didn't light it. At last he said: 'I can't pick another choice, Frannie, because you don't want to discuss this. You want to score points off me.'

That touched her a little bit. She nodded. 'Maybe you're right. I've had a few scored off me in the last couple of weeks. Now you, Jess, you're Joe College all the way. If a mugger came at you with a knife, you'd want to convene a seminar on the spot.'

'Oh for God's sake.'

'Pick another choice.'

'No. You've got your reasons all figured out. Maybe I need a little time to think, too.'

'Okay. Would you take us back to the parking lot? I'll drop you off and do some errands.'

He gazed at her, startled. 'Frannie, I rode my bike all the way down from Portland. I've got a room at a motel outside of town. I thought we were going to spend the weekend together.'

'In your motel room. No, Jess. The situation has changed. You just get back on your ten-speed and bike back to Portland and you get in touch when you've thought about it a little more. No great hurry.'

'Stop riding me, Frannie.'

'No, Jess, you were the one who rode me,' she jeered in sudden, furious anger, and that was when he slapped her lightly backhand on the cheek.

He stared at her, stunned.

'I'm sorry, Fran.'

'Accepted,' she said colorlessly. 'Drive on.'

They didn't talk on the ride back to the public beach parking lot. She sat with her hands folded in her lap, watching the slices of ocean layered between the cottages just west of the seawall. They looked like slum apartments, she thought. Who owned these houses, most of them still shuttered blindly against the summer that would begin officially in less than a week? Professors from MIT. Boston doctors. New York lawyers. These houses weren't the real biggies, the coast estates owned by men who counted their fortunes in seven and eight figures. But when the families who owned them moved in here, the lowest IQ on Shore Road would be Gus the parking attendant. The kids would have ten-speeds like Jess's. They would have bored expressions and they would go with their parents to have lobster dinners and to attend the Ogunquit Playhouse. They would idle up and down the main street, masquerading after soft summer twilight as street people. She kept looking out at the lovely flashes of cobalt between the crammed-together houses, aware that the vision was blurring with a new film of tears. The little white cloud that cried.

They reached the parking lot, and Gus waved. They waved back.

'I'm sorry I hit you, Frannie,' Jess said in a subdued voice. 'I never meant to do that.'

'I know. Are you going back to Portland?'

'I'll stay here tonight and call you in the morning. But it's your decision, Fran. If you decide, you know, that an abortion is the thing, I'll scrape up the cash.'

'Pun intended?'

'No,' he said. 'Not at all.' He slid across the seat and kissed her chastely. 'I love you, Fran.'

I don't believe you do, she thought. Suddenly I don't believe it at all . . . but I'll accept in good grace. I can do that much.

'All right,' she said quietly.

'It's the Lighthouse Motel. Call if you want.'

'Okay.' She slid behind the wheel, suddenly feeling very tired. Her tongue ached miserably where she had bitten it.

He walked to where his bike was locked to the iron railing and coasted it back to her. 'Wish you'd call, Fran.'

She smiled artificially. 'We'll see. So long, Jess.'

She put the Volvo in gear, turned around, and drove across the lot to the Shore Road. She could see Jess standing by his bike yet, the ocean at his back, and for the second time that day she mentally accused him of knowing exactly what kind of picture he was making. This time, instead of being irritated, she felt a little bit sad. She drove on, wondering if the ocean would ever look the way it had looked to her before all of this had happened. Her tongue hurt miserably. She opened her window wider and spat. All white and all right this time. She could smell the salt of the ocean strongly, like bitter tears.

CHAPTER 3

Norm Bruett woke up at quarter past ten in the morning to the sound of kids fighting outside the bedroom window and country music from the radio in the kitchen.

He went to the back door in his saggy shorts and undershirt, threw it open, and yelled: 'You kids shutcha heads!'

A moment's pause. Luke and Bobby looked around from the old and rusty dump truck they had been arguing over. As always when he saw his kids, Norm felt dragged two ways at once. His heart ached to see them wearing hand-me-downs and Salvation Army giveouts like the ones you saw the nigger children in east Arnette wearing; and at the same time a horrible, shaking anger would sweep through him, making him want to stride out there and beat the living shit out of them.

'Yes, Daddy,' Luke said in a subdued way. He was nine.

'Yes, Daddy,' Bobby echoed. He was seven going on eight.

Norm stood for a moment, glaring at them, and slammed the door shut. He stood for a moment, looking indecisively at the pile of clothes he had worn yesterday. They were lying at the foot of the sagging double bed where he had dropped them.

That slutty bitch, he thought. She didn't even hang up my duds.

'Lila!' he bawled.

There was no answer. He considered ripping the door open again and asking Luke where the hell she had gone. It wasn't donated commodities day until next week and if she was down at the employment office in Braintree again she was an even bigger fool than he thought.

He didn't bother to ask the kids. He felt tired and he had a queasy, thumping headache. Felt like a hangover, but he'd only had three beers down at Hap's the night before. That accident had been a hell of a thing. The woman and the baby dead in the car, the man, Campion, dying on the way to the hospital. By the time Hap had gotten back, the State Patrol had come and gone, and the wrecker, and the Braintree undertaker's hack. Vic Palfrey had given the Laws a statement for all five of them. The undertaker, who was also the county coroner, refused to speculate on what might have hit them.

'But it ain't cholera. And don't you go scarin people sayin it is. There'll be an autopsy and you can read about it in the paper.'

Miserable little pissant, Norm thought, slowly dressing himself in yesterday's clothes. His headache was turning into a real blinder. Those kids had better be quiet or they were going to have a pair of broken arms to mouth off about. Why the hell couldn't they have school the whole year round?

He considered tucking his shirt into his pants, decided the President probably wouldn't be stopping by that day, and shuffled out into the kitchen in his sock feet. The bright sunlight coming in the east windows made him squint.

The cracked Philco radio over the stove sang:

> But bay-yay-yaby you can tell me if anyone can,
> Baby, can you dig your man?
> He's a righteous man,
> Tell me baby, can you dig your man?

Things had come to a pretty pass when they had to play nigger rock and roll music like that on the local country music station. Norm turned it off before it could split his head. There was a note by the radio and he picked it up, narrowing his eyes to read it.

> Dear Norm,
>   Sally Hodges says she needs somebody to sit her kids this morning and says shell give me a dolar. Ill be back for luntch. Theres sassage if you want it. I love you honey.
>   Lila.

Norm put the note back and just stood there for a moment, thinking it over and trying to get the sense of it in his mind. It was goddam hard to think past the headache. Babysitting . . . a dollar. For Ralph Hodges's wife.

The three elements slowly came together in his mind. Lila had gone off to sit Sally Hodges's three kids to earn a lousy dollar and had stuck him with Luke and Bobby. By God it was hard times when a man had to sit home and wipe his kids' noses so his wife could go and scratch out a lousy buck that wouldn't even buy them a gallon of gas. That was hard fucking times.

Dull anger came to him, making his head ache even worse. He shuffled slowly to the Frigidaire, bought when he had been making good overtime, and opened it. Most of the shelves were empty, except for leftovers Lila had put up in refrigerator dishes. He hated those little plastic Tupperware dishes. Old beans, old corn, a left-over dab of chili . . . nothing a man liked to eat. Nothing in there but little Tupperware dishes and three little old sausages done up in Handi-Wrap. He bent, looking at them, the familiar helpless anger now compounded by the dull throb in his head. Those sausages looked like somebody had cut the cocks off'n three of those pygmies they had down in Africa or South America or wherever the fuck it was they had them. He didn't feel like eating anyway. He felt damn sick, when you got right down to it.

He went over to the stove, scratched a match on the piece of sandpaper nailed to the wall beside it, lit the front gas ring, and put on the coffee. Then he sat down and waited dully for it to boil. Just before it did, he had to scramble his snotrag out of his back pocket to catch a big wet sneeze. Coming down with a cold, he thought. Isn't that something nice on top of everything else? But it never occurred to him to think of the phlegm that had been running out of that fellow Campion's pump the night before.

Hap was in the garage bay putting a new tailpipe on Tony Leominster's Scout and Vic Palfrey was rocking back on a folding camp chair, watching him and drinking a Dr Pepper when the bell dinged out front.

Vic squinted. 'It's the State Patrol,' he said. 'Looks like your cousin, there. Joe Bob.'

'Okay.'

Hap came out from beneath the Scout, wiping his hands on a ball of waste. On his way through the office he sneezed heavily. He hated summer colds. They were the worst.

Joe Bob Brentwood, who was almost six and a half feet tall, was standing by the back of his cruiser, filling up. Beyond him, the three pumps Campion had driven over the night before were neatly lined up like dead soldiers.

'Hey Joe Bob!' Hap said, coming out.

'Hap, you sumbitch,' Joe Bob said, putting the pump handle on automatic and stepping over the hose. 'You lucky this place still standin this mornin.'

'Shit, Stu Redman saw the guy coming and switched off the pumps. There was a load of sparks, though.'

'Still damn lucky. Listen, Hap, I come over for somethin besides a fill-up.'

'Yeah?'

Joe Bob's eyes went to Vic, who was standing in the station door. 'Was that old geezer here last night?'

'Who? Vic? Yeah, he comes over most every night.'

'Can he keep his mouth shut?'

'Sure, I reckon. He's a good enough old boy.'

The automatic feed kicked off. Hap squeezed off another twenty cents' worth, then put the nozzle back on the pump and switched it off. He walked back to Joe Bob.

'So? What's the story?'

'Well, let's go inside. I guess the old fella ought to hear, too. And if you get a chance, you can phone the rest of them that was here.'

They walked across the tarmac and into the office.

'A good mornin to you, Officer,' Vic said.

Joe Bob nodded.

'Coffee, Joe Bob?' Hap asked.

'I guess not.' He looked at them heavily. 'Thing is, I don't know how my superiors would like me bein here at all. I don't think they would. So when those guys come here, you don't let them know I tipped you, right?'

'What guys, Officer?' Vic asked.

'Health Department guys,' Joe Bob said.

Vic said, 'Oh Jesus, it *was* cholera. I *knowed* it was.'

Hap looked from one to the other. 'Joe Bob?'

'I don't know nothing,' Joe Bob said, sitting down in one of the plastic Woolco chairs. His bony knees came nearly up to his neck. He took a pack of Chesterfields from his blouse pocket and lit up. 'Finnegan, there, the coroner –'

'That was a smartass,' Hap said fiercely. 'You should have seen him struttin around in here, Joe Bob. Just like a pea turkey that got its first hardon. Shushin people and all that.'

'He's a big turd in a little bowl, all right,' Joe Bob agreed. 'Well, he got Dr James to look at this Campion, and the two of them called in another doctor that I don't know. Then they got on the phone to Houston. And around three this mornin they come into that little airport outside of Braintree.'

'Who did?'

'Pathologists. Three of them. They were in there with the bodies until about eight o'clock. Cuttin on em is my guess, although I dunno for sure. Then they got on the phone to the Plague Center in Atlanta, and those guys are going to be here this afternoon. But they said in the meantime that the State Health Department was to send some fellas out here and see all the guys that were in the station last night, and the guys that drove the rescue unit to Braintree. I dunno, but it sounds to me like they want you quarantined.'

'Moses in the bulrushes,' Hap said, frightened.

'The Atlanta Plague Center's federal,' Vic said. 'Would they send out a planeload of federal men just for cholera?'

'Search me,' Joe Bob said. 'But I thought you guys had a right to know. From all I heard, you just tried to lend a hand.'

'It's appreciated, Joe Bob,' Hap said slowly. 'What did James and this other doctor say?'

'Not much. But they looked scared. I never seen doctors look scared like that. I didn't much care for it.'

A heavy silence fell. Joe Bob went to the drink machine and got a bottle of Fresca. The faint hissing sound of carbonation was audible as he popped the cap. As Joe Bob sat down again, Hap took a Kleenex from the box next to the cash register, wiped his runny nose, and folded it into the pocket of his greasy overall.

'What have you found out about Campion?' Vic asked. 'Anything?'

'We're still checking,' Joe Bob said with a trace of importance. 'His ID says he was from San Diego, but a lot of the stuff in his wallet was two and three years out of date. His driver's license was expired. He had a BankAmericard that was issued in 1986 and that was expired, too. He had an army card so we're checking with them. The captain has a hunch that Campion hadn't lived in San Diego for maybe four years.'

'AWOL?' Vic asked. He produced a big red bandanna, hawked, and spat into it.

'Dunno yet. But his army card said he was in until 1997, and he was in civvies, and he was with his family, and he was a fuck of a long way from California, and listen to my mouth run.'

'Well, I'll get in touch with the others and tell em what you said, anyway,' Hap said. 'Much obliged.'

Joe Bob stood up. 'Sure. Just keep my name out of it. I sure wouldn't want to lose my job. Your buddies don't need to know who tipped you, do they?'

'No,' Hap said, and Vic echoed it.

As Joe Bob went to the door, Hap said a little apologetically: 'That's five even for gas, Joe Bob. I hate to charge you, but with things the way they are –'

'That's okay.' Joe Bob handed him a credit card. 'State's payin. And I got my credit slip to show why I was here.'

While Hap was filling out the slip he sneezed twice.

'You want to watch that,' Joe Bob said. 'Nothin any worse than a summer cold.'

'Don't I know it.'

Suddenly, from behind them, Vic said: 'Maybe it ain't a cold.'

They turned to him. Vic looked frightened.

'I woke up this morning sneezin and hackin away like sixty,' Vic said. 'Had a mean headache, too. I took some aspirins and it's gone back some, but I'm still full of snot. Maybe we're coming down with it. What that Campion had. What he died of.'

Hap looked at him for a long time, and as he was about to put forward all his reasons why it couldn't be, he sneezed again.

Joe Bob looked at them both gravely for a moment and then said, 'You know, it might not be such a bad idea to close the station, Hap. Just for today.'

Hap looked at him, scared, and tried to remember what all his reasons had been. He couldn't think of a one. All he could remember was that he had also awakened with a headache and a runny nose. Well, everyone caught a cold once in a while. But before that guy Campion had shown up, he had been fine. Just fine.

The three Hodges kids were six, four, and eighteen months. The two youngest were taking naps, and the oldest was out back digging a hole. Lila Bruett was in the living room, watching 'The Young and the Restless.' She hoped Sally wouldn't return until it was over. Ralph Hodges had bought a big color TV when times had been better in

Arnette, and Lila loved to watch the afternoon stories in color. Everything was so much prettier.

She drew on her cigarette and then let the smoke out in spasms as a racking cough seized her. She went into the kitchen and spat the mouthful of crap she had brought up down the drain. She had gotten up with the cough, and all day it had felt like someone was tickling the back of her throat with a feather.

She went back to the living room after taking a peek out the pantry window to make sure Bert Hodges was okay. A commercial was on now, two dancing bottles of toilet bowl cleaner. Lila let her eyes drift around the room and wished her own house looked this nice. Sally's hobby was doing paint-by-the-numbers pictures of Christ, and they were all over the living room in nice frames. She especially liked the big one of the Last Supper mounted in back of the TV; it had come with sixty different oil colors, Sally had told her, and it took almost three months to finish. It was a real work of art.

Just as her story came back on, Baby Cheryl started to cry, a whooping, ugly yell broken by bursts of coughing.

Lila put out her cigarette and hurried into the bedroom. Eva, the four-year-old, was still fast asleep, but Cheryl was lying on her back in her crib, and her face was going an alarming purple color. Her cries began to sound strangled.

Lila, who was not afraid of the croup after seeing both of her own through bouts with it, picked her up by the heels and swatted her firmly on the back. She had no idea if Dr Spock recommended this sort of treatment or not, because she had never read him. It worked nicely on Baby Cheryl. She emitted a froggy croak and suddenly spat an amazing wad of yellow phlegm out onto the floor.

'Better?' Lila asked.

'Yeth,' said Baby Cheryl. She was almost asleep again.

Lila wiped up the mess with a Kleenex. She couldn't remember ever having seen a baby cough up so much snot all at once.

She sat down in front of 'The Young and the Restless' again, frowning. She lit another cigarette, sneezed over the first puff, and then began to cough herself.

CHAPTER 4

It was an hour past nightfall.

Starkey sat alone at a long table, sifting through sheets of yellow flimsy. Their contents dismayed him. He had been serving his country for thirty-six years, beginning as a scared West Point plebe. He had won medals. He had spoken with Presidents, had offered them advice, and on occasion his advice had been taken. He had been through dark moments before, plenty of them, but this . . .

He was scared, so deeply scared he hardly dared admit it to himself. It was the kind of fear that could drive you mad.

On impulse he got up and went to the wall where the five blank TV monitors looked into the room. As he got up, his knee bumped the table, causing one of the sheets of flimsy to fall off the edge. It seesawed lazily down through the mechanically purified air and landed on the tile, half in the table's shadow and half out. Someone standing over it and looking down would have seen this:

OT CONFIRMED
SEEMS REASONABLY
STRAIN CODED 848-AB
CAMPION, (W.) SALLY
ANTIGEN SHIFT AND MUTATION.
HIGH RISK/EXCESS MORTALITY
AND COMMUNICABILITY ESTIMATED
REPEAT 99.4%. ATLANTA PLAGUE
CENTER
UNDERSTANDS. TOP SECRET BLUE FOLDER.
ENDS
P-T-222312A

Starkey pushed a button under the middle screen and the picture flashed on with the unnerving suddenness of solid state components. It showed the western California desert, looking east. It was desolate, and the desolation was rendered eerie by the reddish-purple tinge of infrared photography.

It's out there, straight ahead, Starkey thought. Project Blue.

The fright tried to wash over him again. He reached into his pocket and brought out a blue pill. What his daughter would call a 'downer.' Names didn't matter; results did. He dry-swallowed it, his hard, unseamed face wrinkling for a moment as it went down.

Project Blue.

He looked at the other blank monitors, and then punched up pictures on all of them. 4 and 5 showed labs. 4 was physics, 5 was viral biology. The vi-bi lab was full of animal cages, mostly for guinea pigs, rhesus monkeys, and a few dogs. None of them appeared to be sleeping. In the physics lab a small centrifuge was still turning around and around. Starkey had complained about that. He had complained *bitterly*. There was something spooky about that centrifuge whirling gaily around and around and around while Dr Ezwick lay dead on the floor nearby, sprawled out like a scarecrow that had tipped over in a high wind.

They had explained to him that the centrifuge was on the same circuit as the lights, and if they turned off the centrifuge, the lights would go, too. And the cameras down there were not equipped for infrared. Starkey understood. Some more brass might come down from Washington and want to look at the dead Nobel Prize winner who was lying four hundred feet under the desert less than a mile away. If we turn off the centrifuge, we turn off the professor. Elementary. What his daughter would have called a 'Catch-22.'

He took another 'downer' and looked into monitor 2. This was the one he liked least of all. He didn't like the man with his face in the soup. Suppose someone walked up to you and said: *You will spend eternity with your phiz in a bowl of soup.* It's like the old pie-in-the-face routine: it stops being funny when it starts being you.

Monitor 2 showed the Project Blue cafeteria. The accident had occurred almost perfectly between shifts, and the cafeteria had been only lightly populated. He supposed it hadn't mattered much to them, whether they had died in the cafeteria or in their bedrooms or their labs. Still, the man with his face in the soup . . .

A man and a woman in blue coveralls were crumpled at the foot of the candy machine. A man in a white coverall lay beside the Seeburg jukebox. At the tables themselves were nine men and fourteen women, some of them slumped beside Hostess Twinkies, some with spilled cups of Coke and Sprite still clutched in their stiff hands. And at the second table, near the end, there was a man who had been identified as Frank D. Bruce. His face was in a bowl of what appeared to be Campbell's Chunky Sirloin Soup.

The first monitor showed only a digital clock. Until June 13, all the numbers on that clock had been green. Now they had turned bright red. They had stopped. The figures read 06:13:90:02:37:16.

June 13, 1990. Thirty-seven minutes past two in the morning. And sixteen seconds.

From behind him came a brief burring noise.

Starkey turned off the monitors one by one and then turned around. He saw the sheet of flimsy on the floor and put it back on the table.

'Come.'

It was Creighton. He looked grave and his skin was a slaty color. More bad news, Starkey thought serenely. Someone else has taken a long high dive into a cold bowl of Chunky Sirloin Soup.

'Hi, Len,' he said quietly.

Len Creighton nodded. 'Billy. This . . . Christ, I don't know how to tell you.'

'I think one word at a time might go best, soldier.'

'Those men who handled Campion's body are through their prelims at Atlanta, and the news isn't good.'

'All of them?'

'Five for sure. There's one – his name is Stuart Redman – who's negative so far. But as far as we can tell, Campion himself was negative for over fifty hours.'

'If only Campion hadn't run,' Starkey said. 'That was sloppy security, Len. Very sloppy.'

Creighton nodded.

'Go on.'

'Arnette has been quarantined. We've isolated at least sixteen cases of constantly shifting A-Prime flu there so far. And those are just the overt ones.'

'The news media?'

'So far, no problem. They believe it's anthrax.'

'What else?'

'One very serious problem. We have a Texas highway patrolman named Joseph Robert Brentwood. His cousin owns the gas station where Campion ended up. He dropped by yesterday morning to tell Hapscomb the health people were coming. We picked Brentwood up three hours ago and he's en route to Atlanta now. In the meantime he's been patrolling half of East Texas. God knows how many people he's been in contact with.'

'Oh, shit,' Starkey said, and was appalled by the watery weakness in his voice and the skin-crawl that had started near the base of his testicles and was now working up into his belly. 99.4% communicability, he thought. It played insanely over and over in his mind. And that meant 99.4% excess mortality, because the human body couldn't produce the antibodies necessary to stop a constantly shifting antigen virus. Every time the body *did* produce the right antibody, the virus simply shifted to a slightly new form. For the same reason a vaccine was going to be almost impossible to create.

99.4%.

'Christ,' he said. 'That's it?'

'Well –'

'Go on. Finish.'

Softly, then, Creighton said: 'Hammer's dead, Billy. Suicide. He shot himself in the eye with his service pistol. The Project Blue specs were on his desk. I guess he thought leaving them there was all the suicide note anybody would need.'

Starkey closed his eyes. Vic Hammer was . . . had been . . . his son-in-law. How was he supposed to tell Cynthia about this? I'm sorry, Cindy. Vic took a high dive into a cold bowl of soup today. Here, have a 'downer.' You see, there was a goof. Somebody made a mistake with a box. Somebody else forgot to pull a switch that would have sealed off the base. The lag was only forty-some seconds, but it was enough. The box is known in the trade as a 'sniffer.' It's made in Portland, Oregon, Defense Department Contract 164480966. The boxes are put together in separate circuits by female technicians, and they do it that way so none of them really know what they're doing. One of them was maybe thinking about what to make for supper, and whoever was supposed to check her work was maybe thinking about trading the family car. Anyway, Cindy, the last coincidence was that a man at the Number Four security post, a man named Campion, saw the numbers go red just in time to get out of the room before the doors shut and mag-locked. Then he got his family and ran. He drove through the main gate just four minutes before the sirens started going off and we sealed the whole base. And no one started looking for him until nearly an hour later because there are no monitors in the security posts – somewhere along the line you have to stop guarding the guardians or everyone in the world would be a goddam turnkey – and everybody just assumed he was in there, waiting for the sniffers to sort out the clean areas from the dirty ones. So he got him some running room and he was smart enough to use the ranch trails and lucky enough not to pick any of the ones where his car could get bogged down. Then someone had to make a command decision on whether or not to bring in the State Police, the FBI, or both of them and that fabled buck got passed hither, thither, and yon, and by the time someone decided the Shop ought to handle it, this happy asshole – this happy *diseased* asshole – had gotten to Texas, and when they finally caught him he wasn't running anymore because he and his wife and his baby daughter were all laid out on cooling boards in some pissant little town called Braintree. Braintree, Texas. Anyway, Cindy, what I'm trying to say is that this was a chain of coincidence on the order of winning the Irish Sweepstakes. With a little incompetence thrown in for good luck – for bad luck, I mean, please excuse me – but mostly it was just a thing that happened. None of it was your man's fault. But he was the head of the project, and he saw the situation start to escalate, and then –

'Thanks, Len,' he said.

'Billy, would you like –'

'I'll be up in ten minutes. I want you to schedule a general staff meeting fifteen minutes from now. If they're in bed, kick em out.'

'Yes, sir.'

'And Len . . .'

'Yes?'

'I'm glad you were the one who told me.'

'Yes, sir.'

Creighton left. Starkey glanced at his watch, then walked over to the monitors set into the wall. He turned on 2, put his hands behind his back, and stared thoughtfully into Project Blue's silent cafeteria.

CHAPTER 5

Larry Underwood pulled around the corner and found a parking space big enough for the Datsun Z between a fire hydrant and somebody's trashcan that had fallen into the gutter. There was something unpleasant in the trashcan and Larry tried to tell himself that he really hadn't seen the stiffening dead cat and the rat gnawing at its white-furred belly. The rat was gone so fast from the sweep of his headlights that it really might not have been there. The cat, however, was fixed in stasis. And, he supposed, killing the Z's engine, if you believed in one you had to believe in the other. Didn't they say that Paris had the biggest rat population in the world? All those old sewers. But New York did well, too. And if he remembered his misspent youth well enough, not all the rats in New York City went on four legs. And what the hell was he doing parked in front of this decaying brownstone, thinking about rats anyway?

Five days ago, on June 14, he had been in sunny Southern California, home of hopheads, freak religions, the only c/w nightclubs in the world with gogo dancers, and Disneyland. This morning at quarter of four he had arrived on the shore of the other ocean, paying his toll to go across the Triborough Bridge. A sullen drizzle had been falling. Only in New York can an early summer drizzle seem so unrepentantly sullen. Larry could see the drops accreting on the Z's windshield now, as intimations of dawn began to creep into the eastern sky.

Dear New York: I've come home.

Maybe the Yankees were in town. That might make the trip worthwhile. Take the subway up to the Stadium, drink beer, eat hotdogs, and watch the Yankees wallop the piss out of Cleveland or Boston . . .

His thoughts drifted off and when he wandered back to them he saw that the light had gotten much stronger. The dashboard clock read 6:05. He had been dozing. The rat had been real, he saw. The rat was back. The rat had dug himself quite a hole in the dead cat's guts. Larry's empty stomach did a slow forward roll. He considered beeping the horn to scare it away for good, but the sleeping brownstones with their empty garbage cans standing sentinel duty daunted him.

He slouched lower in the bucket seat so he wouldn't have to watch the rat eating breakfast. Just a bite, my good man, and then back to the subway system. Going out to Yankee Stadium this evening? Perhaps I'll see you, old chum. Although I really doubt that you'll see me.

The front of the building had been defaced with spray can slogans, cryptic and ominous: CHICO 116, ZORRO 93, LITTLE ABIE #1! When he had been a boy, before his father died, this had been a good neighborhood. Two stone dogs had guarded the steps leading up to the double doors. A year before he took off for the coast, vandals had demolished the one on the right from the forepaws up. Now they were both entirely gone, except for one rear paw of the left dog. The body it had been called into creation to support had entirely vanished, perhaps decorating some Puerto Rican junkie's crash-pad. Maybe ZORRO 93 or LITTLE ABIE #1! had taken it. Maybe the rats had carried it away to some deserted subway tunnel one dark night. For all he knew, maybe they had taken his mother along, too. He supposed he should at least climb the steps and make sure her name was still there under the Apartment 15 mailbox, but he was too tired.

No, he would just sit here and nod off, trusting to the last residue of reds in his system to wake him up around seven. Then he would go see if his mother still lived here. Maybe it would be best if she was gone. Maybe then he wouldn't even bother with the Yankees. Maybe he would just check into the Biltmore, sleep for three days, and then head back into the golden West. In this light, in this drizzle, with his legs and head still throbbing from the bring-down, New York had all the charm of a dead whore.

His mind began to drift away again, mulling over the last nine weeks or so, trying to find some sort of key that would make everything clear and explain how you could butt yourself against stone walls for six long years, playing the clubs, making demo tapes, doing sessions, the whole bit, and then suddenly make it in nine weeks. Trying to get that straight in your mind was like trying to swallow a doorknob. There had to be an answer, he thought, an explanation that would allow him to reject the ugly notion that the whole thing had been a whim, a simple twist of fate, in Dylan's words.

He dozed deeper, arms crossed on his chest, going over it and over it, and mixed up in all of it was this new thing, like a low and sinister counterpoint, one note at the threshold of audibility played on a synthesizer, heard in a migrainy sort of way that acted on you like a premonition: the rat, digging into the dead cat's body, munch, munch, just looking for something tasty here. It's the law of the jungle, my man, if you're in the trees you got to swing . . .

It had really started eighteen months ago. He had been playing with the Tattered Remnants in a Berkeley club, and a man from Columbia had called. Not a biggie, just another toiler in the vinyl vineyards. Neil Diamond was thinking of recording one of his songs, a tune called 'Baby, Can You Dig Your Man?'

Diamond was doing an album, all his own stuff except for an old Buddy Holly tune, 'Peggy Sue Got Married,' and maybe this Larry Underwood tune. The question was, would Larry like to come up and cut a demo of the tune, then sit in on the session? Diamond wanted a second acoustic guitar, and he liked the tune a lot.

Larry said yes.

The session lasted three days. It was a good one. Larry met Neil Diamond, also Robbie Robertson, also Richard Perry. He got mention on the album's inner sleeve and got paid union scale. But 'Baby, Can You Dig Your Man?' never made the album. On the second evening of the session, Diamond had come up with a new tune of his own and that made the album instead.

Well, the man from Columbia said, that's too bad. It happens. Tell you what – why don't you cut the demo anyway. I'll see if there's anything I can do. So Larry cut the demo and then found himself back out on the street. In LA times were hard. There were a few sessions, but not many.

He finally got a job playing guitar in a supper club, crooning things like 'Softly as I Leave You' and 'Moon River' while elderly cats talked business and sucked up Italian food. He wrote the lyrics on scraps of notepaper, because otherwise he tended to mix them up or forget them altogether, chording the tune while he went 'hmmmm-hmmmm, ta-da-hmmmm,' trying to look suave like Tony Bennett vamping and feeling like an asshole. In elevators and super-markets he had become morbidly aware of the low Muzak that played constantly.

Then, nine weeks ago and out of the blue, the man from Columbia had called. They wanted to release his demo as a single.

Could he come in and back it? Sure, Larry said. He could do that. So he had gone into Columbia's LA studios on a Sunday afternoon, double-tracked his own voice on 'Baby, Can You Dig Your Man?' in about an hour, and then backed it with a song he had written for the Tattered Remnants, 'Pocket Savior.' The man from Columbia presented him with a check for five hundred dollars and a stinker of a contract that bound Larry to more than it did the record company. He shook Larry's hand, told him it was good to have him aboard, offered him a small, pitying smile when Larry asked him how the single would be promoted, and then took his leave. It was too late to deposit the check, so Larry ran through his repertoire at Gino's with it in his pocket. Near the end of his first set, he sang a subdued version of 'Baby, Can You Dig Your Man?' The only person who noticed was Gino's proprietor, who told him to save the nigger bebop for the cleanup crew.

Seven weeks ago, the man from Columbia called again and told him to go get a copy of *Billboard*. Larry ran. 'Baby, Can You Dig Your Man?' was one of three hot prospects for that week. Larry called the man from Columbia back, and he had asked Larry how he would like to lunch with some of the real biggies. To discuss the album. They were all pleased with the single, which was getting airplay in Detroit, Philadelphia, and Portland, Maine, already. It looked as if it was going to catch. It had won a late-night Battle of the Sounds contest for four nights running on one Detroit soul station. No one seemed to know that Larry Underwood was white.

He had gotten drunk at the luncheon and hardly noticed how his salmon tasted. No one seemed to mind that he had gotten loaded. One of the biggies said he wouldn't be surprised to see 'Baby, Can You Dig Your Man?' carry off a Grammy next year. It all rang gloriously in Larry's ears. He felt like a man in a dream, and going back to his apartment he felt strangely sure that he would be hit by a truck and that would end it all. The Columbia biggies had presented him with another check, this one for $2,500. When he got home, Larry picked up the telephone and began to make calls. The first one was to Mort 'Gino' Green. Larry told him he'd have to find someone else to play 'Yellow Bird' while the customers ate his lousy undercooked pasta. Then he called everyone he could think of, including Barry Grieg of the Remnants. Then he went out and got standing-up falling-down drunk.

Five weeks ago the single had cracked *Billboard*'s Hot One

Hundred. Number eighty-nine. With a bullet. That was the week spring had really come to Los Angeles, and on a bright and sparkling May afternoon, with the buildings so white and the ocean so blue that they could knock your eyes out and send them rolling down your cheeks like marbles, he had heard his record on the radio for the first time. Three or four friends were there, including his current girl, and they were moderately done up on cocaine. Larry was coming out of the kitchenette and into the living room with a bag of Toll House cookies when the familiar KLMT slogan – *Nyoooooo . . . meee-USIC!* – came on. And then Larry had been transfixed by the sound of his own voice coming out of the Technics speakers:

> I know I didn't say I was comin down,
> I know you didn't know I was here in town,
> But bay-yay-yaby you can tell me if anyone can,
> Baby, can you dig your man?
> He's a righteous man,
> Tell me baby, can you dig your man?

'Jesus, that's me,' he had said. He dropped the cookies onto the floor and then stood gape-mouthed and stone-flabbergasted as his friends applauded.

Four weeks ago his tune had jumped to seventy-three on the *Billboard* chart. He began to feel as if he had been pushed rudely into an old-time silent movie where everything was moving too fast. The phone rang off the hook. Columbia was screaming for the album, wanting to capitalize on the single's success. Some crazy rat's ass of an A & R man called three times in one day, telling him he *had* to get in to Record One, not now but *yesterday*, and record a remake of the McCoys' 'Hang On, Sloopy' as the follow-up. Monster! this moron kept shouting. Only follow-up that's possible, Lar! (He had never met this guy and already he wasn't even Larry but Lar.) It'll be a monster! I mean a fucking *monster*!

Larry at last lost his patience and told the monster-shouter that, given a choice between recording 'Hang On, Sloopy' and being tied down and receiving a Coca-Cola enema, he would pick the enema. Then he hung up.

The train kept rolling just the same. Assurances that this could be the biggest record in five years poured into his dazed ears. Agents called by the dozen. They all sounded hungry. He began to take uppers, and it seemed to him that he heard his song everywhere.

One Saturday morning he heard it on 'Soul Train' and spent the rest of the day trying to make himself believe that, yes, that had actually happened.

It became suddenly hard to separate himself from Julie, the girl he had been dating since his gig at Gino's. She introduced him to all sorts of people, few of them people he really wanted to see. Her voice began to remind him of the prospective agents he heard over the telephone. In a long, loud, acrimonious argument, he split with her. She had screamed at him that his head would soon be too big to fit through a recording studio door, that he owed her five hundred dollars for dope, that he was the 1990s' answer to Zagar and Evans. She had threatened to kill herself. Afterward Larry felt as if he had been through a long pillow-fight in which all the pillows had been treated with a low-grade poison gas.

They had begun cutting the album three weeks ago, and Larry had withstood most of the 'for your own good' suggestions. He used what leeway the contract gave him. He got three of the Tattered Remnants — Barry Grieg, Al Spellman, and Johnny McCall — and two other musicians he had worked with in the past, Neil Goodman and Wayne Stukey. They cut the album in nine days, absolutely all the studio time they could get. Columbia seemed to want an album based on what they thought would be a twenty-week career, beginning with 'Baby, Can You Dig Your Man?' and ending with 'Hang On, Sloopy.' Larry wanted more.

The album cover was a photo of Larry in an old-fashioned clawfoot tub full of suds. Written on the tiles above him in a Columbia secretary's lipstick were the words POCKET SAVIOR and LARRY UNDERWOOD. Columbia had wanted to call the album *Baby, Can You Dig Your Man?* but Larry absolutely balked, and they had finally settled for a CONTAINS THE HIT SINGLE sticker on the shrink-wrap.

Two weeks ago the single hit number forty-seven, and the party had started. He had rented a Malibu beachhouse for a month, and after that things got a little hazy. People wandered in and out, always more of them. He knew some, but mostly they were strangers. He could remember being huckstered by even more agents who wanted to 'further his great career.' He could remember a girl who had bumtripped and gone screaming down the bone-white beach as naked as a nuthatch. He could remember being shaken awake on Saturday morning, it must have been a week or so ago, to hear Kasey

Kasem spin his record as a debut song at number thirty-six on 'American Top Forty'. He could remember taking a great many reds and, vaguely, dickering for the Datsun Z with a four-thousand-dollar royalty check that had come in the mail.

And then it was June 13, six days ago, the day Wayne Stukey asked Larry to go for a walk with him down the beach. It had only been nine in the morning but the stereo was on, both TVs, and it sounded like an orgy was going on in the basement playroom. Larry had been sitting in an overstuffed living room chair, wearing only underpants, and trying owlishly to get the sense from a *Superboy* comic book. He felt very alert, but none of the words seemed to connect to anything. There was no gestalt. A Wagner piece was thundering from the quad speakers, and Wayne had to shout three or four times to make himself understood. Then Larry nodded. He felt as if he could walk for miles.

But when the sunlight struck Larry's eyeballs like needles, he suddenly changed his mind. No walk. Uh-uh. His eyes had been turned into magnifying glasses, and soon the sun would shine through them long enough to set his brains on fire. His poor old brains felt tinder-dry.

Wayne, gripping his arm firmly, insisted. They went down to the beach, over the warming sand to the darker brown hardpack, and Larry decided it had been a pretty good idea after all. The deepening sound of the breakers coming home was soothing. A gull, working to gain altitude, hung straining in the blue sky like a sketched white letter M.

Wayne tugged his arm firmly. 'Come on.'

Larry got all the miles he had felt he could walk. Except that he no longer felt that way. He had an ugly headache and his spine felt as if it had turned to glass. His eyeballs were pulsing and his kidneys ached dully. An amphetamine hangover is not as painful as the morning after the night you got through a whole fifth of Four Roses, but it is not as pleasant as, say, balling Raquel Welch would be. If he had another couple of uppers, he could climb neatly on top of this eight-ball that wanted to run him down. He reached in his pocket to get them and for the first time became aware that he was clad only in skivvies that had been fresh three days ago.

'Wayne, I wanna go back.'

'Let's walk a little more.' He thought that Wayne was looking at him strangely, with a mixture of exasperation and pity.

'No, man, I only got my shorts on. I'll get picked up for indecent exposure.'

'On this part of the coast you could wrap a bandanna around your wingwang and let your balls hang free and still not get picked up for indecent exposure. Come on, man.'

'I'm tired,' Larry said querulously. He began to feel pissed at Wayne. This was Wayne's way of getting back at him, because Larry had a hit and he, Wayne, only had a keyboard credit on the new album. He was no different than Julie. Everybody hated him now. Everyone had the knife out. His eyes blurred with easy tears.

'Come on, man,' Wayne repeated, and they struck off up the beach again.

They had walked perhaps another mile when double cramps struck the big muscles in Larry's thighs. He screamed and collapsed onto the sand. It felt as if twin stilettos had been planted in his flesh at the same instant.

'Cramps!' he screamed. 'Oh man, cramps!'

Wayne squatted beside him and pulled his legs out straight. The agony hit again, and then Wayne went to work, hitting the knotted muscles, kneading them. At last the oxygen-starved tissues began to loosen.

Larry, who had been holding his breath, began to gasp. 'Oh man,' he said. 'Thanks. That was . . . that was bad.'

'Sure,' Wayne said, without much sympathy. 'I bet it was, Larry. How are you now?'

'Okay. But let's just sit, huh? Then we'll go back.'

'I want to talk to you. I had to get you out here and I wanted you straight enough so you could understand what I was laying on you.'

'What's that, Wayne?' He thought: Here it comes. The pitch. But what Wayne said seemed so far from a pitch that for a moment he was back with the *Superboy* comic, trying to make sense of a six-word sentence.

'The party's got to end, Larry.'

'Huh?'

'The party. When you go back. You pull all the plugs, give everybody their car keys, thank everyone for a lovely time, and see them out the front door. Get rid of them.'

'I can't do that!' Larry said, shocked.

'You better,' Wayne said.

'But why? Man, this party's just getting going!'

'Larry, how much has Columbia paid you up front?'

'Why would you want to know?' Larry asked slyly.

'Do you think I want to suck off you, Larry? Think.'

Larry thought, and with dawning bewilderment he realized there was no reason why Wayne Stukey would want to put the arm on him. He hadn't really made it yet, was scuffling for jobs like most of the people who had helped Larry cut the album, but unlike most of them, Wayne came from a family with money and he was on good terms with his people. Wayne's father owned half of the country's third-largest electronic games company, and the Stukeys had a modestly palatial home in Bel Air. Bewildered, Larry realized that his own sudden good fortune probably looked like small bananas to Wayne.

'No, I guess not,' he said gruffly. 'I'm sorry. But it seems like every tinhorn cockroach-chaser west of Las Vegas —'

'So how much?'

Larry thought it over. 'Seven grand up front. All told.'

'They're paying you quarterly royalties on the single and biannually on the album?'

'Right.'

Wayne nodded. 'They hold it until the eagle screams, the bastards. Cigarette?'

Larry took one and cupped the end for a light.

'Do you know how much this party's costing you?'

'Sure,' Larry said.

'You didn't rent the house for less than a thousand.'

'Yeah, that's right.' It had actually been $1,200 plus a $500 damage deposit. He had paid the deposit and half the month's rent, a total of $1,100 with $600 owing.

'How much for dope?' Wayne asked.

'Aw, man, you got to have something. It's like cheese for Ritz crackers —'

'There was pot and there was coke. How much, come on?'

'The fucking DA,' Larry said sulkily. 'Five hundred and five hundred.'

'And it was gone the second day.'

'The hell it was!' Larry said, startled. 'I saw two bowls when we went out this morning, man. Most of it was gone, yeah, but —'

'Man, don't you remember the Deck?' Wayne's voice suddenly

dropped into an amazingly good parody of Larry's own drawling voice. 'Just put it on my tab, Dewey. Keep em full.'

Larry looked at Wayne with dawning horror. He *did* remember a small, wiry guy with a peculiar haircut, a whiffle cut they had called it ten or fifteen years ago, a small guy with a whiffle haircut and a T-shirt reading JESUS IS COMING & IS HE PISSED. This guy seemed to have good dope practically falling out of his asshole. He could even remember telling this guy, Dewey the Deck, to keep his hospitality bowls full and put it on his tab. But that had been . . . well, that had been *days* ago.

Wayne said, 'You're the best thing to happen to Dewey Deck in a long time, man.'

'How much is he into me for?'

'Not bad on pot. Pot's cheap. Twelve hundred. Eight grand on coke.'

For a minute Larry thought he was going to puke. He goggled silently at Wayne. He tried to speak and he could only mouth: *Ninety-two hundred?*

'Inflation, man,' Wayne said. 'You want the rest?'

Larry didn't want the rest, but he nodded.

'There was a color TV upstairs. Someone ran a chair through it. I'd guess three hundred for repairs. The wood paneling downstairs had been gouged to hell. Four hundred. With luck. The picture window facing the beach got broken the day before yesterday. Three hundred. The shag rug in the living room is totally kaput – cigarette burns, beer, whiskey. Four hundred. I called the liquor store and they're just as happy with their tab as the Deck is with his. Six hundred.'

'Six hundred for booze?' Larry whispered. Blue horror had encased him up to the neck.

'Be thankful most of them have been scoffing beer and wine. You've got a four-hundred-dollar tab down at the market, mostly for pizza, chips, tacos, all that good shit. But the worst is the noise. Pretty soon the cops are going to land. *Les flics.* Disturbing the peace. And you've got four or five heavies doing up on heroin. There's three or four ounces of Mexican brown in the place.'

'Is that on my tab, too?' Larry asked hoarsely.

'No. The Deck doesn't mess with heroin. That's an Organization item and the Deck doesn't like the idea of cement cowboy boots. But if the cops land, you can bet the *bust* will go on your tab.'

'But I didn't know —'

'Just a babe in the woods, yeah.'

'But —'

'Your total tab for this little shindy so far comes to over twelve thousand dollars,' Wayne said. 'You went out and picked that Z off the lot . . . how much did you put down?'

'Twenty-five,' Larry said numbly. He felt like crying.

'So what have you got until the next royalty check? Couple thousand?'

'That's about right,' Larry said, unable to tell Wayne he had less than that: about eight hundred, split evenly between cash and checking.

'Larry, you listen to me because you're not worth telling twice. There's always a party waiting to happen. Out here the only two constants are the constant bullshitting and the constant party. They come running like dickey birds looking for bugs on a hippo's back. Now they're here. Pick them off your carcass and send them on their way.'

Larry thought of the dozens of people in the house. He knew maybe one person in three at this point. The thought of telling all those unknown people to leave made his throat want to close up. He would lose their good opinion. Opposing this thought came an image of Dewey Deck refilling the hospitality bowls, taking a notebook from his back pocket, and writing it all down at the bottom of his tab. Him and his whiffle haircut and his trendy T-shirt.

Wayne watched him calmly as he squirmed between those two pictures.

'Man, I'm gonna look like the asshole of the world,' Larry said finally, hating the weak and petulant words as they fell from his mouth.

'Yeah, they'll call you a lot of names. They'll say you're going Hollywood. Getting a big head. Forgetting your old friends. Except none of them are your friends, Larry. Your friends saw what was happening three days ago and split the scene. It's no fun to watch a friend who's, like, pissed his pants and doesn't even know it.'

'So why tell me?' Larry asked, suddenly angry. The anger was prodded out of him by the realization that all his really good friends had taken off, and in retrospect all their excuses seemed lame. Barry Grieg had taken him aside, had tried to talk to him, but Larry had been really flying, and he had just nodded and smiled indulgently at

Barry. Now he wondered if Barry had been trying to lay this same rap on him. It made him embarrassed and angry to think so.

'Why tell me?' he repeated. 'I get the feeling you don't like me so very goddam much.'

'No . . . but I really don't dislike you, either. Beyond that, man, I couldn't say. I could have let you get your nose punched on this. Once would have been enough for you.'

'What do you mean?'

'You'll tell them. Because there's a hard streak in you. There's something in you that's like biting on tinfoil. Whatever it takes to make success, you've got it. You'll have a nice little career. Middle-of-the-road pop no one will remember in five years. The junior high boppers will collect your records. You'll make money.'

Larry balled his fists on his legs. He wanted to punch that calm face. Wayne was saying things that made him feel like a small pile of dogshit beside a stop sign.

'Go on back and pull the plug,' Wayne said softly. 'Then you get in that car and go. Just go, man. Stay away until you know that next royalty check is waiting for you.'

'But Dewey –'

'I'll find a man to talk to Dewey. My pleasure, man. The guy will tell Dewey to wait for his money like a good little boy, and Dewey will be happy to oblige.' He paused, watching two small children in bright bathing suits run up the beach. A dog ran beside them, rowfing loudly and cheerily at the blue sky.

Larry stood up and forced himself to say thanks. The sea breeze slipped in and out of his aging shorts. The word came out of his mouth like a brick.

'You just go away somewhere and get your shit together,' Wayne said, standing up beside him, still watching the children. 'You've got a lot of shit to get together. What kind of manager you want, what kind of tour you want, what kind of contract you want after *Pocket Savior* hits. I think it will; it's got that neat little beat. If you give yourself some room, you'll figure it all out. Guys like you always do.'

Guys like you always do.

Guys like me always do.

Guys like –

Somebody was tapping a finger on the window.

Larry jerked, then sat up. A bolt of pain went through his neck and he winced at the dead, cramped feel of the flesh there. He had been asleep, not just dozing. Reliving California. But here and now it was gray New York daylight, and the finger tapped again.

He turned his head cautiously and painfully and saw his mother, wearing a black net scarf over her hair, peering in.

For a moment they just stared at each other through the glass and Larry felt curiously naked, like an animal being looked at in the zoo. Then his mouth took over, smiling, and he cranked the window down.

'Mom?'

'I knew it was you,' she said in a queerly flat tone. 'Come on out of there and let me see what you look like standing up.'

Both legs had gone to sleep; pins and needles tingled up from the balls of his feet as he opened the door and got out. He had never expected to meet her this way, unprepared and exposed. He felt like a sentry who had fallen asleep at his post suddenly called to attention. He had somehow expected his mother to look smaller, less sure of herself, a trick of the years that had matured him and left her just the same.

But it was almost uncanny, the way she had caught him. When he was ten, she used to wake him up on Saturday mornings after she thought he had slept long enough by tapping one finger on his closed bedroom door. She had wakened him this same way fourteen years later, sleeping in his new car like a tired kid who had tried to stay up all night and got caught by the sandman in an undignified position.

Now he stood before her, his hair corkscrewed, a faint and rather foolish grin on his face. Pins and needles still coursed up his legs, making him shift from foot to foot. He remembered that she always asked him if he had to go to the bathroom when he did that and now he stopped the movement and let the needles prick him at will.

'Hi, Mom,' he said.

She looked at him without saying anything, and a dread suddenly roosted in his heart like an evil bird coming back to an old nest. It was a fear that she might turn away from him, deny him, show him the back of her cheap coat, and simply go off to the subway around the corner, leaving him.

Then she sighed, the way a man will sigh before picking up a heavy bundle. And when she spoke, her voice was so natural and so mildly – rightly – pleased that he forgot his first impression.

'Hi, Larry,' she said. 'Come on upstairs. I knew it was you when I looked out the window. I already called in sick at my building. I got sick time coming.'

She turned to lead him back up the steps, between the vanished stone dogs. He came three steps behind her, catching up, wincing at the pins and needles. 'Mom?'

She turned back to him and he hugged her. For a moment an expression of fright crossed her features, as if she expected to be mugged rather than hugged. Then it passed and she accepted his embrace and gave back her own. The smell of her sachet slipped up his nose, evoking unexpected nostalgia, fierce, sweet, and bitter. For a moment he thought he was going to cry, and was smugly sure that she would; it was A Touching Moment. Over her sloped right shoulder he could see the dead cat, lying half in and half out of the garbage can. When she pulled away, her eyes were dry.

'Come on, I'll make you some breakfast. Have you been driving all night?'

'Yes,' he said, his voice slightly hoarse with emotion.

'Well, come on. Elevator's broken, but it's only two floors. It's worse for Mrs Halsey with her arthritis. She's on five. Don't forget to wipe your feet. If you track in, Mr Freeman will be on me like a shot. I swear Goshen he can smell dirt. Dirt's his enemy, all right.' They were on the stairs now. 'Can you eat three eggs? I'll make toast, too, if you don't mind pumpernickel. Come on.'

He followed her past the vanished stone dogs and looked a little wildly at where they had been, just to reassure himself that they were really gone, that he had not shrunk two feet, that the whole decade of the 1980s had not vanished back into time. She pushed the doors open and they went in. Even the dark brown shadows and the smells of cooking were the same.

Alice Underwood fixed him three eggs, bacon, toast, juice, coffee. When he had finished all but the coffee, he lit a cigarette and pushed back from the table. She flashed the cigarette a disapproving look but said nothing. That restored some of his confidence – some, but not much. She had always been good at biding her time.

She dropped the iron spider skillet into the gray dishwater and it hissed a little. She hadn't changed much, Larry was thinking. A little older – she would be fifty-one now – a little grayer, but there was still plenty of black left in that sensibly netted head of hair. She was wearing a plain gray dress, probably the one she worked in. Her bosom was still the same large comber blooming out of the bodice of the dress – a little larger, if anything. Mom, tell me the truth, has your bosom gotten bigger? Is that the fundamental change?

He started to tap cigarette ashes into his coffee saucer; she jerked it away and replaced it with the ashtray she always kept in the cupboard. The saucer had been sloppy with coffee and it had seemed okay to tap in it. The ashtray was clean, reproachfully spotless, and he tapped into it with a slight pang. She could bide her time and she could keep springing small traps on you until your ankles were all bloody and you were ready to start gibbering.

'So you came back,' Alice said, taking a used Brill from a Table Talk pie dish and putting it to work on the skillet. 'What brought you?'

Well, Ma, this friend of mine clued me in to the facts of life – the assholes travel in packs and this time they were after me. I don't know if friend is the right word for him. He respects me musically about as much as I respect The 1910 Fruitgum Company. But he got me to put on my traveling shoes and wasn't it Robert Frost who said home is a place that when you go there they have to take you in?

Aloud he said, 'I guess I got to missing you, Mom.'

She snorted. 'That's why you wrote me often?'

'I'm not much of a letter-writer.' He pumped his cigarette slowly up and down. Smoke rings formed from the tip and drifted off.

'You can say that again.'

Smiling, he said: 'I'm not much of a letter-writer.'

'But you're still smart to your mother. That hasn't changed.'

'I'm sorry,' he said. 'How have you been, Mom?'

She put the skillet in the drainer, pulled the sink stopper, and wiped the lace of soapsuds from her reddened hands. 'Not so bad,' she said, coming over to the table and sitting down. 'My back pains me some, but I got my pills. I make out all right.'

'You haven't thrown it out of whack since I left?'

'Oh, once. But Dr Holmes took care of it.'

'Mom, those chiropractors are –' *just frauds*. He bit his tongue.

'Are what?'

He shrugged uncomfortably in the face of her hooked smile. 'You're free, white, and twenty-one. If he helps you, fine.'

She sighed and took a roll of wintergreen Life Savers from her dress pocket. 'I'm a lot more than twenty-one. And I feel it. Want one?' He shook his head at the Life Saver she had thumbed up. She popped it into her own mouth instead.

'You're just a girl yet,' he said with a touch of his old bantering flattery. She had always liked it, but now it brought only a ghost of a smile to her lips. 'Any new men in your life?'

'Several,' she said. 'How bout you?'

'No,' he said seriously. 'No new men. Some girls, but no new men.'

He had hoped for laughter, but got only the ghost smile again. I'm troubling her, he thought. That's what it is. She doesn't know what I want here. She hasn't been waiting for three years for me to show up after all. She only wanted me to stay lost.

'Same old Larry,' she said. 'Never serious. You're not engaged? Seeing anyone steadily?'

'I play the field, Mom.'

'You always did. At least you never came home to tell me you'd got some nice Catholic girl in a family way. I'll give you that. You were either very careful, very lucky, or very polite.'

He strove to keep a poker face. It was the first time in his life that she had ever mentioned sex to him, directly or obliquely.

'Anyway, you're gonna learn,' Alice said. 'They say bachelors have all the fun. Not so. You just get old and full of sand, nasty, the way that Mr Freeman is. He's got that sidewalk-level apartment and he's always standing there in the window, hoping for a strong breeze.'

Larry grunted.

'I hear that song you got on the radio. I tell people, that's my son. That's Larry. Most of them don't believe it.'

'You've heard it?' He wondered why she hadn't mentioned that first, instead of going into all this piddling shit.

'Sure, all the time on that rock and roll station the young girls listen to. WROK.'

'Do you like it?'

'As well as I like any of that music.' She looked at him firmly. 'I think some of it sounds suggestive. Lewd.'

He found himself shuffling his feet and forced himself to stop. 'It's just supposed to sound . . . passionate, Mom. That's all.' His face suffused with blood. He had never expected to be sitting in his mother's kitchen, discussing passion.

'The place for passion's the bedroom,' she said curtly, closing off any aesthetic discussion of his hit record. 'Also, you did something to your voice. You sound like a nigger.'

'Now?' he asked, amused.

'No, on the radio.'

'That brown soun, she sho do get aroun,' Larry said, deepening his voice to Bill Withers level and smiling.

'Just like that,' she nodded. 'When I was a girl, we thought Frank Sinatra was daring. Now they have this *rap*. Rap, they call it. *Screaming*, I call it.' She looked at him grudgingly. 'At least there's no screaming on your record.'

'I get a royalty,' he said. 'A certain percent of every record sold. It breaks down to –'

'Oh, go on,' she said, and made a shooing gesture with her hand. 'I flunked all my maths. Have they paid you yet, or did you get that little car on credit?'

'They haven't paid me much,' he said, skating up to the edge of the lie but not quite over it. 'I made a down payment on the car. I'm financing the rest.'

'Easy credit terms,' she said balefully. 'That's how your father ended up bankrupt. The doctor said he died of a heart attack, but it wasn't that. It was a *broken* heart. Your dad went to his grave on easy credit terms.'

This was an old rap, and Larry just let it flow over him, nodding at the right places. His father had owned a haberdashery. A Robert Hall had opened not far away, and a year later his business had failed. He had turned to food for solace, putting on 110 pounds in three years. He had dropped dead in the corner luncheonette when Larry was nine, a half-finished meatball sandwich on his plate in front of him. At the wake, when her sister tried to comfort a woman who looked absolutely without need of comfort, Alice Underwood said it could have been worse. It could, she said, looking past her sister's shoulder and directly at her brother-in-law, have been drink.

Alice brought Larry the rest of the way up on her own, dominating his life with her proverbs and prejudices until he left home. Her last remark to him as he and Rudy Schwartz drove off in Rudy's old Ford was that they had poorhouses in California, too. Yessir, that's my mamma.

'Do you want to stay here, Larry?' she asked softly.

Startled, he countered, 'Do you mind?'

'There's room. The rollaway's still in the back bedroom. I've been storing things back there, but you could move some of the boxes around.'

'All right,' he said slowly. 'If you're sure you don't mind. I'm only in for a couple of weeks. I thought I'd look up some of the old guys. Mark . . . Galen . . . David . . . Chris . . . those guys.'

She got up, went to the window, and tugged it up.

'You're welcome to stay as long as you like, Larry. I'm not so good at expressing myself, maybe, but I'm glad to see you. We didn't say goodbye very well. There were harsh words.' She showed him her face, still harsh, but also full of a terrible, reluctant love. 'For my part, I regret them. I only said them because I love you. I never knew how to say that just right, so I said it in other ways.'

'That's all right,' he said, looking down at the table. The flush was back. He could feel it. 'Listen, I'll chip in for stuff.'

'You can if you want. If you don't want to, you don't have to. I'm working. Thousands aren't. You're still my son.'

He thought of the stiffening cat, half in and half out of the trashcan, and of Dewey the Deck, smilingly filling the hospitality bowls, and he suddenly burst into tears. As his hands blurred double in the wash of them, he thought that this should be her bit, not his – nothing had gone the way he thought it would, nothing. She had changed after all. So had he, but not as he had suspected. An unnatural reversal had occurred; she had gotten bigger and he had somehow gotten smaller. He had not come home to her because he had to go somewhere. He had come home because he was afraid and he wanted his mother.

She stood by the open window, watching him. The white curtains fluttered in on the damp breeze, obscuring her face, not hiding it entirely but making it seem ghostly. Traffic sounds came in through the window. She took the handkerchief from the bodice of her dress and walked over to the table and put it in one of his groping hands. There was something hard in Larry. She could have taxed him with it, but to what end? His father had been a softie, and in her heart of hearts she knew it was that which had really sent him to the grave; Max Underwood had been done in more by lending credit than taking it. So when it came to that hard streak? Who did Larry have to thank? Or blame?

His tears couldn't change that stony outcropping in his character any more than a single summer cloudburst can change the shape of rock. There were good uses for such hardness – she knew that, had known it as a woman raising a boy on her own in a city that cared little for mothers and less for their children – but Larry hadn't found any yet. He was just what she had said he was: the same old Larry. He would go along, not thinking, getting people – including himself – into jams, and when the jams got bad enough, he would call upon that hard streak to extricate himself. As for the others? He would leave them to sink or swim on their own. Rock was tough, and there was toughness in his character, but he still used it destructively. She could see it in his eyes, read it in every line of his posture . . . even in the way he bobbed his cancer-stick to make those little rings in the air. He had never sharpened that hard piece of him into a blade to cut people with, and that was something, but when he needed it, he was still calling on it as a child did – as a bludgeon to beat his way out of traps he had dug for himself. Once, she had told herself Larry would change. *She* had; he *would*.

But this was no boy in front of her; this was a grown-up man, and she feared that his days of change – the deep and fundamental sort her minister called a change of soul rather than one of heart – were behind him. There was something in Larry that gave you the bitter zing of hearing chalk screech on a blackboard. Deep inside, looking out, was only Larry. He was the only one allowed inside his heart. But she loved him.

She also thought there was good in Larry, great good. It was there, but this late on it would take nothing short of a catastrophe to bring it out. There was no catastrophe here; only her weeping son.

'You're tired,' she said. 'Clean up. I'll move the boxes, then you can sleep. I guess I'll go in today after all.'

She went down the short hall to the back room, his old bedroom, and Larry heard her grunting and moving boxes. He wiped his eyes slowly. The sound of traffic came in the window. He tried to remember the last time he had cried in front of his mother. He thought of the dead cat. She was right. He was tired. He had never been so tired. He went to bed and slept for nearly eighteen hours.

CHAPTER 6

It was late afternoon when Frannie went out back to where her father was patiently weeding the peas and beans. She had been a late child and he was in his sixties now, his white hair coming out from under the baseball cap he always wore. Her mother was in Portland, shopping for white gloves. Fran's best childhood friend, Amy Lauder, was getting married early next month.

She looked down at her dad's back for a peaceful moment, just loving him. At this time of day the light took on a special quality that she loved, a timeless quality that belonged only to that most fleeting Maine genus, early summer. She could think of that particular tone of light in the middle of January and it would make her heart ache fiercely. The light of an early summer afternoon as it slipped toward dark had so many good things wrapped up in it: baseball at the Little League park, where Fred had always played third and batted clean-up; watermelon; first corn; iced tea in chilled glasses; childhood.

Frannie cleared her throat a little. 'Need a hand?'

He turned and grinned. 'Hello, Fran. Caught me diggin, didn't you?'

'I guess I did.'

'Is your mother back yet?' He frowned vaguely, and then his face cleared. 'No, that's right, she just went, didn't she. Sure, pitch a hand if you want to. Just don't forget to wash up afterward.'

'A lady's hands proclaim her habits,' Fran mocked lightly and snorted. Peter tried to look disapproving and did a poor job of it.

She got down in the row next to him and began to weed. Sparrows were twittering and there was a constant hum of traffic on US 1, less than a block from here. It hadn't reached the volume it would in July, when there would be a fatal accident nearly every day between here and Kittery, but it was building.

Peter told her about his day and she responded with the right questions, nodding in places. Intent on his work, he wouldn't see her nods, but the corner of his eye would catch her *shadow* nodding. He was a machinist in a large Sanford auto parts firm, the largest auto firm north of Boston. He was sixty-four and about to start on his last year of work before retirement. A short year at that, because he had four weeks' vacation time stockpiled, which he planned to take in September, after the 'ijits' went home. The retirement was much on his mind. He was trying not to look at it as a never-ending vacation, he told her; he had enough friends in retirement now who had brought back the news that it wasn't like *that* at all. He didn't think he would be as bored as Harlan Enders or as shamefully poor as the Carons – there was poor Paul, hardly ever missed a day at the shop in his life, and yet he and his wife had been forced to sell their house and move in with their daughter and her husband.

Peter Goldsmith hadn't been content with Social Security; he had never trusted it, even in the days before the system began to break down under recession, inflation, and the steadily increasing number of people on the books. There hadn't been many Democrats in Maine during the thirties and forties, he told his listening daughter, but her grandfather had been one, and her grandfather had by-God made one out of her father. In Ogunquit's palmiest days, that had made the Goldsmiths pariahs of a kind. But his father had had one saying as rock-ribbed as the stoniest Maine Republican's philosophy: Put not your trust in the princes of this world, for they will frig thee up and so shalt their governments, even unto the end of the earth.

Frannie laughed. She loved it when her dad talked this way. It wasn't a way he talked often, because the woman that was his wife and her mother would (and had) all but cut the tongue out of his head with the acid which could flow so quickly and freely from her own.

You had to trust yourself, he continued, and let the princes of this world get along as best they could with the people who had elected them. Most times that wasn't very well, but that was okay; they deserved each other.

'Hard cash is the answer,' he told Frannie. 'Will Rogers said it was land, because that's the only thing they're not making any more of, but the same goes for gold and silver. A man who loves money is a bastard, someone to be hated. A man who can't take care of it is a fool. You don't hate him, but you got to pity him.'

Fran wondered if he was thinking of poor Paul Caron, who

had been his friend since before Fran herself was born, and decided not to ask.

At any rate, she didn't need him to tell her that he had socked away enough in the good years to keep them rolling. What he did tell her was that she had never been a burden to them, in good times or in bad, and he was proud to tell his friends he had sent her through school. What his money and her brains hadn't been able to take care of, he told them, she had done the old-fashioned way: by bending her back and shucking her buns. Working, and working hard, if you wanted to cut through the country bullshit. Her mother didn't always understand that. Changes had come for women, whether the women always liked them or not, and it was hard for Carla to get it through her head that Fran wasn't down there at UNH husband-hunting.

'She sees Amy Lauder getting married,' Peter said, 'and she thinks, "That should be my Fran. Amy's pretty, but when you put my Fran beside her, Amy Lauder looks like an old dish with a crack in it." Your mother has been using the old yardsticks all her life, and she can't change now. So if you n her scrape together a bit and make some sparks from time to time, like steel against flint, that's why. No one is to blame. But you have to remember, Fran, she's too old to change, but you are getting old enough to understand that.'

From this he rambled back to his job again, telling her about how one of his co-workers had almost lost his thumb in a small press because his mind was down at the pool-hall while his damn thumb was under the stamp. Good thing Lester Crowley had pulled him away in time. But, he added, someday Lester Crowley wouldn't be there. He sighed, as if remembering he wouldn't be either, then brightened and began telling her about an idea he'd had for a car antenna concealed in the hood ornament.

His voice switched from topic to topic, mellow and soothing. Their shadows grew longer, moving up the rows before them. She was lulled by it, as she always had been. She had come here to tell something, but since earliest childhood she had often come to tell and stayed to listen. He didn't bore her. So far as she knew, he didn't bore anyone, except possibly her mother. He was a story-teller, and a good one.

She became aware that he had stopped talking. He was sitting on a rock at the end of his row, tamping his pipe and looking at her.

'What's on your mind, Frannie?'

She looked at him dumbly for a moment, not sure how she should proceed. She had come out here to tell him, and now she wasn't sure if she could. The silence hung between them, growing larger, and at last it was a gulf she couldn't stand. She jumped.

'I'm pregnant,' she said simply.

He stopped filling his pipe and just looked at her. 'Pregnant,' he said, as if he had never heard the word before. Then he said: 'Oh, Frannie . . . is it a joke? Or a game?'

'No, Daddy.'

'You better come over here and sit with me.'

Obediently, she came up the row and sat next to him. There was a rock wall that divided their land from the town common next door. Beyond the rock wall was a tangled, sweet-smelling hedge that had long ago run wild in the most amiable way. Her head was pounding and she felt a little sick to her stomach.

'For sure?' he asked her.

'For sure,' she said, and then – there was no artifice in it, not a trace, she simply couldn't help it – she began to cry in great, braying sobs. He held her with one arm for what seemed to be a very long time. When her tears began to taper off, she forced herself to ask the question that troubled her the most.

'Daddy, do you still like me?'

'What?' He looked at her, puzzled. 'Yes. I still like you fine, Frannie.'

That made her cry again, but this time he let her tend herself while he got his pipe going. Borkum Riff began to ride slowly off on the faint breeze.

'Are you disappointed?' she asked.

'I don't know. I never had a pregnant daughter before and am not sure just how I should take it. Was it that Jess?'

She nodded.

'You told him?'

She nodded again.

'What did he say?'

'He said he would marry me. Or pay for an abortion.'

'Marriage or abortion,' Peter Goldsmith said, and drew on his pipe. 'He's a regular two-gun Sam.'

She looked down at her hands, splayed on her jeans. There was dirt in the small creases of the knuckles and dirt under the nails. A lady's hands proclaim her habits, the mental mother spoke up. A pregnant daughter. I'll have to resign my membership in the church. A lady's hands —

Her father said: 'I don't want to get any more personal than I have to, but wasn't he . . . or you . . . being careful?'

'I had birth control pills,' she said. 'They didn't work.'

'Then I can't put any blame, unless it's on both of you,' he said, looking at her closely. 'And I can't do that, Frannie. I can't lay blame. Sixty-four has a way of forgetting what twenty-one was like. So we won't talk about blame.'

She felt a great relief come over her, and it was a little like swooning.

'Your mother will have plenty to say about blame,' he said, 'and I won't stop her, but I won't be with her. Do you understand that?'

She nodded. Her father never tried to oppose her mother anymore. Not out loud. There was that acid tongue of hers. When she was opposed, it sometimes got out of control, he had told Frannie once. And when it was out of control, she just might take a notion to cut anyone with it and think of sorry too late to do the wounded much good. Frannie had an idea that her father might have faced a choice many years ago: continued opposition resulting in divorce, or surrender. He had chosen the latter — but on his own terms.

She asked quietly: 'Are you sure you can stay out of this one, Daddy?'

'You asking me to take your part?'

'I don't know.'

'What are you going to do about it?'

'With Mom?'

'No. With you, Frannie.'

'I don't know.'

'Marry him? Two can live as cheap as one, that's what they say, anyway.'

'I don't think I can do that. I think I've fallen out of love with him, if I was ever in.'

'The baby?' His pipe was drawing well now, and the smoke was sweet on the summer air. Shadows were gathering in the garden's hollows, and the crickets were beginning to hum.

'No, the baby isn't the reason why. It was happening anyway. Jesse is . . .' She trailed off, trying to put her finger on what was wrong with Jesse, the thing that could be overlooked by the rush the baby was putting on her, the rush to decide and get out from under the threatening shadow of her mother, who was now at a shopping mall buying gloves for the wedding of Fran's childhood friend. The thing that could be buried now but would nonetheless rest unquiet for six months, sixteen months, or twenty-six, only to rise finally from its grave and attack them both. Marry in haste, repent in leisure. One of her mother's favorite sayings.

'He's weak,' she said. 'I can't explain better than that.'

'You don't really trust him to do right by you, do you, Frannie?'

'No,' she said, thinking that her father had just gotten closer to the root of it than she had. She didn't trust Jesse, who came from money and wore blue chambray workshirts. 'Jesse *means* well. He wants to do the right thing; he really does. But . . . we went to a poetry reading two semesters ago. It was given by a man named Ted Enslin. The place was packed. Everyone was listening very solemnly . . . very carefully . . . so as not to miss a word. And me . . . you know me . . .'

He put a comfortable arm around her and said, 'Frannie got the giggles.'

'Yeah. That's right. I guess you know me pretty well.'

'I know a little,' he said.

'They – the giggles, I mean – just came out of nowhere. I kept thinking, "The scruffy man, the scruffy man, we all came to listen to the scruffy man." It had a beat, like a song you might hear on the radio. And I got the giggles. I didn't mean to. It really didn't have anything to do with Mr Enslin's poetry, it was pretty good, or even with the way he looked. It was the way *they* were looking at *him*.'

She glanced at her father to see how he was taking this. He simply nodded for her to go on.

'Anyway, I had to get out of there. I mean I really *had* to. And Jesse was furious with me. I'm sure he had a right to be mad . . . it was a childish thing to do, a childish way to *feel*, I'm sure . . . but that's the way I often am. Not always. I can get a job done –'

'Yes, you can.'

'But sometimes –'

'Sometimes King Laugh knocks and you're one of those people who can't keep him out,' Peter said.

'I guess I must be. Anyway, Jess isn't one of those people. And if we were married . . . he'd keep coming home to that unwanted guest that I had let in. Not every day, but often enough to make him mad. Then I'd try, and . . . and I guess . . .'

'I guess you'd be unhappy,' Peter said, hugging her tighter against his side.

'I guess I would,' she said.

'Don't let your mother change your mind, then.'

She closed her eyes, her relief even greater this time. He had understood. By some miracle.

'What do you think of me getting an abortion?' she asked after a while.

'My guess is that's really what you wanted to talk about.'

She looked at him, startled.

He looked back, half-quizzical, half-smiling, one bushy eyebrow – the left – cocked. Yet the overall impression she took from him was one of great gravity.

'Maybe that's true,' she said slowly.

'Listen,' he said, and then fell paradoxically silent. But she *was* listening and she heard a sparrow, crickets, the far high hum of a plane, someone calling for Jackie to come on in now, a power mower, a car with a glasspack muffler accelerating down US 1.

She was just about to ask him if he was all right when he took her hand and spoke.

'Frannie, you've no business having such an old man for a father, but I can't help it. I never married until 1956.'

He looked at her thoughtfully in the dusklight.

'Carla was different in those days. She was . . . oh, hellfire, she was young herself, for one thing. She didn't change until your brother Freddy died. Until then, she was young. She stopped growing after Freddy died. That . . . you mustn't think I'm talking against your mother, Frannie, even if it sounds a little like I am. But it seems to me that Carla stopped . . . growing . . . after Freddy died. She slapped three coats of lacquer and one of quick-dry cement on her way of looking at things and called it good. Now she's like a guard in a museum, and if she sees anyone tampering with the ideas on display there, she gives them a lot of look-out-below. But she wasn't always like that. You'll just have to take my word for it, but she wasn't.'

'What was she like, Daddy?'

'Why . . .' He looked vaguely out across the garden. 'She was a lot like you, Frannie. She got the giggles. We used to go down to Boston to see the Red Sox play and during the seventh-inning stretch she'd go out with me to the concession and have a beer.'

'Mamma . . . drank beer?'

'Yes, she did. And she'd spend most of the ninth in the ladies' and come out cussing me for making her miss the best part of the game when all the time it was she tellin *me* to go on down to the concession stand and get em.'

Frannie tried to imagine her mother with a cup of Narragansett beer in one hand, looking up at her father and laughing, like a girl on a date. She simply couldn't do it.

'She never kindled,' he said, bemused. 'We went to a doctor, she and I, to see which of us was wrong. The doctor said neither one. Then, in '60, there came your brother Fred. She just about loved that boy to death, Fran. Fred was her father's name, you know. She had a miscarriage in '65, and we both figured that was the end of it. Then you came along in '69, a month early but just fine. And I just about loved you to death. We each had one of our own. But she lost hers.'

He fell silent, brooding. Fred Goldsmith had died in 1973. He had been thirteen, Frannie four. The man who hit Fred had been drunk. He had a long list of traffic violations, including speeding, driving so as to endanger, and driving under the influence. Fred had lived seven days.

'I think abortion's too clean a name for it,' Peter Goldsmith said. His lips moved slowly over each word, as if they pained him. 'I think it's infanticide, pure and simple. I'm sorry to say so, to *be* so . . . inflexible, set, whatever it is I'm being . . . about something which you now have to consider, if only because the law says you may consider it. I told you I was an old man.'

'You're not old, Daddy,' she murmured.

'I am, I am!' he said roughly. He looked suddenly distraught. 'I'm an old man trying to give a young daughter advice, and it's like a monkey trying to teach table manners to a bear. A drunk driver took my son's life seventeen years ago and my wife has never been the same since. I've always seen the question of abortion in terms of Fred. I seem to be helpless to see it any other way, just as helpless as you were to stop your giggles when they came on you at that poetry reading, Frannie. Your mother would argue against it for all the standard reasons. Morality, she'd say. A morality that goes back two thousand years. The right to life. All our Western morality is based on that idea. I've read the

philosophers. I range up and down them like a housewife with a divi-
dend check in the Sears and Roebuck store. Your mother sticks with
the *Reader's Digest*, but it's me that ends up arguing from feeling and
her from the codes of morality. I just see Fred. He was destroyed inside.
There was no chance for him. These right-to-life biddies hold up their
pictures of babies drowned in salt, and arms and legs scraped out onto
a steel table, so what? The end of a life is never pretty. I just see Fred,
lying in that bed for seven days, everything that was ruined pasted over
with bandages. Life is cheap, abortion makes it cheaper. I read more
than she does, but she is the one who ends up making more sense on
this one. What we do and what we think . . . those things are so often
based on arbitrary judgments when they are right. I can't get over that.
It's like a block in my throat, how all true logic seems to proceed from
irrationality. From faith. I'm not making much sense, am I?'

'I don't want an abortion,' she said quietly. 'For my own
reasons.'

'What are they?'

'The baby is partly me,' she said, lifting her chin slightly. 'If
that's ego, I don't care.'

'Will you give it up, Frannie?'

'I don't know.'

'Do you want to?'

'No. I want to keep it.'

He was silent. She thought she felt his disapproval.

'You're thinking of school, aren't you?' she asked.

'No,' he said, standing up. He put his hands in the small of his
back and grimaced pleasurably as his spine crackled. 'I was thinking
we've talked enough. And that you don't have to make that decision
just yet.'

'Mom's home,' she said.

He turned to follow her gaze as the station wagon turned into
the drive, the chrome winking in the day's last light. Carla saw them,
beeped the horn, and waved cheerily.

'I have to tell her,' Frannie said.

'Yes. But give it a day or two, Frannie.'

'All right.'

She helped him pick up the gardening tools and then they
walked up toward the station wagon together.

CHAPTER 7

In the dim light that comes over the land just after sunset but before true dark, during one of those very few minutes that moviemakers call 'the magic hour,' Vic Palfrey rose out of green delirium to brief lucidity.

I'm dying, he thought, and the words clanged strangely through his mind, making him believe he had spoken aloud, although he had not.

He gazed around himself and saw a hospital bed, now cranked up to keep his lungs from drowning in themselves. He had been tightly secured with brass laundry-pins, and the sides of the bed were up. *Been thrashing some, I guess*, he thought with faint amusement. *Been kicking up dickins.* And belatedly: *Where am I?*

There was a bib around his neck and the bib was covered with clots of phlegm. His head ached. Queer thoughts danced in and out of his mind and he knew he had been delirious . . . and would be again. He was sick and this was not a cure or the beginning of one, but only a brief respite.

He put the inside of his right wrist against his forehead and pulled it away with a wince, the way you pull your hand off a hot stove. Burning up, all right, and full of tubes. Two small clear plastic ones were coming out of his nose. Another one snaked out from under the hospital sheet to a bottle on the floor, and he surely knew where the other end of *that* one was connected. Two bottles hung suspended from a rack beside the bed, a tube coming from each one and then joining to make a Y that ended by going into his arm just below the elbow. An IV feed.

You'd think that would be enough, he thought. But there were wires on him as well. Attached to his scalp. And chest. And left arm. One seemed to be plastered into his sonofabitching belly-button. And to cap it all off, he was pretty sure something was jammed up his ass. What in God's name could that one be? Shit radar?

'Hey!'

He had intended a resonant, indignant shout. What he produced was the humble whisper of a very sick man. It came out surrounded on all sides by the phlegm on which he seemed to be choking.

Mamma, did George put the horse in?

That was the delirium talking. An irrational thought, zooming boldly across the field of more rational cogitation like a meteor. All the same, it almost fooled him for a second. He wasn't going to be up for long. The thought filled him with panic. Looking at the scrawny sticks of his arms, he guessed he had lost as much as thirty pounds, and there hadn't been all that much of him to start with. This . . . this whatever-it-was . . . was going to kill him. The idea that he might die babbling insanities and inanities like a senile old man terrified him.

Georgie's gone courting Norma Willis. You get that horse your ownself, Vic, and put his nosebag on like a good boy.

Ain't my job.

Victor, you love your mamma, now.

I do. But it ain't –

You got to love your mamma, now. Mamma's got the flu.

No you don't, Mamma. You got TB. It's the TB that's going to kill you. In nineteen and forty-seven. And George is going to die just about six days after he gets to Korea, time enough for just one letter and then bang bang bang. George is –

Vic, you help me now and put that horse in and that is my last word ON it.

'I'm the one with the flu, not her,' he whispered, surfacing again. 'It's *me*.'

He was looking at the door, and thinking it was a damn funny door even for a hospital. It was round at the corners, outlined with pop-rivets, and the lower jamb was set six inches or more up from the tile floor. Even a jackleg carpenter like Vic Palfrey could

(gimme the funnies Vic you had em long enough)

(Mamma he took my funnypages! Give em back! Give em baaaack!)

build better than that. It was

(steel)

Something in the thought drove a nail deep into his brain and Vic struggled to sit up so he could see the door better. Yes, it was. It definitely was. A steel door. Why was he in a hospital behind a steel door? What had happened? Was he really dying? Had he best be thinking of just how he was going to meet his God? God, what had *happened*? He tried desperately to pierce the hanging gray fog, but only voices came through, far away, voices he could put no names against.

Now what I say is this . . . they just got to say . . . 'fuck this inflation shit . . .'

Better turn off your pumps, Hap.

(Hap? Bill Hapscomb? Who was he? I know *that name)*

Holy moly . . .

They're dead, okay . . .

Gimme your hand and I'll pull you up outta there . . .

Gimme the funnies Vic you had —

At that moment the sun sank far enough below the horizon to cause a light-activated circuit (or in this case, an absence-of-light-activated circuit) to kick in. The lights went on in Vic's room. As the room lit up, he saw the row of faces observing him solemnly from behind two layers of glass and he screamed, at first thinking these were the people who had been holding conversations in his mind. One of the figures, a man in doctor's whites, was gesturing urgently to someone outside Vic's field of vision, but Vic was already over his scare. He was too weak to stay scared long. But the sudden fright that had come with the silent bloom of light and this vision of staring faces (like a jury of ghosts in their hospital whites) had cleared away some of the blockage in his mind and he knew where he was. Atlanta. Atlanta, Georgia. They had come and taken him away — him and Hap and Norm and Norm's wife and Norm's kids. They had taken Hank Carmichael. Stu Redman. God alone knew how many others. Vic had been scared and indignant. Sure, he had the snuffles and sneezes, but he surely wasn't coming down with cholera or whatever it was that poor man Campion and his family had had. He'd been running a low-grade fever, too, and he remembered that Norm Bruett had stumbled and needed help getting up the steps to the plane. His wife had been scared, crying, and little Bobby Bruett had been crying too — crying and coughing. A raspy, croupy cough. The plane had been at the small landing strip outside of Braintree, but to get beyond the Arnette town limits they had had to pass a roadblock on US 93, and men had been stringing bobwire . . . stringing bobwire right out into the desert . . .

A red light flashed on over the strange door. There was a hissing sound, then a sound like a pump running. When it kicked off, the door opened. The man who came in was dressed in a huge white pressure suit with a transparent faceplate. Behind the faceplate, the man's head bobbed like a balloon enclosed in a capsule. There were pressure tanks on his back, and when he spoke, his voice was metallic and clipped, devoid of all human quality. It might have been a voice coming from one of those video games, like the one that said 'Try again, Space Cadet' when you fucked up your last go.

It rasped: 'How are you feeling, Mr Palfrey?'

But Vic couldn't answer. Vic had gone back down into the green depths. It was his mamma he saw behind the faceplate of the white suit. Mamma had been dressed in white when Poppa took him and George to see her for the last time in the sanny-tarium. She had to go to the sanny-tarium so everybody else in the fambly wouldn't catch what she had. TB was catching. You could die.

He talked to his mamma . . . said he would be good and put in the horse . . . told her George had taken the funnies . . . asked her if she felt better . . . asked her if she thought she would be home soon . . . and the man in the white suit gave him a shot and he sank deeper and his words became incoherent. The man in the white suit glanced back at the faces behind the glass wall and shook his head.

He clicked an intercom switch inside his helmet with his chin and said, 'If this one doesn't work, we'll lose him by midnight.'

For Vic Palfrey, magic hour was over.

'Just roll up your sleeve, Mr Redman,' the pretty nurse with the dark hair said. 'This won't take a minute.' She was holding the blood pressure cuff in two gloved hands. Behind the plastic mask she was smiling as if they shared an amusing secret.

'No,' Stu said.

The smile faltered a little. 'It's only your blood pressure. It won't take a minute.'

'No.'

'Doctor's orders,' she said, becoming businesslike. 'Please.'

'If it's doctor's orders, let me talk to the doctor.'

'I'm afraid he's busy right now. If you'll just –'

'I'll wait,' Stu said equably, making no move to unbutton the cuff of his shirtsleeve.

'This is only my job. You don't want me to get in trouble, do you?' This time she gave him a charming-waif smile. 'If you'll only let me –'

'I won't,' Stu said. 'Go back and tell them. They'll send somebody.'

Looking troubled, the nurse went across to the steel door and turned a square key in a lockplate. The pump kicked on, the door shooshed open, and she stepped through. As it closed, she gave Stu a final reproachful look. Stu gazed back blandly.

When the door was closed, he got up and went restlessly to the window – double-paned glass and barred on the outside – but it was full dark now and there was nothing to see. He went back and sat down. He was wearing faded jeans and a checked shirt and his brown boots with the stitching beginning to bulge up the sides. He ran a hand up the side of his face and winced disapprovingly at the prickle. They wouldn't let him shave, and he haired up fast.

He had no objection to the tests themselves. What he objected to was being kept in the dark, kept scared. He wasn't sick, at least not yet, but scared plenty. There was some sort of snow job going on here, and he wasn't going to be a party to it anymore until somebody told him something about what had happened in Arnette and what that fellow Campion had to do with it. At least then he could base his fears on something solid.

They had expected him to ask before now, he could read it in their eyes. They had certain ways of keeping things from you in hospitals. Three years ago his wife had died of cancer at the age of twenty-seven, it had started in her womb and then just raced up through her like wildfire, and Stu had observed the way they got around her questions, either by changing the subject or giving her information in large, technical lumps. So he simply hadn't asked, and he could see it had worried them. Now it was time to ask, and he would get some answers. In words of one syllable.

He could fill in some of the blank spots on his own. Campion and his wife and child had something pretty bad. It hit you like the flu or a summer cold, only it kept on getting worse, presumably until you choked to death on your own snot or until the fever burned you down. It was highly contagious.

They had come and got him on the afternoon of the seventeenth, two days ago. Four army men and a doctor. Polite but firm. There was no question of declining; all four of the army men had been wearing sidearms. That was when Stu Redman started being seriously scared.

There had been a regular caravan going out of Arnette and over to the airstrip in Braintree. Stu had been riding with Vic Palfrey, Hap, the Bruetts, Hank Carmichael and his wife, and two army noncoms. They were all crammed into an army station wagon, and the army guys wouldn't say aye, nay, or maybe no matter how hysterical Lila Bruett got.

The other wagons were crammed, too. Stu hadn't seen all the people in them, but he had seen all five of the Hodges family, and Chris Ortega, brother of Carlos, the volunteer ambulance driver. Chris was the bartender down at the Indian Head. He had seen Parker Nason and his wife, the elderly people from the trailer park near Stu's house. Stu guessed that they had netted up everyone who had been in the gas station and everyone that the people from the gas station said they'd talked to since Campion crashed into the pumps.

At the town limits there had been two olive-green trucks blocking the road. Stu guessed the other roads going into Arnette were most likely blocked off, too. They were stringing barbed wire, and when they had the town fenced off they would probably post sentries.

So it was serious. Deadly serious.

He sat patiently in the chair by the hospital bed he hadn't had to use, waiting for the nurse to bring someone. The first someone would most likely be no one. Maybe by morning they would finally send in a someone who would have enough authority to tell him the things he needed to know. He could wait. Patience had always been Stuart Redman's strong suit.

For something to do, he began to tick over the conditions of the people who had ridden to the airstrip with him. Norm had been the only obvious sick one. Coughing, bringing up phlegm, feverish. The rest seemed to be suffering to a greater or lesser degree from the common cold. Luke Bruett was sneezing. Lila Bruett and Vic Palfrey had mild coughs. Hap had the sniffles and kept blowing his nose. They hadn't sounded much different from the first- and second-grade classes Stu remembered attending as a little boy, when at least two thirds of the kids present seemed to have some kind of a bug.

But the thing that scared him most of all – and maybe it was only coincidence – was what had happened just as they were turning onto the airstrip. The army driver had let out three sudden bellowing sneezes. Probably just coincidence. June was a bad time in east-central Texas for people with allergies. Or maybe the driver was just coming down with a common, garden-variety cold instead of the weird shit the rest of them had. Stu wanted to believe that. Because something that could jump from one person to another that quickly . . .

Their army escort had boarded the plane with them. They rode stolidly, refusing to answer any questions except as to their destination. They were going to Atlanta. They would be told more there (a bald-faced lie). Beyond that, the army men refused to say.

Hap had been sitting next to Stu on the flight, and he was pretty well sloshed. The plane was army too, strictly functional, but the booze and the food had been first-class airline stuff. Of course, instead of being served by a pretty stewardess, a plank-faced sergeant took your order, but if you could overlook that, you could get along pretty well. Even Lila Bruett had calmed down with a couple of grass-hoppers in her.

Hap leaned close, bathing Stu in a warm mist of Scotch fumes. 'This is a pretty funny bunch of ole boys, Stuart. Ain't one of em under fifty, nor one with a weddin ring. Career boys, low rank.'

About half an hour before they touched down, Norm Bruett had some kind of a fainting spell and Lila began to scream. Two of the hard-faced stewards bundled Norm into a blanket and brought him around in fairly short order. Lila, no longer calm, continued to scream. After a while she threw up her grasshoppers and the chicken salad sandwich she had eaten. Two of the good ole boys went expressionlessly about the job of cleaning it up.

'What is all this?' Lila screamed. 'What's wrong with my man? Are we going to die? Are my babies going to die?' She had one 'baby' in a headlock under each arm, their heads digging into her plentiful breasts. Luke and Bobby looked frightened and uncomfortable and rather embarrassed at the fuss she was making. 'Why won't somebody answer me? Isn't this America?'

'Can't somebody shut her up?' Chris Ortega had grumbled from the back of the plane. 'Christly woman's worse'n a jukebox with a broken record inside it.'

One of the army men had forced a glass of milk on her and Lila *did* shut up. She spent the rest of the ride looking out the window at the countryside passing far below and humming. Stu guessed there had been more than milk in that glass.

When they touched down, there had been four Cadillac limousines waiting for them. The Arnette folks got into three of them. Their army escort had gotten into the fourth. Stu guessed that those good old boys with no wedding rings – or close relatives, probably – were now somewhere right in this building.

The red light went on over his door. When the compressor

or pump or whatever it was had stopped, a man in one of the white space-suits stepped through. Dr Denninger. He was young. He had black hair, olive skin, sharp features, and a mealy mouth.

'Patty Greer says you gave her some trouble,' Denninger's chest-speaker said as he clopped over to Stu. 'She's quite upset.'

'No need for her to be,' Stu said easily. It was hard to sound easy, but he felt it was important to hide his fear from this man. Denninger looked and acted like the kind of man who would ride his help and bullyrag them around but lick up to his superiors like an egg-suck dog. That kind of man could be pushed a ways if he thought you held the whip hand. But if he smelled fear on you, he would hand you the same old cake: a thin icing of 'I'm sorry I can't tell you more' on top and a lot of contempt for stupid civilians who wanted to know more than what was good for them underneath.

'I want some answers,' Stu said.

'I'm sorry, but –'

'If you want me to cooperate, give me some answers.'

'In time you will be –'

'I can make it hard for you.'

'We know that,' Denninger said peevishly. 'I simply don't have the authority to tell you anything, Mr Redman. I know very little myself.'

'I guess you've been testing my blood. All those needles.'

'That's right,' Denninger said warily.

'What for?'

'Once more, Mr Redman, I can't tell you what I don't know.' The peevish tone was back again, and Stu was inclined to believe him. He was nothing but a glorified technician on this job, and he didn't like it much.

'They put my home town under quarantine.'

'I know nothing about that, either.' But Denninger cut his eyes away from Stu's and this time Stu thought he was lying.

'How come I haven't seen anything about it?' He pointed to the TV set bolted to the wall.

'I beg your pardon?'

'When they roadblock off a town and put bobwire around it, that's news,' Stu said.

'Mr Redman, if you'll only let Patty take your blood pressure –'

'No. If you want any more from me, you better send two big strong men to get it. And no matter how many you send, I'm gonna try to rip some holes in those germ-suits. They don't look all that strong, you know it?'

He made a playful grab at Denninger's suit, and Denninger skipped backward and nearly fell over. The speaker of his intercom emitted a terrified squawk and there was a stir behind the double glass.

'I guess you could feed me something in my food to knock me out, but that'd mix up your tests, wouldn't it?'

'Mr Redman, you're not being reasonable!' Denninger was keeping a prudent distance away. 'Your lack of cooperation may do your country a grave disservice. Do you understand me?'

'Nope,' Stu said. 'Right now it looks to me like it's my country doing *me* a grave disservice. It's got me locked up in a hospital room in Georgia with a buttermouth little pissant doctor who doesn't know shit from Shinola. Get your ass out of here and send somebody in to talk to me or send enough boys to take what you need by force. I'll fight em, you can count on that.'

He sat perfectly still in his chair after Denninger left. The nurse didn't come back. Two strong orderlies did not appear to take his blood pressure by force. Now that he thought about it, he supposed that even such a small thing as a blood-pressure reading wouldn't be much good if obtained under duress. For the time being they were leaving him to simmer in his own juices.

He got up and turned on the TV and watched it unseeingly. His fear was big inside him, a runaway elephant. For two days he had been waiting to start sneezing, coughing, hawking black phlegm and spitting it into the commode. He wondered about the others, people he had known all his life. He wondered if any of them were as bad off as Campion had been. He thought of the dead woman and her baby in that old Chevy, and he kept seeing Lila Bruett's face on the woman and little Cheryl Hodges's face on the baby.

The TV squawked and crackled. His heart beat slowly in his chest. Faintly, he could hear the sound of an air purifier sighing air into the room. He felt his fear twisting and turning inside him beneath his poker face. Sometimes it was big and panicky, trampling everything: the elephant. Sometimes it was small and gnawing, ripping with sharp teeth: the rat. It was always with him.

But it was forty hours before they sent him a man who would talk.

CHAPTER 8

On June 18, five hours after he had talked to his cousin Bill Hapscomb, Joe Bob Brentwood pulled down a speeder on Texas Highway 40 about twenty-five miles east of Arnette. The speeder was Harry Trent of Braintree, an insurance man. He had been doing sixty-five miles per in a fifty-mile-an-hour zone. Joe Bob gave him a speeding ticket. Trent accepted it humbly and then amused Joe Bob by trying to sell him insurance on his house and his life. Joe Bob felt fine; dying was the last thing on his mind. Nevertheless, he was already a sick man. He had gotten more than gas at Bill Hapscomb's Texaco. And he gave Harry Trent more than a speeding summons.

Harry, a gregarious man who liked his job, passed the sickness to more than forty people during that day and the next. How many those forty passed it to is impossible to say – you might as well ask how many angels can dance on the head of a pin. If you were to make a conservative estimate of five apiece, you'd have two hundred. Using the same conservative formula, one could say those two hundred went on to infect a thousand, the thousand five thousand, the five thousand *twenty*-five thousand.

Under the California desert and subsidized by the taxpayers' money, someone had finally invented a chain letter that really worked. A very lethal chain letter.

On June 19, the day Larry Underwood came home to New York and the day that Frannie Goldsmith told her father about her impending Little Stranger, Harry Trent stopped at an East Texas café called Babe's Kwik-Eat for lunch. He had the cheeseburger platter and a piece of Babe's delicious strawberry pie for dessert. He had a slight cold, an allergy cold, maybe, and he kept sneezing and having to spit. In the course of the meal he infected Babe, the dishwasher, two truckers in a corner booth, the man who came in to deliver bread, and the man who came in to change the records on the juke. He left the sweet thang that waited his table a dollar tip that was crawling with death.

On his way out, a station wagon pulled in. There was a roof-rack on top, and the wagon was piled high with kids and luggage. The wagon had New York plates and the driver, who rolled down his window to ask Harry how to get to US 21 going north, had a New York accent. Harry gave the New York fellow very clear directions on how to get to Highway 21. He also served him and his entire family their death-warrants without even knowing it.

The New Yorker was Edward M. Norris, lieutenant of police, detective squad, in the Big Apple's 87th Precinct. This was his first real vacation in five years. He and his family had had a fine time. The kids had been in seventh heaven at Disney World in Orlando, and not knowing the whole family would be dead by the second of July, Norris planned to tell that sour sonofabitch Steve Carella that it *was* possible to take your wife and kids someplace by car and have a good time. Steve, he would say, you may be a fine detective, but a man who can't police his own family ain't worth a pisshole drilled in a snowbank.

The Norris family had a kwik-eat at Babe's, then followed Harry Trent's admirable directions to Highway 21. Ed and his wife Trish marveled over southern hospitality while the three kids colored in the back seat. Christ only knew, Ed thought, what *Carella's* pair of monsters would have been up to.

That night they stayed in a Eustace, Oklahoma, travel court. Ed and Trish infected the clerk. The kids, Marsha, Stanley, and Hector, infected the kids they played with on the tourist court's playground – kids bound for west Texas, Alabama, Arkansas, and Tennessee. Trish infected the two women who were washing clothes at the Laundromat two blocks away. Ed, on his way down the motel corridor to get some ice, infected a fellow he passed in the hallway. Everybody got into the act.

Trish woke Ed up in the early morning hours to tell him that Heck, the baby, was sick. He had an ugly, rasping cough and was running a fever. It sounded to her like the croup. Ed Norris groaned and told her to give the kid some aspirin. If the kid's goddam croup could only have held off another four or five days, he could have had it in his very own house and Ed would have been left with the memory of a perfect vacation (not to mention the anticipation of all that gloating he planned to do). He could hear the poor kid through the connecting door, hacking away like a hound dog.

Trish expected that Hector's symptoms would abate in the morning – croup was a lying-down sickness – but by noon of the twentieth, she admitted to herself that it wasn't happening. The aspirin wasn't controlling the fever; poor Heck was just glass-eyed with it. His cough had taken on a booming note she didn't like, and his respiration sounded labored and phlegmy. Whatever it was, Marsha seemed to be coming down with it, too, and Trish had a nasty little tickle in the back of her own throat that was making her cough, although so far it was only a light cough she could smother in a small hankie.

'We've got to get Heck to a doctor,' she said finally.

Ed pulled into a service station and checked the map paper-clipped to the station wagon's sun-visor. They were in Hammer Crossing, Kansas. 'I don't know,' he said. 'Maybe we can at least find a doctor who'll give us a referral.' He sighed and ran an aggravated hand through his hair. 'Hammer Crossing, Kansas! Jesus! Why'd he have to get sick enough to need a doctor at some goddam nothing place like *this*?'

Marsha, who was looking at the map over her father's shoulder, said: 'It says Jesse James robbed the bank here, Daddy. Twice.'

'Fuck Jesse James,' Ed grumped. 'Ed!' Trish cried. 'Sorry,' he said, not feeling sorry in the least. He drove on.

After six calls, during each of which Ed Norris carefully held his temper with both hands, he finally found a doctor in Polliston who would look at Hector if they could get him there by three. Polliston was off their route, twenty miles west of Hammer Crossing, but now the important thing was Hector. Ed was getting very worried about him. He'd never seen the kid with so little oomph in him.

They were waiting in the outer office of Dr Brenden Sweeney by two in the afternoon. By then Ed was sneezing, too. Sweeney's waiting room was full; they didn't get in to see the doctor until nearly four o'clock. Trish couldn't rouse Heck to more than a sludgy semiconsciousness, and she felt feverish herself. Only Stan Norris, age nine, still felt good enough to fidget.

During their wait in Sweeney's office they communicated the sickness which would soon be known across the disintegrating country as Captain Trips to more than twenty-five people, including a matronly woman who just came in to pay her bill before going on to pass the disease to her entire bridge club.

This matronly woman was Mrs Robert Bradford, Sarah Bradford

to the bridge club, Cookie to her husband and close friends. Sarah played well that night, possibly because her partner was Angela Dupray, her best friend. They seemed to enjoy a happy kind of telepathy. They won all three rubbers resoundingly, making a grand slam during the last. For Sarah, the only fly in the ointment was that she seemed to be coming down with a slight cold. It wasn't fair, arriving so soon on the heels of the last one.

She and Angela went out for a quiet drink in a cocktail bar after the party broke up at ten. Angela was in no hurry to get home. It was David's turn to have the weekly poker game at their house, and she just wouldn't be able to sleep with all that noise going on . . . unless she had a little self-prescribed sedative first, which in her case would be two sloe gin fizzes.

Sarah had a Ward 8 and the two women rehashed the bridge game. In the meantime they managed to infect everyone in the Polliston cocktail bar, including two young men drinking beer nearby. They were on their way to California – just as Larry Underwood and his friend Rudy Schwartz had once gone – to seek their fortunes. A friend of theirs had promised them jobs with a moving company. The next day they headed west, spreading the disease as they went.

Chain letters don't work. It's a known fact. The million dollars or so you are promised if you'll just send one single dollar to the name at the top of the list, add yours to the bottom, and then send the letter on to five friends never arrives. This one, the Captain Trips chain letter, worked very well. The pyramid was indeed being built, not from the bottom up but from the tip down – said tip being a deceased army security guard named Charles Campion. All the chickens were coming home to roost. Only instead of the mailman bringing each participant bale after bale of letters, each containing a single dollar bill, Captain Trips brought bales of bedrooms with a body or two in each one, and trenches, and dead-pits, and finally bodies slung into the oceans on each coast and into quarries and into the foundations of unfinished houses. And in the end, of course, the bodies would rot where they fell.

Sarah Bradford and Angela Dupray walked back to their parked cars together (infecting four or five people they met on the street), then pecked cheeks and went their separate ways. Sarah went home to infect her husband and his five poker buddies and her teenaged daughter, Samantha. Unknown to her parents, Samantha was terribly afraid she had caught a dose of the clap from her boyfriend. As a matter of fact, she had. As a *further* matter of fact, she had nothing to worry about; next to what her mother had given her, a good working dose of the clap was every bit as serious as a little eczema of the eyebrows.

The next day Samantha would go on to infect everybody in the swimming pool at the Polliston YWCA.

And so on.

CHAPTER 9

They set on him sometime after dusk, while he was walking up the shoulder of US Route 27, which was called Main Street a mile back, where it passed through town. A mile or two farther on, he had been planning to turn west on 63, which would have taken him to the turnpike and the start of his long trip north. His senses had been dulled, maybe, by the two beers he had just downed, but he had known something was wrong. He was just getting around to remembering the four or five heavyset townies down at the far end of the bar when they broke cover and ran at him.

Nick put up the best fight he could, decking one of them and bloodying another's nose – breaking it, too, by the sound. For one or two hopeful moments he thought there was actually a chance that he might win. The fact that he fought without making any sound at all was unnerving them a little. They were soft, maybe they had done this before with no trouble, and they certainly hadn't expected a serious fight from this skinny kid with the knapsack.

Then one of them caught him just over the chin, shredding his lower lip with some sort of a school ring, and the warm taste of blood gushed into his mouth. He stumbled backward and someone pinned his arms. He struggled wildly and got one hand free just as a fist looped down into his face like a runaway moon. Before it closed his right eye, he saw that ring again, glittering dully in the starlight. He saw stars and felt his consciousness start to diffuse, drifting away into parts unknown.

Scared, he struggled harder. The man wearing the ring was back in front of him now and Nick, afraid of being cut again, kicked him in the belly. School Ring's breath went out of him and he doubled over, making a series of breathless whoofing sounds, like a terrier with laryngitis.

The others closed in. To Nick they were only shapes now, beefy men – good old boys, they called themselves – in gray shirts with the sleeves rolled up to show their big sunfreckled biceps. They wore blocky workshoes. Tangles of oily hair fell over their brows. In the last fading light of day all of this began to seem like a malign dream. Blood ran in his open eye. The knapsack was torn from his back. Blows rained down on him and he became a boneless, jittering puppet on a fraying string. Consciousness would not quite desert him. The only sounds were their out-of-breath gasps as they pistoned their fists into him and the liquid twitter of a nightjar in the deep stand of pine close by.

School Ring had staggered to his feet. 'Hold im,' he said. 'Hold im by the har.'

Hands grasped his arms. Somebody else twined both hands into Nick's springy black hair.

'Why don't he yell out?' one of the others asked, agitated. 'Why don't he yell out, Ray?'

'I tole you not to use any names,' Signet Ring said. 'I don't *give* a fuck why he don't yell out. I'm gonna mess im up. Sucker kicked me. Goddam dirty-fighter, that's what he is.'

The fist looped down. Nick jerked his head aside and the ring furrowed his cheek.

'Hold im, I tole you,' Ray said. 'What are y'all? Bunch of pussies?'

The fist looped down again and Nick's nose became a squashed and dripping tomato. His breath clogged to a snuffle. Consciousness was down to a narrow pencil beam. His mouth dropped open and he scooped in night air. The nightjar sang again, sweet and solus. Nick heard it this time no more than he had the last.

'Hold im,' Ray said. 'Hold im, goddammit.'

The fist looped down. Two of his front teeth shattered as the school ring snowplowed through them. It was an agony he couldn't scream about. His legs unhinged and he sagged, held like a grainsack now by the hands behind him.

'Ray, that's enough! You wanna kill im?'

'Hold im. Sucker kicked me. I'm gonna mess im up.'

Then lights were splashing down the road, which was bordered here by underbrush and interlaced with huge old pines.

'Oh, Jesus!'

'Dump im, dump im!'

That was Ray's voice, but Ray was no longer in front of him. Nick was dimly grateful, but most of what little consciousness he had left was taken up with the agony in his mouth. He could taste flecks of his teeth on his tongue.

Hands pushed him, propelling him out into the center of the road. Oncoming circles of light pinned him there like an actor on a stage. Brakes screamed. Nick pinwheeled his arms and tried to make his legs go but his legs wouldn't oblige; they had given him up for dead. He collapsed on the composition surface and the screaming sound of brakes and tires filled the world as he waited numbly to be run over. At least it would put an end to the pain in his mouth.

Then a splatter of pebbles struck his cheek and he was looking at a tire which had come to a stop less than a foot from his face. He could see a small white rock embedded between two of the treads like a coin held between a pair of knuckles.

Piece of quartz, he thought disjointedly, and passed out.

When Nick came to, he was lying on a bunk. It was a hard one, but in the last three years or so he had lain on harder. He struggled his eyes open with great effort. They seemed gummed shut and the right one, the one that had been hit by the runaway moon, would only come to halfmast.

He was looking at a cracked gray cement ceiling. Pipes wrapped in insulation zigzagged beneath it. A large beetle was trundling busily along one of these pipes. Bisecting his field of vision was a chain. He raised his head slightly, sending a monstrous bolt of pain through it, and saw another chain running from the outside foot of the bunk to a bolt in the wall.

He turned his head to the left (another bolt of pain, this one not so killing) and saw a rough concrete wall. Cracks ran through it. It had been extensively written on. Some of the writing was new, some old, most illiterate. THIS PLACE HAS BUGS. LOUIS DRAGONSKY, 1987. I LIKE IT IN MY ASSHOLE. DTS CAN BE FUN. GEORGE RAMPLING IS A JERK-OFF. I STILL LOVE YOU SUZANNE. THIS PLACE SUX, JERRY. CLYDE D. FRED 1981. There were pictures of large dangling penises, gigantic breasts, crudely drawn vaginas. It all gave Nick a sense of place. He was in a jail cell.

Carefully, he propped himself on his elbows, let his feet (clad in paper slippers) drop over the edge of the cot, and then swung up to a sitting position. The large economy-size pain rocked his head again and his backbone gave out an alarming creak. His stomach rolled alarmingly in his gut, and a fainting kind of nausea seized him, the most dismaying and unmanning kind, the kind that makes you feel like crying out to God to make it stop.

Instead of crying out – he couldn't have done that – Nick leaned over his knees, one hand on each cheek, and waited for it to pass. After a while, it did. He could feel the Band-Aids that had been placed over the furrow on his cheek, and by wrinkling that side of his face a couple of times he decided that some sawbones had sunk a couple of stitches in there for good measure.

He looked around. He was in a small cell shaped like a Saltine box stood on end. Beyond the end of the cot was a barred door. At the head of the cot was a lidless, ringless toilet. Behind and above him – he saw this by craning his stiff neck very, very carefully – was a small barred window.

After he had sat on the edge of the cot long enough to feel sure he wasn't going to pass out, he hooked the shapeless gray pajama pants he was wearing down around his knees, squatted on the can, and urinated for what seemed at least an hour. When he was finished he stood up, holding on to the edge of the cot like an old man. He looked apprehensively into the bowl for signs of blood, but his urine had been clear. He flushed it away.

He walked carefully over to the barred door and looked out into a short corridor. To his left was the drunk tank. An old man was lying on one of its five bunks, a hand like driftwood dangling on the floor. To the right the corridor ended in a door that was chocked open. In the center of the corridor was a dangling green-shaded light like the kind he had seen in pool-halls.

A shadow rose, danced on the propped-open door, and then a large man in khaki suntans walked into the corridor. He was wearing a Sam Browne belt and a big pistol. He hooked his thumbs into his pants pockets and looked at Nick for almost a full minute without speaking. Then he said, 'When I was a boy we caught ourselves a mountain lion up in the hills and shot it and then drug it twenty mile back to town over dirt hardpan. What was left of that creature when we got home was the sorriest-lookin sight I ever saw. You the second-sorriest, boy.'

Nick thought it had the feel of a prepared speech, carefully honed and treasured, saved for out-of-towners and vags that occupied the barred Saltine boxes from time to time.

'You got a name, Babalugah?'

Nick put a finger to his swelled and lacerated lips and shook his head. He put a hand over his mouth, then cut the air with it in a soft diagonal hashmark and shook his head again.

'What? Cain't talk? What's this happy horseshit?' The words were amiable enough, but Nick couldn't follow tones or inflections. He plucked an invisible pen from the air and wrote with it.

'You want a pencil?'

Nick nodded.

'If you're mute, how come you don't have none of those cards?'

Nick shrugged. He turned out his empty pockets. He balled his fists and shadowboxed the air, which sent another bolt of pain through his head and another wave of nausea through his stomach. He finished by tapping his own temples lightly with his fists, rolling his eyes up, and sagging on the bars. Then he pointed to his empty pockets.

'You were robbed.'

Nick nodded.

The man in khaki turned away and went back into his office. A moment later he returned with a dull pencil and a notepad. He thrust them through the bars. Written across the top of each notesheet was MEMO and *From The Desk Of Sheriff John Baker.*

Nick turned the pad around and tapped the pencil eraser at the name. He raised questioning eyebrows.

'Yeah, that's me. Who are you?'

'Nick Andros,' he wrote. He put his hand through the bars.

Baker shook his head. 'I ain't gonna shake with you. You deaf, too?'

Nick nodded.

'What happened to you tonight? Doc Soames and his wife almost ran you down like a woodchuck, boy.'

'Beat up & robbed. A mile or so from a rdhouse on Main St Zack's Place.'

'That hangout's no place for a kid like you, Babalugah. You surely aren't old enough to drink.'

Nick shook his head indignantly. 'I'm twenty-two,' he wrote. 'I can have a couple of beers without getting beaten up & robbed for them, can't I?'

Baker read this with a sourly amused look on his face. 'It don't appear you can in Shoyo. What you doing here, kid?'

Nick tore the first sheet off the memo pad, crumpled it in a ball, dropped it on the floor. Before he could begin to write his reply, an arm shot through the bars and a steel hand clutched his shoulder. Nick's head jerked up.

'My wife neatens these cells,' Baker said, 'and I don't see any need for you to litter yours up. Go throw that in the john.'

Nick bent over, wincing at the pain in his back, and fished the ball of paper off the floor. He took it over to the toilet, tossed it in, and then looked up at Baker with his eyebrows raised. Baker nodded.

Nick came back. This time he wrote longer, pencil flying over the paper. Baker reflected that teaching a deaf-mute kid to read and write was probably quite a trick, and this Nick Andros must have some pretty good equipment upstairs to have caught the hang of it. There were fellows here in Shoyo, Arkansas, who had never properly caught the hang of it, and more than a few of them hung out in Zack's. But he supposed you couldn't expect a kid who just blew into town to know that.

Nick handed the pad through the bars.

'I've been traveling around but I'm not a vag. Spent today working for a man named Rich Ellerton about 6 miles west of here. I cleaned his barn & put up a load of hay in his loft. Last week I was in Watts, Okla., running fence. The man who beat me up got my week's pay.'

'You sure it was Rich Ellerton you was working for? I can check that, you know.' Baker had torn off Nick's explanation, folded it to wallet-photo size, and tucked it into his shirt pocket.

Nick nodded.

'You see his dog?'

Nick nodded.

'What kind was it?'

Nick gestured for the pad. 'Big Doberman,' he wrote. 'But nice. Not mean.'

Baker nodded, turned away, and went back into his office. Nick stood at the bars, watching anxiously. A moment later, Baker returned with a big keyring, unlocked the holding cell, and pushed it back on its track.

'Come on in the office,' Baker said. 'You want some breakfast?'

Nick shook his head, then made pouring and drinking motions.

'Coffee? Got that. You take cream and sugar?'

Nick shook his head.

'Take it like a man, huh?' Baker laughed. 'Come on.'

Baker started up the hallway, and although he was speaking,

Nick was unable to hear what he was saying with his back turned and his lips hidden. 'I don't mind the company. I got insomnia. It's got so I can't sleep more'n three or four hours most nights. M'wife wants me to go see some big-shot doctor up in Pine Bluff. If it keeps on, I just might do it. I mean, looka this – here I am, five in the morning, not even light out, and there I sit eatin aigs and greazy home fries from the truck stop up the road.'

He turned on the last phrase and Nick caught '. . . truck stop up the road.' He raised his eyebrows and shrugged his shoulders to indicate his puzzlement.

'Don't matter,' Baker said. 'Not to a young kid like you, anyway.'

In the outer office, Baker poured him a cup of black coffee out of a huge thermos. The sheriff's half-finished breakfast plate stood on his desk blotter, and he pulled it back to himself. Nick sipped the coffee. It hurt his mouth, but it was good.

He tapped Baker on the shoulder, and when he looked up, Nick pointed to the coffee, rubbed his stomach, and winked soberly.

Baker smiled. 'You better say it's good. My wife Jane puts it up.' He tucked half a hard-fried egg into his mouth, chewed, and then pointed at Nick with his fork. 'You're pretty good. Just like one of those pantomimers. Bet you don't have much trouble makin yourself understood, huh?'

Nick made a seesawing gesture with his hand in midair. *Comme çi, comme ça.*

'I ain't gonna hold you,' Baker said, mopping up grease with a slice of toasted Wonder Bread, 'but I tell you what. If you stick around, maybe we can get the guy who did this to you. You game?'

Nick nodded and wrote: 'You think I can get my week's pay back?'

'Not a chance,' Baker said flatly. 'I'm just a hick sheriff, boy. For somethin like that, you'd be wantin Oral Roberts.'

Nick nodded and shrugged. Putting his hands together, he made a bird flying away.

'Yeah, like that. How many were there?'

Nick held up four fingers, shrugged, then held up five.

'Think you could identify any of them?'

Nick held up one finger and wrote: 'Big & blond. Your size, maybe a little heavier. Gray shirt & pants. He was wearing a big ring. 3rd finger right hand. Purple stone. That's what cut me.'

As Baker read this, a change came over his face. First concern, then anger. Nick, thinking the anger was directed against him, became frightened again.

'Oh Jesus Christ,' Baker said. 'This here's a full commode slopping over for sure. You sure?'

Nick nodded reluctantly.

'Anything else? You see anything else?'

Nick thought hard, then wrote: 'Small scar. On his forehead.'

Baker looked at the words. 'That's Ray Booth,' he said. 'My brother-in-law. Thanks, kid. Five in the morning and my day's wrecked already.'

Nick's eyes opened a little wider, and he made a cautious gesture of commiseration.

'Well, all right,' Baker said, more to himself than to Nick. 'He's a bad actor. Janey knows it. He beat her up enough times when they was kids together. Still, they're brother n sister and I guess I can forget my lovin for this week.'

Nick looked down, embarrassed. After a moment Baker shook his shoulder so that Nick would see him speaking.

'It probably won't do any good anyway,' he said. 'Ray 'n his jerk-off buddies'll just swear each other up. Your word against theirs. Did you get any licks in?'

'Kicked this Ray in the guts,' Nick wrote. 'Got another one in the nose. Might have broken it.'

'Ray chums around with Vince Hogan, Billy Warner, and Mike Childress, mostly,' Baker said. 'I might be able to get Vince alone and break him down. He's got all the spine of a dyin jellyfish. If I could get him I could go after Mike and Billy. Ray got that ring in a fraternity at LSU. He flunked out his sophomore year.' He paused, drumming his fingers against the rim of his breakfast plate. 'I guess we could give it a go, kid, if you wanted to. But I'll warn you in advance, we probably won't get them. They're as vicious and cowardly as a dogpack, but they're town boys and you're just a deaf-mute drifter. And if they got off, they'd come after you.'

Nick thought about it. In his mind he kept coming back to the image of himself, being shoved from one of them to the next like a bleeding scarecrow, and to Ray's lips forming the words: *I'm gonna mess im up. Sucker kicked me.* To the feel of his knapsack, that old friend of the last two wandering years, being ripped from his back.

On the memo pad he wrote and underlined two words: '*Let's try.*'

Baker sighed and nodded. 'Okay. Vince Hogan works down to the sawmill . . . well, that ain't just true. What he does mostly is fucks off down to the sawmill. We'll take a ride down there about nine, if that's fine with you. Maybe we can get him scared enough to spill the beans.'

Nick nodded.

'How's your mouth? Doc Soames left some pills. He said it would probably be a misery to you.'

Nick nodded ruefully.

'I'll get em. It . . .' He broke off, and in Nick's silent movie world, he watched the sheriff explode several sneezes into his handkerchief. 'That's another thing,' he went on, but he had turned away now and Nick caught only the first word. 'I'm comin down with a real good cold. Jesus Christ, ain't life grand? Welcome to Arkansas, boy.'

He got the pills and came back to where Nick sat. After he passed them and a glass of water to Nick, Baker rubbed gently under the angle of his jaw. There was a definite painful swelling there. Swollen glands, coughing, sneezing, a low fever, felt like. Yeah, it was shaping up to be a wonderful day.

CHAPTER 10

Larry woke up with a hangover that was not too bad, a mouth that tasted as if a baby dragon had used it for a potty chair, and a feeling that he was somewhere he shouldn't be.

The bed was a single, but there were two pillows on it. He could smell frying bacon. He sat up, looked out the windows at another gray New York day, and his first thought was that they had done something horrible to Berkeley overnight: turned it dirty and sooty, had aged it. Then last night began coming back and he realized he was looking at Fordham, not Berkeley. He was in a second-floor flat on Tremont Avenue, not far from the Concourse, and his mother was going to wonder where he had been last night. Had he called her, given her any kind of excuse, no matter how thin?

He swung his legs out of bed and found a crumpled pack of Winstons with one crazy cigarette left in it. He lit it with a green plastic Bic lighter. It tasted like dead horseshit. Out in the kitchen the sound of frying bacon went on and on, like radio static.

The girl's name was Maria and she had said she was a . . . what? Oral hygienist, was that it? Larry didn't know how much she knew about hygiene, but she was great on oral. He vaguely remembered being gobbled like a Perdue drumstick. Crosby, Stills, and Nash on the crappy little stereo in the living room, singing about how much water had gone underneath the bridge, time we had wasted on the way. If his memory was correct, Maria sure hadn't wasted much time. She had been a little overwhelmed to discover he was *that* Larry Underwood. At one point in the evening's festivities, hadn't they gone out reeling around looking for an open record store so they could buy a copy of 'Baby, Can You Dig Your Man?'

He groaned very softly and tried to retrace yesterday from its innocuous beginnings to its frantic, gobbling finale.

The Yankees weren't in town, he remembered that. His mother had been gone to work when he woke up, but she had left a Yankees schedule on the kitchen table along with a note: 'Larry. As you can see, the Yankees won't be back until Jul 1. They are playing a doubleheader the 4th of July. If you're not doing anything that day, why not take your mom to the ball park. I'll buy the beer and hotdogs. There are eggs and sausage in the fridge or sweetrolls in the breadbox if you like them better. Take care of yourself kiddo.' There was a typical Alice Underwood PS: 'Most of the kids you hung around with are gone now and good riddance to that bunch of hoods but I think Buddy Marx is working at that print shop on Stricker Avenue.'

Just thinking of that note was enough to make him wince. No 'Dear' before his name. No 'Love' before her signature. She didn't believe in phony stuff. The real stuff was in the refrigerator. Sometime while he had been sleeping off his drive across America, she had gone out and stocked up on every goddam thing in the world that he liked. Her memory was so perfect it was frightening. A Daisy canned ham. Two pounds of real butter – how the hell could she afford that on her salary? Two six-packs of Coke. Deli sausages. A roast of beef already marinating in Alice's secret sauce, the contents of which she refused to divulge even to her son, and a gallon of Baskin-Robbins Peach Delight ice cream in the freezer. Along with a Sara Lee cheesecake. The kind with strawberries on top.

On impulse, he had gone into the bathroom, not just to take care of his bladder but to check the medicine cabinet. A brand-new Pepsodent toothbrush was hanging in the old holder, where all of his childhood toothbrushes had hung, one after another. There was a package of disposable razors in the cabinet, a can of Barbaso shave cream, even a bottle of Old Spice cologne. Not fancy, she would have said – Larry could actually *hear* her – but smelly enough, for the money.

He had stood looking at these things, then had taken the new tube of toothpaste out and held it in his hand. No 'Dear,' no 'Love, Mom.' Just a new toothbrush, new tube of toothpaste, new bottle of cologne. Sometimes, he thought, real love is silent as well as blind. He began brushing his teeth, wondering if there might not be a song in that someplace.

The oral hygienist came in, wearing a pink nylon halfslip and nothing else. 'Hi, Larry,' she said. She was short, pretty in a vague Sandra Dee sort of way, and her breasts pointed at him perkily without a sign of a sag. What was the old joke? That's right, Loot – she had a pair of 38s and a real gun. Ha-ha, very funny. He had come three thousand miles to spend the night being eaten alive by Sandra Dee.

'Hi,' he said, and got up. He was naked but his clothes were at the foot of the bed. He began to put them on.

'I've got a robe you can wear if you want to. We're having kippers and bacon.'

Kippers and bacon? His stomach began to shrivel and fold in on itself.

'No, honey, I've got to run. Someone I've got to see.'

'Oh hey, you can't just run out on me like that –'

'Really, it's important.'

'Well, I'm impawtant, too!' She was becoming strident. It hurt Larry's head. For no particular reason, he thought of Fred Flintstone bellowing '*WIIILMAAA!*' at the top of his cartoon lungs.

'Your Bronx is showing, luv,' he said.

'What's that supposed to mean?' She planted her hands on her hips, the greasy spatula sticking out of one closed fist like a steel flower. Her breasts jiggled fetchingly, but Larry wasn't fetched. He stepped into his pants and buttoned them. 'So I'm from the Bronx, does that make me black? What have you got against the Bronx? What are you, some kind of racist?'

'Nothing and I don't think so,' he said, and walked over to her in his bare feet. 'Listen, the somebody I have to meet is my mother. I just got into town two days ago and I didn't call her last night or anything . . . did I?' he added hopefully.

'You didn't call anybody,' she said sullenly. 'I just *bet* it's your mother.'

He walked back to the bed and stuck his feet in his loafers. 'It is. Really. She works in the Chemical Bank Building. She's a house-keeper. Well, these days I guess she's a floor supervisor.'

'I bet you aren't the Larry Underwood that has that record, either.'

'You believe what you want. I have to run.'

'You cheap prick!' she flashed at him. 'What am I supposed to do with all the stuff I cooked?'

'Throw it out the window?' he suggested.

She uttered a high squawk of anger and hurled the spatula at him. On any other day of his life it would have missed. One of the first laws of physics was, to wit, a spatula will not fly a straight trajec-tory if hurled by an angry oral hygienist. Only this was the exception that proved the rule, flip-flop, up and over, smash, right into Larry's forehead. It didn't hurt much. Then he saw two drops of blood fall on the throw-rug as he bent over to pick the spatula up.

He advanced two steps with the spatula in his hand. 'I ought to paddle you with this!' he shouted at her.

'Sure,' she said, cringing back and starting to cry. 'Why not? Big star. Fuck and run. I thought you were a nice guy. You ain't no nice guy.' Several tears ran down her cheeks, dropped from her jaw, and plopped onto her upper chest. Fascinated, he watched one of them roll down the slope of her right breast and perch on the nipple. It had a magnifying effect. He could see pores, and one black hair sprouting from the inner edge of the aureole. Jesus Christ, I'm going crazy, he thought wonderingly.

'I have to go,' he said. His white cloth jacket was on the foot of the bed. He picked it up and slung it over his shoulder.

'You ain't no nice guy!' she cried at him as he went into the living room. 'I only went with you because I thought you were a nice guy!'

The sight of the living room made him feel like groaning. On the couch where he dimly remembered being gobbled were at least two dozen copies of 'Baby, Can You Dig Your Man?' Three more were on the turntable of the dusty portable stereo. On the far wall was a huge poster of Ryan O'Neal and Ali McGraw. Being gobbled means never having to say you're sorry, ha-ha. Jesus, I *am* going crazy.

She stood in the bedroom doorway, still crying, pathetic in her halfslip. He could see a nick on one of her shins where she had cut herself shaving.

'Listen, give me a call,' she said. 'I ain't mad.'

He should have said, 'Sure,' and that would have been the end of it. Instead he heard his mouth utter a crazy laugh and then, 'Your kippers are burning.'

She screamed at him and started across the room, only to trip over a throw-pillow on the floor and go sprawling. One of her arms knocked over a half-empty bottle of milk and rocked the empty bottle of Scotch standing next to it. *Holy God*, Larry thought, *were we* mixing *those?*

He got out quickly and pounded down the stairs. As he went down the last six steps to the front door, he heard her in the upstairs hall, yelling down: *'You ain't no nice guy! You ain't no —'*

He slammed the door behind him and misty, humid warmth washed over him, carrying the aroma of spring trees and automobile exhaust. It was perfume after the smell of frying grease and stale cigarette smoke. He still had the crazy cigarette, now burned down to the filter, and he threw it into the gutter and took a deep breath of the fresh air. Wonderful to be out of that craziness. Return with us not to those wonderful days of normalcy as we —

Above and behind him a window went up with a rattling bang and he knew what was coming next.

'I hope you rot!' she screamed down at him. The Compleat Bronx Fishwife. *'I hope you fall in front of some fuckin subway train! You ain't no singer! You're shitty in bed! You louse! Pound this up your ass! Take this to ya mother, you louse!'*

The milk bottle came zipping down from her second-floor bedroom window. Larry ducked. It went off in the gutter like a bomb, spraying the street with glass fragments. The Scotch bottle came next, twirling end over end, to crash nearly at his feet. Whatever else she was, her aim was terrifying. He broke into a run, holding one arm over his head. This madness was never going to end.

From behind him came a final long braying cry, triumphant with juicy Bronx intonation: *'KISS MY ASS, YOU CHEAP BAAASTARD!'* Then he was around the corner and on the expressway overpass, leaning over, laughing with a shaky intensity that was nearly hysteria, watching the cars pass below.

'Couldn't you have handled that better?' he said, totally unaware he was speaking out loud. 'Oh man, you coulda done better than that. That was a bad scene. Crap on that, man.' He realized he was speaking aloud, and another burst of laughter escaped him. He suddenly felt a dizzy, spinning nausea in his stomach and squeezed his eyes tightly closed. A memory circuit in the Department of Masochism clicked open and he heard Wayne Stukey saying, *There's something in you that's like biting on tinfoil.*

He had treated the girl like an old whore on the morning after the frathouse gangbang.

You ain't no nice guy.

I am. I am.

But when the people at the big party had protested his decision to cut them off, he had threatened to call the police, and he had meant it. Hadn't he? Yes. Yes, he had. Most of them were strangers, true, he could care if they crapped on a landmine, but four or five of the protestors had gone back to the old days. And Wayne Stukey, that bastard, standing in the doorway with his arms folded like a hanging judge on the big day.

Sal Doria going out, saying: *If this is what it does to guys like you, Larry, I wish you were still playing sessions.*

He opened his eyes and turned away from the overpass, looking for a cab. Oh sure. The outraged friend bit. If Sal was such a big friend, what was he doing there sucking off him in the first place? I was stupid and nobody likes to see a stupid guy wise up. That's the real story.

You ain't no nice guy.

'I am a nice guy,' he said sulkily. 'And whose business is it, anyway?'

A cab was coming and Larry flagged it. It seemed to hesitate a moment before pulling up to the curb, and Larry remembered the blood on his forehead. He opened the back door and climbed in before the guy could change his mind.

'Manhattan. The Chemical Bank Building on Park,' he said.

The cab pulled out into traffic. 'You got a cut on your forehead, guy,' the cabbie said.

'A girl threw a spatula at me,' Larry said absently.

The cabbie offered him a strange false smile of commiseration and drove on, leaving Larry to settle back and try to imagine how he was going to explain his night out to his mother.

CHAPTER 11

Larry found a tired-looking black woman on the lobby level who told him she thought Alice Underwood was up on the twenty-fourth floor, doing an inventory. He got an elevator and went up, aware that the other people in the car were stealing cautious glances at his forehead. The wound there was no longer bleeding, but it had caked over into an unsightly mess.

The twenty-fourth floor was taken up by the executive offices of a Japanese camera company. Larry walked up and down the halls for almost twenty minutes, looking for his mother and feeling like a horse's ass. There were plenty of Occidental executives, but enough of them were Japanese to make him feel, at six-feet-two, like a very *tall* horse's ass. The small men and women with the upslanted eyes looked at his caked forehead and bloody jacket sleeve with unsettling Oriental blandness.

He finally spotted a door with CUSTODIAN & HOUSEKEEPING on it behind a very large fern. He tried the knob. The door was unlocked and he peered inside. His mother was in there, dressed in her shapeless gray uniform, support hose, and crepe-soled shoes. Her hair was firmly caught under a black net. Her back was to him. She had a clipboard in one hand and seemed to be counting bottles of spray cleaner on a high shelf.

Larry felt a strong and guilty impulse to just turn tail and run. Go back to the garage two blocks from her apartment building and get the Z. Fuck the two months' rent he had just laid down on the space. Just get in and *boogie*. Boogie where? Anywhere. Bar Harbor, Maine. Tampa, Florida. Salt Lake City, Utah. Any place would be a good place, as long as it was comfortably over the horizon from Dewey the Deck and from this soap-smelling little closet. He didn't know if it was the fluorescent lights or the cut on his forehead, but he was getting one *fuck* of a headache.

Oh, quit whining, you goddam sissy.

'Hi, Mom,' he said.

She started a little but didn't turn around. 'So, Larry. You found your way uptown.'

'Sure.' He shuffled his feet. 'I wanted to apologize. I should have called you last night –'

'Yeah. Good idea.'

'I stayed with Buddy. We . . . uh . . . we went out steppin. Did the town.'

'I figured it was that. That or something like it.' She hooked a small stool over with her foot, climbed up on it, and began to count the bottles of floor-wax on the top shelf, touching each one lightly with the tips of her right thumb and forefinger as she went. She had to reach, and when she did, her dress pulled up and he could see beyond the brown tops of her stockings to the waffled white flesh of her upper thighs and he turned his eyes away, suddenly and aimlessly recalling what had happened to Noah's third son when he looked at his father as the old man lay drunk and naked on his pallet. Poor guy had ended up being a hewer of wood and fetcher of water ever after. Him and all his descendants. And that's why we have race riots today, son. Praise God.

'Is that all you came to tell me?' she asked, looking around at him for the first time.

'Well, where I was and to apologize. It was crummy of me to forget.'

'Yeah,' she said again. 'But you got your crummy side to you, Larry. Did you think I forgot that?'

He flushed. 'Mom, listen –'

'You're bleeding. Some stripper hit you with a loaded G-string?' She turned back to the shelves, and after she had counted the whole row of bottles on the top one, she made a notation on her clipboard. 'Someone has had themselves two bottles of floor-wax this past week,' she remarked. 'Lucky them.'

'I came to say I was *sorry!*' Larry told her loudly. She didn't jump, but he did. A little.

'Yeah, so you said. Mr Geoghan is gonna be on us like a ton of bricks if the damned floor-wax doesn't stop going out.'

'I didn't get in a barroom fight and I wasn't in a strip-joint. It wasn't anything like that. It was just . . .' He trailed off.

She turned around, eyebrows arched in that old sardonic way he remembered so well. 'Was what?'

'Well . . .' He couldn't think of a convincing lie quick enough. 'It was. A. Uh. Spatula.'

'Someone mistook you for a fried egg? Must have been quite a night you and Buddy had out on the town.'

He kept forgetting that she could run rings around him, had always been able to, probably always would.

'It was a girl, Ma. She threw it at me.'

'She must be a hell of a shot,' Alice Underwood said, and turned away again. 'That dratted Consuela is hiding the requisition forms again. Not that they do much good; we never get all the stuff we need, but we get plenty I wouldn't know what to do with if my life depended on it.'

'Ma, are you mad at me?'

Her hands suddenly dropped to her sides. Her shoulders slumped.

'Don't be mad at me,' he whispered. 'Don't be, okay? Huh?'

She turned around and he saw an unnatural sparkle in her eyes – well, he supposed it was *natural* enough, but it sure wasn't caused by the fluorescents in here, and he heard the oral hygienist say once more, with great finality: *You ain't no nice guy.* Why had he ever bothered to come home if he was going to do stuff like this to her . . . and never mind what she was doing to him.

'Larry,' she said gently. 'Larry, Larry, Larry.'

For a moment he thought she was going to say no more; even allowed himself to hope this was so.

'Is that all you can say? "Don't be mad at me, please, Ma, don't be mad"? I hear you on the radio, and even though I don't like that song you sing, I'm proud it's you singing it. People ask me if that's really my son and I say yes, that's Larry. I tell them you could always sing, and that's no lie, is it?'

He shook his head miserably, not trusting himself to speak.

'I tell them how you picked up Donny Roberts's guitar when you were in junior high and how you were playing better than him in half an hour, even though he had lessons ever since second grade. You got talent, Larry, nobody ever had to tell me that, least of all you. I guess you knew it, too, because it's the only thing I never heard you whine about. Then you went away, and am I beating you about the head and shoulders with that? No. Young men and young women, they go away. That's the nature of the world. Sometimes it stinks, but it's natural. Then you come back. Does somebody have to tell me why that is? No. You come back because, hit record or no hit record, you got in some kind of jam out there on the West Coast.'

'I'm not in any trouble!' he said indignantly.

'Yes you are. I know the signs. I've been your mother for a long time, and you can't bullshit me, Larry. Trouble is something you have always looked around for when you couldn't just turn your head and see it. Sometimes I think you'd cross the street to step in dogshit. God will forgive me for saying it, because God knows it's true. Am I mad? No. Am I disappointed? Yes. I had hoped you would change out there. You didn't. You went away a little boy in a man's body and you came back the same way, except the man got his hair processed. You know why I think you came home?'

He looked at her, wanting to speak, but knowing the only thing he would be able to say if he did would make them both mad: *Don't cry, Mom, huh?*

'I think you came home because you couldn't think where else to go. You didn't know who else would take you in. I never said a mean word about you to anyone else, Larry, not even to my own sister, but since you've pushed me to it, I'll tell you exactly what I think of you. I think you're a taker. You've always been one. It's like God left some part of you out when He built you inside of me. You're not *bad*, that's not what I mean. Some of the places we had to live after your father died, you would have gone bad if there was bad in you, God knows. I think the worst thing I ever caught you doing was writing a nasty word in the downstairs hall of that place on Carstairs Avenue in Queens. You remember that?'

He remembered. She had chalked that same word on his forehead and then made him walk around the block with her three times. He had never written that word or any other word on a building, wall, or stoop.

'The worst part, Larry, is that you *mean* well. Sometimes I think it would almost be a mercy if you were broke worse. As it is, you seem to know what's wrong but not how to fix it. And I don't know how, either. I tried every way *I* knew when you were small. Writing that word on your forehead, that was only one of them . . . and by then I was getting desperate, or I never would have done such a mean thing to you. You're a taker, that's all. You came home to me because you knew that I have to give. Not to everybody, but to you.'

'I'll move out,' he said, and every word was like spitting out a dry ball of lint. 'This afternoon.'

Then it came to him that he probably couldn't *afford* to move out, at least not until Wayne sent him his next royalty check – or whatever was left of it after he finished feeding the hungriest of the LA hounds – on to him. As for current out-of-pocket expenses, there was the rent on the parking slot for the Datsun Z, and a hefty payment he would have to send out by Friday, unless he wanted the friendly neighborhood repo man looking for him, and he didn't. And after last night's revel, which had begun so innocently with Buddy and his fiancée and this oral hygienist the fiancée knew, a nice girl from the Bronx, Larry, you'll love her, great sense of humor, he was pretty low on cash. No. If you wanted to be accurate, he was busted to his heels. The thought made him panicky. If he left his mother's now, where would he go? A hotel? The doorman at any hotel better than a fleabag would laugh his ass off and tell him to get lost. He was wearing good threads, but they knew. Somehow those bastards knew. They could *smell* an empty wallet.

'Don't go,' she said softly. 'I wish you wouldn't, Larry. I bought some food special. Maybe you saw it. And I was hoping maybe we could play some gin rummy tonight.'

'Ma, you can't play gin,' he said, smiling a little.

'For a penny a point, I can beat the tailgate off a kid like you.'

'Maybe if I gave you four hundred points –'

'Listen to the kid,' she jeered softly. 'Maybe if I gave *you* four hundred. Stick around, Larry. What do you say?'

'All right,' he said. For the first time that day he felt good, really good. A small voice inside whispered he was taking again, same old Larry, riding for free, but he refused to listen. This was his *mother*, after all, and she had *asked* him. It was true that she had said some pretty hard things on the way to asking, but asking was asking, true or false? 'Tell you what. I'll pay for our tickets to the game on July fourth. I'll just peel it off the top of whatever I skin you out of tonight.'

'You couldn't skin a tomato,' she said amiably, then turned back to the shelves. 'There's a men's down the hall. Why don't you go wash the blood off your forehead? Then take ten dollars out of my purse and go to a movie. There's some good movie-houses over on Third Avenue, still. Just stay out of those scum-pits around Forty-ninth and Broadway.'

'I'll be giving money to you before long,' Larry said. 'Record's number eighteen on the *Billboard* chart this week. I checked it in Sam Goody's coming over here.'

'That's wonderful. If you're so loaded, why didn't you buy a copy, instead of just looking?'

Suddenly there was some kind of a blockage in his throat. He harrumphed, but it didn't go away.

'Well, never mind,' she said. 'My tongue's like a horse with a bad temper. Once it starts running, it just has to go on running until it's tired out. You know that. Take fifteen, Larry. Call it a loan. I guess I will get it back, one way or the other.'

'You will,' he said. He came over to her and tugged at the hem of her dress like a little boy. She looked down. He stood on tiptoe and kissed her cheek. 'I love you, Ma.'

She looked startled, not at the kiss but either at what he had said or the tone in which he had said it. 'Why, I know that, Larry,' she said.

'About what you said. About being in trouble. I am, a little, but it's not –'

Her voice was cold and stern at once. So cold, in fact, that it frightened him a little. 'I don't want to hear about that.'

'Okay,' he said. 'Listen, Ma – what's the best theater around here?'

'The Lux Twin,' she said, 'but I don't know what's playing there.'

'It doesn't matter. You know what I think? There's three things you can get everyplace in America, but you can only get them good in New York City.'

'Yeah, Mr New York *Times* critic? What are those?'

'Movies, baseball, and hotdogs from Nedick's.'

She laughed. 'You ain't stupid, Larry – you never were.'

So he went down to the men's room. And washed the blood off his forehead. And went back and kissed his mother again. And got fifteen dollars from her scuffed black purse. And went to the movies at the Lux. And watched an insane, malignant revenant named Freddy Krueger suck a number of teenagers into the quicksand of their own dreams, where all but one of them – the heroine – died. Freddy Krueger also appeared to die at the end, but it was hard to tell, and since this movie had a Roman numeral after its name and seemed to be well attended, Larry thought the man with the razors on the tips of his fingers would be back, without knowing that the persistent sound in the row behind him signaled the end to all that: there would be no more sequels, and in a very short time, there would be no more movies at all.

In the row behind Larry, a man was coughing.

CHAPTER 12

There was a grandfather clock standing in the far corner of the parlor. Frannie Goldsmith had been listening to its measured ticks and tocks all of her life. It summed up the room, which she had never liked and, on days like today, actively hated.

Her favorite room in the place was her father's workshop. It was in the shed that connected house and barn. You got there through a small door which was barely five feet high and nearly hidden behind the old kitchen woodstove. The door was good to begin with: small and almost hidden, it was deliciously like the sort of door one encountered in fairy-tales and fantasies. When she grew older and taller, she had to duck through it just as her father did – her mother never went out into the workshop unless she absolutely had to. It was an *Alice in Wonderland* door, and for a while her pretend game, secret even from her father, was that one day when she opened it, she would not find Peter Goldsmith's workshop at all. Instead she would find an underground passageway leading somehow from Wonderland to Hobbiton, a low but somehow cozy tunnel with rounded earthen sides and an earthen ceiling interlaced with sturdy roots that would give your head a good bump if you knocked it against any of them. A tunnel that smelled not of wet soil and damp and nasty bugs and worms, but one which smelled of cinnamon and baking apple pies, one which ended somewhere up ahead in the pantry of Bag End, where Mr Bilbo Baggins was celebrating his eleventy-first birthday party . . .

Well, that cozy tunnel never turned out to be there, but to the Frannie Goldsmith who had grown up in this house, the work-shop (sometimes called 'the toolshop' by her father and 'that dirty place where your dad goes to drink beer' by her mother) had been enough. Strange tools and odd gadgets. A huge chest with a thousand drawers, each of the thousand crammed full. Nails, screws, bits, sandpaper (of three kinds: rough, rougher, and roughest), planes, levels, and all the other things she'd had no name for then and still had no name for. It was dark in the workshop except for the cobwebby forty-watt bulb that hung down by its cord and the bright circle of light from the Tensor lamp that was always focused where her father was working. There were the smells of dust and oil and pipesmoke, and it seemed to her now that there should be a rule: every father must smoke. Pipe, cigar, cigarette, marijuana, hash, lettuce leaves, *something*. Because the smell of smoke seemed an integral part of her own childhood.

'Hand me that wrench, Frannie. No – the little one. What did you do at school today? . . . She did? . . . Well, why would Ruthie Sears want to push you down? . . . Yes, it is nasty. Very nasty scrape. But it goes good with the color of your dress, don't you think? Now if you could only find Ruthie Sears and get her to push you down again and scrape the other leg. Then you'd have a pair. Hand me that big screwdriver, would you? . . . No, the one with the yellow handle.'

'Frannie Goldsmith! You come out of that nasty place right now and change your schoolclothes! RIGHT . . . NOW! You'll be filthy!'

Even now, at twenty-one, she could duck through that doorway and stand between his worktable and the old Ben Franklin stove that gave out such stuperous heat in the wintertime and catch some of what it had felt like to be such a small Frannie Goldsmith growing up in this house. It was an illusory feeling, almost always intermingled with sadness for her barely remembered brother Fred, whose own growing-up had been so rudely and finally interrupted. She could stand and smell the oil that was rubbed into everything, the must, the faint odor of her father's pipe. She could rarely remember what it had been like to be so small, so strangely small, but out there she sometimes could, and it was a glad way to feel.

But the parlor, now.

The parlor.

If the workshop was the goodness of childhood, symbolized by the phantom smell of her father's pipe (he sometimes puffed smoke gently into her ear when she had an earache, always after extracting a promise that she wouldn't tell Carla, who would have had a fit), then the parlor was everything in childhood you wished you could forget. Speak when spoken to! Easier to break it than to fix it! Go right upstairs this minute and change your clothes, don't you know that isn't suitable? Don't you *ever* think? Frannie, don't pick at your clothes, people will think you have fleas. What must your Uncle

Andrew and Aunt Carlene think? You embarrassed me half to death! The parlor was where you were tongue-tied, the parlor was where you itched and couldn't scratch, the parlor was dictatorial commands, boring conversation, relatives pinching cheeks, aches, sneezes that couldn't be sneezed, coughs that couldn't be coughed, and above all, yawns that must not be yawned.

At the center of this room where her mother's spirit dwelt was the clock. It had been built in 1889 by Carla's grandfather, Tobias Downes, and it had ascended to family heirloom status almost immediately, shifting down through the years, carefully packed and insured for moves from one part of the country to another (it had originally come into being in the Buffalo, New York, workshop of Tobias, a place which had undoubtedly been every bit as smoky and nasty as Peter's workshop, although such a comment would have struck Carla as completely irrelevant), sometimes shifting from one section of the family to another when cancer, heart attack, or accident pinched off some branch of the family tree. The clock had been in this parlor since Peter and Carla Goldsmith moved into the house some forty years ago. Here it had been placed and here it had stayed, ticking and tocking, marking off segments of time in a dry age. Someday the clock would be hers, if she wanted, Frannie reflected as she looked into her mother's white, shocked face. But I don't want it! Don't want it and won't have it!

In this room there were dried flowers under glass bells. There was in this room a dove gray carpet with dusky pink roses figured into the nap. There was a graceful bow window that looked down the hill to Route 1, with a big privet hedge between the road and the grounds. Carla had nagged her husband with a grim fervor until he planted that hedge right after the Exxon station on the corner went up. Once it was in, she nagged her husband to make it grow faster. Even radioactive fertilizer, Frannie thought, would have been acceptable to her if it had served that end. The stridency of her remonstrations concerning the privet had lessened as the hedge grew taller, and she supposed it would stop altogether in another two years or so, when the hedge finally grew tall enough to blot out the offending gas station completely and the parlor was inviolate again.

It would stop on *that* subject, at least.

Stencils on the wallpaper, large green leaves and pink flowers almost the same shade as the roses in the carpet. Early American furniture and a dark mahogany set of double doors. A fireplace which was just for show where a birch log sat eternally on a hearth of red brick which was eternally immaculate and untouched by even a speck of soot. Frannie guessed that by now that log was so dry that it would burn like newspaper if lit. Above the log was a pot almost big enough for a child to bathe in. It had been handed down from Frannie's great-grandmother, and it hung eternally suspended over the eternal log. Above the mantel, finishing that part of the picture, was The Eternal Flintlock Rifle.

Segments of time in a dry age.

One of her earliest memories was of peeing on the dove gray rug with the dusky pink roses figured into the nap. She might have been three, not trained for very long, and probably not allowed in the parlor save for special occasions because of the chance of accidents. But somehow she had gotten in, and seeing her mother not just running but *sprinting* to grab her up before the unthinkable could happen had brought the unthinkable on. Her bladder let go, and the spreading stain as the dove gray rug turned to a darker slate gray around her bottom had caused her mother to actually shriek. The stain had finally come out, but after how many patient shampooings? The Lord might know; Frannie Goldsmith did not.

It was in the parlor that her mother had talked to her, grimly, explicitly, and at length, after she caught Frannie and Norman Burstein examining each other in the barn, their clothes piled in one amicable heap on a haybale to one side. How would she like it, Carla asked as the grandfather clock solemnly ticked off segments of time in a dry age, if she took Frannie out for a walk up and down US Route 1 without any clothes on? How would that be? Frannie, then six, had cried, but had somehow managed to avoid the hysterics which impended at this prospect.

When she was ten she had ridden her bike into the mailbox post while looking back over her shoulder to yell something to Georgette McGuire. She cut her head, bloodied her nose, lacerated both knees, and had actually grayed out for a few moments with shock. When she came around she had stumbled up the driveway to the house, weeping and horrified at the sight of so much blood coming out of herself. She would have gone to her father, but since her father was at work, she had stumbled into the parlor where her mother was serving tea to Mrs Venner and Mrs Prynne. *Get out!* her mother had screamed, and the next moment she was running to Frannie, embracing her, crying *Oh Frannie, oh dear, what happened, oh your poor nose!* But she was leading Frannie back into the kitchen, where the floor could safely be bled upon, even as she was comforting her, and Frannie never forgot that her first two words that day hadn't been *Oh, Frannie!* but *Get out!* Her first concern had been for the parlor, where that dry age went on and on and blood was not allowed. Perhaps Mrs Prynne never forgot, either, because even through her tears Frannie had seen a shocked, slapped expression cross the woman's face. After that day, Mrs Prynne had become something of a seldom caller.

In her first year of junior high she had gotten a bad conduct mark on her report card, and of course she was invited into the parlor to discuss this mark with her mother. In her final year of senior high school, she had received three detention periods for passing notes, and that had likewise been discussed with her mother in the parlor. It was there that they discussed Frannie's ambitions, which always ended up seeming a trifle shallow; it was there that they discussed Frannie's hopes, which always ended up seeming a trifle unworthy; it was there that they discussed Frannie's complaints, which always ended up seeming very much unwarranted, not to mention puling, whining, and ungrateful.

It was in the parlor that her brother's coffin had stood on a trestle bedecked with roses, chrysanthemums, and lilies of the valley, their dry perfume filling the room while in the corner the poker-faced clock kept its place, ticking and tocking off segments of time in a dry age.

'You're pregnant,' Carla Goldsmith repeated for the second time.

'Yes, Mother.' Her voice was very dry but she would not allow herself to wet her lips. She pressed them together instead. She thought: *In my father's workshop there is a little girl in a red dress and she will always be there, laughing and hiding under the table with the vise clamped to one edge or all bundled up with her scabby knees clasped against her chest behind the big toolbox with its thousand drawers. That girl is a very happy girl. But in my mother's parlor there is a much smaller girl who can't help piddling on the rug like a bad dog. Like a bad little bitch puppy. And she will always be there, too, no matter how much I wish she would be gone.*

'Oh-Frannie,' her mother said, her words coming very quick. She laid a hand against the side of her cheek like an offended maiden aunt. 'How-did-it-happen?'

It was Jesse's question. That was what really pissed her off; it was the same question *he* had asked.

'Since you had two kids yourself, Mother, I think you know how it happened.'

'Don't be smart!' Carla cried. Her eyes opened wide and flashed the hot fire that had always terrified Frannie as a child. She was on her feet in the quick way she had (and that had also terrified her as a child), a tall woman with graying hair which was nicely upswept and tipped and generally beauty-shopped, a tall woman in a smart green dress and faultless beige hose. She went to the mantelpiece, where she always went in moments of distress. Resting there, below the flintlock, was a large scrapbook. Carla was something of an amateur genealogist, and her entire family was in that book . . . at least, as far back as 1638, when its earliest traceable progenitor had risen out of the nameless crowd of Londoners long enough to be recorded in some very old church records as Merton Downs, Freemason. Her family tree had been published four years ago in *The New England Genealogist*, with Carla herself the compiler of record.

Now she fingered that book of painstakingly amassed names, a safe ground where none could trespass. Were there no thieves in there anyplace? Frannie wondered. No alcoholics? No unwed mothers?

'How could you do something like this to your father and me?' she asked finally. 'Was it that boy Jesse?'

'It was Jesse. Jesse's the father.'

Carla flinched at the word.

'How could you do it?' Carla repeated. 'We did our best to bring you up in the right way. This is just – just –'

She put her hands to her face and began to weep.

'How could you *do* it?' she cried. 'After all we've done for you, this is the thanks we get? For you to go out and . . . and . . . rut with a boy like a bitch in heat? You bad girl! You bad girl!'

She dissolved into sobs, leaning against the mantelpiece for support, one hand over her eyes, the other continuing to slip back and forth over the green cloth cover of the scrapbook. Meantime, the grandfather clock went on ticking.

'Mother –'

'Don't talk to me! You've said enough!'

Frannie stood up stiffly. Her legs felt like wood but must not be, because they were trembling. Tears were beginning to leak out of her own eyes, but let them; she would not let this room defeat her again. 'I'll be going now.'

'You ate at our table!' Carla cried at her suddenly. 'We loved you . . . and supported you . . . and this is what we get for it! Bad girl! *Bad* girl!'

Frannie, blinded by tears, stumbled. Her right foot struck her left ankle. She lost her balance and fell down with her hands splayed out. She knocked the side of her head against the coffee table and one hand sent a vase of flowers pitching onto the rug. It didn't break but water gurgled out, turning dove gray to slate gray.

'Look at that!' Carla screamed, almost in triumph. The tears had put black hollows under her eyes and cut courses through her makeup. She looked haggard and half-mad. 'Look at that, you've spoiled the rug, your grandmother's rug –'

She sat on the floor, dazedly rubbing her head, still crying, wanting to tell her mother that it was only water, but she was completely unnerved now, and not really sure. *Was* it only water? Or was it urine? Which?

Again moving with that spooky quickness, Carla Goldsmith snatched the vase up and brandished it at Frannie. 'What's your next move, miss? Are you planning to stay right here? Are you expecting us to feed you and board you while you sport yourself all around town? That's it, I suppose. Well, no! No! I won't have it. *I will not have it!*'

'I don't want to stay here,' Frannie muttered. 'Did you think I would?'

'Where are you going to go? With him? I doubt it.'

'Bobbi Rengarten in Dorchester or Debbie Smith in Somersworth, I suppose.' Frannie slowly gathered herself together and got up. She was still crying but she was beginning to be mad, as well. 'Not that it's any business of yours.'

'No business of mine?' Carla echoed, still holding the vase. Her face was parchment white. 'No business of *mine*? What you do when you're under my roof is no business of *mine*? You ungrateful little *bitch*!'

She slapped Frannie, and slapped her hard. Frannie's head rocked back. She stopped rubbing her head and started rubbing her cheek, looking unbelievingly at her mother.

'This is the thanks we get for seeing you into a nice school,' Carla said, showing her teeth in a merciless and frightful grin. 'Now you'll *never* finish. After you marry him –'

'I'm not going to marry him. And I'm not going to quit school.'

Carla's eyes widened. She stared at Frannie as if Frannie had lost her mind. 'What are you talking about? An abortion? Having an abortion? You want to be a murderer as well as a tramp?'

'I'm going to have the child. I'll have to take the spring semester off, but I can finish next summer.'

'What do you think you're going to finish *on*? *My* money? If that's it, you've got a lot more thinking to do. A modern girl like you hardly needs support from her parents, does she?'

'Support I could use,' Frannie said softly. 'The money . . . well, I'll get by.'

'There's not a bit of shame in you! Not a single thought for anyone but yourself!' Carla shouted. 'My God, what this is going to do to your father and me! But you don't care a bit! It will break your father's heart, and —'

'It don't feel so broken.' Peter Goldsmith's calm voice came from the doorway, and they both swung around. In the doorway he was, but far back in it; the toes of his workboots stopped just short of the place where the parlor carpet took over from the shabbier one in the hallway. Frannie realized suddenly that it was a place she had seen him in a great many times before. When had he last actually been in the parlor? She couldn't remember.

'What are you doing here?' Carla snapped, suddenly unmindful of any structural damage her husband's heart might have sustained. 'I thought you were working late this afternoon.'

'I switched off with Harry Masters,' Peter said. 'Fran's already told me, Carla. We are going to be grandparents.'

'*Grandparents!*' she shrieked. An ugly, confused sort of laughter jarred out of her. 'You leave this to me. She told you first and you kept it from me. All right. It's what I've come to expect of you. But now I'm going to close the door and the two of us are going to thrash this out.'

She smiled with glittery bitterness at Frannie.

'Just . . . we "girls."'

She put her hand on the knob of the parlor door and began to swing it closed. Frannie watched, still dazed, hardly able to comprehend her mother's sudden gush of fury and vitriol.

Peter put his hand out slowly, reluctantly, and stopped the door halfway through its swing.

'Peter, I want you to leave this to me.'

'I know you do. I have in the past. But not this time, Carla.'

'This is *not* your province.'

Calmly, he replied: 'It is.'

'Daddy –'

Carla turned on her, the parchment white of her face now tattooed red over the cheekbones. '*Don't you speak to him!*' she screamed. 'He's not the one you're dealing with! I know you could always wheedle him around to any crazy idea you had or sweet-talk him into taking your side no matter what you did, *but he is not the one you're dealing with today, miss!*'

'Stop it, Carla.'

'*Get out!*'

'I'm not in. You can see th –'

'Don't you make fun of me! *Get out of my parlor!*'

And with that she began to push the door, lowering her head and getting her shoulders into it until she looked like some strange bull, both human and female. He held her back easily at first, then with more effort. At last the cords stood out on his neck, although she was a woman and seventy pounds lighter than he.

Frannie wanted to scream at them to stop it, to tell her father to go away so the two of them wouldn't have to look at Carla like this, at the sudden and irrational bitterness that had always seemed to threaten but which had now swept her up. But her mouth was frozen, its hinges seemingly rusted shut.

'Get out! Get out of my parlor! Out! Out! Out! *You bastard, let go of the goddamned door and GET OUT!*'

That was when he slapped her.

It was a flat, almost unimportant sound. The grandfather clock did not fly into outraged dust at the sound, but went on ticking just as it had ever since it was set going. The furniture did not groan. But Carla's raging words were cut off as if amputated with a scalpel. She fell on her knees and the door swung all the way open to bang softly against a high-backed Victorian chair with a hand-embroidered slipcover.

'No, oh no,' Frannie said in a hurt little voice.

Carla pressed a hand to her cheek and stared up at her husband.

'You have had that coming for ten years or better,' Peter remarked. His voice had a slight unsteadiness in it. 'I always told myself I didn't do it because I don't hold with hitting women. I still don't. But when a person – man *or* woman – turns into a dog and begins to bite, someone has to shy it off. I only wish, Carla, I'd had the guts to do it sooner. 'Twould have hurt us both less.'

'Daddy –'

'Hush, Frannie,' he said with absent sternness, and she hushed.

'You say she's being selfish,' Peter said, still looking down into his wife's still, shocked face. 'You're the one doing that. You stopped caring about Frannie when Fred died. That was when you decided caring hurt too much and decided it'd be safer just to live for yourself. And this is where you came to do that, time and time and time again. This room. You doted on your dead family and forgot the part of it still living. And when she came in here and told you she was in trouble, asked for your help, I bet the first thing that crossed your mind was to wonder what the ladies in the Flower and Garden Club would say, or if it meant you'd have to stay away from Amy Lauder's weddin. Hurt's a reason to change, but all the hurt in the world don't change facts. You have been selfish.'

He reached down and helped her up. She came to her feet like a sleepwalker. Her expression didn't change; her eyes were still wide and unbelieving. Relentlessness hadn't yet come back into them, but Frannie dully thought that in time it would.

It would.

'It's my fault for letting you go on. For not wanting any unpleasantness. For not wanting to rock the boat. I was selfish, too, you see. And when Fran went off to school I thought, Well, now Carla can have what she wants and won't hurt nobody but herself, and if a person doesn't know they're hurting, why, maybe they're not. I was wrong. I've been wrong before, but never as bad as this.' Gently, but with great force, he reached out and grasped Carla's shoulders. 'Now: I am telling you this as your husband. If Frannie needs a place to stay, this can be the place – same as it always was. If she needs money, she can have it from my purse – same as she always could. And if she decides to keep her baby, you will see that she has a proper baby shower, and you may think no one will come, but she has friends, good ones, and they will. I'll tell you one more thing, too. If she wants it christened, it will be done right here. Right here in this goddamned parlor.'

Carla's mouth had dropped open, and now a sound began to come from it. At first it sounded uncannily like the whistle of a teakettle on a hot burner. Then it became a keening wail.

'Peter, your own son lay in his coffin in this room!'

'Yes. And that's why I can't think of a better place to christen a new life,' he said. 'Fred's blood. *Live* blood. Fred himself, he's been dead a lot of years, Carla. He was worm-food long since.'

She screamed at that and put her hands to her ears. He bent down and pulled them away.

'But the worms haven't got your daughter and your daughter's baby. It don't matter how it was got; it's *alive*. You act like you want to drive her off, Carla. What will you have if you do? Nothing but this room and a husband who'll hate you for what you did. If you do that, why, it might just as well have been all three of us that day – me and Frannie as well as Fred.'

'I want to go upstairs and lie down,' Carla said. 'I feel nauseated. I think I'd better lie down.'

'I'll help you,' Frannie said.

'Don't you touch me. Stay with your father. You and he seem to have this all worked out. How you are going to destroy me in this town. Why don't you just settle into my parlor, Frannie? Throw mud on the carpet, take ashes from the stove and throw them into my clock? Why not? Why not?'

She began to laugh and pushed past Peter, into the hall. She was listing like a drunken woman. Peter tried to put an arm around her shoulders. She bared her teeth and hissed at him like a cat.

Her laughter turned to sobs as she went slowly up the stairs, leaning on the mahogany banister for support; those sobs had a ripping, helpless quality that made Frannie want to scream and throw up at the same time. Her father's face was the color of dirty linen. At the top, Carla turned and swayed so alarmingly that for a moment Frannie believed she would tumble all the way back down to the bottom. She looked at them, seemingly about to speak, then turned away again. A moment later, the closing of her bedroom door muted the stormy sound of her grief and hurt.

Frannie and Peter stared at each other, appalled, and the grandfather clock ticked calmly on.

'This will work itself out,' Peter said calmly. 'She'll come around.'

'Will she?' Frannie asked. She walked slowly to her father, leaned against him, and he put his arm around her. 'I don't think so.'

'Never mind. We won't think about it for now.'

'I ought to go. She doesn't want me here.'

'You ought to stay. You ought to be here when – if – she comes to and finds out she still *needs* you to stay.' He paused. 'Me, I already do, Fran.'

'Daddy,' she said, and put her head against his chest. 'Oh, Daddy, I'm so sorry, just so goddam sorry –'

'Shhh,' he said, and stroked her hair. Over her head he could see the afternoon sunlight streaming duskily in through the bow windows, as it had always done, golden and still, the way sunlight falls into museums and the halls of the dead. 'Shhh, Frannie; I love you. I love you.'

CHAPTER 13

The red light went on. The pump hissed. The door opened. The man who stepped through was not wearing one of the white all-over suits, but a small shiny nose-filter that looked a little bit like a two-pronged silver fork, the kind the hostess leaves on the canape table to get the olives out of the bottle.

'Hi, Mr Redman,' he said, strolling across the room. He stuck out his hand, clad in a thin transparent rubber glove, and Stu, surprised into the defensive, shook it. 'I'm Dick Deitz. Denninger said you wouldn't play ball anymore unless somebody told you what the score was.'

Stu nodded.

'Good.' Deitz sat on the edge of the bed. He was a small brown man, and sitting there with his elbows cocked just above his knees, he looked like a gnome in a Disney picture. 'So what do you want to know?'

'First, I guess I want to know why you're not wearing one of those space-suits.'

'Because Geraldo there says you're not catching.' Deitz pointed to a guinea pig behind the double-paned window. The guinea pig was in a cage, and standing behind the cage was Denninger himself, his face expressionless.

'Geraldo, huh?'

'Geraldo's been breathing your air for the last three days, via convector. This disease that your friends have passes easily from humans to guinea pigs and vice versa. If you were catching, we figure Geraldo would be dead by now.'

'But you're not taking any chances,' Stu said dryly, and cocked a thumb at the nose-filter.

'That,' Deitz said with a cynical smile, 'is not in my contract.'

'What have I got?'

Smoothly, as if rehearsed, Deitz said, 'Black hair, blue eyes, one hell of a suntan . . .' He looked closely at Stu. 'Not funny, huh?'

Stu said nothing.

'Want to hit me?'

'I don't believe it would do any good.'

Deitz sighed and rubbed the bridge of his nose as if the plugs going up the nostrils hurt. 'Listen,' he said. 'When things look serious, I do jokes. Some people smoke or chew gum. It's the way I keep my shit together, that's all. I don't doubt there are lots of people who have better ways. As to what sort of disease you've got, well, so far as Denninger and his colleagues have been able to ascertain, you don't have any at all.'

Stu nodded impassively. Yet somehow he had an idea this little gnome of a man had seen past his poker face to his sudden and deep relief.

'What have the others got?'

'I'm sorry, that's classified.'

'How did that fellow Campion get it?'

'That's classified, too.'

'My guess is that he was in the army. And there was an accident someplace. Like what happened to those sheep in Utah thirty years ago, only a lot worse.'

'Mr Redman, I could go to jail just for telling you you were hot or cold.'

Stu rubbed a hand thoughtfully over his new scrub of beard.

'You should be glad we're not telling you more than we are,' Deitz said. 'You know that, don't you?'

'So I can serve my country better,' Stu said dryly.

'No, that's strictly Denninger's thing,' Deitz said. 'In the scheme of things both Denninger and I are little men, but Denninger is even littler than I am. He's a servomotor, nothing more. There's a more pragmatic reason for you to be glad. You're classified, too, you know. You've disappeared from the face of the earth. If you knew enough, the big guys might decide that the safest thing would be for you to disappear forever.'

Stu said nothing. He was stunned.

'But I didn't come here to threaten you. We want your cooperation very badly, Mr Redman. We need it.'

'Where are the other people I came in here with?'

Deitz brought a paper out of an inside pocket. 'Victor Palfrey, deceased. Norman Bruett, Robert Bruett, deceased. Thomas Wannamaker, deceased. Ralph Hodges, Bert Hodges, Cheryl Hodges, deceased. Christian Ortega, deceased. Anthony Leominster, deceased.'

The names reeled in Stu's head. Chris the bartender. He'd always kept a sawed-off, lead-loaded Louisville Slugger under the bar, and the trucker who thought Chris was just kidding about using it was apt to get a big surprise. Tony Leominster, who drove that big International with the Cobra CB under the dash. Sometimes hung around Hap's station, but hadn't been there the night Campion took out the pumps. Vic Palfrey . . . Christ, he had known Vic his whole life. How could Vic be dead? But the thing that hit him the hardest was the Hodges family.

'*All* of them?' he heard himself ask. 'Ralph's whole *family*?'

Deitz turned the paper over. 'No, there's a little girl. Eva. Four years old. She's alive.'

'Well, how is she?'

'I'm sorry, that's classified.'

Rage struck him with all the unexpectedness of a sweet surprise. He was up, and then he had hold of Deitz's lapels, and he was shaking him back and forth. From the corner of his eye he saw startled movement behind the double-paned glass. Dimly, muffled by distance and soundproofed walls, he heard a hooter go off.

'What did you people do?' he shouted. 'What did you do? What in Christ's name did you *do*?'

'Mr Redman —'

'Huh? What the fuck did you people *do*?'

The door hissed open. Three large men in olive-drab uniforms stepped in. They were all wearing nose-filters.

Deitz looked over at them and snapped, 'Get the hell out of here!'

The three men looked uncertain.

'Our orders —'

'Get out of here and *that's* an order!'

They retreated. Deitz sat calmly on the bed. His lapels were rumpled and his hair had tumbled over his forehead. That was all. He was looking at Stu calmly, even compassionately. For a wild moment Stu considered ripping his nose-filter out, and then he remembered Geraldo, what a stupid name for a guinea pig. Dull despair struck him like cold water. He sat down.

'Christ in a sidecar,' he muttered.

'Listen to me,' Deitz said. 'I'm not responsible for you being here. Neither is Denninger, or the nurses who come in to take your blood pressure. If there was a responsible party it was Campion, but you can't lay it all on him, either. He ran, but under the circumstances, you or I might have run, too. It was a technical slipup that allowed him to run. The situation exists. We are trying to cope with it, all of us. But that doesn't make us responsible.'

'Then who is?'

'Nobody,' Deitz said, and smiled. 'On this one the responsibility spreads in so many directions that it's invisible. It was an accident. It could have happened in any number of other ways.'

'Some accident,' Stu said, his voice nearly a whisper. 'What about the others? Hap and Hank Carmichael and Lila Bruett? Their boy Luke? Monty Sullivan —'

'Classified,' Deitz said. 'Going to shake me some more? If it will make you feel better, shake away.'

Stu said nothing, but the way he was looking at Deitz made Deitz suddenly look down and begin to fiddle with the creases of his pants.

'They're alive,' he said, 'and you may see them in time.'

'What about Arnette?'

'Quarantined.'

'Who's dead there?'

'Nobody.'

'You're lying.'

'Sorry you think so.'

'When do I get out of here?'

'I don't know.'

'Classified?' Stu asked bitterly.

'No, just unknown. You don't seem to have this disease. We want to know why you don't have it. Then we're home free.'

'Can I get a shave? I itch.'

Deitz smiled. 'If you'll allow Denninger to start running his tests again, I'll get an orderly in to shave you right now.'

'I can handle it. I've been doing it since I was fifteen.'

Deitz shook his head firmly. 'I think not.'

Stu smiled dryly at him. 'Afraid I might cut my own throat?'

'Let's just say —'

Stu interrupted him with a series of harsh, dry coughs. He bent over with the force of them.

The effect on Deitz was galvanic. He was up off the bed like a shot and across to the airlock with his feet seeming not to touch the floor at all. Then he was fumbling in his pocket for the square key and ramming it into the slot.

'Don't bother,' Stu said mildly. 'I was faking.'

Deitz turned to him slowly. Now his face had changed. His lips were thinned with anger, his eyes staring. 'You were *what*?'

'Faking,' Stu said. His smile broadened.

Deitz took two uncertain steps toward him. His fists closed, opened, then closed again. 'But why? Why would you want to do something like that?'

'Sorry,' Stu said, smiling. 'That's classified.'

'You shit sonofabitch,' Deitz said with soft wonder.

'Go on. Go on out and tell them they can do their tests.'

He slept better that night than he had since they had brought him here. And he had an extremely vivid dream. He had always dreamed a great deal – his wife had complained about him thrashing and muttering in his sleep – but he had never had a dream like this.

He was standing on a country road, at the precise place where the black hottop gave up to bone-white dirt. A blazing summer sun shone down. On both sides of the road there was green corn, and it stretched away endlessly. There was a sign, but it was dusty and he couldn't read it. There was the sound of crows, harsh and far away. Closer by, someone was playing an acoustic guitar, fingerpicking it. Vic Palfrey had been a picker, and it was a fine sound.

This is where I ought to get to, Stu thought dimly. *Yeah, this is the place, all right.*

What was that tune? 'Beautiful Zion'? 'The Fields of My Father's Home'? 'Sweet Bye and Bye'? Some hymn he remembered from his childhood, something he associated with full immersion and picnic lunches. But he couldn't remember which one.

Then the music stopped. A cloud came over the sun. He began to be afraid. He began to feel that there was something terrible, something worse than plague, fire, or earthquake. Something was in the corn and it was watching him. Something dark was in the corn.

He looked, and saw two burning red eyes far back in the shadows, far back in the corn. Those eyes filled him with the paralyzed, hopeless horror that the hen feels for the weasel. *Him*, he thought. The man with no face. *Oh dear God. Oh dear God no.*

Then the dream was fading and he awoke with feelings of disquiet, dislocation, and relief. He went to the bathroom and then to his window. He looked out at the moon. He went back to bed but it was an hour before he got back to sleep. All that corn, he thought sleepily. Must have been Iowa or Nebraska, maybe northern Kansas. But he had never been in any of those places in his life.

CHAPTER 14

It was quarter of twelve. Outside the small pillbox window, dark pressed evenly against the glass. Deitz sat alone in the office cubicle, tie pulled down, collar button undone. His feet were up on the anonymous metal desk, and he was holding a microphone. On top of the desk, the reels of an old-fashioned Wollensak tape recorder turned and turned.

'This is Colonel Deitz,' he said. 'Located Atlanta facility code PB-2. This is Report 16, subject file Project Blue, subfile Princess/ Prince. This report, file, and subfile are Top Secret, classification 2-2-3, eyes only. If you are not classified to receive this material, fuck off, Jack.'

He stopped and let his eyes fall closed for a moment. The tape reels ran on smoothly, undergoing all the correct electrical and magnetic changes.

'Prince gave me one helluva scare tonight,' he said at last. 'I won't go into it; it'll be in Denninger's report. That guy will be more than willing to quote chapter and verse. Plus, of course, a transcription of my conversation with Prince will be on the telecom- munications disc which also contains the transcription of this tape, which is being made at 2345 hours. I was almost pissed enough to hit him, because he scared the living Jesus out of me. I am not pissed anymore, however. The man put me into his shoes, and for just a second there I knew exactly how it feels to shake in them. He's a fairly bright man once you get past the Gary Cooper exterior, and one independent sonofabitch. If it suits him, he'll find all sorts of novel monkey-wrenches to throw into the gears. He has no close family in Arnette or anyplace else, so we can't put much of a hammerlock on him. Denninger has volunteers – or says he does – who'll be happy to go in and muscle him into a more coopera- tive frame of mind, and it may come to that, but if I may be pardoned another personal observation, I believe it would take more muscle than Denninger thinks. Maybe a whole lot more. For the record, I am still against it. My mother used to say you can catch more flies with honey than you can with vinegar, and I guess I still believe it.

'Again, for the record, he still tests virus-clean. You figure it out.'

He paused again, fighting the urge to doze off. He had managed only four hours of sleep in the last seventy-two.

'Records as of twenty-two-hundred hours,' he said formally, and picked a sheaf of reports off the desk. 'Henry Carmichael died while I was talking with Prince. The cop, Joseph Robert Brentwood, died half an hour ago. This won't be in Dr D's report, but he was all but shitting green apples over that one. Brentwood showed a sudden positive response to the vaccine type . . . uh . . .' He shuffled papers. 'Here it is. 63-A-3. See subfile, if you like. Brentwood's fever broke, the characteristic swellings in the glands of the neck went down, he reported hunger, and ate a poached egg and a slice of unbuttered toast. Spoke rationally, wanted to know where he was, and so on and so on and scooby-dooby-do. Then, around twenty-hundred hours, the fever came back with a bang. Delirious. He broke the restraints on his bed and went reeling around the room, yelling, coughing, blowing snot, the whole bit. Then he fell over and died. Kaboom. The opinion of the team is that the vaccine killed him. It made him better for a while, but he was getting sick again even before it killed him. So, it's back to the old drawing boards.'

He paused.

'I saved the worst for last. We can declassify Princess back to plain old Eva Hodges, female, age four, Caucasian. Her coach-and-four turned back into a pumpkin and a bunch of mice late this afternoon. To look at her, you'd think she was perfectly normal, not even a sniffle. She's downhearted, of course; she misses her mom. Other than that, she appears perfectly normal. She's got it, though. Her post-lunch BP first showed a drop, then a rise, which is the only halfway decent diagnostic tool Denninger's got so far. Before supper Denninger showed me her sputum slides – as an incentive to diet, sputum slides are really primo, believe me – and they're lousy with those wagon-wheel germs he says aren't really germs at all, but incubators. I can't understand how he can know where this thing is and what it looks like and still not be able to

stop it. He gives me a lot of jargon, and I don't think he understands it, either.'

Deitz lit a cigarette.

'So where are we tonight? We've got a disease that's got several
well-defined stages . . . but some people may skip a stage. Some people
may backtrack a stage. Some people may do both. Some people stay
in one stage for a relatively long time and others zoom through
all four as if they were on a rocket-sled. One of our two "clean"
subjects is no longer clean. The other is a thirty-year-old redneck
who seems to be as healthy as I am. Denninger has done about
thirty million tests on him and has succeeded in isolating only four
abnormalities: Redman appears to have a great many moles on his
body. He has a slight hypertensive condition, too slight to medi-
cate right now. He develops a mild tic under his left eye when
he's under stress. And Denninger says he dreams a great deal more
than average – almost all night, every night. They got that from
the standard EEG series they ran before he went on strike. And
that's it. I can't make anything out of it, neither can Dr Denninger,
and neither can the people who check Dr Demento's work.

'This scares me, Starkey. It scares me because nobody but a
very smart doctor with all the facts is going to be able to diagnose
anything but a common cold in the people who are out there carrying
this. Christ, nobody goes to the doctor anymore unless they've got
pneumonia or a suspicious lump on the tit or a bad case of the
dancing hives. Too hard to get one to look at you. So they're going
to stay home, drink fluids and get plenty of bedrest, and then they're
going to die. Before they do, they're going to infect everyone who
comes into the same room with them. All of us are still expecting
the Prince – I think I used his real name here someplace, but at this
juncture I don't really give a fuck – to come down with it tonight
or tomorrow or the day after, at the latest. And so far, no one who's
come down with it has gotten better. Those sonsofbitches out in
California did this job a little too well for my taste.

'Deitz, Atlanta PB facility 2, this report ends.'

He turned off the recorder and stared at it for a long time.
Then he lit another cigarette.

CHAPTER 15

It was two minutes to midnight.

Patty Greer, the nurse who had been trying to take Stu's blood pressure when he went on strike, was leafing through the current issue of *McCall's* at the nurses' station and waiting to go in and check Mr Sullivan and Mr Hapscomb. Hap would still be awake watching Johnny Carson and would be no problem. He liked to josh her about how hard it would be to pinch her bottom through her white all-over suit. Mr Hapscomb was scared, but he was being cooperative, not like that dreadful Stuart Redman, who only looked at you and wouldn't say boo to a goose. Mr Hapscomb was what Patty Greer thought of as a 'good sport.' As far as she was concerned, all patients could be divided into two categories: 'good sports' and 'old poops.' Patty, who had broken a leg roller skating when she was seven and had never spent a day in bed since, had very little patience with the 'old poops.' You were either really sick and being a 'good sport' or you were a hypochondriac 'old poop' making trouble for a poor working girl.

Mr Sullivan would be asleep, and he would wake up ugly. It wasn't her fault that she had to wake him up, and she would think Mr Sullivan would understand that. He should just be grateful that he was getting the best care the government could provide, and all free at that. And she would just tell him so if he started being an 'old poop' again tonight.

The clock touched midnight; time to get going.

She left the nurses' station and walked down the hallway toward the white room where she would first be sprayed and then helped into her suit. Halfway there, her nose began to tickle. She got her hankie out of her pocket and sneezed lightly three times. She replaced the handkerchief.

Intent on dealing with cranky Mr Sullivan, she attached no significance to her sneezes. It was probably a touch of hay fever. The directive in the nurses' station which said in big red letters, REPORT ANY COLD SYMPTOMS <u>NO MATTER HOW MINOR</u> TO YOUR SUPERVISOR <u>AT ONCE</u>, never even crossed her mind. They were worried that whatever those poor people from Texas had might spread outside the sealed rooms, but she also knew it was impossible for even a tiny virus to get inside the self-contained environment of the white-suits.

Nevertheless, on her way down to the white room she infected an orderly, a doctor who was just getting ready to leave, and another nurse on her way to do her midnight rounds.

A new day had begun.

CHAPTER 16

A day later, on June 23, a big white Connie was roaring north on US 180, in another part of the country. It was doing somewhere between ninety and one hundred, its Corinthian white paintjob glittering in the sun, the chrome winking. The opera windows in the rear also gave back the sun, heliographing it viciously.

The trail that Connie had left behind itself since Poke and Lloyd killed its owner and stole it somewhere just south of Hachita was wandering and pretty much senseless. Up 81 to US 80, the turnpike, until Poke and Lloyd began to feel nervous. They had killed six people in the last six days, including the owner of the Continental, his wife, and his smarmy daughter. But it was not the six murders that made them feel antsy about being on the interstate. It was the dope and the guns. Five grams of hash, a little tin snuffbox filled with God knew how much coke, and sixteen pounds of marijuana. Also two .38s, three .45s, a .357 Mag that Poke called his Pokerizer, six shotguns – two of them sawed-off pumps – and a Schmeisser submachine gun. Murder was a trifle beyond their intellectual reach, but they both understood the trouble they were going to be in if the Arizona State Police picked them up in a stolen car full of blow and shootin irons. On top of everything else, they were interstate fugitives. Had been ever since they crossed the Nevada border.

Interstate fugitives. Lloyd Henreid liked the sound of that. Gangbusters. Take that, you dirty rat. Have a lead sandwich, ya lousy copper.

So they had turned north at Deming, now on 180; had gone through Hurley and Bayard and the slightly larger town of Silver City, where Lloyd had bought a bag of burgers and eight milkshakes (why in the name of Christ had he bought eight of the motherfuckers? they would soon be pissing chocolate), grinning at the waitress in an empty yet hilarious way that made her nervous for hours afterward. I believe that man would just as soon killed me as looked at me, she told her boss that afternoon.

Past Silver City and roaring through Cliff, the road now bending west again, just the direction they didn't want to go. Through Buckhorn and then they were back in the country God forgot, two-lane blacktop running through sagebrush and sand, buttes and mesas in the background, all that same old same old made you want to just rare back and puke at it.

'We're gettin low on gas,' Poke said.

'Wouldn't be if you didn't drive so fuckin fast,' Lloyd said. He took a sip of his third milkshake, gagged on it, powered down the window, and threw out all the leftover crap, including the three milkshakes neither of them had touched.

'Whoop! Whoop!' Poke cried. He began to goose the gas pedal. The Connie lurched forward, dropped back, lurched forward.

'Ride em cowboy!' Lloyd yelled.

'Whoop! Whoop!'

'You want to smoke?'

'Smoke em if you got em,' Poke said. 'Whoop! Whoop!'

There was a large green Hefty bag on the floor between Lloyd's feet. It held the sixteen pounds of marijuana. He reached in, got a handful, and began to roll a bomber joint.

'Whoop! Whoop!' The Connie cruised back and forth over the white line.

'Cut the shit!' Lloyd shouted. 'I'm spillin it everywhere!'

'Plenty more where that came from . . . whoop!'

'Come on, we gotta deal this stuff, man. We gotta deal this stuff or we're gonna get caught and wind up in somebody's trunk.'

'Okay, sport.' Poke began to drive smoothly again, but his expression was sulky. 'It was your idea, your fuckin idea.'

'You thought it was a *good* idea.'

'Yeah, but I didn't know we'd end up drivin all over fuckin Arizona. How we ever gonna get to New York this way?'

'We're throwin off pursuit, man,' Lloyd said. In his mind he saw police garage doors opening and thousands of 1940s radio cars issuing forth into the night. Spotlights crawling over brick walls. Come on out, Canarsie, we know you're in there.

'Good fuckin luck,' Poke said, still sulking. 'We're doin a helluva job. You know what we got, besides that dope and the guns? We got sixteen bucks and three hundred fuckin credit cards we don't dare use. What the fuck, we don't even have enough cash to fill this hog's gas tank.'

'God will provide,' Lloyd said, and spit-sealed the bomber. He lit it with the Connie's dashboard lighter. 'Happy fuckin days.'

'And if you want to sell it, what are we doing smokin it?' Poke went on, not much mollified by the thought of God providing.

'So we sell a few short ounces. Come on, Poke. Have a smoke.'

This never failed to break Poke up. He brayed laughter and took the joint. Between them, standing on its wire stock, was the Schmeisser, fully loaded. The Connie blazed on up the road, its gas gauge standing at an eighth.

Poke and Lloyd had met a year before in the Brownsville Minimum Security Station, a Nevada work farm. Brownsville was ninety acres of irrigated farmland and a prison compound of Quonset huts about sixty miles north of Tonopah and eighty northeast of Gabbs. It was a mean place to do short time. Although Brownsville Station was supposed to be a farm, nothing much grew there. Carrots and lettuce got one taste of that blaring sun, chuckled weakly, and died. Legumes and weeds would grow, and the state legislature was fanatically dedicated to the idea that someday soybeans would grow. But the kindest thing that could be said about Brownsville's ostensible purpose was that the desert was taking a Christless long time to bloom. The warden (who preferred to be called 'the boss') prided himself on being a hardass, and he hired only men he considered to be fellow hardasses. And, as he was fond of telling the new fish, Brownsville was mostly minimum security because when it came to escape, it was like the song said: noplace to run to, baby, noplace to hide. Some gave it a shot anyway, but most were brought back in two or three days, sunburned, glareblind, and eager to sell the boss their shriveled raisin souls for a drink of water. Some of them cackled madly, and one young man who was out for three days claimed he saw a large castle some miles south of Gabbs, a castle with a moat. The moat, he said, was guarded by trolls riding big black horses. Some months later when a Colorado revival preacher did a show at Brownsville, this same young man got Jesus in a big way.

Andrew 'Poke' Freeman, in for simple assault, was released in April 1989. He had occupied a bed next to Lloyd Henreid, and had told him that if Lloyd was interested in a big score, he knew about something interesting in Vegas. Lloyd was willing.

Lloyd was released on June 1. His crime, committed in Reno, had been attempted rape. The lady was a showgirl on her way home, and she had shot a load of teargas into Lloyd's eyes. He felt lucky to get only two to four, plus time served, plus time off for good behavior. At Brownsville it was just too fuckin hot to misbehave.

He caught a bus to Las Vegas, and Poke met him at the terminal. This is the deal, Poke told him. He knew this guy, 'one-time business associate' might describe him best, and this guy was known in certain circles as Gorgeous George. He did some piecework for a group of people with mostly Italian and Sicilian names. George was strictly part-time help. What he did mostly for these Sicilian-type people was to take things and bring things. Sometimes he took things from Vegas to LA; sometimes he brought other things from LA to Vegas. Small-time dope mostly, freebies for big-time customers. Sometimes guns. The guns were always a bring, never a take. As Poke understood it (and Poke's understanding never got much beyond what the movie people call 'soft focus'), these Sicilian-type people sometimes sold iron to independent thieves. Well, Poke said, Gorgeous George was willing to tell them the time and place when a fairly good haul of these items would be in the offing. George was asking twenty-five percent of what they realized. Poke and Lloyd would crash in on George, tie him and gag him, take the stuff, and maybe give him a couple of biffs and baffs for good measure. It had to look good, George had cautioned, because these Sicilian-type people were no one to fool around with.

'Well,' Lloyd said, 'it sounds good.'

The next day Poke and Lloyd went to see Gorgeous George, a mild-mannered six-footer with a small head which sat incongruously above his roofbeam shoulders on a neck which did not seem to exist. He had a full head of waved blond hair, which made him look a bit like the famed wrestler.

Lloyd had had second thoughts about the deal, but Poke had changed his mind again. Poke was good at that. George told them to come around to his house the following Friday evening around six. 'Wear masks, for God's sake,' he said. 'And you bloody my nose and black my eye, too. Jesus, I wish I'd never gotten into this.'

The big night came. Poke and Lloyd took a bus to the corner of George's street and put on ski-masks at the foot of his walk. The door was locked, but as George had promised, not too tightly locked. There was a rumpus room downstairs, and there was George, standing in front of a Hefty bag full of pot. The Ping-Pong table was loaded down with guns. George was scared.

'Jesus, oh Jesus, I wish I'd never gotten into this,' he kept saying as Lloyd tied his feet with clothesrope and Poke bound his hands with Scotch brand filament tape.

Then Lloyd biffed George in the nose, bloodying it, and Poke baffed him in the eye, blacking it as per request.

'Jeez!' George cried. 'Did you have to do it so hard?'

'You were the one wanted to make sure it looked good,' Lloyd pointed out.

Poke plastered a piece of adhesive tape across George's mouth. The two of them had begun to gather up the swag.

'You know something, old buddy?' Poke said, pausing.

'Nope,' Lloyd said, giggling nervously. 'Not a thing.'

'I wonder if ole George there can keep a secret.'

For Lloyd, this was a brand-new consideration. He stared thoughtfully at Gorgeous George for a long hard minute. George's eyes bugged back at him in sudden terror.

Then Lloyd said, 'Sure. It's his ass too.' But he sounded as uneasy as he felt. When certain seeds are planted, they nearly always grow.

Poke smiled. 'Oh, he could just say, "Hey guys. I met this old friend and his buddy. We shot the shit for a while, had a few beers, and what do you think, the sonsofbitches came over to the house and took me off. Sure hope you catch em. Lemme tell you what they look like."'

George was shaking his head wildly, his eyes capital Os of terror.

The guns were by then in a heavy canvas laundry sack they had found in the downstairs bathroom. Now Lloyd hefted the bag nervously and said, 'Well, what do you think we ought to do?'

'I think we ought to pokerize him, ole buddy,' Poke said regretfully. 'Only thing we *can* do.'

Lloyd said, 'That seems awful hard, after he put us onto this.'

'Hard old world, buddy.'

'Yeah,' Lloyd sighed, and they walked over to George.

'*Mph*,' George said, shaking his head wildly. '*Mmmmmnh! Mmmmph!*'

'I know,' Poke soothed him. 'Bitch, ain't it? I'm sorry, George, no shit. It ain't a bit personal. Want you to 'member that. Catch on his head, Lloyd.'

That was easier said than done. Gorgeous George was whipping his head wildly from side to side. He was sitting in the corner of his rumpus room and the walls were cinder-block and he kept rapping his head against them. Didn't even seem to feel it.

'Catch him,' Poke said serenely, and ripped another piece of tape from the roll.

Lloyd at last got him by the hair and managed to hold him still long enough for Poke to slap the second strip of adhesive neatly across George's nose, thereby sealing all of his tubes. George went purely crazy. He rolled out of the corner, bellywhopped, and then lay there, humping the floor and making muffled sounds which Lloyd supposed were supposed to be screams. Poor old fellow. It went on for almost five minutes before George was completely still. He bucked and scrabbled and thumped. His face got as red as the side of old Dad's barn. The last thing he did was to lift both legs eight or ten inches straight up off the floor and bring them down with a crash. It reminded Lloyd of something he had seen in a Bugs Bunny cartoon or something, and he chuckled a little, feeling a bit cheered up. Up until then it had been sort of gruesome to see.

Poke squatted beside George and felt for his pulse.

'Well?' Lloyd said.

'Nothin tickin but his watch, ole buddy,' Poke said. 'Speakin of which . . .' He lifted George's meaty arm and looked at his wrist. 'Naw, just a Timex. I was thinkin it might be a Casio, somethin like that.' He let George's arm drop.

George's car keys were in his front pants pocket. And in an upstairs cupboard they found a Skippy peanut butter jar half filled with dimes, and they took those, too. There was twenty dollars and sixty cents in dimes.

George's car was a wheezy old Mustang with a four on the floor and lousy shocks and tires that were as bald as Telly Savalas. They left Vegas on US 93 and went southeast into Arizona. By noon of the next day, day before yesterday, they had skirted Phoenix on the back roads. Yesterday around nine they had stopped at a dusty old general store two miles beyond Sheldon on Arizona Highway 75. They knocked over the store and pokerized the proprietor, an elderly gentleman with mail-order false teeth. They got sixty-three dollars and the old dude-mar's pickup truck.

The pickup truck had blown two tires this morning. Two tires at the same time, and neither of them could find any tacks or nails on the road at all, although they spent nearly half an hour looking, swapping a bomber joint back and forth as they did so. Poke finally said it must have been a coincidence. Lloyd said he had heard of stranger things, by God. Then along came the white Connie, like an answer to their prayers. They had crossed the state line from Arizona into New Mexico earlier on, although neither of them knew it, and so they had become meat for the FBI.

The Connie's driver had pulled over, leaned out, and said: 'Need any help?'

'Sure do,' Poke had said, and pokerized the guy right on the spot. Got him dead-bang between the eyes with the .357 Mag. Poor sucker probably never even knew what had hit him.

'Why don't you turn here?' Lloyd said, pointing to the junction coming up. He was pleasantly stoned.

'Sure could,' Poke said cheerfully. He let the Connie's speed drop from eighty to sixty. Drifted it to the left, right wheels barely leaving the ground, and then a new piece of road was unrolling in front of them. Route 78, due west. And so, not knowing they had ever left it or that they were now the perpetrators of what the newspapers were calling a TRI-STATE KILL-SPREE, they reentered Arizona.

About an hour later a sign came up on their right: BURRACK 6.

'Burlap?' Lloyd said foggily.

'Burrack,' Poke said, and began twisting the Connie's wheel so that the car made big graceful loops back and forth across the road. 'Whoop! Whoop!'

'You want to stop there? I'm hungry, man.'

'You're always hungry.'

'Fuck you. When I get stoned, I get the munchies.'

'You can munch my nine-inch hogleg, how's that? Whoop! Whoop!'

'Seriously, Poke. Let's stop.'

'Okay. Got to get some cash, too. We've thrown off enough fuckin pursuit for a while. We got to get some money and shag ass north. This desert shit makes no sense to me.'

'Okay,' Lloyd said. He didn't know if it was the dope working on him or what, but all of a sudden he felt paranoid as hell, even worse than when they had been on the turnpike. Poke was right. Stop outside this Burrack and pull a score like they had outside of Sheldon. Get some money and some gas station maps, ditch this fuckin Connie for something that would blend into the scenery, then head north and east by the secondary roads. Get the fuck out of Arizona.

'I'll tell you the truth, man,' Poke said. 'All of a sudden I feel as nervous as a longtail cat in a room fulla rockin chairs.'

'I know what you mean, jellybean,' Lloyd said gravely, and then it hit them both funny and they broke up.

Burrack was a wide place in the road. They shot through it and on the other side was a combination café, store, and gas station. There was an old Ford wagon and a dust-streaked Olds with a horse trailer behind it in the dirt parking lot. The horse stared out at them as Poke wheeled the Connie in.

'This looks like just the ticket,' Lloyd said.

Poke agreed. He reached into the back for the .357 and checked the loads. 'You ready?'

'I guess so,' Lloyd said, and took hold of the Schmeisser.

They walked across the baked parking lot. The police had known who they were for four days now; they had left their fingerprints all over Gorgeous George's house, and in the store where the old man with the mail-order dentures had been pokerized. The old man's pickup had been found within fifty feet of the bodies of the three people who belonged with the Continental, and it seemed reasonable to assume that the men who had killed Gorgeous George and the store owner had also killed these three. If they had been listening to the Connie's radio instead of the tape-player, they would have known that Arizona and New Mexico police were coordinating the largest manhunt in forty years, all for a couple of small-time grifters who could not quite comprehend what they might have done to start such a fuss.

The gas was self-service; the clerk had to turn on the pump. So they went up the steps and inside. Three aisles of canned goods went up the room toward the counter. At the counter a man in cowboy clothes was paying for a pack of smokes and half a dozen Slim Jims. Halfway down the middle aisle a tired-looking woman with coarse black hair was trying to decide between two brands of spaghetti sauce. The place smelled of stale licorice and sun and tobacco and age. The proprietor was a freckled man in a gray shirt. He was wearing a company cap that said SHELL in red letters against a white field. He looked up as the screen door slapped shut and his eyes widened.

Lloyd put the wire stock of the Schmeisser against his shoulder and fired a burst at the ceiling. The two hanging lightbulbs shattered like bombs. The man in the cowboy clothes began to turn around.

'Just hold still and nobody'll get hurt!' Lloyd shouted, and Poke immediately made him a liar by blowing a hole through the woman looking at the sauces. She flew out of her shoes.

'Holy gee, Poke!' Lloyd hollered. 'You didn't have to —'

'Pokerized her, ole buddy!' Poke yelled. 'She'll never watch Jerry Falwell again! Whoop! Whoop!'

The man in the cowboy clothes kept turning. He was holding his smokes in his left hand. The harsh light falling through the show window and the screen door pricked out bright stars on the dark lenses of his sunglasses. There was a .45 revolver tucked into his belt, and now he plucked it out unhurriedly as Lloyd and Poke were staring at the dead woman. He aimed, fired, and the left side of Poke's face suddenly disappeared in a spray of blood and tissue and teeth.

'Shot!' Poke screamed, dropping the .357 and flailing backward. His flailing hands raked potato chips and taco chips and Cheez Doodles onto the splintery wooden floor. 'Shot me, Lloyd! Look out! Shot me! Shot me!' He hit the screen door and it slammed open and Poke sat down hard on the porch outside, pulling one of the aged door hinges loose.

Lloyd, stunned, fired more in reflex than in self-defense. The Schmeisser's roar filled the room. Cans flew. Bottles crashed, spilling catsup, pickles, olives. The glass front of the Pepsi cooler jingled inward. Bottles of Dr Pepper and Jolt and Orange Crush exploded like clay pigeons. Foam ran everywhere. The man in the cowboy clothes, cool, calm, and collected, fired his piece again. Lloyd felt rather than heard the bullet as it droned by nearly close enough to part hair. He raked the Schmeisser across the room, from left to right.

The man in the SHELL cap dropped behind the counter with such suddenness that an observer might have thought a trapdoor had been sprung on him. A gumball machine disintegrated. Red, blue, and green chews rolled everywhere. The glass bottles on the counter exploded. One of them had contained pickled eggs; another, pickled pigs' feet. Immediately the room was filled with the sharp odor of vinegar.

The Schmeisser put three bullet holes in the cowboy's khaki shirt and most of his innards exited from the back to splatter all over Spuds MacKenzie. The cowboy went down, still clutching his .45 in one hand and his deck of Luckies in the other.

Lloyd, bullshit with fear, continued to fire. The machine pistol was growing hot in his hands. A box filled with returnable soda bottles tinkled and fell over. A calendar girl wearing hotpants took a bullet hole in one magical peach-colored thigh. A rack of paperbacks with no covers crashed over. Then the Schmeisser was empty, and the new silence was deafening. The smell of gunpowder was heavy and rank.

'Holy gee,' Lloyd said. He looked cautiously at the cowboy. It didn't look like the cowboy was going to be a problem in either the near or distant future.

'*Shot me!*' Poke brayed, and staggered back inside. He clawed the screen door out of his way with such force that the other hinge popped and the door slapped onto the porch. '*Shot me, Lloyd, look out!*'

'I got him, Poke,' Lloyd soothed, but Poke seemed not to hear. He was a mess. His right eye blazed like a baleful sapphire. The left was gone. His left cheek had been vaporized; you could watch his jaw work on that side as he talked. Most of his teeth were gone over there, too. His shirt was soaked with blood. When you got right down to it, Poke was sort of a mess.

'*Stupid fuck blew me up!*' Poke screamed. He bent over and got the .357 Mag. '*I'll teach you to shoot me, you dumb fuck!*'

He advanced on the cowboy, a rural Dr Sardonicus. He put one foot on the cowboy's butt like a hunter posing for a picture with the bear which would soon be decorating the wall of his den, and prepared to empty the .357 into his head. Lloyd stood watching, gape-mouthed, the smoking machine pistol dangling from one hand, still trying to figure out how all of this had happened.

At that moment the man in the SHELL cap popped back up from behind the counter like Jack from his box, his face screwed up in an expression of desperate intent, a double-barreled shotgun clutched in both hands.

'Huh?' Poke said, and looked up just in time to get both barrels. He went down, his face a worse mess than ever and not caring a bit.

Lloyd decided it was time to leave. Fuck the money. There was money everywhere. The time to throw off a little more pursuit had clearly come. He wheeled and exited the store in large shambling strides, his boots barely touching the boards.

He was halfway down the steps when an Arizona State Police

cruiser wheeled into the yard. A trooper got out on the passenger side and pulled his pistol. 'Hold it right there! What's going on in there?'

'Three people dead!' Lloyd cried. 'Hell of a mess! Guy that did it went out the back! I'm gettin the fuck out!'

He ran to the Connie, had actually slipped behind the wheel, and was just remembering that the keys were in Poke's pocket when the trooper yelled: 'Halt! Halt or I'll shoot!'

Lloyd halted. After examining the radical surgery on Poke's face, it didn't take a long time to decide he'd just as soon pass.

'Holy gee,' he said miserably as a second trooper laid a big horse pistol upside his head. The first one cuffed him.

'In the back of the cruiser, Sunny Jim.'

The man in the SHELL cap had come out onto the porch, still clutching his shotgun. 'He shot Bill Markson!' he yelled in a high, queer voice. 'T'other one shot Missus Storm! Hell of a note! I shot t'other one! He's deader'n a shitbug! Like to shoot this one too, iff'n you boys'll stand away!'

'Calm down, pop,' one of the troopers said. 'Fun's over.'

'I'll shoot him where he stands!' the old guy yelled. 'I'll lay him low!' Then he leaned forward like an English butler making a bow and threw up on his shoes.

'You boys get me away from that guy, would you?' Lloyd said. 'I believe he's crazy.'

'You got this comin outta the store, Sunny Jim,' the trooper who had thrown down on him in the first place said. The barrel of his pistol looped up and up, catching the sun, and then it crashed down on Lloyd Henreid's head and he never woke up until that evening in the Apache County Jail's infirmary.

CHAPTER 17

Starkey was standing in front of monitor 2, keeping a close eye on Tech 2nd Class Frank D. Bruce. When we last saw Bruce, he was facedown in a bowl of Chunky Sirloin Soup. No change except for the positive ID. Situation normal, all fucked up.

Thoughtfully, hands locked behind his back like a general reviewing troops, like General Black Jack Pershing, his boyhood idol, Starkey moved down to monitor 4, where the situation had changed for the better. Dr Emmanual Ezwick still lay dead on the floor, but the centrifuge had stopped. At 1940 hours last night, the centrifuge had begun to emit fine tendrils of smoke. At 1995 hours the sound pickups in Ezwick's lab had transmitted a *whunga-whunga-whunga* sort of sound that deepened into a fuller, richer, and more satisfying *ronk! ronk! ronk!* At 2107 hours the centrifuge had ronked its last ronk and had slowly come to rest. Was it Newton who had said that somewhere, beyond the farthest star, there may be a body perfectly at rest? Newton had been right about everything but the distance, Starkey thought. You didn't have to go far at all. Project Blue was perfectly at rest. Starkey was very glad. The centrifuge had been the last illusion of life, and the problem he'd had Steffens run through the main computer bank (Steffens had looked at him as though he were crazy, and yes, Starkey thought he might be) was: How long could that centrifuge be expected to run? The answer, which had come back in 6.6 seconds, was: ±3 YEARS PROBABLE MALFUNCTION NEXT TWO WEEKS .009% AREAS OF PROBABLE MALFUNCTION BEARINGS 38% MAIN MOTOR 16% ALL OTHER 54%. That was a smart computer. Starkey had gotten Steffens to query it again after the actual burnout of Ezwick's centrifuge. The computer communed with the Engineering Systems data bank and confirmed that the centrifuge had indeed burned out its bearings.

Remember that, Starkey thought as his caller began to beep urgently behind him. The sound of burning bearings in the final stages of collapse is *ronk-ronk-ronk.*

He went to the caller and pushed the button that snapped off the beeper. 'Yes, Len.'

'Billy, I've got an urgent from one of our teams in a town called Sipe Springs, Texas. Almost four hundred miles from Arnette. They say they have to talk to you; it's a command decision.'

'What is it, Len?' he asked calmly. He had taken over sixteen 'downers' in the last ten hours, and was, generally speaking, feeling fine. Not a sign of a ronk.

'Press.'

'Oh Jesus,' Starkey said mildly. 'Patch them through.'

There was a muffled roar of static with a voice talking unintelligibly behind it.

'Wait a minute,' Len said.

The static slowly cleared.

'– Lion, Team Lion, do you read, Blue Base? Can you read? One . . . two . . . three . . . four . . . this is Team Lion –'

'I've got you, Team Lion,' Starkey said. 'This is Blue Base One.'

'Problem is coded Flowerpot in the Contingency Book,' the tinny voice said. 'Repeat, Flowerpot.'

'I know what the fuck Flowerpot is,' Starkey said. 'What's the situation?'

The tinny voice coming from Sipe Springs talked uninterrupted for almost five minutes. The situation itself was unimportant, Starkey thought, because the computer had informed him two days ago that just this sort of situation (in some shape or form) was apt to occur before the end of June. 88% probability. The specifics didn't matter. If it had two legs and belt-loops, it was a pair of pants. Never mind the color.

A doctor in Sipe Springs had made some good guesses, and a pair of reporters for a Houston daily had linked what was happening in Sipe Springs with what had already happened in Arnette, Verona, Commerce City, and a town called Polliston, Kansas. Those were the towns where the problem had gotten so bad so fast that the army had been sent in to quarantine. The computer had a list of twenty-five other towns in ten states where traces of Blue were beginning to show up.

The Sipe Springs situation wasn't important because it wasn't unique. They'd had their chance at unique in Arnette – well, maybe – and flubbed it. What was important was that the 'situation' was finally going to see print on something besides yellow military flimsy; was, anyway, unless Starkey took steps. He hadn't decided whether to do that or not. But when the tinny voice stopped talking, Starkey realized that he had made the decision after all. He had perhaps made it as long as twenty years ago.

It came down to what was important. And what was important wasn't the fact of the disease; it wasn't the fact that Atlanta's integrity had somehow been breached and they were going to have to switch the whole preventative operation to much less satisfactory facilities in Stovington, Vermont; it wasn't the fact that Blue spread in such sneaky common-cold disguise.

'What is important –'

'Say again, Blue Base One,' the voice said anxiously. 'We did not copy.'

What was important was that a regrettable incident had occurred. Starkey flashed back in time twenty-two years to 1968. He had been in the officers' club in San Diego when the news came about Calley and what had happened at Mei Lai Four. Starkey had been playing poker with four other men, two of whom now sat on the Joint Chiefs of Staff. The poker game had been forgotten, utterly forgotten, in a discussion of exactly what this was going to do to the military – not any one branch but the entire military – in the witch-hunt atmosphere of Washington's fourth estate. And one of their number, a man who could now dial directly to the miserable worm who had been masquerading as a Chief Executive since January 20, 1989, had laid his cards carefully down on the green felt table and he had said: *Gentlemen, a regrettable incident has occurred. And when a regrettable incident occurs which involves any branch of the United States Military, we don't question the roots of that incident but rather how the branches may best be pruned. The service is mother and father to us. And if you find your mother raped or your father beaten and robbed, before you call the police or begin an investigation, you cover their nakedness. Because you love them.*

Starkey had never heard anyone talk so well before or since.

Now he unlocked the bottom drawer of his desk and fumbled out a thin blue folder bound with red tape. The legend written on the cover read: IF TAPE IS BROKEN NOTIFY ALL SECURITY DIVISIONS AT ONCE. Starkey broke the tape.

'Are you there, Blue Base One?' the voice was asking. 'We do not copy you. Repeat, do not copy.'

'I'm here, Lion,' Starkey said. He had flipped to the last page

of the book and now ran his finger down a column labeled EXTREME
COVERT COUNTERMEASURES.

'Lion, do you read?'

'We read five-by, Blue Base One.'

'Troy,' Starkey said deliberately. 'I repeat, Lion: *Troy*. Repeat
back, please. Over to you.'

Silence. A faraway mumble of static. Starkey was fleetingly
reminded of the walkie-talkies they made as kids, two tin Del Monte
cans and twenty yards of waxed string.

'I say again –'

'Oh Jesus!' a very young voice in Sipe Springs gulped.

'Repeat back, son,' Starkey said.

'T-Troy,' the voice said. Then, more strongly: 'Troy.'

'Very good,' Starkey said calmly. 'God bless you, son. Over
and out.'

'And you, sir. Over and out.'

A click, followed by heavy static, followed by another click,
silence, and Len Creighton's voice. 'Billy?'

'Yes, Len.'

'I copied the whole thing.'

'That's fine, Len,' Starkey said tiredly. 'You make your report
as you see fit. Of course.'

'You don't understand, Billy,' Len said. 'You did the right
thing. Don't you think I know that?'

Starkey let his eyes slip closed. For a moment all the sweet
downers deserted him. 'God bless you, too, Len,' he said, and his
voice was close to breaking. He switched off and went back to stand
in front of monitor 2. He put his hands behind his back like a Black
Jack Pershing reviewing troops. He regarded Frank D. Bruce and his
final resting place. In a little while he felt calm again.

Going southeast out of Sipe Springs, if you get on US 36, you are
headed in the general direction of Houston, a day's drive away. The
car burning up the road was a three-year-old Pontiac Bonneville,
doing eighty, and when it came over the rise and saw the nondescript
Ford blocking the road, there was nearly an accident.

The driver, a thirty-six-year-old stringer for a large Houston
daily, tromped on the power brake and the tires began to screech,
the Pontiac's nose first dipping down toward the road and then
beginning to break to the left.

'Holy Gawd!' the photographer in the shotgun seat cried. He dropped his camera to the floor and began to scramble his seat belt across his middle.

The driver let up on the brake, skirted the Ford on the shoulder, and then felt his left wheels start to drag in the soft dirt. He matted the gas pedal and the Bonneville responded with more traction, dragging back onto the blacktop. Blue smoke squirted from beneath the tires. The radio blared on and on:

> Baby, can you dig your man,
> He's a righteous man,
> Baby, can you dig your man?

He tromped the brake again, and the Bonneville slued to a stop in the middle of the hot and deserted afternoon. He drew in a ragged, terrified breath and then coughed it out in a series of bursts. He began to be angry. He threw the Pontiac into reverse and backed toward the Ford and the two men standing behind it.

'Listen,' the photographer said nervously. He was fat and hadn't been in a fight since the ninth grade. 'Listen, maybe we just better –'

He was thrown forward with a grunt as the stringer brought the Pontiac to another screeching halt, threw the transmission lever into park with one hard thrust of his hand, and got out.

He began to walk toward the two young men behind the Ford, his hands doubled into fists.

'All right, motherfuckers!' he shouted. 'You almost got us fucking killed and I want –'

He had been in the service, four years in the army. Volunteer. He had just time to identify the rifles as the new M-3A's when they brought them up from below the rear deck of the Ford. He stood shocked in the hot Texas sunshine and made water in his pants.

He began to scream and in his mind he was turning to run back to the Bonneville but his feet never moved. They opened up on him, and slugs blew out his chest and groin. As he dropped to his knees, holding both hands out mutely for mercy, a slug struck him an inch over his left eye and tore off the top of his head.

The photographer, who had been twisted over the back seat, found it impossible to comprehend exactly what had happened until the two young men stepped over the stringer's body and began to walk toward him, rifles raised.

He slid across the Pontiac's seat, warm bubbles of saliva collecting at the corners of his mouth. The keys were still in the ignition. He turned the car on and screamed out just as they began shooting. He felt the car lurch to the right as if a giant had kicked the left rear, and the wheel began to shimmy wildly in his hands. The photographer bounced up and down as the Bonneville pogoed up the road on the flat tire. A second later the giant kicked the other side of the car. The shimmy got worse. Sparks flew off the blacktop. The photographer was whining. The Pontiac's rear tires shimmied and flapped like black rags. The two young men ran back to their Ford, whose serial number was listed among the multitude in the Army Vehicles division at the Pentagon, and one of them drove it around in a tight, swaying circle. The nose bounced wildly as it came off the shoulder and drove over the body of the stringer. The sergeant in the passenger seat sprayed a startled sneeze onto the windshield.

Ahead of them, the Pontiac washing-machined along on its two flat rear tires, the nose bouncing up and down. Behind the wheel the fat photographer had begun to weep at the sight of the dark Ford growing in the rear-view mirror. He had the accelerator pressed to the floor but the Pontiac would do no more than forty and it was all over the road. On the radio Larry Underwood had been replaced by Madonna. Madonna was asserting that she was a material girl.

The Ford swung around the Bonneville and for one second of crystal hope the photographer thought it was going to keep right on going, to just disappear over the desolate horizon and let him alone.

Then it pulled back in, and the Pontiac's wildly jittering nose caught its mudguard. There was a scream of pulling metal. The photographer's head flew forward into the wheel and blood sprayed from his nose.

Throwing terrified, creaky-necked glances back over his shoulder, he slid across the warm plastic seat as if it were grease and got out on the passenger's side. He ran down the shoulder. There was a barbed wire fence and he leaped over it, sailing up and up like a blimp, and he thought: *I'm going to make it. I can run forever –*

He fell down on the other side with his leg caught in the barbs. Screaming at the sky, he was still trying to free his pants and dimpled white flesh when the two young men came down the shoulder with their guns in their hands.

Why, he tried to ask them, but all that came out of him was a low and helpless squawk and then his brains exited the back of his head.

There was no published report of disease or any other trouble in Sipe Springs, Texas, that day.

CHAPTER 18

Nick opened the door between Sheriff Baker's office and the jail cells and they started razzing him right off. Vincent Hogan and Billy Warner were in the two Saltine-box cells on Nick's left. Mike Childress was in one of the two on the right. The other was empty and it was empty because Ray Booth, he of the purple LSU fraternity ring, had flown the coop.

'Hey, dummy!' Childress called. 'Hey, you fuckin dummy! What's gonna happen to you when we get outta here? Huh? What the fuck's gonna happen to you?'

'I'm personally gonna rip your balls off and stuff em down your throat until you strangle on em,' Billy Warner told him. 'You understand me?'

Only Vince Hogan didn't participate in the razzing. Mike and Billy didn't have too much use for him on this day, June 23, when they were to be taken up to the Calhoun County seat and jugged pending trial. Sheriff Baker had leaned on Vince and Vince had spilled his yellow guts. Baker had told Nick he could get an indictment against these ole boys, but when it got to a jury trial, it was going to be Nick's word against these three – four, if they picked up Ray Booth.

Nick had gained a healthy respect for Sheriff John Baker these last couple of days. He was a two-hundred-and-fifty-pound ex-farmer who was predictably called Big Bad John by his constituents. The respect Nick felt for him was not because Baker had given him this job swamping out the holding area to make up for his lost week's pay, but because he had gone after the men who had beaten and robbed Nick. He had done it as if Nick were a member of one of the oldest and most respected families in town instead of just a deaf-mute drifter. There were plenty of sheriffs here in the border South, Nick knew, who would have seen him on a work farm or roadgang for six months instead.

They had driven out to the sawmill where Vince Hogan worked, taking Baker's private car, a Power Wagon, instead of the county prowler car. There was a shotgun under the dash ('Always locked up and always loaded,' Baker said) and a bubble light Baker put on the dash when he was on police business. He put it up there when they swung into the lumberyard parking area, two days ago now.

Baker had hawked, spat out the window, blown his nose, and dabbed at his red eyes with a handkerchief. His voice had acquired a nasal foghorn quality. Nick couldn't hear it, of course, but he didn't need to. It was clear enough that the man had a nasty cold.

'Now, when we see him, I'll grab him by the arm,' Baker said. 'I'll ask you, "Is this one of em?" You give me a big nod yes. I don't care if it was or not. You just nod. Get it?'

Nick nodded. He got it.

Vince was working the board planer, feeding rough planks into the machine, standing in sawdust almost to the top of his workboots. He gave John Baker a nervous smile, and his eyes flicked uneasily to Nick standing beside the sheriff. Nick's face was thin and battered and still too pale.

'Hi, Big John, what you doin out with the workin folk?'

The other men in the crew were watching all this, their eyes shifting gravely from Nick to Vince to Baker and then back the other way like men watching some complicated new version of tennis. One of them spat a stream of Honey Cut into the fresh sawdust and wiped off his chin with the heel of his hand.

Baker grabbed Vince Hogan by one flabby, sunburned arm and pulled him forward.

'Hey! What's the idea, Big John?'

Baker turned his head so Nick could see his lips. 'Is this one of em?'

Nick nodded firmly, and pointed at Vince for good measure.

'What *is* this?' Vince protested again. 'I don't know this dummy from Adam.'

'Then how come you know he's a dummy? Come on, Vince, you're going to the cooler. Toot-sweet. You can send one of these boys to get your toothbrush.'

Protesting, Vince was led to the Power Wagon and deposited inside. Protesting, he was taken back to town. Protesting, he was locked up and left to stew for a couple of hours. Baker didn't bother with reading him his rights. 'Damn fool'd just get confused,' he told Nick. When Baker went back around noon, Vince was too hungry and too scared to do any more protesting. He just spilled everything.

Mike Childress was in the jug by one o'clock, and Baker got Billy Warner at his house just as Billy was packing up his old Chrysler to go someplace – a long piece from the look of all the packed liquor-store boxes and strapped-together luggage. But somebody had talked to Ray Booth, and Ray had been just smart enough to move a little quicker.

Baker took Nick home to meet his wife and have some supper. In the car Nick wrote on the memo pad: 'I am sure sorry it's her brother. How is she taking it?'

'She's bearing up,' Baker said, both his voice and the set of his body almost formal. 'I guess she's done some crying over him, but she knew what he was. And she knows you can't pick your relatives like you do your friends.'

Jane Baker was a small, pretty woman who had indeed been crying. Looking at her deeply socketed eyes made Nick uncomfortable. But she shook his hand warmly and said, 'I'm pleased to know you, Nick. And I apologize deeply for your trouble. I feel responsible, with one of mine being a part of it and all.'

Nick shook his head and shuffled his feet awkwardly.

'I offered him a job around the place,' Baker said. 'Station's gone right to hell since Bradley moved up to Little Rock. Painting and picking up, mostly. He's gonna have to stick around for a while anyway – for the . . . you know.'

'The trial, yes,' she said.

There was a moment then in which the silence was so heavy even Nick found it painful.

Then, with forced gaiety, she said, 'I hope you eat redeye ham, Nick. That's what there is, along with some corn and a big bowl of slaw. My slaw's never been up to what his mother used to make. That's what *he* says, anyway.'

Nick rubbed his stomach and smiled.

Over dessert (a strawberry shortcake – Nick, who had been on short rations during the last couple of weeks, had two helpings), Jane Baker said to her husband: 'Your cold sounds worse. You've been taking too much on, John Baker. And you didn't eat enough to keep a fly alive.'

Baker looked guiltily at his plate for a moment, then shrugged. 'I can afford to miss a meal now and then,' he said, and palpated his double chin.

Nick, watching them, wondered how two people of such radically different size got along in bed. I guess they manage, he thought with an interior grin. They sure look comfortable enough with each other. And not that it's any of my business anyway.

'You're flushed, too. You carrying a fever?'

Baker shrugged. 'Nope . . . well. Maybe a touch.'

'Well, you're not going out again tonight. That's final.'

'My dear, I have prisoners. If they don't specially need to be watched, they *do* need to be fed and watered.'

'Nick can do it,' she said with finality. 'You're going to bed. And don't go on about your insomnia; it won't do you any good.'

'I can't send Nick,' he said weakly. 'He's a deaf-mute. Besides, he ain't a deputy.'

'Well then, you just up and deputize him.'

'He ain't a resident!'

'I won't tell if you won't,' Jane Baker said inexorably. She stood up and began clearing the table. 'Now you just go on and do it, John.'

And that was how Nick Andros went from Shoyo prisoner to Shoyo deputy in less than twenty-four hours. As he was preparing to go up to the sheriff's office, Baker came into the downstairs hall, looking large and ghostly in a frayed bathrobe. He seemed embarrassed to be on view in such attire.

'I never should have let her talk me into this,' he said. 'Wouldn't have done, either, if I didn't feel so punk. My chest's all clogged up and I'm as hot as a fire sale two days before Christmas. Weak, too.'

Nick nodded sympathetically.

'I'm stuck between deputies. Bradley Caide and his wife went up to Little Rock after their baby passed away. One of those crib deaths. Awful thing. I don't blame them for going.'

Nick pointed at his own chest and made a circle with his thumb and forefinger.

'Sure, you'll be okay. You just take normal care, you hear? There's a .45 in the third drawer of my desk, but don't you be takin it back there. Nor the keys either. Understand?'

Nick nodded.

'If you go back there, stay out of their reach. If any of em tries playin sick, don't you fall for it. It's the oldest dodge in the world. If one of em *should* get sick, Doc Soames can see them just as easy in the morning. I'll be in then.'

Nick took his pad from his pocket and wrote: 'I appreciate you trusting me. Thanks for locking them up & thanks for the job.'

Baker read this carefully. 'You're a puredee caution, boy. Where you from? How come you're out on your own like this?'

'That's a long story,' Nick jotted. 'I'll write some of it down for you tonight, if you want.'

'You do that,' Baker said. 'I guess you know I put your name on the wire.'

Nick nodded. It was SOP. But he was clean.

'I'll get Jane to call Ma's Truck Stop out by the highway. Those boys'll be hollering police brutality if they don't get their supper.'

Nick wrote: 'Have her tell whoever brings it to come right in. I can't hear him if he knocks.'

'Okay.' Baker hesitated a moment longer. 'You got your cot in the corner. It's hard, but it's clean. You just remember to be careful, Nick. You can't call for help if there's trouble.'

Nick nodded and wrote, 'I can take care of myself.'

'Yeah, I believe you can. Still, I'd get someone from town if I thought any of them would –' He broke off as Jane came in.

'You still jawing this poor boy? You let him go on, now, before my stupid brother comes along and breaks them all out.'

Baker laughed sourly. 'He'll be in Tennessee by now, I guess.' He whistled out a long sigh that broke up into a series of phlegmy, booming coughs. 'I b'lieve I'll go upstairs and lie down, Janey.'

'I'll bring you some aspirin to cut that fever,' she said.

She looked back over her shoulder at Nick as she went to the stairs with her husband. 'It was a pleasure meeting you, Nick. Whatever the circumstances. You be just as careful as he says.'

Nick bowed to her, and she dropped half a curtsy in return. He thought he saw a gleam of tears in her eyes.

A pimply, curious boy in a dirty busboy's jacket brought three dinner trays about half an hour after Nick had gotten down to the jail. Nick motioned for the busboy to put the trays on the cot, and while he did, Nick scribbled: 'Is this paid for?'

The busboy read this with all the concentration of a college freshman tackling *Moby Dick*. 'Sure,' he said. 'Sheriff's office runs a tab. Say, can't you talk?'

Nick shook his head.

'That's a bitch,' the busboy said, and left in a hurry, as if the condition might be catching.

Nick took the trays in one at a time and pushed each one through the slot in the bottom of the cell door with a broomhandle.

He looked up in time to catch '– chickshit bastard, ain't he?' from Mike Childress. Smiling, Nick showed him his middle finger.

'I'll give you the finger, you dummy,' Childress said, grinning unpleasantly. 'When I get out of here I'll –' Nick turned away, missing the rest.

Back in the office, sitting in Baker's chair, he drew the memo pad into the center of the blotter, sat thinking for a moment, and then jotted at the top:

Life History
By Nick Andros

He stopped, smiling a little. He had been in some funny places, but never in his wildest dreams had he expected to be sitting in a sheriff's office, deputized, in charge of three men who had beaten him up, and writing his life story. After a moment he began to write again:

I was born in Caslin, Nebraska, on November 14, 1968. My daddy was an independent farmer. He and my mom were always on the edge of getting squeezed out. They owed three different banks. My mother was six months pregnant with me and my dad was taking her to see the doctor in town when a tie rod on his truck let go and they went into the ditch. My daddy had a heart attack and died.

Anyway, three months after, my mom had me and I was born the way I am. Sure was a tough break on top of losing her husband that way.

She carried on with the farm until 1973 and then lost it to the 'big operators,' as she always called them. She had no family but wrote to some friends in Big Springs, Iowa, and one of them got her a job in a bakery. We lived here until 1977 when she was killed in an accident. A man on a motorcycle hit her while she was crossing the street on her way home from work. It wasn't even his fault but only bad luck as his brakes failed. He wasn't even speeding or anything. The Baptist Church gave my mamma a charity funeral. This same church, the Grace

Baptist, sent me to the Children of Jesus Christ orphanage in Des
Moines. This is a place that all sorts of churches chip together to support.
That was where I learned to read and write . . .

He stopped there. His hand was aching from writing so much, but
that wasn't why. He felt uneasy, hot and uncomfortable at having
to relive all that again. He went back to the jail quarters and looked
in. Childress and Warner were asleep. Vince Hogan was standing
by the bars, smoking a cigarette and looking across the corridor at
the empty cell where Ray Booth would have been tonight if he
hadn't run so quick. Hogan looked as if he might have been crying,
and that led him back in time to that small mute scrap of humanity,
Nick Andros. There was a word he had learned at the movies as
a kid. That word was INCOMMUNICADO. It was a word that had
always had fantastic, Lovecraftian overtones to Nick, a fearful word
that echoed and clanged in the brain, a word that inscribed all the
nuances of fear that live only outside the sane universe and inside
the human soul. He had been INCOMMUNICADO all his life.

He sat down and re-read the last line he'd written. *That was
where I learned to read and write*. But it hadn't been as simple as that.
He lived in a silent world. Writing was code. Speech was the
moving of lips, the rise and fall of teeth, the dance of a tongue.
His mother had taught him to read lips, and had taught him how
to write his name in struggling, sprawling letters. *That's your name*,
she had said. *That's you, Nicky*. But of course she had said it silently,
meaninglessly. The prime connection had come when she tapped
the paper, then tapped his chest. The worst part about being deaf-
mute was not living in the silent movie world; the worst part was
not knowing the names of things. He had not really begun to
understand the concept of naming until he was four. He had not
known that you called the tall green things *trees* until he was six.
He had wanted to know, but no one had thought to tell him and
he had no way to ask: He was INCOMMUNICADO.

When she died he had retreated almost all the way. The
orphanage was a place of roaring silence where grim-faced thin boys
made fun of his silence; two boys would run up to him, one boy
with his hands plastered over his mouth, one boy with his hands
plastered over his ears. If none of the staff happened to be near, they
would punch him out. Why? No reason. Except that maybe in the
vast white class of victims there is a subclass: the victims of victims.

He stopped *wanting* to communicate, and when that happened the thinking process itself began to rust and disintegrate. He began to wander from place to place vacantly, looking at the nameless things that filled the world. He watched groups of children in the play yard move their lips, raise and lower their teeth like white drawbridges, dance their tongues in the ritual mating of speech. He sometimes found himself looking at a single cloud for as long as an hour at a time.

Then Rudy had come. A big man with scars on his face and a bald head. Six feet, five inches tall, might as well have been twenty to runty Nick Andros. They met for the first time in a basement room where there was a table, six or seven chairs, and a TV that only worked when it felt like it. Rudy squatted, putting his eyes on approximately the same level as Nick's. Then he took his huge, scarred hands and put them over his mouth, his ears.

I am a deaf-mute.

Nick turned his face sullenly away: *Who gives a fuck?*

Rudy slapped him.

Nick fell down. His mouth opened and silent tears began to leak from his eyes. He didn't want to be here with this scarred troll, this bald boogey. He was no deaf-mute, it was a cruel joke.

Rudy pulled him gently to his feet and led him to the table. A blank sheet of paper was there. Rudy pointed at it, then at Nick. Nick stared sullenly at the paper and then at the bald man. He shook his head. Rudy nodded and pointed at the empty paper again. He produced a pencil and handed it to Nick. Nick put it down as if it were hot. He shook his head. Rudy pointed at the pencil, then at Nick, then at the paper. Nick shook his head. Rudy slapped him again.

More silent tears. The scarred face looking at him with nothing but deadly patience. Rudy pointed at the paper again. At the pencil. At Nick.

Nick grasped the pencil in his fist. He wrote the four words that he knew, calling them forth from the cobwebby, rusting mechanism that was in his thinking brain. He wrote:

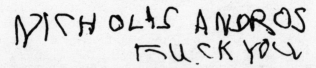

Then he broke the pencil in half and looked sullenly and defiantly at Rudy. But Rudy was smiling. Suddenly he reached across the table and held Nick's head steady between his hard, callused palms. His hands were warm, gentle. Nick could not remember the last time he had been touched with such love. His mother had touched him like that.

Rudy removed his hands from Nick's face. He picked up the half of the pencil with the point on it. He turned the paper over to the blank side. He tapped the empty white space with the tip of the pencil, and then tapped Nick. He did it again. And again. And again. And finally Nick understood.

You are this blank page.

Nick began to cry.

Rudy came for the next six years.

. . . where I learned to read and write. A man named Rudy Sparkman came to help me. I was very lucky to have him. In 1984, the orphanage went broke. They placed as many kids that they could, but I was not one of them. They said I would get in with a family after a while and the state would pay them for keeping me. I wanted to go with Rudy but Rudy was in Africa working for the Peace Corps.

So I ran away. Being sixteen, I don't think they looked for me too hard. I figured if I could stay out of trouble I would be all right, and so far so good. I have been taking the high school correspondence courses one at a time, because Rudy always said education is the most important. When I settle down for a while I'm going to take that high school equivalency test. I will be able to pass it soon. I like school. Maybe I will go to college someday. I know that sounds crazy, a deaf-mute bum like me, but I don't think it's impossible. Anyway, that's my story.

Yesterday morning Baker had come in around seven-thirty while Nick was emptying wastebaskets. The sheriff looked better.

'How you feeling?' Nick wrote.

'Pretty good. I was burnin up until midnight. Worst fever I've had since I was a kid. Aspirin didn't seem to help it. Janey wanted to call the doc, but around twelve-thirty the fever just broke. I slep like a log after that. How are you doing?'

Nick made a thumb-and-forefinger circle.

'How's our guests?'

Nick opened and closed his mouth several times in a mime jabbering. Looked furious. Made banging gestures on invisible bars.

Baker threw back his head and laughed, then sneezed several times.

'You ought to be on TV,' he said. 'Did you write your life story down like you said you was gonna try to do?'

Nick nodded and handed the two sheets of longhand over. The sheriff sat down and read them carefully. When he was done he looked at Nick so long and so piercingly that Nick stared down at his feet for a moment, embarrassed and confused.

When he looked up again Baker said: 'You've been on your own since you were sixteen? For six years?'

Nick nodded.

'And you've really taken all these high school courses?'

Nick wrote for some time on one of the memo sheets. 'I was way behind because I started to read & write so late. When the orphanage closed I was just starting to catch up. I got six h.s. credits from there and another six since then from La Salle in Chicago. I learned about them from a matchbook cover. I need four more credits.'

'What courses do you still need?' Baker asked, then turned his head and shouted: 'Shut up in there! You'll get your hotcakes and coffee when I'm damned good and ready and not before!'

Nick wrote: 'Geometry. Advanced math. Two years of a language. Those are the college requirements.'

'A language. You mean like French? German? Spanish?'

Nick nodded.

Baker laughed and shook his head. 'Don't that beat all. A deaf-mute learning to talk a foreign language. Nothing against you, boy. You understand that.'

Nick smiled and nodded.

'So why you been driftin around so much?'

'While I was still a minor I didn't dare stay in one place for too long,' Nick wrote. 'Afraid they'd try to stick me in another orphanage or something. When I got old enough to look for a steady job, times got worse. They said the stock-market crashed, or something, but since I'm deaf I didn't hear it (ha-ha).'

'Most places would have just let you ramble on,' Baker said. 'In hard times the milk of human kindness don't flow so free, Nick. As for a steady job, I might be able to put you onto something around here, unless those boys soured you on Shoyo and Arkansas for good. But . . . we ain't all like that.'

Nick nodded to show he understood.

'How's your teeth? That was quite a shot in the mouth you took.'

Nick shrugged.

'Take any of those pain pills?'

Nick held up two fingers.

'Well, look, I got some paperwork to do on those boys. You go on with what you were doing. We'll talk more later.'

Dr Soames, the man who had almost hit Nick with his car, came by around 9:30 AM the same morning. He was a man of about sixty with shaggy white hair, a scrawny chicken neck, and very sharp blue eyes.

'Big John tells me you read lips,' he said. 'He also says he wants to see you gainfully employed, so I guess I better make sure you're not going to die on his hands. Take off your shirt.'

Nick unbuttoned his blue workshirt and took it off.

'Holy Jesus, lookitim,' Baker said.

'They did a job of work, all right.' Soames looked at Nick and said dryly, 'Boy, you almost lost your left tit.' He pointed to a crescent-shaped scab just above the nipple. Nick's belly and ribcage looked like a Canadian sunrise. Soames poked and prodded him and looked carefully into the pupils of his eyes. At last he examined the shattered remains of Nick's front teeth, the only part of him that really hurt now, in spite of the spectacular bruises.

'That must hurt like a sonofabitch,' he said, and Nick nodded ruefully. 'You're gonna lose them,' Soames went on. 'You –' He sneezed three times in quick succession. 'Excuse me.'

He began to put his tools back into his black bag. 'The prognosis is favorable, young man, barring strokes of lightning or further trips to Zack's ginmill. Is your speaking problem physical, or does it come from being deaf?'

Nick wrote: 'Physical. Birth defect.'

Soames nodded. 'Damn shame. Got to think positive, though, and thank God that He didn't decide to give your brains a stir while He was at it. Put your shirt on.'

Nick did. He liked Soames; in his way, he was very much like Rudy Sparkman, who had told him once that God had given all deaf-mute males an extra two inches below the waist to make up for the little bit He had subtracted from above the collarbones.

Soames said, 'I'll tell em to give you a refill on that pain medication down at the drugstore. Tell moneybags here to pay for it.'

'Ho-ho,' John Baker said.

'He's got more dough stashed away in fruit jars than a hog has warts,' Soames went on. He sneezed again, wiped his nose, rummaged around in his bag, and brought out a stethoscope.

'You want to look out, Gramps, I'll lock you up for drunk and disorderly,' Baker said with a smile.

'Yeah, yeah, yeah,' Soames said. 'You'll open your mouth too wide one day and fall right in. Take off y'shirt, John, and let's see if your boobs are as big as they used to be.'

'Take off my shirt? Why?'

'Because your wife wants me to look at you, that's why. She thinks you're a sick man and she doesn't want you to get any sicker, God knows why. Ain't I told her enough times that she and I wouldn't have to sneak around anymore if you were underground? Come on, Johnny. Show me some skin.'

'It was just a cold,' Baker said, reluctantly unbuttoning his shirt. 'I feel fine this morning. Honest to God, Ambrose, you sound worse'n I do.'

'You don't tell the doctor, the doctor tells you.' As Baker pulled his shirt off, Soames turned to Nick and said, 'But you know it's funny how a cold will just start making the rounds. Mrs Lathrop is down sick, and the whole Richie family, and most of those no-accounts out on the Barker Road are coughing their brains out. Even Billy Warner in there's hacking away.'

Baker had wormed out of his undershirt.

'There, what'd I tell you?' Soames asked. 'Ain't he got a set of knockers on him? Even an old shit like me could get horny looking at that.'

Baker gasped as the stethoscope touched his chest. 'Jesus, that's cold! What do you do, keep it in a deep freeze?'

'Breathe in,' Soames said, frowning. 'Now let it out.'

Baker's exhale turned into a weak cough.

Soames kept at the sheriff for a long time. Front and back both. At last he put away his stethoscope and used a tongue depressor to look down Baker's throat. Finished, he broke it in two and tossed it into the wastebasket.

'Well?' Baker said.

Soames pressed the fingers of his right hand into the flesh of Baker's neck under the jaw. Baker winced away from it.

'I don't have to ask if that hurt,' Soames said. 'John, you go home and go to bed and that isn't advice, that's an order.'

The sheriff blinked. 'Ambrose,' he said quietly, 'come on. You know I can't do that. I've got three prisoners who have to go up to Camden this afternoon. I left this kid with them last night, but I had no business doing it, and I won't do it again. He's mute. I wouldn't have agreed to it last night if I had been thinking right.'

'You never mind them, John. You got problems of your own. It's some kind of respiratory infection, a damn good one by the sound, and a fever to go with it. Your pipes are sick, Johnny, and to be perfectly frank, that's no joke for a man who's carrying around the extra meat you are. Go to bed. If you still feel okay tomorrow morning, get rid of them then. Better still, call the State Patrol to come down and get them.'

Baker looked apologetically at Nick. 'You know,' he said, 'I *do* feel kind of dragged out. Maybe some rest −'

'Go home and lie down,' Nick wrote. 'I'll be careful. Besides, I have to earn enough to pay for those pills.'

'Nobody works so hard for you as a junkie,' Soames said, and cackled.

Baker picked up the two sheets of paper with Nick's background on them. 'Could I take these home for Janey to read? She took a real shine to you, Nick.'

Nick scrawled on the pad, 'Sure can. She's very nice.'

'One of a kind,' Baker said, and sighed as he buttoned his shirt back up. 'This fever's comin on strong again. Thought I had it licked.'

'Take aspirin,' Soames said, latching his bag. 'It's that glandular infection I don't like.'

'There's a cigar box in the bottom desk drawer,' Baker said. 'Petty cash fund. You can go out for lunch and get your medication on the way. Those boys are more dildoes than desperadoes. They'll be okay. Just leave a voucher for how much money you take. I'll get in touch with the State Police and you'll be shut of them by late this afternoon.'

Nick made a thumb-and-forefinger circle.

'I've been trusting you a lot on short notice,' Baker said soberly, 'but Janey says it's all right. You have a care.'

Nick nodded.

★   ★   ★

Jane Baker had come in around six yesterday evening with a covered dish supper and a carton of milk.

Nick wrote, 'Thanks very much. How's your husband?'

She laughed, a small woman with chestnut brown hair, dressed prettily in a checked shirt and faded jeans. 'He wanted to come down himself, but I talked him out of it. His fever was up so high this afternoon that it scared me, but it's almost normal tonight. I think it's because of the State Patrol. Johnny's never really happy unless he can be mad at the State Patrol.'

Nick looked at her quizzically.

'They told him they couldn't send anybody down for his prisoners until nine tomorrow morning. They've had a bad sick-day, twenty or more troopers out. And a lot of the people who are on have been fetching people to the hospital up at Camden or even Pine Bluff. There's a lot of this sickness around. I think Am Soames is a lot more worried than he's letting on.'

She looked worried herself. Then she took the two folded sheets of memo paper from her breast pocket.

'This is quite a story,' she said quietly, handing the papers back to him. 'You've had just about the worst luck of anyone I ever heard of. I think the way you've risen above your handicaps is admirable. And I have to apologize again for my brother.'

Nick, embarrassed, could only shrug.

'I hope you'll stay on in Shoyo,' she said, standing. 'My husband likes you, and I do, too. Be careful of those men in there.'

'I will,' Nick wrote. 'Tell the sheriff I hope he feels better.'

'I'll take him your good wishes.'

She left then, and Nick passed a night of broken rest, getting up occasionally to check on his three wards. Desperadoes they were not; by ten o'clock they were all sleeping. Two town fellows came in to check and make sure Nick was all right, and Nick noticed that both of them seemed to have colds.

He dreamed oddly, and all he could remember upon waking was that he seemed to have been walking through endless rows of green corn, looking for something and terribly afraid of something else that seemed to be behind him.

This morning he was up early, carefully sweeping out the back of the jail and ignoring Billy Warner and Mike Childress. As he went out, Billy called after him: 'Ray's gonna be back, you know. And when he catches you, you're gonna wish you were *blind* as well as deaf and dumb!'

Nick, his back turned, missed most of this.

Back in the office, he picked up an old copy of *Time* magazine and began to read. He considered putting his feet up on the desk and decided that would be a very good way to get in trouble if the sheriff came by.

By eight o'clock he was wondering uneasily if Sheriff Baker might have had a relapse in the night. Nick had expected him by now, ready to turn the three prisoners in his jail over to the county when the State Patrol came for them. Also, Nick's stomach was rumbling uncomfortably. No one had showed up from the truck-stop down the road, and he looked at the telephone, more with disgust than with longing. He was quite fond of science fiction, picking up falling-apart paperbacks from time to time on the dusty back shelves of antique barns for a nickel or a dime, and he found himself thinking, not for the first time, that it was going to be a great day for the deaf-mutes of the world when the telephone viewscreens the science fiction novels were always predicting finally came into general use.

By quarter of nine he was acutely uneasy. He went to the door which gave on the cells and looked in.

Billy and Mike were both standing at their cell doors. Both of them had been banging on the bars with their shoes ... which just went to show you that people who can't talk only made up a small percentage of the world's dummies. Vince Hogan was lying down. He only turned his head and stared at Nick when he came to the door. Hogan's face was pallid except for a hectic flush on his cheeks, and there were dark patches under his eyes. Beads of sweat were standing out on his forehead. Nick met his apathetic, fevered gaze and realized that the man was sick. His uneasiness deepened.

'Hey, dummy, how about some brefus?' Mike called down to him. 'An ole Vince there seems like he could use a doctor. Tattle-talein' don't agree with him, does it, Bill?'

Bill didn't want to banter. 'I'm sorry I yelled at you before, man. Vince, he's sick, all right. He needs the doctor.'

Nick nodded and went out, trying to figure out what he should do next. He bent over the desk and wrote on the memo pad: 'Sheriff Baker, or Whoever: I've gone to get the prisoners some breakfast and to see if I can hunt Dr Soames up for Vincent Hogan. He appears to be really sick, not just playing possum. Nick Andros.'

He tore the sheet off the pad and left it in the middle of the desk. Then, tucking the pad into his pocket, he went out into the street.

The first thing that struck him was the still heat of the day and the smell of greenery. By afternoon it was going to be a scorcher. It was the sort of day when people like to get their chores and errands done early so they can spend the afternoon as quietly as possible, but to Nick, Shoyo's main street looked strangely indolent this forenoon, more like a Sunday than a workday.

Most of the diagonal parking spaces in front of the stores were empty. A few cars and farm trucks were going up and down the street, but not many. The hardware store looked open, but the shades of the Mercantile Bank were still drawn, although it was past nine now.

Nick turned right, toward the truck-stop, which was five blocks down. He was on the corner of the third block when he saw Dr Soames's car moving slowly up the street toward him, weaving a little from side to side, as if with exhaustion. Nick waved vigorously, not sure if Soames would stop, but Soames pulled in at the curb, indifferently taking up four of the slanted parking spaces. He didn't get out but merely sat behind the wheel. The look of the man shocked Nick. Soames had aged twenty years since he had last seen him bantering casually with the sheriff. It was partly exhaustion, but exhaustion couldn't be the whole explanation – even Nick could see that. As if to confirm his thought, the doctor produced a wrinkled handkerchief from his breast pocket like an old magician doing a creaky trick that does not interest him much anymore, and sneezed into it repeatedly. When he was done he leaned his head back against the car's seat, mouth half-open to draw breath. His skin looked so shiny and yellow that he reminded Nick of a dead person.

Then Soames opened his eyes and said, 'Sheriff Baker's dead. If that's what you flagged me down for, you can forget it. He died a little after two o'clock this morning. Now Janey's sick with it.'

Nick's eyes widened. Sheriff Baker dead? But his wife had been in just last night and said he was feeling better. And she . . . she had been fine. No, it just wasn't possible.

'Dead, all right,' Soames said, as though Nick had spoken his thought aloud. 'And he's not the only one. I've signed twelve death certificates in the last twelve hours. And I know of another twenty that are going to be dead by noon unless God shows mercy. But I doubt if this is God's doing. I suspect He'll keep right out of it as a consequence.'

Nick pulled the pad from his pocket and wrote: 'What's the matter with them?'

'I don't know,' Soames said, crumpling the sheet slowly and tossing the ball into the gutter. 'But everyone in town seems to be coming down with it, and I'm more frightened than I ever have been in my life. I have it myself, although what I'm suffering most from right now is exhaustion. I'm not a young man anymore. I can't go these long hours without paying the price, you know.' A tired, frightened petulance had entered his voice, which Nick fortunately couldn't hear. 'And feeling sorry for myself won't help.'

Nick, who hadn't been aware Soames *was* feeling sorry for himself, could only look at him, puzzled.

Soames got out of his car, holding on to Nick's arm for a minute to help himself. He had an old man's grip, weak and a little frenzied. 'Come on over to that bench, Nick. You're good to talk to. I suppose you've been told that before.'

Nick pointed back toward the jail.

'They're not going anywhere,' Soames said, 'and if they're down with it, right now they're on the bottom of my list.'

They sat on the bench, which was painted bright green and bore an advertisement on the backrest for a local insurance company. Soames turned his face gratefully up to the warmth of the sun.

'Chills and fever,' he said. 'Ever since about ten o'clock last night. Just lately it's been the chills. Thank God there hasn't been any diarrhea.'

'You ought to go home to bed,' Nick wrote.

'So I ought. And will. I just want to rest for a few minutes first . . .' His eyes slipped shut and Nick thought he had gone to sleep. He wondered if he should go on down to the truck-stop and get Billy and Mike some breakfast.

Then Dr Soames spoke again, without opening his eyes. Nick watched his lips. 'The symptoms are all very common,' he said, and began to enumerate them on his fingers until all ten were spread out in front of him like a fan. 'Chills. Fever. Headache. Weakness and general debilitation. Loss of appetite. Painful urination. Swelling of the glands, progressing from minor to acute. Swelling in the armpits and in the groin. Respiratory weakness and failure.'

He looked at Nick.

'They are the symptoms of the common cold, of influenza, of pneumonia. We can cure all of those things, Nick. Unless the patient is very young or very old, or perhaps already weakened by a previous illness, antibiotics will knock them out. But not this. It comes on the patient quickly or slowly. It doesn't seem to matter. Nothing helps. The thing escalates, backs up, escalates again; debilitation increases; the swelling gets worse; finally, death.

'Somebody made a mistake.

'And they're trying to cover it up.'

Nick looked at him doubtfully, wondering if he had picked the words rightly from the doctor's lips, wondering if Soames might be raving.

'It sounds slightly paranoid, doesn't it?' Soames asked, looking at him with weary humor. 'I used to be frightened of the younger generation's paranoia, do you know that? Always afraid someone was tapping their phones . . . following them . . . running computer checks on them . . . and now I find out they were right and I was wrong. Life is a fine thing, Nick, but old age takes an unpleasantly high toll on one's dearly held prejudices, I find.'

'What do you mean?' Nick wrote.

'None of the phones in Shoyo work,' Soames said. Nick had no idea if this was in answer to his question (Soames seemed to have given Nick's last note only the most cursory of glances), or if the doctor had gone off on some new tack – the fever could be making Soames's mind jump around, he supposed.

The doctor observed Nick's puzzled face, and seemed to think the deaf-mute might not believe him. 'Quite true,' he said. 'If you try to dial any number not on this town's circuit, you get a recorded announcement. Furthermore, the two Shoyo exits and entrances from the turnpike are closed off with barriers which say ROAD CONSTRUCTION. But there is no construction. Only the barriers. I was out there. I believe it would be possible to move the barriers aside, but the traffic on the turnpike seems very light this morning. And most of it seems to consist of army vehicles. Trucks and jeeps.'

'What about the other roads?' Nick wrote.

'Route 63 has been torn up at the east end of town to replace a culvert,' Soames said. 'At the west end of town there appears to have been a rather nasty car accident. Two cars across the road, blocking it entirely. There are smudgepots out, but no sign of state troopers or wreckers.'

He paused, removed his handkerchief, and blew his nose.

'The men working on the culvert are going very slowly, according to Joe Rackman, who lives out that way. I was at the Rackmans' about two hours ago, looking at their little boy, who is very ill indeed. Joe said that he thinks that the men at the culvert are in fact soldiers, though they're dressed in state road crew coveralls and driving a state truck.'

Nick wrote: 'How does he know?'

Standing up, Soames said: 'Workmen rarely salute each other.'

Nick got up, too.

'Back roads?' he jotted.

'Possibly.' Soames nodded. 'But I am a doctor, not a hero. Joe said he saw guns in the cab of that truck. Army-issue carbines. If one tried to leave Shoyo by the back roads and if they were watched, who knows? And what might one find beyond Shoyo? I repeat: someone made a mistake. And now they're trying to cover it up. Madness. Madness. Of course the news of something like this will get out, and it won't take long. And in the meantime, how many will die?'

Nick, frightened, only looked at Dr Soames as he went back to his car and climbed slowly in.

'And you, Nick,' Soames said, looking out the window at him. 'How do you feel? A cold? Sneezing? Coughing?'

Nick shook his head to each one.

'Will you try to leave town? I think you could, if you went by the fields.'

Nick shook his head and wrote, 'Those men are locked up. I can't just leave them. Vincent Hogan is sick but the other two seem okay. I'll get them their breakfast and then go see Mrs Baker.'

'You're a thoughtful boy,' Soames said. 'That's rare. A boy in this degraded age who has a sense of responsibility is even rarer. She'd appreciate that, Nick, I know. Mr Braceman, the Methodist minister, also said he would stop by. I'm afraid he'll have a lot of calls to make before the day is over. You'll be careful of those three you have locked up, won't you?'

Nick nodded soberly.

'Good. I'll try to drop by and check on you this afternoon.' He dropped the car into gear and drove away, looking weary and red-eyed and shriveled. Nick stared after him, his face troubled, and then began to walk down to the truck-stop again. It was open, but one of the two cooks was not in and three of the four waitresses hadn't shown up for the seven-to-three shift. Nick had to wait a long time to get his order. When he got back to the jail, both Billy and Mike looked badly frightened. Vince Hogan was delirious, and by six o'clock that evening he was dead.

CHAPTER 19

It had been so long since Larry had been in Times Square that he expected it to look different somehow, magical. Things would look smaller and yet better there, and he would not feel intimidated by the rank, smelly, and sometimes dangerous vitality of the place the way he had as a child, when he and Buddy Marx or just he alone would scuttle down here to see the 99-cent double features or to stare at the glittering junk in the windows of the shops and arcades and poolhalls.

But it all looked just the same – more than it should have because some things really had changed. When you came up the stairs from the subway, the newsstand that had been on the corner as you came out was gone. Half a block down, where there had been a penny arcade full of flashing lights and bells and dangerous-looking young men with cigarettes dangling from the corners of their mouths as they played the Gottlieb Desert Isle or Space Race, where that had been there was now an Orange Julius with a flock of young blacks standing in front of it, their lower bodies moving gently as if somewhere jive played on and on, jive that only black ears could hear. There were more massage parlors and X-rated movies.

Still, it was much the same, and this made him sad. In a way the only real difference made things seem worse: he felt like a tourist here now. But maybe even native New Yorkers felt like tourists in the Square, dwarfed, wanting to look up and read the electronic headlines as they marched around and around up there. He couldn't tell; he had forgotten what it was like to be a part of New York. He had no particular urge to relearn.

His mother hadn't gone to work that morning. She'd been fighting a cold for the last couple of days and had gotten up early this morning with a fever. He had heard her from the narrow, safe bed in his old room, banging around out in the kitchen, sneezing and saying 'Shit!' under her breath, getting ready for breakfast. The sound of the TV being turned on, then the news on the 'Today' program. An attempted coup in India. A power station blown up in Wyoming. The Supreme Court was expected to hand down a landmark decision having to do with gay rights.

By the time Larry came out into the kitchen, buttoning his shirt, the news was over and Gene Shalitt was interviewing a man with a bald head. The man with the bald head was showing a number of small animals he had hand-blown. Glassblowing, he said, had been his hobby for forty years, and his book would be published by Random House. Then he sneezed. 'Excuse you,' Gene Shalitt said, and chuckled.

'You want em fried or scrambled?' Alice Underwood asked. She was in her bathrobe.

'Scrambled,' Larry said, knowing it would do no good to protest the eggs. In Alice's view, it wasn't breakfast without eggs (which she called 'crackleberries' when she was in a good humor). They had protein and nutrition. Her idea of nutrition was vague but all-encompassing. She kept a list of nutritious items in her head, Larry knew, as well as their opposite numbers – Jujubes, pickles, Slim Jims, the slice of pink bubble gum that came with baseball cards, and oh dear God, so many others.

He sat down and watched her make the eggs, pouring them into the same old black skillet, stirring them with the same wire whisk that she had used to stir his eggs when he had been going to the first grade at PS 162.

She pulled her hankie out of her bathrobe pocket, coughed into it, sneezed into it, and muttered 'Shit!' indistinctly into it before putting it back.

'Day off, Mom?'

'I called in sick. This cold wants to break me. I hate to call in sick on Fridays, so many do, but I've got to get off my feet. I'm running a fever. Swollen glands, too.'

'Did you call the doctor?'

'When I was a charming maid, doctors made housecalls,' she said. 'Now if you're sick, you have to go to the hospital emergency room. That, or spend the day waiting for some quack to see you in one of those places where they're supposed to have – ha-ha – walk-in medical care. Walk in and get ready to collect your "Medicare", that's what *I* think. Those places are worse than the Green Stamp Redemption Center a week before Christmas. I'll stay home and take aspirin, and by tomorrow this time I'll be on the downhill side of it.'

He stayed most of the morning, trying to help out. He lugged the TV in by her bed, the cords standing out heroically on his arms ('You're going to give yourself a hernia so I can watch "Let's Make a Deal,"' she sniffed), brought her juice and an old bottle of NyQuil for her stuffiness, and ran down to the market to get her a couple of paperbacks.

After that there wasn't much for them to do except get on each other's nerves. She marveled how much poorer the TV reception was in the bedroom and he had to bite back an acid comment to the effect that poor reception was better than no reception at all. Finally he said he might go out and see some of the city.

'That's a good idea,' she said with obvious relief. 'I'm going to take a nap. You're a good boy, Larry.'

So he had gone down the narrow stairs (the elevator was still broken) and onto the street, feeling guilty relief. The day was his, and he still had some cash in his pocket.

But now, in Times Square, he didn't feel so cheerful. He wandered along, his wallet long since transferred to a front pocket. He paused in front of a discount record store, transfixed by the sound of his own voice coming from the battered overhead speakers. The bridge verse.

> I didn't come to ask you to stay all night
> Or to find out if you've seen the light
> I didn't come to make a fuss or pick a fight
> I just want you to tell me if you think you can
> Baby, can you dig your man?
> Dig him, baby –
> Baby, can you dig your man?

That's me, he thought, looking vacantly in at the albums, but today the sound depressed him. Worse, it made him homesick. He didn't want to be here under this gray washtub sky, smelling New York exhaust, one hand constantly playing pocket pool with his wallet to make sure it was still there. New York, thy name is paranoia. Suddenly where he wanted to be was in a West Coast recording studio, making a new album.

Larry quickened his step and turned in at an arcade. Bells and buzzers jangled in his ears; there was the amplified, ripping growl of a Deathrace 2000 game, complete with the unearthly, electronic screams of the dying pedestrians. Neat game, Larry thought, soon to be followed by Dachau 2000. They'll love that one. He went to the change booth and got ten dollars in quarters. There was a working phone kiosk next to the Beef'n Brew across the street and he direct-dialed Jane's Place from memory. Jane's was a poker parlor where Wayne Stukey sometimes hung out.

Larry plugged quarters into the slot until his hand ached, and the phone began to ring three thousand miles away.

A female voice said, 'Jane's. We're open.'

'To anything?' he asked, low and sexy.

'Listen, wise guy, this isn't . . . hey, is this Larry?'

'Yeah, it's me. Hi, Arlene.'

'Where are you? Nobody's seen you, Larry.'

'Well, I'm on the East Coast,' he said cautiously. 'Somebody told me there were bloodsuckers on me and I ought to get out of the pool until they dropped off.'

'Something about a big party?'

'Yeah.'

'I *heard* about *that*,' she said. 'Big spender.'

'Is Wayne around, Arlene?'

'You mean Wayne Stukey?'

'I don't mean John Wayne – he's dead.'

'You mean you haven't heard?'

'What would I hear? I'm on the other coast. Hey, he's okay, isn't he?'

'He's in the hospital with this flu bug. Captain Trips, they're calling it out here. Not that it's any laughing matter. A lot of people have died with it, they say. People are scared, staying in. We've got six empty tables, and you know Jane's *never* has empty tables.'

'How is he?'

'Who knows? They've got wards and wards of people and none of them can have visitors. It's spooky, Larry. And there are a lot of soldiers around.'

'On leave?'

'Soldiers on leave don't carry guns or ride around in convoy trucks. A lot of people are really scared. You're well off out where you are.'

'Hasn't been anything on the news.'

'Out here there's been a few things in the papers about getting flu boosters, that's all. But some people are saying the army got careless with one of those little plague jars. Isn't that *creepy*?'

'It's just scare talk.'

'There's nothing like it where you are?'

'No,' he said, and then thought of his mother's cold. And hadn't there been a lot of sneezing and hacking going on in the subway? He remembered thinking it sounded like a TB ward. But there were plenty of sneezes and runny noses to go around in any city. Cold germs are gregarious, he thought. They like to share the wealth.

'Janey herself isn't in,' Arlene was saying. 'She's got a fever and swollen glands, she said. I thought that old whore was too tough to get sick.'

'Three minutes are up, signal when through,' the operator broke in.

Larry said: 'Well, I'll be coming back in a week or so, Arlene. We'll get together.'

'Fine by me. I always wanted to go out with a famous recording star.'

'Arlene? You don't by any chance know a guy named Dewey the Deck, do you?'

'Oh!' she said in a very startled way. 'Oh wow! Larry!'

'What?'

'Thank God you didn't hang up! I *did* see Wayne, just about two days before he went into the hospital. I forgot all about it! Oh, gee!'

'Well, what is it?'

'It's an envelope. He said it was for you, but he asked me to keep it in my cash drawer for a week or so, or give it to you if I saw you. He said something like "He's goddam lucky Dewey the Deck isn't collecting it instead of him."'

'What's in it?' He switched the phone from one hand to the other.

'Just a minute. I'll see.' There was a moment of silence, then ripping paper. Arlene said, 'It's a savings account book. First Commercial Bank of California. There's a balance of . . . wow! Just over thirteen thousand dollars. If you ask me to go somewhere dutch, I'll brain you.'

'You won't have to,' he said, grinning. 'Thanks, Arlene. Hang on to that for me, now.'

'No, I'll throw it down a storm-drain. Asshole.'

'It's so good to be loved.'

She sighed. 'You're too much, Larry. I'll put it in an envelope with both our names on it. Then you can't duck me when you come in.'

'I wouldn't do that, sugar.'

They hung up and then the operator was there, demanding three more dollars for Ma Bell. Larry, still feeling the wide and foolish grin on his face, plugged it willingly into the slot.

He looked at the change still scattered on the phone booth's shelf, picked out a quarter, and dropped it into the slot. A moment later his mother's phone was ringing. Your first impulse is to share good news, your second is to club someone with it. He thought – no, he believed – that this was entirely the former. He wanted to relieve both of them with the news that he was solvent again.

The smile faded off his lips little by little. The phone was only ringing. Maybe she had decided to go in to work after all. He thought of her flushed, feverish face, and of her coughing and sneezing and saying 'Shit!' impatiently into her handkerchief. He didn't think she would have gone in. The truth was, he didn't think she was strong enough to go in.

He hung up and absently removed his quarter from the slot when it clicked back. He went out, jingling the change in his hand. When he saw a cab he hailed it, and as the cab pulled back into the flow of traffic it began to spatter rain.

The door was locked and after knocking two or three times he was sure the apartment was empty. He had rapped loud enough to make someone on the floor above rap back, like an exasperated ghost. But he would have to go in and make sure, and he didn't have a key. He turned to go down the stairs to Mr Freeman's apartment, and that was when he heard the low groan from behind the door.

There were three different locks on his mother's door, but she was indifferent about using them all in spite of her obsession with the Puerto Ricans. Larry hit the door with his shoulder and it rattled loudly in its frame. He hit it again and the lock gave. The door swung back and banged off the wall.

'Mom?'

That groan again.

The apartment was dim; the day had grown dark very suddenly, and now there was thick thunder and the sound of rain had swelled. The living room window was half open, the white curtains bellying out over the table, then being sucked back through the opening and into the airshaft beyond. There was a glistening wet patch on the floor where the rain had come in.

'Mom, where are you?'

A louder groan. He went through into the kitchen, and thunder rumbled again. He almost tripped over her. She was lying on the floor, half in and half out of her bedroom.

'Mom! Jesus, Mom!'

She tried to roll over at the sound of his voice, but only her head would move, pivoting on the chin, coming to rest on the left cheek. Her breathing was stertorous and clogged with phlegm. But the worst thing, the thing he never forgot, was the way her visible eye rolled up to look at him, like the eye of a hog in a slaughtering pen. Her face was bright with fever.

'Larry?'

'Going to put you on your bed, Mom.'

He bent, locking his knees, fiercely against the trembling that wanted to start up in them, and got her in his arms. Her housecoat fell open, revealing a wash-faded nightgown and fishbelly-white legs sewn with puffy varicose veins. Her heat was immense. That terrified him. No one could remain so hot and live. Her brains must be frying in her head.

As if to prove this, she said querulously: 'Larry, go get your father. He's in the bar.'

'Be quiet,' he said, distraught. 'Just be quiet and go to sleep, Mom.'

'He's in the bar with that photographer!' she said shrilly into the palpable afternoon darkness, and thunder cracked viciously outside. Larry's body felt as if it was coated with slowly running slime. A cool breeze was moving through the apartment, coming from the half-open window in the living room. As if in response to it, Alice began to shiver and the flesh of her arms humped up in gooseflesh. Her teeth clicked. Her face was a full moon in the bedroom's semidarkness. Larry scrambled the covers down, put her legs in, and pulled the blankets up to her chin. Still she shivered helplessly, making the top blanket quiver and quake. Her face was dry and sweatless.

'*You go tell him I said come outta there!*' she cried, and then was silent, except for the heavy bronchial sound of her breathing.

He went back into the living room, approached the telephone, then detoured around it. He shut the window with a bang and then went back to the phone.

The books were on a shelf underneath the little table it sat on. He looked up the number of Mercy Hospital and dialed it while more thunder cracked outside. A stroke of lightning turned the window he'd just closed into a blue and white X-ray plate. In the bedroom his mother screamed breathlessly, chilling his blood.

The phone rang once, there was a buzzing sound, then a click. A mechanically bright voice said: 'This is a recording made at Mercy General Hospital. Right now all of our circuits are busy. If you will hold, your call will be taken as soon as possible. Thank you. This is a recording made at Mercy General Hospital. At the time of your call –'

'We put the mopheads downstairs!' his mother cried out. Thunder rolled. *'Those Puerto Rickies don't know nothing!'*

'– call will be taken as soon as –'

He thumped the phone down and stood over it, sweating. What kind of goddam hospital was that, where you got a fucking recorded announcement when your mother was dying? What was going on there?

Larry decided to go down and see if Mr Freeman could watch her while he got over to the hospital. Or should he call a private ambulance? Christ, how come nobody knew about these things when they needed to know about them? Why didn't they teach it in school?

In the bedroom his mother's laborious breathing went on and on.

'I'll be back,' he muttered, and went to the door. He was scared, terrified for her, but underneath another voice was saying things like: *These things always happen to me.* And: *Why did it have to happen after I got the good news?* And most despicable of all: *How bad is this going to screw up my plans? How many things am I going to have to change around?*

He hated that voice, wished it would die a quick, nasty death, but it just went on and on.

He ran down the stairs to Mr Freeman's apartment and thunder boomed through the dark clouds. As he reached the first-floor landing the door blew open and a curtain of rain swept in.

CHAPTER 20

The Harborside was the oldest hotel in Ogunquit. The view was not so good since they had built the new yacht club over on the other side, but on an afternoon like this, when the sky had been poxed with intermittent thunderstorms, the view was good enough.

Frannie had been sitting by the window for almost three hours, trying to write a letter to Grace Duggan, a high school chum who was now going to Smith. It wasn't a confessional letter dealing with her pregnancy or the scene with her mother – writing about those things would do nothing but depress her, and she supposed Grace would hear soon enough from her own sources in town. She had only been trying to write a friendly letter. The bicycle trip Jesse and I took to Rangely in May with Sam Lothrop and Sally Wenscelas. The biology final I lucked out on. Peggy Tate's (another high school friend and mutual acquaintance) new job as a Senate page. The impending marriage of Amy Lauder.

The letter just wouldn't allow itself to be written. The interesting pyrotechnics of the day had played a part – how could you write while pocket thunderstorms kept coming and going over the water? More to the point, none of the news in the letter seemed precisely honest. It had twisted slightly, like a knife in the hand that gives you a superficial cut instead of peeling the potato as you had expected it to do. The bicycle trip had been jolly, but she and Jess were no longer on such jolly terms. She had indeed lucked out on her BY-7 final, but had not been lucky at all on the biology final that really counted. Neither she nor Grace had ever cared all that much for Peggy Tate, and Amy's forthcoming nuptuals, in Fran's present state, seemed more like one of those ghastly sick jokes than an occasion of joy. Amy's getting married but I'm having the baby, hah-hah-hah.

Feeling that the letter had to be finished if only so she wouldn't have to wrestle with it anymore, she wrote:

I've got problems of my own, boy do I have problems,
but I just don't have the heart to write them all down.
Bad enough just having to think about them! But I
expect to see you by the Fourth, unless your plans
have changed since your last letter. (One letter in six
weeks? I was beginning to think someone had chopped
your typing fingers off, kid!). When I see you I'll tell
you all. I could sure use your advice.

      Believe in me and I'll believe in you,

               Fran

She signed her name with her customary flamboyant/comic scrawl,
so it took up half of the remaining white space on the notesheet.
Just doing that made her feel more like an imposter than ever. She
folded it into the envelope and addressed it and put it against the
mirror standing up. Finished business.

There. Now what?

The day was darkening again. She got up and walked restlessly
around the room, thinking she ought to go out before it started to rain
again, but where was there to go? A movie? She'd seen the only one
in town. With Jesse. To Portland to look at clothes? No fun. The only
clothes she could look at realistically these days were the ones with the
elastic waistbands. Room for two.

She'd had three calls today, the first one good news, the second
indifferent, the third bad. She wished they'd come in reverse order.
Outside the rain had begun to fall, darkening the marina's pier again.
She decided she'd go out and walk and to hell with the impending
rain. The fresh air, the summer damp, might make her feel better.
She might even stop somewhere and have a glass of beer. Happiness
in a bottle. Equilibrium, anyway.

The first call had been from Debbie Smith, in Somersworth.
Fran was more than welcome, Debbie said warmly. In fact, she was
needed. One of the three girls who had been sharing the apartment
had moved out in May, had gotten a job in a warehousing firm as
a secretary. She and Rhoda couldn't swing the rent much longer
without a third. 'And we both come from big families,' Debbie said.
'Crying babies don't bother us.'

Fran said she'd be ready to move in by the first of July, and
when she hung up she found warm tears coursing down her cheeks.
Relief tears. If she could get away from this town where she had

grown up, she thought she would be all right. Away from her mother, away from her father, even. The fact of the baby and her singleness would then assume some sort of sane proportion in her life. A large factor, surely, but not the only one. There was some sort of animal, a bug or a frog, she thought, that swelled up to twice its normal size when it felt threatened. The predator, in theory at least, saw this, got scared, and slunk off. She felt a little like that bug, and it was this whole town, the total environment (*gestalt* was maybe an even better word), that made her feel that way. She knew that nobody was going to make her wear a scarlet letter, but she also knew that for her mind to finish convincing her nerves of that fact, a break with Ogunquit was necessary. When she went out on the street she could feel people, not looking at her, but *getting ready* to look at her. The year-round residents, of course, not the summer people. The year-round residents always had to have someone to look at – a tosspot, a welfare slacker, The Kid from a Good Family who had been picked up shoplifting in Portland or Old Orchard Beach . . . or the girl with the levitating belly.

The second call, the so-so one, had been from Jess Rider. He had called from Portland and he had tried the house first. Luckily, he had gotten Peter, who gave him Fran's telephone number at the Harborside with no editorial comment.

Still, almost the first thing he'd said was: 'You got a lot of static at home, huh?'

'Well, I got some,' she said cautiously, not wanting to go into it. That would make them conspirators of a kind.

'Your mother?'

'Why do you say that?'

'She looks like the type that might freak out. It's something in the eyes, Frannie. It says if you shoot my sacred cows, I'll shoot yours.'

She was silent.

'I'm sorry. I don't want to offend you.'

'You didn't,' she said. His description was actually quite apt – surface-apt anyway – but she was still trying to get over the surprise of that verb, *offend*. It was a strange word to hear from him. Maybe there's a postulate here, she thought. When your lover begins to talk about 'offending' you, he's not your lover anymore.

'Frannie, the offer still stands. If you say yes, I can get a couple of rings and be there this afternoon.'

On your bike, she thought, and almost giggled. A giggle would be a horrible, unnecessary thing to do to him, and she covered the phone for a second just to be sure it wasn't going to escape. She had done more weeping and giggling in the last six days than she had done since she was fifteen and starting to date.

'No, Jess,' she said, and her voice was quite calm.

'I mean it!' he said with startling vehemence, as if he had seen her struggling with laughter.

'I know you do,' she said. 'But I'm not ready to get married. I know that about me, Jess. It has nothing to do with you.'

'What about the baby?'

'I'm going to have it.'

'And give it up?'

'I haven't decided.'

For a moment he was silent and she could hear other voices in other rooms. They had their own problems, she supposed. Baby, the world is a daytime drama. We love our lives, and so we look for the guiding light as we search for tomorrow.

'I wonder about that baby,' Jesse said finally. She really doubted if he did, but it was maybe the only thing he could have said that would cut her. It did.

'Jess —'

'So where are you going?' he asked briskly. 'You can't stay at the Harborside all summer. If you need a place, I can look around in Portland.'

'I've got a place.'

'Where, or am I not supposed to ask?'

'You're not supposed to,' she said, and bit her tongue for not finding a more diplomatic way of saying it.

'Oh,' he said. His voice was queerly flat. Finally he said cautiously, 'Can I ask you something and not piss you off, Frannie? Because I really want to know. It's not a rhetorical question or anything.'

'You can ask,' she agreed warily. Mentally she did gird herself not to be pissed off, because when Jess prefaced something like that, it was usually just before he came out with some hideous and totally unaware piece of chauvinism.

'Don't I have any rights in this at all?' Jess asked. 'Can't I share the responsibility and the decision?'

For a moment she *was* pissed off, and then the feeling was

gone. Jess was just being Jess, trying to protect his image of himself to himself, the way all thinking people do so they can get to sleep at night. She had always liked him for his intelligence, but in a situation like this, intelligence could be a bore. People like Jess – and herself, too – had been taught all their lives that the good thing to do was commit and be active. Sometimes you had to hurt yourself – and badly – to find out it could be better to lie back in the tall weeds and procrastinate. His toils were kind, but they were still toils. He didn't want to let her get away.

'Jesse,' she said, 'neither of us wanted this baby. We agreed on the pills so the baby wouldn't happen. You don't have any responsibility.'

'But –'

'No, Jess,' she said, quite firmly.

He sighed.

'Will you get in touch when you get settled?'

'I think so.'

'Are you still planning to go back to school?'

'Eventually. I'm going to take the fall semester off. Maybe with something CED.'

'If you need me, Frannie, you know where I'll be. I'm not running out.'

'I know that, Jesse.'

'If you need dough –'

'Yes.'

'Get in touch. I won't press you, but . . . I'll want to see you.'

'All right, Jess.'

'Goodbye, Fran.'

'Goodbye.'

When she hung up the goodbyes had seemed too final, the conversation unfinished. It struck her why. They had not added 'I love you,' and that was a first. It made her sad and she told herself not to be, but the telling didn't help.

The last call had come around noon, and it was from her father. They had had lunch the day before yesterday, and he told her he was worried about the effect this was having on Carla. She hadn't come to bed last night; she had spent it in the parlor, poring over the old genealogical records. He had gone in around eleven-thirty to ask her when she was coming up. Her hair had been down, flowing over her shoulders and the bodice of her nightgown, and

Peter said she looked wild and not strictly in touch with things. That heavy book was on her lap and she hadn't even looked up at him, only continued to turn the pages. She said she wasn't sleepy. She would be up in a while. She had a cold, Peter told her as they sat in a booth at the Corner Lunch, more looking at hamburgers than eating them. The sniffles. When Peter asked her if she would like a glass of hot milk, she didn't answer at all. He had found her yesterday morning asleep in the chair, the book on her lap.

When she finally woke up she had seemed better, more herself, but her cold was worse. She dismissed the idea of having Dr Edmonton in, saying it was just a chest cold. She had put Vicks on her chest, and a flannel square of cloth, and she thought her sinuses were clearing already. But Peter hadn't cared for the way she looked, he told Frannie. Although she refused to let him take her temperature, he thought she was running a couple of degrees of fever.

He had called Fran today just after the first thunderstorm had begun. The clouds, purple and black, had piled up silently over the harbor, and the rain began, at first gentle and then torrential. As they talked she could look out her window and see the lightning stab down at the water beyond the breakwater, and each time it happened there would be a little scratching noise on the wire, like a phonograph needle digging a record.

'She's in bed today,' Peter said. 'She finally agreed to let Tom Edmonton take a look at her.'

'Has he been yet?'

'He just left. He thinks she's got the flu.'

'Oh, Lord,' Frannie said, closing her eyes. 'That's no joke for a woman her age.'

'No, it isn't.' He paused. 'I told him everything, Frannie. About the baby, about the fight you and Carla had. Tom's taken care of you since you were a baby yourself, and he keeps his lip buttoned. I wanted to know if that could have caused this. He said no. Flu is flu.'

'Flu made who,' Fran said bleakly.

'Pardon?'

'Never mind,' Fran said. Her father was amazingly broad-minded, but an AC/DC fan he was not. 'Go on.'

'Well, there's not much further to go, hon. He said there's a lot of it around. A particularly nasty breed. It seems to have migrated out of the south, and New York is swamped with it.'

'But sleeping in the parlor all night –' she began doubtfully.

'Actually, he said being in an upright position was probably better for her lungs and her bronchial tubes. He didn't say anything else, but Alberta Edmonton belongs to all the organizations Carla belongs to, so he didn't have to. Both of us knew she's been inviting something like this, Fran. She's president of the Town Historical Committee, she's spending twenty hours a week in the library, she's secretary of the Women's Club and the Lovers of Literature Club, she's been running the March of Dimes here in town since before Fred died, and last winter she took on the Heart Fund, for good measure. On top of all that she's been trying to drum up interest in a Southern Maine Genealogical Society. She's run down, worn out. And that's part of the reason she blew up at you. All Edmonton said was that she had the welcome mat out for the first evil germ that passed her way. That's all he had to say. Frannie, she's getting old and she doesn't want to. She's been working harder than I have.'

'How sick is she, Daddy?'

'She's in bed, drinking juice and taking the pills that Tom prescribed. I took the day off, and Mrs Halliday is going to come in and sit with her tomorrow. She wants Mrs Halliday so they can work out an agenda for the July meeting of the Historical Society.' He sighed windily and lightning scratched the wire again. 'I sometimes think she wants to die in harness.'

Timidly, Fran said: 'Do you think she'd mind if I –'

'Right now she would. But give her time, Fran. She'll come around.'

Now, four hours later, tying her rain scarf over her hair, she wondered if her mother *would* come around. Maybe if she gave up the baby, no one in town would ever get wind of it. That was unlikely, though. In small towns people scent the wind with noses of uncommon keenness. And of course if she kept the baby . . . but she wasn't really thinking of that, was she? *Was* she?

She could feel guilt working in her as she pulled on her light coat. Her mother was run down, of course she was. Fran had seen that when she came home from college and the two of them exchanged kisses on the cheek. Carla had bags under her eyes, her skin looked too yellow, and the gray in her hair, which was always beauty-shop neat, had progressed visibly in spite of the thirty-dollar rinses. But still . . .

She had been hysterical, absolutely hysterical. And Frannie was left asking herself exactly how she was going to assess responsibility if her mother's flu developed into pneumonia, or if she had some kind of breakdown. Or even died. God, what an awful thought. That couldn't happen, please God no, of course not. The drugs she was taking would knock it out, and once Frannie was out of her line of visibility and incubating her little stranger quietly in Somersworth, her mother would recover from the knock she had been forced to take. She would –

The phone began to ring.

She looked at it blankly for a moment, and outside more lightning flickered, followed by a clap of thunder so close and vicious that she jumped, wincing.

Jangle, jangle, jangle.

But she had had her three calls, who else could it be? Debbie wouldn't need to call her back, and she didn't think Jess would, either. Maybe it was 'Dialing for Dollars.' Or a Saladmaster salesman. Maybe it was Jess after all, giving it the old college try.

As she went to pick it up, she felt sure it was her father and that the news would be worse. It's a pie, she told herself. Responsibility is a pie. Some of the responsibility goes with all the charity work she does, but you're only kidding if you think you're not going to have to cut a big, juicy, bitter piece for yourself. And eat every bite.

'Hello?'

There was nothing but silence for a moment and she frowned, puzzled, and said hello again.

Then her father said, 'Fran?' and made a strange, gulping sound. 'Frannie?' That gulping sound again and Fran realized with dawning horror that her father was fighting back tears. One of her hands crept to her throat and clutched at the knot where the rain scarf was tied.

'Daddy? What is it? Is it Mom?'

'Frannie, I'll have to pick you up. I'll . . . just swing by and pick you up. That's what I'll do.'

'Is Mom all right?' she screamed into the phone. Thunder whacked over the Harborside again and frightened her and she began to cry. 'Tell me, Daddy!'

'She got worse, that's all I know,' Peter said. 'About an hour after I talked to you she got worse. Her fever went up. She started to rave. I tried to get Tom . . . and Rachel said he was out, that a lot of people were really sick . . . so I called the Sanford Hospital and they said their ambulances were out on calls, both of them, but they'd add Carla to the list. The *list*, Frannie, what the hell is this *list*, all of a sudden? I know Jim Warrington, he drives one of the Sanford ambulances, and unless there's a car wreck on 95 he sits around and plays gin rummy all day. What's this *list*?' He was nearly screaming.

'Calm down, Daddy. Calm down. Calm down.' She burst into tears again and her hand left the knot in her scarf and went to her eyes. 'If she's still there, you better take her yourself.'

'No . . . no, they came about fifteen minutes ago. And Christ, Frannie, there were *six people* in the back of that ambulance. One of them was Will Ronson, the man who runs the drugstore. And Carla . . . your mother . . . she came out of it a little as they put her in and she just kept saying, "I can't catch my breath, Peter, I can't catch my breath, why can't I breathe?" Oh, Christ,' he finished in a breaking, childish voice that frightened her.

'Can you drive, Daddy? Can you drive over here?'

'Yes,' he said. 'Yes, sure.' He seemed to be pulling himself together.

'I'll be on the front porch.'

She hung up and went down the stairs quickly, her knees trembling. On the porch she saw that, although it was still raining, the clouds of this latest thundershower were already breaking up and late afternoon sun was beaming through. She looked automatically for the rainbow and saw it, far out over the water, a misty and mystic crescent. Guilt gnawed and worried at her, furry bodies inside her belly, in where that other thing was, and she began to cry again.

Eat your pie, she told herself as she waited for her father to come. It tastes terrible, so eat your pie. You can have seconds, even thirds. Eat your pie, Frannie, eat every bite.

CHAPTER 21

Stu Redman was frightened.

He looked out the barred window of his new room in Stovington, Vermont, and what he saw was a small town far below, miniature gas station signs, some sort of mill, a main street, a river, the turnpike, and beyond the turnpike the granite backbone of far western New England – the Green Mountains.

He was frightened because this was more like a jail cell than a hospital room. He was frightened because Denninger was gone. He hadn't seen Denninger since the whole crazy three-ring circus moved from Atlanta to here. Deitz was gone, too. Stu thought that maybe Denninger and Deitz were sick, perhaps dead already.

Somebody had slipped. Either that, or the disease that Charles D. Campion had brought to Arnette was a lot more communicable than anyone had guessed. Either way, the integrity of the Atlanta Plague Center had been breached, and Stu thought that everyone who had been there was now getting a chance to do a little firsthand research on the virus they called A-Prime or the superflu.

They still did tests on him here, but they seemed desultory. The schedule had become slipshod. Results were scrawled down and he had a suspicion that someone looked at them cursorily, shook his head, and dumped them in the nearest shredder.

That wasn't the worst, though. The worst was the guns. The nurses who came in to take blood or spit or urine were now always accompanied by a soldier in a white-suit, and the soldier had a gun in a plastic Baggie. The Baggie was fastened over the wrist of the soldier's right gauntlet. The gun was an army-issue .45, and Stu had no doubt that, if he tried any of the games he had tried with Deitz, the .45 would tear the end of the Baggie into smoking, burning shreds and Stu Redman would become a Golden Oldie.

If they were just going through the motions now, then he had become expendable. Being under detention was bad. Being under detention and being expendable . . . that was *very* bad.

He watched the six o'clock news very carefully every night now. The men who had attempted the coup in India had been branded 'outside agitators' and shot. The police were still looking for the person or persons who had blown a power station in Laramie, Wyoming, yesterday. The Supreme Court had decided 6–3 that known homosexuals could not be fired from civil service jobs. And for the first time, there had been a whisper of other things.

AEC officials in Miller County, Arkansas, had denied there was any chance of a reactor meltdown. The atomic power plant in the small town of Fouke, about thirty miles from the Texas border, had been plagued with minor circuitry problems in the equipment that controlled the pile's cooling cycle, but there was no cause for alarm. The army units in that area were merely a precautionary measure. Stu wondered what precautions the army could take if the Fouke reactor did indeed go China Syndrome. He thought the army might be in southwestern Arkansas for other reasons altogether. Fouke wasn't all that far from Arnette.

Another item reported that an East Coast flu epidemic seemed to be in the early stages – the Russian strain, nothing to really worry about except for the very old and the very young. A tired New York City doctor was interviewed in a hallway of Brooklyn's Mercy Hospital. He said the flu was exceptionally tenacious for Russian-A, and he urged viewers to get flu boosters. Then he suddenly started to say something else, but the sound cut off and you could only see his lips moving. The picture cut back to the newscaster in the studio, who said: 'There have been some reported deaths in New York as a result of this latest flu outbreak, but contributing causes such as urban pollution and perhaps even the AIDS virus have been present in many of those fatal cases. Government health officials emphasize that this is Russian-A flu, not the more dangerous Swine flu. In the meantime, old advice is good advice, the doctors say: stay in bed, get lots of rest, drink fluids, and take aspirin for the fever.'

The newscaster smiled reassuringly . . . and off-camera, someone sneezed.

The sun was touching the horizon now, tinting it a gold that would turn to red and fading orange soon. The nights were the worst. They had flown him to a part of the country that was alien to him, and it was somehow more alien at night. In this early summer season the amount of green he could see from his window seemed abnormal, excessive, a little scary. He had no friends; as far as he knew all the people who had been on the plane with him when it flew from Braintree to Atlanta were now dead. He was surrounded by automatons who took his blood at gunpoint. He was afraid for his life, although he still felt fine and had begun to believe he wasn't going to catch It, whatever It was.

Thoughtfully, Stu wondered if it would be possible to escape from here.

CHAPTER 22

When Creighton came in on June 24, he found Starkey looking at the monitors, his hands behind his back. He could see the old man's West Point ring glittering on his right hand, and he felt a wave of pity for him. Starkey had been cruising on pills for ten days, and he was close to the inevitable crash. But, Creighton thought, if his suspicion about the phone call was correct, the real crash had already occurred.

'Len,' Starkey said, as if surprised. 'Good of you to come in.'

'*De nada*,' Creighton said with a slight smile.

'You know who that was on the phone.'

'It was really him, then?'

'The President, yes. I've been relieved. The dirty alderman relieved me, Len. Of course I knew it was coming. But it still hurts. Hurts like hell. It hurts coming from that grinning, gladhanding sack of shit.'

Len Creighton nodded.

'Well,' Starkey said, passing a hand over his face. 'It's done. Can't be undone. You're in charge now. He wants you in Washington as soon as you can get there. He'll have you on the carpet and he'll chew your ass to a bloody rag, but you just stand there and yessir him and take it. We've salvaged what we can. It's enough. I'm convinced it's enough.'

'If so, this country ought to get down on its knees to you.'

'The throttle burned my hand, but I . . . I held it as long as I could, Len. I held it.' He spoke with quiet vehemence, but his eyes wandered back to the monitor, and for a moment his mouth quivered infirmly. 'I couldn't have done it without you.'

'Well . . . we go back a country mile or three, Billy, don't we?'

'You can say that again, soldier. Now – listen. One thing is top priority. You've got to see Jack Cleveland, first chance you get. He knows who we've got behind both curtains, iron and bamboo. He knows how to get in touch with them, and he won't stick at what has to be done. He'll know it'll have to be quick.'

'I don't understand, Billy.'

'We have to assume the worst,' Starkey said, and a queer grin came over his face. It lifted his upper lip and made it wrinkle like the snout of a dog protecting a farmyard. He pointed a finger at the sheets of yellow flimsy on the table. 'It's out of control now. It's popped up in Oregon, Nebraska, Louisiana, Florida. Tentative cases in Mexico and Chile. When we lost Atlanta, we lost the three men best equipped to deal with the problem. We're getting exactly nowhere with Mr Stuart 'Prince' Redman. Did you know they actually injected him with the Blue virus? He thought it was a sedative. He killed it, and no one has the slightest idea how. If we had six weeks, we might be able to turn the trick. But we don't. The flu story is the best one, but it is imperative – *imperative* – that the other side never sees this as an artificial situation created in America. It might give them ideas.

'Cleveland has between eight and twenty men and women in the USSR and between five and ten in each of the European satellite countries. Not even I know how many he has in Red China.' Starkey's mouth was trembling again. 'When you see Cleveland this afternoon, all you need tell him is *Rome falls*. You won't forget?'

'No,' Len said. His lips felt curiously cold. 'But do you really expect that they'll do it? Those men and women?'

'Our people got those vials one week ago. They believe they contain radioactive particles to be charted by our Sky-Cruise satellites. That's all they need to know, isn't it, Len?'

'Yes, Billy.'

'And if things do go from bad to . . . to worse, no one will ever know. Project Blue was uninfiltrated to the very end, we're sure of that. A new virus, a mutation . . . our opposite numbers may suspect, but there won't be time enough. Share and share alike, Len.'

'Yes.'

Starkey was looking at the monitors again. 'My daughter gave me a book of poems some years ago. By a man named Yeets. She said every military man should read Yeets. I think it was her idea of a joke. You ever heard of Yeets, Len?'

'I think so,' Creighton said, considering and rejecting the idea of telling Starkey the man's name was pronounced Yates.

'I read every line,' Starkey said, as he peered into the eternal silence of the cafeteria. 'Mostly because she thought I wouldn't. It's a mistake to become too predictable. I didn't understand much of it – I believe the man must have been crazy – but I read it. Funny poetry. Didn't always rhyme. But there was one poem in that book that I've never been able to get out of my mind. It seemed as if that man was describing everything I dedicated my life to, its hopelessness, its damned nobility. He said that things fall apart. He said the center doesn't hold. I believe he meant that things get flaky, Len. That's what I believe he meant. Yeets knew that sooner or later things get goddam flaky around the edges even if he didn't know anything else.'

'Yes, sir,' Creighton said quietly.

'The end of it gave me goosebumps the first time I read it, and it still does. I've got that part by heart. "What rough beast, its hour come round at last, slouches towards Bethlehem to be born?"'

Creighton stood silent. He had nothing to say.

'The beast is on its way,' Starkey said, turning around. He was weeping and grinning. 'It's on its way, and it's a good deal rougher than that fellow Yeets ever could have imagined. Things are falling apart. The job is to hold as much as we can for as long as we can.'

'Yes, sir,' Creighton said, and for the first time he felt the sting of tears in his own eyes. 'Yes, Billy.'

Starkey put out his hand and Creighton took it in both of his own. Starkey's hand was old and cold, like the shed skin of a snake in which some small prairie animal has died, leaving its own fragile skeleton within the husk of the reptile. Tears overspilled the lower arcs of Starkey's eyes and ran down his meticulously shaved cheeks.

'I have business to attend to,' Starkey said.

'Yes, sir.'

Starkey slipped his West Point ring off his right hand and his wedding band off his left. 'For Cindy,' he said. 'For my daughter. See that she gets them, Len.'

'I will.'

Starkey went to the door.

'Billy?' Len Creighton called after him.

Starkey turned.

Creighton stood ramrod straight, the tears still running down his own cheeks. He saluted.

Starkey returned it and then stepped out the door.

★　　★　　★

The elevator hummed efficiently, marking off the floors. An alarm began to hoot — mournfully, as if it somehow knew it was warning of a situation which had already become a lost cause — when he used his special key to open it at the top, so he could enter the motor-pool area. Starkey imagined Len Creighton watching him on a succession of monitors as he first picked out a jeep and then drove it across the desert floor of the sprawling test site and through a gate marked HIGH SECURITY ZONE NO ADMITTANCE WITHOUT SPECIAL CLEARANCE. The checkpoints looked like turnpike toll-booths. They were still manned, but the soldiers behind the yellowish glass were dead and rapidly mummifying in the dry desert heat. The booths were bulletproof, but they hadn't been germproof. Their glazed and sunken eyes stared vacantly at Starkey as he motored past, the only moving thing along the tangle of dirt roads among the Quonset huts and low cinderblock buildings.

He stopped outside a squat blockhouse with a sign reading ABSOLUTELY NO ADMITTANCE WITHOUT A-I-A CLEARANCE on the door. He used one key to get in, and another to summon the elevator. A guard, dead as a doornail and stiff as a poker, stared at him from the glass-encased security station to the left of the elevator doors. When the elevator arrived and the doors opened, Starkey stepped in quickly. He seemed to feel the gaze of the dead guard on him, a small weight of eyes like two dusty stones.

The elevator sank so rapidly his stomach turned over. A bell dinged softly when it came to a halt. The doors slid open, and the sweet odor of decay hit him like a soft slap. It wasn't too strong because the air purifiers were still working, but not even the purifiers could dispose of that smell completely. When a man has died, he wants you to know about it, Starkey thought.

There were almost a dozen bodies sprawled in front of the elevator. Starkey minced among them, not wanting to tread on a decaying, waxy hand or trip over an outstretched leg. That might make him scream, and he most definitely didn't want to do that. You didn't want to scream in a tomb because the sound of it might drive you mad, and that's exactly where he was: in a tomb. It looked like a well-financed scientific research project, but what it really was now was a tomb.

The elevator doors slid shut behind him; there was a hum as it began to go up automatically. It wouldn't come down again unless somebody else keyed it, Starkey knew; as soon as the installation's integrity had been breached, the computers had switched all the elevators to the general containment program. Why were these poor men and women lying here? Obviously they had been hoping the computers would fuck up the switch-over to the emergency procedures. Why not? It even had a certain logic. Everything else had fucked up.

Starkey walked down the corridor which led to the cafeteria, his heels clicking hollowly. Above, the fluorescents embedded in their long fixtures like inverted ice-cube trays threw a hard, shadowless light. There were more bodies. A man and a woman with their clothes off and holes in their heads. They screwed, Starkey thought, and then he shot her, and then he shot himself. Love among the viruses. The pistol, an army-issue .45, was still clutched in his hand. The tile floor was spotted with blood and gray stuff that looked like oatmeal. He felt a terrible and thankfully transient urge to bend down and touch the dead woman's breasts, to see if they were hard or flaccid.

Farther down the hall a man sat with his back propped against a closed door, a sign tied around his neck with a shoelace. His chin had fallen forward, obscuring what was written there. Starkey put his fingers under the man's chin and pushed his head back. As he did so, the man's eyeballs fell back into his head with a meaty little thud. The words on the sign had been written in red Magic Marker. NOW YOU KNOW IT WORKS, the sign said. ANY QUESTIONS?

Starkey let go of the man's chin. The head remained cocked at its stiff angle, the dark eye sockets staring raptly upward. Starkey stepped back. He was crying again. He suspected he was crying because he didn't have any questions.

The cafeteria doors were propped open. Outside them was a large cork bulletin board. There was to have been a league bowl-off on June 20, Starkey saw. The Grim Gutter-ballers vs The First Strikers for the Project championship. Also, Anna Floss wanted a ride to Denver or Boulder on July 9. She would share driving and expenses. Also, Richard Betts wanted to give away some friendly pups, half collie and half St Bernard. Also, there were weekly nondenominational religious services in the caf.

Starkey read every announcement on the bulletin board, and then he went inside.

The smell in here was worse – rancid food as well as dead bodies. Starkey looked around with dull horror.

Some of them seemed to be looking at him.

'Men –' Starkey said, and then choked. He had no idea what he had been about to say.

He walked slowly over to where Frank D. Bruce lay with his face in his soup. He looked down at Frank D. Bruce for several moments. Then he pulled Frank D. Bruce's head up by the hair. The soup bowl came with him, still stuck on his face by soup which had long since congealed, and Starkey struck at it in horror, finally knocking it off. The bowl clunked to the floor, upside down. Most of the soup still clung to Frank D. Bruce's face like moldy jelly. Starkey produced his handkerchief and wiped off as much of it as he could. Frank D. Bruce's eyes appeared to be gummed shut by soup, but Starkey forbore to wipe the lids. He was afraid Frank D. Bruce's eyes would fall back into his skull, like the eyes of the man with the sign. He was even more afraid that the lids, freed of the glue which held them, might roll up like windowshades. He was mostly afraid of what the expression in Frank D. Bruce's eyes might be.

'Private Bruce,' Starkey said softly, 'at ease.'

He put the handkerchief carefully over the face of Frank D. Bruce. It stuck there. Starkey turned and walked out of the cafeteria in long, even strides, as if on a parade ground.

Halfway back to the elevator he came to the man with the sign around his neck. Starkey sat down beside him, loosened the strap over the butt of his pistol, and put the barrel of the gun into his mouth.

When the shot came, it was muffled and undramatic. None of the corpses took the slightest notice. The air purifiers took care of the puff of smoke. In the bowels of Project Blue, there was silence. In the cafeteria, Starkey's handkerchief came unstuck from Private Frank D. Bruce's face and wafted to the floor. Frank D. Bruce did not seem to mind, but Len Creighton found himself looking into the monitor which showed Bruce more and more often, and wondering why in hell Billy couldn't have gotten the soup out of the man's eyebrows while he was at it. He was going to have to face the President of the United States soon, very soon, but the soup congealing in Frank D. Bruce's eyebrows worried him more. Much more.

CHAPTER 23

Randall Flagg, the dark man, strode south on US 51, listening to the nightsounds that pressed close on both sides of this narrow road that would take him sooner or later out of Idaho and into Nevada. From Nevada he might go anywhere. From New Orleans to Nogales, from Portland, Oregon, to Portland, Maine, it was his country, and none knew or loved it better. He knew where the roads went, and he walked them at night. Now, an hour before dawn, he was somewhere between Grasmere and Riddle, west of Twin Falls, still north of the Duck Valley Reservation that spreads across two states. And wasn't it fine?

He walked rapidly, rundown bootheels clocking against the paved surface of the road, and if car lights showed on the horizon he faded back and back, down over the soft shoulder to the high grass where the night bugs made their homes . . . and the car would pass him, the driver perhaps feeling a slight chill as if he had driven through an air pocket, his sleeping wife and children stirring uneasily, as if all had been touched with a bad dream at the same instant.

He walked south, south on US 51, the worn heels of his sharp-toed cowboy boots clocking on the pavement; a tall man of no age in faded, pegged jeans and a denim jacket. His pockets were stuffed with fifty different kinds of conflicting literature – pamphlets for all seasons, rhetoric for all reasons. When this man handed you a tract you took it no matter what the subject: the dangers of atomic power plants, the role played by the International Jewish Cartel in the overthrow of friendly governments, the CIA-Contra-cocaine connection, the farm workers' unions, the Jehovah's Witnesses (*If You Can Answer These Ten Questions 'Yes,' You have been SAVED!*), the Blacks for Militant Equality, the Kode of the Klan. He had them all, and more, too. There was a button on each breast of his denim jacket. On the right, a yellow smile-face. On the left, a pig wearing a policeman's cap. The legend was written beneath in red letters which dripped to simulate blood: HOW'S YOUR PORK?

He moved on, not pausing, not slowing, but alive to the night. His eyes seemed almost frantic with the night's possibilities. There was a Boy Scout knapsack on his back, old and battered. There was a dark hilarity in his face, and perhaps in his heart, too, you would think – and you would be right. It was the face of a hatefully happy man, a face that radiated a horrible handsome warmth, a face to make waterglasses shatter in the hands of tired truck-stop waitresses, to make small children crash their trikes into board fences and then run wailing to their mommies with stake-shaped splinters sticking out of their knees. It was a face guaranteed to make barroom arguments over batting averages turn bloody.

He moved on south, somewhere on US 51 between Grasmere and Riddle, now closer to Nevada. Soon he would camp and sleep the day away, waking up as evening drew on. He would read as his supper cooked over a small, smokeless campfire, it didn't matter what: words from some battered and coverless paperback porno novel, or maybe *Mein Kampf*, or an R. Crumb comic book, or one of the baying reactionary position papers from the America Firsters or the Sons of the Patriots. When it came to the printed word, Flagg was an equal opportunity reader.

After supper he would commence walking again, walking south on this excellent two-lane highway cutting through this godforsaken wilderness, watching and smelling and listening as the climate grew more arid, strangling everything down to sagebrush and tumbleweed, watching as the mountains began to poke out of the earth like dinosaur spines. By dawn tomorrow or the day after that he would pass into Nevada, striking Owyhee first and then Mountain City, and in Mountain City there was a man named Christopher Bradenton who would see that he had a clean car and some clean papers and then the country would come alive in all its glorious possibilities, a body politic with its network of roads embedded in its skin like marvelous capillaries, ready to take him, the dark speck of foreign matter, anywhere or everywhere – heart, liver, lights, brain. He was a clot looking for a place to happen, a splinter of bone hunting a soft organ to puncture, a lonely lunatic cell looking for a mate – they would set up housekeeping and raise themselves a cozy little malignant tumor.

He hammered along, arms swinging by his sides. He was known, well known, along the highways in hiding that are traveled by the poor and the mad, by the professional revolutionaries and by those who have been taught to hate so well that their hate shows on their faces like harelips and they are unwanted except by others like them, who welcome them to cheap rooms with slogans and posters on the walls, to basements where lengths of sawed-off pipe are held in padded vises while they are stuffed with high explosives, to back rooms where lunatic plans are laid: to kill a Cabinet member, to kidnap the child of a visiting dignitary, or to break into a board-room meeting of Standard Oil with grenades and machine guns and murder in the name of the people. He was known there, and even the maddest of them could only gaze upon his dark and grin-ning face at an oblique angle. The women he took to bed with him, even if they reduced intercourse to something as casual as getting a snack from the refrigerator, accepted him with a stiffening of the body, a turning away of countenance. They took him the way they might take a ram with golden eyes or a black dog – and when it was done they were *cold*, so *cold*, it seemed impossible they could ever be warm again. When he walked into a meeting the hysterical babble ceased – the backbiting, recriminations, accusations, the ideological rhetoric. For a moment there would be dead silence and they would start to turn to him and then turn away, as if he had come to them with some old and terrible engine of destruction cradled in his arms, something a thousand times worse than the plastic explosive made in the basement labs of renegade chemistry students or the black market arms obtained from some greedy army post supply sergeant. It seemed that he had come to them with a device gone rusty with blood and packed for centuries in the Cosmoline of screams but now ready again, carried to their meeting like some infernal gift, a birthday cake with nitroglycerine candles. And when the talk began again it would be rational and disciplined – as rational and disciplined as madmen can make it – and things would be agreed upon.

He rocked along, his feet easy in the boots, which were comfortably sprung in all the right places. His feet and these boots were old lovers. Christopher Bradenton in Mountain City knew him as Richard Fry. Bradenton was a conductor on one of the underground railway systems by which fugitives moved. Half a dozen different organizations, from the Weathermen to the Guevara Brigade, saw that Bradenton had money. He was a poet who sometimes taught Free University classes or traveled in the Western states of Utah, Nevada, and Arizona, speaking to high school English classes, stunning middle-class boys and girls (he hoped) with the news that poetry was alive – narcoleptic, to be sure, but still possessed of a certain hideous vitality. He was in his late fifties now, but Bradenton had been dismissed from one California college twenty-some years ago for getting too chummy with the SDS. He had been busted in The Great Chicago Pig Convention of 1968, formed his ties to one radical group after another, first embracing the craziness of these groups, then being swallowed whole.

The dark man walked and smiled. Bradenton represented just one end of one conduit, and there were thousands of them – the pipes the crazies moved through, carrying their books and bombs. The pipes were interconnected, the signposts disguised but readable to the initiate. In New York he was known as Robert Franq, and his claim that he was a black man had never been disputed, although his skin was very light. He and a black veteran of Nam – the black had more than enough hate to make up for his missing left leg – had offed six cops in New York and New Jersey. In Georgia he was Ramsey Forrest; a distant descendant of Nathan Bedford Forrest, and in his white sheet he had participated in two rapes, a castration, and the burning of a nigger shanty town. But that had been long ago, in the early sixties, during the first civil rights surge. He sometimes thought that he might have been born in that strife. He certainly could not remember much that had happened to him before that, except that he came originally from Nebraska and that he had once attended high school classes with a red-haired, bandy-legged boy named Charles Starkweather. He remembered the civil rights marches of 1960 and 1961 better – the beatings, the night rides, the churches that had exploded as if some miracle inside them had grown too large to be contained. He remembered drifting down to New Orleans in 1962, and meeting a demented young man who was handing out tracts urging America to leave Cuba alone. That man had been a certain Mr Oswald, and he had taken some of Oswald's tracts and he still had a couple, very old and crumpled, in one of his many pockets. He had sat on a hundred different Committees of Responsibility. He had walked in demonstrations against the same dozen companies on a hundred different college campuses. He wrote the questions that most discomfited those in power when they came to lecture, but he never asked the questions himself; those power merchants might have seen his grinning, burning face as some cause for alarm and fled from the podium. Likewise he never spoke at rallies because the microphones would scream with hysterical feedback and circuits would blow. But he had written speeches for those who did speak, and on several occasions those speeches had ended in riots, overturned cars, student strike votes, and violent demonstrations. For a while in the early seventies he had been acquainted with a man named Donald DeFreeze, and had suggested that DeFreeze take the name Cinque. He had helped lay plans that resulted in the kidnapping of an heiress, and it had been he who suggested that the heiress be made crazy instead of simply ransomed. He had left the small Los Angeles house where DeFreeze and the others had fried not twenty minutes before the police moved in; he slunk away up the street, his bulging and dusty boots clocking on the pavement, a fiery grin on his face that made mothers grab up their children and pull them into the house, a grin that made pregnant women feel premature labor pains. And later, when a few tattered remnants of the group were swept up, all they knew was there had been someone else associated with the group, maybe someone important, maybe a hanger-on, a man of no age, a man called the Walkin Dude, or sometimes the Boogeyman.

He strode on at a steady, ground-eating pace. Two days ago he had been in Laramie, Wyoming, part of an ecotage group that had blown a power station. Today he was on US 51, between Grasmere and Riddle, on his way to Mountain City. Tomorrow he would be somewhere else. And he was happier than he had ever been, because –

He stopped.

Because something was coming. He could feel it, almost taste it on the night air. He *could* taste it, a sooty hot taste that came from everywhere, as if God was planning a cook-out and all of civilization was going to be the barbecue. Already the charcoal was hot, white and flaky outside, as red as demons' eyes inside. A huge thing, a great thing.

His time of transfiguration was at hand. He was going to be born for the second time, he was going to be squeezed out of the laboring cunt of some great sand-colored beast that even now lay in the throes of its contractions, its legs moving slowly as the birthblood gushed, its sun-hot eyes glaring into the emptiness.

He had been born when times changed, and the times were going to change again. It was in the wind, in the wind of this soft Idaho evening.

It was almost time to be reborn. He knew. Why else could he suddenly do magic?

He closed his eyes, his hot face turning up slightly to the dark sky, which was prepared to receive the dawn. He concentrated. Smiled. The dusty, rundown heels of his boots began to rise off the road. An inch. Two. Three inches. The smile broadened into a grin. Now he was a foot up. And two feet off the ground, he hung steady over the road with a little dust blowing beneath him.

Then he felt the first inches of dawn stain the sky, and he lowered himself down again. The time was not yet.

But the time was soon.

He began to walk again, grinning, now looking for a place to lay up for the day. The time was soon, and that was enough to know for now.

CHAPTER 24

Lloyd Henreid, who had been tagged 'the baby-faced, unrepentant killer' by the Phoenix papers, was led down the hallway of the Phoenix municipal jail's maximum security wing by two guards. One of them had a runny nose, and they both looked sour. The wing's other occupants were giving Lloyd their version of a tickertape parade. In Max, he was a celebrity.

'Heyyy, Henreid!'

'Go to, boy!'

'Tell the DA if he lets me walk I won't letya hurt im!'

'Rock steady, Henreid!'

'Right on, brother! *Rightonrightonrighton!*'

'Cheap mouthy bastards,' the guard with the runny nose muttered, and then sneezed.

Lloyd grinned happily. He was dazzled by his new fame. It sure wasn't much like Brownsville had been. Even the food was better. When you got to be a heavy hitter, you got some respect. He imagined that Tom Cruise must feel something like this at a world première.

At the end of the hall they went through a doorway and a double-barred electric gate. He was frisked again, the guard with the cold breathing heavily through his mouth as if he had just run up a flight of stairs. Then they walked him through a metal detector for good measure, probably to make sure he didn't have something crammed up his ass like that guy Papillon in the movies.

'Okay,' the one with the runny nose said, and another guard, this one in a booth made of bulletproof glass, waved them on. They walked down another hall, this one painted industrial green. It was very quiet in here; the only sounds were the guards' clicking footfalls (Lloyd himself was wearing paper slippers) and the asthmatic wheeze from Lloyd's right. At the far end of the hall, another guard was waiting in front of a closed door. The door had one small window, hardly more than a loophole, with wire embedded in the glass.

'Why do jails always smell so pissy?' Lloyd asked, just to make conversation. 'I mean, even the places where no guys are locked up, it smells pissy. Do you guys maybe do your wee-wees in the corners?' He snickered at the thought, which was really pretty comical.

'Shut up, killer,' the guard with the cold said.

'You don't look so good,' Lloyd said. 'You ought to be home in bed.'

'Shut up,' the other said.

Lloyd shut up. That's what happened when you tried to talk to these guys. It was his experience that the class of prison corrections officers had no class.

'Hi, scumbag,' the door-guard said.

'How ya doin, fuckface?' Lloyd responded smartly. There was nothing like a little friendly repartee to freshen you up. Two days in the joint and he could feel that old stir-stupor coming on him already.

'You're gonna lose a tooth for that,' the door-guard said. 'Exactly one, count it, one tooth.'

'Hey, now, listen, you can't –'

'Yes I can. There are guys on the yard who would kill their dear old mothers for two cartons of Chesterfields, scumbucket. Would you care to try for two teeth?'

Lloyd was silent.

'That's okay, then,' the door-guard said. 'Just one tooth. You fellas can take him in.'

Smiling a little, the guard with the cold opened the door and the other led Lloyd inside, where his court-appointed lawyer was sitting at a metal table, looking at papers from his briefcase.

'Here's your man, counselor.'

The lawyer looked up. He was hardly old enough to be shaving yet, Lloyd judged, but what the hell? Beggars couldn't be choosers. They had him cold-cocked anyway, and Lloyd figured to get twenty years or so. When they had you nailed, you just had to close your eyes and grit your teeth.

'Thank you very –'

'That guy,' Lloyd said, pointing to the door-guard. 'He called me a scumbag. And when I said something back to him, he said he was gonna have some guy knock out one of my *teeth*! How's that for police brutality?'

The lawyer passed a hand over his face. 'Any truth to that?' he asked the door-guard.

The door-guard rolled his eyes in a burlesque *My God, can you believe it?* gesture. 'These guys, counselor,' he said, 'they should write for TV. I said hi, he said hi, that was it.'

'That's a fuckin lie!' Lloyd said dramatically.

'I keep my opinions to myself,' the guard said, and gave Lloyd a stony stare.

'I'm sure you do,' the lawyer said, 'but I believe I'll count Mr Henreid's teeth before I leave.'

A slight, angry discomfiture passed over the guard's face, and he exchanged a glance with the two that had brought Lloyd in. Lloyd smiled. Maybe the kid was okay at that. The last two CAs he'd had were old hacks; one of them had come into court lugging a colostomy bag, could you believe that, a fucking *colostomy* bag? The old hacks didn't give a shit for you. Plead and leave, that was their motto, let's get rid of him so we can get back to swapping dirty stories with the judge. But maybe this guy could get him a straight ten, armed robbery. Maybe even time served. After all, the only one he'd actually poker-ized was the wife of the guy in the white Connie, and maybe he could just roll that off on ole Poke. Poke wouldn't mind. Poke was just as dead as old Dad's hatband. Lloyd's smile broadened a little. You had to look on the sunny side. That was the ticket. Life was too short to do anything else.

He became aware that the guard had left them alone and that his lawyer – his name was Andy Devins, Lloyd remembered – was looking at him in a strange way. It was the way you might look at a rattlesnake whose back has been broken but whose deadly bite is probably still unimpaired.

'You're in deep shit, Sylvester!' Devins exclaimed suddenly.

Lloyd jumped. 'What? What the hell do you mean, I'm in deep shit? By the way, I thought you handled ole fatty there real good. He looked mad enough to chew nails and spit out –'

'Listen to me, Sylvester, and listen very carefully.'

'My name's not –'

'You don't have the slightest idea how big a jam you're in, Sylvester.' Devins's gaze never faltered. His voice was soft and intense. His hair was blond and crewcut, hardly more than a fuzz. His scalp shone through pinkly. There was a plain gold wedding band on the third finger of his left hand and a fancy fraternity ring on the third finger of his right. He knocked them together and they made a funny little click that set Lloyd's teeth on edge. 'You're going to trial in just nine days, Sylvester, because of a decision the Supreme Court handed down four years ago.'

'What was that?' Lloyd was more uneasy than ever.

'It was the case of *Markham vs South Carolina*,' Devins said, 'and it had to do with the conditions under which individual states may best administer swift justice in cases where the death penalty is requested.'

'*Death* penalty!' Lloyd cried, horror-struck. 'You mean the lectric chair? Hey, man, I never killed anybody! Swear to God!'

'In the eyes of the law, that doesn't matter,' Devins said. 'If you were there, you did it.'

'What do you mean, it don't *matter*?' Lloyd nearly screamed. 'It does *so* matter! It *better* fuckin matter! I didn't waste those people, Poke did! He was crazy! He was —'

'Will you shut up, Sylvester?' Devins inquired in that soft, intense voice, and Lloyd shut. In his sudden fear he had forgotten the cheers for him in Maximum, and even the unsettling possibility that he might lose a tooth. He suddenly had a vision of Tweety Bird running a number on Sylvester the Cat. Only in his mind, Tweety wasn't bopping that dumb ole puddy-tat over the head with a mallet or sticking a mousetrap in front of his questing paw; what Lloyd saw was Sylvester strapped into Old Sparky while the parakeet perched on a stool by a big switch. He could even see the guard's cap on Tweety's little yellow head.

This was not a particularly amusing picture.

Perhaps Devins saw some of this in his face, because he looked moderately pleased for the first time. He folded his hands on the pile of papers he had taken from his briefcase. 'There is no such thing as an accessory when it comes to first-degree murder committed during a felony crime,' he said. 'The state has three witnesses who will testify that you and Andrew Freeman were together. That pretty well fries your skinny butt. Do you understand?'

'I —'

'Good. Now to get back to *Markham vs South Carolina*. I am going to tell you, in words of one syllable, how the ruling in that case bears on your situation. But first, I ought to remind you of a fact you doubtless learned during one of your trips through the ninth grade: the Constitution of the United States specifically forbids cruel and unusual punishment.'

'Like the fucking lectric chair, damn right,' Lloyd said righteously.

Devins was shaking his head. 'That's where the law was unclear,' he said, 'and up until four years ago, the courts had gone round and round and up and down, trying to make sense of it. *Does* "cruel and unusual punishment" mean things like the electric chair and the gas chamber? Or does it mean the *wait* between sentencing and execution? The appeals, the delays, the stays, the months and years that certain prisoners – Edgar Smith, Caryl Chessman, and Ted Bundy are probably the most famous – were forced to spend on various Death Rows? The Supreme Court allowed executions to recommence in the late seventies, but Death Rows were still clogged, and that nagging question of cruel and unusual punishment remained. Okay – in *Markham vs South Carolina*, you had a man sentenced to the electric chair for the rape-murder of three college coeds. Premeditation was proved by a diary this fellow, Jon Markham, had kept. The jury sentenced him to death.'

'Bad shit,' Lloyd whispered.

Devins nodded, and gave Lloyd a slightly sour smile. 'The case went all the way to the Supreme Court, which reconfirmed that capital punishment was not cruel and unusual under certain circumstances. The court suggested that sooner was better . . . from a legal standpoint. Are you beginning to get it, Sylvester? Are you beginning to see?'

Lloyd didn't.

'Do you know why you're being tried in Arizona rather than New Mexico or Nevada?'

Lloyd shook his head.

'Because Arizona is one of four states that has a Capital Crimes Circuit Court which sits only in cases where the death penalty has been asked for and obtained.'

'I don't follow you.'

'You're going to trial in four days,' Devins said. 'The state has such a strong case that they can afford to empanel the first twelve men and women that get called to the box. I'll drag it out as long as I can, but we'll have a jury on the first day. The state will present its case on the second day. I'll try to take up three days, and I'll filibuster on my opening and closing statements until the judge cuts me off, but three days is really tops. We'll be lucky to get that. The jury will retire and find you guilty in about three minutes unless a goddamned miracle happens. Nine days from today you'll be sentenced to death, and a week later, you'll be dead as dogmeat. The people of Arizona will love it, and so will the Supreme Court. Because quicker makes everybody happier. I can stretch the week – maybe – but only a little.'

'Jesus Christ, but that's not fair!' Lloyd cried.

'It's a tough old world, Lloyd,' Devins said. 'Especially for "mad dog killers," which is what the newspapers and TV commentators are calling you. You're a real big man in the world of crime. You've got real drag. You even put the flu epidemic back East on page two.'

'I never pokerized nobody,' Lloyd said sulkily. 'Poke, he did it all. He even made up that word.'

'It doesn't matter,' Devins said. 'That's what I'm trying to pound through your thick skull, Sylvester. The judge is going to leave the Governor room for one stay, and *only* one. I'll appeal, and under the new guidelines, my appeal has to be in the hands of the Capital Crimes Circuit Court within seven days or you exit stage left immediately. If they decide not to hear the appeal, I have another seven days to petition the Supreme Court of the United States. In your case, I'll file my appeal brief as late as possible. The Capital Crimes Circuit Court will probably agree to hear us – the system's still new, and they want as little criticism as possible. They'd probably hear Jack the Ripper's appeal.'

'How long before they get to me?' Lloyd muttered.

'Oh, they'll handle it in jig time,' Devins answered, and his smile became slightly wolfish. 'You see, the Circuit Court is made up of five retired Arizona judges. They've got nothing to do but go fishing, play poker, drink bonded bourbon, and wait for some sad sack of shit like you to show up in their courtroom, which is really a bunch of computer modems hooked up to the State House, the Governor's office, and each other. They've got telephones equipped with modems in their cars, cabins, even their boats, as well as in their houses. Their average age is seventy-two –'

Lloyd winced.

'– which means some of them are old enough to have actually ridden the Circuit Line out there in the willywags, if not as judges then as lawyers or law students. They all believe in the Code of the West – a quick trial and then up the rope. It was the way out here until 1950 or so. When it came to multiple murderers, it was the *only* way.'

'Jesus Christ Almighty, do you have to go on about it like that?'

'You need to know what we're up against,' Devins said. 'They just want to make sure you don't suffer cruel and unusual punishment, Lloyd. You ought to thank them.'

'*Thank* them? I'd like to –'

'Pokerize them?' Devins asked quietly.

'No, course not,' Lloyd said unconvincingly.

'Our petition for a new trial will be turned down and all my exceptions will be quickly heaved out. If we're lucky, the court will invite me to present witnesses. If they give me the opportunity, I'll recall everybody that testified at the original trial, plus anyone else I can think of. At that point I'd call your junior high school chums as character witnesses, if I could find them.'

'I quit school in the sixth grade,' Lloyd said bleakly.

'After the Circuit Court turns us down, I'll petition to be heard by the Supreme Court. I expect to be turned down on the same day.'

Devins stopped and lit a cigarette.

'Then what?' Lloyd asked.

'Then?' Devins asked, looking mildly surprised and exasperated at Lloyd's continuing stupidity. 'Why, then you go on to Death Row at state prison and just enjoy all that good food until it's time to ride the lightning. It won't be long.'

'They wouldn't really do it,' Lloyd said. 'You're just trying to scare me.'

'Lloyd, the four states that have the Capital Crimes Circuit Court do it *all the time*. So far, forty men and women have been executed under the *Markham* guidelines. It costs the taxpayers a little extra for the added court, but not all that much, since they only work on a tiny percentage of first-degree murder cases. Also, the taxpayers really don't mind opening their pocket books for capital punishment. They *like* it.'

Lloyd looked ready to throw up.

'Anyway,' Devins said, 'a DA will only try a defendant under *Markham* guidelines if he looks completely guilty. It isn't enough for the dog to have chicken feathers on his muzzle; you've got to catch him in the henhouse. Which is where they caught you.'

Lloyd, who had been basking in the cheers from the boys in Maximum Security not fifteen minutes ago, now found himself staring down a paltry two or three weeks and into a black hole.

'You scared, Sylvester?' Devins asked in an almost kindly way.

Lloyd had to lick his lips before he could answer. 'Christ yes, I'm scared. From what you say, I'm a dead man.'

'I don't want you dead,' Devins said, 'just scared. If you go into that courtroom smirking and swaggering, they'll strap you in the chair and throw the switch. You'll be number forty-one under *Markham*. But if you listen to me, we might be able to squeak through. I don't say we will; I say we might.'

'Go ahead.'

'The thing we have to count on is the jury,' Devins said. 'Twelve ordinary *shleps* off the street. I'd like a jury filled with forty-two-year-old ladies who can still recite *Winnie the Pooh* by heart and have funerals for their pet birds in the back yard, that's what I'd like. Every jury is made very aware of *Markham*'s consequences when they're empaneled. They're not bringing in a verdict of death that may or may not be implemented in six months or six years, long after they've forgotten it; the guy they're condemning in June is going to be pushing up daisies before the All-Star break.'

'You've got a hell of a way of putting things.'

Ignoring him, Devins went on: 'In some cases, just that knowledge has caused juries to bring in verdicts of not guilty. It's one adverse result of *Markham*. In some cases, juries have let blatant murderers go just because they didn't want blood that fresh on their hands.' He picked up a sheet of paper. 'Although forty people have been executed under *Markham*, the death penalty has been asked for under *Markham* a total of *seventy* times. Of the thirty not executed, twenty-six were found "not guilty" by the empaneled juries. Only four convictions were overturned by the Capital Crimes Circuit Courts, one in South Carolina, two in Florida, and one in Alabama.'

'Never in Arizona?'

'Never. I told you. The Code of the West. Those five old men want your ass nailed to a board. If we don't get you off in front of a jury, you're through. I can offer you ninety-to-one on it.'

'How many people have been found not guilty by regular court juries under that law in Arizona?'

'Two out of fourteen.'

'Those are pretty crappy odds, too.'

Devins smiled his wolfish smile. 'I should point out,' he said, 'that one of those two was defended by yours truly. He was guilty as sin, Lloyd, just like you are. Judge Pechert raved at those ten women and two men for twenty minutes. I thought he was going to have apoplexy.'

'If I was found not guilty, they couldn't try me again, could they?'

'Absolutely not.'

'So it's one roll, double or nothing.'

'Yes.'

'Boy,' Lloyd said, and wiped his forehead.

'As long as you understand the situation,' Devins said, 'and where we have to make our stand, we can get down to brass tacks.'

'I understand it. I don't like it, though.'

'You'd be nuts if you did.' Devins folded his hands and leaned over them. 'Now. You've told me and you've told the police that you, uh . . .' He took a stapled sheaf of papers out of the stack by his briefcase and riffled through them. 'Ah. Here we are. "I never killed nobody. Poke did all the killing. Killing was his idea, not mine. Poke was crazy as a bedbug and I guess it is a blessing to the world that he has passed on."'

'Yeah, that's right, so what?' Lloyd said defensively.

'Just this,' Devins said cozily. 'That implies you were *scared* of Poke Freeman. Were you scared of him?'

'Well, I wasn't exactly —'

'You were afraid for your life, in fact.'

'I don't think it was —'

'Terrified. Believe it, Sylvester. You were shitting nickels.'

Lloyd frowned at his lawyer. It was the frown of a lad who wants to be a good student but is having a serious problem grasping the lesson.

'Don't let me lead you, Lloyd,' Devins said. 'I don't want to do that. You might think I was suggesting that Poke was stoned almost all the time —'

'He was! We *both* was!'

'No. *You* weren't, but *he* was. And he got crazy when he got stoned —'

'Boy, you're not shitting.' In the halls of Lloyd's memory, the ghost of Poke Freeman cried *Whoop! Whoop!* merrily and shot the woman in the Burrack general store.

'And he held a gun on you at several points in time —'

'No, he never —'

'Yes he did. You just forgot for a while. In fact, he once threatened to kill you if you didn't back his play.'

'Well, I had a gun —'

'I believe,' Devins said, eyeing him closely, 'that if you search your memory, you'll remember Poke telling you that your gun was loaded with blanks. Do you remember that?'

'Now that you mention it —'

'And nobody was more surprised than you when it actually started firing *real* bullets, right?'

'Sure,' Lloyd said. He nodded vigorously. 'I bout damn near had a hemorrhage.'

'And you were about to turn that gun on Poke Freeman when he was cut down, saving you the trouble.'

Lloyd regarded his lawyer with dawning hope in his eyes.

'Mr Devins,' he said with great sincerity, 'that's just the way the shit went down.'

He was in the exercise yard later that morning, watching a softball game and mulling over everything Devins had told him, when a large inmate named Mathers came over and yanked him up by the collar. Mathers's head was shaved bald, à la Telly Savalas, and it gleamed benignly in the hot desert air.

'Now wait a minute,' Lloyd said. 'My lawyer counted every one of my teeth. Seventeen. So if you —'

'Yeah, that's what Shockley said,' Mathers said. 'So, he told me to —'

Mathers's knee came up squarely in Lloyd's crotch, and blinding pain exploded there, so excruciating that he could not even scream. He collapsed in a hunching, writhing pile, clutching his testicles, which felt crushed. The world was a reddish fog of agony.

After a while, who knew how long, he was able to look up. Mathers was still looking at him, and his bald head was still gleaming. The guards were pointedly looking elsewhere. Lloyd moaned and writhed, tears squirting out of his eyes, a red-hot ball of lead in his belly.

'Nothing personal,' Mathers said sincerely. 'Just business, you understand. Myself, I hope you make out. That *Markham* law's a bitch.'

He strode away and Lloyd saw the door-guard standing atop the ramp in the truck-loading bay on the other side of the exercise yard. His thumbs were hooked in his Sam Browne belt and he was grinning at Lloyd. When he saw he had Lloyd's complete, undivided attention, the door-guard shot him the bird with the middle fingers of both hands. Mathers strolled over to the wall, and the door-guard threw him a pack of Tareytons. Mathers put them in his breast pocket, sketched a salute, and walked away. Lloyd lay on the ground, his knees drawn up to his chest, hands clutching his cramping belly, and Devins's words echoed in his brain: *It's a tough old world, Lloyd, it's a tough old world.*

Right.

CHAPTER 25

Nick Andros pushed aside one of the curtains and looked out into the street. From here, on the second story of the late John Baker's house, you could see all of downtown Shoyo by looking left, and by looking right you could see Route 63 going out of town. Main Street was utterly deserted. The shades of the business establishments were drawn. A sick-looking dog sat in the middle of the road, head down, sides bellowsing, white foam dripping from its muzzle to the heat-shimmering pavement. In the gutter half a block down, another dog lay dead.

The woman behind him moaned in a low, guttural way, but Nick did not hear her. He closed the curtain, rubbed his eyes for a moment, and then went to the woman, who had awakened. Jane Baker was bundled up with blankets because she had been cold a couple of hours ago. Now sweat was streaming from her face and she had kicked off the blankets – he saw with embarrassment that she had sweated her thin nightgown into transparency in some places. But she was not seeing him, and at this point he doubted her seminakedness mattered. She was dying.

'Johnny, bring the basin. I think I'm going to throw up!' she cried.

He brought the basin out from under the bed and put it beside her, but she thrashed and knocked it onto the floor with a hollow bonging sound which he also couldn't hear. He picked it up and just held it, watching her.

'Johnny!' she screamed. 'I can't find my sewing box! It isn't in the closet!'

He poured her a glass of water from the pitcher on the nightstand and held it to her lips but she thrashed again and almost knocked it from his grasp. He set it back down where it would be in reach if she quieted.

He had never been so bitterly aware of his muteness as the last two days had made him. The Methodist minister, Braceman, had been with her on the twenty-third when Nick came over. He was Bible-reading with her in the living room, but he looked nervous and anxious to get away. Nick could guess why. Her fever had given her a rosy, girlish glow that went jarringly with her bereavement. Perhaps the minister had been afraid she was going to make a pass at him. More likely, though, he had been anxious to gather up his family and melt away over the fields. News travels fast in a small town, and others had already decided to get out of Shoyo.

Since the time Braceman had left the Baker living room some forty-eight hours ago, everything had turned into a waking nightmare. Mrs Baker had gotten worse, so much worse that Nick had feared she would die before the sun went down.

Worse, he couldn't sit with her constantly. He had gone down to the truck stop to get his three prisoners lunch, but Vince Hogan hadn't been able to eat. He was delirious. Mike Childress and Billy Warner wanted out, but Nick couldn't bring himself to do it. It wasn't fear; he didn't believe they would waste any time working him over to settle their grievance; they would want to make fast tracks away from Shoyo, like the others. But he had a responsibility. He had made a promise to a man who was now dead. Surely, sooner or later the State Patrol would get things in hand and come to take them away.

He found a .45 rolled up in its holster in the bottom drawer of Baker's desk, and after a few moments of debate he put it on. Looking down and seeing the woodgrip butt of the gun lying against his skinny hip had made him feel ridiculous – but its weight was comforting.

He had opened Vince's cell on the afternoon of the twenty-third and had put makeshift icepacks on the man's forehead, chest, and neck. Vince had opened his eyes and looked at Nick with such silent, miserable appeal that Nick wished he could say anything – as he wished it now, two days later, with Mrs Baker – anything that would give the man a moment's comfort. Just *You'll be okay* or *I think the fever's breaking* would be enough.

All the time he was tending to Vince, Billy and Mike were yelling at him. While he was bent over the sick man they didn't matter, but he saw their scared faces every time he looked up, their lips forming words that all came down to the same thing: *Please let us out.* Nick was careful to keep away from them. He wasn't grown, but he was old enough to know that panic makes men dangerous.

That afternoon he had shuttled back and forth on nearly empty streets, always expecting to find Vince Hogan dead on one end or Jane Baker dead on the other. He looked for Dr Soames's car but didn't see it. That afternoon a few of the shops had still been open, and the Texaco, but he became more and more convinced that the town was emptying out. People were taking paths through the woods, logging roads, maybe even wading up Shoyo Stream, which passed through Smackover and eventually came out in the town of Mount Holly. More would leave after dark, Nick thought.

The sun had just gone down when he arrived at the Baker house to find Jane moving shakily around the kitchen in her bathrobe, brewing tea. She looked at Nick gratefully when he came in, and he saw her fever was gone.

'I want to thank you for watching after me,' she said calmly. 'I feel ever so much better. Would you like a cup of tea?' And then she burst into tears.

He went to her, afraid she might faint and fall against the hot stove.

She held his arm to steady herself and laid her head against him, her hair a dark flood against the light blue robe.

'Johnny,' she said in the darkening kitchen. 'Oh, my poor Johnny.'

If he could speak, Nick thought unhappily. But he could only hold her, and guide her across the kitchen to a chair by the table.

'The tea —'

He pointed to himself and then made her sit down.

'All right,' she said. 'I do feel better. Remarkably so. It's just that . . . just . . .' She put her hands over her face.

Nick made them hot tea and brought it to the table. They drank for a while without speaking. She held her cup in both hands, like a child. At last she put her cup down and said: 'How many in town have this, Nick?'

'I don't know anymore,' Nick wrote. 'It's pretty bad.'

'Have you seen the doctor?'

'Not since this morning.'

'Am will wear himself out if he's not careful,' she said. 'He'll be careful, won't he, Nick? Not to wear himself out?'

Nick nodded and tried a smile.

'What about John's prisoners? Has the patrol come for them?'

'No,' Nick wrote. 'Hogan is very sick. I'm doing what I can. The others want me to let them out before Hogan can make them sick.'

'Don't you let them out!' she said with some spirit. 'I hope you're not thinking of it.'

'No,' Nick wrote, and after a moment he added: 'You ought to go back to bed. You need rest.'

She smiled at him, and when she moved her head Nick could see the dark smudges under the angles of her jaw – and he wondered uneasily if she was out of the woods yet.

'Yes. I'm going to sleep the clock right around. It seems wrong, somehow, to sleep with John dead . . . I can hardly believe he is, you know. I keep stumbling over the idea like something I forgot to put away.' He took her hand and squeezed it. She smiled wanly. 'There may be something else to live for, in time. Have you gotten your prisoners their supper, Nick?'

Nick shook his head.

'You ought to. Why don't you take John's car?'

'I can't drive,' Nick wrote, 'but thank you. I'll just walk down to the truckstop. It isn't far. & check on you in the morning, if that's all right.'

'Yes,' she said. 'Fine.'

He got up and pointed sternly at the teacup.

'Every drop,' she promised.

He was going out the screen door when he felt her hesitant touch on his arm.

'John –' she said, stopped, and then forced herself to go on. 'I hope they . . . took him to the Curtis Mortuary. That's where John's folks and mine have always buried out of. Do you think they took him there all right?'

Nick nodded. The tears brimmed over her cheeks and she began to sob again.

When he left her that night he had gone directly to the truck-stop. A CLOSED sign hung crookedly in the window. He had gone around to the house trailer in back, but it was locked and dark. No one answered his knock. Under the circumstances he felt he was justified in a little breaking and entering; there would be enough in Sheriff Baker's petty cash box to pay any damages.

He hammered in the glass by the restaurant's lock and let himself in. The place was spooky even with all the lights on, the jukebox dark and dead, no one at the bumper-pool table or the video games, the booths empty, the stools unoccupied. The hood was over the grille.

Nick went out back and fried some hamburgers on the gas stove and put them in a sack. He added a bottle of milk and half an apple pie that stood under a plastic dome on the counter. Then he went back to the jail, after leaving a note on the counter explaining who had broken in and why.

Vince Hogan was dead. He lay on the floor of his cell amid a clutter of melting ice and wet towels. He had clawed at his neck at the end, as if he had been resisting an invisible strangler. The tips of his fingers were bloody. Flies were lighting on him and buzzing off. His neck was as black and swollen as an inner-tube some heedless child has pumped up to the point of bursting.

'*Now* will you let us out?' Mike Childress asked. 'He's dead, ya fuckin mutie, are you satisfied? You feel revenged yet? Now he's got it, too.' He pointed to Billy Warner.

Billy looked terrified. There were hectic red splotches on his neck and cheeks; the arm of his workshirt, with which he had repeatedly swiped at his nose, was stiff with snot. 'That's a lie!' he chanted hysterically. 'A lie, a lie, a fuckin lie! that's a l –' He began to sneeze suddenly, doubling over with the force of them, expelling a heavy spray of saliva and mucus.

'See?' Mike demanded. 'Huh? Y'happy, ya fuckin mutie dimwit? Let me out! You can keep him if you want to, but not me. It's murder, that's all it is, cold-blooded murder!'

Nick shook his head, and Mike had a tantrum. He began to throw himself against the bars of his cell, bruising his face, bloodying the knuckles of both hands. He stared at Nick with bulging eyes while he banged his forehead repeatedly.

Nick waited until he got tired and then pushed the food through the slots in the bottoms of the cells with the broom-handle. Billy Warner looked at him dully for a moment, then began to eat.

Mike threw his glass of milk against the bars. It shattered and milk sprayed everywhere. He slammed his two burgers against the graffiti-covered rear wall of his cell. One of them stuck in a splat of mustard, ketchup, and relish that was grotesquely cheery, like a Jackson Pollock painting. He jumped up and down on his slice of apple pie, boogying on it. Apple chunks flew every which way. The white plastic plate splintered:

'I'm on a hunger strike!' he yelled. 'Fuckin hunger strike! I won't eat nothing! You'll eat my dingle before I eat anything you bring me, you fuckin deaf-mute retard asshole! You'll –'

Nick turned away and silence immediately descended. He went back out into the office, not knowing what to do, scared. If he could drive, he would take them up to Camden himself. But he couldn't drive. And there was Vince to think about. He couldn't just let him lie there, drawing flies.

There were two doors opening off the office. One was a coat closet. The other led down a flight of stairs. Nick went down and saw it was a combination cellar and storage room. It was cool down there. It would do, at least for a while.

He went back upstairs. Mike was sitting on the floor, morosely picking up squashed apple slices, brushing them off and eating them. He didn't look up at Nick.

Nick gathered the body up in his arms and tried to lift it. The sick smell coming off the corpse was making his stomach do cartwheels and handstands. Vince was too heavy for him. He looked at the body helplessly for a moment, and became aware that both of the others were now standing at their cell doors, watching with a dreadful fascination. Nick could guess what they were thinking. Vince had been one of them, a whiny gasbag, maybe, but someone they hung with, just the same. He had died like a rat in a trap with some horrible swelling sickness they didn't understand. Nick wondered, not for the first time that day, when *he* would start to sneeze and run a fever and develop those peculiar swellings on his neck.

He laid hold of Vince Hogan's meaty forearms and dragged him out of the cell. Vince's head leaned toward him because of the weight on his shoulders, and he seemed to be looking at Nick, wordlessly telling him to be careful, not to joggle him too much.

It took ten minutes to get the big man's remains down the steep stairs. Panting, Nick laid him on the concrete under the fluorescents, and then covered him quickly with a frayed army blanket from the cot in his cell.

He tried to sleep then, but sleep only came in the early hours of the morning after June twenty-third had become the twenty-fourth, yesterday. His dreams had always been very vivid, and sometimes he was afraid of them. He rarely had out-and-out nightmares, but more and more often lately they were ominous, giving him the feeling that no one in them was exactly as they seemed, and that the normal world had skewed into a place where babies were sacrificed behind closed blinds and stupendous black machines roared on and on in locked basements.

And, of course, there was the very personal terror – that he would wake up with it himself.

He did sleep a little, and the dream that came was one he had had before recently: the cornfield, the smell of warm growing things, the feel that something – or someone – very good and safe was close. A sense of *home*. And that began to fade into cold terror as he became aware that something was in the corn, watching him. He thought: *Ma, weasel's got in the henhouse!* and awoke to early morning light, sweat standing out on his body.

He put coffee on and went in to check on his two prisoners.

Mike Childress was in tears. Behind him, the hamburger was still stuck on the wall in its drying glue of condiments.

'You satisfied now? I got it too. Ain't that what you wanted? Ain't that your revenge? Listen to me, I sound like a fuckin freight train goin up a hill!'

But Nick's first concern had been for Billy Warner, who lay comatose on his bunk. His neck was swelled and black, his chest rising in fits and starts.

He hurried back to the office, looked at the telephone, and in a fit of rage and guilt he knocked it off the desk and onto the floor, where it lay meaninglessly at the end of its cord. He turned the hotplate off and ran down the street to the Baker house. He pushed the bell for what seemed an hour before Jane came down, wrapped in her robe. The fever-sweat was back on her face. She was not delirious, but her words were slow and slurry and her lips were blistered.

'Nick. Come in. What is it?'

'V. Hogan died last night. Warner's dying, I think. He's awful sick. Have you seen Dr Soames?'

She shook her head, shivered in the light draft, sneezed, and then swayed on her feet. Nick put an arm around her shoulders and led her to a chair. He wrote: 'Can you call his office for me?'

'Yes, of course. Bring me the phone, Nick. I seem . . . to have had a setback in the night.'

He brought the phone over and she dialed Soames's number. After she had held the receiver to her ear for more than half a minute, he knew there was going to be no answer.

She tried his home, then the home of his nurse. No answer.

'I'll try the State Patrol,' she said, but put the phone back in the cradle after dialing a single number. 'The long-distance is still out of service, I guess. After I dial 1, it just goes wah-wah-wah in my ear.' She gave him a pallid smile and then the tears began to flow helplessly. 'Poor Nick,' she said. 'Poor me. Poor everybody. Could you help me upstairs? I feel so weak, and I can't catch my breath. I think I'll be with John soon.' He looked at her, wishing he could speak. 'I think I'll lie down, if you can help me.'

He helped her upstairs, then wrote: 'I'll be back.'

'Thank you, Nick. You're a good boy . . .' She was already drifting off to sleep.

Nick left the house and stood on the sidewalk, wondering what to do next. If he could drive, he might be able to do something. But . . .

He saw a child's bicycle lying on the lawn of a house across the street. He went to it, looked at the house it belonged to with its drawn shades (so much like the houses in his confused dreams), then went and knocked on the door. There was no answer, although he knocked several times.

He went back to the bike. It was small, but not too small for him to ride, if he didn't mind his knees whamming the handlebars. He would look ludicrous, of course, but he was not at all sure there was anyone left in Shoyo to see . . . and if there was, he didn't think many of them would be in a laughing frame of mind.

He got on the bike and pedaled clumsily up Main Street, past the jail, then east on Route 63, toward where Joe Rackman had seen the soldiers masquerading as a road crew. If they were still there, and if they really were soldiers, Nick would get them to take care of Billy Warner and Mike Childress. If Billy was still alive, that was. If those men had quarantined Shoyo, then surely the sick of Shoyo were their responsibility.

It took him an hour to pedal out to the roadwork, the bike weaving crazily back and forth across the center line, his knees thumping the handlebars with monotonous regularity. But when he got there the soldiers, or road crew, or whatever they had been, were gone. There were a few smudgepots, one of them still flickering. There were two orange saw-horses. And the road had been torn up, although Nick judged it would still be passable, if you weren't too choosy about the springs of your car.

Black flickering movement caught the tail of his eye, and at the same instant the wind stirred around a little, just a soft summer breath, but enough to bring a ripe and sickening odor of corruption to his nostrils. The black movement was a cloud of flies, constantly forming and re-forming itself. He walked the bike over to the ditch at the far side of the road. In it, next to a shiny new corrugated culvert pipe, were the bodies of four men. Their necks and swollen faces were black. Nick didn't know if they were soldiers or not, and he didn't go any closer. He told himself he would walk back to the bike, there was nothing here to be scared about, they were dead, and dead people couldn't hurt you. He was running by the time he was twenty feet from the ditch, anyway, and he was in a panic as he rode back toward Shoyo. On the outskirts of town he hit a rock and crashed the bike. He went over the handlebars, bumped his head, and scraped his hands. He only hunkered there for a moment in the middle of the road, shivering all over.

For the next hour and a half of that morning, yesterday morning, Nick knocked on doors and rang bells. There would be someone well, he told himself. He himself felt all right, and surely he could not be the only one. There would be someone, a man, a woman, maybe a teenager with a learner's permit, and he or she would say: *Oh, hey, yes. Let's get them to Camden. We'll take the station wagon.* Or words to that effect.

But his knocking and ringing were answered less than a dozen times. The door would open to the length of a latch-chain, a sick but hopeful face would look out, see Nick, and hope would die. The face would move back and forth in negation, and then the door would shut. If Nick could talk, he would have argued if they could still walk, they could drive. That if they took his prisoners to Camden, they could go themselves, and there would be a hospital. They would be made well. But he couldn't speak.

Some asked if he had seen Dr Soames. One man, in a delirious rage, threw the door of his small ranch-house wide open, staggered out on the porch dressed only in his underpants, and tried to grab Nick. He said he was going to do 'what I should have done to you back in Houston.' He seemed to think Nick was someone named Jenner. He lurched back and forth along the porch after Nick like a zombie in a third-rate horror picture. His crotch had swelled terribly; his underpants looked as if someone had stuffed a honeydew melon into them. At last he crashed to the porch and Nick watched him from the lawn below, his heart thumping rapidly. The man shook his fist weakly, then crawled back inside, not bothering to shut the door.

But most of the houses were only silent and cryptic, and at last he could do no more. That dream-sense of ominousness was creeping up on him and it became impossible to dismiss the idea that he was knocking on the doors of tombs, knocking to wake the dead, and that sooner or later the corpses might begin to answer. It didn't help much to tell himself that most of the houses were empty, their occupants already fled to Camden or El Dorado or Texarkana.

He went back to the Baker house. Jane Baker was sleeping deeply, her forehead cool. But this time he wasn't as hopeful.

It was noon. Nick went back to the truck-stop, feeling his night's broken rest now. His body seemed to throb all over from his spill off the bike. Baker's .45 banged his hip. At the truck-stop he heated two cans of soup and put them in thermos jugs. The milk in the fridge still seemed fine, so he took a bottle of that, too.

Billy Warner was dead, and when Mike saw Nick, he began to giggle hysterically and point his finger. 'Two down and one to go! Two down and one to go! You're gettin your revenge! Right? Right?'

Nick carefully pushed the thermos of soup through the slot with the broomhandle, and then a big glass of milk. Mike began to drink soup directly from the thermos in small sips. Nick took his own thermos and sat down in the hallway. He would take Billy downstairs, but first he would have lunch. He was hungry. As he drank his soup he looked at Mike thoughtfully.

'You wondering how I am?' Mike asked.

Nick nodded.

'Just the same as when you left this morning. I must have hawked out a pound of snot.' He looked at Nick hopefully. 'My mom always said that when you hawked snot like that, you was gettin better. Maybe I just got a mild case, huh? You think that might be?'

Nick shrugged. Anything was possible.

'I got the constitution of a brass eagle,' Mike said. 'I think it's nothing. I think I'll throw it off. Listen, man, let me out. Please. I'm fuckin beggin you now.'

Nick thought about it.

'Hell, you got the gun. I don't want you for nothing, anyway.

I just want to get out of this town. I want to check on my wife first –'

Nick pointed to Mike's left hand, which was bare of rings.

'Yeah, we're divorced, but she's still here in town, out on the Ridge Road. I'd like to look in on her. What do you say, man?' Mike was crying. 'Give me a chance. Don't keep me locked up in this rat-trap.'

Nick stood up slowly, went out into the office, and opened the desk drawer. The keys were there. The man's logic was inexorable; there was no sense in believing that someone was going to come and bail them out of this terrible mess. He got the keys and went back. He held up the one Big John Baker had shown him, with the tag of white tape on it, and tossed it through the bars to Mike Childress.

'Thanks,' Mike babbled. 'Oh, thanks. I'm sorry we beat up on you, I swear to God, it was Ray's idea, me and Vince tried to stop him but he gets drinkin and he gets crazy –' He rattled the key in the lock. Nick stood back, his hand on the gunbutt.

The cell door opened and Mike stepped out. 'I meant it,' he said. 'All I want to do is get out of this town.' He sidled past Nick, a grin twitching at his lips. Then he bolted through the door between the small cellblock and the office. Nick followed just in time to see the office door closing behind him.

Nick went outside. Mike was standing on the curb, his hand on a parking meter, looking at the empty street.

'My God,' he whispered, and turned his stunned face to look at Nick. 'All this? All *this*?'

Nick nodded, his hand still on the gunbutt.

Mike started to say something, and it turned into a coughing spasm. He covered his mouth, then wiped his lips.

'I'm getting to Christ out of here,' he said. 'You're wise, you'll do the same thing, mutie. This is like the black death, or somethin.'

Nick shrugged, and Mike started down the sidewalk. He moved faster and faster until he was nearly running. Nick watched him until he was out of sight, and then went back inside. He never saw Mike again. His heart felt lighter, and he was suddenly sure that he had done the right thing. He lay down on the cot and went to sleep almost at once.

He slept all afternoon on the blanketless couch and awoke sweaty but feeling a little better. Thunderstorms were beating the hills – he couldn't hear the thunder, but he could see the blue-white forks of light stabbing the hills – but none had come to Shoyo that night.

At dusk he walked down Main Street to Paulie's Radio & TV and committed another of his apologetic break-ins. He left a note by the cash register and lugged a Sony portable back to the jail. He turned it on and flipped through the channels. The CBS affiliate was broadcasting a sign which read MICROWAVE RELAY DIFFICULTY PLEASE STAY TUNED. The ABC station was showing 'I Love Lucy,' and the NBC feed was a rerun episode in a current series about a perky young girl trying to be a mechanic on the stock-car circuit. The Texarkana station, an independent specializing mostly in old movies, game shows, and religious zanies of the Jack Van Impe stripe, was off the air.

Nick snapped the TV off, went down to the truck-stop, and fixed enough soup and sandwiches for two. He thought there was something eerie about the way all the streetlights still came on, stretching out both ways along Main Street in spotlit pools of white light. He put the food in a hamper, and on the way to Jane Baker's house three or four dogs, obviously unfed and ravenous, advanced on him in a pack, drawn by the smell from the hamper. Nick drew the .45 but couldn't summon up the heart to use it until one of the dogs was getting ready to bite him. Then he pulled the trigger and the bullet whined off the cement five feet in front of him, leaving a silvery streak of lead. The sound of the report did not come to him, but he felt the dull thud of vibration. The dogs broke and ran.

Jane was asleep, her forehead and cheeks hot, her breathing slow and labored. She looked dreadfully wasted to Nick. He got a cold washcloth and wiped her face. He left her share of food on the night table, and then went down into the living room and turned on the Bakers' TV, a big console color job.

CBS didn't come on all night. NBC kept to a regular broadcast schedule, but the picture on the ABC affiliate kept going hazy, sometimes fading out to snow and then snapping back suddenly. The ABC channel showed only old syndication programs, as if its line to the network had been severed. It didn't matter. What Nick was waiting for was the news.

When it came on, he was dumbfounded. The 'superflu epidemic,' as it was now being called, was the lead story, but the newscasters on both stations said it was being brought under control. A flu vaccine had been developed at the Atlanta Centers for Disease Control, and you could get a shot from your doctor by early the following week.

Outbreaks were reportedly serious in New York, San Francisco, LA, and London, but all were being contained. In some areas, the newscaster went on, public gatherings had been canceled temporarily.

In Shoyo, Nick thought, the entire *town* had been canceled. Who was kidding who?

The newscaster concluded by saying that travel to most of the large city areas was still restricted, but the restrictions would be lifted as soon as the vaccine was in general release. He then went on to a plane crash in Michigan and some congressional reactions to the latest Supreme Court gay-rights decision.

Nick turned off the TV and went out onto the Bakers' porch. There was a glider and he sat down in it. The back-and-forth motion was soothing, and he couldn't hear the rusty squeak that John Baker had kept forgetting to oil. He watched fireflies as they hemmed irregular seams in the dark. Lightning flashed dully inside the clouds on the horizon, making them look as if they held fireflies of their own, monster fireflies the size of dinosaurs. The night was sticky and close.

Because television was a completely visual medium for Nick, he had noticed something about the news broadcast that others might have missed. There had been no film-clips, none at all. There had been no baseball scores, maybe because no ball games had been played. A vague weather report and no weather map showing the highs and lows – it was as if the US Bureau of Meteorology had closed up shop. For all Nick knew to the contrary, they had.

Both newscasters had seemed nervous and upset. One of them had a cold; he had coughed once on mike and had excused himself. Both newscasters had kept cutting their eyes to the left and right of the camera they were facing . . . as if someone was in the studio with them, someone who was there to make sure they got it right.

That was the night of June 24, and he slept raggedly on the Bakers' front porch, and his dreams were very bad. And now, on the afternoon of the following day, he was officiating at the death of Jane Baker, this fine woman . . . *and he couldn't say a word to comfort her.*

She was tugging at his hand. Nick looked down at her pale, drawn face. Her skin was dry now, the sweat evaporated. He took no hope or comfort in that, however. She was going. He had come to know the look.

'Nick,' she said, and smiled. She clasped one of his hands in both of hers. 'I wanted to thank you again. No one wants to die all alone, do they?'

He shook his head violently, and she understood this was not in agreement with her statement but rather in vehement contradiction of its premise.

'Yes I am,' she contradicted. 'But never mind. There's a dress in that closet, Nick. A white one. You'll know it because of . . .' A fit of coughing interrupted her. When she had it under control, she finished, '. . . because of the lace. It's the one I wore on the train when we left for our honeymoon. It still fits . . . or did. I suppose it will be a little big on me now – I've lost some weight – but it doesn't really matter. I've always loved that dress. John and I went to Lake Pontchartrain. It was the happiest two weeks of my life. John always made me happy. Will you remember the dress, Nick? It's the one I want to be buried in. You wouldn't be too embarrassed to . . . to dress me, would you?'

He swallowed hard and shook his head, looking at the coverlet. She must have sensed his mixture of sadness and discomfort, because she didn't mention the dress again. She talked of other things instead – lightly, almost coquettishly. How she had won an elocution contest in high school, had gone on to the Arkansas state finals, and how her halfslip had fallen down and puddled around her shoes just as she reached the ringing climax of Shirley Jackson's 'The Daemon Lover.' About her sister, who had gone to Viet Nam as part of a Baptist mission group, and had come back with not one or two but three adopted children. About a camping trip she and John had taken three years ago, and how an ill-tempered moose in rut had forced them up a tree and kept them there all day.

'So we sat up there and spooned,' she said sleepily, 'like a couple of high school kids in a balcony. My goodness, he was in a state when we got down. He was . . . we were . . . in love . . . very much in love . . . love is what moves the world, I've always thought . . . it is the only thing which allows men and women to stand in a world where gravity always seems to want to pull them down . . . bring them low . . . and make them crawl . . . we were . . . so much in love . . .'

She drowsed off and slept until he wakened her into fresh delirium by moving a curtain or perhaps just by treading on a squeaky board.

'*John!*' she screamed now, her voice choked with phlegm. '*Oh, John, I'll never get the hang of this dad-ratted stick shift! John, you got to help me! You got to help me* –'

Her words trailed off in a long, rattling exhalation he could not hear but sensed all the same. A thin trickle of dark blood issued from one nostril. She fell back on the pillow, and her head snapped back and forth once, twice, three times, as if she had made some kind of vital decision and the answer was negative.

Then she was still.

Nick put his hand timidly against the side of her neck, then her inner wrist, then between her breasts. There was nothing. She was dead. The clock on her bedtable ticked importantly, unheard by either of them. He put his head against his knees for a minute, crying a little in the silent way he had. *All you can do is have sort of a slow leak*, Rudy had told him once, *but in a soap opera world, that can come in handy*.

He knew what came next and didn't want to do it. It wasn't fair, part of him cried out. It wasn't his responsibility. But since there was no one else here – maybe no one else well for miles around – he would have to shoulder it. Either that or leave her here to rot, and he couldn't do that. She had been kind to him, and there had been too many people along the way who hadn't been able to spare that, sick or well. He supposed he would have to get going. The longer he sat here and did nothing, the more he would dread the task. He knew where the Curtis Funeral Home was – three blocks down and one block west. It would be hot out there, too.

He forced himself to get up and go to the closet, half hoping that the white dress, the honeymoon dress, would turn out to have been just another part of her delirium. But it was there. A little yellowed with the years now, but he knew it, all the same. Because of the lace. He took it down and laid it across the bench at the foot of the bed. He looked at the dress, looked at the woman, and thought, *It's going to be more than just a* little *big on her now. The disease, whatever it is, was crueler to her than she knew . . . and I guess that's just as well.*

Unwillingly, he went around to her and began to remove the nightgown. But when it was off and she lay naked before him, the dread departed and he felt only pity – a pity lodged so deep in him that it made him ache and he began to cry again as he washed her body and then dressed it as it had been dressed when she wore it on the way to Lake Pontchartrain. And when she was dressed as she had been on that day, he took her in his arms and carried her down to the funeral home in her lace, oh, in her lace: he carried her like a bridegroom crossing an endless threshold with his beloved in his arms.

CHAPTER 26

Some campus group, probably either Students for a Democratic Society or the Young Maoists, had been busy with a ditto machine during the night of June 25–26. In the morning, these posters were plastered all over the University of Kentucky at Louisville campus:

ATTENTION! ATTENTION! ATTENTION! ATTENTION!

YOU ARE BEING LIED TO! THE GOVERNMENT IS LYING TO YOU! THE PRESS, WHICH HAS BEEN CO-OPTED BY THE FORCES OF THE PIG PARAMILITARY, IS LYING TO YOU! THE ADMINISTRATION OF THIS UNIVERSITY IS LYING TO YOU, AS ARE THE INFIRMARY DOCTORS UNDER THE ADMINISTRATION'S ORDERS!

1. THERE IS NO SUPERFLU VACCINE.
2. SUPERFLU IS NOT A SERIOUS DISEASE, IT IS A DEADLY DISEASE.
3. SUSCEPTIBILITY MAY RUN AS HIGH AS 75%.
4. SUPERFLU WAS DEVELOPED BY THE FORCES OF THE US PIG PARAMILITARY AND DISBURSED BY ACCIDENT.
5. THE US PIG PARAMILITARY NOW MEANS TO COVER UP THEIR MURDEROUS BLUNDER EVEN IF IT MEANS 75% OF THE POPULATION WILL DIE!

ALL REVOLUTIONARY PEOPLE, GREETINGS! THE TIME OF OUR STRUGGLE IS NOW! UNITE, STRIVE, CONQUER!

MEETING IN GYM AT 7:00 PM!

STRIKE! STRIKE! STRIKE! STRIKE! STRIKE! STRIKE!

What happened at WBZ-TV in Boston had been planned the night before by three newscasters and six technicians, all operating in Studio 6. Five of these men played poker regularly, and six of the nine were already ill. They felt they had nothing to lose. They collected nearly a dozen handguns. Bob Palmer, who anchored the morning news, brought them upstairs inside a flight bag where he usually carried his notes, pencils, and several legal-sized notepads.

The entire broadcast facility was cordoned off by what they had been told were National Guardsmen, but as Palmer had told George Dickerson the night before, they were the only over-fifty guardsmen he had ever seen.

At 9:01 AM, just after Palmer had begun to read the soothing copy he had been handed ten minutes before by an army noncom, a coup took place. The nine of them effectively captured the television station. The soldiers, who hadn't expected any real trouble from a soft bunch of civilians accustomed to reporting tragedy at long distance, were taken completely by surprise and disarmed. Other station personnel joined the small rebellion, and cleared the sixth floor quickly and locked all the doors. The elevators were brought to six before the soldiers on the lobby level quite knew what was happening. Three soldiers tried to come up the east fire stairs, and a janitor named Charles Yorkin, armed with an army-issue carbine, fired a shot over their heads. It was the only shot fired.

Viewers in the WBZ-TV broadcast area saw Bob Palmer stop his newscast in the middle of a sentence, and heard him say, 'Okay, right now!' There were scuffling sounds off-camera. When it was over, thousands of bemused viewers saw Bob Palmer was now holding a snub-nosed pistol in his hand.

A hoarse, off-mike voice yelled jubilantly: 'We got em, Bob! We got the bastards! We got em all!'

'Okay, that's good work,' Palmer said. He then faced into the camera again. 'Fellow citizens of Boston, and Americans in our broadcast area. Something both grave and terribly important has just happened in this studio, and I am very glad it has happened here first, in Boston, the cradle of American independence. For the last seven days, this broadcast facility has been under guard by men purporting to be National Guardsmen. Men in army khaki, armed with guns, have been standing beside our cameramen, in our control rooms, beside our teletypes. Has the news been managed? I am sorry to say that this is the case. I have been given copy and forced to read it, almost literally with gun to my head. The copy I have been reading was to do with the so-called "superflu epidemic," and all of it is patently false.'

Lights began to flicker on the switchboard. Within fifteen seconds every light was on.

'Our cameramen have taken film that has either been confiscated or deliberately exposed. Our reporters' stories have disappeared. Yet we *do* have film, ladies and gentlemen, and we have correspondents right here in the studio – not professional reporters, but eyewitnesses to what may be the greatest disaster this country has ever faced . . . and I do not use those words lightly. We are going to run some of this film for you now. All of it was taken clandestinely, and some of it is of poor quality. Yet we here, who have just liberated our own television station, think you may see enough. More, indeed, than you might have wished.'

He looked up, took a handkerchief from his sport-coat pocket, and blew his nose. Those with good color TVs could see that he looked flushed and feverish.

'If it's ready, George, go ahead and run it.'

Palmer's face was replaced with shots of Boston General Hospital. Wards were crammed. Patients lay on the floors. The halls were full; nurses, many of them obviously sick themselves, wove in and out, some of them weeping hysterically. Others looked shocked to the point of coma.

Shots of guards standing on street corners with cradled rifles. Shots of buildings that had been broken into.

Bob Palmer appeared again. 'If you have children, ladies and gentlemen,' he said quietly, 'we would advise that you ask them to leave the room.'

A grainy shot of a truck backing down a pier jutting out over Boston Harbor, a big olive-colored army truck. Below it, riding uncertainly, was a barge covered with canvas tarps. Two soldiers, rugose and alien in gas masks, jumped down from the truck's cab. The picture jiggled and joggled, then became steady again as they pulled back the canvas sheet covering the open rear end of the truck. Then they jumped up inside, and bodies began to cascade out onto the barge: women, old men, children, police, nurses; they came in a cartwheeling flood that seemed never to end. At some point during the film-clip it became clear that the soldiers were using pitchforks to get them out.

Palmer went on broadcasting for two hours, his steadily hoarsening voice reading clippings and bulletins, interviewing other members of the crew. It went on until somebody on the ground floor realized that they didn't have to retake the sixth floor to stop it. At 11:16, the WBZ transmitter was shut down permanently with twenty pounds of *plastique*.

Palmer and the others on the sixth floor were summarily executed on charges of treason to their government, the United States of America.

It was a small-town, once-weekly West Virginia newspaper called the Durbin *Call-Clarion*, put out by a retired lawyer named James D. Hogliss, and its circulation figures had always been good because Hogliss had been a fiery defender of the miners' right to organize in the late 1940s and in the 1950s, and because his anti-establishment editorials were always filled with hellfire and brimstone missiles aimed at the government hacks at every level, from town to federal.

Hogliss had a regular bunch of paperboys, but on this clear summer morning he took the papers around himself in his 1948 Cadillac, the big whitewall tires whispering up and down the streets of Durbin . . . and the streets were painfully empty. The papers were piled on the Cadillac's seats and in its trunk. It was the wrong day for the *Call-Clarion* to come out, but the paper was only one page of large type set inside a black border. The word at the top proclaimed EXTRA, the first extra edition Hogliss had put out since 1980, when the Ladybird mine had exploded, entombing forty miners for all time.

The headline read: GOV'T FORCES TRY TO CONCEAL PLAGUE OUTBREAK!

Beneath: 'Special to the *Call-Clarion* by James D. Hogliss'

Below that: 'It has been revealed to this reporter by a reliable source that the flu epidemic (sometimes called Choking Sickness or Tube Neck here in West Virginia) is in reality a deadly mutation of the ordinary flu virus created by this government, for purposes of war – and in direct disregard of the revised Geneva accords concerning germ and chemical warfare, accords which representatives of the United States signed seven years ago. The source, who is an army official now stationed in Wheeling, also said that promises of a soon-forthcoming vaccine are "a baldfaced lie." No vaccine, according to this source, has yet been developed.

'Citizens, this is more than a disaster or a tragedy; it is the end of all hope in our government. If we have indeed done such a thing to ourselves, then . . .'

Hogliss was sick, and very weak. He seemed to have used the last of his strength composing the editorial. It had gone from him into the words and had not been replaced. His chest was full of phlegm, and even normal breathing was like running uphill. Yet he went methodically from house to house, leaving his broadsides, not even knowing if the houses were still occupied, or if they were, if anyone inside had enough strength left to go out and pick up what he had left.

Finally he was on the west end of town, Poverty Row, with its shacks and trailers and its rank septic-tank smell. Only the papers in the trunk remained and he left it open, its lid flopping slowly up and down as he went over the washboards in the road. He was trying to cope with a fearsome headache, and his vision kept doubling on him.

When the last house, a tumbledown shack near the Rack's Crossing town line, was taken care of, he still had a bundle of perhaps twenty-five papers. He slit the string which bound them with his old pocketknife and then let the wind take them where the wind would, thinking of his source, a major with dark, haunted eyes who had been transferred from something top secret in California called Project Blue only three months before. The major had been charged with outside security there, and he kept fingering the pistol on his hip as he told Hogliss everything he knew. Hogliss thought it would not be long before the major used the gun, if he hadn't used it already.

He climbed back behind the wheel of the Cadillac, the only car he had owned since his twenty-seventh birthday, and discovered he was too tired to drive back to town. So he leaned back sleepily, listened to the drowning sounds coming from his chest, and watched the wind blow his extra editions lazily up the road toward Rack's Crossing. Some of them had caught in the overhanging trees, where they hung like strange fruit. Nearby, he could hear the bubbling, racing sound of Durbin Stream, where he had fished as a boy. There were no fish in it now, of course – the coal companies had seen to that – but the sound was still soothing. He closed his eyes, slept, and died an hour and a half later.

The Los Angeles *Times* ran only 26,000 copies of their one-page extra before the officers in charge discovered that they were not printing an advertising circular, as they had been told. The reprisal was swift and bloody. The official FBI story was that 'radical revolutionaries,' the old bugaboo, had dynamited the LA *Times'* presses, causing the death of twenty-eight workers. The FBI didn't have to explain how the explosion had put bullets in each of the twenty-eight heads, because the bodies were mingled with those of thousands of others, epidemic victims who were being buried at sea.

Yet 10,000 copies got out, and that was enough. The headline, in 36-point-type, screamed:

WEST COAST IN GRIP OF PLAGUE EPIDEMIC

Thousands Flee Deadly Superflu
Government Coverup Certain

LOS ANGELES – Some of the soldiers purporting to be National Guardsmen helping out during the current ongoing tragedy are career soldiers with as many as four ten-year pips on their sleeves. Part of their job is to assure terrified Los Angeles residents that the superflu, known as Captain Trips by the young in most areas, is 'only slightly more virulent' than the London or Hong Kong strains . . . but these assurances are made through portable respirators. The President is scheduled to speak tonight at 6:00 PST and his press secretary, Hubert Ross, has branded reports that the President will speak from a set mocked up to look like the Oval Office but actually deep in the White House bunker 'hysterical, vicious, and totally unfounded.' Advance copies of the President's speech indicate that he will 'spank' the American people for overreacting, and compare the current panic to that which followed Orson Welles's 'War of the Worlds' radio broadcast in the early 30s.

The *Times* has five questions it wishes the President would answer in his speech.

1. Why has the *Times* been enjoined from printing the news by thugs in army uniforms, in direct violation of its Constitutional right to do so?
2. Why have the following highways – US 5, US 10, and US 15 – been blocked off by armored cars and troop carriers?
3. If this is a 'minor outbreak of flu,' why has martial law been declared for Los Angeles and surrounding areas?
4. If this is a 'minor outbreak of flu,' then why are barge-trains being towed out into the Pacific and dumped? And do these barges contain what we are afraid they contain and what informed sources have assured us they do contain – the dead bodies of plague victims?

5. Finally, if a vaccine really is to be distributed to doctors and area hospitals early next week, why has *not one* of the forty-six physicians that this newspaper contacted for further details heard of any delivery plans? Why has *not one* clinic been set up to administer flu shots? Why has *not one* of the ten pharmaceutical houses we called gotten freight invoices or government fliers on this vaccine?

   We call upon the President to answer these questions in his speech, and above all we call upon him to end these police-state tactics and this insane effort to cover up the truth . . .

In Duluth a man in khaki shorts and sandals walked up and down Piedmont Avenue with a large smear of ash on his forehead and a hand-lettered sandwich board hanging over his scrawny shoulders.

The front read:

THE TIME OF THE DISAPPEARANCE IS HERE
CHRIST THE LORD RETURNETH SOON
PREPARE TO MEET YOUR GOD!

The back read:

BEHOLD THE HEARTS OF THE SINNERS WERE BROKEN
THE GREAT SHALL BE ABASED AND THE ABASED MADE GREAT
THE EVIL DAYS ARE AT HAND
WOE TO THEE O ZION

Four young men in motorcycle jackets, all of them with bad coughs and runny noses, set upon the man in the khaki shorts and beat him unconscious with his own sandwich board. Then they fled, one of them calling back hysterically over his shoulder: 'Teach you to scare people! Teach you to scare people, you half-baked freak!'

The highest-rated morning program in Springfield, Missouri, was KLFT's morning phone-in show, 'Speak Your Piece,' with Ray Flowers. He had six phone lines into his studio booth, and on the morning of June 26, he was the only KLFT employee to show up for work. He was aware of what was going on in the outside world and it scared him. In the last week or so, it seemed to Ray that everyone he knew had come down sick. There were no troops in Springfield, but he had heard that the National Guard had been called into KC and St Louis to 'stop the spread of panic' and 'prevent looting.' Ray Flowers himself felt fine. He looked thoughtfully at his equipment – phones, time-delay device to edit those callers who lapsed into profanity from time to time, racks of commercials on cassettes ('*If your toilet overflows/And you don't know just what goes/Call for the man with the big steel hose/Call your Kleen-Owt Man!*'), and of course, the mike.

He lit a cigarette, went to the studio door, and locked it. Went into his booth and locked that. He turned off the canned music that had been playing from a tape reel, turned on his own theme music, and then settled in at the microphone.

'Hi, y'all,' he said, 'this is Ray Flowers on "Speak Your Piece," and this morning I guess there's only one thing to call about, isn't there? You can call it Tube Neck or superflu or Captain Trips, but it all means the same thing. I've heard some horror stories about the army clamping down on everything, and if you want to talk about that, I'm ready to listen. It's still a free country, right? And since I'm here by myself this morning, we're going to do things just a little bit differently. I've got the time-delay turned off, and I think we can dispense with the commercials. If the Springfield you're seeing is anything like the one I'm seeing from the KLFT windows, no one feels much like shopping, anyway.

'Okay – if you're spo's to be up and around, as my mother used to say, let's get going. Our toll-free numbers are 555–8600 and 555–8601. If you get a busy, just be patient. Remember, I'm doing it all myself.'

There was an army unit in Carthage, fifty miles from Springfield, and a twenty-man patrol was dispatched to take care of Ray Flowers. Two men refused the order. They were shot on the spot.

In the hour it took them to get to Springfield, Ray Flowers took calls from: a doctor who said people were dying like flies and who thought the government was lying through its teeth about a vaccine; a hospital nurse who confirmed that bodies were being removed from Kansas City hospitals by the truckload; a delirious woman who claimed it was flying saucers from outer space; a farmer who said that an army squad with two payloaders had just finished digging a hell of a long ditch in a field near Route 71 south of Kansas City; half a dozen others with their own stories to tell.

Then there was a crashing sound on the outer studio door. 'Open up!' a muffled voice cried. 'Open up in the name of the United States!'

Ray looked at his watch. Quarter to twelve.

'Well,' he said, 'it looks like the Marines have landed. But we'll just keep taking calls, shall w –'

There was a rattle of automatic rifle fire, and the knob of the studio door thumped onto the rug. Blue smoke drifted out of the ragged hole. The door was shouldered inward and half a dozen soldiers, wearing respirators and full battle-dress, burst in.

'Several soldiers have just broken into the outer office,' Ray said. 'They're fully armed . . . they look like they're ready to start a mop-up operation in France fifty years ago. Except for the respirators on their faces . . .'

'Shut it down!' a heavyset man with sergeant's stripes on his sleeves yelled. He loomed outside the broadcast booth's glass walls and gestured with his rifle.

'I think not!' Ray called back. He felt very cold, and when he fumbled his cigarette out of his ashtray, he saw that his fingers were trembling. 'This station is licensed by the FCC and I'm –'

'I'm *revokin* ya fuckin license! Now shut *down*!'

'I think not,' Ray said again, and turned back to his microphone. 'Ladies and gentlemen, I have been ordered to shut down the KLFT transmitter and I have refused the order, quite properly, I think. These men are acting like Nazis, not American soldiers. I am not –'

'Last chance!' The sergeant brought his gun up.

'Sergeant,' one of the soldiers by the door said, 'I don't think you can just –'

'If that man says anything else, waste him,' the sergeant said.

'I think they're going to shoot me,' Ray Flowers said, and the next moment the glass of his broadcast booth blew inward and he fell over his control panel. From somewhere there came a terrific feedback whine that spiraled up and up. The sergeant fired his entire clip into the control panel and the feedback cut off. The lights on the switchboard continued to blink.

'Okay,' the sergeant said, turning around. 'I want to get back to Carthage by one o'clock and I don't –'

Three of his men opened up on him simultaneously, one of them with a recoilless rifle that fired seventy gas-tipped slugs per second. The sergeant did a jigging, shuffling death-dance and then fell backward through the shattered remains of the broadcast booth's glass wall. One leg spasmed and his combat boot kicked shards of glass from the frame.

A PFC, pimples standing out in stark relief on his whey-colored face, burst into tears. The others only stood in stunned disbelief. The smell of cordite was heavy and sickening in the air.

'We scragged him!' the PFC cried hysterically. 'Holy God, we done scragged Sergeant Peters!'

No one replied. Their faces were still dazed and uncomprehending, although later they would only wish they had done it sooner. All of this was some deadly game, but it wasn't their game.

The phone, which Ray Flowers had put in the amplifier cradle just before he died, gave out a series of squawks.

'Ray? You there, Ray?' The voice was tired, nasal. 'I listen to your program all the time, me and my husband both, and we just wanted to say keep up the good work and don't let them bully you. Okay, Ray? Ray? . . . Ray? . . .'

COMMUNIQUE 234 ZONE 2 SECRET SCRAMBLE

FROM: LANDON ZONE 2 NEW YORK

TO: CREIGHTON COMMANDING

RE: OPERATION CARNIVAL

FOLLOWS: NEW YORK CORDON STILL OPERATIVE DISPOSAL OF BODIES PROCEEDING CITY RELATIVELY QUIET X COVER STORY UNRAVELING FASTER THAN EXPECTED BUT SO FAR NOTHING WE CAN'T HANDLE FROM CITY POPULATION SUPERFLU IS KEEPING MOST OF THEM INSIDE XX NOW ESTIMATE THAT 50% OF TROOPS MANNING BARRICADES AT POINTS OF EGRESS/INGRESS [GEORGE WASH BRIDGE TRIBOROUGH BRIDGE BROOKLYN BRIDGE LINCOLN AND HOLLAND TUNNELS PLUS LIMITED ACCESS HIGHWAYS IN THE OUTER BOROUGHS] NOW ILL W/ SUPERFLU MOST TROOPS STILL CAPABLE OF ACTIVE DUTY AND PERFORMING WELL XXX THREE FIRES OUT OF CONTROL IN CITY HARLEM 7TH AVENUE SHEA STADIUM XXXX DESERTION FROM RANKS BECOMING A GREATER PROBLEM DESERTERS NOW BEING SUMMARILY SHOT XXXXX PERSONAL SUMMARY IS THAT SITUATION IS STILL VIABLE BUT DETERIORATING SLOWLY XXXXXX COMMUNICATION ENDS

LANDON ZONE 2 NEW YORK

In Boulder, Colorado, a rumor that the US Meteorological Air Testing Center was really a biological warfare installation began to spread. The rumor was repeated on the air by a semidelirious Denver FM disc jockey. By 11 PM on the night of June 26, a vast, lemminglike exodus from Boulder had begun. A company of soldiers was sent out from Denver-Arvada to stop them, but it was like sending a man with a whisk-broom to clean out the Augean stables. Better than eleven thousand civilians – sick, scared, and with no other thought but to put as many miles between themselves and the Air Testing Center as possible – rolled over them. Thousands of other Boulderites fled to other points of the compass.

At quarter past eleven a shattering explosion lit the night at the Air Testing Center's location on Broadway. A young radical named Desmond Ramage had planted better than sixteen pounds of plastique, originally earmarked for various Midwestern courthouses and state legislatures, in the ATC lobby. The explosive was great; the timer was cruddy. Ramage was vaporized along with all sorts of harmless weather equipment and particle-for-particle pollution-measuring gadgets.

Meanwhile, the exodus from Boulder went on.

COMMUNIQUE 771 ZONE 6 SECRET SCRAMBLE

FROM: GARETH ZONE 6 LITTLE ROCK

TO: CREIGHTON COMMANDING

RE: OPERATION CARNIVAL

FOLLOWS: BRODSKY NEUTRALIZED REPEAT BRODSKY NEUTRALIZED HE WAS FOUND WORKING IN A STOREFRONT CLINIC HERE TRIED AND SUMMARILY EXECUTED FOR TREASON AGAINST THE UNITED STATES OF AMERICA SOME OF THOSE BEING TREATED ATTEMPTED TO INTER- FERE 14 CIVILIANS SHOT, 6 KILLED 3 OF MY MEN WOUNDED, NONE SERIOUSLY X ZONE 6 FORCES THIS AREA WORKING AT ONLY 40% CAPACITY ESTIMATE 25% OF THOSE STILL ON ACTIVE DUTY NOW ILL W SUPERFLU 15% AWOL XX MOST SERIOUS INCIDENT IN REGARD TO CONTINGENCY PLAN F FOR FRANK XXX SERGEANT T. L. PETERS STATIONED CARTHAGE MO ON EMERGENCY DUTY SPRINGFIELD MO APPARENTLY ASSASSINATED BY OWN MEN XXXX OTHER INCIDENTS OF SIMILAR NATURE POSSIBLE BUT UNCONFIRMED SITUATION DETERI- ORATING RAPIDLY XXXXX COMMUNICATION ENDS

GARFIELD ZONE 6 LITTLE ROCK

When the evening was spread out against the sky like a patient etherized upon a table, two thousand students attending Kent State

University in Ohio went on the warparth – big time. The two thousand rioters consisted of first mini-semester summer students, members of a symposium on the future of college journalism, one hundred and twenty attendees of a drama workshop, and two hundred members of the Future Farmers of America, Ohio branch, whose convention happened to coincide with the grassfire spread of the superflu. All of them had been cooped up on the campus since June 22, four days ago. What follows is a transcription of police-band communications in the area, spanning the time period 7:16–7:22 PM.

'Unit 16, unit 16, do you copy? Over.'

'Ah, copy, unit 20. Over.'

'Ah, we got a group of kids coming down the mall here, 16. About seventy warm bodies, I'd say, and . . . ah, check that, unit 16, we got another group coming the other way . . . Jesus, two hundred or more in that one, looks like. Over.'

'Unit 20, this is base. Do you copy? Over.'

'Read you five-by, base. Over.'

'I'm sending Chumm and Halliday over. Block the road with your car. Take no other action. If they go over you, spread your legs and enjoy it. No resistance, do you copy? Over.'

'I copy no resistance, base. What are those soldiers doing over on the eastern side of the mall, base? Over.'

'What soldiers? Over.'

'That's what I asked you, base. They're –'

'Base, this is Dudley Chumm. Oh shit, this is unit 12. Sorry, base. There's a bunch of kids coming down Burrows Drive. About a hundred and fifty. Headed for the mall. Singing or chanting or some damn thing. But Cap, Jesus Christ, we see soldiers, too. They're wearing gas masks, I think. Ah, they look to be in a skirmish line. That's what it looks like, anyway. Over.'

'Base to unit 12. Join unit 20 at the foot of the mall. Same instructions. No resistance. Over.'

'Roger, base. I am rolling. Over.'

'Base, this is unit 17. This is Halliday, base. Do you copy? Over.'

'I copy, 17. Over.'

'I'm behind Chumm. There's another two hundred kids coming west to east toward the mall. They've got signs, just like in the sixties. One says SOLDIERS THROW DOWN YOUR GUNS. I see another one that says THE TRUTH THE WHOLE TRUTH AND NOTHING BUT THE TRUTH. They –'

'I don't give a shit *what* the signs say, unit 17. Get down there with Chumm and Peters and block them off. It sounds like they're headed into a tornado. Over.'

'Roger. Over and out.'

'This is Campus Security Chief Richard Burleigh now speaking to the head of the military forces encamped on the south side of this campus. Repeat: this is Campus Security Chief Burleigh. I know you've been monitoring our communications, so please spare me the ducking and fucking and acknowledge. Over.'

'This is Colonel Albert Philips, US Army. We are listening, Chief Burleigh. Over.'

'Base, this is unit 16. The kids are coming together at the war memorial. They appear to be turning toward the soldiers. This looks nasty. Over.'

'This is Burleigh, Colonel Philips. Please state your intentions. Over.'

'My orders are to contain those present on campus *to* the campus. My only intention is to follow my orders. If those people are just demonstrating, they are fine. If they intend to try breaking out of quarantine, they are not. Over.'

'You surely don't mean –'

'I mean what I said, Chief Burleigh. Over and out.'

'Philips! Philips! Answer me, goddamn you! Those aren't commie guerrillas out there! They're kids! American kids! They aren't armed! They –'

'Unit 13 to base. Ah, those kids are walking right toward the soldiers, Cap. They're waving their signs. Singing that song. The one the Baez crotch used to sing. Oh. Shit, I think some of them are throwing rocks. They . . . Jesus! Oh Jesus Christ! They can't do that!'

'Base to unit 13! What's going on out there? What's happening?'

'This is Chumm, Dick. I'll tell you what's happening out here. It's a slaughter. I wish I was blind. Oh, the fuckers! They . . . ah, they're mowing those kids down. With machine guns, it looks like. As far as I can tell, there wasn't even any warning. The kids that are still on their feet . . . ah, they are breaking up . . . running to all points of the compass. Oh Christ! I just saw a girl cut in half by gunfire! Blood . . . there must be seventy, eighty kids lying out there on the grass. They –'

'Chumm! Come in! Come in, unit 12!'

'Base, this is unit 17. Do you copy? Over.'

'I copy *you*, goddammit, but where's fucking *Chumm*? Fucking *over!*'

'Chumm and . . . Halliday, I think . . . got out of their cars for a better look. We're coming back, Dick. Now it looks like the soldiers are shooting each other. I don't know who's winning, and I don't care. Whoever it is will probably start on us next. When those of us who can get back *do* get back, I suggest that we all go down in the basement and wait for them to use up their ammo. Over.'

'Goddammit —'

'The turkey shoot's still going on, Dick. I'm not kidding. Over. Out.'

Through most of the running exchange transcribed above, the listener can hear faint popping sounds in the background, not unlike horse chestnuts in a hot fire. One may also hear thin screams . . . and, in the last forty seconds or so, the heavy, coughing thump of mortar rounds exploding.

Following is a transcription taken from a special high-frequency radio band in Southern California. The transcription was made from 7:17 to 7:20 PM, PST.

'Massingill, Zone 10. Are you there, Blue Base? This message is coded Annie Oakley, Urgent-plus-10. Come in, if you're there. Over.'

'This is Len, David. We can skip the jargon, I think. Nobody's listening.'

'It's out of control, Len. Everything. LA is going up in flames. Whole fucking city and everything around it. All my men are sick or rioting or AWOL or looting right along with the civilian population. I'm in the Skylight Room of the Bank of America, main branch. There's over six hundred people trying to get in and get at me. Most of them are regular army.'

'Things fall apart. The center does not hold.'

'Say again. I didn't copy.'

'Never mind. Can you get out?'

'Hell no. But I'll give the first of the scum something to think about. I've got a recoilless rifle here. Scum. Fucking scum!'

'Luck, David.'

'You too. Hold it together as long as you can.'

'Will do.'

'I'm not sure –'

Verbal communication ends at this point. There is a splintering, crashing sound, the screech of giving metal, the tinkle of breaking glass. A great many yelling voices. Small-arms fire, and then, very close to the radio transmitter, close enough to distort, the heavy, thudding explosions of what might very well be a recoilless rifle. The yelling, roaring voices draw closer. There is the whining sound of a ricochet, a scream very close to the transmitter, a thud, and silence.

Following is a transcription taken from the regular army band in San Francisco. The transcription was made from 7:28 to 7:30 PM, PST.

'Soldiers and brothers! We have taken the radio station, and the command HQ! Your oppressors are dead! I, Brother Zeno, until moments ago Sergeant First Class Roland Gibbs, proclaim myself first President of the Republic of Northern California! We are in control! We are in control! If your officers in the field try to counter-mand my orders, shoot them like dogs in the street! Like dogs! Like bitches with shit drying on their rumps! Take down name, rank, and serial numbers of deserters! List those that speak sedition or treason against the Republic of Northern California! A new day is dawning! The day of the oppressor is ended! We are –'

A rattle of machine-gun fire. Screams. Thumps and thuds. Pistol shots, more screams, a sustained burst of machine-gun fire. A long, dying moan. Three seconds of dead air.

'This is Major Alfred Nunn, United States Army. I am taking provisional and temporary control of United States forces in the San Francisco area. The handful of traitors present in this HQ have been dealt with. I am in command, repeat, in command. The holding operation will go on. Deserters and defectors will be dealt with as before: extreme prejudice, repeat, extreme prejudice. I am now –'

More gunfire. A scream.

Background: '– them all! Get them all! Death to the war-pigs –'

Heavy gunfire. Then silence on the band.

At 9:16 PM, EST, those still well enough to watch television in the Portland, Maine, area, tuned in WCSH-TV and watched with numbed horror as a huge black man, naked except for a pink leather loincloth and a Marine officer's cap, obviously ill, performed a series of sixty-two public executions.

His colleagues, also black, also nearly naked, all wore loincloths and some badge of rank to show they had once belonged in the military. They were armed with automatic and semi-automatic weapons. In the area where a studio audience had once watched local political debates and 'Dialing for Dollars,' more members of this black 'junta' covered perhaps two hundred khaki-clad soldiers with rifles and handguns.

The huge black man, who grinned a lot, showing amazingly even and white teeth in his coal-black face, was holding a .45 automatic pistol and standing beside a large glass drum. In a time that already seemed long ago, that drum had held scraps of cut-up telephone books for the 'Dialing for Dollars' program.

Now he spun it, pulled out a driver's license, and called, 'PFC Franklin Stern, front and center, *puh-leeze*.'

The armed men flanking the audience on all sides bent to look at name tags while a cameraman obviously new to the trade panned the audience in jerky sweeps.

At last a young man with light blond hair, no more than nineteen, was jerked to his feet, screaming and protesting, and led up to the set area. Two of the blacks forced him to his knees.

The black man grinned, sneezed, spat phlegm, and put the .45 automatic to PFC Stern's temple.

'No!' Stern cried hysterically. 'I'll come in with you, honest to God I will! I'll –'

'Inthenameofthefathersonandholyghost,' the big black man intoned, grinning, and pulled the trigger. There was a large smear of blood and brains behind the spot where PFC Stern was being forced to kneel, and now he added his own contribution.

Splat.

The black man sneezed again and almost fell over. Another black man, this one in the control room (he was wearing a green long-billed fatigue cap and pristine white jockey shorts), pushed the APPLAUSE button, and in front of the studio audience, the sign flashed on. The blacks guarding the audience/prisoners raised their weapons threateningly, and the captive white soldiers, their faces glistening with perspiration and terror, applauded wildly.

'Next!' the black man in the loincloth proclaimed hoarsely, and delved into the drum again. He looked at the slip and announced:

'Master Tech Sergeant Roger Petersen, front n center, *puh-leeze!*'

A man in the audience began to howl and made an abortive dive for the back doors. Seconds later he was up on stage. In the confusion one of the men in the third row tried to remove the name tag pinned to his blouse. One shot banged out and he slumped down in his seat, his eyes glazed as if such a tawdry show had bored him into a deathlike semi-doze.

This spectacle went on until almost quarter of eleven, when four squads of regular army, wearing respirators and carrying sub-machine guns, crashed into the studio. The two dying groups of soldiers immediately went to war.

The black man in the loincloth went down almost immediately, cursing, sweating, riddled with bullets, and firing his automatic pistol crazily into the floor. The renegade who had been operating the #2 camera was shot in the belly, and as he leaned forward to catch his spilling guts, his camera pivoted slowly around, giving the audience a leisurely pan shot of hell. The semi-naked guards were returning fire, and the soldiers in the respirators were spraying the entire audience area. The unarmed soldiers in the middle, instead of being rescued, found that their executions had only been speeded up.

A young man with carroty hair and a wild expression of panic on his face climbed over the backs of six rows of seats like a circus performer on stilts before his legs were chewed away by a stream of .45-caliber bullets. Others crawled up the carpeted aisles between rows, their noses to the floor, the way they had been taught to crawl under live machinegun fire in basic training. An aging sergeant with gray hair stood up, arms spread wide like a TV host, and screamed, '*STAWWWWP!*' at the top of his lungs. Heavy fire from both sides homed in on him and he began to jig-a-jig like a disintegrating puppet. The roar of the guns and the screams of the dying and wounded made the audio needles in the control room jump over to +50 dB.

The camera operator fell forward over the handle that controlled his camera, and those watching were now given only a merciful view of the studio ceiling for the rest of the exchange. The gunfire dimin-ished over a period of five minutes to isolated explosions, then to nothing. Only the screams went on.

At five minutes past eleven, the studio ceiling was replaced on home screens by a picture of a cartoon man who was staring glumly at a cartoon TV. On the cartoon TV was a sign that said: SORRY, WE'RE HAVING PROBLEMS!

As the evening wound toward its close, that was true of almost everyone.

In Des Moines, at 11:30 PM, CST, an old Buick covered with religious stickers – HONK IF YOU LOVE JESUS, among others – cruised the deserted downtown streets relentlessly. There had been a fire in Des Moines earlier in the day that had burned most of the south side of Hull Avenue and Grandview Junior College; later there had been a riot that gutted most of the downtown area.

When the sun went down, these streets had been filled with restlessly circling crowds of people, most of them under twenty-five, many riding choppers. They had broken windows, stolen TV sets, filled their gas tanks at service stations while watching for anyone who might have a gun. Now the streets were empty. Some of them – the bikers, mainly – were kicking out their remaining jams on Interstate 80. But most of them had crept into houses and locked the doors, already suffering with superflu or only terror of it as daylight left this flat green land. Now Des Moines looked like the aftermath of some monster New Year's Eve party after sodden sleep had claimed the last of the revelers. The Buick's tires whispered and crunched over the broken glass in the street and turned west from Fourteenth onto Euclid Avenue, passing two cars that had crashed head-on and now lay on their sides with their bumpers interlaced like lovers after a successful double homicide. There was a loudspeaker on top of the Buick's roof, and now it began to give off amplified boops and beeps, followed by the scratchy sounds of an old record's opening grooves, and then, blaring up and down the spectral, deserted streets of Des Moines, came the sweetly droning voice of Mother Maybelle Carter, singing 'Keep on the Sunny Side.'

> Keep on the sunny side,
> Always on the sunny side,
> Keep on the sunny side of life,
> Though your problems may be many
> It will seem you don't have any
> If you keep on the sunny side of life . . .

The old Buick cruised on and on, making figure-eights, loops, sometimes circling the same block three or four times. When it hit a bump (or rolled over a body), the record would skip.

At twenty minutes to midnight, the Buick pulled over to the

curb and idled. Then it began to roll again. The loudspeaker blared
Elvis Presley singing 'The Old Rugged Cross,' and a night wind
soughed through the trees and stirred a final whiff of smoke from
the smoldering ruins of the junior college.

From the President's speech, delivered at 9 PM, EST, not seen in
many areas.

'. . . a great nation such as this must do. We cannot afford to
jump at shadows like small children in a dark room; but neither can
we afford to take this serious outbreak of influenza lightly. My fellow
Americans, I urge you to stay at home. If you feel ill, stay in bed,
take aspirin, and drink plenty of clear liquids. Be confident that you
will feel better in a week *at most*. Let me repeat what I said at the
beginning of my talk to you this evening: There is no truth – *no
truth* – to the rumor that this strain of flu is fatal. In the greatest
majority of cases, the person afflicted can expect to be up and around
and feeling fine within a week. Further –'

[a spasm of coughing]

'Further, there has been a vicious rumor promulgated by
certain radical anti-establishment groups that this strain of influenza
has been somehow bred by this government for some possible
military use. Fellow Americans, this is a flat-out falsehood, and I
want to brand it as such right here and now. This country signed
the revised Geneva Accords on poison gas, nerve gas, and germ
warfare in good conscience and in good faith. We have not now
nor have we ever –'

[a spasm of sneezes]

'– have we ever been a party to the clandestine manufacture
of substances outlawed by the Geneva Convention. This is a moderately serious outbreak of influenza, no more and no less. We have
reports tonight of outbreaks in a score of other countries, including
Russia and Red China. Therefore we –'

[a spasm of coughs and sneezes]

'– we ask you to remain calm and secure in the knowledge
that late this week or early next, a flu vaccine will be available for
those not already on the mend. National Guardsmen have been
called out in some areas to protect the populace against hooligans,
vandals, and scare-mongers, but there is absolutely no truth to the
rumors that some cities have been "occupied" by regular army
forces or that the news has been managed. My fellow Americans,

this is a flat-out falsehood, and I want to brand it as such right here and . . .'

Graffito written on the front of the First Baptist Church of Atlanta in red spray paint:

'Dear Jesus. I will see you soon. Your friend, America. PS. I hope you will still have some vacancies by the end of the week.'

CHAPTER 27

Larry Underwood sat on a bench in Central Park on the morning of June 27, looking into the menagerie. Behind him, Fifth Avenue was crazily jammed with cars, all of them silent now, their owners dead or fled. Farther down Fifth, many of the posh shops were smoking rubble.

From where Larry sat he could see a lion, an antelope, a zebra, and some sort of monkey. All but the monkey were dead. They had not died of the flu, Larry judged; they had gotten no food or water for God knew how long, and that had killed them. All but the monkey, and in the three hours that Larry had been sitting here, the monkey had moved only four or five times. The monkey had been smart enough to outwit starvation or death by thirst — so far — but it surely had a good case of superflu. That was one monkey who was hurtin for certain. It was a hard old world.

To his right, the clock with all the animals chimed the hour of eleven. The clockwork figures which had once delighted all children now played to an empty house. The bear tooted his horn, a clockwork monkey who would never get sick (but who might eventually run down) played a tambourine, the elephant beat his drum with his trunk. Heavy tunes, baby, heavy fucking tunes. *End of the World Suite Arranged for Clockwork Figures.*

After a bit the clock fell silent and he could hear the hoarse shouting again, now mercifully faint with distance. The monster-shouter was somewhere off to Larry's left this fine forenoon, perhaps in the Heckscher Playground. Maybe he would fall into the wading pool there and drown.

'Monsters coming!' the faint, hoarse voice cried. The overcast had broken this morning, and the day was bright and hot. A bee cruised past Larry's nose, circled one of the nearby flowerbeds, and made a three-point landing on a peony. From the menagerie came the soothing, soporific drone of the flies as they landed on the dead animals.

'Monsters coming now!' The monster-shouter was a tall man who looked to be in his middle sixties. Larry had first heard him the night before, which he had spent in the Sherry-Netherland. With night lying over the unnaturally quiet city, the faint, howling voice had seemed sonorous and dark, the voice of a lunatic Jeremiah floating through the streets of Manhattan, echoing, rebounding, distorting. Larry, lying sleepless in a queen-sized double with every light in the suite blazing, had become irrationally convinced that the monster-shouter was coming for him, seeking him out, the way the creatures of his frequent bad dreams sometimes did. For a long time it had seemed that the voice was drawing ever closer – *Monsters coming! Monsters on the way! They're in the suburbs!* – and Larry became convinced that the suite's door, which he had triple-locked, would burst inward and that the monster-shouter would be there . . . not a human being at all but a gigantic troll-thing with the head of a dog and saucer-sized fly eyes and champing teeth.

But earlier this morning Larry had seen him in the park and he was only a crazy old man wearing corduroy pants and zoris and horn-rimmed glasses with one bow taped. Larry had tried to speak to him and the monster-shouter had run in terror, crying back over his shoulder that the monsters would be in the streets at any moment. He had tripped over an ankle-high wire fence and went sprawling on one of the bikepaths with a loud comic *thwap!* sound, his glasses flying off but not shattering. Larry had gone to him, but before he could get there, the monster-shouter had scooped up his glasses and was gone toward the mall, crying his endless warning. So Larry's opinion of him had swung from extreme terror to utter boredom and mild annoyance in the space of twelve hours.

There were other people in the park; Larry had spoken to a few of them. They were all pretty much the same, and Larry supposed that he himself wasn't much different. They were dazed, their speech disjointed, and they seemed helpless to stop reaching for your sleeve with their hands as they talked. They had stories to tell. All the stories were the same. Their friends and relatives were dead or dying. There had been shooting in the streets, there had been an inferno on Fifth Avenue, was it true that Tiffany's was gone, could that be true? Who was going to clean up? Who was going to collect the garbage? Should they get out of New York? They had heard that troops were guarding all the places where one could hope to do this. One woman was terrified that the rats were going to rise up out of the subways and inherit the earth, reminding Larry uneasily of his own thoughts on the day he had first returned to New York. A young man munching Fritos from a gigantic bag told Larry conversationally that he was going to fulfill a lifetime ambition. He was going to Yankee Stadium, run around the outfield naked, and then masturbate on home plate. 'Chance of a lifetime, man,' he told Larry, winked with both eyes, and then wandered off, eating Fritos.

Many of the people in the park were sick, but not many had died there. Perhaps they had uneasy thoughts of being munched for dinner by the animals, and they had crawled indoors when they felt the end was near. Larry had had only one confrontation with death this morning, and one was all he wanted. He had walked up Transverse Number One to the comfort station there. He had opened the door and a grinning dead man with maggots crawling briskly hither and yon on his face had been seated inside, his hands settled on his bare thighs, his sunken eyes staring into Larry's own. A sickening sweet smell bloated out at Larry as if the man sitting there was a rancid bonbon, a sweet treat which, in all the confusion, had been left for the flies. Larry slammed the door shut, but belatedly: he lost the cornflakes he had eaten for breakfast and then dry-heaved until he was afraid he might rupture some of his inner workings. God, if You're there, he had prayed as he stumbled back toward the menagerie, if You're taking requests today, Big Fella, mine is not to have to look at anything else like that today. The kooks are bad enough, something like that is more than I can take. Thank You so much.

Now, sitting on this bench (the monster-shouter had moved out of earshot, at least temporarily), Larry found himself thinking about the World Series five years ago. It was good to remember that because, it now seemed to him, that was the last time he had been completely happy, his physical condition tiptop, his mind resting easily and not working against itself.

That had been just after he and Rudy split up. That had been a damn piss-poor thing, that split-up, and if he ever saw Rudy again (never happen, his mind told him with a sigh), Larry was going to apologize. He would get down and kiss Rudy's shoetops, if that was what Rudy needed to make it okay again.

They had started off across the country in a wheezy old 1968 Mercury that had shat its transmission in Omaha. From there on they would work for a couple of weeks, hitchhike west for a while, work another couple of weeks, then hitchhike some more. For a while they worked on a farm in western Nebraska, just below the panhandle, and one night Larry had lost sixty dollars in a poker game. The next day he'd had to ask Rudy for a loan to tide him over. They had arrived in LA a month later, and Larry had been the first to land a job – if you wanted to call washing dishes for the minimum wage working. One night about three weeks later, Rudy had broached the subject of the loan. He said he'd met a guy who'd recommended a really good employment agency, never miss, but the fee was twenty-five bucks. Which happened to be the amount of the loan he had made to Larry after the poker game. Ordinarily, Rudy said, he never would have asked, but –

Larry had protested that he'd paid the loan back. They were square. If Rudy wanted the twenty-five, okay, but he just hoped Rudy wasn't trying to get him to pay off the same loan twice.

Rudy said he didn't want a *gift*; he wanted the money he was *owed*, and he wasn't interested in a lot of Larry Underwood bullshit, either. Jesus Christ, Larry said, trying a good-humored laugh. I never thought I'd need a receipt from you, Rudy. Guess I was wrong.

It had escalated into a full-scale argument, almost to the point of blows. At the end Rudy's face had been flushed. That's you, Larry, he'd shouted. That's you all over. That's how you are. I used to think I'd never learn my lesson, but I think I finally did. Fuck off, Larry.

Rudy left, and Larry followed him to the stairs of the cheap rooming house, digging his wallet out of his back pocket. There were three tens neatly folded into the secret compartment behind the photos and he had heaved them after Rudy. *Go on, you cheap little lying fuck! Take it! Take the goddamn money!*

Rudy had slammed the outer door open with a bang and had gone out into the night, toward whatever tin destiny the Rudys of this world can expect. He didn't look back. Larry had stood at the top of the stairs, breathing hard, and after a minute or so he had looked around for his three ten-dollar bills, gathered them up, and put them away again.

Thinking of the incident now and then over the years, he had become more and more sure that Rudy had been right. Actually, he was positive. Even if he *had* paid Rudy back, the two of them had been friends since grade school, and it seemed (looking back) that Larry had always been a dime short for the Saturday matinee because

he'd bought some licorice whips or a couple of candy bars on the way over to Rudy's, or borrowing a nickel to round out his school lunch money or getting seven cents to make up carfare. Over the years he must have bummed fifty dollars in change from Rudy, maybe a hundred. When Rudy had braced him for that twenty-five, Larry could remember the way he had tightened up. His brain had subtracted twenty-five dollars from the three tens, and had said to him: *That only leaves five bucks. Therefore, you already paid him back. I'm not sure just when, but you did. Let's have no more discussion of the matter.* And no more there had been.

But after that he had been alone in the city. He had no friends, hadn't even attempted to make any at the café on Encino where he worked. The fact was, he'd believed everyone who worked there, from the evil-tempered head cook to the ass-wiggling, gum-chewing waitresses, had been a dipstick. Yes, he had really believed everyone at Tony's Feed Bag was a dipstick but him, the sainted, soon-to-succeed (and you better believe it) Larry Underwood. Alone in a world of dipsticks, he felt as achy as a whipped dog and as homesick as a man marooned on a desert island. He began to think more and more of buying a Greyhound AmeriPass and dragging himself back to New York.

In another month, maybe even another two weeks, he would have done it, too . . . except for Yvonne.

He met Yvonne Wetterlen at a movie theater two blocks from the club where she worked as a topless dancer. When the second show let out, she had been weeping and searching around her seat on the aisle for her purse. It had her driver's license in it, also her checkbook, her union card, her one credit card, a photostat of her birth certificate, and her Social Security card. Although he was positive it had been stolen, Larry did not say so and helped her look for it. And sometimes it seemed they really must live in a world of wonders, because he had found it three rows down just as they were about to give up. He guessed it had probably migrated down there as a result of people shuffling their feet as they watched the picture, which had really been pretty boring. She had hugged him and wept as she thanked him. Larry, feeling like Captain America, told her he wished he could take her out for burgers or something to celebrate, only he was really strapped for cash. Yvonne said she'd treat. Larry, that great prince, had been pretty sure she would.

They started to see each other; in less than two weeks they had a regular thing going. Larry found a better job, clerking in a bookstore, and had gotten a gig singing with a group called The Hotshot Rhythm Rangers & All-Time Boogie Band. The name was the best thing about the group, actually, but the rhythm guitarist had been Johnny McCall, who later went on to form the Tattered Remnants, and that was actually a pretty good band.

Larry and Yvonne moved in together, and for Larry everything changed. Part of it was just having a place, his own place, that he was paying half the rent for. Yvonne put up some curtains, they got some cheap thrift-shop furniture and refinished it together, other members of the band and some of Yvonne's friends started to drop around. The place was bright in the daytime, and at night a fragrant California breeze, which seemed redolent with oranges even when the only thing it was really redolent with was smog, would drift in through the windows. Sometimes no one would come and he and Yvonne would just watch television, and sometimes she would bring him a can of beer and sit on the arm of his chair and rub his neck. It was his own place, a *home*, goddammit, and sometimes he'd lie awake in bed at night with Yvonne sleeping beside him, and marvel at how good he felt. Then he would slip smoothly into sleep, and it was the sleep of the just, and he never did think of Rudy Marks at all. At least, not much.

They lived together for fourteen months, all of it fine until the last six weeks or so, when Yvonne got to be kind of a bitch, and the part of it that summed it all up for Larry was that World Series. He would put in his day at the bookstore, then go over to Johnny McCall's house and the two of them – the whole group only practiced on weekends, because the other two boys had night jobs – would work on some new stuff or maybe just hack away at the great oldies, the ones Johnny called 'real bar-rippers,' tunes like 'Nobody but Me' and 'Double Shot of My Baby's Love.'

Then he'd go home, to *his* home, and Yvonne would have dinner all ready. Not just TV dinners, shit like that, either. Real home cooking. Girl was well trained. And afterward they would go into the living room and turn on the tube and watch the Series. Later, love. It had seemed all right, it had all seemed his. There hadn't been one single thing hassling his mind. Nothing had been so good since then. Nothing.

He realized he was crying a little bit, and he felt a momentary disgust that he should be sitting here on a bench in Central Park, crying in the sun like some wretched old man on a pension. Then it occurred to him that he had a right to cry for the things he had lost, that he had a right to be in shock if that was what this was.

His mother had died three days ago. She had been lying on a cot in the hallway of Mercy Hospital when she died, crammed in with thousands of others who were also busy dying. Larry had been kneeling beside her when she went, and he had thought he might go mad, watching his mother die while all around him rose the stench of urine and feces, the hell's babble of the delirious, the choking, the insane, the screams of the bereaved. She hadn't known him at the end; there had been no final moment of recognition. Her chest had finally just stopped in mid-heave and had settled very slowly, like the weight of an automobile settling down on a flat tire. He had crouched beside her for ten minutes or so, not knowing what to do, thinking in a confused way that he ought to wait until a death certificate was signed or someone asked him what had happened. But it was obvious what had happened, it was happening everywhere. It was just as obvious that the place was a madhouse. No sober young doctor was going to come along, express sympathy, and then start the machinery of death. Sooner or later his mother would just be carried away like a sack of oats, and he didn't want to watch that. Her purse was under the cot. He found a pen and a bobby pin and her checkbook. He tore a deposit slip from the back of her book and wrote on it her name, her address, and after a moment's calculation, her age. He clipped it to her blouse pocket with the bobby pin and began to cry. He kissed her cheek and fled, crying. He felt like a deserter. Being on the street had been a little better, although at that time the streets had been full of crazy people, sick people, and circling army patrols. And now he could sit on this bench and grieve for more general things: his mother's loss of her retirement, the loss of his own career, for that time in LA when he had sat watching the World Series with Yvonne, knowing there would be bed and love later, and for Rudy. Most of all he grieved for Rudy and wished he had paid Rudy his twenty-five dollars with a grin and a shrug, saving the six years that had been lost.

The monkey died at quarter of twelve.

It was on its perch, just sitting there apathetically with its hands drawn up under its chin, and then its eyelids fluttered and it fell forward and hit the cement with a final horrid smack.

Larry didn't want to sit there anymore. He got up and began to walk aimlessly down toward the mall with its large bandshell. He had heard the monster-shouter some fifteen minutes ago, very far away, but now the only sound in the park seemed to be his own heels clicking on the cement and the twitter of the birds. Birds apparently didn't catch the flu. Good for them.

When he neared the bandshell, he saw that a woman was sitting on one of the benches in front of it. She was maybe fifty, but had taken great pains to look younger. She was dressed in expensive-looking gray-green slacks and a silk off-the-shoulder peasant blouse . . . except, Larry thought, as far as he knew, peasants can't afford silk. She looked around at the sound of Larry's footsteps. She had a pill in one hand and tossed it casually into her mouth like a peanut.

'Hi,' Larry said. Her face was calm, her eyes blue. Sharp intelligence gleamed in them. She was wearing gold-rimmed glasses, and her pocketbook was trimmed with something that certainly looked like mink. There were four rings on her fingers: a wedding band, two diamonds, and a cat's-eye emerald.

'Uh, I'm not dangerous,' he said. It was a ridiculous thing to say, he supposed, but she looked like she might be wearing about $20,000 on her fingers. Of course, they might be fakes, but she didn't look like a woman who would have much use for paste and zircons.

'No,' she said, 'you don't look dangerous. You're not sick, either.' Her voice rose a little on the last word, making her statement into a polite half-question. She wasn't as calm as she looked at first glance; there was a little tic working on the side of her neck, and behind the lively intelligence in the blue eyes was the same dull shock that Larry had seen in his own eyes this morning as he shaved.

'No, I don't think I am. Are you?'

'Not at all. Did you know you have an ice cream wrapper on your shoe?'

He looked down and saw that he did. It made him blush because he suspected that she would have informed him that his fly was open in that same tone. He stood on one leg and tried to pull it off.

'You look like a stork,' she said. 'Sit down and try it. My name is Rita Blakemoor.'

'Pleased to know you. I'm Larry Underwood.'

He sat down. She offered her hand and he shook it lightly, his fingers pressing against her rings. Then he gingerly removed the ice cream wrapper from his shoe and dropped it primly into a can beside the bench that said IT'S *YOUR* PARK SO KEEP IT CLEAN! It struck him as funny, the whole operation. He threw his head back and laughed. It was the first real laugh since the day he had come home to find his mother lying on the floor of her apartment, and he was enormously relieved to find that the good feel of laughing hadn't changed. It rose from your belly and escaped from between your teeth in the same jolly go-to-hell way.

Rita Blakemoor was smiling both at him and with him, and he was struck again by her casual yet elegant handsomeness. She looked like a woman from an Irwin Shaw novel. *Nightwork*, maybe, or the one they had made for TV when he was just a kid.

'When I heard you coming, I almost hid,' she said. 'I thought you were probably the man with the broken glasses and the queer philosophy.'

'The monster-shouter?'

'Is that what you call him or what he calls himself?'

'What I call him.'

'Very apt,' she said, opening her mink-trimmed (maybe) bag and taking out a package of menthol cigarettes. 'He reminds me of an insane Diogenes.'

'Yeah, just lookin for an honest monster,' Larry said, and laughed again.

She lit her cigarette and chuffed out smoke.

'He's not sick, either,' Larry said. 'But most of the others are.'

'The doorman at my building seems very well,' Rita said. 'He's still on duty. I tipped him five dollars when I came out this morning. I don't know if I tipped him for being very well or for being on duty. What do you think?'

'I really don't know you well enough to say.'

'No, of course you don't.' She put her cigarettes back in her bag and he saw that there was a revolver in there. She followed his gaze. 'It was my husband's. He was a career executive with a major New York bank. That's just how he put it when anyone asked what he did to keep himself in cocktail onions. I-am-a-career-executive-with-a-major-New-York-bank. He died two years ago. He was at a luncheon with one of those Arabs who always look as if they have rubbed all the visible areas of their skin with

Brylcreem. He had a massive stroke. He died with his tie on. Do you think that could be our generation's equivalent of that old saying about dying with your boots on? Harry Blakemoor died with his tie on. I like it, Larry.'

A finch landed in front of them and pecked the ground.

'He was insanely afraid of burglars, so he had this gun. Do guns really kick and make a loud noise when they go off, Larry?'

Larry, who had never fired a gun in his life, said, 'I don't think one that size would kick much. Is it a .38?'

'I believe it's a .32.' She took it out of her bag and he saw there were also a good many small pill bottles in there. This time she didn't follow his gaze; she was looking at a small chinaberry tree about fifteen paces away. 'I believe I'll try it. Do you think I can hit that tree?'

'I don't know,' he said apprehensively. 'I don't really think –'

She pulled the trigger and the gun went off with a fairly impressive bang. A small hole appeared in the chinaberry tree. 'Bull's-eye,' she said, and blew smoke from the pistol barrel like a gunfighter.

'Real good,' Larry said, and when she put the gun back in her purse, his heart resumed something like its normal rhythm.

'I couldn't shoot a person with it. I'm quite sure of that. And soon there won't be anyone to shoot, will there?'

'Oh, I don't know about that.'

'You were looking at my rings. Would you like one?'

'Huh? No!' He began to blush again.

'As a banker, my husband believed in diamonds. He believed in them the way the Baptists believe in Revelations. I have a great many diamonds, and they are all insured. We not only owned a piece of the rock, my Harry and I, I sometimes believed we held a lien on the whole goddamn thing. But if someone should want my diamonds, I would hand them over. After all, they're only rocks again, aren't they?'

'I guess that's right.'

'Of course,' she said, and the tic on the side of her neck jumped again. 'And if a stick-up man wanted them, I'd not only hand them over, I would give him the address of Cartier's. Their selection of rocks is much better than my own.'

'What are you going to do now?' Larry asked her.

'What would you suggest?'

'I just don't know,' Larry said, and sighed.

'My answer exactly.'

'You know something? I saw a guy this morning who said he was going out to Yankee Stadium and je . . . and masturbate on home plate.' He could feel himself blushing again.

'What an awful walk for him,' she said. 'Why didn't you suggest something closer?' She sighed, and the sigh turned into a shudder. She opened her purse, took out a bottle of pills, and popped a gel capsule into her mouth.

'What's that?' Larry asked.

'Vitamin E,' she said with a glittering, false smile. The tic in her neck jumped once or twice and then stopped. She became serene again.

'There's nobody in the bars,' Larry said suddenly. 'I went into Pat's on Forty-third and it was totally empty. They have that great big mahogany bar and I went behind it and poured myself a water glass full of Johnnie Walker. Then I didn't even want to be there. So I left it sitting on the bar and got out.'

They sighed together, like a chorus.

'You're very pleasant to be with,' she said. 'I like you very much. And it's wonderful that you're not crazy.'

'Thank you, Mrs Blakemoor.' He was surprised and pleased.

'Rita. I'm Rita.'

'Okay.'

'Are you hungry, Larry?'

'As a matter of fact, I am.'

'Perhaps you'd take the lady to lunch.'

'That would be a pleasure.'

She stood up and offered him her arm with a slightly deprecatory smile. As he linked his through it, he caught a whiff of her sachet, a smell that was at once comforting and disquietingly adult in its associations for him, almost old. His mother had worn a sachet on their many trips to the movies together.

Then he forgot about it as they walked out of the park and up Fifth Avenue, away from the dead monkey, the monster-shouter, and the dark sweet treat sitting endlessly inside the comfort station on Transverse Number One. She chattered incessantly, and later he could remember no one thing she had chattered about (yes, just one: she had always dreamed, she said, of strolling up Fifth Avenue on the arm of a handsome young man, a man who was young enough to have been her own son but who wasn't), but he recalled the walk often just the same, especially after she began to jitter apart like some indifferently made toy. Her beautiful smile, her light, cynical, casual chatter, the whisper of her slacks.

They went into a steak house and Larry cooked, a trifle clumsily, but she applauded each course: the steak, the french fries, the instant coffee, the strawberry-rhubarb pie.

CHAPTER 28

There was a strawberry pie in the fridge. It was covered with Saran Wrap and after looking at it for a long time with dull and bemused eyes, Frannie took it out. She set it on the counter and cut a wedge. A strawberry fell to the counter with a fat plop as she was transferring the piece of pie to a small plate. She picked the berry up and ate it. She wiped up the small splotch of juice on the counter with a dishrag. She put the Saran Wrap back over the remains of the pie and stuck it back in the refrigerator.

She was turning back to get her pie when she happened to glance at the knife-rack beside the cupboards. Her father had made it. It was two magnetized runners. The knives hung from them, blades down. The early afternoon sun was gleaming on them. She stared at the knives for a long time, the dull, half-curious cast of her eyes never changing, her hands working restlessly in the folds of the apron tied around her waist.

At last, some fifteen minutes later, she remembered that she had been in the middle of something. What? A line of scripture, a paraphrase, occurred to her for no good reason: *Before removing the mote in thy neighbor's eye, attend the beam in thine own.* She considered it. Mote? Beam? That particular image had always bothered her. What sort of beam? Moonbeam? Roofbeam? There were also flashlight beams and beaming faces and there had been a New York mayor named Abe Beame, not to mention a song she had learned in Vacation Bible School – 'I'll Be a Sunbeam for Him.'

– before removing the mote in thy neighbor's eye –

But it wasn't an eye; it was a pie. She turned to it and saw there was a fly crawling on her pie. She waved a hand at it. Bye-bye, Mr Fly, say so long to Frannie's pie.

She regarded the piece of pie for a long time. Her mother and father were both dead, she knew. Her mother had died in the Sanford Hospital and her father, who had once made a little girl feel welcome

in his shop, was lying dead in bed above her head. Why did everything have to keep coming in rhymes? Coming and going in such
dreadful cheap jingles and jangles, like the idiot mnemonics that recur
in fevers? *My dog has fleas, they bite his knees* –

She came to her senses suddenly, and a kind of terror twisted
through her. There was a hot smell in the room. Something was
burning.

Frannie jerked her head around, saw a skillet of french fries in
oil she had put on the stove and then forgotten. Smoke was billowing
up from the pan in a stinking cloud. Grease was flying out of the
pan in angry splatters, and the splatters that landed on the burner
were flaring alight and then going out, as if an invisible butane lighter
was being flicked by an invisible hand. The cooking surface of the
pan was black.

She touched the handle of the pan and drew her fingers back
with a little gasp. It was now too hot to touch. She grabbed a
dishtowel, wrapped it around the handle, and quickly carried the
utensil, sizzling like a dragon, out through the back door. She set it
down on the top step of the porch. The smell of honeysuckle and
the droning of the bees came to her, but she barely noticed. For a
moment the thick, dull blanket which had swaddled all her emotional
responses for the last four days was pierced, and she was acutely
frightened. Frightened? No – in a state of low terror, only a pace
away from panic.

She could remember peeling the potatoes and putting them
into the Wesson Oil to cook. *Now* she could remember. But for a
while there she had just . . . whew! She had just forgotten.

Standing on the porch, dishtowel still clutched in one hand,
she tried to remember exactly what her train of thought had been
after she had put the french fries on to cook. It seemed very
important.

Well, first she had thought that a meal which consisted of
nothing but french fries wasn't very nutritious. Then she'd thought
that if the McDonald's down on Route 1 had still been open, she
wouldn't have had to cook them herself, and she could have had a
burger, too. Just take the car and cruise up to the take-out window.
She would get a Quarter Pounder and the large-size fries, the ones
that came in the bright red cardboard container. Little grease-spots
on the inside. Undoubtedly unhealthy, indubitably comforting. And
besides – pregnant women get strange cravings.

That brought her to the next link in the chain. Thoughts of strange cravings had led to thoughts of the strawberry pie lurking in the fridge. Suddenly it had seemed to her that she wanted a piece of that strawberry pie more than she wanted anything in the world. So she had gotten it, but somewhere along the line her eye had been caught by the knife-rack her father had made for her mother (Mrs Edmonton, the doctor's wife, had been so envious of that knife-rack that Peter had made one for her two Christmases ago), and her mind had just . . . short-circuited. Motes . . . beams . . . flies . . .

'Oh God,' she said to the empty back yard and her father's unweeded garden. She sat down and put the apron over her face and cried.

When the tears dried up, she seemed to feel a little better . . . but she was still frightened. Am I losing my mind? she asked herself. Is this the way it happens, the way it feels, when you have a nervous breakdown or whatever you want to call it?

Since her father had died at half past eight the night before, her ability to focus mentally seemed to have gotten fragmented. She would forget things she had been doing, her mind would go off on some dreamy tangent, or she would simply sit, not thinking of anything at all, no more aware of the world than a head of cabbage.

After her father died she had sat beside his bed for a long time. At last she had gone downstairs and turned on the TV. No particular reason; like the man said, it just seemed like a good idea at the time. The only station broadcasting had been the NBC affiliate in Portland, WCSH, and they seemed to be broadcasting some sort of crazy trial show. A black man, who looked like a Ku Klux Klansman's worst nightmare of headhunting Africans, had been pretending to execute white men with a pistol while other men in the audience applauded. It had to be pretend, of course – they didn't show things like that on TV if they were real – but it hadn't *looked* like pretend. It reminded her crazily of *Alice in Wonderland*, only it wasn't the Red Queen yelling 'Off with their heads!' in this case, but . . . what? Who? The Black Prince, she had supposed. Not that the beef in the loincloth had looked much like Prince.

Later in the program (how much later she could not have said), some other men broke into the studio and there was a firefight which was even more realistically staged than the executions had been. She saw men, nearly decapitated by heavy-caliber bullets, thrown backward with blood bursting from their shredded necks in gaudy arterial pumps. She remembered thinking in her disorganized way that they should have put one of those signs on the screen from time to time, the ones that warned parents to put the kiddies to bed or change the channel. She also remembered thinking that WCSH might get their license to broadcast lifted all the same; it really was an *awfully* bloody program.

She switched it off when the camera swung up, showing only the studio-lights hanging down from the ceiling, and lay back on the couch, looking at her own ceiling. She had fallen asleep there, and this morning she was more than half convinced that she had dreamed the entire program. And that was the nub, really: *everything* had come to seem like a nightmare filled with free-floating anxieties. It had begun with the death of her mother; the death of her father had only intensified what had already been there. As in *Alice*, things just got curiouser and curiouser.

There had been a special town meeting which her father had attended even though he had been getting sick by then himself. Frannie, feeling drugged and unreal – but physically no different than ever – had gone with him.

The town hall had been crowded, much more crowded than it was for town meetings in late February or early March. There was a lot of sniffling and coughing and kerchooing. The attendees were frightened and ready to be angry at the least excuse. They spoke in loud, hoarse voices. They stood up. They shook their fingers. They pontificated. Many of them – not just the women, either – had been in tears.

The upshot had been a decision to close off the town entirely. No one would be allowed in. If people wanted to leave, that was fine, as long as they understood that they couldn't come in again. The roads leading in and out of town – most notably US 1 – were to be barricaded with cars (after a shouting match that lasted half an hour, that was amended to town-owned Public Works trucks), and volunteers would stand watches at these roadblocks with shotguns. Those trying to use US 1 to go north or south would be directed up north to Wells or down south to York, where they could get on Interstate 95 and thus detour around Ogunquit. Anyone who still tried to get through would be shot. Dead? Someone asked. You bet, several others answered.

There was a small contingent of about twenty which maintained that those already sick should be put out of town at once. They were overwhelmingly voted down because by the evening of the twenty-fourth, when the meeting was held, almost everyone in town who was not sick had close relatives or friends who were. Many of them believed the newscasts, which said that a vaccine would be available soon. How, they argued, would they ever be able to look each other in the face again if it all turned out to be just a scary close call, and they had overreacted to it by putting their own out like pariah dogs?

It was suggested that all the sick *summer* people be put out, then.

The summer people, a large contingent of them, pointed out grimly that they had supported the town's schools, roads, indigent, and public beaches for years with the taxes they paid on their cottages. Businesses that couldn't break even from mid-September to mid-June stayed afloat because of their summer dollars. If they were to be treated in such a cavalier fashion, the people of Ogunquit could be sure that they would never come back. They could go back to lobstering and clamming and grubbing quahogs out of the dirt for a living. The motion to escort sick summer people out of town was defeated by a comfortable margin.

By midnight the barriers were set up, and by dawn the next morning, the morning of the twenty-fifth, several people had been shot at the barriers, most just wounded, but three or four killed. Almost all of them were people coming north, streaming out of Boston, stricken with fear, panic-stupid. Some of them went back to York to get on the turnpike willingly enough, but others were too crazy to understand and tried to either ram the barriers or swing around them on the soft shoulders of the road. They were dealt with.

But by that evening, most of the men manning the barricades were sick themselves, glowing bright with fever, constantly propping their shotguns between their feet so they could blow their noses. Some, like Freddy Delancey and Curtis Beauchamp, simply fell down unconscious and were later driven back to the jackleg infirmary that had been set up over the town hall, and there they died.

By yesterday morning Frannie's father, who had opposed the whole idea of the barricades, had taken to his bed and Frannie was staying in to nurse him. He wouldn't allow her to take him to the infirmary. If he was going to die, he told Frannie, he wanted to do it here at home, decently, in private.

By afternoon, the flow of traffic had mostly dried up. Gus Dinsmore, the public beach parking lot attendant, said he guessed that so many cars must be just stopped dead along the road that even those manned (or womaned) by able drivers would be unable to move. It was just as well, because by the afternoon of the twenty-fifth there had been less than three dozen men capable of standing watch. Gus, who felt perfectly fine until yesterday, had come down with a runny nose himself. In fact, the only person in town besides herself who seemed all right was Amy Lauder's sixteen-year-old brother Harold. Amy herself had died just before that first town meeting, her wedding dress still hung in the closet, unworn.

Fran hadn't been out today, hadn't seen anyone since Gus had come by yesterday afternoon to check on her. She had heard engines a few times this morning, and once the close-together double explosions of a shotgun, but that was all. The steady, unbroken silence added to her sense of unreality.

And now there were these questions to consider. Flies . . . eyes . . . pies. Frannie found herself listening to the refrigerator. It had an automatic icemaker attachment, and every twenty seconds or so there would be a cold thump somewhere inside as it made another cube.

She sat there for almost an hour, her plate before her, the dull, half-questioning expression on her face. Little by little another thought began to surface in her mind – two thoughts, actually, that seemed at once connected and totally unrelated. Were they maybe interlocking parts of a bigger thought? Keeping an ear open for the sound of dropping icecubes inside the refrigerator's icemaking gadget, she examined them. The first thought was that her father was dead; he had died at home, and he might have liked that.

The second thought had to do with the day. It was a beautiful summer's day, flawless, the kind that the tourists came to the Maine seacoast for. You don't come to swim because the water's never really warm enough for that; you come to be knocked out by the day.

The sun was bright and Frannie could read the thermometer outside the back kitchen window. The mercury stood just under 80.

It was a beautiful day and her father was dead. Was there any connection, other than the obvious tear-jerky one?

She frowned over it, her eyes confused and apathetic. Her mind circled the problem, then drifted away to think of other things. But it always drifted back.

It was a beautiful *warm* day and her father was dead.

That brought it home to her all at once and her eyes squeezed shut, as if from a blow.

At the same time her hands jerked involuntarily on the tablecloth, yanking her plate off onto the floor. It shattered like a bomb and Frannie screamed, her hands going to her cheeks, digging furrows there. The wandering, apathetic vagueness disappeared from her eyes, which were suddenly sharp and direct. It was as if she had been slapped hard or had an open bottle of ammonia waved under her nose.

You can't keep a corpse in the house. Not in high summer.

The apathy began to creep back in, blurring the outlines of the thought. The full horror of it began to be obscured, cushioned. She began to listen for the clunk and drop of the icecubes again –

She fought it off. She got up, went to the sink, ran the cold water on full, and then splatted cupped handfuls against her cheeks, shocking her lightly perspiring skin.

She could drift away all she wanted, but first this thing had to be solved. It *had* to be. She couldn't just let him lie in bed up there as June melted into July. It was too much like that Faulkner story that was in all the college anthologies. 'A Rose for Emily.' The town fathers hadn't known what that terrible smell was, but after a while it had gone away. It . . . it . . .

'No!' she cried out loud to the sunny kitchen. She began to pace, thinking about it. Her first thought was the local funeral home. But who would . . . would . . .

'Stop backing away from it!' she shouted furiously into the empty kitchen. 'Who's going to *bury* him?'

And at the sound of her own voice, the answer came. It was perfectly clear. She was, of course. Who else? She was.

It was two-thirty in the afternoon when she heard the car turn into the driveway, its heavy motor purring complacently, low with power. Frannie put the spade down on the edge of the hole – she was digging in the garden, between the tomatoes and the lettuce – and turned around, a little afraid.

The car was a brand-new Cadillac Coupe de Ville, bottle green, and stepping out of it was fat sixteen-year-old Harold Lauder. Frannie felt an instant surge of distaste. She didn't like Harold and didn't know anyone who did, including his late sister Amy. Probably his mother had. But it struck Fran with a tired sort of irony that the only person left in Ogunquit besides herself should be one of the very few people in town she honestly didn't like.

Harold edited the Ogunquit High School literary magazine and wrote strange short stories that were told in the present tense or with the point of view in the second person, or both. *You come down the delirious corridor and shoulder your way through the splintered door and look at the race-track stars* – that was Harold's style.

'He whacks off in his pants,' Amy had once confided to Fran. 'How's that for nasty? Whacks off in his pants and wears the same pair of undershorts until they'll just about stand up by themselves.'

Harold's hair was black and greasy. He was fairly tall, about six-one, but he was carrying nearly two hundred and forty pounds. He favored cowboy boots with pointed toes, wide leather garrison belts that he was constantly hitching up because his belly was considerably bigger than his butt, and flowered shirts that billowed on him like staysails. Frannie didn't care how much he whacked off, how much weight he carried, or if he was imitating Wright Morris this week or Hubert Selby, Jr. But looking at him, she always felt uncomfortable and a little disgusted, as if she sensed by low-grade telepathy that almost every thought Harold had was coated lightly with slime. She didn't think, even in a situation like this, that Harold could be dangerous, but he would probably be as unpleasant as always, perhaps more so.

He hadn't seen her. He was looking up at the house. 'Anybody home?' he shouted, then reached through the Cadillac's window and honked the horn. The sound jagged on Frannie's nerves. She would have kept silent, except that when Harold turned around to get back into the car, he would see the excavation, and her sitting on the end of it. For a moment she was tempted to crawl deeper into the garden and just lie low among the peas and beans until he got tired and went away.

Stop it, she told herself, just stop it. He's another living human being, anyway.

'Over here, Harold,' she called.

Harold jumped, his large buttocks joggling inside his tight pants. Obviously he had just been going through the motions, not really expecting to find anyone. He turned around and Fran walked to the edge of the garden, brushing at her legs, resigned to being stared at in her white gym shorts and halter. Harold's eyes crawled over her with great avidity as he came to meet her.

'Say, Fran,' he said happily.

'Hi, Harold.'

'I'd heard that you were having some success in resisting the dread disease, so I made this my first stop. I'm canvassing the township.' He smiled at her, revealing teeth that had, at best, a nodding acquaintance with his toothbrush.

'I was awfully sorry to hear about Amy, Harold. Are your mother and father –?'

'I'm afraid so,' Harold said. He bowed his head for a moment, then jerked it up, making his clotted hair fly. 'But life goes on, does it not?'

'I guess it does,' Fran said wanly. His eyes were on her breasts again, dancing across them, and she wished for a sweater.

'How do you like my car?'

'It's Mr Brannigan's, isn't it?' Roy Brannigan was a local realtor.

'It was,' Harold said indifferently. 'I used to believe that, in these days of shortages, anyone who drove such a thyroidal monster ought to be hung from the nearest Sunoco sign, but all of that has changed. Less people means more petrol.' *Petrol*, Fran thought dazedly, he actually said *petrol*. 'More everything,' Harold finished. His eyes took on a fugitive gleam as they dropped to the cup of her navel, rebounded to her face, dropped to her shorts, and bounced to her face again. His smile was both jolly and uneasy.

'Harold, if you'll excuse me –'

'But whatever can you be doing, my child?'

The unreality was trying to creep back in again, and she found herself wondering just how much the human brain could be expected to stand before snapping like an overtaxed rubber band. My parents are dead, but I can take it. Some weird disease seems to have spread across the entire country, maybe the entire *world*, mowing down the righteous and the unrighteous alike – I can take it. I'm digging a hole in the garden my father was weeding only last week, and when it's deep enough I guess I'm going to put him in it – I *think* I can take it. But Harold Lauder in Roy Brannigan's Cadillac, feeling me up with his eyes and calling me 'my child'? I don't know, my Lord. I just don't know.

'Harold,' she said patiently. 'I am not your child. I am five years older than you. It is physically *impossible* for me to be your child.'

'Just a figure of speech,' he said, blinking a little at her controlled ferocity. 'Anyway, what is it? That hole?'

'A grave. For my father.'

'Oh,' Harold Lauder said in a small, uneasy voice.

'I'm going in to get a drink of water before I finish up. To be blunt, Harold, I'd just as soon you went away. I'm upset.'

'I can understand that,' he said stiffly. 'But Fran . . . in the garden?'

She had started toward the house, but now she rounded on him, furious. 'Well, what would you suggest? That I put him in a coffin and drag him out to the cemetery? What in the name of God for? He *loved* his garden! And what's it to you, anyway? What business is it of yours?'

She was starting to cry. She turned and ran for the kitchen, almost running into the Cadillac's front bumper. She knew Harold would be watching her jiggling buttocks, storing up the footage for whatever X-rated movie played constantly in his head, and that made her angrier, sadder, and more weepy than ever.

The screen door whacked flatly shut behind her. She went to the sink and drank three cold glasses of water, too quickly, and a silver spike of pain sank deeply into her forehead. Her surprised belly cramped and she hung over the porcelain sink for a moment, eyes slitted closed, waiting to see if she was going to throw up. After a moment her stomach told her it would take the cold water, at least on a trial basis.

'Fran?' The voice was low and hesitant.

She turned and saw Harold standing outside the screen, his hands dangling limply at his sides. He looked concerned and unhappy, and Fran suddenly felt badly for him. Harold Lauder tooling around this sad, ruined town in Roy Brannigan's Cadillac, Harold Lauder who had probably never had a date in his life and so affected what he probably thought of as worldly disdain. For dates, girls, friends, everything. Including himself, most likely.

'Harold, I'm sorry.'

'No, I didn't have the right to say anything. Look, if you want me to, I can help.'

'Thank you, but I'd rather do it alone. It's . . .'

'It's personal. Of course, I understand.'

She could have gotten a sweater from the kitchen closet, but of course he would have known why and she didn't want to embarrass him again. Harold was trying hard to be a good guy – something which must have been a little like speaking a foreign language. She went back out on the porch and for a moment they stood there looking at the garden, at the hole with the dirt thrown up around it. And the afternoon buzzed somnolently around them as if nothing had changed.

'What are you going to do?' she asked Harold.

'I don't know,' he said. 'You know . . .' He trailed off.

'What?'

'Well, it's hard for me to say. I am not one of the most loved persons in this little patch of New England. I doubt if a statue would ever have been erected in my memory on the local common, even if I had become a famous writer, as I had once hoped. Parenthetically speaking, I believe I may be an old man with a beard down to my beltbuckle before there is another famous writer.'

She said nothing; only went on looking at him.

'So!' Harold exclaimed, and his body jerked as if the word had exploded out. 'So I am forced to wonder at the unfairness of it. The unfairness seems, to me at least, so monstrous that it is easier to believe that the louts who attend our local citadel of learning have finally succeeded in driving me mad.'

He pushed his glasses up on his nose, and she noticed with sympathy how really horrible his acne problem was. Had anyone ever told him, she wondered, that soap and water would take care of some of that? Or had they all been too busy watching pretty, petite Amy as she zoomed through the University of Maine with a 3.8 average, graduating twenty-third in a class of over a thousand? Pretty Amy, who was so bright and vivacious where Harold was just abrasive.

'Mad,' Harold repeated softly. 'I've been driving around town in a Cadillac on my learner's permit. And look at these boots.' He pulled up the legs of his jeans a little, disclosing a gleaming pair of cowboy boots, complexly stitched. 'Eighty-six dollars. I just went into the Shoe Boat and picked out my size. I feel like an imposter. An actor in a play. There have been moments today when I've been *sure* I was mad.'

'No,' Frannie said. He smelled like he hadn't had a bath in three or four days, but this no longer disgusted her. 'What's that line? I'll be in your dream if you'll be in mine? We're not crazy, Harold.'

'Maybe it would be better if we were.'

'Someone will come,' Frannie said. 'After a while. After this disease, whatever it is, burns itself out.'

'Who?'

'Somebody in authority,' she said uncertainly. 'Somebody who will . . . well . . . put things back in order.'

He laughed bitterly. 'My dear child . . . sorry, Fran. Fran, it was the people in authority who *did* this. They're good at putting things back in order. They've solved the depressed economy, pollution, the oil shortage, and the cold war, all at a stroke. Yeah, they put things in order, all right. They solved everything the same way Alexander solved the Gordian knot – by cutting it in two with his sword.'

'But it's just a funny strain of the *flu*, Harold. I heard it on the radio –'

'Mother Nature just doesn't work that way, Fran. Your somebody in authority got a bunch of bacteriologists, virologists, and epidemiologists together in some government installation to see how many funny bugs they could dream up. Bacteria. Viruses. Germ plasm, for all I know. And one day some well-paid toady said, "Look what *I* made. It kills almost *everybody*. Isn't it great?" And they gave him a medal, and a pay-raise, and a time-sharing condo, and then somebody spilled it.

'What are you going to do, Fran?'

'Bury my father,' she said softly.

'Oh . . . of course.' He looked at her for a moment and then said, very swiftly, 'Look, I'm going to get out of here. Out of Ogunquit. If I stay much longer, I really will go crazy. Fran, why don't you come with me?'

'Where?'

'I don't know. Not yet.'

'Well, if you think of a place, come ask me again.'

Harold brightened. 'All right, I will. It . . . you see, it's a matter of . . .' He trailed off and began to walk down the porch steps in a kind of daze. His new cowboy boots gleamed in the sun. Fran watched him with sad amusement.

He waved just before climbing behind the wheel of the Caddy. Fran lifted a hand in return. The car jerked unprofessionally when he put it in reverse, and then he was backing down the driveway in fits and starts. He wandered to the left, crushing some of Carla's flowers under the offside wheels, and nearly thumped into the culvert ditch as he turned out onto the road. Then he honked twice and was gone. Fran watched until he was out of sight, and then went back to her father's garden.

Sometime after four o'clock she went back upstairs with dragging footsteps, forcing herself along. There was a dull headache in her temples and forehead, caused by heat and exertion and tension. She had told herself to wait another day, but that would only make it worse. Under her arm she carried her mother's best damask tablecloth, the one kept strictly for company.

It did not go as well as she had hoped, but it was also nowhere near as bad as she had feared. There were flies on his face, lighting, rubbing their hairy little forelegs together and then taking off again, and his skin had gone a dusky dark shade, but he was so tanned from working in the garden that it was hardly noticeable . . . if you made your mind up not to notice it, that was. There was no smell, and that was what she had been most afraid of.

The bed he had died in was the double he had shared for years with Carla. She laid the tablecloth out on her mother's half, so that its hem touched her father's arm, hip, and leg. Then, swallowing hard (her head was pounding worse than ever), she prepared to roll her father onto his shroud.

Peter Goldsmith was wearing his striped pajamas, and that struck her as jarringly frivolous, but they would have to do. She could not even entertain the thought of first undressing and then dressing him again.

Steeling herself, she grasped his left arm — it was as hard and unyielding as a piece of furniture — and pushed, rolling him over. As she did so, a hideous long burping sound escaped him, a belch that seemed to go on and on, rasping in his throat as if a locust had crawled down there and had now come to life in the dark channel, calling and calling.

She screeched, stumbling away and knocking over the bedtable. His combs, his brushes, the alarm clock, a little pile of change and some tieclips and cufflinks all jingled and fell to the floor. *Now* there was a smell, a corrupted, gassy smell, and the last of the protective fog which had wrapped her dissipated and she knew the truth. She fell to her knees and wrapped her arms around her head and wailed. She was not burying some life-sized doll; it was her *father* she was burying, and the last of his humanity, the very last, was the juicy, gassy smell that now hung on the air. And it would be gone soon enough.

The world went gray and the sound of her own grief, braying and constant, began to seem distant, as if someone else was uttering those sounds, perhaps one of the little brown women you see on the TV newsclips. Some length of time went by, she had no idea how long, and then, little by little, she came back to herself and to the knowledge of all that still remained to be done. They were the things she could not have brought herself to do before.

She went to him and turned him over. He uttered another belch, this one small and dwindling. She kissed his forehead.

'I love you, Daddy,' she said. 'I love you, Frannie loves you.' Her tears fell on his face and gleamed there. She removed his pajamas and dressed him in his best suit, hardly noticing the dull throb in her back, the ache in her neck and arms as she lifted each part of his weight, dressed it, dropped it, and went on to the next part. She propped his head up with two volumes of *The Book of Knowledge* to get his tie right. In his bottom drawer, under the socks, she found his army medals – Purple Heart, good conduct medals, campaign ribbons . . . and the Bronze Star he had won in Korea. She pinned them to his lapel. In the bathroom she found Johnson's Baby Powder and powdered his face and neck and hands. The smell of the powder, sweet and nostalgic, brought the tears on again. Sweat slicked her body. There were pitted dark circles of exhaustion under her eyes.

She folded the tablecloth over him, got her mother's sewing kit, and closed the seam. Then she doubled the seam and sewed again. With a sobbing, whistling grunt, she managed to get his body to the floor without dropping it. Then she rested, half-swooning. When she felt she could go on, she lifted the top half of the corpse, got it to the head of the stairs, and then, as carefully as she could, down to the first floor. She stopped again, her breath coming in quick, whining gasps. Her headache was sharp now, needling into her with quick hard bursts of pain.

She dragged the body down the hall, through the kitchen, and out onto the porch. Down the porch steps. Then she had to rest again. The golden light of early evening was on the land now. She gave way again and sat beside him, her head on her knees, rocking back and forth, weeping. Birds twittered. Eventually she was able to drag him into the garden.

At last it was done. By the time the last sods were back in place (she had fitted them together down on her knees, as if doing a jigsaw puzzle) it was a quarter of nine. She was filthy. Only the flesh around her eyes was white; that area had been washed clean by her tears. She was reeling with exhaustion. Her hair hung against her cheeks in matted strings.

'Please be at peace, Daddy,' she muttered. 'Please.'

She dragged the spade back to her father's workshop and slung it inside indifferently. She had to rest twice as she climbed the six steps to the back porch. She crossed the kitchen without turning on the lights and kicked off her low-topped sneakers as she entered the living room. She dropped to the couch and slept immediately.

In the dream she was climbing the stairs again, going to her father, to do her duty and see him decently under the ground. But when she entered the room the tablecloth was already over the body and her sense of grief and loss changed to something else . . . something like fear. She crossed the darkened room, not wanting to, suddenly wanting only to flee, but helpless to stop. The tablecloth glimmered in the shadows, ghostly, ghastly, and it came to her:

It wasn't her father under there. And what was under there was not dead.

Something – someone – filled with dark life and hideous good cheer was under there, and it would be more than her life was worth to pull that tablecloth back, but she . . . couldn't . . . stop her feet.

Her hand reached out, floated over the tablecloth – and snatched it back.

He was grinning, but she couldn't see his face. A wave of frigid cold blasting up at her from that awful grin. No, she couldn't see his face, but she could see the gift this terrible apparition had brought for her unborn baby: a twisted coathanger.

She fled, fled from the room, from the dream, coming up, surfacing briefly –

Surfacing briefly in the three o'clock darkness of the living room, her body floating on a foam of dread, the dream already tattering and unraveling, leaving behind it only a sense of doom like the rancid aftertaste of some rotten meal. She thought, in that moment of half-sleeping and half-waking: *Him, it's him, the Walkin Dude, the man with no face.*

Then she slept again, this time dreamlessly, and when she woke the next morning she didn't remember the dream at all. But when she thought of the baby in her belly, a feeling of fierce protectiveness swept over her all at once, a feeling that perplexed her and frightened her a little with its depth and strength.

CHAPTER 29

That same evening, as Larry Underwood slept with Rita Blakemoor and as Frannie Goldsmith slept alone, dreaming her peculiarly ominous dream, Stuart Redman was waiting for Elder. He had been waiting for three days – and this evening Elder did not disappoint him.

At just past noon on the twenty-fourth, Elder and two male nurses had come and taken away the television. The nurses had removed it while Elder stood by, holding his revolver (neatly wrapped in a Baggie) on Stu. But by then Stu hadn't wanted or needed the TV – it was just putting out a lot of confused shit anyway. All he had to do was stand at his barred window and look out at the town on the river below. Like the man on the record said, 'You don't need a weatherman to know which way the wind blows.'

Smoke was no longer billowing from the stacks of the textile mill. The gaudy stripes and eddies of dye in the river had dissipated and the water ran clear and clean again. Most of the cars, glittering and toylike from this distance, had left the mill's parking lot and hadn't come back. By yesterday, the twenty-sixth, there had been only a few cars still moving on the turnpike, and those few had to weave between the stalls like skiers in a slalom race. No wreckers had come to remove the abandoned vehicles.

The downtown area was spread out below him like a relief map, and it seemed totally deserted. The town clock, which had chimed off the hours of his imprisonment here, had not tolled since nine this morning, when the little tune that preceded the striking had sounded draggy and weird, like a tune played underwater by a drowned music box. There had been a fire at what looked like a roadside café or maybe a general store just outside of town. It had burned merry hell all this afternoon, black smoke etched against the blue sky, but no fire engines had come to put it out. If the building hadn't been set in the middle of an asphalt parking lot, Stu supposed that half the town might have gone up. Tonight the ruins were still smoldering in spite of an afternoon spat of rain.

Stu supposed that Elder's final orders were to kill him – why not? He would only be one more corpse, and he knew their little secret. They had been unable to find a cure or to discover how his bodily makeup varied from all those who had succumbed. The thought that there would be precious few left he could tell their secret to had probably never even entered their computations. He was a loose thread held hostage by a bunch of tight assholes.

Stu was sure that a hero in a television program or a novel could have thought of a way to escape, hell, even some people in real life, but he wasn't one of them. In the end he had decided with a certain panicky resignation that the only thing to do would be to wait for Elder and just try to be ready.

Elder was the clearest sign that this installation had been breached by what the help sometimes called 'Blue' and sometimes the 'superflu.' The nurses called him Dr Elder, but he was no doctor. He was in his mid-fifties, hard-eyed and humorless. None of the doctors before Elder had felt a need to hold a gun on him. Elder scared Stu because there would be no reasoning or pleading with such a man. Elder was waiting for orders. When they came, he would carry them out. He was a spear-carrier, the army version of a Mafia button-man, and it would never occur to him to question his orders in the light of ongoing events.

Three years ago Stu had gotten a book called *Watership Down* to send to a nephew of his in Waco. He had gotten out a box to put the book in, and then, because he hated to wrap presents even more than he hated to read, he had thumbed to the first page, thinking he would scan a little of it to see what it was about. He read that first page, then the second . . . and then he was enthralled. He had stayed up all night, drinking coffee and smoking cigarettes and plowing steadily along, the way a man does when he's not much used to reading just for the pleasure of it. The thing turned out to be about rabbits, for Christ's sake. The stupidest, most cowardly animals of God's earth . . . except the guy who wrote that book made them seem different. You really cared about them. It was a pretty damn good story, and Stu, who read at a snail's pace, finished it two days later.

The thing he remembered most from that book was a phrase: 'going tharn,' or just 'tharn.' He understood it at once, because he had seen plenty of tharn animals, and run down a few on the highway.

An animal which had gone tharn would crouch in the middle of the road, its ears flattened, watching as a car rushed toward it, unable to move from the certain oncoming death. A deer could be driven tharn simply by shining a flashlight in its eyes. Loud music would do it to a raccoon, and constant tapping on its cage would do it to a parrot.

Elder made Stu feel like that. He would look into Elder's flat blue eyes and feel all the will drain out of him. Elder probably wouldn't even need the pistol to dispose of him. Elder probably had had courses in karate, savate, and general dirty tricks. What could he possibly do against a man like that? Just thinking about Elder made his will to even try to want to drain away. Tharn. It was a good word for a bad state of mind.

The red light went on over the door at just past 10 PM, and Stu felt light perspiration break on his arms and face. It was this way every time the red light went on, because one of these times Elder would be alone. He would be alone because he wouldn't want witnesses. There would be a furnace somewhere to cremate plague victims. Elder would bundle him into it. Snip. No more loose ends.

Elder stepped through the door. Alone.

Stu was sitting on his hospital bed, one hand resting on the back of his chair. At the sight of Elder he felt the familiar sickening drop in his belly. He felt the familiar urge to spill out a flood of loose, pleading words, in spite of his knowledge that such pleas would avail him nothing. There was no mercy in the face behind the white-suit's transparent visor.

Now everything seemed very clear to him, very colorful, very slow. He could almost hear his eyes rolling in their bed of lubrication as he followed Elder's progress into the room. He was a big man, stocky, and his white-suit was stretched too tight over him. The hole at the end of the pistol he held looked tunnel-size.

'How are you feeling?' Elder asked, and even through the tinny speaker Stu could hear the nasal quality of Elder's voice. Elder was sick.

'Just the same,' Stu said, surprised at the evenness of his voice. 'Say, when do I get out of here?'

'Very soon now,' Elder said. He was pointing the gun in Stu's general direction, not precisely at him, but not precisely away, either. He uttered a muffled sneeze. 'You don't talk much, do you?'

Stu shrugged.

'I like that in a man,' Elder said. 'Your big talkers, they're your whimperers and whiners and belly-achers. I just got the word on you about twenty minutes ago, Mr Redman. They're not such hot orders, but I think you'll do okay.'

'What orders?'

'Well, I've been ordered to —'

Stu's eyes flicked past Elder's shoulder, toward the high, riveted sill of the airlock door. 'Christ Jesus!' he exclaimed. 'That's a fucking rat, what kind of place are you running with rats in it?'

Elder turned, and for a moment Stu was almost too surprised by the unexpected success of his ruse to go on. Then he slid off the bed and grasped the back of his chair in both hands as Elder began to pivot toward him again. Elder's eyes were wide and suddenly alarmed. Stu lifted the chair over his head and stepped forward, swinging it down, getting every ounce of his one-eighty behind it.

'Get back there!' Elder cried. 'Don't —'

The chair crashed down on his right arm. The gun went off, disintegrating the Baggie, and the bullet screamed off the floor. Then the gun fell to the carpet, where it discharged again.

Stu was afraid he could count on only one more blow with the chair before Elder fully recovered himself. He determined to make it a good one. He brought it around in a high hard arc, a Henry Aaron home run swing. Elder tried to get his broken right arm up and couldn't. The legs of the chair crashed into the hood of the white-suit. The plastic faceplate splintered in Elder's eyes and nose. He screamed and fell backward.

He rolled onto all fours and scrambled for the gun lying on the carpet. Stu swung the chair one last time, bringing it down on the back of Elder's head. Elder collapsed. Panting, Stu reached down and grabbed the gun. He stepped away, pointing it at the prone body, but Elder didn't move.

For a moment a nightmarish thought tormented him: What if Elder's orders had not been to kill him but to release him? But that made no sense, did it? If his orders had been to release him, why the talk about no whimpering and whining? Why would he have termed the orders 'not so hot'?

No — Elder had been sent here to kill him.

Stu looked at the prone body, trembling all over. If Elder got up now, Stu thought he would probably miss him with all five bullets at point-blank range. But he didn't think Elder was going to get up. Not now, not ever.

Suddenly the need to get out of there was so strong that he almost bolted blindly through the airlock door and into whatever lay beyond. He had been locked up for over a week, and all he wanted now was to breathe fresh air and then get far, far away from this terrible place.

But it had to be done carefully.

Stu walked to the airlock, stepped in, and pushed a button marked CYCLE. An air-pump went on, ran briefly, and the outer door opened. Beyond it was a small room furnished only with a desk. On it was a thin stack of medical charts . . . and his clothes. The ones he had been wearing on the airplane from Braintree to Atlanta. The cold finger of dread touched him again. Those things would have gone into the crematorium with him, no doubt. His charts, his clothes. So long, Stuart Redman. Stuart Redman would have become an unperson. In fact –

There was a slight noise behind him and Stu turned around fast. Elder was staggering toward him, crouched over, his hands swinging loosely. A jagged splinter of plastic was lodged in one oozing eye. Elder was smiling.

'Don't move,' Stu said. He pointed the gun, steadying it with both hands – and still the barrel jittered.

Elder gave no sign that he had heard. He kept coming.

Wincing, Stu pulled the trigger. The pistol bucked in his hands and Elder stopped. The smile had turned into a grimace, as if he had been struck with a sudden gas pain. There was now a small hole in the breast of his white-suit. For a moment he stood, swaying, and then he crashed forward. For a moment Stu could only stare at him, frozen, and then he blundered into the room where his personal effects were piled on the desk.

He tried the door at the far end of the office, and it opened. Beyond the door was a hallway lit by muted fluorescents. Halfway down to the elevator bank, an abandoned gurney cart stood by what was probably the nurses' station. He could hear faint groaning. Someone was coughing, a harsh, ratcheting sound that seemed to have no end.

He went back into the room, gathered his clothes up, and put them under one arm. Then he went out, closed the door behind him, and started down the hall. His hand was sweating against the grip of Elder's gun. When he reached the gurney he looked behind him, unnerved by the silence and the emptiness. The cougher had stopped. Stu kept expecting to see Elder creeping or crawling after him, intent on carrying out his final directive. He found himself longing for the closed and known dimensions of his room.

The groaning began again, louder this time. At the elevators another corridor ran at right angles to this one, and leaning against the wall was a man Stu recognized as one of his nurses. His face was swelled and blackened, his chest rising and falling in quick spurts. As Stu looked at him, he began to groan again. Behind him, curled in a fetal position, was a dead man. Farther down the hall there were another three bodies, one of them female. The male nurse – Vic, Stu remembered, his name is Vic – began to cough again.

'Jesus,' Vic said. 'Jesus, what are you doing out? You're not supposed to be out.'

'Elder came to take care of me and I took care of him instead,' Stu said. 'I was lucky he was sick.'

'Sweet bleeding Jesus, you better believe you was lucky,' Vic said, and another coughing fit, this one weaker, tore loose from his chest. 'That hurts, man, you wouldn't believe how that hurts. What a fuckup this turned out to be. Bleeding *Christ*.'

'Listen, can I do anything for you?' Stu asked awkwardly.

'If you're serious, you can put that gun in my ear and pull the trigger. I'm ripping myself to pieces inside.' He began to cough again, and then to groan helplessly.

But Stu couldn't do that, and as Vic's hollow groans continued, Stu's nerve broke. He ran for the elevators, away from the blackish face like the moon in partial eclipse, half expecting Vic to call after him in that strident and helplessly righteous voice that the sick always seem to use when they need something from the well. But Vic only went on groaning and that was somehow worse.

The elevator door had shut and the car was already moving downward when it occurred to Stu that it might be booby-trapped. That would be just their speed. Poison gas, maybe, or a cutout circuit that would disengage the cables and send the elevator careering down the shaft to crash at the bottom. He stepped into the middle of the car and looked around nervously for hidden vents or loopholes. Claustrophobia caressed him with a rubber hand and suddenly the elevator seemed no more than telephone-booth-size, then coffin-size. Premature burial, anyone?

He reached out a finger to push the STOP button, and then wondered what good that would do if he was between floors. Before he could answer the question, the elevator slid to a smooth, normal stop.

What if there are men with guns out there?

But the only sentinel when the door slid back was a dead woman in a nurse's uniform. She was curled up in a fetal position by a door marked LADIES.

Stu stared at her so long that the door began to slide shut again. He put his arm out and the door bounced obediently back. He stepped out. The hallway led down to a T-junction and he walked toward it, giving the dead nurse a wide berth.

There was a noise behind him and he whirled, bringing the gun up, but it was only the elevator door sliding shut for the second time. He looked at it for a moment, swallowed hard, then walked on. The rubber hand was back, playing tunes on the base of his spine, telling him to hell with this walk-don't-run bit, let's get out quick before someone . . . some*thing* . . . can get us. The echoes of his footfalls in this semidark corridor of the administration wing was too much like macabre company – *Coming to play, Stuart? Very good.* Doors with frosted glass panels marched past him, each with its own tale to tell: DR SLOANE. RECORDS AND TRANSCRIPTS. MR BALLINGER. MICROFILM. COPYFILE. MRS WIGGS. Perhaps of the cabbage patch, Stu thought.

There was a drinking fountain at the T-junction, but the warm, chlorinated taste of the water made his stomach turn. There was no exit to his left; a sign on the tile wall with an orange arrow beneath read LIBRARY WING. The corridor seemed to stretch away for miles that way. Some fifty yards down was the body of a man in a white-suit, like some strange animal cast up on a sterile beach.

His control was getting bad. This place was much, much bigger than he had first assumed. Not that he'd had a right to assume much of anything from what he'd seen when he was admitted – which had been two halls, one elevator, and one room. Now he guessed it to be the size of a largish metropolitan hospital. He could stumble around in here for hours, his footfalls echoing and rebounding, coming across a corpse every now and then. They were strewn about like prizes in some ghastly treasure hunt. He remembered taking Norma, his wife, to a big hospital in Houston when they diagnosed the cancer. Everyplace you went in there they had little maps on the walls with little arrows pointing at a dot. The words written on each arrow said: YOU ARE HERE. They put those up so people wouldn't get lost. Like he was now. *Lost.* Oh baby, this was bad. This was so bad.

'Don't go tharn now, you're almost home free,' he said, and his words echoed back, flat and strange. He hadn't meant to speak aloud, and that made it worse.

He turned to the right, setting his back to the library wing, walked past more offices, came to another corridor, and turned down that. He began to look behind himself frequently, assuring himself that no one – Elder, maybe – was following him, but unable to believe it. The hallway ended in a closed door that said RADIOLOGY. A hand-lettered sign hung on the knob: CLOSED UNTIL FURTHER NOTICE RANDALL.

Stu went back and peered around the corner and back where he had come from. The dead body in the white-suit was tiny with distance now, hardly more than a speck, but seeing it there so changeless and eternal made him want to run away as fast as he could.

He turned right, setting his back to it again. Twenty yards farther up, the corridor branched into another T-junction. Stu turned right and went past more offices. The corridor ended at the micro-biology lab. In one of the lab carrels a young man clad in jockey shorts lay sprawled over his desk. He was comatose, bleeding from the nose and mouth. His breath rattled in and out with a sound like October wind in dead cornhusks.

And then Stu did begin to run, turning from one corridor to another, becoming more and more convinced that there was no way out, at least not from this level. The echo of his footfalls chased him, as if either Elder or Vic had lived just long enough to put a squad of ghostly MPs on his trail. Then another fancy crowded that out, one he somehow associated with the queer dreams he had been having the last few nights. The idea grew so strong that he became afraid to turn around, afraid that if he did he would see a white-suited figure striding after him, a white-suited figure with no face but only blackness behind a Plexiglas plate. Some dreadful apparition, a hit-man from beyond sane time and space.

Panting, Stu rounded a corner, sprinted ten feet before he realized the corridor was a dead end, and crashed into a door with a sign over it. The sign read EXIT.

He pushed at the bar, convinced it would not move, but it did, and the door opened easily. He went down four steps to another door. To the left of this landing, more stairs went down into thick darkness. The top half of this second door was clear glass reinforced with crisscrossed safety wire. Beyond it was only the night, the beautiful mellow summer night, and all the freedom a man ever dreamed of.

Stu was still staring out, transfixed, when the hand slipped out of the darkness of the stairwell and grasped his ankle. A gasp tore at Stu's throat like a thorn. He looked around, his belly a freezing floe of ice, and beheld a bloody, grinning face upturned in the darkness.

'Come down and eat chicken with me, beautiful,' it whispered in a cracked and dying voice. 'It's *soooo* dark −'

Stu screamed and tried to pull free. The grinning thing from the darkness held on, talking and grinning and chuckling. Blood or bile was trickling from the corners of its mouth. Stu kicked at the hand holding his ankle, then stomped it. The face hanging in the darkness of the stairwell disappeared. There was a series of thudding crashes . . . and then the screams began. Of pain or of rage, Stu could not tell. He didn't care. He battered against the outside door with his shoulder. It banged open and he tottered out, whirling his arms to keep his balance. He lost it anyway and fell down on the cement path.

He sat up slowly, almost warily. Behind him, the screams had stopped. A cool evening breeze touched his face, dried the sweat on his brow. He saw with something very like wonder that there was grass, and flowerbeds. Night had never smelled as fragrantly sweet as this. A crescent moon rode the sky. Stu turned his face up to it thankfully, and then walked across the lawn toward the road which led to the town of Stovington below. The grass was dressed with dewfall. He could hear wind whispering in the pines.

'I'm alive,' Stu Redman said to the night. He began to cry. 'I'm alive, thank God I'm alive, thank You, God, thank You, God, thank You −'

Tottering a little, he began to walk down the road.

CHAPTER 30

Dust blew straight across the Texas scrubland, and at twilight it created a translucent curtain that made the town of Arnette seem like a sepia ghost-image. Bill Hapscomb's Texaco sign had blown down and lay in the middle of the road. Someone had left the gas on in Norm Bruett's house, and the day before, a spark from the air conditioner had blown the whole place sky-high, rattling lumber and shingles and Fisher-Price toys all over Laurel Street. On Main Street, dogs and soldiers lay dead together in the gutter. In Randy's Sooperette a man in pj's lay draped over the meat counter, his arms hanging down. One of the dogs now lying in the gutter had been at this man's face before losing its appetite. Cats did not catch the flu, and dozens of them wove in and out of the twilit stillness like smoky shades. From several houses the sound of television snow ran on and on. A random shutter banged back and forth. A red wagon, old and faded and rusty, the words SPEEDAWAY EXPRESS barely legible on its sides, stood in the middle of Durgin Street in front of the Indian Head Tavern. There were a number of returnable beer and soda bottles in the wagon. On Logan Lane, in Arnette's best neighborhood, wind chimes played on the porch of Tony Leominster's house. Tony's Scout stood in the driveway, its windows open. A family of squirrels had nested in the back seat. The sun deserted Arnette; the town grew dark under the wing of the night. The town was, except for the chirr and whisper of small animals and the tinkle of Tony Leominster's wind chimes, silent. And silent. And silent.

CHAPTER 31

Christopher Bradenton struggled out of delirium like a man struggling out of quicksand. He ached all over. His face felt alien, as if someone had injected it with silicone in a dozen places and it was now the size of a blimp. His throat was raw pain, and more frightening, the opening there seemed to have closed from ordinary throat-size to something no larger than the bore of a boy's air pistol. His breath whistled in and out through this horribly tiny connection he needed to maintain contact with the world. Still it wasn't enough, and worse than the steady, throbbing soreness there was a feeling like drowning. Worst of all, he was hot. He could not remember ever having been this hot, not even two years ago when he had been driving two political prisoners who had jumped bail in Texas west to Los Angeles. Their ancient Pontiac Tempest had died on Route 190 in Death Valley and he had been hot then, but this was worse. This was an *inside* hot, as if he had swallowed the sun.

He moaned and tried to kick the covers off, but he had no strength. Had he put himself to bed? He didn't think so. Someone or something had been in the house with him. Someone or something . . . he should remember, but he couldn't. All Bradenton could remember was that he had been afraid even before he got sick, because he knew someone (or something) was coming and he would have to . . . what?

He moaned again and rocked his head from side to side on the pillow. Delirium was all he remembered. Hot phantoms with sticky eyes. His mother had come into this plain log bedroom, his mother who had died in 1969, and she had talked to him: 'Kit, oh Kit, I tole you, "Don't get mixed up with those people," I said. "I don't care nothing about politics," I said, "but those men you hang around with are crazy as mad dogs and those girls are nothing but hoors." I tole you, Kit . . .' And then her face had broken apart, letting through a horde of grave beetles from the splitting yellow parchment fissures and he had screamed until blackness wavered and there was confused shouting, the slap of shoe-leather as people ran . . . lights, flashing lights, the smell of gas, and he was back in Chicago, the year was 1968, somewhere voices were chanting *The whole world is watching! The whole world is watching! The whole world* . . . and there was a girl lying in the gutter by the entrance to the park, her body clad in overall jeans, her feet bare, her long hair full of glass-fragments, her face a glittering mask of blood that was black in the heartless white glow of the streetlights, the mask of a crushed insect. He helped her to her feet and she screamed and shrank against him because an outer-space monster was advancing out of the drifting gas, a creature clad in shining black boots and a flak-jacket and a walleyed gas mask, holding a truncheon in one hand, a can of Mace in the other, and grinning. And when the outer-space monster pushed its mask back, revealing its grinning, flaming face, they had both screamed because it was the somebody or something he had been waiting for, the man Kit Bradenton had always been terrified of. It had been the Walkin Dude. Bradenton's screams had shattered the fabric of that dream like high C shatters fine crystal and he was in Boulder, Colorado, an apartment on Canyon Boulevard, summer and hot, so hot that even in your skivvy shorts your body was trickling sweat, and across from you stands the most beautiful boy in the world, tall and tanned and straight, he is wearing lemon-yellow bikini briefs which cling lovingly to every ridge and hollow of his precious buttocks and you know if he turns his face will be like a Raphael angel and he will be hung like the Lone Ranger's horse. Hiyo Silver, away. Where did you pick him up? A meeting to discuss racism on the CU campus, or in the cafeteria? Hitchhiking? Does it matter? Oh, it's so hot, but there's water, a pitcher of water, an urn of water carved with strange figures which stand out in bas-relief, and beside it the pill, no – ! THE PILL! The one that will send him off to what this angel in the light yellow briefs calls Huxleyland, the place where the moving finger writes and doesn't move on, the place where flowers grow on dead oak trees, and boy, what an erection is tenting out your skivvies! Has Kit Bradenton ever been so horny, so ready for love? 'Come to bed,' you say to that smooth brown back, 'come to bed and do me and then I'll do you. Just the way you like.' 'Take your pill first,' he says without turning. 'Then we'll see.' You take the pill, the water is cool in your throat, and little by little the strangeness comes over your sight, the weirdness that makes every angle in the place a little more or a little less than ninety degrees. For some time you find yourself looking at the fan on the cheap Grand Rapids bureau and then you're looking at your own reflection in the wavy looking glass above it. Your face looks black and swelled but you don't let it worry you because it's just the pill, only !!! THE PILL!! 'Trips,' you murmur, 'oh boy, Captain Trips and I am sooo horny . . .' He begins to run and at first you have to look at those smooth hips where the elastic of his briefs rides so low, and then your gaze moves up the flat, tanned belly, then to the beautiful hairless chest, and finally from the slimly corded neck to the face . . . and it is *his* face, sunken and happy and ferociously grinning, not the face of a Raphael angel but of a Goya devil and from each blank eyesocket there peers the reptilian face of an adder; he is coming toward you as you scream, he is whispering: *Trips, baby, Captain Trips . . .*

Then murkiness, faces and voices that he didn't remember, and at last he had surfaced here, in the small house he had built with his own hands on the outskirts of Mountain City. Because now was now, and the great wave of revolt which had engulfed the country had long since withdrawn, the young Turks were now mostly old lags with gray in their beards and big coke-burned holes where their septa used to be, and this was the wreckage, baby. The boy in the yellow briefs had been long ago, and in Boulder Kit Bradenton had been little more than a boy himself.

My God, am I dying?

He beat at the thought with agonized horror, the heat rolling and billowing in his head like a sandstorm. And suddenly his short, quick respiration stopped as a sound began to rise from somewhere beyond and below the closed bedroom door.

At first Bradenton thought it was a fire-siren, or a police-car siren. It rose and grew louder as it grew closer; beneath it he could hear the jagged pounding of footfalls clocking along his downstairs hall and then through his living room and then battering up the stairs in a Goth's stampede.

He pushed himself back against his pillow, his face drawing down in a rictus of terror even as his eyes widened to circles in his puffy, blackish face and the sound neared. Not a siren any more but a scream, high and ululating, a scream that no human throat could make or sustain, surely the scream of a banshee or of some black

Charon, come to take him across the river that separates the land of the living from that of the dead.

Now the running footsteps clattered straight toward him along the upstairs hall, boards groaning and creaking and protesting under the weight of those merciless rundown bootheels and suddenly Kit Bradenton knew who it was and he shrieked as the door burst inward and the man in the faded jeans jacket ran in, his murderer's grin flashing on his face like a whirring white circle of knives, his face as jolly as that of a lunatic Santa Claus, carrying a galvanized steel bucket high over his right shoulder.

'HEEEEEEEOOOOOOWWWWWWWWWW!'

'No!' Bradenton screamed, crossing his arms weakly across his face. 'No! Noo —!'

The bucket tipped forward and the water flew out, all of it seeming to hang suspended for a moment in the yellow lamplight like the largest uncut diamond in the universe, and he saw the dark man's face through it, reflected and refracted into the face of a supremely grinning troll who had just made its way up from hell's darkest shit-impacted bowels to rampage on the earth; then the water fell on him, so cold that his swelled throat sprang momentarily open again, squeezing blood from its walls in big beads, shocking breath into him and making him kick the covers all the way over the foot of the bed in one convulsive spasm so that his body would be free to jackknife and sunfish as bitter cramps from these involuntary struggles whipped through him like greyhounds biting on the run.

He screamed. He screamed again. Then lay trembling, his feverish body soaked from toe to crown, his head thumping, his eyes bulging. His throat closed to a raw slit and he began to struggle for breath miserably again. His body began to shake and shiver.

'I *knew* that'd cool you off!' the man he knew as Richard Fry cried cheerily. He set the bucket down with a clang. 'Ah say, Ah say Ah *knew* dat wuz goan do de trick, Kingfish! Thanks are in order, my good man, thanks from you tendered to me. Do you thank me? Can't talk? No? Yet in your heart I know you do.

'Yeee-GAAAHHH!'

He sprang into the air like Bruce Lee in a Run Run Shaw kungfu epic, knees spread, for a moment seeming to hang suspended directly over Kit Bradenton as the water had done, his shadow a blob on the chest of Bradenton's soaked pajamas, and Bradenton screamed weakly. Then one knee came down on either side of his ribcage and Richard

Fry's bluejeaned groin was the crotch of a fork suspended above his chest by inches, and his face burned down at Bradenton's like a cellar torch in a gothic novel.

'Had to wake you up, man,' Fry said. 'I didn't want you to boogie off without a chance for us to talk a bit.'

'. . . off . . . off . . . off me . . .'

'I'm not *on* you, man, come on. I'm just hanging suspended above you. Like the great invisible world.'

Bradenton, in an agony of fear, could only pant and shake and roll his trapped eyeballs away from that jolly, fuming face.

'We got to talk about ships and seals and sailing wax, and whether bees have stings. Also about the papers you're supposed to have for me, and the car, and the keys to the car. Now all I see in your gay-radge is a Chevy pickup, and I know that's yours, Kitty-Kitty, so how bout it?'

'. . . they . . . papers . . . can't . . . can't talk . . .' He gasped harshly for air. His teeth chittered together like small birds in a tree.

'You *better* be able to talk,' Fry said, and stuck out his thumbs. They were both double-jointed (as were all his fingers), and he wiggled them back and forth at angles that seemed to deny biology and physics. ''Cause if you aren't, I'm going to have your baby blues for my keychain and you're going to have to trot around hell with a seeing-eye dog.' He jammed his thumbs at Bradenton's eyes and Bradenton jerked back against the pillow helplessly.

'You tell me,' Fry said, 'and I'll leave you the right pills. In fact, I'll hold you up so you can swallow them. Make you well, man. Pills to take care of everything.'

Bradenton, now trembling with fear as much as with cold, forced the words out through his clacking teeth. 'Papers . . . in the name of Randall Flagg. Welsh dresser downstairs. Under the . . . contact paper.'

'Car?'

Bradenton tried desperately to think. Had he gotten this man a car? It was so far away, all the flames of delirium were in between, and the delirium seemed to have done something to his thought processes, burned out whole banks of memory. Whole sections of his past were scorched cabinets filled with smoldering wires and blackened relays. Instead of the car this awful man wanted to know about, an image of the first car he'd ever owned drifted up, a 1953 Studebaker with a bullet nose that he had painted pink.

Gently, Fry put one hand over Bradenton's mouth and pinched

his nostrils shut with the other. Bradenton began to buck beneath him. Furry moans escaped around Fry's hand. Fry took both hands away and said, 'Does that help you remember?'

Strangely, it did.

'Car . . .' he said, and then panted like a dog. The world swirled, steadied, and he was able to go on. 'Car's parked . . . behind the Conoco station . . . just outside of town. Route 51.'

'North or south of town?'

'Suh . . . suh . . .'

'Yes suh! I got it. Go on.'

'Covered with a tarp. Byoo . . . Byoo . . . Buick. Registration's on the steering post. Made out . . . Randall Flagg.' He collapsed into panting again, unable to say more or do anything except look at Fry with dumb hope.

'Keys?'

'Floormat. Under . . .'

Fry's backside cut off any further words by settling on Bradenton's chest. He settled there the way he might have settled on a comfortable hassock in a friend's apartment and suddenly Bradenton couldn't even get a small breath.

He expelled the last of his tidal breath on a single word: '. . . please . . .'

'And thank you,' Richard Fry/Randall Flagg said with a prim grin. 'Say goodnight, Kit.'

Unable to speak, Kit Bradenton could only roll his eyes whitely in their puffed sockets.

'Don't think unkindly of me,' the dark man said softly, looking down at him. 'It's just that we have to hurry now. The carnival is opening early. They're opening all the rides, and the Pitch-til-U-Win, and the Wheel of Fortune. And it's my lucky night, Kit. I feel that. I feel that very strongly. So we have to hurry.'

It was a mile and a half to the Conoco station, and by the time he got there it was quarter past three in the morning. The wind had picked up, whining along the street, and on his way here he had seen the corpses of three dead dogs and one dead man. The man had been wearing some sort of uniform. Above, the stars shone hard and bright, sparks struck off the dark skin of the universe.

The tarp which covered the Buick had been pegged tautly to the ground, and the wind made the canvas flap. When Flagg pulled the pegs the tarpaulin went cartwheeling off into the night like a large brown ghost, moving east. The question was, in which direction was *he* heading?

He stood beside the Buick, which was a well-preserved 1975 model (cars did well out here: there was little moisture and rust had a hard time starting), scenting the summer night air like a coyote. There was desert perfume on it, the kind you can only smell clearly at night. The Buick stood whole in an automobile mortuary of dismembered parts, Easter Island monoliths in the windy silence. An engine block. An axle looking like some muscle-boy's dumbbell. A pile of tires for the wind to make hooting sound effects in. A cracked windshield. More.

He thought best in scenes like these. In scenes like these, any man could be Iago.

He walked past the Buick and ran his hand across the dented hood of what might once have been a Mustang. 'Hey little Cobra, don't ya know ya gonna shut em down . . .' he sang softly. He kicked over a stove-in radiator with one dusty boot and disclosed a nest of jewels, winking back at him with dim fire. Rubies, emeralds, pearls the size of goose eggs, diamonds to rival the stars. Snapped his finger at them. They were gone. Where was *he* to go?

The wind moaned through the shattered wing window of an old Plymouth and tiny living things rustled inside.

Something else rustled behind him. He turned and it was Kit Bradenton, clad only in absurd yellow underpants, his poet's pot hanging over the waistband like an avalanche held in suspended animation. Bradenton walked toward him over the heaped remains of Detroit rolling iron. A leafspring pierced through his foot like crucifixion, but the wound was bloodless. Bradenton's navel was a black eye.

The dark man snapped his fingers and Bradenton was gone.

He grinned and walked back to the Buick. Laid his forehead against the slope of roof on the passenger's side. Time passed. At some length he straightened, still grinning. He knew.

He slipped behind the wheel of the Buick, and pumped the gas a couple of times to prime up the carburetor. The motor purred into life and the needle on the gas gauge swung over to F. He pulled out and drove around the side of the gas station, his headlight beams for a moment catching another pair of emeralds, cat's eyes glistening warily from the tall grass by the Conoco station's Ladies Room door. In the cat's mouth was the small limp body of a mouse. At the sight of his grinning, moonlike face peering down at it from the driver's side window, the cat dropped its morsel and ran. Flagg laughed aloud, heartily, the laugh of a man with nothing on his mind but lots of good things. Where the Conoco's tarmac became highway, he turned right and began to run south.

CHAPTER 32

Someone had left the door open between Maximum Security and the cellblock beyond it; the steel-walled length of corridor acted as a natural amplifier, blowing up the steady, monotonous hollering that had been going on all morning to monster size, making it echo and re-echo until Lloyd Henreid thought that, between the cries and the very natural fear that he felt, he would go utterly and completely bugshit.

'Mother,' the hoarse, echoing cry came. 'Mootherr!'

Lloyd was sitting crosslegged on the floor of his cell. Both of his hands were slimed with blood; he looked like a man who has drawn on a pair of red gloves. The light blue cotton shirt of his prison uniform was smeared with blood because he kept wiping his hands dry on it in order to get a better purchase. It was ten o'clock in the morning, June 29. Around seven this morning he had noticed that the front right leg of his bunk was loose, and since then he had been trying to unthread the bolts that held it to the floor and to the underside of the bedframe. He was trying to do this with only his fingers for tools, and he had actually gotten five of the six bolts. As a result his fingers now looked like a spongy mess of raw hamburger. The sixth bolt was the one that had turned out to be the bitch-kitty, but he was beginning to think he might actually get it. Beyond that, he hadn't allowed himself to think. The only way to keep back brute panic was not to think.

'Mootherr –'

He leaped to his feet, drops of blood from his wounded, throbbing fingers splattering on the floor, and shoved his face out into the corridor as far as he could, eyes bulging furiously, hands gripping the bars.

'Shut up, cock-knocker!' he screamed. 'Shut up, ya drivin me fuckin batshit!'

There was a long pause. Lloyd savored the silence as he had once savored a piping hot Quarter Pounder with Cheese from McD's.

Silence is golden, he had always thought that was a stupid saying, but it sure had its points.

'MOOOOTHERRRR –' The voice came drifting up at the steel throat of the holding cells again, as mournful as a foghorn.

'Jesus,' Lloyd muttered. 'Holy Jesus. *SHUT UP! SHUT UP! SHUT UP, YA FUCKIN DIMWIT!*'

'MOOOOOOOTHERRRRRRRRRR –'

Lloyd turned back to the leg of his bunk and attacked it savagely, wishing again that there was something in the cell to pry with, trying to ignore the throbbing in his fingers and the panic in his mind. He tried to remember exactly when he had seen his lawyer last – things like that grew hazy very soon in Lloyd's mind, which retained a chronology of past events about as well as a sieve retains water. Three days ago. Yes. The day after that prick Mathers had socked him in the balls. Two guards had taken him down to the conference room again and Shockley was still on the door and Shockley had greeted him: *Why, here's the wise-ass pusbag, what's the story, pusbag, got anything smart to say?* And then Shockley had opened his mouth and sneezed right into Lloyd's face, spraying him with thick spit. *There's some cold germs for you, pusbag, everybody else has got one from the warden on down, and I believe in share the wealth. In America even scummy douchebags like you should be able to catch a cold.* Then they had taken him in, and Devins had looked like a man who is trying to conceal some pretty good news lest it should turn out to be bad news, after all. The judge who was supposed to hear Lloyd's case was flat on his back with the flu. Two other judges were also ill, either with the flu that was going around or with something else, so the remaining benchwarmers were swamped. Maybe they could get a postponement. Keep your fingers crossed, the lawyer had said. When would we know? Lloyd had asked. Probably not until the last minute, Devins had replied. I'll let you know, don't worry. But Lloyd hadn't seen him since then and now, thinking back on it, he remembered that the lawyer had had a runny nose himself and –

'*Owwwwooo Jesus!*'

He slipped the fingers of his right hand into his mouth and tasted blood. But that frigging bolt had given a little bit, and that meant he was going to get it for sure. Even the mother-shouter down there at the end of the hall could no longer bother him . . . at least not so badly. He was going to get it. After that he would just have to wait and see what happened. He sat with his fingers in his mouth, giving them a rest. When this was done, he'd rip his shirt into strips and bandage them.

'Mother?'

'I know what you can do with your mother,' Lloyd muttered.

That night, after he had talked to Devins for the last time, they had begun taking sick prisoners out, *carrying* them out, not to put too fine a point on it, because they weren't taking anyone that wasn't already far gone. The man in the cell on Lloyd's right, Trask, had pointed out that most of the guards sounded pretty snotty themselves. Maybe we can get something outta this, Trask said. What? Lloyd had asked. I dunno, Trask said. He was a skinny man with a long bloodhound face who was in Maximum Security while awaiting trial on charges of armed robbery and assault with a deadly weapon. Postponements, he said. I dunno.

Trask had six joints under the thin mattress of his bunk, and he gave four of them to one of the screws who still seemed okay to tell him what was going on outside. The guard said people were leaving Phoenix, bound for anyplace. There was a lot of sickness, and people were croaking faster than a horse could trot. The government said a vaccine was going to be available soon, but most people seemed to think that was crap. A lot of the radio stations from California were broadcasting really terrible things about martial law, army blockades, home-boys with automatic weapons on the rampage, and rumors of people dying by the tens of thousands. The guard said he wouldn't be surprised to find out that the longhaired comsymp pervos had done it by putting something into the water.

The guard said he was feeling fine himself, but he was going to get the Christ out just as soon as his shift was over. He had heard the army was going to roadblock US 17 and 1-10 and US 80 by tomorrow morning, and he was going to load up his wife and kid and all the food he could get his hands on and stay up in the mountains until it all blew over. He had a cabin up there, the guard said, and if anyone tried to get within thirty yards of it, he would put a bullet in his head.

The next morning Trask had a runny nose and said he felt feverish. He had been nearly gibbering with panic, Lloyd remembered as he sucked his fingers. Trask had yelled at every guard who passed to get him the fuck out before he got really sick or something. The guards never even looked at him, or at any of the other prisoners, who were now as restless as underfed lions in the zoo. That was when Lloyd started to feel scared. Usually there were as many as twenty different screws on the floor at any given time. So how come he had seen only four or five different faces on the other side of the bars?

That day, the twenty-seventh, Lloyd had begun eating only half of the meals that were thrust through the bars at him, and saving the other half – precious little – under his bunk mattress.

Yesterday Trask had gone into sudden convulsions. His face had turned as black as the ace of spades and he had died. Lloyd had looked longingly at Trask's half-eaten lunch, but he had no way to reach it. Yesterday afternoon there had still been a few guards on the floor, but they weren't carrying anyone down to the infirmary anymore, no matter how sick. Maybe they were dying down in the infirmary, too, and the warden decided to stop wasting the effort. No one came to remove Trask's body.

Lloyd napped late yesterday afternoon. When he woke, the Maximum Security corridors were empty. No supper had been served. Now the place really *did* sound like the lion house at the zoo. Lloyd wasn't imaginative enough to wonder how much more savage it would have sounded if Maximum Security had been filled to its capacity. He had no idea how many were still alive and lively enough to yell for their supper, but the echoes made it sound like more. All Lloyd knew for sure was that Trask was gathering flies on his right, and the cell on his left was empty. The former occupant, a young jive-talking black guy who had tried to mug an old lady and had killed her instead, had been taken to the infirmary days back. Across the way he could see two empty cells and the dangling feet of a man who was in for killing his wife and his brother-in-law during a penny Pokeno game. The Pokeno Killer, as he had been called, had apparently opted out with his belt, or if they had taken that, his own pair of pants.

Later that night, after the lights had come on automatically, Lloyd had eaten some of the beans he had saved from two days ago. They tasted horrible but he ate them anyway. He washed them down with water from the toilet bowl and then crawled up on his bunk and clasped his knees against his chest, cursing Poke for getting him into such a mess. It was all Poke's fault. On his own, Lloyd never would have been ambitious to get into more than small-time trouble.

Little by little, the roaring for food had quieted down, and Lloyd suspected he wasn't the only one who had been squirreling away some insurance. But he didn't have much. If he had really believed this was going to happen, he would have put away more. There was something in the back of his mind that he didn't want to see. It was as if there was a set of flapping drapes in the back of his mind, with something behind them. You could only see that thing's bony, skeletal feet below the hem of the drapes. That's all you wanted to see. Because the feet belonged to a nodding, emaciated corpse, and his name was STARVATION.

'Oh no,' Lloyd said. 'Someone's gonna come. Sure they are. Just as sure as shit sticks to a blanket.'

But he kept remembering the rabbit. He couldn't help it. He had won the rabbit and a cage to keep him in at a school raffle. His daddy didn't want him to keep it, but Lloyd had somehow persuaded him that he would take care of it and feed it out of his own allowance. He loved that rabbit, and he did take care of it. At first. The trouble was, things slipped his mind after a while. It had always been that way. And one day while he was swinging idly in the tire that hung from the sickly maple behind their scraggy little house in Marathon, Pennsylvania, he had suddenly sat bolt upright, thinking of that rabbit. He hadn't thought of his rabbit in . . . well, in better than two weeks. It had just completely slipped his mind.

He ran to the little shed tacked onto the barn, and it had been summer just like it was now, and when he stepped into that shed, the bland smell of the rabbit had struck him in the face like a big old roundhouse slap. The fur he had liked so much to stroke was matted and dirty. White maggots crawled busily in the sockets that had once held his rabbit's pretty pink eyes. The rabbit's paws were ragged and bloody. He tried to tell himself that the paws were bloody because it had tried to scratch its way out of the cage, and that was undoubtedly how it had happened, but some sick, dark part of his mind spoke up in a whisper and said that maybe the rabbit, in the final extremity of its hunger, had tried to eat itself.

Lloyd had taken the rabbit away, dug a deep hole, and buried it, still in its cage. His father had never asked him about the rabbit, might even have forgotten that his boy *had* a rabbit – Lloyd was not terribly bright, but he was a mental giant when stacked up against his daddy – but Lloyd had never forgotten. Always plagued by vivid dreams, the death of the rabbit had occasioned a series of terrible nightmares. And now the vision of the rabbit returned as he sat on his bunk with his knees drawn up to his chest, telling himself that someone would come, someone would surely come and let him go free. He didn't have this Captain Trips flu; he was just hungry. Like his rabbit had been hungry. Just like that.

Sometime after midnight he had fallen asleep, and this morning he had begun to work on the leg of his bunk. And now, looking at his bloody fingers, he thought with fresh horror about the paws of that long-ago rabbit, to whom he had meant no harm.

By one o'clock on the afternoon of June 29, he had the cotleg free. At the end the bolt had given with stupid ease and the leg had clanged to the floor of his cell and he had just looked at it, wondering what in God's name he had wanted it for in the first place. It was about three feet long.

He took it to the front of the cell and began to hammer furiously against the blued-steel bars. 'Hey!' he yelled, as the clanging bar gave off its deep, gonglike notes. 'Hey, I want out! I want to get the fuck out of here, understand? Hey, goddammit, *hey!*'

He stopped and listened as the echoes faded. For a moment there was total silence and then from the holding cellblock came the rapturous, hoarse answer: 'Mother! Down here, Mother! I'm down here!'

'Jeeesus!' Lloyd cried, and threw the cotleg into the corner. He had struggled for hours, practically destroyed his fingers, just so he could wake that asshole up.

He sat on his bunk, lifted the mattress, and took out a piece of rough bread. He debated adding a handful of dates, told himself he should save them, and snatched them up anyway. He ate them one by one, grimacing, saving the bread for last to take that slimy, fruity taste out of his mouth.

When he was done with this miserable excuse for a meal, he walked aimlessly to the right side of his cell. He looked down and stifled a cry of revulsion. Trask was sprawled half on his cot and half off it, and his pants legs had pulled up a little. His ankles were bare above the prison slippers they gave you to wear. A large, sleek rat was lunching up on Trask's leg. Its repulsive pink tail was neatly coiled around its gray body.

Lloyd walked to the other corner of his own cell and picked up the cotleg. He went back and stood for a moment, wondering if the rat would see him and decide to go off where the company wasn't quite so lively. But the rat's back was to him, and as far as Lloyd could tell, the rat didn't even know he was there. Lloyd measured the distance with his eye and decided the cotleg would reach admirably.

'Huh!' Lloyd grunted, and swung the leg. It squashed the rat against Trask's leg, and Trask fell off his bunk with a stiff thump. The rat lay on its side, dazed, aspirating weakly. There were beads of blood on its whiskers. Its rear legs were moving, as if its ratty little brain was telling it to run somewhere but along the spinal cord the signals were getting all scrambled up. Lloyd hit it again and killed it.

'There you are, you cheap fuck,' Lloyd said. He put the cotleg down and wandered back to his bunk. He was hot and scared and felt like crying. He looked back over his shoulder and cried: 'How do you like rat hell, you scuzzy little cocksucker?'

'Mother!' the voice cried happily in answer. '*Moootherrr!*'

'*Shut up!*' Lloyd screamed. '*I ain't your mother! Your mother's in charge of blowjobs at a whorehouse in Asshole, Indiana!*'

'Mother?' the voice said, now full of weak doubt. Then it fell silent.

Lloyd began to weep. As he cried he rubbed his eyes with his fists like a small boy. He wanted a steak sandwich, he wanted to talk to his lawyer, he wanted to get *out* of here.

At last he lay down on his cot, put one arm over his eyes, and masturbated. It was as good a way of getting to sleep as any.

When he woke up again it was 5 PM and Maximum Security was dead quiet. Blearily, Lloyd got off his cot, which now leaned drunkenly toward the spot where one of its supports had been taken away. He got the cotleg, steeled himself for the cries of '*Mother!*' and began hammering on the bars like a farm cook calling the hired hands in for a big country supper. *Supper.* Now there was a word, had there ever been a finer? Ham steaks and potatoes with redeye gravy and fresh new peas and milk with Hershey's chocolate syrup to dump in it. And a great big old dish of strawberry ice cream for dessert. No, there had never been a word to match *supper.*

'Hey, ain't nobody there?' Lloyd cried, his voice breaking.

No answer. Not even a cry of '*Mother!*' At this point, he might have welcomed it. Even the company of the mad was better than the company of the dead.

Lloyd let the cotleg drop with a crash. He stumbled back to his bunk, turned up the mattress, and made inventory. Two more hunks of bread, two more handfuls of dates, a half-gnawed pork chop, one piece of bologna. He pulled the slice of bologna in two and ate the big half, but that only whetted his appetite, brought it raging up.

'No more,' he whispered, then gobbled the rest of the pork off the chopbone and called himself names and wept some more. He was going to die in here, just as his rabbit had died in its cage, just as Trask had died in his.

Trask.

He looked into Trask's cell for a long, thoughtful time, watching the flies circle and land and take off. There was a regular LA International Airport for flies right on ole Trask's face. At long last, Lloyd got the cotleg, went to the bars, and reached through with it. By standing on tiptoe he could get just enough length to catch the rat's body and drag it toward his cell.

When it was close enough, Lloyd got on his knees and pulled the rat through to his side. He picked it up by the tail and held the dangling body before his eyes for a long time. Then he put it under his mattress where the flies could not get at it, segregating the limp body from what remained of his food-stash. He looked fixedly at the rat for a long time before letting the mattress fall back, mercifully hiding it from sight.

'Just in case,' Lloyd Henreid whispered to the silence. 'Just in case, is all.'

Then he climbed up on the other end of the bunk, drew his knees up to his chin, and sat still.

CHAPTER 33

At twenty-two minutes of nine by the clock over the sheriff's office doorway, the lights went off.

Nick Andros had been reading a paperback he had taken from the rack in the drugstore, a gothic novel about a frightened governess who thought the lonely estate where she was supposed to be teaching the handsome master's sons was haunted. Although he wasn't even halfway through the book, Nick already knew the ghost was really the handsome master's wife, who was probably locked up in the attic, and crazy as a loon.

When the lights went out he felt his heart lurch in his chest and a voice whispered to him from deep in his mind, from the place where the nightmares which now haunted him every time he fell asleep lay in wait: *He's coming for you . . . he's out there now, on the highways of the night . . . the highways in hiding . . . the dark man . . .*

He dropped the paperback on the desk and went out into the street. The last of the daylight hadn't gone out of the sky yet, but twilight was nearly over. All the streetlights were dark. The fluorescents in the drugstore, which had burned night and day, were also gone. The subdued thrum of the junction boxes atop the power poles was also gone; this was something Nick verified by putting his hand on one and feeling nothing but wood. The vibration, which was to him a kind of hearing, had ceased.

There were candles in the office supply cabinet, a whole box of them, but the thought of candles did not comfort Nick very much. The fact of the lights going out had hit him very hard and now he stood looking to the west, silently begging the light not to desert him and leave him in this dark graveyard.

But the light did go. Nick could no longer even pretend there was a little light left in the sky by ten past nine, and he went back to the office and fumbled his way to the cabinet where the candles were. He was feeling around on one of the shelves for the right box when the door behind him burst open and Ray Booth staggered inside, his face black and puffy, his LSU ring still glistening on his finger. He had been laid up in the woods close to town ever since the night of June twenty-second, a week ago. By the morning of the twenty-fourth, he had been feeling sick, and at last, this evening, hunger and fear for his life had driven him down to town, where he had seen no one at all but the goddamn mutie freak who had gotten him into this fix in the first place. The mutie had been crossing the town square just as big as Billy-be-damned, walking as if he owned the town where Ray had lived most of his life, the sheriff's pistol holstered at his right hip and secured to his thigh with a gunslinger's tie-down. Maybe he thought he *did* own the town. Ray suspected he was going to die of whatever had taken everyone else off, but first he was going to show the goddamn freak that he didn't own jack-shit.

Nick's back was turned, and he had no idea he was no longer alone in Sheriff Baker's office until the hands closed around his neck and locked there. The box he had just picked up fell out of his hands, wax candles breaking and rolling everywhere on the floor. He was half-strangled before he got over his first terror and he felt sudden certainty that the black creature from his dreams had come to life: some fiend from the basement of hell was behind him, and had wrapped its scaled claws around his neck as soon as the power had failed.

Then, convulsively, instinctively, he put his own hands over the hands that were throttling him and tried to pull them free. Hot breath blew against his right ear, making a windtunnel there which he could feel but not hear. He caught one clogged and rasping breath before the hands clamped tight again.

The two of them swayed in the black like dark dancers. Ray Booth could feel his strength ebbing as the kid struggled. His head was pounding. If he didn't finish the mutie quick, he would never finish him at all. He throttled the scrawny kid's neck with all the force left in his hands.

Nick felt the world going away. The pain in his throat, which had been sharp at first, was now numb and far off – almost pleasant. He stamped his booted heel down hard on one of Booth's feet, and leaned his weight back against the big man at the same time. Booth was forced back a step. One of his feet came down on a candle. It rolled away under him and he crashed to the floor with Nick back-to on top of him. His hands were finally jarred loose.

Nick rolled away, breathing in harsh rasps. Everything seemed far off and floating, except for the pain in his throat, which had returned in slow, thudding bursts. He could taste slick blood in the back of his throat.

The large humped shape of whoever it was who had jumped him was lurching to its feet. Nick remembered the gun and clawed for it. It was there, but it wouldn't come free. It was stuck in the holster somehow. He pulled at it mightily, now crazed with panic. It went off. The slug furrowed the side of his leg and embedded itself in the floor.

The shape fell on him like dead fate.

Nick's breath exploded out of him, and then large white hands were groping at his face, the thumbs gouging at his eyes. Nick saw a purple gleam on one of those hands in the faint moonlight and his surprised mouth formed the word '*Booth!*' in the darkness. His right hand continued to pull at the gun. He had barely felt the hot sizzle of pain along the length of his thigh.

One of Ray Booth's thumbs jammed into Nick's right eye. Exquisite pain flared and sparkled in his head. He jerked the gun free at last. Booth's thumb, work-callused and hard, turned briskly clock and counterclock, grinding Nick's eyeball.

Nick uttered an amorphous scream which was little more than a violent susurrus of air and jammed the gun into Booth's flabby side. He pulled the trigger and the gun made a muffled *whump!* which Nick felt as a violent recoil that went nowhere but up his arm; the gunsight had snagged in Booth's shirt. Nick saw a muzzle-flash, and a moment later smelled powder and Booth's charring shirt. Ray Booth stiffened, then slumped on top of him.

Sobbing with pain and terror, Nick heaved against the weight on top of him and Booth's body half fell, half slithered off him. Nick crawled out from underneath, one hand clapped over his wounded eye. He lay on the floor for a long time, his throat on fire. His head felt as if giant, merciless calipers had been screwed into his temples.

At last he felt around, found a candle, and lit it with the desk lighter. By its weak yellow glow he could see Ray Booth lying facedown on the floor. He looked like a dead whale cast up on a beach. The gun had made a blackened circle on the side of his shirt the size of a flapjack. There was a great deal of blood. Booth's shadow stretched away to the far wall in the candle's uncertain flicker, huge and unshaped.

Moaning, Nick stumbled into the small bathroom, his hand still clapped over his eye, and then looked into the mirror. He saw blood seeping out from between his fingers and took his hand away reluctantly. He wasn't sure, but he thought he might now be one-eyed as well as deaf and dumb.

He walked back into the office and kicked Ray Booth's limp body.

You fixed me, he told the dead man. First my teeth and now my eye. Are you happy? You would have taken both eyes if you could have done it, wouldn't you? Taken my eyes and left me deaf, dumb, and blind in a world of the dead. How do you like this, home-boy?

He kicked Booth again, and the feel of his foot sinking into that dead meat made him feel ill. After a little bit he retreated to the bunk and sat on it and put his head in his hands. Outside, the dark held hard. Outside, all the lights of the world were going out.

CHAPTER 34

For a long time, for days (how many days? who knew? not the Trashcan Man, that was for sure), Donald Merwin Elbert, known to the intimates of his dim and confusing grade-school past as the Trashcan Man, had wandered up and down the streets of Powtanville, Indiana, cringing from the voices in his head, dodging away and putting up his hands to shield against stones thrown by ghosts.

Hey, Trashcan!

Hey, Trashcan Man, digging you, Trash! Lit any good fires this week? What'd ole lady Semple say when you lit up her pension check, Trash? Hey, Trash-baby, wanna buy some kerosene?

How'd you like those shock treatments down in Terre Haute, Trashie? Trash –

– Hey, Trashcan –

Sometimes he knew those voices weren't real, but sometimes he would cry out loud for them to stop, only to realize that the only voice was his voice, hitting back at him from the houses and store-fronts, bouncing off the cinderblock wall of the Scrubba-Dubba Car Wash where he used to work and where he now sat on the morning of June 30, eating a big sloppy sandwich of peanut butter and jelly and tomatoes and Gulden's Diablo mustard. No voice but his voice, hitting the houses and stores and being turned away like an unwanted guest and thus returning to his own ears. Because, somehow, Powtanville was empty. Everyone was gone . . . or were they? They had always said he was crazy, and that's something a crazy man would think, that his home town was empty except for himself. But his eyes kept returning to the oil tanks on the horizon, huge and white and round, like low clouds. They stood between Powtanville and the road to Gary and Chicago, and he knew what he wanted to do and *that* wasn't a dream. It was bad but not a dream and he wasn't going to be able to help himself.

Burn your fingers, Trash?

Hey, Trashcan Man, don't you know playin with fire makes you wet the bed?

Something seemed to whistle past him and he sobbed and held up his hands, dropping his sandwich into the dust, cringing his cheek into his neck, but there was nothing, there was no one. Beyond the cinderblock wall of the Scrubba-Dubba Car Wash there was only Indiana Highway 130, going to Gary, but first going past the huge Cheery Oil Company storage tanks. Sobbing a little, he picked up his sandwich, brushed the gray dirt off the white bread as best he could, and began to munch it again.

Were they dreams? Once his father had been alive, and the sheriff had cut him down in the street right outside the Methodist Church, and he had had to live with that his whole life.

Hey, Trash, Sheriff Greeley cut your old man down just like a mad dog, you know that, ya fuckin weirdo?

His father had been in O'Toole's and there was some bad talk, and Wendell Elbert had a gun and he murdered the bartender with it, then went home and murdered Trashcan's two older brothers and his sister with it – oh, Wendell Elbert was a strange fellow with a badass temper and he had been getting flaky for a long time before that night, anyone in Powtanville would tell you so, and they would tell you like father like son – and he would have murdered Trashcan's mother, too, only Sally Elbert had fled screaming into the night with five-year-old Donald (later to be known as the Trashcan Man) in her arms. Wendell Elbert had stood on the front steps, shooting at them as they fled, the bullets whining and striking on the road, and on the last shot the cheap pistol, which Wendell had bought from a nigger in a bar located on Chicago's State Street, had exploded in his hand. The flying shrapnel had erased most of his face. He had gone wandering up the street with blood running in his eyes, screaming and waving the remainder of the cheap pistol in one hand, the barrel mushroomed and split like the remains of a novelty exploding cigar, and just as he got to the Methodist Church, Sheriff Greeley pulled up in Powtanville's only squad car and commanded him to stand still and drop the gun. Wendell Elbert pointed the remains of his Saturday night special at the sheriff instead, and Greeley either did not notice that the barrel of the Saturday night special was ruptured or *pretended* not to notice, and either way the result was the same. He gave Wendell Elbert both barrels of his over and under.

Hey, Trash, ya burned ya COCK off yet?

He looked around for whoever had yelled that – it sounded like Carley Yates or one of the kids who hung out with him – except Carley wasn't a kid anymore, any more than he was himself.

Maybe now he could be just Don Elbert again instead of the Trashcan Man, the way Carley Yates was now just Carl Yates who sold cars at the Stout Chrysler-Plymouth dealership here in town. Except that Carl Yates was gone, *everyone* was gone, and maybe it was too late for him to be anyone anymore.

And he wasn't sitting against the wall of the Scrubba-Dubba anymore; he was a mile or more to the northwest of town, walking along 130, and the town of Powtanville was laid out below him like a scale-model community on a kid's HO railroad table. The tanks were only half a mile away and he had a toolkit in one hand and a five-gallon can of gas in the other.

Oh it was so bad but –

So after Wendell Elbert was underground, Sally Elbert had gotten a job at the Powtanville Café and sometime, in the first or second grade, her one remaining chick, Donald Merwin Elbert, had started lighting fires in people's trashcans and running away.

Look out girls here comes the Trashcan Man, he'll burn up ya dresses!

Eeeek! A freeeak!

It wasn't until he was in the third grade or so that the grown-ups found out who was doing it and then the sheriff came around, good old Sheriff Greeley, and he guessed that was how the man who cut his father down in front of the Methodist Church ended up being his stepfather.

Hey, Carley, got a riddle for ya: How can your father kill your father?

I dunno, Petey, how?

I dunno either, but it helps if you're the Trashcan Man!

HeeheehahahaHawHawHaw!

He was standing at the head of the graveled drive now, his shoulders aching from carrying the toolkit and the gas. The sign on the gate read CHEERY PETROLEUM COMPANY, INC. ALL VISITORS MUST CHECK IN AT THE OFFICE! THANKS!

A few cars were parked in the lot, not many. Many were standing on flats. Trashcan Man walked up the drive and slipped through the gate, which was standing ajar. His eyes, blue and strange, were fixed on the spidery stairs that wound around the nearest tank in a spiral, all the way to the top. There was a chain across the bottom of these stairs and another sign swung from the chain. This one said KEEP OFF! PUMPING STATION CLOSED. He stepped over the chain and started up the stairs.

It wasn't right, his mother marrying that Sheriff Greeley. The year he was in the fourth grade he had started lighting fires in mailboxes, that was the year he burned up old Mrs Semple's pension check, and he got caught again. Sally Elbert Greeley went into hysterics the one time her new husband mentioned sending the boy to that place down in Terre Haute *(You think he's crazy! How can a ten-year-old boy be crazy? I think you just want to get rid of him! You got rid of his father and now you want to get rid of him!)*. The only other thing Greeley could do was to bring the boy up on charges and you can't send a kid of ten to reform school, not unless you want him to come out with a size eleven asshole, not unless you wanted your new wife to divorce you.

Up the stairs and up the stairs. His feet made little ringing noises on the steel. He had left the voices down below and no one could throw a stone this high; the cars in the parking lot looked like twinkling Corgi toys. There was only the wind's voice, talking low in his ear and moaning in a vent somewhere; that, and the far-off call of a bird. Trees and open fields spread out all around, all in shades of green only slightly blued by a dreaming morning haze. He was smiling now, happy, as he followed the steel spiral up and up, around and around.

When he got to the tank's flat, circular cap, it seemed that he must be standing directly under the roof of the world, and if he reached up he could scratch blue chalk from the bottom of the sky with his fingernails. He put the gascan and the toolkit down and just looked. From here you could actually see Gary, because the industrial smokes that usually poured from its factory stacks were absent and the air up that way was as clear as it was down here. Chicago was a dream wrapped in summer haze, and there was a faint blue glint to the far north that was either Lake Michigan or just wishful thinking. The air had a soft, golden aroma that made him think of a calm breakfast in a well-lighted kitchen. And soon the day would burn.

Leaving the gas where it was, he took the toolkit over to the pumping machinery and began to puzzle it out. He had an intuitive grasp of machinery; he could handle it the way certain *idiots savants* can multiply and divide seven-digit numbers in their heads. There was nothing thoughtful or cognitive about it; he simply let his eyes wander here and there for a few moments, and then his hands would move with quick, effortless confidence.

Hey, Trashcan, whydja want to burn up a church? Why dintcha burn up the SCHOOL?

When he was in the fifth grade he had started a fire in the living room of a deserted house in the neighboring town of Sedley, and the house burned flat. His stepfather Sheriff Greeley put him in the cooler because a gang of kids had beaten him up and now the grownups wanted to start *(Why, if it hadn't rained, we could have lost half the township thanks to that goddamn firebug kid!)*. Greeley told Sally that Donald would have to go down to that place in Terre Haute and have the tests. Sally said she would leave him if he did that to her baby, her only chick and child, but Greeley went ahead and got the judge to sign the order and so the Trashcan Man left Powtanville for a while, for two years, and his mother divorced the sheriff and later that year the voters disowned the sheriff and Greeley ended up going to Gary to work on an auto assembly line. Sally came to see Trash every week and always cried.

Trashcan whispered: 'There you are, motherfuck,' and then looked around furtively to see if anyone had heard him say that bad swear. Of course no one had, because he was on top of Cheery Oil's #1 storage tank, and even if he had been down on the ground, there was no one left. Except for ghosts. Above him, fat white clouds floated by.

A large pipe projected out of the tangle of pumping machinery, its bore better than two feet, its end threaded to take what the oil people called a clutch-hose. It was strictly for outflow or overflow, but the tank was now full of unleaded gasoline and some of it had trickled out, perhaps a pint, cutting shiny tracks through the light fall of dust on the tank. Trashcan stood back, eyes bright, still gripping a large wrench in one hand and a hammer in the other. He dropped them and they clanged.

He wouldn't need the gasoline he'd brought after all. He

picked up the can, yelled 'Bombs away!' and dropped it over the side. He watched its tumbling, glinting progress with great interest. A third of the way down it hit the stairs, bounced off, and then fell all the way to the ground, turning over and over, spraying amber gas from the side that had been punched open when it hit the stairs.

He turned back to the outflow pipe. He looked at the shiny puddles of gasoline. He took a package of paper matches from his breast pocket and looked at them, guilty and fascinated and excited. There was an ad on the front that said you could get an education in most anything you wanted at the La Salle Correspondence School in Chicago. *I'm standing on a bomb*, he thought. He closed his eyes, trembling in fear and ecstasy, the old cold excitement on him, making his toes and fingers feel numb.

Hey, Trash, ya fuckin firebug!

The place in Terre Haute let him go when he was thirteen. They didn't know if he was cured or not, but they said he was. They needed his room so they could put some other crazy kid in it for a couple of years. Trashcan went home. He was way behind in his schoolwork now, and he couldn't seem to catch the hang of it. They had given him shock treatments in Terre Haute, and when he got back to Powtanville, he couldn't remember things. He would study for a test and then forget half the stuff and flunk with a 60 or 40 or something like that.

For a while he didn't light any fires, though; there was that, at least. Everything had gone back to the way it should be, it seemed. The father-killing sheriff was gone; he was up there in Gary putting headlights on Dodges ('Putting wheels on miscarriages,' his mother sometimes said). His mother was back working in the Powtanville Café. It was all right. Of course, there was CHEERY OIL, the white tanks rising on the horizon like oversized whitewashed tin cans, and behind them the industrial smokes from Gary – where the father-killing sheriff was – as if Gary was already on fire. He often wondered how the Cheery Oil tanks would go up. Three single explosions, loud enough to rip your eardrums to tatters and bright enough to fry your eyeballs in their sockets? Three pillars of fire (father, son, and holy father-killing sheriff) that would burn day and night for months? Or would they maybe not burn at all?

He would find out. The soft summer breeze puffed out the first two matches he lit, and he dropped their blackened stumps onto the riveted steel. Off to his right, near the knee-high railing that circled the edge of the tank, he saw a bug struggling weakly in a puddle of gasoline. I'm like that bug, he thought resentfully, and wondered what kind of a world it was where God would not only let you be caught in a big sticky mess like a bug in a puddle of gas, but leave you there alive and struggling for hours, maybe days . . . or in his case, for years. It was a world that deserved to burn, that was what. He stood, head bowed, a third match ready to strike when the breeze died.

For a while when he came back he was called *loony* and *halfwit* and *torchy*, but Carley Yates, who was by then three grades ahead, remembered the trashcans and it was Carley's name that stuck. When he turned sixteen he left school with his mother's permission (*What do you expect? They roont him down there in Terre Haute. I'd sue em if I had the money. Shock treatments, they call it. Goddamned electric chair, I call it!*) and went to work at the Scrubba-Dubba Car Wash: soap the headlights/soap the rocker panels/knock the wipers/wipe the mirrors/hey mister you want hotwax with that? And for a little while longer things went their appointed course. People would yell at him from street corners or passing cars, would want to know what ole lady Semple (now four years in her grave) had said when he lit up her pension check, or if he had wet the bed after he torched that house over in Sedley; and they'd catcall to each other as they lounged in front of the candy store or leaned in the doorway of O'Toole's; they'd holler to each other to hide their matches or butt their smokes because the Trashcan Man was on his way. The voices all became phantom voices, but the rocks were impossible to ignore when they came whizzing from the mouths of dark alleys or from the other side of the street. Once someone had pegged a half-full can of beer at him from a passing car and the beer can had struck him on the forehead and had driven him to his knees.

That was life: the voices, the occasional flying rock, the Scrubba-Dubba. And on his lunch break he would sit where he had been sitting today, eating the BLT his mother had made for him, looking at the Cheery Oil tanks and wondering which way it would be.

That was life, anyway, until one night he found himself in the vestibule of the Methodist Church with a five-gallon can of gasoline, splashing it everywhere – especially on the heaps of old hymnals in the corner – and he had *stopped* and thought, *This is bad, and maybe worse than that, it's STUPID, they'll know who did it, they'd know who did it even if someone else did it, and they'll 'put you away';* he thought about it and smelled gas while the voices fluttered and circled in his head like bats in a haunted belfry. Then a slow smile came to his face and he had upended the gascan and he had run straight up the center aisle with it, the gas spraying out, all the way from the vestibule to the altar he had run, like a groom late to his own wedding and so eager that he had begun to spray hot fluid more properly meant for his soon-to-be marriage bed.

Then he had run back to the vestibule, pulled a single wooden match from his breast pocket, scratched it on the zipper of his jeans, flung the match on the pile of dripping hymnals, direct hit, *kaflump!*, and the next day he was riding to the Northern Indiana Correctional Center for Boys past the black and smoldering ribs of the Methodist Church.

And there was Carley Yates leaning against the light standard across from the Scrubba-Dubba, a Lucky Strike pasted in the corner of his mouth, and Carley had yelled his valedictory, his epitaph, his hail and farewell: *Hey, Trashcan, whydja wanta burn up a church? Why dintcha burn up the SCHOOL?*

He was seventeen when he went to the jail for kids, and when he turned eighteen they sent him over to the state prison, and how long was he there? Who knew? Not the Trashcan Man, that was for sure. No one in stir cared that he had burned the Methodist Church down. There were people in stir who had done much worse. Murder. Rape. Breaking open the heads of old lady librarians. Some of the inmates wanted to do something to him, and some of them wanted him to do something to them. He didn't mind. It happened after the lights were out. One man with a bald head had said he loved him – *I love you, Donald* – and that was sure better than dodging rocks. Sometimes he would think, just as long as I can stay in here forever. But sometimes at night he would dream of CHEERY OIL, and in the dreams it was always a single, thundering explosion followed by two others, and the sound was WHAM! . . . . WHAM! WHAM! Huge, toneless explosions slamming their way into bright daylight, shaping the daylight like the blows of a hammer shaping thin copper. And everyone in town would stop what they were doing and look north, toward Gary, toward where the three tanks stood against the sky like oversized whitewashed tin cans. Carley Yates would be trying to sell a two-year-old Plymouth to a young couple with a baby, and he would stop in mid-spiel and look. The idlers in O'Toole's and in the candy store would crowd outside, leaving their beers and chocolate malteds behind. In the café his mother would pause in front of the cash register. The new boy at the Scrubba-Dubba would straighten from the headlights he had been soaping, the sponge glove still on his hand, looking north as that huge and portentous sound sledge-hammered its way into the thin copper routine of the day: WHAMM! That was his dream.

He became a trusty somewhere along the line, and when the strange sickness came they sent him to the infirmary and some days ago there had been no more sick people because all of those who had been sick were now dead. Everybody was dead or had run off, except for a young guard named Jason Debbins, who sat behind the wheel of a prison laundry truck and shot himself.

And where else did he have to go then, except home?

The breeze pressed softly against his cheek and then died.

He struck another match and dropped it. It landed in a small pool of gasoline and the gas caught. The flames were blue. They spread out delicately, a kind of corona with the burned match stub at its center. Trashcan watched for a moment, paralyzed with fascination, and then he stepped quickly to the stairs that circled around the tank to the bottom, looking back over his shoulder. He could see the pumping machinery through a heat haze now, flickering back and forth like a mirage. The blue flames, no more than two inches high, spread toward the machinery and toward the open pipe in a widening semicircle. The bug's struggles had ended. It was nothing but a blackened husk.

I could let that happen to me.

But he didn't seem to want to. It seemed, vaguely, that there might be another purpose in his life now, something very grand and great. So he felt a touch of fear and he began to descend the steps on the run, his shoes clanging, his hand slipping quickly over the steep, rust-pitted railing.

Down and down, circling, wondering how long until the vapor hanging around the mouth of the outflow pipe would catch, how long before heat great enough for ignition would rush down the pipe's throat and into the tank's belly.

Hair flying back from his forehead, a terrified grin pasted to his face, the wind roaring in his ears, he rushed down. Now he was halfway, racing past the letters CH, letters twenty feet high and lime green against the white of the tank. Down and down, and if his flying feet stuttered or caught on anything, he would tumble like the gascan had tumbled, his bones breaking like dead branches.

The ground came closer, the white gravel circles around the tanks, the green grass beyond the gravel. The cars in the parking lot began to regain their normal size. And still he seemed to be floating, floating in a dream, and he would never reach the bottom, only run and run and get nowhere. He was next to a bomb and the fuse was lit.

From far overhead there came a sudden bang, like a five-inch Fourth of July firecracker. There was a dim clang, and then something whirred past him. It was part of the outflow pipe, he saw with a sharp and almost delicious fear. It was totally black and twisted into a new and excitingly senseless shape by the heat.

He placed one hand on the railing and vaulted over, hearing something snap in his wrist. Sickening pain flowed up his arm to the elbow. He dropped the last twenty-five feet, landed on the gravel, and went sprawling. The gravel scraped skin from his forearms, but he hardly felt it. He was full of moaning, grinning panic now, and the day seemed very bright.

Trashcan Man scrambled up, craning his head around and back, sending his gaze up even as he began to run again. The top of this middle tank had grown yellow hair, and the hair was growing at an amazing rate. The whole thing could blow at any second.

He ran, his right hand flopping on its broken wrist. He leaped over the parking lot curb, and his feet slapped on asphalt. Now he was across the parking lot, his shadow trailing at his feet, and now he was running straight down the wide gravel access road and bolting through the half-open gate and back onto Highway 130. He ran straight across it and flung himself into the ditch on the far side, landing on a soft bed of dead leaves and wet moss, his arms wrapped around his head, the breath tearing in and out of his lungs like stabbing jackknives.

The oil tank blew. Not *WHAMM!* but KA-*WHAP!*, a sound

so huge, yet at the same time so short and guttural, that he felt his eardrums actually press in and his eyeballs press out as the air somehow changed. A second explosion followed, then a third, and Trashcan writhed on the dead leaves and grinned and screamed soundlessly. He sat up, holding his hands over his ears, and sudden wind struck him and slapped him flat with such power that he might have been no more than a piece of litter.

The young saplings behind him bent over backward and their leaves made a frantic whirring sound, like the pennants over a used car lot on a windy day. One or two snapped with small cracking sounds, as if someone was shooting a target pistol. Burning pieces of the tank started to fall on the other side of the road, some actually on the road. They hit with a clanging noise, the rivets still hanging in some of the chunks of metal, twisted and black, as the outflow pipe had been.

KA-WHAMMM!

Trashcan sat up again and saw a gigantic firetree beyond the Cheery Oil parking lot. Black smoke was billowing from its top, rising straight to an amazing height before the wind could disrupt it and rafter it away. You couldn't look at it without squinting your eyes almost shut and now there was radiant heat baking across the road at him, tightening his skin, making it feel shiny. His eyes were gushing water in protest. Another burning chunk of metal, this one better than seven feet across at its widest and shaped like a diamond, fell out of the sky, landed in the ditch twenty feet to his left, and the dry leaves on top of the wet moss were instantly ablaze.

KA-WHAMM-KA-WHAMM!

If he stayed here he would go up in a jigging, screaming blaze of spontaneous combustion. He scrambled to his feet and began to run along the shoulder of the highway in the direction of Gary, the breath getting hotter and hotter in his lungs. The air had begun to taste like heavy metal. Presently he began to feel his hair to see if he had started burning. The sweet stench of gasoline filled the air, seeming to coat him. Hot wind ripped his clothes. He felt like something trying to escape from a microwave oven. The road doubled before his watering eyes, then trebled.

There was another coughing roar as rising air pressure caused the Cheery Oil Company office building to implode. Scimitars of glass whickered through the air. Chunks of concrete and cinderblock rained out of the sky and hailed on the road. A whizzing piece of steel about the size of a quarter and the thickness of a Mars Bar sliced through Trashcan's shirtsleeve and made a thin scrape on his skin. A piece big enough to have turned his head to guava jelly struck in front of his feet and then bounded away, leaving a good-sized crater behind. Then he was beyond the fallout zone, still running, the blood beating in his head as if his very brain had been sprayed with #2 heating oil and then set ablaze.

KA-WHAMM!

That was another one of the tanks, and the air resistance in front of him seemed to disappear and a large warm hand pushed him firmly from behind, a hand that fitted every contour of his body from heels to head; it *shoved* him forward with his toes barely touching the road, and now his face bore the terrified, pants-wetting grin of someone who has been attached to the world's biggest kite in a high cap of wind and let loose to fly, fly, baby, up into the sky until the wind goes somewhere else, leaving him to scream all the way down in a helpless power-dive.

From behind a perfect fusillade of explosions, God's ammunition dump going up in the flames of righteousness, Satan storming heaven, his artillery captain a fiercely grinning fool with red, flayed cheeks, Trashcan Man by name, never to be Donald Merwin Elbert again.

Sights jittering by: cars wrecked off the road, Mr Strang's blue mailbox with the flag up, a dead dog with its legs up, a powerline down in a cornfield.

The hand was not pushing him quite so hard now. Resistance had come back in front. Trash risked a glance back over his shoulder and saw that the knoll where the oil tanks had stood was a mass of fire. Everything was burning. The road itself seemed to be on fire back there, and he could see the summer trees going up like torches.

He ran another quarter mile, then dropped into a puffing, blowing, shambling walk. A mile farther on he rested, looking back, smelling the glad smell of burning. With no firetrucks and firefighters to put it out, it would go whatever way the wind took it. It might burn for months. Powtanville would go and the fireline would march south, destroying houses, villages, farms, crops, meadows, forests. It might get as far south as Terre Haute, and it would burn that place he had been in. It might burn farther! In fact –

His eyes turned north again, toward Gary. He could see the town now, its great stacks standing quiet and blameless, like strokes of chalk on a light blue blackboard. Chicago beyond that. How many oil tanks? How many gas stations? How many trains standing silent on sidings, full of LP gas and flammable fertilizer? How many slums, as dry as kindling? How many cities beyond Gary and Chicago?

There was a whole country ripe for burning under the summer sun.

Grinning, Trashcan Man got to his feet and began to walk. His skin was already going lobster red. He didn't feel it, although that night it would keep him awake in a kind of exaltation. There were bigger and better fires ahead. His eyes were soft and joyful and utterly crazy. They were the eyes of a man who has discovered the great axle of his destiny and has laid his hands upon it.

CHAPTER 35

'I want to get out of the city,' Rita said without turning around. She was standing on the small apartment balcony, the early morning breeze catching the diaphanous nightgown she wore, blowing yards of the material back through the sliding doors.

'All right,' Larry said. He was sitting at the table, eating a fried egg sandwich.

She turned to him, her face haggard. If she had looked an elegant forty in the park the day he had met her, she now looked like a woman dancing on the chronological knife edge that separates the early sixties from the late. There was a cigarette between her fingers and the tip trembled, making jitters of smoke, as she brought it to her lips and puffed without inhaling.

'I mean it, I'm serious.'

He used his napkin. 'I know you are,' he said, 'and I can dig it. We have to go.'

Her facial muscles sagged into something like relief, and with an almost (but not quite) subconscious distaste, Larry thought it made her look even older.

'When?'

'Why not today?' he asked.

'You're a dear boy,' she said. 'Would you like more coffee?'

'I can get it.'

'Nonsense. You sit right where you are. I always used to get my husband a second cup. He insisted on it. Although I never saw more than his hairline at breakfast. The rest of him was behind *The Wall Street Journal* or some dreadful heavy piece of literature. Something not just meaningful, or deep, but positively gravid with meaning. Böll. Camus. *Milton*, for God's sake. You're a welcome change.' She looked back over her shoulder on the way to the kitchenette; her expression was arch. 'It would be a shame to hide *your* face behind a newspaper.'

He smiled vaguely. Her wit seemed forced this morning, as it had all yesterday afternoon. He remembered meeting her in the park, and how he had thought her conversation seemed like a careless spray of diamonds on the green felt of a billiard table. Since yesterday afternoon it had seemed more like the glitter of zircons, near-perfect pastes that were, after all, only pastes.

'Here you are.' She went to set the cup down, and her hand, still trembling, caused hot coffee to slop out onto the side of his forearm. He jerked back from her with an indrawn feline hiss of pain.

'Oh, I'm sorry –' Something more than consternation on her face; there was something there which could almost be terror.

'It's all right –'

'No, I'll just . . . a cold rag . . . don't . . . sit right there . . . clumsy . . . stupid . . .'

She burst into tears, harsh caws escaping her as if she had witnessed the messy death of her best friend instead of burning him slightly.

He got to his feet and held her, and didn't much care for the convulsive way she hugged him in return. It was almost a clutch. *Cosmic Clutch*, the new album by Larry Underwood, he thought unhappily. Oh shit. You ain't no nice guy. Here we go again.

'I'm sorry, I don't know what's the matter with me, I'm never like this, I'm so sorry . . .'

'It's all right, it's nothing.' He went on soothing her automatically, brushing his hand over her salt-and-pepper hair that would look so much better (all of her would look better, as a matter of fact) after she had put in some heavy time in the bathroom.

Of course he knew what part of the trouble was. It was both personal and impersonal. It had affected him too, but not so suddenly or deeply. With her, it was as if some internal crystal had shattered in the last twenty hours or so.

Impersonally, he supposed, it was the smell. It was coming in through the opening between the apartment living room and the balcony right now, riding the cool early morning breeze that would later give way to still, humid heat if this day was anything like the last three or four. The smell was hard to define in any way that could be correct yet less painful than the naked truth. You could say it was like moldy oranges or spoiled fish or the smell you sometimes got in subway tunnels when the windows were open; none of them were exactly right. That it was the smell of rotting people, thousands of them, decomposing in the heat behind closed doors was putting it right, but you wanted to shy away from that.

The power was still on in Manhattan, but Larry didn't think it would be for much longer. It had gone out in most other places already. Last night he had stood on the balcony after Rita was asleep and from this high up you could see that the lights were out in better than half of Brooklyn and all of Queens. There was a dark pocket across 110th all the way to that end of Manhattan Island. Looking the other way you could still see bright lights in Union City and – maybe – Bayonne, but otherwise, New Jersey was black.

The blackness meant more than the loss of lights. Among other things it meant the loss of the air conditioning, the modern convenience that made it possible to live in this particular hardcore urban sprawl after the middle of June. It meant that all the people who had died quietly in their apartments and tenements were now rotting in ovens, and whenever he thought of that his mind returned to the thing he had seen in the comfort station on Transverse Number One. He had dreamed about that, and in his dreams that black, sweet treat came to life and beckoned him.

On a more personal level, he supposed she was troubled by what they had found when they walked down to the park yesterday. She had been laughing and chatty and gay when they started out, but coming back she had begun to be old.

The monster-shouter had been lying on one of the paths in a huge pool of his own blood. His glasses lay with both lenses shattered beside his stiff and outstretched left hand. Some monster had been abroad after all, apparently. The man had been stabbed repeatedly. To Larry's sickened eyes he looked like a human pincushion.

She had screamed and screamed, and when her hysteria had finally quieted, she insisted that they bury him. So they had. And going back to the apartment, she had been the woman he had found this morning.

'It's all right,' he said. 'Just a little scald. The skin's hardly red.'

'I'll get the Unguentine. There's some in the medicine cabinet.'

She started away, and he grabbed her firmly by the shoulders and made her sit down. She looked up at him from darkly circled eyes.

'What you're going to do is eat,' he said. 'Scrambled eggs, toast, coffee. Then we're going to get some maps and see what's the best way to get off Manhattan. We'll have to walk, you know.'

'Yes . . . I suppose we will.'

He went into the kitchenette, not wanting to look at the mute need in her eyes anymore, and got the last two eggs from the refrigerator. He cracked them into a bowl, tossed the eggshells into the disposal, and began to beat them.

'Where do you want to go?' he asked.

'What? I don't . . .'

'Which way?' he said with a touch of impatience. He added milk to the eggs and put the skillet back on the stove. 'North? New England's that way. South? I don't really see the point in that. We could go –'

A strangled sob. He turned and saw her looking at him, her hands warring with each other in her lap, her eyes shiny. She was trying to control herself and having no luck.

'What's the matter?' he asked, going to her. 'What is it?'

'I don't think I can eat,' she sobbed. 'I know you want me to . . . I'll try . . . but the *smell* . . .'

He crossed the living room, trundled the glass doors closed along their stainless steel tracks, then latched them firmly.

'There,' he said lightly, hoping the annoyance he felt with her didn't show. 'Better?'

'Yes,' she said eagerly. 'That's a lot better. I can eat now.'

He went back to the kitchenette and stirred the eggs, which had begun to bubble. There was a grater in the utensil drawer and he ran a block of American cheese along it, making a small pile that he sprinkled into the eggs. Behind him she moved and a moment later Debussy filled the apartment, too light and pretty for Larry's taste. He didn't care for light classical music. If you were going to have classical shit, you ought to go whole hog and have your Beethoven or your Wagner or someone like that. Why fuck around?

She had asked him in a casual manner what he did for a living . . . the casual manner, he reflected with some resentment, of a person for whom anything so simple as 'a living' had never been a problem. I was a rock and roll singer, he told her, slightly amazed at how painless that past tense was. Sing with this band for a while, then that one. Sometimes a studio gig. She had nodded and that was the end of it. He had no urge to tell her about 'Baby, Can You Dig Your Man?' – that was the past now. The gap between that life and this was so large he hadn't really comprehended it yet. In that life he had been running away from a cocaine dealer; in this one he could bury a man in Central Park and accept that (more or less) as a matter of course.

He put the eggs on a plate, added a cup of instant coffee with a lot of cream and sugar, the way she liked it (Larry himself subscribed to the trucker's credo of 'if you wanted a cup of cream and sugar, whydja ask for coffee?'), and brought it to the table. She was sitting on a hassock, holding her elbows and facing the stereo. Debussy strained out of the speakers like melted butter.

'Soup's on,' he called.

She came to the table with a wan smile, looked at the eggs the way a track and field runner might look at a series of hurdles, and began to eat.

'Good,' she said. 'You were right. Thank you.'

'You're more than welcome,' he said. 'Now look. What I'm going to suggest is this. We go down Fifth to Thirty-ninth and turn west. Cross to New Jersey by the Lincoln Tunnel. We can follow 495 northwest to Passaic and . . . those eggs okay? They're not spoiled?'

She smiled. 'They're fine.' She forked more into her mouth, followed it with a sip of coffee. 'Just what I needed. Go ahead, I'm listening.'

'From Passaic we just ankle it west until the roads are clear enough for us to drive. Then I thought we could turn northeast and head up to New England. Make kind of a buttonhook, do you see what I mean? It looks longer, but I think it'll end up saving us a lot of hassles. Maybe take a house on the ocean in Maine. Kittery, York, Wells, Ogunquit, maybe Scarborough or Boothbay Harbor. How does that sound?'

He had been looking out the window, thinking as he spoke, and now he turned back to her. What he saw frightened him badly for a moment – it was as if she'd gone insane. She was smiling, but it was a rictus of pain and horror. Sweat stood out on her face in big round droplets.

'Rita? Jesus, Rita, what –'

'– sorry –' She scrambled up, knocking her chair over, and fled across the living room. One foot hooked the hassock she had been sitting on and it rolled on its side like an oversized checker. She almost fell herself.

'Rita?'

Then she was in the bathroom and he could hear the industrial grinding sound of her breakfast coming up. He slammed his hand flat on the table in irritation, then got up and went in after her. God, he hated it when people puked. It always made you feel like puking yourself. The smell of slightly used American cheese in the bathroom made him want to gag. Rita was sitting on the robin's-egg-blue tile of the floor, her legs folded under her, her head still hanging weakly over the bowl.

She wiped her mouth with a swatch of toilet paper and then looked up at him supplicatingly, her face as pale as paper.

'I'm sorry, I just couldn't eat it, Larry. Really. I'm so sorry.'

'Well Jesus, if you knew it was going to make you do that, why did you *try*?'

'Because you wanted me to. And I didn't want you to be angry with me. But you are, aren't you? You are angry with me.'

His mind went back to last night. She had made love to him with such frantic energy that for the first time he had found himself thinking of her age and had been a little disgusted. It had been like being caught in one of those exercise machines. He had come quickly, almost in self-defense it seemed, and a long while later she had fallen back, panting and unfulfilled. Later, while he was on the borderline of sleep, she had drawn close to him and once again he had been able to smell her sachet, a more expensive version of scent his mother had always worn when they went out to the movies, and she had murmured the thing that had jerked him back from sleep and had kept him awake for another two hours: *You won't leave me, will you? You won't leave me alone?*

Before that she had been good in bed, so good that he was stunned. She had taken him back to this place after their lunch on the day they had met, and what had happened had happened quite naturally. He remembered an instant of disgust when he saw how her breasts sagged, and how the blue veins were prominent (it made him think of his mother's varicose veins), but he had forgotten all about that when her legs came up and her thighs pressed against his hips with amazing strength.

Slow, she had laughed. *The last shall be first and the first last.*

He had been on the verge when she had pushed him off and gotten cigarettes.

What the hell are you doing? he asked, amazed, while old John Thomas waved indignantly in the air, visibly throbbing.

She had smiled. *You've got a free hand, don't you? So do I.*

So they had done that while they smoked, and she chatted

lightly about all manner of things – although the color had come up in her cheeks and after a while her breath had shortened and what she was saying began to drift off, forgotten.

Now, she said, taking his cigarette and her own and crushing them both out. *Let's see if you can finish what you started. If you can't, I'll likely tear you apart.*

He finished it, quite satisfactorily for both of them, and they had slipped off to sleep. He woke up sometime after four and watched her sleeping, thinking that there was something to be said for experience after all. He had done a lot of screwing in the last ten years or so, but what had happened earlier hadn't been screwing. It had been something much better than that, if a little decadent.

Well, she's had lovers, of course.

This had excited him again, and he woke her up.

And so it had been until they had found the monster-shouter, and last night. There had been other things before then, things that troubled him, but which he had accepted. Something like this, he had rationalized it, *if it only makes you a little bit psycho, you're way ahead.*

Two nights ago he had awakened sometime after two and had heard her running a glass of water in the bathroom. He knew she was probably taking another sleeping pill. She had the big red-and-yellow gelatine capsules that were known as 'yellowjackets' on the West Coast. Big downers. He told himself she'd probably been taking them long before the superflu had happened.

And there was the way she followed him from place to place in the apartment, too, even standing in the bathroom door and talking to him while he was showering or relieving himself. He was a private bathroom person, but he told himself that some weren't. A lot of it depended on your upbringing. He would have a talk with her . . . sometime.

But now . . .

Was he going to have to carry her on his back? Christ, he hoped not. She had seemed stronger than that, at least she had at first. It was one of the reasons she had appealed to him so strongly that day in the park . . . the main reason, really. *There's no more truth in advertising*, he thought bitterly. How the hell was he qualified to take care of her when he couldn't even watch out for himself? He'd shown that pretty conclusively after the record had broken out. Wayne Stukey hadn't been shy about pointing it out, either.

'No,' he told her, 'I'm not angry. It's just that . . . you know, I'm not your boss. If you don't feel like eating, just say so.'

'I told you . . . I said I didn't think I could —'

'The fuck you did,' he snapped, startled and angry.

She bent her head and looked at her hands and he knew she was struggling to keep from sobbing because he wouldn't like that. For a moment it made him angrier than ever and he almost shouted: *I'm not your father or your fat-cat husband! I'm not going to take care of you! You've got thirty years on me, for Christ's sake!* Then he felt the familiar surge of self-contempt and wondered what the hell could be the matter with him.

'I'm sorry,' he said. 'I'm an insensitive bastard.'

'No you're not,' she said, and sniffled. 'It's just that . . . all of this is starting to catch up with me. It . . . yesterday, that poor man in the park . . . I thought: no one is ever going to catch the people who did that to him, and put them in jail. They'll just go on and do it again and again. Like animals in the jungle. And it all began to seem very real. Do you understand, Larry? Can you see what I mean?' She turned her tearwet eyes up to him.

'Yes,' he said, but he was still impatient with her, and just a trifle contemptuous. It was a real situation, how could it not be? They were in the middle of it and had watched it develop this far. His own mother was dead; he had watched her die, and was she trying to say that she was somehow more sensitive to all this than he was? He had lost his mother and she had lost the man who brought her Mercedes around, but somehow her loss was supposed to be the greater. Well, that was bullshit. Just bullshit.

'Try not to be angry with me,' she said. 'I'll do better.'

I hope so. I sure do hope so.

'You're fine,' he said, and helped her to her feet. 'Come on, now. What do you say? We've got a lot to do. Feel up to it?'

'Yes,' she said, but her expression was the same as it had been when he offered her the eggs.

'When we get out of the city, you'll feel better.'

She looked at him nakedly. 'Will I?'

'Sure,' Larry said heartily. 'Sure you will.'

They went first-cabin.

Manhattan Sporting Goods was locked, but Larry broke a hole in the show window with a long iron pipe he had found. The burglar alarm brayed senselessly into the deserted street. He selected a large pack for himself and a smaller one for Rita. She had packed two changes of clothes for each of them – it was all he would allow – and he was carrying them in a PanAm flight bag she had found in the closet, along with toothbrushes. The toothbrushes struck him as slightly absurd. Rita was fashionably attired for walking, in white silk deckpants and a shell blouse. Larry wore faded bluejeans and a white shirt with the sleeves rolled up.

They loaded the packs with freeze-dried foods and nothing else. There was no sense, Larry told her, in weighting themselves down with a lot of other stuff – including more clothes – when they could simply take what they wanted on the other side of the river. She agreed wanly, and her lack of interest nettled him again.

After a short interior debate with himself, he also added a .30–.30 and two hundred rounds of ammunition. It was a beautiful gun, and the pricetag he pulled from the trigger-guard and dropped indifferently on the floor said four hundred and fifty dollars.

'Do you really think we'll need that?' she asked apprehensively. She still had the .32 in her purse.

'I think we'd better have it,' he told her, not wanting to say more but thinking about the monster-shouter's ugly end.

'Oh,' she said in a small voice, and he guessed from her eyes that she was thinking about that, too.

'That pack's not too heavy for you, is it?'

'Oh, no. It isn't. Really.'

'Well, they have a way of getting heavier as you walk along. You just say the word and I'll carry it for a while.'

'I'll be all right,' she said, and smiled. After they were on the sidewalk again, she looked both ways and said, 'We're leaving New York.'

'Yes.'

She turned to him. 'I'm glad. I feel like . . . oh, when I was a little girl. And my father would say, "We're going on a trip today." Do you remember how that was?'

Larry smiled a little in return, remembering the evenings his mother would say, 'That Western you wanted to see is down at the Crest, Larry. Clint Eastwood. What do you say?'

'I guess I do remember,' he said.

She stretched up on her toes, and readjusted the pack a little bit on her shoulders.

'The beginning of a journey,' she said, and then so softly he wasn't sure he'd heard her correctly: '*The way leads ever on . . .*'

'What?'

'It's a line from Tolkien,' she said. '*The Lord of the Rings*. I've always thought of it as sort of a gateway to adventure.'

'The less adventure the better,' Larry said, but almost unwillingly he knew what she meant.

Still she was looking at the street. Near this intersection it was a narrow canyon between high stone and stretches of sun-reflecting thermopane, clogged with cars backed up for miles. It was as if everyone in New York had decided at the same time to park in the streets.

She said: 'I've been to Bermuda and England and Jamaica and Montreal and Saigon and to Moscow. But I haven't been on a journey since I was a little girl and my father took my sister Bess and me to the zoo. Let's go, Larry.'

It was a walk that Larry Underwood never forgot. He found himself thinking that she hadn't been so wrong to quote Tolkien at that, Tolkien with his mythic lands seen through the lens of time and half-mad, half-exalted imaginings, peopled with elves and ents and trolls and orcs. There were none of those in New York, but so much had changed, so much was out of joint, that it was impossible not to think of it in terms of fantasy. A man hung from a lamppost at Fifth and East Fifty-fourth, below the park and in a once-congested business district, a placard with the single word LOOTER hung around his neck. A cat lying on top of a hexagonal litter basket (the basket still had fresh-looking advertisements for a Broadway show on its sides) with her kittens, giving them suck and enjoying the midmorning sun. A young man with a big grin and a valise who strolled up to them and told Larry he would give him a million dollars for the use of the woman for fifteen minutes. The million, presumably, was in the valise. Larry unslung the rifle and told him to take his million elsewhere. 'Sure, man. Don't hold it against me, you dig it? Can't blame a guy for tryin, can you? Have a nice day. Hang loose.'

They reached the corner of Fifth and East Thirty-ninth shortly after meeting that man (Rita, with a hysterical sort of good humor, insisted on referring to him as John Bearsford Tipton, a name which meant nothing to Larry). It was nearly noon, and Larry suggested lunch. There was a delicatessen on the corner, but when he pushed the door open, the smell of rotted meat that came out made her draw back.

'I'd better not go in there if I want to save what appetite I have,' she said apologetically.

Larry suspected he could find some cured meat inside – salami, pepperoni, something like that – but after running across 'John Bearsford Tipton' four blocks back, he didn't want to leave her alone for even the short time it would take to go in and check. So they found a bench half a block west, and ate dehydrated fruit and dehydrated strips of bacon. They finished with cheese spread on Ritz crackers and passed a thermos of iced coffee back and forth.

'This time I was really hungry,' she said proudly.

He smiled back, feeling better. Just to be on the move, to be taking some positive action – that was good. He had told her she would feel better when they got out of New York. At the time it had just been something to say. Now, consulting the rise in his own spirits, he guessed it was true. Being in New York was like being in a graveyard where the dead were not yet quiet. The sooner they got out, the better it would be. She would perhaps revert to the way she had been that first day in the park. They would go to Maine on the secondary roads and set up housekeeping in one of those rich-bitch summer houses. North now, and south in September or October. Boothbay Harbor in the summer, Key Biscayne in the winter. It had a nice ring. Occupied with his thoughts, he didn't see her grimace of pain as he stood up and shouldered the rifle he had insisted on bringing.

They were moving west now, their shadows behind them – at first as squat as frogs, beginning to lengthen out as the afternoon progressed. They passed the Avenue of the Americas, Seventh Avenue, Eighth, Ninth, Tenth. The streets were crammed and silent, frozen rivers of automobiles in every color, predominated by the yellow of the taxicabs. Many of the cars had become hearses, their decaying drivers still leaning behind the wheels, their passengers slumped as if, weary of the traffic jam, they had fallen asleep. Larry started to think that maybe they'd want to pick up a couple of motorcycles once they got out of the city: That would give them both mobility and a fighting chance to skirt the worst of the clots of dead vehicles which must litter the highways everywhere.

Always assuming she can run a bike, he thought. And the way things were going, it would turn out she couldn't. Life with Rita was turning out to be a real pain in the butt, at least in some of its aspects. But if push came down to shove, he supposed she could ride pillion behind him.

At the intersection of Thirty-ninth and Seventh, they saw a young man wearing cutoff denim shorts and nothing else lying atop a Ding-Dong Taxi.

'Is he dead?' Rita asked, and at the sound of her voice the young man sat up, looked around, saw them, and waved. They waved back. The young man lay placidly back down.

It was just after two o'clock when they crossed Eleventh Avenue. Larry heard a muffled cry of pain behind him and realized Rita was no longer walking on his left.

She was down on one knee, holding her foot. With something like horror, Larry noticed for the first time that she was wearing expensive open-toed sandals, probably in the eighty-dollar range, just the thing for a four-block stroll along Fifth Avenue while window-shopping, but for a long walk – a hike, really – like the one they had been making . . .

The ankle-straps had chafed through her skin. Blood was trickling down her ankles.

'Larry, I'm s –'

He jerked her abruptly to her feet. 'What were you thinking about?' he shouted into her face. He felt a moment's shame at the miserable way she recoiled, but also a mean sort of pleasure. 'Did you think you could cab back to your apartment if your feet got tired?'

'I never thought –'

'Well, Christ!' He ran his hands through his hair. 'I guess you didn't. You're *bleeding*, Rita. How long has it been hurting?'

Her voice was so low and husky that he had trouble hearing her even in the preternatural silence. 'Since . . . well, since about Fifth and Forty-ninth, I guess.'

'Your feet have been hurting you for twenty fucking blocks and you didn't say anything?'

'I thought . . . it might . . . go away . . . not hurt anymore . . . I didn't want to . . . we were making such good time . . . getting out of the city . . . I just thought . . .'

'You didn't think at all,' he said angrily. 'How much good time are we going to make with you like this? Your fucking feet look like you got fucking crucified.'

'Don't swear at me, Larry,' she said, beginning to sob. 'Please don't . . . it makes me feel so bad when you . . . please don't swear at me.'

He was in an ecstasy of rage now, and later he would not be able to understand why the sight of her bleeding feet had blown all his circuits that way. For the moment it didn't matter. He screamed into her face: 'Fuck! Fuck! Fuck!' The word echoed back from the high-rise apartment buildings, dim and meaningless.

She put her hands over her face and leaned forward, crying. It made him even angrier, and he supposed that part of it was that she really didn't *want* to see: she would just as soon put her hands over her face and let him lead her, why not, there had always been someone around to take good care of Our Heroine, Little Rita. Someone to drive the car, do the marketing, wash out the toilet bowl, do the taxes. So let's put on some of that gagging-sweet Debussy and put our well-manicured hands over our eyes and leave it all up to Larry. Take care of me, Larry, after seeing what happened to the monster-shouter, I've decided I don't want to see anymore. It's all rawther sordid for one of my breeding and background.

He yanked her hands away. She cringed and tried to put them over her eyes again.

'Look at me.'

She shook her head.

'Goddammit, you look at me, Rita.'

She finally did in a strange, flinching way, as if thinking he would now go to work on her with his fists as well as his tongue. The way a part of him felt now, that would be just fine.

'I want to tell you the facts of life because you don't seem to understand them. The fact is, we may have to walk another twenty or thirty miles. The fact is, if you get infected from those scrapes, you could get blood poisoning and die. The fact is, you've got to get your thumb out of your ass and start helping me.'

He had been holding her by the upper arms, and he saw that his thumbs had almost disappeared into her flesh. His anger broke when he saw the red marks that appeared when he let her go. He stepped away, feeling uncertain again, knowing with sick certainty that he had overreacted. Larry Underwood strikes again. If he was so goddamn smart, why hadn't he checked out her footgear before they started out?

Because that's her problem, part of him said with surly defensiveness. No, that wasn't true. It had been *his* problem. Because she didn't know. If he was going to take her with him (and it was only today that he had begun to think how much simpler life would be if he hadn't), he was just going to have to be responsible for her.

Be damned if I will, the surly voice said.

His mother: *You're a taker, Larry.*

The oral hygienist from Fordham, crying out her window after him: *I thought you were a nice guy! You ain't no nice guy!*

There's something left out of you, Larry. You're a taker.

That's a lie! That is a goddamned LIE!

'Rita,' he said, 'I'm sorry.'

She sat down on the pavement in her sleeveless blouse and her white deckpants, her hair looking gray and old. She bowed her head and held her hurt feet. She wouldn't look at him.

'I'm sorry,' he repeated. 'I . . . look, I had no right to say those things.' He did, but never mind. If you apologized, things got smoothed over. It was how the world worked.

'Go on, Larry,' she said, 'don't let me slow you down.'

'I *said* I was sorry,' he told her, his voice a trifle petulant. 'We'll get you some new shoes and some white socks. We'll . . .'

'We'll nothing. Go on.'

'Rita, I'm sorry –'

'If you say that one more time, I'll scream. You're a shit and your apology is *not* accepted. Now go on.'

'I said I was –'

She threw back her head and shrieked. He took a step backward, looking around to see if anyone had heard her, to see if maybe a policeman was running over to see what kind of awful thing that young fellow was doing to the old lady who was sitting on the sidewalk with her shoes off. Culture lag, he thought distractedly, what fun it all is.

She stopped screaming and looked at him. She made a flicking gesture with her hand, as if he was a bothersome fly.

'You better stop,' he said, 'or I really will leave you.'

She only looked at him. He couldn't meet her eyes and so dropped his gaze, hating her for making him do that.

'All right,' he said, 'have a good time getting raped and murdered.'

He shouldered the rifle and started off again, now angling left toward the car-packed 495 entrance ramp, sloping down toward the tunnel's mouth. At the foot of the ramp he saw there had been one hell of a crash; a man driving a Mayflower moving van had tried to butt his way into the main traffic flow and cars were scattered around the van like bowling pins. A burned-out Pinto lay almost beneath the van's body. The van's driver hung halfway out of the cab window, head down, arms dangling. There was a fan of dried blood and puke sprayed out below him on the door.

Larry looked around, sure he would see her walking toward him or standing and accusing him with her eyes. But Rita was gone.

'Fuck you,' he said with nervous resentment. 'I tried to apologize.'

For a moment he couldn't go on; he felt impaled by hundreds of angry dead eyes, staring out at him from all these cars. A snatch of Dylan occurred to him: *'I waited for you inside the frozen traffic . . . when you knew I had some other place to be . . . but where are you tonight, sweet Marie?'*

Ahead, he could see four lanes of westbound traffic disappearing into the black arch of the tunnel, and with something like real dread he saw that the overhead fluorescent bars inside the Lincoln were out. It would be like going into an automobile graveyard. *They would let him get halfway and then they would all begin to stir . . . to come alive . . . he would hear car doors clicking open and then softly chunking closed . . . their shuffling footsteps . . .*

A light sweat broke on his body. Overhead a bird called raucously and he jumped. You're being stupid, he told himself. Kid's stuff, that's what this is. All you have to do is stay on the pedestrian catwalk and in no time at all you'll be –

– *strangled by the walking dead.*

He licked his lips and tried to laugh. It came out badly. He walked five paces toward the place where the ramp joined the highway and then stopped again. To his left was a Caddy, an El Dorado, and a woman with a blackened troll face was staring out at him. Her nose was pressed into a bulb against the glass. Blood and snot had trickled out onto the window. The man who had been driving the Caddy was slumped over the wheel as if looking for something on the floor. All the Caddy's windows were rolled up; it would be like a greenhouse in there. If he opened the door the woman would spill out and break open on the pavement like a sack of rotten melons and the smell would be warm and steamy, wet and crawling with decay.

The way it would smell in the tunnel.

Abruptly Larry turned around and trotted back the way he had come, feeling the breeze he was making cool the sweat on his forehead.

'Rita! Rita, listen! I want to –'

The words died as he reached the top of the ramp. Rita was still gone. Thirty-ninth Street dwindled away to a point. He ran from the south sidewalk to the north, squeezing between bumpers and scrambling over hoods almost hot enough to blister his skin. But the north sidewalk was also empty.

He cupped his hands around his mouth and cried: 'Rita! *Rita!*'

His only answer a dead echo: '*Rita . . . ita . . . ita . . . ita . . .*'

By four o'clock dark clouds had begun to build over Manhattan and the sound of thunder rolled back and forth between the city's cliffs. Lightning forked down at the buildings. It was as if God were trying to frighten the few remaining people out of hiding. The light had become yellow and strange, and Larry didn't like it. His belly was cramped and when he lit a cigarette it trembled in his hand the way the coffee cup had trembled in Rita's this morning.

He was sitting at the street end of the access ramp, leaning his back against the lowest bar of the railing. His pack was on his lap, and the .30–.30 was leaning against the railing beside him. He had thought she would get scared and come back before long, but she hadn't. Fifteen minutes ago he had given up calling her name. The echoes freaked him out.

Thunder rolled again, close this time. A chilly breeze ran its hand over the back of his shirt, which was pasted to his skin with sweat. He was going to have to get inside somewhere or else stop shitting around and go through the tunnel. If he couldn't work up the guts to go through, he'd have to spend another night in the city and go over the George Washington Bridge in the morning, and that was 140 blocks north.

He tried to think rationally about the tunnel. There was nothing in there that was going to bite him. He'd forgotten to pick up a good big flashlight – Christ, you never remembered *everything* – but he did have his butane Bic, and there was a guardrail between the catwalk and the road. Anything else . . . thinking about all those dead people in their cars, for instance . . . that was just panic talking, comic-book stuff, about as sensible as worrying about the boogeyman in the closet.

If that's all you can think about, Larry [he lectured himself], then you're not going to get along in this brave new world. Not at all. You're –

A stroke of lightning split the sky almost directly overhead, making him wince. It was followed by a heavy caisson of thunder. He thought randomly, July 1, this is the day you're supposed to take your sweetie to Coney Island and eat hotdogs by the score. Knock down the three wooden milk bottles with one ball and win the Kewpie doll. The fireworks at night –

A cold splash of rain struck the side of his face and then another hit the back of his neck and trickled inside the collar of his shirt. Dime-sized drops began to hit around him. He stood up, slung the pack over his shoulders, and hoisted the rifle. He was still not sure which way to go – back to Thirty-ninth or into the Lincoln Tunnel. But he had to get undercover somewhere because it was starting to pour.

Thunder broke overhead with a gigantic roar, making him squeal in terror – a sound no different than those made by Cro-Magnon men two million years before.

'You fucking coward,' he said, and trotted down the ramp toward the maw of the tunnel, his head bent forward as the rain began to come harder. It dripped from his hair. He passed the woman with her nose against the El Dorado's passenger window, trying not to look but catching her out of the tail of his eye just the same. The rain drummed on the car roofs like jazz percussion. It was coming down so hard it bounced back up again, causing a light mist-haze.

Larry stopped for a moment just outside the tunnel, undecided and frightened again. Then it began to hail, and that decided him. The hailstones were big, stinging. Thunder bellowed again.

Okay, he thought. *Okay, okay, okay, I'm convinced.* He stepped into the Lincoln Tunnel.

It was much blacker inside than he had imagined it would be. At first the opening behind him cast dim white light ahead and he could see yet more cars, jammed in bumper to bumper (it must have been bad, dying in here, he thought, as claustrophobia wrapped its stealthy banana fingers lovingly around his head and began to first caress and then to squeeze his temples, it must have been really bad, it must have been fucking *horrible*), and the greenish-white tiles that dressed the upward-curving walls. He could see the pedestrian railing to his right, stretching dimly ahead. On his left, at thirty- or forty-foot intervals, were big support pillars. A sign advised him DO NOT CHANGE LANES. There were dark fluorescents embedded in the tunnel's roof, and the blank glass eyes of closed-circuit TV cameras. And as he negotiated the first slow, banked curve, bearing gently to the right, the light grew dimmer until all he could see were muted flashes of chrome. After that the light simply ceased to exist at all.

He fumbled out his Bic, held it up, and spun the wheel. The light it provided was pitifully small, feeding his unease rather than assuaging it. Even with the flame turned up all the way it only gave him a circle of visibility about six feet in diameter.

He put it back in his pocket and kept walking, trailing his hand lightly along the railing. There was an echo in here, too, one he liked even less than the one outside. The echo made it sound like someone was behind him . . . stalking him. He stopped several times, head cocked, eyes wide (but blind), listening until the echo had died off. After a bit he began to shuffle along, not lifting his heels from the concrete, so the echo wouldn't recur.

Sometime after that he stopped again and flicked the lighter close to his wristwatch. It was four-twenty, but he wasn't sure what to make of that. In this blackness time seemed to have no objective meaning. Neither did distance, for that matter; how long was the Lincoln Tunnel, anyway? A mile? Two? Surely it couldn't be two miles under the Hudson River. Let's say a mile. But if a mile was all it was, he should have been at the other end already. If the average man walks four miles an hour, he can walk one mile in fifteen minutes and he'd already been in this stinking hole five minutes longer than that.

'I'm walking a lot slower,' he said, and jumped at the sound of his own voice. The lighter dropped from his hand and clicked onto the catwalk. The echo spoke back, changed into the dangerously jocular voice of an approaching lunatic:

'. . . lot slower . . . lower . . . lower . . .'

'Jesus,' Larry muttered, and the echo whispered back: 'zuss . . . zuss . . . zuss . . .'

He wiped a hand across his face, fighting panic and the urge to give up thought and just run blindly forward. Instead he knelt (his knees popped like pistol shots, frightening him again) and walked his fingers over the miniature topography of the pedestrian catwalk – the chipped valleys in the cement, the ridge of an old cigarette butt, the hill of a tiny tinfoil ball – until at last he happened on his Bic. With an inner sigh he squeezed it tightly in his hand, stood up, and walked on.

Larry was beginning to get himself under control again when his foot struck something stiff and barely yielding. He uttered an inhalatory sort of scream and took two staggering steps backward. He made himself hold steady as he pulled the Bic lighter from his pocket and flicked it. The flame wavered crazily in his trembling grasp.

He had stepped on a soldier's hand. He was sitting with his back against the tunnel wall, his legs splayed across the walkway, a horrible sentinel left here to bar passage. His glazed eyes stared up at Larry. His lips had fallen away from his teeth and he seemed to be grinning. A switchblade knife jutted jauntily from his throat.

The lighter was growing warm in his hand. Larry let it go out. Licking his lips, holding the railing in a deathgrip, he forced himself forward until the toe of his shoe struck the soldier's hand again. Then he stepped over, making a comically large stride, and a kind of nightmarish certainty came over him. He would hear the scrape of the soldier's boots as he shifted, and then the soldier would reach out and clasp his leg in a loose cold grip.

In a shuffling sort of run, Larry went another ten paces and then made himself stop, knowing that if he didn't stop, the panic would win and he would bolt blindly, chased by a terrible regiment of echoes.

When he felt he had himself under some sort of control, he began to walk again. But now it was worse; his toes shrank inside his shoes, afraid that at any second they might come in contact with another body sprawled on the catwalk . . . and soon enough, it happened.

He groaned and fumbled the lighter out again. This time it was much worse. The body his foot had struck was that of an old man in a blue suit. A black silk skullcap had fallen from his balding head into his lap. There was a six-pointed star of beaten silver in his lapel. Beyond him were another half a dozen corpses: two women, a man of middle age, a woman who might have been in her late seventies, two teenage boys.

The lighter was growing too hot to hold any longer. He snapped it off and slipped it back into his pants pocket, where it glowed like a warm coal against his leg. Captain Trips hadn't taken this group off any more than it had taken the soldier back there. He had seen the blood, the torn clothes, the chipped tiles, the bullet holes. They had been gunned down. Larry remembered the rumors that soldiers had blocked off the points of exit from Island Manhattan. He hadn't known whether to believe them or not; he had heard so many rumors last week as things were breaking down.

The situation here was easy enough to reconstruct. They had been caught in the tunnel, but they hadn't been too sick to walk. They got out of their car and began to make their way toward the Jersey side, using the catwalk just as he was doing. There had been a command post, machine-gun emplacement, something.

Had been? Or was now?

Larry stood sweating, trying to make up his mind. The solid darkness provided the perfect theater screen on which the mind could play out its fantasies. He saw: grim-eyed soldiers in germproof suits crouched behind a machine gun equipped with an infrared peeper-scope, their job to cut down any stragglers who tried to come through the tunnel; one single soldier left behind, a suicide volunteer, wearing infrared goggles and creeping toward him with a knife in his teeth; two soldiers quietly loading a mortar with a single poison gas canister.

Yet he couldn't bring himself to go back. He was quite sure that these imaginings were only vapors, and the thought of retracing his steps was insupportable. Surely the soldiers were now gone. The dead one he'd stepped over seemed to support that. But . . .

But what was really troubling him, he supposed, were the bodies directly ahead. They were sprawled all over each other for eight or nine feet. He couldn't just step over them as he had stepped over the soldier. And if he went off the catwalk to go around them, he risked breaking his leg or his ankle. If he was to go on, he would have to . . . well . . . he would have to walk over them.

Behind him, in the darkness, something moved.

Larry wheeled around, instantly engulfed with fear at that single gritting sound . . . a footstep.

'Who's there?' he shouted, unslinging his rifle.

No answer but the echo. When it faded he heard – or thought he did – the quiet sound of breathing. He stood bug-eyed in the dark, the hairs along the nape of his neck turning into hackles. He held his breath. There was no sound. He was beginning to dismiss it as imagination when the sound came again . . . a sliding, quiet footstep.

He fumbled madly for his lighter. The thought that it would make him a target never occurred to him. As he pulled it from his pocket the striker wheel caught on the lining momentarily and the lighter tumbled from his hand. He heard a clink as it struck the railing, and then there was a soft *bonk* as it struck the hood or trunk of a car below.

The sliding footstep came again, a little closer now, impossible to tell how close. Someone coming to kill him and his terror-locked mind gave him a picture of the soldier with the switchblade in his neck, moving slowly toward him in the dark –

The soft, gritting step again.

Larry remembered the rifle. He threw the butt against his shoulder, and began to fire. The explosions were shatteringly loud in the closed space; he screamed at the sound of them but the scream was lost in the roar. Flashbulb images of tile and frozen lanes of traffic exploded one after another like a string of black and white snapshots as fire licked from the muzzle of the .30-.30. Ricochets whined like banshees. The gun whacked his shoulder again and again until it was numb, until he knew that the force of the recoils had turned him on his feet and he was shooting out over the roadway instead of back along the catwalk. He was still unable to stop. His finger had taken over the function of the brain, and it spasmed mindlessly until the hammer began to fall with a dry and impotent clicking sound.

The echoes rolled back. Bright afterimages hung before his eyes in triple exposures. He was faintly aware of the stench of cordite and of the whining sound he was making deep in his chest.

Still clutching the gun he whirled around again, and now it was not the soldiers in their sterile *Andromeda Strain* suits that he saw on the screen of his interior theater but the Morlocks from the Classic Comics version of H. G. Wells's *The Time Machine*, humped and blind creatures coming out of their holes in the ground where engines ran on and on in the bowels of the earth.

He began to struggle across the soft yet stiff barricade of bodies, stumbling, almost falling, clutching the railing, going on. His foot punched through into some dreadful sliminess and there was a gassy, putrid smell that he barely noticed. He went on, gasping.

Then, from behind him, a scream rose in the darkness, freezing him on the spot. It was a desperate, wretched sound, close to the limits of sanity: '*Larry! Oh, Larry, for God's sake –*'

It was Rita Blakemoor.

He turned around. There was sobbing now, wild sobbing that filled the place with fresh echoes. For one wild moment he decided to go on anyway, to leave her. She would find her way out eventually, why burden himself with her again? Then he got hold of himself and shouted, 'Rita! Stay where you are! Do you hear me?'

The sobbing continued.

He stumbled back across the bodies, trying not to breathe, his face twisted in an expression of grimacing disgust. Then he ran toward her, not sure how far he had to go because of the distorting quality of the echo. In the end he almost fell over her.

'Larry —' She threw herself against him and clutched his neck with a strangler's force. He could feel her heart skidding along at a breakneck pace under her shirt. 'Larry Larry don't leave me alone here don't leave me alone in the dark —'

'No.' He held her tightly. 'Did I hurt you? Are . . . are you shot?'

'No . . . I felt the wind . . . one of them went by so close I felt the wind of it . . . and chips . . . tile-chips, I think . . . on my face . . . cut my face . . .'

'Oh Jesus, Rita, I didn't know. I was freaking out in here. The dark. And I lost my lighter . . . you should have called. I could have killed you.' The truth of it came home to him. *'I could have killed you,'* he repeated in stunned revelation.

'I wasn't sure it was you. I went into an apartment house when you went down the ramp. And you came back and called and I almost . . . but I couldn't . . . and then two men came after the rain started . . . I think they were looking for us . . . or for me. So I stayed where I was and when they were gone I thought, maybe they're not gone, maybe they're hiding and looking for me and I didn't dare go out until I started to think you'd get to the other side, and I'd never see you again . . . so I . . . I . . . Larry, you won't leave me, will you? You won't go away?'

'No,' he said.

'I was wrong, what I said, that was wrong, you were right, I should have told you about the sandals, I mean the shoes, I'll eat when you tell me to . . . I . . . I . . . *oooohhhowww —*'

'Shh,' he said, holding her. 'It's all right now. All right.' But in his mind he saw himself firing at her in a blind panic, and thought how easily one of those slugs could have smashed her arm or blown out her stomach. Suddenly he had to go to the bathroom very badly and his teeth wanted to chatter. 'We'll go when you feel like you can walk. Take your time.'

'There was a man . . . I think it was a man . . . I stepped on him, Larry.' She swallowed and her throat clicked. 'Oh, I almost screamed then, but I didn't because I thought it might be one of those men up ahead instead of you. And when you called out . . . the echo . . . I couldn't tell if it was you . . . or . . . or . . .'

'There are more dead people up ahead. Can you stand that?'

'If you're with me. Please . . . if you're with me.'

'I will be.'

'Let's go, then. I want to get out of here.' She shuddered convulsively against him. 'I never wanted anything so badly in my life.'

He felt for her face and kissed her, first her nose, then each eye, then her mouth.

'Thank you,' he said humbly, having not the slightest idea what he meant. 'Thank you. Thank you.'

'Thank you,' she repeated. 'Oh dear Larry. You won't leave me, will you?'

'No,' he said. 'I won't leave you. Just tell me when you feel like you can, Rita, and we'll go together.'

When she felt she could, they did.

They got over the bodies, their arms slung about each other's necks like drunken chums coming home from a neighborhood tavern. Beyond that they came to a blockage of some sort. It was impossible to see, but after running her hands over it, Rita said it might be a bed standing on end. Together they managed to tip it over the catwalk railing. It crashed onto a car below with a loud, echoing bang that made them both jump and clutch each other. Behind where it had been there were more sprawled bodies, three of them, and Larry guessed that these were the soldiers that had shot down the Jewish family. They got over them and went on, holding hands.

A short time later Rita stopped short.

'What's the matter?' Larry asked. 'Is there something in the way?'

'No. I can see, Larry! It's the end of the tunnel!'

He blinked and realized that he could see, too. The glow was dim and it had come so gradually that he hadn't been aware of it until Rita had spoken. He could make out a faint shine on the tiles, and the pale blur of Rita's face closer by. Looking over to the left he could see the dead river of automobiles.

'Come on,' he said, jubilant.

Sixty paces farther along there were more bodies sprawled on the walkway, all soldiers. They stepped over them.

'Why would they only close off New York?' she asked. 'Unless maybe . . . Larry, maybe it only happened in New York!'

'I don't think so,' he said, but felt a touch of irrational hope anyway.

They walked faster. The mouth of the tunnel was ahead of them now. It was blocked by two huge army convoy trucks parked nose to nose. The trucks blotted out much of the daylight; if they hadn't been there, Larry and Rita would have had some light much farther back in the tunnel. There was another sprawl of bodies where the catwalk descended to join the ramp leading outside. They squeezed between the convoy trucks, scrambling over the locked bumpers. Rita didn't look inside, but Larry did. There was a half-assembled tripod machine gun, boxes of ammunition, and canisters of stuff that looked like teargas. Also, three dead men.

As they came outside, a rain-dampened breeze pressed against them, and its wonderfully fresh smell seemed to make it all worth-while. He said so to Rita, and she nodded and put her head against his shoulder for a moment.

'I wouldn't go through there again for a million dollars, though,' she said.

'In a few years you'll be using money for toilet paper,' he said. 'Please don't squeeze the greenbacks.'

'But are you sure —'

'That it wasn't just New York?' He pointed. 'Look.'

The tollbooths were empty. The middle one stood in a heap of broken glass. Beyond them, the westbound lanes were empty for as far as they could see, but the eastbound lanes, the ones which fed into the tunnel and the city they had just left, were crowded with silent traffic. There was an untidy pile of bodies in the breakdown lane, and a number of seagulls stood watch over it.

'Oh dear God,' she said weakly.

'There were as many people trying to get into New York as there were trying to get out of it. I don't know why they bothered blockading the tunnel on the Jersey end. Probably they didn't know why, either. Just somebody's bright idea, busywork —'

But she had sat down on the road and was crying.

'Don't,' he said, kneeling beside her. The experience in the tunnel was still too fresh for him to feel angry with her. 'It's all right, Rita.'

'What is?' she sobbed. 'What is? Just tell me one thing.'

'We're out, anyway. That's something. And there's fresh air. In fact, New Jersey never smelled so good.'

That earned him a wan smile. Larry looked at the scratches on her cheek and temple where the shards of tile had cut her.

'We ought to get you to a drugstore and put some peroxide on those cuts,' he said. 'Do you feel up to walking?'

'Yes.' She was looking at him with a dumb gratitude that made him feel uneasy. 'And I'll get some new shoes. Some sneakers. I'll do just what you tell me, Larry. I want to.'

'I shouted at you because I was upset,' he said quietly. He brushed her hair back and kissed one of the scratches over her right eye. 'I'm not such a bad guy,' he added quietly.

'Just don't leave me.'

He helped her to her feet and slipped an arm around her waist. Then they walked slowly toward the tollbooths and slipped through them, New York behind them and across the river.

CHAPTER 36

There was a small park in the center of Ogunquit, complete with a Civil War cannon and a War Memorial, and after Gus Dinsmore died, Frannie Goldsmith went there and sat beside the duck pond, idly throwing stones in and watching the ripples spread in the calm water until they reached the lily pads around the edges and broke up in confusion.

She had taken Gus to the Hanson house down on the beach the day before yesterday, afraid that if she waited any longer Gus wouldn't be able to walk and would have to spend his 'final confinement,' as her ancestors would have termed it with such grisly yet apt euphemism, in his hot little cubicle near the public beach parking lot.

She had thought Gus would die that night. His fever had been high and he had been crazily delirious, falling out of bed twice and even staggering around old Mr Hanson's bedroom, knocking things over, falling to his knees, getting up again. He cried out to people who were not there, answered them, and watched them with emotions varying from hilarity to dismay until Frannie began to feel that Gus's invisible companions were the real ones and she was the phantom. She had begged Gus to get back into bed, but for Gus she wasn't there. She had to keep stepping out of his way; if she hadn't, he would have knocked her over and walked over her.

At last he had fallen onto the bed and had passed from energetic delirium to a gasping, heavy-breathing unconsciousness that Fran supposed was the final coma. But the next morning when she looked in on him, Gus had been sitting up in bed and reading a paperback Western he had found on one of the shelves. He thanked her for taking care of him and told her earnestly that he hoped he hadn't said or done anything embarrassing the night before.

When she said he hadn't, Gus had looked doubtfully around

the wreckage of the bedroom and told her she was good to say so, anyway. She made some soup, which he ate with gusto, and when he complained of how hard it was to read without his spectacles, which had been broken while he had been taking his turn on the barricade at the south end of town the week before, she had taken the paperback (over his weak protests) and had read him four chapters in a Western by that woman who lived up north in Haven. *Rimfire Christmas*, it was called. Sheriff John Stoner was having problems with the rowdier element in the town of Roaring Rock, Wyoming, it seemed – and, worse, he just couldn't find anything to give his lovely young wife for Christmas.

Fran had gone away more optimistic, thinking that Gus might be recovering. But last night he had been worse again, and he had died at quarter to eight this morning, only an hour and a half ago. He had been rational at the end, but unaware of just how serious his condition was. He had told her longingly that he'd like to have an ice cream soda, the kind his daddy had treated Gus and his brothers to every Fourth of July and again at Labor Day when the fair came to Bangor. But the power was off in Ogunquit by then – it had gone at exactly 9:17 PM on the evening of June 28 by the electric clocks – and there was no ice cream to be had in town. She had wondered if someone in town might not have a gasoline generator with a freezer hooked up to it on an emergency circuit, and even thought of hunting up Harold Lauder to ask him, but then Gus began to breathe his final whooping, hopeless breaths. That went on for five minutes while she held his head up with one hand and a cloth under his mouth with the other to catch the thick expectorations of mucus. Then it was over.

Frannie covered him with a clean sheet and had left him on old Jack Hanson's bed, which overlooked the ocean. Then she had come here and since then had been skipping rocks across the pond, not thinking about much of anything. But she unconsciously realized that it was a *good* kind of not thinking; it wasn't like that strange apathy that had shrouded her on the day after her father had died. Since then, she had been more and more herself. She had gotten a rosebush down at Nathan's House of Flowers and had carefully planted it at the foot of Peter's grave. She thought it would take hold real well, as her father would have said. Her lack of thought now was a kind of rest, after seeing Gus through the last of it. It was nothing like the prelude to madness she had gone through before.

That had been like passing through some gray, foul tunnel full of shapes more sensed than seen; it was a tunnel she never wanted to travel again.

But she would have to think soon about what to do next, and she supposed that thinking would have to include Harold Lauder. Not just because she and Harold were now the last two people in the area, but because she had no idea what would become of Harold without someone to watch out for him. She didn't suppose that she was the world's most practical person, but since she was here she would have to do. She still didn't particularly like him, but at least he had tried to be tactful and had turned out to have some decency. Quite a bit, even, in his own queer way.

Harold had left her alone since their meeting four days ago, probably respecting her wish to grieve for her parents. But she had seen him from time to time in Roy Brannigan's Cadillac, cruising aimlessly from place to place. And twice, when the wind was right, she had been able to hear the clacking of his typewriter from her bedroom window – the fact that it was quiet enough to hear that sound, although the Lauder house was nearly a mile and a half away, seemed to underline the reality of what had happened. She was a little amused that although Harold had latched on to the Cadillac, he hadn't thought of replacing his manual typewriter with one of those quiet humming electric torpedoes.

Not that he could have it now, she thought as she stood up and brushed off the seat of her shorts. Ice cream and electric typewriters were things of the past. It made her feel sadly nostalgic, and she found herself wondering again with a sense of deep bewilderment how such a cataclysm could have taken place in only a couple of weeks.

There *would* be other people, no matter what Harold said. If the system of authority had temporarily broken down, they would just have to find the scattered others and re-form it. It didn't occur to her to wonder why 'authority' seemed to be such a necessary thing to have, any more than it occurred to her to wonder why she had automatically felt responsible for Harold. It just was. Structure was a necessary thing.

She left the park and walked slowly down Main Street toward the Lauder house. The day was warm already, but the air was freshened by a sea breeze. She suddenly wanted to go down to the beach, find a nice piece of kelp, and nibble on it.

'God, you're disgusting,' she said aloud. Of course she wasn't disgusting; she was just pregnant. That was it. Next week it would be Bermuda onion sandwiches. With creamy horseradish on top.

She stopped on the corner, still a block from Harold's, surprised at how long it had been since she had thought of her 'delicate condition.' Before, she had always been discovering that *I'm-pregnant* thought around odd corners, like some unpleasant mess she kept forgetting to clean up: I ought to be sure and get that blue dress to the cleaners before Friday (a few more months and I can hang it in the closet because *I'm-pregnant*); I guess I'll take my shower now (in a few months it'll look like there's a whale in the shower stall because *I'm-pregnant*). I ought to get the oil changed in the car before the pistons fall right out of their sockets or whatever (and I wonder what Johnny down at the Citgo would say if he knew *I'm-pregnant*). But maybe now she had become accustomed to the thought. After all, she was nearly three months along, nearly a third of the way there.

For the first time she wondered with some unease who would help her have her baby.

From behind the Lauder house there came a steady ratcheting *click-clickclick* of a hand mower, and when Fran came around the corner, what she saw was so strange that only her complete surprise kept her from laughing out loud.

Harold, clad only in a tight and skimpy blue bathing suit, was mowing the lawn. His white skin was sheened with sweat; his long hair flopped against his neck (although to do Harold credit it did appear to have been washed in the not-too-distant past). The rolls of fat above the waistband of his trunks and below the legbands jounced up and down wildly. His feet were green with cut grass to above the ankle. His back had gone reddish, although with exertion or incipient sunburn she couldn't tell.

But Harold wasn't just *mowing*; he was *running*. The Lauders' back lawn sloped down to a picturesque, rambling stone wall, and in the middle of it was an octagonal summer-house. She and Amy used to hold their 'teas' there when they were little girls, Frannie remembered with a sudden stab of nostalgia that was unexpectedly painful, back in the days when they could still cry over the ending of *Charlotte's Web* and moan happily over Chuckie Mayo, the cutest boy in school. The Lauders' lawn was somehow English in its greenness and peace, but now a dervish in a blue bathing suit had invaded this pastoral scene. She could hear Harold panting in a way that was alarming to listen to as he turned the northeast corner where the Lauders' back lawn was divided from the Wilsons' by a row of mulberry bushes. He roared down the slope of the lawn, bent over the mower's T-handle. The blades whirred. Grass flew in a green jet, coating Harold's lower legs. He had mowed perhaps half of the lawn; what was left was a diminishing square with the summerhouse in the middle. He turned the corner at the bottom of the hill and then roared back, for a moment obscured from view by the summerhouse, and then reappearing, bent over his machine like a Formula One race driver. About halfway up, he saw her. At exactly the same instant Frannie said timidly: 'Harold?' And she saw that he was in tears.

'Huh!' Harold said – squeaked, actually. She had startled him out of some private world, and for a moment she feared that the startle on top of his exertion would give him a heart attack.

Then he ran for the house, his feet kicking through drifts of mown grass, and she was peripherally aware of the sweet smell it made on the hot summer air.

She took a step after him. 'Harold, what's wrong?'

Then he was bounding up the porch steps. The back door opened, Harold ran inside, and it slammed behind him with a jarring crash. In the silence that descended afterward, a jay called stridently and some small animal made rattling noises in the bushes behind the stone wall. The mower, abandoned, stood with cut grass behind it and high grass before it a little way from the summerhouse where she and Amy had once drunk their Kool-Aid in Barbie's kitchen cups with their little fingers sticking elegantly off into the air.

Frannie stood indecisive for a while and at last walked up to the door and knocked. There was no answer, but she could hear Harold crying somewhere inside.

'Harold?'

No answer. The weeping went on.

She let herself into the Lauders' back hall, which was dark, cool, and fragrant – Mrs Lauder's cold-pantry opened off the hall to the left, and for as long as Frannie could remember there had been the good smell of dried apples and cinnamon back here, like pies dreaming of creation.

'Harold?'

She walked up the hall to the kitchen and Harold was there, sitting at the table. His hands were clutched in his hair, and his green feet rested on the faded linoleum that Mrs Lauder had kept so spotless.

'Harold, what's wrong?'

'Go away!' he yelled tearfully. 'Go away, you don't like me!'

'Yes I do. You're okay, Harold. Maybe not great, but okay.' She paused. 'In fact, considering the circumstances and all, I'd have to say that right now you're one of my favorite people in the whole world.'

This seemed to make Harold cry harder.

'Do you have anything to drink?'

'Kool-Aid,' he said. He sniffed, wiped his nose, and still looking at the table, added: 'It's warm.'

'Of course it is. Did you get the water at the town pump?' Like many small towns, Ogunquit still had a common pump in back of the town hall, although for the last forty years it had been more of an antiquity than a practical source of water. Tourists sometimes took pictures of it. This is the town pump in the little seaside town where we spent our vacation. Oh, isn't that quaint.

'Yeah, that's where I got it.'

She poured them each a glass and sat down. *We should be having it in the summerhouse*, she thought. *We could drink it with our little fingers sticking off into the air.* 'Harold, what's wrong?'

Harold uttered a strange, hysterical laugh and fumbled his Kool-Aid to his mouth. He drained the glass and set it down. 'Wrong? Now what could be wrong?'

'I mean, is it something specific?' She tasted her Kool-Aid and fought down a grimace. It wasn't that warm, Harold must have drawn the water only a short time ago, but he had forgotten the sugar.

He looked up at her finally, his face tear-streaked and still wanting to blubber. 'I want my mother,' he said simply.

'Oh, Harold –'

'I thought when it happened, when she died, "Now that wasn't so bad."' He was gripping his glass, staring at her in an intense, haggard way that was a little frightening. 'I know how terrible that must sound to you. But I never knew *how* I would take it when they passed away. I'm a very sensitive person. That's why I was so persecuted by the cretins at that house of horrors the town fathers saw fit to call a high school. I thought it might drive me mad with grief, their passing, or at least prostrate me for a year . . . my interior sun, so to speak, would . . . would . . . and when it happened, my mother . . . Amy . . . my father . . . I said to myself, "Now that wasn't so bad." I . . . they . . .' He brought his fist down on the table, making her flinch. 'Why can't I say what I mean?' he screamed. 'I've *always* been able to say what I meant! It's a writer's job to carve with language, to hew close to the bone, *so why can't I say what it feels like?*'

'Harold, don't. I know how you feel.'

He stared at her, dumbstruck. 'You know . . . ?' He shook his head. 'No. You couldn't.'

'Remember when you came to the house? And I was digging the grave? I was half out of my mind. Half the time I couldn't even remember what I was doing. I tried to cook some french fries and almost burned the house down. So if it makes you feel better to mow the grass, fine. You'll get a sunburn if you do it in your bathing trunks, though. You're already getting one,' she added critically, looking at his shoulders. To be polite, she sipped a little more of the dreadful Kool-Aid.

He wiped his hands across his mouth. 'I never even liked them that well,' he said, 'but I thought grief was something you felt anyway. Like your bladder's full, you have to urinate. And if close relatives die, you have to be grief-stricken.'

She nodded, thinking that was strange but not inapt.

'My mother was always taken with Amy. She was Amy's friend,' he amplified with unconscious and nearly pitiful childishness. 'And I horrified my father.'

Fran saw how that could be. Brad Lauder had been a huge, brawny man, a foreman at the woolen mill in Kennebunk. He would have had very little idea of what to make of the fat, peculiar son that his loins had produced.

'He took me aside once,' Harold resumed, 'and asked me if I was a queerboy. That's just how he said it. I got so scared I cried, and he slapped my face and told me if I was going to be such a goddamned baby all the time, I'd best ride right out of town. And Amy . . . I think it would be safe to say that Amy just didn't give a shit. I was just an embarrassment when she brought her friends home. She treated me like I was a messy room.'

With an effort, Fran finished her Kool-Aid.

'So when they were gone and I didn't feel too much one way or the other, I just thought I was wrong. "Grief is not a knee-jerk reaction," I said to myself. But I got fooled. I missed them more and more every day. Mostly my mother. If I could just see her . . . a lot of times she wasn't around when I wanted her . . . needed her . . . she was too busy doing things for Amy, or with Amy, but she was never mean to me. So this morning when I got thinking about it, I said to myself, "I'll mow the grass. Then I won't think about it." But I did. And I started to mow faster and faster . . . as if I could outrun it . . . and I guess that's when you came in. Did I look as crazy as I felt, Fran?'

She reached across the table and touched his hand. 'There's nothing wrong with the way you feel, Harold.'

'Are you sure?' He was looking at her again in that wide-eyed, childish stare.

'Yes.'

'Will you be my friend?'

'Yes.'

'Thank God,' Harold said. 'Thank God for that.' His hand was sweaty in hers, and as she thought it, he seemed to sense it, and pulled his hand reluctantly away. 'Would you like some more Kool-Aid?' he asked her humbly.

She smiled her best diplomatic smile. 'Maybe later,' she said.

They had a picnic lunch in the park: peanut butter and jelly sand-wiches, Hostess Twinkies, and a large bottle of Coke each. The Cokes were fine after they had been cooled in the duck pond.

'I've been thinking about what I'm going to do,' Harold said. 'Don't you want the rest of that Twinkie?'

'No, I'm full.'

Her Twinkie disappeared into Harold's mouth in a single bite. His belated grief hadn't affected his appetite, Frannie observed, and then decided that was a rather mean way to think.

'What?' she said.

'I was thinking of going to Vermont,' he said diffidently. 'Would you like to come?'

'Why Vermont?'

'There's a government plague and communicable diseases center there, in a town called Stovington. It's not as big as the one in Atlanta, but it's sure a lot closer. I was thinking that if there were still people alive and working on this flu, a lot of them would be there.'

'Why wouldn't they be dead, too?'

'Well, they might be, they might be,' Harold said rather prissily. 'But in places like Stovington, where they're used to dealing with communicable diseases, they're also used to taking precautions. And if they are still in operation, I would imagine they are looking for people like us. People who are immune.'

'How do you know all that, Harold?' She was looking at him with open admiration, and Harold blushed happily.

'I read a lot. Neither of those places are secret. So what do you think, Fran?'

She thought it was a wonderful idea. It appealed to that uncoalesced need for structure and authority. She immediately dismissed Harold's disclaimer that the people running such an institution might all be dead. They would get to Stovington, they would be taken in, tested, and out of all the tests would come some discrepancy, some difference between them and all the people who had gotten sick and died. It didn't occur to her just then to wonder what earthly good a vaccine could do at this point.

'I think we ought to find a road atlas and see how to get there yesterday,' she said.

His face lit up. For a moment she thought he was going to kiss her, and in that single shining moment she probably would have allowed it, but then the moment passed. In retrospect she was glad.

By the road atlas, where all distance was reduced to finger-lengths, it looked simple enough. Number 1 to 1–95, 1–95 to US 302, and then northwest on 302 through the lake country towns of western Maine, across the chimney of New Hampshire on the same road, and then into Vermont. Stovington was only thirty miles west of Barre, accessible either by Vermont Route 61 or 1–89.

'How far is that, altogether?' Fran asked.

Harold got a ruler, measured, and then consulted the mileage scale.

'You won't believe this,' he said glumly.

'What is it? A hundred miles?'

'Over three hundred.'

'Oh God,' Frannie said. 'That kills my idea. I read somewhere that you could walk through most of the New England states in a single day.'

'It's a gimmick,' Harold said in his most scholarly voice. 'It *is* possible to walk in four states – Connecticut, Rhode Island,

Massachusetts, and just across the Vermont state line – in twenty-four hours, if you do it in just the right way, but it's like solving that puzzle where you have two interlocked nails – it's easy if you know how, impossible if you don't.'

'Where in the world did you get that?' she asked, amused.

'Guinness Book of World Records,' he said disdainfully. 'Otherwise known as the Ogunquit High School Study Hall Bible. Actually, I was thinking of bikes. Or . . . I don't know . . . maybe motor scooters.'

'Harold,' she said solemnly, 'you're a genius.'

Harold coughed, blushing and pleased again. 'We could bike as far as Wells, tomorrow morning. There's a Honda dealership there . . . can you drive a Honda, Fran?'

'I can learn, if we can go slow for a while.'

'Oh, I think it would be very unwise to speed,' Harold said seriously. 'One would never know when one might come around a blind curve and find a three-car smashup blocking the road.'

'No, one never would, would one? But why wait until tomorrow? Why don't we go today?'

'Well, it's past two now,' he said. 'We couldn't get much farther than Wells, and we'd need to outfit ourselves. That would be easier to do here in Ogunquit, because we know where everything is. And we'll need guns, of course.'

It was queer, really. As soon as he mentioned that word, she had thought of the baby. 'Why do we need guns?'

He looked at her for a moment, then dropped his eyes. A red blush was creeping up his neck.

'Because the police and courts are gone and you're a woman and you're pretty and some people . . . some men . . . might not be . . . be gentlemen. That's why.'

His blush was so red now it was almost purple.

He's talking about rape, she thought. *Rape*. But how could anybody want to rape me, *I'm-pregnant*. But no one knew that, not even Harold. And even if you spoke up, said to the intended rapist: *Will you please not do that because I'm-pregnant*, could you reasonably expect the rapist to reply, *Jeez, lady, I'm sorry, I'll go rape some other goil?*

'All right,' she said. 'Guns. But we could still get as far as Wells today.'

'There's something else I want to do here,' Harold said.

★ ★ ★

The cupola atop Moses Richardson's barn was explosively hot. Sweat had been trickling down her body by the time they got to the hayloft, but by the time they reached the top of the rickety flight of stairs leading from the loft to the cupola, it was coursing down her body in rivers, darkening her blouse and molding it to her breasts.

'Do you really think this is necessary, Harold?'

'I don't know.' He was carrying a bucket of white paint and a wide brush with the protective cellophane still on it. 'But the barn overlooks US 1, and that's the way most people would come, I think. Anyway, it can't hurt.'

'It will hurt if you fall off and break your bones.' The heat was making her head ache, and her lunchtime Coke was sloshing around her stomach in a way that was extremely nauseating. 'In fact, it would be the end of you.'

'I won't fall,' Harold said nervously. He glanced at her. 'Fran, you look sick.'

'It's the heat,' she said faintly.

'Then go downstairs, for goodness' sake. Lie under a tree. Watch the human fly as he does his death-defying act on the precipitous ten-degree slope of Moses Richardson's barn roof.'

'Don't joke. I still think it's silly. And dangerous.'

'Yes, but I'll feel better if I go through with it. Go on, Fran.'

She thought: *Why, he's doing it for me.*

He stood there, sweaty and scared, old cobwebs clinging to his naked, blubbery shoulders, his belly cascading over the waistband of his tight bluejeans, determined to not miss a bet, to do all the right things.

She stood on tiptoe and kissed his mouth lightly. 'You be careful,' she said, and then went quickly down the stairs with the Coke sloshing in her belly, up-down-all-around, yeeeecchh; she went quickly, but not so quickly that she didn't see the stunned happiness come up in his eyes. She went down the nailed rungs from the hayloft to the straw-littered barn floor even faster because she knew she was going to puke now, and while *she* knew that it was the heat and the Coke and the baby, what might Harold think if he heard? So she wanted to get outside where he couldn't hear. And she made it. Just.

Harold came down at a quarter to four, his sunburn now flaming red, his arms splattered with white paint. Fran had napped uneasily under an elm in Richardson's dooryard while he worked, never quite going under completely, listening for the rattle of shingles giving way and poor fat Harold's despairing scream as he fell the ninety feet from the barn's roof to the hard ground below. But it never came – thank God – and now he stood proudly before her – lawn-green feet, white arms, red shoulders.

'Why did you bother to bring the paint back down?' she asked him curiously.

'I wouldn't want to leave it up there. It might lead to spontaneous combustion and we'd lose our sign.' And she thought again how determined he was not to miss a single bet. It was just a little bit scary.

They both gazed up at the barn roof. The fresh paint gleamed out in sharp contrast to the faded green shingles, and the words painted there reminded Fran of the signs you sometimes came upon down South, painted across barn roofs – JESUS SAVES or CHEW RED INDIAN. Harold's read:

HAVE GONE TO STOVINGTON, VT. PLAGUE CENTER
US 1 TO WELLS
INTERSTATE 95 TO PORTLAND
US 302 TO BARRE
INTERSTATE 89 TO STOVINGTON
LEAVING OGUNQUIT JULY 2, 1990
         HAROLD EMERY LAUDER
            FRANCES GOLDSMITH

'I didn't know your middle name,' Harold said apologetically.

'That's fine,' Frannie said, still looking up at the sign. The first line had been written just below the cupola window; the last, her name, just above the rain-gutter. 'How did you get that last line on?' she asked.

'It wasn't hard,' he said self-consciously. 'I had to dangle my feet over a little, that's all.'

'Oh, Harold. Why couldn't you have just signed for yourself?'

'Because we're a team,' he said, and then looked at her a little apprehensively. 'Aren't we?'

'I guess we are . . . as long as you don't kill yourself. Hungry?'

He beamed. 'Hungry as a bear.'

'Then let's go eat. And I'll put some baby oil on your sunburn. You're just going to have to wear your shirt, Harold. You won't be able to sleep on that tonight.'

'I'll sleep fine,' he said, and smiled at her. Frannie smiled back. They ate a supper of canned food and Kool-Aid (Frannie made it, and added sugar), and later, when it had begun to get dark, Harold came over to Fran's house with something under his arm.

'It was Amy's,' he said. 'I found it in the attic. I think Mom and Dad gave it to her when she graduated from junior high. I don't even know if it still works, but I got some batteries from the hardware store.' He patted his pockets, which were bulging with EverReady batteries.

It was a portable phonograph, the kind with the plastic cover, invented for teenage girls of thirteen or fourteen to take to beach and lawn parties. The kind of phonograph constructed with 45 singles in mind – the ones made by the Osmonds, Leif Garrett, John Travolta, Shaun Cassidy. She looked at it closely, and felt her eyes filling with tears.

'Well,' she said, 'let's see if it does.'

It did work. And for almost four hours they sat at the opposite ends of the couch, the portable phonograph on the coffee table before them, their faces lit with silent and sorrowful fascination, listening as the music of a dead world filled the summer night.

CHAPTER 37

At first Stu accepted the sound without question; it was such a typical part of a bright summer morning. He had just passed through the town of South Ryegate, New Hampshire, and now the highway wound through a pretty country of overhanging elms that dappled the road with coins of moving sunlight. The underbrush on either side was thick – bright sumac, blue-gray juniper, lots of bushes he couldn't name. The profusion of them was still a wonder to his eyes, accustomed as they were to East Texas, where the roadside flora had nothing like this variety. On the left, an ancient rock wall meandered in and out of the brush, and on the right a small brook gurgled cheerily east. Every now and then small animals would move in the underbrush (yesterday he had been transfixed by the sight of a large doe standing on the white line of 302, scenting the morning air), the birds called raucously. And against that background of sound, the barking dog sounded like the most natural thing in the world.

He walked almost another mile before it occurred to him that the dog – closer now, by the sound – might be out of the ordinary after all. He had seen a great many dead dogs since leaving Stovington, but no live ones. Well, he supposed, the flu had killed most but not all of the people. Apparently it had killed most but not all of the dogs, as well. Probably it would be extremely people-shy by now. When it scented him, it would most likely crawl back into the bushes and bark hysterically at him until Stu left its territory.

He adjusted the straps of the Day-Glo pack he was wearing and refolded the handkerchiefs that lay under the straps at each shoulder. He was wearing a pair of Georgia Giants, and three days of walking had rubbed most of the new from them. On his head was a jaunty, wide-brimmed red felt hat, and there was an army carbine slung across his shoulder. He did not expect to run across marauders, but he had a vague idea that it might be a good idea to have a gun. Fresh meat, maybe. Well, he had seen fresh meat yesterday, still on the hoof, and he had been too amazed and pleased to even think about shooting it.

The pack riding easily again, he went on up the road. The dog sounded as if it was just beyond the next bend. Maybe I'll see him after all, Stu thought.

He had picked up 302 going east because he supposed that sooner or later it would take him to the ocean. He had made a kind of compact with himself: When I get to the ocean, I'll decide what I'm going to do. Until then, I won't think about it at all. His walk, now in its fourth day, had been a kind of healing process. He had thought about taking a ten-speed bike or maybe a motorcycle with which he could thread his way through the occasional crashes that blocked the road, but instead had decided to walk. He had always enjoyed hiking, and his body cried out for exercise. Until his escape from Stovington he had been cooped up for nearly two weeks, and he felt flabby and out of shape. He supposed that sooner or later his slow progress would make him impatient and he would get the bike or motorcycle, but for now he was content to hike east on this road, looking at whatever he wanted to look at, taking five when he wanted to, or in the afternoon, dropping off for a snooze during the hottest part of the day. It was good for him to be doing this. Little by little the lunatic search for a way out was fading into memory, just something that had happened instead of a thing so vivid it brought cold sweat out onto his skin. The memory of that feeling of someone following him had been the hardest to shake. The first two nights on the road he had dreamed again and again of his final encounter with Elder, when Elder had come to carry out his orders. In the dreams Stu was always too slow with the chair. Elder stepped back out of its arc, pulled the trigger of his pistol, and Stu felt a heavy but painless boxing glove weighted with lead shot land on his chest. He dreamed this over and over until he woke unrested in the morning, but so glad to be alive that he hardly realized it. Last night the dream hadn't come. He doubted if the willies would stop all at once, but he thought he might be walking the poison out of his system little by little. Maybe he would never get rid of all of it, but when most of it was gone he felt sure he would be able to think better about what came next, whether he had reached the ocean by then or not.

He came around the bend and there was the dog, an auburn-colored Irish setter. It barked joyously at the sight of Stu and ran up the road, toenails clicking on the composition surface, tail wagging frantically back and forth. It jumped up, placing its forepaws on Stu's belly, and its forward motion made him stagger back a step. 'Whoa, boy,' he said, grinning.

The dog barked happily at the sound of his voice and leaped up again.

'Kojak!' a stern voice said, and Stu jumped and stared around. 'Get down! Leave that man alone! You're going to track all over his shirt! Miserable dog!'

Kojak put all four feet on the road again and walked around Stu with his tail between his legs. The tail was still flipping back and forth in suppressed joy despite its confinement, however, and Stu decided this one would never make much of a canine put-on artist.

Now he could see the owner of the voice – and of Kojak, it seemed like. A man of about sixty wearing a ragged sweater, old gray pants . . . and a beret. He was sitting on a piano stool and holding a palette. An easel with a canvas on it stood before him.

Now he stood up, placed the palette on the piano stool (under his breath Stu heard him mutter, 'Now don't forget and sit on that'), and walked toward Stu with his hand extended. Beneath the beret his fluffy grayish hair bounced in a small and mellow breeze.

'I hope you intend no foul play with that rifle, sir. Glen Bateman, at your service.'

Stu stepped forward and took the outstretched hand (Kojak was growing frisky again, bouncing around Stu but not daring to renew his leaps – not yet, at least). 'Stuart Redman. Don't worry about the gun. I ain't seen enough people to start shootin em. In fact, I ain't seen any, until you.'

'Do you like caviar?'

'Never tried it.'

'Then it's time you did. And if you don't care for it, there's plenty of other things. Kojak, don't jump. I know you're thinking of renewing your crazed leaps – I can read you like a book – but control yourself. Always remember, Kojak, that control is what separates the higher orders from the lower. Control!'

His better nature thus appealed to, Kojak shrank down on his haunches and began to pant. He had a big grin on his doggy face. It had been Stu's experience that a grinning dog is either a biting dog or a damned good dog. And this didn't look like a biting dog.

'I'm inviting you to lunch,' Bateman said. 'You're the first human being I've seen, at least in the last week. Will you stay?'

'I'd be glad to.'

'Southerner, aren't you?'

'East Texas.'

'An Easterner, my mistake.' Bateman cackled at his own wit and turned back to his picture, an indifferent watercolor of the woods across the road.

'I wouldn't sit down on that piano stool, if I were you,' Stu said.

'Shit, no! Wouldn't do at all, would it?' He changed course and headed toward the back of the small clearing. Stu saw there was an orange and white cooler chest in the shade back there, with what looked like a white lawn tablecloth folded on top of it. When Bateman fluffed it out, Stu saw that was just what it was.

'Used to be part of the communion set at the Grace Baptist Church in Woodsville,' Bateman said. 'I liberated it. I don't think the Baptists will miss it. They've all gone home to Jesus. At least all the Woodsville Baptists have. They can celebrate their communion in person now. Although I think the Baptists are going to find heaven a great letdown unless the management allows them television – or perhaps they call it heavenvision up there – on which they can watch Jerry Falwell and Jack van Impe. What we have here is an old pagan communing with nature instead. Kojak, don't step on the tablecloth. Control, always remember that, Kojak. In all you do, make control your watchword. Shall we step across the road and have a wash, Mr Redman?'

'Make it Stu.'

'All right, I will.'

They went down the road and washed in the cold, clear water. Stu felt happy. Meeting this particular man at this particular time seemed somehow exactly right. Downstream from them Kojak lapped at the water and then bounded off into the woods, barking happily. He flushed a wood pheasant and Stu watched it explode up from the brush and thought with some surprise that just maybe everything would be all right. Somehow all right.

He didn't care much for the caviar – it tasted like cold fish jelly – but Bateman also had a pepperoni, a salami, two tins of sardines, some slightly mushy apples, and a large box of Keebler fig bars.

Wonderful for the bowels, fig bars, Bateman said. Stu's bowels had been giving him no grief at all since he'd gotten out of Stovington and started walking, but he liked fig bars anyway, and helped himself to half a dozen. In fact, he ate hugely of everything.

During the meal, which was eaten largely on Saltines, Bateman told Stu he had been an assistant professor of sociology at Woodsville Community College. Woodsville, he said, was a small town ('famous for its community college and its four gas stations,' he told Stu) another six miles down the road. His wife had been dead ten years. They had been childless. Most of his colleagues had not cared for him, he said, and the feeling had been heartily mutual. 'They thought I was a lunatic,' he said. 'The strong possibility that they were right did nothing to improve our relations.' He had accepted the superflu epidemic with equanimity, he said, because at last he would be able to retire and paint full-time, as he had always wanted to do.

As he divided the dessert (a Sara Lee poundcake) and handed Stu his half on a paper plate, he said, 'I'm a horrible painter, horrible. But I simply tell myself that this July there is no one on earth painting better landscapes than Glendon Pequod Bateman, BA, MA, MFA. A cheap ego trip, but mine own.'

'Was Kojak your dog before?'

'No – that would have been a rather amazing coincidence, wouldn't it? I believe Kojak belonged to someone across town. I saw him occasionally, but since I didn't know what his name was, I have taken the liberty of rechristening him. He doesn't seem to mind. Excuse me for a minute, Stu.'

He trotted across the road and Stu heard him splashing in the water. He came back shortly, pantslegs rolled to his knees. He was carrying a dripping six-pack of Narragansett beer in each hand.

'This was supposed to go with the meal. Stupid of me.'

'It goes just as well after,' Stu said, pulling a can off the template. 'Thanks.'

They pulled their ringtabs and Bateman raised his can. 'To us, Stu. May we have happy days, satisfied minds, and little or no low back pain.'

'Amen to that.' They clicked their cans together and drank. Stu thought that a swallow of beer had never tasted so good to him before and probably never would again.

'You're a man of few words,' Bateman said. 'I hope you don't feel that I'm dancing on the grave of the world, so to speak.'

'No,' Stu said.

'I was prejudiced against the world,' Bateman said. 'I admit that freely. The world in the last quarter of the twentieth century had, for me at least, all the charm of an eighty-year-old man dying of cancer of the colon. They say it's a malaise which has struck all Western peoples as the century – any century – draws to a close. We have always wrapped ourselves in mourning shrouds and gone around crying woe to thee, O Jerusalem . . . or Cleveland, as the case may be. The dancing sickness took place during the latter part of the fifteenth century. Bubonic plague – the black death – decimated Europe near the end of the fourteenth. Whooping cough near the end of the seventeenth, and the first known outbreaks of influenza near the end of the nineteenth. We've become so used to the idea of the flu – it seems almost like the common cold to us, doesn't it? – that no one but the historians seems to know that *a hundred years ago it didn't exist.*

'It's during the last three decades of any given century that your religious maniacs arise with facts and figures showing that Armageddon is finally at hand. Such people are always there, of course, but near the end of a century their ranks seem to swell . . . and they are taken seriously by great numbers of people. Monsters appear. Attila the Hun, Genghis Khan, Jack the Ripper, Lizzie Borden. Charles Manson and Richard Speck and Ted Bundy in our own time, if you like. It's been suggested by colleagues even more fanciful than I that Western Man needs an occasional high colonic, a purging, and this occurs at the end of centuries so that he can face the new century clean and full of optimism. And in this case, we've been given a super-enema, and when you think about it, that makes perfect sense. We are not, after all, simply approaching the centenary this time. We are approaching a whole new millennium.'

Bateman paused, considering.

'Now that I think about it, I *am* dancing on the grave of the world. Another beer?'

Stu took one, and thought over what Bateman had said.

'It's not really the end,' he said at last. 'At least, I don't think so. Just . . . intermission.'

'Rather apt. Well said. I'm going back to my picture, if you don't mind.'

'Go ahead.'

'Have you seen any other dogs?' Bateman asked as Kojak came bounding joyously back across the road.

'No.'

'Nor have I. You're the only other person I've seen, but Kojak seems to be one of a kind.'

'If he's alive, there will be others.'

'Not very scientific,' Bateman said kindly. 'What kind of an American are you? Show me a second dog – preferably a bitch – and I'll accept your thesis that somewhere there is a third. But don't show me one and from that posit a second. It won't do.'

'I've seen cows,' Stu said thoughtfully.

'Cows, yes, and deer. But the horses are all dead.'

'You know, that's right,' Stu agreed. He had seen several dead horses on his walk. In some cases cows had been grazing upwind of the bloating bodies. 'Now why should that be?'

'No idea. We all respire in much the same way, and this seems to be primarily a respiratory disease. But I wonder if there isn't some other factor? Men, dogs, and horses catch it. Cows and deer don't. And rats were down for a while but now seem to be coming back.' Bateman was recklessly mixing paint on his palette. 'Cats everywhere, a plague of cats, and from what I can see, the insects are going on pretty much as they always have. Of course, the little *faux pas* mankind commits rarely seem to affect them, anyway – and the thought of a mosquito with the flu is just too ridiculous to consider. None of it makes any surface sense. It's crazy.'

'It sure is,' Stu said, and uncorked another beer. His head was buzzing pleasantly.

'We're apt to see some interesting shifts in the ecology,' Bateman said. He was making the horrible mistake of trying to paint Kojak into his picture. 'Remains to be seen if *Homo sapiens* is going to be able to reproduce himself in the wake of this – it very much remains to be seen – but at least we can get together and try. But is Kojak going to find a mate? Is he ever going to become a proud papa?'

'Jesus, I guess he might not.'

Bateman stood, put his palette on his piano stool, and got a fresh beer. 'I think you're right,' he said. 'There probably are other people, other dogs, other horses. But many of the animals may die without ever reproducing. There may be some animals of those susceptible species who were pregnant when the flu came along, of course. There may be dozens of healthy women in the United States right now who – pardon the crudity – have cakes baking in the oven. But some of the animals are apt to just sink below the point of no return. If you take the dogs out of the equation, the deer – who seem immune – are going to run wild. Certainly there aren't enough men left around to keep the deer population down. Hunting season is going to be canceled for a few years.'

'Well,' Stu said, 'the surplus deer will just starve.'

'No they won't. Not all of them, not even most of them. Not up here, anyway. I can't speak for what might happen in East Texas, but in New England, all the gardens were planted and growing nicely before this flu happened. The deer will have plenty to eat this year and next. Even after that, our crops will germinate wild. There won't be any starving deer for maybe as long as seven years. If you come back this way in a few years, Stu, you'll have to elbow deer out of your way to get up the road.'

Stu worked this over in his mind. Finally he said, 'Aren't you exaggerating?'

'Not on purpose. There may be a factor or factors I haven't taken into consideration, but I honestly don't think so. And we could take my hypothesis about the effect of the complete or almost complete subtraction of the dog population on the deer population and apply it to the relationships between other species. Cats breeding without check. What does that mean? Well, I said rats were down on the Ecological Exchange but making a comeback. If there are enough cats, that may change. A world without rats sounds good at first, but I wonder.'

'What did you mean when you said whether or not people could reproduce themselves was open to question?'

'There are two possibilities,' Bateman said. 'At least two that I see now. The first is that the babies may not be immune.'

'You mean, die as soon as they get into the world?'

'Yes, or possibly *in utero*. Less likely but still possible, the superflu may have had some sterility effect on those of us that are left.'

'That's crazy,' Stu said.

'So's the mumps,' Glen Bateman said dryly.

'But if the mothers of the babies that are . . . are *in utero* . . . if the mothers are immune –'

'Yes, in some cases immunities can be passed on from mother to child just as susceptibilities can. But not in all cases. You just can't bank on it. I think the future of babies now *in utero* is very uncertain. Their mothers are immune, granted, but statistical probability says that most of the fathers were not, and are now dead.'

'What's the other possibility?'

'That we may finish the job of destroying our species ourselves,' Bateman said calmly. 'I actually think that's *very* possible. Not right away, because we're all too scattered. But man is a gregarious, social animal, and eventually we'll get back together, if only so we can tell each other stories about how we survived the great plague of 1990. Most of the societies that form are apt to be primitive dictatorships run by little Caesars unless we're very lucky. A few may be enlightened, democratic communities, and I'll tell you exactly what the necessary requirement for that kind of society in the 1990s and early 2000s is going to be: a community with enough technical people in it to get the lights back on. It could be done, and very easily. This isn't the aftermath of a nuclear war, with everything laid to waste. All the machinery is just sitting there, waiting for someone to come along – the right someone, who knows how to clean the plugs and replace a few burned-out bearings – and start it up again. It's all a question of how many of those who have been spared understand the technology we all took for granted.'

Stu sipped his beer. 'Think so?'

'Sure.' Bateman took a swallow of his own beer, then leaned forward and smiled grimly at Stu. 'Now let me give you a hypothetical situation, Mr Stuart Redman from East Texas. Suppose we have Community A in Boston and Community B in Utica. They are aware of each other, and each community is aware of the conditions in the other community's camp. Society A is in good shape. They are living on Beacon Hill in the lap of luxury because one of their members just happens to be a Con Ed repairman. This guy knows just enough to get the power plant which serves Beacon Hill running again. It would mostly be a matter of knowing which switches to pull when the plant went into an automatic shutdown. Once it's running, it's almost all automated anyhow. The repairman can teach other members of Society A which levers to pull and which gauges to watch. The turbines run on oil, of which there is a glut, because everybody who used to use it is as dead as old Dad's hatband. So in Boston, the juice is flowing. There's heat against the cold, light so you can read at night, refrigeration so you can have your Scotch on the rocks like a civilized man. In fact, life is pretty damn near idyllic. No pollution. No drug problem. No race problem. No shortages. No money or barter problem, because all the goods, if not the services, are out on display and there are enough of them to last a radically reduced society for three centuries. Sociologically speaking, such a group would probably become communal in nature. No dictatorship here. The proper breeding ground for dictatorship, conditions of want, need, uncertainty, privation . . . they simply wouldn't exist. Boston would probably end up being run by a town meeting form of government again.

'But Community B, up there in Utica. There's no one to run the power plant. The technicians are all dead. It's going to take a long time for them to figure out how to make things go again. In the meantime, they're cold at night (and winter is coming), they're eating out of cans, they're miserable. A strongman takes over. They're glad to have him because they're confused and cold and sick. Let *him* make the decisions. And of course he does. He sends someone to Boston with a request. Will they send their pet technician up to Utica to help them get their power plant going again? The alternative is a long and dangerous move south for the winter. So what does Community A do when they get this message?'

'They send the guy?' Stu asked.

'Christ's testicles, *no!* He might be held against his will, in fact it would be extremely likely. In the post-flu world, technological know-how is going to replace gold as the most perfect medium of exchange. And in those terms, Society A is rich and Society B is poor. So what does Society B do?'

'I guess they go south,' Stu said, then grinned. 'Maybe even to East Texas.'

'Maybe. Or maybe they threaten the Boston people with a nuclear warhead.'

'Right,' Stu said. 'They can't get their power plant going, but they can fire a nuclear missile at Beantown.'

Bateman said, 'If it was me, I wouldn't bother with a missile. I'd just try to figure out how to detach the warhead, then drive it to Boston in a station wagon. Think that would work?'

'Dogged if I know.'

'Even if it didn't, there are plenty of conventional weapons around. That's the point. *All* of that stuff is lying around, waiting to be picked up. And if Communities A and B both have pet technicians, they might work up some kind of rusty nuclear exchange over religion, or territoriality or some paltry ideological difference. Just think, instead of six or seven world nuclear powers, we may end up with sixty or seventy of them right here in the continental United States. If the situation were different, I'm sure that there would be fighting with rocks and spiked clubs. But the fact is, all the old soldiers have faded away and left their playthings behind. It's a grim thing to be thinking about, especially after so many grim things have already happened . . . but I'm afraid it's entirely possible.'

A silence fell between them. Far off they could hear Kojak barking in the woods as the day turned on its noontime axis.

'You know,' Bateman said finally, 'I'm fundamentally a cheerful man. Maybe because I have a low threshold of satisfaction. It's made me greatly disliked in my field. I have my faults; I talk too much, as you've heard, and I'm a terrible painter, as you've seen, and I used to be terribly unwise with money. I sometimes spent the last three days before payday eating peanut butter sandwiches and I was notorious in Woodsville for opening savings accounts and then closing them out a week later. But I never really let it get me down, Stu. Eccentric but cheerful, that's me. The only bane of my life has been my dreams. Ever since boyhood I've been plagued by amazingly vivid dreams. A lot of them have been nasty. As a youngster it was trolls under bridges that reached up and grabbed my foot or a witch that turned me into a bird . . . I would open my mouth to scream, and nothing but a string of caws would come out. Do you ever have bad dreams, Stu?'

'Sometimes,' Stu said, thinking of Elder, and how Elder lurched after him in his nightmares, and of the corridors that never ended but only switched back on themselves, lit by cold fluorescents and filled with echoes.

'Then you know. When I was a teenager, I had the regular quota of sexy dreams, both wet and dry, but these were sometimes interspersed with dreams in which the girl I was with would change into a toad, or a snake, or even a decaying corpse. As I grew older I had dreams of failure, dreams of degradation, dreams of suicide, dreams of horrible accidental death. The most recurrent was one where I was slowly being crushed to death under a gas station lift. All simple permutations of the troll-dream, I suppose. I really believe that such dreams are a simple psychological emetic, and the people who have them are more blessed than cursed.'

'If you get rid of it, it doesn't pile up.'

'Exactly. There are all sorts of dream interpretations, Freud's being the most notorious, but I have always believed they served a simple eliminatory function, and not much more — that dreams are the psyche's way of taking a good dump every now and then. And that people who don't dream – or don't dream in a way they can often remember when they wake up – are mentally constipated in some way. After all, the only practical compensation for having a nightmare is waking up and realizing it was all just a dream.'

Stu smiled.

'But lately, I've had an extremely bad dream. It recurs, like my dream of being crushed to death under the lift, but it makes that one look like a pussycat in comparison. It's like no other dream I've ever had, but somehow it's like all of them. As if . . . as if it were the *sum* of all bad dreams. And I wake up feeling bad, as if it wasn't a dream at all, but a vision. I know how crazy that must sound.

'What is it?'

'It's a man,' Bateman said quietly. 'At least, I think it's a man. He's standing on the roof of a high building, or maybe it's a cliff that he's on. Whatever it is, it's so high that it sheers away into mist thousands of feet below. It's near sunset, but he's looking the other way, east. Sometimes he seems to be wearing bluejeans and a denim jacket, but more often he's in a robe with a cowl. I can never see his face, but I can see his eyes. He has red eyes. And I have a feeling that he's looking for *me* – and that sooner or later he will find me or I will be forced to go to him . . . and that will be the death of me. So I try to scream, and . . .' He trailed off with an embarrassed little shrug.

'That's when you wake up?'

'Yes.' They watched Kojak come trotting back, and Bateman patted him while Kojak nosed in the aluminum dish and cleaned up the last of the poundcake.

'Well, it's just a dream, I suppose,' Bateman said. He stood up, wincing as his knees popped. 'If I were being psychoanalyzed, I suppose the shrink would say the dream expresses my unconscious fear of some leader or leaders who will start the whole thing going again. Maybe a fear of technology in general. Because I do believe that all the new societies which arise, at least in the Western world, will have technology as their cornerstone. It's a pity, and it needn't be, but it *will* be, because we are hooked. They won't remember – or won't choose to remember – the corner we had painted ourselves into. The dirty rivers, the hole in the ozone layer, the atomic bomb, the atmospheric pollution. All they'll remember is that once upon a time they could keep warm at night without expending much effort to do it. I'm a Luddite on top of my other failings, you see. But this dream . . . it preys on me, Stu.'

Stu said nothing.

'Well, I want to get back,' Bateman said briskly. 'I'm halfway drunk already, and I believe there will be thunder-showers this afternoon.' He walked to the back of the clearing and rummaged there. A few moments later he came back with a wheelbarrow. He screwed the piano stool down to its lowest elevation, put it in, added his palette, the picnic cooler, and, balanced precariously on top of everything else, his mediocre painting.

'You wheeled that all the way out here?' Stu asked.

'I wheeled it until I saw something I wanted to paint. I go different ways on different days. It's good exercise. If you're going east, why don't you come back to Woodsville and spend the night at my house? We can take turns wheeling the barrow, and I've got yet another six-pack of beer cooling in yonder stream. That ought to get us home in style.'

'I accept,' Stu said.

'Good man. I'll probably talk all the way home. You are in the arms of the Garrulous Professor, East Texas. When I bore you, just tell me to shut up. I won't be offended.'

'I like to listen,' Stu said.

'Then you are one of God's chosen. Let's go.'

So they walked on down 302, one of them wheeling the barrow while the other drank a beer. No matter which was which, Bateman talked, an endless monologue that jumped from topic to topic with hardly a pause. Kojak bounced alongside. Stu would listen for a while, then his thoughts would trail off for a while, following their own tangents, and then his mind would come back. He was disquieted by Bateman's picture of a hundred little enclaves of people, some of them militaristic, living in a country where thousands of doomsday weapons had been left around like a child's set of blocks. But oddly, the thing his mind kept returning to was Glen Bateman's dream, the man with no face on top of the high building – or the cliff-edge – the man with the red eyes, his back to the setting sun, looking restlessly to the east.

He woke up sometime before midnight, bathed in sweat, afraid he had screamed. But in the next room, Glen Bateman's breathing was slow and regular, undisturbed, and in the hallway he could see Kojak sleeping with his head on his paws. Everything was picked out in moonlight so bright it was surreal.

When he woke, Stu had been up on his elbows, and now he lowered himself back to the damp sheet and put an arm over his eyes, not wanting to remember the dream but helpless to avoid it.

He had been in Stovington again. Elder was dead. Everyone was dead. The place was an echoing tomb. He was the only one alive, and he couldn't find the way out. At first he tried to control his panic. *Walk, don't run*, he told himself over and over, but soon he would have to run. His stride was becoming quicker and quicker, and the urge to look back over his shoulder and make sure that it was only the echoes behind him was becoming insuperable.

He walked past closed office doors with names written in black on milky frosted glass. Past an overturned gurney. Past the body of a nurse with her white skirt rucked up to her thighs, her blackened, grimacing face staring at the cold white inverted icecube trays that were the ceiling fluorescents.

At last he began to run.

Faster, faster, the doors slipping by him and gone, his feet pounding on the linoleum. Orange arrows oozing on white cinderblock. Signs. At first they seemed right: RADIOLOGY and CORRIDOR B TO LABS and DO NOT PROCEED BEYOND THIS POINT WITHOUT VALID PASS. And then he was in another part of the installation, a part he had never seen and had never been meant to see. The paint on these walls had begun to peel and flake. Some of the fluorescents were out; others buzzed like flies caught in a screen. Some of the frosted glass office windows were shattered, and through the stellated holes he had been able to see wreckage and bodies in terrible positions of pain. There was blood. These people had not died of the flu. These people had been murdered. Their bodies had sustained punctures and gunshot wounds and the grisly traumas which could only have been inflicted by blunt instruments. Their eyes bulged and stared.

He plunged down a stopped escalator and into a long dark tunnel lined with tile. At the other end there were more offices, but now the doors were painted dead black. The arrows were bright red. The fluorescents buzzed and flickered. The signs read THIS WAY TO COBALT URNS and LASER ARMORY and SIDEWINDER MISSILES and PLAGUE ROOM. Then, sobbing with relief, he saw an arrow pointing around a right-angled turn, and the single blessed word above it: EXIT.

He went around the corner and the door was standing open. Beyond it was the sweet, fragrant night. He plunged toward the door and then, stepping into it, blocking his way, was a man in jeans and a denim jacket. Stu skidded to a stop, a scream locked in his throat like rusty iron. As the man stepped into the glow of the flickering fluorescents, Stu saw that there was only a cold black shadow where his face should have been, a blackness punched by two soulless red eyes. No soul, but a sense of humor. There was that; a kind of dancing, lunatic glee.

The dark man put out his hands, and Stu saw that they were dripping blood.

'Heaven and earth,' the dark man whispered from that empty hole where his face should have been. 'All of heaven and earth.'

Stu had awakened.

Now Kojak moaned and growled softly in the hall. His paws twitched in his sleep, and Stu supposed that even dogs dreamed. It was a perfectly natural thing, dreaming, even an occasional nightmare.

But it was a long time before he could get back to sleep.

CHAPTER 38

As the superflu epidemic wound down, there was a second epidemic that lasted roughly two weeks. This epidemic was most common in technological societies such as the United States, least common in under-developed countries such as Peru or Senegal. In the US the second epidemic took about 16 percent of the superflu survivors. In places like Peru and Senegal, no more than 3 percent. The second epidemic had no name because the symptoms differed wildly from case to case. A sociologist like Glen Bateman might have called this second epidemic 'natural death' or 'those ole emergency room blues.' In a strictly Darwinian sense, it was the final cut – the unkindest cut of all, some might have said.

Sam Tauber was five and a half years old. His mother had died on June the twenty-fourth in the Murfreesboro, Georgia, General Hospital. On the twenty-fifth, his father and younger sister, two-year-old April, had died. On June the twenty-seventh, his older brother Mike died, leaving Sam to shift for himself.

Sam had been in shock ever since the death of his mother. He wandered carelessly up and down the streets of Murfreesboro, eating when he was hungry, sometimes crying. After a while he stopped crying, because crying did no good. It didn't bring the people back. At night his sleep was broken by horrible nightmares in which Papa and April and Mike died over and over, their faces swollen black, a terrible rattling sound in their chests as they strangled on their own snot.

At quarter of ten on the morning of July 2, Sam wandered into a field of wild blackberries behind Hattie Reynold's house. Bemused and vacant-eyed, he zigzagged among blackberry bushes that were almost twice as tall as he was, picking the berries and eating them until his lips and chin were smeared black. The thorns ripped at his clothes and sometimes at his bare flesh, but he barely noticed. Bees hummed drowsily around him. He never saw the old and rotted well-cover half buried in tall grass and blackberry creepers. It gave under his weight with a grinding, splintering crash, and Sam plunged twenty feet down the rock-lined shaft to the dry bottom, where he broke both legs. He died twenty hours later, as much from fear and misery as from shock and hunger and dehydration.

Irma Fayette lived in Lodi, California. She was a lady of twenty-six, a virgin, morbidly afraid of rape. Her life had been one long nightmare since June twenty-third, when looting had broken out in town and there had been no police to stop the looters. Irma had a small house on a side street; her mother had lived there with her until she had died of a stroke in 1985. When the looting began, and the gunshots, and the horrifying sound of drunken men roaring up and down the streets of the main business section on motorcycles, Irma had locked all the doors and then had hidden in the spare room downstairs. Since then she had crept upstairs periodically, quiet as a mouse, to get food or to relieve herself.

Irma didn't like people. If everyone on earth had died but her, she would have been perfectly happy. But that wasn't the case. Only yesterday, after she had begun cautiously to hope that no one was left in Lodi but her, she had seen a gross and drunken man, a hippie man in a T-shirt that said I GAVE UP SEX AND DRINKING AND IT WAS THE SCARIEST 20 MINUTES OF MY LIFE, wandering up the street with a bottle of whiskey in his hand. He had long blond hair which cascaded out from under the gimme cap he was wearing and all the way down to his shoulders. Tucked into the waistband of his tight bluejeans was a pistol. Irma had peeked around the bedroom curtain at him until he was out of sight and then had scurried downstairs to the barricaded spare room as if she had been released from a malign spell.

They were not all dead. If there was one hippie man left, there would be other hippie men. And they would all be rapers. They would rape *her*. Sooner or later they would find her and rape her.

This morning, before first light, she had crept up to the attic where her father's few possessions were stored in cardboard boxes. Her father had been a merchant seaman. He had deserted Irma's mother in the late sixties. Irma's mother had told Irma all about it.

She had been perfectly frank. Her father had been a beast who got drunk and then wanted to rape her. They all did. When you got married, that gave a man the right to rape you anytime he wanted. Even in the daytime. Irma's mother always summed up her husband's desertion in three words, the same words Irma could have applied to the death of almost every man, woman, and child on the face of the earth: 'No great loss.'

Most of the boxes contained nothing but cheap trinkets bought in foreign ports – Souvenir of Hong Kong, Souvenir of Saigon, Souvenir of Copenhagen. There was a scrapbook of photographs. Most of them showed her father on ship, sometimes smiling into the camera with his arms about the shoulders of his fellow beasts. Well, probably the disease that they were calling Captain Trips out here had struck him down in whatever place he had run off to. No great loss.

But there was one wooden box with small gold hinges on it, and in this box was a gun. A .45 caliber pistol. It lay on red velvet, and in a secret compartment below the red velvet were some bullets. They were green and mossy-looking, but Irma thought they would work all right. Bullets were metal. They didn't spoil like milk or cheese.

She loaded the gun under the single cobwebby attic bulb, and then went down to eat her breakfast at her own kitchen table. She would not hide like a mouse in a hole any longer. She was armed. Let the rapers beware.

That afternoon she went out on the front porch to read her book. The name of the book was *Satan Is Alive and Well on the Planet Earth*. It was grim and joyful stuff. The sinners and the ingrates had gotten their just deserts, just as the book said they would. They were all gone. Except for a few hippie rapers, and she guessed she could handle *them*. The gun was by her side.

At two o'clock the man with the blond hair came back. He was so drunk he could hardly stand up. He saw Irma and his face lighted, no doubt thinking of how lucky he had been to finally discover some 'pussy.'

'Hey, baby!' he cried. 'It's just you and me! How long –' Then terror clouded his face as he saw Irma put down her book and raise the .45.

'Hey, listen, put that thing down . . . is it loaded? *Hey –!*'

Irma pulled the trigger. The pistol exploded, killing her instantly. No great loss.

George McDougall lived in Nyack, New York. He had been a teacher of high school mathematics, specializing in remedial work. He and his wife had been practicing Catholics, and Harriett McDougall had borne him eleven children, nine boys and two girls. So between June twenty-second, when his nine-year-old son Jeff had succumbed to what was then diagnosed as 'flu-related pneumonia' and June twenty-ninth, when his sixteen-year-old daughter Patricia (and oh God she had been so young and so achingly beautiful) had succumbed to what everyone – those that were left – was then calling tube-neck, he had seen the twelve people he loved best in the world pass away while he himself remained healthy and feeling fine. He had joked at school about not being able to remember all his kids' names, but the order of their passing was engraved on his memory: Jeff on the twenty-second, Marty and Helen on the twenty-third, his wife Harriett and Bill and George, and Robert and Stan on the twenty-fourth, Richard on the twenty-fifth, Danny on the twenty-seventh, three-year-old Frank on the twenty-eighth, and finally Pat – and Pat had seemed to be getting better, right up to the end.

George thought he would go mad.

He had begun jogging ten years before, on his doctor's advice. He didn't play tennis or handball, paid a kid (one of his, of course) to mow the lawn, and usually drove to the corner store when Harriett needed a loaf of bread. You're putting on weight, Dr Warner had said. Lead in the seat. No good for your heart. Try jogging.

So he had gotten a sweatsuit and had gone jogging every night, for short distances at the start, then longer and longer ones. At first he'd felt self-conscious, sure that the neighbors must be tapping their foreheads and rolling their eyes, and then a couple of the men that he had only known to wave to when they were out watering their lawns came and asked if they could join him – probably there was safety in numbers. By that time, George's two oldest boys had also joined in. It became a sort of neighborhood thing, and although the membership was always evolving as people dropped in and dropped out, it stayed a neighborhood thing.

Now that everyone was gone, he still jogged. Every day. For hours. It was only when he was jogging, concentrating on nothing more than the thud of his tennis shoes on the sidewalk and the swing of his arms and his steady, harsh respiration, that he lost that feeling of impending madness. He could not commit suicide because as a practicing

Catholic he knew that suicide was a mortal sin and God must be saving him for something, so he jogged. Yesterday he had jogged for almost six hours, until he was completely out of breath and almost retching with exhaustion. He was fifty-one, not a young man anymore, and he supposed that so much running was not good for him, but in another, more important way, it was the only thing that *was* any good.

So he had gotten up this morning at first light after a mostly sleepless night (the thought that played over and over in his mind was: Jeff-Marty-Helen-Harriett-Bill-George-Junior-Robert-Stanley-Richard-Danny-Frank-Patty-and-I-thought-she-was-getting-better) and put on his sweatsuit. He went out and began to jog up and down the deserted streets of Nyack, his feet sometimes gritting on broken glass, once leaping over a TV set that lay shattered on the pavement, taking him past residential streets where the shades were drawn and also past the horrible three-car crash at the Main Street intersection.

He jogged at first, but it became necessary to run faster and faster to keep the thoughts behind him. He jogged and then he trotted and then he ran and finally he sprinted, a fifty-one-year-old man with gray hair in a gray sweatsuit and white tennis shoes, fleeing up and down empty streets as if all the devils of hell were after him. At quarter past eleven he suffered a massive coronary thrombosis and fell down dead on the corner of Oak and Pine, near a fire plug. The expression on his face was very like gratitude.

Mrs Eileen Drummond of Clewiston, Florida, got very drunk on DeKuyper crème de menthe on the afternoon of July 2. She wanted to get drunk because if she was drunk she wouldn't have to think about her family, and crème de menthe was the only kind of alcohol she could stand. She had found a baggie filled with marijuana in her sixteen-year-old's room the day before and had succeeded in getting stoned, but being stoned only seemed to make things worse. She had sat in her living room all afternoon, stoned and crying over photographs in her scrapbook.

So this afternoon she drank a whole bottle of crème de menthe and then got sick and threw up in the bathroom and then went to bed and lit a cigarette and fell asleep and burned the house down and she didn't have to think about it anymore, ever. The wind had freshened, and she also burned down most of Clewiston. No great loss.

            ★   ★   ★

Arthur Stimson lived in Reno, Nevada. On the afternoon of the twenty-ninth, after swimming in Lake Tahoe, he stepped on a rusty nail. The wound turned gangrenous. He diagnosed the trouble by smell and tried to amputate his foot. Halfway through the operation he fainted and died of shock and blood loss in the lobby of Toby Harrah's gambling casino, where he had attempted the operation.

In Swanville, Maine, a ten-year-old girl named Candice Moran fell off her bike and died of a fractured skull.

Milton Craslow, a rancher in Harding County, New Mexico, was bitten by a rattlesnake and died half an hour later.

In Milltown, Kentucky, Judy Horton was quite pleased with events. Judy was seventeen years old and pretty. Two years before she had made two serious mistakes: she had allowed herself to get pregnant, and she had allowed her parents to talk her into marrying the boy responsible, a four-eyes engineering student from the state university. At fifteen she had been flattered just to be asked out by a college man (even if he was only a freshman) and for the life of her she couldn't remember why she had allowed Waldo – Waldo Horton, what a yuck name – to 'work his will' on her. And if she was going to be knocked up, why did it have to be him? Judy had also allowed Steve Phillips and Mark Collins to 'work their will' on her; they were both on the Milltown High football team (the Milltown Cougars, to be exact, fight-fight-fight-fight-for-the-dear-blue-and-white) and she was a cheerleader. If it hadn't been for yucky old Waldo Horton, she would have made head cheerleader her junior year, easy. And, getting back to the point, either Steve or Mark would have made more acceptable husbands. They both had broad shoulders and Mark had stone bitchin shoulder-length blond hair. But it was Waldo, it could have been no one but Waldo. All she had to do was look in her diary and do the arithmetic. And after the baby came she wouldn't have even had to do that. It looked just like him. Yucky.

So for two long years she had struggled along, through a variety of crummy jobs in fast food restaurants and motels, while Waldo went to school. It got so she hated Waldo's school most of all, even more than the baby and Waldo himself. If he wanted a family so bad, why couldn't he get out and work? *She* had. But her parents and his wouldn't allow it. Alone, Judy could have sweet-talked him into it (she would have gotten him to promise before she let him touch her in bed), but all four of the in-laws had their noses in things all the time. Oh Judy, things will be so much better when Waldo has a good job. Oh Judy, things would look so much brighter if you'd go to church more often. Oh Judy, eat shit and keep smiling until you get it down. Until you get it *all* down.

Then the superflu had come along and had solved all her problems. Her parents had died, her little boy Petie had died (that was sort of sad, but she got over it in a couple of days), then Waldo's parents had died, and finally Waldo himself had died and she was free. The thought that she herself might die had never crossed her mind, and of course she didn't.

They had been living in a large and rambling apartment house in downtown Milltown. One of the features of the place that sold Waldo on it (Judy, of course, didn't have a say) was a large walk-in meat freezer in the basement. They had taken the apartment in September of 1988, and their apartment was on the third floor, and who always seemed to get stuck taking the roast and the hamburger down to the freezer? Three guesses and the first two don't count. Waldo and Petie had died at home. By that time you couldn't get hospital service unless you were a bigwig and the mortuaries were swamped (creepy old places anyway, Judy wouldn't go near one on a bet), but the power was still on. So she had taken them downstairs and put them in the freezer.

The power had gone off in Milltown three days ago, but it was still fairly cool down there. Judy knew because she went down to look at their dead bodies three or four times a day. She told herself she was just checking. What else could it be? Surely she wasn't gloating?

She went down on the afternoon of July 2 and forgot to put the rubber wedge under the freezer door. The door swung shut behind her and latched. It was then that she noticed, after two years of coming and going down here, that there was no inside knob on the freezer door. By then it was too warm to freeze, but not too cold to starve. So Judy Horton died in the company of her son and husband after all.

Jim Lee of Hattiesburg, Mississippi, hooked up all the electrical outlets in his house to a gasoline generator and then electrocuted himself trying to start it up.

★ ★ ★

Richard Hoggins was a young black man who had lived his entire life in Detroit, Michigan. He had been addicted to the fine white powder he called 'hehrawn' for the last five. During the actual superflu epidemic, he had gone through extreme withdrawal as all the pushers and users he knew died or fled.

On this bright summer afternoon he was sitting on a littered stoop, drinking a warm 7-Up and wishing he had a pop, just a small, minor skinpop.

He began to think about Allie McFarlane, and something he had heard about Allie on the streets, just before the shit hit the fan. People were saying that Allie, who was about the third-biggest in Detroit, had just gotten a fine shipment. Everybody was going to get well. None of that brown shit. China White, all kinds of the stuff.

Richie didn't know for sure where McFarlane would keep a big order like that – it wasn't healthy to know about such things – but he had heard it said at different times in passing that if the cops ever got a search-writ for the Grosse Pointe house that Allie had bought for his great-uncle, Allie would go away until the new moon turned to gold.

Richie decided to take a walk up to Grosse Pointe. After all, there was nothing better to do.

He got the Lake Shore Drive address of one Erin D. McFarlane from the Detroit phone book and walked out there. It was almost dark by the time he made it and his feet hurt. He was no longer trying to tell himself that this was just a casual stroll; he wanted to shoot and he wanted to bad.

There was a gray fieldstone wall around the estate and Richie went over it like a black shadow, cutting his hands on the broken glass embedded in the top. When he broke a window to gain entry, a burglar alarm went off, causing him to flee halfway down the lawn before he remembered there were no cops to answer. He came back, jittery and slicked with sweat.

The main power was off, and there were easily twenty rooms in the fucking place. He'd have to wait until tomorrow to look properly, and it would still take three weeks to dump the place upside down in the proper way. And the stuff probably wasn't even here. Christ. Richie felt sick despair wave through him. But he would at least look in the obvious places.

And in the upstairs bathroom; he found a dozen large plastic bags bulging with white powder. They were in the toilet tank, that old standby. Richie stared at them, sick with desire, dimly thinking that Allie must have been greasing all the right people if he could afford to leave a stash like this in a fucking toilet tank. There was enough dope here to last one man sixteen centuries.

He took one bag into the master bedroom and broke it open on the bedspread. His hands trembled as he got his works out and cooked up. It never occurred to him to wonder how much this stuff was cut. On the street the heaviest hit Richie had ever taken was 12 percent pure, and that had put him into a sleep so deep it was nearly a coma. He hadn't even nodded. Just bang and off he went, outta the blue and into the black.

He injected himself above the elbow and pushed the plunger of his spike home. The stuff was almost 96 percent pure. It hit his bloodstream like a highballing freight and Richie fell down on the bags of heroin, flouring the front of his shirt with it. He was dead six minutes later.

No great loss.

CHAPTER 39

Lloyd Henreid was down on his knees. He was humming and grinning. Every now and then he would forget what he had been humming and the grin would fade and he would sob a little bit, and then he would forget he was crying and go on humming. The song he was humming was 'Camptown Races.' Every now and then, instead of humming or sobbing, he would whisper 'Doo-dah, doo-dah' under his breath. The holding cellblock was utterly quiet except for the humming, the sobbing, the occasional doo-dah, and the soft scrape of the cotleg as Lloyd fumbled with it. He was trying to turn Trask's body around so he could get at the leg. Please, waiter, bring me some more of that cole slaw and another leg.

Lloyd looked like a man who had embarked upon a radical crash diet. His prison coverall hung on his body like a limp sail. The last meal served in the holding cellblock had been lunch eight days ago. Lloyd's skin was stretched tightly across his face, limning every curve and angle of the skull beneath. His eyes were bright and glittering. His lips had drawn back from his teeth. He had an oddly piebald look, because his hair had begun to fall out in clumps. He looked crazy.

'Doo-dah, doo-dah,' Lloyd whispered as he fished with his cotleg. Once upon a time he hadn't known why he had bothered hurting his fingers to unscrew the damn thing. Once upon a time he had thought he had known what real hunger was. That hunger had been nothing but a slight edge to the appetite when compared with this.

'Ride around all night . . . ride around all day . . . doo-dah . . .'

The cotleg snagged the calf of Trask's pantsleg and then pulled free. Lloyd put his head down and sobbed like a child. Behind him, tossed indifferently in one corner, was the skeleton of the rat he had killed in Trask's cell on June 29, five days ago. The rat's long pink tail was still attached to the skeleton. Lloyd had tried repeatedly to eat the tail but it was too tough. Almost all the water in the toilet bowl was gone despite his efforts to conserve it. The cell was filled with the reek of urine; he had been peeing out into the corridor so as not to contaminate his water supply. He had not – and this was understandable enough, considering the radically reduced conditions of his diet – had to move his bowels.

He had eaten the food he had squirreled away too fast. He knew that now. He had thought someone would come. He hadn't been able to believe –

He didn't want to eat Trask. The thought of eating Trask was horrible. Just last night he had managed to slap one of his slippers over a cockroach and had eaten it alive; he had felt it scuttering madly around inside his mouth just before his teeth had crunched it in two. Actually, it hadn't been half bad, much tastier than the rat. No, he didn't want to eat Trask. He didn't want to be a cannibal. It was like the rat. He would get Trask over within reaching distance . . . but just in case. Just in case. He had heard a man could go a long time without food as long as he had water.

(not much water but I won't think about that now not just now no not just now)

He didn't want to die. He didn't want to starve. He was too full of hate.

The hate had built up at a fairly leisurely pace over the last three days, growing with his hunger. He supposed that, if his long-dead pet rabbit had been capable of thought, it would have hated him in the same way (he slept a great deal now, and his sleep was always troubled with dreams of his rabbit, its body swollen, its fur matted, the maggots squirming in its eyes, and worst of all, those bloody paws: when he awoke he would look at his own fingers in dread fascination). Lloyd's hate had coalesced around a simple imagistic concept, and this concept was THE KEY.

He was locked in. Once upon a time it had seemed right that he should be. He was one of the bad guys. Not a *really* bad guy; Poke had been the really bad guy. Small shit was the worst he would have done without Poke. Still, he shared a certain amount of the blame. There had been Gorgeous George in Vegas, and the three people in the white Continental – he had been in on that, and he supposed he had owned some of that heat. He supposed he deserved to take a fall, do a little time. It wasn't something you volunteered for, but when they had you cold they gave you the bullet and you ate it. Like he had told the lawyer, he thought he deserved about twenty for his part in the 'tri-state killspree.' Not in the electric chair, Christ no. The thought of Lloyd Henreid riding the lightning was just . . . it was crazy.

But they had THE KEY, that was the thing. They could lock you up and do what they wanted with you.

In the last three days, Lloyd had vaguely begun to grasp the symbolic, talismanic power of THE KEY. THE KEY was your reward for playing by the rules. If you didn't, they could lock you up. It was no different than the *Go to Jail* card in Monopoly. Do not pass Go, do not collect two hundred dollars. And with THE KEY went certain prerogatives. They could take away ten years of your life, or twenty, or forty. They could hire people like Mathers to beat on you. They could even take away your life in the electric chair.

But having THE KEY didn't give them the right to go away and leave you locked up to starve. It didn't give them the right to force you into eating a dead rat and to try to eat the dry ticking of your mattress. It didn't give them the right to leave you in a spot where you might just have to eat the man in the next cell to stay alive (if you can get ahold of him, that is – doo-dah, doo-dah).

There were certain things you just couldn't do to people. Having THE KEY only took you so far and no farther. They had left him here to die a horrible death when they could have let him out. He wasn't a mad dog killer who was going to waste the first person he saw, in spite of what the papers had said. Small shit was the worst he had ever gotten into before meeting Poke.

So he hated, and the hate commanded him to live . . . or at least to try. For a while it seemed to him that the hate and the determination to go on living were useless things, because all of those who had THE KEY had succumbed to the flu. They were beyond the reach of his vengeance. Then, little by little, as he grew hungrier, he realized that the flu wouldn't kill *them*. It would kill the losers like him; it would kill Mathers but not that scumbag screw who had hired Mathers because the screw had THE KEY. It wasn't going to kill the governor or the warden – the guard who said the warden was sick had obviously been a fucking liar. It wasn't going to kill the parole officers, the county sheriffs, or the FBI agents. The flu would not touch those who had THE KEY. It wouldn't dare. But Lloyd would touch them. If he lived long enough to get out of here, he would touch them plenty.

The cotleg snagged in Trask's cuff again.

'Come on,' Lloyd whispered. 'Come on. Come on over here . . . camptown ladies sing dis song . . . all doo-dah day.'

Trask's body slid slowly, stiffly, along the floor of his cell. No fisherman ever played a bonita more carefully or with greater wile than Lloyd played Trask. Once Trask's trousers ripped and Lloyd had to hook on in a new place. But at last his foot was close enough so that Lloyd could reach through the bars and grab it . . . if he wanted to.

'Nothing personal,' he whispered to Trask. He touched Trask's leg. He caressed it. 'Nothing personal, I ain't going to eat you, old buddy. Not less I have to.'

He was not even aware that he was salivating.

Lloyd heard someone in the ashy afterglow of dusk, and at first the sound was so far away and so strange – the clash of metal on metal – that he thought he must be dreaming it. The waking and sleeping states had become very similar to him now; he crossed back and forth across that boundary almost without knowing it.

But then the voice came and he snapped upright on his cot, his eyes flaring wide, huge and lambent in his starved face. The voice came floating down the corridors from God knew how far up in the Administration Wing and then down the stairwell to the hallways which connected the visiting areas to the central cellblock, where Lloyd was. It bobbed serenely through the twice-barred doors and finally reached Lloyd's ears:

'Hooooo-hoooo! Anybody home?'

And strangely, Lloyd's first thought was: *Don't answer. Maybe he'll go away.*

'Anybody home? Going once, going twice? . . . Okay, I'm on my way, just about to shake the dust of Phoenix from my boots –'

At that, Lloyd's paralysis broke. He catapulted off the cot, snatched up the cotleg, and began to beat it frantically on the bars; the vibrations raced up the metal and shivered in the bones of his clenched fist.

'No!' he screamed. 'No! Don't go! Please don't go!'

The voice, closer now, coming from the stairway between the Administration and this floor: 'We'll eat you up, we love you so . . . and oh, someone sounds *so . . . hungry.*' This was followed by a lazy chuckle.

Lloyd dropped the cotleg on the floor and wrapped both hands around the bars of the cell door. Now he could hear the footfalls somewhere up in the shadows, clocking steadily down the hall that led to the holding cellblock. Lloyd wanted to burst into tears of relief . . . after all, he was saved . . . yet it was not joy but fear he felt in his heart, a growing dread that made him wish he had stayed silent. Stayed silent? My God! What could be worse than starvation?

Starvation made him think of Trask. Trask lay sprawled on his back in the ashy afterglow of dusk, one leg stretched stiffly into Lloyd's cell, and an essential subtraction had occurred in the region of that leg's calf. The *fleshy* part of that leg's calf. There were teeth-marks there. Lloyd knew whose teeth had made those marks, but he had only the vaguest memory of lunching on filet of Trask. All the same, powerful feelings of revulsion, guilt, and horror filled him. He rushed across to the bars and pushed Trask's leg back into his own cell. Then, looking over his shoulder to make sure the owner of the voice was not yet in sight, he reached through, and with the dividing bars pressed against his face, he pulled Trask's pantsleg down, hiding what he had done.

Of course there was no great hurry, because the barred gates at the head of the cellblock were shut, and with the power off, the pushbutton wouldn't work. His rescuer would have to go back and find THE KEY. He would have to –

Lloyd grunted as the electric motor which operated the barred gates whined into life. The silence of the cellblock magnified the sound, which ceased with the familiar *clickslam!* of the gates locking open.

Then the steps were clocking steadily up the cellblock walkway.

Lloyd had gone to his cell door again after neatening up Trask; now he involuntarily fell back two steps. He dropped his gaze to the floor outside and what he saw first was a pair of dusty cowboy boots with pointed toes and rundown heels and his first thought was that Poke had had a pair like that.

The boots stopped in front of his cell.

His gaze rose slowly, taking in the faded jeans snugged down over the boots, the leather belt with the brass buckle (various astro-logical signs inside a pair of concentric circles), the jeans jacket with a button pinned to each of the breast pockets – a smiley-smile face on one, a dead pig and the words HOW'S YOUR PORK on the other.

At the same instant Lloyd's eyes reluctantly reached Randall Flagg's darkly flushed face, Flagg screamed *'Boo!'* The single sound floated down the dead cellblock and then rushed back. Lloyd shrieked, stumbled over his own feet, fell down, and began to cry.

'That's all right,' Flagg soothed. 'Hey, man, that's all right. Everything's purely all right.'

Lloyd sobbed: 'Can you let me out? Please let me out. I don't want to be like my rabbit, I don't want to end up like that, it's not fair, if it wasn't for Poke I never would have got into anything but small shit, please let me out, mister, I'll do anything.'

'You poor guy. You look like an advertisement for a summer vacation at Dachau.'

Despite the sympathy in Flagg's voice, Lloyd could not bring himself to raise his eyes beyond the knees of the newcomer's jeans. If he looked into that face again, it would kill him. It was the face of a devil.

'Please,' Lloyd mumbled. 'Please let me out. I'm starving.'

'How long you been shitcanned, my friend?'

'I don't know,' Lloyd said, wiping his eyes with thin fingers. 'A long time.'

'How come you're not dead already?'

'I knew what was coming,' Lloyd told the bluejeaned legs as he drew the last tattered shreds of his cunning around him. 'I saved up my food. That's what.'

'Didn't happen to have a chomp on this fine fellow in the next cell, by any chance?'

'What?' Lloyd croaked. '*What?* No! Christ's sake! What do you think I *am*? Mister, mister, please –'

'His left leg there looks a little thinner than his right one. That's the only reason I asked, my good friend.'

'I don't know nothing about that,' Lloyd whispered. He was trembling all over.

'How about Br'er Rat? How did he taste?'

Lloyd put his hands over his face and said nothing.

'What's your name?'

Lloyd tried to say, but all that came out was a moan.

'What's your name, soldier?'

'Lloyd Henreid.' He tried to think what to say next, but his mind was a chaotic jumble. He had been afraid when his lawyer told him he might go to the electric chair, but not *this* afraid. He had never been *this* afraid in his entire life.

'It was all Poke's idea!' he screamed. 'Poke should be here, not me!'

'Look at me, Lloyd.'

'No,' Lloyd whispered. His eyes rolled wildly.

'Why not?'

'Because . . .'

'Go on.'

'Because I don't think you're real,' Lloyd whispered. 'And if you are real . . . mister, if you're real, you're the devil.'

'Look at me, Lloyd.'

Helplessly, Lloyd turned his eyes up to that dark, grinning face that hung behind an intersection of bars. The right hand held something up beside the right eye. Looking at it made Lloyd feel cold and hot all over. It looked like a black stone, so dark it seemed almost resinous and pitchy. There was a red flaw in the center of it, and to Lloyd it looked like a terrible eye, bloody and half-open, peering at him. Then Flagg turned it slightly between his fingers, and the red flaw in the dark stone looked like . . . a key. Flagg turned it back and forth between his fingers. Now it was the eye, now it was the key.

The eye, the key.

He sang: 'She brought me coffee . . . she brought me tea . . . she brought me . . . damn near everything . . . but the workhouse key. Right, Lloyd?'

'Sure,' Lloyd said huskily. His eyes never left the small dark stone. Flagg began to walk it from one finger to the next like a magician doing a trick.

'Now you're a man who must appreciate the value of a good key,' the man said. The dark stone disappeared in his clenched fist and suddenly reappeared in his other hand, where it began to finger-walk again. 'I'm sure you are. Because what a key is for is opening doors. Is there anything more important in life than opening doors, Lloyd?'

'Mister, I'm awfully hungry . . .'

'Sure you are,' the man said. An expression of concern spread over his face, an expression so magnified that it became grotesque. 'Jesus Christ, a rat isn't anything to eat! Why, do you know what I had for lunch? I had a nice rare roast beef sandwich on Vienna bread with a few onions and a lot of Gulden's Spicy Brown. Sound good?'

Lloyd nodded his head, tears oozing slowly out of his overbright eyes.

'Had some homefries and chocolate milk to go with it, and then for dessert . . . holy crow, I'm *torturing* you, ain't I? Someone ought to take a hosswhip to me, that's what they ought to do. I'm sorry. I'll let you right out and then we'll go get something to eat, okay?'

Lloyd was too stunned to even nod. He had decided that the man with the key was indeed a devil, or even more likely a mirage, and the mirage would stand outside his cell until Lloyd finally dropped dead, talking happily about God and Jesus and Gulden's Spicy Brown Mustard as he made the strange black stone appear and disappear. But now the compassion on the man's face seemed real enough, and he sounded genuinely disgusted with himself. The black stone disappeared into his clenched fist again. And when the fist opened, Lloyd's wondering eyes beheld a flat silver key with an ornate grip lying on the stranger's palm.

'My – dear – *God!*' Lloyd croaked.

'You like that?' the dark man asked, pleased. 'I learned that trick from a massage parlor honey in Secaucus, New Jersey, Lloyd. Secaucus, home of the world's greatest pig farms.'

He bent and seated the key in the lock of Lloyd's cell. And that was strange, because as well as his memory served him (which right now was not very well), these cells *had* no keyways, because they were all opened and shut electronically. But he had no doubt that the silver key would work.

Just as it rattled home, Flagg stopped and looked at Lloyd, grinning slyly, and Lloyd felt despair wash over him again. It was all just a trick.

'Did I introduce myself? The name is Flagg, with the double g. Pleased to meet you.'

'Likewise,' Lloyd croaked.

'And I think, before I open this cell and we go get some dinner, we ought to have a little understanding, Lloyd.'

'Sure thing,' Lloyd croaked, and began to cry again.

'I'm going to make you my righthand man, Lloyd. Going to put you right up there with Saint Peter. When I open this door, I'm going to slip the keys to the kingdom right into your hand. What a deal, right?'

'Yeah,' Lloyd whispered, growing frightened again. It was almost full dark now. Flagg was little more than a dark shape, but his eyes were still perfectly visible. They seemed to glow in the dark like the eyes of a lynx, one to the left of the bar that ended in the lockbox, one to the right. Lloyd felt terror, but something else as well: a kind of religious ecstasy. A pleasure. The pleasure of being *chosen*. The feeling that he had somehow won through . . . to something.

'You'd like to get even with the people who left you here, isn't that right?'

'Boy, that sure is,' Lloyd said, forgetting his terror momentarily. It was swallowed up by a starving, sinewy anger.

'Not just those people, but everyone who would do a thing like that,' Flagg suggested. 'It's a type of person, isn't it? To a certain type of person, a man like you is nothing but garbage. Because they are high up. They don't think a person like you has a right to live.'

'That's just right,' Lloyd said. His great hunger had suddenly been changed into a different kind of hunger. It had changed just as surely as the black stone had changed into the silver key. This man had expressed all the complex things he had felt in just a handful of sentences. It wasn't just the gate-guard he wanted to get even with – *why, here's the wise-ass pusbag, what's the story, pusbag, got anything smart to say?* – because the gate-guard wasn't the one. The gate-guard had had THE KEY, all right, but the gate-guard had not *made* THE KEY. Someone had given it to him. The warden, Lloyd supposed, but the warden hadn't made THE KEY, either. Lloyd wanted to find the makers and forgers. They would be immune to the flu, and he had business with them. Oh yes, and it was *good* business.

'You know what the Bible says about people like that?' Flagg asked quietly. 'It says the exalted shall be abased and the mighty shall be brought low and the stiffnecked shall be broken. And you know what it says about people like you, Lloyd? It says blessed are the meek, for they shall inherit the earth. And it says blessed are the poor in spirit, for they shall see God.'

Lloyd was nodding. Nodding and crying. For a moment it seemed that a blazing corona had formed around Flagg's head, a light so bright that if Lloyd looked at it for long it would burn his eyes to cinders. Then it was gone . . . if it had ever been there at all, and it must not have been, because Lloyd had not even lost his night vision.

'Now you aren't very bright,' Flagg said, 'but you are the first. And I have the feeling you might be very loyal. You and I, Lloyd, we're going to go far. It's a good time for people like us. Everything is starting up for us. All I need is your word.'

'W-word?'

'That we're going to stick together, you and me. No denials. No falling asleep on guard duty. There will be others very soon – they're on their way west already – but for now, there's just us. I'll give you the key if you give me your promise.'

'I . . . promise,' Lloyd said, and the words seemed to hang in the air, vibrating strangely. He listened to that vibration, his head cocked to one side, and he could almost see those two words, glowing as darkly as the aurora borealis reflected in a dead man's eye.

Then he forgot about them as the tumblers made their half-turns inside the lockbox. The next moment the lockbox fell at Flagg's feet, tendrils of smoke seeping from it.

'You're free, Lloyd. Come on out.'

Unbelieving, Lloyd touched the bars hesitantly, as if they might burn him; and indeed, they did seem warm. But when he pushed, the door slid back easily and soundlessly. He stared at his savior, those burning eyes.

Something was placed in his hand. The key.

'It's yours now, Lloyd.'

'Mine?'

Flagg grabbed Lloyd's fingers and closed them around it . . . and Lloyd felt it move in his hand, felt it *change*. He uttered a hoarse cry and his fingers sprang open. The key was gone and in its place was the black stone with the red flaw. He held it up, wondering, and turned it this way and that. Now the red flaw looked like a key, now like a skull, now like a bloody, half-closed eye again.

'Mine,' Lloyd answered himself. This time he closed his hand with no help, holding the stone savagely tight.

'Shall we get some dinner?' Flagg asked. 'We've got a lot of driving to do tonight.'

'Dinner,' Lloyd said. 'All right.'

'There's such a lot to do,' Flagg said happily. 'And we're going to move very fast.' They walked toward the stairs together, past the dead men in their cells. When Lloyd stumbled in weakness, Flagg seized his arm above the elbow and bore him up. Lloyd turned and looked into that grinning face with something more than gratitude. He looked at Flagg with something like love.

CHAPTER 40

Nick Andros lay sleeping but not quiet on the bunk in Sheriff Baker's office. He was naked except for his shorts and his body was lightly oiled with sweat. His last thought before sleep had taken him the night before was that he would be dead by morning; the dark man that had consistently haunted his feverish dreams would somehow break through that last thin barrier of sleep and take him away.

It was strange. The eye which Ray Booth had gouged into darkness had hurt for two days. Then, on the third, the feeling that giant calipers had been screwed into his head had faded down to a dull ache. There was nothing but a gray blur when he looked through that eye now, a gray blur in which shapes sometimes moved, or seemed to move. But it wasn't the eye injury which was killing him; it was the bullet-graze down his leg.

He had gone without disinfecting it. The pain in his eye had been so great that he had barely been aware of it. The graze ran shallowly along his right thigh and ended at the knee; he had examined the bullet hole in his pants where the slug had exited the next day with some wonder. And on that next day, June thirtieth, the wound had been red along the edges and all the muscles of that leg seemed to ache.

He had limped down to Dr Soames's office and had gotten a bottle of hydrogen peroxide. He had poured the whole bottle of peroxide over the bullet wound, which was about ten inches long. It had been a case of locking the barn door after the horse had been stolen. By that evening his entire right leg was throbbing like a rotten tooth, and under the skin he could see the telltale red lines of blood poisoning radiating out from the wound, which had only begun to scab over.

On July first he had gone down to Soames's office again and had rummaged through his drug closet, looking for penicillin. He found some, and after a moment's hesitation, he swallowed both of the pills in one of the sample packets. He was well aware that he would die if his body reacted strongly against the penicillin, but he thought the alternative might be an even nastier death. The infection was racing, racing. The penicillin did not kill him, but there was no noticeable improvement, either.

By yesterday noon he had been running a high fever, and he suspected he had been delirious a great deal of the time. He had plenty of food but didn't want to eat it; all he seemed to want to do was drink cup after cup of the distilled water in the cooler which stood in Baker's office. That water had been almost gone when he fell asleep (or passed out) last night, and Nick had no idea how he might get more. In his feverish state, he didn't care much. He would die soon, and there would be nothing to worry about anymore. He was not crazy about the idea of dying, but the thought of having no more pain or worry was a great relief. His leg throbbed and itched and burned.

His sleep those days and nights after the killing of Ray Booth had not seemed like sleep at all. His dreams were a flood. It seemed that everyone he had ever known was coming back for a curtain call. Rudy Sparkman, pointing at the white sheet of paper: *You are this blank page.* His mother, tapping lines and circles she had helped him make on another white page, marring its purity: *It says Nick Andros, honey. That's you.* Jane Baker, her face turned aside on the pillow, saying, *Johnny, my poor Johnny.* In his dreams Dr Soames asked John Baker again and again to take off his shirt, and again and again Ray Booth said, *Hold im . . . I'm gonna mess im up . . . sucker hit me . . . hold im . . .* Unlike all the other dreams he had had in his life, Nick did not have to lip-read these. He could actually hear what people were saying. The dreams were incredibly vivid. They would fade as the pain in his leg brought him close to waking. Then a new scene would appear as he sank down into sleep again. There were people he had never seen in two of the dreams, and these were the dreams he remembered the most clearly when he woke up.

He was on a high place. The land was spread out below him like a relief map. It was desert land, and the stars above had the mad clarity of altitude. There was a man beside him . . . no, not a man but the *shape* of a man. As if the figure had been cut from the fabric of reality and what really stood beside him was a negative man, a black hole in the shape of a man. And the voice of this shape whispered: *Everything you see will be yours if you fall down on your knees and worship me.* Nick shook his head, wanting to step away from that awful drop, afraid the shape would stretch out its black arms and push him over the edge.

Why don't you speak? Why do you just shake your head?

In the dream Nick made the gesture he had made so many times in the waking world: a laying of his finger over his lips, then the flat of his hand against his throat . . . and then he heard himself say in a perfectly clear, rather beautiful voice: 'I can't talk. I am mute.'

But you can. If you want to, you can.

Nick reached out to touch the shape then, his fear momentarily swept away in a flood of amazement and burning joy. But as his hand neared that figure's shoulder it turned ice cold, so cold it seemed that he had burned it. He jerked it away with ice crystals forming on the knuckles. And it came to him. He could hear. The dark shape's voice; the far-off cry of a hunting night-bird; the endless whine of the wind. He was struck mute all over again by the wonder of it. There was a new dimension to the world he had never missed because he had never experienced it, and now it had fallen into place. He was hearing *sounds*. He seemed to know what each was without being told. They were pretty. Pretty *sounds*. He ran his fingers back and forth across his shirt and marveled at the swift whisper of his nails on the cotton.

Then the dark man was turning toward him, and Nick was terribly afraid. This creature, whatever it was, performed no free miracles.

– if you fall down on your knees and worship me.

And Nick put his hands over his face because he wanted all the things the black manshape had shown him from this high desert place: cities, women, treasure, power. But most of all he wanted to hear the entrancing sound his fingernails made on his shirt, the tick of a clock in an empty house after midnight, and the secret sound of rain.

But the word he said was *No* and then that freezing cold was on him again and he had been *pushed*, he was falling end over end, screaming soundlessly as he tumbled through these cloudy depths, tumbled into the smell of –

– corn?

Yes, corn. This was the other dream, they blended together like this, with hardly a seam to show the difference. He was in the corn, the green corn, and the smell was summer earth and cow manure and growing things. He got to his feet and began to walk up the row he had found himself in, stopping momentarily as he realized he could hear the soft whicker of the wind flowing between the July corn's green, swordlike blades . . . and something else.

Music?

Yes – some sort of music. And in the dream he thought, 'So *that's* what they mean.' It was coming from straight ahead and he walked toward it, wanting to see if this particular succession of pretty sounds came from what was called 'piano' or 'horn' or 'cello' or what.

The hot smell of summer in his nostrils, the overarching blue sky above, that lovely sound. In this dream, Nick had never been happier. And as he neared the source, a voice joined the music, an old voice like dark leather, slurring the words a little as if the song was a stew, often reheated, that never lost its old savor. Mesmerized, Nick walked toward it.

> I come to the garden alone
> While the dew is still on the roses
> And the voice I hear, falling on my ear
> The son . . . of God . . . disclo-o-ses
> And he walks with me and he talks with me
> Tells me I am his own
> And the joy we share as we tarry there
> None other . . . has ever . . . known.

As the verse ended, Nick pushed through to the head of the row and there in the clearing was a shack, not much more than a shanty, with a rusty trash barrel to the left and an old tire swing to the right. It hung from an apple tree that was gnarled but still green with lovely life. A porch slanted out from the house, a splintery old thing held up with old, oil-clotted jacklifters. The windows were open, and the kind summer breeze blew ragged white curtains in and out of them. From the roof a peaked chimney of galvanized tin, dented and smoky, jutted at its own old, odd angle. This house sat in its clearing and the corn stretched away in all four directions as far as the eye could see; it was broken only on the north by a dirt road that dwindled away to a point on the flat horizon. It was always then that Nick knew where he was: Polk County, Nebraska, west of Omaha and a little north of Osceola. Far up that dirt road was US 30 and Columbus sitting on the north bank of the Platte.

Sitting on the porch is the oldest woman in America, a black woman with fluffy white thin hair – she is thin herself, wearing a housedress and specs. She looks thin enough for the high afternoon wind to just blow her away, tumble her into the high blue sky and carry her perhaps all the way to Julesburg, Colorado. And the instrument she is playing (perhaps that's what is holding her down, keeping her on the earth) is a 'guitar,' and Nick thinks in the dream: *That's what a 'guitar' sounds like. Nice.* He feels he could just stand where he is for the rest of the day, watching the old black woman sitting on her porch held up by jacklifters in the middle of all this Nebraska corn, stand here west of Omaha and a little north of Osceola in the county of Polk, listening. Her face is seamed with a million wrinkles like the map of a state where the geography hasn't settled down – rivers and canyons along her brown leather cheeks, ridges below the knob of her chin, the sinuous raised drumlin of bone at the base of her forehead, the caves of her eyes.

She has begun to sing again, accompanying herself on the old guitar.

> Jee-sus, won't you kun-bah-yere
> Oh Jee-sus, won't you kun-bah-yere,
> Jesus, won't you come by here?
> Cause now . . . is the needy time
> Oh now . . . is the needy time
> Now is the –

Say, boy, who nailed you to that spot?

She puts the guitar across her lap like a baby and gestures him forward. Nick comes. He says he just wanted to listen to her sing, the singing was beautiful.

Well, singing's God's foolishness, I do it most the day now . . . how you making out with that black man?

He scares me. I'm afraid –

Boy, you got to be afraid. Even a tree at dusk, if you see it the right way, you got to be afraid. We're all mortal, praise God.

But how do I tell him no? How do I –

How do you breathe? How do you dream? No one knows. But you come see me. Anytime. Mother Abagail is what they call me. I'm the oldest woman in these parts, I guess, and I still make m'own biscuit. You come see me anytime, boy, and bring your friends.

But how do I get out of this?

God bless you; boy, no one ever does. You just look up to the best and come see Mother Abagail anytime you take a mind to. I be right here, I guess; don't move around much anymore. So you come see me. I be right –

– here, right here –

He came awake bit by bit until Nebraska was gone, and the smell of the corn, and Mother Abagail's seamed, dark face. The real world filtered in, not so much replacing that dream world as overlaying it until it was out of sight.

He was in Shoyo, Arkansas, his name was Nick Andros, he had never spoken nor heard the sound of a 'guitar' . . . but he was still alive.

He sat up on the cot, swung his legs over, and looked at the scrape. The swelling had gone down some. The ache was only a throb. I'm healing, he thought with great relief. I think I'm going to be okay.

He got up from the cot and limped over to the window in his shorts. The leg was stiff, but it was the kind of stiffness you know will work out with a little exercise. He looked out at the silent town, not Shoyo anymore but the corpse of Shoyo, and knew he would have to leave today. He wouldn't be able to get far, but he would make a start.

Where to go? Well, he supposed he knew that. Dreams were just dreams, but for a start he supposed he could go northwest. Toward Nebraska.

Nick pedaled out of town at about quarter past one on the afternoon of July 3. He packed a knapsack in the morning, putting in some more of the penicillin pills in case he needed them, and some canned goods. He went heavy on the Campbell's tomato soup and the Chef Boy-ar-dee ravioli, two of his favorites. He put in several boxes of bullets for the pistol and took a canteen.

He walked up the street, looking in garages until he found what he wanted: a ten-speed bike that was just about right for his height. He pedaled carefully down Main Street, in a low gear, his hurt leg slowly warming to the work. He was moving west and his shadow followed him, riding its own black bike. He went past the gracious, cool-looking houses on the outskirts of town, standing in the shade with their curtains drawn for all time.

He camped that night in a farmhouse ten miles west of Shoyo. By nightfall on July fourth he was nearly to Oklahoma. That evening before he went to sleep he stood in another farmyard, his face turned up to the sky, watching a meteor shower scratch the night with cold white fire. He thought he had never seen anything so beautiful. Whatever lay ahead, he was glad to be alive.

CHAPTER 41

Larry woke up at half past eight to sunlight and the sound of birds. They both freaked him out. Every morning since they had left New York City, sunlight and the sound of birds. And as an extra added attraction, a Bonus Free Gift, if you like, the air smelled clean and fresh. Even Rita had noticed it. He kept thinking: Well, that's as good as it's going to get. But it kept getting better. It got better until you wondered what they had been doing to the planet. And it made you wonder if this was the way the air had *always* smelled in places like upstate Minnesota and in Oregon and on the western slope of the Rockies.

Lying in his half of the double sleeping bag under the low canvas roof of the two-man tent they had added to their traveling kit in Passaic on the morning of July second, Larry remembered when Al Spellman, one of the Tattered Remnants, had tried to persuade Larry to go on a camping trip with him and two or three other guys. They were going to go east, stop in Vegas for a night, then go on to a place called Loveland, Colorado. They were going to camp out in the mountains above Loveland for five days or so.

'You can leave all that Rocky Mountain High shit for John Denver,' Larry had scoffed. 'You'll all come back with mosquito bites and probably with a good case of poison ivy up the kazoo from shitting in the woods. Now, if you change your mind and decide to camp out at the Dunes in Vegas for five days, give me a jingle.'

But maybe it had been like this. On your own, with nobody hassling you (except for Rita, and he guessed he could put up with her hassle), breathing good air and sleeping at night with no tossing and turning, just bang, fast asleep, like somebody had hit you on the head with a hammer. No problems, except which way you were going tomorrow and how much time you could make. It was pretty wonderful.

And this morning in Bennington, Vermont, now headed due

east along Highway 9, this morning was something special. It was the by-God Fourth of July, Independence Day.

He sat up in the sleeping bag and looked over at Rita, but she was still out like a light, nothing showing but the lines of her body under the bag's quilted fabric and a fluff of her hair. Well, he would wake her up in style this morning.

Larry unzipped his side of the bag and got out, buck naked. For a moment his flesh marbled into goosebumps and then the air felt naturally warm, probably seventy already. It was going to be another peach of a day. He crawled out of the tent and stood up.

Parked beside the tent was a 1200-cc Harley-Davidson cycle, black and chrome. Like the sleeping bag and the tent, it had been acquired in Passaic. By that time they had already gone through three cars, two blocked by terrible traffic jams, the third stuck in the mud outside of Nutley when he had tried to swing around a two-truck smashup. The bike was the answer. It could be trundled around accidents, pulling itself along in low gear. When the traffic was seriously piled up it could be ridden along the breakdown lane or the sidewalk, if there was one. Rita didn't like it – riding pillion made her nervous and she clung to Larry desperately – but she had agreed it was the only practical solution. Mankind's final traffic jam had been a dilly. And since they had left Passaic and gotten into the country, they had made great time. By the evening of July second they had recrossed into New York State and had pitched their tent on the outskirts of Quarryville, with the hazed and mystic Catskills to the west. They turned east on the afternoon of the third, crossing into Vermont just as dusk fell. And here they were in Bennington.

They had camped on a rise outside of town, and now as Larry stood naked beside the cycle, urinating, he could look down and marvel at the picture-postcard New England town below him. Two clean white churches, their steeples rising as if to poke through the blue morning sky; a private school, gray fieldstone buildings shackled with ivy; a mill; a couple of red brick school buildings; plenty of trees dressed in summer greengowns. The only thing that made the picture subtly wrong was the lack of smoke from the mill and the number of twinkling toy cars parked at weird angles on the main street, which was also the highway they were following. But in the sunny silence (silent, that was, except for an occasional twittering bird), Larry might have echoed the sentiments of the late Irma Fayette, had he known the lady: no great loss.

Except it was the Fourth of July, and he supposed he was still an American.

He cleared his throat, spat, and hummed a little to find his pitch. He drew breath, very much aware of the light morning breeze on his naked chest and buttocks, and burst into song.

> Oh! say, can you see,
> by the dawn's early light,
> What so proudly we hailed,
> at the twilight's last gleaming . . .

He sang it all the way through, facing Bennington, doing a little burlesque bump and grind at the end, because by now Rita would be standing at the flap of the tent, smiling at him.

He finished with a snappy salute at the building he thought might be the Bennington courthouse, then turned around, thinking the best way to start another year of independence in the good old US of A would be with a good old all-American fuck.

'Larry Underwood, Boy Patriot, wishes you a very good m –'

But the tent-flap was still closed, and he felt a momentary irritation with her again. He squashed it resolutely. She couldn't be on his wavelength all the time. That's all. When you could recognize that and deal with it, you were on your way to an adult relationship. He had been trying very hard with Rita since that harrowing experience in the tunnel, and he thought he'd been doing pretty well.

You had to put yourself in her place, that was the thing. You had to recognize that she was a lot older, she had been used to having things a certain way for most of her life. It was natural for her to have a harder job adapting to a world that had turned itself upside down. The pills, for instance. He hadn't been overjoyed to discover that she had brought her whole fucking pharmacy along with her in a jelly jar with a screw-on lid. Yellowjackets, Quaaludes, Darvon, and some other stuff that she called 'my little pick-me-ups.' The little pick-me-ups were reds. Three of those with a shot of tequila and you would jitter and jive all the live-long day. He didn't like it because too many ups and downs and all-arounds added up to one mean monkey on your back. A monkey roughly the size of King Kong. And he didn't like it because, when you got right down to where the cheese binds, it was a kind of slap in the face at him, wasn't it? What did she have to be nervous about? Why should she have trouble dropping off at night? He sure as hell didn't. And wasn't he taking care of her? You were damned tooting he was.

He went back to the tent, then hesitated for a moment. Maybe he ought to let her sleep. Maybe she was worn out. But . . .

He looked down at Old Sparky, and Old Sparky didn't really want to let her sleep. Singing the old Star-Speckled Banana had turned him right on. So Larry turned back the tent-flap and crawled in.

'Rita?'

And it hit him right away after the fresh morning cleanness of the air outside; he must have been mostly asleep before to have missed it. The smell was not overpoweringly strong because the tent was fairly well ventilated, but it was strong enough: the sweet-sour smell of vomit and sickness.

'Rita?' He felt mounting alarm at the still way she was lying, just that dry fluff of her hair sticking out of the sleeping bag. He crawled toward her on his hands and knees, the smell of vomit stronger now, making his stomach knot. 'Rita, you all right? Wake up, Rita!'

No movement.

So he rolled her over and the sleeping bag was halfway unzipped as if she had tried to struggle out of it in the night, maybe realizing what was happening to her, struggling and failing, and he all the time sleeping peacefully beside her, old Mr Rocky Mountain High himself. He rolled her over and one of her pill bottles fell out of her hand and her eyes were cloudy dull marbles behind half-closed lids and her mouth was filled with the green puke she had strangled on.

He stared into her dead face for what seemed a very long time. They were almost nose to nose, and the tent seemed to be getting hotter and hotter until it was like an attic on a late August afternoon just before the cooling thundershowers hit. His head seemed to be swelling and swelling. Her mouth was full of that shit. He couldn't take his eyes off that. The question that ran around and around in his brain like a mechanical rabbit on a dogtrack rail was: *How long was I sleeping with her after she died?* Repulsive, man. *Reeee-*pulsive.

The paralysis broke and he scrambled out of the tent, scraping both knees when they came off the groundsheet and onto the naked earth. He thought he was going to puke himself and he struggled with it, willing himself not to, he hated to puke worse than anything, and then he thought *But I was going back in there to FUCK her, man!*

and everything came up in a loose rush and he crawled away from the steaming mess crying and hating the cruddy taste in his mouth and nose.

He thought about her most of the morning. He felt a measure of relief that she had died – a great measure, actually. He would never tell anyone that. It confirmed everything his mother had said about him, and Wayne Stukey, and even that silly bit of fluff with the apartment near Fordham University. Larry Underwood, the Fordham Flasher.

'I ain't no nice guy,' he said aloud, and having said it, he felt better. It became easier to tell the truth, and truth-telling was the most important thing. He had made an agreement with himself, in whatever back room of the subconscious where the Powers Behind the Throne wheel and deal, that he was going to take care of her. Maybe he wasn't no nice guy, but he was no murderer either and what he had done in the tunnel was pretty close to attempted murder. So he was going to take care of her, he wasn't going to shout at her no matter how pissed he got sometimes – like when she grabbed him with her patented Kansas City Clutch as they mounted the Harley – he wasn't going to get mad no matter how much she held him back or how stupid she could be about some things. The night before last she had put a can of peas in the coals of their fire without ventilating the top and he had fished it out all charred and swelled, about three seconds before it would have gone off like a bomb, maybe blinding them with flying hooks of tin shrapnel. But had he read her out about it? No. He hadn't. He had made a light joke and passed it off. Same with the pills. He had figured the pills were her business.

Maybe you should have discussed it with her. Maybe she wanted you to.

'It wasn't a friggin encounter session,' he said aloud. It was survival. And she hadn't been able to cut it. Maybe she had known it, ever since the day in Central Park when she had taken a careless shot at a chinaberry tree with a cheap-looking .32 that might have blown up in her hand. Maybe –

'Maybe, *shit!*' Larry said angrily. He tipped the canteen up to his mouth but it was empty and he still had that slimy taste in his mouth. Maybe there were people like her all over the country. The flu didn't just leave survivor types, why the hell should it? There might be a young guy somewhere in the country right now, perfect physical condition, immune to the flu but dying of tonsillitis. As Henny Youngman might have said, hey, folks, I got a million of em.

Larry was sitting on a paved scenic turnout just off the highway. The view of Vermont marching away to New York in the golden morning haze was breathtaking. A sign announced that this was Twelve-Mile Point. Actually Larry thought he could see a lot farther than twelve miles. On a clear day you could see forever. At the far side of the turnout there was a knee-high rock wall, the rocks cemented together, and a few smashed Budweiser bottles. Also a used condom. He supposed that high school kids used to come up here at twilight and watch the lights come on in the town below. First they would get exalted and then they would get laid. BFD, as they used to say: big fucking deal.

So why was he feeling so bad, anyway? He was telling the truth, wasn't he? Yes. And the worst of the truth was that he felt relief, wasn't it? That the stone around his neck was gone?

No, the worst is being alone. Being lonely.

Corny but true. He wanted someone to share this view with. Someone he could turn to and say with modest wit: *On a clear day you can see forever.* And the only company was in a tent a mile and a half back with a mouthful of green puke. Getting stiff. Drawing flies.

Larry put his head on his knees and closed his eyes. He told himself he wouldn't cry. He hated to cry almost as bad as he hated to puke.

In the end he was chicken. He couldn't bury her. He summoned up the worst thoughts he could – maggots and beetles, the wood-chucks that would smell her and come in for a munch, the unfairness of one human being leaving another like a candy wrapper or a discarded Pepsi can. But there also seemed to be something vaguely illegal about burying her and to tell the truth (and he was telling the truth now, wasn't he?), that was just a cheap rationalization. He could face going down to Bennington and breaking into the Ever Popular hardware store, taking the Ever Popular spade and a matching Ever Popular pick; he could even face coming back up here where it was still and beautiful and digging the Ever Popular grave near the Ever Popular Twelve-Mile Point. But to go back into that tent (which would now smell very much like the comfort station on Transverse Number One in Central Park, where the Ever Popular dark sweet treat would be sitting for eternity) and unzip her side of the sleeping bag the rest of the way and pull out her stiff and baggy body and drag it up to the hole by the armpits and tumble it in and then shovel the dirt over it, watching the earth patter on her white legs with their bulging nodules of varicose veins and stick in her hair . . .

Uh-uh, buddy. Guess I'll sit this one out. If I'm a chicken, so be it. Plucka-plucka-plucka.

He went back to where the tent was pitched and turned back the flap. He found a long stick. He took a deep breath of fresh air, held it, and hooked his clothes out with the stick. Backed away with them, put them on. Took another deep breath, held it, and used the stick to fish out his boots. He sat on a fallen tree and put them on, too.

The smell was in his clothes.

'Bullshit,' he whispered.

He could see her, half in and half out of the sleeping bag, her stiff hand held out and still curled around the pill bottle that was no longer there. Her half-lidded eyes seemed to be staring at him accusingly. It made him think of the tunnel again; and his visions of the walking dead. Quickly he used the stick to close the tent-flap.

But he could still smell her on him.

So he made Bennington his first stop after all, and in the Bennington Men's Shop he stripped off all his clothes and got new ones, three changes plus four pairs of socks and shorts. He even found a new pair of boots. Looking at himself in the three-way mirror he could see the empty store spread out behind him and the Harley leaning raffishly at the curb.

'Sharp threads,' he murmured. 'Heavy-heavy.' But there was no one to admire his taste.

He left the store and gunned the Harley into life. He supposed he should stop at the hardware store and see if they had a tent and another sleeping bag, but all he wanted now was to get out of Bennington. He would stop farther up the line.

He looked up toward where the land made its slow rise as he guided the Harley out of town, and he could see Twelve-Mile Point, but not where they had pitched the tent. That was really all for the best, it was —

Larry looked back at the road and terror jumped nimbly down his throat. An International-Harvester pickup towing a horse trailer had swerved to avoid a car and the horse trailer had overturned. He was going to drive the Harley right into it because he hadn't been looking where he was going.

He turned hard right, his new boot dragging on the road, and he almost got around. But the left footrest clipped the trailer's rear bumper and yanked the bike out from under him. Larry came to rest on the highway's verge with a bone-rattling thump. The Harley chattered on for a moment behind him and then stalled out.

'You all right?' he asked aloud. Thank God he'd only been doing twenty or so. Thank God Rita wasn't with him, she'd be bullshit out of her mind with hysterics. Of course if Rita had been with him he wouldn't have been looking up there in the first place, he would have been TCB, taking care of business to the cubistic among you.

'I'm all right,' he answered himself, but he still wasn't sure he was. He sat up. The quiet impressed itself upon him as it did from time to time – it was so quiet that if you thought about it you could go crazy. Even Rita bawling would have been a relief at this point. Everything seemed suddenly full of bright twinkles, and with sudden horror he thought he was going to pass out. He thought, *I really am hurt, in just a minute I'll feel it, when the shock wears off, that's when I'll feel it, I'm cut bad or something, and who's going to put on a tourniquet?*

But when the instant of faintness had passed, he looked at himself and thought he was probably all right after all. He had cut both hands and his new pants had shredded away at the right knee – the knee was also cut – but they were all just scrapes and what the fuck was the big deal, anybody could dump their cycle, it happens to everybody once in a while.

But he knew what the big deal was. He could have hit his head the right way and fractured his skull and he would have lain there in the hot sun until he died. Or strangled to death on his own puke like a certain now-deceased friend of his.

He walked shakily over to the Harley and stood it up. It didn't seem to be damaged in any way, but it looked different. Before, it had just been a machine, a rather charming machine that could serve the dual purpose of transporting him and making him feel like James Dean or Jack Nicholson in *Hell's Angels on Wheels*. But now its chrome seemed to grin at him like a sideshow barker, seeming to invite him to step right up and see if he was man enough to ride the two-wheeled monster.

It started on the third kick, and he putted out of Bennington at no more than walking speed. He was wearing bracelets of cold sweat on his arms and suddenly he had never, no never, in his whole life wanted so badly to see another human face.

But he didn't see one that day.

In the afternoon he made himself speed up a little, but he could not force himself to twist the throttle any farther once the speedometer needle had reached twenty, not even if he could see the road was clear ahead. There was a sporting goods and cycle shop on the outskirts of Wilmington, and he stopped there and got some heavy gloves and a helmet, and even with them on he could not force himself to go faster than twenty-five. On blind corners he slowed down until he was walking the big cycle along. He kept having visions of lying unconscious at the side of the road and bleeding to death unattended.

At five o'clock, as he was approaching Brattleboro, the Harley's overheat light went on. Larry parked it and turned it off with mingled feelings of relief and disgust.

'You might as well have pushed it,' he said. 'It's meant to run at sixty, you goddamn fool!'

He left it and walked into town, not knowing if he would come back for it.

He slept on the Brattleboro Municipal Common that evening, under the partial shelter of the bandshell. He turned in as soon as it was dark, and fell asleep instantly. Some sound woke him with a jerk a time later. He looked at his watch. The thin radium lines on the dial scratched out 11:20. He got up on one elbow and stared into the darkness, feeling the bandshell huge around him, missing the little tent that had held in body heat. What a fine little canvas womb it had been!

If there had been a sound, it was gone now; even the crickets had fallen silent. Was that right? Could it be right?

'Is someone there?' Larry called, and the sound of his own voice frightened him. He groped for the .30-.30 and for a long and increasingly panicky moment could not find it. When he did, he squeezed the trigger without thinking, just as a man drowning in the ocean will squeeze a thrown life preserver. If the safety hadn't been on, he would have fired it. Possibly into himself.

There was something in the silence, he was sure of it. Perhaps a person, perhaps some large and dangerous animal. Of course, a person could be dangerous, too. A person like the one who had repeatedly stabbed the poor monster-shouter or like John Bearsford Tipton, who had offered him a million in cold cash for the use of his woman.

'Who is it?'

He had a flashlight in his pack, but in order to hunt for it, he would have to let go of the rifle, which he had drawn across his lap. Besides . . . did he really want to see who it was?

So he just sat there, willing movement or a repetition of the sound which had awakened him (*had* it been a sound? or just something he had dreamed?), and after a little while he first nodded, then dozed off.

Suddenly his head jerked up, his eyes wide, his flesh shrinking against his bones. *Now* there was a sound, and if the night hadn't been cloudy, the moon, nearly full, would have shown him –

But he didn't want to see. No, he most definitely didn't want to see. Yet he sat forward, head cocked, listening to the sound of dusty bootheels clocking away from him down the sidewalk of Main Street, Brattleboro, Vermont, moving west, fading, until they were lost in the open hum of things.

Larry felt a sudden mad urge to stand up, letting the sleeping bag slither down around his ankles, to shout: *Come back, whoever you are! I don't care! Come back!* But did he really want to issue such a blank check to Whoever? The bandshell would amplify his shout – his plea. And what if those bootheels actually *did* return, growing louder in a stillness where not even the crickets sang?

Instead of standing, he lay back down and curled up in the fetal position with his hands wrapped around the rifle. *I won't sleep again tonight*, he thought, but he was asleep in three minutes and quite sure the next morning that he had dreamed the whole thing.

CHAPTER 42

While Larry Underwood was taking his Fourth of July spill only a state away, Stuart Redman was sitting on a large rock at the side of the road and eating his lunch. He heard the sound of approaching engines. He finished his can of beer at a swallow and carefully folded over the top of the waxed-paper tube the Ritz crackers were in. His rifle was leaning against the rock beside him. He picked it up, flicked off the safety catch, and then put it down again, a little closer to hand. Motorcycles coming, small ones by the sound. Two-fifties? In this great stillness it was impossible to tell how far away they were. Ten miles, maybe, but only maybe. Plenty of time to eat more if he wanted to, but he didn't. In the meantime, the sun was warm and the thought of meeting fellow creatures pleasant. He had seen no living people since leaving Glen Bateman's house in Woodsville. He glanced at the rifle again. He had flicked the safety because the fellow creatures might turn out to be like Elder. He had left the rifle leaning against the rock because he hoped they would be like Bateman – only not quite so glum about the future. *Society will reappear*, Bateman had said. *Notice I didn't use the word 'reform.' That would have been a ghastly pun. There's precious little reform in the human race.*

But Bateman himself hadn't wanted to get in on the ground floor of society's reappearance. He seemed perfectly content – at least for the time being – to go for his walks with Kojak, paint his pictures, putter around his garden, and think about the sociological ramifications of nearly total decimation.

If you come back this way and renew your invitation to 'jine up,' Stu, I'll probably agree. That is the curse of the human race. Sociability. What Christ should have said was 'Yea, verily, whenever two or three of you are gathered together, some other guy is going to get the living shit knocked out of him.' Shall I tell you what sociology teaches us about the human race? I'll give it to you in a nutshell. Show me a man or woman alone and I'll show you a saint. Give me two and they'll fall in love. Give me three and they'll invent the charming thing we call 'society.' Give me four and they'll build a pyramid. Give me five and they'll make one an outcast. Give me six and they'll reinvent prejudice. Give me seven and in seven years they'll reinvent warfare. Man may have been made in the image of God, but human society was made in the image of His opposite number, and is always trying to get back home.

Was that true? If it was, then God help them. Just lately Stu had been thinking a great deal about old friends and acquaintances. In his memory there was a great tendency to downplay or completely forget their unlovable characteristics – the way Bill Hapscomb used to pick his nose and wipe the snot on the sole of his shoe, Norm Bruett's heavy hand with his kids, Billy Verecker's unpleasant method of controlling the cat population around his house by crushing the thin skulls of the new kittens under the heels of his Range Rider boots.

The thoughts that came wanted to be wholly good. Going hunting at dawn, bundled up in quilted jackets and Day-Glo orange vests. Poker games at Ralph Hodges's house and Willy Craddock always complaining about how he was four dollars in the game, even if he was twenty ahead. Six or seven of them pushing Tony Leominster's Scout back onto the road that time he went down into the ditch drunk out of his mind, Tony staggering around and swearing to God and all the saints that he had swerved to avoid a U-Haul full of Mexican wetbacks. Jesus, how they had laughed. Chris Ortega's endless stream of ethnic jokes. Going down to Huntsville for whores, and that time Joe Bob Brentwood caught the crabs and tried to tell everybody they came from the sofa in the parlor and not from the girl upstairs. They had been goddamn good times. Not what your sophisticates with their nightclubs and their fancy restaurants and their museums would think of as good times, maybe, but good times just the same. He thought about those things, went over them and over them, the way an old recluse will lay out hand after hand of solitaire from a greasy pack of cards. Mostly he wanted to hear other human voices, get to know someone, be able to turn to someone and say, *Did you see that?* when something happened like the meteor shower he had watched the other night. He was not a talkative man, but he did not care much for being alone, and never had.

So he sat up a little straighter when the motorcycles finally swept around the bend, and he saw they were a couple of Honda 250s, ridden by a boy of about eighteen and a girl who was maybe older than the boy. The girl was wearing a bright yellow blouse and light blue Levi's.

They saw him sitting on the rock, and both Hondas swerved a little as their drivers' surprise caused control to waver briefly. The boy's mouth dropped open. For a moment it was unclear whether they would stop or just speed by heading west.

Stu raised an empty hand and said 'Hi!' in an amiable voice. His heart was beating heavily in his chest. He wanted them to stop. They did.

For a moment he was puzzled by the tenseness in their postures. Particularly the boy; he looked as if a gallon of adrenalin had just been dumped into his blood. Of course Stu had a rifle, but he wasn't holding it on them and they were armed themselves; he was wearing a pistol and she had a small deer-rifle slung across her back on a strap, like an actress playing Patty Hearst with no great conviction.

'I think he's all right, Harold,' the girl said, but the boy she called Harold continued to stand astride his bike, looking at Stu with an expression of surprise and considering antagonism.

'I said I think −' she began again.

'How are we supposed to know that?' Harold snapped without taking his eyes off Stu.

'Well, I'm glad to see you, if that makes any difference,' Stu said.

'What if I don't believe you?' Harold challenged, and Stu saw that he was scared green. Scared by him and by his responsibility to the girl.

'Well, then, I don't know.' Stu climbed off the rock. Harold's hand jittered toward his holstered pistol.

'Harold, you leave that alone,' the girl said. Then she fell silent and for a moment they all seemed helpless to proceed further − a group of three dots which, when connected, would form a triangle whose exact shape could not yet be foreseen.

'Ouuuu,' Frannie said, easing herself down on a mossy patch at the base of an elm beside the road. 'I'm never going to get the calluses off my fanny, Harold.'

Harold uttered a surly grunt.

She turned to Stu. 'Have you ever ridden a hundred and seventy miles on a Honda, Mr Redman? *Not* recommended.'

Stu smiled. 'Where are you headed?'

'What business is it of yours?' Harold asked rudely.

'And what kind of attitude is that?' Fran asked him. 'Mr Redman is the first person we've seen since Gus Dinsmore died! I mean, if we didn't come looking for other people, what did we come for?'

'He's watching out for you, is all,' Stu said quietly. He picked a piece of grass and put it between his lips.

'That's right, I am,' Harold said, unmollified.

'I thought we were watching out for each other,' she said, and Harold flushed darkly.

Stu thought: *Give me three people and they'll form a society.* But were these the right two for his one? He liked the girl, but the boy impressed him as a frightened blowhard. And a frightened blowhard could be a very dangerous man, under the right circumstances . . . or the wrong ones.

'Whatever you say,' Harold muttered. He shot Stu a lowering look and took a box of Marlboros from his jacket pocket. He lit one. He smoked on it like a fellow who had only recently taken up the habit. Like maybe the day before yesterday.

'We're going to Stovington, Vermont,' Frannie said. 'To the plague center there. We – what's wrong? Mr Redman?' He had gone pale all of a sudden. The stem of grass he had been chewing fell onto his lap.

'Why there?' Stu asked.

'Because there happens to be an installation there for the study-ing of communicable diseases,' Harold said loftily. 'It was my thought that, if there is any order left in this country, or any persons in authority who escaped the late scourge, they would likely be at Stovington or Atlanta, where there is another such center.'

'That's right,' Frannie said.

Stu said: 'You're wasting your time.'

Frannie looked stunned. Harold looked indignant; the red began to creep out of his collar again. 'I hardly think you're the best judge of that, my man.'

'I guess I am. I came from there.'

Now they both looked stunned. Stunned and astonished.

'You knew about it?' Frannie asked, shaken. 'You checked it out?'

'No, it wasn't like that. It –'

'You're a liar!' Harold's voice had gone high and squeaky.

Fran saw an alarming cold flash of anger in Redman's eyes, then they were brown and mild again. 'No. I ain't.'

'I say you are! I say you're nothing but a —'

'Harold, you shut up!'

Harold looked at her, wounded. 'But Frannie, how can you believe —'

'How can you be so rude and antagonistic?' she asked hotly. 'Will you at least listen to what he has to say, Harold?'

'I don't trust him.'

Fair enough, Stu thought, that makes us even.

'How can you not trust a man you just met? Really, Harold, you're being disgusting!'

'Let me tell you how I know,' Stu said quietly. He told an abridged version of the story that began when Campion had crashed into Hap's pumps. He sketched his escape from Stovington a week ago. Harold glared dully down at his hands, which were plucking up bits of moss and shredding them. But the girl's face was like an unfolding map of tragic country, and Stu felt bad for her. She had set off with this boy (who, to give him credit, had had a pretty good idea), hoping against hope that there was something of the old taken-for-granted ways left. Well, she had been disappointed. Bitterly so, from her look.

'Atlanta too? The plague got both of them?' she asked.

'Yes,' he said, and she burst into tears.

He wanted to comfort her, but the boy would not take to that. Harold glanced uncomfortably at Fran, then down at the litter of moss on his cuffs. Stu gave her his handkerchief. She thanked him distractedly, without looking up. Harold glared sullenly at him again, the eyes those of a piggy little boy who wants the whole cookie jar to himself. Ain't he going to be surprised, Stu thought, when he finds out a girl isn't a jar of cookies.

When her tears had tapered down to sniffles, she said, 'I guess Harold and I owe you our thanks. At least you saved us a long trip with disappointment at the end.'

'You mean you believe him? Just like that? He tells you a big story and you just . . . you buy it?'

'Harold, why would he lie? For what gain?'

'Well, how do I know what he's got on his mind?' Harold asked truculently. 'Murder, could be. Or rape.'

'I don't believe in rape myself,' Stu said mildly. 'Maybe you know something about it I don't.'

'Stop it,' Fran said. 'Harold, won't you try not to be so awful?'

'*Awful?*' Harold shouted. 'I'm trying to watch out for you – us – and that's so bloodydamn *awful?*'

'Look,' Stu said, and brushed his sleeve up. On the inside of his elbow were several healing needle marks and the last remains of a discolored bruise. 'They injected me with all kinds of stuff.'

'Maybe you're a junkie,' Harold said.

Stu rolled his sleeve back down without replying. It was the girl, of course. He had gotten used to the idea of owning her. Well, some girls could be owned and some could not. This one looked like the latter type. She was tall and pretty and very fresh-looking. Her dark eyes and hair accentuated a look that could be taken for dewy helplessness. It would be easy to miss that faint line (the *I-want* line, Stu's mother had called it) between her eyebrows that became so pronounced when she was put out, the swift capability of her hands, even the forthright way she tossed her hair from her forehead.

'So now what do we do?' she asked, ignoring Harold's last contribution to the discussion entirely.

'Go on anyway,' Harold said, and when she looked over at him with that line furrowing her brow, he added hastily: 'Well, we have to go *somewhere*. Sure, he's probably telling the truth, but we could double-check. Then decide what's next.'

Fran glanced at Stu with an I-don't-want-to-hurt-your-feelings-but kind of expression. Stu shrugged.

'Okay?' Harold pressed.

'I suppose it doesn't matter,' Frannie said. She picked up a gone-to-seed dandelion and blew away the fluff.

'You didn't see anyone at all back the way you came?' Stu asked.

'There was a dog that seemed to be all right. No people.'

'I saw a dog, too.' He told them about Bateman and Kojak. When he had finished he said, 'I was going toward the coast, but you saying there aren't any people back that way kind of takes the wind out of my sails.'

'Sorry,' Harold said, sounding anything but. He stood up. 'Ready, Fran?'

She looked at Stu, hesitated, then stood up. 'Back to the wonderful diet machine. Thank you for telling us what you know, Mr Redman, even if the news wasn't so hot.'

'Just a second,' Stu said, also standing up. He hesitated, wondering again if they were right. The girl was, but the boy surely was seventeen and afflicted with a bad case of the I-hate-most-everybodies. But were there enough people left to pick and choose? Stu thought not.

'I guess we're both looking for people,' he said. 'I'd like to tag along with you, if you'd have me.'

'No,' Harold said instantly.

Fran looked from Harold to Stu, troubled. 'Maybe we —'

'You never mind. I say no.'

'Don't I get a vote?'

'What's the matter with you? Can't you see he only wants one thing? Christ, Fran!'

'Three's better than two if there's trouble,' Stu said, 'and I know it's better than one.'

'No,' Harold repeated. His hand dropped to the butt of his gun.

'Yes,' Fran said. 'We'd be glad to have you, Mr Redman.'

Harold rounded on her, his face angry and hurt. Stu tightened for just a moment, thinking that perhaps he was going to strike her, and then relaxed again. 'That's the way you feel, is it? You were just waiting for some excuse to get rid of me, I get it.' He was so angry that tears had sprung to his eyes, and that made him angrier still. 'If that's the way you want it, okay. You go on with him. I'm done with you.' He stamped off toward where the Hondas were parked.

Frannie looked at Stu with stricken eyes, then turned toward Harold.

'Just a minute,' Stu said. 'Stay here, please.'

'Don't hurt him,' Fran said. 'Please.'

Stu trotted toward Harold, who was astride his Honda and trying to start it up. In his anger he had twisted the throttle all the way over and it was a good thing for him it was flooded, Stu thought; if it actually started up with that much throttle, it would rear back on its rear wheel like a unicycle and pile old Harold into the first tree and land on top of him.

'You stay away!' Harold screamed angrily at him, and his hand fell onto the butt of the gun again. Stu put his hand on top of Harold's, as if they were playing slapjack. He put his other hand on Harold's arm. Harold's eyes were very wide, and Stu believed he was only an inch or so from becoming dangerous. He wasn't just jealous of the girl, that had been a bad oversimplification on his part. His personal dignity was wrapped up in it, and his new image of himself as the girl's protector. God knew what kind of a fuckup he had been before all of this, with his wad of belly and his pointy-toed boots and his stuck-up way of talking. But underneath the new image was the belief that he was still a fuckup and always would be. Underneath was the certainty that there was no such thing as a fresh start. He would have reacted the same way to Bateman, or to a twelve-year-old kid. In any triangle situation he was going to see himself as the lowest point.

'Harold,' he said, almost into Harold's ear.

'Let me *go*.' His heavy body seemed light in its tension; he was thrumming like a live wire.

'Harold, are you sleeping with her?'

Harold's body gave a shivering jerk and Stu knew he was not.

'None of your business!'

'No. Except to get things out where we can see them. She's not mine, Harold. She's her own. I'm not going to try to take her away from you. I'm sorry to have to speak so blunt, but it's best for us to know where we stand. We're two and one now and if you go off, we're two and one again. No gain.'

Harold said nothing, but his trembling hand subsided.

'I'll be just as plain as I have to,' Stu went on, still speaking very nearly into Harold's ear (which was clotted with brown wax), and taking the trouble to speak very, very calmly. 'You know and I know that there's no need for a man to be rapin women. Not if he knows what to do with his hand.'

'That's –' Harold licked his lips and then looked over at the side of the road where Fran was still standing, hands cupping elbows, arms crossed just below her breasts, watching them anxiously. 'That's pretty disgusting.'

'Well maybe it is and maybe it isn't, but when a man's around a woman who doesn't want him in bed, that man's got his choice. I pick the hand every time. I guess you do too since she's still with you of her own free will. I just want to speak plain, between you and me. I'm not here to squeeze you out like some bully at a country fair dance.'

Harold's hand relaxed on the gun and he looked at Stu. 'You mean that? I . . . you promise you won't tell?'

Stu nodded.

'I love her,' Harold said hoarsely. 'She doesn't love me, I know that, but I'm speaking plainly, like you said.'

'That's best. I don't want to cut in. I just want to come along.'

Compulsively, Harold repeated: 'You promise?'

'Yeah, I do.'

'All right.'

He got slowly off the Honda. He and Stu walked back to Fran.

'He can come,' Harold said. 'And I . . .' He looked at Stu and said with difficult dignity, 'I apologize for being such an asshole.'

'Hooray!' Fran said, and clapped her hands. 'Now that that's settled, where are we going?'

In the end they went in the direction Fran and Harold had been headed in, west. Stu said he thought Glen Bateman would be glad to have them overnight, if they could reach Woodsville by dark – and he might agree to tag along with them in the morning (at this Harold began to glower again). Stu drove Fran's Honda, and she rode pillion behind Harold. They stopped in Twin Mountain for lunch and began the slow, cautious business of getting to know each other. Their accents sounded funny to Stu, the way they broadened their a's and dropped or modified their r's. He supposed he sounded just as funny to them, maybe funnier.

They ate in an abandoned lunchroom and Stu found his gaze was drawn again and again to Fran's face – her lively eyes, the small but determined set of her chin, the way that line formed between her eyes, indexing her emotions. He liked the way she looked and talked; he even liked the way her dark hair was drawn back from her temples. And that was the beginning of his knowing that he did want her, after all.

BOOK II

ON THE BORDER

July 5 – September 6, 1990

We come on the ship they call the Mayflower
We come on the ship that sailed the moon
We come in the age's most uncertain hour
and sing an American tune
But it's all right, it's all right
You can't be forever blessed . . .

Paul Simon

Lookin hard for a drive-in
Searching for a parking space
Where hamburgers sizzle on an open
grille night and day
Yes! Juke-box is jumpin with records back in the USA
Well I'm so glad I'm living in the USA
Anything you want we got it right here in the USA.

Chuck Berry

CHAPTER 43

There was a dead man lying in the middle of Main Street in May, Oklahoma.

Nick wasn't surprised. He had seen a lot of corpses since leaving Shoyo, and he suspected he hadn't seen a thousandth of all the dead people he must have passed. In places, the rich smell of death on the air was enough to make you feel like swooning. One more dead man, more or less, wasn't going to make any difference.

But when the dead man sat up, such an explosion of terror rose in him that he again lost control of his bike. It wavered, then wobbled, then crashed, spilling Nick violently onto the pavement of Oklahoma Route 3. He cut his hands and scraped his forehead.

'Holy gee, mister, but you took a tumble,' the corpse said, coming toward Nick at a pace best described as an amiable stagger. 'Didn't you just? My laws!'

Nick got none of this. He was looking at a spot on the pavement between his hands where drops of blood from his cut forehead were falling, and wondering how badly he had been cut. When the hand touched him on the shoulder he remembered the corpse and scrambled away on the palms of his hands and the soles of his shoes, the eye not covered with the patch bright with terror.

'Don't you take on so,' the corpse said, and Nick saw he wasn't a corpse at all but a young man who was looking happily at him. He had most of a bottle of whiskey in one hand, and now Nick understood. Not a corpse but a man who had gotten drunk and had passed out in the middle of the road.

Nick nodded at him and made a circle with his thumb and forefinger. Just then a drop of blood oozed warmly into the eye that Ray Booth had worked over, making it smart. He raised the eyepatch and swiped his forearm across it. He had a little more vision on that side today, but when he closed his good eye, the world still retreated to something which was little more than a colorful blur. He replaced the patch and then walked slowly to the curb and sat beside a Plymouth with Kansas plates which was slowly settling on its tires. He could see the gash on his forehead reflected in the Plymouth's bumper. It looked ugly but not deep. He would find the local drugstore, disinfect it, and slap a Band-Aid over it. He thought he still must have enough penicillin in his system to fight off almost anything, but his close call from the bullet-scrape on his leg had given him a horror of infection. He picked scraps of gravel out of his palms, wincing.

The man with the bottle of whiskey had been watching all of this with no expression at all. If Nick had looked up, it would have struck him as queer immediately. When he had turned away to examine his wound in the bumper's reflection, the animation had leaked out of the man's face. It became empty and clean and unlined. He was wearing bib-alls that were clean but faded and heavy workshoes. He stood about five-nine, and his hair was so blond it was nearly white. His eyes were a bright, empty blue, and with the cornsilk hair, his Swedish or Norwegian descent was unmistakable. He looked no more than twenty-three, but Nick found out later he had to be forty-five or close to it because he could remember the end of the Korean War, and how his daddy had come home in uniform a month later. There was no question that he might have made that up. Invention was not Tom Cullen's long suit.

He stood there, empty of face, like a robot whose plug has been pulled. Then, little by little, animation seeped back into his face. His whiskey-reddened eyes began to twinkle. He smiled. He had remembered again what this situation called for.

'Holy gee, mister, but you took a tumble. Didn't you just? My laws!' He blinked at the amount of blood on Nick's forehead.

Nick had a pad of paper and a Bic in his shirt pocket; neither had been jarred loose by the fall. He wrote: 'You just scared me. Thought you were dead until you sat up. I'm okay. Is there a drugstore in town?'

He showed the pad to the man in the bib-alls. The man took it. Looked at what was written there. Handed it back. Smiling, he said, 'I'm Tom Cullen. But I can't read. I only got to third grade but then I was sixteen and my daddy made me quit. He said I was too big.'

Retarded, Nick thought. I can't talk and he can't read. For a moment he was utterly nonplussed.

'Holy gee, mister, but you took a tumble!' Tom Cullen

exclaimed. In a way, it was the first time for both of them. 'My laws, didn't you just!'

Nick nodded. Replaced the pad and pen. Put a hand over his mouth and shook his head. Cupped his hands over his ears and shook his head. Placed his left hand against his throat and shook his head.

Cullen grinned, puzzled. 'Got a toothache? I had one once. Gee, it hurt. Didn't it just? My laws!'

Nick shook his head and went through his dumbshow again. Cullen guessed earache this time. Nick threw his hands up and went over to his bike. The paint was scraped, but it didn't seem hurt. He got on and pedaled a little way up the street. Yes, it was all right. Cullen jogged alongside, smiling happily. His eyes never left Nick. He hadn't seen anyone for most of a week.

'Don't you feel like talkin?' he asked, but Nick didn't look around or appear to have heard. Tom tugged at his sleeve and repeated his question.

The man on the bike put his hand over his mouth again and shook his head. Tom frowned. Now the man had put his bike on its kickstand and was looking at the storefronts. He seemed to see what he wanted, because he went over to the sidewalk and then to Mr Norton's drugstore. If he wanted to go in there it was just too bad, because the drug was locked up. Mr Norton had left town. Just about everybody had locked up and left town, it seemed like, except for Mom and her friend Mrs Blakely, and they were both dead.

Now the no-talking-man was trying the door. Tom could have told him it was no use even though the OPEN sign was on the door. The OPEN sign was a liar. Too bad, because Tom would dearly have loved an ice cream soda. It was a lot better than the whiskey, which had made him feel good at first and then made him sleepy and then had made his head ache fit to split. He had gone to sleep to get away from the headache but he had had a lot of crazy dreams about a man in a black suit like the one that Revrunt Deiffenbaker always wore. The man in the black suit chased him through the dreams. He seemed like a very bad man to Tom. The only reason he had gone to drinking in the first place was because he wasn't supposed to, his daddy had told him that, and Mom too, but now everyone was gone, so what? He would if he wanted to.

But what was the no-talking-man doing now? Picked up the litter basket from the sidewalk and he was going to . . . what? Break

Mr Norton's window? CRASH! By God and by damn if he didn't! And now he was reaching through, unlocking the door . . .

'Hey, mister, you can't do that!' Tom cried, his voice throbbing with outrage and excitement. 'That's illegal! M-O-O-N and that spells *il*-legal. Don't you know –'

But the man was already inside and he never turned around.

'What are you, anyway, deaf?' Tom called indignantly. 'My laws! Are you . . .'

He trailed off. The animation and excitement left his face. He was the robot with the pulled plug again. In May it had not been an uncommon sight to see Feeble Tom like this. He would be walking along the street, looking into shop windows with that eternally happy expression on his slightly rounded Scandahoovian face, and all of a sudden he would stop dead and go blank. Someone might shout, '*There goes Tom!*' and there would be laughter. If Tom's daddy was with him he would scowl and elbow Tom, perhaps even sock him repeatedly on the shoulder or the back until Tom came to life. But Tom's daddy had been around less and less over the first half of 1988 because he was stepping out with a redheaded waitress who worked at Boomer's Bar & Grille. Her name was DeeDee Packalotte (and weren't there some jokes about that name), and about a year ago she and Don Cullen had run off together. They had been seen just once, in a cheap fleabag motel not far away, in Slapout, Oklahoma, and that had been the last of them.

Most folks took Tom's sudden blankouts as a further sign of retardation, but they were actually instances of nearly normal thinking. The human thinking process is based (or so the psychologists tell us) on deduction and induction, and the retarded person is incapable of making these deductive and inductive leaps. There are lines down somewhere inside, circuits shorted out, fouled switches. Tom Cullen was not severly retarded, and he was capable of making simple connections. Every now and then – during his blankouts – he would be capable of making a more sophisticated inductive or deductive connection. He would feel the possibility of making such a connection the way a normal person will sometimes feel a name dancing 'right on the tip of his tongue.' When it happened, Tom would dismiss his real world, which was nothing more or less than an instant-by-instant flow of sensory input, and go into his mind. He would be like a man in a darkened unfamiliar room who holds the plug-end of a lampcord in one hand and who goes crawling around on the floor, bumping into things and feeling with his free hand for the electrical socket. And if he found it – he didn't always – there would be a burst of illumination and he would see the room (or the idea) plain. Tom was a sensory creature. A list of his favorite things would have included the taste of an ice cream soda at Mr Norton's fountain, watching a pretty girl in a short dress waiting on the corner to cross the street, the smell of lilac, the feel of silk. But more than any of these things he loved the intangible, he loved that moment when the connection would be made, the switch cleared (at least momentarily), the light would go on in the dark room. It didn't always happen; often the connection eluded him. This time it didn't.

He had said, *What are you, anyway, deaf?*

The man hadn't acted like he heard what Tom was saying except for those times he had been looking right at him. And the man hadn't said anything to him, not even hi. Sometimes people didn't answer Tom when he asked questions because something in his face told them he was soft upstairs. But when that happened, the person who wouldn't answer looked mad or sad or kind of blushy. This man didn't act like that – he had given Tom a circle made of his thumb and forefinger and Tom knew that meant Okey Dokey . . . but still he didn't talk.

Hands over his ears and a shake of his head.

Hands over his mouth and the same.

Hands over his neck and the same again.

The room lit up: connection made.

'My laws!' Tom said, and the animation came back into his face. His bloodshot eyes glowed. He rushed into Norton's Drugstore, forgetting that it was illegal to do so. The no-talking-man was squirting something that smelled like Bactine onto cotton and was then wiping the cotton on his forehead.

'Hey mister!' Tom said, rushing up. The no-talking-man didn't turn around. Tom was momentarily puzzled, and then he remembered. He tapped Nick on the shoulder and Nick turned. 'You're deaf n dumb, right? Can't hear! Can't talk! Right?'

Nick nodded. And to him, Tom's reaction was nothing short of amazing. He jumped into the air and clapped his hands wildly.

'I thought of it! Hooray for me! I thought of it myself! Hooray for Tom Cullen!'

Nick had to grin. He couldn't remember when his disability had brought someone so much pleasure.

★　　★　　★

There was a small town square fronting on the courthouse, and in this square was a statue of a Marine tricked out in World War II kit and weaponry. The plaque beneath announced that this monument was dedicated to the boys from Harper County who had made the ULTIMATE SACRIFICE FOR THEIR COUNTRY. In the shade of this monument Nick Andros and Tom Cullen sat, eating Underwood Deviled Ham and Underwood Deviled Chicken on potato chips. Nick had an *x* of Band-Aids on his forehead above his left eye. He was reading Tom's lips (which was a little tough, because Tom kept stuffing food through what he was saying) and reflecting to himself that he was getting damned tired of eating stuff which came out of cans. What he would really like was a big steak with all the trimmings.

Tom hadn't stopped talking since they sat down. It was pretty repetitious stuff, with many ejaculations of *My laws!* and *Wasn't it just?* thrown in for seasoning. Nick didn't mind. He hadn't really known how much he missed other people until he met Tom, or how much he had been secretly afraid that he was the only one left, out of all the earth. It had even crossed his mind at one point that maybe the disease had killed everyone in the world but deaf-mutes. Now, he thought with an interior smile, he could speculate on the possibility that it had killed everyone in the world but deaf-mutes and the mentally retarded. That thought, which seemed amusing in the two o'clock light of a summer's afternoon, would come back to haunt him that night and not seem funny at all.

He wondered where Tom thought all the people had gone. He had already heard about Tom's daddy, who had run off a couple of years before with a waitress, and about Tom's job as a handyman out on the Norbutt farm and how, two years ago, Mr Norbutt had decided Tom was 'getting on well enough' to be trusted handling an axe, and about the 'big boys' who had jumped Tom one night and how Tom had 'fought em all off 'til they was just about dead, and I put one of em in the hospital with ruptures, M-O-O-N, that spells ruptures, that's what Tom Cullen did,' and he had heard about how Tom had found his mother at Mrs Blakely's house and they were both dead in the living room and so Tom had stolen away. Jesus wouldn't come and take dead people up to heaven if anyone was watching, Tom said (Nick reflected that Tom's Jesus was a kind of Santa Claus in reverse, taking dead people up the chimney instead of bringing presents down). But he had said nothing at all about

May's total emptiness, or the road arrowing in and out of town on which nothing moved.

He put his hands lightly on Tom's chest, stopping the flow of words.

'What?' Tom asked.

Nick waved his arm in a large circle at the buildings of the downtown area. He put a burlesque expression of puzzlement on his face, wrinkling his brow, cocking his head, scratching the back of his skull. Then he made walking motions with his fingers on the grass and finished by looking up at Tom questioningly.

What he saw was alarming. Tom might have died sitting up for all the animation on his face. His eyes, which had been sparkling a moment before with all the things he wanted to tell, were now cloudy blue marbles. His mouth hung ajar so Nick could see the soggy potato chip crumbs lying on his tongue. His hands were lax in his lap.

Concerned, Nick reached out to touch him. Before he could, Tom's body gave a jerk. His eyelids fluttered, and the animation flowed back into his eyes like water filling a pail. He began to grin. If a balloon containing the word EUREKA had appeared over his head, what had happened would not have been more plain.

'You want to know where all the people went!' Tom exclaimed.

Nick nodded his head strongly.

'Well, I guess they went to Kansas City,' Tom said. 'My laws, yes. Everybody's always talkin about what a little town this is. Nothin happens. No fun. Even the roller-skating place went bust. Now there's nothin but the drive-in, and that doesn't show anything but those diddly-daddly pitchers. My mom always says people leaves but no people comes back. Just like my dad, he run off with a waitress from Boomer's Café, her name was M-O-O-N, that spells DeeDee Packalotte. So I guess everybody just got fed up and went at the same time. To Kansas City it must have been, my laws, didn't they just? That's where they must have gone. Except for Mrs Blakely and my mom. Jesus is going to take them up to heaven up above and rock them in the everlasting harms.'

Tom's monologue recommenced.

Gone to Kansas City, Nick thought. For all *I* know, that could be it, too. Everybody left on the poor sad planet picked up by the Hand of God and either rocked in the everlasting harms of Same or set down again in Kansas City.

He leaned back and his eyelids fluttered so that Tom's words broke up into the visual equivalent of a modern poem, sans caps, like a work by e. e. cummings:

> mother said
> ain't got no
> but i said to them i said you better
> not mess with

The dreams had been bad the night before, which he had spent in a barn, and now, with his belly full, all he wanted was . . .

> my laws
> M-O-O-N that spells
> sure do wish

Nick fell asleep.

Waking up, he first wondered in that dazed way you have when you sleep heavily in the middle of the day why he was sweating so much. Sitting up, he understood. It was quarter to five in the afternoon; he had slept over two and a half hours and the sun had moved out from behind the war memorial. But that was not all. Tom Cullen, in a perfect orgy of solicitude, had covered him so he would not take a chill. With two blankets and a quilt.

He threw them aside, stood up, stretched. Tom was not in sight. Nick walked slowly toward the main entrance to the square, wondering what – if anything – he was going to do about Tom . . . or with him. The retarded fellow had been feeding himself from the A&P on the far side of the town square. He had felt no compunction about going in there and picking out what he wanted to eat by the pictures on the labels of the cans because, Tom said, the supermarket door had been unlocked.

Nick wondered idly what Tom would have done if it hadn't been. He supposed that, when he'd gotten hungry enough, he would have forgotten his scruples, or laid them aside for the nonce. But what would become of him when the food was gone?

But that wasn't what really bothered him about Tom. It was the pathetic eagerness with which the man had greeted him. Retarded he might be, Nick thought, but he was not too retarded to feel loneliness. Both his mother and the woman who had served as his commonlaw aunt were dead. His dad had run off long before. His employer, Mr Norbutt, and everyone else in May had stolen off to Kansas City one night while Tom slept, leaving him behind to wander up and down Main Street like a gently unhinged ghost. And he was getting into things he had no business getting into – like the whiskey. If he got drunk again, he might hurt himself. And if he got hurt with no one to take care of him, it would probably mean the end of him.

But . . . a deaf-mute and a man who was mentally retarded? Of what possible use could they be to each other? Here you got one guy who can't talk and another guy who can't think. Well, that wasn't fair. Tom could think at least a little, but he couldn't read, and Nick had no illusions about how long it would take him to get tired of playing charades with Tom Cullen. Not that *Tom* would get tired of it. Laws, no.

He stopped on the sidewalk just outside the park's entrance, hands stuffed in his pockets. Well, he decided, I can spend the night here with him. One night won't matter. I can cook him a decent meal at the very least.

Cheered a little by this, he went to find Tom.

Nick slept in the park that night. He didn't know where Tom slept, but when he woke up the next morning, slightly dewy but feeling pretty good otherwise, the first thing he saw when he crossed the town square was Tom, crouched over a fleet of toy Corgi cars and a large plastic Texaco station.

Tom must have decided that if it was all right to break into Norton's Drug Store, it was all right to break into another place. He was sitting on the curb of the five-and-ten, his back to Nick. About forty model cars were lined up along the edge of the sidewalk. Next to them was the screwdriver Tom had used to jimmy the display case open. There were Jaguars, Mercedes-Benzes, Rolls-Royces, a scale-model Bentley with a long, lime-green cowling, a Lamborghini, a Cord, a four-inch-long customized Pontiac Bonneville, a Corvette, a Maserati, and, God watch over us and protect us, a 1933 Moon. Tom was hunched over these studiously, driving them in and out of the garage, gassing them up at the toy pump. One of the lifts in the repair bay worked, Nick saw, and from time to time Tom would raise one of the cars up on it and pretend to do something underneath. If he had been able to hear, he would have heard, in the nearly perfect silence, the sound of

Tom Cullen's imagination at work – the lip-vibrating *brrrrr* as he drove the cars onto the Fisher-Price tarmac, the *chk-chk-chk-ding!* of the gas-pump at work, the *ssshhhhhh* as the lift inside went up and down. As it was, he could catch some of the conversation between the station proprietor and the little people in the little cars: *Fill that up, sir? Regular? You bet! Just let me get that windshield, ma'am. I think it's your carb. Let's put her up in the air and take a look at the bass-tud. Restrooms? You bet! Right around the side there!*

And over this, arching for miles in every direction, the sky God had allocated to this little bit of Oklahoma.

Nick thought: *I can't leave him. I can't do that.* And he was suddenly swept by a bitter and totally unexpected sadness, a feeling so deep he thought for a moment he would weep.

They've gone to Kansas City, he thought. *That's what's happened. They've all gone to Kansas City.*

Nick walked across the street and tapped Tom on the arm. Tom jumped and looked over his shoulder. A large and guilty smile stretched his lips, and a blush climbed out of his shirt collar.

'I know it's for little boys and not for grown men,' he said. 'I know that, laws yes, Daddy tole me.'

Nick shrugged, smiled, spread his hands. Tom looked relieved.

'It's mine now. Mine if I want it. If you could go in the drug and get something, I could go into the five-and-dime and get something. My laws, couldn't I just? I don't have to put it back, do I?'

Nick shook his head.

'Mine,' Tom said happily, and turned back to the garage. Nick tapped him again and Tom looked back. 'What?'

Nick tugged his sleeve and Tom stood up willingly enough. Nick led him down the street to where his bike leaned on its kickstand. He pointed to himself. Then at the bike. Tom nodded.

'Sure. That bike is yours. That Texaco garage is mine. I won't take your bike and you won't take my garage. Laws, no!'

Nick shook his head. He pointed at himself. At the bike. Then down Main Street. He waved his fingers: byebye.

Tom became very still. Nick waited. Tom said hesitantly: 'You movin on, mister?'

Nick nodded.

'I don't want you to!' Tom burst out. His eyes were wide and very blue, sparkling with tears. 'I like you! I don't want you to go to Kansas City, too!'

Nick pulled Tom next to him and put an arm around him. Pointed to himself. To Tom. To the bike. Out of town.

'I don't getcha,' Tom said.

Patiently, Nick went through it again. This time he added the byebye wave, and in a burst of inspiration he lifted Tom's hand and made it wave byebye, too.

'Want me to go with you?' Tom asked. A smile of disbelieving delight lit up his face.

Relieved, Nick nodded.

'Sure!' Tom shouted. 'Tom Cullen's gonna go! Tom's –' He halted, some of the happiness dying out of his face, and looked at Nick cautiously. 'Can I take my garage?'

Nick thought about it a moment and then nodded his head yes.

'Okay!' Tom's grin reappeared like the sun from behind a cloud. 'Tom Cullen's going!'

Nick led him to the bike. He pointed at Tom, then at the bike.

'I never rode one like that,' Tom said doubtfully, eyeing the bike's gearshift and the high, narrow seat. 'I guess I better not. Tom Cullen would fall off a fancy bike like that.'

But Nick was provisionally encouraged. *I never rode one like that* meant that he had ridden some sort of bike. It was only a question of finding a nice simple one. Tom was going to slow him down, that was inevitable, but perhaps not too much after all. And what was the hurry, anyway? Dreams were only dreams. But he did feel an inner urge to hurry, something so strong yet indefinable that it amounted to a subconscious command.

He led Tom back to his filling station. He pointed at it, then smiled and nodded at Tom. Tom squatted down eagerly, and then his hands paused in the act of reaching for a couple of cars. He looked up at Nick, his face troubled and transparently suspicious. 'You ain't gonna go without Tom Cullen, are you?'

Nick shook his head firmly.

'Okay,' Tom said, and turned confidently to his toys. Before he could stop himself, Nick had ruffled the man's hair. Tom looked up and smiled shyly at him. Nick smiled back. No, he couldn't just leave him. That was sure.

It was almost noon before he found a bike which he thought would suit Tom. He hadn't expected it to take anywhere near as long as it did, but a surprising majority of people had locked their houses, garages, and outbuildings. In most cases he was reduced to peering into shadowy garages through dirty, cobwebby windows, hoping to spot the right bike. He spent a good three hours trudging from street to street with the sweat pouring off him and the sun pounding steadily against the back of his neck. At one point he had gone back to recheck the Western Auto, but that was no good; the two bikes in the show window were his-and-hers three-speeds and everything else was unassembled.

In the end he found what he was looking for in a small detached garage at the southern end of town. The garage was locked, but it had one window big enough to crawl through. Nick broke the glass with a rock and carefully picked the remaining slivers out of the old, crumbling putty. Inside, the garage was explosively hot and furry with a thick oil-and-dust smell. The bike, an old-fashioned boy's Schwinn, stood next to a ten-year-old Merc station wagon with balding tires and flaking rocker panels.

The way my luck's running the damn bike'll be busted, Nick thought. No chain, flat tires, something. But this time his luck was in. The bike rolled easily. The tires were up and had good tread; all the bolts and sprockets seemed tight. There was no bike basket, he would have to remedy that, but there was a chainguard and hung neatly on the wall between a rake and a snowshovel was an unexpected bonus: a nearly new Briggs hand-pump.

He hunted further and found a can of 3-in-One Oil on a shelf. Nick sat down on the cracked cement floor, now unmindful of the heat, and carefully oiled the chain and both sprockets. That done, he recapped the 3-in-One and carefully put it in his pants pocket.

He tied the bike-pump to the package carrier on the Schwinn's back fender with a hank of hayrope, then unlocked the garage door and ran it up. Fresh air had never smelled so sweet. He closed his eyes, inhaled it deeply, wheeled the bike out to the road, got on, and pedaled slowly down Main Street. The bike rode fine. It would be just the ticket for Tom . . . assuming he really could ride it.

He parked it beside his Raleigh and went into the five-and-dime. He found a good-sized wire bike basket in a jumble of sporting goods near the back of the store and was turning to leave with it under his arm when something else caught his eye: a Klaxon horn with a chrome bell and a large red rubber bulb. Grinning, Nick put the horn in the basket and then went over to the hardware section for a screwdriver and an adjustable wrench. He went back outside. Tom was sprawled peacefully in the shade of the old World War II Marine in the town square, napping.

Nick put the basket on the Schwinn's handlebars and attached the Klaxon horn beside it. He went back into the five-and-dime and came out with a good-sized tote-bag.

He took it up to the A&P and filled it with canned meat, fruit, and vegetables. He was pausing over some canned chili beans when he saw a shadow flit by on the aisle facing him. If he had been able to hear, he would already have been aware that Tom had discovered his bike. The Klaxon's hoarse and drawn-out cry of *Howww-OOO-Gah!* floated up and down the street, punctuated by Tom Cullen's giggles.

Nick pushed out through the supermarket's doors and saw Tom speeding grandly down Main, his blond hair and his shirttail whipping out behind him, squeezing the bulb of the Klaxon horn for all it was worth. At the Arco station that marked the end of the business section he whirled around and pedaled back. There was a huge and triumphant grin on his face. The Fisher-Price garage sat in the bike's basket. His pants pockets and the flap pockets of his khaki shirt bulged with scale-model Corgi cars. The sun flashed bright, revolving circles in the wheelspokes. A little wistfully Nick wished he could hear the sound of the horn, just to see if it pleased him as much as it was pleasing Tom.

Tom waved to him and continued on up the street. At the far end of the business section he swerved around again and rode back, still squeezing the horn. Nick held his hand out, a policeman's order to stop. Tom brought the bike to a skidding halt in front of him. Sweat stood out on his face in great beads. The bike-pump's rubber hose flopped. Tom was panting and grinning.

Nick pointed out of town and waved byebye.

'Can I still take my garage?'

Nick nodded and slipped the strap of the tote-bag over Tom's bull neck.

'We going right now?'

Nick nodded again. Made a circle with his thumb and forefinger.

'To Kansas City?'

Nick shook his head.

'To anywhere we want?'

Nick nodded. Yes. Anywhere they wanted, he thought, but anywhere would most likely turn out to be somewhere in Nebraska.

'Wow!' Tom said happily. 'Okay! Yeah! Wow!'

They got on Route 283 going north and had ridden only two and a half hours when thunderheads began to build up in the west. The storm came at them quickly, riding on a gauzy caul of rain. Nick couldn't hear the thunderclaps, but he could see forks of lightning stabbing down from the clouds. They were bright enough to dazzle the eyes with bluish-purple afterimages. As they approached the outskirts of Rosston, where Nick meant to turn east on Route 64, the veil of rain under the clouds disappeared and the sky turned a still and queerly ominous shade of yellow. The wind, which had been freshening against his left cheek, died away altogether. He began to feel extremely nervous without knowing why, and oddly clumsy. No one had ever told him that one of the few instincts man still shares with the lower animals is exactly that response to a sudden and radical drop in the air pressure.

Then Tom was tugging at his sleeve, tugging him frantically. Nick looked over at him. He was startled to see that all the color had gone out of Tom's face. His eyes were huge, floating saucers.

'Tornado!' Tom screamed. 'There's a tornado coming!'

Nick looked for a funnel and saw none. He turned back to Tom, trying to think of a way to reassure him. But Tom was gone. He was riding his bike into the field at the right of the road, beating a twisted, flattened path through the high grass.

Goddamned fool, Nick thought angrily. You're going to break your fucking axle!

Tom was making for a barn with an attached silo which stood at the end of a dirt road about a quarter of a mile long. Nick, still feeling nervous, pedaled his own bike up the highway, lifted it over the cattle-gate, and then pedaled up the dirt feeder road to the barn. Tom's bike lay on the dirt fill outside. He hadn't even bothered to put the kickstand down. Nick would have chalked this up to simple forgetfulness if he hadn't seen Tom use the kickstand several times before. He's scared right out of what little mind he has, Nick thought.

His own uneasiness made him take one last look over his shoulder, and what he saw coming froze him coldly in his tracks.

A horrible darkness was coming out of the west. It was not a cloud; it was more like a total absence of light. It was in the shape of a funnel, and at first glance it looked a thousand feet high. It was wider at the top than at the bottom; the bottom was not quite touching the earth. At its summit, the very clouds seemed to be fleeing from it, as if it possessed some mysterious power of repulsion.

As Nick watched, it touched down about three quarters of a mile away and a long blue building with a roof made of corrugated metal – an auto supply place, or perhaps a lumber storage shed – exploded with a loud bang. He could not hear this, of course, but the vibration struck him, rocking him back on his feet. And the building seemed to explode *inward*, as if the funnel had sucked all the air out of it. The next moment the tin roof broke in two. The sections whirled upward, spinning and spinning like a top gone insane. Fascinated, Nick craned his neck to follow their progress.

I am looking at whatever it is in my worst dreams, Nick thought, *and it is not a man at all, although it may sometimes look like a man. What it really is is a tornado. One almighty big black twister ripping out of the west, sucking up anything and everything unlucky enough to be in its path. It's –*

Then he was grabbed by both arms and literally jerked off his feet and into the barn. He looked around at Tom Cullen and was momentarily surprised to see him. In his fascination with the storm, he had quite forgotten that Tom Cullen existed.

'Downstairs!' Tom panted. 'Quick! Quick! Oh my laws, yes! Tornado! *Tornado!*'

At last Nick was fully, consciously afraid, ripped out of the half-entranced state he had been in and aware again of where he was and who he was with. As he let Tom lead him to the stairs going down into the barn's storm cellar, he became aware of a strange, thrumming vibration. It was the closest thing to sound he had ever experienced. It was like a nagging ache in the center of his brain. Then, as he went down the stairs behind Tom, he saw something he would never forget: the plank siding of the barn being pulled out board by board, pulled out and whirled up into the cloudy air, like rotted brown teeth being pulled out by invisible forceps. The hay littered on the floor began to rise and whirl in a dozen miniature tornado funnels, nodding and dipping and skipping. That thrumming vibration grew ever more persistent.

Then Tom was pushing open a heavy wooden door, thrusting him through. Nick smelled wet mold and decay. In the last instant of light he saw they were sharing the storm cellar with a family of rat-gnawed corpses. Then Tom slammed the door shut and they were in perfect darkness. The vibration lessened but did not cease completely even then.

Panic crept up on him with its cloak open and gathered him in. The blackness reduced his senses to touch and smell, and neither of them sent messages which were comforting. He could feel the constant vibration of the boards beneath his feet, and the smell was death.

Tom clutched his hand blindly and Nick drew the retarded man next to him. He could feel Tom trembling, and he wondered if Tom was crying, or perhaps trying to speak to him. The thought eased some of his own fear and he slung an arm about Tom's shoulders. Tom reciprocated and they stood bolt upright in the dark, clinging to each other.

The vibration grew stronger under Nick's feet; even the air seemed to be trembling lightly against his face. Tom held him more tightly still. Blind and deaf, he waited for what might happen next and reflected that if Ray Booth had gotten his other eye, all of life would be like this. If that had happened, he believed he would have shot himself in the head days ago and had done with it.

Later he would be almost unable to believe his watch, which insisted that they had spent only fifteen minutes in the darkness of the storm cellar, although logic told him that since the watch was still running, it must be so. Never before in his life had he understood how subjective, how plastic, time really is. It seemed that it must have been at least an hour, probably two or three. And as the time passed, he became convinced that he and Tom were not alone in the storm cellar. Oh, there were the bodies – some poor guy had brought his family down here near the end, perhaps on the fevered assumption that, since they had weathered other natural disasters down here, they could weather this here one, too – but it wasn't the bodies that he meant. To Nick's mind, a corpse was just a thing, no different than a chair or a typewriter or a rug. A corpse was just an inanimate thing which filled space. What he felt was the presence of another being, and he became more and more convinced who – or what – it was.

It was the dark man, the man who came to life in his dreams, the creature whose spirit he had sensed in the black heart of the cyclone.

Somewhere . . . over in the corner or perhaps right behind them . . . *he* was watching them. And waiting. At the right moment he would touch them and they would both . . . what? Go mad with fear, of course. Just that. He could see them. Nick was sure he could see them. He had eyes which could see in the dark like a cat's eyes, or those of some weird alien creature. Like the one in that movie, *Predator*, perhaps. Yes — like that. The dark man could see tones of the spectrum that human eyes could never attain to, and to him everything would look slow and red, as if the whole world had been tie-dyed in a vat of gore.

At first Nick was able to divide this fantasy from reality, but as time passed, he became more and more sure that the fantasy *was* reality. He fancied he could feel the dark man's breath on the back of his neck.

He was about to make a lunge at the door, open it and flee upstairs no matter what, when Tom did it for him. The arm around Nick's shoulders was suddenly gone. The next instant the door of the storm cellar banged open, letting in a flood of dazzling white light that made Nick raise a hand to shield his good eye. He caught just a ghostly, wavering glimpse of Tom Cullen staggering and stumbling up the stairs, and then he followed, groping his way in the dazzle. By the time he got to the top, his eye had adjusted.

He thought that the light hadn't been so bright when they went down, and saw why immediately. The roof had been torn off the barn. It seemed to have been almost surgically removed; the job was so clean that there were no splinters and hardly any litter lying on the floor it had once sheltered. Three roofbeams hung down from the sides of the loft, and almost all the boards had been stripped off the sides. Standing here was like standing inside the picked skeleton of a prehistoric monster.

Tom had not stopped to inventory the damage. He was fleeing the barn as if the devil himself was at his heels. He looked back just once, his eyes huge and almost comically terrified. Nick could not resist a look back over his shoulder and into the storm cellar. The stairs pitched and yawed downward into shadow, old wood, splintered and sunken in the center of each riser. He could see littered straw on the floor and two sets of hands protruding from the shadow. The fingers had been stripped down to the bone by rats.

If there was anyone else down there, Nick did not see him.

Nor did he want to.

He followed Tom outside.

Tom was standing by his bicycle, shivering. Nick was momentarily bemused by the freaky choosiness of the tornado, which had taken most of the barn but had disdained their bikes, when he saw that Tom was weeping. Nick went over to him and put an arm about his shoulders. Tom was staring, wide-eyed, at the sagging double doors of the barn. Nick made a thumb-and-forefinger circle. Tom's eyes dropped to this briefly, but the smile Nick had hoped for did not surface on Tom's face. He simply went back to staring at the barn. His eyes had a vacant, fixated cast Nick didn't like at all.

'Someone was in there,' Tom said abruptly.

Nick smiled, but the smile felt cold on his lips. He had no idea how good the imitation looked, but it felt crappy. He pointed to Tom, to himself, and then made a sharp cutting gesture through the air with the side of his hand.

'No,' Tom said. '*Not* just us. Someone else. Someone who came out of the twister.'

Nick shrugged.

'Can we go now? Please?'

Nick nodded.

They trundled their bicycles back to the highway, using the path of uprooted grass and torn soil that the tornado had made. It had touched down on the west side of Rosston, had cut across US 283 on a west-to-east course, throwing guardrails and connecting cable into the air like piano wire, had skirted the barn to their left and ploughed directly through the house which stood – *had* stood – in front of it. Four hundred yards farther along, its track through the field abruptly ceased. Now the clouds had begun to break up (although it was still showering, lightly and refreshingly) and birds were singing unconcernedly.

Nick watched the hefty muscles under Tom's shirt work as he lifted his bike over the jumble of guardrail cable on the verge of the highway. That guy saved my life, he thought. I never saw a twister in my life before today. If I'd left him behind back there in May like I thought about doing, I'd be as dead as a doornail right about now.

He lifted his bike over the frayed cables and clapped Tom on the back and smiled at him.

We've got to find somebody else, Nick thought. We've *got* to, just so I can tell him thanks. And my name. He doesn't even know my name, because he can't read.

He stood there for a moment, bemused by this, and then they mounted their bikes and rode away.

★   ★   ★

They camped that night in left field of the Rosston Jaycees' Little League ballfield. The evening was cloudless and starry. Nick's sleep came quickly and was dreamless. He woke up at dawn the next morning, thinking how good it was to be with someone again, what a difference it made.

There really was a Polk County, Nebraska. At first that had given him a start, but he had traveled all over the last few years. He must have talked to somebody who mentioned Polk County, or who had come from Polk County, and his conscious mind had just forgotten it. There was a Route 30, too. But he couldn't really believe, at least not in the bright day of this early morning, that they were actually going to find an old Negro woman sitting on her porch in the middle of a field of corn and accompanying herself on a guitar while she sang hymns. He didn't believe in precognition or in visions. But it seemed important to go somewhere, to look for people. In a way he shared Fran Goldsmith's and Stu Redman's urge to regroup. Until that could be done, everything would remain alien and out of joint. There was danger everywhere. You couldn't see it but you could feel it, the way he thought he had felt the presence of the dark man in that cellar yesterday. You felt that danger was everywhere, inside the houses, around the next bend in the highway, maybe even hiding beneath the cars and trucks littered all over the main roads. And if it wasn't there, it was in the calendar, hidden just two or three leaves down. Danger, every particle of his being seemed to whisper it. BRIDGE OUT. FORTY MILES OF BAD ROAD. WE ARE NOT RESPONSIBLE FOR PERSONS PROCEEDING BEYOND THIS POINT.

Part of it was the tremendous, walloping psychological shock of the empty countryside. As long as he had been in Shoyo, he had been partially protected from it. It didn't matter if Shoyo was empty, at least not too much, because Shoyo was so small in the scheme of things. But when you got moving, it was as if . . . well, he remembered a Walt Disney movie he had seen as a kid, a nature thing. Filling the screen was this tulip, this one tulip, so beautiful it just made you want to hold your breath. Then the camera pulled back with dizzying suddenness and you saw a whole field filled with tulips. It knocked you flat. It produced total sensory overload and some internal circuit breaker fell with a sizzle, cutting off the input. It was too much. And that was how this trip had been. Shoyo was empty and he could adjust to that. But McNab was empty, too, and Texarkana, and Spencerville; Ardmore had burned right to the ground. He had come north on Highway 81 and had only seen deer. Twice he had seen what were probably signs of living people: a campfire perhaps two days old, and a deer that had been shot and neatly cleaned out. But no people. It was enough to screw you all up, because the enormity of it was steadily creeping up on you. It wasn't just Shoyo or McNab or Texarkana; it was *America*, lying here like a huge discarded tin can with a few forgotten peas rolling around in the bottom. And beyond America was the *whole world*, and thinking of that made Nick feel so dizzy and sick that he had to give up.

He bent over the atlas instead. If they kept rolling, maybe they would be like a snowball going downhill, getting bigger. With any luck they would pick up a few more people between here and Nebraska (or be picked up themselves, if they met a larger group). After Nebraska he supposed they would go somewhere else. It was like a quest with no object in view at the end of it – no Grail, no sword plunged into an anvil.

We'll cut northeast, he thought, up into Kansas. Highway 35 would take them to another version of 81, and 81 would take them all the way to Swedeholm, Nebraska, where it intersected Nebraska Route 92 at a perfect right angle. Another highway, Route 30, connected the two, the hypotenuse of a right triangle. And somewhere in that triangle was the country of his dream.

Thinking about it gave him a queer, anticipatory thrill.

Movement at the top of his vision made him look up. Tom was sitting, both fists screwed into his eyes. A cavernous yawn seemed to make the whole bottom half of his face disappear. Nick grinned at him and Tom grinned back.

'We gonna ride some more today?' Tom asked, and Nick nodded. 'Gee, that's good. I like to ride my bike. Laws, yes! I hope we never stop!'

Putting the atlas away Nick thought: And who knows? You may get your wish.

They turned east that morning and ate their lunch at a crossroads not far from the Oklahoma–Kansas border. It was July 7, and hot.

Shortly before they stopped to eat, Tom brought his bike to its customary skidding halt. He was staring at a signpost which had been sunk into a cement plug half-buried in the soft shoulder at the side of the road. Nick looked at it. The sign said: YOU ARE LEAVING

HARPER COUNTY, OKLAHOMA — YOU ARE ENTERING WOODS COUNTY, OKLAHOMA.

'I can read that,' Tom said, and if Nick had been able to hear, he would have been partly amused and partly touched by the way Tom's voice climbed into a high, reedy, and declamatory register: '*You are now going out of Harper County. You are now going into Woods County.*' He turned to Nick. 'You know what, mister?'

Nick shook his head.

'I never been out of Harper County in my life, laws, no, not Tom Cullen. But once my daddy took me out here and showed me this sign. He told me if he ever caught me t'other side of it, he'd whale the tar out of me. I sure hope he don't catch us over there in Woods County. You think he will?'

Nick shook his head emphatically.

'Is Kansas City in Woods County?'

Nick shook his head again.

'But we're going into Woods County before we go anyplace else, ain't we?'

Nick nodded.

Tom's eyes gleamed. 'Is it the world?'

Nick didn't understand. He frowned . . . raised his eyebrows . . . shrugged.

'The *world* is the place I mean,' Tom said. 'Are we going into the *world*, mister?' Tom hesitated and then asked with hesitant gravity: 'Is Woods the word for world?'

Slowly, Nick nodded his head.

'Okay,' Tom said. He looked at the sign for a moment, then wiped his right eye, from which a single tear had trickled. Then he hopped back onto his bike. 'Okay, let's go.' He biked over the county line without another word, and Nick followed.

They crossed into Kansas just before it got too dark to ride any farther. Tom had turned sulky and tired after supper; he wanted to play with his garage. He wanted to watch TV. He didn't want to ride anymore because his bum hurt from the seat. He had no conception of state lines and felt none of the lift Nick did when they passed another sign, this one saying YOU ARE NOW ENTERING KANSAS. By then the dusk was so thick that the white letters seemed to float inches above the brown sign, like spirits.

They camped a quarter of a mile over the line, beneath a water tower standing on tall steel legs like an H. G. Wells Martian. Tom was asleep as soon as he crawled into his sleeping bag. Nick sat awhile, watching the stars come out. The land was utterly dark, and for him, utterly still. Shortly before crawling in himself, a crow fluttered down to a fencepost nearby and seemed to be watching him. Its small black eyes were rimmed with half-circles of blood – reflection from a bloated orange summer moon that had risen silently. There was something about the crow Nick didn't like; it made him uneasy. He found a big dirt-clod and pegged it at the crow. It fluttered its wings, seemed to fix him with a baleful glare, and was gone into the night.

That night he dreamed of the man with no face standing on the high roof, his hands stretched out to the east, and then of the corn – corn higher than his head – and the sound of the music. Only this time he *knew* it was music and this time he knew it was a guitar. He awoke near dawn with a painfully full bladder and her words ringing in his ears: *Mother Abagail is what they call me . . . you come see me anytime.*

Late that afternoon, moving east through Comanche County on Highway 160, they sat astride their bikes in amazement, watching a small herd of buffalo – a dozen in all, perhaps – walking calmly back and forth across the road in search of good graze. There had been a barbed-wire fence on the north side of the road, but it appeared the buffalo had butted it down.

'What are they?' Tom asked fearfully. 'Those ain't cows!'

And because Nick couldn't talk and Tom couldn't read, Nick couldn't tell him. That day was July 8, 1990, and they slept that night in flat open farm country forty miles west of Deerhead.

It was July 9, and they were eating their lunch in the shade of an old, graceful elm in the front yard of a farmhouse which had partially burned down. Tom was eating sausages from a tin with one hand and driving a car in and out of his service station with the other. And singing the refrain of a popular song over and over again. Nick knew the shape it made on Tom's lips by heart: 'Baby, can you dig your man – he's a raht-eous ma-yun – baby, can you dig your man?'

Nick was depressed and slightly overawed by the size of the country; never before had he realized how easy it was to stick out your thumb, knowing that sooner or later the law of averages was going to favor you. A car was going to stop, usually with a man driving, and with a can of beer resting comfortably in the fork of his crotch more often than not. He would want to know how far you were going and you would hand him a slip of paper which you'd kept handy in your breast pocket, a slip of paper which read: 'Hello, my name is Nick Andros. I'm a deaf-mute. Sorry about that. I'm going to——. Thanks very much for the ride. I can read lips.' And that would be that. Unless the guy had a thing about deaf-mutes (and some people did, although they were a minority), you hopped in and the car took you where you wanted to go, or a good piece in that direction. The car ate road and blew miles out its tailpipe. The car was a form of teleportation. The car defeated the map. But now there *was* no car, although on many of these roads a car would have been a practical mode of transportation for seventy or eighty miles at a stretch, if you were careful. And when you were finally blocked, you would only have to abandon your vehicle, walk for a while, and then take another. With no car, they were like ants crawling across the chest of a fallen giant, ants trundling endlessly from one nipple to the other. And so Nick half wished, half daydreamed, that when they finally *did* meet someone else (always assuming that would happen), it would be as it had been in those mostly carefree days of hitchhiking: there would be that familiar twinkle of chrome rising over the top of the next hill, that sunflare which simultaneously dazzled and pleased the eye. It would be some perfectly ordinary American car, a Chevy Biscayne or a Pontiac Tempest, sweet old Detroit rolling iron. In his dreams it was never a Honda or Mazda or Yugo. That American beauty would pull over and he would see a man behind the wheel, a man with a sunburned elbow cocked cockily out the window. This man would be smiling and he would say, 'Holy Joe, boys! Ain't I some glad sumbitch to see you guys! Hop in here! Hop in and let's us see where we're goin!'

But they saw no one that day, and on the tenth it was Julie Lawry they ran across.

The day was another scorcher. They had pedaled most of the afternoon with their shirts tied around their waists, and both of them were getting brown as Indians. They hadn't been making very good time, not today, because of the apples. The green apples.

They had found them growing on an old apple tree in a farmyard, green and small and sour, but they had both been deprived of fresh fruit for a long time, and they tasted ambrosial. Nick made himself stop after two, but Tom ate six, greedily, one after the other, right down to the cores. He had ignored Nick's motions that he should stop; when he got an idea in his head, Tom Cullen could be every bit as attractive as a wayward child of four.

So, beginning around eleven in the morning and continuing through the rest of the afternoon, Tom had the squats. Sweat ran off him in small creeks. He groaned. He had to get off his bike and walk it up even shallow hills. Despite his irritation at the poor time they were making, Nick couldn't help a certain rueful amusement.

When they reached the town of Pratt around 4 PM, Nick decided that was it for the day. Tom collapsed gratefully on a bus-stop bench in the shade and dozed off at once. Nick left him there and went along the deserted business section in search of a drugstore. He would get some Pepto-Bismol and force Tom to drink it when he woke up, whether Tom wanted to or not. If it took a whole bottle to cork Tom up, so be it. Nick wanted to make up some time tomorrow.

He found a Rexall between the Pratt Theater and the local Norge. He slipped in through the open door, and stood for a moment smelling the familiar hot, unaired, stale smell. There were other odors mixed in, strong and cloying. Perfume was the strongest. Perhaps some of the bottles had burst in the heat.

Nick glanced around, looking for the stomach medicines, trying to remember if Pepto-Bismol went over in the heat. Well, the label would say. His eyes slipped past a mannequin and two rows to the right he saw what he wanted. He had taken two steps that way when he realized that he had never before seen a mannequin in a drugstore.

He looked back and what he saw was Julie Lawry.

She was standing perfectly still, a bottle of perfume in one hand, the small glass wand you used to daub the stuff on in the other. Her china-blue eyes were wide in stunned, disbelieving suspense. Her brown hair was drawn back and tied with a brilliant silk scarf that hung halfway down her back. She was wearing a pink middy sweater and bluejeans shorts that were almost abbreviated enough to be mistaken for panties. There was a rash of pimples on her forehead and a hell of a good one right in the middle of her chin.

She and Nick stared at each other across half the length of the deserted drugstore, both frozen now. Then the bottle of perfume dropped from her fingers, shattered like a bomb, and a hothouse reek filled the store, making it smell like a funeral parlor.

'Jesus, are you real?' she asked in a trembling voice.

Nick's heart had begun to race, and he could feel his blood thudding crazily in his temples. Even his eyesight had begun to wham in and out a little, making dots of light race across his field of vision.

He nodded.

'You ain't a ghost?'

He shook his head.

'Then say somethin. If you ain't a ghost, say somethin.'

Nick put a hand across his mouth, then on his throat.

'What's *that* s'posed to mean?' Her voice had taken on a slightly hysterical tone. Nick couldn't hear it . . . but he could sense it, see it on her face. He was afraid to step toward her, because if he did, she would run. He didn't think she was afraid of seeing another person; what she was afraid of was that she was seeing a hallucination, and she was cracking up. Again, he felt that wave of frustration. If he could only *talk* –

Instead, he went through his pantomime again. It was, after all, the only thing he could do. This time understanding dawned.

'You can't *talk*? You're a *mute*?'

Nick nodded.

She gave a high laugh that was mostly frustration. 'You mean somebody finally showed up and it's a *mute* guy?'

Nick shrugged and gave a slanting smile.

'Well,' she said, coming down the aisle to him, 'you ain't bad-looking. That's something.' She put a hand on his arm, and the swell of her breasts almost touched his arm. He could smell at least three different kinds of perfume, and under all of them the unlovely aroma of her sweat.

'My name's Julie,' she said. 'Julie Lawry. What's yours?' She giggled a little. 'You can't tell me, can you? Poor *you*.' She leaned a little closer, and her breasts brushed him. He began to feel very warm. What the hell, he thought uneasily, she's only a kid.

He broke away from her, took the pad from his pocket, and began to write. A line or so into his message she leaned over his shoulder to see what he was writing. No bra. Jesus. She had sure gotten over her scare quick. His writing became a little uneven.

'Oh, wow,' she said as he wrote – it was as if he was a monkey capable of doing a particularly sophisticated trick. Nick was looking down at his pad and didn't 'read' her words, but he could feel the tickling warmth of her breath.

'I'm Nick Andros. I'm a deaf-mute. I'm traveling with a man named Tom Cullen, who is lightly retarded. He can't read or understand many of the things I can act out unless they're very simple. We're on our way to Nebraska because I think there might be people there. Come with us, if you want.'

'Sure,' she said immediately, and then, remembering that he was deaf and shaping her words very carefully, she asked, 'Can you read lips?'

Nick nodded.

'Okay,' she said. 'I'm so glad to see someone, who cares if it's a deaf-mute and a retard. Spooky here. I can hardly sleep nights since the power went off.' Her face set in martyred lines of grief more appropriate to a soap opera heroine than a real person. 'My mom and dad died two weeks ago, you know. Everybody died but me. I've been so lonely.' With a sob she threw herself into Nick's arms and began to undulate against him in an obscene parody of grief.

When she drew back from him, her eyes were dry and shiny.

'Hey, let's make it,' she said. 'You're sort of cute.'

Nick gawped at her. I can't believe this, he thought.

But it was real enough. She was tugging at his belt. 'Come on. I'm on the pill. It's safe.' She paused for a moment. 'You can, can't you? I mean, just because you can't talk, that doesn't mean you can't –'

He put his hands out, perhaps meaning to take her by the shoulders, but he found her breasts instead. That was the end of any resistance he might have had. Coherent thought left his mind as well. He lowered her to the floor and had her.

Afterwards he went to the door and looked out as he buckled his belt again, checking on Tom. He was still on the park bench, dead to the world. Julie joined him, fiddling with a fresh bottle of perfume.

'That the retard?' she asked.

Nick nodded, not liking the word. It seemed like a cruel word.

She began to talk about herself, and Nick discovered to his relief that she was seventeen, not much younger than he was. Her mamma and her friends had always called her Angel-Face or just Angel for short, she said, because she looked so young. She told him a great deal more in the following hour, and Nick found it next to impossible to separate the truth from the lies ... or the wish-fulfillment, if you preferred. She might have been waiting for someone like him, who could never interrupt the endless flow of her monologue, all her life. Nick's eyes got tired just watching her pink lips push out the shapes of words. But if his eyes wandered for more than just a moment, to check on Tom or to consider the crashed-out plate-glass window of the dress shop across the street, her hand would touch his cheek, bringing his eyes back to her mouth. She wanted him to 'hear' everything, ignore nothing. He was annoyed with her at first, then bored with her. In the space of an hour, incredibly, he found himself wishing he hadn't found her in the first place, or that she would change her mind about coming with them.

She was 'into' rock music and marijuana and had a taste for what she called 'Colombian short rounds' and 'fry-daddies.' She'd had a boyfriend, but he'd gotten so pissed off at the 'establishment system' running the local high school that he had quit to join the Marines last April. She hadn't seen him since then, but still wrote him every week. She and her two girlfriends, Ruth Honinger and Mary Beth Gooch, went to all the rock concerts in Wichita and had hitched all the way to Kansas City last September to see Van Halen and the Monsters of Heavy Metal in concert. She claimed to have 'made it' with the Dokken bassist, and said it had been 'the most bitchin-groovy experience of my life'; she had just 'cried and cried' after the deaths of her mother and father within twenty-four hours of each other, even though her mother was a 'bitchy prude' and her father 'had a stick up his ass' about Ronnie, her boyfriend who had left town to join the Marines; she had plans to become either a beautician in Wichita when she graduated high school, or to 'truck on out to Hollywood and get a job with one of those companies that do the homes of the stars, I'm bitchin-groovy at interior decoration, and Mary Beth said she'd come with me.'

At this point she suddenly remembered Mary Beth Gooch was dead, and that her opportunity to become a beautician or an interior decorator to the stars had passed with her . . . and everyone and everything else. This seemed to strike her with a more genuine sort of grief. It was not a storm, however, but only a brief squall.

When the flow of words had begun to dry up a little – at least for the time being – she wanted to 'do it' (as she so coyly put it) again. Nick shook his head and she pouted briefly. 'Maybe I don't want to go with you after all,' she said.

Nick shrugged.

'Dummy-dummy-dummy,' she said with sudden sharp

viciousness. Her eyes shone with spite. Then she smiled. 'I didn't mean that. I was just kidding.'

Nick looked at her, expressionless. He had been called worse names, but there was something in her that he very much did not like. Some restless instability. If she got angry with you, she wouldn't yell or slap your face; not this one. This one would claw you. It came to him with sudden surety that she had lied about her age. She wasn't seventeen, or fourteen, or twenty-one. She was any age you wanted her to be . . . as long as you wanted her more than she wanted you, needed her more than she needed you. She came across as a sexual creature, but Nick thought that her sexuality was only a manifestation of something else in her personality . . . a symptom. *Symptom* was a word you used for someone who was sick, though, wasn't it? Did he think she was sick? In a way he did, and he was suddenly afraid of the effect she might have on Tom.

'Hey, your friend's waking up!' Julie said.

Nick looked around. Yes – Tom was now sitting on the park bench, scratching his crow's-nest hair and goggling around pallidly. Nick suddenly remembered the Pepto-Bismol.

'Hi, y'all!' Julie trilled, and ran down the street toward Tom, her breasts bouncing sweetly under her tight middy top. Tom's goggle had been big to begin with; now it grew bigger still.

'Hi?' he said-asked slowly, and looked at Nick for confirmation and/or explanation.

Masking his own unease, Nick shrugged and nodded.

'I'm Julie,' she said. 'How you doin, cutie-pie?'

Deep in thought – and unease – Nick went back into the drugstore to get what Tom needed.

'Uh-uh,' Tom said, shaking his head and backing away.

'Uh-uh, I ain't gonna. Tom Cullen doesn't like medicine, laws no, tastes bad.'

Nick looked at him with frustration and disgust, holding the three-sided bottle of Pepto-Bismol in one hand. He looked to Julie and she caught his gaze, but in it he saw that same teasing light as when she had called him dummy – it was not a twinkle but a hard mirthless shine. It is the look that a person with no essential sense of humor gets in his or her eye when he or she is getting ready to tease.

'That's right, Tom,' she said. 'Don't drink it, it's poison.'

Nick gaped at her. She grinned back, hands on hips, challenging him to convince Tom otherwise. This was her petty revenge, perhaps, for having her second offer of sex turned down.

He looked back at Tom and swigged from the Pepto-Bismol bottle himself. He could feel the dull pressure of anger at his temples. He held the bottle out to Tom, but Tom was not convinced.

'No, uh-uh, Tom Cullen doesn't drink poison,' he said, and with rising fury at the girl Nick saw that Tom was terrified. 'Daddy said don't. Daddy said if it'll kill the rats in the barn, it'll kill Tom! No poison!'

Nick suddenly half turned to Julie, unable to bear her smug grin. He hit her open-handed, hit her hard. Tom stared, eyes wide and scared.

'You . . .' she began, and for a moment she couldn't find the words. Her face flushed thinly, and she suddenly looked scrawny and spoiled and vicious. *'You dummy freak bastard! It was just a joke, you shithead! You can't hit me! You can't hit me, goddamn you!'*

She lunged at him and he pushed her backward. She fell on the seat of her denim shorts and stared up at him, lips pulled back in a snarl. 'I'll tear your balls off,' she breathed. 'You can't *do* that.'

Hands trembling, head pounding now, Nick took his pen out and scrawled a note out in large, jagged letters. He tore it off and held it out to her. Eyes glaring and furious, she batted it aside. He picked it up, grabbed the back of her neck, and shoved the note into her face. Tom had withdrawn, whimpering.

She screamed: 'All right! I'll read it! I'll read your crappy note!'

It was four words: 'We don't need you.'

'Fuck *you!*' she cried, tearing herself out of his grasp. She backed several steps down the sidewalk. Her eyes were as wide and blue as they had been in the drugstore when he almost literally stumbled over her, but now they were spitting with hate. Nick felt tired. Of all the possible people, why her?

'I'm not staying here,' Julie Lawry said. 'I'm coming. And you can't stop me.'

But he could. Didn't she realize that yet? No, Nick thought, she didn't. To her all of this was some sort of Hollywood scenario, a living disaster movie in which she had the starring part. It was a movie where Julie Lawry, also known as Angel-Face, always got what she wanted.

He drew the revolver from its holster and pointed it at her

feet. She became very still, and the flush evaporated from her face. Her eyes changed, and she looked very different, somehow real for the first time. Something had entered her world that she could not, at least in her own mind, manipulate to her advantage. A gun. Nick suddenly felt sick as well as tired.

'I didn't mean it,' she said rapidly. 'I'll do anything you want, honest to God.'

He motioned her away with the gun.

She turned and began to walk, looking back over her shoulder. She walked faster and faster, then broke into a run. She turned the corner a block up and was gone. Nick holstered the gun. He was trembling. He felt soiled and depressed, as if Julie Lawry had been something inhuman, more kin to the trundling and coldblooded beetles you find under dead trees than to other human beings.

He turned around, looking for Tom, but Tom wasn't in sight.

He trotted back down the sunstruck street, his head pounding monstrously, the eye Ray Booth had gouged throbbing. It took him almost twenty minutes to find Tom. He was crouched on a back porch two streets down from the business section. He was sitting on a rusty porch glider, his Fisher-Price garage cradled to his chest. When he saw Nick he began to cry.

'Please don't make me drink it, please don't make Tom Cullen drink poison, laws no, Daddy said if it would kill the rats it would kill me . . . *pleeease!*'

Nick saw that he was still holding the bottle of Pepto-Bismol. He threw it away and spread his empty hands in front of Tom. His diarrhea would just have to run its course. Thanks a lot, Julie.

Tom came down the porch steps, blubbering. 'I'm sorry,' he said over and over. 'I'm sorry, Tom Cullen's sorry.'

They walked back to Main Street together . . . and came to a halt, staring. Both bikes were overturned. The tires had been slashed. The contents of their packs had been strewn from one side of the street to the other.

Just then something passed at high speed close to Nick's face – he felt it – and Tom shrieked and began to run. Nick stood puzzled for a moment, looking around, and happened to be looking in the right direction to see the muzzle-flash of the second shot. It came from a second-story window of the Pratt Hotel. Something like a high-speed darning needle tugged at the fabric of his shirt collar.

He turned and ran after Tom.

He had no way of knowing if Julie fired again; all he knew for sure when he caught up to Tom was that neither of them had been shot. At least we're shut of that hellion, he thought, but that turned out to be only half-true.

They slept in a barn three miles north of Pratt that evening, and Tom kept waking up with nightmares and then waking Nick to be reassured. They reached Iuka the next morning around eleven, and found two good bicycles in a shop called Sport and Cycle World. Nick, who was beginning to recover at last from the encounter with Julie, thought they could finish re-outfitting themselves in Great Bend, which they should reach by the fourteenth at the latest.

But at just about quarter to three on the afternoon of July twelfth, he saw a twinkle in the rear-view mirror mounted near his left handgrip. He stopped (Tom, who was riding behind him and woolgathering, ran over his foot but Nick barely noticed) and looked back over his shoulder. The twinkle that had risen over the hill directly behind them like a daystar pleased and dazzled his eye – he could hardly believe it. It was a Chevy pickup of an ancient vintage, good old Detroit rolling iron, picking its way slowly, slaloming from one lane of US 281 to the other, avoiding a scatter of stalled vehicles.

It pulled up beside them (Tom was waving wildly, but Nick could only stand with his legs apart and his bike's crossbar between them, frozen) and came to a stop. Nick's last thought before the driver's head appeared was that it would be Julie Lawry, smiling her vicious, triumphant smile. She would have the gun with which she had tried to kill them before, and at a range this close, there would be no chance she would miss. Hell hath no fury like a woman scorned.

But the face that appeared belonged to a fortyish man wearing a straw hat with a feather cocked into the blue velvet band at a rakish angle, and when he grinned, his face became a drywash of agreeable sunwrinkles.

And what he said was: 'Holy Christ on a carousel, am I glad to see you boys? I guess I am. Climb on up here and let's see where we're going.'

That was how Nick and Tom met Ralph Brentner.

CHAPTER 44

He was cracking up – baby, don't you just know it?

That was a line from Huey 'Piano' Smith, now that he thought of it. Went way back. A blast from the past. Huey 'Piano' Smith, remember how that one went? *Ah-ah-ah-ah, daaaay-o . . . gooba-gooba-gooba-gooba . . . ah-ah-ah-ah.* Et cetera. The wit, wisdom, and social commentary of Huey 'Piano' Smith.

'Fuck the social commentary,' he said. 'Huey Piano Smith was before my time.'

Years later Johnny Rivers had recorded one of Huey's songs, 'Rockin Pneumonia and the Boogie-Woogie Flu.' Larry Underwood could remember that one very clearly, and he thought it very appropriate to the situation. Good old Johnny Rivers. Good old Huey 'Piano' Smith.

'Fuck it,' Larry opined once again. He looked terrible – a pale, frail phantom stumbling up a New England highway. 'Gimme the sixties.'

Sure, the sixties, those were the days. Mid-sixties, late sixties. Flower Power. Getting clean for Gene. Andy Warhol with his pink-rimmed glasses and his fucking Brillo boxes. Velvet Underground. The Return of the Creature from Yorba Linda. Norman Spinrad, Norman Mailer, Norman Thomas, Norman Rockwell, and good old Norman Bates of the Bates Motel, heh-heh-heh. Dylan broke his neck. Barry McGuire croaked 'The Eve of Destruction.' Diana Ross raised the consciousness of every white kid in America. All those wonderful groups, Larry thought dazedly, give me the sixties and cram the eighties up your ass. When it came to rock and roll, the sixties had been the Last Hurrah of the Golden Horde. Cream. Rascals. Spoonful. Airplane with Grace Slick on vocals, Norman Mailer on lead guitar, and good old Norman Bates on drums. Beatles. Who. Dead –

He fell over and hit his head.

The world swam away blackly and then came back in bright

fragments. He wiped his hand across his temple and it came away with a thin foam of blood on it. Didn't even matter. Whafuck, as they used to say back in the bright and glorious mid-sixties. What was falling down and hitting your head when he had spent the last week unable to sleep without waking up from nightmares, and the good nights were the nights when the scream got no farther than the middle of his throat? If you screamed out loud and woke up to *that*, you scared yourself even worse.

Dreams of being back in the Lincoln Tunnel. There was somebody behind him, only in the dreams it wasn't Rita. It was the devil, and he was stalking Larry with a lightless grin frozen on his face. The black man wasn't the walking dead; he was *worse* than the walking dead. Larry ran with the slow sludgy panic of bad dreams, tripping over unseen corpses, knowing they were staring at him with the glassy eyes of stuffed trophies from the crypts of their cars, which had stalled inside the frozen traffic even though they had some other place to be, he ran, but what good was running when the black devil man, the black magic man, could see in the dark with eyes like snooperscopes? And after a while the dark man would begin to croon to him: *Come on, Laarry, come on, we'll get it togeeeether Laaarry –*

He would feel the black man's breath on his very shoulder and that was when he would struggle up from sleep, escaping sleep, and the scream would be stuck in his throat like a hot bone or actually escaping his lips, loud enough to wake the dead.

Daytimes, the vision of the dark man would recede. The dark man strictly worked the night shift. Daytimes, it was the Big Alone that went to work on him, gnawing its way into his brain with the sharp teeth of some tireless rodent – a rat, or a weasel, maybe. During the days, his thoughts would dwell on Rita. Lovely Rita, meter-maid. Over and over in his mind he would turn her over and over, seeing those slitted eyes, like the eyes of an animal which has died in surprise and pain, that mouth he had kissed now filled with stale green puke. She had died so easy, in the night, *in the same fucking sleeping bag*, and now he was . . .

Well, cracking up. That was it, wasn't it? That was what was happening to him. He was cracking up.

'Cracking,' he moaned. 'Oh Jeez, I'm going out of my mind.'

A part of him that still retained a measure of rationality asserted that that might be true, but what he was suffering from right this minute was heat prostration. After what had happened to Rita, he hadn't been able to ride the motorcycle anymore. He just hadn't been able to; it was like a mental block. He kept seeing himself smeared all over the highway. So finally he had ditched it. Since then he had been walking – how many days? four? eight? nine? He didn't know. It had been in the nineties since ten this morning, it was now nearly four, the sun was right behind him, and he wasn't wearing a hat.

He couldn't remember how many days ago he had ditched the motorcycle. Not yesterday, and probably not the day before (maybe, but probably not), and what did it matter? He had gotten off it, snapped it into gear, twisted the throttle, and let go of the clutch. It had torn itself out of his trembling, sick hands like a dervish and had gone plunging and rearing over the embankment of US 9 some-where just east of Concord. He thought the name of the town in which he had murdered his motorcycle might have been Gossville, although that didn't matter much, either. The fact was, the bike had been no more good to him. He hadn't dared drive it over fifteen miles an hour, and even at fifteen he would have nightmare visions of being thrown over the handlebars and fracturing his skull or going around a blind corner and slamming into an overturned truck and going up in a fireball. And after a while the motherfucking overheat light had come on, of *course* it had, and it seemed he could almost read the word COWARD printed in small no-nonsense letters on the plastic housing over the little red bulb. Had there been a time when he had not only taken the cycle for granted but had actually *enjoyed* it, the sensation of speed as the wind rushed by on both sides of his face, the pavement blurring by six cold inches below the footposts? Yes. When Rita had been with him, before Rita had turned into nothing but a mouthful of green puke and a pair of slitted eyes, he *had* enjoyed it.

So he'd sent the motorcycle crashing over the embankment and into a weed-choked gully and then he had peered at it with a kind of cautious terror, as if it could somehow rise up and smite him. *Come on*, he had thought, *come on and stall out, ya sucker.* But for a long time, the motorcycle wouldn't. For a long time it raved and bellowed down there in that gully, the rear wheel spinning fruitlessly, the hungry chain gobbling up last fall's leaves and spitting out clouds of brown, bitter-smelling dust. Blue smoke belched from the chromed exhaust pipe. And even then he had been far enough gone to think there was something supernatural about it, that the cycle would right itself, rise out of its grave, and chew *him* up . . . either that or he would look back one afternoon at the rising sound of an engine and see his cycle, this damned cycle which wouldn't just stall out and die decently, roaring straight down the highway at him, doing eighty, and bent over the handlebars would be that dark man, that hardcase, and riding pillion behind him, with her white silk deckpants rippling in the breeze, would be Rita Blakemoor, her face chalk white, her eyes slitted, her hair as dry and dead as a cornpatch in the wintertime. Then, at last, the cycle began to spit and chug and seizure and misfire, and when it finally stopped he had looked down at it and felt sad, as if it had been some part of himself he had killed. Without the cycle there was no way in which he could mount a serious assault on the silence, and the silence was, in a way, worse than his fears of dying or being seriously hurt in an accident. Since then he had been walking. He had gone through several small towns along Route 9 which had cycle shops, showroom models with the keys hanging right in them, but if he looked at them too long, the visions of himself lying beside the road in a pool of blood would rise up in vivid, unhealthy Technicolor, like something from one of those awful but somehow fascinating Charles Band horror movies, the ones where people kept dying under the wheels of large trucks or as a consequence of large, nameless bugs which had bred and grown in their warm vitals and finally burst free in a gut-busting display of flying flesh, and he would pass by, enduring the silence, pallid, shivering. He would pass by with exquisite little clusters of perspiration growing on his upper lip and in the hollows of his temples.

He had lost weight – why not? He walked all day long, every day, from sunrise to sunset. He wasn't sleeping. The nightmares would wake him up by four and he would light his Coleman lamp and crouch by it, waiting for the sun to come up enough so he dared to walk. And he would go on walking until it was almost too dark to see and then make camp with the sneaky, urgent speed of a chain-gang fugitive. With camp made he would lie awake late, feeling like a man with about two grams of cocaine chasing itself through his system. Oh baby, shake, rattle, and roll. Also like a heavy coke user, he wasn't eating much; he never felt hungry. Cocaine does not enhance the appetite, and neither does terror. Larry hadn't touched coke since the long-ago party in California, but he was terrified all the time. The squawk of a bird in the woods made him twitch. The deathcry of some small animal as a larger one took it made him almost jump out of his skin. He had passed through slimness and skinniness, had traveled through scrawniness. He was now poised on some metaphoric (or metabolic) fence between scrawniness and emaciation. He had grown a beard and it was actually rather striking, a tawny red-gold two shades lighter than his hair. His eyes were sunken deep in his face; they glittered out of their sockets like small, desperate animals that had been trapped in twin pit-snares.

'Cracking up,' he moaned again. The broken desperation in this splintery whine horrified him. Had it gotten that bad? Once there had been a Larry Underwood who'd had a moderate hit record, who had visions of becoming the Elton John of his time . . . oh my dear, how Jerry Garcia would laugh at *that* . . . and now that fellow had been transmuted into this broken thing crawling on the black hottop of Route 9 somewhere in southeastern New Hampshire, crawling, just a crawling kingsnake, that was him. That other Larry Underwood could surely bear no relation to this crawling cheapskate . . . this . . .

He tried to get up and couldn't.

'Oh this is so ridiculous,' he said, half laughing and half weeping.

Across the road on a hill two hundred yards away, glimmering like a beautiful mirage, was a white and rambling New England farmhouse. It had green siding, green trim, and a green shingled roof. Rolling down from it was a green lawn just beginning to look shaggy. At the foot of the lawn, a small rill of brook ran; he could hear it gurgling and chuckling, an entrancing sound. A rock wall meandered along beside it, probably marking the edge of the property, and leaning over the wall at spaced intervals were big, shady elms. He would just do his World-Famous Crawling Cheapskate Wriggle over there and sit in the shade for a while, that's what he would do. And when he felt a little better about . . . about things in general . . . he would make it to his feet and go down to the brook and have a drink and a wash-up. Probably he smelled bad. Who cared, though? Who was there to smell him now that Rita was dead?

Was she still lying there in that tent? he wondered morbidly. Swelling up? Gathering flies? Looking more and more like the black sweet treat in the comfort station on Transverse Number One? Where the hell else would she be? Golfing at Palm Springs with Bob Hope?

'Christ, that's horrible,' he whispered, and crawled across the road. Once he was in the shade he felt sure he could get to his feet, but it seemed like too much effort. He did spare enough energy, however, to glance slyly back the way he had come to make sure his cycle wasn't bearing down on him.

It was at least fifteen degrees cooler in the shade, and Larry let out his breath in a long sigh of pleasure and relief. He put a hand to the back of his neck where the sun had been beating most of the day and pulled it back with a little hiss of pain. Sunburn pain? Get Xylocaine. And all that good shit. Get these men out of the hot sun. Burn, baby, burn. Watts. Remember Watts? Another blast from the past. The whole human race, just one big heavy blast from the past, a great big golden gasser.

'Man, you're sick,' he said, and leaned his head against the rough trunk of the elm tree and closed his eyes. Sun-dappled shade made moving patterns of red and black on the inside of his eyelids. The sound of water, chuckling and gurgling, was sweet and soothing. In a minute he would go down there and get a drink of water and wash up. In just a minute.

He dozed.

The minutes flowed by and his doze deepened into his first deep and dreamless sleep in days. His hands rested limply in his lap. His thin chest rose and fell, and his beard made his face look even thinner, the troubled face of a lone refugee who had escaped from a terrible slaughter none would believe. Little by little, the lines carved in his sunbaked face began to smooth out. He spiraled down to the deepest levels of unconsciousness and rested there like a small river creature dreamily estivating the summer away in cool mud. The sun moved lower in the sky.

Near the creek's edge, the luxuriant screen of bushes rattled a little as something moved stealthily through them, paused, moved again. After a time, a boy emerged. He was perhaps thirteen, perhaps ten and tall for his age. He was naked except for Fruit of the Loom shorts. His body was tanned an even mahogany, except for the startling white band that began just above the waistband of his shorts. His skin was covered with the bumps of mosquito and chigger bites, some new, mostly old. In his right hand he held a butcher knife. The blade was a foot long, the edge serrated. It glittered hotly in the sun.

Softly, bent forward slightly at the waist, he approached the elm and the rock wall until he stood right behind Larry. His eyes were greenish blue, a seawater color, slightly turned up at the corners, giving him a Chinese look. They were expressionless eyes, mildly savage. He raised the knife.

A woman's voice, soft but firm, said: 'No.'

He turned to her, head cocked and listening, the knife still raised. His attitude was both questioning and disappointed.

'We'll watch and see,' the woman's voice said.

The boy paused, looking from the knife to Larry and then back to the knife again with a clear expression of longing, and then he retreated back the way he had come.

Larry slept on.

When he woke up, the first thing Larry was aware of was that he felt good. The second thing was that he felt hungry. The third thing was that the sun was wrong – it seemed to have traveled backward across the sky. The fourth thing was that he had to, you should pardon the expression, piss like a racehorse.

Standing and listening to the delicious crackle of his tendons as he stretched, he realized that he had not just napped; he had slept all night. He looked down at his watch and saw why the sun was wrong. It was nine-twenty in the morning. Hungry. There would be food in the big white house. Canned soup, maybe corned beef. His stomach rumbled.

Before going up he knelt by the stream with his clothes off and splashed water all over himself. He noticed how scrawny he was getting – that was no way to run a railroad. He stood up, dried himself with his shirt, and pulled his trousers back on. A couple of stones poked their wet black backs out of the stream and he used them to cross. On the far side he suddenly froze and gazed toward the thick stand of bushes. The fear, which had been dormant in him ever since waking up, suddenly blazed up like an exploding pine knot and then subsided just as quickly. It had been a squirrel or a woodchuck that he had heard, possibly a fox. Nothing else. He turned away indifferently and began to walk up the lawn toward the big white house.

Halfway there a thought rose to the surface of his mind like a bubble and popped. It happened casually, with no fanfare, but the implications brought him to a dead halt.

The thought was: *Why haven't you been riding a bicycle?*

He stood in the middle of the lawn, equidistant from the stream and the house, flabbergasted by the simplicity of it. He had been walking ever since he had ditched the Harley. Walking, wearing himself out, finally collapsing with sun-stroke or something so close to it that it made no difference. And he could have been pedaling along, doing no more than a fast run if that's what he felt like, and he would probably be on the coast now, picking out his summer house and stocking it.

He began to laugh, gently at first, a little bit spooked by the sound of it in all the quiet. Laughing when there was no one else around to laugh with was just another sign that you were taking a one-way trip to that fabled land of bananas. But the laughter sounded so real and hearty, so goddamned *healthy*, and so much like the old Larry Underwood that he just let it come. He stood with his hands on his hips and cocked his head back to the sky and just bellowed with laughter at his own amazing foolishness.

Behind him, where the screening bushes by the creek were thickest, greenish-blue eyes watched all of this, and they watched as Larry at last continued up the lawn to the house, still laughing a little and shaking his head. They watched as he climbed the porch and tried the front door, and found it open. They watched as he disappeared inside. Then the bushes began to shake and make the rattling sound that Larry had heard and dismissed. The boy forced his way through, still naked except for his shorts, brandishing the butcher knife.

Another hand appeared and caressed his shoulder. The boy stopped immediately. The woman came out – she was tall and imposing, but seemed not to move the bushes at all. Her hair was a thick, luxuriant black streaked with thick blazes of purest white; attractive, startling hair. It was twisted into a cable that hung over one shoulder and trailed away only as it reached the swell of her breast. When you looked at this woman you first noticed how tall she was, and then your eyes would be dragged away to that hair and you would consider it, you would think how you could almost feel its rough yet oily texture with your eyes. And if you were a man, you would find yourself wondering what she would look like with that hair unpinned, freed, spread over a pillow in a spill of moonlight. You would wonder what she would be like in bed. But she had never taken a man into herself. She was pure. She was waiting. There had been dreams. Once, in college, there had been the Ouija board. And she wondered again if this man might be the one.

'Wait,' she told the boy.

She turned his agonized face up to her calm one. She knew what the trouble was.

'The house will be all right. Why would he hurt the house, Joe?'

He turned back and looked at the house, longingly, worriedly.

'When he goes, we'll follow him.'

He shook his head viciously.

'Yes; we have to. *I* have to.' And she felt that strongly. He was not the one, perhaps, but even if he was not, he was a link in a chain she had followed for years, a chain that was now nearing its end.

Joe – that was not really his name – raised the knife wildly, as if to plunge it into her. She made no move to protect herself or to flee, and he lowered it slowly. He turned toward the house and jabbed the knife at it.

'No, you won't,' she said. 'Because he's a human being, and he'll lead us to . . .' She fell silent. *Other human beings*, she had meant to finish. *He's a human being, and he'll lead us to other human beings.* But she was not sure that was what she meant, or even if it was, that it was *all* she meant. Already she felt pulled two ways at once, and she began to wish they had never seen Larry. She tried to caress the boy again but he jerked away angrily. He looked up at the big white house and his eyes were burning and jealous. After a while he slipped back into the bushes, glaring at her reproachfully. She followed him to make sure he would be all right. He lay down and curled up in a fetal position, cradling the knife to his chest. He put his thumb in his mouth and closed his eyes.

Nadine went back to where the brook had made a small pool and knelt down. She drank from cupped hands, then settled in to watch the house. Her eyes were calm, her face very nearly that of a Raphael Madonna.

Late that afternoon, as Larry biked along a tree-lined section of Route 9, a green reflectorized sign loomed ahead and he stopped to read it, slightly amazed. The sign said he was entering MAINE, VACATION-LAND. He could hardly believe it; he must have walked an incredible distance in his semidaze of fear. Either that or he had lost a couple of days somewhere. He was about to start riding again when something – a noise in the woods or perhaps only in his head – made him look sharply back over his shoulder. There was nothing, only Route 9 running back into New Hampshire, deserted.

Since the big white house, where he had breakfasted on dry cereal and cheese spread from an aerosol can squeezed onto slightly stale Ritz crackers, he had several times had the strong feeling that he was being watched and followed. He was *hearing* things, perhaps even *seeing* things out of the corners of his eyes. His powers of observation, just starting to come fully to life in this strange situation, kept triggering at stimuli so slight as to be subliminal, nagging his nerve-endings with things so small that even in the aggregate they only formed a vague hunch, a feeling of 'watched-ness.' This feeling didn't frighten him as the others had. It had no feeling of hallucination or delirium about it. If someone was watching him and just lying back, it was probably because they were scared of him. And if they were scared of poor old skinny Larry Underwood, who was now too chicken even to go putting along on a motorcycle at twenty-five miles an hour, they were probably nothing to worry about.

Now, standing astride the bike he had taken from a sporting goods shop some four miles east of the big white house, he called out clearly: 'If someone's there, why don't you come on out? I won't hurt you.'

There was no answer. He stood on the road by the sign marking the border, watching and waiting. A bird twittered and then swooped across the sky. Nothing else moved. After a while he pushed on.

By six o'clock that evening he had reached the little town of North Berwick, at the junction of Routes 9 and 4. He decided to camp there and push on to the seacoast in the morning.

There was a small store at the North Berwick crossroads of 9 and 4, and inside he took a six-pack of beer from the dead cooler. It was Black Label, a brand he had never tried before – a regional beer, presumably. He also took a large bag of Humpty Dumpty Salt 'n Vinegar potato chips, and two cans of Dinty Moore Beef Stew. He put these goods in his pack and went back out the door.

Across the street was a restaurant, and for just a moment he thought he saw two long shadows trailing back behind it and out of sight. It might have been his eyes playing him tricks, but he didn't think so. He considered running across the highway and seeing if he could surprise them out of hiding: Allee-allee-in-free, game's over, kids. He decided not to. He knew what fear was.

He walked a little way down the highway instead, pushing his bike with the loaded knapsack swinging from the handlebars. He saw a large brick school with a stand of trees behind it. He gathered enough wood from the grove to make a fire of decent size and built it in the middle of the school's asphalt-paved playground. There was a creek nearby, flowing past a textile mill and under the highway. He cooled his beer in the water and cooked one of the cans of beef stew in its tin. He ate it from his Boy Scout messkit, sitting on one of the playground swings and rocking slowly back and forth with his shadow trailing out long across the faded lines of the basketball court.

It occurred to him to wonder why he was so little afraid of the people who were following him – because he was sure now that there *were* people following him, at least two, maybe more. As a corollary, it occurred to him to wonder why he had felt so good all day long, as if some black poison had leaked out of his system during his long sleep the previous afternoon. Was it just that he had needed rest? That, and nothing more? It seemed too simple.

He supposed, looking at it logically, that if the followers had meant to do him harm, they would have already tried to do it. They would have shot at him from ambush or at least covered him with their weapons and forced him to surrender his. They would have taken what they wanted . . . but again thinking logically (it was *good* to think logically, too, because for the last few days all the thinking he had done had been etched in a corrosive acid-bath of terror), what could he possibly have that anybody would want? As far as worldly goods went, there was now plenty for everybody, because there were precious few everybodies left. Why go to the trouble of stealing and killing and risking your life when everything you'd ever dreamed of having as you sat in the shithouse with the Sears catalogue in your lap was now available behind every shop window in America? Just break the glass, walk in, and take it.

Everything, that was, except the companionship of your fellows. *That* was at a premium, as Larry knew very well. And the real reason he didn't feel afraid was because he thought that was what these people must want. Sooner or later their desire would overcome their fear. He would wait until it did. He wasn't going to flush them out like a covey of quail; that would only make things worse. Two days ago, he would probably have done a fade himself if he had seen someone. Just too freaked to do anything else. So he could wait. But, man, he really wanted to see somebody again. He really did.

He walked back to the stream and rinsed out his messkit. He fished the six-pack out of the water and went back to his swing. He snapped the top on the first one and held the can up in the direction of the restaurant where he had seen the shadows.

'Your very good health,' Larry said, and drank half the can at a draught. Talk about going down smooth!

By the time he had finished the six-pack it was after seven o'clock and the sun was getting ready to go down. He kicked the last few embers of the campfire apart and gathered his stuff together. Then, half-drunk and feeling pleasant, he rode up Route 9 a quarter of a mile and found a house with a screened-in porch. He parked the bike on the lawn, took his sleeping bag, and forced the porch door with a screwdriver.

He looked around once more, hoping to see him or her or them – they were still keeping up with him, he felt it – but the street was quiet and empty. He went inside with a shrug.

It was still early and he expected to lie restless for a while at least, but apparently he still had some sleep to catch up on. Fifteen minutes after lying down he was out, breathing slowly and evenly, his rifle close by his right hand.

Nadine was tired. This now seemed like the longest day of her life. Twice she felt sure they had been spotted, once near Strafford, and again at the Maine–New Hampshire state line, when he had looked back over his shoulder and called out. For herself, she didn't care if they were spotted or not. This man wasn't crazy, like the man who had passed by the big white house ten days ago. That man had been a soldier loaded down with guns and grenades and bandoliers of ammunition. He had been laughing and crying and threatening to blow the balls off someone named Lieutenant Morton. Lieutenant Morton had been nowhere in sight, which was probably a good thing for him, if he was still alive. Joe had been frightened of the soldier, too, and in that case it was probably a very good thing.

'Joe?'

She looked around.

Joe was gone.

And she had been on the edge of sleep and slipping over. She pushed the single blanket back and stood up, wincing at a hundred different aches. How long had it been since she had spent so much time on a bicycle? Never, probably. And then there was the constant, nerve-racking effort to find the golden mean. If they got too close, he would see them and that would upset Joe. If they dropped back too far, he might leave Route 9 for another road and they would lose him. That would upset *her*. It had never occurred to her that Larry might circle back and get behind them. Luckily (for Joe, at least), it had never occurred to Larry, either.

She kept telling herself that Joe would get used to the idea that they needed him . . . and not just him. They could not be alone. If they stayed alone, they would die alone. Joe would get used to the idea; he had not lived his previous life in a vacuum any more than she had. Other people got to be a habit.

'Joe,' she called again, softly.

He could be as quiet as a Viet Cong guerrilla creeping through the bush, but her ears had gotten attuned to him over the last three weeks, and tonight, as a bonus, there was a moon. She heard a faint scrape and clatter of gravel, and she knew where he was going. Ignoring her aches, she followed. It was quarter after ten.

They had made camp (if you wanted to call two blankets in the grass 'camp') behind the North Berwick Grille across from the general store, storing the bikes in a shed behind the restaurant. The man they were following had eaten in the school playground across the street ('If we went over there, I'll bet he would give us some of his supper, Joe,' she had said tactfully. 'It's hot . . . and doesn't it smell nice? I'll bet it's lots nicer than this bologna.' Joe's eyes had gone wide, showing a lot of the white, and he shook his knife balefully in Larry's direction) and then he had gone up the road to a house with a screened-in porch. She thought from the way he was steering his bike that he was maybe a little drunk. He was now asleep on the porch of the house he had chosen.

She went faster, wincing as random pebbles bit into the balls of her feet. There were houses on the left and she crossed to their lawns, which were now growing into fields. The grass, heavy with dew and smelling sweet, came all the way to her bare shins. It made her think of a time she had run with a boy through grass like this, under a moon that had been full, instead of waning like this one was. There had been a hot sweet ball of excitement in her lower belly, and she had been very conscious of her breasts as sexual things, full and ripe and standing out from her chest. The moon had made her feel drunk, and so had the grass, wetting her legs with its night moisture. She had known that if the boy caught her she would let the boy have her maidenhead. She had run like an Indian through the corn. Had he caught her? What did it matter now?

She ran faster, leaping a cement driveway that glimmered like ice in the darkness.

And there was Joe, standing at the edge of the screened porch where the man slept. His white underpants were the brightest thing in the darkness; in fact, the boy's skin was so dark that at first glance you almost thought the underpants were there alone, suspended in space, or else worn by H. G. Wells's invisible man.

Joe was from Epsom, she knew that, because that was where she had found him. Nadine was from South Barnstead, a town fifteen miles northeast of Epsom. She had been searching methodically for other healthy people, reluctant to leave her own house in her own home town. She worked in concentric circles which grew larger and larger. She had found only Joe, delirious and fevered from some sort of animal bite . . . rat or squirrel, from the size of it. He had been sitting on the lawn of a house in Epsom naked except for his underpants, butcher knife clutched in his hand like an old Stone Age savage or a dying but still vicious pygmy. She had had experience with infections before. She had carried him into the house. Had it been his own? She thought it likely, but would never be sure unless Joe told her. There had been dead people in the house, a lot of them: mother, father, three other children, the oldest about fifteen. She had found a doctor's office where there was disinfectant and antibiotics and bandages. She was not sure which antibiotics would be right, and she knew she might kill him if she chose wrongly, but if she did nothing he would die anyway. The bite was on the ankle, which had puffed to the size of an innertube. Fortune was with her. In three days the ankle was down to normal size and the fever was gone. The boy trusted her. No one else, apparently, but her. She would wake up mornings and he would be clinging to her. They had gone to the big white house. She called him Joe. It wasn't his name, but in her life as a teacher, any little girl whose name she hadn't known had always been a Jane, any little boy a Joe. The soldier had come by, laughing and crying and cursing Lieutenant Morton. Joe had wanted to rush out and kill him with the knife. Now this man. She was afraid to take the knife away from him, because it was Joe's talisman. Attempting to do that might be the one thing that could make him turn on her. He slept with it clutched in his hand, and the one night she had attempted to pull it free, more to see if it could actually be done than to actually remove it for good, he had been awake instantly, with no movement. One moment fast asleep. The next, those unsettling blue-gray eyes with their Chinese shape had been staring at her with mild savagery. He had pulled the knife back with a low growl. He didn't talk.

Now he was raising the knife, lowering it, raising it again. Making those low growling noises in his throat and jabbing the knife at the screen. Working himself up to actually rushing in the door, perhaps.

She came up behind him, not making any special effort to be quiet, but he didn't hear her; Joe was lost in his own world. In an instant, unaware that she was going to do it, she clapped her hand over his wrist and twisted it violently in an anticlockwise direction.

Joe uttered a hissing gasp and Larry Underwood stirred a little in his sleep, turned over, and was quiet again. The knife fell to the grass between them, its serrated blade holding splintered reflections of the silver moon. They looked like luminous snowflakes.

He stared at her with angry, reproachful, and distrusting eyes. Nadine stared back uncompromisingly. She pointed back the way they had come. Joe shook his head viciously. He pointed at the screen and the dark lump in the sleeping bag beyond the screen. He made a horribly explicit gesture, drawing his thumb across his throat at the Adam's apple. Then he grinned. Nadine had never seen him grin before and it chilled her. It could not have been more savage if those gleaming white teeth had been filed to points.

'No,' she said softly. 'Or I'll wake him up now.'

Joe looked alarmed. He shook his head rapidly.

'Then come back with me. Sleep.'

He looked down at the knife, then up at her again. The savagery, for now at least, was gone. He was only a lost little boy who wanted his teddy, or the scratchy blanket which had graduated with him from the crib. Nadine recognized vaguely that this might be the time to make him leave the knife, to just shake her head firmly 'No.' But then what? Would he scream? He had screamed after the lunatic soldier had passed out of sight. Screamed and screamed, huge, inarticulate sounds of terror and rage. Did she want to meet the man in the sleeping bag at night, and with such screams ringing in her ears and his?

'Will you come back with me?'

Joe nodded.

'All right,' she said quietly. He bent quickly and picked it up.

They went back together, and he crawled next to her trustingly, the interloper forgotten, at least temporarily. Wrapped his arms around her and went to sleep. She felt the old familiar ache in her belly, the one so much deeper and all-pervading than those caused by the exercise. It was a womanache, and nothing could be done about it. She fell asleep.

She woke up sometime in the early hours of the morning – she wore no watch – cold and stiff and terrified, afraid suddenly that Joe had cunningly waited until she was asleep to creep back to the house and cut the man's throat in his sleep. Joe's arms were no longer around her. She felt responsible for the boy, she had always felt responsible for the little ones who had not asked to be in the world, but if he had done that, she would cut him adrift. To take life when so much had been lost was the one unpardonable sin. And she could not be alone with Joe much longer without help; being with him was like being in a cage with a temperamental lion. Like a lion, Joe could not (or would not) speak; he could only roar in his lost little boy's voice.

She sat up and saw that the boy was still with her. In his sleep he had drawn away from her a little, that was all. He had curled up like a fetus, his thumb in his mouth, his hand wrapped around the shaft of the knife.

Mostly asleep again already, she walked to the grass, urinated, and went back to her blanket. The next morning she was not sure if she had really awakened in the night or only dreamed she had.

If I dreamed, Larry thought, they must have been good dreams. He couldn't remember any of them. He felt like his old self, and he thought today would be a good day. He would see the ocean today. He rolled up his sleeping bag, tied it to the bike-carrier, went back to get his pack . . . and stopped.

A cement path led up to the porch steps, and on both sides the grass was long and violently green. To the right, close by the porch itself, the dewy grass was beaten down. When the dew evaporated, the grass would spring back up, but now it held the shape of footprints. He was a city boy and no kind of woodsman (he had been more into Hunter Thompson than James Fenimore Cooper), but you would have to be blind, he thought, not to see by the tracks that there had been two of them: a big one and a small one. Sometime during the night they had come up to the screen and looked in at him. It gave him a chill. It was the stealth he didn't like, and he liked the first touch of returning fear even less.

If they don't show themselves pretty quick, he thought, I'm going to try and flush them out. Just the thought that he could do that brought most of his self-confidence back. He slipped into his pack and got going.

By noon he had reached US 1 in Wells. He flipped a coin and it came up tails. He turned south on 1, leaving the coin to gleam indifferently up from the dust. Joe found it twenty minutes later and stared at it as if it were a hypnotist's crystal. He put it in his mouth and Nadine made him spit it out.

Two miles down the road Larry saw it for the first time, the huge blue animal, lazy and slow this day. It was completely different from the Pacific or the Atlantic that lay off Long Island. That part of the ocean looked complacent, somehow, almost tame. This water was a darker blue, nearly cobalt, and it came up to the land in one rushing swell after another and bit at the rocks. Spume as thick as eggwhite jumped into the air and then splattered back. The waves made a constant growling boom against the shore.

Larry parked his bike and walked toward the ocean, feeling a deep excitement that he couldn't explain. He was *here*, he had made it to the place where the sea took over. This was the end of east. This was land's end.

He crossed a marshy field, his shoes squishing through water standing around hummocks and clumps of reeds. There was a rich and fecund tidal smell. As he drew closer to the headland, the thin skin of earth was peeled away and the naked bone of granite poked through – granite, Maine's final truth. Gulls rose, clean white against the blue sky, crying and wailing. He had never seen so many birds in one place before. It occurred to him that, despite their white beauty, gulls were carrion eaters. The thought that followed was nearly unspeakable, but it had formed fully in his mind before he could push it away: *The pickings must be real good just lately.*

He begun to walk again, his shoes now clicking and scraping on sun-dried rock which would always be wet in its many seams from the spray. There were barnacles growing in those cracks, and scattered here and there like shrapnel bursts of bone were the shells the gulls had dropped to get at the soft meat inside.

A moment later he stood upon the naked headland. The seawind struck him full force, lifting his heavy growth of hair back from his forehead. He lifted his face into it, into the harsh-clean salt-smell of the blue animal. The combers, glassy blue-green, moved slowly in, their slopes becoming more pronounced as the bottom shallowed up beneath them, their peaks gaining first a curl of foam, then a curdly topping. Then they crashed suicidally against the rocks as they had since the beginning of time, destroying themselves, destroying an infinitesimal bit of the land at the same time. There was a ramming, coughing boom as water was forced deep into some half-submerged channel of rock that had been carved out over the millennia.

He turned first left, then right, and saw the same thing happening in each direction, as far as he could see . . . combers, waves, spray, most of all an endless glut of *color* that took his breath away.

He was at land's end.

He sat down with his feet dangling over the edge, feeling a little overcome. He sat there for half an hour or better. The sea breeze honed his appetite and he rummaged in his pack for lunch. He ate heartily. Thrown spray had turned the legs of his bluejeans black. He felt cleaned out, fresh.

He walked back across the marsh, still so full of his own thoughts that he first supposed the rising scream to be the gulls again. He had even started to look up at the sky before he realized with a nasty jolt of fear that it was a human scream. A warcry.

His eyes jerked downward again and he saw a young boy running across the road toward him, muscular legs pumping. In one hand he held a long butcher knife. He was naked except for underpants and his legs were crisscrossed with bramble welts. Behind him, just coming out of the brush and nettles on the far side of the highway, was a woman. She looked pale, and there were circles of weariness under her eyes.

'*Joe!*' she called, and then began to run as if it hurt her to do so.

Joe came on, never heeding, his bare feet splashing up thin sheets of marsh water. His entire face was drawn back in a tight and murderous grin. The butcher knife was high over his head, catching the sun.

He's coming to kill me, Larry thought, entirely poleaxed by the idea. *This boy . . . what did I ever do to him?*

'*Joe!*' the woman screamed, this time in a high, weary, despairing voice. Joe ran on, closing the distance.

Larry had time to realize he had left his rifle with his bike, and then the screaming boy was upon him.

As he brought the butcher knife down in a long, sweeping arc, Larry's paralysis broke. He stepped aside and, not even thinking, brought his right foot up and sent the wet yellow workboot it was wearing into the boy's midriff. And what he felt was pity: there was nothing to the kid – he went over like a candlepin. He looked fierce but was no heavyweight.

'Joe!' Nadine called. She tripped over a hummock and fell to her knees, splashing her white blouse with brown mud. 'Don't hurt him! He's only a little boy! Please, don't hurt him!' She got to her feet and struggled on.

Joe had fallen flat on his back. He was splayed out like an *x*, his arms making a *v*, his open legs making a second, inverted *v*. Larry took a step forward and tromped on his right wrist, pinning the hand holding the knife to the muddy ground.

'Let go of the sticker, kid.'

The boy hissed and then made a grunting, gobbling sound like a turkey. His upper lip drew back from his teeth. His Chinese eyes glared into Larry's. Keeping his foot on the boy's wrist was like standing on a wounded but still vicious snake. He could feel the boy trying to yank his hand free, and never mind if it was at the expense of skin, flesh, or even a broken bone. He jerked into a half-sitting position and tried to bite Larry's leg through the heavy wet denim of his jeans. Larry stepped down even harder on the thin wrist and Joe uttered a cry – not of pain but defiance.

'Let it *go*, kid.'

Joe continued to struggle.

The stalemate would have continued until Joe got the knife free or until Larry broke his wrist if Nadine had not finally arrived, muddy, breathless, and staggering with weariness.

Without looking at Larry she dropped to her knees. 'Let it go!' she said quietly but with great firmness. Her face was sweaty but calm. She held it only inches above Joe's contorted, twisting features. He snapped at her like a dog and continued to struggle. Grimly, Larry strove to keep his balance. If the boy got free now, he would probably strike at the woman first.

'Let . . . it . . . go!' Nadine said.

The boy growled. Spit leaked between his clenched teeth. There was a smear of mud in the shape of a question mark on his right cheek.

'We'll leave you, Joe. *I'll* leave you. I'll go with him. Unless you're good.'

Larry felt a further tensing of the arm under his foot, then a loosening. But the boy was looking at her grievingly, accusingly, reproachfully. When he shifted his gaze slightly to look at Larry, Larry could read the hot jealousy in those eyes. Even with the sweat running off him in buckets, Larry felt cold under that stare.

She continued to speak calmly. No one would hurt him. No one would leave him. If he let go of the knife, everyone could be friends.

Gradually Larry became aware that the hand under his shoe had relaxed and let go. The boy lay dormant, staring up at the sky. He had opted out. Larry took his foot off Joe's wrist, bent quickly, and picked up the knife. He turned and scaled it up and out toward the headland. The blade whirled and whirled, throwing off spears of sunlight. Joe's strange eyes followed its course and he gave one long, hooting wail of pain. The knife bounced on the rocks with a thin clatter and skittered over the edge.

Larry turned back and regarded them. The woman was looking at Joe's right forearm where the waffled shape of Larry's boot was deeply embedded and turning an angry, exclamatory red. Her dark eyes looked up from that to Larry's face. They were full of sorrow.

Larry felt the old defensive and self-serving words rise – *I had to do it, it wasn't my fault, listen lady, he wanted to kill me* – because he thought he could read the judgment in those sorrowing eyes: *You ain't no nice guy.*

But in the end he said nothing. The situation was what the situation was, and his actions had been forced by the kid's. Looking at the boy, who had now curled himself up desolately over his own knees and put a thumb in his mouth, he doubted if the boy himself had initiated the situation. And it could have ended in a worse way, with one of them cut or even killed.

So he said nothing, and he met the woman's soft gaze and thought: *I think I've changed. Somehow. I don't know how much.* He found himself thinking of something Barry Grieg had once said to him about a rhythm guitar player from LA, a guy named Jory Baker who was always on time, never missed a practice session, or fucked up an audition. Not the kind of guitar player that caught your eye, no showboat like Angus Young or Eddie Van Halen, but competent. Once, Barry had said, Jory Baker had been the driving wheel of a group called Sparx, a group everybody seemed to think that year's Most Likely to Succeed. They had a sound something like early Creedence: hard solid guitar rock and roll. Jory Baker had done most of the writing and all of the vocals. Then a car accident, broken bones, lots of dope in the hospital. He had come out, as the John Prine song says, with a steel plate in his head and a monkey on his back. He progressed from Demerol to heroin. Got busted a couple of times. After a while he was just another street-druggie with fumble fingers, spare-changing down at the Greyhound station and hanging out on the strip. Then, somehow, over a period of eighteen months, he had gotten clean, and stayed clean. A lot of him was gone. He was no longer the driving wheel of any group, Most Likely to Succeed or otherwise, but he was always on time, never missed a practice session, or fucked up an audition. He didn't talk much, but the needle highway on his left arm had disappeared. And Barry Greig had said: *He's come out the other side.* That was all. No one can tell what goes on in between the person you were and the person you become. No one can chart that blue and lonely section of hell. There are no maps of the change. You just . . . come out the other side.

Or you don't.

I've changed somehow, Larry thought dimly. I've come out the other side, too.

She said: 'I'm Nadine Cross. This is Joe. I'm happy to meet you.'

'Larry Underwood.'

They shook hands, both smiling faintly at the absurdity.

'Let's walk back to the road,' Nadine said.

They started off side by side, and after a few steps Larry looked back over his shoulder at Joe, who was still sitting over his knees and sucking his thumb, apparently unaware they were gone.

'He'll come,' she said quietly.

'Are you sure?'

'Quite sure.'

As they came to the highway's gravel shoulder she stumbled and Larry took her arm. She looked at him gratefully.

'Can we sit down?' she asked.

'Sure.'

So they sat down on the pavement, facing each other. After a little bit Joe got up and plodded toward them, looking down at his bare feet. He sat a little way apart from them. Larry looked at him warily, then back at Nadine Cross.

'You were the two following me.'

'You knew? Yes. I thought you did.'

'How long?'

'Two days now,' Nadine said. 'We were staying in the big house at Epsom.' Seeing his puzzled expression she added: 'By the creek. You fell asleep by the rock wall.'

He nodded. 'And last night the two of you came to peek at me while I was sleeping on that porch. Maybe to see if I had horns or a long red tail.'

'That was Joe,' she said quietly. 'I came after him when I found he was gone. How did you know?'

'You left tracks in the dew.'

'Oh.' She looked at him closely, examining him, and although he wanted to, Larry didn't drop his eyes. 'I don't want you to be angry with us. I suppose that sounds ridiculous after Joe just tried to kill you, but Joe isn't responsible.'

'Is that his real name?'

'No, just what I call him.'

'He's like a savage in a *National Geographic* TV show.'

'Yes, just like that. I found him on the lawn of a house – his house, maybe, the name was Rockway – sick from a bite. A rat bite, maybe. He doesn't talk. He growls and grunts. Until this morning I've been able to control him. But I . . . I'm tired, you see . . . and . . .' She shrugged. Marsh-mud was drying on her blouse in what could have been a series of Chinese ideograms. 'I dressed him at first. He took everything off but his underpants. Eventually I got tired of trying. The minges and mosquitoes don't seem to bother him.' She paused. 'I want us to come with you. I guess there is no way to be coy about it, under the circumstances.'

Larry wondered what she would think if he told her about the last woman who had wanted to come with him. Not that he ever would; that episode was deeply buried, even if the woman in question was not. He was no more anxious to bring up Rita than a murderer would be to drag his victim's name into parlor conversation.

'I don't know where I'm going,' he said. 'I came up from New

York City, the long way around, I guess. The plan was to find a nice house on the coast and just lie up there until October or so. But the longer I go, the more I want other people. The longer I go, the more all of this seems to hit me.'

He was expressing himself badly and didn't seem to be able to do better without bringing up Rita or his bad dreams about the dark man.

'I've been scared a lot of the time,' he said carefully, 'because I'm on my own. Pretty paranoid. It's like I expected Indians to just swoop down and scalp me.'

'In other words, you've stopped looking for houses and started looking for people.'

'Yes, maybe.'

'You've found us. That's a start.'

'I do believe you found me. And that boy worries me, Nadine. I have to be up front about that. His knife's gone, but the world is full of knives just lying around waiting to be picked up.'

'Yes.'

'I don't want to sound brutal . . .' He trailed off, hoping she would say it for him, but she said nothing at all, only looked at him with those dark eyes.

'Would you consider leaving him?' There it was, spat out like a lump of rock, and he still didn't sound like much of a nice guy . . . but was it right, was it fair to either of them, to make a bad situation worse by burdening themselves with a ten-year-old psychopath? He had told her he was going to sound brutal, and he supposed he had. But they were in a brutal world now.

Meanwhile, Joe's odd seawater-colored eyes bored into him.

'I couldn't do that,' Nadine said calmly. 'I understand the danger, and I understand that the danger would be primarily to you. He's jealous. He's afraid that you might become more important to me than he is. He might very well try to . . . try to get at you again unless you can make friends with him or at least convince him you don't mean to . . .' She trailed off, leaving that part vague. 'But if I left him, that would be the same as murder. And I won't be a party to that. Too many have died to kill more.'

'If he cuts my throat in the middle of the night, you'll be a party to *that*.'

She bowed her head.

Speaking so quietly that only she could hear (he didn't know

if Joe, who was watching them, understood what they were talking
about or not), Larry said, 'He probably would have done it last night
if you hadn't come after him. Isn't that the truth?'

Softly she replied: 'Those are things that might be.'

Larry laughed. 'The Ghost of Christmas Yet-to-Come?'

She looked up. 'I want to come with you, Larry, but I can't
leave Joe. You will have to decide.'

'You don't make it easy.'

'These days it's no easy life.'

He thought about it. Joe sat on the soft shoulder of the road,
watching them with his seawater eyes. Behind them, the real sea
moved restlessly against the rocks, booming in its secret channels
where it had infiltrated the land.

'All right,' he said. 'I think you're being dangerously softhearted,
but . . . all right.'

'Thank you,' Nadine said. 'I will be responsible for his actions.'

'That will be a great comfort if he kills me.'

'That would be on my heart for the rest of my life,' Nadine
said, and a sudden certainty that all her words about the sanctity of
life would someday not too distant rise up to mock her swept her
like a cold wind, and she shuddered. No, she told herself. I'll not
kill. Not that. Never that.

They camped that night on the soft white sand of the Wells public
beach. Larry built a large fire above the strand of kelp that marked
the last high tide and Joe sat on the other side, away from him and
Nadine, feeding small sticks into the blaze. Occasionally he would
hold a bigger stick into the flames until it caught like a torch and
then tear away down the sand, holding it aloft like a single flaming
birthday candle. They were able to see him until he was beyond the
thirty-foot glow of the fire and then only his moving torch, drawn
back in the wind manufactured by his wild sprinting. The sea breeze
had come up a little, and it was cooler than it had been for days.
Vaguely, Larry remembered the spell of rain that had occurred the
afternoon he had found his mother dying, just before the superflu
had hit New York like a highballing freight train. Remembered the
thunderstorm and the white curtains blowing wildly into the apartment. He shivered a little, and the wind danced a spiral of fire out
of the fire and up toward the black starshot sky. Embers cycloned
up even higher and flickered out. He thought of fall, still distant but

not so far as it had been on that day in June when he had discovered
his mother lying on the floor, delirious. He shivered a little. North,
far down on the beach, Joe's torch bobbed up and down. It made
him feel lonely and all the colder – that single light flickering in the
large and silent darkness. The surf rolled and boomed.

'Do you play?'

He jumped a little at her voice and looked at the guitar case
lying beside them on the sand. It had been leaning against a Steinway
piano in the music room of the big house they had broken into to
get their supper. He had loaded his pack with enough cans to replace
what they had eaten this day, and had taken the guitar on impulse,
not even looking inside the case to see what it was – coming from
a house like that, it was probably a good un. He hadn't played since
that crazy Malibu party, and that had been six weeks ago. In another
life.

'Yeah, I do,' he said, and discovered that he *wanted* to play,
not for her but because sometimes it felt good to play, it eased your
mind. And when you had a bonfire on the beach, someone was
supposed to play the guitar. That was practically graven in stone.

'Let's see what we got here,' he said, and unsnapped the catches.

He had expected something good, but what lay inside the case
was still a happy surprise. It was a Gibson twelve-string, a beautiful
instrument, perhaps even custom-made. Larry wasn't enough of a
judge of guitars to be sure. He did know that the fretboard inlays
were real mother-of-pearl, catching reddish-orange glints from the
fire and waxing them into prisms of light.

'It's beautiful,' she said.

'It sure is.'

He strummed it and liked the sound it made, even open and
not quite in tune. The sound was fuller and richer than the sound
you got from a six-string. A harmonic sound, but tough. That was
the good thing about a steel-string guitar, you got a nice tough
sound. And the strings were Black Diamonds, wrapped and a little
hokey, but you got an honest sound, a trifle rough when you changed
chords – *zing!* He smiled a little, remembering Barry Greig's contempt
for the smooth flat guitar strings. He had always called them 'dollar
slicks.' Good old Barry, who wanted to be Steve Miller when he
grew up.

'What are you smiling about?' Nadine asked.

'Old times,' he said, and felt a little sad.

He tuned by ear, getting it just right, still thinking about Barry and Johnny McCall and Wayne Stukey. As he was finishing she tapped him lightly on the shoulder and he looked up.

Joe was standing by the fire, a burned-out stick held forgotten in one hand. Those strange eyes were staring at him with frank fascination, and his mouth was open.

Very quietly, so quietly that it might have been a thought in his own head, Nadine said: 'Music hath charms . . .'

Larry began to pick out a rough melody on the guitar, an old blues he had picked up off an Elektra folk album as a teenager. Something originally done by Koerner, Ray, and Glover, he thought. When he thought he had the melody right, he let it walk off down the beach and then sang . . . his singing was always going to be better than his playing.

> Well you see me comin baby from a long ways away
> I will turn the night mamma right into day
> Cause I'm here
> A long ways from my home
> But you can hear me comin baby
> By the slappin on my black cat bone.

The boy was grinning now, grinning in the amazed way of someone who has discovered a glad secret. Larry thought he looked like someone who had been suffering from an unreachable itch between his shoulderblades for a long, long time and had finally found someone who knew exactly where to scratch. He scruffed through long-unused archives of memory, hunting a second verse, and found one.

> I can do some things mamma that other men can't do
> They can't find the numbers baby, can't work the
> Conqueror root
> But I can, cause I'm a long way from my home
> And you know you'll hear me comin
> By the whackin on my black cat bone.

The boy's open, delighted grin lit those eyes up, made them into something, Larry realized, that would be apt to make the muscles in any young girl's thighs loosen a little. He reached for an instrumental bridge and fumbled through it, not too badly, either. His fingers wrung the right sounds out of the guitar: hard, flashy, a little bit tawdry, like a display of junk jewelry, probably stolen, sold out of a paper bag on a street corner. He made it swagger a little and then retreated quickly to a good old three-finger E before he could fuck it all up. He couldn't remember all of the last verse, something about a railroad track, so he repeated the first verse again and quit.

When the silence hit again, Nadine laughed and clapped her hands. Joe threw his stick away and jumped up and down on the sand, making fierce hooting sounds of joy. Larry couldn't believe the change in the kid, and had to caution himself not to make too much of it. To do so would be to risk disappointment.

Music hath charms to soothe the savage beast.

He found himself wondering with unwilling distrust if it could be something as simple as that. Joe was gesturing at him and Nadine said: 'He wants you to play something else. Would you? That was wonderful. It makes me feel better. So much better.'

So he played Geoff Muldaur's 'Goin Downtown' and his own 'Sally's Fresno Blues'; he played 'The Springhill Mine Disaster' and Arthur Crudup's 'That's All Right, Mamma.' He switched to primitive rock and roll – 'Milk Cow Blues,' 'Jim Dandy,' 'Twenty Flight Rock' (doing the boogie-woogie rhythm of the chorus as well as he could, although his fingers were getting slow and numb and painful by now), and finally a song he had always liked, 'Endless Sleep,' originally done by Jody Reynolds.

'I can't play anymore,' he said to Joe, who had stood without moving through this entire recital. 'My fingers.' He held them out, showing the deep grooves the strings had made in his fingers, and the chips in his nails.

The boy held out his own hands.

Larry paused for a moment, then shrugged inside. He handed the guitar to the boy neck first. 'It takes a lot of practice,' he said.

But what followed was the most amazing thing he had ever heard in his life. The boy struck up 'Jim Dandy' almost flawlessly, hooting at the words rather than singing them, as if his tongue was plastered to the roof of his mouth. At the same time it was perfectly obvious that he had never played a guitar in his life before; he couldn't bear down hard enough on the strings to make them ring out properly and his chord changes were slurred and sloppy. The sound that came out was muted and ghostly – as if Joe was playing a guitar stuffed full of cotton – but otherwise it was a perfect carbon copy of the way Larry had played the tune.

When he had finished, Joe looked curiously down at his own fingers, as if trying to understand why they could make the substance of the music Larry had played but not the sharp sounds themselves.

Numbly, as if from a distance, Larry heard himself say: 'You're not bearing down hard enough, that's all. You have to build up calluses – hard spots – on the ends of your fingers. And the muscles in your left hand, too.'

Joe looked at him closely as he spoke, but Larry didn't know if the boy really understood or not. He turned to Nadine. 'Did you know he could do that?'

'No. I'm as surprised as you are. It's as if he is a prodigy or something, isn't it?'

Larry nodded. The boy ran through 'That's All Right, Mamma,' again getting almost every nuance of the way Larry had played it. But the strings sometimes thudded like wood as Joe's fingers blocked the vibration of the strings rather than making it come true.

'Let me show you,' Larry said, and held out his hands for the guitar. Joe's eyes immediately slanted down with distrust. Larry thought he was remembering the knife going down into the sea. He backed away, holding the guitar tightly. 'All right,' Larry said. 'All yours. When you want a lesson, come see me.'

The boy made a hooting sound and ran off along the beach, holding the guitar high over his head like a sacrificial offering.

'He's going to smash it to hell,' Larry said.

'No,' Nadine answered, 'I don't think he is.'

Larry woke up sometime in the night and propped himself up on one elbow. Nadine was only a vaguely female shape wrapped up in three blankets a quarter of the way around the dead fire. Directly across from Larry was Joe. He was also under several blankets, but his head stuck out. His thumb was corked securely in his mouth. His legs were drawn up and between them was the body of the Gibson twelve-string. His free hand was wrapped loosely around the guitar's neck. Larry stared at him, fascinated. He had taken the boy's knife and thrown it away; the boy had adopted the guitar. Fine. Let him have it. You couldn't stab anybody to death with a guitar, although, Larry supposed, it would make a pretty fair blunt instrument. He dropped off to sleep again.

When he woke up the next morning, Joe was sitting on a rock with the guitar on his lap and his bare feet in the run of the surf, playing

'Sally's Fresno Blues.' He had gotten better. Nadine woke up twenty minutes later, and smiled at him radiantly. It occurred to Larry that she was a lovely woman, and a snatch of song occurred to him, something by Chuck Berry: Nadine, honey is that you?

Aloud, he said: 'Let's see what we've got for breakfast.'

He built up the fire and the three of them sat close to it, working the nightchill out of their bones. Nadine made oatmeal with powdered milk and they drank strong tea brewed in a can, hobo fashion. Joe ate with the Gibson across his lap. And twice Larry found himself smiling at the boy and thinking you couldn't not like someone who liked the guitar.

They cycled south on US 1. Joe rode his bike straight down the white line, sometimes ranging as far as a mile ahead. Once they caught up to him placidly walking his bike along the verge of the road and eating blackberries in an amusing way – he would toss each berry into the air, unerringly catching them in his mouth as they came down. An hour after that, they found him seated on a historic Revolutionary War marker and playing 'Jim Dandy' on the guitar.

Just before eleven o'clock they came to a bizarre roadblock at the town line of a place called Ogunquit. Three bright orange town dump trucks were driven across the road, blocking it from shoulder to shoulder. Sprawled in the back of one of the dump-bins was the crow-picked body of what had once been a man. The last ten days of solid heat had done their work. Where the body was not clothed, a fever of maggots boiled.

Nadine turned away. 'Where's Joe?' she asked.

'I don't know. Somewhere up ahead.'

'I wish he hadn't seen that. Do you think he did?'

'Probably,' Larry said. He had been thinking that, for a main artery, Route 1 had been awfully deserted ever since they left Wells, with no more than two dozen stalled cars along the way. Now he understood why. They had blocked the road. There would probably be hundreds, maybe thousands, of cars stacked up on the far side of this town. He knew how she felt about Joe. It would have been good to spare the boy this.

'Why did they block the road?' she asked him. 'Why would they do that?'

'They must have tried to quarantine their town. I imagine we'll find another roadblock on the other end.'

'Are there other bodies?'

Larry put his bike on its stand and looked. 'Three,' he said.

'All right. I'm not going to look at them.'

He nodded. They wheeled their bikes past the trucks and then rode on. The highway had turned close to the sea again and it was cooler. Summer cottages were jammed together in long and sordid rows. People took their vacations in those tenements? Larry wondered. Why not just go to Harlem and let your kids play under the hydrant spray?

'Not very pretty, are they?' Nadine asked. On either side of them the essence of honky-tonk beach resort had now enclosed them: gas stations, fried clam stands, Dairy Treets, motels painted in feverish pastel colors, mini-golf.

Larry was drawn two painful ways by these things. Part of him clamored at their sad and blatant ugliness and at the ugliness of the minds that had turned this section of a magnificent, savage coastline into one long highway amusement park for families in station wagons. But there was a more subtle, deeper part of him that whispered of the people who had filled these places and this road during other summers. Ladies in sunhats and shorts too tight for their large behinds. College boys in red-and-black-striped rugby shirts. Girls in beach shifts and thong sandals. Small screaming children with ice cream spread over their faces. They were American people and there was a kind of dirty, compelling romance about them whenever they were in groups – never mind if the group was in an Aspen ski lodge or performing their prosaic-arcane rites of summer along US 1 in Maine. And now all those Americans were gone. A thunderstorm had ripped a branch from a tree and it had knocked the gigantic plastic Dairy Treet sign into the ice cream stand's parking lot, where it lay on its side like a pallid duncecap. The grass was starting to get long on the mini-golf course. This stretch of highway between Portland and Portsmouth had once been a seventy-mile amusement park and now it was only a haunted funhouse where all the clockwork had run down.

'Not very pretty, no,' he said, 'but once it was ours, Nadine. Once it was ours, even though we were never here before. Now it's gone.'

'But not forever,' she said calmly, and he looked at her, her clean and shining face. Her forehead, from which her amazing white-streaked hair was drawn back, glowed like a lamp. 'I am not a religious person, but if I was I would call what has happened a judgment of God. In a hundred years, maybe two hundred, it will be ours again.'

'Those trucks won't be gone in two hundred years.'

'No, but the road will be. The trucks will be standing in the middle of the field or a forest, and there will be louse-wort and ladies' slipper growing where their tires used to be. They won't really be trucks anymore. They will be artifacts.'

'I think you're wrong.'

'How can I be wrong?'

'Because we're looking for other people,' Larry said. 'Now why do you think we're doing that?'

She gazed at him, troubled. 'Well . . . because it's the right thing to do,' she said. 'People *need* other people. Didn't you feel that? When you were alone?'

'Yes,' Larry said. 'If we don't have each other, we go crazy with loneliness. When we do, we go crazy with togetherness. When we get together we build miles of summer cottages and kill each other in the bars on Saturday night.' He laughed. It was a cold and unhappy sound with no humor in it at all. It hung on the deserted air for a long time. 'There's no answer. It's like being stuck inside an egg. Come on – Joe'll be way ahead of us.'

She stood astride her bike a moment longer, her troubled gaze on Larry's back as it pulled away. Then she rode after him. He couldn't be right. *Couldn't* be. If such a monstrous thing as this had happened for no good reason at all, what sense did anything make? Why were they even still alive?

Joe wasn't so far ahead after all. They came upon him sitting on the back bumper of a blue Ford parked in a driveway. He was looking at a girlie magazine he had found somewhere, and Larry observed uncomfortably that the boy had an erection. He shot a glance at Nadine, but she was looking elsewhere – perhaps on purpose.

When they reached the driveway Larry asked, 'Coming?'

Joe put the magazine aside and instead of standing up made a guttural interrogative sound and pointed up in the air. Larry glanced up wildly, for a moment thinking the boy had seen an airplane. Then Nadine cried: 'Not the sky, the barn!' Her voice was close and tight with excitement. 'On the barn! Thank God for you, Joe! We never would have seen it!'

She went to Joe, put her arms around him, and hugged him.

Larry turned to the barn, where white letters stood out clearly on the faded shingle roof:

HAVE GONE TO STOVINGTON, VT. PLAGUE CENTER

Below that were a series of road directions. And at the bottom:

LEAVING OGUNQUIT JULY 2, 1990
HAROLD EMERY LAUDER
FRANCES GOLDSMITH

'Jesus Christ, his ass must have been out to the wind when he put that last line on,' Larry said.

'The plague center!' Nadine said, ignoring him. 'Why didn't I think of it? I read an article about it in the Sunday supplement magazine not three months ago! They've gone there!'

'If they're still alive.'

'Still alive? Of course they are. The plague was *over* by July second. And if they could climb up on that barn roof, they surely weren't feeling sick.'

'One of them was surely feeling pretty frisky,' Larry agreed, feeling a half-reluctant excitement building in his own stomach. 'And to think I came right across Vermont.'

'Stovington is north of Highway 9 by quite a ways,' Nadine said absently, still looking up at the barn. 'Still, they must be there by now. July second was two weeks ago today.' Her eyes were alight. 'Do you think there might be others at that plague center, Larry? There might be, don't you think? Since they know all about quarantines and sterile clothing? They would have been working on a cure, wouldn't they?'

'I don't know,' Larry said cautiously.

'Of course they would,' she said impatiently and a trifle wildly. Larry had never seen her so excited, not even when Joe performed his amazing feat of mimicry on the guitar. 'I'll bet Harold and Frances have found *dozens* of people, maybe *hundreds*. We'll go right away. The quickest route —'

'Wait a minute,' Larry said, taking her by the shoulder.

'What do you mean, wait? Do you realize —'

'I realize that sign's waited two weeks for us to come by, and this can wait a little longer. In the meantime, let's have some lunch. And ole Joe the Guitar-Picking Fool is falling asleep on his feet.'

She glanced around. Joe was looking at the girlie magazine

again, but he had started to nod and blink over it in a glassy way. There were circles under his eyes.

'You said he just got over an infection,' Larry said. 'And you've done a lot of hard traveling, too . . . not to mention Stalking the Blue-Eyed Guitar-Player.'

'You're right . . . I never thought.'

'All he needs is a good meal and a good nap.'

'Of course. Joe, I'm sorry. I wasn't thinking.'

Joe made a sleepy and mostly disinterested grunt.

Larry felt a lump of residual fear rise up in him at what he had to say next, but it ought to be said. If he didn't, Nadine would as soon as she had a chance to think . . . and besides, it was time, maybe, to find out if he had changed as much as he thought.

'Nadine, can you drive?'

'Drive? Do you mean do I have a license? Yes, but a car really isn't that practical with all the stalls in the road, is it? I mean –'

'I wasn't thinking about a car,' he said, and the image of Rita riding pillion behind the mysterious black man (his mind's symbolic representation of death, he supposed) suddenly rose up behind his eyes, the two of them dark and pale, bearing down on him astride a monstrous Harley hog like weird horsemen of the apocalypse. The thought dried out the moisture in his mouth and made his temples pound, but when he went on, his voice was steady. If there was a break in it, Nadine did not seem to notice. Oddly, it was Joe who looked up at him out of his half-doze, seeming to notice some change.

'I was thinking about motorbikes of some kind. We could make better time with less effort and walk them around any . . . well, any messes in the road. Like we walked our bikes around those town trucks back there.'

Dawning excitement in her eyes. 'Yes, we could do that. I've never driven one, but you could show me what to do, couldn't you?'

At the words *I've never driven one*, Larry's dread intensified. 'Yes,' he said. 'But most of what I'd teach you would be to drive slowly until you get the hang of it. *Very* slowly. A motorcycle – even a little motorbike – doesn't forgive human error, and I can't take you to a doctor if you get wrecked up on the highway.'

'Then that's what we'll do. We'll . . . Larry, were you riding a cycle before we came across you? You must have been, to make it up here from New York City so quickly.'

'I ditched it,' he said steadily. 'I got nervous about riding alone.'

'Well, you won't be alone anymore,' Nadine said, almost gaily. She whirled to Joe. 'We're going to Vermont, Joe! We're going to see some other people! Isn't it nice? Isn't it just *great*?'

Joe yawned.

Nadine said she was too excited to sleep but she would lie down with Joe until he was under. Larry rode into Ogunquit to look for a motorcycle dealership. There was none, but he thought that he had seen a cycle shop on their way out of Wells. He went back to tell Nadine and found them both asleep in the shade of the blue Ford where Joe had been perusing *Gallery*.

He lay down a little way from them but couldn't sleep. At last he crossed the highway and made his way through the knee-high timothy grass to the barn where the sign was painted. Thousands of grasshoppers jumped wildly to get out of his way as he walked toward them, and Larry thought: *I'm their plague. I'm their dark man.*

Near the barn's wide double doors he spotted two empty Pepsi cans and a crust of sandwich. In more normal times the gulls would have had the remains of sandwich long ago, but times had changed and the gulls were no doubt used to richer food. He toed the crust, then one of the cans.

Get these right down to the crime lab, Sergeant Briggs. I think our killer has finally made a mistake.

Right-o, Inspector Underwood. The day Scotland Yard decided to send you was a lucky day for Squinchly-on-the-Green.

Don't mention it, Sergeant. All part of the job.

Larry went inside – it was dark, hot, and alive with the softly whirring wings of the barnswallows. The smell of hay was sweet. There were no animals in the stalls; the owner must have let them out to live or die with the superflu rather than face certain starvation.

Mark that down for the coroner's inquest, Sergeant.

I will indeed, Inspector Underwood.

He glanced down at the floor and saw a candy wrapper. He picked it up. A chocolate Payday candy bar had once been stowed inside it. The signpainter had had guts, maybe. Good taste, no. Anyone with a taste for chocolate Paydays had been spending too much time in the hot sun.

Steps leading to the loft were nailed to one of the loft's supporting beams. Greasy with sweat already, not even knowing why he was here, Larry climbed up. In the center of the loft (he was walking slowly and keeping an eye out for rats), a more conventional flight of stairs went up to the cupola, and these stairs were splattered with drips of white paint.

We've stumbled on another find, I believe, Sergeant.

Inspector, I stand amazed – your deductive acumen is exceeded only by your good looks and the extraordinary length of your reproductive organ.

Don't mention it, Sergeant.

He went up to the cupola. It was even hotter up here, explosively so, and Larry reflected that if Frances and Harold had left their paint up here when the job was done, the barn would have burned merrily to the ground a week ago. The windows were dusty and festooned with decaying cobwebs which had no doubt been freshly spun when Gerald Ford was President. One of these windows had been forced up, and when Larry leaned out, he had a breathtaking view of the country for miles around.

This side of the barn faced east, and he was high enough for the roadside concessions, which seemed so monstrously ugly when seen at ground level, to look as inconsequential as a little strewing of roadside litter. Beyond the highway, magnificent, was the ocean, with the incoming waves neatly broken in two by the breakwater stretching out from the northern side of the harbor. The land was an oil painting depicting high summer, all green and gold, wrapped in a still haze of afternoon. He could smell salt and brine. And looking down along the slope of the roof, he could read Harold's sign, upside down.

Just the thought of crawling around on that roof, so high above the ground, made Larry's guts feel dauncy. And he really must have hung his legs right over the raingutter to get the girl's name on.

Why did he go to the trouble, Sergeant? That, I think, is one of the questions to which we must address ourselves.

If you say so, Inspector Underwood.

He went back down the stairs, going slowly and watching his footing. This was no time for a broken leg. At the bottom, something else caught his eye, something carved into one of the support beams, startlingly white and fresh and in direct contrast to all the rest of the barn's old dusty darkness. He went over to the beam and peered at the carving, then ran the ball of his thumb over it, part in amusement, part in wonder that another human being had done it on the day he and Rita had been trekking north. He ran his nail along the carved letters again.

In a heart. With an arrow.

I believe, Sergeant, that the bloke must have been in love.

'Good for you, Harold,' Larry said, and left the barn.

The cycle shop in Wells was a Honda dealership, and from the way the showroom bikes were lined up, Larry deduced that two of them were missing. He was more proud of a second find – a crumpled candy wrapper near one of the wastebaskets. A chocolate Payday. It looked as if someone – lovesick Harold Lauder probably – had finished his candy bar while deciding which bikes he and his inamorata would be happiest with. He had balled up his wrapper and shot it at the wastebasket. And missed.

Nadine thought his deductions were good, but she was not as fetched by them as Larry was. She was eyeing the remaining bikes, in a fever to be off. Joe sat on the showroom's front step, playing the Gibson twelve-string and hooting contentedly.

'Listen,' Larry said, 'it's five o'clock now, Nadine. There's absolutely no way to get going until tomorrow.'

'But there's three hours of daylight left! We can't just sit around! We might miss them!'

'If we miss them, that's that,' he said. 'Harold Lauder left instructions once, right down to the roads they were going to take. If they move on, he'll probably do it again.'

'But –'

'I know you're anxious,' he said, and put his hands on her shoulders. He could feel the old impatience building up and forced himself to control it. 'But you've never been on a motorcycle before.'

'I can ride a bike, though. And I know how to use a clutch, I told you that. *Please*, Larry. If we don't waste time we can camp in New Hampshire tonight and be halfway there by tomorrow night. We –'

'It's not *like* a bike, goddammit!' he burst out, and the guitar came to a jangling stop behind him. He could see Joe looking back at them over his shoulder, his eyes narrowed and instantly distrustful. Gee, I sure do have a way with people, Larry thought. That made him even angrier.

Nadine said mildly: 'You're hurting me.'

He looked and saw that his fingers were buried in the soft flesh of her shoulders, and his anger collapsed into dull shame.

'I'm sorry,' he said.

Joe was still looking at him, and Larry recognized that he had just lost half the ground he had gained with the boy. Maybe more. Nadine had said something.

'What?'

'I said, tell me why it's not like a bike.'

His first impulse was to shout at her, *If you know so much, go on and try it. See how you like looking at the world with your head on backward.* He controlled that, thinking it wasn't only the boy he had lost ground with. He'd lost some with himself. Maybe he had come out the other side, but some of the old childish Larry had come out with him, tagging along at his heels like a shadow which has shrunk in the noonday sun but has not entirely disappeared.

'They're heavier,' he said. 'If you overbalance, you can't get rebalanced as easily as you can with a bicycle. One of these 360s goes three hundred and fifty pounds. You get used to controlling that extra weight very quickly, but it *does* take some getting used to. In a standard shift car, you operate the gearshift with your hand and the throttle with your foot. On a cycle it's reversed: the gearshift is foot-operated, the throttle hand-operated, and that takes a *lot* of getting used to. There are two brakes instead of one. Your right foot brakes the rear wheel, your right hand brakes the front wheel. If you forget and just use the hand-brake, you're apt to fly right over the handlebars. And you're going to have to get used to your passenger.'

'Joe? But I thought he'd ride with you!'

'I'd be glad to take him,' Larry said. 'But right now I don't think he'd have me. Do you?'

Nadine looked at Joe for a long, troubled time. 'No,' she said, and then sighed. 'He may not even want to ride with me. It may scare him.'

'If he does, you're going to be responsible for him. And I'm responsible for both of you. I don't want to see you spill.'

'Did that happen to you, Larry? Were you with someone?'

'I was,' Larry said, 'and I took a spill. But by then the lady I was with was already dead.'

'She crashed her motorcycle?' Nadine's face was very still.

'No. What happened, I'd say it was seventy percent accident and thirty percent suicide. Whatever she needed from me . . . friendship, understanding, help, I don't know . . . she wasn't getting enough.' He was upset now, his temples pounding thickly, his throat tight, the tears close. 'Her name was Rita. Rita Blakemoor. I'd like to do better by you, that's all. You and Joe.'

'Larry, why didn't you tell me before?'

'Because it hurts to talk about it,' he said simply. 'It hurts a lot.' That was the truth, but not the whole truth. There were the dreams. He found himself wondering if Nadine had bad dreams – last night he had awakened briefly and she had been tossing restlessly and muttering. But she had said nothing today. And Joe. Did Joe have bad dreams? Well, he didn't know about *them*, but fearless Inspector Underwood of Scotland Yard was afraid of the dreams . . . and if Nadine took a spill on the motorcycle, they might come back.

'We'll go tomorrow, then,' she said. 'Teach me how tonight.'

But first there was the matter of getting the two small bikes Larry had picked out gassed up. The dealership had a pump, but without electricity it wouldn't run. He found another candy wrapper by the plate covering the underground tank and deduced that it had recently been pried up by the ever-resourceful Harold Lauder. Lovesick or no, Payday freak or not, Larry had gained a lot of respect for Harold, almost a liking in advance. He had already developed his own mental picture of Harold. Probably in his mid-thirties, a farmer maybe, tall and suntanned, skinny, not too bright in the book sense, maybe, but plenty canny. He grinned. Building up a mental picture of someone you had never seen was a fool's game, because they were never the way you had imagined. Everybody knows the one about the three-hundred-pound disc jockey with the whipcord-thin voice.

While Nadine got a cold supper together, Larry prowled around the side of the dealership. There he found a large steel wastecan. Leaning against it was a crowbar and curling over the top was a piece of rubber tubing.

I've found you again, Harold! Take a look at this, Sergeant Briggs. Our man siphoned some gas from the underground tank to get going. I'm surprised he didn't take his hose with him.

Perhaps he cut off a piece and that's what's left, Inspector Underwood – begging your pardon, but it *is* in the wastecan.

By jove, Sergeant, you're right. I'm going to write you up for a promotion.

He took the crowbar and rubber hose back around to the plate covering the tank.

'Joe, can you come here for a minute and help me?'

The boy looked up from the cheese and crackers he was eating and gazed distrustfully at Larry.

'Go on, now, that's all right,' Nadine said quietly.

Joe came over, his feet dragging a little.

Larry slipped the crowbar into the plate's slot. 'Throw your weight on that and let's see if we can get it up,' he said.

For a moment he thought the boy either didn't understand him or didn't want to do it. Then he grasped the far end of the crowbar and pushed on it. His arms were thin but belted with a scrawny sort of muscle, the kind of muscle that working men from poor families always seem to have. The plate tilted a little but didn't come up enough for Larry to get his fingers under.

'Lay over it,' he said.

Those half-savage, uptilted eyes studied him coolly for a moment and then Joe balanced on the crowbar, his feet coming off the ground as his whole weight was thrown onto the lever.

The plate came up a little farther than before, enough so that Larry could squirm his fingers under it. While he was struggling for purchase he happened to think that if the boy still didn't like him, this was the best chance he could have to show it. If Joe took his weight off the crowbar the plate would come down with a crash and he'd lose everything on his hands but the thumbs. Nadine had realized this, Larry saw. She had been peering at one of the bikes but now had turned to watch, her body angled into a posture of tension. Her dark eyes went from Larry, down on one knee, to Joe, who was watching Larry as he leaned his weight on the bar. Those seawater eyes were inscrutable. And still Larry couldn't find purchase.

'Need help?' Nadine asked, her normally calm voice now just a little highpitched.

Sweat ran into one eye and he blinked it away. Still no joy. He could smell gasoline.

'I think we can handle it,' Larry said, looking directly at her.

A moment later his fingers slipped into a short groove on the underside of the plate. He threw his shoulders into it and the plate came up and crashed over on the tarmac with a dull clang. He heard Nadine sigh, and the crowbar fall to the pavement. He wiped his perspiring brow and looked back at the boy.

'That's good work, Joe,' he said. 'If you'd let that thing slip, I would've spent the rest of my life zipping my fly with my teeth. Thank you.'

He expected no response (except perhaps an uninterpretable hoot as Joe walked back to inspect the motorcycles again), but Joe said in a rusty, struggling voice: 'Weck-come.'

Larry flashed a glance at Nadine, who stared back at him and then at Joe. Her face was surprised and pleased, yet somehow she looked – he couldn't have said just how – as if she had expected this. It was an expression he had seen before, but not one he could put his finger on right away.

'Joe,' he said, 'did you say "welcome"?'

Joe nodded vigorously. 'Weck-come. You weck-come.'

Nadine was holding her arms out, smiling. 'That's good, Joe. Very, very good.' Joe trotted to her and allowed himself to be hugged for a moment or two. Then he began to peer at the bikes again, hooting and chuckling to himself.

'He can talk,' Larry said.

'I knew he wasn't mute,' Nadine answered. 'But it's wonderful to know he can recover. I think he needed two of us. Two halves. He . . . oh, I don't know.'

He saw that she was blushing and thought he knew why. He began to slip the length of rubber hose into the hole in the cement, and suddenly realized that what he was doing could easily be inter-preted as a symbolic (and rather crude) bit of dumbshow. He looked up at her, sharply. She turned away quickly, but not before he had seen how intently she was watching what he was doing, and the high color in her cheeks.

The nasty fear rose in his chest and he called: 'For Chrissake, Nadine, *look out!*' She was concentrating on the hand controls, not looking where she was going, and she was going to drive the Honda directly into a pine tree at a wobbling five miles an hour.

She looked up and he heard her say '*Oh!*' in a startled voice. Then she swerved, much too sharply, and fell off the bike. The Honda stalled.

He ran to her, his heart in his throat. 'Are you all right? Nadine! Are you —'

Then she was picking herself up shakily, looking at her scraped hands. 'Yes, I'm fine. Stupid me, not looking where I was going. Did I hurt the motorcycle?'

'Never mind the goddamn motorcycle, let me take a look at your hands.'

She held them out and he took a plastic bottle of Bactine from his pants pocket and sprayed them.

'You're shaking,' she said.

'Never mind that either,' Larry answered, more roughly than he had intended. 'Listen, maybe we had better just stick to the bicycles. This is dangerous —'

'So is breathing,' she answered calmly. 'And I think Joe should ride with you, at least at first.'

'He won't —'

'I think he will,' Nadine said, looking into his face. 'And so do you.'

'Well, let's stop for tonight. It's almost too dark to see.'

'Once more. Haven't I read that if your horse throws you, you should get right back on?'

Joe strolled by, munching blueberries from a motorcycle helmet. He had found a number of wild blueberry bushes behind the dealership and had been picking them while Nadine had her first lesson.

'I guess so,' Larry said, defeated. 'But will you please watch where you're going?'

'Yes, sir. Right, sir.' She saluted and then smiled at him. She had a beautiful slow smile that lit up her whole face. Larry smiled back; there was nothing else to do. When Nadine smiled, even Joe smiled back.

This time she putted around the lot twice and then turned out into the road, swinging over too sharply, bringing Larry's heart into his mouth again. But she brought her foot down smartly as he had shown her, and went up the hill and out of sight. He saw her switch carefully up to second gear, and heard her switch to third as she dropped behind the first rise. Then the bike's engine faded to a drone that melted away to nothing. He stood anxiously in the twilight, absently slapping at an occasional mosquito.

Joe strolled by again, his mouth blue. 'Weck-come,' he said, and grinned. Larry managed a strained smile in return. If she didn't come back soon, he would go after her. Visions of finding her lying in a ditch with a broken neck danced blackly in his head.

He was just walking over to the other cycle, debating whether or not to take Joe with him, when the droning hum came to his ears again and swelled to the sound of the Honda's engine, clocking smoothly along in fourth. He relaxed . . . a little. Dismally he realized he would never be able to relax completely while she was riding that thing.

She came back into sight, the cycle's headlamp now on, and pulled up beside him.

'Pretty good, huh?' She switched off.

'I was getting ready to come after you. I thought you'd had an accident.'

'I sort of did.' She saw the way he stiffened and added, 'I went too slow turning around and forgot to push the clutch in. I stalled.'

'Oh. Enough for tonight, huh?'

'Yes,' she said. 'My tailbone hurts.'

He lay in his blankets that night wondering if she might come to him when Joe was asleep, or if he should go to her. He wanted her and thought, from the way she had looked at the absurd little pantomime with the rubber hose earlier, that she wanted him. At last he fell asleep.

He dreamed he was in a field of corn, lost there. But there was music, guitar music. Joe playing the guitar. If he found Joe he would be all right. So he followed the sound, breaking through one row of corn to the next when he had to, at last coming out in a ragged clearing. There was a small house there, more of a shack really, the porch held up with rusty old jacklifters. It wasn't Joe playing the guitar, how could it have been? Joe was holding his left hand and Nadine his right. They were with him. An old woman was playing the guitar, a jazzy sort of spiritual that had Joe smiling. The old woman was black, and she was sitting on the porch, and Larry guessed she was just about the oldest woman he had ever seen in his life. But there was something about her that made him feel good . . . good in the way his mother had once made him feel good when he was very little and she would suddenly hug him and say, *Here's the best boy, here's Alice Underwood's all-time best boy.*

The old woman stopped playing and looked up at them.

Well say, I got me comp'ny. Step on out where I can see you, my peepers ain't what they once was.

So they came closer, the three of them hand in hand, and Joe reached out and set a bald old tire swing to slow pendulum movement as they passed it. The tire's doughnut-shaped shadow slipped back and forth on the weedy ground. They were in a small clearing, an island in a sea of corn. To the north, a dirt road stretched away to a point.

You like to have a swing on this old box o mine? she asked Joe, and Joe came forward eagerly and took the old guitar from her gnarled hands. He began to play the tune they had followed through the corn, but better and faster than the old woman.

Bless im, he plays good. Me, I'm too old. Cain't make my fingers go that fast now. It's the rheumatiz. But in 1902 I played at the County Hall. I was the first Negro to ever play there, the very first.

Nadine asked who she was. They were in a kind of forever place where the sun seemed to stand still one hour from darkness and the shadow of the swing Joe had set in motion would always travel back and forth across the weedy yard. Larry wished he could stay here forever, he and his family. This was a *good* place. The man with no face could never get him here, or Joe, or Nadine.

Mother Abagail is what they call me. I'm the oldest woman in eastern Nebraska, I guess, and I still make my own biscuits. You come see me as quick as you can. We got to go before he gets wind of us.

A cloud came over the sun. The swing's arc had decreased to nothing. Joe stopped playing with a jangling rattle of strings, and Larry felt the hackles rise on the back of his neck. The old woman seemed not to notice.

Before who gets wind of us? Nadine asked, and Larry wished he could speak, cry out for her to take the question back before it could leap free and hurt them.

That black man. That servant of the devil. We got the Rockies between us n him, praise God, but they won't keep him back. That's why we got to knit together. In Colorado. God come to me in a dream and showed me where. But we got to be quick, quick as we can, anyway. So you come see me. There's others coming, too.

No, Nadine said in a cold and fearful voice. *We're going to Vermont, that's all. Only to Vermont — just a short trip.*

Your trip will be longer than ours, if'n you don't fight off his power, the old woman in Larry's dream replied. She was looking at Nadine with great sadness. *This could be a good man you got here, woman. He wants to make something out of himself. Why don't you cleave to him instead of using him?*

No! We're going to Vermont, to VERMONT!

The old woman looked at Nadine pityingly. *You'll go straight to hell if you don't watch close, daughter of Eve. And when you get there, you are gonna find that hell is cold.*

The dream broke up then, splitting into cracks of darkness that swallowed him. But something in that darkness was stalking him. It was cold and merciless, and soon he would see its grinning teeth.

But before that could happen he was awake. It was half an hour after dawn, and the world was swaddled in a thick white ground fog that would burn off when the sun got up a little more. Now the motorcycle dealership rose out of it like some strange ship's prow constructed of cinderblock instead of wood.

Someone was next to him, and he saw that it wasn't Nadine who had joined him in the night, but Joe. The boy lay next to him, thumb corked in his mouth, shivering in his sleep, as if his own nightmare had gripped him. Larry wondered if Joe's dreams were so different from his own . . . and he lay on his back, staring up into the white fog and thinking about that until the others woke up an hour later.

The fog had burned off enough to travel by the time they had finished breakfast and packed their things on the cycles. As Nadine had said, Joe showed no qualms about riding behind Larry; in fact, he climbed on Larry's cycle without having to be asked.

'Slow,' Larry said for the fourth time. 'We're not going to hurry and have an accident.'

'Fine,' Nadine said. 'I'm really excited. It's like being on a quest!'

She smiled at him, but Larry could not smile back. Rita Blakemoor had said something very much like that when they were leaving New York City. Two days before she died, she had said it.

They stopped for lunch in Epsom, eating fried ham from a can and drinking orange soda under the tree where Larry had fallen asleep and Joe had stood over him with the knife. Larry was relieved to find that riding the motorcycles wasn't as bad as he had thought it would be; in most of the places they could make fairly decent time, and even going through the villages it was only necessary to putt along the sidewalks at walking speed. Nadine was being extremely careful about slowing down on blind curves, and even on the open road she did not urge Larry to go any faster than the steady thirty-five-miles-an-hour pace he was setting. He thought that, barring bad weather, they could be in Stovington by the nineteenth.

They stopped for supper west of Concord, where Nadine said they could save time on Lauder and Goldsmith's route by going directly northwest on the thruway, I-89.

'There will be a lot of stalled traffic,' Larry said doubtfully.

'We can weave in and out,' she said with confidence, 'and use the breakdown lane when we have to. The worst that can happen is we'll have to backtrack to an exit and go around on a secondary road.'

They tried it for two hours after supper, and did indeed come upon a blockage from one side of the northbound lanes to the other. Just beyond Warner a car-and-housetrailer combo had jackknifed; the driver and his wife, weeks dead, lay like grainsacks in the front seat of their Electra.

The three of them, working together, were able to hoist the bikes over the buckled hitch between the car and the trailer. Afterward they were too tired to go any farther, and that night Larry didn't ponder whether or not to go to Nadine, who had taken her blankets ten feet farther down from where he had spread his (the boy was between them). That night he was too tired to do anything but fall asleep.

The next afternoon they came upon a block they couldn't get around. A trailer truck had overturned and half a dozen cars had crashed behind it. Luckily, they were only two miles beyond the Enfield exit. They went back, took the exit ramp, and then, feeling tired and discouraged, stopped in the Enfield town park for a twenty-minute rest.

'What did you do before, Nadine?' Larry asked. He had been thinking about the expression in her eyes when Joe had finally spoken (the boy had added 'Larry, Nadine, fanks,' and 'Go baffroom' to his working vocabulary), and now he made a guess based on that. 'Were you a teacher?'

She looked at him with surprise. 'Yes. That's a good guess.'

'Little kids?'

'That's right. First and second graders.'

That explained something about her complete unwillingness to leave Joe behind. In mind at least, the boy had regressed to a seven-year-old age level.

'How *did* you guess?'

'A long time ago I used to date a speech therapist from Long Island,' Larry said. 'I know that sounds like the start of one of those involved New York jokes, but it's the truth. She worked for the Ocean View school system. Younger grades. Kids with speech impediments, cleft palates, harelips, deaf kids. She used to say that correcting speech defects in children was just showing them an alternative way of getting the right sounds. Show them, say the word. Show them, say the word. Over and over until something in the kid's head clicked. And when she talked about that click happening, she looked the way you did when Joe said "You're welcome."'

'Did I?' She smiled a little wistfully. 'I loved the little ones. Some of them were bruised, but none of them at that age are irrevocably spoiled. The little ones are the only good human beings.'

'Kind of a romantic idea, isn't it?'

She shrugged. 'Children *are* good. And if you work with them, you get to be a romantic. That's not so bad. Wasn't your speech therapist friend happy in her work?'

'Yeah, she liked it,' Larry agreed. 'Were you married? Before?' There it was again – that simple, ubiquitous word. *Before*. It was only two syllables, but it had become all-encompassing.

'Married? No. Never married.' She began to look nervous again. 'I'm the original old maid schoolteacher, younger than I look but older than I feel. Thirty-seven.' His eyes had moved to her hair before he could stop them and she nodded as if he had spoken out loud. 'It's premature,' she said matter-of-factly. 'My grandmother's hair was totally white by the time she was forty. I think I'm going to last at least five years longer.'

'Where did you teach?'

'A small private school in Pittsfield. Very exclusive. Ivy-covered walls, all the newest playground equipment. Damn the recession, full speed ahead. The car pool consisted of two Thunderbirds, three Mercedes-Benzes, a couple of Lincolns, and a Chrysler Imperial.'

'You must have been very good.'

'Yes, I think I was,' she said artlessly, then smiled. 'Doesn't matter much now.'

He put an arm around her. She started a little and he felt her stiffen. Her hand and shoulder were warm.

'I wish you wouldn't,' she said uncomfortably.

'You don't want me to?'

'No. I don't.'

He drew his arm back, baffled. She *did* want him to, that was the thing; he could feel her wanting coming off her in mild but clearly receivable waves. Her color was very high now, and she was looking desperately down at her hands, which were fiddling together in her lap like a couple of hurt spiders. Her eyes were shiny, as if she might be on the verge of tears.

'Nadine –'

(honey, is that you?)

She looked up at him and he saw she was past the verge of tears. She was about to speak when Joe strolled up, carrying his guitar case in one hand. They looked at him guiltily, as if he had found them doing something rather more personal than talking.

'Lady,' Joe said conversationally.

'What?' Larry asked, startled and not tracking very well.

'Lady!' Joe said again, and jerked his thumb back over his shoulder.

Larry and Nadine looked at each other.

Suddenly there was a fourth voice, highpitched and choking with emotion, as startling as the voice of God.

'Thank heaven!' it cried. 'Oh thank heaven!'

They stood up and looked at the woman who was now half running up the street toward them. She was smiling and crying at the same time.

'Glad to see you,' she said. 'I'm so glad to see you, thank heaven –'

She swayed and might have fainted if Larry hadn't been there to steady her until her dizziness passed. He guessed her age at about twenty-five. She was dressed in bluejeans and a plain white cotton blouse. Her face was pale, her blue eyes unnaturally fixed. Those eyes stared at Larry as if trying to convince the brain behind them that this was not a hallucination, that the three people she saw were really here.

'I'm Larry Underwood,' he said. 'The lady is Nadine Cross. The boy is Joe. We're very happy to meet you.'

The woman continued to stare at him wordlessly for a moment, and then walked slowly away from him and toward Nadine.

'I'm so pleased . . .' she began, '. . . so pleased to meet you.' She stumbled a little. 'Oh my God, are you really people?'

'Yes,' Nadine said.

The woman put her arms around Nadine and sobbed. Nadine held her. Joe stood in the street by a stalled pickup truck, his guitar case in one hand, his free thumb in his mouth. At last he went to Larry and looked up at him. Larry held his hand. The two of them stood that way and watched the women solemnly. And that was how they met Lucy Swann.

She was eager to go with them when they told her where they were headed, and that they had reason to believe there were at least two other people there, and possibly more. Larry found a medium-sized knapsack for her in the Enfield Sporting Goods, and Nadine went down to her house on the outskirts of town to help her pack . . . two changes of clothes, some underwear, an extra pair of shoes, a raincoat. And pictures of her late husband and daughter.

They camped that night in a town called Quechee, now over the state line and into Vermont. Lucy Swann told a tale which was short and simple and not much different from the others they would hear. The grief came built-in, and the shock, which had driven her at least within hailing distance of madness.

Her husband had sickened on the twenty-fifth of June, her daughter the next day. She had nursed them as well as she had been able, fully expecting to come down with the rales, as they were calling the sickness in her corner of New England, herself. By the twenty-seventh, when her husband had gone into a coma, Enfield was pretty much cut off from the outside world. Television reception had become spotty and queer. People were dying like flies. During the previous week they had seen extraordinary movements of army troops along the turnpike, but none of them had business in such a little place as Enfield, New Hampshire. In the early morning hours of June twenty-eighth, her husband had died. Her daughter had seemed a little bit better for a while on the twenty-ninth, and then had taken an abrupt turn for the worst that evening. She had died around eleven o'clock. By July third, everyone in Enfield except her and an old man named Bill Dadds had died. Bill had been sick, Lucy said, but he seemed to have thrown it off entirely. Then, on the morning of Independence Day, she had found Bill dead on Main Street, swollen up and black, like everyone else.

'So I buried my people, and Bill too,' she said as they sat around the crackling fire. 'It took all of one day, but I put them to rest.

And then I thought that I better go on down to Concord, where my mother and father live. But I just . . . never got around to it.' She looked at them appealingly. 'Was it so wrong? Do you think they would have been alive?'

'No,' Larry said. 'The immunity sure wasn't hereditary in any direct way. My mother . . .' He looked into the fire.

'Wes and me, we had to get married,' Lucy said. 'That was the summer after I graduated high school – 1984. My mom and dad didn't want me to marry him. They wanted me to go away to have the baby and just give her up. But I wouldn't. My mom said it would end in divorce. My dad said Wes was a no-account man and he'd always be shiftless. I just said, "That may be, but we'll see what happens." I just wanted to take the chance. You know?'

'Yes,' Nadine said. She was sitting next to Lucy, looking at her with great compassion.

'We had a nice little home, and I sure never thought it would end like this,' Lucy said with a sigh that was half a sob. 'We settled down real good, the three of us. It was more Marcy than me that settled Wes down. He thought the sun rose and set on that baby. He thought . . .'

'Don't,' Nadine said. 'All that was before.'

That word again, Larry thought. That little two-syllable word.

'Yes. It's gone now. And I guess I could have gotten along. I was, anyway, until I started to have all those bad dreams.'

Larry's head jerked up. 'Dreams?'

Nadine was looking at Joe. A moment before, the boy had been nodding out in front of the fire. Now he was staring at Lucy, his eyes gleaming.

'Bad dreams, nightmares,' Lucy said. 'They're not always the same. Mostly it's a man chasing me, and I can never see exactly what he looks like because he's all wrapped up in a, what do you call it, a cloak. And he stays in the shadows and alleys.' She shivered. 'I got so I was afraid to go to sleep. But now maybe I'll –'

'Brrr-ack man!' Joe cried suddenly, so fiercely they all jumped. He leaped to his feet and held his arms out like a miniature Bela Lugosi, his fingers hooked into claws. 'Brrack man! Bad dreams! Chases! Chases me! 'Cares me!' And he shrank against Nadine and stared untrustingly into the darkness.

A little silence fell among them.

'This is crazy,' Larry said, and then stopped. They were all looking at him. Suddenly the darkness seemed very dark indeed, and Lucy looked frightened again.

He forced himself to go on. 'Lucy, do you ever dream about . . . well, about a place in Nebraska?'

'I had a dream one night about an old Negro woman,' Lucy said, 'but it didn't last very long. She said something like, "You come see me." Then I was back in Enfield and that . . . that scary guy was chasing me. Then I woke up.'

Larry looked at her so long that she colored and dropped her eyes.

He looked at Joe. 'Joe, do you ever dream about . . . uh, corn? An old woman? A guitar?' Joe only looked at him from Nadine's encircling arm.

'Leave him alone, you'll upset him more,' Nadine said, but she was the one who sounded upset.

Larry thought. 'A house, Joe? A little house with a porch up on jacks?'

He thought he saw a gleam in Joe's eyes.

'Stop it; Larry!' Nadine said.

'A swing, Joe? A swing made out of a tire?'

Joe suddenly jerked in Nadine's arms. His thumb came out of his mouth. Nadine tried to hold him, but Joe broke through.

'The swing!' Joe said exultantly. 'The swing! The swing!' He whirled away from them and pointed first at Nadine, then at Larry. 'Her! You! Lots!'

'Lots?' Larry asked, but Joe had subsided again.

Lucy Swann looked stunned. 'The swing,' she said. 'I remember that, too.' She looked at Larry. 'Why are we all having the same dreams? Is somebody using a ray on us?'

'I don't know.' He looked at Nadine. 'Have you had them, too?'

'I don't dream,' she said sharply, and immediately dropped her eyes. He thought: *You're lying. But why?*

'Nadine, if you –' he began.

'I told you *I don't dream!*' Nadine cried sharply, almost hysterically. 'Can't you just leave me alone? Do you have to badger me?'

She stood up and left the fire, almost running.

Lucy looked after her uncertainly for a moment and then stood up. 'I'll go after her.'

'Yes, you better. Joe, stay with me, okay?'

'Kay,' Joe said, and began to unsnap the guitar case.

Lucy came back with Nadine ten minutes later. They had both been crying, Larry saw, but they seemed to be on good terms now.

'I'm sorry,' Nadine said to Larry. 'It's just that I'm always upset. It comes out in funny ways.'

'It's all right.'

The subject did not come up again. They sat and listened to Joe run through his repertoire. He was getting very good indeed now, and in with the hootings and grunts, fragments of the lyrics were coming through.

At last they slept, Larry on one end, Nadine on the other, Joe and Lucy between.

Larry dreamed first of the black man on the high place, and then of the old black woman sitting on her porch. Only in this dream he knew the black man was coming, striding through the corn, knocking his own twisted swathe through the corn, his terrible hot grin spot-welded to his face, coming toward them, closer and closer.

Larry woke up in the middle of the night, out of breath, his chest constricted with terror. The others slept like stones. Somehow, in that dream he had known. The black man had not been coming empty handed. In his arms, borne like an offering as he strode through the corn, he held the decaying body of Rita Blakemore, now stiff and swollen, the flesh ripped by woodchucks and weasels. A mute accusation to be thrown at his feet to scream his guilt at the others, to silently proclaim that he wasn't no nice guy, that something had been left out of him, that he was a loser, that he was a taker.

At last he slept again, and until he woke up the next morning at seven, stiff, cold, hungry, and needing to go to the bathroom, his sleep was dreamless.

'Oh God,' Nadine said emptily. Larry looked at her and saw a disappointment too deep for tears. Her face was pale, her remarkable eyes clouded and dull.

It was quarter past seven, July nineteenth, and the shadows were drawing long. They had ridden all day, their few rest stops only five minutes long, their lunch break, which they had taken in Randolph, only half an hour. None of them had complained, although after six hours on a cycle Larry's whole body felt numb and achy and full of pins.

Now they stood together in a line outside a wrought-iron fence. Below and behind them lay the town of Stovington, not much changed from the way Stu Redman had seen it on his last couple of days in this institution. Beyond the fence and a lawn that had once been well kept but which was now shaggy and littered by sticks and leaves that had blown onto it during afternoon thunderstorms, was the institution itself, three stories high, more of it buried underground, Larry surmised.

The place was deserted, silent, empty.

In the center of the lawn was a sign which read:

STOVINGTON PLAGUE CONTROL CENTER
THIS IS A GOVERNMENT INSTALLATION!
VISITORS MUST CHECK IN AT MAIN DESK

Beside it was a second sign, and this was what they were looking at.

ROUTE 7 TO RUTLAND	EVERYONE HERE IS DEAD
ROUTE 4 TO SCHUYLER- VILLE	WE ARE MOVING WEST TO NE- BRESKA
ROUTE 29 TO I-87	STAY ON OUR ROUTE
I-87 SOUTH TO I-90	WATCH FOR SIGNS
I-90 WEST	

HAROLD EMERY LAUDER
FRANCES GOLDSMITH
STUART REDMAN
GLENDON PEQUOD BATEMAN
JULY 8, 1990

'Harold, my man,' Larry murmured. 'Can't wait to shake your hand and buy you a beer . . . or a Payday.'

'Larry!' Lucy said sharply.

Nadine had fainted.

CHAPTER 45

She tottered out onto her porch at twenty to eleven on the morning of July twentieth, carrying her coffee and her toast with her as she did every day that the Coca-Cola thermometer outside the sink window read over fifty degrees. It was high summer, the finest summer Mother Abagail could recollect since 1955, the year her mother had died at the goodish age of ninety-three. Too bad there ain't more folks around to enjoy it, she thought as she sat carefully down in her armless rocking chair. But did they ever enjoy it? Some did, of course; young folks in love did, and old folks whose bones remembered so clearly what the death-clutch of winter was. Now most of the young folks and old folks were gone, and most of those in between. God had brought down a harsh judgment on the human race.

Some might argue with such a harsh judgment, but Mother Abagail was not among their number. He had done it once with water, and sometime further along, He would do it with fire. Her place was not to judge God, although she wished He hadn't seen fit to set the cup before her lips that He had. But when it came to matters of *judgment*, she was satisfied with the answer God had given Moses from the burning bush when Moses had seen fit to question. Who are *you*? Mose asks, and God comes back from that bush just as pert as you like: I *Am*, Who I *AM*. In other words, Mose, stop beatin around this here bush and get your old ass in gear.

She wheezed laughter and nodded her head and dipped her toast into the wide mouth of her coffee cup until it was soft enough to chew. It had been sixteen years since she had bid hail and farewell to her last tooth. Toothless she had come from her mother's womb, and toothless she would go into her own grave. Molly, her great-granddaughter, and her husband had given her a set of false teeth for Mother's Day just a year later, the year she herself had been ninety-three, but they hurt her gums and now she only wore them when she knew Molly and Jim were coming. Then she would take them from the box in the drawer and rinse them off good and stick them in. And if she had time before Molly and Jim came, she would make faces at herself in the spotty kitchen mirror and growl through all those big white fake teeth and laugh fit to split. She looked like an old black Everglades gator.

She was old and feeble, but her mind was pretty much in order. Abagail Freemantle was her name, born in 1882 and with the birth certificate to prove it. She'd seen a heap during her time on the earth, but nothing to match the goings-on of the last month or so. No, there never had been such a thing, and now her time was coming to be a part of it and she hated it. She was old. She wanted to rest and enjoy the cycle of the seasons between now and whenever God got tired of watching her make her daily round and decided to call her home to Glory. But what happened when you questioned God? The answer you got was I *Am, Who I AM*, and that was the end. When His own Son prayed that the cup be taken from His lips, God never even answered . . . and she wasn't up to that snuff, no how, no way. Just an ordinary sinner was all she was, and at night when the wind came up and blew through the corn it frightened her to think that God had looked down at a little baby girl poking out between her mother's legs back in early 1882 and had said to Himself: *I got to keep her around a goodish time. She's got work in 1990, on the other side of a whole heap of calendar pages.*

Her time here in Hemingford Home was coming to an end, and her final season of work lay ahead of her in the West, near the Rocky Mountains. He had sent Moses to mountain-climbing and Noah to boatbuilding; He had seen His own Son nailed up on a Tree. What did He care how miserably afraid Abby Freemantle was of the man with no face, *he* who stalked her dreams?

She never saw him; she didn't have to see him. He was a shadow passing through the corn at noon, a cold pocket of air, a gore-crow peering down at you from the phone lines. His voice called to her in all the sounds that had ever frightened her – spoken soft, it was the tick of a deathwatch beetle under the stairs, telling that someone loved would soon pass over; spoken loud it was the afternoon thunder rolling amid the clouds that came out of the west like boiling Armageddon. And sometimes there was no sound at all but the lonely rustle of the nightwind in the corn but she would know *he* was there and that was the worst of all, because then the man with no face seemed only a little less than God Himself; at those times it seemed that she was within touching distance of the dark angel that had flown silently over Egypt, killing the firstborn of every house where the doorpost wasn't daubed with blood. That frightened her most of all. She became a child again in her fear and knew that while others knew of him and were frightened *by* him, only she had been given a clear vision of his terrible power.

'Welladay,' she said, and popped the last bite of toast into her mouth. She rocked back and forth, drinking her coffee. This was a bright, fine day, and no part of her body was giving her particular misery, and she offered up a brief prayer of thanksgiving for what she had got. God is great, God is good; the littlest child could learn those words, and they encompassed the whole world and all the world held, good and evil.

'God is great,' Mother Abagail said, 'God is good. Thank You for the sunshine. For the coffee. For the fine *BM* I had last night, You was right, those dates turned the trick, but my God, they taste nasty to me. Ain't I the one? God is great . . .'

Her coffee was about gone. She set the cup down and rocked, her face turned up to the sun like some strange living rockface, seamed with veins of coal. She dozed, then slept. Her heart, its walls now almost as thin as tissue paper, beat on and on as it had every minute for the last 39,630 days. Like a baby in a crib, you would have had to put your hand on her chest to assure yourself that she was breathing at all.

But the smile stayed on.

Things had surely changed in all the years since she had been a girl. The Freemantles had come to Nebraska as freed slaves, and Abagail's own great-granddaughter Molly laughed in a nasty, cynical way and suggested the money Abby's father had used to buy the home place – money paid to him by Sam Freemantle of Lewis, South Carolina, as wages for the eight years her daddy and his brothers had stayed on after the States War had ended – had been 'conscience money.' Abagail had held her tongue when Molly said that – Molly and Jim and the others were young and didn't understand anything but the veriest good and the veriest bad – but inside she had rolled her eyes and said to herself: *Conscience money? Well, is there any money cleaner than that?*

So the Freemantles had settled in Hemingford Home and Abby, the last of Daddy and Mamma's children, had been born right here on the home place. Her father had bested those who would not buy from niggers and those who would not sell to them; he had bought land a little smidge at a time so as not to alarm those who were worried about 'those black bastards over Columbus way'; he had been the first man in Polk County to try crop rotation; the first man to try chemical fertilizer; and in March of 1902 Gary Sites had come to the house to tell John Freemantle that he had been voted into the Grange. He was the first black man to belong to the Grange in the whole state of Nebraska. That year had been a topper.

She reckoned that anyone, looking back over her life, could pick out one year and say, 'That was the best.' It seemed that, for everyone, there was one spell of seasons when everything came together, smooth and glorious and full of wonder. It was only later on that you might wonder why it had happened that way. It was like putting ten different savory things in the cold-pantry all at once, so each took on a bit of the others' flavors; the mushrooms had a taste of ham and the ham of mushrooms; the venison had the slightest wild taste of partridge and the partridge had the tiniest hint of cucumbers. Later on in life, you might wish that the good things which all befell in your one special year had spread themselves out a little more, that you could maybe take one of the golden things and kind of transplant it right down in the middle of a three-year stretch you couldn't remember a blessed good thing about, or even a bad one, and so you knew that things had just gone on the way they were supposed to in the world God had created and Adam and Eve had half uncreated – the washing had gone out, the floors had been scrubbed, the babies had been cared for, the clothes had been mended; three years with nothing to break up the gray even flow of time but Easter and the Fourth of July and Thanksgiving and Christmas. But there was no answering the ways God set about His wonders to perform, and for Abby Freemantle as well as her father, '02 had been a topper.

Abby thought she was the only one in the family – other than her daddy, that was – that understood what a great, nearly unprecedented thing it was to be invited into the Grange. He would be the first Negro Granger in Nebraska, and very possibly the first Negro Granger in the United States. He had no illusions about the price he and his family would pay in the form of crude jokes and racial slurs from those men – Ben Conveigh chief among them – who were set against the idea. But he also saw that Gary Sites was handing him something more than a chance at survival: Gary was giving him a chance to prosper with the rest of the corn belt.

As a member of the Grange, his problems buying good seed would end. The necessity of taking his crops all the way to Omaha to find a buyer would likewise end. It might mean the end of the water-rights squabble he had been having with Ben Conveigh, who was rabid on the subjects of niggers like John Freemantle and nigger-lovers like Gary Sites. It might even mean that the county tax assessor would stop his endless gouging. So John Freemantle accepted the invitation, and the vote went his way (by quite a comfortable margin, too), and there *were* nasty cracks, and jokes about how a coon had got caught in the Grange Hall loft, and about how when a nigger-baby went to heaven and got its little black wings you called it a bat instead of an angel, and Ben Conveigh went around for a while telling people that the only reason the Mystic Tie Grange had voted John Freemantle in was because the Children's Fair was coming up pretty soon and they needed a nigger to play the African orangutan. John Freemantle pretended not to hear these things, and at home he would quote from the Bible – 'A soft answer turneth away wrath' and 'Brethren, as ye reap so shalt ye surely sow' and his favorite, spoken not in humility but in grim expectation: 'The meek shall inherit the earth.'

And little by little he had brought his neighbors around. Not all of them, not the rabid ones like Ben Conveigh and his half-brother George, not the Arnolds and the Deacons, but all the others. In 1903 they had taken dinner with Gary Sites and his family, right in the parlor, just as good as white.

And in 1902 Abagail had played her guitar at the Grange Hall, and not in the minstrel show, either; she had played in the white folks' talent show at the end of the year. Her mother had been deadset against that; it was one of the few times in her life when she let her opposition to one of her husband's ideas out in front of the children (except by then the boys were damned near middle-aged and John himself had a good deal more than a touch of snow on the mountain). ·

'I know how it was,' she said, weeping. 'You and Sites and that Frank Fenner, you whipped this up together. That's fine for them, John Freemantle, but what's got into your head? They're *white!* You go hunker down with them in the back yard and talk about plowin! You can even go downtown and have a spot of beer with them, if that Nate Jackson will let you into his saloon. Fine! I know what you've been through these last years – none better. I know you've kep a smile on your face when it must have hurt like a grassfire in your heart. *But this is different!* This is *your own daughter!* What you gonna say if she gets up there in her pretty white dress and they laughs at her? What you gonna do if they throws rotten tomatas at her like they did at Brick Sullivan when he tried to sing in the minstrel show? And what are you going to say if she comes to you with those tomatas all over the front of her dress and asks, "Why, Daddy? Why did they do it, and why did you *let* them do it?"'

'Well, Rebecca,' John had answered, 'I guess we better leave it up to her and David.'

David had been her first husband; in 1902 Abagail Freemantle had become Abagail Trotts. David Trotts was a black farmhand from over Valparaiso way, and he had come pretty nearly thirty miles one way to court her. John Freemantle had once said to Rebecca that the bear had caught ole Davy right and proper, and he had been Trotting plenty. There were plenty who had laughed at her first husband and said things like, 'I guess I know who wears the pants in *that* family.'

But David had not been a weakling, only quiet and thoughtful. When he told John and Rebecca Freemantle, 'Whatever Abagail thinks is right, why, I reckon that's what's to do,' she had blessed him for it and told her mother and father she intended to go ahead.

So on December 27, 1902, already three months gone with her first, she had mounted the Grange Hall stage in the dead silence that had ensued when the master of ceremonies had announced her name. Just before her Gretchen Tilyons had been on and had done a racy French dance, showing her ankles and petticoats to the raucous whistles, cheers, and stamping feet of the men in the audience.

She stood in the thick silence, knowing how black her face and neck must look in her new white dress, and her heart was thudding terribly in her chest and she was thinking, *I've forgot every word, every single word, I promised Daddy I wouldn't cry no matter what, I wouldn't cry, but Ben Conveigh's out there and when Ben Conveigh yells NIGGER, then I guess I'll cry, oh why did I ever get into this? Mamma was right, I've got above my place and I'll pay for it –*

The hall was filled with white faces turned up to look at her. Every chair was filled and there were two rows of standees at the back of the hall. Kerosene lanterns glowed and flared. The red velvet curtains were pulled back in swoops of cloth and tied with gold ropes.

And she thought: *I'm Abagail Freemantle Trotts, I play well and I sing well; I do not know these things because anyone told me.*

And so she began to sing 'The Old Rugged Cross' into the moveless silence, her fingers picking melody. Then picking up a strum, the slightly stronger melody of 'How I Love My Jesus,' and then stronger still, 'Camp Meeting in Georgia.' Now people were swaying back and forth almost in spite of themselves. Some were grinning and tapping their knees.

She sang a medley of Civil War songs: 'When Johnny Comes Marching Home,' 'Marching Through Georgia,' and 'Goober Peas' (more smiles at that one; many of these men, Grand Army of the Republic veterans, had eaten more than a few goober peas during their time in the service). She finished with 'Tenting Tonight on the Old Campground,' and as the last chord floated away into a silence that was now thoughtful and sad, she thought: *Now if you want to throw your tomatas or whatever, you go on and do it. I played and sang my best, and I was real fine.*

When the last chord floated into silence, that silence held for a long, almost enchanted instant, as though the people in those seats and the others standing at the back of the hall had been taken far away, so far they could not find their way back all at once. Then the applause broke and rolled over her in a wave, long and sustained, making her blush, making her feel confused, hot and shivery all over. She saw her mother, weeping openly, and her father, and David, beaming at her.

She had tried to leave the stage then, but cries of '*Encore! Encore!*' broke out, and so, smiling, she played 'Digging My Potatoes.' That song was just a tiny bit risky, but Abby guessed that if Gretchen Tilyons could show her ankles in public, then she could sing a song that was the teeniest bit bawdy. She was, after all, a married woman.

> Someone's been diggin my potatoes
> They've left em in my bin,
> And now that someone's gone
> And see the trouble I've got in.

There were six more verses like that (some even worse) and she sang every one, and at the last line of each the roar of approval was louder. And later she thought that if she had done anything wrong that night, it was singing that song, which was exactly the kind of song they probably expected to hear a nigger sing.

She finished to another thunderous ovation and fresh cries of 'Encore!' She remounted the stage, and when the crowd had quietened, she said: 'Thank you all very much. I hope you won't think I am bein forward if I ask to sing just one more song, which I have learned special but never ever expected to sing here. But it is just about the best song I know, on account of what President Lincoln and this country did for me and mine, even before I was born.'

They were very quiet now, listening closely. Her family sat stock still, all together near the left aisle, like a spot of blackberry jam on a white handkerchief.

'On account of what happened back in the middle of the States War,' she went steadily on, 'my family was able to come here and live with the fine neighbors that we have.'

Then she played and sang 'The Star-Spangled Banner,' and everyone stood up and listened, and some of the handkerchiefs came out again, and when she had finished, they applauded fit to raise the roof.

That was the proudest day of her life.

She stirred awake a little after noon and sat up, blinking in the sunlight, an old woman of a hundred and eight. She had slept wrong on her back and it was a pure misery to her. Would be all day, if she knew anything about it.

'Welladay,' she said, and stood up carefully. She began to go down the porch steps, holding carefully to the rickety railing, wincing at the daggers of pain in her back and the prickles in her legs. Her circulation was not what it had once been . . . why should it be? Time after time she had warned herself about the consequences of falling asleep in that rocker. She would doze off and all the old times would come back and that was wonderful, oh yes it was, better than watching a play on the television, but there was hell to pay when she woke up. She could lecture herself all she liked, but she was like an old dog that splays itself out by a fireplace. If she sat in the sun, she went to sleep, that was all. She no longer had a say in the matter.

She reached the bottom of the steps, paused to 'let her legs catch up with her,' then hawked up a goodish gob of snot and spat it into the dirt. When she felt about as usual (except for the misery in her back), she walked slowly around to the privy her grandson Victor had put behind the house in 1931. She went inside, primly shut the door and put the hook through the eye just as if there was a whole crowd of folks out there instead of a few blackbirds, and sat down. A moment later she began to make water and sighed contentedly. Here was another thing about being old no one ever thought to tell you (or was it just that you never listened?) – you stopped knowing when you had to make water. Seemed like you lost all the feeling down there in your bladder, and if you weren't careful, first thing you knew you had to be changing your clothes. It wasn't like her to be dirty, and so she came out here to squat six or seven times a day, and at night she kept the chamberpot beside the bed. Molly's Jim told her once that she was like a dog that couldn't pass a fireplug without at least lifting one leg to salute it, and that had made her laugh until tears spouted from her eyes and streamed down her cheeks. Molly's Jim was an advertising executive in Chicago and getting along a right smart . . . had been, anyway. She supposed he was gone with the rest of them. Molly too. Bless their hearts, they were with Jesus now.

The last year or so, Molly and Jim were about the only ones who came out to the place to see her anymore. The rest seemed to have forgot she was alive, but she could understand that. She had lived past her time. She was like a dinosaur which had no business still wearing its flesh over its bones, a thing whose proper place was in a museum (or a graveyard). She could understand them not wanting to come see *her*, but what she couldn't understand was why they didn't want to come back and see the *land*. There wasn't much left, no; just a matter of acres out of the original large freehold. It was still theirs, however; still *their land*. But black folks didn't seem to care so much about land anymore. There were, in fact, those that actually seemed ashamed of it. They had gone off to make their way in the cities, and most of them, like Jim, came along real well . . . but how it made her heart ache, to think of all those black folks with their faces set away from the land!

Molly and Jim had wanted to put in a flushing toilet for her the year before last, and had been hurt when she refused. She tried to explain so they could understand, but all Molly had been able to say, over and over again, was, 'Mother Abagail, you are a hundred and six years old. How do you think I feel, knowing you are going out there to squat down some days when it's only ten degrees above zero? Don't you know that the shock of the cold could do your heart in?'

'When the Lord wants me, the Lord will take me,' Abagail

said, and she was knitting, and so of course they thought that was what she was looking at and couldn't see the way they rolled their eyes at each other.

Some things you couldn't let go of. It seemed like that was another thing the young people didn't know. Now, back in '82, when she had turned a hundred, Cathy and David had offered her a TV set and she had taken them up on that one. The TV was a marvelous machine for passing the time when you were by your onesome. But when Christopher and Susy came and said they wanted to get her on the city water, she had turned them down just as she had turned down Molly and Jim on their kind offer of a flushing toilet. They had argued that her dug well was shallow, and it could go dry if there was another summer like 1988, when the drought came. It was true, but she just went on saying no. They thought she had flipped her wig, of course, that she was taking coat after coat of senility the way a floor takes varnish, but she herself believed her mind was pretty nigh as good as it had ever been.

She hoisted herself off the privy's seat, dusted lime down through the hole, and slowly let herself out into the sunlight again. She kept her privy sweet, but they were dank old places no matter how sweet they smelled.

It was as if the voice of God had been whispering in her ear when Chris and Susy offered to see that she was put on the city water . . . the voice of God even way back when Molly and Jim wanted to get her that china throne with the flush-lever on the side. God *did* speak to folks; hadn't He talked to Noah about the ark, telling him how many cubits long and how many deep and how many wide? Yes. And she believed He had spoken to her as well, not from a burning bush or out of a pillar of fire, but in a still, small voice that said: *Abby, you are going to need your hand-pump. You enjoy your lectricity all you want, Abby, but you keep those oil-lamps of yours full and keep the wicks trimmed. You keep the cold-pantry just the way your mother kept it before you. And mind you don't let any of the young folks talk you into anything you know to be against My will, Abby. They are your kin, but I am your Father.*

She paused in the middle of the yard, looking out at the sea of corn, broken only by the dirt road going north toward Duncan and Columbus. Three miles up from her house it went to tar. The corn was going to be fine this year, and it was such a shame that no one would be around to harvest it but the rooks. It was sad to think that the big red harvesting machines were going to stay in their barns this September, sad to think there would be no husking bees and barn dances. Sad to think that, for the first time in the last one hundred and eight years, she would not be here in Hemingford Home to see the time of the change as summer gave in to pagan, jocund autumn. She would love this summer all the more because it was to be her last – she felt that clearly. And she would not be laid to rest here but farther west, in a strange country. It was bitter.

She shuffled over to the tire swing and set it to moving. It was an old tractor tire that her brother Lucas had hung here in 1922. The rope had been changed many times between then and now, but never the tire. Now the canvas showed through in many places, and on the inside rim there was a deep depression where generations of young buttocks had set themselves down. Below the tire was a deep and dusty groove in the earth where the grass had long since given up trying to grow, and on the limb where the rope was tied, the bark had been rubbed away to show the branch's white bone. The rope creaked slowly and this time she spoke aloud.

'Please, my Lord, my Lord, not unless I have to, I'd have You take this cup from my lips if You can. I'm old and I'm scared and mostly I'd just like to lie right here on the home place. I'm ready to go right now if You want me. Thy will be done, my Lord, but Abb's one tired shufflin old black woman. Thy will be done.'

No sound but the creak of the rope against the branch and the crows off in the corn. She put her old seamed forehead against the old seamed bark of the apple tree her father had planted so long ago and she wept bitterly.

That night she dreamed she was mounting the steps to the Grange Hall stage again, a young and pretty Abagail, three months quick with child, a dusky Ethiopian jewel in her white dress, holding her guitar by the neck, climbing, climbing into that stillness, her thoughts a millrace, yet holding above all to one thought: *I am Abagail Freemantle Trotts, and I play well and I sing well. I do not know these things because anyone told me.*

In the dream she turned slowly, facing those white faces turned up to her like moons, faced the hall so richly alight with its lamps and the mellow glow thrown back from the darkened, slightly steamed windows and the red velvet swags with their gold ropes.

She held firmly to that one thought and began to play 'Rock of Ages.' She played and her voice came out, not nervous and restrained, but exactly as it had come out when she had been practicing, rich and mellow, like the yellow lamplight itself, and she thought: *I am going to win them. With the help of God I am going to win them over. Oh my people, if you are thirsty, will I not bring water from the rock? I will win them over, and I will make David proud of me and Mamma and Daddy proud of me, I will make myself proud of myself, I will bring music from the air and water from the rock —*

And that was when she saw him for the first time. He was standing far back in the corner, behind all the seats, his arms folded across his chest. He was wearing jeans and a denim jacket with buttons on the pockets. He was wearing dusty black boots with rundown heels, boots that looked as if they had walked many a dark and dusty mile. His forehead was white as gaslight, his cheeks red with jolly blood, his eyes blazing blue diamond chips, sparkling with infernal good cheer, as if the Imp of Satan had taken over the job of Kris Kringle. A hot and fleering grin had pulled his lips back from his teeth into something close to a snarl. The teeth were white and sharp and neat, like the teeth of a weasel.

He raised his hands out from his body. Both of them were curled into fists, as tight and hard as knots on an apple tree. His grin remained, jolly and utterly hideous. Drops of blood began to fall from his fists.

The words dried up in her mind. Her fingers forgot how to play; there was a final discordant jangle and then silence.

God! God! she cried, but God had turned His face away.

Then Ben Conveigh was standing up, his face red and flaming, his small pig's eyes glittering. *Nigger bitch!* he shouted. *What's that nigger bitch doing up on our stage? No nigger bitch ever brought music from the air! No nigger bitch ever brought water from the rock!*

Answering cries of savage agreement. People surging forward. She saw her husband stand up and attempt to mount the stage. A fist hit him in the mouth, bowling him over backward.

Get those dirty coons in the back of the hall! Bill Arnold hollered, and somebody pushed Rebecca Freemantle into the wall. Someone else — Chet Deacon, by the looks — wrapped one of the red velvet window curtains around Rebecca and then tied her in with one of the gold ropes. He was yelling: *Looka here! Dressed coon! Dressed coon!*

Others rushed over to where Chet Deacon was, and they all began to punch and pummel the struggling woman under the velvet drape.

Mamma! Abby screamed.

The guitar was plucked from her nerveless fingers and smashed to strips and strings on the edge of the stage.

She looked wildly for the dark man at the back of the hall, but his engine had been set in motion and was running sweet and hot; he had gone on to some other place.

Mamma! she screamed again, and then rough hands were hauling her from the stage, they were under her dress, pawing her, tweaking her, pinching her bottom. Her hand was pulled sharply by someone, yanking her arm in her socket. It was put against something hard and hot.

Ben Conveigh's voice in her ear: *How do you like MY rock of ages, you nigger slut?*

The room was whirling. She saw her father struggling to get at the limp form of her mother, and she saw a white hand holding a bottle come down on the back of a folding camp chair. There was a rattle and a smash, and then the jagged neck of the bottle, twinkling in the warm glow of all those lamps, was thrust into her father's face. She saw his staring, bulging eyes pop like grapes.

She screamed and the force of her cry seemed to break the room apart, to let in darkness, and she was Mother Abagail again, one hundred and eight years old, too old, my Lord, too old (but let Thy will be done), and she was walking in the corn, the mystic corn that was rooted shallow in the earth but wide, lost in the corn that was silver with moonglow and black with shadow; she could hear the summer night-wind rustling gently through it, she could smell its growing, wholly alive smell as she had smelled it all her long, long life (and she had thought many times that this was the plant closest to all life, the corn, and its smell was the smell of life itself, the start of life, oh she had married and buried three husbands, David Trotts, Henry Hardesty, and Nate Brooks, and she had had three men in bed, had welcomed them as a woman must welcome a man, by giving way before him, and there had always been the yearning pleasure, the thought *Oh my God how I love to be sexy with my man and how I love him to be sexy with me when he gets me what he gets me what he shoots in me* and sometimes at the instant of her climax she would think of the corn, the bland corn with its roots planted not deep but wide, she would think of flesh and then the corn, when it was all over and her husband lay beside her the sex smell would be in the room, the smell of the spunk the man had shot into her, the smell of the juices she made to smooth his way, and it was a smell like husked corn, mild and sweet, a goodish smell).

And yet she was afraid, ashamed of this very intimacy with soil and summer and growing things, because she was not alone. *He* was here with her, two rows to the right or left, trailing just behind or ranging just ahead. The dark man was here, his dusty boots digging into the meat of the soil and throwing it away in clouts, grinning in the night like a stormlamp.

Then he spoke, for the first time he spoke aloud, and she could see his moonshadow, tall and hunched and grotesque, falling into the row she was walking. His voice was like the night wind that begins to moan through the old and fleshless cornstalks in October, like the very rattling of those old white infertile cornstalks themselves as they seem to speak of their end. It was a soft voice. It was the voice of doom.

It said: *I have your blood in my fists, old Mother. If you pray to God, pray He takes you before you ever hear my feet coming up your steps. It was not you who brought music from the air, not you who brought water from the rock, and your blood is in my fists.*

Then she was awake, awake in the hour before dawn, and at first she thought she had peed the bed, but it was only a night sweat, heavy as May dew. Her thin body was shuddering helplessly, and every part of her ached for rest.

My Lord, my Lord, take this cup from my lips.

Her Lord did not answer. There was only the light knocking of the early morning wind at the windowpanes, which were loose and rattling and in need of fresh putty. At last she got up and poked up the fire in her old woodburning stove and put on the coffee.

She had a great deal to do in the next few days, because she was going to have company. Dreams or not, tired or not, she had never been one to slight company and she didn't intend to start now. But she would have to go very slowly or she would get forgetting things – she forgot a lot these days – and misplacing things until she ended up chasing her own tail.

The first thing was to get down to Addie Richardson's henhouse, and that was a goodish way, four or five miles. She found herself wondering if the Lord was going to send her an eagle to fly her those four miles, or send Elijah in his fiery chariot to give her a lift.

'Blasphemy,' she told herself complacently. 'The Lord provides strength, not taxicabs.'

When her few dishes were washed, she put on her heavy shoes and took her cane. Even now she rarely used the cane, but today she would need it. Four miles going, four miles coming back. At sixteen she could have dashed one way and trotted the other, but sixteen was far behind her now.

She set off at eight o'clock in the morning, hoping to reach the Richardson farm by noon and sleep through the hottest part of the day. In the late afternoon she would kill her chickens and then come home in the gloaming. She wouldn't arrive until after dark, and that made her think of her dream of the night before, but that man was still far away. Her company was much closer.

She walked very slowly, even more slowly than she felt she had to, because even at eight-thirty the sun was fat and powerful. She didn't sweat much – there wasn't enough excess flesh on her bones to wring the sweat out of – but by the time she'd reached the Goodells' mailbox, she had to rest a bit. She sat in the shade of their pepper tree and ate a few fig bars. Not an eagle or a taxicab in sight, either. She cackled a little at that, got up, brushed the crumbs off her dress, and went on. Nope, no taxicabs. The Lord helped those that helped themselves. All the same, she could feel all of her joints tuning up; tonight there would be a concert.

She hunched more and more over her cane as she went, even though her wrists began to be a misery to her. Her brogans with the yellow rawhide lacings shuffled in the dust. The sun beat down on her, and as the time passed, her shadow got shorter and shorter. She saw more wild animals that morning than she had seen since the twenties: fox, coon, porcupine, fisher. Crows were everywhere, squalling and cawing and circling in the sky. If she had been around to hear Stu Redman and Glen Bateman discussing the capricious – it had seemed capricious to them, anyhow – way the superflu had taken some animals while leaving others alone, she would have laughed. It had taken the domestic animals and left the wild ones alone, it was as simple as that. A few species of domestics had been spared, but as a general rule, the plague had taken man and man's best friends. It had taken the dogs but left the wolves, because the wolves were wild and the dogs weren't.

A red-hot sparkplug of pain had settled deep into each of her hips, behind each knee, in her ankles, in the wrists she was using to support herself on the cane. She walked and she talked to her God, sometimes silently, sometimes aloud, unaware of any difference between the two. And she fell to thinking about her own past again. 1902 had been the best year, all right. After that it seemed that time sped up, the pages of some big fat calendar ruffling over and over, hardly ever pausing. A body's life went by so fast . . . how was it a body could get so tired of living it?

She'd had five children by Davy Trotts; one of them, Maybelle, had choked to death on a piece of apple in the back yard of the Old Place. Abby had been hanging clothes and she had turned around to see the baby lying on her back, clawing at her throat and turning purple. She had gotten the chunk of apple out at last, but by then little Maybelle had been still and cold, the only girl she had ever borne and the only one of her many children to die an accidental death.

Now she sat in the shade of an elm just inside the Nauglers' fence, and two hundred yards up the road she could see where dirt gave way to tar – this was the place where Freemantle Road became Polk County Road. The heat of the day made a shimmer over the tar, and at the horizon was quicksilver, shining like water in a dream. On a hot day you always saw that quicksilver just at the end of where your eye could see, but you never quite caught up to it. Or at least *she* never had.

David had died in 1913, of an influenza not so very different from this one, which had wiped out so many. In 1916, when she had been thirty-four, she had married Henry Hardesty, a black farmer from Wheeler County up north. He had come to court her special. Henry was a widower with seven children, all but two of them grown up and gone away. He was seven years older than Abagail. He had given her two boys before his tractor turned turtle on him and killed him in the late summer of 1925.

A year after that she had married Nate Brooks, and people had talked – oh yes, people talk, how people do love to talk, sometimes it seemed that was all they had to do. Nate had been Henry Hardesty's hired man, and he had been a good husband to her. Not as sweet as David, perhaps, and surely not as tenacious as Henry, but a good man who had pretty much done as she had told him. When a woman began to get a trifle along in years, it was a comfort to know who had the upper hand.

Her six boys had produced a crop of thirty-two grandchildren for her. Her thirty-two grandchildren had produced ninety-one great-grandchildren that she knew of, and at the time of the superflu, she had had three great-great-grandchildren. Would have had more, if not for the pills the girls took these days to keep the babies away. It seemed like for them, being sexy was just another playground to be in. Abagail felt sorry for them in their modern ways, but she never spoke of it. It was up to God to judge whether or not they were sinning by taking those pills (and not to that baldheaded old fart in Rome – Mother Abagail had been a Methodist all her life, and she was damned proud of not having any truck with those mackerel-snapping Catholics), but Abagail knew what they were missing: the ecstasy which comes when you stand on the lip of the Valley of the Shadow, the ecstasy that comes when you gave yourself up to your man and your God, when you say thy will be done and *Thy* will be done; the final ecstasy of sex in the sight of the Lord, when a man and a woman relive the old sin of Adam and Eve, only now washed and sanctified in the Blood of the Lamb.

Ah, welladay . . .

She wanted a drink of water, she wanted to be home in her rocker, she wanted to be left alone. Now she could see the sun glinting off the henhouse roof ahead to her left. A mile, no more. It was quarter past ten, and she wasn't doing too badly for an old gal. She would let herself in and sleep until the cool of the evening. No sin in that. Not at her age. She shuffled along the shoulder, her heavy shoes now coated with road-dust.

Well, she had had a lot of kin to bless her in her old age, and that was something. There were some, like Linda and that no-account salesman she had married, who didn't care to come calling, but there were the good ones like Molly and Jim and David and Cathy, enough to make up for a thousand Lindas and no-account salesmen who went door to door selling waterless cookware. The last of her brothers, Luke, had died in 1949, at the age of eightysomething, and the last of her children, Samuel, in 1974, at the age of fifty-four. She had outlived all of her children, and that was not the way it was supposed to be, but it seemed like the Lord had special plans for her.

In 1982, when she had turned one hundred, her picture had been in the Omaha paper and they had sent out a TV reporter to do a story on her. 'To what do you attribute your great age?' the young man had asked her, and he had looked disappointed at her brief, almost curt answer: 'To God.' They wanted to hear about how she ate beeswax, or stayed away from fried pork, or how she kept her legs up when she slept. But she did none of those things, and was she to lie? God gives life and He takes it away when He wants.

Cathy and David had given her her TV so she could watch herself on the news, and she got a letter from President Reagan (no spring chicken himself) congratulating her on her 'advanced age' and the fact that she had voted Republican for as long as she'd had a vote to cast. Well, who else would she vote for? Roosevelt and his crowd had all been Communists. And when she turned the century, the town of Hemingford Home had repealed her taxes 'in perpetuity' because of that same advanced age Ronald Reagan had congratulated her for. She got a paper certifying her as the oldest living person in Nebraska, as if that was something little children grew up hoping to be. It was a good thing about the taxes, though, even if the rest of it had been purest foolishness – if they hadn't done that, she would have lost what little land she still had. Most of it had been long gone anyway; the Freemantle holdings and the power of the Grange had both reached high water in that magic year of 1902 and had been declining ever since. Four acres was all that was left. The rest had either been taken for taxes or sold off for cash over the years . . . and most of the selling had been done by her own sons, she was ashamed to say.

Last year she had been sent a paper by some New York combination that called itself the American Geriatrics Society. The paper said she was the sixth-oldest human being in the United States, and the third-oldest woman. The oldest of them all was a fellow in Santa Rosa, California. The fellow in Santa Rosa was a hundred and twenty-two. She had gotten Jim to put that letter in a frame for her and hang it beside the letter from the President. Jim hadn't got around to doing that until this February. Now that she thought about it, that had been the last time she saw Molly and Jim.

She had reached the Richardson farm. Almost completely exhausted, she leaned for a moment against the fencepost closest to the barn and looked longingly at the house. It would be cool inside there, cool and nice. She felt she could sleep an age. Yet before she could do that, there was one more thing she had to do. A lot of animals had died with this disease – horses, dogs, and rats – and she had to know if chickens were among them. It would be a bitter laugh on her to discover she had come all this way to find only dead chickens.

She shuffled toward the henhouse, which was attached to the

barn, and stopped when she could hear them cackling inside. A moment later a cock crowed irritably.

'All right,' she muttered. 'That's good, then.'

She was turning around when she saw the body sprawled by the woodpile, one hand thrown over his face. It was Bill Richardson, Addie's brother-in-law. He had been well picked over by foraging animals.

'Poor man,' Abagail said. 'Poor, poor man. Flights of angels sing you to y'rest, Billy Richardson.'

She turned back to the cool, inviting house. It seemed miles away, although in reality it was only across the dooryard. She wasn't sure she could make it that far; she was utterly exhausted.

'Lord's will be done,' she said, and began to walk.

The sun was shining in the window of the guest bedroom, where she had lain down and fallen asleep as soon as her brogans were off. For a long time she couldn't understand why the light was so bright; it was much the feeling Larry Underwood had had upon awakening beside the rock wall in New Hampshire.

She sat up, every strained muscle and fragile bone in her body crying out. 'God A'mighty, done slep the afternoon and the whole night through!'

If that was so, she must have been tired indeed. She was so lamed up now that it took her almost ten minutes to get out of bed and go down the hall to the bathroom; another ten to get her shoes on her feet. Walking was agony, but she knew she must walk. If she didn't, that stiffness would settle in like iron.

Limping and hobbling, she crossed to the henhouse and went inside, wincing at the explosive hotness, the smell of fowls, and the inevitable smell of decomposition. The water supply was automatic, fed from the Richardsons' artesian well by a gravity pump, but most of the feed had been used up and the heat itself had killed many of the birds. The weakest had long ago been starved or pecked to death, and they lay around the feed- and droppings-spotted floor like small drifts of sadly melting snow.

Most of the remaining chickens fled before her approach with a great flapping of wings, but those that were broody only sat and blinked at her slow, shuffling approach with their stupid eyes. There were so many diseases that killed chickens that she had been afraid that the flu might have carried them off, but these looked all right. The Lord had provided.

She took three of the plumpest and made them stick their heads under their wings. They went immediately to sleep. She bundled them into a sack and then found she was too stiff to actually lift it. She had to drag it along the floor.

The other chickens watched her cautiously from their high vantage points until the old woman was gone, then went back to their vicious squabbling over the diminishing feed.

It was now close to nine in the morning. She sat down on the bench that ran in a circle around the Richardsons' dooryard oak to think. It seemed to her that her original idea, to go home in the cool of dusk, was still best. She had lost a day, but her company was still coming. She could use this day to take care of the chickens and rest.

Her muscles were already riding a little easier against her bones, and there was an unfamiliar but rather pleasant gnawing sensation below her breastbone. It took her several moments to realize what it was . . . she was hungry! This morning she was actually *hungry*, praise God, and how long had it been since she had eaten for any reason other than force of habit? She'd been like a locomotive fireman stoking coal, no more. But when she had parted these three chickens from their heads, she would see what Addie had left in her pantry, and by the blessed Lord, she would *enjoy* what she found. You see? she lectured herself. The Lord knows best. Blessed assurance, Abagail, blessed assurance.

Grunting and puffing, she dragged her towsack around to the chopping block that stood between the barn and the woodshed. Just inside the woodshed door she found Billy Richardson's Son House hanging on a couple of pegs, its rubber glove snugged neatly down over the blade. She took it and went back out.

'Now Lord,' she said, standing over the towsack in her dusty yellow workshoes and looking up at the cloudless midsummer sky, 'You have given me the strength to walk up here, and I'm believin You'll give me the strength to walk back. Your prophet Isaiah says that if a man or woman believes in the Lord God of Hosts, he shall mount up with wings as eagles. I don't know nothin much about eagles, my Lord, except they are mostly ugly-natured birds who can see a long ways, but I got three broilers in this bag and I should like to whack off their heads and not m'own hand. Thy will be done, amen.'

She picked up the towsack, opened it, and peered down. One of the hens still had her head under her wing, fast asleep. The other two had squashed against each other, not moving much. It was dark in the sack and the hens thought it was nighttime. The only thing dumber than a broody hen was a New York Democrat.

Abagail plucked one out and laid it across the block before it knew what was happening. She brought the hatchet down hard, wincing as she always had at the final mortal thud of the blade biting through to wood. The head fell into the dust on one side of the chopping block. The headless chicken strutted off into the Richardsons' dooryard, blood spouting, wings fluttering. After a bit it found out it was dead and lay down decently. Broody hens and New York Democrats, my Lord, my Lord.

Then the job was done and all her worrying that she might botch it or hurt herself doing it had been for nothing. God had heard her prayer. Three good chickens, and now all she had to do was get home with them.

She put the birds back into the towsack and then hung Billy Richardson's Son House hatchet back up. Then she went into the farmhouse again to see what there might be to eat.

She napped during the early part of the afternoon and dreamed that her company was getting closer now; they were just south of York, coming along in an old pickup truck. There were six of them, one of them a boy who was deaf and dumb. But a powerful boy, all the same. He was one of the ones she would have to talk to.

She woke around three-thirty, a little stiff but otherwise feeling rested and refreshed. For the next two and a half hours she plucked the chickens, resting when the work put too much misery into her arthritic fingers, then going on. She sang hymns while she worked – 'Seven Gates to the City (My, Lord Hallelu'),' 'Trust and Obey,' and her own favorite, 'In the Garden.'

When she finished the last chicken, each of her fingers had a migraine headache and the daylight had begun to take on that still and golden hue that means twilight's outrider has arrived. Late July now, and the days were shortening down again.

She went inside and had another bite. The bread was stale but not moldy – no mold would ever dare show its green face in Addie Richardson's kitchen – and she found a half-used jar of smooth peanut butter. She ate a peanut butter sandwich and made up another, which she put in her dress pocket in case she got hungry later.

It was now twenty to seven. She went back out again, gathered up her towsack, and went carefully down the porch steps. She had plucked neatly into another sack, but a few feathers had escaped and now fluttered from the Richardsons' hedge, which was drying for lack of water.

Abagail sighed heavily and said: 'I'm off, Lord. Headed home. I'll be going slow, don't reckon to get there until midnight or so, but the Book says fear neither the terror of night nor that which flieth at noonday. I'm in the way of doing Your will as best I know it. Walk with me, please. Jesus' sake, amen.'

By the time she reached the place where the tar stopped and the road went to dirt, it was full dark. Crickets sang and frogs croaked down in some wet place, probably Cal Goodell's cowpond. There was going to be a moon, a big red one, the color of blood until it got up in the sky a ways.

She sat down to rest and eat half of her peanut butter sandwich (and what she would have done for some nice black-currant jelly to cut that sticky taste, but Addie kept her preserves down cellar and that was just too many stairs). The towsack was beside her. She ached again and her strength seemed just about gone with two and a half miles before her still to walk . . . but she felt strangely exhilarated. How long since she had been out after dark, under the canopy of the stars? They shone just as bright as ever, and if her luck was in she might see a falling star to wish on. A warm night like this, the stars, the summer moon just peeking his red lover's face over the horizon, it made her remember her girlhood again with all its strange fits and starts, its heats, its gorgeous vulnerability as it stood on the edge of the Mystery. Oh, she had been a girl. There were those who would not believe it, just as they were unable to believe that the giant sequoia had ever been a green sprout. But she had been a girl, and in those times the childhood fears of the night had faded a little and the adult fears that came in the night when everything is silent and you can hear the voice of your eternal soul, those fears were yet down the road. In that brief time between, the night had been a fragrant puzzle, a time when, looking up at the star-strewn sky and listening to the breeze that brought such intoxicating smells, you felt close to the heartbeat of the universe, to love and life. It seemed you would be forever young and that –

Your blood is in my fists.

There was a sudden sharp tug at her sack, making her heart jump. 'Hi!' she shrieked in her cracked and startled old woman's voice. She yanked the bag back to her with a small rip in the bottom.

There was a low growling sound. Crouched on the verge of the road, between the gravel shoulder and the corn, was a large brown weasel. Its eyes rolled at her, picking up red glints of moonlight. It was joined by another. And another. And another.

She looked at the other side of the road and saw that it was lined with them, their mean eyes speculative. They were smelling the chickens in the bag. How could so many of them have crept around her? she wondered with mounting fear. She had been bitten by a weasel once; she had reached under the porch of the Big House to get a red rubber ball that had rolled under there, and something which felt like a mouthful of needles had fastened on her forearm. The unexpected viciousness of it, agony jumping red-hot and vital out of the humdrum order of things, had made her shriek as much as the actual pain. She had drawn her arm back and the weasel had been hanging from it with her blood beaded on its smooth brown fur, its body whipping back and forth in the air like a snake's body. She had screamed and waved her arm, but the weasel had not let go; it seemed to have become a part of her.

Her brothers Micah and Matthew had been in the yard; her father had been on the porch, looking at a mail-order catalogue. They had all come running and for a moment they had been struck frozen by the sight of Abagail, then just twelve, tearing around the clearing where the barn was to shortly go up, the brown weasel hanging down from her arm like a stole with its back paws digging for purchase in the thin air. Blood had fallen onto her dress, legs, and shoes in a pattering shower.

It was her father who had acted first. John Freemantle had picked up a chunk of stovewood from beside the chopping block and had bawled: 'Stand still, Abby!' His voice, which had been the voice of ultimate command ever since her babyhood, had cut through the yatter and babble of panic in her mind when probably nothing else could have done. She stood still and the stovelength came whistling down and a jolting agony went all the way up to her shoulder (she had thought her arm was broken for sure) and then the brown Thing which had caused her such agony and surprise – in the horrid heat of those few moments the two feelings had been completely interchangeable – was lying on the ground, its fur streaked and matted with her blood and then Micah jumped straight up into the air and came down on it with both feet and there was a horrid final crunching sound like the sound hard candy made in your head when you crunched it between your teeth and if it hadn't been dead before, it surely was then. Abagail had not fainted, but she had gone into sobbing, screaming hysterics.

By then Richard, the oldest son, had come running, his face pale and scared. He and his father exchanged a sober, frightened glance.

'I never saw a weasel do nothing like that in all my life,' John Freemantle said, holding his sobbing daughter by the shoulders. 'Thank God your mother was up the road with them beans.'

'Maybe it was r –' Richard began.

'You hesh your mouth,' his father rode in before Richard could go any further. His voice had been cold and furious and frightened all at the same time. And Richard *did* hesh his mouth – closed it so fast and hard, in fact, that Abby had heard it snap shut. Then her father said to her, 'Let's take you on over to the pump, Abagail, honey, and wash that mess out.'

It was a year later that Luke told her what their father hadn't wanted Richard to say right out loud: that the weasel must almost surely have been rabid to do a thing like that, and if it had been, she would have died one of the most horrible deaths, aside from outright torture, of which men knew. But the weasel had not been rabid; the wound had healed clean. All the same, she had been terrified of the creatures from that day to this, terrified in the way some people are terrified of rats and spiders. If only the plague had taken *them* instead of the dogs! But it hadn't, and she was –

Your blood is in my fists.

One of them darted forward and tore at the rough hem of the towsack.

'*Hi!*' she screamed at it. The weasel darted away, seeming to grin, a thread of the bag hanging from its chops.

He had sent them – the dark man.

Terror engulfed her. There were hundreds of them now, gray ones, brown ones, black ones, all of them smelling chicken. They lined both sides of the road, squirming over each other in their eagerness to get at some of what they smelled.

I got to give it to them. It was all for nothing. If I don't give it to them, they'll rip me to pieces to get it. All for nothing.

In the darkness of her mind she could see the dark man's grin, she could see his fists held out and the blood dripping from them.

Another tug at the bag. And another.

The weasels on the far side of the road were now squirming across toward her, low, their bellies in the dust. Their little savage eyes glinted like icepicks in the moonlight.

But whosoever believeth on Me, behold, he shall not perish . . . for I have put My sign on him and no thing shall touch him . . . he is Mine, saith the Lord . . .

She stood up, still terrified, but now sure of what she must do. 'Get out!' she cried. 'It's chicken, all right, but it's for my company! Now you all *git!*'

They drew back. Their little eyes seemed to fill with unease. And suddenly they were gone like drifting smoke. *A miracle*, she thought, and exultation and praise for the Lord filled her. Then, suddenly, she was cold.

Somewhere, far to the west, beyond the Rockies that were not even visible on the horizon, she felt an eye – some glittering Eye – suddenly open wide and turn toward her, searching. As clearly as if the words had been spoken aloud she heard him: *Who's there? Is it you, old woman?*

'He knows I'm here,' she whispered in the night. 'Oh help me, Lord. Help me now, help all of us.'

Dragging the towsack, she began to walk home again.

They showed up two days later, on July 24. She hadn't got as much done as she would have liked in the way of preparations; once again she was lame and almost laid up, able to hobble from one place to another only with the aid of her cane and hardly able to pump water up from the well. The day after killing the chickens and standing off the weasels, she had fallen asleep for a long time in the afternoon, exhausted. She dreamed she was in some high cold pass in the middle of the Rockies, west of the Continental Divide. Highway 6 stretched and twisted between high rock walls that shaded this gap all day long, except from about eleven forty-five in the morning until about twelve-fifty in the afternoon. It was not daylight in her dream but full, moonless dark. Somewhere, wolves were howling. And suddenly an Eye had opened in all that darkness, rolling horribly from one side to the other while the wind moved lonesomely through the pines and the blue mountain spruce. It was him, and he was looking for her.

She had awakened from that long, heavy nap feeling less rested than she had when she lay down, and again she prayed to God to let her off, or at least change the direction He wanted her to go in.

North, south, or east, Lord, and I'll leave Hemingford Home singing Your praises. But not west, not toward that dark man. The Rockies ain't enough to have between him and us. The Andes wouldn't be enough.

But it didn't matter. Sooner or later, when that man felt he was strong enough, he would come looking for those who would stand against him. If not this year, then next. The dogs were gone, carried off by the plague, but the wolves remained in the high mountain country, ready to serve the Imp of Satan.

And it was not just the wolves that would serve him.

On the morning of the day her company finally arrived she had begun at seven, lugging wood two sticks at a time until the stove was hot and her woodbox full. God had favored her with a cool, cloudy day, the first in weeks. By nightfall there might be rain. The hip she'd broken in 1958 said so, anyway.

She baked her pies first, using the canned fillings from the shelves in her pantry and the fresh rhubarb and strawberries from the garden. The strawberries had just come on, praise God, and it was good to know they weren't going to go to waste. Just the act of cooking made her feel better, because cooking was life. A blueberry pie, two strawberry-rhubarb, and one apple. The smell of them filled the morning kitchen. She set them on the kitchen windowsills to cool as she had all her life.

She made the best batter she could, although it was hard going with no fresh eggs – there she'd been, right in the henhouse, and she had no one to blame but herself. Eggs or no, by early afternoon the small kitchen with its hilly floor and faded linoleum was filled with the smell of frying chicken. It had gotten pretty toasty inside and so she hobbled out to the porch to read her daily lesson, using her dog-eared last copy of *The Upper Room* to fan her face.

The chicken came out just as light and nice as you could want. One of those fellows could go out and pick her two dozen butter-and-sugar ears of corn, and they would have themselves a good sit-down feed outside.

After the chicken was put on paper towels, she went on out to the back porch with her guitar, sat down, and began to play. She sang all her favorite hymns, her high and quivering voice drifting into the still air.

Have we trials and temptations,
Are we cumbered with a load of care?
We must never be discouraged,
Take it to the Lord in prayer.

The music sounded so fine to her (even though her ear had failed to a degree where she could never be sure her old git was in tune) that she played another hymn, and another, and another.

She was settling down to 'We Are Marching to Zion' when she heard the sound of an engine off to the north, coming down County Road toward her. She stopped singing but her fingers continued to twiddle absently on the strings as she cocked her head and listened. Coming, yes Lord, they found their way just fine, and now she could see the spume of dust the truck was throwing as it left the tar and came onto the dirt track that stopped in her dooryard. A great, welcoming excitement filled her and she was glad she had put on her for-best. She put her git between her knees and shaded her eyes, although there was still no sun.

Now the engine sound was much louder and in a moment, where the corn gave way for Cal Goodell's cattle wade –

Yes, she could see it, an old Chevrolet farm truck, moving slow. The cab was full; four people crammed in there by the looks (there was nothing wrong with her long vision, even at a hundred and eight), and three more in the truckbed, standing up and looking over the cab. She could see a thinnish blond man, a girl with red hair, and in the middle . . . yes, that was him, a boy who was just finishing up learning about being a man. Dark hair, narrow face, high forehead. He saw her sitting on her porch and began to wave frantically. A moment later the blond man copied him. The redheaded girl just looked. Mother Abagail raised her own hand and waved back.

'Praise God for bringin em through,' she muttered hoarsely. Tears coursed warmly down her cheeks. 'My Lord, I thank You so.'

The pickup, rattling and jouncing, turned into the yard. The man behind the wheel was wearing a straw hat with a blue velvet band and a big feather tucked into it.

'Yeeeeee-haw!' he shouted, and waved. 'Hi there, Mother! Nick said he thought you might be here and here you be! Yeeeeee-haw!' He laid on the horn. Sitting with him in the cab was a man of about fifty, a woman of the same age, and a little girl in a red corduroy jumper. The little girl waved shyly with one hand; the thumb of the other was corked securely in her mouth.

The young man with the eyepatch and the dark hair – Nick – jumped over the side of the truck even before it had stopped. He caught his balance and then walked slowly toward her. His face was solemn, but his eye was alight with joy. He stopped at the porch steps and then looked around wonderingly . . . at the yard, the house, the old tree with its tire swing. Most of all at her.

'Hello, Nick,' she said. 'I'm glad to see you. God bless.'

He smiled, now beginning to shed his own tears. He came up the steps toward her and took her hands. She turned her wrinkled cheek toward him and he kissed it gently. Behind him, the truck had stopped and everyone got out. The man who had been driving was holding the girl in the red jumper, who had a cast on her right leg. Her arms were linked firmly around the driver's sunburned neck. Next to him stood the fiftyish woman, next to her the redhead and the blond boy with the beard. No, not a boy, Mother Abagail thought; he's feeble. Last in line stood the other man who had been riding in the cab. He was polishing the lenses of his steel-rimmed eyeglasses.

Nick was looking at her urgently, and she nodded.

'You done just right,' she said. 'The Lord has brought you and Mother Abagail is going to feed you.

'You're *all* welcome here!' she added, raising her voice. 'We can't stay long, but before we do any moving on, we'll rest, and break bread together, and have some fellowship one with the other.'

The little girl piped up from the safety of the driver's arms: 'Are you the oldest lady in the world?'

The fiftyish woman said: 'Shhhh, Gina!'

But Mother Abagail only put a hand on her hip and laughed. 'Mayhap I am, child. Mayhap I am.'

She got them to spread her red-checked tablecloth on the far side of the apple tree and the two women, Olivia and June, spread the picnic lunch while the men went off to pick corn. It was short work to boil it up, and while there was no real butter, she had plenty of oleo and salt.

There was little talk during the meal – mostly the sound of chomping jaws and little grunts of pleasure. It did her heart good to see folks dig into a meal, and these folks were doing her spread full justice. It made her walk to Richardsons' and her tussle with those weasels seem more than worthwhile. It wasn't that they were hungry, exactly, but when you've spent a month eating almost nothing that hasn't come out of a can, you get a powerful hunger for something fresh and just cooked special. She herself put away three pieces of chicken, an ear of corn, and a little smidge of that strawberry-rhubarb pie. When it was all gone, she felt as full as a bedtick in a mattress.

When they got settled and the coffee was poured, the driver, a pleasant, open-faced man named Ralph Brentner, told her: 'That was one dilly of a meal, ma'am. I can't remember when anything hit the spot so good. Thanks are in order.'

The others murmured agreement. Nick smiled and nodded.

The little girl said, 'Can I come and sit with you, grammy-lady?'

'I think you'd be too heavy, honey,' the older woman, Olivia Walker, said.

'Nonsense,' Abagail said. 'The day I can't take a little one on my lap for a spell will be the day they wind me in my shroud. Come on over, Gina.'

Ralph carried her over and set her down. 'When she gets too heavy, you just tell me.' He tickled Gina's face with the feather in his hatband. She put up her hands and giggled. 'Don't tickle me, Ralph! Don't you dare tickle me!'

'Don't worry,' Ralph said, relenting. 'I'm too full to tickle anyone for long.' He sat down again.

'What happened to your leg, Gina?' Abagail asked.

'I broke it when I fell out of the barn,' Gina said. 'Dick fixed it. Ralph says Dick saved my life.' She blew a kiss to the man with the steel-rimmed glasses, who blushed a bit, coughed, and smiled.

Nick, Tom Cullen, and Ralph had happened on Dick Ellis halfway across Kansas, walking along the side of the road with a pack on his back and a hiking staff in one hand. He was a veterinarian. The next day, passing through the small town of Lindsborg, they had stopped for lunch and heard weak cries coming from the south side of town. If the wind had been blowing the other way, they never would have heard the cries at all.

'God's mercy,' Abby said complacently, stroking the little girl's hair.

Gina had been on her own for three weeks. She'd been playing in the hayloft of her uncle's barn a day or two before when the rotted flooring gave way, spilling her forty feet into the lower haymow. There had been hay in it to break her fall, but she had cartwheeled off it and broken her leg. At first Dick Ellis had been pessimistic about her chances. He gave her a local anesthetic to set the leg; she had lost so much weight and her overall physical condition was so poor he had been afraid a general would kill her (the key words in this conversation were spelled out while Gina McCone played unconcernedly with the buttons on Mother Abagail's dress).

Gina had bounced back with a speed that had surprised them all. She had formed an instant attachment for Ralph and his jaunty hat. Speaking in a low, diffident voice, Ellis said he suspected that a lot of her problem had been crushing loneliness.

'Course it was,' Abagail said. 'If you'd missed her, she would have just pined away.'

Gina yawned. Her eyes were large and glassy.

'I'll take her now,' Olivia Walker said.

'Put her in the little room at the end of the hall,' Abby said. 'You can sleep with her, if that's what you want. This other girl . . . what did you say your name was, honey? It's slipped my mind for sure.'

'June Brinkmeyer,' the redhead said.

'Well, you c'n sleep with me, June, unless you've some other mind. The bed ain't big enough for two, and I don't think you'd want to sleep with an old bundle of sticks like me even if it was, but there's a mattress put away overhead that should do you if the bugs ain't got into it. One of these big men will get it down for you, I guess.'

'Sure,' Ralph said.

Olivia carried Gina, who had already fallen asleep, away to bed. The kitchen, now more populated than it had been for years, was filling up with dusk. Grunting, Mother Abagail got to her feet and lit three oil-lamps, one for the table, one which she set on the stove (the cast-iron Black-wood was now cooling and ticking contentedly to itself), and one for the porch windowsill. The darkness was pushed back.

'Maybe the old ways are best,' Dick said abruptly, and they all looked at him. He blushed and coughed again, but Abagail only chuckled.

'I mean,' Dick went on a little defensively, 'that's the first home-cooked meal I've had since . . . well, since June thirtieth, I guess. The day the power went off. And I cooked that myself. What I do could hardly be called home cooking. My wife, now . . . she was one hell of a good cook. She . . .' He trailed off blankly.

Olivia came back in. 'Fast asleep,' she said. 'That was a tired girl.'

'Do you bake your own bread?' Dick asked Mother Abagail.

'Course I do. Always have. Of course, it ain't yeast bread; all the yeast has gone over. But there's other kinds.'

'I crave bread,' he said simply. 'Helen . . . my wife . . . used to make bread twice a week. Just lately it seems to be all I want. Give me three slices of bread and some strawberry jam and I think I could die happy.'

'Tom Cullen's tired,' Tom said abruptly. 'M-O-O-N, that spells tired.' He yawned bone-crackingly.

'You can bed down in the shed,' Abagail said. 'It smells a bit musty, but it's dry.'

For a moment they listened to the steady rustle of the rain, which had been falling for almost an hour now. Alone, it would have been a desolate sound. In company it was a pleasant, secret sound, closing them in together. It gurgled from the galvanized tin gutters and plopped in the rain barrel Abby still kept on the far side of the house. Thunder muttered far away, back over Iowa.

'I guess you got your campin gear?' she asked them.

'All kinds,' Ralph said. 'We'll be fine. Come on, Tom.' He stood up.

'I wonder,' Abagail said, 'if you and Nick would stay a bit, Ralph.'

Nick had been sitting at the table through all of this, on the far side of the room from her rocking chair. You would think, she mused, that if a man couldn't talk he would get lost in a roomful of people, that he would just sink from view. But something about Nick kept that from happening. He sat perfectly still, following the conversation as it traveled around the room, his face reacting to whatever was being said. That face was open and intelligent, but careworn for one so young. Several times as the talk went on she saw people look at him, as if Nick could confirm what he or she was saying. They were very much aware of him, too. And several times she had seen him looking out the window into the dark, his expression troubled.

'Could you get me that mattress?' June asked softly.

'Nick and I will get it,' Ralph said, standing up.

'I don't want to go out in that back shed all by myself,' Tom said. 'Laws, no!'

'I'll go out with you, hoss,' Dick said. 'We'll light the Coleman lamp and bed down.' He rose. 'Thanks again, ma'am. Can't tell you how good all this has been.'

The others echoed his thanks. Nick and Ralph got the mattress, which proved to be bug-free. Tom and Dick – needing only a Harry to fill em up, Abagail thought – went out to the shed, where the Coleman lantern soon flared. Not long after, Nick, Ralph, and Mother Abagail were left alone in the kitchen.

'Mind if I smoke, ma'am?' Ralph asked.

'Not so long as you don't tap ashes on the floor. There's an ashtray in that cupboard right behind you.'

Ralph got up to get it, and Abby was left looking at Nick. He was wearing a khaki shirt, bluejeans, and a faded drill vest. There was something about him that made her feel she had known him before, or had always been meant to know him. Looking at him, she felt a quiet sense of knowledge and completion, as if this moment had been simple fate. As if, at one end of her life there had been her father, John Freemantle, tall and black and proud, and this man at the other end, young, white, and mute, with that one brilliant, expressive eye looking at her from that careworn face.

She looked out the window and saw the glow of the Coleman battery lamp drifting out of the shed window and lighting a little piece of her dooryard. She wondered if that shed still smelled of cow; she hadn't been out there for close on to three years. No need to. Her last cow, Daisy, had been sold in 1975, but in 1987 the shed had still smelled of cow. Probably did to this day. No matter; there were worse smells.

'Ma'am?'

She looked back. Ralph was sitting next to Nick now, holding a sheet of notepaper and squinting at it in the lamplight. On his lap, Nick was holding a pad of paper and a ballpoint pen. He was still looking at her closely.

'Nick says . . .' Ralph cleared his throat, embarrassed.

'Go ahead.'

'His note says it's hard to read your lips because –'

'I guess I know why,' she said. 'No fear.'

She got up and shuffled over to the bureau. On the second shelf above it was a plastic jar, and in it two denture plates floated in cloudy liquid like a medical exhibit.

She fished them out and rinsed them with a dipper of water.

'Lord God I have suffered,' Mother Abagail said balefully, and popped the plates in.

'We got to talk,' she said. 'You two are the head ones, and we got some things to sort out.'

'Well,' Ralph said, 'it ain't me. I was never much more than a full-time factory worker and a part-time farmer. I've raised a helluva lot more calluses than idears in my time. Nick, I guess he's in charge.'

'Is that right?' she asked, looking at Nick.

Nick wrote briefly and Ralph read it aloud, as he continued to do.

'It was my idea to come up this way, yes. About being in charge, I don't know.'

'We met June and Olivia about ninety miles south of here,' Ralph said. 'Day before yesterday, wasn't it, Nick?'

Nick nodded.

'We was on our way to you even then, Mother. The women were headed north, too. So was Dick. We all just threw in together.'

'Have you seen any other folks?' she asked.

'No,' Nick wrote. 'But I've had a feeling – Ralph has, too – that there are other people hiding, watching us. Afraid, I guess. Still getting over the shock of what's happened.'

She nodded.

'Dick said that the day before he joined us, he heard a motor-cycle somewhere south. So there are other people around. I think what scares them is seeing a fairly big group all together.'

'Why did you come here?' Her eyes, caught in their nets of wrinkles, stared at him keenly.

Nick wrote: 'I have dreamed of you. Dick Ellis says he has once. And the little girl, Gina, was calling you "grammylady" long before we got here. She described your place. The tire swing.'

'Bless the child,' Mother Abagail said absently. She looked at Ralph. 'You?'

'Once or twice, ma'am,' Ralph said. He wet his lips. 'Mostly what I dreamed about was just . . . just that other fella.'

'What other fella?'

Nick wrote. Circled what he had written. Handed it to her directly. Her eyes were not much good for close work without her specs or the lighted magnifying glass she'd gotten in Hemingford Center last year, but she could read this. It was writ large, like the writing God had put on the wall of Belshazzar's palace. Circled, it gave her a cold chill just looking at it. She thought of weasels squirming across the road on their bellies, yanking at her towsack

with their needle-sharp killers' teeth. She thought of a single red
eye opening, disclosing itself in the darkness, looking, searching,
now not just for an old woman but a whole party of men and
women . . . and one little girl.

The two circled words were: *dark man*.

'I've been told,' she said, folding the paper, straightening it, then folding
it again, for the time being unmindful of the misery of her arthritis,
'that we're to go west. I've been told in a dream, by the Lord God.
I didn't want to listen. I'm an old woman, and all I want to do is die
on this little piece of land. It's been my family's freehold for a hundred
and twelve years, but I wasn't meant to die here any more than Moses
was meant to go over into Canaan with the Children of Israel.'

She paused. The two men watched her soberly in the lamplight,
and outside the rain continued to fall, slow and ceaseless. There was
no more thunder. Lord, she thought, these dentures hurt my mouth.
I want to take them out and go to bed.

'I started having dreams two years before this plague ever fell. I've
always dreamed, and sometimes my dreams have come true. Prophecy
is the gift of God and everyone has a smidge of it. My own grandmother
used to call it the shining lamp of God, sometimes just the shine. In my
dreams I saw myself going west. At first with just a few people, then a
few more, then a few more. West, always west, until I could see the
Rocky Mountains. It got so there was a whole caravan of us, two
hundred or more. And there would be signs . . . no, not signs from God
but regular road-signs, and every one of them saying things like BOULDER,
COLORADO, 609 MILES or THIS WAY TO BOULDER.'

She paused.

'Those dreams, they scared me. I never told a soul I was havin
em, that's how scared I was. I felt the way I guess Job must have
felt when God spoke to him out of the whirlwind. I even tried to
pretend they was just dreams, foolish old woman runnin from God
the way Jonah did. But the big fish has swallowed us up just the
same, you see! And if God says to Abby, *You got to tell*, then tell I
must. And I always felt like someone would come to me, someone
special, and that's how I'd be in the way of knowin the time had
come.'

She looked at Nick, who sat at the table and regarded her
solemnly with his good eye through the haze of Ralph Brentner's
cigarette smoke.

'I knew when I saw you,' she said. 'It's you, Nick. God has put His finger on your heart. But He has more fingers than one, and there's others out there, still comin on, praise God, and He's got a finger on them, too. I dream of *him*, how he's lookin for us even now, and God forgive my sick spirit, I curse him in my heart.' She began to weep and got up to have a drink of water and a splash. Her tears were the human part of her, weak and flagging.

When she turned back, Nick was writing. At last he ripped the page off his pad and handed it to Ralph.

'I don't know about the God part, but I know something is working here. Everyone we've met has been moving north. As if you had the answer. Have you dreamed about any of the others? Dick? June or Olivia? Maybe the little girl?'

'Not any of these others. A man who doesn't talk much. A woman who is with child. A man of about your age who comes to me with a guitar of his own. And you, Nick.'

'And you think going to Boulder is the right thing?'

Mother Abagail said, 'It's what we're *meant* to do.'

Nick doodled aimlessly on his pad for a moment and then wrote, 'How much do you know about the dark man? Do you know who he is?'

'I know what he's about but not who he is. He's the purest evil left in the world. The rest of the bad is little evil. Shoplifters and sexfiends and people who like to use their fists. But he'll call them. He's started already. He's getting them together a lot faster than we are. Before he's ready to make his move, I guess he'll have a lot more. Not just the evil ones that are like him, but the weak ones . . . the lonely ones . . . and the ones that have left God out of their hearts.'

'Maybe he's not real,' Nick wrote. 'Maybe he's just . . .' He had to nibble at the top of his pen and think. At last he added: '. . . the scared, bad part of all of us. Maybe we are dreaming of the things we're afraid we might do.'

Ralph frowned over this as he read it aloud, but Abby grasped what Nick meant right off. It wasn't much different from the talk of the new preachers who had got on the land in the last twenty years or so. There wasn't really any Satan, that was their gospel. There was evil, and it probably came from original sin, but it was in all of us and getting it out was as impossible as getting an egg out of its shell without cracking it. According to the way these new preachers had it, Satan was like a jigsaw puzzle – and every man, woman, and child on earth added his or her little piece to make up the whole. Yes, all that had a good modern sound to it; the trouble with it was that it wasn't true. And if Nick was allowed to go on thinking that, the dark man would eat him for dinner.

She said: 'You dreamed of me. Ain't I real?'

Nick nodded.

'And I dreamed you. Ain't you real? Praise God, you're sittin right over there with a pad o paper on your knee. This other man, Nick, he's as real as you are.' Yes, he was real. She thought of the weasels, and of the red eye opening in the darkness. And when she spoke up again, her voice was husky. 'He ain't Satan,' she said, 'but he and Satan know of each other and have kept their councils together of old.

'The Bible, it don't say what happened to Noah and his family after the flood went down. But I wouldn't be surprised if there was some awful tussle for the souls of those few people – for their souls, their bodies, *their way of thinking*. And I wouldn't be surprised if that was what was on for us.

'He's west of the Rockies now. Sooner or later he'll come east. Maybe not this year, no, but when he's ready. And it's our lot to deal with him.'

Nick was shaking his head, disturbed.

'Yes,' she said quietly. 'You'll see. There's bitter days ahead. Death and terror, betrayal and tears. And not all of us will be alive to see how it ends.'

'I don't like any of this,' Ralph muttered. 'Aren't things hard enough without this guy you and Nick are talkin about? Ain't we got enough problems, with no doctors or electricity or nothing? Why did we have to get stuck with this damn doorprize?'

'I don't know. It's God's way. He don't explain to the likes of Abby Freemantle.'

'If this is His way,' Ralph said, 'why, I wish He'd retire and let somebody younger take over.'

'If the dark man is west,' Nick wrote, 'maybe we ought to pick up stakes and move east.'

She shook her head patiently. 'Nick, all things serve the Lord. Don't you think this black man serves Him, too? He does, no matter how mysterious His purpose may be. The black man will follow you no matter where you run, because he serves the purpose of God, and God wants you to treat with him. It don't do no good to run from the will of the Lord God of Hosts. A man or woman who tries that only ends up in the belly of the beast.'

Nick wrote briefly. Ralph studied the note, rubbed the side of his nose, and wished he didn't have to read it. Old ladies like this didn't cotton to stuff like what Nick had just written. She'd likely call it a blasphemy, and shout it loud enough to wake everyone in the place, too.

'What's he say?' Abagail asked.

'He says . . .' Ralph cleared his throat; the feather stuck in the band of his hat jiggled. 'He says that he don't believe in God.' The message relayed, he looked unhappily down at his shoes and waited for the explosion.

But she only chuckled, got up, and walked across to Nick. She took one of his hands and patted it. 'Bless you, Nick, but that don't matter. *He* believes in *you*.'

They stayed at Abby Freemantle's place the next day, and it was the best day any of them could remember since the superflu had drawn away, like the waters going down from Mount Ararat. The rain had stopped sometime during the early hours of the morning, and by nine o'clock the sky was a pleasant Midwest mural of sun and broken clouds. The corn twinkled away in all directions like a ransom of emeralds. It was cooler than it had been for weeks.

Tom Cullen spent the morning running up and down the rows of corn, his arms outstretched, scaring up droves of crows. Gina McCone sat contentedly in the dirt by the tire swing, playing with a large number of paper dolls Abagail had found at the bottom of a trunk in her bedroom closet. A little earlier, she and Tom had had a pleasant game of cars and trucks around the Fisher-Price garage Tom had taken from the five-and-dime in May, Oklahoma. Tom did what Gina wanted him to do willingly enough.

Dick Ellis, the vet, came diffidently to Mother Abagail and asked her if anyone in the area had kept pigs.

'Why, the Stoners always had pigs,' she said. She was sitting on the porch in her rocker, chording her guitar and watching Gina at play in the yard, her broken leg in its cast stuck out stiffly in front of her.

'Think any of them might still be alive?'

'You'd have to go see. Might be. Might be they've bust down their pens and gone hogwild.' Her eyes gleamed. 'Might *also* be I know a fella who dreamed about pork chops last night.'

'Could be you do,' Dick said.

'You ever slaughtered a hog?'

'No, ma'am,' he said, grinning broadly now. 'Wormed a few, but haven't slaughtered any hog. I was always what you'd call nonviolent.'

'Do you think you and Ralph there could stand a woman foreman?'

'Could be,' he said.

Twenty minutes later the three of them were off, Abagail riding between the two men in the Chevy's cab with her cane planted regally between her knees. At the Stoners' they found two yearling pigs in the back pen, healthy and full of beans. It appeared that, when the feed had given out, they had taken to dining on their weaker and less fortunate pen-mates.

Ralph set up Reg Stoner's chainfall in the barn, and at Abagail's direction, Dick was finally able to get a rope firmly around the back leg of one of the yearlings. Squealing and thrashing, it was yanked into the barn and hung upside down from the chainfall.

Ralph came out of the house with a butcher knife three feet long – That ain't a knife, that's a regular bayernet, praise God, Abby thought.

'You know, I don't know if I can do this,' he said.

'Well, give her here, then,' Abagail said, and then held out her hand. Ralph looked doubtfully at Dick. Dick shrugged. Ralph handed the knife over.

'Lord,' Abagail said, 'we thank Thee for the gift we are about to receive from Thy bounty. Bless this pig that it might nourish us, amen. Stand clear, boys, she's gonna go a gusher.'

She cut the pig's throat with one practiced sweep of the knife – some things you never forgot, no matter how old you got – and then stepped back as quick as she could.

'You got that fire going under the kettle?' she asked Dick. 'Nice hot fire out there in the dooryard?'

'Yes, ma'am,' Dick said respectfully, unable to take his eyes from the pig.

'You got those brushes?' she asked Ralph.

Ralph displayed two big scrub brushes with stiff yellow bristles.

'Well then, you want to haul him over and dump him in. After he's boiled awhile, those bristles will scrub right off. After that you can peel old Mr Hog just like a banana.'

They both looked a trifle green at the prospect.

'Lively,' she said. 'You can't eat him with his jacket on. Got to get him undressed first.'

Ralph and Dick Ellis looked at each other, gulped, and began to lower the pig from the chainfall. They were done by three that afternoon, back at Abagail's by four with a truckload of meat, and there were fresh pork chops for dinner. Neither of the men ate very well, but Abagail put away two chops all by herself, relishing the way the crisp fat crackled between her dentures. There was nothing like fresh meat you'd seen to yourself.

It was sometime after nine o'clock. Gina was asleep, and Tom Cullen had dozed off in Mother Abagail's rocker on the porch. Soundless lightning flickered against the sky far to the west. The other adults were gathered in the kitchen, except for Nick, who had gone for a walk. Abagail knew what the boy was wrestling with, and her heart went out to him.

'Say, you're not really a hundred and eight, are you?' Ralph asked, remembering something she had said that morning as they set out on the hog-slaughtering expedition.

'You wait right there,' Abagail said. 'I've got something to show you, Mister Man.' She went into the bedroom and got her framed letter from President Reagan out of the top drawer of her bureau. She brought it back to Ralph and put it in his lap. 'Read *that*, sonny,' she said pridefully.

Ralph read it. '. . . occasion of your one hundredth birthday . . . one of seventy-two proven centenarians in the United States of America . . . fifth oldest registered Republican in the United States of America . . . greetings and congratulations from President Ronald Reagan, January 14, 1982.' He looked up at her with wide eyes. 'Well, I'll be dipped in sh –' He stopped, blushing and in confusion. 'Pardon me, ma'am.'

'All the things you must have seen!' Olivia marveled.

'None of it's very much compared to what I've seen in the last month or so.' She sighed. 'Or what I expect to see.'

The door opened and Nick came in – conversation broke off as if they had all been marking time, waiting for him. She could see in his face that he had made his decision, and she thought she knew what it was. He handed her a note that he had written out on the porch, standing by Tom. She held the note at arm's length to read it.

'We'd better start for Boulder tomorrow,' Nick had written.

She looked from the note to Nick's face and nodded slowly. She passed the note on to June Brinkmeyer, who passed it to Olivia. 'I guess we had,' Abagail said. 'I don't want to any more than you, but I guess we had better. What made up your mind?'

He shrugged almost angrily and pointed at her.

'So be it,' Abagail said. 'My faith's in the Lord.'

Nick thought: *I wish mine was.*

The next morning, July 26, after a brief conference, Dick and Ralph set off for Columbus in Ralph's truck. 'I hate to trade her in,' Ralph said, 'but if it's the way you say it is, Nick, okay.'

Nick wrote, 'Be back as soon as you can.'

Ralph uttered a short laugh and looked around the yard. June and Olivia were washing clothes in a large tub with a scrub board stuck in one end. Tom was in the corn, scaring crows – an occupation he seemed to find endlessly diverting. Gina was playing with his Corgi cars and his garage. The old woman sat dozing in her rocker, dozing and snoring.

'You're in one tearin hurry to stick your head in the lion's mouth, Nicky.'

Nick wrote: 'Have we got anyplace better to go to?'

'That's true. It's no good just wandering around. It makes you feel kind of worthless. A person don't hardly feel right unless he's lookin forward, you ever notice that?'

Nick nodded.

'Okay.' Ralph clapped Nick on the shoulder and turned away. 'Dick, you ready to take a ride?'

Tom Cullen came running out of the corn, silk clinging to his shirt and pants and long blond hair. 'Me too! Tom Cullen wants to go on the ride, too! Laws, yes!'

'Come on, then,' Ralph said. 'Here, lookit you, cornsilk from top to bottom and fore to aft. And you ain't caught a crow yet! Better let me brush you off.'

Grinning vacantly, Tom allowed Ralph to brush off his shirt and pants. For Tom, Nick reflected, these last two weeks had probably been the happiest of his life. He was with people who accepted and wanted him. Why shouldn't they? He might be feeble, but he was still a comparative rarity in this new world, a living human being.

'See you, Nicky,' Ralph said, and climbed up behind the wheel of the Chevy.

'See you, Nicky,' Tom Cullen echoed, still grinning.

Nick watched the truck out of sight, then went into the shed and found an old crate and a can of paint. He broke out one of the crate's panels and nailed a long piece of picket fence to it. He took the sign and the paint out into the yard and carefully daubed on it while Gina looked over his shoulder with interest.

'What does it say?' she asked.

'It says, "We have gone to Boulder, Colorado. We are taking secondary roads to avoid traffic jams. Citizen's Band Channel 14,"' Olivia read.

'What does that mean?' June asked, coming over. She picked Gina up and they both watched as Nick carefully planted the sign so that it faced the area where the dirt road became Mother Abagail's driveway. He buried the bottom three feet of the picket. Nothing but a big wind would knock it over now. Of course there *were* big winds out in this part of the world; he thought of the one which had almost carried him and Tom away, and of the scare they'd had in the cellar.

He wrote a note and handed it to June.

'One of the things Dick and Ralph are supposed to get in Columbus is a CB radio. Someone will have to monitor Channel 14 all the time.'

'Oh,' Olivia said. 'Smart.'

Nick tapped his forehead gravely, then smiled.

The two women went back to hang their clothes. Gina returned to the toy cars, hopping nimbly on one leg. Nick walked across the yard, mounted the porch steps, and sat down next to the dozing old woman. He looked out over the corn and wondered what was going to become of them.

If that's the way you say it is, Nick, okay.

They had turned him into a leader. They had done that and he couldn't even begin to understand why. You couldn't take orders from a deaf-mute; it was like a bad joke. Dick should have been their leader. His own place was as spear-carrier, third from the left, no lines, recognized only by his mother. But from the time they had met Ralph Brentner pottering up the road in his truck, not really going anywhere, that business of saying something and then glancing quickly at Nick, as if for confirmation, had begun. A fog of nostalgia had already begun to creep over those few days between Shoyo and May, before Tom and responsibility. It was easy to forget how lonely he had been, the fear that the constant bad dreams might mean he was going crazy.

Easy to remember how there had been only yourself to look out for, a spear-carrier, third from the left, a bit player in this terrible play.

I knew when I saw you. It's you, Nick. God has put His finger on your heart . . .

No, I don't accept that. I don't accept God either, for that matter. Let the old woman have her God, God was as necessary for old women as enemas and Lipton tea bags. He would concentrate on one thing at a time, planting one foot ahead of the other. Get them to Boulder, then see what came next. The old woman said the dark man was a real man, not just a psychological symbol, and he didn't want to believe that, either . . . but in his heart he did. In his heart he believed everything she had said, and it scared him. He didn't want to be their leader.

It's you, Nick.

A hand squeezed his shoulder and he jumped with surprise, then turned around. If she had been dozing, she wasn't anymore. She was smiling down at him from her armless rocker.

'I was just sittin here and thinkin on the Great Depression,' she said. 'Do you know my daddy once owned all this land for miles around? It's true. No small trick for a black man. And I played my guitar and sang down at the Grange Hall in nineteen and oh-two. Long ago, Nick. Long, long ago.'

Nick nodded.

'Those were good days, Nick – most of em were, anyway. But nothin lasts, I guess. Only the love of the Lord. My daddy died, and the land was split between his sons with a piece for my first husband, sixty acres, not much. This house stands on part o that sixty, you know. Four acres, that's all that's left. Oh, I guess now I could lay claim to all of it again, but t'wouldn't be the same, somehow.'

Nick patted her scrawny hand and she sighed deeply.

'Brothers don't always work so well together; they almost always fall to squabblin. Look at Cain n Abel! Everyone wanted to be a foreman and nobody wanted to be a fielhand! Comes 1931, and the bank called its paper home. Then they all pulled together, but by then it was most too late. By 1945 everything was gone but my sixty and forty or fifty more where the Goodell place is now.'

She fumbled her handkerchief from her dress pocket and wiped her eyes with it, slowly and thoughtfully.

'Finally there was only me left, with no money nor nothing. And each year when tax-time came round, they'd take a little more to pay it off, and I'd come out here to look at the part that wasn't my own anymore, and I'd cry over it like I'm crying now. A little more each year for taxes, that's how it happened. A whack here, a whack there. I rented out what was left, but it was never enough to cover what they had to have for their cussed taxes. Then, when I got to be a hundred years old, they remanded the taxes in perpetuity. Yes, they give it over after they'd taken everything but this little piece o scratch that's here. Big o them, wa'n't it?'

He squeezed her hand lightly and looked at her.

'Oh, Nick,' Mother Abagail said, 'I have harbored hate of the Lord in my heart. Every man or woman who loves Him, they hate Him too, because He's a hard God, a jealous God, He Is, what He *Is*, and in this world He's apt to repay service with pain while those who do evil ride over the roads in Cadillac cars. Even the joy of serving Him is a bitter joy. I do His will, but the human part o me has cursed Him in my heart. "Abby," the Lord says to me, "there's work for you far up ahead. So I'll let you live an live, until your flesh is bitter on your bones. I'll let you see all your children die ahead of you and still you'll walk the earth. I'll let you see your daddy's lan taken away piece by piece. And in the end, your reward will be to go away with strangers from all the things you love best and you'll die in a strange land with the work not yet finished. That's My will, Abby," says He, and "Yes, Lord," says I. "Thy will be done," and in my heart I curse Him and ask, "Why, why, why?" and the only answer I get is "Where were you when I made the world?"'

Now her tears came in a bitter flood, running down her cheeks and wetting the bodice of her dress, and Nick marveled that there could be so many tears in such an old woman, who seemed as dry and thin as a dead twig.

'Help me along, Nick,' she said. 'I only want to do what's right.'

He held her hands tightly. Behind them Gina giggled and held one of the toy cars up to the sky for the sun to shine and sparkle on.

Dick and Ralph came back at noon, Dick behind the wheel of a new Dodge van and Ralph driving a red wrecker truck with a push-board on the front and the crane and hook dangling from the back. Tom stood in the rear, waving grandly. They pulled up by the porch and Dick got out of the van.

'There's a helluva nice CB in that wrecker,' he told Nick. 'Forty-channel job. I think Ralph's in love with it.'

Nick grinned. The women had come over and were looking at the trucks. Abagail's eyes noted the way Ralph squired June over to the wrecker so she could look at the radio equipment, and approved. The woman had a good set of hips on her, there would be a fine porch door down there between them. She could have just about as many little ones as she wanted.

'So when do we go?' Ralph asked.

Nick scribbled, 'Soon as we eat. Did you try the CB?'

'Yeah,' Ralph said. 'I had it on all the way back. Horrible static; there's a squelch button, but it doesn't seem to work very well. But you know, I swear I did hear something, static or no static. Far off. Might not have been voices at all. But I'll say the truth, Nicky, I didn't care for it much. Like those dreams.'

A silence fell among them.

'Well,' Olivia said, breaking it. 'I'll get something cooking. Hope nobody minds pork two days in a row.'

No one did. And by one o'clock the camping things – and Abagail's rocker and guitar – had been stowed in the van and they were off, the wrecker now lumbering ahead to move anything blocking the road. Abagail sat up front in the van as they drove westbound on Route 30. She did not cry. Her cane was planted between her legs. Crying was done. She was set in the center of the Lord's will and His will would be done. The Lord's will would be done, but she thought of that red Eye opening in the dark heart of the night and she was afraid.

CHAPTER 46

It was late evening, July 27. They were camped on what the sign, now half-demolished by summer storms, proclaimed to be the Kunkle Fairgrounds. Kunkle itself, Kunkle, Ohio, was south of them. There had been some sort of fire there, and most of Kunkle was gone. Stu said it had probably been lightning. Harold had of course disputed that. These days if Stu Redman said a firetruck was red, Harold Lauder would produce facts and figures proving that most of them these days were green.

She sighed and rolled over. Couldn't sleep. She was afraid of the dream.

To her left the five motorcycles stood in a row, heeled over on their kickstands, moonlight twinkling along their chromed exhaust pipes and fittings. As if a band of Hell's Angels had picked this particular spot to crash for the night. Not that the Angels ever would have ridden such a pussycat bunch of bikes as these Hondas and Yamahas, she supposed. They had driven 'hogs' . . . or was that just something she had picked up from the old American-International bike epics she'd seen on TV? *The Wild Angels. The Devil's Angels. Hell's Angels on Wheels.* The bike pictures had been very big at the drive-ins when she had been in high school, Wells Drive-In, Sandford Drive-In, South Portland Twin, you pays your money and you takes your choice. Now kaput, all the drive-ins were kaput, not to mention the Hell's Angels and good old American-International Pictures.

Put it in your diary, Frannie, she told herself, and rolled over on her other side. Not tonight. Tonight she was going to sleep, dreams or no dreams.

Twenty paces from where she was lying, she could see the others, zonked out in their sleeping bags like Hell's Angels after a big beer party, the one where everybody in the picture got laid except for Peter Fonda and Nancy Sinatra. Harold, Stu, Glen Bateman,

Mark Braddock, Perion McCarthy. Take Sominex tonight and *sleep . . .*

It wasn't Sominex they were on but half a grain of Veronal apiece. It had been Stu's idea when the dreams got really bad and they all began to get flaky and hard to live with. He had taken Harold aside before mentioning it to the rest of them because the way to flatter Harold was to soberly ask his opinion and also because Harold *knew* things. It was good that he did, but it was also rather spooky, as if they had a fifth-rate god traveling with them – more or less omniscient, but emotionally unstable and likely to fragment at any time. Harold had picked up a second gun in Albany, where they had met Mark and Perion, and now he wore the two pistols criss-crossed low on his hips like a latterday Johnny Ringo. She felt badly for Harold, but Harold had also begun to frighten her. She had begun to wonder if Harold might not just go crackers some night and start blazing away with his two pistols. She often found herself remembering the day she had come upon Harold in his back yard, all his emotional defenses demolished, mowing the lawn in his bathing suit and crying.

She knew just how Stu would have put it to him, very quietly, almost conspiratorially: *Harold, these dreams are a problem. I've got an idea, but I don't know exactly how to carry it out . . . a mild sedative . . . but it would have to be just the right dose. Too much and nobody would wake up if there was trouble. What do you suggest?*

Harold had suggested they try a whole grain of Veronal, available at any drugstore, and if that interrupted the dream-cycle, that they cut back to three quarters of a grain, and if that worked to half. Stu had gone privately to Glen, had gotten a concurring opinion, and the experiment had been tried. At a quarter grain the dreams had begun to creep back in, so they held the dosage at a half.

At least for the others.

Frannie accepted her drug each night, but palmed it. She didn't know if Veronal would hurt the baby or not, but she was taking no chances. They said that even aspirin could break the chromosome chain. So she suffered the dreams – *suffered*, that was the right word. One of them predominated; if the others were different, they would sooner or later blend into this one. She was in her Ogunquit house, and the dark man was chasing her. Up and down shadowy corridors, through her mother's parlor where the clock continued to tick off seasons in a dry age . . . she could get away from him, she knew, if she didn't have to carry the body. It was her father's body, wrapped in a bedsheet, and if she dropped it the dark man would do something to it, perform some awful desecration on it. So she ran, knowing that he was getting closer and closer, and at last his hand would fall on her shoulder, his hot and sickening hand. She would go boneless and weak, her father's shrouded corpse would slither out of her arms, she would turn, ready to say: *Take him, do anything, I don't care, just don't chase me anymore.*

And there he would be, dressed in some dark stuff like a hooded monk's robe, nothing visible of his features save his huge and happy grin. And in one hand he held the bent and twisted coathanger. That was when the horror struck her like a padded fist and she struggled up from sleep, her skin clammy with sweat, her heart thudding, wanting never to sleep again.

Because it wasn't the dead body of her father he wanted; it was the living child in her womb.

She rolled over again. If she didn't go to sleep soon she really would take her diary out and write in it. She had been keeping the journal since July 5. In a way she was keeping it for the baby. It was an act of faith — faith that the baby would live. She wanted it to know what it had been like. How the plague had come to a place called Ogunquit, how she and Harold had escaped, what became of them. She wanted the child to know how things had been.

The moonlight was strong enough to write by, and two or three pages of diary were always enough to make her feel snoozy. Didn't say much for her literary talents, she supposed. She would give sleep one more fair chance first, though.

She closed her eyes.

And went on thinking of Harold.

The situation might have eased with the coming of Mark and Perion if the two of them hadn't already been committed to each other. Perion was thirty-three, eleven years older than Mark, but in this world such things made little difference. They had found each other, they had been looking out for each other, and they were content to stick together. Perion had confided to Frannie that they were trying to make a baby. Thank God I was on the pill and didn't have a loop, Peri said. How in God's name would I ever have gotten it out?

Frannie had almost told her about the baby she was carrying

(she was over a third of the way along now) but something held her back. She was afraid it might make a bad situation even worse.

So now there were six of them instead of four (Glen refused utterly to try driving a motorcycle and always rode pillion behind Stu or Harold), but the situation hadn't changed with the addition of another woman.

What about *you*, Frannie? What do *you* want?

If she *had* to exist in a world like this, she thought, with a biological clock inside her set to go off in six months, she wanted someone like Stu Redman to be her man – no, not someone like. She wanted *him*. There it was, stated with complete baldness.

With civilization gone, all the chrome and geegaws had been stripped from the engine of human society. Glen Bateman held forth on this theme often, and it always seemed to please Harold inordinately.

Women's lib, Frannie had decided (thinking that if she was going to be bald, she might as well go totally bald), was nothing more nor less than an outgrowth of the technological society. Women were at the mercy of their bodies. They were smaller. They tended to be weaker. A man couldn't get with child, but a woman could – every four-year-old knows it. And a pregnant woman is a vulnerable human being. Civilization had provided an umbrella of sanity that both sexes could stand beneath. *Liberation* – that one word said it all. Before civilization, with its careful and merciful system of protections, women had been slaves. Let us not gild the lily; slaves was what we were, Fran thought. Then the evil days ended. And the Women's Credo, which should have been hung in the offices of *Ms* magazine, preferably in needlepoint, was just this: *Thank you, Men, for the railroads. Thank you, Men, for inventing the automobile and killing the red Indians who thought it might be nice to hold on to America for a while longer, since they were here first. Thank you, Men, for the hospitals, the police, the schools. Now I'd like to vote, please, and have the right to set my own course and make my own destiny. Once I was chattel, but now that is obsolete. My days of slavery must be over; I need to be a slave no more than I need to cross the Atlantic Ocean in a tiny boat with sails. Jet planes are safer and quicker than little boats with sails and freedom makes more sense than slavery. I am not afraid of flying. Thank you, Men.*

And what was there to say? Nothing. The rednecks could grunt about burning bras, the reactionaries could play intellectual little games, but the truth only smiles. Now all that had changed, in a matter of weeks it had changed — how much only time would tell. But lying here in the night, she knew that she needed a man. Oh God, she badly needed a man.

Nor was it all a matter of preserving herself and her baby, of looking out for number one (and, she supposed, number two). Stu attracted her, especially after Jess Rider. Stu was calm, capable, and most of all he was not what her father would have called 'twenty pounds of bullshit in a ten-pound bag.'

He was attracted to her as well. She knew that perfectly well, had known it since that first lunch together on the Fourth of July in that deserted restaurant. For a moment — just one moment — their eyes had met and there had been that instant of heat, like a power surge when all the needles swing over to overload. She guessed Stu knew how things were, too, but he was waiting on her, letting her make her decision in her own time. She had been with Harold first, therefore she was Harold's chattel. A stinking macho idea, but she was afraid this was going to be a stinking macho world again, at least for a while.

If only there was someone else, someone for Harold, but there wasn't, and she was afraid she could not wait long. She thought of the day Harold, in his clumsy way, had tried to make love to her, to make his claim of ownership irrevocable. How long ago? Two weeks? It seemed longer. All the past seemed longer now. It had pulled out like warm Bonomo's Turkish taffy. Between her worry of what to do about Harold — and her fears of what he might do if she did go to Stuart — and her fears of the dreams, she would never get to sleep.

So thinking, she drifted off.

When she woke up, it was still dark. Someone was shaking her.

She muttered some protest — her sleep had been restful and without dreams for the first time in a week — and then came reluctantly out of it, thinking that it must be morning, and time to get going. But why would they want to get going in the dark? As she sat up, she saw that even the moon was down.

It was Harold shaking her, and Harold looked scared.

'Harold? Is something wrong?'

Stu was also up, she saw. And Glen Bateman. Perion was kneeling on the far side of the place where their small fire had been.

'It's Mark,' Harold said. 'He's sick.'

'Sick?' she said, and then a low moan came from the other side of the campfire's ashes, where Perion was kneeling and the two men were standing. Frannie felt dread rise up inside her like a black column. Sickness was the thing they were all most afraid of.

'It isn't . . . the flu, is it, Harold?' Because if Mark came down with a belated case of Captain Trips, that meant any of them could. Perhaps the germ was still hanging around. Perhaps it had even mutated. The better to feed on you, my dear.

'No, it's not the flu. It's nothing like the flu. Fran, did you eat any of the canned oysters tonight? Or maybe when we stopped for lunch?'

She tried to think, her mind still fuzzy with sleep. 'Yes, I had some both times,' she said. 'They tasted fine. I love oysters. Is it food poisoning? Is that what it is?'

'Fran, I'm just asking. None of us *know* what it is. There isn't a doctor in the house. How do you feel? Do you feel all right?'

'Fine, just sleepy.' But she wasn't. Not anymore. Another groan floated over from the other side of the camp, as if Mark were accusing her of feeling well while he did not.

Harold said, 'Glen thinks it might be his appendix.'

'*What?*'

Harold only grinned sickly and nodded.

Fran got up and walked across to where the others were gathered. Harold trailed her like an unhappy shadow.

'We've got to help him,' Perion said. She spoke mechanically, as if she had said it many times before. Her eyes went from one of them to the next relentlessly, eyes so full of terror and helplessness that Frannie once again felt accused. Her thoughts went selfishly to the baby she was carrying and she tried to push the thoughts away. Inappropriate or not, they wouldn't go. *Get away from him*, part of her screamed at the rest of her. *You get away from him right now, he might be catching.* She looked at Glen, who was pale and old-looking in the steady glow of the Coleman lantern.

'Harold says you think it's his appendix?' she asked.

'I don't know,' Glen said, sounding upset and scared. 'He's got the symptoms, certainly; he's feverish, his belly is hard and swelled, painful to touch –'

'We've got to help him,' Perion said again, and burst into tears.

Glen touched Mark's belly and Mark's eyes, which had been half-lidded and glazed, opened wide. He screamed. Glen jerked his hand away as if he had put it on a hot stove and looked from Stu to Harold and then back to Stu again with barely concealed panic. 'What would you two gentlemen suggest?'

Harold stood with his throat working convulsively, as if something was stuck in there, and choking him. At last he blurted, 'Give him some aspirin.'

Perion, who had been gazing down at Mark through her tears, now whirled to look at Harold. 'Aspirin?' she asked. Her tone was one of furious astonishment. '*Aspirin?*' This time she shrieked it. 'Is *that* the best you can do with all your big-talk smartassery? *Aspirin?*'

Harold stuffed his hands into his pockets and looked at her miserably, accepting the rebuke.

Stu said very quietly, 'But Harold's right, Perion. For now, aspirin's just about the best we can do. What time is it?'

'You don't *know* what to do!' she screamed at them. 'Why don't you just admit it?'

'It's quarter of three,' Frannie said.

'What if he *dies*?' Peri pushed a sheaf of dark auburn hair away from her face, which was puffed from crying.

'Leave them alone, Peri,' Mark said in a dull, tired voice. It startled them all. 'They'll do what they can. If it goes on hurting as bad as this, I think I'd rather be dead anyway. Give me some aspirin. Anything.'

'I'll get it,' Harold said, eager to be away. 'There's some in my knapsack. Extra Strength Excedrin,' he added, as if hoping for their approval, and then he went for it, nearly scuttling in his hurry.

'We've got to help him,' Perion said, returning to her old scripture.

Stu drew Glen and Frannie off to one side.

'Any ideas on what to do about this?' he asked them quietly. '*I* don't have any, I can tell you. She was mad at Harold, but his aspirin idea was just about twice as good as any I've had.'

'She's upset, that's all,' Fran said.

Glen sighed. 'Maybe it's just his bowels. Too much roughage. Maybe he'll have a good movement and it'll clear up.'

Frannie was shaking her head. 'I don't think that's it. He wouldn't be running a fever if it was his bowels. And I don't think his belly would have swelled up that way, either.' It had almost looked as if a tumor had swelled up there overnight. It made her feel ill to think about it. She could not remember when (except for when she was dreaming the dreams) she had been so badly frightened. What was it Harold had said? There's no doctor in the house. How true it was. How horribly true. God, it was all coming at her at once, crashing down all around her. How horribly alone they were. How horribly far out on the wire they were, and somebody had forgotten the safety net. She looked from Glen's strained face to Stu's. She saw deep concern in both of them, but no answers in either of them.

Behind them, Mark screamed again, and Perion echoed his cry as if she felt his pain. In a way, Frannie supposed that she did.

'What are we going to do?' Frannie asked helplessly.

She was thinking of the baby, and over and over again the question which dinned its way into her mind was: *What if it has to be cesarean? What if it has to be cesarean? What if —*

Behind her, Mark screamed again like some horrible prophet, and she hated him.

They looked at each other in the trembling dark.

From Fran Goldsmith's Diary

July 6, 1990
After some persuasion Mr Bateman has agreed to come along with us. He sez that after all his articles ('I write them in big words so no one will really know how simpleminded they are,' he sez) and boring twenty years of students to death in SY-1 and SY-2, not to mention the Sociology of Deviant Behavior and Rural Sociology, he has decided he can't afford to turn down this opportunity.

Stu wanted to know what opportunity he meant.

'I should think that would be clear,' sez Harold in that INSUFFERABLY SNOTTY way of his (sometimes Harold can be a dear but he can also be a real *boogersnot* and tonight he was being the latter). 'Mr Bateman —'

'Please call me Glen,' sez he, very quietly, but the way Harold glared at him, you would have thought he had accused Harold of having some social disease.

'*Glen*, as a sociologist, sees the opportunity to study the formation of a society first-hand, I believe. He wants to see how fact compares with theory.'

Well, to make a long story short, Glen (which I will call him from now on, since that's what he likes) agreed that was mostly it but added: 'I also have certain theories which I've written down and hope to prove or disprove. I don't believe that man arising from the ashes of the superflu is going to be anything like man arising from the cradle of the Nile with a bone in his nose and a woman by the hair. That's one of the theories.'

Stu said, in that quiet way he has, 'Because everything is lying around, waiting to be picked up again.' He looked so grim when he said it that I was surprised, and even Harold looked at him sort of funny.

But Glen just nodded and said, 'That's right. The technological society has walked off the court, so to speak, but they've left all the basketballs behind. Someone will come along who remembers the game and teach it to the rest again. That's rather neat, isn't it? I ought to write it down later.'

[But I've written it down myself, just in case he forgets. Who knows? The Shadow do, hee-hee.]

So then Harold sez, 'You sound as if you believe the whole thing will start up again – the arms race, the pollution, and so on. Is that another of your theories? Or a corollary to the first one?'

'Not exactly,' Glen started to say, but before he could go any further, Harold burst in with his own chicken-bone to pick. I can't put it down word for word, because when he gets excited Harold talks fast, but what he said amounted to how, even though he had a pretty low opinion of people in general, he didn't think they could be *that* stupid. He said he thought that this time around, certain laws would be made. One would be no fiddling around with badass stuff like nuclear fission and fleurocarbon (probably spelled that one wrong, oh well) sprays and stuff like that. I *do* remember one thing he said, because it was a very vivid image. 'Just because the Gordian knot has been cut for us is no reason for us to go to work and tie it back up.'

I could see he was just spoiling for an argument – one of the things that makes Harold hard to like is how eager he is to show off how much he knows (and he sure does know a lot, I can't take that away from him, Harold is superbright) – but all Glen said was, 'Time will tell, won't it?'

That all finished up about an hour ago, and now I am in an upstairs bedroom with Kojak lying on the floor beside me. Good dog! It is all rawther cozy, reminds me of home, but I am trying not to think about home too much because it makes me weepy. I know this must sound awful but I really wish I had someone to help me warm this bed. I even have a candidate in mind.

Put it *out* of your mind, Frannie!

So tomorrow we're off for Stovington and I know Stu doesn't like the idea much. He's scared of that place. I like Stu *very* much, only wish Harold liked him more. Harold is making everything very hard, but I suppose he can't help his nature.

Glen has decided to leave Kojak behind. He is sorry to have to do that, even though Kojak will have no trouble finding forage. Still there is nothing else for it unless we could find a motorcycle with a sidecar, and even then poor Kojak might get scared and jump out. Hurt or kill himself.

Anyway tomorrow we'll be going.

Things to Remember: The Texas Rangers (baseball team) had a pitcher named Nolan Ryan who pitched all kinds of no-hitters and things with his famous fastball, and a no-hitter is very good. There were TV comedies with laugh-tracks, and a laugh-track was people on tape laughing at the funny parts, and they were supposed to make you have a better time watching. You used to be able to get frozen cakes and pies at the supermarket and just thaw them out and eat them. Sara Lee strawberry cheesecake was my personal favorite.

July 7, 1990

Can't write long. Cycled all day. My fanny feels like hamburger & my back feels like there's a rock in it. I had that bad dream again last night. Harold has also been dreaming about that ?man? and it upsets the hell out of him because he can't explain how both of us can be having what is essentially the same dream.

Stu sez he is still having that dream about Nebraska and the old black woman there. She keeps saying he should come and see her anytime. Stu thinks she lives in a town called Holland Home or Hometown or something like that. Sez he thinks he could find it. Harold sneered at him and went into a long spiel about how dreams were psycho-Freudian manifestations of things we didn't dare think about when we were awake. Stu was angry, I think, but kept his temper. I'm so afraid that the bad feeling between them may break out into the open, I WISH IT DIDN'T HAVE TO BE THIS WAY!

Anyway, Stu said, 'So how come you and Frannie are having the same dream?' Harold muttered something about coincidence and just stalked off.

Stu told Glen and I that he would like us to go to Nebraska after Stovington. Glen shrugged and said, 'Why not? We have to go somewhere.'

Harold, of course, will object on general principles. Damn you, Harold, grow up!

Things to Remember: There were gasoline shortages in the early 80s because everybody in America was driving something and we had used up most of our oil supplies and the Arabs had us by the short hairs. The Arabs had so much money they literally couldn't spend it. There was a rock and roll group called The Who that sometimes used to finish their live performances by smashing their guitars and amplifiers. This was known as 'conspicuous consumption.'

July 8, 1990

It's late and I'm tired again but I should try to get as much down as I possibly can before my eyelids just SLAM SHUT. Harold finished his sign about an hour ago (with much bad grace I must say) and put it on the front lawn of the Stovington installation. Stu helped him put it up and held his peace in spite of all Harold's mean little jibes.

I had tried to prepare myself for the disappointment. I never believed Stu was lying, and I really don't think Harold believed he was, either. So I was sure everybody was dead, but still it was an upsetting experience and I cried. I couldn't help myself.

But I wasn't the only one who was upset. When Stu saw the place he turned almost dead white. He had on a short-sleeved shirt, and I could see he had goosebumps all up and down his arms. His eyes are normally blue but they had gone a slaty color, like the ocean on a gray day.

He pointed up to the third floor and said, 'That was my room.'

Harold turned toward him, and I could see him getting ready with one of his patented Harold Lauder Smartass Comments, but then he saw Stu's face and shut up. I think that was very wise of him, actually.

So after a little while Harold sez, 'Well, let's go in and look around.'

'What would you want to do that for?' Stu answers, and he sounded almost hysterical, but keeping it under a tight rein. It scared me, more so because he is usually as cool as icewater. Witness what little success Harold has had getting under his skin.

'Stuart –' Glen starts, but Stu interrupts with,

'What *for*? Can't you see it's a dead place? No brass bands, no soldiers, no nothing. Believe it,' he says, 'if they were here they'd be all over us by now. We'd be up in those white rooms like a bunch of fucking guinea pigs.' Then he looks at me and says, 'Sorry, Fran – I didn't mean to talk that way. I guess I'm upset.'

'Well, *I'm* going in,' Harold sez, 'who's coming with me?' But I could see that even though Harold was trying to be BIG & BOLD, he was really scared himself.

Glen said he would, and Stu said: 'You go in, too, Fran. Have a look. Satisfy yourself.'

I wanted to say I'd stay outside with him, because he looked so uptight (and because I really didn't want to go in, either, you know), but that would have made more trouble with Harold, so I said okay.

If we – Glen and I – had really had any doubts about Stu's story, we could have dropped them as soon as we opened the door. It was the smell. You can smell the same thing in any of the fair-sized towns we've traveled thru, it's a smell like decayed tomatoes, and oh God I'm crying *again*, but is it right for people not just to die but then to stink like

Wait

(later)

There, I've had my second GOOD CRY of the day, whatever can be happening to L'il Fran Goldsmith, Our Gal Sal, who used to be able to chew up nails and spit out carpet tacks, ha-ha, as the old saying goes. Well, no more tears tonite, and that's a promise.

We went inside anyway, morbid curiosity, I guess. I don't know about the others, but I kind of wanted to see the room where Stu was held prisoner. Anyway, it wasn't just the smell, you know, but how *cool* the place was after the outside. A lot of granite and marble and probably really fantastic insulation. It was warmer on the top 2 floors, but down below was that smell . . . and the cool . . . it was like a tomb. YUCK.

It was also spooky, like a haunted house – the three of us were all huddled together like sheep, and I was glad I had my rifle, even if it *is* only a .22. Our footsteps kept echoing back to us as if there was someone creeping along, following us, you know, and I started thinking about that dream again, the one starring the man in the black robe. No wonder Stu didn't want to come with us.

We wandered around to the elevators at last and went up to the 2nd floor. Nothing there but offices . . . and several bodies. The 3rd floor was made up like a hospital, but all the rooms had airlock doors (both Harold and Glen said that's what they were) and special viewing windows. There were *lots* of bodies up there, in the rooms and in the hallways, too. Very few women. Did they try to evacuate them at the end, I wonder? There's so much we'll never know. But then, why would we want to?

Anyway, at the end of the hall leading down from the main corridor where the elevator core was, we found a room with its airlock door open. There was a dead man in there, but he wasn't a patient (*they* were all wearing white hospital johnnies) and he sure didn't die of the flu. He was lying in a big pool of dried blood, and he looked like he'd been trying to crawl out of the room when he died. There was a broken chair, and things were all messed up, as if there'd been a fight.

Glen looked around for a long time and then said, 'I don't think we'd better say anything about this room to Stu. I believe he came very close to dying in here.'

I looked at that sprawled body and felt creepier than ever.

'What do you mean?' Harold asked, and even *he* sounded hushed. It was one of the few times I ever heard Harold talk as if what he was saying wasn't going out on a public address system.

'I believe that gentleman came in here to kill Stuart,' Glen said, 'and that Stu somehow got the better of him.'

'But why?' I asked. 'Why would they want to kill Stu if he was *immune*? It doesn't make any sense!'

He looked at me, and his eyes were scary. His eyes looked almost dead, like a mackerel's eyes.

'*That* doesn't matter, Fran,' he said. 'Sense didn't have much to do with this place, from the way it looks. There is a certain mentality that believes in covering up. They believe in it with the sincerity and fanaticism that members of some religious groups believe in the divinity of Jesus. Because, for some people, the necessity to continue covering up even after the damage is done is all-important. It makes me wonder how many immunes they killed in Atlanta and San Francisco and the Topeka Viral Center before the plague finally killed *them* and made an end to their butchery. This asshole? I'm glad he's dead. I'm only sorry for Stu, who'll probably spend the rest of his life having nightmares about him.'

And do you know what Glen Bateman did then? That nice man who paints the horrible pictures? He went over and kicked that dead man in the face. Harold made a muffled sort of grunt, as if he was the one who had been kicked. Then Glen drew his foot back again.

'No!' Harold yells, but Glen kicked the dead man again just the same. Then he turned around and he was wiping his mouth with the back of his hand, but at least his eyes had lost that awful dead-fish look.

'Come on,' he sez, 'let's get out of here. Stu was right. It's a dead place.'

So we went out, and Stu was sitting with his back to the iron gate in the high wall that ran around the place, and I wanted to . . . oh go ahead, Frannie, if you can't tell your diary, who *can* you tell? I wanted to run to him and kiss him and tell him I was ashamed for all of us not believing him. And ashamed of how all of us had gone on about what a hard time *we'd* had when the plague was on, and him hardly saying anything when all the time that man had almost killed him.

Oh dear, I'm falling in love with him, I think I've got the world's most crushable crush, if only it wasn't for Harold I'd take my damn chances!

Anyway (there's always an anyway, even tho by now my fingers are so numb they are just about falling off), that was when Stu told us for the first time that he wanted to go to Nebraska, that he wanted to check out his dream. He had a stubborn, sort of embarrassed look on his face, as if he knew he was going to have to take some more patronizing shit from Harold, but Harold was too unnerved from our 'tour' of the Stovington facility to offer more than token resistance. And even that stopped when Glen said, in a very reticent way, that he had also dreamed of the old woman the night before.

'Of course, it might only be because Stu told us about *his* dream,' he said, kind of red in the face, 'but it *was* remarkably similar.'

Harold said that of course that was it, but Stu said, 'Wait a minute, Harold – I've got an idea.'

His idea was that we all take a sheet of paper and write down everything we could remember of our dreams over the last week, then compare notes. This was just scientific enough so that Harold couldn't grumble too much.

Well, the only dream I've had is the one I've already written down, and I won't repeat it. I'll just say I wrote it down, leaving in the part about my father but leaving out the part about the baby and the coathanger he always has.

The results when we compared our papers were rather amazing.

Harold, Stu, and I had all dreamed about 'the dark man,' as I call him. Both Stu & I visualized him as a man in a monk's robe with no visible features – his face is always in a shadow. Harold's paper said that he was always standing in a dark doorway, beckoning to him 'like a pimp.' Sometimes he could just see his feet and the shine of his eyes – 'like weasel's eyes' is how he put it.

Stu and Glen's dreams of the old woman are very similar. The points of similarity are almost too many to go into (which is my 'literary' way of saying my fingers are going numb). Anyway, they both agree she is in Polk County, Nebraska, altho they couldn't get together on the actual name of the town – Stu says Hollingford Home, Glen says Hemingway Home. Close either way. They both seemed to feel they could find it. (Note Well, diary: My guess is 'Hemingford Home.')

Glen said, 'This is really remarkable. We all seem to be sharing an authentic psychic experience.' Harold pooh-poohed, of course, but he looked like he'd been given lots of food for thought. He would only agree to go on the basis of 'we have to go somewhere.' We leave in the morning. I'm scared, excited, and mostly happy to be leaving Stovington, which is a death-place. And I'll take that old woman over the dark man anytime.

Things to Remember: 'Hang loose' meant don't get upset. 'Rad' and 'gnarly' were ways of saying a thing was good. 'No sweat' meant you weren't worried. To 'boogie down' was to have a good time, and lots of people wore T-shirts which said SHIT HAPPENS, which it certainly did . . . and still does. 'I got grease' was a pretty current expression (I first heard it just this year) that meant everything was going well. 'Digs,' an old British expression, was just replacing 'pad' or 'crashpad' as an expression for the place you were living in before the superflu hit. It was very cool to say 'I dig your digs.' Stupid, huh? But that was life.

It was just after twelve noon.

Perion had fallen into an exhausted sleep beside Mark, who they had moved carefully into the shade two hours earlier. He was in and out of consciousness, and it was easier on all of them when he was out. He had held against the pain for the remainder of the night, but after daybreak he had finally given in to it and when he was conscious, his screams curdled their blood. They stood looking at each other, helpless. No one had wanted any lunch.

'It's his appendix,' Glen said. 'I don't think there's any doubt about it.'

'Maybe we ought to try . . . well, operating on him,' Harold said. He was looking at Glen. 'I don't suppose you . . .'

'We'd kill him,' Glen said flatly. 'You know that, Harold. If we could open him up without having him bleed to death, which we couldn't, we wouldn't know his appendix from his pancreas. The stuff in there isn't labeled, you know.'

'We'll kill him if we don't,' Harold said.

'Do *you* want to try?' Glen asked waspishly. 'Sometimes I wonder about you, Harold.'

'I don't see that *you're* being much help in our current situation, either,' Harold said, flushing.

'No, stop, come on,' Stu said. 'What good are either of you doing? Unless one of you plans to saw him open with a jackknife, it's out of the question, anyway.'

'*Stu!*' Frannie almost gasped.

'Well?' he asked, and shrugged. 'The nearest hospital would be back in Maumee. We could never get him there. I don't even think we could get him back to the turnpike.'

'You're right, of course,' Glen muttered, and ran a hand over his sandpapery cheek. 'Harold, I apologize. I'm very upset. I knew this sort of thing could happen – pardon me, *would* happen – but I guess I only knew it in an academic way. This is a lot different than sitting in the old study, blue-skying things.'

Harold muttered an ungrateful acknowledgment and walked off with his hands stuffed deep into his pockets. He looked like a sulky, overgrown ten-year-old.

'Why can't we move him?' Fran asked desperately, looking from Stu to Glen.

'Because of how much his appendix must have swelled by now,' Glen said. 'If it bursts, it's going to dump enough poison into his system to kill ten men.'

Stu nodded. 'Peritonitis.'

Frannie's head whirled. Appendicitis? That was nothing these days. *Nothing.* Why sometimes, if you were in the hospital for gallstones or something, they would just lift out your appendix on general principles while they still had you open. She remembered that one of her grammar school friends, a boy named Charley Biggers whom everyone had called Biggy, had had his appendix out during the summer between fifth and sixth grades. He was only in the hospital for two or three days. Having your appendix out was just nothing, medically speaking.

Just like having a baby was nothing, medically speaking.

'But if you leave him alone,' she asked, 'won't it burst anyway?'

Stu and Glen looked at each other uncomfortably and said nothing.

'Then you're just as bad as Harold says!' she burst out wildly. 'You've got to do *something*, even if it *is* with a jackknife! You've *got* to!'

'Why *us*?' Glen asked angrily. 'Why not *you*? We don't even have a medical book, for Christ's sweet sake!'

'But you . . . he . . . it can't happen this way! *Having your appendix out is supposed to be nothing!*'

'Well, maybe not in the old days, but it's sure something now,' Glen said, but by then she had blundered off, crying.

She came back around three o'clock, ashamed of herself and ready to apologize. But neither Glen nor Stu was in camp. Harold was sitting dejectedly on the trunk of a fallen tree. Perion was sitting crosslegged by Mark, sponging his face with a cloth. She looked pale but composed.

'Frannie!' Harold said, looking up and brightening visibly.

'Hi, Harold.' She went on to Peri. 'How is he?'

'Sleeping,' Perion said, but he wasn't sleeping; even Fran could see that. He was unconscious.

'Where have the others gone, Peri? Do you know?'

It was Harold who answered her. He had come up behind her, and Fran could feel him wanting to touch her hair or put a hand on her shoulder. She didn't want him to. Harold had begun to make her acutely uncomfortable almost all of the time.

'They've gone to Kunkle. To look for a doctor's office.'

'They thought they could get some books,' Peri said. 'And some . . . some instruments.' She swallowed and her throat made an audible click. She went on cooling Mark's face, occasionally dipping her cloth into one of the canteens and wringing it out.

'We're really sorry,' Harold said uncomfortably. 'I guess that doesn't sound like jack-shit, but we really are.'

Peri looked up and offered Harold a strained, sweet smile. 'I know that,' she said. 'Thank you. This is no one's fault. Unless there's a God, of course. If there's a God, then it's *His* fault. And when I see Him, I intend to kick Him in the balls.'

She had a horsey sort of face and a thick peasant's body. Fran, who saw everyone's best features long before she saw the less fortunate ones (Harold, for instance, had a lovely pair of hands for a boy), noticed that Peri's hair, a soft auburn shade, was almost gorgeous, and that her dark indigo eyes were fine and intelligent. She had taught anthropology at NYU, she had told them, and she had also been active in a number of political causes, including women's rights and equal treatment under the law for AIDS victims. She had never been married. Mark, she told Frannie once, had been better to her than she had ever expected a man to be. The others she had known had either ignored her or lumped her in with other girls as a 'pig' or a 'scag.' She admitted Mark might have been in the group which had always just ignored her if conditions had been normal, but they hadn't been. They had met each other in Albany, where Perion had been summering with her parents, on the last day of June, and after some talk they had decided to get out of the city before all the germs incubating in all the decomposing bodies could do to them what the superflu hadn't been able to do.

So they had left, and the next night they had become lovers, more out of desperate loneliness than any real attraction (this was girl-talk, and Frannie hadn't even written it down in her diary). He was good to her, Peri had told Fran in the soft and slightly amazed way of all plain women who have discovered a nice man in a hard world. She began to love him, a little more each day she had begun to love him.

And now this.

'It's funny,' she said. 'Everybody here but Stu and Harold are college graduates, and you certainly would have been if things had gone on in their normal course, Harold.'

'Yes, I guess that's true,' Harold said.

Peri turned back to Mark and began to sponge his forehead again, gently, with love. Frannie was reminded of a color plate in their family Bible, a picture that showed three women making the body of Jesus ready for burial – they were anointing him with oils and spices.

'Frannie was studying English, Glen was a teacher of sociology, Mark was getting his doctorate in American history, Harold, you'd be in English, too, wanting to be a writer. We could sit around and have some wonderful bull sessions. We did, as a matter of fact, didn't we?'

'Yes,' Harold agreed. His voice, normally penetrating, was almost too low to hear.

'A liberal arts education teaches you how to think – I read that somewhere. The hard facts you learn are secondary to that. The big thing you take away from school with you is how to induct and deduct in a constructive way.'

'That's good,' Harold said. 'I like that.'

Now his hand *did* drop on Fran's shoulder. She didn't shrug it away, but she was unhappily conscious of its presence.

'But it *isn't* good,' Peri said fiercely, and in his surprise, Harold took his hand off Fran's shoulder. She felt lighter immediately.

'No?' he asked, rather timidly.

'He's *dying*!' Peri said, not loudly but in an angry, helpless way. 'He's dying because we've all been spending our time learning how to bullshit each other in dorms and the living rooms of cheap apartments in college towns. Oh, I could tell you about the Midi Indians of New Guinea, and Harold could explain the literary technique of the later English poets, but what good does any of that do my Mark?'

'If we had somebody from med school –' Fran began tentatively.

'Yes, if we did. But we don't. We don't even have a car mechanic with us, or someone who went to ag college and might have at least *watched* once when a vet was working on a cow or a horse.' She looked at them, her indigo eyes growing even darker. 'Much as I like you all, I think at this point I'd trade the whole bunch of you for Mr Goodwrench. You're all so afraid to touch him, even though you know what's going to happen if you don't. And I'm the same way – I'm not excluding myself.'

'At least the two . . .' Fran stopped. She had been about to say *At least the two men went*, then decided that might be unfortunate phrasing, with Harold still here. 'At least Stu and Glen went. That's something, isn't it?'

Peri sighed. 'Yes – that's something. But it was Stu's decision to go, wasn't it? The only one of us who finally decided it would be better to try anything than to just stand around wringing our hands.' She looked at Frannie. 'Did he tell you what he did for a living before?'

'He worked in a factory,' Fran said promptly. She did not notice that Harold's brow clouded at how quickly she was able to come up with this information. 'He put circuits in electronic calculators. I guess you could say he was a computer technician.'

'Ha!' Harold said, and smiled sourly.

'He's the only one of us who understands taking things apart,' Peri said. 'What he and Mr Bateman do will kill Mark, I'm almost sure it will, but it's better that he be killed while somebody is trying to make him well than it would be for him to die while we just stand around watching . . . as if he were a dog that had been run over in the street.'

Neither Harold nor Fran could find a reply to that. They only stood behind her and watched Mark's pale, still face. After a while Harold put his sweaty hand on Fran's shoulder again. It made her feel like screaming.

Stu and Glen got back at quarter to four. They had taken one of the cycles. Tied behind it was a doctor's black bag of instruments and several large black books.

'We'll try,' was all Stu said.

Peri looked up. Her face was white and strained, her voice calm. 'Would you? Please. We both want you to,' she said.

'Stu?' Perion said.

It was ten minutes past four. Stu was kneeling on a rubber sheet that had been spread under the tree. Sweat was pouring from his face in rivers. His eyes looked bright and haunted and frantic. Frannie was holding a book open in front of him, switching back and forth between two colored plates whenever Stu raised his eyes and nodded at her. Beside him, horribly white, Glen Bateman held a spool of fine white thread. Between them was an open case of stainless steel instruments. The case was now splashed with blood.

'It's here!' Stu cried. His voice was suddenly high and hard and exultant. His eyes had narrowed to two points. 'Here's the little bastard! Here! Right here!'

'Stu?' Perion said.

'Fran, show me that other plate again! Quick! Quick!'

'Can you take it out?' Glen asked. 'Jesus, East Texas, do you really think you can?'

Harold was gone. He had left the party early, holding one hand cupped over his mouth. He had been standing in a small grove of trees to the east, his back to them, for the last fifteen minutes. Now he turned back, his large round face hopeful.

'I don't know,' Stu said, 'but I might. I just might.'

He stared at the color plate Fran was showing him. He was wearing blood up to his elbows, like scarlet evening gloves.

'Stu?' Perion said.

'It's self-containing above and below,' Stu whispered. His eyes glittered fantastically. 'The appendix. It's its own little unit. It . . . wipe my forehead, Frannie, Jesus, I'm sweating like a fucking pig . . . thanks . . . God, I don't want to cut his doins any worse than I have to . . . that's his everfucking intestines . . . but Christ, I gotta. I gotta.'

'Stu?' Perion said.

'Give me the scissors, Glen. No – not those. The small pair.'

'*Stu.*'

He looked at her at last.

'You don't need to.' Her voice was calm, soft. 'He's dead.'

Stu looked at her, his narrowed eyes slowly widening.

She nodded. 'Almost two minutes ago. But thank you. Thank you for trying.'

Stu looked at her for a long time. 'You're sure?' he whispered at last.

She nodded again. Tears were spilling silently down her face.

Stu turned away from them, dropping the small scalpel he had been holding, and put his hands over his eyes in a gesture of utter despair. Glen had already gotten up and walked off, not looking back, his shoulders hunched, as if from a blow.

Frannie put her arms around Stu and hugged him.

'That's that,' he said. He said it over and over again, speaking in a slow and toneless way that frightened her. 'That's that. All over. That's that. That's that.'

'You did the best you could,' she said, and hugged him even tighter, as if he might fly away.

'That's that,' he said again, with dull finality.

Frannie hugged him. Despite all her thoughts of the last three and a half weeks, despite her 'crushable crush,' she had not made a single overt move. She had been almost painfully careful not to show the way she felt. The situation with Harold was just too much on a hair trigger. And she was not showing the true way she felt about Stu even now, not really. It was not a lover's hug she was bestowing on him. It was simply one survivor clinging to another. Stu seemed to understand this. His hands came up to her shoulders and pressed them firmly, leaving bloody handprints on her khaki shirt, marking her in a way which seemed to make them partners in some unhappy crime. Somewhere a jay cawed harshly, and closer at hand Perion began to weep.

Harold Lauder, who did not know the difference between the hugs survivors and lovers may bestow on each other, gazed at Frannie and Stu with dawning suspicion and fear. After a long moment he crashed furiously off into the brush and didn't come back until long after supper.

She woke up early the next morning. Someone was shaking her. I'll open my eyes and it'll be Glen or Harold, she thought sleepily. We're going to go through it again, and we'll *keep* going through it until we get it right. Those who do not learn from history –

But it was Stu. And it was already daylight of a sort; creeping dawn, muffled in early mist like fresh gold wrapped in thin cotton. The others were sleeping humps.

'What is it?' she asked, sitting up. 'Is something wrong?'

'I was dreaming again,' he said. 'Not the old woman, the . . . the other one. The dark man. I was scared, so I . . .'

'Stop it,' she said, frightened by the look on his face. 'Say what you mean, *please.*'

'It's Perion. The Veronal. She got the Veronal out of Glen's pack.'

She hissed in breath.

'Oh boy,' Stu said brokenly. 'She's dead, Frannie. Oh Lord, ain't this some mess.'

She tried to speak and found she could not.

'I guess I've got to wake the other two up,' Stu said in an absent sort of way. He rubbed at his cheek, which was sandpapery with beard. Fran could still remember how it had felt against her own cheek yesterday, when she had hugged him. He turned back to her, bewildered. 'When does it end?'

She said softly: 'I don't think it ever will.'

Their eyes locked in the early dawn.

From Fran Goldsmith's Diary

July 12, 1990
We're camped just west of Guilderland (NY) tonight, have finally made it onto the Big Highway, Route 80/90. The excitement of meeting Mark and Perion (don't you think that's a pretty name? I do) yesterday afternoon has more or less abated. They have agreed to throw in with us . . . in fact, they made the suggestion before any of us could.

Not that I'm sure Harold would have offered. You know how he is. And
he was a little put off (I think Glen was, too) by all the hardware they were
carrying, including semiautomatic rifles (two). But mostly Harold just had to
have his little song and dance . . . he has to register his presence, you know.

I guess I have filled up pages and pages with THE PSYCHOLOGY OF
HAROLD, and if you don't know him by now, you never will. Underneath
his swagger and all those pompous pronouncements, there is a very insecure
little boy. He can't really believe that things have changed. Part of him –
quite a large part, I think – has to go on believing that all his high school
tormentors are going to rise out of their graves one fine day and start
shooting spitballs at him again or maybe calling him Whack-Off Lauder,
as Amy said they used to do. Sometimes I think it would have been better
for him (and maybe me too) if we hadn't hooked up back in Ogunquit.
I'm part of his old life, I was best friends with his sister once upon a time,
and so on and so on. What sums up my weird relationship with Harold is
this: strange as it may seem, knowing what I know now, I would probably
pick *Harold* to be friends with instead of Amy, who was mostly dizzy about
boys with nice cars and clothes from Sweetie's, and who was (God forgive
me for saying Cruddy Things about the Dead but it's true) a real Ogunquit
Snob, the way only a year-round townie can be one. Harold is, in his own
weird way, sort of cool. When he's not concentrating all his mental ener-
gies on being an asshole, that is. But, you see, Harold could never believe
that anyone could think he was cool. Part of him has such a *huge* investment
in being square. He is determined to carry all of his problems right along
with him into this not-so-brave new world. He might as well have them
packed right inside his knapsack along with those chocolate Payday candy
bars he likes to eat.

Oh Harold, jeez, I just don't know.

Things to Remember: The Gillette parrot. 'Please don't squeeze the Charmin.'
The walking Kool-Aid pitcher that used to say, 'Oh . . . YEAAAAHHH!' 'O.
B. Tampons . . . created by a woman gynecologist.' Converse All-Stars. *Night
of the Living Dead*. Brrrr! That last one hits too close to home. I quit.

July 14, 1990
We had a very long and very sober talk about these dreams today at lunch,
stopping much longer than we should have, probably. We're just north of
Batavia, New York, by the way.

Yesterday, Harold very diffidently (for him) suggested we start stocking up
on Veronal and hitting ourselves with very light doses to see if we couldn't
'disrupt the dream-cycle,' as he put it. I went along with the idea so no one
would start to wonder if something might be wrong with me, but I plan to
palm my dose because I don't know what it might do to the Lone Ranger
(I hope he's Lone; I'm not sure I could face twins).

With the Veronal proposal adopted, Mark had a comment. 'You know,' he sez, 'things like this really don't bear too much thinking about. The next thing you know, we'll all be thinking we're Moses or Joseph, getting telephone calls from God.'

'That dark man isn't calling from heaven,' Stu sez. 'If it's a toll-call, I think it's comin from someplace a lot lower down.'

'Which is Stu's way of saying Old Scratch is after us,' Frannie pipes up.

'And that's as good an explanation as any other,' Glen sez. We all looked at him. 'Well,' he went on, a little on the defensive, I think, 'if you look at it from a theological point of view, it does rather seem as if we're the knot in a tug-o-war rope between heaven and hell, doesn't it? If there are any Jesuit survivors of the superflu, they must be going absolutely bananas.'

That made Mark laugh his head off. I didn't really get it, but kept my mouth shut.

'Well, *I* think the whole thing is ridiculous,' Harold put in. 'You'll be getting around to Edgar Cayce and the transmigration of souls before we know it.'

He pronounced Cayce *Case*, and when I corrected him (you say it like the initials for Kansas City), he gave me a really HORRID HAROLD-FROWN. He isn't the type of guy who swamps you with gratitude when you point out his little flaws, diary!

'Whenever something overtly paranormal occurs,' Glen said, 'the only explanation that really fits well and holds its interior logic is the theological one. That's why psychics and religion have always gone hand in hand, right up to your modern-day faith-healers.'

Harold was grumbling, but Glen went on anyway.

'My own gut feeling is that everyone's psychic . . . and it's so ingrained a part of us that we very rarely notice it. The talent may be largely preventative, and that keeps it from being noticed, too.'

'Why?' I asked.

'Because it's a negative factor, Fran. Have any of you ever read James D. L. Staunton's 1958 study of train and airplane crashes? It was originally published in a sociology journal, but the tabloid newspapers rake it up every now and again.'

We all shook our heads.

'You ought to,' he said. 'James Staunton was what my students of twenty years ago would have called "a real good head" – a mild-mannered clinical sociologist who studied the occult as a kind of hobby. He wrote any number of articles on the combined subjects before going over to the other side to do some first-hand research.'

Harold snorted, but Stu and Mark were grinning. I fear I was, too.

'So tell us about the planes and trains,' Peri sez.

'Well, Staunton got the stats on over fifty plane crashes since 1925 and over two hundred train crashes since 1900. He fed all the data into a computer. Basically, he was correlating three factors: those present on any such conveyance that met with disaster, those killed, and the *capacity* of the vehicle.'

'Don't see what he was trying to prove,' Stu said.

'To see that, you have to understand that he fed a second series of figures into the computer – this time an equal number of planes and trains which *didn't* meet with disaster.'

Mark nodded. 'A control group and an experimental group. That seems solid enough.'

'What he found was simple enough, but staggering in its implications. It's a shame one has to stagger through sixteen tables to get at the underlying statistical fact.'

'*What* fact?' I asked.

'Full planes and trains rarely crash,' Glen said.

'Oh fucking *BULLSHIT!*' Harold just about screams.

'Not at all,' Glen sez calmly. 'That was Staunton's theory, and the computer bore him out. In cases where planes or trains crash, the vehicles are running at 61 percent capacity, as regards passenger loads. In cases where they don't, the vehicles are running at 76 per cent capacity. That's a difference of 15 percent over a large computer run, and that sort of across-the-board deviation is *significant*. Staunton points out that, statistically speaking, a 3 percent deviation would be food for thought, and he's right. It's an anomaly the size of Texas. Staunton's deduction was that people *know* which planes and trains are going to crash . . . that they are unconsciously predicting the future.

'Your Aunt Sally gets a bad stomach ache just before Flight 61 takes off from Chicago bound for San Diego. And when the plane crashes in the Nevada desert, everyone says, "Oh Aunt Sally, that bellyache was really the grace of God." But until James Staunton came along, no one had realized that there were really *thirty* people with bellyaches . . . or headaches . . . or just that funny feeling you get in your legs when your body is trying to tell your head that something is getting ready to go *way* off-course.'

'I just can't believe that,' Harold sez, shaking his head rather woefully.

'Well, you know,' Glen said, 'about a week after I finished the Staunton article for the first time, a Majestic Airlines jet crashed at Logan Airport. It killed everyone on board. Well, I called the Majestic office at Logan after things had settled down a bit. I told them I was a reporter from the Manchester *Union-Leader* – a small lie in a good cause. I said we were getting a sidebar on airline crashes together and asked if they could tell me how many no-shows there were on that flight. The man sounded kind of surprised, because he said the airline personnel had been talking about that. The number was sixteen. Sixteen no-shows. I asked him what the average was on 747 flights from Denver to Boston, and he said it was three.'

'Three,' Perion sez in a marveling kind of way.

'Right. But the guy went further. He said they'd also had fifteen *cancelations*, and the average number is eight. So, although the headlines after the fact screamed LOGAN AIR CRASH KILLS 94, it could just as well have read 31 AVOID DEATH IN LOGAN AIRPORT DISASTER.'

Well . . . there was a lot more talk about psychic stuff, but it wandered pretty far afield from the subject of *our* dreams and whether or not they come from the Big Righteous in the sky. One thing that did come up (this was after Harold had wandered away in utter disgust) was Stu asking Glen, 'If we're all so psychic, then how come we don't know when a loved one has just died or that our house just blew away in a tornado, or something?'

'There are cases of exactly that sort of thing,' Glen said, 'but I will admit they are nowhere near as common . . . or as easy to prove with the aid of a computer. It's an interesting point. I have a theory –'

(Doesn't he always, diary?)

'– that has to do with evolution. You know, once men – or their progenitors – had tails and hair all over their bodies, and much sharper senses than they do now. Why don't we have them anymore? Quick, Stu! This is your chance to go to the head of the class, mortarboard and all.'

'Why, for the same reason people don't wear goggles and dusters when they drive anymore, I guess. Sometimes you outgrow a thing. It gets to a point where you don't need it anymore.'

'Exactly. And what is the point of having a psychic sense that's useless in any practical way? What earthly good would it do you to be working in your office and suddenly know that your wife had been killed in a car-smash coming back from the market? Someone is going to call you on the telephone and tell you, right? That sense may have atrophied long ago, if we ever had it. It may have gone the way of our tails and our pelts.

'What interests me about these dreams,' he went on, 'is that they seem to presage some future struggle. We seem to be getting cloudy pictures of a protagonist . . . and an antagonist. An adversary, if you like. If that's so, it may be like looking at a plane on which we're scheduled to fly . . . and getting a bellyache. We're being given the means to help shape our own futures, perhaps. A kind of fourth-dimensional free will: the chance to choose in advance of events.'

'But we don't know what the dreams *mean*,' I said.

'No, we don't. But we may. I don't know if a little tickle of psychic ability means we are divine; there are plenty of people who can accept the miracle of eyesight without believing that eyesight proves the existence of God, and I am one of them; but I do believe these dreams are a constructive force in spite of their ability to frighten us. I'm having second thoughts about the Veronal as a result. Taking it is very much like swallowing some Pepto-Bismol to quiet the bellyache, and then getting on the plane anyway.'

Things to Remember: Recessions, shortages, the prototype Ford Growler that could go sixty miles of highway on a single gallon of gas. Quite the wonder car. That's all; I quit. If I don't shorten my entries, this diary will be as long as *Gone with the Wind* even before the Lone Ranger arrives (although please not on a white horse named Silver). Oh yes, one other Thing to Remember. Edgar Cayce. Can't forget him. He supposedly saw the future in his dreams.

July 16, 1990

Only two notes, both of them relating to the dreams (see entry two days ago). First, Glen Bateman has been very pale and silent these last two days, and tonight I saw him take an extra-large dose of Veronal. My suspicion is that he skipped his last two doses and the result was some VERY bad dreams. That worries me. I wish I knew a way to approach him about it, but can think of nothing.

Second, my own dreams. Nothing night before last (the night after our discussion); slept like a baby and can't remember a thing. Last night I dreamed of the old woman for the first time. Have nothing to add beyond what has already been said except to say she seems to exude an aura of NICENESS, of KINDNESS. I think I can understand why Stu was so set on going to Nebraska even in the face of Harold's sarcasm. I woke up this morning completely refreshed, thinking that if we could just get to that old woman, Mother Abigail, everything would be A-OK. I hope she's really there. (By the way, I'm quite sure that the name of the town is Hemingford Home.)

Things to remember: Mother Abigail!

CHAPTER 47

When it happened, it happened fast.

It was around quarter of ten on July 30 and they had been on the road only an hour. Going was slow because there had been heavy showers the night before and the road was still slippery. There had been little talk among the four of them since yesterday morning, when Stu had awakened first Frannie, then Harold and Glen, to tell them about Perion's suicide. He was blaming himself, Fran thought miserably, blaming himself for something that was no more his fault than a thunderstorm would have been.

She would have liked to have told him so, partly because he needed to be scolded for his self-indulgence and partly because she loved him. This latter was a fact she could no longer conceal from herself. She thought she could convince him that Peri's death wasn't his fault . . . but the convincing would entail showing him what her own true feelings were. She thought she would have to pin her heart to her sleeve, where he could see it. Unfortunately, Harold would be able to see it, too. So that was out . . . but only for the time being. She thought she would have to do it soon, Harold or no Harold. She could only protect him so long. Then he would have to know . . . and either accept or not accept. She was afraid Harold might opt for the second choice. A decision like that could lead to something horrible. They were, after all, carrying a lot of shooting irons.

She was mulling these thoughts over when they swept around a curve and saw a large housetrailer overturned in the middle of the road, blocking it from one end to the other. Its pink corrugated side still glistened with last night's rain. This was surprising enough, but there was more – three cars, all station wagons, and a big auto-wrecker were parked along the sides of the road. There were people standing around, too, at least a dozen of them.

Fran was so surprised she braked too suddenly. The Honda she was riding skidded on the wet road, and almost dumped her before she was able to get it under control. Then all four of them had stopped, more or less in a line which crossed the road, blinking and more than a little stunned at the sight of so many people who were still alive.

'Okay, dismount,' one of the men said. He was tall, sandy-bearded, and wearing dark sunglasses. Fran time-traveled for a moment inside her head, back to the Maine Turnpike and being hauled down by a state trooper for speeding.

Next he'll ask to see our drivers' licenses, Fran thought. But this was no lone State Trooper, bagging speeders and writing tickets. There were four men here, three of them standing behind the sandy-bearded man in a short skirmish line. The rest were all women. At least eight of them. They looked pale and scared, clustered around the parked station wagons in little groups.

The sandy-bearded man was carrying a pistol. The men behind him all had rifles. Two of them were wearing bits and pieces of army kit.

'*Dismount*, goddamn you,' the bearded man said, and one of the men behind him levered a round into the breech of his rifle. It was a loud, bitterly imperative sound in the misty morning air.

Glen and Harold looked puzzled and apprehensive. That, and no more. *They're sitting ducks*, Frannie thought with rising panic. She did not fully understand the situation herself yet, but she knew the equation here was all wrong. *Four men, eight women*, her brain said, and then repeated it, louder, in tones of alarm: *Four men! Eight women!*

'Harold,' Stu said in a quiet voice. Something had come up in his eyes. Some realization. 'Harold, don't –' And then everything happened.

Stu's rifle was slung over his back. He dropped one shoulder so that the strap slid down his arm, and then the rifle was in his hands.

'Don't do it!' the bearded man shouted furiously. 'Garvey! Virge! Ronnie! Get them! Save the woman!'

Harold began to grab for his pistols, at first forgetting they were still strapped into their holsters.

Glen Bateman still sat behind Harold in stunned surprise.

'*Harold!*' Stu yelled again.

Frannie began to unsling her own rifle. She felt as if the air around her had suddenly been packed with invisible molasses, treacly stuff she would never be able to struggle through in time. She realized they were probably going to die here.

One of the girls screamed: '*NOW!*'

Frannie's gaze switched to this girl even as she continued to struggle with her rifle. Not really a girl; she was at least twenty-five. Her hair, ash-blond, lay against her head in a ragged helmet, as if she had recently lopped it off with a pair of hedge-clippers.

Not all of the women moved; some of them appeared to be nearly catatonic with fright. But the blond girl and three of the others did.

All of this happened in the space of seven seconds.

The bearded man had been pointing his pistol at Stu. When the young blond woman screamed, '*Now!*', the barrel jerked slightly toward her, like a divining rod sensing water. It went off, making a loud noise like a piece of steel being punched through cardboard. Stu fell off his bike and Frannie screamed his name.

Then Stu was up on both elbows (both were scraped from hitting the road, and the Honda was lying on one of his legs), firing. The bearded man seemed to dance backward like a vaudeville hoofer leaving the stage after his encore. The faded plaid shirt he was wearing puffed and billowed. His pistol, an automatic, jerked up toward the sky and that steel-punching-through-cardboard sound happened four more times. He fell over on his back.

Two of the three men behind him had jerked around at the blond woman's cry. One pulled both triggers of the weapon he was holding, an old-fashioned Remington twelve-gauge. The stock of the gun was not resting against anything – he was holding it outside his right hip – and when it went off with a sound like a thunderclap in a small room, it flew backward out of his hands, ripping skin from his fingers as it went. It clattered on the road. The face of one of the women who had not reacted to the blond woman's shout dissolved in an unbelievable fury of blood, and for a moment Frannie could actually hear blood raining down on the pavement, as if there had been a sudden shower. One eye peered unharmed through the mask of blood this woman now wore. It was dazed and unknowing. Then the woman fell forward onto the road. The Country Squire station wagon behind her was peppered with buckshot. One of the windows was a cataract of milky cracks.

The blond girl grappled with the second man who had turned

toward her. The rifle the man held went off between their bodies. One of the girls scrambled for the lost shotgun.

The third man, who had *not* turned toward the women, began to fire at Fran. Frannie sat astride her bike, her rifle in her hands, blinking stupidly at him. He was an olive-skinned man who looked Italian. She felt a bullet drone by her left temple.

Harold had finally gotten one of his pistols free. He raised it and fired at the olive-skinned man. The distance was about fifteen paces. He missed. A bullet hole appeared in the skin of the pink housetrailer just to the left of the olive-skinned man's head. The olive-skinned man looked at Harold and said, 'Now I gonna keel-a you, you sonnabeesh.'

'Don't do that!' Harold screamed. He dropped his pistol and held out his open hands.

The olive-skinned man fired three times at Harold. All three shots missed. The third round came the closest to doing damage; it screamed off the exhaust pipe of Harold's Yamaha. It fell over, spilling Harold and Glen off.

Now twenty seconds had passed. Harold and Stu lay flat. Glen sat cross-legged on the road, still looking as if he didn't know exactly where he was, or what was going on. Frannie was trying desperately to shoot the olive-skinned man before he could shoot Harold or Stu, but her gun wouldn't fire, the trigger wouldn't even pull, because she had forgotten to thumb the safety catch to its off position. The blond woman continued to struggle with the second man, and the woman who had gone after the dropped shotgun was now fighting with a second woman for possession of it.

Cursing in a language which was undoubtedly Italian, the olive-skinned man aimed at Harold again and then Stu fired and the olive-skinned man's forehead caved in and he went down like a sack of potatoes.

Another woman had now joined the fray over the shotgun. The man who had lost it tried to throw her aside. She reached between his legs, grabbed the crotch of his jeans, and squeezed. Fran saw her hamstrings pop out all the way up her forearm to the elbow. The man screamed. The man lost interest in the shotgun. The man grabbed his privates and stumbled away bent-over.

Harold crawled to where his dropped pistol lay on the road and pounced on it. He raised it and fired at the man holding his privates. He fired three times and missed every time.

It's like Bonnie and Clyde, Frannie thought. *Jesus, there's blood everywhere!*

The blond woman with the ragged hair had lost her struggle for possession of the second man's rifle. He jerked it free and kicked her, perhaps aiming for her stomach, catching her in the thigh with one of his heavy boots instead. She went quick-stepping backward, whirling her arms for balance, and landed on her fanny with a wet splat.

Now he'll shoot her, Frannie thought, but the second man whirled around like a drunken soldier doing an about-face and began to fire rapidly into the group of three women still cringing against the side of the Country Squire.

'Yaaah! You bitches!' this gentleman screamed. 'Yaaaah! You bitches!'

One of the women fell over and began to flop on the pavement between the station wagon and the overturned trailer like a stabbed fish. The other two women ran. Stu fired at the shooter and missed. The second man fired at one of the running women and did not. She threw her hands up to the sky and fell down. The other button-hooked left and ran behind the pink trailer.

The third man, the one who had lost and failed to regain the shotgun, was still staggering around and holding his crotch. One of the women pointed the shotgun at him and pulled both triggers, her eyes squeezed shut and her mouth grimacing in anticipation of that thunder. The thunder didn't come. The shotgun was dry. She reversed it so she was holding it by the barrels and brought the stock down in a hard arc. She missed his head, but got the place where his neck joined his right shoulder. The man was driven to his knees. He began to crawl away. The woman, who was wearing a blue sweatshirt which said KENT STATE UNIVERSITY and tattered bluejeans, walked along after him, bludgeoning him with the shotgun as she went. The man continued to crawl, blood now running off him in rivers, and the woman in the Kent State sweatshirt continued to whale on him.

'Yaaaaah, you *bitches*!' the second man screamed, and fired at a dazed and muttering middle-aged woman. The distance between muzzle and woman was at the most three feet; she could almost have reached out and plugged the barrel with her pinky finger. He missed. He pulled the trigger again, but this time the rifle only dry-fired.

Harold was now holding his pistol in both hands, as he had

seen cops do in the movies. He pulled the trigger and his bullet smashed the second man's elbow. The second man dropped his rifle and began to dance up and down, making high jabbering noises. To Frannie, he sounded a little like Roger Rabbit saying '*P-P-Pleeeeze!*'

'I got im!' Harold cried ecstatically. 'Got im! By God, I got im!'

Frannie finally remembered the safety catch on her rifle. She thumbed it off just as Stu fired again. The second man fell down, now clutching his stomach instead of his elbow. He went on screaming.

'My God, my God,' Glen said mildly. He put his face into his hands and began to weep.

Harold fired his pistol again. The second man's body jumped. He stopped screaming.

The woman in the Kent State University sweatshirt brought the stock of the shotgun down again, and this time she connected solidly with the crawling man's head. It sounded like Jim Rice connecting solidly with a high, hard fastball. The shotgun's walnut stock and the man's head both shattered.

For a moment there was silence. A bird called in it: *Whitwhit . . . whitwhit . . . whitwhit.*

Then the girl in the sweatshirt stood astride the third man's body and gave a long, primeval scream of triumph that haunted Fran Goldsmith for the rest of her life.

The blond girl was Dayna Jurgens, from Xenia, Ohio. The girl in the Kent State sweatshirt was Susan Stern. A third woman, the one who had squeezed Shotgun's crotch, was Patty Kroger. The other two were quite a bit older. The eldest, Dayna said, was Shirley Hammett. They didn't know the name of the other woman, who looked to be in her mid-thirties; she had been in shock, wandering, when Al, Garvey, Virge, and Ronnie had picked her up in the town of Archbold, two days before.

The nine of them got off the highway and camped in a farmhouse somewhere just west of Columbia, now over the Indiana state line. They were all in shock, and Fran thought in later days that their walk across the field from the overturned pink trailer on the turnpike to the farmhouse would have looked to an observer like a fieldtrip sponsored by the local lunatic asylum. The grass, thigh-high and still wet from the previous night's rain, had soon soaked their pants. White butterflies, sluggish in the air because their wings were still heavy with moisture, swooped toward them and then away in drugged circles and figure-eights. The sun was struggling to break through but hadn't made it yet; it was a bright smear feebly illuminating a uniform white cloud cover that stretched from horizon to horizon. But cloud cover or no cloud cover, the day was hot already, wringing with humidity, and the air was filled with whirling flocks of crows and their raucous, ugly cries. There are more crows than people now, Fran thought dazedly. If we don't watch out, they'll peck us right off the face of the earth. Revenge of the blackbirds. Were crows meat-eaters? She very much feared that they were.

Below this steady trickle of nonsense, barely visible, like the sun behind the melting cloud cover (but full of power, as the sun was on this awful, humid morning, the thirtieth of July, 1990), the gunbattle played over and over in her mind. The woman's face disintegrating under the shotgun blast. Stu falling over. The instant of stark terror when she had been sure he was dead. One man crying out *Yaaah, you bitches!* and then sounding like Roger Rabbit when Harold plugged him. The steel-punching-through-cardboard sound of the bearded man's pistol. Susan Stern's primitive cry of victory as she stood astride the body of her enemy while his brains, still warm, leaked out of his cloven skull.

Glen walked beside her, his thin, rather sardonic face now distraught, his gray hair flying wispily around his head as if in imitation of the butterflies. He held her hand, and he kept patting it compulsively.

'You mustn't let it affect you,' he said. 'Such horrors . . . bound to occur. Best protection is in numbers. Society, you know. Society is the keystone of the arch we call civilization, and it is the only real antidote to outlawry. You must take . . . things . . . things like this . . . as a matter of course. This was an isolated occurrence. Think of them as trolls. Yes! Trolls or yogs or affrits. Monsters of a generic sort. I accept that. I hold that truth to be self-evident, a socioconstitutional ethic, one might say. Ha! Ha!'

His laugh was half moan. She punctuated each of his elliptical sentences with 'Yes, Glen,' but he seemed not to hear. Glen smelled a trifle vomitous. The butterflies banged against them and then banged off again on their butterfly errands. They were almost to the farmhouse. The battle had lasted less than a minute. Less than a minute, but she suspected it was going to be held over by popular demand inside her head. Glen patted her hand. She wanted to tell him to please stop doing that, but she was afraid that he might cry if she did. She could stand the patting. She wasn't sure she could stand to see Glen Bateman weeping.

Stu was walking with Harold on one side and the blond girl, Dayna Jurgens, on the other. Susan Stern and Patty Kroger flanked the unnamed catatonic woman who had been picked up in Archbold. Shirley Hammett, the woman who had been missed at pointblank range by the man who had imitated Roger Rabbit before he died, walked a little way off to the left, muttering and making the occasional grab at the passing butterflies. The party was walking slowly, but Shirley Hammett was slower. Her gray hair hung untidily about her face, and her dazed eyes peered out at the world like frightened mice peering out of a temporary bolthole.

Harold looked at Stu uneasily. 'We wiped them out, didn't we, Stu? We blew them up. Scragged their asses.'

'I guess so, Harold.'

'Man, but we *had* to,' Harold said earnestly, as if Stu had suggested things might have been otherwise. 'It was them or us!'

'They would have blown your heads off,' Dayna Jurgens said quietly. 'I was with two guys when they hit us. They shot Rich and Damon from ambush. After it was over, they put a round in each of their heads, just to make sure. You had to, all right. By rights you should be dead now.'

'By rights we should be dead now!' Harold exclaimed to Stu.

'It's all right,' Stu said. 'Take her easy, Harold.'

'Sure! Negative perspiration!' Harold said heartily. He fumbled jerkily in his pack, got a chocolate Payday, and almost dropped it while stripping off the wrapper. He cursed it bitterly and then began to gobble it, holding it in both hands like a lollypop.

They had reached the farmhouse. Harold had to keep touching himself furtively as he ate his candy bar – had to keep making sure he wasn't hurt. He felt very sick. He was afraid to look down at his crotch. He was pretty sure he had wet himself shortly after the festivities back at the pink trailer got into high gear.

Dayna and Susan did most of the talking over a distraught brunch which some picked at but none really ate. Patty Kroger, who was seventeen and absolutely beautiful, occasionally added something. The woman with no name scrunched herself into the farthest corner of the dusty farmhouse kitchen. Shirley Hammett sat at a table, ate stale Nabisco Honey Grahams, and muttered.

Dayna had left Xenia in the company of Richard Darliss and Damon Bracknell. How many others had been alive in Xenia after the flu? Only three that she had seen, a very old man, a woman, and a little girl. Dayna and her friends asked the trio to join them, but the old man waved them off, saying something about 'having business in the desert.'

By the eighth of July, Dayna, Richard, and Damon had begun to suffer bad dreams about a sort of boogeyman. Very scary dreams. Rich had actually gotten the idea that the boogeyman was real, Dayna said, and living in California. He had an idea that this man, if he really was a man, was the business the other three people they'd met had in the desert. She and Damon had begun to fear for Rich's sanity. He called the dream-man 'the hardcase' and said he was getting an *army* of hardcases together. He said this army would soon sweep out of the west and enslave everyone left alive, first in America, then in the rest of the world. Dayna and Damon had begun to privately discuss the possibility of slipping away from Rich some night, and had begun to believe that their own dreams were the result of Rich Darliss's powerful delusion.

In Williamstown, they had come around a curve in the highway to discover a large dump truck lying on its side in the middle of the road. There was a station wagon and a wrecker parked nearby.

'We assumed it was just another smashup,' Dayna said, crumbling a graham cracker nervously between her fingers, 'which was, of course, exactly what we were *supposed* to think.'

They got off their cycles in order to trundle them around the dump truck, and that was when the four hardcases – to use Rich's word – opened up from the ditch. They had murdered Rich and Damon and had taken Dayna prisoner. She was the fourth addition to what they sometimes called 'the zoo' and sometimes 'the harem.' One of the others had been the muttering Shirley Hammett, who at that time had still been almost normal, although she had been repeatedly raped, sodomized, and forced to perform fellatio on all four. 'And once,' Dayna said, 'when she couldn't hold on until it was time for one of them to take her into the bushes, Ronnie wiped her ass with a handful of barbed wire. She bled from her rectum for three days.'

'Jesus Christ,' Stu said. 'Which one was he?'

'The man with the shotgun,' Susan Stern said. 'The one I

brained. I wish he was right here, lying on the floor, so I could do it again.'

The man with the sandy beard and sunglasses they had known only as Doc. He and Virge had been part of an army detachment which had been sent to Akron when the flu broke out. Their job had been 'media relations,' which was an army euphemism for 'media suppression.' When that job was pretty well in hand, they had gone on to 'crowd control,' which was an army euphemism for shooting looters who ran and hanging looters who didn't. By the twenty-seventh of June, Doc had told them, the chain of command had a lot more holes than it did links. A good many of their own men were too ill to patrol, but by then it didn't matter anyway, as the citizens of Akron were too weak to read or write the news, let alone loot banks and jewelry stores.

By June 30, the unit was gone – its members dead, dying, or scattered. Doc and Virge were the only two scatterees, as a matter of fact, and that was when they had begun their new lives as zoo-keepers. Garvey had come along on the first of July, and Ronnie on the third. At that point they had closed their peculiar little club to further memberships.

'But after a while you must have outnumbered them,' Glen said.

Unexpectedly, it was Shirley Hammett who spoke to this.

'Pills,' she said, her trapped-mice eyes staring out at them from behind the fringe of her graying bangs. 'Pills every morning to get up, pills every night to go down. Ups and downs.' Her voice had been sinking, and this last was barely audible. She paused, then began to mutter again.

Susan Stern took up the thread of the story. She and one of the dead women, Rachel Carmody, had been picked up on July 17, outside Columbus. By then the party was traveling in a caravan which consisted of two station wagons and the wrecker. The men used the wrecker to move crashed vehicles out of their way or to roadblock the highway, depending on what opportunities offered. Doc kept the pharmacy tied to his belt in an outsized poke. Heavy downers for bedtime; tranks for travel; reds for recess.

'I'd get up in the morning, be raped two or three times, and then wait for Doc to hand out the pills,' Susan said matter-of-factly. 'The daytime pills, I mean. By the third day I had abrasions on my . . . well, you know, my vagina, and any sort of normal intercourse was very painful. I used to hope for Ronnie, because all Ronnie ever wanted was a blowjob. But after the pills, you got very calm. Not sleepy, just calm. Things didn't seem to matter after you got yourself wrapped around a few of those blue pills. All you wanted to do was sit with your hands in your lap and watch the scenery go by or sit with your hands on your lap and watch them use the wrecker to move something out of the way. One day Garvey got mad because this one girl, she couldn't have been any more than twelve, she wouldn't do . . . well, I'm not going to tell you. It was that bad. So Garvey blew her head off. I didn't even care. I was just . . . calm. After a while, you almost stopped thinking about escape. What you wanted more than getting away was those blue pills.'

Dayna and Patty Kroger were nodding.

But they seemed to recognize eight women as their effective limit, Patty said. When they took her on July 22 after murdering the fiftyish man she had been traveling with, they had killed a very old woman who had been a part of 'the zoo' for about a week. When the unnamed girl sitting in the corner had been picked up near Archbold, a sixteen-year-old girl with strabismus had been shot and left in a ditch. 'Doc used to joke about it,' Patty said. 'He'd say, "I don't walk under ladders, I don't cross black cats' paths, and I'm not going to have thirteen people traveling with me."'

On the twenty-ninth, they had caught sight of Stu and the others for the first time. The zoo had been camped in a picnic area just off the interstate when the four of them passed by.

'Garvey was very taken with you,' Susan said, nodding toward Frannie. Frannie shuddered.

Dayna leaned closer to them and spoke softly. 'And they'd made it pretty clear whose place you were going to take.' She nodded her head almost imperceptibly at Shirley Hammett, who was still muttering and eating graham crackers.

'That poor woman,' Frannie said.

'It was Dayna who decided you guys might be our best chance,' Patty said. 'Or maybe our last chance. There were three men in your party – both she and Helen Roget had seen that. Three *armed* men. And Doc had gotten just the teeniest bit over-confident about the trailer-overturned-in-the-road bit. Doc would just act like somebody official, and the men in the parties they met

– when there *were* men – just caved in. And got shot. It had been working like a charm.'

'Dayna asked us to try and palm our pills this morning,' Susan went on. 'They'd gotten sort of careless about making sure we really took them, too, and we knew that this morning they'd be busy pulling that big trailer out into the road and tipping it over. We didn't tell everyone. The only ones in on it were Dayna and Patty and Helen Roget . . . one of the girls Ronnie shot back there. And me, of course. Helen said, "If they catch us trying to spit the pills into our hands, they're going to kill us." And Dayna said they would kill us anyway, sooner or later, and only sooner if we were lucky, and of course we knew that was true. So we did it.'

'I had to hold mine in my mouth for quite a while,' Patty said. 'It was starting to dissolve by the time I got a chance to spit it out.' She looked at Dayna. 'I think Helen actually had to swallow hers. I think that's why she was so slow.'

Dayna nodded. She was looking at Stu with a clear warmth that made Frannie uneasy. 'It still would have worked if you hadn't gotten wise, big fella.'

'I didn't get wise near soon enough, looks like,' Stu said. 'Next time I will.' He stood up, went to the window, and looked out. 'You know, that's half of what scares me,' he said. 'How wise we're all getting.'

Fran cared even less for the sympathetic way Dayna looked after him. She had no right to look sympathetic after all she'd been through. *And she's much prettier than I am, in spite of everything*, Fran thought. *Also, I doubt if she's pregnant.*

'It's a get-wise world, big fella,' Dayna said. 'Get wise or die.'

Stu turned to look at her, really seeing her for the first time, and Fran felt a stab of pure jealous agony. *I waited too long*, she thought. *Oh my God, I went and did it, I went and waited too long.*

She happened to glance at Harold and saw that Harold was smiling in a guarded way, one hand up to his mouth to conceal it. It looked like a smile of relief. She suddenly felt that she would like to stand up, walk casually over to Harold, and hook his eyes out of his head with her fingernails.

Never, Harold! she would scream as she did it. *Never!*

Never?

From Fran Goldsmith's Diary

July 19, 1990

Oh Lord. The worst has happened. At least in the books when it happens it's over, something at least *changes*, but in real life it just seems to go on and on, like a soap opera where nothing ever comes to a head. Maybe I should move to clear things up, take a chance, but I'm so afraid something might happen between them and. You can't end a sentence with 'and,' but I'm afraid to put down what might come after the conjunction.

Let me tell you everything, dear diary, even though it's no great treat to write it down. I even hate to think about it.

Glen and Stu went into town (which happens to be Girard, Ohio, tonight) near dusk to look for some food, hopefully concentrates and freeze-dried stuff. They're easy to carry and some of the concentrates are really tasty, but as far as I am concerned all the freeze-dried food has the same flavor, namely dried turkey turds. And when have you ever had dried turkey turds to serve as your basis for a comparison? Never mind, diary, some things will never be told, ha-ha.

They asked Harold and me if we wanted to come, but I said I'd had enough motorcycling for one day if they could do without me, and Harold said no, he would fetch some water and get it boiled up. Probably already laying his plans. Sorry to make him sound so scheming, but the simple fact is, he is.

[A note here: We are all fantastically sick of boiled water, which tastes flat and TOTALLY DEVOID of oxygen, but both Mark and Glen say the factories, etc., have not been shut down nearly long enough for the streams & rivers to have purified themselves, especially in the industrial Northeast & what they call the Rust Belt, so we all boil to be safe. We all keep hoping we'll find a large supply of bottled mineral water sooner or later, and should have already – so Harold says – but a lot of it seems to have mysteriously disappeared. Stu thinks that a lot of people must have decided it was the tapwater that was making them sick and used up a lot of mineral water before they died.]

Well, Mark and Perion were off somewhere, supposedly hunting for wild berries to supplement our diet, probably doing something else – they are quite modest about it & bully for them, say I – and so I was first gathering wood for a fire and then getting one going for Harold's kettle of water . . . and pretty soon he came back with one (he'd pretty obviously stayed at the stream long enough to have a bath and wash his hair). He hung it on the whatdoyoucallit that goes over the fire. Then he comes & sits down beside me.

We were sitting on a log, talking about one thing and another, when he suddenly put his arms around me and tried to kiss me. I say tried but he actually succeeded, at least at first, because I was so surprised. Then I jerked away from him – looking back it seems sorta comic altho I'm still sore – and fell backward right off the log. It rucked up the back of my blouse and scraped about a yard of skin off. I let out a yell. Talk about history repeating, that was too much like the time with Jess out on the breakwater when I bit my tongue . . . too much like it for comfort.

In a second Harold's on one knee beside me, asking if I'm all right, blushing right down to the roots of his clean hair. Harold tries sometimes to be so icy, so sophisticated – he always seems to me like a jaded young writer constantly searching for that special Sad Café on the West Bank where he can idle the day away talking about Jean-Paul Sartre and drinking cheap plonk – but underneath, well covered, is a teenager with a far less mature set of fantasies. Or so I believe. Saturday matinee fantasies for the most part: Tyrone Power in *Captain from Castile*, Humphrey Bogart in *Dark Passage*, Steve McQueen in *Bullitt*. In times of stress it's always this side of him which seems to come out, maybe because he repressed it so severely as a child, I don't know. Anyway, when he regresses to Bogie, he only succeeds in reminding me of that guy who played Bogie in that Woody Allen movie, *Play It Again, Sam*.

So when he knelt beside me and said, 'Are you all right, baby?,' I started to giggle. Talk about history repeating itself! But it was more than the humor of the situation, you know. If that had been all, I could have held it in. No, it was more in the line of hysterics. The bad dreams, the worrying about the baby, what to do about my feelings for Stu, the traveling every day, the stiffness, the soreness, losing my parents, everything changed for good . . . it came out in giggles at first, then in hysterical laughter I just couldn't stop.

'What's so funny?' Harold asked, getting up. I think it was supposed to come out in this terribly righteous voice, but by then I had stopped thinking about Harold and got this crazy image of Donald Duck in my head. Donald Duck waddling through the ruins of Western civilization quacking angrily: *What's so funny, hah? What's so funny? What's so fucking funny?* I put my hands over my face & just giggled & sobbed & giggled until Harold must have thought I'd gone absolutely crackers.

After a little bit I managed to stop. I wiped the tears off my face and wanted to ask Harold to look at my back and see how badly it was scraped. But I didn't because I was afraid he might take it as a LIBERTY. Life, liberty, and the pursuit of Frannie, oh-ho, that's not so funny.

'Fran,' Harold sez, 'I find this very hard to say.'

'Then maybe you better not say it,' I said.

'I have to,' he answers, and I began to see he wasn't going to take no for an answer unless it was hollered at him. 'Frannie,' he says, 'I love you.'

I guess I knew all along it was just as bald as that. It would be easier if he only wanted to sleep with me. Love's more dangerous than just balling, and I was in a spot. How to say no to Harold? I guess there's only one way, no matter who you have to say it to.

'I don't love you, Harold,' is what I said.

His face cracked all to pieces. 'It's him, isn't it?' he said, and his face got an ugly grimace on it. 'It's Stu Redman, isn't it?'

'I don't know,' I said. Now I have a temper, which I have not always been able to control – a gift from my mother's side, I think. But I have struggled womanfully with it as applies to Harold. I could feel it straining its leash, however.

'I know.' His voice had gotten shrill and self-pitying. 'I know, all right. The day we met him, I knew it then. I didn't want him to come with us, because I *knew*. And he said . . .'

'What did he say?'

'That he didn't want you! That you could be mine!'

'Just like giving you a new pair of shoes, right, Harold?'

He didn't answer, maybe realizing he had gone too far. With a little effort I remembered back to that day in Fabyan. Harold's instant reaction to Stu was the reaction of a dog when a new dog, a strange dog, comes into the first dog's yard. Into his domain. I could almost see the hackles bristling on the back of Harold's neck. I understood that what Stu said, he said it to take us out of the class of dogs and put us back in the class of people. And isn't that what it's really all about? This hellacious struggle we're in now, I mean? If it isn't, why are we even bothering to try and be decent?

'No one owns me, Harold,' I said.

He muttered something.

'What?'

'I said, you may have to change that idea.'

A sharp retort came to mind, but I didn't let it out. Harold's eyes had gone far away, and his face was very still and open. He said: 'I've seen that guy before. You better believe it, Frannie. He's the guy that's the quarterback on the football team but who just sits there in class throwing spitballs and flipping people the bird because he knows the teacher's got to pass him with at least a C so he can keep on playing. He's the guy who goes steady with the prettiest cheerleader and she thinks he's Jesus Christ with a bullet. The guy who farts when the English teacher asks you to read your composition because it's the best one in the class.

'Yeah, I know fuckers like him. Good luck, Fran.'

Then he just walked off. It wasn't the GRAND, TRAMPLING EXIT that he'd meant to make, I feel quite sure. It was more like he'd had some secret dream, and I'd just shot it full of holes – the dream being that things had changed, the reality being that nothing really had. I felt terrible for him, God's truth, because when he walked off he wasn't playing at jaded cynicism but feeling REAL cynicism, not jaded but as sharp & hurtful as a knife-blade. He was whipped. Oh, but what Harold will never see is that his *head* has got to change a little first, he's got to see that the world is going to stay the same as long as *he* does. He stores up rebuffs the way pirates were supposed to store up treasure . . .

Well. Now everyone is back, supper eaten, smokes smoked, Veronal handed out (mine is in my pocket instead of dissolving in my stomach), people settling down. Harold and I have gone through a painful confrontation which has left me with the feeling that nothing has really been resolved, except that he is watching Stu and me to see what happens next. It makes me feel sick and pointlessly angry to write that. What right does he have to watch us? What right does he have to complicate this miserable situation we are in?

Things to Remember: I'm sorry, diary. It must be my state of mind. I can't remember a single thing.

When Frannie came upon him, Stu was sitting on a rock and smoking a cigar. He had scraped a small round circle of bare earth with his boot heel and was using it for an ashtray. He was facing west, where the sun was just going down. The clouds had rifted enough to allow the red sun to poke its head through. Although they had met the four women and taken them into their party only yesterday, it already seemed distant. They had gotten one of the station wagons out of the ditch easily enough and now, with the motorcycles, they made quite a caravan as they moved slowly west on the turnpike.

The smell of his cigar made her think of her father and her father's pipe. What came with the memory was sorrow that had almost mellowed into nostalgia. I'm getting over losing you, Daddy, she thought. I don't think you'd mind.

Stu looked around. 'Frannie,' he said with real pleasure. 'How are you?'

She shrugged. 'Up and around.'

'Want to share my rock and watch the sun go down?'

She joined him, her heartbeat quickening a little. But after all, why else had she come out here? She had known which way he left camp, just as she knew that Harold and Glen and two of the girls had gone into Brighton to look for a CB radio (Glen's idea instead of Harold's for a change). Patty Kroger was back in camp babysitting their two combat-fatigue patients. Shirley Hammett showed some signs of coming out of her daze, but she had awakened them all around one this morning, shrieking in her sleep, her hands clawing at the air in warding-off gestures. The other woman, the one with no name, seemed to be going in the other direction. She sat. She would eat if she was fed. She would perform the functions of elimination. She would not answer questions. She only really came alive in her sleep. Even with a heavy dose of Veronal, she often moaned and sometimes shrieked. Frannie thought she knew what the poor woman was dreaming of.

'It seems like a long way still to go, doesn't it?' she said.

He didn't answer for a moment, and then he said: 'It's further than we thought. That old woman, she's not in Nebraska anymore.'

'I know –' she began, and then bit down on her words.

He glanced at her with a faint grin. 'You've been skippin your medication, ma'am.'

'My secret's out,' she said with a lame smile.

'We're not the only ones,' Stu said. 'I was talkin to Dayna this afternoon' (she felt that interior dig of jealousy – and fear – at the familiar way he used her name) 'and she said neither she nor Susan wanted to take it.'

Fran nodded. 'Why did you stop? Did they drug you . . . in that place?'

He tapped ashes into his bare earth ashtray. 'Mild sedatives at night, that was all. They didn't need to drug me. I was locked up nice and tight. No, I stopped three nights ago because I felt . . . out of touch.' He meditated for a moment and then expanded. 'Glen and Harold going to get that CB radio, that was a real good idea. What's a two-way for? To put you in touch. This buddy of mine back in Arnette, Tony Leominster, he had one in his Scout. Great gadget. You could talk to folks, or you could holler for help if you got in a jam of trouble. These dreams, they're almost like having a CB in your head, except the transmit seems to be broken and we're only receiving.'

'Maybe we *are* transmitting,' Fran said quietly.

He looked at her, startled.

They sat quiet for a while. The sun peered through the clouds, as if to say a quick goodbye before sinking below the horizon. Fran could understand why primitive people worshiped it. As the gigantic quiet of the nearly empty country accumulated on her day by day, imprinting its truth on her brain by its very weight, the sun – the moon, too, for that matter – began to seem bigger and more important. More personal. Those bright skyships began to look to you as they had when you were a child.

'Anyway, I stopped,' Stu said. 'Last night I dreamed about that black man again. It was the worst yet. He's setting up somewhere

out in the desert. Las Vegas, I think. And Frannie . . . I think he's
crucifying people. The ones who give him trouble.'

'He's doing *what?*'

'That's what I dreamed. Lines of crosses along Highway 15
made out of barn-beams and telephone poles. People hanging off
them.'

'Just a dream,' she said uneasily.

'Maybe.' He smoked and looked west at the red-tinged clouds.
'But the other two nights, just before we run on those maniacs holding
the women, I dreamed about her – the woman who calls herself
Mother Abagail. She was sitting in the cab of an old pickup truck
parked on the shoulder of Highway 76. I was standing on the ground
with one arm leaning on the window, talking to her just as natural as
I'm talking to you. And she says, "You got to move em along faster
still, Stuart; if an old lady like me can do it, a big tough fella from
Texas like you should be able to.'" Stu laughed, threw down his cigar,
and crushed it under his heel. In kind of an absent way, as if not
knowing what he was doing, he put an arm around Frannie's shoulders.

'They're going to Colorado,' she said.

'Why, yes, I think they are.'

'Has . . . has either Dayna or Susan dreamed of her?'

'Both. And last night Susan dreamed of the crosses. Just like I
did.'

'There's a lot of people with that old woman now.'

Stu agreed. 'Twenty, maybe more. You know, we're passing
people nearly every day. They just hunker down and wait for us to
go by. They're scared of us, but her . . . they'll come to her, I guess.
In their own good time.'

'Or to the other one,' Frannie said.

Stu nodded. 'Yeah, or to him. Fran, why did you stop taking
the Veronal?'

She uttered a trembling sigh and wondered if she should tell
him. She wanted to, but she was afraid of what his reaction might
be.

'There's no counting on what a woman will do,' she said at
last.

'No,' he agreed. 'But there are ways to find out what they're
thinking, maybe.'

'What –' she began, and he stopped her mouth with a kiss.

*   *   *

They lay on the grass in the last of the twilight. Flagrant red had given way to cooler purple as they made love, and now Frannie could see stars shining through the last of the clouds. It would be good riding weather tomorrow. With any luck they would be able to get most of the way across Indiana.

Stu slapped lazily at a mosquito hovering over his chest. His shirt was hung on a nearby bush. Fran's shirt was on but unbuttoned. Her breasts pushed at the cloth and she thought, *I'm getting bigger, just a little right now, but it's noticeable . . . at least to me.*

'I've wanted you for a pretty long time now,' Stu said without looking directly at her. 'I guess you know that.'

'I wanted to avoid trouble with Harold,' she said. 'And there's something else that —'

'Harold's got a ways to go,' Stu said, 'but he's got the makings of a fine man somewhere inside him if he'll toughen up. You like him, don't you?'

'That's not the right word. There isn't a word in English for how I feel about Harold.'

'How do you feel about me?' he asked.

She looked at him and found she couldn't say she loved him, couldn't say it right out, although she wanted to.

'No,' he said, as if she'd contradicted him, 'I just like to get things straight. I guess you'd just as soon not have Harold know anything about this yet. Isn't that right?'

'Yes,' she said gratefully.

'It's just as well. If we lie low, it may take care of itself. I've seen him lookin at Patty. She's about his age.'

'I don't know . . .'

'You feel a debt of gratitude to him, don't you?'

'I suppose so. We were the only two left in Ogunquit, and —'

'That was luck, no more, Frannie. You don't want to let anyone put you in a headhold over something that was pure luck.'

'I suppose.'

'I guess I love you,' he said. 'That's not so easy for me to say.'

'I guess I love you, too. But there's something else . . .'

'I knew that.'

'You asked me why I stopped taking the pills.' She plucked at her shirt, not daring to look at him. Her lips felt unnaturally dry. 'I thought they might be bad for the baby,' she whispered.

'For the.' He stopped. Then he grasped her and turned her to face him. 'You're *pregnant*?'

She nodded.

'And you didn't tell anyone?'

'No.'

'Harold. Does Harold know?'

'No one but you.'

'God-almighty-damn,' he said. He was peering into her face in a concentrated way that scared her. She had imagined one of two things: he would leave her immediately (as Jess undoubtedly would have done if he had discovered she was pregnant with another man's child) or he would hug her, tell her not to worry, that he would take care of everything. She had never expected this startled, close scrutiny, and she found herself remembering the night she had told her father in the garden. His look had been very much like this one. She wished she had told Stu what her situation was before they had made love. Maybe then they wouldn't have made love at all, but at least he wouldn't have been able to feel he had somehow been taken advantage of, that she was . . . what was the old phrase? Damaged goods. Was he thinking that? She simply could not tell.

'Stu?' she said in a frightened voice.

'You didn't tell anyone,' he repeated.

'I didn't know how.' Her tears were close to the surface now.

'When are you due?'

'January,' she said, and the tears came.

He held her and made her know it was all right without saying anything. He didn't tell her not to worry or that he would take care of everything, but he made love to her again and she thought that she had never been so happy.

Neither of them saw Harold, as shadowy and as silent as the dark man himself, standing in the bushes and looking at them. Neither of them knew that his eyes squinted down into small, deadly triangles as Fran cried out her pleasure at the end of it, as her good orgasm burst through her.

By the time they had finished, it was full dark.

Harold slipped away silently.

From Fran Goldsmith's Diary

August 1, 1990

No entry last night, too excited, too happy. Stu and I are together.

He has agreed that I'd better keep the secret of my Lone Ranger as long as possible, hopefully until we are settled. If it's to be Colorado, that's okay with me. The way I feel tonight, the mountains of the moon would be okay with me. Do I sound like a dizzy schoolgirl? Well – if a lady can't sound like a dizzy schoolgirl in her diary, where *can* she sound like one?

But I must say one other thing before I drop the subject of the Lone Ranger. It has to do with my 'maternal instinct.' *Is* there such a thing? I think yes. Probably hormonal. I have not felt my old self for some weeks now, but it's very hard to separate the changes caused by my pregnancy from the changes caused by the terrible disaster which has overtaken the world. But there IS a certain jealous feeling ('jealousy' isn't really the right word, but it's the closest I can seem to come to the right word tonight), a feeling that you have moved a little closer to the center of the universe and must protect your position there. That's why the Veronal seems a greater risk than the bad dreams, although my rational mind believes that Veronal would not hurt the baby at all – not, at least, at the low levels the others have been maintaining. And I suppose that jealous feeling is also a part of the love I feel for Stu Redman. I feel I am loving, as well as eating, for two.

Otherwise, I must be quick. I need my sleep, no matter what dreams may come. We haven't made it all the way across Indiana as quickly as we had hoped – a horrible clog of vehicles near the Elkhart interchange slowed us down. A good many of the vehicles were army. There were dead soldiers. Glen, Susan Stern, Dayna, and Stu took as much firepower as they could find – about 2 dozen rifles, some grenades, and – yes, folks, it's true – a rocket launcher. As I write now, Harold and Stu are trying to figure out the rocket launcher, for which there are 17 or 18 rockets. Please God they don't blow themselves up.

Speaking of Harold, I must tell you, dear diary, that he doesn't SUSPECT A THING (sounds like a line from an old Bette Davis movie, doesn't it). When we catch up with Mother Abigail's party I suppose he will have to be told; it would not be fair to hide it any longer, come what may.

But today he was brighter & more cheerful than I have ever seen him. He grinned so much I thought his face would crack! He was the one who suggested Stu help him with that dangerous rocket launcher, and

But here they come back now. Will finish later.

Frannie slept heavily and dreamlessly. So did they all, with the exception of Harold Lauder. Sometime shortly after midnight he rose and walked softly to where Frannie lay, and stood looking down at her. He was not smiling now, although he had smiled all day. At times he had felt that the smile would crack his face right up the middle and spill out his whirling brains. That might have been a relief.

He stood looking down at her, listening to the chirr of summer crickets. *We're in dog days now*, he thought. Dog days, from July the twenty-fifth to August twenty-eighth, according to Webster's. So named because rabid dogs were supposed to be the most common then. He looked down at Fran, sleeping so sweetly, using her sweater for a pillow. Her pack was beside her.

Every dog has his day, Frannie.

He knelt, freezing at the gunshots of his bending knees, but no one stirred. He unbuckled her pack, untied the drawstring, and reached inside. He trained a small pencil flash on the pack's contents. Frannie muttered from deep down in sleep, stirred, and Harold held his breath. He found what he wanted way at the bottom, behind three clean blouses and a lap-eared pocket road atlas. A Spiral notebook. He pulled it out, opened to the first page, and shone his light on Frannie's close but extremely legible handwriting.

July 6, 1990 – After some persuasion, Mr Bateman has agreed to come along with us . . .

Harold shut the book and crept back to his sleeping bag with it. He was feeling like the little boy he had once been, the boy with few friends (he had enjoyed a brief period of babyhood beauty until about age three, had been a fat and ugly joke ever since) but many enemies, the boy who had been more or less taken for granted by his parents – their eyes had been trained on Amy as she began her long walk down the Miss America/Atlantic City runway of her life – the boy who had turned to books for solace, the boy who had escaped never being picked for baseball or always being passed over for School Patrol Boy by becoming Long John Silver or Tarzan or Philip Kent . . . the boy who had become these people late at night under his covers with a flashlight trained on the printed page, his eyes wide with excitement, barely smelling his own bedfarts; this boy now crawled upside down to the bottom of his sleeping bag with Frannie's diary and his flashlight.

As he trained its beam on the front cover of the Spiral, there was a moment of sanity. For just a moment part of his mind cried out *Harold! Stop!* so strongly that he was shaken to his heels. And stop he almost did. For just a moment it seemed *possible* to stop, to put the diary back where he had found it, to give her up, to let them go their own way before something terrible and irrevocable happened. For that moment it seemed he could put the bitter drink away, pour it out of the cup, and refill it with whatever there was for him in this world. *Give it over, Harold*, this sane voice begged, but maybe it was already too late.

At age sixteen he had given up Burroughs and Stevenson and Robert Howard in favor of other fantasies, fantasies that were both well loved and much hated – not of rockets or pirates but of girls in silk see-through pajamas kneeling before him on satin pillows while Harold the Great lolled naked on his throne, ready to chastise them with small leather whips, with silver-headed canes. They were bitter fantasies through which every pretty girl at Ogunquit High School had strolled at one time or another. These daydreams always ended with a gathering expletive in his loins, an explosion of seminal fluid that was more curse than pleasure. And then he would sleep, the sperm drying to a scale on his belly. Every doggy has his day.

And now it was those bitter fantasies, the old hurts, that he gathered around him like yellowed sheets, the old friends who never died, whose teeth never dulled, whose deadly affection never wavered.

He turned to that first page, trained his flashlight on the words, and began to read.

In the hour before dawn, he replaced the diary in Fran's pack and secured the buckles. He took no special precautions. If she woke, he thought coldly, he would kill her and then run. Run where? West. But he would not stop in Nebraska or even in Colorado, oh no.

She didn't wake.

He went back to his sleeping bag. He masturbated bitterly. When sleep came, it was thin. He dreamed he was dying halfway down a steep grade of tumbled rocks and moonscape boulders. High above, riding the night thermals, were cruising buzzards, waiting for him to make them a meal. There was no moon, no stars –

And then a frightful red Eye opened in the dark: vulpine, eldritch. The Eye terrified him yet held him.

The Eye beckoned him.

To the west, where the shadows were even now gathering, in their twilight dance of death.

When they made camp at sundown that evening, they were west of Joliet, Illinois. There was a case of beer, good talk, laughter. They felt they had put the rain behind them with Indiana. Everyone remarked specially on Harold, who had never been so cheerful.

'You know, Harold,' Frannie said later that evening, as the party began to break up, 'I don't think I've ever seen you feeling so good. What is it?'

He gave her a jolly wink. 'Every dog has his day, Fran.'

She smiled back at him, a little puzzled. But she supposed it was just Harold, being elliptical. It didn't matter. What mattered was that things were finally coming right.

That night Harold began his own journal.

CHAPTER 48

He came staggering and flapping up a long upgrade, the heat of the sun stewing his stomach and baking his brains. The Interstate shimmered with reflected radiant heat. He had been Donald Merwin Elbert once, now he was Trashcan Man forever and ever, and he beheld the fabled City, Seven-in-One, Cibola.

How long had he been traveling west? How long since The Kid? God might know; Trashcan Man did not. It had been days. Nights. Oh, he remembered the nights!

He stood, swaying in his rags, looking down at Cibola, the City that is Promised, the City of Dreams. He was a wreck. The wrist that he had broken when he leaped the railing of the stairway bolted to the Cheery Oil tank had not healed right, and that wrist was a grotesque lump wrapped in a dirty, unraveling Ace bandage. All the bones in the fingers of that hand had pulled up somehow, turning the hand into a Quasimodo claw. His left arm was a slowly healing mass of burn tissue from elbow to shoulder. It no longer smelled bad and suppurated, but the new flesh was hairless and pink, like the skin of a cheap doll. His grinning, mad face was sunburned, peeling, scruffy-bearded, and covered with scabs from the header he had taken when the front wheel of his bike had parted company from the frame. He wore a faded blue J. C. Penney workshirt that was marked with expanding rings of sweatstain and a dirty pair of corduroy trousers. His pack, which had been new not so long ago, had now taken on the style and substance of its owner – one strap had broken. Trash had knotted it as best he could, and the pack now hung askew on his back like a shutter on a haunted house. It was dusty, its creases filled with desert sand. On his feet were Keds now bound together with hanks of twine, and from them his scratched and sand-chafed ankles rose innocent of socks.

He stared at the city far ahead and below. He turned his face up to the savage gunmetal sky and to the sun that blared down, coating him with furnace heat. He screamed. It was a savage, triumphant scream, very much like the one Susan Stern had uttered when she split Roger Rabbit's skull with the butt of his own shotgun.

He began to do a shuffling, victorious dance on the hot, shimmering surface of Interstate 15 while the desert sirocco blew sand across the highway and the blue peaks of the Pahranagat and Spotted ranges sawed their teeth indifferently at the brilliant sky as they had done for millennia. Off the other side of the highway, a Lincoln Continental and a T-Bird were now almost buried in sand, their occupants mummified behind safety glass. Up ahead on Trashcan's side was an overturned pickup, everything covered but the wheels and the rocker panels.

He danced. His feet, clad in the lashed and bulging Keds, bumped up and down on the highway in a drunken sort of hornpipe. The tattered tail of his shirt flapped. His canteen clunked against his pack. The unraveling ends of the Ace bandage fluttered in the hot breath of the wind. Pink, smooth burn tissue gleamed rawly. Clocksprings of veins bulged at his temples. He had been in God's frying pan for a week now, moving southwest across Utah, the tip of Arizona, and then into Nevada, and he was just as mad as a hatter.

As he danced, he sang monotonously, the same words over and over, to a tune that had been popular when he was in the Terre Haute institution, a song called 'Down to the Nightclub' that had been done by a black group called Tower of Power. But the words were his own. He sang:

'Ci-a-bola, Ci-a-bola, bump-ty, bump-ty, *bump!* Ci-a-bola, Ci-a-bola, bump-ty, bump-ty, *bump!*' Each final '*bump!*' was followed by a little skipping leap until the heat made everything swim and the harsh bright sky went twilight gray and he collapsed on the road, half fainting, his taxed heart thundering crazily in his arid chest. With the last of his strength, blubbering and grinning, he pulled himself over the overturned pickup truck and lay in its diminishing shade, shivering in the heat and panting.

'Cibola!' He croaked. 'Bumpty-bumpty-*bump!*'

He fumbled his canteen off his shoulder with his claw hand and shook it. The canteen was nearly empty. Didn't matter. He would drink every single drop and lay up here until the sun went down, and then he would walk down the highway and into Cibola, fabled City, Seven-in-One. Tonight he would drink from ever-springing fountains faced in gold. But not until the killer sun went down. God was the greatest firebug of them all. A long time ago a boy named Donald Merwin Elbert had burned up old lady Semple's pension check. That same boy had torched the Methodist Church in Powtanville, and if there had been anything left of Donald Merwin Elbert in this shell, it had surely been cremated with the oiltanks in Gary, Indiana. Over nine dozen of them, and they had gone up like a walloping string of firecrackers. Just in time for the Fourth of July, too. Nice. And in the wake of that conflagration, only the Trashcan Man had been left, his left arm a cracked and boiling stew, a fire inside his body that was never going to go out . . . at least not until his body was so much blackened charcoal.

And tonight he would drink the water of Cibola, yes, and it would taste like wine.

He upended the canteen and his throat worked as the last of his water, pisswarm, gurgled down into his belly. When it was gone, he threw the canteen out into the desert. Sweat had broken on his forehead like dew. He lay shivering deliciously with water cramps.

'Cibola!' he muttered. 'Cibola! I'm coming! I'm coming! I'll do whatever you want! My life for you! Bumpty-bumpty-*bump!*'

Drowsiness began to steal over him now that his thirst was a little slaked. He was nearly asleep when a polar thought slipped up through the floor of his mind like an icy stiletto blade:

What if Cibola had been a mirage?

'No,' he muttered. 'No, uh-uh, no.'

But simple denial would not drive the thought off. The blade probed and poked, keeping sleep at arm's length. What if he had drunk the last of his water in celebration of a mirage? In his own way he recognized his madness, and that was the sort of thing mad people did, right enough. If it had been a mirage, he would die here in the desert and the buzzards would dine on him.

At last, unable to bear the hideous possibility any longer, he staggered to his feet and made his way back to the road, fighting off the waves of faintness and nausea that wanted to take him down. At the breast of the hill he stared out anxiously into the long flat plain below, studded with yucca and tumbleweed and devil's mantilla. His breath caught in his throat and unraveled into a sigh, like a sleeve of fabric on a spike.

It was there!

Cibola, fabled of old, searched for by many, found by the Trashcan Man!

Far down in the desert, surrounded by blue mountains, blue itself in the haze of distance, its towers and avenues gleamed in the desert day. There were palm trees . . . he could see palm trees . . . and movement . . . and *water*!

'Oh, Cibola . . .' he crooned, and staggered back to the shade of the pickup. It was farther than it looked, he knew that. Tonight, after God's torch had left the sky, he would walk as he never had before. He would reach Cibola and his first act would be to plunge headlong into the first fountain he came to. Then he would find *him*, the man who had bade him come here. The man who had drawn him across the plains and the mountains and finally into the desert, all in a month's time and despite his horribly burned arm.

He who *Is* – the dark man, the hardcase. He waited for Trashcan Man in Cibola, and *his* were the armies of the night, *his* were the white-faced riders of the dead who would sweep out of the west and into the very face of the rising sun. They would come raving and grinning and stinking of sweat and gunpowder. There would be shrieks, and Trashcan cared very little for shrieks, there would be rape and subjugation, things about which he cared even less, there would be murder, which was immaterial –

– and there would be a Great Burning.

About that he cared very much. In the dreams the dark man came to him and spread out his arms from a high place and showed Trashcan a country in flames. Cities going up like bombs. Cultivated fields drawn in lines of fire. The very rivers of Chicago and Pittsburgh and Detroit and Birmingham ablaze with floating oil. And the dark man had told him a very simple thing in his dreams, a thing which had brought him running: *I will set you high in my artillery. You are the man I want.*

He rolled on his side, his cheeks and eyelids chafed and irritated from the blowing sand. He had been losing hope – yes, ever since the wheel had fallen off his bike he had been losing hope. God, the God of father-killing sheriffs, the God of Carley Yates, was stronger than the dark man after all, it seemed. Yet he had kept his faith and had kept on. And at last, when it seemed he was going to burn up in this desert before he ever got to Cibola where the dark man waited, he had seen it far below, dreaming in the sun.

'Cibola!' he whispered, and slept.

*　　*　　*

The first dream had come to him in Gary, over a month ago, after he had burned his arm. He had gone to sleep that night sure that he was going to die; no one could be burned as badly as he was and live. A refrain had beaten its way into his head: *Live by the torch, die by the torch. Live by it, die by it.*

His legs had given out in a small city park and he had fallen down, his left arm sprawled out and away from him like a dead thing, the shirtsleeve smoked off. The pain was giant, incredible. He had never dreamed there could be such pain in the world. He had been running gleefully from one set of oil tanks to the next, setting up crude timing devices, each constructed of a steel pipe and a flammable paraffin mixture separated from a little pool of acid by a steel tab. He had been pushing these devices into the outflow pipes on top of the tanks. When the acid ate through the steel the paraffin would ignite, and that would cause the tanks to blow. He had planned to get over to the west side of Gary, near the confusion of interchanges leading various roads toward Chicago or Milwaukee, before any of them blew. He wanted to watch the show as the entire dirty city went up in a firestorm.

But he had misjudged the last device or constructed it badly. It had gone off while he worked at opening the cap on the outflow with a pipewrench. There had been a blinding white flare as burning paraffin belched out of the tube, coating his left arm with fire. This was no painless flameglove of lighter fluid, to be waved in the air and then shaken out like a big match. This was agony, like having your arm in a volcano.

Shrieking, he had run wildly around the top of the oiltank, careering off the waist-high railings like a human pinball. If the railings had not been there, he would have plunged over the side and fallen, turning over and over, like a torch dropped down a well. Only accident saved his life; his feet tangled in each other and he fell with his left arm pinned under him, smothering the flames.

He sat up, still half-crazy with the pain. Later he would think that only blind luck – or the dark man's purpose – had saved him from being burned to death. Most of the paraffin jet had missed him. So he was thankful – but his thankfulness only came later. At the time he could only cry out and rock back and forth, holding his crisped arm out from his body as the skin smoked and crackled and contracted.

Vaguely, as the light faded from the sky, it occurred to him that he had already set a dozen of the time devices. They might go anytime. Dying and being out of his exquisite misery would be wonderful; dying in flames would be utter horror.

Somehow he had crawled down from the tank and had staggered away, weaving and lunging in and out of the dead traffic, holding his barbecued left arm away from his body.

By the time he reached a small park near the center of town, it was sunset. He sat on the grass between two shuffleboard courts, trying to think what you did for burns. Put butter on them, that's what Donald Merwin Elbert's mother would have said. But that was for a scald, or when the bacon fat jumped extra high and spattered you with hot grease. He couldn't imagine putting butter on the cracked and blackened mess between his elbow and shoulder; couldn't even imagine touching it.

Kill himself. That was it, that was the ticket. He would put himself out of his misery like an old dog –

There was a sudden gigantic explosion on the east side of town, as if the fabric of existence had been torn briskly in two. A liquid pillar of fire shot up against dusk's deepening indigo. He had to squeeze his eyes to watering, protesting slits against it.

Even in his agony, the fire pleased him . . . more, it delighted, fulfilled him. The fire was the best medicine, even better than the morphine he found the next day (as a trusty in prison he had worked in the infirmary as well as the library and the motorpool, and he knew about morphine and Elavil and Darvon Complex). He did not connect his present agony to the pillar of fire. He only knew that the fire was good, the fire was beautiful, the fire was something he needed and would always need. Wonderful fire!

Moments later a second oiltank exploded and even here, three miles away, he could feel the warm push of expanding air. Another tank went, and another. A slight pause, and then six of them went up in a rattling string and now it was too bright over there to look at but he looked anyway, grinning, his eyes full of yellow flames, his wounded arm forgotten, thoughts of suicide forgotten.

It took better than two hours for all of them to go up, and by then dark had fallen but it wasn't dark, the night was yellow and orange and feverish with flames. The entire eastern arc of the horizon danced with fire. It reminded him of a Classic funnybook he had owned as a child, an adaptation of H. G. Wells's *The War of the Worlds*. Now, years later, the boy who had owned that funnybook was gone, but the Trashcan Man was here, and Trash owned the wonderful, terrible secret of the Martians' deathray.

It was time to leave the park. Already the temperature had risen ten degrees. He ought to go west, stay ahead of the fire the way he had in Powtanville, racing the expanding arc of destruction. But he was in no condition to race. And so he fell asleep on the grass, and the firelight played over the face of a tired, ill-used child.

In his dream, the dark man came in his hooded robe, his face invisible . . . yet the Trashcan Man thought he had seen this man before. When the loungers in the candy store and the beer parlor back in Powtanville catcalled at him, it seemed that this man had been among them, silent and thoughtful. When he had worked at the Scrubba-Dubba (soap the headlights, knock the wipers, soap the rocker panels, hey mister you want hotwax on that?), wearing the sponge glove on his right hand until the hand beneath looked like a pale dead fish, the nails as white as fresh ivory, it seemed he had seen this man's face, fiery and grinning with lunatic joy from beneath the rippling film of water rolling down the windshield. When the sheriff had sent him away to the nuthatch in Terre Haute, he had been the grinning psych aide standing above his head in the room where they gave you the shocks, his hands on the controls (*I'm gonna fry your brains out, boy, help you on your way as you change from Donald Merwin Elbert into the Trashcan Man, would you like hotwax on that?*), ready to send about a thousand volts zizzing into his brain. He knew this dark man all right, his was the face you could never quite see, his the hands which dealt all spades from a dead deck, his the eyes beyond the flames, his the grin from beyond the grave of the world.

'I'll do whatever you want,' he said gratefully in the dream. 'My life for you!'

The dark man had lifted his arms inside his robe, turning the robe into the shape of a black kite. They stood on a high place, and below them, America lay in flames.

I will set you high in my artillery. You are the man I want.

Then he saw an army of ten thousand raggle-taggle castoff men and women driving east, driving across the desert and into the mountains, a rough beast of an army whose time had come round at last; they loaded down trucks and jeeps and Wagoneers and campers and tanks; each man and woman wore a dark stone about his or her neck, and deep in some of those stones was a red shape that might have been an Eye or might have been a Key. And riding in their van, atop a giant tanker with pillow tires, he saw himself, and knew that the truck was filled with jellied napalm . . . and behind him, in column, were trucks loaded with pressure bombs and Teller mines and plastic explosive; flame throwers and flares and heat-seeking missiles; grenades and machine guns and rocket launchers. The dance of death was about to begin, and already the strings of the fiddles and guitars were smoking and the stench of brimstone and cordite filled the air.

The dark man lifted his arms again and when he dropped them everything was cold and silent, the fires gone, even the ashes cold, and for just a moment he was only Donald Merwin Elbert again, small and afraid and confused. For just that moment he suspected he was just another pawn in the dark man's huge chess game, that he had been deceived.

Then he saw the dark man's face was no longer entirely hidden; two dark red coals burned in the sunken pits where his eyes should have been, and illuminated a nose as narrow as a blade.

'I'll do whatever you want,' Trash said gratefully in the dream. 'My life for you! My soul for you!'

'I will set you to burn,' the dark man said gravely. 'You must come to my city and there all will be made clear.'

'Where? Where?' He was in an agony of hope and expectation.

'West,' the dark man said, fading. 'West. Beyond the mountains.'

He woke up then, and it was still night and still bright. The flames were closer. The heat was stifling. Houses were exploding. The stars were gone, shrouded in a thick pall of oilsmoke. A fine rain of soot had begun. The shuffleboard courts were dusted with black snow.

Now that he had a purpose, he found he could walk. He limped west, and from time to time he saw a few others leaving Gary, looking back over their shoulders at the conflagration. Fools, Trash thought, almost affectionately. You'll burn. In good time, you'll burn. They took no notice of him; to them, the Trashcan Man was only another survivor. They disappeared into the smoke and sometime after dawn Trashcan Man limped across the Illinois state line. Chicago was north of him, Joliet to the southwest, the fire lost in its own horizon-blotting smoke behind. That had been the dawn of July 2.

He had forgotten his dreams of burning Chicago to the

ground – his dreams of more oiltanks and freightcars full of LP gas tucked away on railroad sidings and the tinder-dry tenements. He didn't care a fig for the Windy City. That afternoon he broke into a Chicago Heights doctor's office and stole a case of morphine syrettes. The morphine drove back the pain a little, but it had a more important side-effect: it made him care less about the pain he *did* feel.

He took a huge jar of Vaseline from a drugstore that night and packed the burned part of his arm in an inch of the jelly. He was very thirsty; it seemed he wanted to drink all of the time. Fantasies of the dark man buzzed in and out of his mind like blowflies. When he collapsed at dusk, he had already begun to think that the city the dark man was directing him to must be Cibola, Seven-in-One, the City that is Promised.

That night the dark man came to him again in his dreams, and with a sardonic giggle confirmed that this was so.

Trashcan Man awoke from these confused dream-memories of what had been to shivering desert cold. In the desert it was always ice or fire; there was no in-between.

Moaning a little, he stood up, holding himself as close to himself as he could. Overhead a trillion stars gleamed, seeming almost close enough to touch, bathing the desert in their cold witchlight.

He walked back to the road, wincing at his chafed and tender skin, and his many aches and pains. They were little to him now. He paused for a moment looking down at the city, dreaming in the night (there were little sparks of light here and there, like electric campfires). Then he began to walk.

When dawn began to color the sky hours later, Cibola seemed almost as distant as it had when he first came over the rise and saw it. And he had foolishly drunk all of his water, forgetting how magnified things looked out here. He didn't dare walk for long after sunrise because of the dehydration. He would have to lie up again before the sun rose in all its power.

An hour past dawn he came to a Mercedes-Benz off the road, its right side drifted in sand up to the door panels. He opened one of the left side doors and pulled the two wrinkled, monkeylike occupants out – an old woman wearing a lot of bangled jewelry, an old man with theatrical-looking white hair. Muttering, Trash took the keys from the ignition, went around, and opened the trunk. Their suitcases were not locked. He hung a variety of clothes over the windows of the Mercedes, weighting them down with rocks. Now he had a cool, dim cave.

He crawled in and went to sleep. Miles to the west, the city of Las Vegas gleamed in the light of the summer sun.

He couldn't drive a car, they had never taught him that in prison, but he could ride a bike. On July 4, the day that Larry Underwood discovered Rita Blakemoor had overdosed and died in her sleep, Trashcan Man took a ten-speed and began to ride. At first his progress was slow, because his left arm wasn't much good to him. He fell off twice that first day, once squarely on his burn, causing terrible agony. By then the burn was suppurating freely through the Vaseline and the smell was terrific. He wondered from time to time about gangrene but would not allow himself to wonder for long. He began to mix the Vaseline with an antiseptic ointment, not knowing if it would help, but feeling it certainly couldn't hurt any. It made a milky, viscous gloop that looked like semen.

Little by little he adjusted to riding the bike mostly one-handed and found that he could make good speed. The land had flattened out and most of the time he could keep the bike speeding giddily along. He drove himself steadily in spite of the burn and the light-headedness that came from being constantly stoned on morphine. He drank gallons of water and ate prodigiously. He pondered the dark man's words: *I will set you high in my artillery. You are the man I want.* How lovely those words were – had anyone really wanted him before? The words played over and over in his mind as he pedaled under the hot Midwestern sun. And he began to hum the melody of a little tune called 'Down to the Nightclub' under his breath. The words ('Ci-a-bola! Bumpty-bumpty-*bump!*') came in their own good time. He was not then as insane as he was to become, but he was advancing.

On July 8, the day Nick Andros and Tom Cullen saw buffalo grazing in Comanche County, Kansas, Trashcan Man crossed the Mississippi at the Quad Cities of Davenport, Rock Island, Bettendorf, and Moline. He was in Iowa.

On the fourteenth, the day Larry Underwood woke up near the big white house in eastern New Hampshire, Trashy crossed the Missouri north of Council Bluffs and entered Nebraska. He had regained some use of his left hand, his leg muscles had toned up, and he pressed on, feeling a huge need to hurry, hurry.

It was on the west side of the Missouri that Trash first suspected that God Himself might intervene between Trashcan Man and his destiny. There was something wrong about Nebraska, something dreadfully wrong. Something that made him afraid. It looked about the same as Iowa . . . but it wasn't. The dark man had come to him every previous night in dreams, but when Trashy crossed into Nebraska, the dark man came no more.

Instead, he began to dream about an old woman. In these dreams he would find himself belly-down in a cornfield, almost paralyzed with hate and fear. It was bright morning. He could hear flocks of crows cawing. In front of him was a screen of broad, sword-like corn-leaves. Not wanting to, but powerless to stop himself, he would spread the leaves with a shaking hand and peer between them. He saw an old house in the middle of a clearing. The house was up on blocks or jacks or something. There was an apple tree with a tire swing hanging from one of the branches. And sitting on the porch was an old black woman playing a guitar and singing some old-time spiritual song. The song varied from dream to dream and Trashcan knew most of them because he had once known a woman, the mother of a boy named Donald Merwin Elbert, who had sung many of the same songs as she did her housework.

This dream was a nightmare, but not just because something exceedingly horrible happened at the end of it. At first you would have said there wasn't a frightening element in the whole dream. Corn? Blue sky? Old woman? Tire swing? What could be frightening about those things? Old women didn't throw rocks and jeer, especially not old women that sang old-home Jesus-jumping songs like 'In That Great Getting-Up Morning' and 'Bye-and-Bye, Sweet Lord, Bye-and-Bye.' It was the Carley Yateses of the world who threw rocks.

But long before the dream ended he was paralyzed with fear, as if it wasn't an old woman at all he was peeking at but at some secret, some barely concealed light that seemed ready to break out all around her, to play over her with a fiery brilliance that would make the flaming oiltanks of Gary seem like so many candles in the wind − a light so bright it would chalk his eyes to cinders. And during this part of the dream all he thought was: *Oh please get me*

*away from her, I don't want no part of that old biddy, please oh please get
me out of Nebraska!*

Then whatever song she had been playing would come to a
discordant, jangling stop. She would look right at the place where
he was peeping through a tiny loophole in the broad lattice of leaves.
Her face was old and seamed with wrinkles, her hair was thin enough
to show her brown skull, but her eyes were bright as diamonds, full
of the light he feared.

In an old, cracked, but strong voice she would cry out: *Weasels
in the corn!* and he would feel the change in himself and would look
down to see he had become a weasel, a furry, brownish-black slinking
thing, his nose grown long and sharp, his eyes melted down to beady
black points, his fingers turned into claws. He was a weasel, a cowardly
nocturnal thing preying on the weak and the small.

He would begin to scream then, and eventually he would
scream himself awake, streaming with sweat and buggy-eyed. His
hands would fly over his body, reassuring himself that all his human
parts were still there. At the end of this panicky check he would
grip his head, making sure it was still a *human* head and not something long and sleek and streamlined, furry and bullet-shaped.

He crossed four hundred miles of Nebraska in three days,
running mostly on high octane terror. He crossed into Colorado near
Julesburg, and the dream began to fade and grow sepia-toned.

(For Mother Abagail's part, she woke on the night of July 15
– shortly after Trashcan Man had passed north of Hemingford Home
– with a terrible chill and a feeling that was both fear and pity; pity
for whom or for what she did not know. She thought she might
have been dreaming of her grandson Anders, who had been killed
senselessly in a hunting accident when he was but six.)

On July 18, then southwest of Sterling, Colorado, and still
some miles from Brush, he had met The Kid.

Trash woke up just as twilight was falling. In spite of the clothes
he had hung over the windows, the Mercedes had gotten hot. His
throat was a dry well which had been faced with sandpaper. His
temples thumped and jumped. He ran his tongue out, and when
he stroked it with his finger, it felt like a dead treebranch. Sitting
up, he put his hand on the Mercedes' steering wheel and then drew
it back with a scalded hiss of pain. He had to wrap his shirttail
around the doorhandle to let himself out. He thought he would

just *step* out, but he had overestimated his strength and underestimated how far the dehydration had advanced on this August evening: his legs collapsed and he fell onto the road, which was also hot. Moaning, he scrabbled his way into the shadow of the Mercedes like a crippled crawdad. He sat there, arms and head dangling between his cocked knees, panting. He stared morbidly at the two bodies he had pulled out of the car, she with her bangles on her shriveled arms and he with his shock of theatrical white hair above his mummified monkey-face.

He must get to Cibola before the sun came up tomorrow morning. If he didn't, he would die . . . and in sight of his goal! Surely the dark man could not be as cruel as that – surely not!

'My life for you,' Trashcan Man whispered, and when the sun had dropped below the line of the mountains, he gained his feet and began to walk toward the towers, minarets, and avenues of Cibola, where the sparks of the lights were coming on again.

As the heat of the day segued into the cool of the desert night, he found himself more able to walk. His sprung and rope-tied sneakers flapped and thudded against the surface of 1–15. He was plodding along, his head hanging like the bloom of a dying sunflower, and did not see the green, reflectorized sign which read LAS VEGAS 30 when he passed it.

He was thinking about The Kid. By rights The Kid should have been with him now. They should be driving into Cibola together, with the straightpipes of The Kid's deuce coupe blatting back echoes from the desert. But The Kid had proved unworthy, and Trash had been sent on alone into the wilderness.

His feet rose and fell on the pavement. 'Ci-a-bola!' he croaked. 'Bumpty-bumpty-*bump!*'

Around midnight he collapsed by the side of the road and fell into an uneasy doze. The city was closer now.

He would make it.

He was quite sure he would make it.

He heard The Kid a long time before he saw him. It was the heavy, crackling roar of unmuffled straightpipes thundering toward him from the east, branding the day. The sound was coming up Highway 34 from the direction of Yuma, Colorado. His first impulse was to hide, the way he'd hidden from the few other survivors he'd seen since Gary. But this time something made him stay where he was, astride his bike on the shoulder of the road, looking back apprehensively over his shoulder.

The thunder grew louder and louder, and then the sun was reflecting off chrome and

(??FIRE??)

something bright and orange.

The driver saw him. Downshifted in a machine-gun burst of backfires. Goodyear rubber peeled off on the highway in hot swatches. And then the car was beside him, not idling but panting like a deadly animal which may or may not be tamed, and the driver was getting out. But at first Trashcan only had eyes for the car. He knew about cars, he liked cars, even though he had never gotten so much as a learner's permit. This one was a beauty, a car someone had worked on for years, put thousands of dollars into, the kind of thing you usually only saw at funnycar shows, a labor of love.

It was a 1932 Ford deuce coupe, but the owner had not stinted nor stopped with the usual deuce coupe customizing innovations. He had gone on and on, turning it into a parody of all American cars, a glittering science fiction vehicle with hand-painted flames billowing out of the manifold pipes. The paintjob was flake gold. The chrome headpipes, which stretched almost the whole length of the car, reflected the sun fiercely. The windshield was a convex bubble. The back tires were gigantic Goodyear Wide Ovals, the wheel-wells cut to an exaggerated height and depth to accommodate them. Growing out of the hood like a weird heating duct was a supercharger. Growing out of the roof, solid black but shot with red flecks like embers, was a steel sharkfin. Written on both sides were two words, raked backward to indicate speed. THE KID, they said.

'Hey, youall long tall an *ogly*,' the driver drawled, and Trash shifted his attention from the painted flames to the driver of this rolling bomb.

He stood about five feet three inches. His hair was piled and swirled and pomaded and brilliantined. The hair alone gave him another three inches of height. The swirls all met above his collar in what was not just a duck's ass but the avatar of all the duck's-ass hairdos ever affected by the punks and hoods of the world. He was wearing black boots with pointed toes. The sides were elasticized. The heels, which gave The Kid another three inches, bringing him up to a respectable five-nine total, were stacked Cubans. His pegged and faded jeans were tight enough to read the dates of the coins in his pockets. They limned each nifty little buttock into a kind of blue sculpture and made his crotch look like he'd maybe stuffed a chamois bag full of Spalding golfballs in there. He wore a Western-style silk shirt of an off-burgundy color. It was decorated with yellow trim and imitation sapphire buttons. The cufflinks looked like polished bone, and Trash later found out that was just what they were. The Kid had two sets, one made from a pair of human molars, the other from the incisors of a Doberman pinscher. Over this wonder of a shirt, in spite of the heat of the day, he wore a black leather motorcycle jacket with an eagle on the back. It was crisscrossed with zippers, the teeth glimmering like diamonds. From the shoulder-flaps and waistbelt three rabbits' feet dangled. One was white, one brown, one bright St Paddy's Day green. This jacket, even more wonderful than the shirt, creaked smugly with rich oil. Above the eagle, this time written in white silk thread, were the words THE KID. The face now looking up at the Trashcan Man from between the high pile of gleaming hair and the upturned collar of the gleaming motorcycle jacket was tiny and pallid, a doll's face, with heavy but flawlessly sculpted pouting lips, dead gray eyes, a wide forehead without a mark or a seam, and strange full cheeks. He looked like Baby Elvis.

Two gunbelts were crisscrossed on his flat belly, and a giant .45 leaned out of each of the sagging holsters on his hips.

'Hey, boy, whatchall *say*?' The Kid drawled.

And the only thing Trashcan could *think* of to say was, 'I like your car.'

It was the right thing. Maybe the *only* thing. Five minutes later Trash was in the passenger seat and the deuce coupe was accelerating up to The Kid's cruising speed, which was about ninety-five. The bike Trash had ridden all the way from eastern Illinois was fading to a speck on the horizon.

Timidly, Trashcan Man suggested that at such a speed The Kid would not be able to see a wreck or a stall in the road if they came to one (they had already come to several, as a matter of fact; The Kid simply slalomed around them, the Wide Ovals shrieking unheeded protest).

'Hey, boy,' The Kid said. 'I got the reflexes. I got the timin. I got three-fiffs of a second. You believe that?'

'Yes, sir,' Trash said faintly. He felt like a man who has just used a stick to stir up a nest of snakes.

'I like you, boy,' The Kid said in his odd, droning voice. His doll's eyes stared out over the fluorescent orange steering wheel at the shimmering road. Large Styrofoam dice with death's heads for pips dangled and bounced from the rear-view mirror. 'Getchall a beer out'n the back seat.'

They were Coors and they were warm and Trashcan Man hated beer and he drank one fast and said how good it was.

'Hey, boy,' The Kid said. 'Coors beer's the *only* beer. I'd *piss* Coors if I could. You believe that happy crappy?'

Trashcan said he did indeed believe that happy crappy.

'They call me The Kid. Outta Shreveport, Looseyanna. You know that? This here beast won every major carshow award in the South. You believe that happy crappy?'

Trashcan Man said he did and got another warm beer. It seemed like the best move under the circumstances.

'What they call you, boy?'

'The Trashcan Man.'

'The *whut?*' For one horrible moment the dead doll's eyes rested on Trashcan's face. 'You jokin me, boy? Ain't nobody jokes The Kid. An you better believe *that* happy crappy.'

'I do believe it,' Trashcan said earnestly, 'but that's what they call me. Because I used to light fires in people's trashcans and mailboxes and stuff. I set old lady Semple's pension check on fire. I got sent to the reformatory for it. I also burned down the Methodist Church in Powtanville, Indiana.'

'*Didja?*' The Kid asked, delighted. 'Boy, you sound as crazy as a rat in a shithouse. That's okay. I like crazy people. I'm crazy myself. Tripped right outta my fuckin gourd. Trashcan Man, huh? I like that. We make a pair. The fucking Kid and the fucking Trashcan Man. Shake, Trash.'

The Kid offered his hand and Trash shook it as quick as he could so that The Kid could put both hands back on the wheel. They whizzed around a bend and there was a Bekins semi nearly blocking the whole highway and Trashcan put his hands over his face, prepared to make an immediate transition to the astral plane. The Kid never turned a hair. The deuce coupe skittered along the left side of the highway like a waterbug and they skinned by the cab of the truck with a coat of paint to spare.

'Close,' Trashcan said when he felt he could speak without a quaver in his voice.

'Hey, boy,' The Kid said flatly. Then one of his doll's eyes closed in a solemn wink. 'Don't tell me — I'll tell you. How's that beer? Pretty fuckin gnarly, ain't it? Hits the spot after ridin that kiddy-bike, don't it?'

'It sure does,' Trashcan Man said, and took another big swallow of warm Coors. He was insane, but not yet insane enough to disagree with The Kid while he was driving. Nowhere near.

'Well, no sense beatin around the motherfuckin bush,' The Kid said, reaching back over the seat to get his own can of suds. 'I guess we're goin to the same place.'

'I guess so,' Trash said cautiously.

'Gonna jine up,' The Kid said. 'Goin west. Gonna get in on the motherfuckin ground floor. You believe that happy crappy?'

'I guess so.'

'You been gettin dreams about that boogeyman in the black flight-suit, ain'tcha?'

'You mean the priest.'

'I always mean what I say an say what I mean,' The Kid said flatly. 'Don't tell me, ya fuckin bug, I'll tell you. It's a black flight-suit, and the guy's got goggles. Like in a John Wayne movie about Big Two. Goggles so big you can't see his motherfuckin face. Spooky old cock-knocker, ain't he?'

'Yeah,' Trashcan said, and sipped his warm beer. His head was beginning to buzz.

The Kid hunched over the orange steering wheel and began to imitate a fighter pilot — one who had done his stuff in Big Two, presumably — in a dogfight. The deuce coupe rollercoastered alarmingly from one side of the road to the other as he imitated loops and dives and barrel rolls.

'*Neeeeyaaaahhhh . . . eheheheheheh . . . budda-budda-budda . . .* take that, ya fuckin kraut . . . Cap'n! Bandits at twelve o'clock! . . . Turn the air-cooled cannon on em, ya fuckin dipstick . . . takka . . . takka . . . takka-takka-takka! We got em, sir! All clear . . . HowOOOGAH! *Stand down, fellers! HowOOOOOOOGAH!*'

His face gained no expression as he went through this fantasy; not a single well-oiled hair fell from grace as he jerked the car back into its lane and pounded on up the road. Trashcan Man's heart thudded heavily in his chest. A light sheen of sweat had oiled his body. He drank his beer. He had to make wee-wee.

'But he don't scare me,' The Kid said, as if the former topic of conversation had never lapsed. 'Fuck no. He's a hard baby, but The Kid has handled hard babies before. I shut em up and then I shut em down, just like The Boss says. You believe that happy crappy?'

'Sure,' Trash said.

'You dig The Boss?'

'Sure,' Trash said. He hadn't the slightest idea who The Boss was or had been.

'Fuckin *better* dig The Boss. Listen, you know what I'm gonna do?'

'Go west?' Trashcan Man hazarded. It seemed safe.

The Kid looked impatient. '*After* I get there, I mean. *After.* You know what I'm gonna do after?'

'No. What?'

'I'm gonna lay low for a while. Check out the situation. Can you dig that happy crappy?'

'Sure,' Trash said.

'Fuckin A. Don't tell me, I'll fuckin tell you. Just check it out. Check out the big man. Then . . .'

The Kid fell silent, brooding over the top of his orange steering wheel.

'Then what?' Trashcan asked hesitantly.

'Gonna shut him down. Send him around dead man's curve. Put him out to pasture on the motherfuckin Cadillac Ranch. You believe it?'

'Yeah, sure.'

'I'm gonna take over,' The Kid said confidently. 'Gonna strip his gears and leave him at the Cadillac Ranch. You stick with me, Trashman or whatever the fuck ya call yaself. We ain't gonna eat no pork and beans. We're gonna eat more chicken than any man ever seen.'

The deuce coupe roared down the highway with painted flames shooting up from the manifold. Trashcan Man sat in the passenger seat, a warm beer in his lap and troubled in his mind.

It was almost dawn on the morning of August 5 when Trashcan Man entered Cibola, otherwise known as Vegas. Somewhere in the last five miles he had lost his left sneaker and now, as he walked down the curving exit ramp, his footfalls sounded like this: *slap-THUMP, slap-THUMP, slap-THUMP.* They sounded like the flap of a flat tire.

He was almost done in, but a little wonder came back as he made his way down the Strip, which was jammed with dead cars and quite a few dead people, most of them well picked over by the buzzards. He had made it. He was here in Cibola. He had been tested and he had passed the test.

He saw a hundred honky-tonk nightclubs. There were signs that read LIBERAL SLOTS, signs that said BLUEBELL WEDDING CHAPEL and 60-SECOND WEDDING BUT IT'LL LAST A LIFETIME! He saw a Silver Ghost Rolls-Royce halfway through a plate glass window of an adult bookstore. He saw a naked woman hanging upside down from a lamppost. He saw two pages of the Las Vegas *Sun* go riffling by. The headline that revealed itself over and over again as the paper flapped and turned was PLAGUE GROWS <u>WORSE</u> WASHINGTON MUTE. He saw a gigantic billboard which said NEIL DIAMOND! THE AMERICANA HOTEL JUNE 15-AUGUST 30! Someone had scrawled the words DIE LAS VEGAS FOR YOUR SINS! across the show window of a jewelry store seeming to specialize in nothing but wedding and engagement rings. He saw an overturned grand piano lying in the street like a large dead wooden horse. His eyes were full of these wonders.

As he walked on he began to see other signs, their neon dead this midsummer for the first time in years. Flamingo. The Mint. Dunes. Sahara. Glass Slipper. Imperial. But where were the people? Where was the water?

Hardly knowing what he was doing, letting his feet pick their own path, Trashcan turned off the Strip. His head dropped forward, his chin resting on his chest. He dozed as he walked. And when his feet tripped over the curbing, when he fell forward and gave himself a bloody nose on the pavement, when he looked up and beheld what was there, he could hardly believe it. Blood ran unnoticed from his nose to his tattered blue shirt. It was as if he was still dozing and this was his dream.

A tall white building stretched up to the desert sky, a monolith in the desert, a needle, a monument, every bit as magnificent as the Sphinx or the Great Pyramid. The windows of its eastern face gave off the fire of the rising sun like an omen. In front of this bonewhite desert edifice, flanking its entranceway, were two huge gold pyramids. Over the canopy was a great bronze medallion, and carved on it in bas-relief was the snarling head of a lion.

Above this, also in bronze, the simple but mighty legend: MGM GRAND HOTEL.

But what captured his eyes was what stood on the grassy quadrangle between the parking lot and the entranceway. Trashcan stared, an orgasmic shivering consuming him so fiercely that for a moment he could only prop himself on his bloody hands, the unraveling end of the Ace bandage trailing between them, and stare at the fountain with his faded blue eyes, eyes that were halfway to being glareblind by now. A little groaning noise began to escape him.

The fountain was working. It was a gorgeous construction of stone and ivory, chased and inlaid with gold. Colored lights played over the spray, making the water purple, then yellow-orange, then red, then green. The constant ticking patter as the spray fell back into the pool was very loud.

'Cibola,' he muttered, and struggled to his feet. His nose was still dripping blood.

He began to stagger toward the fountain. His stagger became a trot. The trot became a run, the run a sprint, the sprint a mad dash. His scabbed knees rose, pistonlike, almost to his neck. A word began to fly out of his mouth, a long word like a paper streamer that rose to the sky, bringing people to the windows high above (and who saw them? God, perhaps, or the devil, but certainly not the Trashcan Man). The word grew higher and shriller, longer and longer as he approached the fountain and that word was:

'CIIIIIIIBOLAAAAAAAA!'

The final 'aahh' sound drew out and out, a sound of all the pleasures that all the people who have ever lived on the earth have ever known, and it ended only when he struck the lip of the fountain chest-high and yanked himself up and over and into a bath of incredible coolness and mercy. He could feel the pores of his body open like a million mouths and slurp the water in like a sponge. He screamed. He lowered his head, snorted in water, and blew it back out in a combined sneeze and cough that sent blood and water and snot against the side of the fountain in a splat. He lowered his head and drank like a cow.

'Cibola! Cibola!' Trash cried rapturously. 'My life for you!'

He dogpaddled his way around the fountain, drank again, then climbed over the edge and fell onto the grass with an awkward thump. It had all been worth it, everything had been worth it. Water cramps struck him and he suddenly threw up with a loud grunt. Even throwing up felt grand.

He got to his feet, and holding on to the lip of the fountain with his claw hand, he drank again. This time his belly accepted the gift gratefully.

Sloshing like a filled goatskin, he staggered toward the alabaster steps which led to the doors of this fabulous place, steps that led between the golden pyramids. Halfway up the steps, a water cramp struck him and doubled him over. When it passed he lurched gamely onward. The doors were of the revolving type, and it took all his feeble strength to get one of them in motion. He pushed through into a plushy carpeted lobby that seemed miles long. The rug underfoot was thick and lush and cranberry-colored. There was a registration desk, a mail desk, a key desk, the cashiers' windows. All empty. To his right, beyond an ornamental grilled railing, was the casino. Trashcan Man stared at it in awe – the serried ranks of slot machines like soldiers standing at parade rest, beyond them the roulette and crap tables, the marble railings enclosing the baccarat tables.

'Who's here?' Trash croaked, but no answer came back.

He was afraid then, because this was a place of ghosts, a place where monsters might lurk, but the fear was weakened by his weariness. He stumbled down the steps and into the casino, passing the Cub Bar, where Lloyd Henreid sat silently in the deep shadows, watching him and holding a glass of Poland water.

He came to a table upholstered in green baize, the mystic legend DEALER MUST HIT 16 AND STAND ON 17 inscribed thereon. Trash climbed up on it and fell instantly asleep. Soon nearly half a dozen men stood around the sleeping ragamuffin that was the Trashcan Man.

'What do we do with him?' Ken DeMott asked.

'Let him sleep,' Lloyd answered. 'Flagg wants him.'

'Yeah? Where the Christ *is* Flagg, anyway?' another asked.

Lloyd turned to look at the man, who was balding and stood a full foot taller than Lloyd. Nonetheless, he drew back a step at Lloyd's gaze. The stone around Lloyd's neck was the only one that was not solid jet; in the center gleamed a small and disquieting red flaw.

'Are you that anxious to see him, Hec?' Lloyd asked.

'No,' the balding man said. 'Hey, Lloyd, you know I didn't –'

'Sure.' Lloyd looked down at the man sleeping on the blackjack table. 'Flagg will be around,' he said. 'He's been waiting for this guy. This guy is something special.'

On the table, oblivious of all this, Trashcan Man slept on.

★　　★　　★

Trash and The Kid spent the night of July 18 in a motel in Golden, Colorado. The Kid picked two rooms with a connecting door. The connecting door was locked. The Kid, now well in the bag, solved this minor problem by blowing the lock off with three bullets from one of his .45s.

The Kid raised one tiny boot and kicked the door. It shuddered open in a fine blue haze of gunsmoke.

'Betcha fuckin A,' he said. 'Which room? Take your pick, Trashy.'

Trashcan Man opted for the room on the right, and for a while was left alone. The Kid had gone out someplace. Trashcan Man was slowly considering the idea of simply fading away into the gloom before something really bad could happen – trying to balance that possibility against his lack of transportation – when The Kid returned. Trashcan Man was alarmed to see that he was pushing a shopping cart which was full of six-packs of Coors beer. The doll's eyes were now bloodshot and rimmed with red. The pompadour hairdo was coming unraveled like a broken and expanding clock-spring, and greasy bunches of hair now hung down over The Kid's ears and cheeks, making him look like some dangerous (albeit absurd) caveman who had found a leather jacket left by a time-traveler and put it on. The rabbits' feet bobbed back and forth on the belt of the jacket.

'It's warm,' The Kid said, 'but who gives a rip, am I right?'

'Right, absolutely,' Trashcan Man said.

'Have a beer, asshole,' The Kid said, and tossed him a can. When Trashcan pulled the ringtab, he got a faceful of foam and The Kid roared with oddly diminutive laughter, holding his flat belly with both hands. Trash smiled weakly. He decided that later tonight, after this small monster had succumbed to sleep, he would slip away. He had had enough. And what The Kid had said about the dark priest . . . Trashcan Man's fears about that were so big he could not even get them to coalesce. Saying things like that, even if you were joking, was like shitting on the altar of a church or holding your face up to the sky in a thunderstorm and begging the lightning to come hit you.

The worst thing was that he didn't think The Kid had been joking.

Trashcan Man had no intention of going up into the mountains and around all those hairpin turns with this crazy dwarf who drank all day (and apparently all night) and who talked about overthrowing the dark man and putting himself in his place.

Meanwhile, The Kid had put away two beers in two minutes, crushed the cans, and tossed them indifferently on one of the room's twin beds. He was looking morosely at the RCA Chromacolor, a fresh Coors in his left hand and the .45 he had used to blow open the connecting door in his right.

'No fuckin lectricity, so there ain't no fuckin TV,' he said. As he grew more drunk, his Southern accent grew more pronounced, putting fur on his words. 'Don't I hate that. I love it that all the assholes got wasted, but Jesus-jumped-up-baldheaded-ole-Christ, where's HBO? Where's the goddam rasslin matches? Where's the Playboy Channel? That was a good one, Trashy. I mean, they never showed guys gettin right down and eating hair pie, munchin the ole bearded clam, you know what I mean, but some of those ladies had laigs went right up to their *chins*, you know what the motherfuck I'm talkin about?'

'Sure,' Trashcan said.

'You're fuckin A. Don't tell me, I'll tell you.'

The Kid stared at the dead TV. 'You numb cunt,' he said, and shot the TV. The picture tube imploded with a great hollow bang. Glass belched out onto the carpet. Trashcan Man raised his arm to shield his eyes, and his beer gurgled out onto the green nylon shag when he did.

'Oh looka that, you dumb dork!' The Kid exclaimed. His tone was one of great outrage. Suddenly the .45 was pointed at Trash, its bore as big and dark as an ocean liner's smokestack. Trashcan felt his groin go numb. He thought he might be pissing himself, but had no way of telling for sure.

'I'm gonna venilate your thinkin-machine for that,' The Kid said. 'You done spilt the beer. If it was any other kind I wun't do it, but that was *Coors* you spilled. I'd *piss* Coors if I could, you believe that happy crappy?'

'Sure,' Trashcan whispered.

'And do you think they're makin any more Coors these days, Trash? That seem very fuckin likely to you?'

'No,' Traschcan whispered. 'Guess not.'

'You're fuckin right. It's a dangered spee-shees.' He raised the gun slightly. Trashcan Man thought it was the end of his life, the end of his life for sure. Then The Kid lowered the gun again . . . slightly. He had an absolutely vacant look on his face. Trashcan guessed this expression indicated deep thought. 'I'll tell you what, Trash. You get you another can, and you chug it. If you can chug the whole thing, I won't send you to the Cadillac Ranch. You believe that happy crappy?'

'What's . . . what's chugging?'

'Jesus Christ, boy, you as dumb as a stone *boat!* Drink the whole can without *stoppin*, that's what chuggin is! Where you been spendin your time, motherfuckin Africa? You want to get on the stick, Trashy. If I have to put one inya, it goes right in your eye. I got this sucker loaded up with dumdums. Open you right the fuck up, turn you into a fuckin buffet dinner for the cockroaches in this dump.' He gestured with the pistol, his red eyes fixed on Trash. There was a speckle of beer-foam on his upper lip.

Trashcan went to the cardboard carton, selected a beer, and popped the top.

'Go on. Ever drop. And if you puke it back up, you're a gone fuckin goose.'

Trashcan Man upended the can. Beer gurgled out. He swallowed convulsively, his Adam's apple going up and down like a monkey on a stick. When the can was empty he dropped it between his feet, fought a seemingly endless battle with his gorge, and won his life back in one long, echoing belch. The Kid threw his small head back and laughed with tinkling delight. Trash swayed on his feet, grinning sickly. All at once he was a lot drunk instead of a little.

The Kid holstered his piece.

'Okay. Not bad, Trashcan Man. Not too motherfuckin shabby.'

The Kid continued to drink. Squashed cans piled up on the motel bed. Trash held a can of Coors between his knees and sipped on it whenever The Kid seemed to be looking at him with disapproval. The Kid muttered on and on, his voice growing ever lower and more Southern as the empties piled up. He talked of places he had been. Races he had won. A load of dope he had run across the border from Mexico in a laundry truck with a 442 hemi engine under the hood. Nasty stuff, he said. All dope was nasty motherfuckin stuff. He never touched it himself, but boy-howdy, after you muled a few loads of that shit, you could wipe your ass with gold toilet paper. At last he began to nod off, the little red eyes closing for longer and longer periods, then coming reluctantly back to halfmast.

'Gonna get him, Trashy,' The Kid muttered. 'I'll go out there, check it out, keep kissin his motherfuckin ass until I see how the land lays. But nobody orders this Kid around. No-fuckin-body. Not for long. I don't do piecework. If I'm on a job, I run it. That's just my style. I dunno who he is or where he comes from or how he can broadcast into our motherfuckin thinkin-machines, but I'm gonna run him right the fuck' – huge yawn – 'outta town. Gonna shut him down. Gonna send him to the Cadillac Ranch. Stick with me, Crash, or whoever the fuck y'are.'

He collapsed slowly backward onto the bed. His can of beer, freshly opened, fell from his relaxing hand. More Coors puddled on the rug. The case was gone, and by Trashcan's reckoning, The Kid had gotten through twenty-one cans of it himself. Trashcan Man couldn't understand how such a little man could drink so much beer, but he *did* understand what time it was: time for him to go. He *knew* that, but he felt drunk and weak and ill. What he wanted more than anything was to sleep for a little while. That would be all right, wouldn't it? The Kid was apt to sleep like a log all night, maybe half of tomorrow morning, too. Plenty of time for him to take a little nap.

So he went into the other room (tiptoeing in spite of The Kid's comatose state) and closed the connecting door as well as he could – which wasn't very well. The force of the bullets had warped it somehow. There was a wind-up alarm clock on the dresser. Trash wound it, set it for midnight since he didn't know (and didn't care) what time it really was, and then set the alarm for five o'clock. He lay down on one of the twin beds without even stopping to take off his sneakers. He was asleep in five minutes.

He woke up sometime later, in the dark grave of the morning, with the smell of beer and puke blowing across his face in a dry little gale. Something was in bed with him, something hot and smooth and squirmy. His first panicky thought was that a weasel had somehow gotten right out of his Nebraska dream and into reality. A whimpery little moan came out of him as he realized that the animal in bed with him, while not big, was too big to be a weasel. He had a headache from the beer; it drilled mercilessly at his temples.

'Grab on me,' The Kid whispered in the dark. Trashcan's hand was seized and led to something hard and cylindrical and throbbing like a piston. 'Jerk me off. Go on, jerk me off, you know what to do, I saw that the first time I looked atcha. Come on, ya motherfuckin jerkoff, jerk me off.'

Trashcan Man knew how to do it. In many ways it was a relief.

He knew about it from the long nights in stir. They said it was bad, that it was queer, but what the queers did was better than what some of the others did, the ones who spent their nights sharpening spoon-handles into shanks, and the ones who just lay there on their bunks, cracking their knuckles and looking at you and grinning.

The Kid had put Trashcan's hand on the kind of gun he understood. He closed his hand around it and began. After it was over The Kid would fall asleep again. Then he would creep out.

The Kid's breath was becoming ragged. He began to bump his hips in time with Trashcan's strokes. Trash did not at first realize The Kid was also unbuckling his belt, then slipping his jeans and underpants down to his knees. Trash let him. It didn't matter if The Kid wanted to slip it to him. Trash had had it slipped to him before. You didn't die. It wasn't poison.

Then his hand froze. Whatever it was suddenly pressing against his anus, it wasn't flesh. It was cold steel.

And suddenly he *knew* what it was.

'No,' he whispered. His eyes were wide and terrified in the dark. Now he could dimly see that homicidal doll's face in the mirror, hanging over his shoulder with its hair in its red eyes.

'Yes,' The Kid whispered back. 'And you don't want to lose a stroke, Trashy. Not one motherfuckin *stroke*. Or I might just pull the trigger on this thang. Blow your shit-factory all to hell and gone. Dumdums, Trashy. You believe that happy crappy?'

Whining, Trashcan began to stroke him again. His whines became little gasps of pain as the barrel of the .45 worked its way into him, rotating, gouging, tearing. And could it be that this was exciting him? It was.

Eventually his excitement became apparent to The Kid.

'Like it, dontcha?' The Kid panted. 'I knew you would, you bag of pus. You like having it up your ass, dontcha? Say yes, pusbag. Say yes or right to hell you go.'

'Yes,' Trashcan Man whimpered.

'Want me to do it to you?'

He didn't. Excited or not, he didn't. But he knew better than to say so. 'Yes.'

'I wouldn't touch your dick if it was diamonds. Do it yaself. Why you think God gave you two hands?'

How long did it go on? God might know; the Trashcan Man did not. A minute, an hour, an age – what was the difference? He became sure that at the instant of The Kid's orgasm he would feel two things simultaneously: the hot jet of the small monster's semen on his belly and the mushrooming agony of a dumdum bullet roaring up through his vitals. The ultimate enema.

Then The Kid's hips froze and his penis went through its convulsions in Trashcan Man's hand. His fist became slick, like a rubber glove. An instant later, the pistol was withdrawn. Silent tears of relief gushed down Trashcan's cheeks. He was not afraid to die, at least not in the service of the dark man, but he did not want to die in this dark motel room at the hands of a psychopath. Not before he had seen Cibola. He would have prayed to God, but he knew instinctively that God would not lend a sympathetic ear to those who had thrown their allegiance to the dark man. And what had God ever done for the Trashcan Man, anyway? Or for Donald Merwin Elbert either, for that matter?

In the breathing silence The Kid's voice rose in song, offkey, cracking, trailing down toward sleep:

'My buddies an me are gettin real well known . . . yeah, the bad guys know us an they leave us alone . . .'

He began to snore.

Now I'll leave, Trashcan Man thought, but he was afraid that if he moved, he would wake The Kid up. *I'll leave just as soon as I'm sure he's really asleep. Five minutes. Shouldn't take any longer than that.*

But no one knows how long five minutes is in the dark; it might be fair to say that, in the dark, five minutes does not exist. He waited. He rolled in and out of a doze without knowing he had dozed. Before long he had slipped down the slide of sleep.

He was on a dark road that was very high. The stars seemed close enough to reach up and touch; it seemed you could just pick them off the sky and pop them into a jar, like fireflies. It was bitterly cold. It was dark. Dimly, frosted with starshine, he could see the living rockfaces through which this highway had been cut.

And in the darkness, something was walking toward him.

And then *his* voice, coming from nowhere, coming from everywhere: *In the mountains I'll give you a sign. I'll show you my power. I'll show you what happens to those who would set themselves against me. Wait. Watch.*

Red eyes began to open in the dark, as if someone had set out three dozen danger lamps with hoods on them and now that someone was pulling the hoods off in pairs. They were eyes, and they surrounded the Trashcan Man in a fey ring. At first he thought they were the eyes of weasels, but as the ring tightened around him he saw they were great gray mountain wolves, their ears cocked forward, foam dripping from their dark muzzles.

He was afraid.

They are not for you, my good and faithful servant. See?

And they were gone. Just like that, the panting gray timber-wolves were gone.

Watch, the voice said.

Wait, the voice said.

The dream ended. He woke to discover bright sunshine falling in through the motel room window. The Kid was standing in front of it, seeming none the worse for wear from his bout with the now-defunct Adolph Coors Company the night before. His hair was combed into its former shining swirls and eddies, and he was admiring his reflection in the glass. He had slipped his leather jacket over the back of a chair. The rabbits' feet dangled from the belt like tiny corpses from a gibbet.

'Hey, pusbag! I thought I was gonna hafta grease your hand again to wake you up. Come on, we got us a big day ahead. Lotta stuff gonna happen today, am I right?'

'You sure are,' the Trashcan Man replied with a queer smile.

When the Trashcan Man swam out of sleep on the evening of August 5, he was still lying on the blackjack table in the casino of the MGM Grand Hotel. Sitting backward on a chair in front of him was a young man with lank straw-blond hair and mirror sunglasses. The first thing Trash noticed was the stone which hung about his neck in the V of his open sport-shirt. Black, with a red flaw in the center. Like the eye of a wolf in the night.

He tried to say he was thirsty and managed only a weak 'Gaw!' sound.

'You sure did spend some time in the hot sun, I guess,' Lloyd Henreid said.

'Are you *him*?' Trash whispered. 'Are you –'

'The big guy? No, I'm not him. Flagg's in LA. He knows you're here, though. I talked to him on the radio this afternoon.'

'Is he coming?'

'What, just to see *you*? Hell, no! He'll be here in his own good time. You and me, guy, we're just little people. He'll be here in his own good time.' And he reiterated the question he had asked the tall man that morning, not long after Trashcan Man had stumbled in. 'Are you that anxious to see him?'

'Yes . . . no . . . I don't know.'

'Well, whichever way it turns out to be, you'll get your chance.'

'Thirsty . . .'

'Sure. Here.' He handed over a large thermos filled with cherry Kool-Aid. Trashcan drained it at a draught, then leaned over, holding his belly and groaning. When the cramp had passed, he looked at Lloyd with dumb gratitude.

'Think you could eat something?' Lloyd asked.

'Yes, I think so.'

Lloyd turned to a man standing behind them. The man was idly whirling a roulette wheel, then letting the little white ball bounce and rattle.

'Roger, go tell Whitney or Stephanie-Ann to rustle this man up some fries and a couple of hamburgers. Naw, shit, what am I thinking about? He'll ralph all over the place. Soup. Get him some soup. That okay, man?'

'Anything,' Trash said gratefully.

'We got a guy here,' Lloyd said, 'name of Whitney Horgan, used to be a butcher. He's a fat, loud sack of shit, but don't that man know how to cook! Jesus! And they got everything here. The gennies were still running when we moved in, and the freezers're full. Fucking Vegas! Ain't it the goddamndest place you ever saw?'

'Yeah,' Trash said. He liked Lloyd already, and he didn't even know his name. 'It's Cibola.'

'Say what?'

'Cibola. Searched for by many.'

'Yeah, been plenty people searchin for it over the years, but most of em go away sort of sorry they found it. Well, you call it whatever you want, buddy – looks like you almost cooked yourself gettin here. What's your name?'

'Trashcan Man.'

Lloyd didn't seem to think this a strange name at all. 'Name like that, I bet you used to be a biker.' He stuck out a hand. The tips of his fingers still bore the fading marks of his stay in the Phoenix jail where he had almost died of starvation. 'I'm Lloyd Henreid. Pleased to meet you, Trash. Welcome aboard the good ship *Lollypop*.'

Trashcan Man shook the offered hand and had to struggle to

keep from weeping with gratitude. So far as he could remember, this was the first time in his life someone had offered to shake his hand. He was here. He had been accepted. At long last he was *on the inside of something.* He would have walked through twice as much desert as he had for this moment, would have burned the other arm and both legs as well.

'Thanks,' he muttered. 'Thanks, Mr Henreid.'

'Shit, brother – if you don't call me Lloyd, we'll have to throw that soup out.'

'Lloyd, then. Thanks, Lloyd.'

'That's better. After you eat, I'll take you upstairs and put you in a room of your own. We'll get you doing something tomorrow. The big guy's got something of his own for you, I think, but until then there's plenty for you to do. We've got some of the place running again, but nowhere near all of it. There's a crew up at Boulder Dam, trying to get all the power back on. There's another one working on water supplies. We've got scout parties out, we've been pulling in six or eight people a day, but we'll keep you off that detail for a while. Looks like you've had enough sun to last you a month.'

'I guess I have,' Trashcan Man said with a weak smile. He was already willing to lay down his life for Lloyd Henreid. Gathering up all of his courage, he pointed at the stone which lay in the hollow of Lloyd's throat. 'That –'

'Yeah, us guys who are sort of in charge all wear em. *His* idea. It's jet. Not really a rock at all, you know. It's like an oil bubble.'

'I mean . . . the red light. The eye.'

'Looks like that to you too, huh? It's a flaw. Special from *him.* I'm not the smartest guy he's got, not even the smartest guy in good ole Lost Wages, not by a long shot. But I'm . . . shit, I guess you'd say I'm his mascot.' He looked closely at Trash. 'Maybe you too, who knows? Not me, that's for sure. He's a close one, Flagg is. Anyway, we heard about you special. Me and Whitney. That's not the regular drill at all. Too many comin in to take special notice of many.' He paused. 'Although I guess *he* could, if he wanted to. I guess *he* could take notice of just about anybody.'

Trashcan Man nodded.

'He can do magic,' Lloyd said, his voice becoming slightly hoarse. 'I seen it. I'd hate to be the people against him, you know?'

'Yes,' Trashcan said. 'I saw what happened to The Kid.'

'What kid?'

'The guy I was with until we got into the mountains.' He shuddered. 'I don't want to talk about it.'

'Okay, man. Here comes your soup. And Whitney put a burger on the side after all. You'll love it. The guy makes great burgers, but try not to puke, okay?'

'Okay.'

'Me, I got places to go and people to see. If my old buddy Poke could see me now, he'd never believe it. I'm busier'n a one-legged man in an ass-kickin contest. Catch you later.'

'Sure,' Trashcan said, and then added, almost timidly: 'Thanks. Thanks for everything.'

'Don't thank *me*,' Lloyd said amiably. 'Thank *him*.'

'I do,' Trashcan Man said. 'Every night.' But he was talking to himself. Lloyd was already halfway down the lobby, talking with the man who had brought the soup and the hamburger. Trashcan Man watched them fondly until they were out of sight, and then he began to chow down, eating ravenously until almost everything was gone. He would have been fine if he hadn't looked down into the soup bowl. It was tomato soup, and it was the color of blood.

He pushed the bowl aside, his appetite suddenly gone. It was all very well for him to tell Lloyd Henreid he didn't want to talk about The Kid; it was quite another thing to stop *thinking* about what had happened to him.

He walked over to the roulette wheel, sipping at the glass of milk that had come with his food. He gave the wheel an idle twist and dropped the little white marble into the dish. It rolled around the rim, then hit the slots below and began to racket back and forth. He thought about The Kid. He wondered if someone would come and show him which room was his. He thought about The Kid. He wondered if the ball would fetch up on a red number or a black one . . . but mostly he thought about The Kid. The bouncing, jittering ball caught in one of the slots, this time for good. The wheel came to a stop. The ball was sitting under the green double zero.

House spin.

On the cloudless, eighty-degree day when they headed west from Golden directly into the Rockies along Interstate 70, The Kid had given up Coors in favor of a bottle of Rebel Yell whiskey. Two more bottles sat between the two of them on the driveshaft hump, each neatly packed into an empty cardboard milk carton so the bottles wouldn't roll around and break. The Kid would nip at the bottle, chase the nip with a swallow of Pepsi-Cola, and then holler *hot-damn!* or *yahoo!* or *sex-machine!* at the top of his lungs. He remarked several times that he would *piss* Rebel Yell if he could. He asked Trashcan Man if he believed that happy crappy. Trashcan Man, pale with fright and still hung over from his three beers of the night before, said he did.

Even The Kid couldn't stampede along at ninety on these roads. He lowered his speed to sixty and muttered about the goddam fucking mountains under his breath. Then he brightened. 'When we get over in Utah n Nevada, we'll make up plenty of lost time, Trashy. This little darlin'll do a hunnert n sixty on the flat. You believe that happy crappy?'

'Sure is a nice car,' Trashcan said with a sick-doggy smile.

'Bet your ass.' He nipped Rebel Yell. Chased it with Pepsi. Yelled *yahoo!* at the top of his lungs.

Trash stared morbidly out at the passing scenery, which was now washed with midmorning sunshine. The Interstate had been blasted right into the shoulder of the mountain, and at times they were traveling between huge cliffs of rock. The cliffs he had seen in his dream of the night before. After dark, would those red eyes open again?

He shuddered.

A short while later he became aware that their speed had dropped from sixty to forty. Then to thirty. The Kid was swearing monotonously and horribly under his breath. The deuce coupe wove in and out of steadily thickening traffic, all of it stalled and deadly silent.

'What the fuck *is* this?' The Kid raged. 'What did they all decide to die at ten thousand motherfuckin feet? *Hey, you stupid fucks, out my way! You hear me? Get the fuck out my way!*'

Trashcan Man cringed.

They rounded a curve and faced a horrendous four-car pileup which blocked the westbound lanes of I-70 completely. A dead man covered with blood which had dried to an uneven crack-glaze long since lay spreadeagled facedown in the road. Near him was a broken Chatty Cathy doll. Any way around the jam on the left was blocked by steel guardrail posts six feet high. On the right, the land fell away into cloudy distance.

The Kid gulped Rebel Yell and swung the deuce coupe toward the dropoff. 'Hang on, Trashy,' he whispered, 'we're goin around.'

'There's no room,' Trashcan Man rasped. His throat felt like the side of a steel file.

'Yeah, just enough,' The Kid whispered. His eyes were glittering. He began to edge the car off the road. The righthand wheels were now hissing in the dirt of the shoulder.

'Count me out,' Trashcan said hurriedly, and grabbed for the doorhandle.

'You sit,' said The Kid, 'or you're gonna be one dead pusbag.'

Trash turned his head and looked into the bore of a .45. The Kid giggled tensely.

Trashcan Man sat back. He wanted to close his eyes but could not. On his side of the car, the last six inches of shoulder dropped from view. Now he was looking straight down at a long vista of blue-gray pines and huge tumbled boulders. He could imagine the deuce coupe's Wide Oval tires now four inches from the edge . . . now two . . .

'Another inch,' The Kid crooned, his eyes huge, his grin enormous. Sweat stood out on that pale doll's forehead in perfect clear drops. 'Just . . . one . . . *more*.'

It ended in a hurry. Trashcan Man felt the right rear of the car slip suddenly outward and sharply downward. He heard a falling millrace, first of pebbles, then of larger stones. He screamed. The Kid cursed horribly, changed down to first gear, and floored the accelerator. From the left, where they had been inching by the overturned corpse of a VW Microbus, came a squall of grinding metal.

'*Fly!*' The Kid screamed. '*Just like a bigass bird! Fly! Goddammit, FLY!*'

The deuce coupe's rear wheels spun. For a moment their shift toward the drop seemed to be increasing. Then the car jerked forward, lurched up, and they were back on the road on the far side of the pileup, laying rubber.

'*I told you she'd do it!*' The Kid screamed triumphantly. '*Goddam! Did we do it? Did we do it, Trashy, ya fuckin chickenshit suckhole?*'

'We did it,' Trashcan Man said quietly. He was twitching all over. He couldn't seem to control it. And then, for the second time since meeting The Kid, he unwittingly said the one thing that could have saved his life – had he not said it, The Kid surely would have killed him; it would have been his queer way of celebrating. 'Good driving, champ,' he said. He had never called anyone 'champ' in his whole life before now.

'Ahhh . . . not that great,' The Kid said patronizingly. 'There's at least two other guys in the country coulda done it. You believe that happy crappy?'

'If you say so, Kid.'

'Don't tell me, sweetheart, I'll fuckin tell you. Well, on we go. All in a day's work.'

But they did not go on for long. The Kid's deuce coupe was stopped for good fifteen minutes later, eighteen hundred miles or more from its point of origin in Shreveport, Louisiana.

'I don't believe it,' The Kid said. 'I don't . . . mother-fuckin . . . *B'LEEVE* it!'

He threw open the driver's side door and jumped out, the quarter-full bottle of Rebel Yell still clutched in his left hand.

'*GET OUTTA MY ROAD!*' The Kid roared, dancing about in his grotesquely high-heeled boots, a tiny natural force of destruction, like an earthquake in a bottle. '*GET OUTTA MY ROAD, MOTHERFUCKERS, YOU'RE DEAD, Y'ALL B'LONG IN THE MOTHERFUCKIN BONEYARD, YOU GOT NO BUSINESS IN MY FUCKIN ROAD!*'

He threw the Rebel Yell bottle and it flew end over end, spraying amber droplets. It crashed into a hundred pieces against the side of an old Porsche. The Kid stood silent, panting and reeling a little on his feet.

The problem was nothing so simple as a four-car pileup this time. This time the problem was nothing but traffic. The eastbound lanes were here divided from those westbound by a grassy median strip about ten yards across, and the deuce coupe probably could have made it from one side of the highway to the other, but the condition of both arteries was the same: the four lanes were crowded with six lanes of traffic, bumper to bumper and side to side. The breakdown lanes were as full as the travel lanes. Some drivers had even attempted to use the median itself, although it was rough and ungraded and full of rocks which punched out of the thin gray soil like dragon's teeth. Perhaps there had been high-hung four-wheel-drive vehicles which had had some success there, but what Trashcan saw on the median strip was an automobile graveyard of crashed, bashed, and mashed Detroit rolling iron. It was as if a mass madness had infected all the drivers and they had decided to hold an apocalyptic demolition derby or lunatic gymkhana here high up on I-70. Colorado Rocky Mountain high, Trashcan Man thought, I've seen it raining Chevies in the sky. He almost giggled and hurriedly covered his mouth. If The Kid heard him giggling now, he would most likely never giggle again.

The Kid came striding back in his high-heeled boots, his carefully coiffed hair gleaming. His face was that of a dwarf basilisk. His eyes were bulging with fury. 'I'm not leavin my fuckin car,' he said. 'You hear me? No way. I'm not leavin it. You get walkin, Trashy. You walk up there and see how far this motherfuckin traffic jam goes. Maybe it's a truck in the road, I don't know. I know we can't fuckin backtrack. We lost the shoulder. We'd go all the way down. But if it's just a stalled truck or somethin, I don't give a rat's ass. I'll jump these sonsofwhores one at a time and run em right the fuck over the edge. I can do it, and you better believe *that* happy crappy. Get movin, son.'

Trash didn't argue. He began to walk carefully up the road, weaving in and out between the packed cars. He was ready to duck and run if The Kid started shooting. But The Kid didn't. When Trashcan had walked what he judged to be a safe distance (i.e., out of pistol range), he climbed atop a tanker truck and looked back. The Kid, miniature streetpunk from hell, truly doll-sized at this half-a-mile distance, was leaning against the side of his deucey, having a drink. Trashcan Man thought of waving and then decided it might be a bad idea.

The Trashcan Man started his walk that day at about ten-thirty in the morning, MDT. Walking was slow – he often had to scramble over the hoods and roofs of cars and trucks, they were so tightly packed together – and by the time he got to the first TUNNEL CLOSED sign, it was already quarter past three in the afternoon. He had made about twelve miles. Twelve miles wasn't so much – not to someone who'd crossed twenty percent of the country on a bicycle – but considering the obstacles, he thought twelve miles was pretty awesome. He could have gone back long ago to tell The Kid it was impossible . . . if, that was, he'd ever had any intentions of going back. He didn't, of course. Trashcan Man had never read much history (after the electroshock therapy, reading had gotten sort of tough for him), but he didn't need to know that, in times of old, kings and emperors had often killed the bearers of bad news out of simple pique. What he did know was enough: he had seen enough of The Kid to know he didn't ever want to see any more.

He stood pondering the sign, black letters on an orange diamond-shaped field. It had been knocked over and was lying beneath one wheel of what looked like the world's oldest Yugo. TUNNEL CLOSED. *What* tunnel? He peered ahead, shading his eyes, and thought he could see *something*. He walked on another three hundred yards, scrambling over cars when he had to, and came to an alarming confusion of crashed vehicles and dead bodies. Some of the cars and trucks had been burned to the axles. Many were army vehicles. Many of the bodies were dressed in khaki. Beyond the scene of this battle – Trash was pretty sure that's what it had been – the traffic jam began again. And beyond it, east and west, the traffic disappeared into the twin bores of what a huge sign bolted to the living rock proclaimed to be THE EISENHOWER TUNNEL.

He walked closer, heart bumping, not knowing just what he intended. Those twin bores punching their way into the rock intimidated him, and as he drew closer, intimidation became outright terror. He would have understood Larry Underwood's feelings about the Lincoln Tunnel perfectly; in that instant they were unknowing soul brothers, the shared soul emotion one of stark fear.

The main difference was that, while the Lincoln Tunnel's pedestrian catwalk was set high off the roadbed, here it was low enough so that some cars had actually attempted to run along the side, with one pair of wheels up on the catwalk and the other on the road. The tunnel was two miles long. The only way to negotiate it would be to crawl along from car to car in the pitch dark. It would take hours.

Trashcan Man felt his bowels turn to water.

He stood looking at the tunnel for a long time. Larry Underwood, over a month before, had gone into his tunnel in spite of his fear. After a long contemplation, Trashcan Man turned away and began to walk back toward The Kid, his shoulders slumped, the corners of his mouth trembling. It was not just the absence of any easy place to walk which made him turn back, or the length of the tunnel (Trash, who had lived his whole life in Indiana, had no idea how long the Eisenhower Tunnel was). Larry Underwood had been moved (and perhaps controlled) by an underlying streak of self-interest, by the simple logic of survival: New York was an island, and he had to get off. The tunnel was the quickest way. So he would walk through as quick as he could; he would do it the way you held your nose and swallowed fast when you knew the medicine was going to taste bad. Trashcan Man was a beaten thing, used to accepting the punchings and pummelings of both fate and his own inexplicable nature . . . and doing so with a bowed head. He had been further unmanned, brainwashed almost, by his cataclysmic encounter with The Kid. He had been whooshed along at speeds high enough to induce brain-damage. He had been threatened with extinction if he could not drink a whole can of beer without stopping and without throwing up afterward. He had been sodomized with a pistol barrel. He had been nearly dumped a thousand feet straight down from the edge of the turnpike. On top of this, could he summon enough courage to crawl through a hole bored straight through the base of a mountain, a hole where he might encounter who knew what horrors in the dark? He could not. Others, maybe, but not the Trashcan Man. And there was also a certain logic in the idea of turning back. It was the logic of the beaten and the half-mad, true, but it still had its own perverse charm. He was *not* on an island. If he had to backtrack the rest of today and all day tomorrow in order to find a road that went over the mountains instead of through them, he would do it. He'd have to get by The Kid, it was true, but he thought The Kid might have changed his mind and left already, in spite of his declarations to the contrary. He might be dead drunk. He might even (although Trash really doubted that such extraordinarily good luck would ever come his way) be simply dead. At the worst, if The Kid was still there, watching and waiting, Trashcan could wait until dark and then creep past him like

(a weasel)

some small animal in the underbrush. Then he would just continue on to the east until he found the road he was looking for.

He arrived back at the tanker truck from whose top he had last seen The Kid and The Kid's mythic deuce coupe, making better time on the return trip. This time he did not climb up to where he would be clearly silhouetted against the evening sky but began to crawl from car to car on his hands and knees, trying to be very quiet. The Kid might be alert and on watch. With a guy like The Kid, you just couldn't tell . . . and it didn't pay to take chances. He found himself wishing he had taken one of the soldiers' guns, even though he had never used a gun in his life. He kept crawling, the road-pebbles biting painfully into his claw hand. It was eight o'clock, and the sun had gone behind the mountains.

Trashcan stopped behind the hood of the Porsche The Kid had thrown his liquor bottle at and carefully raised his eyes over it. Yes, there was The Kid's deuce coupe, with its flamboyant flake-gold paint, its convex windshield and sharkfin cutting at the bruise-colored evening sky. The Kid was slumped behind the Day-Glo steering wheel, his eyes closed, his mouth open. Trashcan Man's heart thundered a percussive victory song in his chest. *Dead drunk!* his heartbeat proclaimed in syllables of two. *Dead drunk! By God! Dead drunk!* Trash thought he could be twenty miles east of here before The Kid even woke up to his hangover.

Still, he was careful. He skittered from car to car like a waterbug crossing the still surface of a pond, skirting the deuce coupe on his left, hurrying across the increasing gaps. Now the deucey was at nine o'clock on his left, now seven, now six and directly behind him. Now to put distance between him and that crazy –

'You prick-stupid cocksucker, you hold still.'

Trash froze on his hands and knees. He made wee-wee in his pants, and his mind dissolved into a madly fluttering black bird of panic.

He turned around little by little, the tendons in his neck creaking like the hinges of a door in a haunted house. And there stood The Kid, resplendent in an iridescent shirt of green and gold and a pair of sunfaded cords. There was a .45 in each hand and a horrible grimace of hate and rage on his face.

'I was just chuh-checkin down this way,' Trashcan Man heard himself saying. 'To make sure the cuh-cuh-coast was clear.'

'Sure – on your hands and knees you was checkin, dinkweed. I'll clear your motherfuckin coast. Stand up here.'

Trashcan somehow gained his feet and kept them by holding on to the doorhandle of a car on his right. The twin bores of The Kid's matched set of .45s looked every bit as big as the twin bores of the Eisenhower Tunnel. He was looking at death now. He knew that. There were no right words to avert it this time.

He offered up a silent prayer to the dark man: *Please . . . if it be your will . . . my life for you!*

'What's up there?' The Kid asked. 'A wreck?'

'A tunnel. It's jammed solid. That's why I came back, to tell you. Please –'

'A tunnel,' The Kid groaned. 'Jesus-hairy-ole-baldheaded-*Christ!*' The scowl returned. 'Are you lying to me, you fuckin fairy?'

'*No!* I swear I'm not! The sign said Eeesenhoover Tunnel. I think that's what it said, but I have trouble with long words. I –'

'Shut your dough-hole. How far?'

'Eight miles. Maybe even more.'

The Kid was silent for a moment, looking west along the turnpike. Then he fixed Trashcan Man with a glittery gaze. 'You trine to tell me this traffic jam's *eight miles long?* You lyin sack of shit!' The Kid thumbed the triggers on both guns up to half-cock. Trashcan, who wouldn't have known half-cock from full cock and full cock from a bag of frogs, screeched like a woman and put his hands over his eyes.

'*No kidding!*' he screamed. '*No kidding! I swear! I swear!*'

The Kid looked at him for a long time. At last he lowered the hammers on his guns.

'I'm gonna kill you, Trashy,' he said, smiling. 'I'm gonna take your motherfuckin life. But first we're gonna walk back to that pileup we squeaked by this morning. You're gonna push the van over the edge. Then I'm gonna go back and find another way around. Not gonna leave my fuckin car,' he added petulantly. 'Nohow no *way.*'

'Please don't kill me,' Trashcan whispered. 'Please don't.'

'If you can get that VW van over the side in less'n fifteen minutes, maybe I won't,' The Kid said. 'You believe that happy crappy?'

'Yes,' Trash said. But he had gotten a good look into those preternaturally glittering eyes, and he did not believe it at all.

They walked back to the pileup, Trashcan Man walking in front of The Kid on wobbling rubber legs. The Kid walked mincingly, his leather jacket creaking softly in its secret folds. There was a vague, almost sweet smile on his doll-like lips.

By the time they got to the pileup, dusk was almost gone. The VW Microbus was on its side, the corpses of the three or four occupants a tangle of arms and legs that was mercifully hard to see in the fast-failing light. The Kid walked past the van and stood on the shoulder, looking at the place they had edged by some ten hours before. One of the deucey's tire tracks was still there, but the other had crumbled away with the embankment.

'Nope,' The Kid said with finality. 'Never make it by here again unless we do some movin and groovin first. Don't tell me, I'll tell you.'

For one brief moment, Trashcan Man entertained the notion of rushing at The Kid and trying to push him over the edge. Then The Kid turned around. His guns were drawn and pointing casually at Trashcan's midriff.

'Say, Trashy. You was thinkin evil thoughts. Don't try to tell me no different. I can read you like a motherfuckin book.'

Trashcan shook his head violently back and forth in protest.

'Don't you make a mistake with me, Trashy. That's the one thing in this wide world you don't want to do. Now get pushing on that van. You got fifteen minutes.'

There was an Austin parked nearby on the broken center-line. The Kid pulled open the passenger door, casually ripped out the bloated corpse of a teenage girl (her arm came off in his hand and he tossed it aside with the absent air of a man who has finished with the turkey drumstick he has been nibbling on), and sat down on the bucket seat with his feet out on the pavement. He gestured good-humoredly with his guns at the slumped, shuddering form of the Trashcan Man.

'Time's a-wastin, good buddy.' He threw back his head and sang: 'Oh . . . here comes Johnny with his pecker in his hand, he's a one-ball man and he's *OFF* to the ro-dee-*OH* . . . that's right, Trashy, ya fuckin wet end, getcha back into it, only twelve minutes left . . . alamand left an alamand right, come on, ya fuckin dummy, getcha right foot right . . .'

Trash leaned against the Microbus. Bunched his legs and pushed. The Microbus moved perhaps two inches toward the drop. In his heart, hope – that indestructible weed of the human heart – had begun to bloom again. The Kid was irrational, impulsive, what Carley Yates and his poolhall buddies would have called crazier than a shithouse rat. Maybe if he actually got the van over the side and cleared the way for The Kid's precious deuce coupe, the lunatic would let him live.

Maybe.

He lowered his head, gripped the edge of the VW's frame, and shoved with all his might. Pain flared in his recently burned arm, and he knew that the fragile new tissue would soon rip open. Then the pain would become agony.

The bus moved three inches. Sweat dripped from Trashcan's brow and ran into his eyes, stinging like warm engine oil.

'Oh, here comes Johnny with his pecker in his hand, he's a one-ball man and he's *OFF* to the ro-dee-*OH!*' The Kid sang. 'Well, alamand left an alamand r −'

The song broke off like a brittle twig. Trashcan Man looked up apprehensively. The Kid had come out of the Austin's passenger seat. He was standing in profile to Trash, staring across their half of the turnpike toward the eastbound lanes. A rocky, brushy slope rose beyond them, blotting out half the sky.

'What the fuck was *that?*' The Kid whispered.

'I didn't hear anyth −'

Then he *did* hear something. He heard a small rattle of pebbles and stones on the other side of the highway. His dream recurred to him in sudden, total recall that froze his blood and evaporated all the spit in his mouth.

'*Who's there?*' The Kid shouted. '*You better answer me! Answer, goddammit, or I start shooting!*'

And he *was* answered, but not by any human voice. A howl rose up in the night like a hoarse siren, first climbing and then dropping rapidly down to a guttural growl.

'Holy Jesus!' The Kid said, and his voice was suddenly thin.

Coming down the slope on the far side of the turnpike and crossing the median strip were wolves, gaunt gray timberwolves, their eyes red, their jaws gaping and adrip. There were more than two dozen of them. Trashcan, in an ecstasy of terror, made wee-wee in his pants again.

The Kid stepped around the trunk of the Austin, leveled his .45s, and began firing. Flame licked from the barrels; the sound of the shots echoed and reechoed from the mountain faces, making it sound as if artillery were at work. Trashcan Man cried out and poked his index fingers in his ears. The night breeze tattered the gunsmoke, fresh and ripe and hot. Its cordite aroma stung his nose.

The wolves came on, no faster and no slower, at a fast walk. Their eyes . . . Trashcan Man found himself unable to look away from their eyes. They were not the eyes of ordinary wolves; of that he was quite convinced. They were the eyes of their Master, he thought. Their Master and *his* Master. Suddenly he remembered his prayer and he was afraid no longer. He took his fingers out of his ears. He ignored the wetness spreading at his crotch. He began to smile.

The Kid had emptied both of his guns, dropping three of the wolves in so doing. He holstered the .45s without making an attempt to reload and turned west. He went about ten paces and then stopped. More wolves were padding down the westbound lanes, weaving in and out of the dark hulks of the stalled cars like tattered streamers of mist. One of them raised its snout to the sky and howled. Its cry was joined by a second, the second by a third, the third by a whole chorus. Then they came on again.

The Kid began to back up. He was trying to load one of his guns now, but the shells were spilling out between his nerveless fingers. Suddenly he gave up. The gun fell out of his hand and clunked on the road. As if it had been a signal, the wolves rushed him.

With a high, reedy scream of fear, The Kid turned and ran for the Austin. As he ran, his second pistol tumbled from its low holster and bounced off the road. With a low, ripping growl, the wolf closest to him sprang just as The Kid dove into the Austin and slammed the door.

He just made it. The wolf bounced off the door, growling, its red eyes rolling horribly. It was joined by the others, and in moments the Austin was ringed with wolves. From inside, The Kid's face was a small white moon looking out.

Then one of the wolves was coming toward the Trashcan Man, its triangular head held low, its eyes glowing like stormlamps.

My life for you . . .

Steadily, now not in the least afraid, Trash went to meet it. He held out his burned hand and the wolf licked it. After a moment it sat at his feet, curling its ragged, brushy tail about its withers.

The Kid was staring at him, his mouth hanging open.

Smiling into his eyes, Trashcan Man gave him the finger.

Both fingers.

And he screamed: 'Fuck you! You're shut down! Do you hear me? *DO YOU BELIEVE THAT HAPPY CRAPPY? SHUT DOWN! DON'T TELL ME, I'LL TELL YOU!'*

The wolf's mouth closed gently on Trashcan's good hand. He looked down. It was standing again, tugging him lightly. Tugging him west.

'All right,' Trashcan said serenely. 'Okay, boy.'

He began to walk and the wolf fell in right behind him, walking like a well-trained dog at heel. As they walked away, five others joined them from amid the stalled cars. Now he walked with one wolf ahead of him, one behind him, and two on each side, like an escorted dignitary.

He paused once and looked back over his shoulder. He never forgot what he saw: a ring of wolves sitting patiently in a gray circle around the little Austin, and the pale circle of The Kid's face staring out, his mouth working behind the windowglass. The wolves seemed to grin up at The Kid, their tongues lolling out of their mouths. They seemed to be asking him just how long it would be before he kicked the dark man out of ole Lost Wages on his ass. Just how long?

Trashcan Man wondered how long those wolves would sit around the little Austin, ringing it in a circle of teeth. The answer, of course, was as long as it took. Two days, three, maybe even four. The Kid would sit there, looking out. Nothing to eat (unless the teenage girl had had a passenger, that was), nothing to drink, the afternoon temperature in the car's small interior maybe as high as a hundred and thirty degrees, what with the greenhouse effect. The dark man's lapdogs would wait until The Kid starved to death, or until he got crazy enough to open the door and try to make a run for it. Trashcan Man giggled in the darkness. The Kid wasn't very big. He wouldn't make much more than a mouthful for each of them. And what they *did* get might well poison them.

'Am I right?' he cried, and cackled up at the bright stars. 'Don't tell *me* if you believe that happy crappy! I'll motherfuckin tell *YOU*!'

His gray-ghostly companions padded gravely along all about him, taking no notice of Trashcan Man's shouts. When they reached The Kid's deuce coupe, the wolf at his heel padded over to it, sniffed at one of the Wide Ovals, and then, grinning sardonically, lifted his leg and made wee-wee on it.

Trashcan Man had to laugh. He laughed until tears squirted from his eyes and ran down his cracked, stubbled cheeks. His madness, like a fine skillet dish, now wanted only for the desert sun to simmer it and complete it, to give it that final subtle touch of flavor.

They walked, the Trashcan Man and his escorts. As the traffic grew thicker, the wolves either squirmed under cars with their bellies dragging on the road or padded over hoods and roofs near him – sanguine, silent companions with red eyes and bright teeth. When, sometime after midnight, they reached the Eisenhower Tunnel,

Trashcan did not hesitate but worked his way steadily into the maw of the westbound side. How could he be afraid now? How could he be afraid with guardians like these?

It was a long trip, and he had lost all track of time before it had little more than begun. He groped blindly forward from one car to the next. Once his hand plunged into something wet and sickeningly soft, and there was a horrible whoosh of stinking gas. Even then he did not falter. From time to time he saw red eyes in the dark, always up ahead, always leading him forward.

A time later he sensed a new freshness in the air and began to hurry, once losing his balance and plunging from the hood of one car to crack his skull painfully on the bumper of the next. A short time after that, he looked up and saw the stars again, now paling before the onset of dawn. He was out.

His guardians had faded away. But Trashcan fell to his knees and gave thanks in a long, rambling, disjointed prayer. He had seen the hand of the dark man at work, and he had seen it plain.

In spite of all he had been through since he had awakened the previous morning to see The Kid admiring his hairdo in the mirror of the Golden Motel room, Trash was too exalted to sleep. He walked instead, putting the tunnel behind him. The traffic was choked on the westbound side of the tunnel too, but it had cleared out enough to walk comfortably before he had gone two miles. Across the median, in the eastbound lanes, the stream of cars that had been waiting to use the tunnel stretched on and on.

At noon he began to come down from Vail Pass into Vail itself, passing the condominiums and the singles apartment complexes. Now weariness had almost overcome him. He broke a window, unlocked a door, found a bed. And that was all he remembered until early the next morning.

The beauty of religious mania is that it has the power to explain everything. Once God (or Satan) is accepted as the first cause of everything which happens in the mortal world, nothing is left to chance . . . or change. Once such incantatory phrases as 'we see now through a glass darkly' and 'mysterious are the ways He chooses His wonders to perform' are mastered, logic can be happily tossed out the window. Religious mania is one of the few infallible ways of responding to the world's vagaries, because it totally eliminates pure accident. To the true religious maniac, it's *all* on purpose.

It was quite likely for this reason that the Trashcan Man talked to a crow for nearly twenty minutes on the road west of Vail, convinced it was either an emissary of the dark man . . . or the dark man himself. The crow regarded him silently from its perch on a high telephone wire for a long time, not flying away until it was bored or hungry . . . or until Trashcan's outpouring of praise and promises of loyalty were complete.

He got another bike near Grand Junction, and by July 25 he had been speeding across western Utah on Route 4, which connects 1–89 on the east to the great southwestern-tending 1–15, which goes from north of Salt Lake City all the way to San Bernadino, California. And when the front wheel of his new bike suddenly decided to part company from the rest of the machine and go speeding off into the desert on its own, Trashcan Man was pitched over the handlebars to land on his head, a crash that should have fractured his skull (he was doing forty when it happened, and wearing no helmet). Yet he was able to stand up less than five minutes later, with blood streaming over his face from half a dozen cuts and lacerations, able to do his shuffling, grimacing little dance, able to chant: '*Cii-a-bo-la, my life for you, Ci-a-bola, bumpty, bumpty, bump!*'

There is really nothing so comforting to the beaten of spirit or the broken of skull than a good strong dose of 'Thy will be done.'

On August 7, Lloyd Henreid came to the room in which the dehydrated and semidelirious Trashcan Man had been installed the day before. It was a fine room, on the thirtieth floor of the MGM Grand. There was a round bed with silk sheets, and a round mirror which looked to be the exact same size as the bed, mounted on the ceiling.

Trashcan Man looked at Lloyd.

'How you feeling, Trash?' Lloyd asked, looking back.

'Good,' Trashcan Man said. 'Better.'

'Some food and water and rest, that's all you needed,' Lloyd said. 'I brought you some clean clothes. Had to guess at the sizes.'

'They look fine.' Trash had never really been able to remember his sizes. He took the jeans and the workshirt Lloyd offered.

'Come on down to breakfast when you're dressed,' Lloyd said. He spoke almost deferentially. 'Most of us eat in the deli.'

'Okay. Sure.'

The deli hummed with conversation, and he paused outside and around the corner, suddenly overcome with fright. They would

look up at him when he came in. They would look up and laugh.
Someone would start giggling in the back of the room, someone else
would join in, and then the whole place would be an uproar of
laughter and pointing fingers.

Hey, put away ya matches, here comes the Trashcan Man!

Hey, Trash! What did ole lady Semple say when you torched her pension check?

Wet the bed much, Trashy?

Sweat popped out on his skin, making him feel slimy in spite
of the shower he'd taken after Lloyd left. He remembered his face
in the bathroom mirror, covered with slowly healing scabs, his body,
too gaunt, his eyes, too small for their yawning sockets. Yes, they
would laugh. He listened to the hum of conversation, the clink of
silverware, and thought he should just slink away.

Then he thought of the way the wolf had taken his hand, so
gently, and had led him away from The Kid's metal tomb, and Trash
squared his shoulders and walked inside.

A few people looked up briefly, then went back to their meals
and their conversations. Lloyd, at a big table in the middle of the
room, raised an arm and waved him over. Trash threaded his way
among the tables and under a darkened electronic Keno toteboard.
There were three other people at the table. They were all eating
ham and scrambled eggs.

'Serve yourself,' Lloyd said. 'It's a steam-table kinda thing.'

Trashcan Man got a tray and served himself. The man behind
the counter, large and dressed in dirty cook's whites, watched him.

'Are you Mr Horgan?' Trashcan Man asked timidly.

Horgan grinned, exposing gapped teeth. 'Yeah, but we won't
get nowhere with you callin me that, boy. You call me Whitey.
You feelin a little better? When you came in, you looked like the
wratha God.'

'Much better, sure.'

'Dig in those aigs. All you want. Go light on the home fries,
though. I would, at least. Them taters is old and tough. Good to
have you here, boy.'

'Thanks,' Trash said.

He went back to Lloyd's table.

'Trash, this here is Ken DeMott. The fella with the bald spot
is Hector Drogan. And this kid tryin to grow on his face what springs
up wild in his asshole calls himself Ace High.'

They all nodded at him.

'This is our new boy,' Lloyd said. 'Name's Trashcan Man.'

Hands were shaken all around. Trash started to dig into his eggs. He looked up at the young man with the scraggly beard and said in a low, polite voice: 'Would you pass the salt, please, Mr High?'

There was a moment of surprise as they looked at each other, and then they all burst into laughter. Trash stared at them, feeling the panic rise in his chest, and then he heard the laughter, really *heard* it, with his mind as well as his ears, and understood that there was no meanness in it. No one here was going to ask him why he hadn't burned down the school instead of the church. No one here was going to dun him about old lady Semple's pension check. He could smile too, if he wanted. And he did.

'Mr *High*,' Hector Drogan was giggling. 'Oh, Ace, you just been had. Mr *High*, I love it. *Meeestair Haaaaah*. Man, that is so fuckin rich.'

Ace High handed Trashcan the salt. 'Just Ace, my man. That'll get me every time. You don't call me Mr High and I won't call you Mr Man, that a deal?'

'Okay,' Trashcan Man said, still smiling. 'That's fine.'

'Oh, Mr *Hiiiigh*?' Heck Drogan said in a coy falsetto. Then he burst into laughter again. 'Ace, you never gonna live that down. I swear you won't.'

'Maybe not, but I'm sure-God gonna live it up,' Ace High said, and got up with his plate for more eggs. His hand closed for a moment on Trashcan Man's shoulder as he went. The hand was warm and solid. It was a friendly hand that did not squeeze or pinch.

Trashcan Man dug into his eggs, feeling warm and good inside. This warmth and goodness was so foreign to his nature that it almost felt like a disease. As he ate he tried to isolate it, understand it. He looked up, looked at the faces around him, and thought he might understand what it was.

Happiness.

What a good bunch of people, he thought.

And on the heels of that: *I'm home.*

That day he was left on his own to sleep, but the next day he was bussed up to Boulder Dam with a lot of other people. There they spent the day wrapping copper core wire around the spindles of burned-out motors. He worked at a bench with a view of the water

– Lake Mead – and no one supervised him. Trashcan Man assumed that there was no foreman or anyone like that around because everyone was as in love with what they were doing as he was himself.

He learned differently the next day.

It was quarter past ten in the morning. Trashcan Man was sitting on his bench, wrapping copper wire, his mind a million miles away as his fingers did their work. He was composing a psalm of praise to the dark man in his mind. It had occurred to him that he should get a large book (a Book, actually) and begin to write some of his thoughts about *him* down. It would be the sort of Book people might want to read someday. People who felt about *him* as Trash did.

Ken DeMott came to his bench, and Ken looked pale and frightened under his desert tan. 'Come on,' he said. 'Work's over. We're going back to Vegas. Everyone. The buses are outside.'

'Huh? Why?' Trashcan blinked up at him.

'I don't know. It's *his* order. Lloyd passed it along. Get your ass in gear, Trashy. It's best not to ask questions when the hardcase is involved.'

So he didn't. Outside, on Hoover Drive, three Las Vegas Public School buses were parked with their engines idling. Men and women were climbing aboard. There was little talk; the midmorning ride back to Vegas was the antithesis of the usual commutes to and from work. There was no horseplay, little conversation, and none of the usual light banter that passed between the twenty or so women and the thirty or so men. Everyone had drawn into himself or herself.

As they neared the city, Trashcan Man heard one of the men sitting across the aisle from him say quietly to his seatmate: 'It's Heck. Heck Drogan. Goddammit, how does that spook find things out?'

'Shut up,' the other said, and gave Trashcan Man a mistrustful glance.

Trash averted his gaze and looked out the window at the passing desert. He was once again troubled in his mind.

'Oh Jesus,' one of the women said as they filed off the bus, but hers was the only comment.

Trashcan looked around, puzzled. Everyone was here, it looked like, everyone in Cibola. They had all been called back, with the exception of a few scouts that might be anywhere from the Mexican peninsula to west Texas. They were gathered in a loose semicircle around the fountain, six and seven deep, more than four hundred in all. Some of those in the back were standing on hotel chairs so they could see, and until Trashcan drew closer, he thought it was the fountain they were looking at. Craning his neck, he could see there was something lying on the lawn in front of the fountain, but he couldn't see what it was.

A hand grasped his elbow. It was Lloyd. His face looked white and strained. 'I been lookin for you. *He* wants to see you later. Meantime, we got this. God, I hate these. Come on. I need help and you're elected.'

Trashcan Man's head was whirling. *He* wanted to see him! *Him!* But in the meantime there was this . . . whatever *this* was.

'What, Lloyd? What is it?'

Lloyd didn't answer. Still holding lightly to Trashcan Man's arm, he led him toward the fountain. The crowd parted before them, almost shrank from them. The narrow corridor they passed through seemed to be insulated with a still cold layer of loathing and fear.

Standing at the front of the crowd was Whitney Horgan. He was smoking a cigarette. One of his Hush Puppies was propped on the object Trash hadn't been quite able to make out before. It was a wooden cross. Its vertical piece was about twelve feet long. It looked like a crude lowercase *t.*

'Everyone here?' Lloyd asked.

'Yeah,' Whitey said, 'I guess they are. Winky took roll-call. We got nine guys out of state. Flagg said never mind about them. How are you holding up, Lloyd?'

'I'll be fine,' Lloyd said. 'Well . . . not fine, but you know – I'll get through it.'

Whitey cocked his head toward Trashcan Man. 'How much does the kid know?'

'I don't know anything,' Trashcan said, more confused than ever. Hope, awe, and dread were all in dubious battle within him. 'What is this? Someone said something about Heck –'

'Yeah, it's Heck,' Lloyd said. 'He's been freebasing. Fucking blow, don't I hate the goddam fucking blow. Go on, Whitey, tell em to bring him out.'

Whitey moved away from Lloyd and Trash, stepping over a rectangular hole in the ground. The hole had been throated with cement. It looked just the right size and depth to take the butt end of the cross. As Whitney 'Whitey' Horgan trotted up the wide steps between the gold pyramids, Trashcan Man felt all the spit in his mouth dry up. He suddenly turned, first to the silent crowd, waiting in its crescent formation under the blue sky, then to Lloyd, who stood pale and silent, looking at the cross and picking the white head of a pimple on his chin.

'You . . . we . . . nail him up?' Trashcan managed at last. 'Is that what this is about?'

Lloyd reached suddenly into the pocket of his faded shirt. 'You know, I got something for you. *He* gave it to me to give to you. I can't make you take it, but it's a goddam good thing for me that I remembered to at least make the offer. Do you want it?'

From his breast pocket he drew a fine gold chain with a black jet stone on the end of it. The stone was flawed with a tiny red spot, as was Lloyd's own. He dangled it before Trashcan Man's eyes like a hypnotist's amulet.

The truth was in Lloyd's eyes, too clear not to be recognized, and Trashcan Man knew he could never weep and grovel – not before *him*, not before anybody, but especially not before him – and claim he hadn't understood. *Take this and you take everything*, Lloyd's eyes said. *And what's a part of everything? Why, Heck Drogan, of course. Heck and the cement-lined hole in the ground, the hole just big enough to take the butt end of Heck's cross-tree.*

He reached for it slowly. His hand paused just before the outstretched fingers could touch the gold chain.

This is my last chance. My last chance to be Donald Merwin Elbert.

But another voice, one which spoke with greater authority (but with a certain gentleness, like a cool hand on a fevered brow), told him that the time of choices had long since passed. If he chose Donald Merwin Elbert now, he would die. He had sought the dark man of his own free will (if there *is* such a thing for the Trashcan Men of the world), had accepted the dark man's favors. The dark man had saved him from dying at the hands of The Kid (that the dark man might have *sent* The Kid for just that purpose never crossed Trashcan Man's mind), and surely that meant his life was now a debt he owed to that same dark man . . . the man some of them here called the Walkin Dude. His life! Had he not himself offered it again and again?

But your soul . . . did you offer your soul as well?

In for a penny, in for a pound, the Trashcan Man thought, and gently put one hand around the gold chain and the other around the dark stone. The stone was cold and smooth. He held it in his fist for a moment just to see if he could warm it up. He didn't think he would be able to, and he was right. So he put it around his neck, where it lay against his skin like a tiny ball of ice.

But he didn't mind that icy feeling.

That icy feeling counterbalanced the fire which was always in his mind.

'Just tell yourself you don't know him,' Lloyd said. 'Heck, I mean. That's what I always do. It makes it easier. It −'

Two of the wide hotel doors banged open. Frantic, terrified screams floated across to them. The crowd sighed.

A party of nine came down the steps. Hector Drogan was in the center. He was fighting like a tiger caught in a net. His face was dead pale except for two hectic blots of color riding high up on his cheekbones. Sweat was pouring off every inch of skin in rivers. He was mother-naked. Five men were holding on to him. One of them was Ace High, the kid Heck had been ribbing about his name.

'Ace!' Hector was babbling. 'Hey, Ace, what do you say? Little help for the kid, okay? Tell them to quit this, man − I can get clean, I swear to God I can clean up my act. What do you say? Little help here! *Please*, Ace!'

Ace High said nothing; simply tightened his grip on Heck's thrashing arm. It was answer enough. Hector Drogan began to scream again. He was dragged relentlessly across the pavilion and toward the fountain.

Behind him, walking in line like a solemn undertaker's party, were three men: Whitney Horgan, carrying a large carpetbag; a man named Roy Hoopes, with a stepladder; and Winky Winks, a bald man whose eyes twitched constantly. Winky was carrying a clipboard with a typed sheet of paper on it.

Heck was dragged to the foot of the cross. A horrible yellow smell of fear was radiating out from him; his eyes rolled, showing the muddy whites, like the eyes of a horse left out in a thunderstorm.

'Hey, Trashy,' he said hoarsely as Roy Hoopes set up the stepladder behind him. 'Trashcan Man. Tell em to cut it out, buddy. Tell them I can get clean. Tell them a scare like this is better'n all the fuckin rehabs in the world. Tell em, man.'

Trashcan stared down at his feet. As he bent his neck, the black stone swung out from his chest and into his field of vision. The red flaw, the eye, seemed to be staring up at him fixedly.

'I don't know you,' he mumbled.

From the tail of his eye he saw Whitey down on one knee, a cigarette dangling from the corner of his mouth, his left eye squinted against the smoke. He opened the carpetbag. He was taking out sharp wooden nails. To Trashcan Man's horrified gaze, they looked almost as big as tentpegs. He laid the nails on the grass and then removed a large wooden mallet from the carpetbag.

In spite of the murmuring voices all around them, Trashcan Man's words seemed to have penetrated the panicky haze in Hector Drogan's mind. 'What do you *mean*, you don't know me?' he cried wildly. 'We had breakfast together just two days ago! You called the kid there Mr High. *What do you mean you don't know me, you chickenshit little liar?*'

'I don't know you at all,' Trash repeated, a little more clearly this time. And what he felt was almost a sense of relief. All he saw here in front of him was a stranger, a stranger who looked a bit like Carley Yates. His hand went to the stone and curled around it. Its coolness reassured him further.

'*You liar!*' Heck screamed. He began to struggle again, his muscles flexing and pumping, the sweat trickling down his bare chest and arms. '*You liar! You do so know me! You do so, you liar!*'

'No I don't. I don't know you and I don't *want* to know you.'

Heck began to scream again. The four men holding him bore down, panting and out of breath.

'Go ahead,' Lloyd said.

Heck was dragged backward. One of the men holding him stuck out a leg and tripped him. He landed half on the cross and half off it. Meanwhile, Winky had begun to read the typed sheet on his clipboard in a high voice that sliced through Heck's screams like the howl of a buzz-saw.

'Attention attention attention! By the order of Randall Flagg, Leader of the People and First Citizen, this man, Hector Alonzo Drogan by name, is ordered executed by an act of crucifixion, this penalty so ordered for the crime of drug use.'

'*No! No! No!*' Heck screamed in frenzied counterpoint. His left arm, greasy with sweat, escaped Ace High's hold, and instinctively Trash knelt and pinned the arm back down, forcing the wrist against an arm of the cross. A second later, Whitey was kneeling beside Trashcan with the wooden mallet and two of the crude nails. The cigarette still hung from the corner of his mouth. He looked like a man about to do a little job of carpentering in his back yard.

'Yeah, good, hold him just like that, Trash. I'll staple him. Won't take a minute.'

'Drug use is not allowed in this Society of the People because it impairs the user's ability to contribute fully to the Society of the People,' Winky was proclaiming. He spoke fast, like an auctioneer, and his eyes bunched and scrunched and wiggled. 'Specifically in this case, the accused Hector Drogan was found with freebasing paraphernalia and a large supply of cocaine.'

Now Heck's screams had reached a pitch that might well have shattered crystal, if there had been any crystal around to shatter. His head lashed from side to side. There was foam on his lips. Ribbons of blood coursed down his arms as six of them, Trashcan Man included, lifted the cross into the cement pit. Now Hector Drogan was silhouetted against the sky with his head thrown back in a rictus of pain.

'– is done for the good of this Society of the People,' Winky screamed relentlessly. 'This communication ends with a solemn warning and greetings to the People of Las Vegas. Let this bill of true facts be nailed above the miscreant's head, and let it be marked with the seal of the First Citizen, *RANDALL FLAGG* by name.'

'*Oh my God it HURTS!*' Hector Drogan screamed from above them. '*Oh my God my God oh God God God!*'

The crowd remained for almost an hour, each person afraid to be remarked upon as having been the first to leave. There was disgust on many faces, a drowsy kind of excitement on many others . . . but if there was a common denominator, it was fear.

Trashcan Man wasn't frightened, though. Why should he have been frightened? He hadn't known the man.

He hadn't known him at all.

It was quarter past ten that night when Lloyd came back to Trashcan Man's room. He glanced at Trash and said, 'You're dressed. Good. I thought you might have gone to bed already.'

'No,' Trashcan Man said, 'I'm up. Why?'

Lloyd's voice dropped. 'It's now, Trashy. He wants to see you. Flagg.'

'He – ?'

'Yeah.'

Trashcan Man was transported. 'Where is he? My life for him, oh yes –'

'Top floor,' Lloyd said. 'He got in just after we finished burning Drogan's body. From the Coast. He was just here when Whitey and I got back from the landfill. No one ever sees him come or go, Trash, but they always know when he's taken off again. Or when he comes back. Come on, let's go.'

Four minutes later the elevator arrived at the top floor and Trashcan Man, his face alight and his eyes goggling, stepped out. Lloyd did not.

Trash turned toward him. 'Aren't you – ?'

Lloyd managed a smile, but it was a sorry affair. 'No, he wants to see you alone. Good luck, Trash.'

And before he could say anything else, the elevator door had slid shut and Lloyd was gone.

Trashcan Man turned around. He was in a wide, sumptuous hallway. There were two doors . . . and the one at the end was slowly opening. It was dark in there. But Trash could see a form standing in the doorway. And eyes. Red eyes.

Heart thudding slowly in his chest, mouth dry, Trashcan Man started to walk toward that form. As he did, the air seemed to grow steadily cooler and cooler. Goosebumps rashed out on his sunbaked arms. Somewhere deep inside him, the corpse of Donald Merwin Elbert rolled over in its grave and seemed to cry out.

Then it was still again.

'The Trashcan Man,' a low and charming voice said. 'How good it is to have you here. How very good.'

The words fell like dust from his mouth: 'My . . . my life for you.'

'Yes,' the shape in the doorway said soothingly. Lips parted and white teeth showed in a grin. 'But I don't think it will come to that. Come in. Let me look at you.'

His eyes overbright, his face as slack as the face of a sleepwalker, Trashcan Man stepped inside. The door closed, and they were in dimness. A terribly hot hand closed over Trashcan Man's icy one . . . and suddenly he felt at peace.

Flagg said: 'There's work for you in the desert, Trash. Great work. If you want it.'

'Anything,' Trashcan Man whispered. 'Anything.'

Randall Flagg slipped an arm around his wasted shoulders. 'I'm going to set you to burn,' he said. 'Come, let's have something to drink and talk about it.'

And in the end, that burning was very great.

CHAPTER 49

When Lucy Swann woke up it was fifteen minutes to midnight by the ladies' Pulsar watch she wore. There was silent heat lightning in the west where the mountains were – the *Rocky* Mountains, she amended with some awe. Before this trip she had never been west of Philadelphia, where her brother-in-law lived. Had lived.

The other half of the double sleeping bag was empty; that was what had wakened her. She thought of just rolling over and going back to sleep – he would come back to bed when he was ready – and then she got up and went quietly toward where she thought he would be, on the west side of camp. She went lithely, without disturbing a soul. Except for the Judge, of course; ten to midnight was his watch, and you'd never catch Judge Farris nodding off on duty. The Judge was seventy, and he'd joined them in Joliet. There were nineteen of them now, fifteen adults, three children, and Joe.

'Lucy?' the Judge said, his voice low.

'Yes. Did you see –'

A low chuckle. 'Sure did. He's out by the highway. Same place as last night and the night before that.'

She drew closer to him and saw that his Bible was open on his lap. 'Judge, you'll strain your eyes doing that.'

'Nonsense. Starlight's the best light for this stuff. Maybe the only light. How's this? "*Is there not an appointed time to man upon earth? are not his days like the days of an hireling? As a servant earnestly desireth the shadow, and as an hireling looketh for the reward of his work: So am I made to possess months of vanity, and wearisome nights are appointed to me. When I lie down, I say, When shall I arise, and the night be gone? and I am full of tossings to and fro unto the dawning of the day.*"'

'Far out,' Lucy said without much enthusiasm. 'Real nice, Judge.'

'It's not nice, it's Job. There's nothing very nice in the Book of Job, Lucy.' He closed the Bible. ' "*I am full of tossings to and fro unto the dawning of the day."* That's your man, Lucy: that's Larry Underwood to a *t*.'

'I know,' she said, and sighed. 'Now if I only knew what was wrong with him.'

The Judge, who had his suspicions, kept silent.

'It can't be the dreams,' she said. 'No one has them anymore, unless Joe does. And Joe's . . . different.'

'Yes. He is. Poor boy.'

'And everyone's healthy. At least since Mrs Vollman died.' Two days after the Judge joined them, a couple who introduced themselves as Dick and Sally Vollman had thrown in with Larry and his assorted company of survivors. Lucy thought it extremely unlikely that the flu had spared a man and wife, and suspected that their marriage was common-law and of extremely short duration. They were in their forties, and obviously very much in love. Then, a week ago, at the old woman's house in Hemingford Home, Sally Vollman had gotten sick. They camped for two days, waiting helplessly for her to get better or die. She had died. Dick Vollman was still with them, but he was a different man – silent, thoughtful, pale.

'He's taken that to heart, hasn't he?' she asked Judge Farris.

'Larry is a man who found himself comparatively late in life,' the Judge said, clearing his throat. 'At least, that is how he strikes me. Men who find themselves late are never sure. They are all the things the civics books tell us the good citizens should be: partisans but never zealots, respecters of the facts which attend each situation but never benders of those facts, uncomfortable in positions of leadership but rarely able to turn down a responsibility once it has been offered . . . or thrust upon them. They make the best leaders in a democracy because they are unlikely to fall in love with power. Quite the opposite. And when things go wrong . . . when a Mrs Vollman dies . . .

'Could it have been diabetes?' the Judge interrupted himself. 'I think it likely. The cyanosed skin, the fast drop into a coma . . . possibly, possibly. But if so, where was her insulin? Might she have let herself die? Could it have been suicide?'

The Judge lapsed into a thinking pause, hands clasped under his chin. He looked like a brooding black bird of prey.

'You were going to say something about when things go wrong,' Lucy prompted gently.

'When they go wrong – when a Sally Vollman dies, of diabetes or internal bleeding or whatever – a man like Larry blames himself. The men the civics books idolize rarely come to good ends. Melvin Purvis, the super G-man of the thirties, shot himself with his own service pistol in 1959. When Lincoln was assassinated, he was a prematurely old man tottering on the edge of a nervous breakdown. We used to watch Presidents decay before our very eyes from month to month and even week to week on national TV – except for Nixon, of course, who thrived on power the way that a vampire bat thrives on blood, and Reagan, who seemed a little too stupid to get old. I guess Gerald Ford was that way, too.'

'I think there's something more,' Lucy said sadly.

He looked at her, inquiring.

'How did it go? I am full of tossings and turnings unto the dawning of the day?'

He nodded.

Lucy said, 'Pretty good description of a man in love, isn't it?'

He looked at her, surprised that she had known all along about the thing he wouldn't say. Lucy shrugged, smiled – a bitter quirk of the lips. 'Women know,' she said. 'Women almost always know.'

Before he could reply, she had drifted away toward the road, where Larry would be, sitting and thinking about Nadine Cross.

'Larry?'

'Here,' he said briefly. 'What are you doing up?'

'I got cold,' she said. He was sitting cross-legged on the shoulder of the road, as if in meditation. 'Room for me?'

'Sure.' He moved over. The boulder still held a bit of warmth from the day which was now passing. She sat down. He slipped an arm around her. According to Lucy's estimation, they were about fifty miles east of Boulder tonight. If they could get on the road by nine tomorrow, they could be in the Boulder Free Zone for lunch.

It was the man on the radio who called it the Boulder Free Zone; his name was Ralph Brentner, and he said (with some embarrassment) that the Boulder Free Zone was mostly a radio call-sign, but Lucy liked it just for itself, for the way it sounded. It sounded right. It sounded like a fresh start. And Nadine Cross had adopted the name with an almost religious zeal, as if it was talismanic.

Three days after Larry, Nadine, Joe, and Lucy had arrived at Stovington and found the plague center deserted, Nadine had suggested they pick up a CB radio and start conning the forty channels. Larry had accepted the idea wholeheartedly – the way he accepted most of her ideas, Lucy thought. She didn't understand Nadine Cross at all. Larry was stuck on her, that was obvious, but Nadine didn't want to have much to do with him outside of each day's routine.

Anyway, the CB idea had been a good one, even if the brain that had produced it was icelocked (except when it came to Joe). It would be the easiest way to locate other groups, Nadine had said, and to agree upon a rendezvous.

This had led to some puzzled discussion in their group, which at that time had numbered half a dozen with the addition of Mark Zellman, who had been a welder in upstate New York, and Laurie Constable, a twenty-six-year-old nurse. And the puzzled discussion had led to yet another upsetting argument about the dreams.

Laurie had begun by protesting that they knew *exactly* where they were going. They were following the resourceful Harold Lauder and his party to Nebraska. Of course they were, and for the same reason. The force of the dreams was simply too powerful to be denied.

After some back and forth on this, Nadine had gotten hysterical. She had had no dreams – repeat: *no goddam dreams*. If the others wanted to practice autohypnosis on each other, fine. As long as there was some rational basis for pushing on to Nebraska, such as the sign at the Stovington installation, fine. But she wanted it understood that she wasn't going along on the basis of a lot of metaphysical bullshit. If it was all the same to them, she would place her faith in radios, not visions.

Mark had turned a friendly, gapped grin on Nadine's strained countenance and said, 'If you ain't had no dreams, how come you woke me up last night talkin in your sleep?'

Nadine had gone paper white. 'Are you calling me a liar?' she nearly screamed. 'Because if you are, one of us had better leave right now!' Joe shrank close to her, whimpering.

Larry had smoothed it over, agreeing with the CB idea. And in the last week or so, they had begun to pick up broadcasts, not from Nebraska (which had been abandoned even before they got there – the dreams had told them that, but even then the dreams had been fading, losing their urgency), but from Boulder, Colorado, six hundred miles farther west – signals boosted by Ralph's powerful transmitter.

Lucy could still remember the joyous, almost ecstatic faces of the others as Ralph Brentner's drawling, Oklahoma accent had cut nasally through the static: 'This is Ralph Brentner, Boulder Free Zone. If you hear me, reply on Channel 14. Repeat, Channel 14.'

They could hear Ralph, but had no transmitter powerful enough to acknowledge, not then. But they had drawn closer, and since that first transmission they had found out that the old woman, Abagail Freemantle by name (but Lucy herself would always think of her as Mother Abagail), and her party had been the first to arrive, but since then people had been straggling in by twos and threes and in groups as large as thirty. There had been two hundred people in Boulder when Brentner first got in contact with them; this evening, as they chattered back and forth – their own CB now in easy reaching distance – there were over three hundred and fifty. Their own group would send that number well on the way to four hundred.

'Penny for your thoughts,' Lucy said to Larry, and put her hand on his arm.

'I was thinking about that watch and the death of capitalism,' he said, pointing at her Pulsar. 'It used to be root, hog, or die – and the hog who rooted the hardest ended up with the red, white, and blue Cadillac and the Pulsar watch. Now, true democracy. Any lady in America can have a Pulsar digital and a blue haze mink.' He laughed.

'Maybe,' she said. 'But I'll tell you something, Larry. I may not know much about capitalism, but I know something about this thousand-dollar watch. I know it's no damned good.'

'No?' He looked at her, surprised and smiling. It was just a little one, but it was genuine. She was glad to see his smile – a smile that was for her. 'Why not?'

'Because no one knows what time it is,' Lucy said pertly. 'Four or five days ago I asked Mr Jackson, and Mark, and you, one right after another. And you all gave me different times and you all said that your watches had stopped least once . . . remember that place where they kept the world's time? I read an article about it in a magazine one time when I was in the doctor's office. It was tremendous. They had it right down to the micro-micro-second. They had pendulums and solar clocks and everything. Now I think about that place sometimes and it just makes me mad. All the clocks there must be stopped and I have a thousand-dollar Pulsar watch that I hawked from a jewelry store and it can't keep time down to the solar second like it's supposed to. Because of the flu. The goddamned flu.'

She fell silent and they sat together awhile without talking. Then Larry pointed at the sky. 'See there!'

'What? Where?'

'Three o'clock high. Two, now.'

She looked but didn't see what he had pointed at until he pressed his warm hands to the sides of her face and tilted it toward the right quadrant of the sky. Then she did see and her breath caught in her throat. A bright light, starbright, but hard and unwinking. It fled rapidly across the sky on an east-to-west course.

'My God,' she cried, 'it's a plane, isn't it, Larry? A plane?'

'No. An earth satellite. It will be going around and around up there for the next seven hundred years, probably.'

They sat and watched it until it was out of sight behind the dark bulk of the Rockies.

'Larry?' she said softly. 'Why didn't Nadine admit it? About the dreams?'

There was a barely perceptible stiffening in him, making her wish she hadn't brought it up. But now that she had, she was determined to pursue it . . . unless he cut her off entirely.

'She says she doesn't have any dreams.'

'She does have them, though – Mark was right about that. And she talks in her sleep. She was so loud one night she woke me up.'

He was looking at her now. After a long time he asked, 'What was she saying?'

Lucy thought, trying to get it just right. 'She was thrashing around in her sleeping bag and she was saying over and over, "Don't, it's so cold, don't, I can't stand it if you do, it's so cold, so cold." And then she started to pull her hair. She started to pull her own hair in her sleep. And moan. It gave me the creeps.'

'People can have nightmares, Lucy. That doesn't mean they're about . . . well, about *him*.'

'It's better not to say much about him after dark, isn't it?'

'Better, yes.'

'She acts as if she's coming unraveled, Larry. Do you know what I mean?'

'Yes.' He knew. In spite of her insistence that she didn't dream, there had been brown circles under her eyes by the time they reached

Hemingford Home. That magnificent cable of heavy hair was noticeably whiter. And if you touched her, she jumped. She *flinched*.

Lucy said, 'You love her, don't you?'

'Oh, Lucy,' he said reproachfully.

'No, I just want you to know . . .' She shook her head violently
at his expression. 'I have to say this. I see the way you look at
her . . . the way she looks at you sometimes, when you're busy with
something else and it's . . . it's safe. She loves you, Larry. But she's
afraid.'

'Afraid of what? Afraid of *what*?'

He was remembering his attempt to make love to her, three
days after the Stovington fiasco. Since then she had grown quiet –
she was still cheerful on occasion, but now she was quite obviously
laboring to be cheerful. Joe had been asleep. Larry had gone to sit
beside her, and for a while they had talked, not about their current
situation but about the old things, the safe things. Larry had tried to
kiss her. She pushed him away, turning her head, but not before he
had felt the things Lucy had just told him. He had tried again, being
rough and gentle at the same time, wanting her so damn badly. And
for just one moment she had given in to him, had shown him what
it *could* be like, if . . .

Then she broke from him and moved away, her face pale, her
arms strapped across her breasts, hands cupping elbows, head lowered.

*Don't do that again, Larry. Please don't. Or I'll have to take Joe
and leave.*

*Why? Why, Nadine? Why does it have to be such a goddam big
deal?*

She hadn't answered. Simply stood in that head-down posture,
the brown bruised places already beginning beneath her eyes.

If I could tell you I would, she said finally, and walked away
without looking back.

'I had a girlfriend once who acted a little like her,' Lucy said.
'My senior year in high school. Her name was Joline. Joline Majors.
Joline wasn't in high school. She dropped out to marry her boyfriend.
He was in the Navy. She was pregnant when they got married, but
she lost the baby. Her man was gone a lot, and Joline . . . she liked
to party down. She liked that, and her man was a regular jealous
bear. He told her if he ever found out she was doing anything behind
his back, he'd break both of her arms and spoil her face. Can you
imagine what that life must have been like? Your husband comes

home and says, "Well, I'm shipping out now, love. Give me a kiss, and then we'll have a little roll in the hay, and by the way, if I come back and someone tells me you've been messing around, I'll break both your arms and spoil your face."'

'Yeah, that's not so great.'

'So after a while she met this guy,' Lucy said. 'He was the assistant phys ed coach at Burlington High. They snuck around, always looking over their shoulders, and I don't know if her husband had set someone up to spy on them, but after a while it didn't matter. After a while Joline got really flaky. She'd think that some guy waiting for a bus on the corner was one of her husband's friends. Or the salesman checking in behind her and Herb at some fleabag motel was. She'd think that even if the motel was somewhere way down in New York State. Or even the cop who gave them directions to a picnic spot when they were together. It got so bad that she'd give a little scream if a door slammed in the wind, and she'd jump every time someone came up her stairs. And since she was living in a place that was split up into seven little apartments, someone was almost always coming up the stairs. Herb got scared and left her. He didn't get scared of Joline's husband – he got scared of *her*. And just before her husband came back on leave, Joline had a nervous breakdown. All because she liked to love a little too much . . . and because he was crazy jealous. Nadine reminds me of that girl, Larry. I'm sorry for her. I don't like her that much, I guess, but I sure am sorry for her. She looks terrible.'

'Are you saying Nadine is afraid of me the way that girl was afraid of her husband?'

Lucy said: 'Maybe. I'll tell you this – wherever Nadine's husband is, he's not here.'

He laughed a little uneasily. 'We ought to go back to bed. Tomorrow's going to be a heavy day.'

'Yes,' she said, thinking he hadn't understood a word she said. And suddenly she burst into tears.

'Hey,' he said. 'Hey.' He tried to put an arm around her.

She struck it off. 'You're getting what you want from me, you don't have to do that!'

There was still enough of the old Larry in him to wonder if her voice would carry back to camp.

'Lucy, I never twisted your arm,' he said grimly.

'Oh, you're so *stupid*!' she cried, and beat at his leg. 'Why are men so stupid, Larry? All you can see is what's in black and white. No, you never twisted my arm. I ain't like *her*. You could twist her arm and she'd still spit in your eye and cross her legs. Men have names for girls like me; they write them on bathroom stalls, I've heard. But all it is, is needing someone warm, needing to *be* warm. Needing to love. Is that so bad?'

'No. No, it isn't. But Lucy –'

'But you don't believe that,' she said scornfully. 'So you go on chasing Miss Highpockets and in the meantime you got Lucy to do the horizontal bop with when the sun goes down.'

He sat quietly, nodding. It was true, every word of it. He was too tired, too Christless beat, to argue against it. She seemed to see that; her face softened and she put a hand on his arm.

'If you catch her, Larry, I'll be the first to throw you a bouquet. I never held a grudge in my life. Just . . . try not to be too disappointed.'

'Lucy –'

Her voice rose suddenly, rough with unexpected power, and for a moment his arms goosefleshed. 'I just happen to think love is very important, only love will get us through this, good connections; it's hate against us, worse, it's emptiness.' Her voice dropped. 'You're right. It's late. I'm going back to bed. Coming?'

'Yes,' he said, and as they stood up, he took her in his arms with no calculation at all and kissed her firmly. 'I love you as much as I can, Lucy.'

'I know that,' she said, and gave him a tired smile. 'I know that, Larry.'

This time when he put his arm around her she let it stay. They walked back to camp together, made diffident love, slept.

Nadine came awake like a cat in the dark some twenty minutes after Larry Underwood and Lucy Swann had come back to camp, ten minutes after they had finished their act of love and drifted off to sleep.

The high iron of terror sang in her veins.

Someone wants me, she thought, listening as the millrace of her heart slowed. Her eyes, wide and full of darkness, stared up to where the overhanging branches of an elm laced the sky with shadows. *There's that. Someone wants me. It's true.*

But . . . it's so cold.

Her parents and her brother had been killed in a car accident when she was six; she hadn't gone along that day to see her aunt and uncle, staying behind instead to play with a friend from down the street. They had liked brother best anyway, she could remember that. Brother hadn't been like *her*, little halfling stolen from an orphanage cradle at the age of four and a half months. Brother's origins had been clear. Brother had been – trumpets, please – *Their Own*. But Nadine had always and forever belonged only to Nadine. She was the earth's child.

After the accident she had gone to live with the aunt and uncle, because they were the only two relatives. The White Mountains of eastern New Hampshire. She remembered that they had taken her for a ride on the Cog Railway up Mount Washington for her eighth birthday and the altitude had caused a bloody nose and they had been angry with her. Aunt and Uncle were too old, they had been in their mid-fifties when she turned sixteen, the year she had run fleetly through the dewy grass under the moon – the night of wine, when dreams condensed out of thin air like the nightmilk of fantasy. A lovenight. And if the boy caught her she would have given him whatever prizes were hers to give, and what did it matter if he caught her? They had run, wasn't that the important thing?

But he hadn't caught her. A cloud had drifted over the moon. The dew began to feel clammy and unpleasant, frightening. The taste of wine in her mouth had somehow changed to the taste of electric spit, slightly sour. A kind of metamorphosis had taken place, a feeling that she should, *must* wait.

And where had he been then, her intended, her dark bridegroom? On what streets, what back roads, clocking along in outside suburban darkness while inside the brittle clink of cocktail chatter broke the world into neat and rational sections? What cold winds were his? How many sticks of dynamite in his frayed packsack? Who knew what his name had been when she was sixteen? How ancient was he? Where had been his home? What sort of mother had held him to her breast? She was only sure that he was an orphan as she was, his time still to come. He walked mostly on roads that hadn't even been laid down yet, while she had but one foot on those same roads. The junction where they would meet was far ahead. He was an American man, she knew that, a man who would have a taste for milk and apple pie, a man who would appreciate the homely beauty of red check and gingham. His home was America, and his ways were the secret ways, the highways in hiding, the underground railways where directions are written in runes. He was the other man, the other face, the hardcase, the dark man, the Walkin Dude, and his rundown bootheels clocked along the perfumed ways of the summer night.

Who knoweth when the bridegroom comes?

She had waited for him, the unbroken vessel. At sixteen she had almost fallen, and again in college. Both of them had gone away angry and perplexed, the way Larry was now, sensing the crossroads inside her, the sense of some preordained, mystic junction point.

Boulder was the place where the roads diverged.

The time was close. *He* had called, bid her come.

After college she had buried herself in her work, had shared a rented house with two other girls. What two girls? Well, they came and went. Only Nadine stayed, and she was pleasant to the young men her changing roommates brought home, but she never had a young man herself. She supposed they talked about her, called her spinster-in-waiting, maybe even conjectured that she might be a carefully circumspect lesbian. It wasn't true. She was simply –

Unbroken.

Waiting.

It had seemed to her sometimes that a change was coming. She would be putting toys away in the silent classroom at the end of the day and suddenly she would pause, her eyes lambent and watchful, a jack-in-the-box held forgotten in one hand. And she would think: *A change is coming . . . a great wind is going to blow.* Sometimes, when such a thought came to her, she would find herself looking back over her shoulder like something pursued. Then it would break and she would laugh uneasily.

Her hair had begun to gray in her sixteenth year, the year she had been chased and not caught – just a few strands at first, startlingly visible in all the black, and not gray, no, that was the wrong word . . . *white*, it had been *white*.

Years later she had attended a party in the basement lounge of a frathouse. The lights had been low and after a while the people had drifted away by twos. Many of the girls – Nadine among them – had signed out for overnight from their dorms. She had fully intended to go through with it . . . but something that was still buried beneath the months and years had held her back. And the next morning, in the cold light of 7 AM, she had looked at herself in one of a long line of dormitory bathroom mirrors and saw that the white had advanced again, seemingly overnight – although that, of course, was impossible.

And so the years had passed, ticking away like seasons in a dry age, and there had been feelings, yes, *feelings*, and sometimes in the dead grave of night she had awakened both hot and cold, bathed in sweat, deliciously alive and aware in the trench of her bed, thinking of weird dark sex in a kind of gutter ecstasy. Rolling in hot liquid. Coming and biting at the same time. And the mornings after she would go to the mirror and she would fancy that she saw more white there.

Through those years she was, outwardly, only Nadine Cross: sweet, good with the children, good at her job, single. Once such a woman would have caused comment and curiosity in the community, but times had changed. And her beauty was so singular that it somehow seemed perfectly right for her to be just as she was.

Now times were going to change again.

Now the change was coming, and in her dreams she had begun to know her bridegroom, to understand him a little, even though she had never seen his face. He was the one she had been waiting for. She wanted to go to him . . . but she didn't want to. She was meant for him, but he terrified her.

Then Joe had come, and after him, Larry. Things had become terribly complicated then. She began to feel like a prize ring in a tug-of-war rope. She knew that her purity, her virginity, was somehow important to the dark man. That if she let Larry have her (or if she let any man have her), the dark enchantment would end. And she was attracted to Larry. She had set out, quite deliberately, to let him have her – again, she had intended to go through with it. Let him have her, let it end, let it all end. She was tired, and Larry was right. She had waited too long for the other one, through too many dry years.

But Larry was *not* right . . . or so it had seemed at first. She had brushed his initial advances away with a kind of contempt, the way a mare might switch at a fly with her tail. She could remember thinking: *If that's all there is to him, who could blame me for rejecting his suit?*

She had followed him, though. That was a fact. But she had been frantic to reach other people, not just because of Joe but because she had come almost to the point of deserting the boy and striking west on her own to find the man. Only years of ingrained responsibility to the children who had been placed under her care had kept her from doing that . . . and her knowledge that, left on his own, Joe would die.

In a world where so many have died, to parcel out more death is surely the gravest sin.

So she had gone with Larry, who was, after all, better than nothing or no one.

But it had turned out that there was a great deal more to Larry Underwood than nothing or no one – he was like one of those optical illusions (maybe even to himself) where the water looks shallow, only an inch or two deep, but when you put your hand in you've suddenly got your arm wet to the shoulder. The way he had gotten to know Joe, that was one thing. The way Joe had taken to him was another, her own jealous reaction to the growing relationship between Joe and Larry was a third. At the motorcycle dealership in Wells, Larry had bet the fingers of both hands on the boy, and he had won.

If they had not been concentrating their full attention on the lid covering the gasoline tank, they would have seen her mouth drop open in a slack *o* of surprise. She had stood watching them, unable to move, her gaze concentrated on the bright metal line of the crowbar, waiting for it to first jitter and then fall away. She only realized after it was over that she had been waiting for the screams to begin.

Then the lid was up and over and she was faced with her own error in judgment, an error so deep it was fundamental. In that case he had known Joe better than she, and without any special training, and on much shorter notice. Only hindsight allowed her to understand how important the guitar episode had been, how quickly and fundamentally it had defined Larry's relationship with Joe. And what was at the center of that relationship?

Why, dependence, of course – what else could have caused that sudden jangle of jealousy all through her system? If Joe had depended on Larry, that would have been one thing, normal and acceptable. What had upset her was that Larry also depended on Joe, needed Joe in a way she didn't . . . *and Joe knew it.*

Had her judgment been that wrong about Larry's character? She thought now that the answer was yes. That nervous, self-serving exterior was a veneer, and it was being worn away by hard use. Just the fact that he had held them all together on this long trip spoke for his determination.

The conclusion seemed clear. Beneath her decision to let Larry make love to her, a part of her was still committed to the other man . . . and making love to Larry would be like killing that part of herself forever. She wasn't sure she could do that.

And she wasn't the only one who had dreamed of the dark man now.

That had disturbed her at first, then frightened her. Fright was all it was when she had only Joe and Larry to compare notes with; when they met Lucy Swann and she said she'd had the same sort of dream, fright became a kind of frenzied terror. It was no longer possible to tell herself their dreams only *sounded* like hers. What if everyone left was having them? What if the dark man's time had come around at last – not just for her, *but for everyone left on the planet?*

This idea more than any other raised the conflicting emotions of utter terror and strong attraction within her. She had held to the idea of Stovington with a nearly panicky grip. It stood, by nature of its function, as a symbol of sanity and rationality against the rising tide of dark magic she felt around her. But Stovington had been deserted, a mockery of the safe haven she had built it up to be in her mind. The symbol of sanity and rationality was a deathhouse.

As they moved west, picking up survivors, her hope that it could somehow end for her without confrontation had gradually died. It died as Larry grew in her estimation. He was sleeping with Lucy Swann now, but what did that matter? She was spoken for. The others had been having two opposing dreams: the dark man and the old woman. The old woman seemed to stand for some sort of elemental force, just as the dark man did. The old woman was the nucleus the others were gradually cohering around.

Nadine had never dreamed of her.

Only of the dark man. And when the dreams of the others had suddenly faded away as inexplicably as they had come, her own dreams had seemed to grow in power and in clarity.

She knew many things which they did not. The dark man's name was Randall Flagg. Those in the West who opposed him or went against his way of doing things had either been crucified or driven mad somehow and set free to wander in the boiling sink of Death Valley. There were small groups of technical people in San

Francisco and Los Angeles, but they were only temporary; very soon they would be moving to Las Vegas, where the main concentration of people was growing. For him there was no hurry. Summer was on the downside now. Soon the Rocky Mountain passes would be filling with snow, and while there were plows to clear them, they would not be able to spare enough warm bodies to man the plows. There would be a long winter in which to consolidate. And next April . . . or May . . .

Nadine lay in the dark, looking up at the sky.

Boulder was her last hope. The old woman was her last hope. The sanity and rationality she had hoped to find at Stovington had begun to form in Boulder. They were good, she thought, the good guys, and if only it could be that simple for her, caught in her crazy web of conflicting desires.

Played over and over again, like a dominant chord, was her own firm belief that murder in this decimated world was the gravest sin, and her heart told her firmly and without question that death was Randall Flagg's business. But oh how she wanted his cold kiss – more than she had wanted the kisses of the high school boy, or the college boy . . . even more, she feared, than Larry Underwood's kiss and embrace.

We'll be in Boulder tomorrow, she thought. *Maybe I'll know then if the trip is over or . . .*

A shooting star scratched its fire across the sky, and like a child, she wished on it.

CHAPTER 50

Dawn was coming up, painting the eastern sky a delicate rose color. Stu Redman and Glen Bateman were about halfway up Flagstaff Mountain in West Boulder, where the first foothills of the Rockies rise up out of the flat plains like a vision of prehistory. In the dawnlight Stu thought that the pines crawling between the naked and nearly perpendicular stone faces looked like the veins ridging some giant's hand that had poked out of the earth. Somewhere to the east, Nadine Cross was at last falling into a thin, unsatisfactory sleep.

'I'm going to have a headache this afternoon,' Glen said. 'I don't believe I've stayed up drinking all night since I was an undergrad.'

'Sunrise is worth it,' Stu said.

'Yes, it is. Beautiful. Have you ever been in the Rockies before?'

'Nope,' Stu said. 'But I'm glad I came.' He hoisted the jug of wine and had a swallow. 'I got quite a buzz on myself.' He looked out over the view in silence for a few moments and then turned to Glen with a slanted smile. 'What's going to happen now?'

'Happen?' Glen raised his eyebrows.

'Sure. That's why I got you up here. Told Frannie, "I'm gonna get him good n drunk and then pick his brains." She said fine.'

Glen grinned. 'There are no tea-leaves in the bottom of a wine bottle.'

'No, but she explained to me just what it is you used to be. Sociology. The study of group interaction. So make some educated guesses.'

'Cross my palm with silver, O aspirant to knowledge.'

'Never mind the silver, baldy. I'll take you down to the First National Bank of Boulder tomorrow and give you a million dollars. How's that?'

'Seriously, Stu – what do you want to know?'

'Same things that mute guy Andros wants to know, I guess. What's going to happen next. I don't know how to put it any better than that.'

'There's going to be a society,' Glen said slowly. 'What kind? Impossible to say right now. There are almost four hundred people here now. I'd guess from the rate they've been coming in – more every day – that by the first of September there'll be fifteen hundred of us. Forty-five hundred by the first of October, and maybe as many as eight thousand by the time the snow flies in November and closes the roads. Write that down as prediction number one.'

To Glen's amusement, Stu did indeed produce a notebook from the back pocket of his jeans and jotted down what he had just said.

'Hard for me to believe,' Stu said. 'We came all the way across the country and didn't see a hundred people all told.'

'Yes, but they're coming in, aren't they?'

'Yes . . . in dribs and drabs.'

'In what and whats?' Glen asked, grinning.

'Dribs and drabs. My mother used to say that. You shitting on my mom's way of talking?'

'The day will never come in when I lose enough respect for my own hide to shit on a Texan's mother, Stuart.'

'Well, they're comin in, sure. Ralph's in touch with five or six groups right now that will bring us up to five hundred by the end of the week.'

Glen smiled again. 'Yes, and Mother Abagail sits right there with him in his "radio station," but she won't talk on the CB. Says she's afraid she'll get an electroshock.'

'Frannie loves that old woman,' Stu said. 'Part of it is because she knows so much about delivering babies, but part of it is just . . . loving her. You know?'

'Yes. Most everybody feels the same.'

'Eight thousand people by winter,' Stu said, returning to the original topic. 'Man oh man.'

'It's just arithmetic. Let's say the flu wiped out ninety-nine percent of the population. Maybe it wasn't that bad, but let's use that figure just so we have a place to put our feet. If the flu was ninety-nine percent fatal, that means it wiped out damned near two hundred and eighteen million people, just in this country.' He looked at Stu's shocked face and nodded grimly. 'Maybe it wasn't that bad, but we can make a pretty good guess that figure's in the ballpark. Makes the Nazis look like pikers, doesn't it?'

'My Lord,' Stu said in a dry voice.

'But that would still leave over two million people, a fifth of the pre-plague population of Tokyo, a fourth of the pre-plague population of New York. That's in this country alone. Now, I believe that ten percent of that two million might not have survived the aftermath of the flu. Folks who fell victims to what I'd call the aftershock. People like poor Mark Braddock with his burst appendix, but also the accidents, the suicides, yes, and murder, too. That takes us down to 1.8 million. But we suspect there's an Adversary, don't we? The dark man that we dreamed about. West of us somewhere. There are seven states over there that could legitimately be called his territory . . . *if* he really exists.'

'I guess he exists, all right,' Stu said.

'My feeling, too. But is he simply in dominion of all the people over there? I don't think so, any more than Mother Abagail is automatically in dominion over the people in the other forty-one continental United States. I think things have been in a state of slow flux and that that state of affairs is beginning to end. People are cohering. When you and I first discussed this back in New Hampshire, I envisioned dozens of little tinpot societies. What I didn't count on — because I didn't know about it — was the all but irresistible pull of these two opposing dreams. It was a new fact that no one could have foreseen.'

'Are you saying that we'll end up with nine hundred thousand people and *he'll* end up with nine hundred thousand?'

'No. First, the coming winter is going to take its toll. It's going to take it here, and it's going to be even tougher for the small groups that don't make it here before the snow. You realize we don't even have one doctor in the Free Zone yet? Our medical staff consists of a veterinarian and Mother Abagail herself, who's forgotten more valid folk medicine than you or I will ever have a chance to learn. Still, they'd look cute trying to put a steel plate in your skull after you took a fall and bashed in the back of your head, wouldn't they?'

Stu snickered. 'That ole boy Rolf Dannemont would probably drag out his Remington and let daylight through me.'

'I'd guess the total American population might be down to 1.6 million by next spring — and that's a kind estimate. Of that number, I'd like to hope we'd get the million.'

'A million people,' Stu said, awed. He looked out over the sprawling, mostly deserted city of Boulder, now brightening as the sun began to hoist itself over the flat eastern horizon. 'I just can't picture that. This town would be busting at the seams.'

'Boulder couldn't hold them. I know that boggles the mind when you walk around the empty streets downtown and out toward Table Mesa, but it just couldn't. We'd have to seed the communities around us. The situation you'd have is this one giant community and the rest of the country east of here absolutely empty.'

'Why do you think we'd get most of the people?'

'For a very unscientific reason,' Glen said, riffling his tonsure of hair with one hand. 'I like to believe most people are good. And I believe that whoever is running the show west of us is really bad. But I have a hunch . . .' He trailed off.

'Go on, spill it.'

'I will because I'm drunk. But it stays between us, Stuart.'

'All right.'

'Your word?'

'My word,' Stu said.

'I think he's going to get most of the techies,' Glen said finally. 'Don't ask me why; it's just a hunch. Except that tech people like to work in an atmosphere of tight discipline and linear goals, for the most part. They like it when the trains run on time. What we've got here in Boulder right now is mass confusion, everyone bopping along and doing his own thing . . . and we've got to do something about what my students would have called "getting our shit together." But that other fellow . . . I'll bet *he's* got the trains running on time and all his ducks in a row. And techies are just as human as the rest of us; they'll go where they're wanted the most. I've a suspicion that our Adversary wants as many as he can get. Fuck the farmers, he'd just as soon have a few men who can dust off those Idaho missile silos and get them operational again. Ditto tanks and helicopters and maybe a B-52 bomber or two just for chuckles. I doubt if he's gotten that far yet – in fact, I'm sure of it. We'd know. Right now he's probably still concentrating on getting the power back on, re-establishing communications . . . maybe he's even had to indulge in a purge of the fainthearted. Rome wasn't built in a day, and he'll know that. He has time. But when I watch the sun go down at night – this is no shit, Stuart – I get scared. I don't need bad dreams to scare me anymore. All I have to do is think of them over there on the other side of the Rockies, busy as little bees.'

'What should we be doing?'

'Should I give you a list?' Glen responded, grinning.

Stuart gestured at his battered notebook. There were two dancers in silhouette and the words BOOGIE DOWN! on its hot pink cover. 'Yup,' he said.

'You're kidding.'

'No, I ain't. You said it, Glen, we got to start getting our shit together someplace. I feel it, too. It's getting later every day. We can't just sit here jacking off and listening to the CB. We may wake up some morning to find that hardcase waltzing into Boulder at the head of an armored column, complete with air support.'

'Don't look for him tomorrow,' Glen said.

'No. But what about next May?'

'Possible,' Glen said in a low voice. 'Yes, quite possible.'

'And what do you think would happen to us?'

Glen didn't reply with words. He made an explicit little trigger-pulling gesture with the forefinger of his right hand and then hurriedly scoffed the last of the wine.

'Yeah,' Stu said. 'So let's start getting it together. Talk.'

Glen closed his eyes. The brightening day touched his wrinkled cheeks and forehead.

'Okay,' he said. 'Here it is, Stu. First: Re-create America. Little America. By fair means and by foul. Organization and government come first. If it starts now, we can form the sort of government we want. If we wait until the population triples, we are going to have grave problems.

'Let's say we call a meeting a week from today, that would make it August eighteenth. Everyone to attend. Before the meeting there should be an ad hoc Organization Committee. A committee of seven, let us say. You, me, Andros, Fran, Harold Lauder, maybe, a couple more. The job of the committee would be to create an agenda for the August eighteenth meeting. And I can tell you right now what some of the items on that agenda should be.'

'Shoot.'

'First, reading and ratification of the Declaration of Independence. Second, r and r of the Constitution. Third, r and r of the Bill of Rights. All ratification to be done by voice vote.'

'Christ, Glen, we're all Americans —'

'No, that's where you're wrong,' Glen said, opening his eyes. They looked socketed and bloodshot. 'We're a bunch of survivors with no government at all. We're a hodgepodge collection from every age group, religious group, class group, and racial group. Government is an *idea*, Stu. That's really all it is, once you strip away the bureaucracy and the bullshit. I'll go further. It's an inculcation, nothing but a memory path worn through the brain. What we've got going for us now is culture lag. Most of these people still believe in government by representation – the Republic – what they think of as "democracy." But culture lag never lasts long. After a while they'll start having the gut reactions: the President is dead, the Pentagon is for rent, nobody is debating anything in the House and the Senate except maybe for the termites and the cockroaches. Our people here are very soon going to wake up to the fact that the old ways are gone, and that they can restructure society any old way they want. We want – we *need* – to catch them before they wake up and do something nutty.'

He leveled his finger at Stu.

'If someone stood up at the August eighteenth meeting and proposed that Mother Abagail be put in absolute charge, with you and me and that fellow Andros as her advisers, those people would pass the item by acclamation, blissfully unaware that they had just voted the first operating American dictatorship into power since Huey Long.'

'Oh, I can't believe that. There are college graduates here, lawyers, political activists –'

'Maybe they used to be. Now they're just a bunch of tired, scared people who don't know what's going to happen to them. Some might squawk, but they'd shut up when you told them that Mother Abagail and her advisers were going to get the power back on in sixty days. No, Stu, it's very important that the first thing we do is ratify the *spirit* of the old society. That's what I meant about re-creating America. It has to be that way as long as we're operating under direct threat of the man we're calling the Adversary.'

'Go on.'

'All right. The next item on the agenda would be that we run the government like a New England township. Perfect democracy. As long as we're relatively small, it'll work fine. Only instead of a board of selectmen we'll have seven . . . representatives, I guess. Free Zone Representatives. How does that sound?'

'It sounds fine.'

'I think so, too. And we'll see to it that the people who get elected are the same people who were on the ad hoc committee. We'll put the rush on everybody and get the vote taken before people can do any tub-thumping for their friends. We can handpick people to nominate us and then second us. The vote'll go through as slick as shit through a goose.'

'That's neat,' Stu said admiringly.

'Sure,' Glen said glumly. 'If you want to short-circuit the democratic process, ask a sociologist.'

'What's next?'

'This is going to be very popular. The item would read: "Resolved: Mother Abagail is to be given absolute veto power over any action proposed by the Board."'

'Jesus! Will she agree to that?'

'I think so. But I don't think she'd ever be apt to exercise her veto power, not in any circumstances I can foresee. We just can't expect to have a workable government here unless we make her its titular head. She's the thing we all have in common. We've all had a paranormal experience that revolves around her. And she has a . . . a kind of aura about her. People all use the same loose bunch of adjectives to describe her: good, kind, old, wise, clever, nice. These people have had one dream that frightens the bejesus out of them and one that makes them feel safe and secure. They love and trust the source of the good dream all the more because of the dream that frightened them. And we can make it clear to her that she's our leader in name only. I think that's how she'd want it. She's old, tired . . .'

Stu was shaking his head. 'She's old and tired, but she sees this problem of the dark man as a religious crusade, Glen. And she's not the only one, either. You know that.'

'You mean she might decide to take the bit in her teeth?'

'Maybe that wouldn't be so bad,' Stu remarked. 'After all, it was *her* we dreamed of, not a Representative Board.'

Glen was shaking his head. 'No, I can't accept the idea that we're all pawns in some post-Apocalypse game of good and evil, dreams or not. Goddammit, it's irrational!'

Stu shrugged. 'Well, let's not get bogged down in it now. I think your idea of giving her veto power is a good one. In fact, I don't think it goes far enough. We ought to give her the power to propose as well as dispose.'

'But not absolute power on that side of the slate,' Glen said hastily.

'No, her ideas would have to be ratified by the Representative Board,' Stu said, and then added slyly: 'But we might find ourselves a rubber stamp for her instead of the other way around.'

There was a long silence. Glen had put his forehead into one hand. At last he said, 'Yeah, you're right. She can't just be a figure-head . . . at the very least we have to accept the possibility that she may have her own ideas. And that's where I pack up my cloudy crystal ball, East Texas. Because she's what those of us who ride the sociology range call other-directed.'

'Who's the other?'

'God? Thor? Allah? Pee-wee Herman? It doesn't matter. What it means is that what she says won't necessarily be directed by what this society needs or by what its mores turn out to be. She'll be listening to some other voice. Like Joan of Arc. What you've made me see is that we just might wind up with a theocracy on our hands here.'

'Theoc-what?'

'On a God trip,' Glen said. He didn't sound too happy about it. 'When you were a little boy, Stu, did you ever dream that you might grow up to be one of seven high priests and/or priestesses to a one-hundred-and-eight-year-old black woman from Nebraska?'

Stu stared at him. Finally he said: 'Is there any more of that wine?'

'All gone.'

'Shit.'

'Yes,' Glen said. They studied each other's face in silence and then suddenly burst out laughing.

It was surely the nicest house Mother Abagail had ever lived in, and sitting here on the screened-in porch put her in mind of a traveling salesman who had come around Hemingford back in 1936 or '37. Why, he had been the sweetest-talking fellow she had ever met in her life; he could have charmed the birdies right down from the trees. She had asked this young man, Mr Donald King by name, what his business was with Abby Freemantle, and he had replied: 'My business, ma'am, is pleasure. *Your* pleasure. Do you like to read? Listen to the radio, perchance? Or maybe just put your tired old dogs up on a foot hassock and listen to the world as it rolls down the great bowling alley of the universe?'

She had admitted she enjoyed all those things, not admitting that the Motorola had been sold a month before to pay for ninety bales of hay.

'Well, those are the things I'm selling,' this sweet-talking road-merchant had told her. 'It may be called an Electrolux vacuum cleaner complete with all the attachments, but what it really is, is spare time. Plug her in and you open up whole new vistas of relaxation for yourself. And the payments are almost as easy as your housework's going to be.'

They had been deep in the Depression then, she hadn't even been able to raise twenty cents for hair ribbons for her granddaughters' birthdays, and there was no chance for that Electrolux. But say, didn't that Mr Donald King of Peru, Indiana, talk sweet. My! She had never seen him again, but she had never forgotten his name, either. She just bet he had gone on to break some white lady's heart. She never did own a vacuum cleaner until the end of the Nazi war, when it seemed like all of a sudden anybody could afford anything and even poor white trash had a Mercury hidden away in their back shed.

Now this house, which Nick had told her was in the Mapleton Hill section of Boulder (Mother Abagail just bet there hadn't been many blacks living up *here* before the smiting plague), had every gadget she'd ever heard of and some she hadn't. Dishwasher. *Two* vacuums, one strictly for the upstairs work. Dispos-All in the sink. Microwave oven. Clothes washer and dryer. There was a gadget in the kitchen, looked like nothing more than a steel box, and Nick's good friend Ralph Brentner told her it was a 'trash masher,' and you could put about a hundred pounds of swill into it and get back a little block of garbage about the size of a footstool. Wonders never ceased.

But come to think of it, some of them had.

Sitting, rocking on the porch, her eye happened to fall upon an electrical plug-in plate set into the baseboard. Probably so folks could come out here in the summertime and listen to the radio or even have the baseball on that cute little round TV. Nothing in the whole country more common than those little wall-plates with the prong-slits in them. She'd even had them back in her squatter's shack in Hemingford. You didn't think nothing of those plates . . . unless they didn't work anymore. Then you realized that one hell of a lot of a person's life came out of them. All that spare time, that pleasure which the long-ago Don King had extolled her on . . . it came out of those switchplates set into the wall. With their potency taken away, you might as well use all those gadgets like the microwave oven and the 'trash masher' to hang your hat and coat on.

Say! Her own little house had been better equipped to handle the death of those little switchplates than this one was. Here, someone had to bring her water fetched all the way from Boulder Creek, and it had to be boiled before you could use it, just for safety's sake. Back home she'd had her own handpump. Here, Nick and Ralph had had to truck up an ugly gadget called a Port-O-San; they had put it in the back yard. At home she'd had her own outhouse. She would have traded the Maytag washer-dryer combination in a second for her own washtub, but she had gotten Nick to find her a new one, and Brad Kitchner had found her a scrub-board somewhere and some good old lye soap. They probably thought she was a good old pain in the ass, wanting to do her own washing – and so much of it – but cleanly went next to Godly, she had never sent her washing out in her whole life, and she didn't mean to start now. She had her little accidents from time to time, too, as old folks often did, but as long as she could do her own wash, those accidents didn't have to be anybody's business but her own.

They would get the power back on, of course. It was one of the things God had shown her in her dreams. She knew a goodish number of things about what was to come here – some from the dreams, some from her own common sense. The two were too intertwined to tell apart.

Soon all these people would stop running around like chickens with their heads cut off and start pulling together. She was not a sociologist like that Glen Bateman (who always eyed her like a racetrack agent looking at a phony ten), but she knew that people always did pull together after a while. The curse and blessing of the human race was its chumminess. Why, if six people went floating down the Mississippi on a church roof in a flood, they'd start a bingo game as soon as the roof grounded on a sandbar.

First they'd want to form some sort of government, probably one they'd want to run around her. She couldn't allow that, of course, as much as she would like to; that would not be God's will. Let them run all the things that had to do with this earth – get the power back on? Fine. First thing she was going to do was try out that 'trash masher.' Get the gas running so they wouldn't freeze their bee-hinds off this winter. Let them pass their resolutions and make their plans, that was fine. She would keep her nose right out of that part. She would insist that Nick have a part in the running of it, and maybe Ralph. That Texan seemed all right, he knew enough to shut off his mouth when his brains weren't running. She supposed they might want that fat boy, that Harold, and she wouldn't stop them, but she didn't like him. Harold made her nervous. All the time grinning, but the grin never touched his eyes. He was pleasant, he said the right things, but his eyes were like two cold flints poking out of the ground.

She thought that Harold had some kind of secret. Some smelly, nasty thing all wrapped up in a stinking poultice in the middle of his heart. She had no idea what it might be; it was not God's will for her to see that, so it must not matter to His plan for this community. All the same, it troubled her to think that fat boy might be a part of their high councils . . . but she would say nothing.

Her business, she thought rather complacently in her rocker, her place in their councils and deliberations had only to do with the dark man.

He had no name, although it pleased him to call himself Flagg . . . at least for the time being. And on the far side of the mountains, his work was already well begun. She did not know his plans; they were as veiled from her eyes as whatever secrets lay in that fat boy Harold's heart. But she did not have to know the specifics. His goal was clear and simple: to destroy all of them.

Her understanding of him was surprisingly sophisticated. The people who had been drawn to the Free Zone all came to see her in this place, and she received them, although they sometimes made her tired . . . and they all wanted to tell her that they had dreamed of her and of *him*. They were terrified of him, and she nodded and comforted and soothed as best she could, but privately she thought that most of them wouldn't know this Flagg if they met him on the street . . . unless he *wanted* to be noticed. They might *feel* him – a cold chill, the kind you got when a goose walked over your grave, a sudden hot feeling like a fever-flash, or a sharp and momentary drilling pain in the ears or the temples. But these people were wrong to think he had two heads, or six eyes, or big spike horns growing out of his temples. He probably didn't look much different than the man who used to bring the milk or the mail.

She guessed that behind the conscious evil there was an unconscious blackness. That was what distinguished the earth's children of darkness; they couldn't make things but only break them. God the Creator had made man in His own image, and that meant that every man and woman who dwelt under God's light was a creator of some kind, a person with an urge to stretch out his hand and shape the world into some rational pattern. The black man wanted – was able – only to unshape. Anti-Christ? You might as well say anti-creation.

He would have his followers, of course; *that* was nothing new. He was a liar, and his father was the Father of Lies. He would be like a big neon sign to them, standing high to the sky, dazzling their sight with fizzing fireworks. They would not be apt to notice, these apprentice unshapers, that like a neon sign, he only made the same simple patterns over and over again. They would not be apt to realize that, if you release the gas which makes the pretty patterns from its complex assortment of tubes, it floats silently away and dissipates, leaving not a taste or so much as a whiff of smell behind.

Some would make the deduction for themselves in time – his kingdom would never be one of peace. The sentry posts and barbed wire at the frontiers of his land would be there as much to keep the converts in as to keep the invader out.

Would he win?

She had no assurance that he would not. She knew he must be as aware of her as she was of him, and nothing would give him more pleasure than to see her scrawny black body hung up to the sky on a cross of telephone poles for the crows to pick. She knew that a few of them besides herself had dreamed of crucifixions, but only a few. Those who did had told her but no one else, she suspected. And none of that answered the question:

Would he win?

That was not for her to know, either. God worked discreetly, and in the ways that pleased Him. It had pleased Him that the Children of Israel should sweat and strain under the Egyptian yoke for generations. It had pleased Him to send Joseph into slavery, his fine coat of many colors ripped rudely from his back. It had pleased Him to allow the visitation of a hundred plagues on hapless Job, and it had pleased Him to allow His only Son to be hung up on a tree with a bad joke written over His head.

God was a gamesman – if He had been a mortal, He would have been at home hunkering over a checkerboard on the porch of Pop Mann's general store back in Hemingford Home. He played red to black, white to black. She thought that, for Him, the game was more than worth the candle, the game *was* the candle. He would prevail in His own good time. But not necessarily this year, or in the next thousand . . . and she would not overestimate the dark man's craft and cozening. If he was neon gas, then she was the tiny dark dust particle a great raincloud forms about over the parched land. Only another private soldier – long past retirement age, it was true! – in the service of the Lord.

'Thy will be done,' she said, and reached into her apron pocket for a packet of Planters peanuts. Her last doctor, Dr Staunton, had told her to steer clear of salty foods, but what did he know? She had outlived both of the doctors who had presumed to advise her on her health since her eighty-sixth birthday, and she would have a few peanuts if she wanted to. They hurt her gums mortal bad, but my! weren't they tasty?

As she munched, Ralph Brentner came up her walk, his hat with the feather in the band cocked back well on his head. As he tapped on the porch door, he took the hat off.

'You awake, Mother?'

'That I am,' she said through a mouthful of peanuts. 'Step in, Ralph, I ain't chewin these nuts, I'm gummin em to death.'

Ralph laughed and came in. 'There's some folk out past the gate that'd like to say howdy, if you ain't too tired. They just got in about an hour ago. A pretty good crew, I'd say. The fella in charge is one of these longhairs, but he seems well about it. Name's Underwood.'

'Well, bring em up, Ralph, that's fine,' she said.

'Good enough.' He turned to go.

'Where's Nick?' she asked him. 'Haven't seen him today nor yesterday neither. He gettin too good for homefolks?'

'He's been out at the reservoir,' Ralph said. 'Him and that electrician, Brad Kitchner, have been looking at the power plant.' He rubbed the side of his nose. 'I was out this morning. Figured all those chiefs orta have at least one Indian to order around.'

Mother Abagail cackled. She *did* like Ralph. He was a simple soul, but canny. He had a feel for how things worked. She was not surprised that he had been the one to get what everybody now called Free Zone Radio going. He was the kind of man who wouldn't be afraid to try epoxy on your tractor battery when it started to split open, and if the epoxy did the job, why, he'd just take off his shapeless hat and scratch his balding head and grin that grin, like he was an eleven-year-old kid with the chores done and his fishing pole leaned against his shoulder. He was a good sort to have around when things weren't going just right and the type of man who always somehow ended up on relief when times were flush for just about everyone else. He could put the right sort of valve on your bicycle pump when it wouldn't mate to a tire bigger than the kind that went on a bike and he'd know what was making that funny buzzing noise in your oven just by looking at it, but when he had to deal with a company time-clock, he'd somehow always end up punching in late and punching out early and get fired for it before very long. He'd know you could fertilize corn with pigshit if you mixed it right, and he'd know how to pickle cukes, but he would never be able to understand a car loan agreement, or to figure out how the dealers managed to rook him every time. A job application form filled out by Ralph Brentner would look as if it had been through a Hamilton-Beach blender . . . misspelled, dog-eared, dotted with blots of ink and greasy fingerprints. His employment history would look like a checkerboard which had been around the world on a tramp steamer. But when the very fabric of the world began to tear open, it was the Ralph Brentners who were not afraid to say, 'Let's slap a little epoxy in there and see if *that'll* hold her.' And more often than not, it did.

'You're a good fella, Ralph, you know it? You're a one.'

'Why, you are too, Mother. Not that you're a fella, but you know what I mean. Anyhow, that fella Redman came by while we were workin. Wanted to talk to Nick about being on some kind of committee.'

'And what did Nick say?'

'Aw, he wrote a couple of pages. But what it came down to was fine by me if it's fine by Mother Abagail. Is it?'

'Well now, what would an old lady like myself have to say about such doings?'

'A lot,' Ralph said in a serious, almost shocked manner. 'You're the reason we're here. I guess we'll do whatever you want.'

'What I want is to go on livin free like I always have, like an American. I just want my say when it's time for me to have it. Like an American.'

'Well, you'll have all of that.'

'The rest feel that way, Ralph?'

'You bet they do.'

'Then that's fine.' She rocked serenely. 'Time everyone got

going. There's people lollygaggin around. Mostly just waitin for somebody to tell em where to squat and lean.'

'Then I can go ahead?'

'With what?'

'Well, Nick and Stu ast me if I could find a printing press and maybe get her going, if they got me some electricity to run it. I said I didn't need any electricity, I'd just go down to the high school and find the biggest hand-crank mimeograph I could lay my hands on. They want some fliers.' He shook his head. 'Do they! Seven hundred. Why, we only got four hundred and some here.'

'And nineteen out by the gate, probably getting heatstroke while you and me chin. You go bring them in.'

'I will.' Ralph started away.

'And Ralph?'

He turned back.

'Print a thousand,' she said.

They filed in through the gate that Ralph opened and she felt her sin, the one she thought of as the mother of sin. The father of sin was theft; every one of the Ten Commandments boiled down to 'Thou shalt not steal.' Murder was the theft of a life, adultery the theft of a wife, covetousness the secret, slinking theft that took place in the cave of the heart. Blasphemy was the theft of God's name, swiped from the House of the Lord and sent out to walk the streets like a strutting whore. She had never been much of a thief; a minor pilferer from time to time at worst.

The mother of sin was pride.

Pride was the female side of Satan in the human race, the quiet egg of sin, always fertile. Pride had kept Moses out of Canaan, where the grapes were so big the men had to carry them in slings. *Who brought the water from the rock when we were thirsty?* the Children of Israel asked, and Moses had answered, *I did it.*

She had always been a proud woman. Proud of the floor she washed on her hands and knees (but Who had provided the hands, the knees, the very water she washed with?), proud that all her children had turned out all right – none in jail ever, none caught by dope or the bottle, none of them frigging around on the wrong side of the sheets – but the mothers of children were the daughters of God. She was proud of her life, but she had not made her life. Pride was the curse of will, and like a woman, pride had its wiles. At her great age she had not learned all its illusions yet, or mastered its glamors.

And when they filed through the gate she thought: *It's me they've come to see.* And on the heels of that sin, a series of blasphemous metaphors, rising unbidden in her mind: how they filed through one by one like communicants, their young leader with his eyes mostly cast down, a light-haired woman by his side, a little boy just behind him with a dark-eyed woman whose black hair was shot with twists of gray. The others behind them in a line.

The young man climbed the porch steps, but his woman stopped at the foot. His hair was long, as Ralph had said, but it was clean. He had a considerable growth of reddish-gold beard. He had a strong face with freshly etched lines of care in it, around the mouth and across the forehead.

'You're really real,' he said softly.

'Why, I have always thought so,' she said. 'I am Abagail Freemantle, but most folks round here just call me Mother Abagail. Welcome to our place.'

'Thank you,' he said thickly, and she saw he was struggling with tears. 'I'm . . . we're glad to be here. My name's Larry Underwood.'

She held her hand out and he took it lightly, with awe, and she felt that twinge of pride again, that stiffneckedness. It was as if he thought she had a fire in her that would burn him.

'I . . . dreamed of you,' he said awkwardly.

She smiled and nodded and he turned stiffly, almost stumbling. He went back down the steps, shoulders hunched. He would unwind, she thought. Now that he was here and when he found out he didn't have to take the whole weight of the world on his shoulders. A man who doubts himself shouldn't have to try too hard for too long, not until he's seasoned, and this man Larry Underwood was still a little green and apt to bend. But she liked him.

His woman, a pretty little thing with eyes like violets, came next. She looked boldly at Mother Abagail, but not scornfully. 'I'm Lucy Swann. Pleased to make your acquaintance.' And although she was wearing pants, she sketched a little curtsy.

'Glad you could come by, Lucy.'

'Would you mind if I asked . . . well . . .' Now her eyes dropped and she began to blush furiously.

'A hundred and eight at last count,' she said kindly. 'Feels more like two hundred and sixteen some days.'

'I dreamed about you,' Lucy said, and then retired in some confusion.

The woman with the dark eyes and the boy came next. The woman looked at her gravely and unflinchingly; the boy's face showed frank wonder. The boy was all right. But something about the woman made her feel grave-cold. *He's here*, she thought. *He's come in the shape of this woman . . . for behold he comes in more forms than his own . . . the wolf . . . the crow . . . the snake.*

She was not above feeling fear for herself, and for one instant she felt this strange woman with the white in her hair would reach out, almost casually, and snap her neck. For the one instant the feeling held, Mother Abagail actually fancied that the woman's face was gone and she was looking into a hole in time and space, a hole from which two eyes, dark and damned, stared out at her − eyes that were lost and haggard and hopeless.

But it was just a woman, and not *him*. The dark man would never dare come to her here, even in a shape that was not his own. This was just a woman − a very pretty one, too − with an expressive, sensitive face and one arm about her little boy's shoulders. She had only been daydreaming for a moment. Surely that was all.

For Nadine Cross, the moment was a confusion. She had been all right when they came in through the gate. She had been all right until Larry had begun talking to the old lady. Then an almost swooning sense of revulsion and terror had come over her. The old woman could . . . could what?

Could see.

Yes. She was afraid that the old woman could see inside her, to where the darkness was already planted and growing well. She was afraid the old woman would rise from her place on the porch and denounce her, demand that she leave Joe and go to those (to *him*) for whom she was intended.

The two of them, each with their own murky fears, looked at each other. They measured each other. The moment was short, but it seemed very long to the two of them.

He's in her − the Devil's Imp, Abby Freemantle thought.

All of their power is right here, Nadine thought in her own turn. *She's all they've got, although they may think differently.*

Joe was growing restive beside her, tugging at her hand.

'Hello,' she said in a thin, dead voice. 'I'm Nadine Cross.'

The old woman said: 'I know who you are.'

The words hung in the air, cutting suddenly through the other chatter. People turned, puzzled, to see if something was happening.

'Do you?' Nadine said softly. Suddenly it seemed that Joe was her protection, her only one.

She moved the boy slowly in front of her, like a hostage. Joe's queer seawater eyes looked up at Mother Abagail.

Nadine said: 'This is Joe. Do you know him as well?'

Mother Abagail's eyes remained locked on the eyes of the woman who called herself Nadine Cross, but a thin shine of perspiration had broken out on the back of her neck.

'I don't think Joe's his name any more than mine's Cassandra,' she said, 'and I don't think you're his mom.' She dropped her eyes to the boy with something like relief, unable to suppress a queer feeling that the woman had somehow won – that she had put the little chap between them, used him to keep her from doing whatever her duty was . . . ah, but it had come so sudden, and she hadn't been ready for it!

'What's your name, chap?' she asked the boy.

The boy struggled as if a bone were caught in his throat. 'He won't tell you,' Nadine said, and put a hand on the boy's shoulder. 'He can't tell you. I don't think he remem –'

Joe threw it off and that seemed to break the block. '*Leo!*' he said with sudden force and great clarity. 'Leo Rockway, that's me! I'm Leo!' And he sprang into Mother Abagail's arms, laughing. That generated laughter and some applause from the crowd. Nadine became virtually unnoticed, and Abby felt again that some vital focus, some vital chance, had ebbed away.

'Joe,' Nadine called. Her face was remote, under control again.

The boy drew away a bit from Mother Abagail and looked at her.

'Come away,' Nadine said, and now she looked unflinchingly at Abby, speaking not to the boy but directly at her. 'She's old. You'll hurt her. She's very old and . . . not very strong.'

'Oh, I think I'm strong enough to love a chap like him a bit,' Mother Abagail said, but her voice sounded oddly uncertain in her own ears. 'He looks like he's had a hard road.'

'Well, he's tired now. And you are, too, from the look. Come on, Joe.'

'I love her,' the boy said, not moving.

Nadine seemed to flinch at that. Her voice sharpened. 'Come away, Joe!'

'That's not my name! Leo! Leo! That's my name!'

The little crowd of new pilgrims quieted again, aware that something unexpected had happened, might be happening still, but unable to know what.

The two women locked eyes again like sabers.

I know who you are, Abby's eyes said.

Nadine's answered: *Yes. And I know you.*

But this time it was Nadine who dropped her eyes first.

'All right,' she said. 'Leo, or whatever you like. Just come away before you tire her any more.'

He left Mother Abagail's arms, but reluctantly.

'You come back and see me whenever you want,' Abby said, but she did not raise her eyes to include Nadine.

'Okay,' the boy said, and blew her a kiss. Nadine's face was stony. She didn't speak. As they went back down the porch steps, the arm Nadine had around his shoulders seemed more like a drag-chain than a comfort. Mother Abagail watched them go, aware that she was losing the focus again. With the woman's face out of her sight, the sense of revelation began to grow fuzzy. She became unsure of what she had felt. She was only another woman, surely . . . wasn't she?

The young man, Underwood, was standing at the base of the steps, and his face was like a thundercloud.

'Why were you like that?' he asked the woman, and although he'd lowered his voice, Mother Abagail could still hear perfectly well.

The woman paid no attention. She went by him without a word. The boy looked at Underwood in a beseeching way, but the woman was in charge, at least for the time being, and the little boy let her bear him along, bear him away.

There was a moment of silence, and she suddenly felt at a loss to fill it, although it needed to be filled —

— didn't it?

Wasn't it her *job* to fill it?

And a voice asked softly, *Is it? Is that your job? Is that why God brought you here, woman? To be the Official Greeter at the gates of the Free Zone?*

I can't think, she protested. *The woman was right: I AM tired.*

He comes in more shapes than his own, the small interior voice persisted. *Wolf, crow, snake . . . woman.*

What did it mean? What had happened here? What, in God's name?

I was sitting here complacently, waiting to be kowtowed to – yes, that's what I was doing, no use denying it – and now that woman has come and something has happened and I'm losing what it was. But there was something about that woman . . . wasn't there? Are you sure? Are you sure?

There was an instant of silence, and in it they all seemed to be looking at her, waiting for her to prove herself. And she wasn't doing it. The woman and the boy were gone from sight; they had left as if they were the true believers and she nothing but a shoddy, grinning Sanhedrin they had seen through immediately.

Oh, but I'm old! It's not fair!

And on the heels of that came another voice, small and low and rational, a voice that was not her own: *Not too old to know the woman is –*

Now another man had approached her in hesitant, deferential fashion. 'Hi, Mother Abagail,' he said. 'The name's Zellman. Mark Zellman. From Lowville, New York. I dreamed about you.'

And she was faced with a sudden choice that was clearcut for only an instant in her groping mind. She could acknowledge this man's hello, banter with him a little to set him at his ease (but not too much at ease; that was not precisely what she wanted), and then go on to the next and the next and the next, receiving their homage like new palm leaves, or she could ignore him and the rest. She could follow the thread of her thought down into the depths of herself, searching for whatever it was that the Lord meant her to know.

The woman is –

– what?

Did it matter? The woman was gone.

'I had me a great-nephew lived in upstate New York one time,' she said easily to Mark Zellman. 'Town named Rouse's Point. Backed right up against Vermont on Lake Champlain, it is. Probably never heard of it, have you?'

Mark Zellman said he sure had heard of it; just about everyone in New York State knew that town. Had he ever been there? His face broke tragically. No, never had. Always meant to.

'From what Ronnie wrote in his letters, you didn't miss much,' she said, and Zellman went away beaming broadly.

The others came up to make their manners as the other parties had done before them, as still others would do in the days and weeks to come. A teenage boy named Tony Donahue. A fellow named Jack Jackson, who was a car mechanic. A young RN named Laurie Constable – she would come in handy. An old man named Richard Farris whom everyone called the Judge; he looked at her keenly and almost made her feel uncomfortable again. Dick Vollman. Sandy DuChiens – pretty name, that, French. Harry Dunbarton, a man who had sold spectacles for a living only three months ago. Andrea Terminello. A Smith. A Rennett. And a great many others. She spoke to them all, nodded, smiled, and put them at their ease, but the pleasure she had felt on other days was gone today and she felt only the aches in her wrists and fingers and knees, plus the gnawing suspicion that she had to go use the Port-O-San and if she didn't get there soon she was going to stain her dress.

All of that and the feeling, fading now (and it would be entirely gone by nightfall), that she had missed something of great significance and might later be very sorry.

He thought better when he wrote, and so he jotted down everything which might be of importance in outline, using two felt-tip pens: a blue and a black. Nick Andros sat in the study of the house on Baseline Drive that he shared with Ralph Brentner and Ralph's woman, Elise. It was almost dark. The house was a beauty, sitting below the bulk of Flagstaff Mountain but quite a bit above the town of Boulder proper, so that from the wide living room window the streets and roads of the municipality appeared spread out like a gigantic gameboard. That window was treated on the outside with some sort of silvery reflective stuff, so that the squire could look out but passersby could not look in. Nick guessed that the house was in the $450,000–$500,000 range . . . and the owner and his family were mysteriously absent.

On his own long journey from Shoyo to Boulder, first by himself, then with Tom Cullen and the others, he had passed through tens of dozens of towns and cities, and all of them had been stinking charnel houses. Boulder had no business being any different . . . but it was. There were corpses here, yes, thousands of them, and something was going to have to be done about them before the hot, dry days ended and the fall rains began, causing quicker decomposition and possible disease . . . but there were not *enough* corpses. Nick wondered if anyone other than he and Stu Redman had noticed it . . . Lauder, maybe. Lauder noticed almost everything.

For every house or public building you found littered with corpses, there were ten others completely empty. Sometime, during the last spasm of the plague, most of Boulder's citizens, sick or well, had blown town. Why? Well, he supposed it really didn't matter, and maybe they would never know. The awesome fact remained that Mother Abagail, sight unseen, had managed to lead them to maybe the one small city in the United States that had been cleared of plague victims. It was enough to make even an agnostic like himself wonder where she was getting her information.

Nick had taken three rooms on the basement level of the house, and nice rooms they were, furnished in knotty pine. No urging on Ralph's part had moved him to enlarge his living space – he felt like an interloper already, but he liked them . . . and until his trip from Shoyo to Hemingford Home, he hadn't realized how much he had come to miss other faces. He hadn't gotten his fill yet.

And the place was the finest one he'd ever lived in, just as it was. He had his own entrance by the back door, and he kept his ten-speed parked under the door's low, overhanging eave, where it stood axle-deep in generations of fragrantly rotting aspen leaves. He had the beginnings of a book collection, something he had always wanted and never been able to have in his years of wandering. He had been a great reader in those days (during these new days, there rarely seemed to be time to sit and have a good long conversation with a book), and some of the books on the shelves – shelves which were still largely empty – were old friends, most of them originally borrowed from lending libraries at two cents a day; in the last few years he had never spent enough time in one town to get a regular library card. Others were books he hadn't yet read, books the lending library books had led him to look for. As he sat here with his felt-tip pens and paper, one of these books sat on the desk beside his right hand – *Set This House on Fire*, by William Styron. He had marked his place with a ten-dollar bill he had found on the street. There was a lot of money in the streets, blowing along the gutters in the wind, and he was still surprised and amused at how many people – himself among them – still stopped to pick them up. And why?

The books were free now. The *ideas* were free. Sometimes that thought exhilarated him. Sometimes it frightened him.

The paper he was writing on came from a ring-binder in which he kept all his thoughts – the contents of the binder were half diary, half shopping list. He had discovered a deep fondness in himself for making lists; he thought one of his forebears must have been an accountant. When your mind was troubled, he had discovered that making a list often set it at ease again.

He went back to the fresh page before him, doodling formlessly in the margin.

It seemed to him that all the things they wanted or needed from the old life were stored in the silent East Boulder power plant, like dusty treasure in a dark cupboard. An unpleasant feeling seemed to run through the people who had gathered in Boulder, a feeling just submerged below the surface – they were like a scared bunch of kids knocking around in the local haunted house after dark. In some ways, the place was like a rancid ghost town. There was a sense that being here was a strictly temporary thing. There was one man, a fellow named Impening, who had once lived in Boulder and worked on one of the custodial crews at the IBM plant out on the Boulder–Longmont Diagonal. Impening seemed determined to stir up unrest. He was going around telling people that in 1974 there had been an inch and a half of snow in Boulder by September 14, and that by November it would be cold enough to freeze the balls off a brass monkey. That was the kind of talk Nick would like to put a quick stop to. Never mind that if Impening had been in the army he would have been cashiered for such talk; that was an empty logic, if it was logic at all. The important thing was that Impening's words would have no power if people could move into houses where the lights worked and where the furnaces blew hot air up through grates at the touch of a finger on a button. If that didn't happen by the time the first coldsnap arrived, Nick was afraid that people would begin simply to slip away, and all the meetings, representatives, and ratifications in the world wouldn't stop that.

According to Ralph, there wasn't that much wrong at the power plant, at least not that much visible. The crews who ran it had shut some of the machinery down; other machinery had shut itself down. Two or three of the big turbine engines had blown, perhaps as the result of some final power surge. Ralph said that some of the wiring would have to be replaced, but he thought that he and Brad Kitchner and a crew of a dozen warm bodies could do that. A much bigger work crew was needed to remove fused and blackened copper wire from the blown turbine generators and then install new copper wire by the yard. There was plenty of copper wire in the Denver supply houses for the taking; Ralph and Brad had gone one day last week to check for themselves. With the manpower, they thought they could have the lights on again by Labor Day.

'And then we'll throw the biggest fucking party this town ever saw,' Brad said.

Law and Order. That was something else that troubled him. Could Stu Redman be handed that particular package? He wouldn't want the job, but Nick thought he could perhaps persuade Stu to take it . . . and if push came to shove, he could get Stu's friend Glen to back him up. What really bothered him was the memory, still too fresh and hurtful to look at more than briefly, of his own brief and terrible tour as Shoyo's jailkeeper. Vince and Billy dying, Mike Childress jumping up and down on his supper and crying out in wretched defiance: *Hunger strike! I'm on a fuckin hunger strike!*

It made him ache inside to think they might need courts and jails . . . maybe even an executioner. Christ, these were Mother Abagail's people, not the dark man's! But he supposed the dark man would not bother with such trivialities as courts and jails. His punishment would be swift and sure and heavy. He would not need the threat of jail when the corpses hung on the telephone pole crosses along I-15 for the birds to pick.

Nick hoped most of the infractions would be small ones. There had been several cases of drunk and disorderly already. One kid, really too young to drive, had been rodding a big dragging machine up and down Broadway, scaring people out of the street. He had finally driven into a stalled bread truck and had gashed his forehead – and lucky to get off so cheaply, in Nick's opinion. The people who had seen him knew he was too young, but no one had felt he or she had the authority to put a stop to it.

Authority. Organization. He wrote the words on his pad and put them inside a double circle. Being Mother Abagail's people gave them no immunity to weakness, stupidity, or bad companions. Nick didn't know if they were the children of God or not, but when Moses had come down from the mountain, those not busy worshipping the golden calf had been busy shooting craps, he knew that. And they had to face the possibility that someone might get cut over a card game or decide to shoot someone else over a woman.

Authority. Organization. He circled the words again and now they were like prisoners behind a triple stockade. How well they went together . . . and what a sorry sound they made.

Not long after, Ralph came in. 'We got some more folks coming in tomorrow, Nicky, and a whole parade the day after. Over thirty in that second one.'

'Good,' Nick wrote. 'We'll get a doc before long, I bet. Law of averages says so.'

'Yeah,' Ralph said. 'We're turnin into a regular by-God city.' Nick nodded.

'I had a talk with the fella leadin the party that came in today. His name's Larry Underwood. Smart man, Nick. Sharp as a tack.'

Nick raised his eyebrows and drew a ? in the air.

'Well, let's see,' Ralph said. He knew what the question mark meant: give more information, if you can. 'He's six or seven years older'n you, I think, and maybe eight or nine younger than Redman. But he's the kind of man you said we ought to be on the lookout for. He asks the right questions.'

?

'Who's in charge, for one,' Ralph said. 'What comes next, for another. Who does it, for a third.'

Nick nodded. Yes – the right questions. But was he the right man? Ralph might be right. He also might not be.

'I'll try to meet up with him tomorrow & say hello,' he wrote on a fresh sheet of paper.

'Yeah, you oughtta. He's all right.' Ralph shuffled his feet. 'And I talked to Mother a little bit before this Underwood and his folks came up to be innerduced. Talked to her like you wanted me to.'

?

'She says we ought to go ahead. Get moving. She says there's people lollygaggin, and they need some folks to be in charge and tell em where to squat and lean.'

Nick leaned back in his chair and laughed silently. Then he wrote, 'I was pretty sure she'd feel that way. I'll talk to Stu & Glen tomorrow. Did you print the handbills?'

'Oh! Those! Shit, yeah,' Ralph said. 'That's where I been most of the afternoon, for Christ's sake.' He showed Nick a sample poster. Still smelling strongly of mimeograph ink, the print was large and eyecatching. Ralph had done the graphics himself:

MASS MEETING!!!
REPRESENTATIVE BOARD
TO BE NOMINATED AND ELECTED!

8:30 PM, August 18, 1990
Place: Canyon Boulevard Park & Bandshell if FINE
Chautauqua Hall in Chautauqua Park if FOUL

REFRESHMENTS WILL BE SERVED
FOLLOWING THE MEETING

Below this were two rudimentary street maps for newcomers and those who hadn't spent much time exploring Boulder. Below, in rather fine print, were the names he and Stu and Glen had agreed upon after some discussion earlier in the day:

> *Ad Hoc Committee*
> Nick Andros
> Glen Bateman
> Ralph Brentner
> Richard Ellis
> Fran Goldsmith
> Stuart Redman
> Susan Stern

Nick pointed to the line on the flier about refreshments and raised his eyebrows.

'Oh yeah, well, Frannie came by and said we'd be more apt to get everybody if we had something. She and her friend there, Patty Kroger, they're going to see to it. Cookies and Za-Rex.' Ralph made a face. 'If it came down to a choice between drinking Za-Rex and bullpiss, I'd have to sit down and think her over. You c'n have mine, Nicky.'

Nick grinned.

'The only thing about this,' Ralph went on more seriously, 'is you guys putting me on this committee. I know what that word means. It means "Congratulations, you get to do all the hard work." Well, I don't really mind that, I been workin hard all my life. But committees are supposed to have idears, and I ain't much of an idear man.'

On his pad, Nick quickly sketched a big CB setup, and in the background a radio tower with bolts of electricity coming from its top.

'Yeah, but that's a lot different,' Ralph said glumly.

'You'll be fine,' Nick wrote. 'Believe it.'

'If you say so, Nicky. I'll give her a try. I still think you'd be better off with this Underwood fella, though.'

Nick shook his head and clapped Ralph on the shoulder. Ralph bid him goodnight and went upstairs. When he was gone, Nick looked thoughtfully at the handbill for a long time. If Stu and Glen had seen copies – and he was sure they had by now – they knew that he had unilaterally stricken Harold Lauder's name from their list of ad hoc committee members. He didn't know how they might be taking it, but the fact that they hadn't shown up at his door yet was probably a good sign. They might want him to do some horsetrading of his own, and if he had to, he would do it, just to keep Harold out at the top. If he had to, he would give them Ralph. Ralph didn't really want the position anyway, although, goddammit, Ralph had great native wit and the nearly priceless ability to think around the corners of problems. He would be a good man to have on the permanent committee, and he felt that Stu and Glen had already packed the committee with their friends. If he, Nick, wanted Lauder out, they would just have to go along. To pull off this leadership coup smoothly, there had to be no dissension at all among them. Say, Ma, how did that man get a rabbit to come out of that hat? Well, son, I'm not sure, but I think he *might* have used the old 'misdirect em with cookies and Za-Rex' trick. It works just about every time.

He turned back to the page he had been doodling on when Ralph came in. He stared at the words he had circled not just once but three times, as if to keep them in. *Authority. Organization.* He suddenly wrote another one below them – there was just room. Now the words in the triple circle read:

Authority. Organization. Politics.

But he wasn't trying to knock Lauder out of the picture just because he felt Stu and Glen Bateman were trying to hog what was really his football. He felt a certain amount of pique, sure. It would have been odd if he hadn't. In a way, he, Ralph, and Mother Abagail had *founded* the Boulder Free Zone.

There's hundreds of people here now and thousands more on their way if Bateman's right, he thought, tapping his pencil against the circled words. The longer he looked at them, the uglier they seemed. *But when Ralph and I and Mother and Tom Cullen and the rest in our party got here, the only living things in Boulder were the cats and the deer that had come down here from the state park to forage in people's gardens . . . and even in the stores. Remember that one that got into the Table Mesa Supermarket somehow and then couldn't get out? It was crazy, running up and down the aisles, knocking things over, falling down, then getting up and running again.*

We're Johnny-come-latelies, sure, we haven't even been here a month yet, but we were first! So there's a little pique, but pique isn't the reason I want Harold out. I want him out because I don't trust him. He smiles all the time, but there's a watertight

(smiletight?)

compartment between his mouth and his eyes. There was some friction between him and Stu at one time, over Frannie, and all three of them say it's over, but I wonder if it really is over. Sometimes I see Frannie looking at Harold, and she looks uneasy. She looks as if she's trying to figure out how 'over' this over really is. He's bright enough, but he strikes me as unstable.

Nick shook his head. That wasn't all. On more than one occasion he had wondered if Harold Lauder might not be crazy.

Mostly it's that grin. I don't want to have to share secrets with anyone who grins like that and looks as if he isn't sleeping well at night.

No Lauder. They'll have to go along with that.

Nick closed his ring-binder and put it away in the bottom drawer of his desk. Then he stood up and began taking off his clothes. He wanted a shower. He felt obscurely dirty.

The world, he thought, not according to Garp but according to the superflu. This brave new world. But it didn't seem particularly brave to him, or particularly new. It was as if someone had put a large cherry bomb into a child's toybox. There had been a big bang and everything had gone everywhere. Toys had scattered from one end of the playroom to the other. Some things were shattered beyond repair, other things would be fixable, but most of the stuff had just been scattered. Those things were still a little too hot to handle, but they would be fine once they had cooled off.

Meanwhile, the job was to sort things out. Throw away the things which were no longer good. Set aside the toys which could be fixed. List everything which was still okay. Get a new toybox to put the things in, a nice new toybox. A *strong* toybox. There is a frightening, sickening ease – and a clear attraction – to the way in which things can be blown apart. The hard job is bringing things together again. The sorting. The fixing. The listing. And discarding the things which are no good, of course.

Except . . . can you *ever* bring yourself to throw away the things which are no good?

Nick paused halfway to the bathroom, naked, his clothes held in his arms.

Oh, the night was so silent . . . but weren't all his nights symphonies of silence? Why had his body suddenly broke out in gooseflesh?

Why, because he suddenly felt that it was not toys the Free Zone Committee would be in charge of picking up, not toys at all. He suddenly felt that he had joined some bizarre sewing circle of the human spirit – he and Redman and Bateman and Mother Abagail, yes, even Ralph with his big radio and his boosting equipment that sent the Free Zone signal flying far and wide across the dead continent. They each had a needle and perhaps they were working together to make a warm blanket to keep off the winter chill . . . or perhaps they had only, after a brief pause, begun once again to make a large shroud for the human race, beginning their work at the toes and working their way up.

After love, Stu had gone to sleep. He had been on short sleep rations lately, and the night before he had been up all night with Glen Bateman, getting drunk and planning for the future. Frannie had put on her robe and come out here on the balcony.

The building they lived in was downtown, on the corner of Pearl Street and Broadway. Their apartment was on the third floor, and below her she could see the intersection, Pearl running east-west, Broadway running north-south. She liked it here. They had the compass boxed. The night was warm and windless, the black stone of the sky flawed with a million stars. In their faint and frosty glow, Fran could see the slabs of the Flatirons rising in the west.

She passed a hand down from her neck to her thighs. The dressing gown she wore was silk, and she was naked underneath. Her hand passed smoothly over her breasts and then, instead of continuing on flat and straight to the mild rise of her pubis, her hand traced an arc of belly, following a curve that had not been this pronounced even two weeks ago.

She was beginning to show, not a lot yet, but Stu had commented on it this evening. His question had been casual enough, even comic: *How long can we do it without me, uh, squeezing him?*

Or her, she had answered, amused. *How does four months sound, Chief?*

Fine, he had answered, and slipped deliciously into her.

Earlier talk had been much more serious. Not long after they got to Boulder, Stu had told her he had discussed the baby with Glen and Glen had advanced the idea, very cautiously, that the superflu germ or virus might still be around. If so, the baby might die. It was an unsettling thought (you could always, she thought, count on Glen Bateman for an Unsettling Thought or two), but surely if the mother was immune, the baby . . . ?

Yet there were plenty of people here who had lost children to the plague.

Yes, but that would mean –

Would mean what?

Well, for one thing, it might mean that all these people here were just an epilogue to the human race, a brief coda. She didn't want to believe that, *couldn't* believe it. If that were true –

Someone was coming up the street, turning sideways to slip between a dump truck that had stalled with two of its wheels on the pavement and the wall of a restaurant called the Pearl Street Kitchen. He had a light jacket slung over one shoulder and was carrying something in one hand that was either a bottle or a gun with a long barrel. In the other hand he had a sheet of paper, probably with an address written on it from the way he was checking street numbers. At last he stopped in front of their building. He was looking at the door as if trying to decide what to do next. Frannie thought he looked a little like a private detective in some old TV series. She was standing less than twenty feet above his head, and she found herself in one of those situations. If she called him, she might scare him. If she didn't, he might start knocking and wake Stuart up. And what was he doing with a gun in his hand anyway . . . if it *was* a gun?

He suddenly craned his neck and looked up, probably to see if any lights were on in the building. Frannie was still looking down. They peered directly into each other's eyes.

'Holy God!' the man on the sidewalk cried. He took an involuntary step backward, went off the sidewalk into the gutter, and sat down hard.

'Oh!' Frannie said at the same moment, and took her own step backward on the balcony. There was a spider-plant in a large pottery vase on a pedestal behind her. Frannie's behind struck it. It tottered, almost decided to live a little longer, and then defenestrated itself on the balcony's slate flags with a loud crash.

In the bedroom, Stu grunted, turned over, and was still again.

Frannie, perhaps predictably, was seized with the giggles. She put both hands over her mouth and pinched viciously at her lips, but the giggles came out anyway in a series of hoarse little whispers. *Grace strikes again*, she thought, and whisper-giggled madly into her cupped hands. *If he'd had a guitar I could have dropped the damned vase on his head. O sole mio . . . CRASH!* Her belly hurt from trying to hold in the giggles.

A conspiratorial whisper wafted its way up from below: 'Hey, you . . . you on the balcony . . . *psssst!*'

'*Pssst*,' Frannie whispered to herself. '*Pssst*, oh great.'

She had to get out before she started hee-hawing away like a donkey. She had never been able to hold in her laughter once it got hold of her. She ran fleetly across the darkened bedroom, snatched a more substantial – and demure – wrapper from the back of the bathroom door, and went down the hall struggling it on, her face working like a rubber mask. She let herself out onto the landing and got down one flight before the laughter escaped her and flew free. She went down the lower two flights cackling wildly.

The man – a young man, she saw now – had picked himself up and was brushing himself off. He was slim and well built, most of his face covered with a beard that might be blond or possibly sandy-red by daylight. There were dark circles under his eyes, but he was smiling a rueful little smile.

'What did you knock over?' he asked. 'It sounded like a piano.'

'It was a vase,' she said. 'It . . . it . . .' But then the giggles caught her again and she could only point a finger at him and laugh quietly and shake her head and then hold her aching belly again. Tears rolled down her cheeks. 'You really looked funny . . . I know that's a hell of a thing to say to somebody you just met but . . . oh, my! You *did*!'

'If this was the old days,' he said, grinning, 'my next move would be to sue you for at least a quarter of a million. Whiplash.

Judge, I looked up and this young woman was peering down at me. Yes, I believe she was making a face. Her face was on, at any rate. We find for the plaintiff, this poor boy. Also for the bailiff. There will be a ten-minute recess.'

They laughed together a little. The young man was wearing clean faded jeans and a dark blue shirt. The summer night was warm and kind, and Frannie was beginning to be glad she had come out.

'Your name wouldn't happen to be Fran Goldsmith, would it?'

'It so happens. But I don't know you.'

'Larry Underwood. We just came in today. Actually, I was looking for a fellow named Harold Lauder. They said he was living at 261 Pearl along with Stu Redman and Frannie Goldsmith and some other people.'

That dried her giggles up. 'Harold was in the building when we first got to Boulder, but he split quite a while ago. He's on Arapahoe now, on the west side of town. I can give you his address if you want it, and directions.'

'I'd appreciate that. But I'll wait until tomorrow to go over, I guess. I'm not risking this action again.'

'Do you know Harold?'

'I do and I don't – the same way I do and don't know you. Although I have to be honest and say you don't look the way I pictured you. In my mind I saw you as a Valkyrie-type blonde right out of a Frank Frazetta painting, probably with a .45 on each hip. But I'm pleased to meet you anyway.' He stuck out his hand and Frannie shook it with a bewildered little smile.

'I'm afraid I don't have the slightest idea what you're talking about.'

'Sit down on the curb a minute and I'll tell you.'

She sat. A ghost of a breeze riffled up the street, shuffling scraps of paper and making the old elms move on the courthouse lawn three blocks farther down.

'I've got some stuff for Harold Lauder,' Larry said. 'But it's supposed to be a surprise, so if you see him before I do, mum's the word and all that.'

'Okay, sure,' Frannie said. She was more mystified than ever.

He held up the long-barreled gun and it wasn't a gun at all; it was a wine bottle with a long neck. She tilted the label to the starlight and could just barely read the large print – BORDEAUX at the top, and at the bottom, the date: *1947*.

'The best vintage Bordeaux in this century,' he said. 'At least that's what an old friend of mine used to say. His name was Rudy. God love and rest his soul.'

'But 1947 . . . that's forty-three years ago. Won't it be . . . well, gone over?'

'Rudy used to say a good Bordeaux never went over. Anyway, I've carried it all the way from Ohio. If it's bad wine, it'll be well-traveled bad wine.'

'And that's for Harold?'

'That and a bunch of these.' He took something out of his jacket pocket and handed it to her. She didn't have to turn this up to the starlight to read the print. She burst out laughing. 'A Payday candy bar!' she exclaimed. 'Harold's favorite . . . but how could you know that?'

'That's the story.'

'Then tell me!'

'Well, then. Once upon a time there was a fellow named Larry Underwood who came from California to New York to see his dear old mother. That wasn't the only reason he came, and the other reasons were a little less pleasant, but let's stick to the nice-guy reason, shall we?'

'Why not?' Fran agreed.

'And behold, the Wicked Witch of the West, or some Pentagon assholes, visited the country with a great plague, and before you could say "Here comes Captain Trips," just about everyone in New York was dead. Including Larry's mother.'

'I'm sorry. My mom and dad, too.'

'Yeah – everybody's mom and dad. If we all sent each other sympathy cards, there wouldn't be any left. But Larry was one of the lucky ones. He made it out of the city with a lady named Rita who wasn't very well equipped to deal with what had happened. And unfortunately, Larry wasn't very well equipped to help her deal with it.'

'No one had the equipment.'

'But some developed it quicker than others. Anyhow, Larry and Rita headed for the coast of Maine. They made it as far as Vermont, and there the lady OD'd on sleeping pills.'

'Oh, Larry, that is too bad.'

'Larry took it very hard. In fact, he took it as a more or less divine judgment on his strength of character. In *further* fact, he had been told by one or two people who should have known that his most incorruptible character trait was a splendid streak of self-interest, which came shining through like a Day-Glo madonna sitting on the dashboard of a '59 Cadillac.'

Frannie shifted a bit on the curb.

'I hope I'm not making you uncomfortable, but all of this has been sloshing around inside for a long time, and it *does* have some bearing on the Harold part of the story. Okay?'

'Okay.'

'Thanks. I think that ever since we stopped by and met that old woman today I've been looking for a friendly face so I could spill this. I just thought it would be Harold's. Anyway – Larry continued on to Maine because there didn't seem to be anyplace else to go. He was having very bad dreams by then, but since he was alone he had no way of knowing that other people were having them, too. He simply assumed it was another symptom of his continuing mental breakdown. But eventually he made it to a small coastal town named Wells, where he met a woman named Nadine Cross and a strange little boy whose name turns out to be Leo Rockway.'

'Wells,' she marveled softly.

'Anyway, the three travelers sort of flipped a coin to see which way they should head on US 1, and since it came up tails, they headed down south where they eventually came to –'

'Ogunquit!' Frannie said, delighted.

'Just so. And there, on a barn, in huge letters, I made my first acquaintance with Harold Lauder and Frances Goldsmith.'

'Harold's sign! Oh, Larry, he *will* be pleased!'

'We followed the directions on the barn to Stovington, and the directions at Stovington to Nebraska and the directions at Mother Abagail's house to Boulder. We met people along the way. One of them was a girl named Lucy Swann, who's my woman. I'd like you to meet her sometime. I think you'd like her.

'By then something had happened that Larry didn't really want. His little party of four grew to six. The six met four more in upstate New York, and our party absorbed theirs. By the time we made it to Harold's sign in Mother Abagail's dooryard there were sixteen of us, and we picked up another three just as we were leaving. Larry was in charge of this brave band. There was no vote or anything like that. It just *was*. And he really didn't want the responsibility. It was a drag. It was keeping him awake nights. He started popping Tums and Rolaids. But it's funny the way your mind boxes your mind. I couldn't let it go. It got to be a self-respect thing. And I – *he* – was always afraid he was going to fuck it up righteously, that he'd get up some morning and someone would be dead in their sleeping bag the way Rita was that time in Vermont and everyone would be standing around pointing their fingers and saying, "It's your fault. You didn't know any better and it's your fault." And that was something I couldn't talk about, not even to the Judge –'

'Who's the Judge?'

'Judge Farris. An old guy from Peoria. I guess he really was a judge at one time back in the early fifties, circuit judge or something, but he'd been retired a long time when the flu hit. He's plenty sharp, though. When he looks at you, you'd swear he has X-ray eyes. Anyhow, Harold was important to me. He got to be more important as there got to be more people. In direct ratio, you might say.' He chuckled a little. 'That barn. Man! The last line of that sign, the one with your name, was so low I figured he really must have been hanging ass out to the wind when he painted it on.'

'Yes. I was sleeping when he did that. I would have made him stop.'

'I started to get a sense of him,' Larry said. 'I found a Payday wrapper in the cupola of that barn in Ogunquit, and then the carving on the beam –'

'What carving?'

She felt that Larry was studying her in the dark, and she pulled her robe a little closer around her . . . not a gesture of modesty, because she felt no threat from this man, but one of nervousness.

'Just his initials,' Larry said casually. 'H. E. L. If that had been the end of it, I wouldn't be here now. But then at the motorcycle dealership in Wells –'

'We were there!'

'I know you were. I saw a couple of bikes gone. What made an even bigger impression was that Harold had siphoned some gas from the underground tank. You must have helped him, Fran. I damn near lost my fingers.'

'No, I didn't have to. Harold hunted around until he found something he called a plug-vent –'

Larry groaned and slapped his forehead. 'Plug-vent! Jesus! I never even looked for where they were venting the tank! You mean he just hunted around . . . pulled a plug . . . and put his hose in?'

'Well . . . yes.'

'Oh, Harold,' Larry said in a tone of admiration that she had never heard before, at least not in connection with Harold Lauder's name. 'Well, that's one of his tricks I missed. Anyway, we got to Stovington. And Nadine was so upset she fainted.'

'I cried,' Fran said. 'I bawled until it seemed I'd never stop. I just had my mind made up that when we got there, someone would welcome us in and say, "Hi! Step inside, delousing on the right, cafeteria's on your left."' She shook her head. 'That seems so silly now.'

'I was not dismayed. Dauntless Harold had been there before me, left his sign, and gone on. I felt like a tenderfoot Easterner following that Indian from *The Pathfinder*.'

His view of Harold both fascinated and amazed her. Hadn't Stu really been leading the party by the time they left Vermont and struck out for Nebraska? She couldn't honestly remember. By then they had all been preoccupied with the dreams. Larry was reminding her of things she had forgotten . . . or worse, taken for granted. Harold risking his life to put that sign on the barn – it had seemed like a foolish risk to her, but it had done some good after all. And getting gas from that underground tank . . . it had apparently been a major operation for Larry, but Harold had seemed to take it purely as a matter of course. It made her feel small and made her feel guilty. They all more or less assumed that Harold was nothing but a grinning supernumerary. But Harold had turned quite a few tricks in the last six weeks. Had she been so much in love with Stu that it took this total stranger to point out some home truths about Harold? What made the feeling even more uncomfortable was the fact that, once he had gotten his feet under him, Harold had been completely adult about herself and Stuart.

Larry said, 'So here's another neat sign, complete with route numbers, at Stovington, right? And fluttering in the grass next to it, another Payday candy wrapper. I felt like instead of following broken sticks and bent grasses, I was following Harold's trail of chocolate Paydays. Well, we didn't follow your route the whole way. We bent north near Gary, Indiana, because there was one hell of a fire, still burning in places. It looked like every damn oiltank in the city went up. Anyhow, we picked up the Judge on the detour, stopped by Hemingford Home – we knew she was gone by then, the dreams you know, but we all wanted to *see* that place just the same. The corn . . . the tire swing . . . you know what I mean?'

'Yes,' Frannie said quietly. 'Yes, I do.'

'And all the time I'm going crazy, thinking that something is going to happen, we're going to get attacked by a motorcycle gang or something, run out of water, I don't know.

'There used to be a book my mom had, she got it from her grandmother or something. *In His Steps*, that was the name of it. And there were all these little stories about guys with horrible problems. Ethical problems, most of them. And the guy who wrote the book said that to solve the problems, all you had to do was ask, "What would Jesus do?" It always cleared the trouble right up. You know what I think? It's a Zen question, not really a question at all but a way to clear your mind, like saying Om and looking at the tip of your nose.'

Fran smiled. She knew what her mother would have said about something like *that*.

'So when I really started to get wound up, Lucy – that's my girl, did I tell you? – Lucy would say, "Hurry up, Larry, ask the question."'

'What would Jesus do?' Fran said, amused.

'No, what would *Harold* do?' Larry answered seriously. Fran was nearly dumbfounded. She could not help wishing to be around when Larry actually met Harold. Whatever in the world would his reaction be?

'We camped in this farmyard one night and we really were almost out of water. The place had a well, but no way of drawing it up, naturally, because the power was off and the pump wouldn't work. And Joe – Leo, I'm sorry, his real name is Leo – Leo kept walking by and saying, "Firsty, Larry, pwetty firsty now." And he was driving me bugshit. I could feel myself tightening up, and the next time he came by I probably would have hit him. Nice guy, huh? Getting ready to hit a disturbed child. But a person can't change all at once. I've had plenty of time to work that out for myself.'

'You brought them all across from Maine intact,' Frannie said. 'One of ours died. His appendix burst. Stu tried to operate on him, but it was no good. All in all, Larry, I'd say you did pretty well.'

'Harold and I did pretty well,' he corrected. 'Anyway, Lucy said, "Quick, Larry, ask the question." So I did. There was a windmill on the place that ran water up to the barn. It was turning pretty good, but there wasn't any water coming out of the barn faucets either. So I opened the big case at the foot of the windmill, where all the machinery was, and I saw that the main driveshaft had popped out of its hole. I got it back in and bingo! All the water you could want. Cold and tasty. Thanks to Harold.'

'Thanks to *you*. Harold wasn't really there, Larry.'

'Well, he was in my head. And now I'm here and I brought him the wine and the candy bars.' He looked at her sideways. 'You know, I kind of thought he might be your man.'

She shook her head and looked down at her clasped fingers. 'No. He . . . not Harold.'

He didn't say anything for a long time, but she felt him looking at her. At last he said, 'Okay, how have I got it wrong? About Harold?'

She stood up. 'I ought to go in now. It's been nice to meet you, Larry. Come by tomorrow and meet Stu. Bring your Lucy, if she's not busy.'

'What is it about him?' he insisted, standing with her.

'Oh, I don't know,' she said thickly. Suddenly the tears were very close. 'You make me feel as if . . . as if I've treated Harold very shabbily and I don't know . . . why or how I did it . . . can I be blamed for not loving him the way I do Stu? Is that supposed to be my fault?'

'No, of course not.' Larry looked taken aback. 'Listen, I'm sorry. I barged in on you. I'll go.'

'He's *changed*!' Frannie burst out. 'I don't know how or why, and sometimes I think it might be for the better . . . but I don't . . . don't really know. And sometimes I'm afraid.'

'Afraid of Harold?'

She didn't answer; only looked down at her feet. She thought she had already said too much.

'You were going to tell me how I could get there?' he asked gently.

'It's easy. Just go straight out Arapahoe until you come to the little park . . . the Eben G. Fine Park, I think it is. The park's on the right. Harold's little house is on the left, just across from it.'

'All right, thanks. Meeting you was a pleasure, Fran, busted vase and all.'

She smiled, but it was perfunctory. All of the dizzy good humor had gone out of the evening.

Larry raised the bottle of wine and offered his slanted little smile. 'And if you see him before I do . . . keep a secret, huh?'

'Sure.'

'Night, Frannie.'

He walked back the way he had come. She watched him out of sight, then went upstairs and slipped into bed next to Stu, who was still out like a light.

Harold, she thought, pulling the covers up to her chin. How was she supposed to tell this Larry, who seemed so nice in his strangely lost way (but weren't they all lost now?), that Harold Lauder was fat and juvenile and lost himself? Was she supposed to tell him that one day not so long ago she had happened upon wise Harold, resourceful Harold, what-would-Jesus-do Harold, mowing the back lawn in his bathing suit and weeping? Was she supposed to tell him that the sometimes sulky, often frightened Harold that had come to Boulder from Ogunquit had turned into a stout politician, a backslapper, a hail-fellow-well-met type of guy who nonetheless looked at you with the flat and unsmiling eyes of a gila monster?

She thought her wait for sleep might be very long tonight. Harold had fallen hopelessly in love with her and she had fallen hopelessly in love with Stu Redman, and it certainly was a tough old world. And now every time I see Harold I get such a case of the *creeps*. Even though he looks like he's lost ten pounds or so and he doesn't have quite so many pimples, I get the –

Her breath caught audibly in her throat and she sat up on her elbows, eyes wide in the dark.

Something had moved inside her.

Her hands went to the slight swelling of her middle. Surely it was too early. It had only been her imagination. Except –

Except it hadn't been.

She lay back down slowly, her heart beating hard. She almost woke Stu up and then didn't. If only he had put the baby inside her, instead of Jess. If he had, she would have awakened him and shared the moment with him. The next baby she would. If there *was* a next baby, of course.

And then the movement came again, so slight it might only have been gas. Except she knew better. It was the baby. And the baby was alive.

'Oh glory,' she murmured to herself, and lay back. Larry Underwood and Harold Lauder were forgotten. Everything that had happened to her since her mother had fallen ill was forgotten. She waited for it to move again, listening for that presence inside herself, and fell asleep listening. Her baby was alive.

Harold sat in a chair on the lawn of the little house he had picked out for himself, looking up at the sky and thinking of an old rock and roll song. He hated rock, but he could remember this one almost line-for-line and even the name of the group that had sung it: Kathy Young and the Innocents. The lead singer, songstress, whatever, had a high, yearning, reedy voice that had somehow caught his full attention. A golden goody, the DJs called it. A Blast from the Past. A Platter that Matters. The girl singing lead sounded sixteen years old, pallid, blond, and plain. She sounded as if she might be singing to a picture that spent most of its time buried in a dresser drawer, a picture that was taken out only late at night when everyone else in the house was asleep. She sounded hopeless. The picture she sang to had perhaps been clipped from her big sister's yearbook, a picture of the local Big Jock – captain of the football team and president of the Student Council. The Big Jock would be slipping it to the head cheerleader on some deserted lovers' lane while far away in suburbia this plain girl with no breasts and a pimple in the corner of her mouth sang:

'*A thousand stars in the sky . . . make me realize . . . you are the one love that I'll adore . . . tell me you love me . . . tell me you're mine, all mine . . .*'

There were a lot more than a thousand stars in his sky tonight, but they weren't lovers' stars. No soft caul of Milky Way here. Here, a mile above sea-level they were as sharp and cruel as a billion holes in black velvet, stabs from God's icepick. They were haters' stars, and because they were, Harold felt well qualified to wish on them. Wish-I-may, wish-I-might, have-the-wish-I-wish-tonight. Drop dead, folks.

He sat silently with his head cocked back, a brooding astronomer. Harold's hair was longer than ever, but it was no longer dirty and clotted and tangled. He no longer smelled like a shootoff in a haymow. Even his blemishes were clearing up, now that he had laid off the candy. And with the hard work and all the walking, he was losing some weight. He was starting to look pretty good. There had been times in the last few weeks when he had strode past some reflective surface only to glance back over his shoulder, startled, as if he had caught a glimpse of a total stranger.

He shifted in his chair. There was a book in his lap, a tall volume with a marbled blue binding and imitation leather covers. He kept it hidden under a loose hearthstone in the house when he was away. If anyone found the book, that would be the end of him in Boulder. There was one word stamped in gold leaf on the book's cover, and the word was LEDGER. It was the journal he had started after reading Fran's diary. Already he had filled the first sixty pages with his close, margin-to-margin handwriting. There were no paragraphs, only a solid block of writing, an outpouring of hate like pus from a skin abscess. He hadn't thought he had so much hate in him. It seemed he should have exhausted the flow by now, yet it seemed he had only tapped it. It was like that old joke. Why was the ground all white after Custer's Last Stand? Because the Indians kept coming and coming and . . .

And why did he hate?

He sat up straight, as if the question had come from the outside. It was a hard question to answer, except maybe to a few, a chosen few. Hadn't Einstein said there were only six people in the world who understood all the implications of $E=mc^2$? What about the equation inside his own skull? The relativity of Harold. The speed of blight. Oh, he could fill twice as many pages as he had already written about that, becoming more obscure, more arcane, until he finally became lost in the clockwork of himself and still nowhere near the mainspring at all. He was perhaps . . . raping himself. Was that it? It was close, anyway. An obscene and ongoing act of buggery. The Indians just kept on coming and coming.

He would be leaving Boulder soon. A month or two, no more. When he finally settled on a method of settling his scores. Then he would head out west. And when he got there he would open his mouth and spill his guts about this place. He would tell them what went on at the public meetings, and much more important, what went on at the private meetings. He was sure to be on the Free Zone Committee. He would be welcomed, and he would be well rewarded by the fellow in charge over there . . . not by an end to hate but by the perfect vehicle for it, a Hate Cadillac, a Fearderado, long and darkly shining. He would climb into it and it would bear him and his hate down on them. He and Flagg would kick this miserable settlement apart like an anthill. But first he would settle with Redman, who had lied to him and stolen his woman.

Yes, Harold, but why do you hate?

No; there was no satisfactory answer to that, only a kind of . . . of endorsement for the hate itself. Was it even a fair question? He thought not. You might as well ask a woman why she gave birth to a defective baby.

There had been a time, an hour or an instant, when he had contemplated jettisoning the hate. That had been after he had finished reading Fran's diary and had discovered she was irrevocably committed to Stu Redman. That sudden knowledge had acted upon him the way a dash of cold water acts on a slug, causing it to contract into a tight little ball instead of a spread-out, loosely questing organism. In that hour or instant, he became aware that he could simply *accept what was*, and that knowledge had both exhilarated and terrified him. For that space of time he knew he could turn himself into a new person, a fresh Harold Lauder cloned from the old one by the sharp intervening knife of the superflu epidemic. He sensed, more clearly than any of the others, that that was what the Boulder Free Zone was all about. People were not the same as they had been. This small-town society was like no other in American pre-plague society. They didn't see it because they didn't stand outside the boundaries as he did. Men and women were living together with no apparent desire to reinstitute the ceremony of marriage. Whole groups of people were living together in small subcommunities like communes. There wasn't much fighting. People seemed to be getting along. And strangest of all, none of them seemed to be questioning the profound theological implications of the dreams . . . and of the plague itself. Boulder itself was a cloned society, a *tabula* so *rasa* that it could not sense its own novel beauty.

Harold sensed it, and hated it.

Far away over the mountains was another cloned creature. A cutting from the dark malignancy, a single wild cell taken from the dying corpus of the old body politic, a lone representative of the carcinoma that had been eating the old society alive. One single cell, but it had already begun to reproduce itself and spawn other wild cells. For society it would be the old struggle, the effort of healthy tissue to reject the malignant incursion. But for each individual cell there was the old, old question, the one that went back to the Garden – did you eat the apple or leave it alone? Over there, in the West, they were already eating them a mess of apple pie and apple cobbler. The assassins of Eden were there, the dark fusiliers.

And he himself, when faced with the knowledge that he was free to *accept what was*, had rejected the new opportunity. To seize it would have been to murder himself. The ghost of every humiliation he had ever suffered cried out against it. His murdered dreams and ambitions came back to eldritch life and asked if he could forget them so easily. In the new Free Zone society he could only be Harold Lauder. Over there he could be a prince.

The malignancy drew him. It was a dark carnival – Ferris wheels with their lights out revolving above a black landscape, a never-ending sideshow filled with freaks like himself, and in the main tent the lions ate the spectators. What called to him was this discordant music of chaos.

He opened his journal and by starlight wrote firmly:

August 12, 1990 (early morning).

It is said that the two great human sins are pride and hate. Are they? I elect to think of them as the two great virtues. To give away pride and hate is to say you will change for the good of the world. To embrace them, to vent them, is more noble; that is to say that the world must change for the good of you. I am on a great adventure.

HAROLD EMERY LAUDER

He closed the book. He went into the house, put the book in its hole in the hearth, and carefully replaced the hearth-stone. He went into the bathroom, set his Coleman lamp on the sink so that it illuminated the mirror, and for the next fifteen minutes he practiced smiling. He was getting very good at it.

CHAPTER 51

Ralph's posters announcing the August 18 meeting went up all over Boulder. There was a great deal of excited conversation, most of it having to do with the good and bad qualities of the seven-person ad hoc committee.

Mother Abagail went to bed exhausted before the light was even gone from the sky. The day had been a steady stream of callers, all of them wanting to know what her opinion was. She allowed as how she thought most of the choices for the committee were pretty good. The people were anxious to know if she would serve on a more permanent committee, if one should be formed at the big meeting. She replied that that would be a spot too tiring, but she sure would give a committee of elected representatives whatever help she could, if people wanted her to help out. She was assured again and again that any permanent committee that refused her help would be turned out en masse, and that right early. Mother Abagail went to bed tired but satisfied.

So did Nick Andros that night. In one day, by virtue of a single poster turned out on a hand-crank mimeograph machine, the Free Zone had been transformed from a loose group of refugees into potential voters. They liked it; it gave them the sense of a place to stand after a long period of free fall.

That afternoon Ralph drove him out to the power plant. He, Ralph, and Stu agreed to hold a preliminary meeting at Stu and Frannie's place the day after next. It would give all seven of them another two days to listen to what people were saying.

Nick smiled and cupped his own useless ears.

'Lip-reading's even better,' Stu said. 'You know, Nick, I'm starting to think we're really going to get somewhere with those blown motors. That Brad Kitchner's a regular bear for work. If we had ten like him, we'd have this whole town running perfect by the first of September.'

Nick gave him a thumb-and-forefinger circle and they walked inside together.

That afternoon Larry Underwood and Leo Rockway walked west on Arapahoe Street toward Harold's house. Larry was wearing the knapsack he had worn all the way across the country, but all that was in it now was the bottle of wine and a half dozen Paydays.

Lucy was out with a party of half a dozen people who had taken two wrecking trucks and were beginning to clear the streets and roads in and around Boulder of stalled vehicles. Trouble was, they were working on their own – it was a sporadic operation that only ran when a few people felt like getting together and doing it. A wrecking bee instead of a quilting bee, Larry thought, and his eye caught one of the posters headed MASS MEETING, this one nailed to a telephone pole. Maybe that would be the answer. Hell, people around here wanted to work; what they needed was somebody to coordinate things and tell them what to do. He thought that, most of all, they wanted to wipe away the evidence of what had happened here this early summer (and could it be late summer already?) the way you would use an eraser to wipe dirty words off a blackboard. Maybe we can't do it from one end of America to the other, Larry thought, but we should be able to do it here in Boulder before snow flies, if Mother Nature cooperates.

A tinkle of glass made him turn. Leo had lobbed a large stone from someone's rock garden through the rear window of an old Ford. A bumper sticker on the back deck of the Ford's trunk read: GET YO ASS UP THE PASS – COLD CREEK CANYON.

'Don't do that, Joe.'

'I'm Leo.'

'Leo,' he corrected. 'Don't do that.'

'Why not?' Leo asked complacently, and for a long time Larry couldn't think of a satisfactory answer.

'Because it makes an ugly sound,' he said finally.

'Oh. Okay.'

They walked on. Larry put his hands in his pockets. Leo did likewise. Larry kicked a beer can. Leo swerved out of his way to kick a stone. Larry began to whistle a tune. Leo made a whispering chuffling sound in accompaniment. Larry ruffled the kid's hair and Leo looked up at him with those odd Chinese eyes and grinned.

And Larry thought: *For Christ's sake, I'm falling in love with him. Pretty far out.*

They came to the park Frannie had mentioned, and across from it was a green house with white shutters. There was a wheelbarrow full of bricks on the cement path leading up to the front door, and next to it was a garbage can lid filled with that do-it-yourself mortar-mix to which you just add water. Squatting beside it, his back to the street, was a broad-shouldered dude with his shirt off and the peeling remnants of a bad sunburn. He had a trowel in one hand. He was building a low and curving brick wall around a flower bed.

Larry thought of Fran saying: *He's changed . . . I don't know how or why or even if it's for the best . . . and sometimes I'm afraid.*

Then he stepped forward, saying it just the way he had planned on his long days crossing the country: 'Harold Lauder, I presume?'

Harold jerked with surprise, then turned with a brick in one hand and his mortar-dripping trowel in the other, half-raised, like a weapon. Out of the corner of his eye, Larry thought he saw Leo flinch backward. His first thought was, sure enough, Harold didn't look at all as he had imagined. His second thought had to do with the trowel: *My God, is he going to let me have it with that thing?* Harold's face was grimly set, his eyes narrow and dark. His hair fell in a lank wave across his sweaty forehead. His lips were pressed together and almost white.

And then there was a transformation so sudden and complete that Larry was never quite able to believe afterward that he had seen that tense, unsmiling Harold, the face of a man more apt to use a trowel to wall someone up in a basement niche than to construct a garden wall around a flower bed.

He smiled, a broad and harmless grin that made deep dimples at the corners of his mouth. His eyes lost their menacing cast (they were bottle-green, and how could such clear and feckless eyes have seemed menacing, or even dark?). He stuck the trowel blade-down into the mortar – *chunk!* – wiped his hands on the hips of his jeans, and advanced with his hand out. Larry thought: *My God, he's just a kid, younger than I am. If he's eighteen yet I'll eat the candles on his last birthday cake.*

'Don't think I know you,' Harold said, grinning, as they shook. He had a firm grip. Larry's hand was pumped up and down exactly three times and let go. It reminded Larry of the time he had shaken hands with George Bush back when the old bushwhacker had been running for President. It had been at a political rally, which he had attended on the advice of his mother, given many years ago. If you can't afford a movie, go to the zoo. If you can't afford the zoo, go see a politician.

But Harold's grin was contagious, and Larry grinned back. Kid or not, politician's handshake or not, the grin impressed him as completely genuine, and after all this time, after all those candy wrappers, here was Harold Lauder, in the flesh.

'No, you don't,' Larry said. 'But I'm acquainted with you.'

'Is that so!' Harold exclaimed, and his grin escalated. If it got any broader, Larry thought with amusement, the ends would meet around at the back of his skull and the top two thirds of his head would just topple off.

'I followed you across the country from Maine,' Larry said.

'No fooling! You did, really?'

'Really did.' He unslung his packsack. 'Here, I've got some stuff for you.' He took out the bottle of Bordeaux and put it in Harold's hand.

'Say, you shouldn't have,' Harold said, looking at the bottle with some astonishment. 'Nineteen forty-seven?'

'A good year,' Larry said. 'And these.'

He put nearly half a dozen Paydays in Harold's other hand. One of them slipped through his fingers and onto the grass. Harold bent to pick it up, and as he did, Larry caught a glimpse of that earlier expression.

Then Harold bobbed back up, smiling. 'How did you know?'

'I followed your signs . . . and your candy wrappers.'

'Well I be go to hell. Come on in the house. We ought to have a jaw, as my dad was fond of saying. Would your boy drink a Coke?'

'Sure. Wouldn't you, L –'

He looked around, but Leo was no longer beside him. He was all the way back on the sidewalk and looking down at some cracks in the pavement as if they were of great interest to him.

'Hey, Leo! Want a Coke?'

Leo muttered something Larry couldn't hear.

'Talk up!' he said, irritated. 'What did God give you a voice for? I asked you if you wanted a Coke.'

Barely audible, Leo said: 'I think I'll go see if Nadine-mom's back.'

'What the hell? We just got here!'

'I want to go back!' Leo said, looking up from the cement. The sun flashed too strongly back from his eyes and Larry thought, *What in God's name is this? He's almost crying.*

'Just a sec,' he said to Harold.

'Sure,' Harold said, grinning. 'Sometimes kids're shy. I was.'

Larry walked over to Leo and hunkered down, so they would be at eye-level. 'What's the matter, kiddo?'

'I just want to go back,' Leo said, not meeting his gaze. 'I want Nadine-mom.'

'Well, you . . .' He paused helplessly.

'Want to go back.' He looked up briefly at Larry. His eyes flickered over Larry's shoulder toward where Harold stood in the middle of his lawn. Then down at the cement again. 'Please.'

'You don't like Harold?'

'I don't know . . . he's all right . . . I just want to go back.'

Larry sighed. 'Can you find your way?'

'Sure.'

'Okay. But I sure wish you'd come in and have a Coke with us. I've been waiting to meet Harold a long time. You know that, don't you?'

'Ye-es . . .'

'And we could walk back together.'

'I'm not going in that house,' Leo hissed, and for a moment he was Joe again, his eyes going blank and savage.

'Okay,' Larry said hastily. He stood up. 'Go straight home. I'll check to see if you did. And stay out of the street.'

'I will.' And suddenly Leo blurted in that small, hissing whisper: 'Why don't you come back with me? Right now? We'll go together. Please, Larry? Okay?'

'Jeez, Leo, what –'

'Never mind,' Leo said. And before Larry could say anything more, Leo was hurrying away. Larry stood watching him until he was out of sight. Then he turned back to Harold with a troubled frown.

'Say, that's all right,' Harold said. 'Kids are funny.'

'Well, that one sure is, but I guess he's got a right. He's been through a lot.'

'I'll bet he has,' Harold replied, and just for an instant Larry felt distrust, felt that Harold's quick sympathy for a boy he had never met was as ersatz as powdered eggs.

'Well, come in,' Harold said. 'You know, you're just about my first company. Frannie and Stu have been out a few times, but they hardly count.' His grin became a smile, a slightly sad smile, and Larry felt sudden pity for this boy – because a boy was all he was, really. He was lonely and here stood Larry, same old Larry, never a good word for anyone, judging him on vapors. It wasn't fair. It was time for him to stop being so goddam mistrustful.

'Glad to,' he answered.

The living room was small but comfortable. 'I'm going to put in some new furniture when I get around to it,' Harold said. 'Modern. Chrome and leather. As the commercial says. "Fuck the budget. I've got MasterCard."'

Larry laughed heartily.

'There are some good glasses in the basement, I'll just get them. I think I'll pass on the candy bars, if that's all right with you – I'm off the sweets, trying to lose weight, but we've got to try the wine, this is a special occasion. You came all the way across the country from Maine behind us, huh, and following my – our – signs. That's really something. You'll have to tell me all about it. Meanwhile, try that green chair. It's the best of a bad lot.'

Larry had one final doubtful thought during this outpouring: *He even talks like a politician – smooth and quick and glib.*

Harold left, and Larry sat down in the green chair. He heard a door open and then Harold's heavy tread descending a flight of stairs. He looked around. Nope, not one of the world's great living rooms, but with a shag rug and some nice modern furniture, it might be fine. The best feature was the stone fireplace and chimney. Lovely work, carefully done by hand. But there was one loose stone on the hearth. It looked to Larry as if it had come out and had been put back a little carelessly. Leaving it like that would be like leaving one piece out of the jigsaw puzzle or a picture hanging crooked on the wall.

He got up and picked the stone out of the hearth. Harold was still rummaging around downstairs. Larry was about to put it back in when he saw there was a book down in the hole, its front now lightly powdered with rockdust, not enough to obscure the single word stamped there in gold leaf: LEDGER.

Feeling slightly ashamed, as if he had been prying intentionally, he put the rock back in place just as Harold's footfalls began to ascend the stairs again. This time the fit was perfect, and when Harold came back into the living room with a balloon glass in each hand, Larry was seated in the green chair again.

'I took a minute to rinse them out in the downstairs sink,' Harold said. 'They were a bit dusty.'

'They look fine,' Larry said. 'Look, I can't swear that Bordeaux hasn't gone over. We might be helping ourselves to vinegar.'

'Nothing ventured,' Harold said, grinning, 'nothing gained.'

That grin made him feel uncomfortable, and Larry suddenly found himself thinking about the ledger – was it Harold's, or had it belonged to the house's previous owner? And if it was Harold's, what in the world might be written in there?

They cracked the bottle of Bordeaux and found, to their mutual pleasure, that it was just fine. Half an hour later they were both pleasantly squiffed, Harold a little more so than Larry. Even so, Harold's grin remained; broadened, in fact.

His tongue loosened a bit by wine, Larry said: 'Those posters. The big meeting on the eighteenth. How come you didn't get on that committee, Harold? I would have thought a guy like you would have been a natural.'

Harold's smile became large, beatific. 'Well, I'm awfully young. I suppose they thought I didn't have experience enough.'

'I think it's a goddam shame.' But did he? The grin. The dark, barely glimpsed expression of suspicion. Did he? He didn't know.

'Well, who knows what lies in the future?' Harold said, grinning broadly. 'Every dog has its day.'

Larry left around five o'clock. His parting from Harold was friendly; Harold shook his hand, grinned, told him to come back often. But Larry had somehow gotten the feeling that Harold could give a shit if he never came back.

He walked slowly down the cement path to the sidewalk and turned to wave, but Harold had already gone back inside. The door was shut. It had been very cool in the house because the venetian blinds were drawn, and inside that had seemed all right, but standing outside it occurred to him suddenly that it was the only house he'd been inside in Boulder where the blinds and curtains were drawn. But of course, he thought, there were still plenty of houses in Boulder where the shades were drawn. They were the houses of the dead. When they got sick, they had drawn their curtains against the world. They had drawn them and died in privacy, like any animal in its last extremity prefers to do. The living – maybe in subconscious acknowledgment of that fact of death – threw their shutters and their curtains wide.

He had a slight headache from the wine, and he tried to tell himself that the chill he felt came from that, part of a little hangover, righteous punishment administered for guzzling good wine as if it was cheap muscatel. But that wouldn't quite get it – no, it wouldn't. He stared up and down the street and thought: *Thank God for tunnel vision. Thank God for selective perception. Because without it, we might as well all be in a Lovecraft story.*

His thoughts became confused. He became suddenly convinced that Harold was peeping at him from between the slats of his blinds, his hands opening and closing in a strangler's grip, his grin turned into a leer of hatred . . . *Every dog has its day.* At the same time he was remembering the night in Bennington, sleeping on the steps of the bandshell, waking up to the horrible feeling that someone was there . . . and then hearing (or only dreaming it?) the dusty sound of bootheels moving off to the west.

Stop it. Stop freaking yourself out.

Boot Hill, his mind free-associated. *Chrissake, just stop it, wish I'd never thought about the dead people, the dead people behind all those closed blinds and pulled drapes and shut curtains, in the dark, like in the tunnel, the Lincoln Tunnel, Christ, what if they all started to move, to stir around, Holy God, cut it out –*

And suddenly he found himself thinking of a trip to the Bronx Zoo with his mother when he had been small. They had gone into the monkey-house and the smell in there had hit him like a physical thing, a fist driven not just at his nose but into it. He had turned to bolt out of there, but his mother had stopped him.

Just breathe normal, Larry, she had said. *In five minutes you won't notice that nasty smell at all.*

So he had stayed, not believing her, just fighting not to puke (even at the age of seven, he had hated to puke worse than anything), and it turned out she was right. When he looked down at his watch the next time, he saw that they had been in the monkey-house for half an hour, and he couldn't understand why the ladies who came in the door were suddenly clapping their hands over their noses and looking disgusted. He said as much to his mother, and Alice Underwood had laughed.

Oh, it still smells bad, all right. Just not to you.

How come, Mommy?

I don't know. Everybody can do it. Now just say to yourself, 'I'm going to smell how the monkey-house REALLY is again,' and take a deep breath.

So he did, and the stink was there, the stink was even bigger and badder than it had been when they first came in, and his hotdogs and cherry pie started to come up on him again in one big sickening whipped bubble, and he had charged for the door and the fresh air beyond it and managed – barely – to hold everything down.

That's selective perception, he thought now, *and she knew what it was even if she didn't know what it's called.* This thought had no more than completed itself in his mind before he heard his mother's voice saying, *Just say to yourself, 'I'm going to smell how Boulder REALLY smells again.'* And he *was* smelling it – just like that, he *was* smelling it. He was smelling what was behind all the closed doors and drawn shades and pulled blinds, he was smelling the slow corruption that was going on even in this place which had died almost empty.

He walked faster, not running but getting closer and closer to it, smelling that fruity, rich reek which he – and everyone else – had stopped consciously smelling because it was everywhere, it was everything, it was coloring their thoughts, and you didn't pull your shades even if you were making love because the dead lie behind drawn shades and the living still want to look out on the world.

It wanted to come up on him, not hotdogs and cherry pie now but wine and a Payday candy bar. Because this was one monkey-house he was never going to be able to get out of, not unless he moved to an island where no one had ever lived, and even though he still hated to puke worse than anything, he was going to now –

'Larry? Are you okay?'

He was so startled that a little noise – '*Yike!*' squeaked out of his throat and he jumped. It was Leo, sitting on the curb about three blocks down from Harold's. He had a Ping-Pong ball and was bouncing it up and down on the pavement.

'What are you doing here?' Larry asked. His heartbeat was slowly returning to normal.

'I wanted to walk home with you,' Leo said diffidently, 'but I didn't want to go into that guy's house.'

'Why not?' Larry asked. He sat down on the curb beside Leo.

Leo shrugged and turned his eyes back to the Ping-Pong ball. It made a small *whock! whock!* sound as it struck the pavement and bounced back up to his hand.

'I don't know.'

'Leo?'

'What.'

'This is very important to me. Because I like Harold . . . and don't like him. I feel two ways about him. Have you ever felt two ways about a person?'

'I only feel one way about him.' *Whock! Whock!*

'How?'

'Scared,' Leo said simply. 'Can we go home and see my Nadine-mom and my Lucy-mom?'

'Sure.'

They continued down Arapahoe for a while without speaking, Leo still bouncing the Ping-Pong ball and catching it deftly.

'Sorry you had to wait so long,' Larry said.

'Aw, that's okay.'

'No, really, if I'd known I would have hurried up.'

'I had something to do. I found this on a guy's lawn. It's a Pong-Ping ball.'

'Ping-Pong,' Larry corrected absently. 'Why do you think Harold would keep his shades down?'

'So nobody can see in, I guess,' Leo said. 'So he can do secret things. It's like the dead people, isn't it?' *Whock! Whock!*

They walked on, reached the corner of Broadway, and turned south. They saw other people on the streets now; women looking in windows at dresses, a man with a pickaxe returning from somewhere, another man casually sorting through fishing tackle in the broken display window of a sporting goods store. Larry saw Dick Vollman from his party biking in the other direction. He waved at Larry and Leo. They waved back.

'Secret things,' Larry mused aloud, not really trying to draw the boy out anymore.

'Maybe he's praying to the dark man,' Leo said casually, and

Larry jerked as if brushed by a live wire. Leo didn't notice. He was double-bouncing his Ping-Pong ball, first off the sidewalk and then catching it on the rebound from the brick wall they were passing . . . *whock-whap!*

'Do you really think so?' Larry asked, making an effort to sound casual.

'I don't know. But he's not like us. He smiles a lot. But I think there might be worms inside him, making him smile. Big white worms eating up his brain. Like maggots.'

'Joe . . . Leo, I mean . . .'

Leo's eyes – dark, remote, and Chinese – suddenly cleared. He smiled. 'Look, there's Dayna. I like her. Hey, Dayna!' he yelled, waving. 'Got any gum?'

Dayna, who had been oiling the sprocket of a spidery-thin ten-speed bike, turned and smiled. She reached into her shirt pocket and spread out five sticks of Juicy Fruit like a poker hand. With a happy laugh, Leo ran toward her, his long hair flying, Ping-Pong ball clutched in one hand, leaving Larry to stare after him. That idea of white worms behind Harold's smile . . . where had Joe (*no, Leo, he's Leo, at least I think he is*) gotten an idea as sophisticated – and as horrible – as that? The boy had been in a semi-trance. And he wasn't the only one; how many times in the few days he had been here had Larry seen someone just stop dead on the street, looking blankly at nothing for a moment, and then going on? Things had changed. The whole range of human perception seemed to have stepped up a notch.

It was scary as hell.

Larry got his feet moving and walked over to where Leo and Dayna were sharing out the chewing gum.

That afternoon Stu found Frannie washing clothes in the small yard behind their building. She had filled a low wash-tub with water, had shaken in nearly half a box of Tide, and had stirred everything with a mop-handle until a sickly suds had resulted. She doubted if she was going about this in the right way, but she was damned if she was going to go to Mother Abagail and expose her ignorance. She dumped their clothes in the water, which was stone cold, then grimly jumped in and began to stomp and slosh around, like a Sicilian mashing grapes. *Your new model Maytag 5000,* she thought. *The Double-Foot Agitation Method, perfect for all your bright colors, fragile underthings, and –*

She turned around and beheld her man, standing just inside the back yard gate and watching with an expression of amusement. Frannie stopped, a little out of breath.

'Ha-ha, very funny. How long have you been there, smartypants?'

'Couple of minutes. What do you call that, anyway? The mating dance of the wild wood duck?'

'Again, ha-ha.' She looked coolly at him. 'One more crack like that and you can spend the night on the couch, or up on Flagstaff with your friend Glen Bateman.'

'Say, I didn't mean —'

'They're your clothes too, Mr Stuart Redman. You may be a Founding Father and all that, but you still leave an occasional skid-mark in your underdrawers.'

Stu grinned, the grin broadened, and finally he had to laugh. 'That's crude, darlin.'

'Right now I don't feel particularly delicate.'

'Well, pop out for a minute. I need to talk to you.'

She was glad to, even though she would have to wash her feet before getting back in. Her heart was hurrying along, not happily but rather dolefully, like a faithful piece of machinery being misused by someone with a marked lack of good sense. If this was the way my great-great-great-grandmother had to do it, Fran thought, then maybe she was entitled to the room which eventually became my mother's precious parlor. Maybe she thought of it as hazard pay, or something like that.

She looked down at her feet and lower legs with some discouragement. There was still a thin sheath of gray soapsuds clinging to them. She brushed at it distastefully.

'When my wife handwashed,' Stu said, 'she used a . . . what do you call it? Scrub-board, I think. My mother had about three, I remember.'

'I know that,' Frannie said, irritated. 'June Brinkmeyer and I walked over half of Boulder looking for one. We couldn't find a single one. Technology strikes again.'

He was smiling again.

Frannie put her hands on her hips. 'Are you trying to piss me off, Stuart Redman?'

'No'm. I was just thinking I know where I can get you a scrub-board, I think. Juney too, if she wants one.'

'Where?'

'You let me look and see first.' His smile disappeared, and he put his arms around her and his forehead on hers. 'You know I appreciate you washing my clothes,' he said, 'and I know that a woman who is pregnant knows better than her man what she should and shouldn't be doing. But Frannie, why bother?'

'*Why?*' She looked at him, perplexed. 'Well, what are you going to wear? Do you want to go around in dirty clothes?'

'Frannie, the stores are full of clothes. And I'm an easy size.'

'What, throw out old ones just because they're *dirty*?'

He shrugged a little uneasily.

'No way, uh-uh,' she said. 'That's the old way, Stu. Like the boxes they used to put your Big Mac in or the no-deposit-no-return bottles. That's no way to start over.'

He gave her a little kiss. 'All right. Only next washday it's my turn, you hear?'

'Sure.' She smiled a little slyly. 'And how long does that last? Until I deliver?'

'Until we get the power back on,' Stu said. 'Then I'm going to bring you the biggest, shiniest washer you ever saw, and hook it up myself.'

'Offer accepted.' She kissed him firmly and he kissed back, his strong hands moving restlessly in her hair. The result was a spreading warmth (hotness, let's not be coy, I'm hot and he always gets me hot when he does that) that first peaked her nipples, then spread down into her lower belly.

'You better stop,' she said rather breathlessly, 'unless you plan to do more than talk.'

'Maybe we'll talk later.'

'The clothes –'

'Soaking's good for that grimed-in dirt,' he said seriously. She started to laugh and he stopped her mouth with a kiss. As he lifted her, set her on her feet, and led her inside, she was struck by the warmth of the sun on her shoulders and wondered, *Was it ever so hot before? So strong? It's cleared up every last blemish on my back . . . could it be the ultraviolet, I wonder, or the altitude? Is it this way every summer? Is it this hot?*

And then he was doing things to her, even on the stairs he was doing things to her, making her naked, making her hot, making her love him.

★   ★   ★

'No, you sit down,' he said.

'But —'

'I mean it, Frannie.'

'Stuart, they'll *congeal* or something. I put half a box of Tide in there —'

'Don't worry.'

So she sat down in the lawn chair in the building's shady overhang. He had set up two of them when they came back down. Stu took off his shoes and socks and rolled up his pants past the knee. As he stepped into the washtub and began gravely to stomp up and down on the clothes, she began to giggle helplessly.

Stu looked over and said, 'You want to spend the night on the couch?'

'No, Stuart,' she said with grave repentance, and then began to giggle again . . . until tears ran down her cheeks and the little muscles in her stomach felt rubbery and weak. When she had some control again she said, 'For the third and last time, what did you come back to talk about?'

'Oh yeah.' He marched back and forth, and by now he had worked up quite a bed of lather. A pair of bluejeans floated to the surface and he stomped them back down, sending a creamy squirt of soapsuds onto the lawn. Frannie thought: *It looks a little like . . . oh no, away with that, away with that unless you want to laugh yourself into a miscarriage.*

'We've got that first ad hoc meeting tonight,' Stu said.

'I've got two cases of beer, cheese crackers, cheese spread, some pepperoni that should still be —'

'That's not it, Frannie. Dick Ellis came by today and said he wanted off the committee.'

'He did?' She was surprised. Dick had not impressed her as the sort of man who would back away from responsibility.

'He said he'd be glad to serve in any capacity as soon as we get ourselves a real doctor, but just now he can't. We had another twenty-five come in today, and one of them had a gangrenous leg. Came from a scratch she got crawling under a rusty bobwire fence, apparently.'

'Oh, that's bad.'

'Dick saved her . . . Dick and that nurse that came in with Underwood. Tall, pretty girl. Laurie Constable, her name is. Dick said he just would have lost the woman without her. Anyway, they took her leg off at the knee, and they're both exhausted. It took em three hours. Plus they've got a little boy with convulsive fits, and Dick's driving himself crazy trying to figure out if it's epilepsy or cranial pressure of some kind or maybe diabetes. They've had several cases of food poisoning from people eating stuff that's gone over, and he says some people are going to die of it if we don't get out a flier real soon telling people how to pick their supplies. Let's see, where was I? Two broken arms, one case of the flu —'

'My God! Did you say *flu?*'

'Ease up. It's the regular flu. Aspirin knocks down the fever no sweat . . . and it doesn't come back up. No black patches on the neck, either. But Dick isn't sure which antibiotics to use, if any, and he's burning the midnight oil trying to find out. Also, he's scared the flu will spread and people will panic.'

'Who is it?'

'A lady named Rona Hewett. She walked most of the way here from Laramie, Wyoming, and Dick says she was ripe for a bug.'

Fran nodded.

'Lucky for us, this Laurie Constable seems sort of stuck on Dick, even though he's about twice her age. I guess that's all right.'

'How big of you to give them your seal of approval, Stuart.'

He smiled. 'Anyhow, Dick's forty-eight and he's got a minor heart condition. Right now he feels that he can't spread himself too thin . . . he's practically studying to be a doctor, for the Lord's sake.' He looked soberly at Fran. 'I can understand why that Laurie fell for him. He's the closest thing to a hero we've got around here. He's just a country vet and he's scared shitless he's going to kill someone. And he knows there are more people coming in every day, and some of them have been banged around.'

'So we need one more for the committee.'

'Yeah. Ralph Brentner's gung-ho for this Larry Underwood guy, and from what you say, he struck you as being pretty handy.'

'Yes. He did. I think he'd be fine. And I met his lady today downtown, Lucy Swann her name is. She's awfully sweet, and she thinks the world of Larry.'

'I guess every good woman feels that way. But Frannie, I got to be honest with you — I don't like the way he spilled his life's story to someone he just met.'

'I think it was just because I was with Harold from the start. I don't think he understood why I was with you instead of him.'

'I wonder what he made of Harold?'

'Ask him and see.'

'I guess I will.'

'Are you going to invite him onto the committee?'

'More likely than not.' He stood up. 'I'd like to have that old fellow they call the Judge. But he's seventy, and that's too damn old.'

'Have you talked to him about Larry?'

'No, but Nick did. Nick Andros is one sharp guy, Fran. He changed a few things around on Glen and I. Glen was a little bent out of shape about it, but even he had to admit Nick's ideas were good ones. Anyway, the Judge told Nick that Larry's just the kind of person we're looking for. He said Larry was just getting around to finding out he was good for something, and that he was going to get a lot better.'

'I'd call that a pretty strong recommendation.'

'Yes,' Stu said. 'But I'm going to find out what he thought of Harold before I invite him along for the ride.'

'What is it about Harold?' she asked restlessly.

'Might as well ask what it is about *you*, Fran. You still feel responsible for him.'

'Do I? I don't know. But when I think about him, I still feel a little guilty – I can tell you that.'

'Why? Because I cut in on him? Fran, did you ever want him?'

'No. God, no.' She almost shuddered.

'I lied to him once,' Stu said. 'Well . . . it wasn't actually a lie. It was the day the three of us met. July Fourth. I think he might have sensed what was coming even then. I said I didn't want you. How was I to know right then if I wanted you or not? There may be such a thing as love at first sight in books, but in real life . . .'

He stopped, and a slow grin spread across his face.

'What are you grinning about, Stuart Redman?'

'I was just thinkin,' he said, 'that in real life it took me at least . . .' He rubbed his chin consideringly. 'Oh, I'm gonna say four hours.'

She kissed his cheek. 'That's very sweet.'

'It's the truth. Anyway, I think he still holds what I said against me.'

'He never says a mean word against you, Stu . . . or anybody.'

'No,' Stu agreed. 'He *smiles*. That's what I don't like.'

'You don't think he's . . . plotting revenge, or anything?'

Stu smiled and stood up. 'No, not Harold. Glen thinks the Opposition Party may just end up coming together around Harold. That's okay. I just hope he doesn't try to fuck up what we're doing now.'

'Just remember that he's scared and lonely.'

'And jealous.'

'Jealous?' She considered it, then shook her head. 'I don't think so – I really don't. I've talked to him, and I think I'd know. He may be feeling rejected, though. I think he expected to be on the ad hoc committee –'

'That was one of Nick's unilateral – is that the word? – decisions that we all went along with. What it came down to was that none of us quite trusted him.'

'In Ogunquit,' she said, 'he was the most insufferable kid you could imagine. A lot of it was compensation for his family situation, I guess . . . to them it must have seemed like he had hatched from a cowbird egg or something . . . but after the flu, he seemed to change. At least to me, he did. He seemed to be trying to be, well . . . a man. Then he changed again. Like all at once. He started to smile all the time. You couldn't really talk to him anymore. He was . . . in himself. The way people get when they convert to religion or read –' She stopped suddenly, and her eyes took on a momentary startled look that seemed very like fear.

'Read what?' Stu asked.

'Something that changes their lives,' she said. '*Das Kapital. Mein Kampf.* Or maybe just intercepted love letters.'

'What are you talking about?'

'Hmm?' She looked around at him, as if startled out of a deep daydream. Then she smiled. 'Nothing. Weren't you going to go see Larry Underwood?'

'Sure . . . if you're okay.'

'I'm better than okay – I'm ultimately fine. Go on. Shoo. Meeting's at seven. If you hurry, you've got just enough time to get back here for some supper before.'

'All right.'

He was at the gate which separated the front yard from the back when she called after him: 'Don't forget to ask him what he thought of Harold.'

'Don't worry,' Stu said, 'I won't.'

'And watch his eyes when he answers, Stuart.'

When Stu asked casually about his impression of Harold (at this point Stu had not mentioned the vacancy on the ad hoc committee at all), Larry Underwood's eyes grew both wary and puzzled.

'Fran told you about my fixation on Harold, huh?'

'Yep.'

Larry and Stu were in the living room of a small Table Mesa tract house. Out in the kitchen Lucy was rattling dinner together, heating canned stuff on a brazier grill Larry had rigged for her. It ran off bottled gas. She was singing snatches of 'Honky Tonk Women' as she worked, and she sounded very happy.

Stu lit a cigarette. He was down to no more than five or six a day; he didn't fancy having Dick Ellis operating on him for lung cancer.

'Well, all the time I was following Harold I kept telling myself he probably wouldn't be like I pictured him. And he wasn't, but I'm still trying to figure out what it *is* about him. He was pleasant as hell. A good host. He cracked the bottle of wine I brought him and we toasted each other's good health. I had a good time. But . . .'

'But?'

'We came up behind him. Leo and me. He was putting a brick wall around this flower garden and he whirled around . . . didn't hear us coming until I spoke up, I guess . . . and for a minute there I'm saying to myself, "Holy God, this dude is gonna kill me."'

Lucy came into the doorway. 'Stu, can you stay for dinner? There's plenty.'

'Thanks, but Frannie expects me back. I can only stay fifteen minutes or so.'

'Sure?'

'Next time, Lucy, thanks.'

'Okay.' She went back into the kitchen.

'Did you come just to ask about Harold?' Larry asked.

'No,' Stu said, coming to a decision. 'I came to ask if you'd serve on our little ad hoc committee. One of the other guys, Dick Ellis, had to say no.'

'Like that, is it?' Larry went to the window and looked out on the silent street. 'I thought I could go back to being a private again.'

'Your decision, of course. We need one more. You were recommended.'

'By who, if you don't mind me –'

'We asked around. Frannie seems to think you're pretty level. And Nick Andros talked – well, he doesn't talk, but you know – to one of the men that came in with you. Judge Farris.'

Larry looked pleased. 'The Judge gave me a recommendation, huh? That's great. You know, you ought to have him. He's smart as the devil.'

'That's what Nick said. But he's also seventy, and our medical facilities are pretty primitive.'

Larry turned to look at Stu, half smiling. 'This committee isn't quite as temporary as it looks on the face of it, is it?'

Stu smiled and relaxed a little. He still hadn't really decided how he felt about Larry Underwood, but it was clear enough the man hadn't fallen off a hayrick yesterday. 'We-ell, let's put it this way. We'd like to see our committee stand for election to a full term.'

'Preferably unopposed,' Larry said. His eyes on Stu were friendly but sharp – very sharp. 'Can I get you a beer?'

'I better not. Had a few too many with Glen Bateman a couple nights ago. Fran's a patient girl, but her patience only stretches so far. What do you say, Larry? Want to ride along?'

'I guess . . . oh hell, I say yes. I thought nothing in the world would make me happier than to get here and dump my people and let somebody else take over for a change. Instead, pardon my French, I've been just about bored out of my tits.'

'We're having a little meeting tonight at my place to talk over the big meeting on the eighteenth. Think you could come?'

'Sure. Can I bring Lucy?'

Stu shook his head slowly. 'Nor talk to her about it. We want to keep some of this stuff close for a while.'

Larry's smile evaporated. 'I'm not much on cloak-and-dagger, Stu. I better get that up front because it might save a hassle later. I think what happened in June happened because too many people were playing it a little too close. That wasn't any act of God. That was an act of pure human fuckery.'

'That's one you don't want to get into with Mother,' Stu said. He was still smiling, relaxed. 'As it happens, I agree with you. But would you feel the same way if it was wartime?'

'I don't follow you.'

'That man we dreamed about. I doubt if he's just gone away.'

Larry looked startled, considering.

'Glen says he can understand why nobody's talking about that,' Stu went on, 'even though we've all been warned. The people here are still shellshocked. They feel like they've been through hell to get here. All they want to do is lick their wounds and bury their dead. But if Mother Abagail's here, then *he's* there.' Stu jerked his head toward the window, which gave on a view of the Flatirons rising in the high summer haze. 'And most of the people here may not be thinking about him, but I'd bet my bottom dollar that he's thinking about us.'

Larry glanced at the doorway to the kitchen, but Lucy had gone outside to talk to Jane Hovington from next door.

'You think he's after us,' he said in a low voice. 'That's a nice thought to have just before dinner. Good for the appetite.'

'Larry, I'm not sure of anything, myself. But Mother Abagail says it won't be over, one way or the other, until he's got us or we've got him.'

'I hope she's not saying that around. These people would be headed for fucking Australia.'

'Thought you didn't hold much with secrets.'

'Yeah, but this —' Larry stopped. Stu was smiling kindly, and Larry smiled back, rather sourly. 'Okay. Your point. We talk it out and keep our mouths shut.'

'Fine. See you at seven.'

'Sure thing.'

They walked to the door together. 'Thank Lucy for the invite again,' Stu said. 'Frannie and I'll take her up on it before long.'

'Okay.' As Stu reached the door, Larry said, 'Hey.'

Stu turned back, questioning.

'There's a boy,' Larry said slowly, 'that came across from Maine with us. His name is Leo Rockway. He's had his problems. Lucy and I sort of share him with a woman named Nadine Cross. Nadine's a little out of the ordinary herself, you know?'

Stu nodded. There had been some talk about a peculiar little scene between Mother Abagail and the Cross woman when Larry brought his party in.

'Nadine was taking care of Leo before I ran across them. Leo kind of sees into people. He's not the only one, either. Maybe there were always people like that, but there seems to be a little bit more of it around since the flu. And Leo . . . he wouldn't go into Harold's house. Wouldn't even stay on the lawn. That's . . . sort of funny, isn't it?'

'It is,' Stu agreed.

They looked at each other thoughtfully for a moment and then Stu left to go home and get his supper. Fran seemed preoccupied herself during the meal, and didn't talk much. And while she was doing the last of the dishes in a plastic bucket full of warm water, people began arriving for the first meeting of the Free Zone Ad Hoc Committee.

After Stu had gone over to Larry's, Frannie rushed upstairs to the bedroom. In the corner of the closet was the sleeping bag she had carried across the country strapped to the back of her motorcycle. She had kept her personal belongings in a small zipper bag. Most of these belongings were now distributed through the apartment she and Stu shared, but a few still hadn't found a home and rested at the foot of the sleeping bag. There were several bottles of cleansing cream – she had suffered a sudden rash of skin outbreaks after the deaths of her mother and father, but that had now subsided – a box of Stayfree Mini Pads in case she starting spotting (she had heard that pregnant women sometimes did), two boxes of cheap cigars, one marked IT'S A BOY! and the other marked IT'S A GIRL! The last item was her diary.

She drew it out and looked at it speculatively. She had entered in it only eight or nine times since their arrival in Boulder, and most of the entries had been short, almost elliptical. The great outpouring had come and gone while they were still on the road . . . like afterbirth, she thought a little ruefully. She hadn't entered at all in the last four days, and suspected that the diary might eventually have slipped her mind altogether, although she had firmly intended to keep it more fully when things settled down a little. For the baby. Now, however, it was very much on her mind once more.

The way people get when they convert to religion . . . or read something that changes their lives . . . like intercepted love letters . . .

Suddenly it seemed to her that the book had gained weight, and that the very act of turning back the pasteboard cover would cause sweat to pop out on her brow and . . . and . . .

She suddenly looked back over her shoulder, her heart beating wildly. Had something moved in here?

A mouse, scuttering behind the wall, maybe. Surely no more than that. More likely just her imagination. There was no reason, no reason at all, for her to suddenly be thinking of the man in the black robe, the man with the coathanger. Her baby was alive and safe and this was just a book and anyhow there was no way to tell if a book had been read, and even if there was a way, there would be no way to tell if the person who had read it had been Harold Lauder.

Still, she opened the book and began to turn slowly through its pages, getting shutterclicks of the recent past like black-and-white photographs taken by an amateur. Home movie of the mind.

Tonight we were admiring them and Harold was going on about color & texture & tone and Stu gave me a very sober wink. Evil me, I winked back . . .

Harold will object on general principles, of course. Damn you, Harold, grow up!

. . . and I could see him getting ready with one of his Patented Harold Lauder Smartass Comments . . .

(my God, Fran, why did you ever say all those things about him? to what *purpose*?)

Well, you know Harold . . . his swagger . . . all those pompous words & pronouncements . . . an insecure little boy . . .

That was July 12. Wincing, she turned past it rapidly, fluttering through the pages now, in a hurry to get to the end. Phrases still leaped up, seeming to slap at her: *Anyway, Harold smelled pretty clean for a change . . . Harold's breath would have driven away a dragon tonight . . .* And another, seeming almost prophetic: *He stores up rebuffs like pirate treasure.* But to what purpose? To feed his own feelings of secret superiority and persecution? Or was it a matter of retribution?

Oh, he's making a list . . . and checking it twice . . . he's gonna find out . . . who's naughty and nice . . .

Then, on August 1, only two weeks ago. The entry started at the bottom of a page. *No entry last night, I was too happy. Have I ever been this happy? I don't think so. Stu and I are together. We*

End of the page. She turned to the next one. The first words at the top of the page were *made love twice*. But they barely caught her eye before her glance dropped halfway down the page. There, beside some blathering about the maternal instinct, was something that caught her eyes and froze her almost solid.

It was a dark, smeary thumbprint.

She thought wildly: I was riding on a motorcycle all day long, every day. Sure, I took care to clean up every chance I got, but your hands get dirty and . . .

She put out her hand, not at all surprised to see that it was shaking badly. She put her thumb on the smudge. The smudge was a lot bigger.

Well, of course it is, she told herself. When you smear something around, it naturally gets bigger. That's why, that's all *that* is . . .

But this thumbprint wasn't *that* smeared. The little lines and loops and whorls were still clear, for the most part.

And it wasn't grease or oil, there was no use even kidding herself that it was.

It was dried chocolate.

Paydays, Fran thought sickly. *Chocolate-covered Payday candy bars.*

For a moment she was afraid to do so much as turn around — afraid that she might see Harold's grin hanging over her shoulder like the grin of the Cheshire cat in *Alice*. Harold's thick lips moving as he said solemnly: *Every dog has his day, Frannie. Every dog has his day.*

But even if Harold had sneaked a glance into her diary, did it have to mean he was contemplating some secret vendetta against her or Stu or any of the others? Of course not.

But Harold's changed, an interior voice whispered.

'Goddammit, he hasn't changed that much!' she cried to the empty room. She flinched a little at the sound of her own voice, then laughed shakily. She went downstairs and began to get supper. They would be eating early because of the meeting . . . but suddenly the meeting didn't seem as important as it had earlier.

Excerpts from the Minutes of the Ad Hoc Committee Meeting
August 13, 1990

The meeting was held in the apartment of Stu Redman and Frances Goldsmith. All members of the ad hoc committee were present, those being: Stuart Redman, Frances Goldsmith, Nick Andros, Glen Bateman, Ralph Brentner, Susan Stern, and Larry Underwood . . .

Stu Redman was elected moderator of the meeting. Frances Goldsmith was elected recording secretary . . .

These notes (plus complete coverage of every burp, gurgle, and aside, all recorded on Memorex cassettes for anyone crazy enough to want to listen to them) will be placed in a safe deposit box of the First Bank of Boulder . . .

Stu Redman presented a broadside on the subject of food poisoning written by Dick Ellis and Laurie Constable (eyecatchingly titled IF YOU EAT YOU SHOULD READ THIS!). He said Dick wanted to see it printed and nailed up all over Boulder before the big meeting on August 18, because there have already been fifteen cases of food poisoning in Boulder, two of them quite serious. The committee voted 7–0 that Ralph should duplicate a thousand copies of Dick's poster and get ten people to help him put them up all over town . . .

Susan Stern then presented another item that Dick and Laurie wanted to put before the meeting (we all wished one or the other of them could have been here). They both feel that there must be a Burial Committee; Dick's idea was that it should be put on the agenda of the public meeting and that it be presented not as a health hazard – because of the possibility it might cause panic – but as 'the decent thing to do.' We all know there are surprisingly few corpses in Boulder in proportion to its pre-plague population, but we don't know why . . . not that it matters much now. But there are still thousands of dead bodies and they must be gotten rid of if we intend to stay here.

Stu asked how serious the problem was at present and Sue said she thought it would not become really serious until fall, when the dry, hot weather usually turns damp.

Larry made a motion that we add Dick's suggestion that a Burial Committee be formed to the agenda of the August 18 meeting. A motion was carried, 7–0.

Nick Andros was then recognized, and Ralph Brentner read his prepared comments, which I am here quoting verbatim:

'One of the most important questions this committee must deal with is whether or not it will agree to take Mother Abagail into its complete confidence, and shall she be told about everything that goes on at our meetings, both open and closed? The question can also be put the other way: "Shall Mother Abagail agree to take this committee – and the permanent committee that will follow it – into her complete confidence, and shall the committee be told about all that goes on in her meetings with God or Whoever . . . particularly the closed ones?"

'That may sound like gibberish, but let me explain, because it's really a pragmatic question. We have to settle Mother Abagail's place in the community right away, because our problem is not just one of "getting on our feet again." If that was all, we wouldn't really need her in the first place. As we all know there is another problem, that of the man we sometimes call the dark man, or as Glen puts it, the Adversary. My proof for his existence is very simple, and I think most people in Boulder would agree with my reasoning – if they wanted to think of it at all. Here it is: "I dreamed of Mother Abagail and she was; I dreamed of the dark man and therefore he must be, although I have never seen him." The people here love Mother Abagail, and I love her myself. But we won't get far – in fact, we won't get anywhere – if we don't start off with her approval of what we're doing.

'So this early afternoon I went to see the lady and put the question to her directly, with all the bark on it: Will you go along? She said that she would – but not without conditions. She was perfectly blunt. She said we should be perfectly free to guide the community in all "worldly matters" – her phrase. Clearing the streets, allocating housing, getting the power back on.

'But she was also very clear about wanting to be consulted on *all* matters that have to do with the dark man. She believes we are all a part of a chess game between God and Satan; that Satan's chief agent in this game is the Adversary, whose name she says is Randall Flagg ("the name he's using this time," is how she puts it); that for reasons best known to Himself, God has chosen her as *His* agent in this matter. She believes, and in this I happen to agree with her, that a struggle is coming and it's going to be us or him. She thinks this struggle is the most important thing, and she's adamant about being consulted when our deliberations touch on it . . . and on *him*.

'Now I don't want to get into the religious implications of all this, or argue whether she's right or wrong, but it should be obvious that all implications aside, we have a situation we *must* cope with. So I have a series of motions.'

There was some discussion of Nick's statement.

Nick made this motion: Can we, as a committee, agree not to discuss the theological, religious, or supernatural implications of the Adversary matter during our meetings? By a 7–0 vote, the committee agreed to bar discussion on those matters, at least while we're 'in session.'

Nick then made this motion: Can we agree that the main private, secret business of the committee is the question of how to deal with this force known as the dark man, the Adversary, or Randall Flagg? Glen Bateman seconded the motion, adding that from time to time there might be other business – such as the real reason for the Burial Committee – that we should keep close to the vest. The motion carried, 7–0.

Nick then made his original motion, that we keep Mother Abagail informed of all public and private business transacted by the committee.

That motion was passed, 7–0.

Having disposed of the Mother Abagail business for the time being, the committee then moved on to the question of the dark man himself at Nick's request. He proposed that we send three volunteers west to join the dark man's people, the purpose being to gain intelligence about what's really going on over there.

Sue Stern immediately volunteered. After some hot discussion of *that*, Glen Bateman was recognized by Stu and put this motion on the floor: *Resolved*, that no one from our ad hoc committee or from the permanent committee be eligible to volunteer for this reconnaissance. Sue Stern wanted to know why not.

Glen: 'Everyone respects your honest desire to help, Susan, but the fact is, we simply don't know if the people we send will ever come back, or when, or in what shape. In the meantime, we have the not-so-inconsiderable job of getting things in Boulder back on a paying basis, if you'll pardon the slang. If you go, we'll have to fill your seat with someone new who would have to be briefed on the ground we've already covered. I just don't think we can afford all that lost time.'

Sue: 'I suppose you're right . . . or at least being sensible . . . but I *do* wonder sometimes if those two things are always the same. Or even *usually* the same. What you're really saying is that we can't send anyone from the committee because we're all so fucking inexpendable. So we just . . . just . . . I don't know . . .'

Stu: 'Lay back in the buckwheat?'

Sue: 'Yes. Thank you. That's just what I mean. We lay back in the buck-wheat and send somebody over there, maybe to get crucified on a telephone pole, maybe something even worse.'

Ralph: 'What the hell could be worse?'

Sue: 'I don't know, but if anyone *does* know, it will be Flagg. I just hate it.'

Glen: 'You may hate it, but you've stated our position very succinctly. We're politicians here. The first politicians of the new age. We just have to hope that our cause is more just than some of the causes for which politicians have sent people into life-or-death situations before this.'

Sue: 'I never thought I'd be a politician.'

Larry: 'Welcome to the club.'

Glen's motion that no one from the ad hoc committee should be one of the scouts was carried – gloomily – by a 7–0 vote. Fran Goldsmith then asked Nick what sort of qualifications we should look for in prospective undercover agents, and what we should expect them to find out.

Nick: 'We won't know what there is to be learned until they come back. If they do come back. The point is, we have absolutely no idea what he's up to over there. We're more or less like fishermen using human bait.'

Stu said he thought the committee should pick the people it wanted to ask, and there was general agreement on this. By committee vote, most of the discussion from this point on has been transcribed into these excerpts verbatim from the audio tapes. It seemed important to have a permanent record of our deliberations on the matter of the scouts (or spies), because it turned out to be so delicate and so troubling.

Larry: 'I've got a name I'd like to put into nomination, if I could. I suppose it'll sound off the wall to those of you who don't know him, but it might be a really good idea. I'd like to send Judge Farris.'

Sue: 'What, that old man? Larry, you must be nuts!'

Larry: 'He's the sharpest old guy I've ever met. He's only seventy, for the record. Ronald Reagan was serving as President at an older age than that.'

Fran: 'That's not what I'd call a very strong recommendation.'

Larry: 'But he's hale and hearty. And I think the dark man might not suspect we'd send an old crock like Farris to spy on him . . . and we have to take his suspicions into account, you know. He's *got* to be looking for a move like this, and I wouldn't be entirely surprised if he had border guards checking people coming in over there against a potential "spy profile." And – this will sound brutal, I know, especially to Fran – but if we lose him, we haven't lost somebody with fifty good years in front of him.'

Fran: 'You're right. It sounds brutal.'

Larry: 'All I want to add is that I know the Judge would say okay. He really wants to help. And *I* really think he could carry it off.'

Glen: 'A point well taken. What does anybody else think?'

Ralph: 'I'll go either way, because I don't know the gentleman. But I don't think we should throw the guy out just because he's old. After all, look who's in charge of this place – an old lady who's well over a hundred.'

Glen: 'Another point well taken.'

Stu: 'You sound like a tennis ref, baldy.'

Sue: 'Listen, Larry. What if he fools the dark man and then drops dead of a heart attack while he's busting his hump to get back here?'

Stu: 'That could happen to just about anyone. Or an accident.'

Sue: 'I agree . . . but with an old man, the odds go way up.'

Larry: 'That's true, but you don't know the Judge, Sue. If you did, you'd see that the advantages outweigh the disadvantages. He's really smart. Defense rests.'

Stu: 'I think Larry's right. It's the sort of thing Flagg might not expect. I second the motion. Those in favor?'

Committee voted aye, 7–0.

Sue: 'Well, I went along with yours, Larry – maybe you'll go along with mine.'

Larry: 'Yeah, this is politics, all right. [General laughter.] Who is it?'

Sue: 'Dayna.'

Ralph: 'Dayna who?'

Sue: 'Dayna Jurgens. She's got more guts than any woman I ever knew. Of course, I know she isn't seventy, but I think if we put the idea to her, she'd go along.'

Fran: 'Yes – if we really have to do this, I think she'd be good. I second the nomination.'

Stu: 'Okay – it's been moved and seconded that we ask Dayna Jurgens along for the ride. Those in favor?'

Committee voted aye, 7–0.

Glen: 'Okay – who's number three?'

Nick (read by Ralph): 'If Fran disliked Larry's, I'm afraid she's *really* going to dislike mine. I nominate –'

Ralph: 'Nick, you're crazy! You don't mean it!'

Stu: 'Come on, Ralph, just read it.'

Ralph: 'Well . . . it says here he wants to nominate . . . Tom Cullen.'

Uproar from the committee.

Stu: 'Okay. Nick has the floor. He's been writin like a bastard, so you better read it, Ralph.'

Nick: 'First of all, I know Tom just as well as Larry knows the Judge, and probably better. He loves Mother Abagail. He'd do anything for her, including roasting over a slow fire. I really mean that – no hype. He'd set himself on fire for her, if she asked him to.'

Fran: 'Oh, Nick, nobody's arguing that, but Tom is –'

Stu: 'Let it go, Fran – Nick's got the floor.'

Nick: 'My second point is the same one Larry made about the Judge. The Adversary is not going to expect us to send a retarded person as a spy. Your combined reactions to the idea are maybe the best argument in favor of the idea.

'My third – and last – point is that, while Tom may be retarded, he is *not* a halfwit. He saved my life once when a tornado came, and he reacted much faster than anyone else I know would have done. Tom is childish, but even a child can learn to do certain things if he is drilled and taught and then drilled some more. I see no problem at all in giving Tom a very simple story to memorize. In the end, they'll likely assume that we sent him away because –'

Sue: 'Because we didn't want him polluting our genepool? Say, that's good.'

Nick: '– because he *is* retarded. He can even say he's mad at the people who sent him away and would like to get back at them. The one imperative which would have to be drilled into him would be to never change his story, no matter what.'

Fran: 'Oh, no, I can't believe –'

Stu: 'Come on, Nick has the floor. Let's keep it orderly.'

Fran: 'Yes – I'm sorry.'

Nick: 'Some of you may feel that, because Tom is retarded, it would be easier to shake him from his story than it would be someone with a wider intelligence, but –'

Larry: 'Yeah.'

Nick: '– but actually, the reverse is true. If I tell Tom he simply *must* stick to the story I give him, *stick to it no matter what*, he will. A so-called normal person could only stand up to so many hours of water torture or so many electric shocks or splinters under the fingernails –'

Fran: 'It wouldn't come to *that*, would it? *Would* it? I mean, nobody really thinks it would come to *that*, do they?'

Nick: '– before saying, "Okay, I give up. I'll tell you what I know." Tom simply won't do that. If he goes over his story enough times, he won't just have it by heart; he'll come to almost believe it *is* true. Nobody will be able to shake him on it. I just want to make it clear that I think, in a number of ways, Tom's retardation is actually a plus in a mission like this. "Mission" sounds like a pretentious word, but that's just what it is.'

Stu: 'Is that it, Ralph?'

Ralph: 'There's a little more.'

Sue: 'If he actually starts to live his cover story, Nick, how in the hell will he know when it's time to come back?'

Ralph: 'Pardon me, ma'am, but it looks like that's what some of this is about.'

Sue: 'Oh.'

Nick (read by Ralph): 'Tom can be given a post-hypnotic suggestion before we send him out. Again, this is not just blue-skying; when I had this idea, I asked Stan Nogotny if he would try to hypnotize Tom. Stan used to do it as a parlor trick at parties sometimes, I heard him say. Well, Stan didn't think it would work . . . but Tom went under in about six seconds.'

Stu: 'I'll be. Ole Stan knows how to do that, huh?'

Nick: 'The reason I thought Tom might be ultrasusceptible dates back to when I met him in Oklahoma. He's apparently developed the knack, over a long period of years, of hypnotizing *himself* to a degree. It helps him make connections. He couldn't understand what I was up to on the day I met him – why I didn't talk to him or answer any of his questions. I kept putting my hand on my mouth and then my throat to show I was mute, but he didn't get it at all. Then, all at once, he just turned off. I can't explain it any better than that. He became perfectly still. His eyes went far away. Then he came out of it, exactly the way a subject comes out of it when the hypnotist tells him it's time to wake up. And he knew. Just like that. He went into himself and came up with the answer.'

Glen: 'That's really amazing.'

Stu: 'It sure is.'

Nick: 'I had Stan give him a post-hypnotic suggestion when we tried this, about five days ago now. The suggestion was that when Stan said, "I sure would like to see an elephant," Tom would feel a great urge to go into the corner and stand on his head. Stan sprang it on him about half an hour after he woke Tom up, and Tom hustled right over into the corner and stood on his head. All the toys and marbles fell out of his pants pockets. Then he sat down and grinned at us and said, "Now I wonder why Tom Cullen went and did that?"'

Glen: 'I can just hear him, too.'

Nick: 'Anyway, all this elaborate hypnosis stuff is just an introduction to two very simple points. One, we can plant a post-hypnotic suggestion that Tom return at a certain time. The obvious way would be to do this by the moon. The full moon. Two, by putting him into deep hypnosis when he gets back, we'd get almost perfect recall of everything he saw.'

Ralph: 'That's the end of what Nick's got written down. Wow.'

Larry: 'It sounds like that old movie *The Manchurian Candidate* to me.'

Stu: 'What?'

Larry: 'Nothing.'

Sue: 'I have a question, Nick. Would you also program Tom – I guess that's the right word – not to give out any information about what we're doing?'

Glen: 'Nick, let me answer that, and if your reasoning is different, just shake your head. I would say that Tom doesn't need to be programmed at all. Let him spill anything and everything he knows about us. We're keeping our business as it relates to Flagg *in camera* anyway, and we're not doing much else that he couldn't guess on his own . . . even if his crystal ball is on the blink.'

Nick: 'Exactly.'

Glen: 'Okay – I'm going to second Nick's motion right on the spot. I think we have everything to win and nothing to lose. It's a tremendously daring and original idea.'

Stu: 'It's been moved and seconded. We can have a little further discussion if you want, but only a little. We'll be here all night, if we don't look lively. *Is* there any further discussion?'

Fran: 'You bet there is. You said we have everything to win and nothing to lose, Glen. Well, what about Tom? What about our own goddam *souls*? Maybe it doesn't bother you guys to think about people sticking . . . things . . . under Tom's fingernails and giving him electric shocks, but it bothers me. How can you be so cold-blooded? And Nick, hypnotizing him so he'd behave like a . . . a chicken with its head stuck in a bag! You ought to be ashamed! I thought he was your *friend*!'

Stu: 'Fran –'

Fran: 'No, I'm going to have my say. I won't wash my hands of the committee or even walk off in a huff if I'm voted down, but I'm going to have my say. Do you really want to take that sweet, foggy boy and turn him into a human U-2 plane? Don't any of you understand that's the same as starting all the old shit over again? Can't you *see* that? What do we do if they kill him, Nick? What do we do if they kill *all* of them? Breed up some new bugs? An improved version of Captain Trips?'

There was a pause here while Nick wrote out a response.

Nick (read by Ralph): 'The things Fran has brought up have affected me pretty deeply, but I stand by my nomination. No, I don't feel good about standing Tom on his head, and I don't feel good about sending him into a situation where he might be tortured and then killed. I'll only point out again that he would be doing it for *Mother Abagail*, and her ideas, and her God, not for us. I also truly believe that we have to use any means at our disposal to end the threat this being poses. He's crucifying people over there. I'm sure of that from my dreams, and I know some of you others have had that dream, too. Mother Abagail has had it herself. And I know that Flagg is evil. If anyone works up a new strain of Captain Trips, Frannie, it will be him, to use on us. I'd like to stop him while we still can.'

Fran: 'Those things are all true, Nick. I can't argue them. I know he's bad. For all *I* know, he may be Satan's Imp, as Mother Abagail says. But we're putting our hand to the same switch in order to stop him. Remember *Animal Farm*? "They looked from the pigs to the men, and could not tell the difference." I guess what I really want to hear you say – even if it's Ralph who reads it – is that if we *do* have to pull that switch in order to stop him . . . if we *do* . . . that we'll be able to let go once it's over. Can you say that?'

Nick: 'Not for sure, I guess. Not for sure.'

Fran: 'Then I vote no. If we must send people into the West, let's at least send people who know what they are in for.'

Stu: 'Anyone else?'

Sue: 'I'm against it, too, but for more practical reasons. If we go on the way we're headed, we're going to end up with an old man and a feeb. Pardon the expression, I like him too, but that's what he is. I'm against it, and now I'll shut up.'

Glen: 'Call the question, Stu.'

Stu: 'Okay. Let's go around the table. I vote aye. Frannie?'

Fran: 'Nay.'

Stu: 'Glen?'

Glen: 'Aye.'

Stu: 'Suze?'

Sue: 'Nay.'

Stu: 'Nick?'

Nick: 'Aye.'

Stu: 'Ralph?'

Ralph: 'Well – I don't like it that much either, but if Nick's for it, I got to go along. Aye.'

Stu: 'Larry?'

Larry: 'Want me to be frank? I think the idea sucks so bad I feel like a pay toilet. This is the kind of stuff you get when you're at the top, I guess. Neat fucking place to be. I vote aye.'

Stu: 'Motion's carried, 5–2.'

Fran: 'Stu?'

Stu: 'Yes?'

Fran: 'I'd like to change my vote. If we're really going to put Tom into it, we better do it together. I'm sorry I made such a fuss, Nick. I know it hurts you – I can see it on your face. It's so crazy! Why did any of this have to happen? It sure isn't like being on the sorority prom committee, I'll tell you that. Frannie votes aye.'

Sue: 'Me too, then. United front. Nixon Stands Firm, Says I Am Not a Crook. Aye.'

Stu: 'Amended vote is 7–0. Here's a hanky, Fran. And I'd like the record to show that I love you.'

Larry: 'On that note, I think we should adjourn.'

Sue: 'I second that emotion.'

Stu: 'It has been moved and seconded by Zippy and Zippy's mom that we adjourn. Those in favor, raise your hands. Those opposed, be prepared to get a can of beer dumped on your head.'

The vote to adjourn was 7–0.

'Coming to bed, Stu?'

'Yeah. Is it late?'

'Almost midnight. Late enough.'

Stu came in from the balcony. He was wearing jockey shorts and nothing else; their whiteness was nearly dazzling against his tanned skin. Frannie, propped up in bed with a Coleman gas lantern on the night table next to her, found herself amazed again by the confident depth of her love for him.

'Thinking about the meeting?'

'Yes. I was.' He poured himself a glass of water from the pitcher on the night table and grimaced at the flat, boiled taste.

'I thought you made a wonderful moderator. Glen asked you if you'd do it at the public meeting, didn't he? Is it bothering you? Did you decline?'

'No, I said I would. I guess I can do that. I was thinking about sending those three across the mountains. It's a dirty business, sending out spies. You were right, Frannie. Only trouble is, Nick was right, too. In a case like that, what you gonna do?'

'Vote your conscience and then get the best night's sleep you can, I guess.' She reached out to touch the Coleman lamp switch. 'Ready for the light?'

'Yeah.' She put it out and he swung into bed beside her. 'Goodnight, Frannie,' he said. 'I love you.'

She lay looking at the ceiling. She had made her peace with Tom Cullen . . . but that smudged chocolate thumbprint stayed on her mind.

Every dog has its day, Fran.

Maybe I ought to tell Stu right now, she thought. But if there was a problem, it was her problem. She would just have to wait . . . watch . . . and see if anything happened.

It was a long time before she slept.

CHAPTER 52

In the early hours of the morning, Mother Abagail lay sleepless in her bed. She was trying to pray.

She got up without making a light and knelt down in her white cotton nightgown. She pressed her forehead to her Bible, which was open to the Acts of the Apostles. The conversion of dour old Saul on the Damascus road. He had been blinded by the light, and on the Damascus road the scales had fallen from his eyes. Acts was the last book in the Bible where doctrine was backed up by miracles, and what were miracles but the divine hand of God at work upon the earth?

And oh, there were scales on her eyes and would they ever be shaken free?

The only sounds in the room were the faint hiss of the oil lamp, the tick of her windup Westclox, and her low, muttering voice. 'Show me my sin, Lord. I don't know. I know I've gone and missed something You meant for me to see. I can't sleep, I can't take a crap, and I don't feel You, Lord. I feel like I'm prayin into a dead phone, and this is a bad time for that to happen. How have I offended Thee? I'm listenin, Lord. Listenin for the still, small voice in my heart.'

And she did listen. She put her arthritis-bunched fingers over her eyes and leaned forward even farther and tried to clear her mind. But all was dark there, dark like her skin, dark like the fallow earth that waits for the good seed.

Please my Lord, my Lord, please my Lord –

But the image that rose was of a lonely stretch of dirt road in a sea of corn. There was a woman with a gunnysack full of freshly killed chickens. And the weasels came. They darted forward and made snatches at the bag. They could smell the blood – the old blood of sin and the fresh blood of sacrifice. She heard the old woman raise her voice to God, but her tone was weak and whining, a petulant voice, not begging humbly that God's will be done, whatever her place in that will's scheme of things might be, but demanding that God save her so she could finish the work . . . her work . . . as if she knew the Mind of God and could suborn His will to hers. The weasels grew bolder still; the croker sack began to fray as they twitched and pulled it. Her fingers were too old, too weak. And when the chickens were gone the weasels would still be hungry and they would come for her. Yes. They would –

And then the weasels were scattering, they had run squeaking into the night, leaving the contents of the sack half-devoured, and she thought exultantly: *God has saved me after all! Praise His Name! God has saved His good and faithful servant.*

Not God, old woman. Me.

In her vision, she turned, fear leaping hotly into her throat with a taste like fresh copper. And there, shouldering its way out of the corn like a ragged silver ghost, was a huge Rocky Mountain timberwolf, its jaws hanging open in a sardonic grin, its eyes burning. There was a beaten silver collar around its thick neck, a thing of handsome, barbarous beauty, and from it dangled a small stone of blackest jet . . . and in the center was a small red flaw, like an eye. Or a key.

She crossed herself and forked the sign of the evil eye at this dreadful apparition, but its jaws only grinned wider, and between them lolled the naked pink muscle of its tongue.

I'm coming for you, Mother. Not now, but soon. We'll run you like dogs run deer. I am all the things you think, but I'm more. I'm the magic man. I'm the man who speaks for the latter age. Your own people know me best, Mother. They call me John the Conqueror.

Go! Leave me in the name of the Lord God Almighty!

But she was so terrified! Not for the people around her, which were represented in her dream by the chickens in the sack, but for herself. She was afraid in her soul, afraid *for* her soul.

Your God has no power over me, Mother. His vessel is weak.

No! Not true! My strength is the strength of ten, I shall mount up with wings as eagles –

But the wolf only grinned and drew closer. She shrank from its breath, which was heavy and savage. This was the terror at noonday and the terror which flieth at midnight, and she *was* afraid. She was in her extremity of fear. And the wolf, still grinning, began to speak in two voices, asking and then answering itself.

'Who brought water from the rock when we were thirsty?'

'I did,' the wolf answered in a petulant, half-crowing, half-cowering voice.

'Who saved us when we did faint?' asked the grinning wolf, its muzzle now only bare inches from her, its breath that of a living abattoir.

'I did,' the wolf whined, drawing closer still, its grinning muzzle full of sharp death, its eyes red and haughty. *'Oh fall down and praise my name, I am the bringer of water in the desert, praise my name, I am the good and faithful servant who brings water in the desert, and my name is also the name of my Master —'*

The mouth of the wolf opened wide to swallow her.

'. . . my name,' she muttered. 'Praise my name, praise God from whom all blessings flow, praise Him ye creatures here below . . .'

She raised her head and looked around the room in a kind of stupor. Her Bible had fallen to the floor. There was dawnlight in the eastward-facing window.

'O my Lord!' she cried in a great and quavering voice.

Who brought water from the rock when we were thirsty?

Was that it? Dear God, was that it? Was that why the scales had covered her eyes, making her blind to the things she should know?

Bitter tears began to fall from her eyes and she got slowly and painfully to her feet and walked to the window. Arthritis jabbed blunt darning needles into the joints of her hips and knees.

She looked out and knew what she had to do now.

She went back to the closet and pulled the white cotton nightgown over her head. She dropped it on the floor. Now she stood naked, revealing a body so lapped with wrinkles that it might have been the bed of time's great river.

'Thy will be done,' she said, and began to dress.

An hour later she was walking slowly west on Mapleton Avenue toward the wooded tangles and narrow-throated defiles beyond town.

Stu was at the power plant with Nick when Glen burst in. Without preamble he said, 'Mother Abagail. She's gone.'

Nick looked at him sharply.

'What are you talking about?' Stu asked, at the same time drawing Glen away from the crew wrapping copper wire on one of the blown turbines.

Glen nodded. He had ridden a bike the five miles out here, and he was still trying to catch his breath.

'I went over to tell her a little about the meeting last night, and to play her the tape, if she wanted to hear it. I wanted her to know about Tom, because I was uneasy about the whole idea . . . what Frannie had to say kind of worked on me in the wee hours, I guess. I wanted to do it early because Ralph said there's another two parties coming in today and you know she likes to greet them. I went over around eight-thirty. She didn't answer my knock, so I went on in. I thought if she was asleep I'd just leave . . . but I wanted to make sure she wasn't . . . wasn't dead or anything . . . she's so *old*.'

Nick's gaze never left Glen's lips.

'But she wasn't there at all. And I found this on her pillow.' He handed them a paper towel. Written on it in large and trembling strokes was this message:

> I must be gone a bit now. I've sinned and presumed
> to know the Mind of God. My sin has been PRIDE,
> and He wants me to find my place in His work again.
> I will be with you again soon if it is God's will.
> Abby Freemantle

'I'll be a sonofabitch,' Stu said. 'What do we do now? What do you think, Nick?'

Nick took the note and read it again. He handed it back to Glen. The fierceness had died out of his face and he only looked sad.

'I guess we'll have to move up that meeting to tonight,' Glen said.

Nick shook his head. He took out his pad, wrote, tore it off, and handed it to Glen. Stu read it over his shoulder.

'Man proposes, God disposes. Mother A. was fond of that one, used to quote it frequently. Glen, you yourself said she was other-directed; God or her own mind or her delusions or whatever. What's to do? She's gone. We can't change it.'

'But the uproar –' Stu began.

'Sure, there's going to be an uproar,' Glen said. 'Nick, shouldn't we at least have a meeting of the committee and discuss it?'

Nick jotted, 'What purpose? Why have a meeting that can't accomplish anything?'

'Well, we could get up a search-party. She can't have gone far.'

Nick double-circled the phrase *Man proposes, God disposes*. Below it he wrote, 'If you found her, how would you bring her back? Chains?'

'Jesus, no!' Stu exclaimed. 'But we can't just let her wander around, Nick! She's got some crazy idea she's offended God. What if she feels like she has to go off into the frigging wilderness, like some Old Testament guy?'

Nick wrote, 'I'm almost positive that's just what she's done.'

'Well, there you go!'

Glen put a hand on Stu's arm. 'Slow down a minute, East Texas. Let's look at the implications of this.'

'To hell with the implications! I don't see no implications in leaving an old woman to wander around day n night until she dies of exposure!'

'She is *not* just any old woman. She is Mother Abagail and around here she's the Pope. If the Pope decides he has to walk to Jerusalem, do you argue with him if you're a good Catholic?'

'Goddammit, it's not the same thing and you know it!'

'Yes, it *is* the same thing. It *is*. At least, that's how the people in the Free Zone are going to see it. Stu, are you prepared to say for sure that God *didn't* tell her to go out into the bushes?'

'No-oo ... but ...'

Nick had been writing and now he showed the paper to Stu, who had to puzzle out some of the words. Nick's handwriting was usually impeccable, but this was hurried, perhaps impatient.

'Stu, this changes nothing, except that it will probably hurt the Free Zone's morale. Not even sure that will happen. People aren't going to scatter just because she's gone. It does mean we won't have to clear our plans with her right now. Maybe that's best.'

'I'm going crazy,' Stu said. 'Sometimes we talk about her as an obstacle to get around, like she was a roadblock. Sometimes you talk about her like she was the Pope, and she couldn't do anything wrong if she wanted to. And it just so happens that I *like* her. What do you want, Nicky? Someone stumbling over her body this fall in one of those box canyons west of town? You want us to leave her out there so she can make a ... a holy meal for the crows?'

'Stu,' Glen said gently. 'It was her decision to go.'

'Oh, god-*damn*, what a mess,' Stu said.

By noon, the news of Mother Abagail's disappearance had swept the community. As Nick had predicted, the general feeling was more one of unhappy resignation than alarm. The sense of the community was that she must have gone off to 'pray for guidance,' so she could help them pick the right path to follow at the mass meeting on the eighteenth.

'I don't want to blaspheme by calling her God,' Glen said over a scratch lunch in the park, 'but she is a sort of God-by-proxy. You can measure the strength of any society's faith by seeing how much that faith weakens when its empiric object is removed.'

'Run that one by me again.'

'When Moses smashed the golden calf, the Israelites stopped worshipping it. When a flood inundated the temple of Baal, the Malachites decided Baal wasn't such a hot god anyway. But Jesus has been out to lunch for two thousand years, and people not only still follow His teachings, they live and die believing He'll come back eventually, and it will be business as usual when He does. That's the way the Free Zone feels about Mother Abagail. These people are perfectly certain she is going to come back. Have you talked to them?'

'Yeah,' Stu said. 'I can't believe it. There's an old woman wandering around out there and everyone says ho-hum, I wonder if she'll bring back the Ten Commandments on stone tablets in time for the meeting.'

'Maybe she will,' Glen said somberly. 'Anyway, not everyone is saying ho-hum. Ralph Brentner is practically tearing his hair out by the roots.'

'Good for Ralph.' He looked at Glen closely. 'What about you, baldy? Where are you in all of this?'

'I wish you wouldn't call me that. It's not at all dignified. But I'll tell you . . . it's a little bit funny. Ole East Texas turns out to be a lot more immune from the Godspell she's cast over this community than the agnostic old bear sociologist. I think she'll be back. Somehow I just do. What does Frannie think?'

'I don't know. I haven't seen her at all this morning. For all I know she's out there eating locusts and wild honey with Mother Abagail.' He stared at the Flatirons, rising high in the blue haze of early afternoon. 'Jesus, Glen, I hope that old lady is all right.'

Fran didn't even know Mother Abagail was gone. She had spent the morning at the library, reading up on gardening. Nor was she the only student. She saw two or three people with books on farming, a bespectacled young man of about twenty-five poring over a book called *Seven Independent Power Sources for Your Home*, and a pretty blond girl of about fourteen with a battered paperback titled *600 Simple Recipes*.

She left the library around noon and strolled down to Walnut Street. She was halfway home when she met Shirley Hammett, the older woman that had been traveling with Dayna, Susan, and Patty Kroger. Shirley had improved strikingly since then. Now she looked like a brisk and pretty matron-about-town.

She stopped and greeted Fran. 'When do you think she'll be back? I've been asking everybody. If this town had a newspaper, I'd write it up for the People Poll. Like, "What do you think of Senator Bunghole's stand on oil depletion?" That sort of thing.'

'When will who be back?'

'Mother *Abagail*, of course. Where have you been, girl, cold storage?'

'What is all this?' Frannie asked, alarmed. 'What's happened?'

'That's just it. Nobody really knows.' And Shirley told Fran what had been going on while Fran had been at the library.

'She just . . . left?' Frannie asked, frowning.

'Yes. Of course she'll be back,' Shirley added confidently. 'The note said so.'

'"If it is God's will"?'

'That's just a manner of speaking, I'm sure,' Shirley said, and looked at Fran with a touch of coldness.

'Well . . . I hope so. Thanks for telling me, Shirley. Are you still having headaches?'

'Oh no. They're all gone now. I'll be voting for you, Fran.'

'Hmmm?' Her mind was far away, chasing this new information, and for a moment she hadn't the slightest idea what Shirley could be talking about.

'For the permanent *committee*!'

'Oh. Well, thanks. I'm not even sure I want the job.'

'You'll do fine. You and Susy both. Got to get going, Fran. See you.'

They parted. Fran hurried toward the apartment, wanting to see if Stu knew anything else. Coming so soon after their meeting last night, the old woman's disappearance struck her around her heart with a kind of superstitious dread. She didn't like not being able to pass on their major decisions – like the one to send people west – to

Mother Abagail for judgment. With her gone, Fran felt too much of the responsibility on her own shoulders.

When she got home the apartment was empty. She had missed Stu by about fifteen minutes. The note under the sugarbowl said simply: 'Back by 9:30. I'm with Ralph and Harold. No worry. Stu.'

Ralph and Harold? she thought, and felt a sudden twinge of dread that had nothing to do with Mother Abagail. Now why should I be afraid for Stu? My God, if Harold tried to do something . . . well, something funny . . . Stu would tear him apart. Unless . . . unless Harold sneaked up behind him or something and . . .

She clutched at her elbows, feeling cold, wondering what Stu could be doing with Ralph and Harold.

Back by 9:30.

God, that seemed a long time away.

She stood in the kitchen a moment longer, frowning down at her knapsack, which she had put on the counter.

I'm with Ralph and Harold.

So Harold's little house on outer Arapahoe would be deserted until nine-thirty tonight. Unless, of course, they were there, and if they were, she could join them and satisfy her curiosity. She could bike out there in no time. If no one was there, she might find something that would set her mind at rest . . . or . . . but she wouldn't let herself think about that.

Set your mind at rest? the interior voice nagged. *Or just make it crazier? Suppose you DO find something funny? What then? What will you do about it?*

She didn't know. She didn't, in fact, have the least tiny smidgen of an idea.

No worry. Stu.

But there *was* worry. That thumbprint in her diary meant there was worry. Because a man who would steal your diary and pilfer your thoughts was a man without much principle or scruple. A man like that might creep up behind someone he hated and give a push off a high place. Or use a rock. Or a knife. Or a gun.

No worry. Stu.

But if Harold did a thing like that, he would be through in Boulder. What could he do then?

But Fran knew what then. She didn't know if Harold was the

sort of man she had hypothesized – not yet, not for sure – but she knew in her heart that there was a place for people like that now. Oh yes indeedy.

She put her knapsack back on with quick little jerks and went out the door. Three minutes later she was biking up Broadway toward Arapahoe in the bright afternoon sunshine, thinking: *They'll be right in Harold's living room, drinking coffee and talking about Mother Abagail and everybody will be fine. Just fine.*

But Harold's small house was dark, deserted . . . and locked.

That in itself was something of a freak in Boulder. In the old days you locked up when you went out so no one would steal your TV, stereo, your wife's jewels. But now the stereos and TV were free, much good they would do you with no juice to run them, and as for jewels, you could go to Denver and pick up a sackful any old time.

Why do you lock your door, Harold, when everything's free? Because nobody is as afraid of robbery as a thief? Could that be it?

She was no lockpicker. She had resigned herself to leaving when it occurred to her to try the cellar windows. They were set just above ground level, opaque with dirt. The first one she tried slid open sideways on its track, giving way grudgingly and sifting dirt down onto the basement floor.

Fran looked around, but the world was quiet. No one except Harold had settled in this far out on Arapahoe as yet. That was odd, too. Harold could grin until his face cracked and slap people on the back and pass the time of day with folks, he could and did gladly offer his help whenever it was asked for and sometimes when it wasn't, he could and did make people like him – and it was a fact that he was highly regarded in Boulder. But where he had chosen to live . . . that was something else, now wasn't it? That displayed a slightly different aspect of Harold's view of society and his place in it . . . maybe. Or maybe he just liked the quiet.

She wriggled in the window, getting her blouse dirty, and dropped to the floor. Now the cellar window was on a level with her eyes. She was no more a gymnast than she was a lockpicker, and she would have to stand on something to get back out.

Fran looked around. The basement had been finished off into a playroom/rumpus room. The kind of thing her own dad had always talked about but never quite got around to doing, she thought with a little pang of sadness. The walls were knotty pine with quadraphonic speakers embedded in them, there was an Armstrong suspended ceiling overhead, a large case filled with jigsaw puzzles and books, an electric train set, a slotcar racing set. There was also an air-hockey game on which Harold had indifferently set a case of Coke. It had been the kids' room, and posters dotted the walls – the biggest, now old and frayed, showed George Bush coming out of a church in Harlem, hands raised high, a big grin on his face. The caption, in huge red letters, said: YOU DON'T WANT TO LAY NO BOOGIE-WOOGIE ON THE KING OF ROCK AND ROLL!

She suddenly felt sadder than she had since . . . well, since she couldn't remember, to tell the truth. She had been through shocks, and fear, and outright terror, and a perfect numbing savagery of grief, but this deep and aching sadness was something new. With it came a sudden wave of homesickness for Ogunquit, for the ocean, for the good Maine hills and pines. For no reason at all she suddenly thought of Gus, the parking lot attendant of the Ogunquit public beach, and for a moment she thought her heart would break with loss and sorrow. What was she doing here, poised between the plains and the mountains that broke the country in two? It wasn't her place. She didn't belong here.

One sob escaped her and it sounded so terrified and lonely that she clapped both hands over her mouth for the second time that day. *No more, Frannie old kid old sock. You don't get over anything this big so quickly. A little at a time. If you have to have a cry, have it later, not here in Harold Lauder's basement. Business first.*

She walked past the poster on her way to the stairs, and a bitter little smile crossed her face as she passed George Bush's grinning and tirelessly cheerful face. They sure laid some boogie-woogie on you, she thought. Someone did, anyhow.

As she got to the top of the cellar stairs she became certain that the door would be locked, but it opened easily. The kitchen was neat and shipshape, the luncheon dishes done up and drying in the drainer, the little Coleman gas stove washed off and sparkling . . . but a greasy smell of frying still hung in the air, like a ghost of Harold's old self, the Harold who had introduced himself into this part of her life by motoring up to her house behind the wheel of Roy Brannigan's Cadillac as she was burying her father.

Sure would be in a fix if Harold picked right now to come back, she thought. The idea made her look suddenly over her shoulder. She half expected to see Harold standing by the door which led into the living room, grinning at her. There was no one there, but her heart had begun to knock unpleasantly against her ribcage.

There was nothing in the kitchen, so she went into the living room.

It was dark, so dark it made her uneasy. Harold not only kept his doors locked, he kept his shades pulled. Again she felt as if she were witnessing an unconscious outward manifestation of Harold's personality. Why would anyone keep their shades pulled down in a small city where that was the way the living came to know and mark the houses of the dead?

The living room, like the kitchen, was astringently neat, but the furniture was stodgy and a little seedy-looking. The room's nicest feature was the fireplace, a huge stone job with a hearth wide enough to sit on. She did sit down for a moment, looking around thoughtfully. As she shifted, she felt a loose hearthstone under her fanny, and she was about to get up and look at it when someone knocked on the door.

Fear drifted down on her like a smothering weight of feathers. She was paralyzed with sudden terror. Her breath stopped, and she would not be aware until later that she had wet herself a little.

The knock came again, half a dozen quick, firm raps.

My God, she thought. *The shades are down at least, thank heaven for that.*

That thought was followed by a sudden cold certainty that she had left her bike out where anyone could see it. Had she? She tried desperately to think, but for a long moment she could summon nothing to mind except a babble of gibberish that was unsettlingly familiar: *Before removing the mote from thy neighbor's eye, remove the pie from thine own –*

The knock came again, and a woman's voice: 'Anybody home?'

Fran sat stockstill. She suddenly remembered that she had parked her bike around back, under Harold's clothes-line. Not visible from the front of the house. But if Harold's visitor decided to try the back door –

The knob of the front door – Frannie could see it down the short length of hall – began to turn back and forth in frustrated half-circles.

Whoever she is, I hope she's no better at locks than I am, Frannie thought, and then had to squeeze both hands over her mouth to stop an insane bray of laughter. That was when she looked down at her cotton slacks and saw how badly she had been frightened. *At least she didn't scare the shit out of me*, Fran thought. *At least, not yet.* The laughter bubbled up again, hysterical and frightened, just below the surface.

Then, with an indescribable sense of relief, she heard footfalls clicking away from the door and down Harold's concrete path.

What Fran did next she did with no conscious decision at all. She ran quietly down the hall to the front door and put her eye to the small crack between the shade and the edge of the window. She saw a woman with long dark hair that was streaked with white. She climbed onto a small Vespa motorscooter that was parked at the curb. As the motor burped into life, she tossed her hair back and clipped it.

It's the Cross woman – the one who came over with Larry Underwood! Does she know Harold?

Then Nadine had the scooter in gear. She started off with a little jerk and was soon out of sight. Fran uttered a huge sigh, and her legs turned to water. She opened her mouth to let out the laugh that had been bubbling below the surface, knowing already how it would sound – shaky and relieved. Instead, she burst into tears.

Five minutes later, too nervous now to search any further, she was boosting herself back through the cellar window from the seat of a wicker chair she had pulled over. Once out, she was able to push the chair far enough so that it wouldn't be obvious someone had used it to climb out. It was still out of position, but people rarely noticed things like that . . . and it didn't look as if Harold used the basement at all, except to store his Coca-Cola.

She reclosed the window and got her bike. She still felt weak and stunned and a little nauseated from her scare. At least my pants are drying, she thought. Next time you go housebreaking, Frances Rebecca, remember to wear your continence pants.

She pedaled out of Harold's yard and left Arapahoe as soon as she could, coming back to the downtown area on Canyon Boulevard. She was back in her own apartment fifteen minutes later.

The place was utterly silent.

She opened her diary and looked down at the muddy chocolate fingerprint and wondered where Stu was.

She wondered if Harold was with him.

Oh Stu please come home. I need you.

★   ★   ★

After lunch, Stu had left Glen and had come home. He had been sitting blankly in the living room, wondering where Mother Abagail was and also wondering if Nick and Glen could possibly be right about just letting the matter be, when there was a knock.

'Stu?' Ralph Brentner called. 'Hello, Stu, you home?'

Harold Lauder was with him. Harold's smile was muted today but not entirely gone; he looked like a jolly mourner trying to be serious for the graveside service.

Ralph, heartsick over Mother Abagail's disappearance, had met Harold half an hour ago, Harold being on his way home after helping with a water-hauling party at Boulder Creek. Ralph liked Harold, who always seemed to have time to listen and commiserate with whoever had a sad tale to tell . . . and Harold never seemed to want anything in return. Ralph had poured out the whole story of Mother Abagail's disappearance, including his fears that she might suffer a heart attack or break one of her brittle bones or die of exposure if she stayed out overnight.

'And you know it showers just about every damn afternoon,' Ralph finished as Stu poured coffee. 'If she gets soaked, she'd be sure to take a cold. Then what? Pneumonia, I guess.'

'What can we do about it?' Stu asked them. 'We can't force her to come back if she doesn't want to.'

'Well, no,' Ralph conceded. 'But Harold had a real good idea.'

Stu's eyes shifted. 'How you doing, Harold?'

'Pretty good. You?'

'Fine.'

'And Fran? You watching out for her?' Harold's eyes didn't waver from Stu's, and they kept their slightly humorous, pleasant light, but Stu had a momentary feeling that Harold's smiling eyes were like sunshine on the water of Brakeman's Quarry back home – the water looked so pleasant, but it went down and down to black depths where the sun had never reached, and four boys had lost their lives in pleasant-looking Brakeman's Quarry over the years.

'As best I can,' he said. 'What's your thought, Harold?'

'Well, look. I see Nick's point. Glen's, too. They recognize that the Free Zone sees Mother Abagail as a theocratic symbol . . . and they're pretty close to speaking for the Zone now, aren't they?'

Stu sipped his coffee. 'What do you mean, "theocratic symbol"?'

'I'd call it an earthly symbol of a covenant made with God,'

Harold said, and his eyes veiled a little. 'Like Holy Communion, or the Sacred Cows of India.'

Stu kindled a little at that. 'Yeah, pretty good. Those cows . . . they let em walk the streets and cause traffic jams, right? They can go in and out of the stores, or decide to leave town altogether.'

'Yes,' Harold agreed. 'But most of those cows are sick, Stu. They're always near the point of starvation. Some are tubercular. And all because they're an aggregate symbol. The people are convinced God will take care of them, just as our people are convinced God will take care of Mother Abagail. But I have my own doubts about a God that says it's right to let a poor dumb cow wander around in pain.'

Ralph looked momentarily uncomfortable, and Stu knew what he was feeling. He felt it himself, and it gave him a way to measure how he felt about Mother Abagail himself. He felt that Harold was edging into blasphemy.

'Anyway,' Harold said briskly, dismissing the Sacred Cows of India, 'we can't change the way people feel about her −'

'And wouldn't want to,' Ralph added quickly.

'Right!' Harold exclaimed. 'After all, she brought us together, and not exactly by shortwave, either. My idea was that we mount our trusty cycles and spend the afternoon reconnoitering the west side of Boulder. If we stay fairly close, we can keep in touch with each other by walkie-talkie.'

Stu was nodding. This was the sort of thing he had wanted to do all along. Sacred Cows or not, God or not, it just wasn't right to leave her to wander around on her own. That didn't have anything to do with religion; something like that was just callous disregard.

'And if we find her,' Harold said, 'we can ask her if she wants anything.'

'Like a ride back to town,' Ralph chipped in.

'At least we can keep tabs on her,' Harold said.

'Okay,' Stu said. 'I think it's a helluva good idea, Harold. Just let me leave a note for Fran.'

But as he scribbled the note, he kept feeling an urge to look back over his shoulder at Harold − to see what Harold was doing while Stu wasn't looking, and what expression might be in Harold's eyes.

Harold had asked for and gotten the twisting stretch of road between Boulder and Nederland, because he considered it to be the least likely area. He didn't think *he* could walk from Boulder to Nederland in one day, let alone that crazy old cunt. But it made a pleasant ride and gave him a chance to think.

Now, at a quarter to seven, he was on his way back. His Honda was parked in a rest area and he was sitting at a picnic table, having a Coke and a few Slim Jims. The walkie-talkie that hung over the Honda's handlebars with its antenna at full extension crackled faintly with Ralph Brentner's voice. They were short-range radios only, and Ralph was somewhere up on Flagstaff Mountain.

'. . . Sunrise Amphitheater . . . no sign of her . . . storm's over up here.'

Then Stu's voice, stronger and closer. He was in Chautauqua Park, only four miles from Harold's location. 'Say again, Ralph.'

Ralph's voice came back, really bellowing. Maybe he would give himself a stroke. That would be a lovely way to end the day. 'No sign of her up here! I'm going down before it gets dark! Over!'

'Ten-four,' Stu said, sounding discouraged. 'Harold, you there?' Harold got up, wiping Slim Jim grease on his jeans. 'Harold? Calling Harold Lauder! You copy, Harold?'

Harold pointed his middle finger – yer fuckfinger, as the high school Neanderthals back in Ogunquit had called it – at the walkie-talkie; then he depressed the talk button and said pleasantly, but with just the right note of discouragement: 'I'm here. I was off to one side . . . thought I saw something down in the ditch. It was just an old jacket. Over.'

'Yeah, okay. Why don't you come down to Chautauqua, Harold? We'll wait there for Ralph.'

Love to give orders, don't you, suckhole? I might have something for you. Yes, I just might.

'Harold, you copy?'

'Yes. Sorry, Stu, I was woolgathering. I can be there in fifteen minutes.'

'*You copying this, Ralph?*' Stu bellowed, making Harold wince. He gave Stu's voice the finger again, grinning furtively as he did so. *Copy this, you Wild West motherfucker.*

'Roger, you'll be at Chautauqua Park,' Ralph's voice came faintly through the roar of static. 'I'm on my way. Over and out.'

'I'm on my way, too,' Harold said. 'Over and out.'

He turned off the walkie-talkie, collapsed the antenna, and hung the radio on the handlebars again, but he sat astride the Honda for a moment without operating the kickstarter. He was wearing an army surplus flak jacket; the heavy padding was good when you were riding a cycle above six thousand feet, even in August. But the jacket served another purpose. It had a great many zippered pockets and in one of these was a Smith & Wesson .38. Harold took the pistol out and turned it over and over in his hands. It was fully loaded and it was heavy in his hands, as if it realized its purposes were grave ones: death, destruction, assassination.

Tonight?

Why not?

He had initiated this expedition on the chance that he might be alone with Stu long enough to do it. Now it looked as though he was going to have that chance, at Chautauqua Park, in less than fifteen minutes. But the trip had served another purpose, as well.

He hadn't meant to go all the way to Nederland, a miserable little town nestled high above Boulder, a town whose only claim to fame was that Patty Hearst had once allegedly stayed there during her time as a fugitive. But as he drove up and up, the Honda purring smoothly between his legs, the air as cold as a blunt razorblade against his face, something had happened.

If you put a magnet on one end of a table and a steel slug on the other, nothing happens. If you move the slug closer to the magnet in slow increments of distance (he held this image in his mind for a moment, savoring it, reminding himself to put it in his diary when he entered tonight), a time will come when the shove you give the slug seems to propel it farther than it should. The slug stops, but it seems to do so reluctantly, as if it has come alive, and part of its liveliness is a resentment of the physical law which deals with inertia. Another little push or two and you can almost – or perhaps even actually – see the slug trembling on the table, seeming to jitter and vibrate slightly, like one of those Mexican jumping beans you can buy in novelty shops, the ones which look like knuckle-sized knots of wood but which actually have a live worm inside. One more push and the balance between friction/inertia and the attraction of the magnet begins to tip the other way. The slug, wholly alive now, moves on its own, faster and faster, until it finally smacks into the magnet and sticks there.

Horrible, fascinating process.

When the world had ended this June, the force of magnetism had still not been understood, although Harold thought (his mind had never been of the rational-scientific bent) that the physicists who studied such things thought it was intimately entwined with the phenomenon of gravity, and that gravity was the keystone of the universe.

On his way to Nederland, moving west, moving *up*, feeling the air grow chillier, seeing the thunderheads slowly piling up around the still-higher peaks far beyond Nederland, Harold had felt that process begin in himself. He was approaching the point of balance . . . and not far beyond that, he would reach the point of shift. He was the steel slug just that distance from the magnet where a little push sends it farther than the force imparted would do under more ordinary circumstances. He could feel the jittering in himself.

It was the closest thing to a holy experience that he had ever had. The young reject the holy, because to accept it means to accept the eventual death of all empiric objects, and Harold also rejected it. The old woman was some sort of psychic, he had thought, and so was Flagg, the dark man. They were human radio stations, and no more. Their real power would lie in societies that coalesced around their signals, which were so different one from the other. So he had thought.

But parked on his cycle at the end of Nederland's cheesy main street with the Honda's neutral light glowing like a cat's eye, listening to the winterwhine of the wind in the pines and the aspens, he had felt something more than mere magnetic attraction. He had felt a stupendous, irrational power coming out of the West, an attraction so great that he felt to closely contemplate it now would be to go mad. He felt that, if he ventured much farther out on the arm of balance, any self-will would be lost. He would go just as he was, emptyhanded.

And for that, although he could not be blamed, the dark man would kill him.

So he had turned away feeling the cold relief of a presuicidal man coming away from a long period of regarding a long drop. But he could go tonight, if he liked. Yes, he could kill Redman with a single bullet fired at pointblank range. Then just stay put, stay cool until the Oklahoma sodbuster showed up. Another shot to the temple. No one would take alarm at the gunshots; game was plentiful, and lots of people had taken to banging away at the deer that wandered down into town.

It was ten to seven now. He could waste them both by seven-thirty. Fran would not raise the alarm until ten-thirty or later, and by then he could be well away, working his way west on his Honda, with his ledger in his knapsack. But it wouldn't happen if he just sat here on his bike, letting time pass.

The Honda started on the second kick. It was a good bike. Harold smiled. Harold grinned. Harold positively radiated good cheer. He drove off toward Chautauqua Park.

Dusk was starting to close down when Stu heard Harold's bike coming into the park. A moment later he saw the Honda's headlamp flashing in and out between the trees that lined the climbing sweep of the drive. Then he could see Harold's helmeted head turning right and left, looking for him.

Stu, who was sitting on the edge of a rock barbecue pit, waved and shouted. After a minute Harold saw him, waved back, and began to putt over in second gear.

After the afternoon the three of them had put in, Stu felt considerably better about Harold . . . better than he ever had, in fact. Harold's idea had been a damn good one even if it hadn't panned out. And Harold had insisted on taking the Nederland road . . . must have been pretty cold in spite of his heavy jacket. As he pulled up, Stu saw that Harold's perpetual grin looked more like a grimace; his face was strained and too white. Disappointed that things hadn't worked out better, Stu guessed. He felt a sudden flush of guilt at the way he and Frannie had treated Harold, as if his constant grin and his overfriendly way with people was some kind of camouflage. Had they ever really considered the idea that the guy might just be trying to turn over a new leaf, that he might be going at it a little strangely just because he had never tried to do such a thing before? Stu didn't guess they had.

'Nothing at all, huh?' he asked Harold, jumping nimbly down from the top of the barbecue pit.

'De nada,' Harold said. The grin reappeared, but it was automatic, without strength, like a rictus. His face still looked strange and deadly pale. His hands were stuffed in the pockets of his jacket.

'Never mind. It was a good idea. For all we know, she's back in her house right now. If not, we can look again tomorrow.'

'That might be like looking for a body.'

Stu sighed. 'Maybe . . . yeah, maybe. Why don't you come back to supper with me, Harold?'

'What?' Harold seemed to flinch back in the gathering gloom under the trees. His grin looked more strained than ever.

'Supper,' Stu said patiently. 'Look, Frannie'd be glad to see you, too. That's no shit. She really would.'

'Well, maybe,' Harold said, still looking uncomfortable. 'But I'm ... well, I had a thing for her, you know. Maybe it's best if we ... just let it go for now. Nothing personal. The two of you go well together. I know that.' His smile shone forth with renewed sincerity. It was infectious; Stu answered it.

'Your choice, Harold. But the door's open, anytime.'

'Thanks.'

'No, I got to thank you,' Stu said seriously.

Harold blinked. 'Me?'

'For helping us hunt when everybody else decided to let nature take her course. Even if it didn't come to nothing. Will you shake with me?' Stu put his hand out. Harold stared at it blankly for a moment, and Stu didn't think his gesture was going to be accepted. Then Harold took his right hand out of his jacket pocket – it seemed to catch on something, the zipper, maybe – and shook Stu's hand briefly. Harold's hand was warm and a little sweaty.

Stu stepped in front of him, looking down the drive. 'Ralph should be here by now. I hope he didn't have an accident coming down that frigging mountain. He ... there he is now.'

Stu walked out to the side of the road; a second headlamp was now flashing up the drive and playing hide-and-seek through the screening trees.

'Yes, that's him,' Harold said in an odd flat voice behind Stu. 'Someone with him, too.'

'Wh–what?'

'There.' Stu pointed to a second motorcycle headlamp behind the first.

'Oh.' That queerly flat voice again. It caused Stu to turn around.

'You okay, Harold?'

'Just tired.'

The second vehicle belonged to Glen Bateman; it was a low-power moped, the closest to a motorcycle that he would come, and it made Nadine's Vespa look like a Harley. Behind Ralph, Nick Andros was riding pillion. Nick had an invitation for all of them to come back to the house he and Ralph shared to have coffee and/or brandy. Stu agreed but Harold begged off, still looking strained and tired.

He's so goddam disappointed, Stu thought, and reflected that it was not only the first sympathy he had probably ever felt for Harold, but also that it was long overdue. He renewed Nick's invitation himself, but Harold only shook his head and told Stu he was shot for the day. He guessed he would go home and get some sleep.

By the time he got home, Harold was shaking so badly he could barely get his key in the front door. When he did get the door open, he darted in as if he suspected a maniac might be creeping up the walk behind him. He slammed the door, turned the lock, shot the bolt. Then he leaned against the door for a moment with his head back and his eyes shut, feeling on the verge of hysterical tears. When he had a grip on himself again, he felt his way down the hall to the living room and lit all three gas lanterns. The room became bright, and bright was better.

He sat down in his favorite chair and closed his eyes. When his heartbeat had slowed a little he went to the hearth, removed the loose stone, and removed his LEDGER. It soothed him. A ledger was where you kept track of debts owed, bills outstanding, accumulating interest. It was where you finally put paid to all accounts.

He sat back down, flipped to the place where he had stopped, hesitated, then wrote: '*August 14, 1990*.' He wrote for nearly an hour and a half, his pen dashing back and forth line after line, page after page. His face as he wrote was by turns savagely amused and dully righteous, terrified and joyous, hurt and grinning. When he was finished, he read what he had written ('*These are my letters to the world/which never wrote to me . . .*') while he absently massaged his aching right hand.

He replaced the ledger and the covering stone. He was calm; he had written it all out of him; he had translated his terror and his fury to the page and his resolve remained strong. That was good. Sometimes the act of writing things down made him feel more jittery, and those were the times he knew he had written falsely, or without the effort required to hone the dull edge of truth to an edge where it would cut – where it would bring blood. But tonight he could put the book back with a calm and serene mind. The rage and fear and frustration had been safely transferred into the book, with a rock to hold it down while he slept.

Harold ran up one of his shades and looked out into the silent street. Looking up at the Flatirons he thought calmly about how close he had come to just going ahead anyway, just hauling out the .38 and trying to mow down all four of them. That would have fixed their reeking sanctimonious ad hoc committee. When he had finished with them they wouldn't even have had a fucking quorum left.

But at the last moment some fraying cord of sanity had held instead of giving way. He had been able to let go of the gun and shake the betraying cracker's hand. How, he would never know, but thank God he had. The mark of genius is its ability to bide – and so he would.

He was sleepy now; it had been a long and eventful day.

Unbuttoning his shirt, Harold turned out two of the three gaslamps, and picked up the last to take into his bedroom. As he went through into the kitchen he stopped, frozen.

The door to the basement was standing open.

He went to it, holding the lamp aloft, and went down the first three steps. Fear came into his heart, driving the calmness out.

'Who's here?' he called. No answer. He could see the air-hockey table. The posters. In the far corner, a set of gaily striped croquet mallets sat in their rack.

He went down another three steps. 'Is someone here?'

No; he felt there was not. But that did not allay his fear.

He went the rest of the way down and held the lamp high above his head; across the room a monstrous shadow-Harold, as huge and black as the ape in the Rue Morgue, did likewise.

Was there something on the floor over there? Yes. There was.

He crossed behind the slotcar track to beneath the window where Fran had entered. On the floor was a spill of light brown grit. Harold set the light down beside the spill. In the center of it, as clear as a fingerprint, was the track of a sneaker or tennis shoe . . . not a waffle or zigzag pattern, but groups of circles and lines. He stared at it, burning it into his mind, and then kicked the dust into a light cloud, destroying the mark. His face was the face of a living waxwork in the light of the Coleman lamp.

'You'll pay!' Harold cried softly. 'Whichever one of you it was, you'll pay! Yes you will! Yes you will!'

He climbed the stairs again and went through his house from end to end, looking for any other signs of defilement. He found none. He ended in the living room, not sleepy at all now. He was just concluding that someone – a kid, maybe – had broken in out of curiosity, when the thought of his LEDGER exploded in his mind like a flare in a midnight sky. The break-in motive was so clear, so awful, that he had nearly overlooked it completely.

He ran to the hearth, pulled up the stone, and ripped the LEDGER from its place. For the first time it came completely home to him how dangerous the book was. If someone found it, everything was over. He of all people should know that; hadn't all of this begun because of Fran's diary?

The LEDGER. The footprint. Did the latter mean the former had been discovered? Of course not. But how to be sure? There *was* no way, that was the pure and hellish truth of the matter.

He replaced the hearthstone and took the LEDGER into his bedroom with him. He put it under his pillow along with his Smith & Wesson revolver, thinking he should burn it, knowing he never could. The best writing he had ever done in his life was between its covers, the only writing that had ever come as a result of belief and personal commitment.

He lay down, resigned to a sleepless night, his mind running restlessly over possible hiding places. Under a loose board? In the back of a cupboard? Could he perhaps pull the old purloined letter trick, and leave it boldly on one of the bookshelves, a volume among many other volumes, flanked by a Reader's Digest Condensed Book on one side and a copy of *The Total Woman* on the other? No – that was too bold; he would never be able to leave the house and have peace. What about a safety-deposit box at the bank? No, that wouldn't do – he wanted it with him, where he could look at it.

At last he did begin to drift off, and his mind, freed by oncoming sleep, drifted along with no conscious guidance, a pinball in slow motion. He thought: *It's got to be hidden, that's the thing . . . if Frannie had hidden hers better . . . if I hadn't read what she really thought of me . . . her hypocrisy . . . if she had . . .*

Harold sat bolt upright in bed, a little cry in his mouth, his eyes wide.

He sat like that for a long time, and after a while he began to shiver. Did she know? Had it been Fran's footprint? Diaries . . . journals . . . ledgers . . .

At last he lay down again, but it was a long time before he slept. He kept wondering if Fran Goldsmith regularly wore a pair of tennis shoes or sneakers. And if she did, what did the pattern on their soles look like?

Patterns of soles, patterns of souls. When he did sleep, his dreams were uneasy and more than once he cried out miserably in the dark, as if to ward off things that had already been let in forever.

Stu let himself in at quarter past nine. Fran was curled up on the double bed, wearing one of his shirts – it came almost to her knees – and reading a book titled *Fifty Friendly Plants*. She got up when he came in.

'Where have you *been*? I was worried!'

Stu explained Harold's idea that they hunt for Mother Abagail so they could at least keep an eye on her. He didn't mention Sacred Cows. Unbuttoning his shirt, he finished: 'We would have taken you along, kiddo, but you were nowhere to be found.'

'I was at the library,' she said, watching as he took off his shirt and slipped it into the net laundry bag hanging from the back of the door. He was quite hairy, chest and back, and she found herself thinking that, until she met Stu, she had always found hairy men mildly repulsive. She supposed her relief at having him back was making her a little silly in the head.

Harold had read her diary, she knew that now. She had been terribly afraid that Harold might connive to get Stu alone and . . . well, do something to him. But why now, today, just when she had found out? If Harold had let the sleeping dog lie this long, wasn't it more logical to assume that he didn't want to wake the dog up at all? And wasn't it just as possible that by reading her diary Harold had seen the futility of his constant chase after her? Coming on top of the news that Mother Abagail had disappeared, she had been in a ripe mood to see ill omens in chicken entrails, but the fact was, it had simply been her *diary* Harold had read, not a confession to the crimes of the world. And if she told Stu what she had found out, she would succeed only in looking silly and maybe getting him pissed at Harold . . . and probably at herself as well for being so silly in the first place.

'No sign of her at all, Stu?'

'Nope.'

'How did Harold seem?'

Stu was taking off his pants. 'Pretty well racked. Sorry his idea didn't pan out better. I invited him to supper whenever he wanted to come. I hope that's okay by you. You know, I really think I could get to like that sucker. You never could have convinced me of that the day I met you two in New Hampshire. Was it wrong to invite him?'

'No,' she said, after a considering pause. 'No, I'd like to be on good terms with Harold.' *I'm sitting home thinking that Harold might be planning to blow his head off*, she thought, *and Stu's inviting him to dinner. Talk about your cases of the pregnant-woman vapors!*

Stu said, 'If Mother Abagail doesn't show up by daylight, I thought I'd ask Harold if he wanted to go out again with me.'

'I'd like to go, too,' Fran said quickly. 'And there are a few others around here who aren't totally convinced that she's being fed by the ravens. Dick Vollman's one. Larry Underwood's another.'

'Okay, fine,' he said, and joined her on the bed. 'Say, what are you wearing under that shirt?'

'A big strong man like yourself should be able to find that out without my help,' Fran said primly.

It turned out to be nothing.

The next day's search-party started out modestly at eight o'clock with half a dozen searchers – Stu, Fran, Harold, Dick Vollman, Larry Underwood, and Lucy Swann. By noon the party had swelled to twenty, and by dusk (accompanied by the usual brief spat of rain and lightning in the foothills) there were better than fifty people combing the brush west of Boulder, splashing through streams, hunting up and down canyons, and stepping all over each other's CB transmissions.

A strange mood of resigned dread had gradually replaced yesterday's acceptance. Despite the powerful force of the dreams that accorded Mother Abagail a semidivine status in the Zone, most of the people had been through enough to be realists about survival: The old woman was well past a hundred, and she had been out all night on her own. And now a second night was coming on.

The fellow who had struggled across the country from Louisiana to Boulder with a party of twelve summed it up perfectly. He had come in with his people at noon the day before. When told that Mother Abagail was gone, this man, Norman Kellogg by name, threw his Astros baseball cap on the ground and said, 'Ain't that my fucking luck . . . who you got hunting her up?'

Charlie Impening, who had more or less become the Zone's resident doomcrier (he had been the one to pass the cheerful news about snow in September), began to suggest to people that if Mother Abagail had bugged out, maybe that was a sign for all of them to bug out. After all, Boulder was just too damn close. Too close to what? Never mind, you know what it's too close to, and New York or Boston would make Mavis Impening's boy Charlie feel a whole hell of a lot safer. He had no takers. People were tired and ready to sit. If it got cold and there was no heat, they might move, but not before. They were healing. Impening was asked politely if he planned to go alone. Impening said he believed he would wait until a few more people had seen the daylight. Glen Bateman was heard to opine that Charlie Impening would make a hell of a poor Moses.

'Resigned dread' was as far as the community's feelings went, Glen Bateman believed, because they were still rationally minded people in spite of all the dreams, in spite of their deep-seated dread concerning whatever might be going on west of the Rockies. Superstition, like true love, needs time to grow and reflect upon itself. When you finish a barn, he told Nick and Stu and Fran after darkness had put an end to the search for the night, you hang a horseshoe ends up over the door to keep the luck in. But if one of the nails falls out and the horseshoe swings points down, you don't abandon the barn.

'The day may come when we or our children *may* abandon the barn if the horseshoe spills the luck out, but that's years away. Right now all we feel is a little strange and lost. And that will pass, I think. If Mother Abagail is dead — and God knows I hope she isn't — it probably couldn't have come at a better time for the mental health of this community.'

Nick wrote, 'But if she was meant as a check for our Adversary, his opposite number, someone put here to keep the scales in balance . . .'

'Yes, I know,' Glen said gloomily. 'I know. The days when the horseshoe didn't matter may really be passing . . . or already gone. Believe me, I know.'

Frannie said: 'You don't really think our grandchildren are going to be superstitious natives, do you, Glen? Burning witches and spitting through their fingers for luck?'

'I can't read the future, Fran,' Glen said, and in the lamplight his face looked old and worn — the face, perhaps, of a failed magician. 'I couldn't even properly see the effect Mother Abagail was having on the community until Stu pointed it out to me that night on Flagstaff Mountain. But I do know this: We're all in this town because of two events. The superflu we can charge off to the stupidity of the human race. It doesn't matter if we did it or the Russians, or the Latvians. Who emptied the beaker loses importance beside the general truth: *At the end of all rationalism, the mass grave.* The laws of physics, the laws of biology, the axioms of mathematics, they're all part of the deathtrip, because we are what we are. If it hadn't been Captain Trips, it would have been something else. The fashion was to blame it on "technology," but "technology" is the trunk of the tree, not the roots. The roots are rationalism, and I would define that word so: "Rationalism is the idea we can ever understand anything about the state of being." It's a deathtrap. It always has been. So you can charge the superflu off to rationalism if you want. But the other reason we're here is the dreams, and the dreams are *irrational*. We've agreed not to talk about that simple fact while we're in committee, but we're not in committee now. So I'll say what we all know is true: We're here under the fiat of powers we don't understand. For me, that means we may be beginning to accept — only subconsciously now, and with plenty of slips backward due to culture lag — a different definition of existence. The idea that we can never understand *anything* about the state of being. And if rationalism is a deathtrip, then *ir*rationalism might very well be a lifetrip . . . at least unless it proves otherwise.'

Speaking very slowly, Stu said: 'Well, I got my superstitions. I been laughed at for it, but I got em. I know it don't make any difference if a guy lights two cigarettes on a match or three, but two don't make me nervous and three does. I don't walk under ladders and I never care to see a black cat cross my path. But to live with no science . . . worshipping the sun, maybe . . . thinking monsters are rolling bowling balls across the sky when it thunders . . . I can't say any of that turns me on very much, baldy. Why, it seems like a kind of slavery to me.'

'But suppose those things were true?' Glen said quietly.

'What?'

'Assume that the age of rationalism has passed. I myself am almost positive that it has. It's come and gone before, you know; it almost left us in the 1960s, the so-called Age of Aquarius, and it took a damn near permanent vacation during the Middle Ages. And suppose . . . suppose that when rationalism does go, it's as if a bright dazzle has gone for a while and we could see . . .' He trailed off, his eyes looking inward.

'See what?' Fran asked.

He raised his eyes to hers; they were gray and strange, seeming to glow with their own inner light.

'Dark magic,' he said softly. 'A universe of marvels where water flows uphill and trolls live in the deepest woods and dragons live under the mountains. Bright wonders, white power. "Lazarus, come forth." Water into wine. And . . . and just maybe . . . the casting out of devils.'

He paused, then smiled.

'The lifetrip.'

'And the dark man?' Fran asked quietly.

Glen shrugged. 'Mother Abagail calls him the Devil's Imp. Maybe he's just the last magician of rational thought, gathering the tools of technology against us. And maybe there's something more, something much darker. I only know that he *is*, and I no longer think that sociology or psychology or any other *ology* will put an end to him. I think only white magic will do that . . . and our white magician is out there someplace, wandering and alone.' Glen's voice nearly broke, and he looked down quickly.

Outside there was only dark, and a breeze coming down from the mountains threw a fresh spatter of rain against the glass of Stu and Fran's living room. Glen was lighting his pipe. Stu had taken a random handful of change from his pocket and was shaking the coins up and down, then opening his hands to see how many had come up heads, how many tails. Nick was making elaborate doodles on the top sheet of his pad, and in his mind he saw the empty streets of Shoyo and heard – yes, heard – a voice whisper: *He's coming for you, mutie. He's closer now.*

After a while Glen and Stu kindled a blaze in the fireplace and they all watched the flames without saying much.

After they were gone, Fran felt low and unhappy. Stu was also in a brown study. He looks tired, she thought. We ought to stay home tomorrow, just stay home and talk to each other and have a nap in the afternoon. We ought to take it easy. She looked at the Coleman gaslamp and wished for electric light instead, bright electric light you got by just flicking a wall switch.

She felt her eyes sting with tears. She told herself angrily not to start, not to add that to their problems, but the part of herself which controlled the waterworks did not seem inclined to listen.

Then, suddenly, Stu brightened. 'By golly! I damn near forgot, didn't I?'

'Forgot what?'

'I'll show you! Stay right here!' He went out the door and clattered down the hall stairs. She went to the doorway and in a moment she could hear him coming back up. He had something in his hand and it was a . . . a . . .

'Stuart Redman, where did you get *that*?' she asked, happily surprised.

'Folk Arts Music,' he said, grinning.

She picked up the washboard and tilted it this way and that. The gleam of light spilled off its bluing. 'Folk –?'

'Down Walnut Street aways.'

'A washboard in a *music* store?'

'Yeah. There was a helluva good washtub, too, but somebody had already poked a hole through it and turned it into a bass.'

She began to laugh. She put the washboard down on the sofa, came to him, and hugged him tight. His hands came up to her breasts and she hugged him tighter still. 'The doctor said give him jug band music,' she whispered.

'Huh?'

She pressed her face against his neck. 'It seems to make him feel just fine. That's what the song says, anyway. Can you make me feel fine, Stu?'

Smiling, he picked her up. 'Well,' he said, 'I guess I could give it a try.'

At quarter past two the next afternoon, Glen Bateman burst straight into the apartment without knocking. Fran was at Lucy Swann's house, where the two women were trying to get a sourdough sponge started. Stu was reading a Max Brand Western. He looked up and saw Glen, his face pale and shocked, his eyes wide, and tossed the book on the floor.

'Stu,' Glen said. 'Oh, man, Stu. I'm glad you're here.'

'What's wrong?' he asked Glen sharply. 'Is it . . . did someone find her?'

'No,' Glen said. He sat down abruptly as if his legs had just given out. 'It's not bad news, it's good news. But it's very strange.'

'What? What is?'

'It's Kojak. I took a nap after lunch and when I got up, Kojak was on the porch, fast asleep. He's beat to shit, Stu, he looks like he's been through a Mixmaster with a set of blunt blades, but it's him.'

'You mean the *dog? That* Kojak?'

'That's who I mean.'

'Are you sure?'

'Same dog-tag that says Woodsville, N. H. Same red collar. Same *dog*. He's really scrawny, and he's been fighting. Dick Ellis – Dick was overjoyed to have an animal to work on for a change – he says he's lost one eye for good. Bad scratches on his sides and belly, some of them infected, but Dick took care of them. Gave him a sedative and taped up his belly. Dick said it looked like he'd tangled with a wolf, maybe more than one. No rabies, anyhow. He's clean.' Glen shook his head slowly, and two tears spilled down his cheeks. 'That damn dog came back to me. I wish to *Christ* I hadn't left him behind to come on his own, Stu. That makes me feel so friggin bad.'

'It couldn't have been done, Glen. Not with the motorcycles.'

'Yes, but . . . he *followed* me, Stu. That's the kind of thing you read about in *Star Weekly* . . . Faithful Dog Follows Master Two Thousand Miles. How could he do a thing like that? How?'

'Maybe the same way we did. Dogs dream, you know – sure they do. Didn't you ever see one lying fast asleep on the kitchen floor, paws twitching away? There was an old guy in Arnette, Vic Palfrey, and he used to say dogs had two dreams, the good dream and the bad one. The good one's when the paws twitch. The bad one's the growling dream. Wake a dog up in the middle of the bad dream, the growling dream, and he's apt to bite you, like as not.'

Glen shook his head in a dazed way. 'You're saying he *dreamed* –'

'I'm not sayin anything funnier than what you were talking last night,' Stu reproached him.

Glen grinned and nodded. 'Oh, I can talk *that* stuff for hours on end. I'm one of the great all-time bullshitters. It's when something actually *happens*.'

'Awake at the lectern and asleep at the switch.'

'Fuck you, East Texas. Want to come over and see my dog?'

'You bet.'

Glen's house was on Spruce Street, about two blocks from the Boulderado Hotel. The climbing ivy on the porch trellis was mostly dead, as were all the lawns and most of the flowers in Boulder – without daily watering from the city mains, the arid climate had triumphed.

On the porch was a small round table holding up a gin and tonic. ('Ain't that pretty horrible stuff without ice?' Stu asked, and Glen answered, 'You don't notice much one way or the other after the third one.') Beside the drink was an ashtray with five pipes in it, copies of *Zen and the Art of Motorcycle Maintenance, Ball Four*, and *My Gun Is Quick* – all of them open to different places. There was also an open bag of Kraft Cheese Kisses.

Kojak was lying on the porch, his tattered snout laid peacefully on his forepaws. The dog was rack-thin and pitifully chewed, but Stu recognized him, even on short acquaintance. He squatted and began to stroke Kojak's head. Kojak woke up and looked happily at Stu. In the way that dogs have, he seemed to grin.

'Say, that's a good dog,' Stu said, feeling a ridiculous lump in his throat. Like a deck of cards swiftly dealt with the faces up, he seemed to see every dog he'd had since his mom had given him Old Spike, when Stu was only five years old. A lot of dogs. Maybe not one for every card in the deck, but still a lot of dogs. A dog was a good thing to have, and so far as he knew, Kojak was the only dog in Boulder. He glanced up at Glen and glanced down quickly. He guessed even old bald sociologists who read three books at a whack didn't like to get caught leaking around the eyes.

'Good dog,' he repeated, and Kojak thumped his tail against the porch boards, presumably agreeing that he was, indeed, a good dog.

'Going inside for a minute,' Glen said thickly. 'Got to use the bathroom.'

'Yeah,' Stu said, not looking up. 'Hey, good boy, say, ole Kojak, wasn't you a good boy? Ain't you a one?'

Kojak's tail thumped agreeably.

'Can you roll over? Play dead, boy. Roll over.'

Kojak obediently rolled over on his back, rear legs splayed out, front paws in the air. Stu's face grew concerned as he ran his hand gently over the stiff white concertina of bandage Dick Ellis had put on. Farther up, he could see red and puffy-looking scratches that undoubtedly deepened to gores under the bandages. Something had been at him, all right, and it hadn't been some other wandering dog. A dog would have gone for the muzzle or the throat. What had happened to Kojak was the work of something lower than a dog. More sneaking. Wolfpack, maybe, but Stu doubted if Kojak could have gotten away from a pack. Whatever, he had been lucky not to be disemboweled.

The screen banged as Glen came back out on the porch.

'Whatever it was got at him didn't miss his vitals by much,' Stu said.

'The wounds were deep and he lost a lot of blood,' Glen agreed. 'I just can't get over thinking that I was the one who let him in for that.'

'And Dick said wolves.'

'Wolves or maybe coyotes . . . but he thought it was unlikely coyotes would have done such a job, and I agree.'

Stu patted Kojak on the rump and Kojak rolled back onto his belly. 'How is it almost all the dogs are gone and there's still enough wolves in one place – and east of the Rockies, at that – to set on a good dog like this?'

'I guess we'll never know,' Glen said. 'Any more than we'll know why the goddamned plague took the horses but not the cows and most of the people but not us. I'm not even going to think about it. I'm just going to lay in a big supply of Gainesburgers and keep him fed.'

'Yeah.' Stu looked at Kojak, whose eyes had slipped closed. 'He's tore up, but his doings are still intact – I saw that when he rolled over. We could do worse than to keep our eye out for a bitch, you know it?'

'Yes, that's so,' Glen said thoughtfully. 'Want a warm gin and tonic, East Texas?'

'Hell, no. I may never have gone any further than one year of vocational-technical school, but I'm no fucking barbarian. Got a beer?'

'Oh, I think I can scare up a can of Coors. Warm, though.'

'Sold.' He started to follow Glen into the house, then paused with the screen door in his hand to look back at the sleeping dog. 'You sleep good, ole boy,' he told the dog. 'Good to have you here.'

He and Glen went inside.

*   *   *

But Kojak wasn't asleep.

He lay somewhere between, where most living things spend a good deal of time when they are hurt badly, but not badly enough to be in the mortal shadow. A deep itch lay in his belly like heat, the itch of healing. Glen would have to spend a good many hours trying to distract him from that itch so he wouldn't scratch off the bandages, reopen the wounds, and reinfect them. But that was later. Just now Kojak (who still thought of himself occasionally as Big Steve, which had been his original name) was content to drift in the place in between. The wolves had come for him in Nebraska, while he was still sniffing dejectedly around the house on jacklifters in the little town of Hemingford Home. The scent of THE MAN – the *feel* of THE MAN – led to this place and then stopped. Where had he gone? Kojak didn't know. And then the wolves, four of them, had come out of the corn like ragged spirits of the dead. Their eyes blazed at Kojak, and their lips wrinkled back from their teeth to let out the low, ripping growls of their intent. Kojak had retreated before them, growling himself, his paws stiff-out and digging at the dirt of Mother Abagail's dooryard. To the left hung the tire-swing, casting its depthless round shadow. The lead wolf had attacked just as Kojak's hind-quarters slipped into the shadow cast by the porch. It came in low, going for the belly, and the others followed. Kojak sprang up and over the leader's snapping muzzle, giving the wolf his underbelly, and as the leader began to bite and scratch, Kojak fastened his own teeth in the wolf's neck, his teeth sinking deep, letting blood, and the wolf howled and tried to struggle away, its courage suddenly gone. As it pulled away, Kojak's jaws closed with lightning speed on the wolf's tender muzzle, and the wolf uttered a howling, abject scream as its nose was laid open to the nostrils and pulled to strings and tatters. It fled yipping with agony, shaking its head crazily from side to side, spraying droplets of blood to the left and right, and in the crude telepathy that all animals of like kind share, Kojak could read its over-and-over thought clearly enough:

(wasps in me o the wasps the wasps in my head wasps are up my head o)

And then the others hit him, one from the left and another from the right like huge blunt bullets, the last of the trio submarining in low, grinning, snapping, ready to pull out his intestines. Kojak had broken to the right, baying hoarsely, wanting to deal with that one first so he could get under the porch. If he could get under the porch he could stand them off, maybe forever. Lying on the porch now he relived the battle in a kind of slow motion: the growls and howls, the strikes and withdrawals, the smell of blood that had gotten into his brain and gradually turned him into a kind of fighting machine, unaware of his own wounds until later. He sent the wolf that had been on his right the way of the first, one of its eyes dead and a huge, gouting, and probably mortal wound in the side of its throat. But the wolf had done its own damage in return; most of it was superficial, but two of the gores were extremely deep, wounds that would heal to hard and twisting scar-tissue like a scrawling lowercase *t*. Even when he was an old, old dog (and Kojak lived another sixteen years, long after Glen Bateman died), those scars would pain and throb on wet days. He had fought free, had scrambled under the porch, and when one of the two remaining wolves, overcome with bloodlust, tried to wriggle in after him, Kojak sprang on it, pinned it, and ripped its throat out. The other retreated almost to the edge of the corn, whining uneasily. If Kojak had come out to do battle, it would have fled with its tail between its legs. But Kojak didn't come out, not then. He was done in. He could only lie on his side, panting rapidly and weakly, licking his wounds and growling deep in his chest whenever he saw the shadow of the remaining wolf draw near. Then it was dark, and a misty halfmoon rode the sky over Nebraska. And each time the last wolf heard Kojak alive and presumably still ready to fight, it shied away, whining. Sometime after midnight it left, leaving Kojak alone to see if he would live or die. In the early morning hours he had felt the presence of some other animal, something that terrified him into a series of soft whimpers. It was a thing in the corn, a thing walking in the corn, hunting for him, perhaps. Kojak lay shivering, waiting to see if this thing would find him, this horrible thing that felt like a Man and a Wolf and an Eye, some dark thing like an ancient crocodile in the corn. Some unknown time later, after the moon went down, Kojak felt that it was gone. He fell asleep. He had lain up under the porch for three days, coming out only when hunger and thirst drove him out. There was always a puddle of water gathered below the lip of the handpump in the yard, and in the house there were all sorts of rich scraps, many of them from the meal Mother Abagail had cooked for Nick's party. When Kojak felt he could go on, he knew where to go. It was not a scent that told him; it was a deep sense of heat that had come out of his own deep and mortal time, a glowing pocket of heat to the west of him. And so he came, limping most of the last five hundred miles on three legs, the pain always gnawing at his belly. From time to time he was able to smell THE MAN, and thus knew he was on the right track. And at last he was here. THE MAN was here. There were no wolves here. Food was here. There was no sense of that dark Thing . . . the Man with the stink of a wolf and the feel of an Eye that could see you over long miles if it happened to turn your way. For now, things were fine. And so thinking (so far as dogs can think in their careful relating to a world seen almost wholly through feelings), Kojak drifted down deeper, now into real sleep, now into a dream, a good dream of chasing rabbits through the clover and timothy grass that was belly-high and wet with soothing dew. His name was Big Steve. This was the north forty. And oh the rabbits are everywhere this gray and endless morning –

As he dreamed, his paws twitched.

CHAPTER 53

Excerpts from the Minutes of the Ad Hoc Committee Meeting
August 17, 1990

This meeting was held at the home of Larry Underwood on South Forty-second Street in the Table Mesa area. All members of the committee were present . . .

The first item of business concerned having the ad hoc committee elected as the permanent Boulder Committee. Fran Goldsmith was recognized.

Fran: 'Both Stu and I agreed that the best, easiest way for us all to get elected would be if Mother Abagail endorsed the whole slate. It would save us the problem of having twenty people nominated by their friends and possibly upsetting the applecart. But now we'll have to do it another way. I'm not going to suggest anything that isn't perfectly democratic, and you all know the plan anyway, but I just want to re-emphasize that each of us has to make sure we have someone who will nominate and second us. We won't do it for each other, obviously – that would look too much like the Mafia. And if you can't find one person to nominate you and another to second you, you might as well give up anyway.'

Sue: 'Wow! That's sneaky, Fran.'

Fran: 'Yes – it is, a little.'

Glen: 'We're edging back into the subject of the committee's morality, and although I'm sure we all find that an endlessly fascinating topic, I'd like to see it tabled for the next few months. I think we just have to agree that we're serving in the Free Zone's best interest and leave it at that.'

Ralph: 'You sound a little pissed, Glen.'

Glen: 'I *am* a little pissed. I admit it. The very fact that we've spent so much time eating at our own livers on this subject should give a pretty good indication as to where our hearts are.'

Sue: 'The road to hell is paved with –'

Glen: 'Good intentions, yes, and since we all seem so worried about our intentions, we must surely be on the highway to heaven.'

Glen then said that he had intended to address the committee on the subject of our scouts or spies or whatever you want to call them, but that he wanted to make a motion instead that we meet to discuss that on the nineteenth. Stu asked him why.

Glen: 'Because we might not all be here on the nineteenth. Somebody might get voted out. It's a remote possibility, but no one really knows what a large group of people is going to do when they all get together in one place. We ought to be as careful as we can.'

That was good for a moment of silence, and the committee voted, 7–0, to meet on the nineteenth – as a Permanent Committee – to discuss the question of the scouts . . . or spies . . . or whatever.

Stu was recognized to put a third item of business before the committee, concerning Mother Abagail.

Stu: 'As you know, she's gone off for reasons of her own. Her note says she'll "be gone for a while," which is pretty vague, and that she'll be back "if it's God's will." Now, that's not very encouraging. We've had a search-party out for three days now and we haven't found a thing. We don't want to just drag her back, not if she doesn't want to come, but if she's lying up somewhere with a busted leg or if she's unconscious, that's a lot different. Now part of the problem is that there just aren't enough of us to search all the wildlands around here. But another part of it is the same thing that's slowing us down at the power station. There's just no organization. So what I'm looking for is permission to put this search-party on the agenda of the big meeting tomorrow night, same as the power station and the burial crew. And I'd like to see Harold Lauder in charge, because it was his idea in the first place.'

Glen said that he didn't think any search-party was going to find very good news after a week or so. After all, the lady in question is a hundred and eight years old. The committee as a whole agreed with that, and then voted in favor of the motion, 7–0, as Stu had put it. To make this record as honest as possible, I should add there were several expressions of doubt over putting Harold in charge . . . but as Stu pointed out, it had been his idea to begin with, and not to give him command of the search-party would be a direct slap in the face.

Nick: 'I withdraw my objection to Harold, but not my basic reservations. I just don't like him very much.'

Ralph Brentner asked if either Stu or Glen would write out Stu's motion about the search-party so he could add it to the agenda, which he plans to print at the high school tonight. Stu said he'd be glad to.

Larry Underwood then moved that we adjourn, Ralph seconded it, and it was voted, 7–0.

Frances Goldsmith, Secretary

The turnout for the meeting the next evening was almost total, and for the first time Larry Underwood, who had been in the Zone only a week, got an idea of just how large the community was becoming.

It was one thing to see people coming and going on the streets, usually alone or by twos, and quite another thing to see them all gathered together in one place – Chautauqua Auditorium. The place was full, every seat taken and more people sitting in the aisles and standing at the back of the hall. They were a curiously subdued crowd, murmuring but not babbling. For the first time since he had gotten to Boulder it had rained all day long, a soft drizzle that seemed to hang suspended in the air, fogging you rather than wetting you, and even with the assemblage of close to six hundred, you could hear the quiet sound of rain on the roof. The loudest sound inside was the constant riffle of paper as people looked at the mimeographed agendas that had been piled up on two card tables just inside the double doors.

This agenda read:

THE BOULDER FREE ZONE
Open Meeting Agenda
August 18th, 1990

1. To see if the Free Zone will agree to read and ratify the Constitution of the United States of America.
2. To see if the Free Zone will agree to read and ratify the Bill of Rights to the Constitution of the United States of America.
3. To see if the Free Zone will nominate and elect a slate of seven Free Zone representatives to serve as a governing board.
4. To see if the Free Zone will agree to veto power for Abagail Freemantle on any and all matters agreed to by the Free Zone representatives.
5. To see if the Free Zone will approve a Burial Committee of at least twenty persons initially to decently inter those who died of the superflu epidemic in Boulder.
6. To see if the Free Zone will approve a Power Committee of at least sixty persons initially to get the electricity back on before cold weather.
7. To see if the Free Zone will approve a Search Committee of at least fifteen persons, its purpose to find the whereabouts of Abagail Freemantle, if possible.

Larry found that his nervous hands had been busy folding this agenda, which he knew nearly word for word, into a paper airplane. Being on the ad hoc committee was sort of fun, like a game –

children playing at parliamentary process in someone's living room, sitting around and drinking Cokes, having a piece of the cake Frannie had made, talking things over. Even the part about sending spies over the mountains and right into the dark man's lap had seemed like a game, partly because it was a thing he couldn't imagine doing himself. You'd have to have lost most of your marbles to face such a living nightmare. But in their closed sessions, with the room comfortably lit with Coleman gas lanterns, it had seemed okay. And if the Judge or Dayna Jurgens or Tom Cullen got caught, it seemed – in those closed sessions, at least – a thing no more important than losing a rook or a queen in a chess game.

But now, sitting halfway down the hall with Lucy on one side and Leo on the other (he had not seen Nadine all day, and Leo didn't seem to know where she was, either; 'Out' had been his disinterested response), the truth of it came home, and in his guts it felt as if a battering ram was in use. It was no game. There were five hundred and eighty people here and most of them didn't have any idea that Larry Underwood wasn't no nice guy, or that the first person Larry Underwood had attempted to take care of after the epidemic had died of a drug overdose.

His hands were damp and chilly. They were trying to fold the agenda into a paper plane again and he stopped them. Lucy took one of them, squeezed it, and smiled at him. He was able to respond only with something that felt like a grimace, and in his heart he heard his mother's voice: *There's something left out of you, Larry.*

Thinking of that made him feel panicky. Was there a way out of this, or had things already gone too far? He didn't want this millstone. He had already made a motion in closed session that could send Judge Farris to his death. If he was voted out and someone else was voted into his seat, they'd have to take another vote on sending the Judge, wouldn't they? Sure they would. And they'd vote to send someone else. When Laurie Constable nominates me, I'll just stand up and say I decline. Sure, nobody can force me, can they? Not if I decide I want out. And who the fuck needs this kind of hassle?

Wayne Stukey on that long ago beach saying: *There's something in you that's like biting on tinfoil.*

Quietly, Lucy said: 'You'll be fine.'

He jumped. 'Huh?'

'I said you'll be fine. Won't he, Leo?'

'Oh yes,' Leo said, bobbing his head. His eyes never left the audience, as if they had not yet been able to communicate its size to his brain. 'Fine.'

You don't understand, you numb broad, Larry thought. You're holding my hand and you don't understand that I could make a bad decision and wind up killing both of you. I'm well on my way to killing Judge Farris and he's seconding my fucking nomination. What a Polish firedrill this turned out to be. A little sound escaped his throat.

'Did you say something?' Lucy asked.

'No.'

Then Stu was walking across the stage to the podium, his red sweater and bluejeans very bright and clear in the harsh glow of the emergency lights, which were running from a Honda generator that Brad Kitchner and part of his crew from the power station had set up. The applause started somewhere in the middle of the hall, Larry was never sure where, and a cynical part of him was always convinced that it had been a plot arranged by Glen Bateman, their resident expert in the art/craft of crowd management. At any rate, it didn't really matter. The first solitary spats swelled to a thunder of applause. On the stage, Stu paused by the podium, looking comically amazed. The applause was joined by cheers and shrill whistles.

Then the entire audience rose to its feet, the applause swelling to a sound like heavy rain, and people were shouting, *'Bravo! Bravo!'* Stu held up his hands, but they wouldn't stop; if anything, the sound redoubled in intensity. Larry glanced sideways at Lucy and saw she was applauding strenuously, her eyes fixed on Stu, her mouth curved in a trembling but triumphant smile. She was crying. On his other side Leo was also applauding, bringing his hands together again and again with so much force that Larry thought they would fall off if Leo kept on much longer. In the extremity of his joy, Leo's carefully won-back vocabulary had deserted him, the way English will sometimes desert a man or woman who has learned it as his or her second tongue. He could only hoot loudly and enthusiastically.

Brad and Ralph had also run a PA from the generator and now Stu blew into the mike and then spoke: 'Ladies and gentlemen —'

But the applause rolled on.

'Ladies and gentlemen, if you'll take your seats —'

But they were not ready to take their seats. The applause roared on and on, and Larry looked down because his own hands hurt, and he saw that he was applauding as frantically as the rest.

'Ladies and gentlemen –'

The applause thundered and echoed. Overhead, a family of barnswallows that had taken up residence in this fine and private place after the plague struck now flew about crazily, swooping and diving, mad to get away to someplace where people weren't.

We're applauding ourselves, Larry thought. We're applauding the fact that we're here, alive, together. Maybe we're saying hello to the group self again, I don't know. Hello, Boulder. Finally. Good to be here, great to be alive.

'Ladies and gentlemen, if you'd take your seats, please, I sure would appreciate it.'

The applause began to taper off little by little. Now you could hear ladies – and some men, too – sniffing. Noses were honked. Conversations were whispered. There was that rustling auditorium sound of people taking their seats.

'I'm glad you're all here,' Stu said. 'I'm glad to be here myself.' There was a whine of feedback from the PA and Stu muttered, 'Goddam thing,' which was clearly picked up and broadcast. There was a ripple of laughter and Stu colored. 'Guess we're all going to have to get used to this stuff again,' he said, and that set off another burst of applause.

When that had run itself out, Stu said: 'For those of you who don't know me, I'm Stuart Redman, originally from Arnette, Texas, although that seems a far way down the road from where I am now, lemme tell you.' He cleared his throat, feedback whined briefly, and he took a wary step back from the mike. 'I'm also pretty nervous up here, so bear with me –'

'We will, Stu!' Harry Dunbarton yelled exuberantly, and there was appreciative laughter. It's like a camp meeting, Larry thought. Next they'll be singing hymns. If Mother Abagail was here, I bet we would be already.

'Last time I had so many people looking at me was when our little consolidated high school made it to the football playoffs, and then they had twenty-one other guys to look at too, not to mention some girls in those little tiny skirts.'

A hearty burst of laughter.

Lucy pulled at Larry's neck and whispered in his ear, 'What was he worried about? He's a natural!'

Larry nodded.

'But if you'll bear with me, I'll get through it somehow,' Stu said.

More applause. This crowd would applaud Nixon's resignation speech and ask him to encore on the piano, Larry thought.

'First off, I should explain about the ad hoc committee and how I happen to be up here at all,' Stu said. 'There are seven of us who got together and planned for this meeting so we could get organized somehow. There's a lot of things to do, and I'd like to introduce each member of our committee to you now, and I hope you saved some applause for them, because they all pitched together to work out the agenda you've got in your hands right now. First, Miss Frances Goldsmith. Stand up, Frannie, and let em see what you look like with a dress on.'

Fran stood up. She was wearing a pretty kelly-green dress and a modest string of pearls that might have cost two thousand dollars in the old days. She was roundly applauded, the applause accompanied by some good-natured wolf whistles.

Fran sat down, blushing furiously, and before the applause could die away entirely, Stu went on. 'Mr Glen Bateman, from Woodsville, New Hampshire.'

Glen stood, and they applauded him. He flipped a pair of twin *v*'s from each of his closed fists, and the crowd roared its approval.

Stu introduced Larry second-to-last and he stood up, aware that Lucy was smiling up at him, and then that was lost in a warm comber of applause that washed over him. Once, he thought, in another world, there would have been concerts, and this kind of applause would have been reserved for the show-closer, a little nothing tune called 'Baby, Can You Dig Your Man?' This was better. He only stood for a second, but it seemed much longer. He knew he would not decline his nomination.

Stu introduced Nick last, and he got the longest, loudest applause.

When it died away, Stu said: 'This wasn't on the agenda, but I wonder if we could start by singing the National Anthem. I guess you folks remember the words and the tune.'

There was that ruffling, shuffling sound of people getting to their feet. Another pause as everyone waited for someone else to start. Then a girl's sweet voice rose in the air, solo for only the first three syllables: 'Oh, say can —' It was Frannie's voice, but for a moment it seemed to Larry to be underlaid by another voice, his own, and the place was not Boulder but upstate Vermont and the day was July 4, the Republic was two hundred and fourteen years old, and Rita lay dead in the tent behind him, her mouth filled with green puke and a bottle of pills in her stiffening hand.

A chill of gooseflesh passed over him and suddenly he felt that they were being watched, watched by something that could, in the words of that old song by The Who, see for miles and miles and miles. Something awful and dark and alien. For just a moment he felt an urge to run from this place, just run and never stop. This was no game they were playing here. This was serious business; killing business. Maybe worse.

Then other voices joined in. '– can you see, by the dawn's early light,' and Lucy was singing, holding his hand, crying again, and others were crying, most of them were crying, crying for what was lost and bitter, the runaway American dream, chrome-wheeled, fuel-injected, and stepping out over the line, and suddenly his memory was not of Rita, dead in the tent, but of he and his mother at Yankee Stadium – it was September 29, the Yankees were only a game and a half behind the Red Sox, and all things were still possible. There were fifty-five thousand people in the Stadium, all standing, the players in the field with their caps over their hearts, Guidry on the mound, Rickey Henderson was standing in deep left field ('– by the twilight's last gleaming –'), and the light-standards were on in the purple gloaming, moths and night-fliers banging softly against them, and New York was around them, teeming, city of night and light.

Larry joined the singing too, and when it was done and the applause rolled out once more, he was crying a bit himself. Rita was gone. Alice Underwood was gone. New York was gone. *America* was gone. Even if they could defeat Randall Flagg, whatever they might make would never be the same as that world of dark streets and bright dreams.

Sweating freely under the bright emergency lights, Stu called the first items: reading and ratification of the Constitution and the Bill of Rights. The singing of the anthem had also affected him deeply, and he wasn't alone. Half the audience, more, was in tears.

No one asked for an actual reading of either document – which would have been their right under the parliamentary process – for which Stu was profoundly grateful. He wasn't much of a reader. The 'reading' section of each item was approved by the Free Zone citizens. Glen Bateman rose and moved that they accept both documents as governing Free Zone law.

A voice in the back said, 'Second that!'

'Moved and seconded,' Stu said. 'Those in favor say aye.'

'*AYE!*' to the rooftops. Kojak, who had been sleeping by Glen's chair, looked up, blinked, and then laid his muzzle on his paws again. A moment later he looked up again as the crowd gave themselves a thunderous round of applause. They like voting, Stu thought. It makes them feel like they're finally in control of something again. God knows they need that feeling. We all need it.

That preliminary taken care of, Stu felt tension worm into his muscles. Now, he thought, we'll see if there are any nasty surprises waiting for us.

'The third item on your agenda reads,' he began, and then he had to clear his throat again. Feedback whined at him, making him sweat even more. Fran was looking calmly up at him, nodding for him to go on. 'It reads, "To see if the Free Zone will nominate and elect a slate of seven Free Zone representatives." That means –'

'Mr Chairman? Mr Chairman!'

Stu looked up from his jotted notes and felt a real jolt of fear, accompanied by something like a premonition. It was Harold Lauder. Harold was dressed in a suit and a tie, his hair was neatly combed, and he was standing halfway up the middle aisle. Once Glen had said he thought the opposition might coalesce around Harold. But so soon? He hoped not. For just a moment he thought wildly of not recognizing Harold – but both Nick and Glen had warned him of the dangers inherent in making any part of this look like a railroad job. He wondered if he had been wrong about Harold turning over a new leaf. It looked as if he was going to find out right here.

'Chair recognizes Harold Lauder.'

Heads turned, necks craned to see Harold better.

'I'd like to move that we accept the slate of ad hoc committee members in toto as the Permanent Committee. If they'll serve, that is.' Harold sat down.

There was a moment of silence. Stu thought crazily: *Toto? Toto? Wasn't that the dog in* The Wizard of Oz?

Then the applause swelled out again, filling the room, and dozens of cries of 'I second!' rang out. Harold was sitting placidly in his seat again, smiling and talking to the people who were thumping him on the back.

Stu brought his gavel down half a dozen times for order.

He planned this, Stu thought. *These people are going to elect us, but it's Harold they'll remember. Still, he got to the root of the thing in a way none of us thought of, not even Glen. It was pretty damn near a stroke of genius.* So why should he be so upset? Was he jealous, maybe? Were his good resolutions about Harold, made only the day before yesterday, already going by the boards?

'There's a motion on the floor,' he blared into the mike, ignoring the feedback whine this time. 'Motion on the floor, folks!' He pounded the gavel and they quieted to a low babble. 'It's been moved and seconded that we accept the ad hoc committee just as it stands as the Permanent Free Zone Committee. Before we go to a discussion of the motion or to a vote, I ought to ask if anyone now serving on the committee has an objection or would like to step down.'

Silence from the floor.

'Very well,' Stu said. 'Discussion of the motion?'

'I don't think we need any, Stu,' Dick Ellis said. 'It's a grand idea. Let's vote!'

Applause greeted this, and Stu needed no further urging. Charlie Impening was waving his hand to be recognized, but Stu ignored him – a good case of selective perception, Glen Bateman would have said – and called the question.

'Those in favour of Harold Lauder's motion please signify by saying aye.'

'*Aye!!*' they bellowed, sending the barnswallows into another frenzy.

'Opposed?'

But no one was, not even Charlie Impening – at least, vocally. There was not a nay in the chamber. So Stu pushed on to the next item of business, feeling slightly dazed, as if someone – namely, Harold Lauder – had crept up behind him and clopped him one on the head with a large sledgehammer made out of Silly Putty.

'Let's get off and push them awhile, want to?' Fran asked. She sounded tired.

'Sure.' He got off his bike and walked along beside her. 'You okay, Fran? The baby bothering?'

'No. I'm just tired. It's quarter of one in the morning, or hadn't you noticed?'

'Yeah, it's late,' Stu agreed, and they pushed their bikes side by side in companionable silence. The meeting had gone on until an hour ago, most of the discussion centering on the search-party for Mother Abagail. The other items had all passed with a minimum of discussion, although Judge Farris had provided a fascinating piece of information that explained why there were so relatively few bodies in Boulder. According to the last four issues of the *Camera*, Boulder's daily newspaper, a wild rumor had swept the community, a rumor that the superflu had originated in the Boulder Air Testing facility on Broadway. Spokesmen for the center – the few still on their feet – protested that it was utter nonsense, and anyone who doubted it was free to tour the facility, where they would find nothing more dangerous than air pollution indicators and wind-vectoring devices. In spite of this, the rumor persisted, probably fed by the hysterical temper of those terrible days in late June. The Air Testing Center had been either bombed or burned, and much of Boulder's population had fled.

Both the Burial Committee and the Power Committee had been passed with an amendment from Harold Lauder – who had seemed almost awesomely prepared for the meeting – to the effect that each committee be increased by two for each increase of one hundred in the total Free Zone population.

The Search Committee was also voted with no opposition, but the discussion of Mother Abagail's disappearance had been a protracted one. Glen had advised Stu before the meeting not to limit discussion on this topic unless absolutely necessary; it was worrying all of them, especially the idea that their spiritual leader believed she had committed some sort of sin. Best to let them get it off their chests.

On the back of her note, the old woman had scrawled two biblical references: Proverbs 11: 1–3, and Proverbs 21: 28–31. Judge Farris had searched these out with the careful diligence of a lawyer preparing a brief, and at the beginning of the discussion, he rose and read them in his cracked and apocalyptic old man's voice. The verses in the eleventh chapter of Proverbs stated, 'A false balance is an abomination of the Lord: but a just weight is his delight. When pride cometh, then cometh shame: but with the lowly is wisdom. The integrity of the upright shall guide them: but the perverseness of transgressors shall destroy them.' The quotation from the twenty-first chapter was in a similar vein: 'A false witness shall perish, but the man that heareth speaketh constantly. A wicked man hardeneth his face, but as for the upright, he directeth his way. There is no wisdom nor understanding nor counsel against the Lord. The horse is prepared against the day of battle: but safety is of the Lord.'

The talk following the Judge's oration (it could be called nothing else) of these two Scriptural tidbits had ranged over far-reaching – and often comical – ground. One man stated ominously that if the chapter numbers were added, you came out with thirty-one, the number of chapters in the Book of Revelations. Judge Farris rose again to say that the Book of Revelations had only twenty-two chapters, at least in *his* Bible, and that, in any case, twenty-one and eleven added up to thirty-two, not thirty-one. The aspiring numerologist muttered but said no more.

Another fellow stated that he had seen lights in the sky the night before Mother Abagail's disappearance and that the Prophet Isaiah had confirmed the existence of flying saucers . . . so they'd better put that in their collective pipe and smoke it, hadn't they? Judge Farris rose once more, this time to point out that the previous gentleman had mistaken Isaiah for Ezekiel, that the exact reference was not to flying saucers but to 'a wheel within a wheel,' and that the Judge himself was of the opinion that the only flying saucers yet proven were those that sometimes flew during marital spats.

Much of the other discussions was a rehash of the dreams, which had ceased altogether, as far as anyone knew, and now seemed rather dreamlike themselves. Person after person rose to protest the charge that Mother Abagail had laid upon herself, that of pride. They spoke of her courtesy and her ability to put a person at ease with just a word or a sentence. Ralph Brentner, who looked awed by the size of the crowd and was nearly tongue-tied – but determined to speak his piece – rose and spoke in that vein for nearly five minutes, adding at the end that he had not known a finer woman since his mother had died. When he sat down, he seemed very near tears.

When taken together, the discussion reminded Stu uncomfortably of a wake. It told him that in their hearts, they had already come halfway to giving her up. If she did return now, Abby Freemantle would find herself welcomed, still sought after, still listened to . . . but she would also find, Stu thought, that her position was subtly changed. If a showdown between her and the Free Zone Committee came, it was no longer a foregone conclusion that she would win, veto power or not. She had gone away and the community had continued to exist. The community would not forget that, as they had already half forgotten the power the dreams had once briefly held over their lives.

After the meeting, more than two dozen people had sat for a while on the lawn behind Chautauqua Hall; the rain had stopped, the clouds were tattering, and the evening was pleasantly cool. Stu and Frannie had sat with Larry, Lucy, Leo, and Harold.

'You darn near knocked us out of the ballpark this evening,' Larry told Harold. He nudged Frannie with an elbow. 'I told you he was ace high, didn't I?'

Harold had merely smiled and shrugged modestly. 'A couple of ideas, that's all. You seven have started things moving again. You should at least have the privilege of seeing it through to the end of the beginning.'

Now, fifteen minutes after the two of them had left that impromptu gathering and still ten minutes from home, Stu repeated: 'You sure you're feeling okay?'

'Yes. My legs are a little tired, that's all.'

'You want to take it easy, Frances.'

'Don't call me that, you know I hate it.'

'I'm sorry. I won't do it again. Frances.'

'All men are bastards.'

'I'm going to try and improve my act, Frances – honest I am.'

She showed him her tongue, which came to an interesting point, but he could tell her heart wasn't in the banter, and he dropped it. She looked pale and rather listless, a startling contrast to the Frannie who had sung the National Anthem with such heart a few hours earlier.

'Something giving you the blues, honey?'

She shook her head no, but he thought he saw tears in her eyes.

'What is it? Tell me.'

'It's nothing. That's what's the matter. Nothing is what's bothering me. It's over, and I finally realized it, that's all. Less than six hundred people singing "The Star-Spangled Banner." It just kind of hit me all at once. No hotdog stands. The Ferris wheel isn't going around and around at Coney Island tonight. No one's having a nightcap at the Space Needle in Seattle. Someone finally found a way to clean up the dope in Boston's Combat Zone and the chicken-ranch business in Times Square. Those were terrible things, but I think the cure was a lot worse than the disease. Know what I mean?'

'Yeah, I do.'

'In my diary I had a little section called "Things to Remember." So the baby would know . . . oh, all the things he never will. And it gives me the blues, thinking of that. I should have called it "Things That Are Gone." She did sob a little, stopping her bike so she could put the back of her hand to her mouth and try to keep it in.

'It got everybody the same way,' Stu said, putting an arm around her. 'Lot of people are going to cry themselves to sleep tonight. You better believe it.'

'I don't see how you can grieve for a whole country,' she said, crying harder, 'but I guess you can. These . . . these little things keep shooting through my mind. Car salesmen. Frank Sinatra. Old Orchard Beach in July, all crowded with people, most of them from Quebec. That stupid guy on MTV – Randy, I think his name was. The times . . . oh God, I sound like a fuh-fuh-frigging Rod Muh-McKuen poem!'

He held her, patting her back, remembering one time when his Aunt Betty had gotten a crying fit over some bread that didn't rise – she was big with his little cousin Laddie then, seven months or so – and Stu could remember her wiping her eyes with the corner of a dishtowel and telling him to never mind, any pregnant woman was just two doors down from the mental ward because the juices their glands put out were always scrambled up into a stew.

After a while Frannie said, 'Okay. Okay. Better. Let's go.'

'Frannie, I love you,' he said. They resumed pushing their bikes.

She asked him, 'What do you remember best? What's the one thing?'

'Well, you know –' he said, and then stopped with a little laugh.

'No, I don't know, Stuart.'

'It's crazy.'

'Tell me.'

'I don't know if I want to. You'll start looking for the guys with the butterfly nets.'

'*Tell* me!' She had seen Stu in many moods, but this curious, embarrassed uneasiness was new to her.

'I never told anybody,' he said, 'but I *have* been thinking on it the last couple of weeks. Something happened to me back in 1982. I was pumping gas at Bill Hapscomb's gas station then. He used to hire me on, if he could, when I was laid off at the calculator plant in town. He had me on part-time, eleven PM to closing, which was three in the morning back in those days. There wasn't much business after the people getting off the three-to-eleven shift at the Dixie Paper factory stopped to get their gas . . . lots of nights there wasn't a single car stopped between twelve and three. I'd sit there and read a book or a magazine, and lots of nights I'd doze off. You know?'

'Yes.' She did know. In her mind's eye she could see him, the man who would become her man in the fullness of time and the peculiarity of events, a broad-shouldered man sleeping in a plastic Woolco chair with a book open and facedown on his lap. She saw him sleeping in an island of white light, an island surrounded by a great inland sea of Texas night. She loved him in this picture, as she loved him in all the pictures her mind drew.

'Well, this one night it was about quarter past two, and I was sitting behind Hap's desk with my feet up, reading some Western – Louis L'Amour, Elmore Leonard, someone like that, and in pulls this big old Pontiac with all the windows rolled down and the tape-player going like mad, playing Hank Williams. I even remember the song – it was "Movin' On." This guy, not young and not old, is all by himself. He was a good-lookin man, but in a way that was a little scary – I mean, he looked like he might do scary things without thinkin very hard about em. He had bushy, curly dark hair. There was a bottle of wine snugged down between his legs and a pair of Styrofoam dice hanging from the rearview mirror. He says, "High test," and I said okay, but for a minute I just stood there and looked at him. Because he looked familiar. I was playin place the face.'

They were on the corner now; their apartment building was across the street. They paused there. Frannie was looking at him closely.

'So I said, "Don't I know you? Ain't you from up around Corbett or Maxin?" But it didn't really seem like I knew him from those two towns. And he says, "No, but I passed through Corbett once with my family, when I was just a kid. It seems like I passed through just about everyplace in America when I was a kid. My dad was in the Air Force."

'So I went back and filled up his car, and all the time I'm thinkin about him, playin place the face, and all at once it came to me. All at once I knew. And I damned near pissed myself, because the man behind the wheel of that Pontiac was supposed to be dead.'

'Who was he, Stuart? Who *was* he?'

'No, you let me tell it my way, Frannie. Not that it isn't a crazy story no matter what way you tell it. I went back to the window and I says, "That'll be six dollars and thirty cents." He gave me two five-dollar bills and told me I could keep the change. And I says, "I think I might have you placed now." And he says, "Well, maybe you do," and he gives me this weird, chilly smile, and all the time Hank Williams is singin about goin to town. I says, "If you are who I think you are, you're supposed to be dead." He says, "You don't want to believe everything you read, man." I says, "You like Hank Williams all right?" It was all I could think of to say. Because I saw, Frannie, if I didn't say something, he was just going to roll up that power window and go tooling on down the road . . . and I wanted him to go, but I also *didn't* want him to go. Not yet. Not until I was sure. I didn't know then that a person is never sure about a lot of things, no matter how much he wants to be.

'He says, "Hank Williams is one of the best. I like road-house music." Then he says, "I'm going to New Orleans, going to drive all night, sleep all day tomorrow, then barrel-house all night long. Is it the same? New Orleans?" And I say, "As what?" And he says, "Well, you know." And I say, "Well, it's all the South, you know, although there are considerable more trees down that way." And that makes him laugh. He says, "Maybe I'll see you again." But I didn't want to see him again, Frannie. Because he had the eyes of a man who has been trying to look into the dark for a long time and has maybe begun to see what is there. I think, if I ever see that man Flagg, his eyes might look a little like that.'

Stu shook his head as they pushed their bikes across the road and parked them. 'I've been thinking of that. I thought about getting some of his records after that, but I didn't want them. His voice . . . it's a good voice, but it gives me the creeps.'

'Stuart, who are you *talking* about?'

'You remember a rock and roll group called The Doors? The man that stopped that night for gas in Arnette was Jim Morrison. I'm sure of it.'

Her mouth dropped open. 'But he died! He died in France! He —' And then she stopped. Because there had been something funny about Morrison's death, hadn't there? Something secret.

'Did he?' Stu asked. 'I wonder. Maybe he did, and the fellow I saw was just a guy who looked like him, but –'

'Do you really think it was?' she asked.

They were sitting on the steps of their building now, shoulders touching, like small children waiting for their mother to call them in to supper.

'Yeah,' he said. 'Yeah, I do. And until this summer, I thought that would always be the strangest thing that ever happened to me. Boy, was I wrong.'

'And you never told anyone,' she marveled. 'You saw Jim Morrison years after he supposedly died and you never told anyone. Stuart Redman, God should have given you a combination lock instead of a mouth when He sent you out into the world.'

Stu smiled. 'Well, the years rolled by, as they say in the books, and whenever I thought of that night – as I did, from time to time – I got surer and surer it wasn't him after all. Just someone who looked a little bit like him, you know. I had my mind pretty well at rest on the subject. But in the last few weeks, I've found myself puzzling over it again. And I think more and more that it was. Hell, he might even still be alive now. That'd be a real laugh, wouldn't it?'

'If he is,' she said, 'he's not here.'

'No,' Stu agreed, 'I wouldn't expect him to be here. 'I saw his eyes, you see.'

She put her hand on his arm. 'That's some story.'

'Yeah, and there's probably twenty million people in this country with one just like it . . . only about Elvis Presley or Howard Hughes.'

'Not anymore.'

'No – not anymore. Harold was something tonight, wasn't he?'

'I believe that's called changing the subject.'

'I believe you're right.'

'Yes,' she said, 'he was.'

He smiled at her worried tone and the slight frown which had puckered her brow. 'Bothered you a little, didn't it?'

'Yes, but I won't say so. You're in Harold's corner now.'

'Now, that's not fair, Fran. It bothered me, too. There we had those two advance meetings . . . hashed everything over to a fare-thee-well . . . at least we thought so . . . and along comes Harold. He takes a *whack-whack* here and a *whack-whack* there and says, "Ain't that what you really meant?" And we say, "Yeah, thanks, Harold.

It was.'" Stu shook his head. 'Putting everybody up for blanket election, how come we never thought of that, Fran? That was *sharp*. And we never even *discussed* it.'

'Well, none of us knew for sure what kind of mood they'd be in. I thought – especially after Mother Abagail walked off – that they'd be glum, maybe even mean. With that Impening talking to them like some kind of deathcrow –'

'I wonder if he should be shut up somehow,' Stu said thoughtfully.

'But it wasn't like that. They were so . . . *exuberant* just to be together. Did you feel that?'

'Yeah, I did.'

'It was like a tent revival, almost. I don't think it was anything Harold had planned. He just seized the moment.'

'I just don't know how to feel about him,' Stu said. 'That night after we hunted for Mother Abagail, I felt real bad for him. When Ralph and Glen turned up, he looked downright horrible, like he was going to faint, or something. But when we were talking out on the lawn just now and everybody was congratulating him, he seemed puffed up like a toad. Like he was smiling on the outside and on the inside he was saying, "There, you see what your committee's worth, you stupid bunch of fools." He's like one of those puzzles you could never figure out when you were a kid. The Chinese finger-pullers or those three steel rings that would come apart if you pulled them just the right way.'

Fran stuck out her feet and looked at them. 'Speaking of Harold, do you see anything funny about my feet, Stuart?'

Stu looked at them judiciously. 'Nope. Just that you're wearing those funny-looking Earth Shoes from up the street. And they're almighty big, o course.'

She slapped at him. 'Earth Shoes are very good for your feet. All the best magazines say so. And I happen to be a size seven, for your information. That's practically petite.'

'So what have your feet got to do with anything? It's late, honey.' He began to push his bike again and she fell in beside him.

'Nothing, I guess. It's just that Harold kept looking at my feet. After the meeting when we were sitting out on the grass and talking things over.' She shook her head, frowning a little. 'Now why would Harold Lauder be interested in my feet?' she asked.

*　　*　　*

When Larry and Lucy got home they were by themselves, walking hand in hand. Sometime before, Leo had gone into the house where he stayed with 'Nadine-mom.'

Now, as they walked toward the door, Lucy said: 'It was quite a meeting. I never thought –' Her words caught in her throat as a dark form unfolded itself from the shadows of their porch. Larry felt hot fear leap up in his throat. *It's him*, he thought wildly. *He's come to get me . . . I'm going to see his face.*

But then he wondered how he could have thought that, because it was Nadine Cross, that was all. She was wearing a dress of some soft bluish-gray material, and her hair was loose, flowing over her shoulders and down her back, dark hair, shot with skeins of purest white.

She sort of makes Lucy look like a used car on a scalper's lot, he thought before he could help himself, and then hated himself for thinking it. That was the old Larry talking . . . old Larry? You might as well say old Adam.

'Nadine,' Lucy was saying shakily, with one hand pressed to her chest. 'You gave me the fright of my life. I thought . . . well, I don't know what I thought.'

She took no notice of Lucy. 'Can I talk to you?' she asked Larry.

'What? Now?' He looked sideways at Lucy, or thought he did . . . later he was never able to remember what Lucy had looked like in that moment. It was as if she had been eclipsed, but by a dark star rather than by a bright one.

'Now. It has to be now.'

'In the morning would –'

'It has to be now, Larry. Or never.'

He looked at Lucy again and this time he did see her, saw the resignation on her face as she looked from Larry to Nadine and back again. He saw the hurt.

'I'll be right in, Lucy.'

'No you won't,' she said dully. Tears had begun to sparkle in her eyes. 'Oh no, I doubt it.'

'Ten minutes.'

'Ten minutes, ten years,' Lucy said. 'She's come to get you. Did you bring your dog collar and your muzzle, Nadine?'

For Nadine, Lucy Swann did not exist. Her eyes were fixed only on Larry, those dark, wide eyes. For Larry, they would always be the strangest, most beautiful eyes he had ever seen, the eyes that come back to you, calm and deep, when you're hurt or in bad trouble or maybe just about out of your mind with grief.

'I'll be in, Lucy,' he said automatically.

'She –'

'Go on.'

'Yes, I guess I will. She's come. I'm dismissed.'

She ran up the steps, stumbling on the top one, regaining her balance, pulling the door open, closing it behind her with a slam, cutting off the sound of her sobs even as they started.

Nadine and Larry looked at each other for a long time as if entranced. This is how it happens, he thought. When you catch someone's eyes across a room and never forget them, or see someone at the far end of a crowded subway platform that could have been your double, or hear a laugh on the street that could have been the laugh of the first girl you ever made love to –

But something in his mouth tasted so bitter.

'Let's walk down to the corner and back,' Nadine said in a low voice. 'Would you do that much?'

'I better go in to her. You picked one hell of a bad time to come here.'

'Please? Just down to the corner and back? If you want, I'll get down on my knees and beg. If that's what you want. Here. See?'

And to his horror she did get down on her knees, pulling her skirt up a little so she could do it, showing him her bare legs, making him curiously certain that everything else was bare as well. Why should he think that? He didn't know. Her eyes were on him, making his head spin, and there was a sickening feeling of power involved here someplace, involved with having her on her knees before him, her mouth on a level with –

'Get up!' he said roughly. He took her hands and yanked her to her feet, trying not to see the way the skirt rode up even more before falling back into place; her thighs were the color of cream, that shade of white that is not pale and dead but vigorous and healthy and enticing.

'Come on,' he said, almost totally unnerved.

They walked west, in the direction of the mountains, which were a negative presence far ahead, triangular patches of darkness blotting out the stars that had come out after the rain. Walking toward those mountains at night always made him feel queerly uneasy but somehow adventurous, and now, with Nadine by his side, her hand resting lightly in the crook of his elbow, those feelings seemed heightened. He had always had vivid dreams, and three or four nights ago about those mountains; he had dreamed there were trolls in them, hideous creatures with bright green eyes, the oversized heads of hydrocephalic cretins, and short-fingered, powerful hands. Strangler's hands. Idiot trolls, guarding the passes through the mountains. Waiting until *his* time came around – the time of the dark man.

A soft breeze meandered down the street, blowing papers before it. They passed King Sooper's, a few shopping carts standing in the big parking lot like dead sentinels, making him think of the Lincoln Tunnel. There had been trolls in the Lincoln Tunnel. They had been dead, but that didn't mean all the trolls in their new world were dead.

'It's hard,' Nadine said, her voice still low. 'She made it hard because she's right. I want you now. And I'm afraid I'm too late. I want to stay here.'

'Nadine –'

'*No!*' she said fiercely. 'Let me finish. *I want to stay here*, can't you understand that? And if we're with each other, I'll be able to. You're my last chance,' she said, her voice breaking. 'Joe's gone now.'

'No, he hasn't,' Larry said, feeling slow and stupid and bewildered. 'We dropped him off at your place on the way home. Isn't he there?'

'No. There's a boy named Leo Rockway asleep in his bed.'

'What are you –'

'Listen,' she said. 'Listen to me, can't you *listen*? As long as I had Joe, I was all right. I could . . . be as strong as I had to be. But he doesn't need me anymore. And I need to be needed.'

'He does need you!'

'Of course he does,' Nadine said, and Larry felt afraid again. She wasn't talking about Leo anymore; he didn't know *who* she was talking about. 'He needs me. That's what I'm afraid of. That's why I came to you.' She stepped in front of him and looked up, her chin tilted. He could smell her secret clean scent, and he wanted her. But part of him turned back toward Lucy. That was the part of him he needed if he was going to make it here in Boulder. If he let it go and went with Nadine, they might as well slink out of Boulder tonight. It would be finished with him. The old Larry triumphant.

'I have to go home,' he said. 'I'm sorry. You'll have to work it out on your own, Nadine.' *Work it out on your own* – weren't they the words he had been using to people in one form or another all his life? Why did they have to rise up this way when he knew he was right and still catch him, and twist in him, and make him doubt himself?

'Make love to me,' she said, and put her arms around his neck. She pressed her body against his and he knew by its looseness, its warmth and springiness, that he had been right, she was wearing the dress and that was all. Buck naked underneath, he thought, and thinking it excited him blackly.

'That's all right, I can feel you,' she said, and began to wriggle against him – sideways, up and down, creating a delicious friction. 'Make love to me and that will be the end of it. I'll be safe. Safe. I'll be safe.'

He reached up, and later he never knew how he was able to do that when he could have been inside her warmth in only three quick movements and one thrust, the way she wanted it, but somehow he reached up and unlocked her hands and pushed her away with such force that she stumbled and almost fell. A low moan came from her.

'Larry, if you knew –'

'Well, I don't. Why don't you try telling me instead of . . . of raping me?'

'Rape!' she repeated, laughing shrilly. 'Oh, that's funny! Oh, what you said! Me! Rape *you*! Oh, Larry!'

'Whatever you want from me, you could have had. You could have had it last week, or the week before. The week before that I asked you to take it. I wanted you to have it.'

'That was too soon,' she whispered.

'And now it's too late,' he said, hating the brutal sound of his voice but unable to control it. He was still shaking all over from wanting her, how was he supposed to sound? 'What are you gonna do, huh?'

'All right. Goodbye, Larry.'

She was turning away. In that instant she was more than Nadine, turning her back on him forever. She was the oral hygienist. She was Yvonne, with whom he had shared an apartment in LA – she had pissed him off and so he had just slipped into his boogie shoes, leaving her holding the lease. She was Rita Blakemoor.

Worst of all, she was his mother.

'Nadine?'

She didn't turn around. She was a black shape distinguishable from other black shapes only when she crossed the street. Then she disappeared altogether against the black background of the mountains. He called her name once again and she didn't answer. There was something terrifying in the way she had left him, the way she had just melted into that black backdrop.

He stood in front of King Sooper's, hands clenched, brow covered with pearls of sweat in spite of the evening cool. His ghosts were with him now, and at last he knew how you pay off for not being no nice guy: never clear about your own motivations, never able to weigh hurt against help except by rule of thumb, never able to get rid of the sour taste of doubt in your mouth and –

His head jerked up. His eyes widened until they seemed to bulge from his face. The wind had picked up again, it made a strange hooting sound in some empty doorway, and farther away he thought he could hear bootheels pacing off the night, rundown bootheels somewhere in the foothills coming to him on the chilly draft of this early morning breeze.

Dirty bootheels clocking their way into the grave of the West.

Lucy heard him let himself in and her heart leaped up fiercely. She told it to stop, that he was probably only coming back for his things, but it would not stop. *He picked me*, was the thought that hammered into her brain, driven there by her heart's triphammer beat. *He picked me –*

In spite of her excitement and hope, which she was helpless to control, she lay stiffly on her back on the bed, waiting and watching nothing but the ceiling. She had only told him the truth when she had said that, for her and for girls like her friend Joline, the only fault was too much need to love. But she had always been faithful. She was no cheater. She hadn't cheated on her husband and she had never cheated on Larry, and if in the years before she had met them she hadn't exactly been a nun . . . time past was time past. You just couldn't get hold of the things you had done and turn them right again. Such power might be given to the gods, but it was not given to men and women, and that was probably a good thing. Had it been otherwise, people would probably die of old age still trying to rewrite their teens.

If you knew that past was out of reach, maybe you could forgive.
Tears were stealing down her cheeks.

The door clicked open and she saw him in it, just a silhouette.

'Lucy? You awake?'

'Yes.'

'Can I put on the lamp?'

'If you want.'

She heard the minute hiss of gas and then the light came on,
turned down to a thread of flame, revealing him. He looked pale
and shaken.

'I have to say something.'

'No you don't. Just come to bed.'

'I have to say it. I . . .' He pressed his hand against his forehead
and ran it through his hair.

'Larry?' She sat up. 'Are you all right?'

He spoke as if he hadn't heard her, and he spoke without
looking at her. 'I love you. If you want me, you got me. But I don't
know if you're getting much. I'm never going to be your best bet,
Lucy.'

'I'll take the chance. Come to bed.'

He did. And they did. And when the love was over she told
him she loved him, it was true, God knew that, and it seemed to
be what he wanted, needed, to hear, but she didn't think he slept
for a long time. Once in the night she came awake (or dreamed she
did) and it seemed to her that Larry was at the window, looking
out, his head cocked in a listening posture, the lines of light and
shadow giving his face the appearance of a haggard mask. But in the
light of day she was more sure that it must have been a dream; in
the light of day he seemed to be his old self again.

It was only three days later that they heard from Ralph Brentner
that Nadine had moved in with Harold Lauder. At that, Larry's face
seemed to tighten, but it was only for a moment. And although Lucy
disliked herself for it, Ralph's news made her breathe a little easier.
It seemed it must be over.

She went home only briefly after seeing Larry. She let herself in,
went to the living room, and lit the lamp. Carrying it high, she went
to the back of the house, pausing for just a moment to let the light
spill into the boy's room. She wanted to see if she had told Larry
the truth. She had.

Leo lay asprawl in a tangle of bedclothes, dressed only in his undershorts . . . but the cuts and scratches had faded, disappeared altogether in most cases, and the all-over tan he had gotten from going practically naked had also faded. But it was more than that, she thought. Something in his face had changed — she could see the change even though he was asleep. That expression of mute, needful savagery had gone out of it. He was not Joe anymore. This was just a boy sleeping after a busy day.

She thought of the night she had been almost asleep and had come awake to find him gone from her side. That had been in North Berwick, Maine — most of the continent away now. She had followed him to the house where Larry lay sleeping on the porch. Larry sleeping inside, Joe standing outside, brandishing his knife with mute savagery, and nothing between them but the thin and sliceable screen. And she had made him come away.

Hate pounced on Nadine in a surging flash, striking up brilliant sparks as if from flint and steel. The Coleman lamp trembled in her hand, making wild shadows leap and dance. She should have let him do it! She should have held the door for Joe herself, let him in so he could stab and rip and cut and puncture and gut and destroy. She should have —

But now the boy turned over and moaned in his throat, as if waking. His hands came up and batted the air, as if warding off a black shape in a dream. And Nadine with-drew, a pulse beating thickly at her temples. There was still something strange in the boy, and she didn't like the way he had moved just now, as if he had picked up her thoughts.

She had to go ahead now. She had to be quick.

She went into her own room. There was a rug on the floor. There was a single narrow bed — an old maid's bed. That was all. There was not even a picture. The room was totally devoid of character. She opened the closet door and rummaged behind her hanging clothes. She was on her knees now, sweating. She drew out a brightly colored box with a photograph of laughing adults on the front, adults who were playing a party-game. A party-game that was at least three thousand years old.

She had found the planchette in a downtown novelty shop, but she dared not use it in the house, not with the boy here. In fact, she had not dared use it at all . . . until now. Something had impelled her into the shop, and when she had seen the planchette in its gay party box, a terrible struggle had gone on inside her – the sort of struggle psychologists call aversion/compulsion. She had been sweating then as now, wanting two things at the same time: to hurry out of that shop without looking back, and to snatch the box, that dreadful gay box, and carry it home with her. The latter wish frightened her the more, because it did not seem to be her own wish.

At last, she had taken the box.

That had been four days ago. Each night the compulsion had grown stronger until tonight, half insane with fears she didn't understand, she had gone to Larry wearing the blue-gray dress with nothing on underneath. She had gone to put an end to the fears for good. Waiting on the porch for them to get back from the meeting, she had been sure she had finally done the right thing. There had been that feeling in her, that lightly drunk, starstruck feeling, that she'd not properly had since she had run across the dewdrenched grass with the boy behind her. Only this time the boy would catch her. She would let him catch her. It would be the end.

But when he had caught her, he hadn't wanted her.

Nadine stood up, holding the box to her chest, and put out the lamp. He had scorned her, and didn't they say that hell hath no fury –? A scorned woman might well traffic with the devil . . . or his henchman.

She paused only long enough to get the large flashlight from the table in the front hall. From deeper inside the house, the boy cried out in his sleep, freezing her for a moment, making the hair prickle on her scalp.

Then she let herself out.

Her Vespa was at the curb, the Vespa she had used some days ago to motor up to Harold Lauder's house. Why had she gone there? She hadn't passed a dozen words with Harold since she'd gotten to Boulder. But in her confusion about the planchette, and in her terror of the dreams that continued to come to her even after everyone else's had stopped, it had seemed to her that she must talk about it to Harold. She had been afraid of that impulse, too, she remembered as she put the Vespa's ignition key in its slot. Like the sudden urge to pick up the planchette (*Amaze Your Friends! Brighten Up Your Get-togethers!* the box said), it had seemed to be an idea that had come to her from outside herself. *His* thought, maybe. But when she had given in and gone to Harold's, he hadn't been at home. The house was locked, the only locked house she had come upon in Boulder, and the shades were drawn. She had rather liked that, and she'd had a moment's bitter disappointment that Harold was not there. If he had been, he could have let her in and then locked the door behind her. They could have gone into the living room and talked, or made love, or have done unspeakable things together, and no one would have known.

Harold's was a private place.

'What's happening to me?' she whispered to the dark, but the dark had no answer for her. She started the Vespa, and the steady burping pop of its engine seemed to profane the night. She put it in gear and drove away. To the west.

Moving, the cool night air on her face, she felt better at last. Blow away the cobwebs, night wind. You know, don't you? When all the choices have been taken away, what do you do? You choose what's left. You choose whatever dark adventure was meant for you. You let Larry have his stupid little twist of tail with her tight pants and her single-syllable vocabulary and her movie-magazine mind. You go beyond them. You risk . . . whatever there is to be risked.

Mostly you risk yourself.

The road unrolled before her in the baby spotlight of the Vespa's headlamp. She had to switch to second gear as the road began to climb; she was on Baseline Road now, headed up the black mountain. Let them have their meetings. They were concerned with getting the power back on; her lover was concerned with the *world*.

The Vespa's engine lugged and strained and somehow carried on. A horrible yet sexy kind of fear began to grip her, and the vibrating saddle of the motorbike began to heat her up down there (*why, you're horny, Nadine*, she thought with shrill good humor, *naughty, naughty, NAUGHTY*). To her right was a straight dropoff. Nothing but death down there. And up above? Well, she would see. It was too late to turn back, and that thought alone made her feel paradoxically and deliciously free.

An hour later she was in Sunrise Amphitheater – but sunrise was still three or more hours away. The amphitheater was close to the summit of Flagstaff Mountain, and nearly everyone in the Free Zone had made the trip to the camping area at the top before they had been in Boulder very long. On a clear day – which was most days in

Boulder, at least during the summer season – you could see Boulder, and I-25 stretching away south to Denver and then off into the haze toward New Mexico two hundred miles beyond. Due east were the flatlands, stretching away toward Nebraska, and closer at hand was Boulder Canyon, a knife-gash through foothills that were walled in pine and spruce. In summers gone by, gliders had plied the thermals over Sunrise Amphitheater like birds.

Now Nadine saw only what was revealed in the glow of the six-cell flashlight which she put on a picnic table near the dropoff. There was a large artist's sketchpad turned back to a clean sheet, and squatting on it the three-cornered planchette like a triangular spider. Protruding from its belly, like the spider's stinger, was a pencil, lightly touching the pad.

Nadine was in a feverish state that was half-euphoria, half-terror. Coming up here on the back of her gamely laboring Vespa, which had most decidedly not been made for mountain climbing, she had felt what Harold had felt in Nederland. She could feel *him*. But while Harold had felt this in a rather precise and technological way, as a piece of steel attracted by a magnet, a *drawing toward*, Nadine felt it as a kind of mystic event, a border-crossing. It was as if these mountains, of which she was even now only in the foothills, were a no-man's-land between two spheres of influence – Flagg in the West, the old woman in the East. And here the magic flew both ways, mixing, making its own concoction that belonged neither to God nor to Satan but which was totally pagan. She felt she was in a haunted place.

And the planchette . . .

She had tossed the brightly marked box, stamped MADE IN TAIWAN, away indifferently for the wind to take. The planchette itself was only a poorly stamped piece of fiberboard or gypsum. But it didn't matter. It was a tool she would only use once – only *dared* to use once – and even a poorly made tool can serve its purpose: to break open a door, to close a window, to write a Name.

The words on the box recurred: *Amaze Your Friends! Brighten Up Your Get-togethers!*

What was that song Larry sometimes bellowed from the seat of his Honda as they rode along? *Hello, Central, what's the matter with your line? I want to talk to –*

Talk to who? But that was the question, wasn't it?

She remembered the time she had used the planchette in college.

That had been more than a dozen years ago . . . but it might as well have been yesterday. She had gone upstairs to ask someone on the third floor of the dorm, a girl named Rachel Timms, about the assignment in a remedial reading class they shared. The room had been filled with girls, six or eight of them at least, giggling and laughing. Nadine remembered thinking that they acted as if they were high on something, smoke or maybe even blow.

'Stop it!' Rachel said, giggling herself. 'How do you expect the spirits to communicate if you're all acting like a bunch of donkeys?'

The idea of laughing donkeys struck them as deliciously funny, and a fresh feminine gale blew through the room for a while. The planchette had sat then as it sat now, a triangular spider on three stubby legs, pencil pointing down. While they giggled, Nadine picked up a sheaf of oversized pages torn from an artist's sketchbook and shuffled through those 'messages from the astral plane' which had already come in.

Tommy says you have been using that strawberry douche again.

Mother says she's fine.

Chunga! Chunga!

John says you won't fart so much if you stop eating those CAFETERIA BEANS!!!!!

Others, just as silly.

Now the giggles had quieted enough so they could start again. Three girls sat on the bed, each with her fingertips placed on a different side of the planchette. For a moment there was nothing. Then the board quivered.

'You did that, Sandy!' Rachel accused.

'I did not!'

'Shhhh!'

The board quivered again and the girls hushed. It moved, stopped, moved again. It made the letter F.

'Fuh . . .' the girl named Sandy said.

'Fuck you, too,' someone else said, and they were off and giggling again.

'Shhhh!' Rachel said sternly.

The planchette began to move more rapidly, tracing out the letters A, T, H, E, and R.

'Father dear, your baby's here,' a girl named Patty something-or-other said, and giggled. 'It must be my father, he died of a heart attack when I was three.'

'It's writing some more,' Sandy said.

S, A, Y, S, the planchette spelled laboriously.

'What's going on?' Nadine whispered to a tall, horse-faced girl she didn't know. The horse-faced girl was looking on with her hands in her pockets and a disgusted look on her face.

'A bunch of girls playing games with something they don't understand,' the horse-faced girl said. '*That's* what's going on.' She spoke in an even lower whisper.

'FATHER SAYS PATTY,' Sandy quoted. 'It's your dear old dad, all right, Pats.'

Another burst of giggles.

The horse-faced girl was wearing spectacles. Now she took her hands out of the pockets of the overall she was wearing and used them to remove the spectacles from her face. She polished them and explained further to Nadine, still in a whisper. 'The planchette is a tool used by psychics and mediums. Kinestheologists –'

'What ologists?'

'Scientists who study movement, and the interaction of muscles and nerves.'

'Oh.'

'They claim that the planchette is actually responding to tiny muscle movements, probably guided by the subconscious rather than the conscious mind. Of course, mediums and psychics claim that the planchette is moved by entities from the spirit world –'

Another burst of hysterical laughter came from the girls clustered around the board. Nadine looked over the horsefaced girl's shoulder and saw the message now read, FATHER SAYS PATTY SHOULD STOP GOING.

'– to the bathroom so much,' another girl in the circle of spectators suggested, and everyone laughed some more.

'Either way, they're just fooling with it,' the horse-faced girl said with a disdainful sniff. 'It's very unwise. Both mediums and scientists agree that automatic writing can be dangerous.'

'The spirits are unfriendly tonight, you think?' Nadine asked lightly.

'Perhaps the spirits are *always* unfriendly,' the horse-faced girl said, giving her a sharp look. 'Or you might get a message from your subconscious mind which you were totally unprepared to receive. There are documented cases of automatic writing getting entirely out of control, you know. People have gone mad.'

'Oh, that seems awfully farfetched. It's just a *game*.'

'Games have a way of turning serious sometimes.'

The loudest burst of laughter yet tacked a period to the horse-faced girl's comment before Nadine could reply. The girl named Patty something-or-other had fallen off the bed and lay on the floor, holding her stomach and laughing and kicking her feet weakly. The completed message read, FATHER SAYS PATTY SHOULD STOP GOING TO THE SUBMARINE RACES WITH LEONARD KATZ.

'*You* did that!' Patty said to Sandy as she finally sat up again.

'I didn't, Patty! Honest!'

'It was your father! From the Great Beyond! From Out There!' another girl told Patty in a Boris Karloff voice which Nadine thought was actually quite good. 'Just remember that he's watching you the next time you take off your pants in the back seat of Leonard's Dodge.'

Another loud outburst greeted this sally. As it tapered off, Nadine pushed forward and twitched Rachel's arm. She meant to ask for the assignment and then make a quiet escape.

'Nadine!' Rachel cried. Her eyes were sparkling and gay. Her cheeks had bloomed with roses. 'Sit down, let's see if the spirits have a message for you!'

'No, really, I only came to get the assignment in remedial r –'

'Oh, *poop* on the assignment in remedial reading! This is *important*, Nadine! This is big-time! You've got to have a try. Here, sit down next to me. Janey, you take the other side.'

Janey sat down opposite Nadine, and at the repeated urging of Rachel Timms, Nadine found herself with the eight fingers of her hands touching the planchette lightly. For some reason she looked over her shoulder at the horse-faced girl. She shook her head at Nadine once, deliberately, and the overhead fluorescent bounced off the lenses of her spectacles and turned her eyes into a pair of large white flashes of light.

She had felt a moment of fear then, she remembered as she stood looking down at another planchette in the glow of a six-cell flashlight, but her remark to the horse-faced girl had recurred – it was just a *game*, for heaven's sake, and what horrible thing could possibly happen in the middle of a gaggle of giggling girls? If there was a more hostile atmosphere for the production of genuine spirits, hostile or otherwise, Nadine didn't know what it would be.

'Now everybody be quiet,' Rachel commanded. 'Spirits, do

you have a message for our sister and Brownie-in-good-standing Nadine Cross?'

The planchette didn't move. Nadine felt mildly embarrassed.

'Eenie-meenie-chili-beanie,' the girl who had done Boris Karloff said in an equally successful Bullwinkle Moose voice. 'The spirits are about to *speak*!'

More giggles.

'Shhhh!' Rachel commanded.

Nadine decided that if one of the other two girls didn't start moving the planchette soon so it would spell out whatever silly message they had for her, she would do it herself – slide it around to spell out something short and sweet, like BOO!, so she could get her assignment and leave.

Just as she was about to try doing this, the planchette jerked rudely under her fingers. The pencil left a dark black diagonal slash on the fresh page.

'Hey! No fair yanking, spirits,' Rachel said in a vaguely uneasy tone of voice. 'Did you do that, Nadine?'

'No.'

'Janey.'

'Uh-uh. Honestly.'

The planchette jerked again, almost pulling their fingers from it, and skittered to the upper-lefthand corner of the paper.

'Wowie,' Nadine said. 'Did you feel –'

They did, all of them did, although neither Rachel nor Jane Fargood would talk to her about it later. And she had never felt particularly welcome in either girl's room after that night. It was as if they were both a little afraid to get too close to her after that.

The planchette suddenly began to thrum underneath their fingers; it was like lightly touching the fender of a smoothly idling car. The vibration was steady and disquieting. It was not the sort of movement a person could cause without being fairly obvious about it.

The girls had grown quiet. Their faces all wore a peculiar expression, an expression common to the faces of all people who have attended a séance where something unexpectedly genuine has occurred – when the table begins to rock, when unseen knuckles rap on the wall, or when the medium begins to extrude smoky-gray teleplasm from her nostrils. It is a pallid *waiting* expression, half wanting whatever it is that has begun to stop, half wanting it to go on. It is an expression of dreadful, distracted excitement . . . and when it wears that particular look, the human face looks most like the skull which always rests half an inch below the skin.

'Stop it!' the horse-faced girl cried out suddenly. 'Stop it right now or you'll be sorry!'

And Jane Fargood screamed in a fear-filled voice: *'I can't take my fingers off it!'*

Someone uttered a little burping scream. At the same instant Nadine realized that her own fingers were also glued to the board. The muscles of her arms bunched in an effort to pull the tips of her fingers from the planchette, but they remained where they were.

'All right, the joke is over,' Rachel said in a tight, scared voice. 'Who –'

And suddenly the planchette began to write.

It moved with lightning speed, dragging their fingers with it, snapping their arms out and back and around in a way which would have been funny if it weren't for the helpless, caught expressions on all three girls' faces. Nadine thought later that it was as if her arms had been caught in an exercise machine. The writing before had been in stilted, draggling letters – messages that looked as if they had been written by a seven-year-old. This writing was smooth and powerful . . . big, slanting capital letters that slashed across the white page. There was something both relentless and vicious about it.

NADINE, NADINE, NADINE, the whirling planchette wrote. HOW I LOVE NADINE TO BE MY TO LOVE MY NADINE TO BE MY QUEEN IF YOU IF YOU IF YOU ARE PURE FOR ME IF YOU ARE CLEAN FOR ME IF YOU ARE IF YOU ARE DEAD FOR ME DEAD YOU ARE

The planchette swooped, raced, and began again, lower down.

YOU ARE DEAD WITH THE REST OF THEM YOU ARE IN THE DEADBOOK WITH THE REST OF THEM NADINE IS DEAD WITH THEM NADINE IS ROTTEN WITH THEM UNLESS UNLESS

It stopped. Thrummed. Nadine thought, hoped – oh how she hoped – that it was over, and then it raced back to the edge of the paper and began again. Jane shrieked miserably. The faces of the other girls were shocked white *o*'s of wonder and dismay.

THE WORLD THE WORLD SOON THE WORLD IS DEAD AND WE WE WE NADINE NADINE I I I WE WE WE ARE WE ARE WE

Now the letters seemed to *scream* across the page:

WE ARE IN THE HOUSE OF THE DEAD NADINE

The last word howled itself across the page in inch-high capital letters and then the planchette whirled from the tablet, leaving a long streak of graphite behind like a shout. It fell on the floor and snapped in two.

There had been an instant of shocked, immobile silence, and then Jane Fargood had burst into high, weeping hysterics. The thing had ended with the housemother coming upstairs to see what was wrong, Nadine remembered, and she had been about to call the infirmary for Jane when the girl had managed to get hold of herself a little.

Through the whole thing Rachel Timms had sat on her bed, calm and pale. When the housemother and most of the other girls (including the horse-faced girl, who undoubtedly felt that a prophetess is without much honor in her own land) had left, she had asked Nadine in a flat, strange voice: 'Who was it, Nadine?'

'I don't know,' Nadine had answered truthfully. She hadn't had the slightest idea. Not then.

'You didn't recognize the handwriting?'

'No.'

'Well, maybe you just better take that . . . that note from beyond or whatever it is . . . and go back to your room.'

'You asked me to sit down!' Nadine flashed at her. 'How was I supposed to know anything like . . . like that would happen? I did it to be polite, for God's sake!'

Rachel had had the good grace to flush at that; she had even offered a little apology. But Nadine had never seen much of the girl after that, and Rachel Timms had been one of the few girls Nadine had ever felt really close to during her first three semesters at college.

From then until now she had never touched one of these triangular spiders made of pressed fiberboard.

But the time had . . . well, it had slouched around at last, hadn't it?

Yes indeed.

Heart beating loudly, Nadine sat down on the picnic bench and pressed her fingers lightly to two of the planchette's three sides. She could feel it begin to move under the balls of her fingers almost immediately, and she thought of a car with its engine idling. But who was the driver? Who was he, *really*? Who would climb in, and slam the door, and put his sun-blackened hands on the wheel? Whose foot, brutal and heavy, shod in an old and dusty cowboy boot, would come down on the accelerator and take her . . . where?

Driver, where you taking us?

Nadine, beyond help or hope of succor, sat upright on the bench at the crest of Flagstaff Mountain in the black trench of morning, her eyes wide, that feeling of being on the border stronger than ever. She stared east, but felt *his* presence coming from behind her, pressing heavy on her, dragging her down like weights tied to the feet of a dead woman: Flagg's dark presence, coming in steady, inexorable waves.

Somewhere the dark man was abroad in the night, and she spoke two words like an incantation to all the black spirits that had ever been – incantation and invitation:

'Tell me.'

And beneath her fingers, the planchette began to write.

CHAPTER 54

Excerpts from the Minutes of the Permanent Free Zone
Committee Meeting
August 19, 1990

This meeting was held at the apartment of Stu Redman and Fran Goldsmith. All members of the Free Zone Committee were present.

Stu Redman offered congratulations to all of us, including himself, on being elected to the Permanent Committee. He made a motion that a letter of thanks to Harold Lauder be drafted and signed by each member of the Committee. It passed unanimously.

Stu: 'Once we get the old business taken care of, Glen Bateman has a couple of items. I don't know what they are any more than you do, but I suspect one of them has to do with the next public meeting. Right, Glen?'

Glen: 'I'll wait my turn.'

Stu: 'That's baldy for you. The main difference between an old drunk and an old bald college professor is the professor waits his turn before he starts talkin the ears off your head.'

Glen: 'Thank you for those pearls of wisdom, East Texas.'

Fran said she could see Stu and Glen were having a wonderful time but wanted to know if they could get down to business, as all her favorite TV shows started at nine. This comment was greeted with more laughter than it probably deserved.

The first real item of business was our scouts in the West. To recap, the committee has decided to ask Judge Farris, Tom Cullen, and Dayna Jurgens to go. Stu suggested that the people who nominated each of them be the ones to broach the subject to their own nominees – that is, Larry Underwood asks the Judge, Nick will have to talk to Tom – with Ralph Brentner's help – and Sue will talk to Dayna.

Nick said that working with Tom might take a few days, and Stu said that brought up the point of when to send them. Larry said they couldn't be sent together or they might all get caught together. He went on to say that both the Judge and Dayna would probably suspect that we had sent more than one spy, but as long as they didn't know the actual names, they couldn't tattle.

Fran said that tattle was hardly the word, considering what the man`in the West might do to them – if he is a man.

Glen: 'I wouldn't be so gloomy, if I were you, Fran. If we give our Adversary credit for even a modicum of intelligence, he'll know we wouldn't give our – operatives, I guess one could call them – any information we considered vital to his interests. He'll know that torture could do him very little good.'

Fran: 'You mean he'll probably pat them on the head and tell them not to do it anymore? I have an idea he might torture them just because torture is one of the things he *likes*. What do you say to that?'

Glen: 'I guess there's not much I *can* say.'

Stu: 'That decision's been made, Frannie. We've all agreed that we're sending our people into a dangerous situation, and we all know that making the decision sure wasn't any fun.'

Glen suggested that we agree tentatively to this schedule: The Judge would go out on August twenty-sixth, Dayna on the twenty-seventh, and Tom on the twenty-eighth, none of them to know about the others and each to leave on a different road. That would allow the time necessary to work with Tom, he added.

Nick said that, with the exception of Tom Cullen, who will be told when to come back by means of a post-hypnotic suggestion, the other two must be told to come back when their own discretion advises them to, but that the weather could become a factor – there can be heavy snow in the mountains by the first week of October. Nick suggested that each of them should be advised to spend no more than three weeks in the West.

Fran said they could swing around to the south if the snow came early in the mountains but Larry disagreed, pointing out that the Sangre de Cristo chain would be in the way, unless they swung all the way down to Mexico. And if they had to do that, we probably wouldn't see them again until spring.

Larry said if that was the case, perhaps we ought to give the Judge a headstart. He suggested August 21, day after tomorrow.

That closed the subject of the scouts . . . or spies, if you prefer.

Glen was then recognized, and I am now quoting from the taped record:

Glen: 'I want to move that we call another public meeting on August twenty-fifth, and I'm going to suggest a few things that we might cover at that meeting.

'I'd like to start by pointing out something that may surprise you. We've been assuming that we've got about six hundred people in the Zone, and Ralph has kept admirable, accurate records of the number of *large groups* that have come in, and we've based our population assumption on those figures. But there have also been people coming in by dribs and drabs, maybe as many as ten a day. So earlier today I went over to Chautauqua Park auditorium with Leo Rockway, and we counted the seats in the hall. There are six hundred and seven of them. Now does that tell you anything?'

Sue Stern said that couldn't be right, because people had been standing in the back and sitting in the aisles when they couldn't get seats. Then we all saw what Glen was getting at, and I guess it would be appropriate to say the committee was thunderstruck.

Glen: 'We don't have any way of accurately estimating how many standees and sittees we had, but my memory of the gathering is fairly clear and I'd have to say that one hundred would be a terribly conservative estimate. So you see, we really have better than seven hundred people here in the Zone. As a result of Leo's and my findings, I motion that one of the items to go on the big meeting agenda is a Census Committee.'

Ralph: 'Well, I'll be a son of a bitch! That's one on me.'

Glen: 'No, it's not your fault. You've got about a dozen irons in the fire, Ralph, and I think we'd all agree you've kept them turning nicely –'

Larry: 'Boy, I'll say.'

Glen: '– but even if we've only been getting four loners a day, that still adds up to almost thirty a week. And my guess is we're getting more like twelve or fourteen. They don't just run up to one of us and announce themselves, you know, and with Mother Abagail gone, there's no one place where you can count on them going after they arrive.'

Fran Goldsmith then seconded Glen's motion that the committee put a Census Committee on the agenda for the meeting on August 25, said committee to be responsible for keeping a roll of every Free Zone member.

Larry: 'I'm all for that if there's some good, practical reason for doing it. But . . .'

Nick: 'But what, Larry?'

Larry: 'Well . . . don't we have enough other things to worry about without hacking around with a bunch of diddly-shit bureaucracy?'

Fran: 'I can see one valid reason right now, Larry.'

Larry: 'What's that?'

Fran: 'Well, if Glen's right, it means we're going to need to hire a bigger hall for the next meeting. That's one thing. If there are going to be eight hundred people here by the twenty-fifth, we'll never cram them all into Chautauqua Auditorium.'

Ralph: 'Jesus, I never thought of that. I *told* you guys I wasn't cut out for this work.'

Stu: 'Relax, Ralph, you're doing fine.'

Sue: 'So where are we going to hold the goddam meeting?'

Glen: 'Wait a minute, wait a minute. One thing at a time. There's a goddam motion on the goddam floor!'

It was voted 7–0 to put the Census Committee on the agenda of the next public meeting.

Stu then moved that we hold the meeting on August 25 in Munzinger Auditorium at CU, which had a bigger capacity – probably over a thousand.

Glen then asked for and received the floor again.

Glen: 'Before we move on, I'd like to point out that there's another good reason to have a Census Committee, one that's a little more serious than knowing how much dip and how many bags of chips to bring to the party. We *should* know who's coming in . . . but we should also know who is leaving. I think people are, you know. Maybe it's just paranoia, but I could swear that there have been faces I've gotten used to seeing that just aren't around anymore. Anyhow, after we went out to the Chautauqua Auditorium, Leo and I went over to Charlie Impening's house. And guess what? The house is empty, Charlie's things are gone, and so is Charlie's BSA.'

Some uproar from the committee, also profanity which, while colorful, does not have any place in this record.

Ralph then asked what good it would do for us to know who is leaving. He suggested that if people like Impening wanted to go over to the dark man, then we should look at it as a case of good riddance. Several of the committee applauded Ralph, who blushed like a schoolboy, if I may add that.

Sue: 'No, I see Glen's point. It would be like a constant drain of information.'

Ralph: 'Well, what could we do? Put them in jail?'

Glen: 'Ugly as it sounds, I think we have to consider that very strongly.'

Fran: 'No, sir. Sending spies . . . I can stomach that. But locking up people who come here because they don't like the way we're doing things? Jesus, Glen! That's secret police stuff!'

Glen: 'Yes, that's about what it comes down to. But our position here is extremely precarious. You're putting me in the position of having to advocate repression, and I think that's very unfair. I'm asking you if you want to allow a brain-drain to go on, in light of our Adversary.'

Fran: 'I still hate it. In the 1950s, Joe McCarthy had Communism. We've got our dark man. How wonderful for us.'

Glen: 'Fran, are you prepared to take the chance that someone may leave here with a key piece of information in his pocket? That Mother Abagail is gone, for instance?'

Fran: 'Charlie Impening can tell him that. What other key pieces of information do we have, Glen? For the most part, aren't we just wandering around without a clue?'

Glen: 'Do you want him to know our strength of numbers? How we're getting along on the technical side? That we don't even have a doctor yet?'

Fran said she'd rather have it that way than start locking people up because they didn't like the way we were running things. Stu then motioned that we table the whole idea of locking people up for contrary views. This motion was passed, with Glen voting against.

Glen: 'You better get used to the idea that you're going to have to deal with this sooner or later, and probably sooner. Charlie Impening spilling his guts to Flagg is bad enough. You just have to ask yourself if you want to multiply what Impening knows by some theoretical *x*-factor. Well, never mind, you've voted to table. But here's another thing . . . we're elected indefinitely, did any of you think of that? We don't know if we're serving six weeks, six months, or six years. My suggestion would be one year . . . that ought to take us to the end of the beginning, in Harold's phrase. I'd like to see the one-year thing on the agenda for our next public meeting.

'One last item and I'm done. Government by town meeting – which is essentially what we have, with ourselves as town selectmen – is going to be fine for a while, until we've got about three thousand people or so, but when things get too big, most of the people who show up at the public meetings are going to be cliques and folks with axes to grind . . . fluoridation makes you sterile, people who want one sort of flag, things like that. My suggestion would be that we all think very hard about how to turn Boulder into a Republic by late next winter or early spring.'

There was some informal discussion of Glen's last proposal, but no action was taken at this meeting. Nick was recognized and gave Ralph something to read.

Nick: 'I'm writing this on the morning of the nineteenth, in preparation for the meeting tonight, and will get Ralph to read it as the last order of business. Being mute is very difficult sometimes, but I have tried to think of all the possible ramifications of what I'm about to propose. I'd like to see this go on the agenda for our next public meeting: "To see if the Free Zone will create a Department of Law and Order with Stu Redman at its head."'

Stu: 'That's a hell of a thing to spring on me, Nick.'

Glen: 'Interesting. Goes back to what we were just talking about, too. Let him finish, Stuart – you'll get your innings.'

Nick: 'The headquarters of this Department of Law and Order would be in the Boulder County Courthouse. Stu would have the power to deputize men on his own up to thirty, over thirty on a majority vote of the Free Zone Committee, and over seventy on a majority vote of the Free Zone in public session. That's the resolution I'd like to see on the next agenda. Of course we can approve until we're black in the face and it will do no good unless Stu goes along.'

Stu: 'Damn right!'

Nick: 'We've gotten big enough to really *need* some law. Things are going to get flaky without it. There's the case of the Gehringer boy racing that fast car up and down Pearl Street. He finally crashed it and was lucky to walk away with nothing worse than a gash on his forehead. He could have killed himself or someone else. Now everybody who saw him doing that knew it was nothing but trouble, M-O-O-N, that spells trouble, as Tom would say. But nobody felt they could stop him, because they just didn't have the authority. That's one thing. Then there's Rich Moffat. Probably some of you know who Rich is, but for those of you who don't, he's probably the Zone's only practicing alcoholic. He's a half-decent guy when he's sober, but when he's drunk, he's just not accountable for what he does, and he spends a lot of time drunk. Three or four days ago he got a load on and decided he was going to break every plate-glass window on Arapahoe. Now I talked to him about that after he sobered off a little – in my way of talking, you know, by note – and he was pretty ashamed. He pointed back the way he come and said, "Look at that. Look at what I done. Glass all over the sidewalk! What if some kid gets hurt in that? I'll be to blame."'

Ralph: 'I got no sympathy. None.'

Fran: 'Come on, Ralph. Everybody knows alcoholism's a disease.'

Ralph: 'Disease, my ass. It's getting sloppo, that's what it is.'

Stu: 'And you're both out of order. Come on, you two, pipe down.'

Ralph: 'Sorry, Stu. I'll stick to reading Nick's letter here.'

Fran: 'And I'll be quiet for at least two minutes, Mr Chairman. I promise.'

Nick: 'To make a long story short, I found Rich a broom and he swept up most of the mess he'd made. Did a pretty good job, too. But he was right to ask why someone didn't stop him. In the old days a guy like Rich couldn't get anywhere near all the high-tension booze he wanted; guys like Rich were just winos. But now there are incredible amounts of booze just waiting around to be lifted off the shelves. And furthermore, I really do believe that Rich never should have been allowed to get past his second window, but he broke every window on the south side of the street for three blocks. He finally stopped because he got tired. And here is one more example: We had a case where a man whose name I won't mention found out that his woman, who I also won't name, was spending her afternoon sack-time with a third party. I guess we all know who I'm talking about.'

Sue: 'Yeah, I guess we do. Big man with his fists.'

Nick: 'Anyway, the man in question beat up the third party and then the woman in the case. Now I don't think it matters to any of us here who was right and who was wrong –'

Glen: 'You are mistaken there, Nick.'

Stu: 'Let the man finish, Glen.'

Glen: 'I'm going to, but it's a point I want to come back to.'

Stu: 'Fine. Go ahead, Ralph.'

Ralph: 'Yep – getting toward the end now.'

Nick: '– because what matters is that the man in question committed a felony crime, assault and battery, and he is walking around free. Of the three cases, this one worries ordinary citizens the most. We've got a melting-pot society, a real hodgepodge, and there are going to be all kinds of conflicts and abrasions. I don't think any of us want a frontier society here in Boulder. Think of the situation we'd have if the man in question had gotten a .45 out of a pawnshop and had shot them both dead instead of just beating them up. Then we'd have a murderer walking around free.'

Sue: 'My God, Nicky, what's that? The thought for the day?'

Larry: 'Yeah, it's ugly, but he's right. There's an old saying, Navy, I think, that goes, "Whatever *can* go wrong *will* go wrong."'

Nick: 'Stu's already our public and private moderator, which means people already see him as an authority figure. And personally, I think Stu is a good man.'

Stu: 'Thanks for the kind words, Nick. I guess you never noticed that I wear elevator shoes. Seriously, though – I'll accept the nomination, if that's what you want. I don't really want the goddam job – from what I've seen down in Texas, police work is mostly cleaning puke off your shirt when guys like Rich Moffat barf on you, or scraping dummies like that Gehringer boy off the roads. All I ask is that when we put it up to the public meeting, we set the same one-year time limit on it that we're setting on our committee jobs. And I intend to make it clear that I'm stepping down at the end of that year. If that's acceptable, okay.'

Glen: 'I think I can speak for all of us in saying that it is. I want to thank Nick for his motion, and get it on the record that I think it's a stroke of genius. And I second the motion.'

Stu: 'Okay, the motion is on the floor. Any discussion?'

Fran: 'Yes, there's some discussion. I have a question. What if somebody blows your head off?'

Stu: 'I don't think –'

Fran: 'No, you don't *think*. You don't *think* so. Well, what's Nick going to tell me if what you all think is *wrong*? "Oh, I'm sorry, Fran"? Is that what he's going to say? "Your man is down in the county courthouse with a bullet hole in his head and I guess we made a *mistake*"? Jesus Mary and Joseph, I'm going to have a *baby* and you people want him to be *Pat Garrett*!'

There was another ten minutes of discussion, most of which is irrelevant; and Fran, your ob'nt recording secretary, had herself a good cry and then got herself under control. The vote on nominating Stu to be Free Zone Marshal was 6–1, and this time Fran would not change her vote. Glen asked to be recognized for one last thing before we closed the meeting.

Glen: 'This is middle-think again, not a motion, nothing to vote on, but something we ought to chew over. Going back to Nick's third example of law-and-order problems. He described the case and finished by saying we didn't have to be concerned with who was right and who was wrong. I think he was mistaken. I believe Stu is one of the fairest men I've ever met. *But law enforcement without a court system isn't justice.* It's just vigilantism, rule by the fist. Now suppose that fellow we all know *had* gotten a .45 and killed his woman and her lover. And further suppose that Stu, as our marshal, went out and collared him and put him in the calaboose. Then what? How long do we keep him there? Legally, we couldn't keep him at all, at least according to the Constitution we adopted at our meeting last night, because under the document a man's innocent until proven guilty in a court of law. Now, as a matter of *fact*, we all know we'd keep him locked up. We wouldn't feel safe with him walking the streets! So we'd do it even though it would be patently unconstitutional, because when safety and constitutionality are at swords' points, safety must win out. But it behooves us to make safety and constitutionality synonymous as quickly as we can. We need to think about a court system.'

Fran: 'That's very interesting, and I agree that it's something we ought to think about, but right now I'm going to move that we adjourn. It's late, and I'm very tired.'

Ralph: 'Boy, I second that motion. Let's talk about courts next time. My head's got so much in it right now that it's going round and round. This reinventing the country is a lot tougher than it looked at first.'

Larry: 'Amen.'

Stu: 'There's a motion to adjourn on the floor. Do you like it, people?'

The motion to adjourn was voted, 7–0.

Frances Goldsmith, Secretary

'Why are you stopping?' Fran asked as Stu slowly biked over to the curb and put his feet down. 'It's a block further up.' Her eyes were still red from her burst of tears during the meeting, and Stu thought he had never seen her looking so tired.

'This marshal thing –' he began.

'Stu, I don't want to talk about it.'

'Somebody has to do it, honey. And Nick was right. I'm the logical choice.'

'Fuck logic. What about me and the baby? Do you see no logic in us, Stu?'

'I ought to know what you want for the baby,' he said softly. 'Haven't you told me enough times? You want him brought into a world that isn't totally crazy. You want things safe for him – or her. I want that, too. But I wasn't going to say that in front of the rest. It's between you and me. You and the baby are the two main reasons I said okay.'

'I know that,' she said in a low, choked voice.

He put his fingers under her chin and tilted her face up. He smiled at her and she made an effort to smile back. It was a weary smile, and tears were coursing down her cheeks, but it was better than no smile at all.

'Everything's going to be fine,' he said.

She was shaking her head back and forth slowly, and some of her tears flew off into the warm summer night.

'I don't think so,' she said. 'No, I really don't think it is.'

She lay awake long into the night, thinking that warmth can only come from a burning – Prometheus got his eyes pecked out on that one – and that love always comes due in blood.

And a queer certainty stole over her, as numbing as some creeping anesthesia, that they would finish by wading in blood. The thought made her place her hands protectively over her belly, and she found herself thinking for the first time in weeks of her dream: the dark man with his grin . . . and his twisted coathanger.

As well as hunting for Mother Abagail with a picked group of volunteers in his spare time, Harold Lauder was on the Burial Committee, and on August 21 he spent the day in the back of a dump truck with five other men, all of them wearing boots and protective clothing and heavy-duty Playtex rubber gloves. The head of the Burial Committee, Chad Norris, was out at what he referred to, with an almost grisly calm, as Burial Site #1. It was ten miles southwest of Boulder in an area that had once been stripmined for coal. The site lay as bleak and barren as the mountains of the moon under the burning August sun. Chad had accepted the post reluctantly because he had once been an undertaker's assistant in Morristown, New Jersey.

'There's no undertaking about this,' he had said this morning at the Greyhound Bus Terminal between Arapahoe and Walnut, which was the Burial Committee's base of operations. He lit a Winston with a wooden match and grinned at the twenty men sitting around. 'That is, it's an undertaking but not an *undertaking* undertaking, if you get my meaning.'

There were a few strained smiles, Harold's largest among them. His belly had been rumbling constantly because he hadn't dared eat breakfast. He hadn't been sure he could keep it down, considering the nature of the work. He could have stuck with finding Mother Abagail and no one would have murmured a word of protest, even though it had to be obvious to every thinking man in the Zone (if there *were* any thinking men in the Free Zone besides himself – a debatable question) that looking for her with fifteen men was an exercise in comic relief when you considered the thousands of square miles of empty forest and plain around Boulder. And, of course, she might never have *left* Boulder, none of them seemed to have thought of that (which didn't surprise Harold at all). She could be set up in a house just about anywhere beyond the center of town and they'd still never find her without a house-to-house search. Redman and Andros hadn't raised a word of protest between them when Harold suggested that the Search Committee be a weekend and evening sort of thing, which told Harold that they accepted it as a closed case, too.

He could have stuck with it, but who gets to be best-liked in any community? Who is most trusted? Why, the man who does the dirty job, of course, and does it with a smile. The man who does the job you couldn't bring yourself to do.

'It's going to be like burying cordwood,' Chad told them. 'If you can keep it on that level in your mind, you'll be okay. Some of you may have to vomit here at the start. There's no shame in that; just try to go someplace where the rest won't have to look at you do it. Once you've puked, you'll find it easier to think that way: cordwood. Nothing but cordwood.'

The men were eyeing each other uncomfortably.

Chad broke them up into three six-man crews. He and the two odd men out went to prepare a place for those who were brought. Each of the three crews were given a specific area of town to work. Harold's truck had spent the day in the Table Mesa area, working their way slowly west from the Denver-Boulder Turnpike exit ramp. Up Martin Drive to the Broadway intersection. Down Thirty-ninth Street and then back up Fortieth, suburban houses in a tract area now about thirty years old, dating back to the start of Boulder's population boom, houses with one floor aboveground and a second below.

Chad had provided gas masks from the local National Guard armory, but they didn't have to use them until after lunch (lunch? what lunch? Harold's consisted of a can of Berry's apple pie filling; it was all he could bring himself to eat), when they entered the Church of Latter-Day Saints on lower Table Mesa Drive. They had come here, filled with the plague, and they had died there, over seventy of them, and the stink was enormous.

'Cordwood,' one of Harold's mates had said in a high, revolted, laughing voice, and Harold had turned and stumbled out past him. He went around the corner of the handsome brick building that had once been a polling place in election years and up came the Berry's apple pie filling and he discovered that Norris had been right: He really felt better without it.

It took them two trips and most of the afternoon to empty the church. Twenty men, Harold thought, to get rid of all the corpses in Boulder. It's almost funny. A goodly number of Boulder's previous population had run like rabbits because of the Air Testing Center scare, but *still* . . . Harold supposed that, as the Burial Committee grew with the population, it was just barely possible that they might get most of the bodies in the ground by the first heavy snowfall (not that he himself expected to be around by then), and most of the people would never know how real the danger of some new epidemic – one they *weren't* immune to – had been.

The Free Zone Committee was full of bright ideas, he thought with contempt. The committee would be just fine . . . as long as they had good old Harold Lauder to make sure their shoelaces were tied, of course. Good old Harold's good enough for that, but not quite good enough to serve on their fucking Permanent Committee. Heavens, no. He had never been quite good enough, not even quite good enough to get a date for the Class Dance at Ogunquit High School, even with a scag. Good God, no, not Harold. Let's remember, folks, when we get right down to the proverbial place where the ursine mammal evacuated his bowels in the buckwheat, that this is no analytical, logical matter, not even a matter of common sense. When we get right down to it, what we end up with is a frigging beauty contest.

Well, somebody remembers. Somebody is keeping score, kids. And the name of that someone is – could we have a drum-roll, please maestro? – Harold Emery Lauder.

So he came back into the church, wiping his mouth and grinning as best he could, nodding that he was ready to go on. Someone clapped him on the back and Harold's grin widened and he thought: *Someday you're going to lose your hand for that, shitheap.*

They made their last run at 4:15 PM, the body of the dump truck filled with the last of the Latter-Day corpses. In town the truck had to weave laboriously in and out of stalled traffic, but on Colorado 119, three tow trucks had been out all day, latching on to stalled cars and depositing them into the ditches on both sides of the road. They lay there like the overturned toys of some giant-child.

At the burial site, the other two orange trucks were already parked. Men stood around with their rubber gloves off, their fingers white and pruney at the tips from a day of sweating inside rubber. They smoked and talked desultorily. Most of them were very pale.

Norris and his two helpers had it down to a science now. They shook out a huge piece of plastic sheeting on the rocky ground. Norman Kellogg, the Louisianian who was driving Harold's truck, backed up to the edge of the plastic. The tailgate slammed down and the first bodies fell out onto the plastic crawsheet like partially stiffened ragdolls. Harold wanted to turn away but was afraid that the others might construe it as weakness. He did not mind watching them fall out too much; it was the *sound* that got him. The sound they made when they hit what was going to become their shroud.

The note of the dumper's engine deepened and there was a hydraulic whine as the truck's body began to go up. Now the bodies tumbled out in a grotesque human rain. Harold felt an instant of pity, a feeling so deep it was an ache. *Cordwood*, he thought. *How right he was. That's all that's left. Just . . . cordwood.*

'*Ho!*' Chad Norris shouted, and Kellogg pulled the dump truck ahead and shut it off. Chad and his helpers stepped onto the plastic carrying rakes and now Harold did turn away, pretending to scan the sky for rain, and he was not alone – but he heard a sound that would haunt him in his dreams, and that was the sound of change falling from the pockets of the dead men and women as Chad and his helpers worked with their rakes, spreading the corpses evenly. The coins falling on the plastic made a sound that reminded Harold absurdly of tiddledy-winks. The sickly-sweet stench of corruption drifted up in the warm air.

When he looked back, the three of them were pulling the edges of the plastic shroud together, grunting with the strain, arms bulging. A few of the other men, Harold among them, pitched in. Chad Norris produced a huge industrial stapling gun. Twenty minutes later that part of the job was done, and the plastic lay on the ground like a giant gelatin capsule. Norris climbed into the cab of a bright yellow bulldozer and keyed the engine. The scarred blade thudded down. The dozer rolled forward.

A man named Weizak, also on Harold's truck, walked away from the scene with the jerky steps of a badly controlled puppet. A cigarette jittered between his fingers. 'Man, I can't watch that,' he said as he passed Harold. 'It's really kind of funny. I never knew I was Jewish until today.'

The bulldozer shoved and rolled the large plastic package into a long rectangular cut in the ground. Chad backed away, shut down, climbed off. Motioning the men to gather around, he walked over to one of the Public Works trucks and put one booted foot up on the running board.

'No football cheers,' he said, 'but you did damned good. We put away close to a thousand units today, I guess.'

Units, Harold thought.

'I know this kind of work takes something out of a man. Committee's promising us another two men before the end of the week, but I know that don't change the way you guys feel – or the way I feel, for that matter. All I'm saying is that if you've had enough, don't feel like you can take another day of it, you don't have to worry about avoiding me on the street. But if you feel like you can't cut it, its awful-damn important that you find someone to take your place tomorrow. So far as I'm concerned, this is the most important job in the Zone. It isn't too bad now, but if we've still got twenty thousand corpses in Boulder next month when it gets to be wet weather, people are going to get sick. If you feel like you can make it, I'll see you tomorrow morning at the bus station.'

'I'll be there,' someone said.

'Me too,' Norman Kellogg said. 'After a six-hour bath tonight.' There was laughter.

'Count me in,' Weizak chimed in.

'Me too,' Harold said quietly.

'It's a dirty job,' Norris said in a low, emotional voice. 'You're good men. I doubt if the rest of them will ever know just how good.'

Harold felt a sense of drawing-together, a camaraderie, and he fought against it, suddenly afraid. This was no part of the plan.

'See you tomorrow, Hawk,' Weizak said, and squeezed his shoulder.

Harold's grin was startled and defensive. *Hawk?* What kind of joke was that? A bad one, of course. Cheap sarcasm. Calling fat, pimply Harold Lauder Hawk. He felt the old black hate rise, directed at Weizak this time, and then it subsided in sudden confusion. He *wasn't* fat anymore. He couldn't even properly be called stout. His pimples had vanished over the last seven weeks. Weizak didn't know he had once been a school joke. Weizak didn't know that Harold's father had once asked him if he was a homosexual. Weizak didn't know that Harold had been his popular sister's cross to bear. And if he had known, Weizak probably wouldn't have given a sweet shit.

Harold climbed into the back of one of the trucks, his mind churning helplessly. All of a sudden the old grudges, the old hurts, and the unpaid debts seemed as worthless as the paper money choking all the cash registers of America.

Could that be true? Could it possibly be true? He felt panicked, alone, scared. No, he decided at last. It couldn't possibly be true. Because, consider. If you were strong-willed enough to be able to resist the low opinions of others, when they thought you were a queer, or an embarrassment, or just a plain old bag of shit, then you had to be strong-willed enough to resist . . .

Resist what?

Their *good* opinion of you?

Wasn't that kind of logic . . . well, that kind of logic was lunacy, wasn't it?

An old quote surfaced in his troubled mind, some general's defense of interning Japanese-Americans during World War II. It had been pointed out to this general that no acts of sabotage had occurred on the West Coast, where the naturalized Japanese were most heavily concentrated. The general's reply had been: 'The very fact that no sabotage has taken place is an ominous development.'

Was that him?

Was it?

Their truck pulled into the bus station parking lot. Harold jumped over the side, reflecting that even his coordination had improved a thousand percent, either from the weight he had lost, his almost constant exercise, or both.

The thought came to him again, stubborn, refusing to be buried: *I could be an asset to this community.*

But they had shut him out.

That doesn't matter. I've got the brains to pick the lock on the door they slammed in my face. And I believe I've found enough guts to open it once it's unlocked.

But –

Stop it! Stop it! You might as well be wearing handcuffs and legchains with that one word stamped all over them. But! But! But! Can't you stop it, Harold? Can't you for Christ's sake climb down off your high fucking horse?

'Hey, man, you okay?'

Harold jumped. It was Norris, coming out of the dispatcher's office, which he had taken over. He looked tired.

'Me? I'm fine. I was just thinking.'

'Well, you go right along. Seems like every time you do that you coin money for this joint.'

Harold shook his head. 'Not true.'

'No?' Chad let it go. 'Can I drop you somewhere?'

'Huh-uh. I've got my chopper.'

'You wanna know something, Hawk? I think most of these guys are really going to come back tomorrow.'

'Yes, so do I.' Harold walked over to his motorcycle and climbed on. He found himself savoring his new nickname, rather against his will.

Norris shook his head. 'I never would have believed it. I figured that once they actually saw what the job was, they'd think of a hundred other things they had to do.'

'I'll tell you what I think,' Harold said. 'I think it's easier to do a dirty job for yourself than it is to do for somebody else. Some of these guys, it's the first time they ever really worked for themselves in their whole lives.'

'Yeah, there's something in that, I guess. I'll see you tomorrow, Hawk.'

'Eight,' Harold confirmed, and drove out Arapahoe to Broadway. To his right a crew comprised mostly of women was at work with a wrecker and a derrick righting a tractor-trailer truck that had jack-knifed, partially blocking the street. They had drawn a respectable little crowd. *This place is building up,* Harold thought. *I don't recognize half of those people.*

He went on out toward his house, his mind worrying and gnawing at the problem he thought he had solved long ago. When he got home, there was a small white Vespa parked at the curb. And a woman sitting on his front step.

She stood up as Harold came up the walk, and put her hand out. She was one of the most striking women Harold had ever seen – he had seen her before, of course, but rarely this close up.

'I'm Nadine Cross,' she said. Her voice was low, close to being husky. Her grip was firm and cool. Harold's eyes dropped involuntarily to her body for a moment, a habit he knew girls hated, but one he seemed powerless to stop. This one did not seem to mind. She was wearing a pair of light cotton twill slacks that clung to her long legs and a sleeveless blouse of some light blue silky material. No bra under it, either. How old was she? Thirty? Thirty-five? Younger, maybe. She was going prematurely gray.

All over? the endlessly horny (and endlessly virginal, seemingly) part of his mind inquired, and his heart beat a little faster.

'Harold Lauder,' he said, smiling. 'You came in with Larry Underwood's party, didn't you?'

'Yes, that's right.'

'Followed Stu and Frannie and me across the Big Empty, I understand. Larry came to see me last week, brought me a bottle of wine and some candy bars.' His words had a tinkling, false sound to them, and he was suddenly sure that she knew he had been cataloguing her, undressing her in his mind. He fought an urge to lick his lips and won . . . at least temporarily. 'He's a helluva nice guy.'

'Larry?' She laughed a little, a strange and somehow cryptic sound. 'Yes, Larry's a prince.'

They gazed at each other for a moment, and Harold had never been looked at by a woman whose eyes were so frank and speculative. He was again aware of his excitement, and a warm nervousness in his belly.

'Well,' he said. 'What can I do for you this afternoon, Miss Cross?'

'You could call me Nadine, for a start. And you could invite me to stay for supper. That would get us a little further along.'

That sense of nervous excitement began to spread. 'Nadine, would you like to stay for supper?'

'Very much,' she said, and smiled. When she laid her hand on his forearm, he felt a tingle like a low-grade electric shock. Her eyes never left his. 'Thank you.'

He fumbled his latchkey into its slot, thinking: *Now she'll ask me why I lock my door and I'll mumble and stumble around, looking for an answer, and seem like a fool.*

But Nadine never asked.

★   ★   ★

He didn't cook dinner; she did.

Harold had gotten to the point where he considered it impossible to get even a half-decent meal out of cans, but Nadine managed nicely. Suddenly aware of and appalled by what he had spent his day doing, he asked if she could entertain herself for twenty minutes (and she was probably here on some very mundane piece of business, he cautioned himself desperately) while he cleaned up.

When he came back – having splurged and taken a two-bucket shower – she was bustling around in the kitchen. Water was boiling merrily away on the bottled gas stove. As he came into the kitchen, she dumped half a cup of elbow macaroni into the pot. Something mellow was being simmered in a skillet on the other burner; he got a combined aroma of French onion soup, red wine, and mushrooms. His stomach rumbled. The day's grisly work had suddenly lost its power over his appetite.

'It smells fantastic,' he said. 'You shouldn't have, but I'm not complaining.'

'It's a Stroganoff casserole,' she said, turning to smile at him. 'Strictly makeshift, I'm afraid. Tinned beef is not one of the recommended ingredients when they make this dish in the world's finer restaurants, but –' She shrugged to indicate the limitations they all labored under.

'It's nice of you to do it.'

'Not at all.' She gave him that speculative glance again, and turned halfway toward him, the silky material of her blouse pulled taut against her left breast, molding it sweetly. He felt a hot flush creeping up his neck and willed himself not to have an erection. He suspected that his willpower would not be equal to the task. He suspected, in fact, that it wouldn't even be close. 'We're going to be very good friends,' she said.

'We . . . are?'

'Yes.' She turned back to the stove, seeming to close the subject, leaving Harold in a thicket of possibilities.

After that, their conversation consisted strictly of trivialities . . . Free Zone gossip, for the most part. Of this there was already a rich supply. Once, halfway through the meal, he tried again to ask her what had brought her here, but she only smiled and shook her head. 'I like to see a man eat.'

For a moment Harold thought she must be talking about someone else and then realized she meant *him*. And he did eat; he had three helpings of the Stroganoff, and the tinned meat did not detract from the recipe at all, in Harold's opinion. The conversation seemed to make itself, leaving him free to quiet the lion in his belly, and to look at her.

Striking, had he thought? She was beautiful. Ripe and beautiful. Her hair, which she had pulled back into a casual horsetail in order to cook more easily, was twisted with strands of pure white, not gray as he had first thought. Her eyes were grave and dark, and when they focused unhesitatingly on his, Harold felt giddy. Her voice was low and confidential. The sound of it began to affect him in a way that was both uncomfortable and almost excruciatingly pleasant.

When the meal was done, he started to get up but she beat him to it. 'Coffee or tea?'

'Really, I could —'

'You could, but you won't. Coffee, tea . . . or me?' She smiled then, not the smile of someone who has offered a remark of minor risquéness ('risky talk,' as his dear old mum would have said, her mouth set in a disapproving line), but a slow little smile, rich as the dollop of cream on top of a gooey dessert. And again the speculative look.

His brain spinning, Harold replied with insane casualness: 'The latter two,' and was only able to contain a burst of adolescent giggles with a mighty effort.

'Well, we'll start with tea for two,' Nadine said, and went to the stove.

Hot blood crashed into Harold's head the instant her back was turned, undoubtedly turning his face as purple as a turnip. *Some Mr Suave you are!* he hectored himself feverishly. *You misinterpreted a perfectly innocent remark like the goddam fool that you are, and you've probably spoiled a very nice occasion. And it serves you right! It serves you damned well right!*

By the time she brought the steaming mugs of tea back to the table, Harold's violent flush had faded somewhat and he had himself under control. Giddiness had turned just as abruptly to despair, and he felt (not for the first time) that his body and mind had been stuffed willy-nilly into the car of a huge roller-coaster made of pure emotion. He hated it but was powerless to get off the ride.

If she was interested in me at all, he thought (and God knows why she would be, he added gloomily to himself), *I have undoubtedly put paid to that by exposing the full range of my sophomoric wit.*

Well, he had done things like that before, and he supposed he could live with the knowledge that he had done it again.

She looked at him over the rim of her teacup with those disconcertingly frank eyes and smiled again, and the shred of equanimity he had been able to muster up promptly vanished.

'Can I help you with something?' he asked. It sounded like some lumbering double-entendre, but he *had* to say something, because she must have had some purpose in coming here. He felt his own protective smile faltering on his lips in his confusion.

'Yes,' she said, and put her teacup down decisively. 'Yes, you can. Maybe we can help each other. Could you come into the living room?'

'Sure.' His hand was shaking; when he set his cup down and rose, some of it spilled. As he followed her into the living room, he noticed how smoothly her slacks (which aren't very slack at all, his mind gibbered) clung to her buttocks. It was the panty line that broke up the smooth look of most women's slacks, he had read that somewhere, maybe in one of the magazines he had kept in the back of his bedroom closet behind the shoeboxes, and the magazine had gone on to say that if a woman really wanted that smooth and seamless look, she should wear a G-string or no panties at all.

He swallowed; tried to, at least. There seemed to be a huge blockage of some kind in his throat.

The living room was dim, lit only by the glow that filtered through the drawn shades. It was past six-thirty, and outside the evening was drawing toward dusk. Harold went to one of the windows to run the shade up and let more light in, when she put her hand on his arm. He turned toward her, his mouth dry.

'No. I like them down. It gives us privacy.'

'Privacy,' Harold croaked. His voice was that of an age-rusted parrot.

'So I can do this,' she said, and stepped lightly into his arms.

Her body was pressed frankly and completely against him, the first time in his life anything of the sort had happened, and his amazement was total. He could feel the soft and individual press of each breast through his white cotton shirt and her silky blue one. Her belly, firm but vulnerable, against his, not shying away from the feel of his erection. There was a sweet smell to her, perfume maybe, or maybe just *her own smell*, that seemed like a told secret that bursts, revelative, on the listener. His hands found her hair and plunged into it.

At last the kiss broke but she didn't move away. Her body remained against his like soft fire. She was perhaps three inches shorter, and her face was turned up to his. It occurred to him in a dim sort of way that it was one of the most amusing ironies of his life: When love – or a reasonable facsimile – had finally found him, it was as if he had slipped sideways into the pages of a love story in a glossy women's magazine. The authors of such stories, he had once claimed in an unacknowledged letter to *Redbook*, were one of the few convincing arguments in favor of enforced eugenics.

But now her face was turned up to his, her lips were moist and half-parted, her eyes were bright and almost . . . almost . . . yes, almost starry. The only detail not strictly compatible with a *Redbook*'s-eye view of life was his hard-on, which was truly amazing.

'Now,' she said. 'On the couch.'

Somehow they got there, and then they were tangled up there, and her hair had come loose and flowed over her shoulders; her perfume seemed everywhere. His hands were on her breasts and she was *not minding*; in fact she was twisting and squirming around to allow his hands freer access. He did not caress her; in his frantic need what he did was plunder her.

'You're a virgin,' Nadine said. No question there . . . and it was easier not to have to lie. He nodded.

'Then we do this first. Next time it will be slower. Better.'

She unbuttoned his jeans and they snapped open to the zipper-tab of his fly. She traced a light forefinger across his belly just below the navel. Harold's flesh shuddered and jumped at her touch.

'Nadine –'

'Shhh!' Her face was hidden in the fall of her hair, making it impossible to read her expression.

His fly was pulled down and the Ridiculous Thing, made even more ridiculous by the white cotton in which it was swaddled (thank God he had changed clothes after his shower), popped out like Jack from his box. The Ridiculous Thing was unaware of its own comical appearance, for its business was deadly serious. The business of virgins is always deadly serious – not pleasure but experience.

'My blouse –'

'Can I – ?'

'Yes, that's what I want. And then I'll take care of you.'

Take care of you. The words echoed down into his mind like stones flung into a well, and then he was sucking greedily at her breast, tasting the salt and sweet of her.

She drew in breath. 'Harold, that's lovely.'

Take care of you, the words clanged and banged in his mind.

Her hands slipped inside the waistband of his underpants and his jeans slid down to his ankles in a meaningless jingle of keys.

'Raise up,' she whispered, and he did.

It took less than a minute. He cried aloud with the strength of his climax, unable to help himself. It was as if someone had touched a match to a whole network of nerves just under his skin, nerves that plunged deep to form the living webwork of his groin. He could understand why so many of the writers made that connection between orgasm and death.

Then he lay back in the dimness, his head against the sofa, his chest heaving, his mouth open. He was afraid to look down. He felt that quarts of semen must have splattered all over everything.

Young feller, we've struck oil!

He looked at her shamefacedly, embarrassed at the hair-trigger way he had gone off. But she was only smiling at him with those calm, dark eyes that seemed to know everything, the eyes of a very young girl in a Victorian painting. A girl who knows too much, perhaps, about her father.

'I'm sorry,' he muttered.

'Why? For what?' Her eyes never left his face.

'You didn't get much out of that.'

'*Au contraire*, I got a great deal of satisfaction.' But he didn't think that was exactly what he had meant. Before he had a chance to consider this, she went on: 'You're young. We can go as many times as you want to.'

He looked at her without speaking, unable to speak.

'But you must know one thing.' She put a hand lightly on him. 'What you told me about being a virgin? Well, I am, too.'

'You –' His expression of astonishment must have been comical, because she threw back her head and laughed.

'Is there no room for virginity in your philosophy, Horatio?'

'No . . . yes . . . but –'

'I'm a virgin. And I'm going to stay that way. Because it's for someone else to . . . to make me not a virgin anymore.'

'Who?'

'You know who.'

He stared at her, suddenly cold all over. She looked back calmly.

'*Him?*'

She half turned away and nodded.

'But I can show you things,' she said, still not looking at him. 'We can do things. Things you've never even . . . no, I take that back. Maybe you *have* dreamed of them, but you never dreamed you'd do them. We can play. We can make ourselves drunk with it. We can wallow in it. We can . . .' She trailed off, and then did look at him, a look so sly and sensual that he felt himself stirring again. 'We can do anything – *everything* – but that one little thing. And that one thing really isn't so important, is it?'

Images whirled giddily in his mind. Silk scarves . . . boots . . . leather . . . rubber. Oh Jesus. *Fantasies of a Schoolboy*. A weird kind of sexual solitaire. But it was all a kind of dream, wasn't it? A fantasy begotten of fantasy, child of a dark dream. He wanted all those things, wanted *her*, but he also wanted more.

The question was, how much would he settle for?

'You can tell me everything,' she said. 'I'll be your mother, or your sister, or your whore, or your slave. All you have to do is tell me, Harold.'

How that echoed in his mind! How that intoxicated him!

He opened his mouth, and the voice that emerged was as tuneless as the chiming of a cracked bell. 'But for a price. Isn't that right? For a price. Because nothing is for free. Not even now, when everything is lying around, waiting to be picked up.'

'I want what you want,' she said. 'I know what's in your heart.'

'No one knows that.'

'What's in your heart is in your ledger. I could read it there – I know where it is – but I don't need to.'

He started and looked at her with a wild guilt.

'It used to be under that loose stone there,' she said, pointing to the hearth, 'but you moved it. Now it's behind the insulation in the attic.'

'How do you know that? *How do you know?*'

'I know because he told me. He . . . you could say that he wrote me a letter. And what's more important, he told me about *you*, Harold. How the cowboy took your woman and then kept you off the Free Zone Committee. He *wants* us to be together, Harold.

And he's generous. From now until when we leave here, it's recess for you and me.'

She touched him and smiled.

'From now until then it's playtime. Do you understand?'

'I —'

'No,' she answered, 'you don't. Not yet. But you will, Harold. You will.'

Insanely, it came to his mind to tell her to call him Hawk.

'And later, Nadine? What does he want later?'

'What you want. And what I want. What you almost did to Redman on the first night you went out hunting for the old woman . . . but on a much larger scale. And when that's done, we can go to him, Harold. We can be with him. We can stay with him.' Her eyes slipped half-closed in a kind of rapture. Perhaps paradoxically, the fact that she loved the other but would give herself to him — might actually enjoy it — brought his desire up again, hot and close.

'What if I say no?' His lips felt cold, ashy.

She shrugged, and the movement made her breasts sway prettily. 'Life will go on, won't it, Harold? I'll try to find some way of doing the thing I have to do. You'll go on. Sooner or later you'll find a girl who will do that . . . one little thing for you. But that one little thing is very tiresome after a while. Very tiresome.'

'How would you know?' he asked, and grinned crookedly at her.

'I know because sex is life in small, and life is tiresome — time spent in a variety of waiting rooms. You might have your little glories here, Harold, but to what end? On the whole it will be a humdrum, slipping-down life, and you'll always remember me with my shirt off, and you'll always wonder what I would have looked like with everything off. You'll wonder what it would have been like to hear me talking dirty to you . . . or to have me spill honey all over your . . . body . . . and then lick it off . . . and you'll wonder —'

'Stop it,' he said. He was trembling all over.

But she wouldn't.

'I think you'll also wonder what it would have been like on *his* side of the world,' she said. 'That more than anything and everything else, maybe.'

'I —'

'Decide, Harold. Do I put my shirt back on or take everything else off?'

How long did he think? He didn't know. Later, he wasn't even sure he had struggled with the question. But when he spoke, the words tasted like death in his mouth: 'In the bedroom. Let's go in the bedroom.'

She smiled at him, such a smile of triumph and sensual promise that he shuddered from it, and his own eager response to it.

She took his hand.

And Harold Lauder succumbed to his destiny.

CHAPTER 55

The Judge's house overlooked a cemetery.

He and Larry sat on the back porch after dinner, smoking Roi-Tan cigars and watching sunset fade to pale orange around the mountains.

'When I was a boy,' the Judge said, 'we lived within walking distance of the finest cemetery in Illinois. Its name was Mount Hope. Every night after supper, my father, who was then in his early sixties, would take a walk. Sometimes I would walk with him. And if the walk took us past this perfectly maintained necropolis, he would say, "What do you think, Teddy? Is there any hope?" And I would answer, "There's Mount Hope," and each time he'd roar with laughter as if it had been the first time. I sometimes think we walked past that boneyard just so he could share that joke with me. He was a wealthy man, but it was the funniest joke he seemed to know.'

The Judge smoked, his chin low, his shoulders hunched high.

'He died in 1937, when I was still in my teens,' he said. 'I have missed him ever since. A boy does not need a father unless he is a good father, but a good father is indispensable. No hope but Mount Hope. How he enjoyed that! He was seventy-eight years old when he passed on. He died like a king, Larry. He was seated upon the throne in our home's smallest room, with the newspaper in his lap.'

Larry, not sure how to respond to this rather bizarre bit of nostalgia, said nothing.

The Judge sighed. 'This is going to be quite a little operation here before long,' he said. 'If you can get the power on again, that is. If you can't, people are going to get nervous and start heading south before the bad weather can come and hem them in.'

'Ralph and Brad say it's going to happen. I trust them.'

'Then we'll hope that your trust is well founded, won't we?

Maybe it is a good thing that the old woman is gone. Perhaps she knew it would be better that way. Maybe people should be free to judge for themselves what the lights in the sky are, and if one tree has a face or if the face was only a trick of the light and shadow. Do you understand me, Larry?'

'No, sir,' Larry said truthfully. 'I'm not sure I do.'

'I wonder if we need to reinvent that whole tiresome business of gods and saviors and ever-afters before we reinvent the flushing toilet. That's what I'm saying. I wonder if this is the right time for gods.'

'Do you think she's dead?'

'She's been gone six days now. The Search Committee hasn't found a trace of her. Yes, I think she's dead, but even now I am not completely sure. She was an amazing woman, completely outside any rational frame of reference. Perhaps one of the reasons I'm almost glad to have her gone is because I'm such a rational old curmudgeon. I like to creep through my daily round, to water my garden – did you see the way I've brought the begonias back? I'm quite proud of that – to read my books, to write my notes for my own book about the plague. I like to do all those things and then have a glass of wine at bedtime and fall asleep with an untroubled mind. Yes. None of us want to see portents and omens, no matter how much we like our ghost stories and the spooky films. None of us want to *really see* a Star in the East or a pillar of fire by night. We want peace and rationality and routine. If we have to see God in the black face of an old woman, it's bound to remind us that there's a devil for every god – and our devil may be closer than we like to think.'

'That's why I'm here,' Larry said awkwardly. He wished mightily that the Judge hadn't just mentioned his garden, his books, his notes, and his glass of wine before bedtime. He had had a two-bit bright idea at a meeting of friends and had made a blithe suggestion. Now he wondered if there was any possible way of going on without sounding like a cruel and opportunistic halfwit.

'I know why you're here. I accept.'

Larry jerked, making the wicker of his chair strain and whisper. 'Who told you? This is supposed to be very quiet, Judge. If someone on the committee has been leaking, we're in a hell of a jam.'

The Judge raised one liverspotted hand, cutting him off. His eyes twinkled in his time-beaten face. 'Softly, my boy – softly. No one on your committee has been leaking, not that I know of, and I keep my ear close to the ground. No, I whispered the secret to myself. Why did you come here tonight? Your face is an education in itself, Larry. I hope you don't play poker. When I was talking about my few simple pleasures, I could see your face sag and droop . . . a rather comic stricken expression appeared on it –'

'Is that so funny? What should I do, look happy about . . . about . . .'

'Sending me west,' the Judge said quietly. 'To spy out the land. Isn't that about it?'

'That's exactly it.'

'I wondered how long it would be before the idea would surface. It is tremendously important, of course, tremendously necessary if the Free Zone is to be assured its full chance to survive. We have no real idea what he's up to over there. He might as well be on the dark side of the moon.'

'If he's really there.'

'Oh, he's there. In one form or another, he is there. Never doubt it.' He took a nail-clipper from his pants pocket and went to work on his fingernails, the little snipping sound punctuating his speech. 'Tell me, has the committee discussed what might happen if we decided we liked it better over there? If we decided to stay?'

Larry was flabbergasted by the idea. He told the Judge that, to the best of his knowledge, it hadn't occurred to anybody.

'I imagine he's got the lights on,' the Judge said with deceptive idleness. 'There's an attraction in that, you know. Obviously this man Impening felt it.'

'Good riddance to bad rubbish,' Larry said grimly, and the Judge laughed long and heartily.

When he sobered he said, 'I'll go tomorrow. In a Land-Rover, I think. North to Wyoming, and then west. Thank God I can still drive well enough! I'll travel straight across Idaho and toward Northern California. It may take two weeks going, longer coming back. Coming back, there may be snow.'

'Yes. We've discussed that possibility.'

'And I'm old. The old are prone to attacks of heart trouble and stupidity. I presume you are sending backups?'

'Well . . .'

'No, you're not supposed to talk about that. I withdraw the question.'

'Look, you can refuse this,' Larry blurted. 'No one is holding a gun to your hea –'

'Are you trying to absolve yourself of your responsibility to me?' the Judge asked sharply.

'Maybe. Maybe I am. Maybe I think your chances of getting back are one in ten and your chances of getting back with information we can actually base decisions on are one in twenty. Maybe I'm just trying to say in a nice way that I could have made a mistake. You could be too old.'

'I am too old for adventure,' the Judge said, putting his clippers away, 'but I hope I am not too old to do what I feel is right. There is an old woman out there someplace who has probably gone to a miserable death because she felt it was right. Prompted by religious mania, I have no doubt. But people who try hard to do the right thing always seem mad. I'll go. I'll be cold. My bowels will not work properly. I'll be lonely. I'll miss my begonias. But . . .' He looked up at Larry, and his eyes gleamed in the dark. 'I'll also be clever.'

'I suppose you will,' Larry said, and felt the sting of tears at the corners of his eyes.

'How is Lucy?' the Judge asked, apparently closing the subject of his departure.

'Fine,' Larry said. 'We're both fine.'

'No problems?'

'No,' he said, and thought about Nadine. Something about her desperation the last time he had seen her still troubled him deeply. *You're my last chance*, she had said. Strange talk, almost suicidal. And what help was there for her? Psychiatry? That was a laugh, when the best they could do for a GP was a horse doctor. Even Dial-A-Prayer was gone now.

'It's good that you are with Lucy,' the Judge said, 'but you're worried about the other woman, I suspect.'

'Yes, I am.' What followed was extremely difficult to say, but having it out and confessed to another person made him feel much better. 'I think she might be considering, well, suicide.' He rushed on: 'It's not just me, don't get the idea I think any girl would kill herself just because she can't have sexy old Larry Underwood. But the boy she was taking care of has come out of his shell, and I think she feels alone, with no one to depend on her.'

'If her depression deepens into a chronic, cyclic thing, she may indeed kill herself,' the Judge said with chilling indifference.

Larry looked at him, shocked.

'But you can only be one man,' the Judge said. 'Isn't that true?'

'Yes.'

'And your choice is made?'

'Yes.'

'For good?'

'Yes, it is.'

'Then live with it,' the Judge said with great relish. 'For God's sake, Larry, grow up. Develop a little self-righteousness. A lot of that is an ugly thing, God knows, but a little applied over all your scruples is an absolute necessity! It is to the soul what a good sun-block is to the skin during the heat of the summer. You can only captain your own soul, and from time to time some smartass psychologist will question your ability to even do that. Grow up! Your Lucy is a fine woman. To take responsibility for more than her and your own soul is to ask for too much, and asking for too much is one of humanity's more popular ways of courting disaster.'

'I like talking to you,' Larry said, and was both startled and amused by the open ingenuousness of the comment.

'Probably because I am telling you exactly what you want to hear,' the Judge said serenely. And then he added: 'There are a great many ways to commit suicide, you know.'

And before too much time had passed, Larry had occasion to recall that remark in bitter circumstances.

At quarter past eight the next morning, Harold's truck was leaving the Greyhound depot to go back to the Table Mesa area. Harold, Weizak, and two others were sitting in the back of the truck. Norman Kellogg and another man were in the cab. They were at the intersection of Arapahoe and Broadway when a brand-new Land-Rover drove slowly toward them.

Weizak waved and shouted, 'Where ya headed, Judge?'

The Judge, looking rather comic in a woolen shirt and a vest, pulled over. 'I believe I might go to Denver for the day,' he said blandly.

'Will that thing get you there?' Weizak asked.

'Oh, I believe so, if I steer clear of the main-traveled roads.'

'Well, if you go by one of those X-rated bookstores, why don't you bring back a trunkful?'

This sally was greeted with a burst of laughter from everyone

– the Judge included – but Harold. He looked sallow and haggard this morning, as if he had rested ill. In fact, he had hardly slept at all. Nadine had been as good as her word; he had fulfilled quite a few dreams the night before. Dreams of the damp variety, let us say. He was already looking forward to tonight, and Weizak's sally about pornography was only good for a ghost of a smile now that he had had a little first-hand experience. Nadine had been sleeping when he left. Before they dropped off around two, she had told him she wanted to read his ledger. He had told her to go ahead if she wanted to. Perhaps he was putting himself at her mercy, but he was too confused to know for sure. But it was the best writing he had ever done in his life and the deciding factor was his want – no, his *need*. His need to have someone else read, experience, his good work.

Now Kellogg was leaning out of the dump truck's cab toward the Judge. 'You be careful, Pop. Okay? There's funny folks on the roads these days.'

'Indeed there are,' the Judge said with a strange smile. 'And indeed I will. A good day to you, gentlemen. And you too, Mr Weizak.'

That brought another burst of laughter, and they parted.

The Judge did not head toward Denver. When he reached Route 36, he proceeded directly across it and out along Route 7. The morning sun was bright and mellow, and on this secondary route, there was not enough stalled traffic to block the road. The town of Brighton was worse; at one point he had to leave the highway and drive across the local high school football field to avoid a colossal traffic jam. He continued east until he reached I-25. A right turn here would have taken him into Denver. Instead he turned left – north – and nosed onto the feeder ramp. Halfway down he put the transmission in neutral and looked left again, west, to where the Rockies rose serenely into the blue sky with Boulder lying at their base.

He had told Larry he was too old for adventure, and God save him, but that had been a lie. His heart hadn't beat with this quick rhythm for twenty years, the air had not tasted this sweet, colors had not seemed this bright. He would follow I-25 to Cheyenne and then move west toward what-ever waited for him beyond the mountains. His skin, dry with age, nonetheless crawled and goosebumped a little at the thought. I-80 west, into Salt Lake City, then across Nevada to Reno. Then he would head north again, but that hardly mattered. Because somewhere between Salt Lake and Reno, maybe even sooner, he would be stopped, questioned, and probably sent somewhere else to be questioned again. And at some place or other, an invitation might be issued.

It was not even impossible to think that he might meet the dark man himself.

'Get moving, old man,' he said softly.

He put the Rover in gear and crept down to the turnpike. There were three lanes northbound, all of them relatively clear. As he had guessed, traffic jams and multiple accidents back in Denver had effectively dammed the flow of traffic. The traffic was heavy on the other side of the median strip – the poor fools who had been headed south, blindly hoping that south would be better – but here the going was good. For a while at least.

Judge Farris drove on, glad to be making his start. He had slept poorly last night. He would sleep better tonight, under the stars, his old body wrapped firmly in two sleeping bags. He wondered if he would ever see Boulder again and thought the chances were probably against it. And yet his excitement was very great.

It was one of the finest days of his life.

Early that afternoon, Nick, Ralph, and Stu biked out to North Boulder to a small stucco house where Tom Cullen lived by himself. Tom's house had already become a land-mark to Boulder's 'old' residents. Stan Nogotny said it was as if the Catholics, Baptists, and Seventh-Day Adventists had gotten together with the Democrats and the Moonies to create a religious-political Disneyland.

The front lawn of the house was a weird tableau of statues. There were a dozen Virgin Marys, some of them apparently in the act of feeding flocks of pink plastic lawn flamingos. The largest of the flamingos was taller than Tom himself and anchored to the ground on a single leg that ended in a four-foot spike. There was a giant wishing well with a large plastic glow-in-the-dark Jesus standing in the ornamental bucket with His hands outstretched . . . apparently to bless the pink flamingos. Beside the wishing well was a large plaster cow who was apparently drinking from a birdbath.

The front door screen slammed open and Tom came out to meet them, stripped to the waist. Seen from a distance, Nick thought, you would have supposed he was some fantastically virile writer or painter, with his bright blue eyes and that big reddish-blond beard. As he got closer you might have given up that idea in favor of one not quite so intellectual . . . maybe some sort of craftsman from the counterculture who had substituted *kitsch* for originality. And when he got very close, smiling and talking away a mile a minute, you realized for sure that a goodly chunk of Tom Cullen's attic insulation was missing.

Nick knew that one of the reasons he felt a strong sense of empathy for Tom was because he himself had been assumed to be mentally retarded, at first because his handicap had held him back from learning to read and write, later because people just assumed that someone who was both deaf and mute must be mentally retarded. He had heard all the slang terms at one time or another. A few bricks short the load. Soft upstairs. Running on three wheels. The guy's got a hole in his head and his brains done leaked out. This guy ain't traveling with a full seabag. He remembered the night he had stopped for a couple of beers in Zack's, the ginmill on the outskirts of Shoyo – the night Ray Booth and his buddies had jumped him. The bartender had stood at the far end of the bar, leaning confidentially over it to speak to a customer. His hand had been half shielding his mouth, so Nick could only make out fragments of what he had been saying. He didn't need to make out any more than that, however. *Deaf-mute . . . probably retarded . . . almost all those guys're retarded . . .*

But among all the ugly terms for mental retardation, there was one term that *did* fit Tom Cullen. It was one Nick had applied to him often, and with great compassion, in the silence of his own mind. The phrase was: *The guy's not playing with a full deck.* That was what was wrong with Tom. That was what it came down to. And the pity in Tom's case was that so few cards were missing, and low cards at that – a deuce of diamonds, a trey of clubs, something like that. But without those cards, you just couldn't have a good game of anything. You couldn't even win at solitaire with those cards missing from the deck.

'Nicky!' Tom yelled. 'Am I glad to see you! Laws, yes! Tom Cullen is so glad!' He threw his arms around Nick's neck and gave him a hug. Nick felt his bad eye sting with tears behind the black eyepatch he still wore on bright days like this one. 'And Ralph too! And that one. You're . . . let's see . . .'

'I'm –' Stu began, but Nick silenced him with a brusque

chopping gesture of his left hand. He had been practicing mnemonics with Tom, and it seemed to work. If you could associate something you knew with a name you wanted to remember, it often clicked home and stuck. Rudy had turned him on to that, too, all those long years ago.

Now he took his pad from his pocket and jotted on it. Then he handed it to Ralph to read aloud.

Frowning a little, Ralph did so: 'What do you like to eat that comes in a bowl with meat and vegetables and gravy?'

Tom went stockstill. The animation died out of his face. His mouth dropped slackly open and he became the picture of idiocy.

Stu stirred uncomfortably and said, 'Nick, don't you think we ought to –'

Nick shushed him with a finger at his lips, and at the same instant Tom came alive again.

'Stew!' he said, capering and laughing. 'You're Stew!' He looked at Nick for confirmation, and Nick gave him a V-for-victory.

'M–O–O–N, that spells Stew, Tom Cullen knows that, *everybody* knows that!'

Nick pointed to the door of Tom's house.

'Want to come in? Laws, yes! All of us are going to come in. Tom's been decorating his house.'

Ralph and Stu exchanged an amused glance as they followed Nick and Tom up the porch steps. Tom was always 'decorating.' He did not 'furnish,' because the house had of course been furnished when he moved in. Going inside was like entering a madly jumbled Mother Goose world.

A huge gilded birdcage with a green stuffed parrot carefully wired to the perch hung just inside the front door and Nick had to duck under it. The thing was, he thought, Tom's decorations were not just random rickrack. That would have made this house into something no more striking than a rummage sale barn. But there was something more here, something that seemed just beyond what the ordinary mind could grasp as a pattern. In a large square block over the mantel in the living room were a number of credit card signs, all of them centered and carefully mounted. YOUR VISA CARD WELCOME HERE. JUST SAY MASTERCARD. WE HONOR AMERICAN EXPRESS. DINERS CLUB. Now the question occurred: How did Tom know that all those signs were part of a fixed set? He couldn't read, but somehow he had grasped the pattern.

Sitting on the coffee table was a large Styrofoam fireplug. On the windowsill, where it could catch the sunlight and reflect cool fans of blue light onto the wall, was a police car bubble.

Tom toured them through the entire house. The downstairs game room was filled with stuffed birds and animals that Tom had found in a taxidermy shop; he had strung the birds on nearly invisible piano wire and they seemed to cruise, owls and hawks and even a bald eagle with moth-eaten feathers and one yellow glass eye missing. A woodchuck stood on its hind legs in one corner, a gopher in another, a skunk in another, a weasel in the fourth. In the center of the room was a coyote, somehow seeming to be the focus for all the smaller animals.

The banister leading up the stairs had been wrapped in red and white strips of Con-Tact paper so that it resembled a barber pole. The upper hallway was hung with fighter planes on more piano wire – Fokkers, Spads, Stukas, Spitfires, Zeros, Messerschmitts. The floor of the bathroom had been painted a bright electric blue and on it was Tom's extensive collection of toy boats, sailing an enamel sea around four white porcelain islands and one white porcelain continent: the legs of the tub, the base of the toilet.

At last Tom took them back downstairs and they sat below the credit card montage and facing a 3-D picture of John and Robert Kennedy against a background of gold-edged clouds. The legend beneath proclaimed BROTHERS TOGETHER IN HEAVEN.

'You like Tom's decorations? What do you think? Nice?'

'Very nice,' Stu said. 'Tell me. Those birds downstairs . . . do they ever get on your nerves?'

'Laws, no!' Tom said, astounded. 'They're full of sawdust!'

Nick handed a note to Ralph.

'Tom, Nick wants to know if you'd mind being hypnotized again. Like the time Stan did it. It's important this time, not just a game. Nick says he'll explain why afterward.'

'Go ahead,' Tom said. '*Youuu . . . are getting . . .* verrrry sleepy . . . right?'

'Yes, that's it,' Ralph said.

'Do you want me to look at the watch again? I don't mind. You know, when you swing it back and forth? *Verrrry . . . sleeeepy . . .*' Tom looked at them doubtfully. 'Except I don't feel very sleepy. Laws, no. I went to bed early last night. Tom Cullen always goes to bed early because there's no TV to watch.'

Stu said softly: 'Tom, would you like to see an elephant?'

Tom's eyes closed immediately. His head dropped forward loosely. His respiration deepened to long, slow strokes. Stu watched this with great surprise. Nick had given him the key phrase, but Stu hadn't known whether or not to believe it would work. And he had never expected that it could happen so fast.

'Just like putting a chicken's head under its wing,' Ralph marveled.

Nick handed Stu his prepared 'script' for this encounter.

Stu looked at Nick for a long moment. Nick looked back, then nodded gravely that Stu should go ahead.

'Tom, can you hear me?' Stu asked.

'Yes, I can hear you,' Tom said, and the quality of his voice made Stu look up sharply.

It was different from Tom's usual voice, but in a way Stu could not quite put his hand to. It reminded him of something which had happened when he was eighteen, and graduating from high school. They had been in the boys' locker room before the ceremony, all the guys he'd been going to school with since . . . well, since the first day of the first grade in at least four cases, and almost as long in many others. And for just a moment he had seen how much their faces had changed between those old days, those first days, and that moment of insight, standing on the tile floor of the locker room with the black robe in his hands. That vision of change had made him shiver then, and it made him shiver now. The faces he had looked into had no longer been the faces of children . . . but neither had they yet become the faces of men. They were faces in limbo, faces caught perfectly between two well-defined states of being. This voice, coming out of the shadowland of Tom Cullen's subconscious, seemed like those faces, only infinitely sadder. Stu thought it was the voice of the man forever denied.

But they were waiting for him to go on, and go on he must.

'I'm Stu Redman, Tom.'

'Yes. Stu Redman.'

'Nick is here.'

'Yes, Nick is here.'

'Ralph Brentner is here, too.'

'Yes, Ralph is, too.'

'We're your friends.'

'I know.'

'We'd like you to do something, Tom. For the Zone. It's dangerous.'

'Dangerous . . .'

Trouble crossed over Tom's face, like a cloud shadow slowly crossing a midsummer field of corn.

'Will I have to be afraid? Will I have to . . .' He trailed off, sighing.

Stu looked at Nick, troubled.

Nick mouthed: *Yes*.

'It's *him*,' Tom said, and sighed dreadfully. It was like the sound a bitter November wind makes in a stand of denuded oaks. Stu felt that shudder inside him again. Ralph had gone pale.

'Who, Tom?' Stu asked gently.

'Flagg. His name is Randy Flagg. The dark man. You want me to . . .' That sick sigh again, bitter and long.

'How do you know him, Tom?' This wasn't in the script.

'Dreams . . . I see his face in dreams.'

I see his face in dreams. But none of them had seen his face. It was always hidden.

'You see him?'

'Yes . . .'

'What does he look like, Tom?'

Tom didn't speak for a long time. Stu had decided he wasn't going to answer and he was preparing to go back to the 'script' when Tom said: 'He looks like anybody you see on the street. But when he grins, birds fall dead off telephone lines. When he looks at you a certain way, your prostate goes bad and your urine burns. The grass yellows up and dies where he spits. He's always outside. He came out of time. He doesn't know himself. He has the name of a thousand demons. Jesus knocked him into a herd of pigs once. His name is Legion. He's afraid of us. We're inside. He knows magic. He can call the wolves and live in the crows. He's the king of nowhere. But he's afraid of us. He's afraid of . . . inside.'

Tom fell silent.

The three of them stared at each other, pallid as gravestones. Ralph had seized his hat from his head and was kneading it convulsively in his hands. Nick had put one hand over his eyes. Stu's throat had turned to dry glass.

His name is Legion. He is the king of nowhere.

'Can you say anything else about him?' Stu asked in a low voice.

'Only that I'm afraid of him, too. But I'll do what you want. But Tom . . . is so afraid.' That dreadful sigh again.

'Tom,' Ralph said suddenly. 'Do you know if Mother Abagail . . . if she's still alive?' Ralph's face was desperately set, the face of a man who has staked everything on one turn of the cards.

'She's alive.' Ralph leaned against the back of his chair with a great gust of breath. 'But she's not right with God yet,' Tom added.

'Not right with God? Why not, Tommy?'

'She's in the wilderness, God has lifted her up in the wilderness, she does not fear the terror that flies at noon or the terror that creeps at midnight . . . neither will the snake bite her nor the bee sting her . . . but she's not right with God yet. It was not the hand of Moses that brought water from the rock. It was not the hand of Abagail that turned the weasels back with their bellies empty. She's to be pitied. She will see, but she will see too late. There will be death. *His* death. She will die on the wrong side of the river. She –'

'Stop him,' Ralph groaned. 'Can't you stop him?'

'Tom,' Stu said.

'Yes.'

'Are you the same Tom that Nick met in Oklahoma? Are you the same Tom we know when you're awake?'

'Yes, but I am more than that Tom.'

'I don't understand.'

He shifted a little, his sleeping face calm.

'I am God's Tom.'

Completely unnerved now, Stu almost dropped Nick's notes.

'You say you'll do what we want.'

'Yes.'

'But do you see . . . do you think you'll come back?'

'That's not for me to see or say. Where shall I go?'

'West, Tom.'

Tom moaned. It was a sound that made the hair on the nape of Stu's neck stand on end. *What are we sending him into?* And maybe he knew. Maybe he had been there himself, only in Vermont, in mazes of corridors where the echo made it seem as if footsteps were following him. And gaining.

'West,' Tom said. 'West, yes.'

'We're sending you to look, Tom. To look and see. Then to come back.'

'Come back and tell.'

'Can you do that?'

'Yes. Unless they catch and kill me.'

Stu winced; they all winced.

'You go by yourself, Tom. Always west. Can you find west?'

'Where the sun goes down.'

'Yes. And if anyone asks why you're there, this is what you'll say: They drove you out of the Free Zone –'

'Drove me out. Drove Tom out. Put him on the road.'

'– because you were feebleminded.'

'They drove Tom out because Tom is feebleminded.'

'– and because you might have a woman and the woman might have idiot children.'

'Idiot children like Tom.'

Stu's stomach was rolling back and forth helplessly. His head felt like iron that had learned how to sweat. It was as if he was suffering from a terrible, debilitating hangover.

'Now repeat what you'll say if someone asks why you're in the West.'

'They drove Tom out because he was feebleminded. Laws, yes. They were afraid I might have a woman the way you have them with your prick in bed. Make her pregnant with idiots.'

'That's right, Tom. That's –'

'Drove me out,' he said in a soft, grieving voice. 'Drove Tom out of his nice house and put his feet on the road.'

Stu passed a shaking hand over his eyes. He looked at Nick. Nick seemed to double, then treble, in his vision. 'Nick, I don't know as I can finish,' he said helplessly.

Nick looked at Ralph. Ralph, pale as cheese, could only shake his head.

'Finish,' Tom said unexpectedly. 'Don't leave me out here in the dark.'

Forcing himself, Stu went on.

'Tom, do you know what the full moon looks like?'

'Yes . . . big and round.'

'Not the half-moon, or even most of the moon.'

'No,' Tom said.

'When you see that big round moon, you'll come back east. Back to us. Back to your house, Tom.'

'Yes, when I see it, I'll come back,' Tom agreed. 'I'll come back home.'

'And when you come back, you'll walk in the night and sleep in the day.'

'Walk at night, sleep in the day.'

'Right. And you won't let anybody see you if you can help it.'

'No.'

'But, Tom, someone might see you.'

'Yes, someone might.'

'If it's one person that sees you, Tom, kill him.'

'Kill him,' Tom said doubtfully.

'If it's more than one, run.'

'Run,' Tom said, with more certainty.

'But try not to be seen at all. Can you repeat all that back?'

'Yes. Come back when the moon is full. Not the half-moon, not the fingernail moon. Walk at night, sleep in the day. Don't let anybody see me. If one person sees me, kill him. If more than one person sees me, run away. But try not to let anyone see me.'

'That's very good. I want you to wake up in a few seconds. Okay?'

'Okay.'

'When I ask about the elephant, you'll wake up, okay?'

'Okay.'

Stu sat back with a long, shuddery sigh. 'Thank God that's over.'

Nick agreed with his eyes.

'Did you know that might happen, Nick?'

Nick shook his head.

'How could he know those things?' Stu muttered.

Nick was motioning for his pad. Stu gave it to him, glad to be rid of it. His fingers had sweated the page with Nick's script written on it almost to transparency. Nick wrote and handed it to Ralph. Ralph read it, lips moving slowly, and then handed it to Stu.

'Some people through history have considered the insane and the retarded to be close to divine. I don't think he told us anything that can be of practical use to us, but I know he scared the hell out of me. Magic, he said. How do you fight magic?'

'It's over my head, that's all,' Ralph muttered. 'Those things he said about Mother Abagail, I don't even want to think about them. Wake him up, Stu, and let's get out of here as quick as we can.' Ralph was close to tears.

Stu leaned forward again. 'Tom?'

'Yes.'

'Would you like to see an elephant?'

Tom's eyes opened at once and he looked around at them. 'I told you it wouldn't work,' he said. 'Laws, no. Tom doesn't get sleepy in the middle of the day.'

Nick handed a sheet to Stu, who glanced at it and then spoke to Tom. 'Nick says you did just fine.'

'I did? Did I stand on my head like before?'

With a twinge of bitter shame, Nick thought: No, Tom, you did a bunch of even better tricks this time.

'No,' Stu said. 'Tom, we came to ask if you could help us.'

'Me? Help? Sure! I love to help!'

'This is dangerous, Tom. We want you to go west, and then come back and tell us what you saw.'

'Okay, sure,' Tom said without the slightest hesitation, but Stu thought he saw a momentary shadow cross Tom's face . . . and linger behind his guileless blue eyes. 'When?'

Stu put a gentle hand on Tom's neck and wondered just what in the hell he was doing here. How were you supposed to figure these things out if you weren't Mother Abagail and didn't have a hot line to heaven? 'Pretty soon now,' he said gently. 'Pretty soon.'

When Stu got back to the apartment, Frannie was fixing supper.

'Harold was over,' she said. 'I asked him to stay to dinner, but he begged off.'

'Oh.'

She looked more closely at him. 'Stuart Redman, what dog bit you?'

'A dog named Tom Cullen, I guess.' And he told her everything.

They sat down to dinner. 'What does it all mean?' Fran asked. Her face was pale, and she was not really eating, only pushing her food from one side of her plate to the other.

'Damned if I know,' Stu said. 'It's a kind of . . . of seeing, I guess. I don't know why we should balk at the idea of Tom Cullen having visions while he's under hypnosis, not after the dreams we all had on our way here. If they weren't a kind of seeing, I don't know what they were.'

'But they seem so long ago now . . . or at least they do to me.'

'Yeah, to me, too,' Stu agreed, and realized he was pushing his own food around.

'Look, Stu – I know we agreed not to talk about committee business outside the committee's meetings if we could help it. You said we'd be wrangling all the time, and you were probably right. I haven't said word one about you turning into Marshal Dillon after the twenty-fifth, have I?'

He smiled briefly. 'No, you haven't, Frannie.'

'But I have to ask if you still think sending Tom Cullen west is a good idea. After what happened this afternoon.'

'I don't know,' Stu said. He pushed his plate away. Most of the food on it was untouched. He got up, went to the hall dresser, and found a pack of cigarettes. He had cut his consumption to three or four a day. He lit this one, drew harsh, stale tobacco smoke deep into his lungs, and blew it out. 'On the positive side, his story is simple enough and believable enough. We drove him out because he's a halfwit. Nobody is going to be able to shake him from that. And if he gets back okay, we can hypnotize him – he goes under in the time it takes you to snap your fingers, for the Lord's sake – and he'll tell us everything he's seen, the important things and the unimportant things. It's possible that he'll turn out to be a better eyewitness than either of the others. I don't doubt that.'

'*If* he gets back okay.'

'Yeah, *if*. We gave him an instruction to travel east only at night and to hide up in the day. If he sees more than one person, to run. But if he was seen by one person only, to kill him.'

'Stu, you *didn't*!'

'Of course we did!' he said angrily, wheeling on her. 'We're not playing pat-a-cake here, Frannie! You must know what's going to happen to him . . . or the Judge . . . or Dayna . . . if they get caught over there! Why else were you so set against the idea in the first place?'

'Okay,' she said quietly. 'Okay, Stu.'

'No, it's *not* okay!' he said, and slammed the freshly lit cigarette down into a pottery ashtray, sending up a little cloud of sparks. Several of them landed on the back of his hand and he brushed them off with a quick, savage gesture. 'It's not okay to send a feeble kid out to fight our battles, and it's not okay to push people around like pawns on a fuckin chessboard and it's not okay giving orders to kill like a Mafia boss. But I don't know what else we can do. I just don't know. If we don't find out what he's up to, there's a damn fine chance that someday next spring he may turn the whole Free Zone into one big mushroom cloud.'

'Okay. Hey. Okay.'

He clenched his fists slowly. 'I was shouting at you. I'm sorry. I had no right to do that, Frannie.'

'It's all right. You weren't the one who opened Pandora's box.'

'We're all opening it, I guess,' he said dully, and got another cigarette from the pack in the dresser. 'Anyhow, when I gave him that . . . what do you call it? When I said he should kill any one person that got in his way, a kind of frown came over his face. It was gone right away. I don't even know if Ralph or Nick saw it. But I did. It was like he was thinking, "Okay, I understand what you mean, but I'll make up m'own mind on that when the time comes."'

'I've read that you can't hypnotize someone into doing something they wouldn't do when they were awake. A person won't go against his own moral code just because they're told to do it when they're under.'

Stu nodded. 'Yeah, I was thinking of that. But what if this fellow Flagg has got a line of pickets strung down the whole eastern length of his border? I would, if I were him. If Tom runs into that picket line going west, he's got his story to cover him. But if he's coming back east and runs into them, it's going to be kill or get killed. And if Tom won't kill, he's apt to be a dead duck.'

'You may be too worried about that one part of it,' Frannie said. 'I mean, if there *is* a picket line, wouldn't it have to be strung pretty thin?'

'Yeah. One man every fifty miles, something like that. Unless he's got five times the people we do.'

'So unless they've got some pretty sophisticated equipment already set up and running, radar and infrared and all that stuff you see in the spy movies, wouldn't Tom be apt to walk right through them?'

'That's what we're hoping. But –'

'But you've got a bad attack of conscience,' she said softly.

'Is that what it comes down to? Well . . . maybe so. What did Harold want, honey?'

'He left a bunch of those survey maps. Areas where his Search Committee has looked for Mother Abagail. Anyhow, Harold's been working on that burial detail as well as supervising the Search Committee. He looked very tired, but his Free Zone duties aren't the only reason. He's been working on something else as well, it seems.'

'What's that?'

'Harold's got a woman.'

Stu raised his eyebrows.

'Anyway, that's why he begged off on dinner. Can you guess who she is?'

Stu squinted up at the ceiling. 'Now who could Harold be shackin with? Let me see –'

'Well, that's a hell of a way to put it! What do you think we're doing?' She threw a mock-slap at him, and he drew back, grinning.

'Fun, ain't it? I give up. Who is it?'

'Nadine Cross.'

'That woman with the white in her hair?'

'That's her.'

'Gosh, she must be twice his age.'

'I doubt,' Frannie said, 'that it's a concern to Harold at this point in his relationship.'

'Does Larry know?'

'I don't know and care less. The Cross woman isn't Larry's girl now. If she ever was.'

'Yeah,' Stu said. He was glad Harold had found himself a little love-interest, but not terribly interested in the subject. 'How does Harold feel about the Search Committee, anyway? Did he give you any idea?'

'Well, you know Harold. He smiles a lot, but . . . not very hopeful. I guess that's why he's putting in most of his time on the burial detail. They call him Hawk now, did you know that?'

'Really?'

'I heard it today. I didn't know who they were talking about until I asked.' She mused for a moment, then laughed.

'What's funny?' Stu asked.

She stuck out her feet, which were clad in low-topped sneakers. On the soles were patterns of circles and lines. 'He complimented me on my sneakers,' she said. 'Isn't that dippy?'

'*You're* dippy,' Stu said, grinning.

*   *   *

Harold woke up just before dawn with a dull but not entirely unpleasant ache in his groin. He shivered a little as he got up. It was getting noticeably colder in the early mornings, although it was only August 22 and fall was still a calendar month away.

But there was heat below his waist, oh yes. Just looking at the delectable curve of her buttocks in those tiny see-through underpants as she slept was warming him up considerably. She wouldn't mind if he woke her up . . . well, maybe she would mind, but she wouldn't *object*. He still had no real idea of what might lie behind those dark eyes, and he was a little afraid of her.

Instead of waking her up, he dressed quietly. He didn't want to mess around with Nadine, as much as he would have liked to.

What he needed to do was go someplace alone and think.

He paused at the door, fully dressed, carrying his boots in his left hand. Between the slight chilliness of the room and the prosy act of getting dressed, his desire had left him. He could smell the room now, and the smell was not terribly appealing.

It was just a little thing, she had said, a thing they could do without. Perhaps it was true. She could do things with her mouth and hands that were nearly beyond belief. But if it was such a small thing, why did this room have that stale and slightly sour odor that he associated with the solitary pleasure of all his bad years?

Maybe you want it to be bad.

Disturbing thought. He went out, closing the door softly behind him.

Nadine's eyes opened the moment the door was closed. She sat up, looked thoughtfully at the door, and then lay down again. Her body ached in a slow and unrelieved cycle of desire. It felt almost like menstrual cramps. If it was such a small thing, she thought (with no idea of how close to Harold's her own thoughts were), why did she feel this way? At one point last night she'd had to bite her lips together to stifle the cries: *Stop that fooling around and STICK me with that thing! Do you hear me? STICK me with it, cram me FULL of it! Do you think what you're doing is doing anything for me? Stick me with it and let's for Christ's sake — or mine, at least — end this crazy game!*

He had been lying with his head between her legs, making strange noises of lust, noises that might have been comic had they not been so honestly urgent, so nearly savage. And she had looked up, those words trembling behind her lips, and had seen (or only thought she had?) a face at the window. In an instant the fire of her own lust had been damped down to cold ash.

It had been *his* face, grinning savagely in at her.

A scream had risen in her throat . . . and then the face was gone, the face was nothing but a moving pattern of shadows on the darkened glass mingled with smudges of dust. No more than the boogeyman a child imagines he sees in the closet, or curled up slyly behind the chest of toys in the corner.

No more than that.

Except it *was* more, and not even now, in the first cold rational light of dawn, could she pretend otherwise. It would be *dangerous* to pretend otherwise. It had been him, and he had been warning her. The husband-to-be was watching over his intended. And the bride defiled would be the bride unaccepted.

Staring at the ceiling, she thought: *I suck his cock, but that's not defilement. I let him stick himself up my ass, but that isn't defilement, either. I dress for him like a cheap streetwalking slut, but that's perfectly okay.*

It was enough to make you wonder what sort of man your fiancé really was.

Nadine stared up at the ceiling for a long, long time.

Harold made instant coffee, drank it with a grimace, and then took a couple of cold Pop-Tarts out onto the front step. He sat down and ate them while dawn crept across the land.

In retrospect, the last couple of days seemed like a mad carnival ride to him. It was a blur of orange trucks, of Weizak clapping him on the shoulder and calling him Hawk (they all called him that now), of dead bodies, a never-ending moldy stream of them, and then coming home from all that death to a never-ending flow of kinky sex. Enough to blur your head.

But now, sitting here on a front step as cold as a marble headstone, a horrible cup of instant coffee sloshing in his guts, he could munch these sawdust-tasting cold Pop-Tarts and think. He felt clearheaded, sane after a season of insanity. It occurred to him that, for a person who had always considered himself to be a Cro-Magnon man amid a herd of thundering Neanderthals, he had been doing precious little thinking lately. He had been led, not by the nose, but by the penis.

He turned his mind to Frannie Goldsmith even as he turned his gaze out to the Flatirons. It was Frannie who had been at his house that day, he knew it for sure now. He had gone over to the place where she lived with Redman on a pretext, really hoping to get a look at her footgear. As it turned out, she had been wearing the sneakers that matched the print he had found on his cellar floor. Circles and lines instead of the usual waffle or zigzag tread. No question, baby.

He thought he could put it together without too much trouble. Somehow she had found out he had read her diary. He must have left a smudge or mark on one of the pages . . . maybe more than one. So she had come to his house looking for some indication of how he felt about what he had read. Something written down.

There was, of course, his ledger. But she hadn't found it, he could feel positive of that. His ledger said flat-out that he planned to kill Stuart Redman. If she had found something like that, she would have told Stu. Even if she hadn't, he didn't believe she could have been as easy and as natural with him as she had been yesterday.

He finished his last Pop-Tart, grimacing at the taste of its cold frosting and colder jelly center. He decided he would walk to the bus station instead of taking his cycle; Teddy Weizak or Norris could drop him off on the way home. He set off, zipping his light jacket all the way to his chin against the chill that would be gone in an hour or so. He walked past the empty houses with their shades drawn, and about six blocks down Arapahoe, he began to see an x-mark chalked boldly on door after door. Again, his idea. The Burial Committee had checked all those houses where the mark appeared, and had hauled away whatever bodies there were to be hauled away. x, a crossing-out. The people who had lived in those houses where the mark appeared were gone for all time. In another month that x-mark would be all over Boulder, signifying the end of an age.

It was time to think, and to think carefully. It seemed that, since he had met Nadine, he really had stopped thinking . . . but maybe he had really stopped even before that.

I read her diary because I was hurt and jealous, he thought. Then she broke into my house, probably looking for my own diary, but she didn't find it. But just the shock of someone breaking in had maybe been revenge enough. It had certainly bent him out of shape. Maybe they were even and it could be quits.

He didn't really want Frannie anymore, did he? . . . *Did* he?

He felt the sullen coal of resentment glow in his chest. Maybe not. But that didn't change the fact that they had excluded him. Although Nadine had said little about her reasons for coming to him, Harold had an idea that she had been excluded in some way too, rebuffed, turned back. They were a couple of outsiders, and outsiders hatch plots. It's perhaps the only thing that keeps them sane. (*Remember to put that in the ledger*, Harold thought . . . he was almost downtown now.)

There was a whole company of outsiders on the other side of the mountains. And when there are enough outsiders together in one place, a mystic osmosis takes place and you're inside. Inside where it's warm. Just a little thing, being inside where it's warm, but really such a big thing. About the most important thing in the world.

Maybe he didn't want to be quits and even. Maybe he didn't want to settle for a draw, for a career of riding in a twentieth-century deadcart and getting meaningless letters of thanks for his ideas, and waiting five years for Bateman to retire from their precious committee so he could be on it . . . and what if they decided to pass over him again? They might, too, because it wasn't just a question of age. They had taken the goddam deaf-mute, and he was only a few years older than Harold himself.

The coal of resentment was burning brightly now. Think, sure, think – that was easy to say, and sometimes it was even to do . . . but what good was thinking when all it got you from the Neanderthals who ran the world was a horselaugh, or even worse, a thank-you letter?

He reached the bus station. It was still early, and no one was there yet. There was a poster on the door saying there was going to be another public meeting on the twenty-fifth. Public meeting? Public circle jerk.

The waiting room was festooned with travel posters and ads for the Greyhound Ameripass and pictures of big mother-humping Scenicruisers rolling through Atlanta, New Orleans, San Francisco, Nashville, wherever. He sat down and stared with a cold morning eye at the darkened pinball machines, the Coke machine, the coffee machine that would also dispense a Lipton Cup-a-Soup that smelled vaguely like a dead fish. He lit a cigarette and threw the matchstub on the floor.

They had adopted the Constitution. Whooppee. How very-very and too-too. They had even sung The Star-Speckled Banana, for

Christ's sweet sake. But suppose Harold Lauder had gotten up, not to make a few constructive suggestions, but to tell them the facts of life in this first year after the plague?

Ladies and gentlemen, my name is Harold Emery Lauder and I am here to tell you that, in the words of the old song, the fundamental things apply as time goes by. Like Darwin. The next time you stand and sing the National Anthem, friends and neighbors, chew on this: America is dead, dead as a doornail, dead as Jacob Marley and Buddy Holly and the Big Bopper and Harry S. Truman, but the principles just propounded by Mr Darwin are still very much alive – as alive as Jacob Marley's ghost was to Ebenezer Scrooge. While you are meditating on the beauties of constitutional rule, spare a little time to meditate on Randall Flagg, Man of the West. I doubt very much if he has any time to spare for such fripperies as public meetings and ratifications and discussions on the true meaning of a peach in the best liberal mode. Instead he has been concentrating on the basics, on his Darwin, preparing to wipe the great Formica counter of the universe with your dead bodies. Ladies and gentlemen, let me modestly suggest that while we are trying to get the lights on and waiting for a doctor to find our happy little hive, he may be searching eagerly for someone with a pilot's credentials so he can start overflights of Boulder in the best Francis Gary Powers tradition. While we debate the burning question of who will be on the Street Cleaning Committee, he has probably already seen to the creation of a Gun Cleaning Committee, not to mention mortars, missile sites, and possibly even germ warfare centers. Of course we know this country doesn't have any germ or biological warfare centers, that's one of the things that makes this country great – what country, ha-ha – but you should realize that while we're busy getting all the wagons in a circle, he's –

'Hey, Hawk, you pullin overtime?'

Harold looked up, smiling. 'Yeah, I thought I'd get some,' he told Weizak. 'I clocked you when I came in. You made six bucks already.'

Weizak laughed. 'You're a card, Hawk, you know that?'

'I am,' Harold agreed, still smiling. He began to relace his boots. 'A wild card.'

CHAPTER 56

Stu spent the next day at the power station, wrapping motors, and was cycling home at the end of the workday. He had reached the small park opposite the First National Bank when Ralph hailed him over. He parked his cycle and walked over to the bandshell where Ralph was sitting.

'I've kind of been looking for you, Stu. You got a minute?'

'Just one. I'm late for supper. Frannie'll be worried.'

'Yeah. Been up to the power station wrapping copper, from the look of your hands.' Ralph looked absent and worried.

'Yeah. Not even workmen's gloves do much good. My hands are wrecked.'

Ralph nodded. There were maybe half a dozen other people in the park, some of them looking at the narrow-gauge railway train that had once gone between Boulder and Denver. A trio of young women had spread out a picnic supper. Stu found it very pleasant just to sit here with his wounded hands in his lap. Maybe marshaling won't be so bad, he thought. At least it'll get me off that goddam assembly line in East Boulder.

'How's it going out there?' Ralph asked.

'Me, I wouldn't know – I'm just hired help, like the rest. Brad Kitchner says it's going like a house afire. He says the lights will be back on by the end of the first week of September, maybe sooner, and that we'll have heat by the middle of the month. Of course, he's pretty young to be making with the predictions . . .'

'I'll put my money on Brad,' Ralph said. 'I trust im. He's been gettin a lot of what you call on-the-job training.' Ralph tried to laugh; the laugh turned into a sigh which seemed fetched up from the big man's bootheels.

'Why you so down at the mouth, Ralph?'

'I got some news on my radio,' Ralph said. 'Some of it's good, some of it . . . well, some of it's not so good, Stu. I want you to know, because there's no way to keep it secret. Lots of people in the Zone with CBs. I imagine some were listening when I was talking to these new folks coming in.'

'How many?'

'Over forty. One of them's a doctor, name of George Richardson. He sounds like a fine man. Level-headed.'

'Well, that's great news!'

'He's from Derbyshire, Tennessee. Most of the people in this group are sort of mid-Southern. Well, it seems they had a pregnant woman with them, and her time come up ten days ago, on the thirteenth. This doctor delivered her of them – twins, she had – and they were fine. At first they were fine.' Ralph lapsed back into silence, his mouth working.

Stu grabbed him. 'They died? The babies *died*? That what you're trying to tell me? That they *died*? Talk to me, dammit!'

'They died,' Ralph said in a low voice. 'One of them went in twelve hours. Appeared to just choke to death. The other went two days later. Nothing Richardson could do to save them. The woman went loony. Raving about death and destruction and no more babies. You want to make sure Fran isn't around when they come in, Stu. That's what I wanted to tell you. And that you should let her know about this right away. Because if you don't, someone else will.'

Stu let go of Ralph's shirt slowly.

'This Richardson, he wanted to know how many pregnant women we had, and I said only one that we know of right now. He asked how far along she was and I said four months. Is that right?'

'She's five months now. But Ralph, is he sure those babies died of the superflu? Is he *sure*?'

'No, he's not, and you gotta tell Frannie that, too, so she understands it. He said it could have been any number of things . . . the mother's diet . . . something hereditary . . . a respiratory infection . . . or maybe they were just, you know, defective babies. He said it could have been the Rh factor, whatever that is. He just couldn't tell, them being born in the middle of a field beside the doggone Interstate 70. He said that him and about three others who were in charge of their group sat up late at night and talked it over. Richardson, he told them what it might mean if it *was* the Captain Trips that killed those babies, and how important it was for them to find out one way or the other for sure.'

'Glen and I talked about that,' Stu said bleakly, 'the day I met him. July Fourth, that was. It seems so long ago . . . anyway, if it was the superflu that killed those babies it probably means that in forty or fifty years we can leave the whole shebang to the rats and the houseflies and the sparrows.'

'I guess that's pretty much what Richardson told them. Anyway, they were some forty miles west of Chicago, and he persuaded them to turn around the next day so they could take the bodies back to a big hospital where he could do an autopsy. He said he could find out for sure if it was the superflu. He saw enough of it at the end of June. I guess all doctors did.'

'Yeah.'

'But when the morning came, the babies were gone. That woman had buried them, and she wouldn't say where. They spent two days digging, thinking that she couldn't have gone too far away from the camp or buried them too deep, being just over her delivery and all. But they didn't find them, and she couldn't say where no matter how much they tried to explain how important it was. Poor woman was just all the way off'n her chump.'

'I can understand that,' Stu said, thinking of how much Fran wanted her baby.

'The doctor said even if it was the superflu, maybe two immune people could make an immune baby,' Ralph said hopefully.

'The chances that the natural father of Fran's baby was immune are about one in a billion, I guess,' Stu said. 'He sure isn't here.'

'Yeah, I guess it couldn't hardly be, could it? I'm sorry to have to put this on you, Stu. But I thought you'd better know. So you could tell her.'

'I don't look forward to that,' Stu said.

But when he got home he found that someone else had already done it.

'Frannie?'

No answer. Supper was on the stove – burnt on, mostly – but the apartment was dark and quiet.

Stu came into the living room and looked around. There was an ashtray on the coffee table with two cigarette butts in it, but Fran didn't smoke and they weren't his brand.

'Babe?'

He went into the bedroom and she was there, lying on the

bed in the semigloom, looking at the ceiling. Her face was puffy and tearstreaked. 'Hi, Stu,' she said quietly.

'Who told you?' he asked angrily. 'Who just couldn't wait to spread the good news? Whoever it was, I'll break their damn arm.'

'It was Sue Stern. She heard it from Jack Jackson. He's got a CB, and he heard that doctor talking with Ralph. She thought she better tell me before someone else made a bad job of it. Poor little Frannie. Handle with care. Do not open until Christmas.' She uttered a little laugh. There was a desolation in that sound that made Stu feel like crying.

He came across the room and lay down beside her on the bed and stroked her hair off her forehead. 'Honey, it's not sure. No way that it's sure.'

'I know it's not. And maybe we could have our own babies, even so.' She turned to look up at him, her eyes red-rimmed and unhappy. 'But I want this one. Is that so wrong?'

'No. Course not.'

'I've been lying here waiting for him to move, or something. I've never felt him move since that night Larry came looking for Harold. Remember?'

'Yes.'

'I felt the baby move and I didn't wake you up. Now I wish I had. I sure do.' She began to cry again and put an arm over her face so he wouldn't see her doing it.

Stu took the arm away, stretched out beside her, kissed her. She hugged him fiercely and then lay passively against him. When she spoke, the words were half muffled against his neck.

'Not knowing makes it that much worse. Now I just have to wait and see. It seems like such a long time to have to wait and see if your baby is going to die before it's spent a day outside of your body.'

'You won't be waiting alone,' he said.

She hugged him tight again for that and they lay there together without moving for a long time.

Nadine Cross had been in the living room of her old place for almost five minutes, gathering things up, before she saw him sitting in the chair in the corner, naked except for his underpants, his thumb in his mouth, his strange gray-green Chinese eyes watching her. She was so startled – as much by the knowledge that he had been sitting there all the time as by the actual sudden sight of him – that her heart took a high, frightened leap in her chest and she screamed. The paperbacks she had been about to stuff into her packsack tumbled to the floor in a flutter of pages.

'Joe . . . I mean Leo . . .'

She put a hand on her chest above the swell of her breasts as if to quell the crazy beating of her heart. But her heart was not ready to slow yet, hand or no hand. Catching sudden sight of him was bad; catching sight of him dressed and acting the way he had been when she had first made his acquaintance in New Hampshire was even worse. It was too much of a return, as if some irrational god had suddenly bundled her viciously through a time-warp and condemned her to live the last six weeks all over again.

'You scared the dickins out of me,' she finished weakly.

Joe said nothing.

She walked slowly over to him, half expecting to see a long kitchen knife in one of his hands, as in days of yore, but the hand which was not at his mouth was curled blamelessly in his lap. She saw that his body had been milked of its tan. The old scars and bramble-scratches were gone. But the eyes were the same . . . eyes that could haunt you. Whatever had been in them, a little more each day, since he had come to the fire to listen to Larry play the guitar, was now utterly gone. His eyes were as they had been when she first met him, and this filled her with a creeping sort of terror.

'What are you doing here?'

Joe said nothing.

'Why aren't you with Larry and Lucy-mom?'

No reply.

'You can't stay here,' she said, trying to reason with him, but before she could go on, she found herself wondering how long he had *already* been here.

This was the morning of August 24. She had spent the previous two nights at Harold's. The thought that he might have been sitting in that chair with his thumb corked securely in his mouth for the last forty hours came to her. It was a ridiculous idea, of course, he would have to eat and drink (wouldn't he?), but once the thought/image had come, it would not leave. That sense of creepiness came over her again, and she realized with something like despair how much she herself had changed: once she had slept fearlessly next to this little savage, at a time when he had been armed and dangerous. Now he was without weapons, but she found herself in mirror of him. She had thought

(Joe? Leo?)

his previous self had been neatly and completely disposed of. Now he was back. And he was here.

'You can't stay here,' she said. 'I just came back to get some things. I'm moving out. I'm moving in with a . . . with a man.'

Oh, is *that* what Harold is? some interior voice mocked. I thought he was just a tool, a means to an end.

'Leo, listen –'

His head shook, faintly but visibly. His eyes, stern and glittering, fixed upon her face.

'You're not Leo?'

That faint shake came again.

'Are you Joe?'

A nod, just as faint.

'Well, all right. But you have to understand that it really doesn't matter who you are,' she said, trying to be patient. That crazy feeling that she was in a time-warp, that she was back to square one, persisted. It made her feel unreal and frightened. 'That part of our lives – the part where we were together and on our own – that part is gone. You've changed, I've changed, and we can't change back.'

But his strange eyes remained fixed upon hers, seeming to deny this.

'And stop staring at me,' she snapped. 'It's very impolite to stare at people.'

Now his eyes seemed to become faintly accusatory. They seemed to suggest that it was also impolite to leave people on their own, and more impolite still to withdraw one's love from people who still needed and depended on it.

'It's *not* as if you're on your own,' she said, turning and beginning to pick up the books she had dropped. She knelt clumsily and without grace, her knees popping like firecrackers as she did so. She began to stuff the books into the packsack willy-nilly, on top of her sanitary napkins and her aspirin and her underthings – plain cotton underthings, quite different from the ones she wore for Harold's frantic amusement.

'You have Larry and Lucy. You want them, and they want you. Well, *Larry* wants you, and that's all that matters, because she wants all the things he does. She's like a piece of carbon paper.

Things are different for me now, Joe, and that's not my fault. That's not my fault at all. So you can just stop trying to guilt-trip me.'

She began trying to buckle the packsack's clasps but her fingers were trembling uncontrollably and it was hard work. The silence grew heavier and heavier around them.

At last she stood up, shrugging the packsack onto her shoulders.

'Leo.' She tried to speak calmly and reasonably, the way she used to speak to difficult children in her classes when they had tantrums. It just wasn't possible. Her voice was all in jigs and jags, and the little shake of his head which greeted her use of the word *Leo* made it even worse.

'It wasn't Larry and Lucy,' Nadine said viciously. 'I could have understood that, if that was all it was. But it was really that old bag you gave me up for, wasn't it? That stupid old woman in her rocking chair, grinning at the world with her false teeth. But now she's gone, and so you come running back to me. But it won't play, do you hear me? *It won't play!*'

Joe said nothing.

'And when I begged Larry . . . got down on my knees and *begged* him . . . he couldn't be bothered. He was too busy playing big man. So you see, none of this is my fault. *None of it!*'

The boy only stared at her impassively.

Her terror began to return, burying her incoherent rage. She backed away from him to the door and fumbled behind her for the knob. She found it at last, turned it, and jerked the door open. The rush of cool outside air against her shoulders was very welcome.

'Go to Larry,' she muttered. 'Goodbye, kiddo.'

She backed out awkwardly and stood on the top step for a moment, trying to gather her wits. It suddenly occurred to her that the whole thing might have been a hallucination, brought on by her own guilt feelings . . . guilt at abandoning the boy, guilt at making Larry wait too long, guilt at the things she and Harold had done, and the much worse things which were waiting. Perhaps there had been no real boy in that house at all. No more real than the phantasms of Poe – the beating of the old man's heart, sounding like a watch wrapped in cotton, or the raven perched on the bust of Pallas.

'Tapping, ever tapping at my chamber door,' she whispered aloud without thinking, and that made her utter a horrid, croaking little giggle, probably not much different from the sounds ravens actually made.

Still, she had to know.

She went to the window beside the front steps and looked into the living room of what had once been her house. Not that it had ever been hers, not really. When you lived in a place and all you wanted to take out of it when you left would fit in one packsack, it had never really been yours to begin with. Looking in, she saw some dead wife's rug and curtains and wallpaper, some dead husband's pipe-stand and issues of *Sports Illustrated* scattered carelessly on the coffee table. Pictures of dead children on the mantel. And sitting in the corner chair, some dead woman's little boy, clad only in his underpants, sitting, still sitting, sitting as he had sat before –

Nadine fled, stumbling, almost falling over the low wire wickets which protected the flower bed to the left of the window where she had looked in. She flung herself onto her Vespa and got it started. She drove with reckless speed for the first few blocks, slaloming in and out of the stalled cars which still littered these side-streets, but a little at a time she calmed down.

By the time she reached Harold's, she had gotten herself under some kind of control. But she knew it had to end quickly for her here in the Zone. If she wanted to keep her sanity, she must soon be away.

The meeting at Munzinger Auditorium went well. They began by singing the National Anthem again but this time most of them remained dry-eyed; it was simply a part of what would soon become ritual. A Census Committee was voted routinely with Sandy DuChiens in charge. She and her four helpers immediately began going through the audience, counting heads, taking names. At the end of the meeting, to the accompaniment of tremendous cheers, she announced that there were now 814 souls in the Free Zone, and promised (rashly, as it turned out) to have a complete 'directory' by the time the next Zone meeting was called – a directory she hoped to update week by week, containing names in alphabetical order, ages, Boulder addresses, previous addresses, and previous occupations. As it turned out, the flow into the Zone was so heavy and yet so erratic that she was always two or three weeks behind.

The elective period of the Free Zone Committee was brought up, and after some extravagant suggestions (ten years was one, life another, and Larry brought down the house by saying they sounded more like prison terms than those of elective office), the yearly term was voted in. Harry Dunbarton's hand waved near the back of the hall, and Stu recognized him.

Bellowing to make himself heard, Harry said: 'Even a year may be too much. I have nothing at all against the ladies and gentlemen of the committee, I think you're doing a helluva job' – cheers and whistles – 'but this is gonna get out of hand before long if we keep gettin bigger.'

Glen raised his hand, and Stu acknowledged him.

'Mr Chairman, this isn't on the agenda, but I think Mr Dunbarton there has an excellent point.'

I just bet you think he does, baldy, Stu thought, *since you brought it up a week ago.*

'I'd like to make a motion that we have a Representative Government Committee so we can really put the Constitution back to work. I think Harry Dunbarton should head that committee, and I'll serve on it myself, unless someone thinks I've got a conflict of interest.'

More cheers.

In the last row, Harold turned to Nadine and whispered in her ear: 'Ladies and gentlemen, the public love feast is now in session.'

She gave him a slow, dark smile, and he felt giddy.

Stu was elected Free Zone Marshal by roaring acclamation.

'I'll do the best I can by you,' he said. 'Some of you cheerin me now may have cause to change your tunes later if I catch you doin somethin you shouldn't be doin. You hear me, Rich Moffat?'

A large roar of laughter. Rich, who was as drunk as a hootowl, joined in agreeably.

'But I don't see any reason why we should have any real trouble here. The main job of a marshal as I see it is stoppin people from hurtin each other. And there aren't any of us who want to do that. Enough people have been hurt already. And I guess that's all I've got to say.'

The crowd gave him a long ovation.

'Now this next item,' Stu said, 'kind of goes along with the marshaling. We need about five people to serve on a Law Committee, or I'm not going to feel right about locking anyone up, should it come to that. Do I hear any nominations?'

'How about the Judge?' someone shouted.

'Yeah, the Judge, damn right!' someone else yelled.

Heads craned expectantly as people waited for the Judge to

stand up and accept the responsibility in his usual rococo style; a whisper ran around the hall as people retold the story of how he had put a pin in the flying saucer nut's balloon. Agendas were put down as people prepared to clap. Stu's eyes met Glen's with mutual chagrin: someone on the committee should have foreseen this.

'Ain't here,' someone said.

'Who's seen him?' Lucy Swann asked, upset. Larry glanced at her uncomfortably, but she was still looking around the hall for the Judge.

'I seen him.'

A mutter of interest as Teddy Weizak stood up about three quarters of the way back in the auditorium, looking nervous and polishing his steel-rimmed spectacles compulsively with his bandanna.

'Where?'

'Where was he, Teddy?'

'Was it in town?'

'What was he doing?'

Teddy Weizak flinched visibly from this barrage of questions. Stu pounded his gavel. 'Come on, folks. Order.'

'I seen him two days ago,' Teddy said. 'He had himself a Land-Rover. Said he was going to Denver for the day. Didn't say why. We had a joke or two about it. He seemed in real good spirits. That's all I know.' He sat down, still polishing his spectacles and blushing furiously.

Stu rapped for order again. 'I'm sorry the Judge isn't here. I think he would have been just the man for the job, but since he isn't, could we have another nomination –?'

'No, let's not leave it at that!' Lucy protested, getting to her feet. She was wearing a snug denim jumpsuit that brought interested looks to the faces of most of the males in the audience. 'Judge Farris is an old man. What if he got sick in Denver and can't get back?'

'Lucy,' Stu said, 'Denver's a big place.'

An odd silence fell over the meeting hall as people considered this. Lucy sat down, looking pale, and Larry put his arm around her. His eyes met Stu's, and Stu looked away.

A half-hearted motion was made to table the Law Committee until the Judge got back and was voted down after twenty minutes of discussion. They had another lawyer, a young man of about twenty-six named Al Bundell, who had come in late that afternoon with the Dr Richardson party, and he accepted the chairmanship when it was offered, saying only that he hoped no one would do anything too terrible in the next month or so, because it would take at least that long to work out some sort of rotating tribunal system. Judge Farris was voted a place on the committee in absentia.

Brad Kitchner, looking pale, fidgety, and a little ridiculous in a suit and tie, approached the podium, dropped his prepared remarks, picked them up in the wrong order, and contented himself by saying they hoped and expected to have the electricity back on by the second or third of September.

This remark was greeted with such a storm of cheering that he gained enough confidence to finish in style and actually strut a little as he left the podium.

Chad Norris was next, and Stu told Frannie later that he had approached the thing in just the right way: They were burying the dead out of common decency, none of them would feel really good until that was done and life could go on, and if it was finished by the fall rainy season they would all feel so much the better. He asked for a couple of volunteers and could have had three dozen if he wanted them. He finished by asking each member of the current Spade Squad (as he called them) to stand and take a bow.

Harold Lauder barely popped up and then sat back down again, and there were those who left the meeting remarking on what a smart but very modest fellow he was. Actually, Nadine had been whispering things in his ear and he was afraid to do much more than bob and nod. A fairly large pup-tent appeared to have been erected in the crotch of his pants.

When Norris left the podium, Ralph Brentner took his place. He told them that they at last had a doctor. George Richardson stood up (to loud applause; Richardson flipped the peace sign with both hands, and the applause turned to cheers), and then told them that, as far as he could tell, they had another sixty people joining them over the next couple of days.

'Well, that's the agenda,' Stu said. He looked out over the gathered people. 'I want Sandy DuChiens to come up here again and tell us how many we are, but before I do that, is there other business we should take up tonight?'

He waited. He could see Glen's face in the crowd, and Sue Stern's, Larry's, Nick's, and of course, Frannie's. They all looked a bit strained. If someone was going to bring up Flagg, ask what the committee was doing about him, this would be the time. But there was silence. After fifteen seconds of it, Stu turned the meeting over to Sandy, who ended things in style. As people began to file out, Stu thought: *Well, we got by it again.*

Several people came up to congratulate him after the meeting, one of them the new doctor. 'You handled that very well, Marshal,' Richardson said, and for a moment Stu almost looked over his shoulder to see who Richardson was talking to. Then he remembered, and suddenly felt scared. Lawman? He was an imposter.

A year, he told himself. A year and no more. But he still felt scared.

Stu, Fran, Sue Stern, and Nick walked back toward the center of town together, their feet clicking hollowly on the cement sidewalk as they crossed the CU campus toward Broadway. Around them, other people were streaming away, talking quietly, headed home. It was nearly eleven-thirty.

'It's chilly,' Fran said. 'I wish I'd worn my jacket as well as this sweater.'

Nick nodded. He also felt the chill. The Boulder evenings were always cool, but tonight it could be no more than fifty degrees. It served to remind that this strange and terrible summer was nearing its end. Not for the first time he wished that Mother Abagail's God or Muse or whatever It was had been more in favor of Miami or New Orleans. But that might not have been so great, now that he stopped to think about it. High humidity, lots of rain . . . and lots of bodies. At least Boulder was dry.

'They jumped the shit out of me, wanting the Judge for the Law Committee,' Stu said. 'We should have expected that.'

Frannie nodded, and Nick jotted quickly on his pad:

'Sure. People will miss Tom & Dayna, 2. Fax of life.'

'Think people will be suspicious, Nick?' Stu asked.

Nick nodded. 'They'll wonder if they did go west. For real.'

They all considered this as Nick took out his butane match and burned the scrap of paper.

'That's tough,' Stu said finally. 'You really think so?'

'Sure, he's right,' Sue said glumly. 'What else have they got to think? That Judge Farris went to Far Rockaway to ride the Monster Coaster?'

'We were lucky to get away tonight without a big discussion of what's going on in the West,' Fran said.

Nick wrote: 'Sure were. Next time we'll have to tackle it head on, I think. That's why I want to postpone another big meeting as long as possible. Three weeks, maybe. September 15?'

Sue said, 'We can hold off that long if Brad gets the power on.'

'I think he will,' Stu said.

'I'm going home,' Sue told them. 'Big day tomorrow. Dayna's off. I'm going with her as far as Colorado Springs.'

'Do you think that's safe, Sue?' Fran asked.

She shrugged. 'Safer for her than for me.'

'How did she take it?' Fran asked her.

'Well, she's a funny sort of girl. She was a jock in college, you know. Tennis and swimming were her biggies, although she played them all. She went to some small community college down in Georgia, but for the first two years she kept on going with her high school boyfriend. He was a big leather jacket type, me Tarzan, you Jane, so get out in the kitchen and rattle those pots and pans. Then she got dragged along to a couple of female consciousness meetings by her roomie, who was this big libber type.'

'And as an upshot, she got to be an even bigger libber than the roomie,' Fran guessed.

'First a libber, then a lesbian,' Sue said.

Stu stopped as if thunderstruck. Frannie looked at him with guarded amusement. 'Come on, splendor in the grass,' she said. 'See if you can't fix the hinge on your mouth.'

Stu shut his mouth with a snap.

Sue went on: 'She dropped both rocks on the caveman boyfriend at the same time. It blew his wheels, and he came after her with a gun. She disarmed him. She says it was the major turning point of her life. She told me she always knew she was stronger and more agile than he was – she knew it *intellectually*. But it took doing it to put it in her guts.'

'You sayin she hates men?' Stu asked, looking at Sue closely.

Susan shook her head. 'She's bi now.'

'Bye now?' Stu said doubtfully.

'She's happy with either sex, Stuart. And I hope you're not going to start leaning on the committee to institute the blue laws along with "Thou shalt not kill."'

'I got enough to worry about without gettin into who sleeps with who,' he mumbled, and they all laughed. 'I only asked because I don't want anyone goin into this thing as a crusade. We need eyes over there, not guerrilla fighters. This is a job for a weasel, not a lion.'

'She knows that,' Susan said. 'Fran asked me how she took it when I asked her if she'd go over there for us. She took it very well. For one thing, she reminded me that if we'd stayed with those men . . . remember how you found us, Stu?'

He nodded.

'If we'd stayed with them, we would have either wound up dead or in the West anyway, because that's the direction they were going in . . . at least when they were sober enough to read the road-signs. She said she'd been wondering what her place in the Zone was, and guessed that her place in the Zone was out of it. And she said . . .'

'What?' Fran asked.

'That she'd try to come back,' Sue said, rather abruptly, and said no more. What else Dayna Jurgens had said was between the two of them, something not even the other members of the committee were to know. Dayna was going west with a ten-inch switchblade strapped to her arm in a spring-loaded clip. When she bent her wrist sharply, the spring unloaded and hey, presto, she had suddenly grown a sixth finger, one which was ten inches long and double-bladed. She felt that most of them – the men – would not have understood.

If he's a big enough dictator, then maybe he's all that's holding them together. If he was gone, maybe they'd start fighting and squabbling among themselves. It might be the end of them, if he dies. And if I get close to him, Susie, he better have his guardian devil with him.

They'll kill you, Dayna.

Maybe. Maybe not. It might be worth it just to have the pleasure of watching his guts fall out on the floor.

Susan could have stopped her, maybe, but she hadn't tried. She had contented herself with extracting a promise from Dayna that she would stick to the original script unless a near-perfect oppor-tunity came up. To that, Dayna had agreed and Sue didn't think her friend would get that chance. Flagg would be well guarded. Still, in the three days since she had broached the idea of going west as a spy to her friend, Sue Stern had found it very difficult to sleep.

'Well,' she said to the rest of them now, 'I'm home to bed. Night, folks.'

She walked off, hands in the pockets of her fatigue jacket.

'She looks older,' Stu said.

Nick wrote and offered the open pad to both of them.

We all do was written there.

Stu was on his way up to the power station the next morning when he saw Susan and Dayna headed down Canyon Boulevard on a pair of cycles. He waved and they pulled over. He thought he had never seen Dayna looking prettier. Her hair was tied behind her with a bright green silk scarf, and she was wearing a rawhide coat open over jeans and a chambray shirt. A bedroll was strapped on behind her.

'Stuart!' she cried, and waved to him, smiling.

Lesbian? he thought doubtfully.

'I understand you're off on a little trip,' he said.

'For sure. And you never saw me.'

'Nope,' Stu said. 'Never did. Smoke?'

Dayna took a Marlboro and cupped her hands over his match.

'You be careful, girl.'

'I will.'

'And get back.'

'I hope to.'

They looked at each other in the bright late-summer morning.

'You take care of Frannie, big fella.'

'I will.'

'And go easy on the marshaling.'

'That I know I can do.'

She cast the cigarette away. 'What do you say, Suze?'

Susan nodded and put her bike in gear, smiling a strained smile. 'Dayna?'

She looked at him, and Stu planted a soft kiss on her mouth. 'Good luck.'

She smiled. 'You have to do it twice for really good luck. Didn't you know that?'

He kissed her again, more slowly and thoroughly this time. *Lesbian?* he wondered again.

'Frannie's a lucky woman,' Dayna said. 'And you can quote me.'

Smiling, not really knowing what to say, Stu stepped back and said nothing at all. Two blocks up, one of the lumbering orange Burial Committee trucks rumbled through the intersection like an omen and the moment was broken.

'Let's go, kid,' Dayna said. 'Get-em-up-Scout.'

They drove off, and Stu stood on the curbing and watched them.

Sue Stern was back two days later. She had watched Dayna moving west from Colorado Springs, she said, had watched her until she was nothing but a speck that merged with the great still landscape. Then she had cried a little. The first night Sue had made camp at Monument, and had awakened in the small hours, chilled by a low whining sound that seemed to be coming from a culvert that traveled beneath the farm road she had camped by.

Finally summoning up her courage, she had shined her flash into the corrugated pipe and had discovered a gaunt and shivering puppy. It looked to be about six months old. It shied from her touch and she was too big to crawl into the pipe. At last she had gone into the town of Monument, smashed her way into the local grocery, and had come back in the first cold light of false dawn with a knapsack full of Alpo and Cycle One. That did the trick. The puppy rode back with her, neatly tucked into one of the BSA saddlebags.

Dick Ellis went into raptures over the puppy. It was an Irish setter bitch, either purebred or so close as to make no difference. When she got older, he was sure Kojak would be glad to make her acquaintance. The news swept the Free Zone, and for that day the subject of Mother Abagail was forgotten in the excitement over the canine Adam and Eve. Susan Stern became something of a heroine, and as far as any of the committee ever knew, no one even thought to wonder what she had been doing in Monument that night, far south of Boulder.

But it was the morning the two of them left Boulder that Stu remembered, watching them ride off toward the Denver-Boulder Turnpike. Because no one in the Zone ever saw Dayna Jurgens again.

August 27; nearly dusk; Venus shining against the sky.

Nick, Ralph, Larry, and Stu sat on the steps of Tom Cullen's house. Tom was on the lawn, whooping and knocking croquet balls through a set of wickets.

It's time, Nick wrote.

Speaking low, Stu asked if they would have to hypnotize him again, and Nick shook his head.

'Good,' Ralph said. 'I don't think I could take that action.' Raising his voice, he called: 'Tom! Hey, Tommy! Come on over here!'

Tom came running over, grinning.

'Tommy, it's time to go,' Ralph said.

Tom's smile faltered. For the first time he seemed to notice that it was getting dark.

'Go? Now? Laws, no! When it gets dark, Tom goes to bed. M-O-O-N, that spells bed. Tom doesn't like to be out after dark. Because of the boogies. Tom . . . Tom . . .'

He fell silent, and the others looked at him uneasily. Tom had lapsed into dull silence. He came out of it . . . but not in the usual way. It was not a sudden reanimation, life flooding back in a rush, but a slow thing, reluctant, almost sad.

'Go west?' he said. 'Do you mean it's *that* time?'

Stu laid a hand on his shoulder. 'Yes, Tom. If you can.'

'On the road.'

Ralph made a choked, muttering sound and walked around the house. Tom did not seem to notice. His gaze alternated between Stu and Nick.

'Travel at night. Sleep in the day.' Very slowly, in the dusk, Tom added: 'And see the elephant.'

Nick nodded.

Larry brought Tom's pack up from where it had rested beside the steps. Tom put it on slowly, dreamily.

'You want to be careful, Tom,' Larry said thickly.

'Careful. Laws, yes.'

Stu wondered belatedly if they should have given Tom a one-man tent as well, and rejected it. Tom would get all bollixed up trying to set up even a little tent.

'Nick,' Tom whispered. 'Do I really have to do this?'

Nick put an arm around Tom and nodded slowly.

'All right.'

'Just stay on the big four-lane highway, Tom,' Larry said. 'The one that says 70. Ralph is going to drive you down to the start of it on his motorcycle.'

'Yes, Ralph.' He paused. Ralph had come back around the house. He was swabbing at his eyes with his bandanna.

'You ready, Tom?' he asked gruffly.

'Nick? Will it still be my house when I get back?'

Nick nodded vigorously.

'Tom loves his house. Laws, yes.'

'We know you do, Tommy.' Stu could feel warm tears in the back of his own throat now.

'All right. I'm ready. Who am I riding with?'

'Me, Tom,' Ralph said. 'Down to Route 70, remember?'

Tom nodded and began to walk toward Ralph's cycle. After a moment Ralph followed him, his big shoulders slumped. Even the feather in his hatband seemed dejected. He climbed on the bike and kicked it alive. A moment later it pulled out onto Broadway and turned east. They stood together, watching the motorcycle dwindle to a moving silhouette in the purple dusk marked by a moving headlight. Then the light disappeared behind the bulk of the Holiday Twin Drive-in and was gone.

Nick walked away, head down, hands in pockets. Stu tried to join him, but Nick shook his head almost angrily and motioned him away. Stu went back to Larry.

'That's that,' Larry said, and Stu nodded gloomily.

'You think we'll ever see him again, Larry?'

'If we don't, the seven of us – well, maybe not Fran, she was never for sending him – the rest of us are going to be eating and sleeping with the decision to send him for the rest of our lives.'

'Nick more than anyone else,' Stu said.

'Yeah. Nick more than anyone else.'

They watched Nick walking slowly down Broadway, losing himself in the shadows which grew around him. Then they looked at Tom's darkened house in silence for a minute.

'Let's get out of here,' Larry said suddenly. 'The thought of all those stuffed animals . . . all of a sudden I got a grade-A case of the creeps.'

When they left, Nick was still standing on the side lawn of Tom Cullen's house, his hands in his pockets, his head down.

George Richardson, the new doctor, had set up in the Dakota Ridge Medical Center, because it was close to Boulder City Hospital with its medical equipment, its large supplies of drugs, and its operating rooms.

By August 28 he was pretty much in business, assisted by Laurie

Constable and Dick Ellis. Dick had asked leave to quit the world of medicine and had been refused permission to do so. 'You're doing a fine job here,' Richardson said. 'You've learned a lot and you're going to learn more. Besides, there's just too much for me to do by myself. We're going to be out of our minds as it is if we don't get another doctor in a month or two. So congratulations, Dick, you're the Zone's first paramedic. Give him a kiss, Laurie.'

Laurie did.

Around eleven o'clock on that late August morning, Fran let herself into the waiting room and looked around curiously and a little nervously. Laurie was behind the counter, reading an old copy of the *Ladies' Home Journal*.

'Hi, Fran,' she said, jumping up. 'I thought we'd see you sooner or later. George is with Candy Jones right now, but he'll be right with you. How are you feeling?'

'Pretty well, thanks,' Fran said. 'I guess –'

The door to one of the examining rooms opened and Candy Jones came out, following a tall, stooped man in corduroy slacks and a sport shirt with the Izod alligator on the breast. Candy was looking doubtfully at a bottle of pink stuff which she held in one hand.

'Are you sure that's what it is?' she asked Richardson doubtfully. 'I never got it before. I thought I was immune.'

'Well, you're not and you have it now,' George said with a grin. 'Don't forget the starch baths, and stay out of the tall grass after this.'

She smiled ruefully. 'Jack's got it too. Should he come in?'

'No, but you can make the starch baths a family affair.'

Candy nodded dolefully and then spotted Fran. 'Hi, Frannie, how's the girl?'

'Okay. How's by you?'

'Terrible.' Candy held up the bottle so Fran could read the world CALADRYL on the label. 'Poison ivy. And you couldn't *guess* where I got it.' She brightened. 'But I bet you can guess where *Jack's* got it.'

They watched her go with some amusement. Then George said, 'Miss Goldsmith, isn't it? Free Zone Committee. A pleasure.'

She held out her hand to be shaken. 'Just Fran, please. Or Frannie.'

'Okay, Frannie. What's the problem?'

'I'm pregnant,' Fran said. 'And pretty damn scared.' And then, with no warning at all, she was in tears.

George put an arm around her shoulders. 'Laurie, I'll want you in about five minutes.'

'All right, Doctor.'

He led her into the examining room and had her sit on the black-upholstered table.

'Now. Why the tears? Is it Mrs Wentworth's twins?'

Frannie nodded miserably.

'It was a difficult delivery, Fran. The mother was a heavy smoker. The babies were lightweights, even for twins. They came in the late evening, very suddenly. I had no opportunity to make a postmortem. Regina Wentworth is being cared for by some of the women who were in our party. I believe – I *hope* – that she's going to come out of the mental fugue-state she's currently in. But for now all I can say is that those babies had two strikes against them from the start. The cause of death could have been *anything*.'

'Including the superflu.'

'Yes. Including that.'

'So we just wait and see.'

'Hell no. I'm going to give you a complete prenatal right now. I'm going to monitor you and any other woman that gets pregnant or is pregnant now every step of the way. General Electric used to have a slogan, "Progress Is Our Most Important Product." In the Zone, babies are our most important product, and they are going to be treated accordingly.'

'But we really don't know.'

'No, we don't. But be of good cheer, Fran.'

'Yes, all right. I'll try.'

There was a brief rap at the door and Laurie came in. She handed George a form on a clipboard, and George began to ask Fran questions about her medical history.

When the exam was over, George left her for a while to do something in the next room. Laurie stayed with her while Fran dressed.

As she was buttoning her blouse, Laurie said quietly: 'I envy you, you know. Uncertainty and all. Dick and I had been trying to make a baby like mad. It's really funny – I was the one who used to wear a ZERO POPULATION button to work. It meant zero population *growth*, of course, but when I think about that button now, it gives me a really creepy feeling. Oh, Frannie, yours is going to be the *first*. And I know it will be all right. It *has* to be.'

Fran only smiled and nodded, not wanting to remind Laurie that hers would *not* be the first.

Mrs Wentworth's twins had been the first.

And Mrs Wentworth's twins had died.

'Fine,' George said half an hour later.

Fran raised her eyebrows, thinking for a moment he had mispronounced her name. For no good reason she remembered that until the third grade little Mikey Post from down the street had called her Fan.

'The baby. It's fine.'

Fran found a Kleenex and held it tightly. 'I felt it move . . . but that was some time ago. Nothing since then. I was afraid . . .'

'It's alive, all right, but I really doubt if you felt it move, you know. More likely a little intestinal gas.'

'It was the baby,' Fran said quietly.

'Well, whether it did or not, it's going to move a lot in the future. I've got you pegged for early to mid-January. How does that sound?'

'Fine.'

'Are you eating right?'

'Yes, I think so – trying hard, anyway.'

'Good. No nausea now?'

'A little at first, but it's passed.'

'Lovely. Getting plenty of exercise?'

For a nightmare instant she saw herself digging her father's grave. She blinked the vision away. That had been another life. 'Yes, plenty.'

'Have you gained any weight?'

'About five pounds.'

'That's all right. You can have another twelve; I'm feeling generous today.'

She grinned. 'You're the doctor.'

'Yes, and I used to be an OB man, so you're in the right place. Take your doctor's advice and you'll go far. Now, concerning bicycles, motorbikes, and mopeds. All of them a no-no after November fifteenth, let's say. No one's going to be riding them by then anyway. Too damn cold. Don't smoke or drink to excess, do you?'

'No.'

'If you want a nightcap once in a while, I think that's perfectly okay. I'm going to put you on a vitamin supplement; you can pick it up at any drugstore in town –'

Frannie burst into laughter, and George smiled uncertainly. 'Did I say something funny?'

'No. It just came out funny under the circumstances.'

'Oh! Yes, I see. Well, at least there won't be any more complaining about high drug prices, will there? One last thing, Fran. Have you ever been fitted with an intrauterine device . . . an IUD?'

'No, why?' Fran asked, and then she happened to think of her dream: the dark man with his coathanger. She shuddered. 'No,' she said again.

'Good. That's it.' He stood up. 'I won't tell you not to worry –'

'No,' she agreed. The laughter was gone from her eyes. 'Don't do that.'

'But I will ask you to keep it to a minimum. Excess anxiety in the mother can lead to glandular imbalance. And that's not good for the baby. I don't like to prescribe tranquilizers for pregnant women, but if you think –'

'No, that won't be necessary,' Fran said, but going out into the hot midday sunshine, she knew that the entire second half of her pregnancy was going to be haunted by thoughts of Mrs Wentworth's vanished twins.

On the twenty-ninth of August three groups came in, one with twenty-two members, one with sixteen, and one with twenty-five. Sandy DuChiens got around to see all seven members of the committee and tell them that the Free Zone now had over one thousand residents.

Boulder no longer seemed such a ghost town.

On the evening of the thirtieth, Nadine Cross stood in the basement of Harold's house, watching him and feeling uneasy.

When Harold was doing something that didn't involve having some sort of strange sex with her, he seemed to go away to his own private place where she had no control over him. When he was in that place he seemed cold; more than that, he seemed contemptuous of her and even of himself. The only thing that didn't change was his hate of Stuart Redman and the others on the committee.

There was a dead air-hockey game in the basement and Harold

was working on its pinholed surface. There was an open book beside him. On the facing page was a diagram. He would look at the diagram for a while, then look at the apparatus he was working on, and then he would do something to it. Spread out neatly by his right hand were the tools from his Triumph motorcycle kit. Little snips of wire littered the air-hockey table.

'You know,' he said absently, 'you ought to take a walk.'

'Why?' She felt a trifle hurt. Harold's face was tense and unsmiling. Nadine could understand why Harold smiled as much as he did: because when he stopped, he looked insane. She suspected that he *was* insane, or very nearly.

'Because I don't know how old this dynamite is,' Harold said.

'What do you mean?'

'Old dynamite sweats, dear heart,' he said, and looked up at her. She saw that his entire face was running with sweat, as if to prove his point. 'It *perspires*, to be perfectly couth. And what it perspires is pure nitroglycerin, one of the world's great unstable substances. So if it's old, there's a very good chance that this little Science Fair project could blow us right over the top of Flagstaff Mountain and all the way to the Land of Oz.'

'Well, you don't have to sound so snotty about it,' Nadine said.

'Nadine? *Ma chère?*'

'What?'

Harold looked at her calmly and without smiling. 'Shut your fucking trap.'

She did, but she didn't take a walk, although she wanted to. Surely if this was Flagg's will (and the planchette had told her that Harold was Flagg's way of taking care of the committee), the dynamite wouldn't be old. And even if it *was* old, it wouldn't explode until it was supposed to . . . would it? Just how much control over events did Flagg have?

Enough, she told herself, *he has enough*. But she wasn't sure, and she was increasingly uneasy. She had been back to her house and Joe was gone – gone for good this time. She had gone to see Lucy, and had borne the cold reception long enough to learn that since she had moved in with Harold, Joe (Lucy, of course, called him Leo) had 'slipped back some.' Lucy obviously blamed her for that, too . . . but if an avalanche came rumbling down from Flagstaff Mountain or an earthquake ripped Pearl Street apart, Lucy would probably blame her for those things, too. Not that there wouldn't be enough to blame on her and Harold very soon. Still, she had been bitterly disappointed not to have seen Joe once more . . . to kiss him goodbye. She and Harold were not going to be in the Boulder Free Zone much longer.

Never mind, best you let him go completely now that you're embarked on this obscenity. You'd only be doing him harm . . . and possibly harm to yourself as well, because Joe . . . sees things, knows things. Let him stop being Joe, let me stop being Nadine-mom. Let him go back to being Leo, forever.

But the paradox in that was inexorable. She could not believe that any of these Zone people had more than a year's life left in them, and that included the boy. It was not *his* will that they should live . . .

. . . so tell the truth, it isn't just Harold who is his instrument. It's you too. You, who once defined the single unforgivable sin in the postplague world as murder, as the taking of a single life . . .

Suddenly she found herself wishing that the dynamite *was* old, that it would blow up and put an end to both of them. A merciful end. And then she found herself thinking about what would happen afterward, after they had gotten over the mountains, and felt the old slippery warmth kindle in her belly.

'There,' Harold said gently. He had lowered his apparatus into a Hush Puppies shoebox and set it aside.

'It's done?'

'Yes. Done.'

'Will it work?'

'Would you like to try it and find out?' His words were bitterly sarcastic, but she didn't mind. His eyes were working her over in that greedy, crawling little boy's way that she had come to recognize. He had returned from that distant place – the place from which he had written what was in the ledger that she had read and then replaced carelessly under the loose hearthstone where it had originally been. Now she could handle him. Now his talk was just talk.

'Would you like to watch me play with myself first?' she asked. 'Like last night?'

'Yeah,' he said. 'Okay. Good.'

'Let's go upstairs then.' She batted her eyelashes at him. 'I'll go first.'

'Yeah,' he said hoarsely. Little dots of sweat stood out on his brow, but fear hadn't put them there this time. 'Go first.'

So she went up first, and she could feel him looking up the short skirt of the little-girl sailor dress she was wearing. She was bare beneath it.

The door closed, and the thing that Harold had made sat in the open shoebox in the gloom. There was a battery-powered Realistic walkie-talkie handset from Radio Shack. Its back was off. Wired to it were eight sticks of dynamite. The book was still open. It was from the Boulder Public Library, and the title was *65 National Science Fair Prize Winners*. The diagram showed a doorbell wired up to a walkie-talkie similar to the one in the shoebox. The caption beneath said: *Third Prize, 1977 National Science Fair, Constructed by Brian Ball, Rutland, Vermont. Say the word and ring the bell up to twelve miles away!*

Some hours later that evening, Harold came back downstairs, put the cover on the shoebox, and carried it carefully upstairs. He put it on the top shelf of a kitchen cupboard. Ralph Brentner had told him that afternoon that the Free Zone Committee was inviting Chad Norris to speak at their next meeting. When was that going to be? Harold had inquired casually. September 2, Ralph had said.

September 2.

CHAPTER 57

Larry and Leo were sitting on the curb in front of the house. Larry was drinking a warm Hamm's Beer, Leo a warm Orange Spot. You could have anything to drink in Boulder that you wanted these days, as long as it came in a can and you didn't mind drinking it warm. From out back came the steady, gruff roar of the Lawnboy. Lucy was cutting the grass. Larry had offered to do it, but Lucy shook her head. 'Find out what's wrong with Leo, if you can.'

It was the last day of August.

The day after Nadine had moved in with Harold, Leo hadn't appeared for breakfast. Larry had found the boy in his room, dressed only in his underpants, his thumb in his mouth. He was uncommunicative and hostile. Larry had been more frightened than Lucy, because she didn't know how Leo had been when Larry had first encountered him. His name had been Joe then, and he had been brandishing a killer's knife.

The best part of a week had passed since then, and Leo was a little better, but he hadn't come back all the way and he wouldn't talk about what had happened.

'That woman has something to do with it,' Lucy had said, screwing the cap onto the lawnmower's tank.

'Nadine? What makes you think that?'

'Well, I wasn't going to mention it. But she came by the other day while you and Leo were trying the fishing down at Cold Creek. She wanted to see the boy. I was just as glad the two of you were gone.'

'Lucy —'

She gave him a quick kiss, and he had slipped his hand under her halter and given her a friendly squeeze. 'I judged you wrong before,' she said. 'I guess I'll always be sorry for that. But I'm never going to like Nadine Cross. There's something *wrong* with her.'

Larry didn't answer, but he thought Lucy's judgment was

probably a true one. That night up by King Sooper's she had been like a crazy woman.

'There's one other thing – when she was here, she didn't call him Leo. She called him the other name. Joe.'

He looked at her blankly as she turned the automatic starter and got the Lawnboy going.

Now, half an hour after that discussion, he drank his Hamm's and watched Leo bounce the Ping-Pong ball he had found the day the two of them had walked up to Harold's, where Nadine now lived. The small white ball was smudged, but not dented. *Thok-thok-thok against the pavement. Bouncy-bouncy-bally, look-at-the-way-we-play.*

Leo (he *was* Leo now, wasn't he?) hadn't wanted to go inside Harold's house that day.

Into the house where Nadine-mom was now living.

'You want to go fishing, kiddo?' Larry offered suddenly.

'No fish,' Leo said. He looked at Larry with his strange, seawater-green eyes. 'Do you know Mr Ellis?'

'Sure.'

'He says we can drink the water when the fish come back. Drink it without –' He made a hooting noise and waved his fingers in front of his eyes. 'You know.'

'Without boiling it?'

'Yes.'

Thok-thok-thok.

'I like Dick. Him and Laurie. Always give me something to eat. He's afraid they won't be able to, but I think they will.'

'Will what?'

'Be able to make a baby. Dick thinks he may be too old. But I guess he's not.'

Larry started to ask how Leo and Dick had gotten on *that* subject, and then didn't. The answer, of course, was that they hadn't. Dick wouldn't talk to a small boy about something so personal as making a baby. Leo had just . . . had just known.

Thok-thok-thok.

Yes, Leo knew things . . . or intuited them. He hadn't wanted to go in Harold's house and had said something about Nadine . . . he couldn't remember exactly what . . . but Larry had recalled that discussion and had felt very uneasy when he heard that Nadine had moved in with Harold. It had been as if the boy was in a trance, as if –

(– thok-thok-thok –)

Larry watched the Ping-Pong ball bounce up and down, and suddenly he looked into Leo's face. The boy's eyes were dark and faraway. The sound of the lawnmower was a far-off, soporific drone. The daylight was smooth and warm. And Leo was in a trance again, as if he had read Larry's thought and simply responded to it.

Leo had gone to see the elephant.

Very casually Larry said: 'Yes, I think they can make a baby. Dick can't be any more than fifty-five at the outside. Cary Grant made one when he was almost seventy, I believe.'

'Who's Cary Grant?' Leo asked. The ball went up and down, up and down.

(Notorious. North by Northwest.)

'Don't you know?' he asked Leo.

'He was that actor,' Leo said. 'He was in *Notorious*. And *Northwest*.'

(North *by Northwest.*)

'North *by Northwest.* I mean,' Leo said in a tone of agreement. His eyes never left the Ping-Pong ball's bouncing course.

'That's right,' he said. 'How's Nadine-mom, Leo?'

'She calls me Joe. I'm Joe to her.'

'Oh.' A cold chill was weaving its slow way up Larry's back.

'It's bad now.'

'Bad?'

'It's bad with both of them.'

'Nadine and –'

(Harold?)

'Yes, him.'

'They're not happy?'

'He's got them fooled. They think he wants them.'

'He?'

'Him.'

The word hung on the still summer air.

Thok-thok-thok.

'They're going to go west,' Leo said.

'Jesus,' Larry muttered. He was very cold now. The old fear swept him. Did he really want to hear any more of this? It was like watching a tomb door swing slowly open in a silent graveyard, seeing a hand emerge –

Whatever it is, I don't want to hear it, I don't want to know it.

'Nadine-mom wants to think it's your fault,' Leo said. 'She wants to think you drove her to Harold. But she waited on purpose. She waited until you loved Lucy-mom too much. She waited until she was sure. It's like *he's* rubbing away the part of her brain that knows right from wrong. Little by little he's rubbing that part away. And when it's gone she'll be as crazy as everyone else in the West. Crazier maybe.'

'Leo –' Larry whispered, and Leo answered immediately:

'She calls me Joe. I'm Joe to her.'

'Shall I call you Joe?' Larry asked doubtfully.

'No.' There was a note of pleading in the boy's voice. 'No, please don't.'

'You miss your Nadine-mom, don't you, Leo?'

'She's dead,' Leo said with chilling simplicity.

'Is that why you stayed out so late that night?'

'Yes.'

'And why you wouldn't talk?'

'Yes.'

'But you're talking now.'

'I have you and Lucy-mom to talk to.'

'Yes, of course –'

'But not for always!' the boy said fiercely. 'Not for always, unless you talk to Frannie! Talk to Frannie! *Talk to Frannie!*'

'About Nadine?'

'No!'

'About what? About you?'

Leo's voice rose, became even shriller. 'It's all written down! You know! Frannie knows! *Talk to Frannie!*'

'The committee –'

'Not the committee! The committee won't help you, it won't help anyone, the committee is the old way, *he* laughs at your committee because it's the old way and the old ways are *his* ways, you know, Frannie knows, if you talk together you can –'

Leo brought the ball down hard – *THOK!* – and it rose higher than his head and came down and rolled away. Larry watched it, his mouth dry, his heart thudding nastily in his chest.

'I dropped my ball,' Leo said, and ran to get it.

Larry sat watching him.

Frannie, he thought.

★   ★   ★

The two of them sat on the edge of the bandshell stage, their feet dangling. It was an hour before dark, and a few people were walking through the park, some of them holding hands. The children's hour is also the lovers' hour, Fran thought disjointedly. Larry had just finished telling her everything Leo had said in his trance, and her mind was whirling with it.

'So what do you think?' Larry asked.

'I don't know what to think,' she said softly, 'except I don't like any of the things that have been happening. Visionary dreams. An old woman who's the voice of God for a while and then walks off into the wilderness. Now a little boy who seems to be a telepath. It's like life in a fairy tale. Sometimes I think the superflu left us alive but drove us all mad.'

'He said I should talk to you. So I am.'

She didn't reply.

'Well,' Larry said, 'if anything comes to you –'

'Written down,' Frannie said softly. 'He was right, that kid. It's the whole root of the problem, I think. If I hadn't been so stupid, so conceited, as to write it all down . . . oh goddam me!'

Larry stared at her, amazed. 'What are you talking about?'

'It's Harold,' she said, 'and I'm afraid. I haven't told Stu. I've been ashamed. Keeping the diary was so *dumb* . . . and now Stu . . . he actually *likes* Harold . . . everybody in the Free Zone likes Harold, including you.' She uttered a laugh which was choked with tears. 'After all, he was your . . . your spirit-guide on the way out here, wasn't he?'

'I'm not tracking this very well,' Larry said slowly. 'Can you tell me what it is you're afraid of?'

'That's just it – *I don't really know.*' She looked at him, her eyes wet with tears. 'I think I'd better tell you what I can, Larry. I have to talk to someone. God knows I just can't keep it inside anymore, and Stu . . . Stu's maybe not the person who should hear. At least, not the first one.'

'Go ahead, Fran. Shoot.'

So she told him, beginning with the day in June that Harold had driven into the driveway of her Ogunquit home in Roy Brannigan's Cadillac. As she talked, the last bright daylight changed to a bluish shade. The lovers in the park began to drift away. A thin rind of moon rose. In the high-rise condominium on the far side of Canyon Boulevard, a few Coleman gaslamps had come on.

She told him about the sign on the barn roof and how she had been sleeping when Harold risked his life to put her name on the bottom. About meeting Stu in Fabyan, and about Harold's shrill get-away-from-my-bone reaction to Stu. She told him about her diary, and about the thumbprint in it. By the time she finished, it was past nine o'clock and the crickets were singing. A silence fell between them and Fran waited apprehensively for Larry to break it. But he seemed lost in thought.

At last he said, 'How sure are you about that fingerprint? In your own mind are you *positive* it was Harold's?'

She only hesitated a moment. 'Yes. I knew it was Harold's print the first time I saw it.'

'That barn he put the sign on,' Larry said. 'You remember the night I met you I said I'd been up in it? And that Harold had carved his initials on a beam in the loft?'   •

'Yes.'

'It wasn't just his initials. It was yours, too. In a heart. The kind of thing a lovesick little boy would do on his school desk.'

She put her hands over her eyes and wiped them. 'What a mess,' she said huskily.

'You're not responsible for Harold Lauder's actions, keed.' He took her hand in both of his and held it tightly. He looked at her. 'Take it from me, the original dipstick, oilslick, and drippy dick. You can't hold it against yourself. Because if you do . . .' His grip tightened to a degree where it became painful, but his face remained soft. 'If you do, you really will go mad. It's hard enough for a person to keep their own socks pulled up, let alone someone else's.'

He took his hand away and they were quiet for a time.

'You think Harold bears Stu a killing grudge?' he said at last. 'You really think it's that deep?'

'Yes,' she said. 'I really think that's a possibility. Maybe the whole committee. But I don't know what –'

His hand fell on her shoulder and gripped it hard, stilling her. In the darkness his posture had changed, his eyes had widened. His lips moved soundlessly.

'Larry? What –'

'When he went downstairs,' Larry muttered. 'He went down to get a corkscrew or something.'

'What?'

He turned toward her slowly, as if his head was on a rusty hinge. 'You know,' he said, 'there just might be a way to resolve all this. I don't guarantee it, because I didn't look in the book, but . . . it makes such beautiful sense . . . Harold reads your diary and not only gets an earful but an idea. Hell, he might have even been jealous that you thought of it first. Didn't all the best writers keep journals?'

'Are you saying *Harold's* got a diary?'

'When he went down to the basement, the day I brought the wine, I was looking around his living room. He said he was going to put in some chrome and leather, and I was trying to figure out how it would look. And I noticed this loose stone on the hearth —'

'*YES!*' she yelled, so loudly that he jumped. 'The day I snuck in . . . and Nadine Cross came . . . I *sat* on the hearth . . . I remember that loose stone.' She looked at Larry again. 'There it is again. As if something had us by the nose, was leading us to it . . .'

'Coincidence,' he said, but he sounded uneasy.

'Is it? We were both in Harold's house. We both noticed the loose stone. And we're both here now. Is it coincidence?'

'I don't know.'

'What was under that stone?'

'A ledger,' he said slowly. 'At least, that was the word stamped on the cover. I didn't look in it. At the time I thought it could just as easily have belonged to the previous owner of the house as to Harold. But if it did, wouldn't Harold have found it? We both noticed the loose stone. So let's say he finds it. Even if the guy who lived there before the flu had filled it up with little secrets — the amount he cheated on his taxes, his sex fantasies about his daughter, I don't know what all — those secrets wouldn't have been *Harold's* secrets. Do you see that?'

'Yes, but —'

'Don't interrupt while Inspector Underwood is elucidating, you giddy slip of a girl. So if the secrets weren't Harold's secrets, why would he have put the ledger back under the stone? Because they *were* his secrets. That was Harold's *journal.*'

'Do you think it's still there?'

'Maybe. I think we'd better look and see.'

'Now?'

'Tomorrow. He'll be out with the Burial Committee, and Nadine has been helping out at the power station afternoons.'

'All right,' she said. 'Do you think I should tell Stu about this?'

'Why don't we wait? There's no sense stirring things up unless we're sure it's something important. The book might be gone. It might be nothing but a list of things to do. It might be full of perfectly innocent things. Or Harold's master political plan. Or it might be in code.'

'I hadn't thought of that. What will we do if there is . . . something important?'

'Then I guess we'll have to bring it up before the Free Zone Committee. Another reason to get it done quickly. We're meeting on the second. The committee will handle it.'

'Will it?'

'Yes, I think so,' Larry said, but he was also thinking of what Leo had said about the committee.

She slipped off the edge of the bandshell and onto the ground. 'I feel better. Thanks for being here, Larry.'

'Where should we meet?'

'The little park across from Harold's. What about there, at one o'clock tomorrow afternoon?'

'Fine,' Larry said. 'I'll see you then.'

Frannie went home feeling lighter at heart than she had for weeks. As Larry said, the alternatives were now fairly clear. The ledger might prove all of their fears groundless. But if it proved otherwise . . .

Well, if it was otherwise, let the committee decide. As Larry had reminded her, they were meeting on the evening of the second, at Nick and Ralph's place, out near the end of Baseline Road.

When she got home, Stu was sitting in the bedroom, a felt-tip marker in one hand and a weighty leather-bound volume in the other. The title, stamped in gold leaf on the cover, was *An Introduction to the Colorado Code of Criminal Justice*.

'Heavy reading,' she said, and kissed him on the mouth.

'Arg.' He tossed the book across the room and it landed on the dresser with a thump. 'Al Bundell brought it over. He and his Law Committee are really up and in the doins, Fran. He wants to talk to the Free Zone Committee when we meet day after tomorrow. What have you been up to, pretty lady?'

'Talking with Larry Underwood.'

He looked at her closely for a long moment. 'Fran – have you been crying?'

'Yes,' she said, meeting his gaze steadily, 'but I feel better now. Much better.'

'Is it the baby?'

'No.'

'What, then?'

'I'll tell you tomorrow night. I'll tell you everything that's been on what passes for my mind. Until then, no questions. Kay?'

'Is it serious?'

'Stu, I don't know.'

He looked at her for a long, long time.

'All right, Frannie,' he said. 'I love you.'

'I know. And I love you, too.'

'Bed?'

She smiled. 'Race you.'

The first of September dawned gray and rainy, a dull, forgettable day – but one that no resident of the Free Zone ever forgot. That was the day the power came back on in North Boulder . . . briefly, at least.

At ten to noon, in the control room of the power station, Brad Kitchner looked at Stu, Nick, Ralph, and Jack Jackson, who were all standing behind him. Brad smiled nervously and said, 'Hail Mary, fulla grace, help me win this stock-car race.'

He yanked two big switches down hard. In the huge and cavernous hall below them, two trial generators began to whine. The five men walked over to the wall-to-wall polarized glass window and looked below, to where almost a hundred men and women stood, all of them wearing protective goggles as per Brad's order.

'If we did something wrong, I'd rather blow two than fifty-two,' Brad had told them earlier.

The generators began to whine more loudly.

Nick elbowed Stu and pointed to the office ceiling, Stu looked up and began to grin. Behind the translucent panels, the fluorescents had begun to glow weakly. The generators cycled up and up, reached a high, steady hum, and leveled off. Down below, the crowd of assembled workers broke into spontaneous applause, some of them wincing as they did so; their hands were raw and frayed from wrapping copper wire hour after drudging hour.

The fluorescents were shining brightly and normally now.

For Nick, the feeling was the exact opposite of the dread he

had known when the lights went out in Shoyo – not one of entomb-
ment now, but of resurrection.

The two generators supplied power to one small section of North
Boulder in the North Street area. There were people in the area who
hadn't known about the test that morning, and many of these people
fled as if all the devils of hell were after them.

TV sets went on in blares of snow. In a house on Spruce
Street, a blender whirred into life, trying to blend a cheese-and-egg
mixture that had congealed long since. The blender's motor soon
overloaded and blew out. A power saw whined into life in a deserted
garage, puffing sawdust out of its guts. Stove burners began to glow.
Marvin Gaye began to sing from the loudspeakers of an oldies
record shop called the Wax Museum; the words, backed by a jive
disco beat, seemed like a dream of the past come to life: *'Let's
dance . . . let's shout . . . get funky what it's all about . . . let's
dance . . . let's shout . . .'*

A power transformer blew on Maple Street and a gaudy spiral
of purple sparks drifted down, lit on the wet grass, and went out.

At the power station, one of the generators began to whine at
a higher, more desperate note. It began to smoke. People backed
away, poised just below the point of panic. The place began to fill
with the sickish-sweet smell of ozone. A buzzer went off stridently.

'Too high!' Brad roared. 'Bastard's crossing over! Overloading!'

He scrambled across the room and slammed both switches back
up. The whine of the generators began to die, but not before there
was a loud pop and screams, deadened by the safety glass, from below.

'Holy crow,' Ralph said. 'One of em's afire.'

Above them, the fluorescents faded to sullen cores of white
light, then went out completely. Brad jerked open the control room
door and came out on the landing. His words echoed flatly in the
big open space. 'Get the foam to that! Hustle!'

Several foam extinguishers were turned on the generators, and
the fire was doused. The smell of ozone still hung on the air. The
others crowded out on the landing beside Brad.

Stu laid a hand on his shoulder. 'I'm sorry it turned out the
way it did, man,' he said.

Brad turned toward him, grinning. 'Sorry? What for?'

'Well, it caught fire, didn't it?' Jack asked.

'Shit, yes! It surely did! And somewhere around North Street
there's a transformer all blown to shit. We forgot, goddammit, we

forgot! They got sick, they died, but they didn't go around turning off their electrical appliances before they did it! There are TVs on, and ovens, and electric blankets, all over Boulder. Hell of a power drain. These generators, they're built to cross over when the load's heavy in one place and light in another. That one down there tried to cross, but all the others were shut down, see?' Brad was fairly jerking with excitement. 'Gary! You remember the way Gary, Indiana, was burned to the ground?'

They nodded.

'Can't be sure, we'll never be sure, but what happened here could have happened there. Could be the power didn't go off soon enough. One shorted-out electric blanket could have been enough under the right conditions, just like Mrs O'Leary's cow kicking over that lantern in Chicago. These gennies tried to cross and had nothing to cross *to*. So they burned out. We're lucky it happened, that's what I think – take my word for it.'

'If you say so,' Ralph responded doubtfully.

Brad said, 'We've got the job to do all over again, but only on one motor. We'll be in business. But –' Brad had begun to snap his fingers, an unconscious gesture of excitement. 'We don't dare turn the juice back on until we're sure. Can we get another work-crew? A dozen guys or so?'

'Sure, I guess so,' Stu said. 'What for?'

'A Turning-Off Crew. Just a bunch of guys to go around Boulder and turn off everything that was left on. We don't dare turn the juice back on until that gets done. We got no fire department, man.' Brad laughed a little crazily.

'We're having a Free Zone Committee meeting tomorrow night,' Stu said. 'You come on over and explain why you want them, and you'll get your men. But are you sure that overload won't happen again?'

'Pretty damn sure, yeah. It wouldn't have happened today if there hadn't been so much stuff left on. Speaking of that, somebody ought to go over to North Boulder and see if it's burning down.'

Nobody was sure if Brad was joking or not. As it turned out there were several small fires, mostly from hot appliances. None of them spread in the drizzle that was falling. And what people in the Zone remembered later about the first of September 1990 was that it was the day the power came back on – if only for thirty seconds or so.

*　　*　　*

An hour later, Fran pedaled her bike into Eben G. Fine Park across from Harold's. At the park's north end, just beyond the picnic tables, Boulder Stream chuckled mildly along. The morning's drizzly rain was turning into a fine mist.

She looked around for Larry, didn't see him, and parked her bike. She walked through the dewy grass toward the swings and a voice said, 'Over here, Frannie.'

Startled, she looked toward the building that housed the men's and women's toilets, and felt a moment of utter confused fear. A tall figure was standing in the shadows of the short passageway running through the center of the dual comfort station, and for just a moment she thought . . .

Then the figure stepped out and it was Larry, dressed in faded jeans and a khaki shirt. Fran relaxed.

'Did I scare you?' he asked.

'You did, just a little.' She sat down in one of the swings, the thud of her heart beginning to slow. 'I just saw a shape, standing there in the dark . . .'

'I'm sorry. I thought it might be safer, even though there's no direct line of sight from here to Harold's place. I see you rode a bicycle, too.'

She nodded. 'Quieter.'

'I stowed mine out of sight in that shelter.' He nodded to an open-walled, low-roofed building by the playground.

Frannie trundled her bike between the swings and the slide and into the shelter. The odor inside was musty and fetid. The place had been a make-out spot for kids too young or too stoned to drive, she guessed. It was littered with beer bottles and cigarette ends. There was a crumpled pair of panties in the far corner and the remains of a small fire in the near one. She parked her bike next to Larry's and came back outside quickly. In those shadows, with the scent of that long-dead sex-musk in her nose, it was too easy to imagine the dark man standing just behind her, his twisted coathanger in hand.

'Regular Holiday Inn, isn't it?' Larry said dryly.

'Not my idea of pleasant accommodations,' Fran said with a little shiver. 'No matter what comes of this, Larry, I want to tell Stu everything tonight.'

Larry nodded. 'Yeah, and not just because he's on the committee. He's also the marshal.'

Fran looked at him, troubled. Really for the first time she understood that this expedition might end with Harold in jail. They were going to sneak into his house without a warrant or anything and poke around.

'Oh, bad,' she said.

'Not too good, is it?' he agreed. 'You want to call it off?'

She thought for a long time and then shook her head.

'Good. I think we ought to know, one way or the other.'

'Are you sure they're both gone?'

'Yes. I saw Harold driving one of the Burial Committee trucks early this morning. And all the people who were on the Power Committee were invited over for the tryout.'

'You sure she went?'

'It would look damn funny if she didn't, wouldn't it?'

Fran thought that over, then nodded. 'I guess it would. By the way, Stu said they hope to have most of the town electrified again by the sixth.'

'That's going to be a mighty day,' Larry said, and thought how nice it would be to sit down in Shannon's or the Broken Drum with a big Fender guitar and an even bigger amp and play something – anything, as long as it was simple and had a heavy beat – at full volume. 'Gloria,' maybe, or 'Walkin' the Dog.' Just about anything, in fact, except 'Baby, Can You Dig Your Man?'

'Maybe,' Fran said, 'we ought to have a cover story, though. Just in case.'

Larry grinned crookedly. 'Want to say we're selling magazine subscriptions if one of them comes back?'

'Har-har, Larry.'

'Well, we could say we came to tell her what you just told me about getting the juice turned on again. If she's there.'

Fran nodded. 'Yes, that might be okay.'

'Don't kid yourself, Fran. She'd be suspicious if we told her we'd come up because Jesus Christ just appeared and is walking back and forth on top of the City Reservoir.'

'If she's guilty of something.'

'Yes. If she's guilty of something.'

'Come on,' Fran said after a moment's thought. 'Let's go.'

There was no need for the cover story. Steady hard rapping at first the front and then the back door convinced them that Harold's house was indeed empty. It was just as well, Fran thought – the more she thought about the cover they'd worked out, the thinner it seemed.

'How did you get in?' Larry asked.

'The cellar window.'

They went around to the side of the house and Larry pulled and tugged fruitlessly at the window while Fran kept watch.

'Maybe you did,' he said, 'but it's locked now.'

'No, it's just sticking. Let me try.'

But she had no better luck. Sometime between her first clandestine trip out here and now, Harold had locked up tight.

'What do we do now?' she asked him.

'Let's break it.'

'Larry, he'll *see* it.'

'Let him. If he doesn't have anything to hide, he'll think it was just a couple of kids, breaking windows in empty houses. It sure *looks* empty, with all the shades pulled down. And if he *does* have something to hide, it'll worry him plenty and he deserves to be worried. Right?'

She looked doubtful but didn't stop him as he took off his shirt, wrapped it around his fist and forearm, and crunched the basement window. Glass tinkled inward and he felt around for the catch.

'Here tis.' He released it and the window slid back. Larry slipped through and turned to help her. 'Be careful, kiddo. No miscarriages in Harold Lauder's basement, please.'

He caught her under the arms and eased her down. They looked around the rumpus room together. The croquet set stood sentinel. The air-hockey table was littered with little snips of colored electrical wire.

'What's this?' she said, picking up a piece of it. 'This wasn't here before.'

He shrugged. 'Maybe Harold's building a better mousetrap.'

There was a box under the table and he fished it out. The cover said: DELUXE REALISTIC WALKIE-TALKIE SET, BATTERIES NOT INCLUDED. Larry opened the box, but the heft of it had already told him it was empty.

'Building walkie-talkies instead of mousetraps,' Fran said.

'No, this wasn't a kit. You buy this kind ready to go. Maybe he was modifying them somehow. It sounds like Harold. Remember how Stu bitched about the walkie-talkie reception when he and Harold and Ralph were out hunting for Mother Abagail?'

She nodded, but there was still something about those snips of wire that bothered her.

Larry dropped the box back onto the floor and made what he would later think of as the most wildly erroneous statement of his entire life. 'It doesn't matter,' he said. 'Let's go.'

They went up the stairs, but this time the door at the top was locked. She looked at him and Larry shrugged. 'We've come this far, right?'

Fran nodded.

Larry bumped his shoulder against the door a few times to get the feel of the bolt on the other side, and then rammed it hard. There was a snapping-metal sound, a clunk, and the door swung open. Larry bent and picked up a bolt assembly from the linoleum kitchen floor. 'I can put this back on and he'll never know the difference. That is, if there's a screwdriver handy.'

'Why bother? He's going to see the broken window.'

'That's true. But if the bolt's back on the door, he'll . . . what are you smiling about?'

'Put the bolt back on, by all means. But how are you going to draw it from the cellar side of the door?'

He thought about it and said, 'Jeez, I hate a smartass woman worse than anything.' He tossed the bolt onto the Formica kitchen counter. 'Let's go look under the hearth-stone.'

They went into the shadowy living room, and Fran felt anxiety start to creep up. Last time Nadine hadn't had a key. This time, if she came back, she would. And if she did come back, they would be caught red-handed. It would be a bitter joke if Stu's first job as marshal turned out to be arresting his own woman for breaking and entering.

'That's it, isn't it?' Larry asked, pointing.

'Yes. Be as quick as you can.'

'There's a good chance he's moved it, anyway.' And Harold had. It was Nadine who had replaced it under the loose hearthstone. Larry and Fran knew nothing of that, only that when Larry pulled the loose hearthstone aside, the book lay there in the hollow beneath, the word LEDGER gleaming mellowly up at them in gold-filled letters. They both stared at it. The room seemed suddenly hotter, stuffier, darker.

'Well,' Larry said, 'are we going to admire it or read it?'

'You,' Fran said. 'I don't even want to touch it.'

Larry picked it out of the hole and automatically wiped the white stone-dust from the cover. He began to flip through it at random. The writing had been done with a felt-tipped marker of the sort that had been marketed under the pugnacious brand name Hardhead. It had allowed Harold to write in a tiny, perfect script – the handwriting of an intensely conscientious man, perhaps a driven man. There were no paragraph breaks. There was only an eyelash of a margin to the right and left, but that margin was constant, so straight that it might have been drawn with a ruler.

'It'd take me three days to read all this,' Larry said, and went on flipping toward the front of the book.

'Hold it,' Fran said, and reached over his arm to turn back a couple of pages. Here the steady flow of words was broken by a boldly boxed-off area. What had been enclosed seemed to be some sort of motto:

> To follow one's star is to concede the power of some greater Force, some Providence; yet is it still not possible that the act of following itself is the taproot of even greater Power? Your GOD, your DEVIL, owns the keys to the lighthouse; I have grappled with that so long and hard in these last two months; but to each of us he has given the responsibility of NAVIGATION.
>
> HAROLD EMERY LAUDER

'Sorry,' Larry said. 'It's by me. You get it?'

Fran shook her head slowly. 'I guess it's Harold's way of saying following can be as honorable as leading. But as a motto, I don't think it's going to put "Waste not, want not" out of business.'

Larry continued to flip toward the front of the book, coming upon another four or five of the boxed maxims, all of them attributed to Harold in capital letters.

'Whoo,' Larry said. 'Look at this one, Frannie!'

> It is said that the two great human sins are pride and hate. Are they? I elect to think of them as the two great virtues. To give away pride and hate is to say you will change for the good of the world. To vent them is more noble; that is to say the world must change for the good of you. I am on a great adventure.
>
> HAROLD EMERY LAUDER

'That's the work of a profoundly disturbed mind,' Fran said. She felt cold.

'It's the kind of thinking that got us into this mess to start with,' Larry agreed. He flipped rapidly to the start of the book. 'Time's wasting. Let's see what we can make of this.'

Neither of them knew exactly what to expect. They had read nothing of the ledger except the boxed mottos and an occasional phrase or two which, mostly owning to Harold's convoluted style (the compound-complex sentence seemed to have been invented with Harold Lauder in mind), meant little or nothing.

What they saw at the ledger's beginning was therefore a complete shock.

The diary began at the top of the first facing page. It was neatly marked with a 1 in a circle. There was an indent here, the only indent in the whole book, as far as Frannie could tell, excepting those which began each boxed motto. They read that first sentence holding the ledger between them like children at a choir practice and Fran said 'Oh!' in a small, strangled voice and stepped away, her hand pressed lightly to her mouth.

'Fran, we have to take the book,' Larry said.

'Yes –'

'And show it to Stu. I don't know if Leo's right about them being on the dark man's side, but at the very least, Harold is danger-ously disturbed. You can see that.'

'Yes,' she said again. She felt faint, weak. So this was how the matter of the diaries ended. It was as if she had known, as if she had known it all from the moment she saw that big smudged thumbprint, and she had to keep telling herself not to faint, not to faint.

'Fran? Frannie? Are you all right?'

Larry's voice. From far away.

The first sentence in Harold's ledger: *My great pleasure this delightful post-Apocalypse summer will be to kill Mr Stuart Dog-Cock Redman; and just maybe I will kill her, too.*

'Ralph? Ralph Brentner, you home? *Hooo-hooo, anybody home?*'

She stood on the steps, looking at the house. No motorcycles in the yard, only a couple of bikes parked around to one side. Ralph would have heard her, but there was the mute to think about. The deaf-mute. You could holler until you were blue and he wouldn't answer and still he might be there.

Shifting her shopping bag from one arm to the other, Nadine tried the door and found it unlocked. She stepped inside out of the fine mist which was falling. She was in a small foyer. Four steps went up to the kitchen, and a flight of them went down to the basement area where Harold said Andros had his apartment. Putting her most pleasant expression on her face, Nadine went downstairs, fixing her excuse in her mind if he should be there.

I came right in because I didn't think you'd know I was knocking. Some of us wanted to know if there's going to be a late shift wrapping those two motors that blew. Did Brad say anything to you?

There were only two rooms down here. One of them was a bedroom as simple as a monk's cell. The other was a study. There was a desk, a big chair, a wastebasket, a bookcase. The top of the desk was littered with scraps of paper and she looked through them idly. Most of them made little sense to her – she guessed they were Nick's side of some conversation (*I guess so, but shouldn't we ask him if it can be done in some simpler way?* one of them read). Others seemed to be memos to himself, jottings, thoughts. A few of them reminded her of the boxes in Harold's ledger, what he called his 'Guideposts to a Better Life' with a sarcastic smile.

One read: *Talk to Glen about trade. Do any of us know how trade starts? Scarcity of goods, isn't it? Or a modified corner on some market? Skills. That may be a key word. What if Brad Kitchner decides to sell instead of giving away? Or the doc? What would we pay with? Hmmm.*

Another: *Community protection is a two-way street.*

Another: *Every time we talk about the law I spend the night having nightmares about Shoyo. Watching them die. Watching Childress throw his supper around the cell. The law, the law, what do we do about the goddamned law? Capital punishment. Now there's a smiley thought. When Brad gets the power on, how long before someone asks him to rig up an electric chair?*

She turned away from the scraps – reluctantly. It was fascinating to look through papers left by a man who could think wholly only by writing (one of her college profs had been fond of saying that the thought process can never be complete without articulation), but her purpose down here was already completed. Nick was not here, no one was here. To linger overlong would be to press her luck unnecessarily.

She went back upstairs. Harold had told her they would probably meet in the living room. It was a huge room, carpeted with a thick wine-colored shag rug, dominated by a freestanding fireplace that went up through the roof in a column of rock. The entire west wall was glass, giving on a magnificent view of the Flatirons. It made her feel as exposed as a bug on a wall. She knew that the outer surface of the thermoplex was iodized so that anyone outside would only see a mirrorlike reflection, but the psychological feeling was still one of utter exposure. She wanted to finish quickly.

On the southern side of the room she found what she was looking for, a deep closet that Ralph hadn't cleaned out. Coats hung far back inside, and in the rear corner there was a tangle of boots and mittens and winter woolens about three feet deep.

Working quickly, she took the groceries out of her shopping bag. They were camouflage, and there was only a single layer of them. Beneath the cans of tomato paste and sardines was the Hush Puppies shoebox with the dynamite and the walkie-talkie inside.

'If I put it in a closet, will it still work?' she had asked. 'Won't the extra wall muffle the blast?'

'Nadine,' Harold had responded, 'if that device works, and I have no reason whatever to believe it won't, it will take the house and most of the surrounding hillside. Put it anywhere you think it will be unobserved until their meeting. A closet will be fine. The extra wall will blow out and become shrapnel. I trust your judgment, dear. It's going to be just like the old fairy tale about the tailor and the flies. Seven at a blow. Only in this case, we're dealing with a bunch of political cockroaches.'

Nadine pushed aside boots and scarves, made a hole, and slipped the shoebox into it. She covered it over again and then worked her way out of the closet. There. Done. For better or worse.

She left the house quickly, not looking back, trying to ignore the voice that wouldn't stay dead, the voice that was now telling her to go back in there and pull the wires that ran between the blasting caps and the walkie-talkie, telling her to give this up before it drove her mad. Because wasn't that what was really lying somewhere up ahead, now maybe less than two weeks ahead? Wasn't madness the final logical conclusion?

She slipped the bag of groceries into the Vespa's carrier and kicked the machine into life. And all the time she was driving away, that voice went on: *You're not going to leave that there, are you? You're not going to leave that bomb in there, are you?*

In a world where so many have died –

She leaned into a turn, barely able to see where she was going. Tears had begun to blur her eyes.

– the one great sin is to take a human life.

Seven lives here. No, more than that, because the committee was going to hear reports from the heads of several subcommittees.

She stopped at the corner of Baseline and Broadway, thinking she would turn around and go back. She was shuddering all over.

And later she would never be able to explain to Harold precisely what had happened – in truth, she never even tried. It was a foretaste of the horrors to come.

She felt a blackness creeping over her vision.

It came like a dark curtain slowly drawn, flipping and flapping in a mild breeze. Every now and then the breeze would gust, the curtain would flap more vigorously, and she would see a bit of daylight under its hem, a little bit of this deserted intersection.

But the curtain came over her vision in steady blackout drifts and soon she was lost in it. She was blind, she was deaf, she was without the sense of touch. The thinking creature, the Nadine-ego, drifted in a warm black cocoon like seawater, like amniotic fluid.

And she felt him creep into her.

A shriek built up within her, but she had no mouth with which to scream.

Penetration: entropy.

She didn't know what those words meant, put together like that; she only knew that they were right.

It was like nothing she had ever felt before. Later, metaphors occurred to her to describe it, and she rejected them, one by one:

You're swimming and suddenly, in the midst of the warm water, you're treading water in a pocket of deep, numbing cold.

You've been given Novocain and the dentist pulls a tooth. It comes out with a painless tug. You spit blood into the white enamel basin. There's a hole in you; you've been gouged. You can slip your tongue into the hole where part of you was living a second ago.

You stare at your face in the mirror. You stare at it for a long time. Five minutes, ten, fifteen. No fair blinking. You watch with an intellectual sort of horror as your face changes, like the face of Lon Chaney, Jr., in a were wolf epic. You become a stranger to yourself, an olive-skinned *Doppelganger*, a psychotic Vampira with pale skin and fishslit eyes.

It was really none of those things, but there was a taste-trace of all of them.

The dark man entered her, *and he was cold.*

★ ★ ★

When Nadine opened her eyes, her first thought was that she was in hell.

Hell was whiteness, the thesis to the dark man's antithesis. She saw white, ivory, bleached-out nothingness. White-white-white. It was white hell, and it was everywhere.

She stared at the whiteness (it was impossible to stare *into* it), fascinated, agonized, for minutes before she realized she could feel the fork of the Vespa between her thighs, and that there was another color – green – at the periphery of her vision.

With a jerk she pulled her eyes out of their blank, locked stare. She gazed around herself. Her mouth was slack, trembling; the eyes themselves dazed and horror-drugged. The dark man had been in her, Flagg had been in her, and when he had come he had driven her away from the windows of her five senses, her loopholes on reality. He had driven her as a man might drive a car or a truck. And he had brought her . . . where?

She glanced toward the white and saw it was a huge blank drive-in movie screen against a background of white late afternoon rainy sky. Turning around, she saw the snack-bar. It was painted a garish flesh-tone pink. Written across the front was *WELCOME TO THE HOLIDAY TWIN! ENJOY ENTERTAINMENT UNDER THE STARS TO-NITE!*

The darkness had come on her at the intersection of Baseline and Broadway. Now she was far out on Twenty-eighth Street, almost over the town line to . . . Longmont, wasn't it?

There was a taste of him in her still, far back in her mind, like cold slime on a floor.

She was surrounded by poles, steel poles like sentries, each of them five feet high, each bearing a matched set of drive-in speakers. There was gravel underfoot, but grass and dandelions were growing up through it. She guessed the Holiday Twin hadn't been doing much business since the middle of June or so. You could say that it had been kind of a dead summer for the entertainment biz.

'Why am I here?' she whispered.

It was only talking aloud, talking to herself; she expected no answer. So when she *was* answered, a shriek of terror pealed from her throat.

All the speakers fell off the speaker poles at once and onto the weed-strewn gravel. The sound they made was a huge, amplified *CHUNK!* – the sound of a dead body striking gravel.

'*NADINE,*' the speakers blared, and it was *his* voice, and how she shrieked then! Her hands flew to her head, her palms clapped themselves over her ears, but it was all the speakers at once and there was no hiding from that giant voice, which was full of fearful hilarity and dreadful comic lust.

'*NADINE, NADINE, OH HOW I LOVE TO LOVE NADINE, MY PET, MY PRETTY —*'

'*Stop it!*' she shrieked back, straining her vocal cords with the force of her cry, and still her voice was so small compared with that giant's bellow. And yet, for a moment the voice *did* stop. There was silence. The fallen speakers looked up at her from the gravel like the rugose eyes of giant insects.

Nadine's hands slowly came down from her ears.

You've gone insane, she comforted herself. That's all it is. The strain of waiting . . . and Harold's games . . . finally planting the explosive . . . all of it has finally driven you over the edge, dear, and you've gone crazy. It's probably better this way.

But she hadn't gone crazy, and she knew it.

This was far worse than being crazy.

As if to prove this, the speakers now boomed out in the stern yet almost prissy voice of a principal reprimanding the student body over the high school intercom for some prank they had all played together. '*NADINE. THEY KNOW.*'

'They know,' she parroted. She wasn't sure who they were, or what they knew, but she was quite sure it was inevitable.

'*YOU'VE BEEN STUPID. GOD MAY LOVE STUPIDITY: I DO NOT.*'

The words crackled and rolled away into the late afternoon. Her clothes clung soddenly to her skin, her hair lay lankly against her pallid cheeks, and she began to shiver.

Stupid, she thought. Stupid, stupid. I know what that word means. I think. I think it means death.

'*THEY KNOW EVERYTHING . . . EXCEPT THE SHOEBOX. THE DYNAMITE.*'

Speakers. Speakers everywhere, staring up at her from the white gravel, peeking at her from clusters of dandelions closed against the rain.

'*GO TO SUNRISE AMPHITHEATER. STAY THERE. UNTIL TOMORROW NIGHT. UNTIL THEY MEET. AND THEN YOU AND HAROLD MAY COME. COME TO ME.*'

Now Nadine began to feel a simple, shining gratitude. They had been stupid . . . but they had also been granted a second chance. They were important enough to have warranted intervention. And soon, very soon, she would be with him . . . and then she *would* go crazy, she was quite sure of it, and all this would cease to matter.

'Sunrise Amphitheater may be too far,' she said. Her vocal cords had been hurt somehow; she could only croak. 'It may be too far for the . . .' For the what? She pondered. Oh! Oh yes! Right! 'For the walkie-talkie. The signal.'

No answer.

The speakers lay on the gravel, staring at her, hundreds of them.

She pushed the Vespa's starter and the little engine coughed to life. The echo made her wince. It sounded like rifle fire. She wanted to get out of this awful place, away from those staring speakers.

Had to get out.

She overbalanced the motor-scooter going around the concession stand. She might have held it if she'd been on a paved surface, but the Vespa's rear wheel skidded out from under her in the loose gravel and she fell with a thump, biting her lip bloody and cutting her cheek. She got up, her eyes wide and skittish, and drove on. She was trembling all over.

Now she was in the alley the cars drove through to get into the drive-in and the ticket stand, looking like a small toll-booth, was just ahead of her. She was going to get out. She was going to get away. Her mouth softened in gratitude.

Behind her, hundreds of speakers blared into life all at once, and now the voice was *singing*, a horrid, tuneless *singing: 'I'LL BE SEEING YOU . . . IN ALL THE OLD FAMILIAR PLACES . . . THAT THIS HEART OF MINE EMBRACES . . . ALL DAY THROOOOO . . .'*

Nadine screamed in her newly cracked voice.

Huge, monstrous laughter came then, a dark and sterile cackling which seemed to fill the earth.

'*DO WELL, NADINE,*' the voice boomed. '*DO WELL, MY FANCY, MY DEAR ONE.*'

Then she gained the road and fled back toward Boulder at the Vespa's top speed, leaving the disembodied voice and staring speakers behind . . . but carrying them with her in her heart, for then, for always.

★   ★   ★

She was waiting for Harold around the corner from the bus station. When he saw her, his face froze and drained of color. 'Nadine –' he whispered. The lunch bucket dropped from his hand and clacked on the pavement.

'Harold,' she said. 'They know. We've got to –'

'Your *hair*, Nadine, oh my God, your *hair* –' His face seemed to be all eyes.

'Listen to me!'

He seemed to gain some of himself back. 'A-all right. What?'

'They went up to your house and found your book. They took it away.'

Emotions at war on Harold's face: anger, horror, shame. Little by little they drained away and then, like some terrible corpse coming up from deep water, a frozen grin resurfaced on Harold's face. 'Who? Who did that?'

'I don't know all of it, and it doesn't matter anyway. Fran Goldsmith was one of them, I'm sure of that. Maybe Bateman or Underwood. I don't know. But they'll come for you, Harold.'

'How do you know?' He grabbed her roughly by the shoulders, remembering that she had put the ledger back under the hearthstone. He shook her like a ragdoll, but Nadine faced him without fear. She had been face-to-face with more terrible things than Harold Lauder on this long, long day. *'You bitch, how do you know?'*

'He told me.'

Harold's hands dropped away.

'Flagg?' A whisper. 'He told you? He spoke to you? And it did *that?'* Harold's grin was ghastly, the grin of the Reaper on horse-back.

'What are you talking about?'

They were standing next to an appliance store. Taking her by the shoulders again, Harold turned her to face the glass. Nadine looked at her reflection for a long time.

Her hair had gone white. Entirely white. There was not a single black strand left.

Oh how I love to love Nadine.

'Come on,' she said. 'We have to leave town.'

'Now?'

'After dark. We'll hide until then, and pick up what camping gear we need on the way out.'

'West?'

'Not yet. Not until tomorrow night.'

'Maybe I don't want to anymore,' Harold whispered. He was still looking at her hair.

She put his hand on it. 'Too late, Harold,' she said.

CHAPTER 58

Fran and Larry sat at the kitchen table of Stu and Fran's place, sipping coffee. Downstairs, Leo was stretching out on his guitar, one that Larry had helped him pick out at Earthly Sounds. It was a nice $600 Gibson with a handrubbed cherry finish. As an afterthought he had gotten the boy a battery-powered phonograph and about a dozen folk/blues albums. Now Lucy was with him, and a startlingly good imitation of Dave van Ronk's 'Backwater Blues' drifted up to them.

> Well it rained five days
> and the sky turned black as night . . .
> There's trouble takin place,
> on the bayou tonight.

Through the arch that gave on the living room, Fran and Larry could see Stu, sitting in his favorite easy chair, Harold's ledger open on his lap. He had been sitting that way since four in the afternoon. It was now nine, and full dark. He had refused supper. As Frannie watched him, he turned another page.

Down below, Leo finished 'Backwater Blues' and there was a pause.

'He plays well, doesn't he?' Fran said.

'Better than I do or ever will,' Larry said. He sipped his coffee.

From below there suddenly came a familiar chop, a swift running down the frets to a not-quite-standard blues progression that made Larry's coffee cup pause. And then Leo's voice, low and insinuating, adding the vocal to the slow, driving beat:

> Hey baby I come down here tonight
> And I didn't come to get in no fight,
> I just want you to say if you can,
> Tell me once and I'll understand,

> Baby, can you dig your man?
> He's a righteous man,
> Baby, can you dig your man?

Larry spilled his coffee.

'Whoops,' Fran said, and got up to get a dishcloth.

'I'll do it,' he said. 'Jiggled when I should have joggled, I guess.'

'No, sit still.' She got the dishcloth and wiped up the stain quickly. 'I remember that one. It was big just before the flu. He must have picked up the single downtown.'

'I guess so.'

'What was that guy's name? The guy that did it?'

'I can't remember,' Larry said. 'Pop music came and went so fast.'

'Yes, but it was something familiar,' she said, wringing the dishcloth out at the sink. 'It's funny how you get something like that on the tip of your tongue, isn't it?'

'Yeah,' Larry said.

Stu closed the ledger with a soft snap, and Larry was relieved to see her look at him as he came into the kitchen. Her eyes went first to the gun on his hip. He had been wearing it since his election as marshal, and he made a lot of jokes about shooting himself in the foot. Fran didn't think the jokes were all that funny.

'Well?' Larry asked.

Stu's face was deeply troubled. He put the ledger on the table and sat down. Fran started to get him a cup of coffee and he shook his head and put a hand on her forearm. 'No thanks, honey.' He looked at Larry in an absent, distracted sort of way. 'I read it all, and now I've got a damn headache. Not used to reading so much. Last book I just sat down and read all the way through like that was this rabbit story. *Watership Down*. I got it for a nephew of mine and just started to read it . . .'

He trailed off for a moment, thinking.

'I read that one,' Larry said. 'Great book.'

'There was this one bunch of rabbits,' Stu said, 'and they had it soft. They were big and well fed and they always lived in one place. There was something wrong there, but none of the rabbits knew what it was. Seemed like they didn't want to know. Only . . . only, see, there was this farmer . . .'

Larry said, 'He left the warren alone so he could take a rabbit for the stewpot whenever he wanted one. Or maybe he sold them. Either way, he had his own little rabbit farm.'

'Yeah. And there was this one rabbit, Silverweed, and he made up poems about the shining wire – the snare the farmer caught the rabbits in, I guess. The snare the farmer used to catch them and strangle them. Silverweed made up poems about *that*.' He shook his head in slow, tired incredulity. 'And that's what Harold reminds me of. Silverweed the rabbit.'

'Harold's ill,' Fran said.

'Yeah.' Stu lit a cigarette. 'And dangerous.'

'What should we do? Arrest him?'

Stu tapped the ledger. 'He and the Cross woman are planning to do something so they'll be made to feel welcome when they go west. But this book doesn't say what.'

'It mentions a lot of people he's not too crazy about,' Larry said.

'Are we going to arrest him?' Fran asked again.

'I just don't know. I want to talk it over with the rest of the committee first. What's on for tomorrow night, Larry?'

'Well, the meeting's going to be in two halves, public business and then private business. Brad wants to talk about his Turning-Off Crew. Al Bundell wants to present a preliminary report from the Law Committee. Let's see . . . George Richardson on clinic hours at Dakota Ridge, then Chad Norris. After that, they leave and it's just us.'

'If we get Al Bundell to stay after and fill him in on this Harold business, can we be sure he'll keep his lip zipped?'

'I'm sure we can,' Fran said.

Stu said fretfully, 'I wish the Judge was here. I cottoned to that man.'

They were quiet for a moment, thinking about the Judge, wondering where he might be tonight. From below came the sound of Leo playing 'Sister Kate' like Tom Rush.

'But if it's got to be Al, it's got to be. I only see two choices anyway. We have to take the pair of them out of circulation. But I don't want to put them in jail, goddammit.'

'What does that leave?' Larry asked.

It was Fran who answered. 'Exile.'

Larry turned to her. Stu was nodding slowly, looking at his cigarette.

'Just drive him out?' Larry asked.

'Him and her both,' Stu said.

'But will Flagg take them like that?' Frannie asked.

Stu looked up at her then. 'Honey, that ain't our problem.'

She nodded and thought: *Oh, Harold, I didn't want it to come out like this. Never in a million years did I want it to come out this way.*

'Any idea what they might be planning?' Stu asked.

Larry shrugged. 'You'd have to get the whole committee's thoughts on that, Stu. But I can think of some things.'

'Such as?'

'The power plant. Sabotage. An assassination attempt on you and Frannie. Those are just the first two things that occur to me.'

Fran looked pale and dismayed.

Larry went on: 'Although he doesn't come right out and say it, I think he went hunting for Mother Abagail with you and Ralph that time in hopes of getting you alone and killing you.'

Stu said, 'He had his chance.'

'Maybe he chickened.'

'Stop it, can't you?' Fran asked dully. 'Please.'

Stu got up and went back into the living room. There was a CB in there hooked up to a Die-Hard battery. After some tinkering, he got Brad Kitchner.

'Brad, you dog! Stu Redman. Listen. Can you round up some guys to stand watch at the power station tonight?'

'Sure,' Brad's voice came, 'but what in God's name for?'

'Well, this is kind of delicate, Bradley. I heard one way and another that somebody might try doing some mischief up there.'

Brad's reply was blue with profanity.

Stu nodded at the mike, smiling a little. 'I know how you feel. This is just for tonight and maybe tomorrow night, so far as I know. Then I guess things'll be ironed out.'

Brad told him he could muster twelve men from the Power Committee without going two blocks, and any one of them would be happy to geld any would-be mischief-maker. 'This something Rich Moffat's up to?'

'No, it ain't Rich. Listen, I'll be talking to you, okay?'

'Fine, Stu. I'll have them on watch.'

Stu turned off the CB and walked back to the kitchen. 'People let you be just as secret as you want to be. It scares me, you know? The old bald-headed sociologist is right. We could set ourselves up like kings here if we wanted to.'

Fran put her hand over his. 'I want you to promise me something. Both of you. Promise me we'll settle this once and for all at the meeting tomorrow night. I just want it to be over.'

Larry was nodding. 'Exile. Yeah. It never crossed my mind, but it might be the best solution. Well, I'm going to collect Lucy and Leo and get home.'

'I'll see you tomorrow,' Stu said.

'Yeah.' He went out.

In the hour before dawn on September 2, Harold stood on the edge of Sunrise Amphitheater, looking down. The town was in a ditch of blackness. Nadine slept behind him in the small two-man tent they had picked up along with a few other camping supplies as they crept out of town.

We'll come back, though. Driving chariots.

But in his secret heart, Harold doubted that. The darkness was upon him in more ways than one. The vile bastards had stolen everything from him – Frannie, his self-respect, then his ledger, now his hope. He felt that he was going down.

The wind was strong, rippling his hair, making the tight canvas of the tent snap back and forth with a steady machine-gun popping sound. Behind him, Nadine moaned in her sleep. It was a scary sound. Harold thought she was as lost as he was, maybe worse. The sounds she made in her sleep were not the sounds of a person having happy dreams.

But I can keep sane. I can do that. If I can go down to whatever's waiting for me with my mind intact, that will be something. Yes, something.

He wondered if they were down there now, Stu and his friends, surrounding his little house, if they were waiting for him to come home so they could arrest him and throw him in the cooler. He would go down in the history books – if any of those sorry slobs were left to write them, that was – as the Free Zone's first jailbird. Welcome to hard times. HAWK CAGED, wuxtry, wuxtry, read all about it. Well, they would wait a long time. He was on his adventure, and he remembered all too clearly Nadine putting his hand on her white hair and saying, *Too late, Harold.* How like a corpse's her eyes had been.

'All right,' Harold whispered. 'We're going through with it.' Around and above him, the dark September wind drummed through the trees.

*   *   *

The Free Zone Committee meeting was rapped to order some fourteen hours later in the living room of the house Ralph Brentner and Nick Andros shared. Stu was sitting in an easy chair, tapping an end table with the rim of his beer can. 'Okay, folks, we better get started here.'

Glen sat with Larry on the curving lip of the freestanding fireplace, their backs to the modest fire Ralph had kindled there. Nick, Susan Stern, and Ralph himself sat on the couch. Nick held the inevitable pen and pad of notepaper. Brad Kitchner was standing just inside the doorway with a can of Coors in his hand, talking to Al Bundell, who was working a Scotch and soda. George Richardson and Chad Norris were sitting by the large window-wall watching the sunset over the Flatirons.

Frannie was sitting with her back propped comfortably against the door of the closet where Nadine had planted the bomb. Her pack, with Harold's ledger inside it, was between her folded legs.

'Order, I say, order!' Stu said, rapping harder. 'That tape recorder working, baldy?'

'It's fine,' Glen said. 'I see your mouth is in good working order, too, East Texas.'

'I oil her a little and she do just fine,' Stu said, smiling. He glanced around at the eleven people spotted around the big combination living room/dining room area. 'Okay . . . we've got a right smart of business, but first I'd like to thank Ralph for providing the roof over our heads and the booze and the crackers —'

He's really getting good at it, Frannie thought. She tried to judge just how much Stu had changed since the day she and Harold had met him, and couldn't do it. You get too subjective about the behavior of the people you're close to, she decided. But she knew that when she had first met him, Stu would have been stricken at the thought of having to chair a meeting of almost a dozen people . . . and he probably would have jumped straight up to heaven at the thought of chairing a mass Free Zone meeting of over a thousand people. She was now watching a Stu that never would have been without the plague.

It's released you, my darling, she thought. *I can cry for the others and still be so proud of you and love you so much —*

She shifted a little, propping her back more firmly against the closet door.

'We'll have our guests speak first,' Stu said, 'and after that we'll have a short closed meeting. Any objections to that?'

There were none.

'Okay,' Stu said. 'I'll turn the floor over to Brad Kitchner, and you folks want to listen close because he's the guy that's going to put the rocks back in your bourbon in about three days.'

This generated a hearty round of spontaneous applause. Blushing furiously, tugging at his tie, Brad walked to the center of the room. He came very close to tripping over a hassock on his way.

'I'm. Real. Happy. To be. Here,' Brad began in a trembling monotone. He looked as if he would have been happier anywhere else, even at the South Pole, addressing a penguin convention. 'The . . . ah . . .' He paused, examining his notes, and then brightened. 'The power!' he exclaimed with the air of a man making a great discovery. 'The power is almost on. Right.'

He fumbled with his notes some more and then went on.

'We had two of the generators going yesterday, and as you know, one of them overloaded and blew its cookies. So to speak. What I mean is that it overlooked. Overloaded, rather. Well . . . you know what I mean.'

A chuckle ran through them, and it seemed to put Brad a little more at ease.

'That happened because when the plague hit, a lot of stuff got left on and we didn't have the rest of the generators on to take the overload. We can take care of the overload danger by turning on the rest of the generators – even three or four would have absorbed the load easily – but that isn't going to solve the fire danger. So we've got to get everything shut off that we can. Stove burners, electric blankets, all that stuff. In fact, I was thinking like this: The quickest way might be to go into every house where no one lives and just pull all the fuses or turn off the main breaker switches. See? Now, when we get ready to turn on, I think we ought to take some elementary fire precautions. I went to the liberty of checking out the fire station in East Boulder, and . . .'

The fire snapped comfortably. It's going to be all right, Fran thought. Harold and Nadine have taken off without any prompting, and maybe that's best. It solves the problem and Stu is safe from them. Poor Harold, I felt sorry for you, but in the end I felt more fear than pity. The pity is still there, and I'm afraid of what may happen to you, but I'm glad your house is empty and you and Nadine have gone. I'm glad you've left us in peace.

Harold sat atop a graffiti-inlaid picnic table like something out of a lunatic's Zen handbook. His legs were crossed. His eyes were far, hazy, contemplative. He had gone to that cold and alien place where Nadine could not follow and she was frightened. In his hands he held the twin of the walkie-talkie in the shoebox. The mountains fell away in front of them in breathtaking ledges and pine-choked ravines. Miles to the east – maybe ten, maybe forty – the land smoothed into the American Midwest and marched away to the dim blue horizon. Night had already come over that part of the world. Behind them, the sun had just disappeared behind the mountains, leaving them outlined in gold that would flake and fade.

'When?' Nadine asked. She was horribly keyed up, and she had to go to the bathroom badly.

'Pretty soon,' Harold said. His grin had become a mellow smile. It was an expression she could not place right away, because she had never seen it on Harold's face before. It took her a few minutes to place it. Harold looked happy.

The committee voted 7–0 to empower Brad to round up twenty men and women for his Turning-Off Crew. Ralph Brentner had agreed to fill up two of the Fire Department's old tanker trucks at Boulder Reservoir and to have them at the power station when Brad turned on.

Chad Norris was next. Speaking quietly, his hands stuffed into the pockets of his chino pants, he talked about the work the Burial Committee had done over the last three weeks. He told them they had buried an incredible twenty-five thousand corpses, better than eight thousand a week, and that he believed they were now over the bulge.

'We've either been lucky or blessed,' he said. 'This mass exodus – that's all I know to call it – has done most of our work for us. In another town Boulder's size, it would have taken a year to get it done. We're expecting to inter another twenty thousand plague victims by the first of October, and we'll probably keep stumbling over individual victims for a long time after, but I wanted you to know that the job is getting done and I don't think we have to worry too much about diseases breeding in the bodies of the unburied dead.'

Fran shifted her position so she could look out at the last of the day. The gold that had surrounded the peaks was already beginning to fade to a less spectacular lemon color. She felt a sudden wave of homesickness that was totally unexpected and almost sickening in its force.

It was five minutes to eight.

If she didn't go in the bushes, she was going to wet her pants. She went around a stand of scrub, lowered herself a little, and let go. When she came back, Harold was still sitting on the picnic table with the walkie-talkie clasped loosely in his hand. He had pulled up the antenna.

'Harold,' she said. 'It's getting late. It's past eight o'clock.'

He glanced at her indifferently. 'They'll be there half the night, clapping each other on the back. When the time's right, I'll pull the pin. Don't you worry.'

'When?'

Harold's smile widened emptily. 'Just as soon as it's dark.'

Fran stifled a yawn as Al Bundell stepped confidently up beside Stu. They were going to run late, and suddenly she wished she was back in the apartment, just the two of them. It wasn't just tiredness, not precisely that feeling of homesickness, either. All of a sudden she didn't want to be in this house. There was no reason for the feeling, but it was strong. She wanted to get out. In fact, she wanted them all to get out. I've just lost my happy thoughts for the evening, she told herself. Pregnant woman blues, that's all.

'The Law Committee has had four meetings in the last week,' Al was saying, 'and I'll keep this as brief as possible. The system we've decided on is a kind of tribunal. Sitting members would be chosen by lottery, much the same way as young men were once selected for the draft –'

'Hiss! Boo!' Susan said, and there was some companionable laughter.

Al smiled. 'But, I was going to add, I think service on such a tribunal would be a lot more palatable to those who were called upon to serve. The tribunal would consist of three adults – eighteen and over – who would serve for six months. Their names would be picked out of a big drum containing the names of every adult in Boulder.'

Larry's hand waved. 'Could they be excused for cause?'

Frowning a trifle at this interruption, Al said: 'I was just getting to that. There would have to be –'

Fran shifted uneasily and Sue Stern winked at her. Fran didn't wink back. She was frightened – and frightened of her own baseless fear, if such a thing were possible. Where had this stifling, claustrophobic feeling come from? She knew that what you were supposed to do with baseless feelings was to ignore them . . . at least in the old world. But what about Tom Cullen's trance? What about Leo Rockway?

Get out of here, the voice inside suddenly cried. *Get them all out!*

But it was so crazy. She shifted again and decided to say nothing.

' – a brief deposition from the person wanting to be excused, but I don't think –'

'Someone's coming,' Fran said suddenly, getting to her feet.

There was a pause. They could all hear motorcycle engines revving toward them up Baseline, coming fast. Horns were beeping. And suddenly, for Frannie, the panic overflowed.

'Listen,' she said, 'all of you!'

Faces turning toward her, surprised, concerned.

'Frannie, are you –' Stu started toward her.

She swallowed. It felt as if there was a heavy weight on her chest, stifling her. 'We have to get out of here. *Right . . . now.*'

It was eight twenty-five. The last of the light had gone out of the sky. It was time. Harold sat up a little straighter and held the walkie-talkie to his mouth. His thumb rested lightly on the SEND button. He would depress it and blow them all to hell by saying –

'What's that?'

Nadine's hand on his arm, distracting him, pointing. Far below, snaking up Baseline, there was a daisy-chain of lights. In the great silence they could hear the faint roar of a great many motorcycle engines. Harold felt a thin thread of disquiet and threw it off.

'Leave me be,' he said. 'This is it.'

Her hand fell from his shoulder. Her face was a white blur in the darkness. Harold pressed the SEND button.

★   ★   ★

She never knew if it was the motorcycles or her own words that got them moving. But they didn't move fast enough. That would always be on her heart; they didn't move fast enough.

Stu was first out the door, the snarl and echo of the motorcycles enormous. They came across the bridge that spanned the small dry wash below Ralph's house, headlights blazing. Instinctively, Stu's hand dropped to the butt of his gun.

The screen door opened and he turned, thinking it would be Frannie. It wasn't; it was Larry.

'What's up, Stu?'

'Don't know. But we better get them out.'

Then the cycles were winding their way into the driveway and Stu relaxed a little. He could see Dick Vollman, the Gehringer kid, Teddy Weizak, others he recognized. Now he could allow himself to recognize what his chief fear had been: that behind the blazing headlights and snarling motorcycle engines had been the spearhead of Flagg's forces, that the war was about to start.

'Dick,' Stu said. 'What the hell?'

'*Mother Abagail!*' Dick roared over the motors. More and more cycles filled the yard as the members of the committee crowded out of the house. It was a carnival of swinging headlights and merry-go-round shadows.

'*What?*' Larry screamed. Behind him and Stu, Glen, Ralph, and Chad Norris crowded out, forcing Larry and Stu to the foot of the steps.

'*She's come back!*' Dick had to bellow to make himself heard over the cycles. '*Oh, she's in terrible shape! We need a doctor . . . Christ, we need a miracle!*'

George Richardson pushed through them. 'The old woman? Where?'

'Get on, Doc!' Dick shouted at him. 'Don't ask questions! Just for Christ's sake be quick!'

Richardson mounted the cycle behind Dick Vollman. Dick turned in a tight circle and began to weave his way back through the cluster of motorcycles.

Stu's eyes met Larry's. Larry looked as bewildered as Stu felt . . . but there was a gathering cloud in Stu's head, and suddenly a terrible feeling of impending doom engulfed him.

'Nick, come on! *Come on!*' Fran cried, seizing his shoulder. Nick was standing in the middle of the living room, his face still, immobile.

He couldn't talk, but suddenly he knew. He *knew*. It came from nowhere, from everywhere.

There was something in the closet.

He gave Frannie a tremendous push.

'Nick –'

GO!! he waved at her.

She went. He turned to the closet, pulled open the door, and began to rip madly at the tangle of things inside, praying God that he wasn't too late.

Suddenly Frannie was next to Stu, her face pallid, her eyes huge. She clutched at him. 'Stu . . . Nick's still in there . . . something . . . something . . .'

'Frannie, what are you talking about?'

'*Death!*' she screamed at him. '*I'm talking about death and NICK IS STILL IN THERE!*'

He pulled aside a handful of scarves and mittens and felt something. A shoebox. He grabbed it, and as he did, like malign necromancy, Harold Lauder's voice spoke from inside it.

'*What about Nick?*' Stu shouted, grabbing her shoulders.

'We have to get him out – Stu – something's going to happen, something awful –'

Al Bundell shouted: 'What the hell is going on, Stuart?'

'I don't know,' Stu said.

'*Stu, please, we have to get Nick out of there!*' Fran screamed.

That was when the house blew up behind them.

With the SEND button depressed, the background static disappeared and was replaced by a smooth, dark silence. Void, waiting for him to fill it. Harold sat cross-legged on the picnic table, summoning himself up.

Then he raised his arm, and at the end of the arm one finger pointed out of his knotted fist, and in that moment he was like Babe Ruth, old and almost washed up, pointing to the spot where he was going to hit the home run, pointing for all the hecklers and badmouths in Wrigley Field, shutting them up once and for all.

Speaking firmly but not loudly into the walkie-talkie, he said: 'This is Harold Emery Lauder speaking. I do this of my own free will.'

A blue-white spark greeted *This is*. A gout of flame shot up at *Harold Emery Lauder speaking*. A faint, flat bang, like a cherrybomb stuffed into a tin can, reached their ears at *I do this*, and by the time he had spoken the words *of my own free will* and tossed the walkie-talkie away, its purpose served, a fire-rose had bloomed at the base of Flagstaff Mountain.

'Breaker, breaker, that's a big ten-four, over and out,' Harold said softly.

Nadine clutched at him, much as Frannie had clutched Stu only seconds ago. 'We ought to be sure. We ought to be sure that it got them.'

Harold looked at her, then gestured at the blooming rose of destruction below them. 'Do you think anything could have lived through that?'

'I . . . I d–don't kn . . . ooow, Harold, I'm –' Nadine turned away, clutched her belly, and began to retch. It was a deep, constant, raw sound. Harold watched her with mild contempt.

She turned back at last, panting, pale, wiping at her mouth with a Kleenex. Scrubbing at her mouth. 'Now what?'

'Now I guess we go west,' Harold said. 'Unless you plan to go down there and sample the mood of the community.'

Nadine shuddered.

Harold slid off the picnic table and winced at the pins and needles as his feet struck the ground. They had gone to sleep.

'Harold –' She tried to touch him and he jerked away. Without looking at her, he began to strike the tent.

'I thought we'd wait until tomorrow –' she began timidly.

'Sure,' he jeered at her. 'So twenty or thirty of them can decide to fan out on their bikes and catch us. Did you ever see what they did to Mussolini?'

She winced. Harold was rolling the tent up and cinching the ground-cords tight.

'And we don't touch each other. That's over. It got Flagg what he wanted. We wasted their Free Zone Committee. They're washed up. They may get the power on, but as a functioning group, they're washed up. *He'll* give me a woman who makes you look like a potato sack, Nadine. And you . . . you get *him*. Happy days, right?

Only if I were wearing your Hush Puppies, I would be shaking in them plenty.'

'Harold – please –' She was sick, crying. He could see her face in the dim fireglow, and felt pity for her. He forced it out of his heart like an unwelcome drunk who has tried to enter a cozy little suburban tavern where everybody knows everybody else. The irrevocable fact of murder was in her heart forever – that fact shone sickly in her eyes. But so what? It was in his, as well. In it and on it, weighing it down like stones.

'Get used to it,' Harold said brutally. He flung the tent on the back of his cycle and began to tie it down. 'It's over for them down there, and it's over for us, and it's over for everybody that died in the plague. God went off on a celestial fishing trip and He's going to be gone a long time. It's totally dark. The dark man's in the driver's seat now. *Him.* So get used to it.'

She made a squeaking, moaning noise in her throat.

'Come on, Nadine. This stopped being a beauty contest two minutes ago. Help me get this shit packed up. I want to do a hundred miles before sunup.'

After a moment she turned her back on the destruction below – destruction that seemed almost inconsequential from this height – and helped him pack the rest of the camping gear in his saddlebags and her wire carrier. Fifteen minutes later they had left the fire-rose behind and were riding through the cool and windy dark, heading west.

For Fran Goldsmith, that day's ending was painless and simple. She felt a warm push of air at her back and suddenly she was flying through the night. She had been knocked out of her sandals.

Whafuck? she thought.

She landed on her shoulder, landed hard, but there was still no pain. She was in the ravine that ran north-to-south at the foot of Ralph's back yard.

A chair landed in front of her, neatly, on its legs. Its seat-cushion was a smoldering black snarl.

WhaFUCK?

Something landed on the seat of the chair and rolled off. Something that was dripping. With faint and clinical horror, she saw that it was an arm.

Stu? Stu! What's happening?

A steady, grinding roar of sound engulfed her, and stuff began to rain down everywhere. Rocks. Hunks of wood. Bricks. A glass block spiderwebbed with cracks (hadn't the bookcase in Ralph's living room been made of those blocks?). A motorcycle helmet with a horrible, lethal hole punched through the back of it. She could see everything clearly . . . much *too* clearly. It had been dark out only a few seconds ago –

Oh Stu, my God, where are you? What's happening? Nick? Larry?

People were screaming. That grinding roar went on and on. It was now brighter than noontime. Every pebble cast a shadow. Stuff still raining down all around her. A board with a six-inch spike protruding from it came down in front of her nose.

– the baby –

And on the heels of that, another thought came, a reprise of her premonition: *Harold did this, Harold did this, Harold –*

Something struck her on the head, the neck, the back. A huge thing that landed on her like a padded coffin.

OH MY GOD OH MY BABY –

Then darkness sucked her down to a nowhere place where not even the dark man could follow.

CHAPTER 59

Birds.

She could hear birds.

Fran lay in darkness, listening to the birds for a long time before she realized the darkness wasn't really dark. It was reddish, moving, peaceful. It made her think of her childhood. Saturday morning, no school, no church, the day you got to sleep late. The day you could wake up a little at a time, at your leisure. You lay with your eyes shut, and you saw nothing but a red darkness that was Saturday sunshine being filtered through the delicate screen of capillaries in your eyelids. You listened to the birds in the old oaks outside and maybe smelled sea-salt, because your name was Frances Goldsmith and you were eleven years old on a Saturday morning in Ogunquit –

Birds. She could hear birds.

But this wasn't Ogunquit; it was

(Boulder)

She puzzled over it in the red darkness for a long time, and suddenly she remembered the explosion.

(?Explosion?)

(!Stu!)

Her eyes flashed open. There was sudden terror. *'Stu!'*

And Stu was sitting there beside her bed, Stu with a clean white bandage wrapped over one forearm and a nasty-looking cut dried on one cheek and part of his hair burned away, but it was *Stu*, he was *alive*, with her, and when she opened her eyes the great relief came on his face and he said, 'Frannie. Thank God.'

'The baby,' she said. Her throat was dry. It came out a whisper.

He looked blank, and blind fear stole into her body. It was cold and numbing.

'The baby,' she said, forcing the words up her sandpaper throat. 'Did I lose the baby?'

Understanding came over his face then. He hugged her clumsily with his good arm. 'No, Frannie, no. You didn't lose the baby.'

Then she began to cry, scalding tears that flowed down her cheeks, and she hugged him fiercely, not caring that every muscle in her body seemed to cry out in pain. She hugged him. The future was later. Now the things she needed most were here in this sun-washed room.

The sound of birds came through the open window.

Later she said, 'Tell me. How bad is it?'

His face was heavy and sorrowful and unwilling. 'Fran . . .'

'Nick?' she whispered. She swallowed and there was a tiny click in her throat. 'I saw an arm, a severed arm —'

'It might be better to wait —'

'No. I have to know. How bad was it?'

'Seven dead,' he said in a low, husky voice. 'We got off lucky, I figure. It could have been much worse.'

'Who, Stuart?'

He held her hands clumsily. 'Nick was one of them, honey. There was a pane of glass, I guess — you know, that iodized glass — and it . . . it . . .' He stopped for a moment, looked down at his hands, then up at her again. 'He . . . we were able to make identification by . . . certain scars . . .' He turned away from her for a moment. Fran made a harsh sighing noise.

When Stu was able to go on he said, 'And Sue. Sue Stern. She was still inside when it went off.'

'That . . . just doesn't seem possible, does it?' Fran said. She felt stunned, numbed, bewildered.

'It's true.'

'Who else?'

'Chad Norris,' he said, and Fran made that harsh sighing noise again. A single tear slipped from the corner of her eye; she brushed it away almost absently.

'Those were the only three from inside. It's like a miracle. Brad says there must have been eight, nine sticks of dynamite hooked up in that closet. And Nick, he almost . . . when I think he might have had his hands right on that shoebox . . .'

'Don't,' she said. 'There was no way to know.'

'That doesn't help much,' he said.

The other four were people who had come up from town on

motorcycles – Andrea Terminello, Dean Wykoff, Dale Pedersen, and a young girl named Patsy Stone. Stu did not tell Fran that Patsy, who had been teaching Leo how to play the flute, had been struck and nearly beheaded by a whirling chunk of Glen Bateman's Wollensak tape recorder.

Fran nodded, and it hurt her neck. When she shifted her body, even a little, her entire back seemed to scream with pain.

Twenty had been wounded in the blast and one of them, Teddy Weizak of the Burial Committee, had no chance to recover. Two others were in critical condition. A man named Lewis Deschamps had lost an eye. Ralph Brentner had lost the third and fourth fingers on his left hand.

'How badly am I hurt?' Fran asked him.

'Why, you have a whiplash and a sprained back and a broken foot,' Stu said. 'That's what George Richardson told me. The blast threw you all the way across the yard. You got the broken foot and the sprained back when the couch landed on you.'

'Couch?'

'Don't you remember?'

'I remember something like a coffin . . . a padded coffin . . .'

'That was the couch. I yanked it off you myself. I was raving and . . . pretty hysterical, I guess. Larry came over to help me and I punched him in the mouth. That's how bad off I was.' She touched his cheek and he put his hand over hers. 'I thought you had to be dead. I remember thinking that I didn't know what I'd do if you were. Go crazy, I guess.'

'I love you,' she said.

He hugged her – gently, because of her back – and they remained that way for some time.

'Harold?' she said at last.

'And Nadine Cross,' he agreed. 'They hurt us. They hurt us bad. But they didn't do anywhere near the damage they wanted to do. And if we catch him before they get too far west . . .' He held his hands, which were scratched and scabbed over, out in front of him and closed them with a sudden snap that made the joints pop. The hamstrings stood out on the insides of his wrists. A sudden cold grin surfaced on his face that made Fran want to shudder. It was too familiar.

'Don't smile like that,' she said. 'Ever.'

The smile faded. 'People have been scouring the hills for them since daybreak,' he went on, no longer smiling. 'I don't think they'll find them. I told them not to go further than fifty miles west of Boulder no matter what, and I imagine Harold was smart enough to get them further than that. But we know how they did it. They had the explosive hooked up to a walkie-talkie –'

Fran gasped, and Stu looked at her with concern.

'What's wrong, babe? Is it your back?'

'No.' She was suddenly understanding what Stu had meant about Nick having his hands on the shoebox when the explosive was detonated. Suddenly understanding everything. Speaking slowly, she told him about the snips of wire and the walkie-talkie box under the air-hockey table. 'If we'd searched the whole house instead of just taking his damn b-book, we might have found the bomb,' she said, and her voice began to choke and break. 'N-Nick and Sue would be a-a-alive and –'

He held her. 'Is that why Larry seems so down this morning? I thought it was because I punched him. Frannie, how could you know, huh? How could you possibly know?'

'We *should* have! We *should* have known!' She buried her face against the good darkness of his shoulder. More tears, hot and scalding. He held her, bent over awkwardly because the electrically powered hospital bed would not crank up.

'I don't want you blamin yourself, Frannie. It's happened. I'm telling you there's no way anybody – except maybe a bomb-squad detective – could make something out of a few snips of wire and an empty box. If they'd left a couple of sticks of dynamite or a blasting cap around, that would have been a different proposition. But they didn't. I don't blame you, and nobody else in the Zone is going to blame you, either.'

As he spoke, two things were combining, slowly and belatedly, in her mind.

Those were the only three from inside . . . it's like a miracle.

Mother Abagail . . . she's come back . . . oh, she's in terrible shape . . . we need a miracle!

With a little hiss of pain, she drew herself up a little so she could look into Stu's face. 'Mother Abagail,' she said. 'We all would have been inside when it went off if they hadn't come up to tell us –'

'It's like a miracle,' Stu repeated. 'She saved our lives. Even if she is –' He fell silent.

'Stu?'

'She saved our lives by coming back when she did, Frannie. She saved our *lives*.'

'Is she dead?' Fran asked. She grabbed his hand, clutched it. 'Stu, is she dead, too?'

'She came back into town around a quarter of eight. Larry Underwood's boy was leading her by the hand. He'd lost all his words, you know he does that when he gets excited, but he took her to Lucy. Then she just collapsed.' Stu shook his head. 'My God, how she ever walked as far as she did . . . and what she can have been eating or doing . . . I'll tell you something, Fran. There's more in the world – and out of it – than I ever dreamed of back in Arnette. I think that woman is from God. Or was.'

She closed her eyes. 'She died, didn't she? In the night. She came back to die.'

'She's not dead yet. She ought to be, and George Richardson says she'll have to go soon, but she's not dead yet.' He looked at her simply and nakedly. 'And I'm afraid. She saved our lives by coming back, but I'm afraid of her, and I'm afraid of why she came back.'

'What do you mean, Stu? Mother Abagail would never harm –'

'Mother Abagail does what her God tells her to,' he said harshly. 'That's the same God murdered His own boy, or so I heard.'

'Stu?'

The fire died out of his eyes. 'I don't know why she's back, or if she has anything left to tell us at all. I just don't know. Maybe she'll die without regaining consciousness. George says that's the most likely. But I do know that the explosion . . . and Nick dying . . . and her coming back . . . it's taken the blinkers off this town. They're talking about *him*. They know Harold was the one who set off the blast, but they think *he* made Harold do it. Hell, I think so too. There's plenty who are saying Flagg's responsible for Mother Abagail coming back the way she is, too. Me, I don't know. I don't know nothing, seems like, but I feel scared. Like it's going to end bad. I didn't feel that way before, but I do now.'

'But there's us,' she said, almost pleading with him. 'There's us and the baby, isn't there? *Isn't there?*'

He didn't answer for a long time. She didn't think he was going to answer. And then he said, 'Yeah. But for how long?'

*   *   *

Near dusk on that day, the third of September, people began to drift
slowly – almost aimlessly – down Table Mesa Drive toward Larry
and Lucy's house. Singly, by couples, in threes. They sat on the front
steps of houses that bore Harold's x-sign on their doors. They sat
on curbs and lawns that were dry and brown at this long summer's
ending. They talked a little in low tones. They smoked their cigarettes
and their pipes. Brad Kitchner was there, one arm wrapped in a
bulky white bandage and supported in a sling. Candy Jones was there,
and Rich Moffat showed up with two bottles of Black Velvet in a
newsboy's pouch. Norman Kellogg sat with Tommy Gehringer, his
shirtsleeves rolled up to show sunburned, freckled biceps. The
Gehringer boy's sleeves were rolled up in imitation. Harry Dunbarton
and Sandy DuChiens sat on a blanket together, holding hands. Dick
Vollman, Chip Hobart, and sixteen-year-old Tony Donahue sat in
a breezeway half a block up from Larry's tract house, passing a bottle
of Canadian Club back and forth, chasing it with warm 7-Up. Patty
Kroger sat with Shirley Hammett. There was a picnic hamper between
them. The hamper was well filled, but they only nibbled. By eight
o'clock the street was lined with people, all of them watching the
house. Larry's cycle was parked out front, and George Richardson's
big Kawasaki 650 was parked beside it.

Larry watched them from the bedroom window. Behind him,
in his and Lucy's bed, Mother Abagail lay unconscious. The dry,
sickly smell coming from her filled his nose and made him want to
puke – he hated to puke – but he wouldn't move. This was his
penance for escaping while Nick and Susan died. He heard low
voices behind him, the deathwatch around her bed. George would
be leaving for the hospital shortly to check on his other patients.
There were only sixteen now. Three had been released. And Teddy
Weizak had died.

Larry himself had been totally unhurt.

Same old Larry – keeps his head while others all around him
are losing theirs. The blast had thrown him across the driveway and
into a flower bed, but he had not sustained a single scratch. Jagged
shrapnel had rained down all around him, but nothing had touched
him. Nick had died, Susan had died, and he had been unhurt. Yeah;
same old Larry Underwood.

Deathwatch in here, deathwatch out there. All the way up the
block. Six hundred of them, easy. Harold, you ought to come on
back with a dozen hand grenades and finish the job. *Harold*. He had

followed Harold all the way across the country, had followed a trail of Payday candy wrappers and clever improvisations. Larry had almost lost his fingers getting gas back in Wells. Harold had simply found the plug vent and used a siphon. Harold was the one who had suggested the memberships in the various committees slide upward with population. Harold, who had suggested that the ad hoc committee be accepted in toto. Clever Harold. Harold and his ledger. Harold and his grin.

It was all well and good for Stu to say no one could have figured out what Harold and Nadine were up to from a few scraps of wire on an air-hockey table. With Larry that line of reasoning just didn't hold up. He had seen Harold's brilliant improvisations before. One of them had been written on the roof of a barn in letters almost twenty feet high, for Christ's sweet sake. He should have guessed. Inspector Underwood was great at ferreting out candy wrappers, but not so great when it came to dynamite. In point of fact, Inspector Underwood was a bloody asshole.

Larry, if you knew —

Nadine's voice.

If you want, I'll get down on my knees and beg.

That had been another chance to avert the murder and destruction . . . one he could never bring himself to tell anybody about. Had it really been in the works even then? Probably. If not the specifics of the dynamite bomb wired to the walkie-talkie, then at least some general plan.

Flagg's plan.

Yes — in the background there was always Flagg, the dark puppet master, pulling the strings on Harold, Nadine, on Charlie Impening, God knew how many others. The people in the Zone would happily lynch Harold on sight, but it was Flagg's doing . . . and Nadine's. And who had sent her to Harold, if not Flagg? But before she had gone to Harold she had come to Larry. And he had sent her away.

How could he have said yes? There was his responsibility to Lucy. That had been all-important, not just because of her but because of himself — he sensed it would take only one or two more fades to destroy him as a man for good. So he had sent her away, and he supposed Flagg was well pleased with the previous night's work . . . if Flagg was really his name. Oh, Stu was still alive, and he spoke for the committee — he was the mouth that Nick could never use. Glen was alive, and Larry supposed he was the point-man of the committee's mind, but Nick had been the heart of the committee, and Sue, along with Frannie, had served as its moral conscience. Yes, he thought bitterly, all in all, a good evening's work for that bastard. He ought to reward Harold and Nadine well when they got over there.

He turned from the window, feeling a dull throb behind his forehead. Richardson was taking Mother Abagail's pulse. Laurie was fiddling with the IV bottles hung on their T-shaped rack. Dick Ellis was standing by. Lucy sat by the door, looking at Larry.

'How is she?' Larry asked George.

'The same,' Richardson said.

'Will she live through the night?'

'I can't say, Larry.'

The woman on the bed was a skeleton covered with thinly stretched, ash-gray skin. She seemed without sex. Most of her hair was gone; her breasts were gone; her mouth hung unhinged and her breath rasped through it harshly. To Larry, she looked like pictures he had seen of the Yucatán mummies – not decayed but shriveled; cured; dry; ageless.

Yes, that's what she was now, not a mother but a mummy. There was only that harsh sigh of her respiration, like a light breeze through hay-stubble. How could she still be alive? Larry wondered . . . and what God would put her through it? To what purpose? It had to be a joke, a big cosmic horselaugh. George said he had heard of similar cases, but never of one so extreme, and he himself had never expected to see one. She was somehow . . . *eating herself*. Her body had kept running long after it should have succumbed to malnutrition. She was breaking down parts of herself for nourishment that had never been meant to be broken down. Lucy, who had lifted her onto the bed, had told him in a low, marveling voice that she seemed to weigh no more than a child's box kite, a thing only waiting for a puff of wind to blow it away forever.

And now Lucy spoke from her corner by the door, startling all of them: 'She's got something to say.'

Laurie said uncertainly, 'She's in deep coma, Lucy . . . the chances that she can ever regain consciousness . . .'

'She came back to tell us something. And God won't let her go until she does.'

'But what could it be, Lucy?' Dick asked her.

'I don't know,' Lucy said, 'but I'm afraid to hear it. I know that. The dying ain't over. It's just got started. That's what I fear.'

There was a long silence that George Richardson finally broke. 'I've got to get up to the hospital. Laurie, Dick, I'm going to need both of you.'

You aren't going to leave us alone with this mummy, are you? Larry almost asked, and pinched his lips shut to keep it in.

The three of them went to the door, and Lucy got them their coats. The temperature was barely sixty this night, and riding a cycle in shirtsleeves was uncomfortable.

'Is there anything we can do for her?' Larry asked George quietly.

'Lucy knows about the IV drip,' George said. 'There's nothing else. You see . . .' He trailed off. Of course they all saw. It was on the bed, wasn't it?

'Good night, Larry, Lucy,' Dick said.

They went out. Larry drifted back to the window. Outside, everyone had come to their feet, watching. Was she alive? Dead? Dying? Perhaps healed by the power of God? *Had she said anything?*

Lucy slipped an arm around his waist, making him jump a little. 'I love you,' she said.

He groped for her, held her. He put his head down and began to shudder helplessly.

'I love you,' she said calmly. 'It's all right. Let it come. Let it come out, Larry.'

He cried. The tears were as hot and hard as bullets. 'Lucy –'

'Shhh.' Her hands on the back of his neck; her soothing hands.

'Oh Lucy, my God, what is all this?' he cried out against her neck, and she held him as tight as she could, not knowing, not knowing yet, and Mother Abagail breathed harshly behind them, holding on in the depths of her coma.

George drove up the street at walking speed, passing the same message over and over again: Yes, still alive. Prognosis is poor. No, she hasn't said anything and isn't likely to. You might as well go home. If anything happens, you'll hear.

When they reached the corner they accelerated, turning toward the hospital. The exhaust of their bikes crackled and echoed back, hitting buildings and bouncing off them, finally fading away to nothing.

People did not go home. They remained standing for a while, renewing their conversations, examining each word George had said. Prognosis, now what might that mean? Coma. Brain-death. If her brain was dead, that was it. Might as well expect a can of peas to talk as a person with a dead brain. Well, maybe that would be it if this was a *natural* situation, but things were hardly natural anymore, were they?

They sat down again. Darkness came. The glow of Coleman lamps came on in the house where the old woman lay. They would go home later, and lie sleepless.

Talk turned hesitantly to the dark man. If Mother Abagail died, didn't that mean *he* was stronger?

What do you mean, 'not necessarily'?

Well I hold he's Satan, pure and simple.

The Antichrist, that's what I think. We're living out the Book of Revelation right in our own time . . . how can you doubt it? 'And the seven vials were opened . . .' Sure sounds like the superflu to me.

Ah, balls, people said Hitler was the Antichrist.

If those dreams come back, I'll kill myself.

In mine I was in a subway station and he was the ticket-taker, only I couldn't see his face. I was scared. I ran into the subway tunnel. Then I could hear *him*, running after me. And gaining.

In mine I was going down cellar to get a jar of pickled watermelon slices and I saw someone standing by the furnace . . . just a shape. And I knew it was him.

Crickets began to chirrup. Stars spread across the sky. The chill in the air was duly commented on. Drinks were drunk. Pipes and cigarettes glowed in the dark.

I heard the Power people went right ahead turning things off.

Good for them. If they don't get the lights and heat back on pretty quick, we're going to be in a peck of trouble.

Low murmur of voices, now faceless in the gloom.

I guess we're safe for this winter. Sure enough. No way he can get over the passes. Too full of cars and snow. But in the spring . . .

Suppose he's got a few A-bombs?

Fuck the A-bomb, what if he's got a few of those dirty neutron bombs? Or the other six of Sally's seven vials?

Or planes?

What's to do?

I don't know.

Damn if I know.

Ain't got a friggin clue.

Dig a hole, then jump in and pull it over you.

And around ten o'clock Stu Redman, Glen Bateman, and Ralph Brentner came among them, talking quietly and giving out fliers, telling them to pass the word on to those not here tonight. Glen was limping slightly because a flying stove dial had clipped a piece of meat out of his right calf. The mimeographed posters said: FREE ZONE MEETING ★ MUNZINGER AUDITORIUM ★ SEPTEMBER 4 ★ 8:00 PM

That seemed to be the signal to leave. People drifted away silently into the dark. Most of them took the fliers, but quite a few were crumpled into balls and thrown away. All of them went home to get what sleep they could.

Perchance to dream.

The auditorium was crammed but extremely quiet when Stu convened the meeting the following night. Sitting behind him were Larry, Ralph, and Glen. Fran had tried to get up, but her back was still much too painful. Unmindful of the grisly irony, Ralph had patched her through to the meeting by walkie-talkie.

'There's a few things that need talking about,' Stu said with quiet and studied understatement. His voice, although only slightly amplified, carried well in the silent hall. 'I guess there's nobody here who doesn't know about the explosion that killed Nick and Sue and the others, and nobody who doesn't know that Mother Abagail has come back. We need to talk about those things, but we wanted you to have some good news first. Want you to listen to Brad Kitchner for that. Brad?'

Brad walked toward the podium, not nearly as nervous as he had been the night before last, and was greeted by listless applause. When he got there he turned to face them, gripped the lectern in both hands, and said simply: 'We're going to switch on tomorrow.'

This time the applause was much louder. Brad held up his hands, but the applause rode over him in a wave. It held for thirty seconds or more. Later Stu told Frannie that if it hadn't been for the events of the last two days, Brad probably would have been dragged down from the podium and carried around the auditorium on the shoulders of the crowd like a halfback who has scored the winning touchdown of the championship game in the last thirty seconds. It had gotten so close to the end of the summer that, in a way, that was just what he was.

But at last the applause subsided.

'We're going to switch on at noon, and I'd like to have every one of you at home and ready. Ready for what? Four things. Listen up now, this is important. First, turn off every light and electrical appliance in your own house that you're not using. Second, do the same for the unoccupied houses around yours. Third, if you smell gas, track down the smell and shut off whatever is on. Fourth, if you hear a fire siren, go to the source of the sound . . . but go safely and sanely. Let's not have any necks broken in motorcycle accidents. Now – are there any questions?'

There were several, all of them reconfirming Brad's original points. He answered each one patiently, the only sign of nervousness the way he bent his little black notebook ceaselessly back and forth in his hands.

When the questions had slowed to a trickle, Brad said: 'I want to thank the folks who busted their humps getting us going again. And I want to remind the Power Committee that it isn't disbanded. There are going to be lines down, power outages, oil supplies to track down in Denver and haul up here. I hope you'll all stick with it. Mr Glen Bateman says we may have ten thousand people here by the time the snow flies, and a lot more next spring. There's power stations in Longmont and Denver that are going to have to come on line before next year's done with –'

'Not if that hardcase gets his way!' someone shouted out hoarsely in the back of the hall.

There was a moment of dead silence. Brad stood with his hands clutching the lectern in a deathgrip, his face pasty white. *He's not going to be able to finish*, Stu thought, and then Brad did go on, his voice amazingly even:

'My business is power, whoever said that. But I think we'll be here long after that other guy's dead and gone. If I didn't think that, I'd be wrapping motors over on his side. Who gives a shit for him?'

Brad stepped away from the podium and someone else bellowed, 'You're goddam right!'

This time the applause was heavy and hard, nearly savage, but there was a note to it Stu didn't like. He had to pound with his gavel a long time to get the meeting back under control.

'The next thing on the agenda –'

'Fuck your agenda!' a young woman yelled stridently. 'Let's talk about the dark man! Let's talk about *Flagg*! It's long overdue, I'd say!'

Roars of approval. Shouts of 'Out of order!' Disapproving babble at the young woman's choice of words. Rumble of side-chatter.

Stu whacked at the block on the podium so hard that the mallet-head flew off his gavel. 'This is a meeting here!' he shouted. 'You're going to get a chance to talk about whatever you want to talk about, but while I'm chairing this meeting, I want . . . to have . . . some ORDER!' He bellowed the last word so loudly that feedback cut through the auditorium like a boomerang, and they quieted at last.

'Now,' Stu said, his voice purposely low and calm, 'the next thing is to report to you on what happened up at Ralph's on the night of September second, and I guess that falls to me, since I'm our elected law enforcement officer.'

He had quiet again, but like the applause that had greeted Brad's closing remarks, this wasn't a quiet Stu liked. They were leaning forward, intent, their expressions greedy. It made him feel disquieted and bewildered, as if the Free Zone had changed radically over the last forty-eight hours and he didn't know what it was anymore. It made him feel the way he'd felt when he had been trying to find his way out of the Stovington Plague Center – a fly caught and struggling in an invisible spider's web. There were so many faces he didn't recognize out there, so many strangers . . .

But there was no time to think about it now.

He described the events leading up to the explosion briefly, omitting Fran's last-minute premonition; with the mood they were in, they didn't need that.

'Yesterday morning Brad and Ralph and I went up and poked through the ruins for three hours or more. We found what seemed to be a dynamite bomb wired up to a walkie-talkie. It appears that this bomb was planted in the living room closet. Bill Scanlon and Ted Frampton found another walkie-talkie up in Sunrise Amphitheater, and we assume the bomb was set off from there. It –'

'Assume, my ass!' Ted Frampton shouted from the third row. 'It was that bastard Lauder and his little whore!'

An uneasy murmur ran through the room.

These are the good guys? They don't give a shit about Nick and Sue and Chad and the rest. They're like a lynch-mob, and all they care about is catching Harold and Nadine and hanging them . . . like a charm against the dark man.

He happened to catch Glen's eye; Glen offered him a very small, very cynical shrug.

'If one more person yells out from the floor without bein recognized, I'm gonna declare this meeting closed and you can talk to each other,' Stu said. 'This is no bull session. If we don't keep to the rules, where are we?' Ted Frampton was staring up at him angrily, and Stu stared back. After a few moments, Ted dropped his eyes.

'We suspect Harold Lauder and Nadine Cross. We have some good reasons, some pretty convincing circumstantial evidence. But there's no real hard evidence against them yet, and I hope you'll keep that in mind.'

A sullen eddy of conversation rippled and disappeared.

'I only said that to say this,' Stu continued. 'If they happen to wander back into the Zone, I want them brought to me. I'll lock them up and Al Bundell will see to it that they're tried . . . and a trial means they get to tell their side, if they got one. We're . . . we're supposed to be the good guys here. I guess we know where the bad guys are. And being the good guys means we have to be civilized about this.'

He looked out at them hopefully and saw only puzzled resentment. Stuart Redman had seen two of his best friends blown to hell, those eyes said, and here he was, taking up for the ones who did it.

'For what it's worth to you, I think they're the ones,' he said. 'But it's got to be done right. And I'm here to tell you that it will be.'

Eyes boring into him. Over a thousand pairs, and he could feel the thought behind each one: *What's this shit you're talking, anyway? They're gone. Gone west. You act like they were on a two-day bird-watching trip.*

He poured a glass of water and drank some, hoping to get rid of the dryness in his throat. The taste of it, boiled and flat, made him grimace. 'Anyway, that's where we stand on that,' he said lamely. 'What's next, I guess, is filling the committee back up to strength. We're not goin to do that tonight, but you ought to be thinkin about who you want –' A hand shot up on the floor and Stu pointed. 'Go ahead. Just identify yourself so everybody'll know who you are.'

'I'm Sheldon Jones,' a big man in a wool-plaid shirt said. 'Why don't we just go ahead and get two new ones tonight? I nom'nate Ted Frampton over there.'

'Hey, I second that!' Bill Scanlon yelled. 'Beautiful!'

Ted Frampton clasped his hands and shook them over his head to scattered applause, and Stu felt that despairing, disoriented feeling sweep over him again. They were supposed to replace Nick Andros with Ted Frampton? It was like one of those sick jokes. Ted had tried the Power Committee and had found it too much like work. He had drifted over to the Burial Committee and that had seemed to suit him better, although Chad had mentioned to Stu that Ted was one of those fellows who seemed able to stretch a coffee break into a lunch hour and a lunch hour into a half-day vacation. He had been quick to join yesterday's hunt for Harold and Nadine, probably because it offered a change. He and Bill Scanlon had stumbled on the walkie-talkie up at Sunrise through sheer luck (and to give Ted his due, he had admitted that), but since the find he had acquired a swagger that Stu didn't like at all.

Now Stu caught Glen's eyes again, and could almost read Glen's thought in the cynical look there, the slight tuck in the corner of Glen's mouth: *Maybe we could use Harold to stack this one, too.*

A word that Nixon had used a lot suddenly floated into Stu's mind, and as he grasped it, he suddenly understood the source of his despair and feeling of disorientation. The word was 'mandate.' Their mandate had disappeared. It had gone up two nights ago in a flash and a roar.

He said, 'You may know who *you* want, Sheldon, but I imagine some of the other folks would like to have time to think it over. Let's call the question. Those of you who want to elect two new reps tonight say aye.'

Quite a few ayes were shouted out.

'Those of you who'd like a week or so to think it over, say nay.'

The nays were louder, but not by a whole lot. A great many people had abstained altogether, as if the topic had no interest for them.

'Okay,' Stu said. 'We'll plan to meet here in Munzinger Auditorium a week from today, September eleventh, to nominate and vote on candidates for the two empty slots on the committee.'

Pretty crappy epitaph, Nick. I'm sorry.

'Dr Richardson is here to talk to you about Mother Abagail and about those folks that were injured in the explosion. Doc?'

Richardson got a solid blast of applause as he stepped forward, polishing his eyeglasses. He told them that there were nine dead as a result of the explosion, three people still in critical condition, two in serious condition, eight in satisfactory condition.

'Considering the force of the blast, I think that fortune was with us. Now, concerning Mother Abagail.'

They leaned forward.

'I think a very short statement and a brief bit of elaboration should suffice. The statement is this: I can do nothing for her.'

A mutter ran through the crowd and stilled. Stu saw unhappiness but no real surprise.

'I am told by members of the Zone who were here before she left that the lady claimed one hundred and eight years. I can't vouch for that, but I can say she is the oldest human being I myself have ever seen and treated. I'm told she has been gone for two weeks, and my estimation – no, my *guess* – is that her diet during that period contained no prepared foods at all. She seems to have lived on roots, herbs, grass, and other things of a similar nature.' He paused. 'She has had one small bowel movement since she returned. It contained a number of small sticks and twigs.'

'My God,' someone muttered, and it was impossible to tell if the voice belonged to a man or a woman.

'One arm is covered with poison ivy. Her legs are covered with ulcerations which would be running if her condition were not so –'

'Hey, can't you stop it?' Jack Jackson hollered, standing up. His face was white, furious, miserable. 'Don't you have any damn decency?'

'Decency is not my concern, Jack. I'm only reporting her condition as it is. She's comatose, malnourished, and most of all, she's very, very old. I think she's going to die. If she was anyone else, I would state that as a certainty. But . . . like all of you, I dreamed of her. Her and one other.'

The low mutter again, like a passing breeze, and Stu felt the hackles on the nape of his neck first stir and then come to attention.

'To me, dreams of such opposing configurations seem mystical,' George said. 'The fact that we all shared them seems to indicate a telepathic ability at the very least. But I pass on parapsychology and theology just as I pass on decency, and for the same reason: neither of them is my field. If the woman is from God, He may choose to heal her. I cannot. I will tell you that the fact that she is still alive at all seems a miracle of sorts to me. That is my statement. Are there any questions?'

There weren't. They looked at him, stunned, some of them openly weeping.

'Thank you,' George said, and returned to his seat in a dead sea of silence.

'All right,' Stu whispered to Glen. 'You're on.'

Glen approached the podium without introduction and gripped it familiarly. 'We've discussed everything but the dark man,' he said.

That mutter again. Several men and women instinctively made the sign of the cross. An elderly woman on the lefthand aisle placed her hands rapidly across her eyes, mouth, and ears in an eerie imitation of Nick Andros before refolding them over the bulky black purse in her lap.

'We've discussed him to some degree in closed committee meetings,' Glen went on, his tone calm and conversational, 'and the question came up in private as to whether or not we should bring the question up in public. The point was made that no one in the Zone really seemed to want to talk about it, not after the funhouse dreams we all had on the way here. That perhaps a period of recuperation was needed. Now, I think, is the time to bring the subject up. To drag him out into the light, as it were. In police work, they have a handy gadget called an Ident-i-Kit, which a police artist uses to create the face of a criminal from various witnesses' recollections of him. In our case we have no face, but we do have a series of recollections that form at least an outline of our Antagonist. I've talked to quite a few people about this and I would like to present you with my own Ident-i-Kit sketch.

'This man's name seems to be Randall Flagg, although some people have associated the names Richard Frye, Robert Freemont, and Richard Freemantle with him. The initials R. F. may have some significance, but if so, none of us on the Free Zone Committee know what it is. His presence – at least in dreams – produces feelings of dread, disquiet, terror, horror. In case after case, the physical feeling associated with him is one of coldness.'

Heads were nodding, and that excited hum of conversation broke out again. Stu thought they sounded like boys who had just discovered sex, were comparing notes, and were excited to find that all reports put the receptacle in approximately the same place. He covered a slight grin with his hand, and reminded himself to save that one for Fran later on.

'This Flagg is in the West,' Glen continued. 'Equal numbers of people have "seen" him in Las Vegas, Los Angeles, San Francisco, Portland. Some people – Mother Abagail was among them – claim that Flagg is crucifying people who step out of line. All of them seem to believe that there is a confrontation shaping up between this man and ourselves, and that Flagg will stick at nothing to bring us down. And sticking at nothing includes quite a lot. Armored force. Nuclear weapons. Perhaps . . . plague.'

'I'd like to catch hold of that dirty bastard!' Rich Moffat called shrilly. 'I'd give him a dose of the everfucking plague!'

There was a tension-relieving burst of laughter, and Rich got a hand. Glen grinned easily. He had given Rich his cue and his line half an hour before the meeting, and Rich had delivered admirably. Old baldy had been right as rain about one thing, Stu was discovering: a background in sociology often came in handy at large meetings.

'All right, I've outlined what I know about him,' he went on. 'My last contribution before throwing the meeting open to discussion is this: I think Stu is right in telling you that we have to deal with Harold and Nadine in a civilized way if they're caught, but like him, I think that is unlikely. Also like him, I believe they did what they did on this man Flagg's orders.'

His words rang out strongly in the hall.

'This man has got to be dealt with. George Richardson told you mysticism isn't his field of study. It isn't mine, either. But I tell you this: I think that dying old woman somehow represents the forces of good as much as Flagg represents the forces of evil. I think that whatever power controls her used her to bring us together. I don't think that power intends to forsake us now. Maybe we need to talk it over and let some air into those nightmares. Maybe we need to begin deciding what we're going to do about him. But he can't just walk into this Zone next spring and take over, not if you people are standing watch. Now I'll turn the meeting back to Stu, who'll chair the discussion.'

His last sentence was lost in a crash of applause, and Glen went back to his seat feeling pleased. He had stirred them with a big stick . . . or was the phrase played them like a violin? It didn't really matter. They were more mad than scared, they were ready for a challenge (although they might not be so eager next April, after they'd had a long winter to cool off in) . . . and most of all, they were ready to talk.

And talk they did, for the next three hours. A few people left as midnight came and went, but not many. As Larry had suspected, no good hard advice came out of it. There were wild suggestions: a bomber and/or a nuclear stockpile of their own, a summit meeting, trained hit squad. There were few practical ideas.

For the final hour, person after person stood up and recited his or her dream, to the seemingly endless fascination of the others. Stu was once again reminded of the endless bull sessions about sex he had participated in (mostly as a listener) during his teenage years.

Glen was both amazed and heartened by their growing willingness to talk, and by the charged atmosphere of excitement that had taken over the dull blankness with which they had begun the meeting. A large catharsis, long overdue, was going on, and he was also reminded of sex-talk, but in a different way. They talk like people, he thought, who have kept the huddled-up secrets of their guilts and inadequacies to themselves for a long time, only to discover that these things, when verbalized, were only life-sized after all. When the inner terror sowed in sleep was finally harvested in this marathon public discussion, the terror became more manageable . . . perhaps even conquerable.

The meeting broke up at one-thirty in the morning, and Glen left it with Stu, feeling good for the first time since Nick's death. He left feeling they had gone the first hard steps out of themselves and toward whatever battleground there would be.

He felt hope.

The power went on at noon on September 5, as Brad had promised.

The air raid siren atop of the County Courthouse went on with a huge, braying whoop, scaring many people into the streets, where they looked wildly up into the blameless blue sky for a glimpse of the dark man's air force. Some ran for their cellars, where they stayed until Brad found a fused switch and turned the siren off. Then they came up, shame faced.

There was an electrical fire on Willow Street, and a group of a dozen volunteer firepeople promptly rushed over and put it out. A manhole cover exploded into the air at the Broadway-and-

Walnut intersection, went nearly fifty feet, and came down on the roof of the Oz Toyshop like a great rusty tiddledywink.

There was a single fatality on what the Zone came to call Power Day. For some unknown reason, an auto-body shop on outer Pearl Street exploded. Rich Moffat was sitting in a doorway across the street with a bottle of Jack Daniel's in his newsboy's pouch, and a flying panel of corrugated steel siding struck him and killed him instantly. He would break no more plate-glass windows.

Stu was with Fran when the fluorescents buzzed into life in the ceiling of her hospital room. He watched them flicker, flicker, flicker, and finally catch with the old familiar light. He was unable to look away until they had been glowing solidly for nearly three minutes. When he looked at Frannie again, her eyes were shiny with tears.

'Fran? What's wrong? Is it the pain?'

'It's Nick,' she said. 'It's so wrong that Nick isn't alive to see this. Hold me, Stu. I want to pray for him if I can. I want to try.'

He held her, but didn't know if she prayed or not. He suddenly found himself missing Nick very much, and hating Harold Lauder more than he ever had before. Fran was right. Harold had not just killed Nick and Sue; he had stolen their light.

'Shh,' he said. 'Frannie, shh.'

But she cried for a long time. When the tears were finally gone, he used the button to raise her bed and turned on the night table lamp so she could see to read.

Stu was being shaken awake, and it took him a long time to come all the way around. His mind ran over a slow and seemingly endless list of people who might be trying to rob his sleep. It was his mother, telling him it was time to get up and light the stoves and get ready for school. It was Manuel, the bouncer in that sleazy little Nuevo Laredo whorehouse, telling him his twenty dollars was used up and it would be another twenty if he wanted to stay all night. It was a nurse in a white all-over suit who wanted to take his blood pressure and a throat culture. It was Frannie.

It was Randall Flagg.

The last thought brought him up like a dash of cold water in the face. It was none of those people. It was Glen Bateman, with Kojak at his knee.

'You're a hard man to wake up, East Texas,' Glen said. 'Like a stone post.' He was only a vague shape in nearly total darkness.

'Well, you could have turned on the damn light to start with.'

'You know, I clean forgot all about that.'

Stu switched on the lamp, squinted against the sudden bright light, and peered owlishly at the wind-up alarm clock. It was quarter to three in the morning.

'What are you doing here, Glen? I was sleepin, in case you didn't happen to notice.'

He got his first good look at Glen as he put the clock down. He looked pale, scared . . . and old. The lines were drawn deeply into his face and he looked haggard.

'What is it?'

'Mother Abagail,' Glen said quietly.

'Dead?'

'God help me, I almost wish she were. She's awake. She wants us.'

'The two of us?'

'The five of us. She —' His voice roughened, went hoarse. 'She knew Nick and Susan were dead, and she knew Fran was in the hospital. I don't know how, but she did.'

'And she wants the committee?'

'What's left of it. She's dying and she says she has to tell us something. And I don't know if I want to hear it.'

Outside the night was cold — not just chilly but cold. The jacket Stu had pulled from the closet felt good, and he zipped it all the way to the neck. A frosty moon hung overhead, making him think of Tom, who had instructions to come back to them and report when the moon was full. This moon was just a trifle past the first quarter. God knew where that moon was looking down on Tom, on Dayna Jurgens, on Judge Farris. God knew it was looking down on strange doings here.

'I got Ralph up first,' Glen said. 'Told him to go over to the hospital and get Fran.'

'If the doctor wanted her up and around, he would have sent her home,' Stu said angrily.

'This is a special case, Stu.'

'For someone who doesn't want to hear what that old woman has to say, you seem to be in an all-fired hurry to get to her.'

'I'm afraid not to,' Glen said.

★　　★　　★

The jeep drew up in front of Larry's house at ten minutes past three. The place was blazing with light – not gaslamps now, but good electric lights. Every second streetlamp was on, too, not just here but all over town, and Stu had stared at them all the way over in Glen's jeep, fascinated. The last of the summer bugs, sluggish with the cold, were beating lackadaisically against the sodium globes.

They got out of the jeep just as headlights swung around the corner. It was Ralph's clattering old truck, and it pulled up nose to nose with the jeep. Ralph got out, and Stu went quickly around to the passenger side, where Frannie sat with her back resting against a plaid sofa cushion.

'Hey, babe,' he said softly.

She took his hand. Her face was a pale disk in the darkness.

'Bad pain?' Stu asked.

'Not so bad. I took some Advil. Just don't ask me to do the hustle.'

He helped her out of the truck and Ralph took her other arm. They both saw her wince as she stepped away from the cab.

'Want me to carry you?'

'I'll be fine. Just keep your arm around me, huh?'

'Sure will.'

'And walk slow. Us grammies can't go very fast.'

They crossed behind Ralph's truck, more shuffling than walking. When they reached the sidewalk, Stu saw Glen and Larry standing in the doorway, watching them. Against the light they looked like figures cut from black construction paper.

'What is it, do you think?' Frannie murmured.

Stu shook his head. 'I don't know.'

They got up the walk, Frannie very obviously in pain now, and Ralph helped Stu get her in. Larry, like Glen, looked pale and worried. He was wearing faded jeans, a shirt that was untucked and buttoned wrong at the bottom, and expensive mocs on bare feet.

'I'm sorry like hell to have to get you out,' he said. 'I was in with her, dozing off and on. We've been keeping watch. You understand?'

'Yes. I understand,' Frannie said. For some reason the phrase *keeping watch* made her think of her mother's parlor . . . and in a kinder, more forgiving light than she had ever thought of it before.

'Lucy had been in bed about an hour. I snapped out of my doze, and – Fran, can I help you?'

Fran shook her head and smiled with an effort. 'No, I'm fine. Go on.'

'– and she was looking at me. She can't talk above a whisper, but she's perfectly understandable.' Larry swallowed. All five of them were now standing in the hallway. 'She told me the Lord was going to take her home at the sunrise. But that she had to talk to those of us God hadn't taken first. I asked her what she meant and she said God had taken Nick and Susan. She *knew*.' He let out a ragged breath and ran his hands through his long hair.

Lucy appeared at the end of the hall. 'I made coffee. It's here when you want it.'

'Thank you, love,' Larry said.

Lucy looked uncertain. 'Should I come in with you folks? Or is it private, like the committee?'

Larry looked at Stu, who said quietly, 'Come on along. I got an idea that stuff don't cut ice anymore.'

They went up the hall to the bedroom, moving slowly to accommodate Fran.

'She'll tell us,' Ralph said suddenly. 'Mother will tell us. No sense fretting.'

They went in together, and Mother Abagail's bright, dying gaze fell upon them.

Fran knew about the old woman's physical condition, but it was still a nasty shock. There was nothing left of her but a pemmican-tough membrane of skin and tendon binding her bones. There was not even a smell of putrescence and oncoming death in the room; instead there was a dry attic smell . . . no, a *parlor* smell. Half the length of the IV needle hung out of her flesh, simply because there was nowhere for it to go.

Yet the eyes had not changed. They were warm and kind and human. That was a relief, but Fran still felt a kind of terror . . . not strictly fear, but perhaps something more sanctified – awe. Was it awe? An impending feeling. Not doom, but as though some dreadful responsibility was poised above their heads like a stone.

Man proposes – God disposes.

'Little girl, sit down,' Mother Abagail whispered. 'You're in pain.'

Larry led her to an armchair and Fran sat down with a thin, whistling sigh of relief, although she knew even sitting would pain her after a while.

Mother Abagail was still watching her with those bright eyes.

'You're quick with child,' she whispered.

'Yes . . . how . . .'

'Shhhhh . . .'

Silence fell in the room, deep silence. Fascinated, hypnotized, Fran looked at the dying old woman who had been in their dreams before she had been in their lives.

'Look out the window, little girl.'

Fran turned her face to the window, where Larry had stood and looked out at the gathered people two days before. She saw not pressing darkness but a quiet light. It was not a reflection of the room; it was morning light. She was looking at the faint, slightly distorted reflection of a bright nursery with ruffled check curtains. There was a crib – *but it was empty*. There was a playpen – *empty*. A mobile of bright plastic butterflies – *moved only by the wind*. Dread clapped its cold hands around her heart. The others saw it on her face but did not understand it; they saw nothing through the window but a section of lawn lit by a streetlight.

'Where's the baby?' Fran asked hoarsely.

'Stuart is not the baby's father, little girl. But his life is in Stuart's hands, and in God's. This chap will have four fathers. If God lets him draw breath at all.'

'If he draws –'

'God has hidden that from my eyes,' she whispered.

The empty nursery was gone. Fran saw only darkness. And now dread closed its hands into fists, her heart beating between them.

Mother Abagail whispered: 'The Imp has called his bride, and he means to put her with child. Will he let your child live?'

'Stop it,' Frannie moaned. She put her hands over her face.

Silence, deep silence like snow in the room. Glen Bateman's face was an old dull searchlight. Lucy's right hand worked slowly up and down the neck of her bathrobe. Ralph had his hat in his hands, picking absently at the feather in the band. Stu looked at Frannie, but could not go to her. Not now. He thought fleetingly of the woman at the meeting, the one who had put her hands rapidly over her eyes, ears, and mouth at the mention of the dark man's name.

'Mother, father, wife, husband,' Mother Abagail whispered. 'Set against them, the Prince of High Places, the lord of dark mornings. I sinned in pride. So have you all, all sinned in pride. Ain't you heard it said, put not your faith in the lords and princes of this world?'

They watched her.

'Electric lights ain't the answer, Stu Redman. CB radio ain't it, either, Ralph Brentner. Sociology won't end it, Glen Bateman. And you doin penance for a life that's long since a closed book won't stop it from coming, Larry Underwood. And your boy-child won't stop it either, Fran Goldsmith. The bad moon has risen. You propose nothing in the sight of God.'

She looked at each of them in turn. 'God will dispose as He sees fit. You are not the potter but the potter's clay. Mayhap the man in the West is the wheel on which you will be broken. I am not allowed to know.'

A tear, amazing in that dying desert, stole from her left eye and rolled down her cheek.

'Mother, what should we do?' Ralph asked.

'Draw near, all of you. My time is short. I'm going home to glory, and there's never been no human more ready than I am now. Get close to me.'

Ralph sat on the edge of the bed. Larry and Glen stood at the foot of it. Fran got up with a grimace, and Stu dragged her chair up beside Ralph. She sat down again and took his hand with her own cold fingers.

'God didn't bring you folks together to make a committee or a community,' she said. 'He brought you here only to send you further, on a quest. He means for you to try and destroy this Dark Prince, this Man of Far Leagues.'

Ticking silence. In it, Mother Abagail sighed.

'I thought it was Nick to lead you, but He's taken Nick – although not all of Nick is gone yet, it seems to me. No, not all. But you must lead, Stuart. And if it's His will to take Stu, then you must lead, Larry. And if He takes you, it falls to Ralph.'

'Looks like I'm riding drag,' Glen began. 'What –'

'Lead?' Fran asked coldly. '*Lead?* Lead where –?'

'Why, west, little girl,' Mother Abagail said. 'West. You're not to go. Only these four.'

'*No!*' She was on her feet in spite of the pain. 'What are you saying? That the four of them are just supposed to deliver themselves into his hands? The heart and soul and guts of the Free Zone?' Her eyes blazed. 'So he can hang them on crosses and just walk in here next summer and kill everyone? I won't see my man sacrificed to your killer God. Fuck Him.'

'*Frannie!*' Stu gasped.

'Killer God! *Killer God!*' she spat. 'Millions – maybe *billions* – dead in the plague. Millions more afterward. We don't even know if the children will live. Isn't He done yet? Does it just have to go on and on until the earth belongs to the rats and the roaches? He's no God. He's a daemon, and you're His witch.'

'Stop it, Frannie.'

'No problem. I'm done. I want to leave. Take me home, Stu. Not to the hospital but back home.'

'We'll listen to what she has to say.'

'Fine. You listen for both of us. I'm leaving.'

'Little girl.'

'*Don't call me that!*'

Her hand shot out and closed around Frannie's wrist. Fran went rigid. Her eyes closed. Her head snapped back.

'Don't. D-D-Don't . . . OH MY GOD – STU –'

'Here! Here!' Stu roared. 'What are you doing to her?'

Mother Abagail didn't answer. The moment spun out, seemed to stretch into a pocket of eternity, and then the old woman let go.

Slowly, dazedly, Fran began to massage the wrist Mother Abagail had taken, although there was no red ring or dent in the flesh to show that pressure had been applied. Frannie's eyes suddenly widened.

'Hon?' Stu asked anxiously.

'Gone,' Fran muttered.

'What . . . what's she talking about?' Stu looked around at the others in shaken appeal. Glen only shook his head. His face was white and strained but not disbelieving.

'The pain . . . the whiplash. The pain in my back. It's gone.' She looked at Stu, dazed. 'It's *all gone*. Look.' She bent and touched her toes lightly: once, then twice. Then she bent a third time and placed her palms flat on the floor without unlocking her knees.

She stood up again and met Mother Abagail's eyes.

'Is this a bribe from your God? Because if it is, He can take His cure back. I'd rather have the pain if Stu comes with it.'

'God don't lay on no bribes, child,' Mother Abagail whispered. 'He just makes a sign and lets people take it as they will.'

'Stu isn't going west,' Fran said, but now she seemed bewildered as well as frightened.

'Sit down,' Stu said. 'We'll listen to what she has to say.'

Fran sat down, shocked, unbelieving, lost at sea. Her hands kept stealing around to the small of her back.

'You are to go west,' Mother Abagail whispered. 'You are to take no food, no water. You are to go this very day, and in the clothes you stand up in. You are to go on foot. I am in the way of knowing that one of you will not reach your destination, but I don't know which will be the one to fall. I am in the way of knowing that the rest will be taken before this man Flagg, who is not a man at all but a supernatural being. I don't know if it's God's will for you to defeat him. I don't know if it's God's will for you to ever see Boulder again. Those things are not for me to see. But he is in Las Vegas, and you must go there, and it is there that you will make your stand. You will go, and you will not falter, because you will have the Everlasting Arm of the Lord God of Hosts to lean on. Yes. With God's help you will stand.'

She nodded.

'That's all. I've said m'piece.'

'No,' Fran whispered. 'It can't be.'

'Mother,' Glen said in a kind of croak. He cleared his throat. 'Mother, we're not "in the way of understanding," if you see what I mean. We're . . . we're not blessed with your closeness to whatever is controlling this. It just isn't our way. Fran's right. If we go over there we'll be slaughtered, probably by the first pickets we come to.'

'Have you no eyes? You've just seen Fran healed of her affliction by God, through me. Do you think His plan for you is to let you be shot and killed by the Dark Prince's least minion?'

'But, Mother —'

'No.' She raised her hand and waved his words away. 'It's not my place to argue with you, or convince, but only to put you in the way of understanding God's plan for you. Listen, Glen.'

And suddenly, from Mother Abagail's mouth, the voice of Glen Bateman issued, frightening them all and making Fran shrink back against Stu with a little cry.

'Mother Abagail calls him the devil's pawn,' this strong, masculine voice said, originating somehow in the old woman's wasted chest and emerging from her toothless mouth. 'Maybe he's just the last magician of rational thought, gathering the tools of technology against us. Maybe he's something more, something darker. I only know that he is. And I no longer think that sociology or psychology or any other ology will put a stop to him. I think only white magic will do that.'

Glen's mouth hung open.

'Is that a true thing, or are those the words of a liar?' Mother Abagail said.

'I don't know if it's true or not, but they're my words,' Glen said shakily.

'Trust. All of you, *trust*. Larry . . . Ralph . . . Stu . . . Glen . . . Frannie. You most patic'ly, Frannie. Trust . . . and obey the word of God.'

'Do we have a choice?' Larry asked bitterly.

She turned to look at him, surprised. 'A choice? There's always a choice. That's God's way, always will be. Your will is still free. Do as you will. There's no set of leg-irons on you. But . . . *this is what God wants of you.*'

That silence again, like deep snow. At last, Ralph broke it. 'Says in the Bible that David did the job on Goliath,' he said. 'I'll be going along if you say it's right, Mother.'

She took his hand.

'Me,' Larry said. 'Me too. Okay.' He sighed and put his hands on his forehead as if it ached. Glen opened his mouth to say something, but before he could, there was a heavy, tired sigh from the corner and a thud.

It was Lucy, whom they had all forgotten. She had fainted.

Dawn touched the edge of the world.

They sat around Larry's kitchen table, drinking coffee. It was ten to five when Fran came up the hall and stood in the doorway. Her face was puffy from crying, but there was no limp as she walked. She was, indeed, cured. 'She's going, I think,' Fran said.

They went in, Larry with his arm around Lucy.

Mother Abagail's breathing had taken on a heavy, hollow rattle that was horribly reminiscent of the superflu. They gathered around the bed without speaking, deep in awe and afraid. Ralph was sure that something would happen at the end that would cause the wonder of God to stand before all of them, naked and revealed. She would be gone in a flash of light, taken. Or they would see her spirit, transfigured in radiance, leaving by the window and going up into the sky.

But in the end, she simply died.

There was a single final breath, the last of millions. It was drawn in, held, and finally let out. Her chest just didn't rise again.

'She's done,' Stu muttered.

'God have mercy on her soul,' Ralph said, no longer afraid. He crossed her hands on her thin bosom, and his tears fell on them.

'I'll go,' Glen said suddenly. 'She was right. White magic. That's all that's left.'

'Stu,' Frannie whispered. 'Please, Stu, say no.'

They looked at him – all of them.

Now you must lead, Stuart.

He thought of Arnette, of the old car carrying Charles D. Campion and his load of death, crashing into Bill Hapscomb's pumps like some wicked Pandora. He thought of Denninger and Deitz, and how he had begun to associate them in his mind with the smiling doctors who had lied and lied and lied to him and to his wife about her condition – and maybe they had lied to themselves, as well. Most of all, he thought of Frannie. And of Mother Abagail saying, *This is what God wants of you.*

'Frannie,' he said. 'I have to go.'

'And die.' She looked at him bitterly, almost hatefully, and then to Lucy, as if for support. But Lucy was stunned and far-off, no help.

'If we don't go, we'll die,' Stu said, feeling his way along the words. 'She was right. If we wait, then spring comes. Then what? How are we going to stop him? We don't know. We don't have a clue. We never did. We had our heads in the sand, too. We can't stop him except like Glen says. White magic. Or the power of God.'

She began to weep bitterly.

'Frannie, don't do that,' he said, and tried to take her hand.

'Don't touch me!' she cried at him. 'You're a dead man, you're a corpse, so *don't touch me!*'

They stood around the bed in tableau as the sun came up.

Stu and Frannie went to Flagstaff Mountain around eleven o'clock. They parked halfway up, and Stu brought the hamper while Fran carried the tablecloth and a bottle of Blue Nun. The picnic had been her idea, but a strange and awkward silence held between them.

'Help me spread it,' she said. 'And watch out for those spiny things.'

They were in a small, slanting meadow a thousand feet below Sunrise Amphitheater. Boulder was spread out below them in a blue haze. Today it was wholly summer again. The sun shone down with power and authority. Crickets buzzed in the grass. A grasshopper leaped up and Stu caught it with a quick lunge of his right hand. He could feel it inside his fingers, tickling and frightened.

'Spit n I'll let you go,' he said, the old childhood formula, and looked up to see Fran smiling sadly at him. With quick, ladylike precision, she turned her head and spat. It hurt his heart, seeing her do that. 'Fran –'

'No, Stu. Don't talk about it. Not now.'

They spread the white lawn tablecloth, which Fran had glommed from the Hotel Boulderado, and moving with quick economy (it made him feel strange to watch her supple grace as she bent and moved, as if there had never been a whiplash injury and sprained back at all), she set out their early lunch: a cucumber and lettuce salad dressed with vinegar; cold ham sandwiches; the wine; an apple pie for dessert.

'Good food, good meat, good God, let's eat,' she said. He sat down beside her and took a sandwich and some salad. He wasn't hungry. He hurt inside. But he ate.

When they had both finished a token sandwich and most of the salad – the fresh greens had been delicious – and a small sliver of apple pie each, she said: 'When are you going?'

'Noon,' he said. He lit a cigarette, cupping the flame in his hands.

'How long will it take you to get there?'

He shrugged. 'Walking? I don't know. Glen's not young. Neither is Ralph, for that matter. If we can make thirty miles a day, we could do it by the first of October, I guess.'

'And if there's early snow in the mountains? Or in Utah?'

He shrugged, looking at her steadily.

'More wine?' she asked.

'No. It gives me acid indigestion. It always did.'

Fran poured herself another glass and drank it off.

'Was she God's voice, Stu? *Was* she?'

'Frannie, I just don't know.'

'We dreamed of her, and she was. This whole thing is part and parcel of some stupid game, do you know that, Stuart? Have you ever read the Book of Job?'

'I was never much on the Bible, I guess.'

'My mom was. She thought it was very important that my brother Fred and I have a certain amount of religious background. She never said why. All the good it ever did me, so far as I know, was that I was always able to answer the Bible questions on "Jeopardy." Do you remember "Jeopardy," Stu?'

Smiling a little, he said: 'And now here's your host, Alex Trebeck.'

'That's the one. It was backward. They gave you the answer, you supplied the question. When it came to the Bible, I knew all the questions. Job was a bet between God and the Devil. The Devil said, "Sure he worships You. He's got it soft. But if You piss in his face long enough, he'll renounce You." So God took the wager. And God won.' She smiled dully. 'God always wins. God's a Boston Celtics fan, I bet.'

'Maybe it *is* a bet,' Stu said, 'but it's their lives, those folks down there. And the guy inside you. What did she call him? The chap?'

'She wouldn't even promise about him,' Fran said. 'If she could have done that . . . just that . . . it would have been at least a little bit easier to let you go.'

Stu could think of nothing to say.

'Well, it's getting on toward noon now,' Fran said. 'Help me pack up, Stuart.'

The half-eaten lunch went back into the hamper with the tablecloth and the rest of the wine. Stu looked at the spot and thought of how there were only a few crumbs to show where their picnic had been . . . and the birds would get those soon enough. When he glanced up, Frannie was looking at him and crying. He went to her.

'It's all right. It's being pregnant. I'm always running at the eyes. I can't seem to help it.'

'It's okay.'

'Stu, make love to me.'

'Here? Now?'

She nodded, then smiled a little. 'It will be all right. If we watch out for the spiny things.'

They spread the tablecloth again.

*   *   *

At the foot of Baseline Road she made him stop at what had been Ralph and Nick's house until four days ago. The entire rear of the house was blown away. The back yard was littered with debris. A shattered digital clock radio sat atop the shredded back hedge. Nearby was the sofa under which Frannie had been pinned. There was a patch of dried blood on the back steps. She looked at this fixedly.

'Is that Nick's blood?' she asked him. 'Could it be?'

'Frannie, what's the point?' Stu asked uneasily.

'*Is* it?'

'Jesus, I don't know. It could be, I suppose.'

'Put your hand on it, Stu.'

'Frannie, have you gone nuts?'

The frown-line creased her brow, the I-want line that he had first noticed back in New Hampshire.

'Put your hand on it!'

Reluctantly, Stu put his hand on the stain. He didn't know if it was Nick's blood or not (and believed, in fact, that it probably wasn't), but the gesture gave him a ghastly, crawly feeling.

'Now swear you'll come back.'

The step seemed rather too warm here, and he wanted to take his hand away.

'Fran, how can I —'

'God can't run all of it!' she hissed at him. 'Not *all* of it. Swear, Stu, swear it!'

'Frannie, I swear to try.'

'I guess that will have to be good enough, won't it?'

'We have to get down to Larry's.'

'I know.' But she held him more tightly still. 'Say you love me.'

'You know I do.'

'I know, but say it. I want to hear it.'

He took her by the shoulder. 'Fran, I love you.'

'Thank you,' she said, and put her cheek against his shoulder. 'Now I think I can say goodbye. I think I can let you go.'

They held each other in the shattered back yard.

CHAPTER 60

She and Lucy watched the undramatic start of their quest from the steps of Larry's house. The four of them stood there on the sidewalk for a moment, no packs, no bedrolls, no special equipment . . . as per instructions. They had all changed into heavy walking shoes.

''Bye, Larry,' Lucy said. Her face was shiny pale.

'Remember, Stuart,' Fran said. 'Remember what you swore.'

'Yes. I'll remember.'

Glen put his fingers into his mouth and whistled. Kojak, who had been investigating a sewer grating, came running.

'Let's go then,' Larry said. His face was as pale as Lucy's, his eyes unusually bright, almost glittery. 'Before I lose my nerve.'

Stu blew a kiss through his closed fist, something he could not remember doing since the days when his mother saw him off on the school bus. Fran waved back. The tears were coming again, hot and burning, but she did not let them fall. They began. They simply walked away. They were halfway down the block now, and somewhere a bird sang. The midday sun was warm and undramatic. They reached the end of the block. Stu turned and waved again. Larry also waved. Fran and Lucy waved back. They crossed the street. They were gone. Lucy looked almost sick with loss and fear.

'Dear God,' she said.

'Let's go in,' Fran said. 'I want tea.'

They went inside. Fran put the teapot on. They began to wait.

The four of them moved slowly southwest during the afternoon, not talking much. They were headed toward Golden, where they would camp this first night. They passed the burial sites, three of them now, and around four o'clock, when their shadows had begun to trail out long behind them and the heat had begun to sneak out of the day, they came to the township marker spotted beside the road at the southern edge of Boulder. For a moment Stu had a feeling that all of them were on the verge of turning together and going back. Ahead of them was darkness and death. Behind them was a little warmth, a little love.

Glen took a bandanna out of his back pocket, whipped it into a blue paisley rope, and tied it around his head. 'Chapter Forty-three, The Bald-Headed Sociologist Dons His Sweat-Band,' he said hollowly. Kojak was up ahead, over the line into Golden, nosing his way happily through a splash of wildflowers.

'Ah, man,' Larry said, and his voice was almost a sob. 'I feel like this is the end of everything.'

'Yeah,' Ralph said. 'It do feel like that.'

'Anybody want to take five?' Glen asked without much hope.

'Come on,' Stu said, smiling a little. 'Do you dogfaces want to live forever?'

They went on, leaving Boulder behind them. By nine that night they were camped in Golden, half a mile from where Route 6 begins its twisting, turning course along Clear Creek and into the stone heart of the Rockies.

None of them slept that first night. Already they felt far from home, and under the shadow of death.

BOOK III
THE STAND

September 7, 1990 – January 10, 1991

This land is your land,
this land is my land,
from California
to the New York island,
from the redwood forests,
to the Gulf stream waters,
this land was made for you and me.
Woody Guthrie

'Hey Trash, what did old lady Semple say
when you torched her pension check?'
Carley Yates

When the night has come
And the land is dark
And the moon is the only light we'll see,
I won't be afraid
Just as long as you stand by me.
Ben E. King

CHAPTER 61

The dark man had set his guardposts all along the eastern border of Oregon. The largest was at Ontario, where I-80 crosses over from Idaho; there were six men there, quartered in the trailer of a large Peterbilt truck. They had been there for more than a week, playing poker the whole time with twenties and fifties as useless as Monopoly money. One man was almost sixty thousand dollars ahead and another – a man whose working wage in the pre-plague world had been about ten thousand dollars a year – was over forty grand in the bucket.

It had rained almost the whole week, and tempers in the trailer were getting short. They had come out of Portland, and they wanted to get back there. There were women in Portland. Hung from a spike was a powerful two-way radio, broadcasting nothing but static. They were waiting for the radio to broadcast two simple words: *Come home.* That would mean that the man they were looking for had been captured somewhere else.

The man they were looking for was approximately seventy years old, heavyset, balding. He wore glasses and he was driving a white-over-blue four-wheel drive, either a jeep or an International-Harvester. He was to be killed when he was finally spotted.

They were edgy and bored – the novelty of high-stakes poker for real money had worn off two days ago, even for the dullest of them – but not bored enough to just take off for Portland on their own. They had received their orders from the Walkin Dude himself, and even after rain-induced cabin fever had set in, their terror of *him* remained. If they screwed the job up and he found out, God help them all.

So they sat and played cards and watched by turns at the sight-slit which had been carved through the side of the trailer's steel wall. I-80 was deserted in the dull, constant rain. But if the Scout happened along, it would be seen . . . and stopped.

'He's a spy from the other side,' the Walkin Dude had told

them, that horrible grin wreathing his chops. Why it was so horrible none of them could have said, but when it turned your way you felt as if your blood had turned to hot tomato soup in your veins. 'He's a spy and we could welcome him in with open arms, show him everything, and send him back with no harm done. But I want him. I want them both. And we're going to send their heads back over the mountains before the snow flies. Let them chew on that all winter.' And he bellowed hot laughter at the people he had gathered together in one of the conference rooms at the Portland Civic Center. They smiled back, but their smiles were cold and uneasy. Aloud they might congratulate each other on having been singled out for such a responsibility, but inside, they wished that those happy, awful, weasel-like eyes had fixed on anyone but *them*.

There was another large guardpost far south of Ontario, at Sheaville. Here there were four men in a small house just off I-95, which meanders down toward the Alvord Desert, with its weird rock formations and its dark, sullen streams of water.

The other posts were manned by pairs of men, and there were an even dozen of them, ranging from the tiny town of Flora, just off Route 3 and less than sixty miles from the Washington border, all the way down to McDermitt, on the Oregon-Nevada border.

An old man in a blue-and-white four-wheel drive. The instructions to all the sentinels were the same: *Kill him, but don't hit him in the head.* There was to be no blood or bruise above the Adam's apple.

'I don't want to send back damaged goods,' Randy Flagg told them, and clacked and roared his horrible laughter.

The northern border between Oregon and Idaho is marked by the Snake River. If you were to follow the Snake north from Ontario, where the six men sat in their Peterbilt playing spit-in-the-ocean for worthless money, you would eventually come to within spitting distance of Copperfield. The Snake takes a kink here that geologists call an oxbow, and near Copperfield the Snake was dammed by the Oxbow Dam. And on that seventh day of September, as Stu Redman and his party trudged up Colorado Highway 6 over a thousand miles to the east and south, Bobby Terry was sitting inside the Copperfield Five-and-Dime, a stack of comic books by his side, wondering what sort of shape the Oxbow Dam was in, and if the sluice gates had been left open or shut. Outside, Oregon Highway 86 ran past the dime store.

He and his partner, Dave Roberts (now asleep in the apartment overhead), had discussed the dam at great length. It had been raining for a week. The Snake was high. Suppose that old Oxbow Dam decided to let go? Bad news. A rushing wall of water would sweep down on Copperfield and ole Bobby Terry and ole Dave Roberts might be washed all the way down to the Pacific Ocean. They had discussed going over to the dam to look for cracks, but finally just hadn't dared. Flagg's orders had been specific: Stay under cover.

Dave had pointed out that Flagg might be *anywhere*. He was a great traveler, and stories had already sprung up about the way he could suddenly appear in a small, out-of-the-way burg where there were only a dozen people repairing power lines or collecting weapons from some army depot. He *materialized*, like a ghost. Only this was a grinning black ghost in dusty boots with rundown heels. Sometimes he was alone, and sometimes Lloyd Henreid was with him, behind the wheel of a great big Daimler automobile, black as a hearse and just as long. Sometimes he was walking. One moment he wasn't there, and the next moment he was. He could be in LA one day (or so the talk went) and show up in Boise a day later . . . on foot.

But as Dave had also pointed out, not even Flagg could be in six different places at the same time. One of them could just scoot over to that damn dam, have a look, and scoot back. The odds in their favor were a thousand to one.

Good, you do it, Bobby Terry told him. You have my permission. But Dave had declined the invitation with an uneasy grin. Because Flagg had a way of *knowing* things, even if he didn't turn up on the dime. There were some who said he had an unnatural power over the predators of the animal kingdom. A woman named Rose Kingman claimed to have seen him snap his fingers at a number of crows sitting on a telephone wire, and the crows fluttered down onto his shoulders, this Rose Kingman said, and she further testified that they had croaked 'Flagg . . . Flagg . . . Flagg . . .' over and over.

That was just ridiculous, and he knew it. Morons might believe it, but Bobby Terry's mother Delores had never raised any morons. He knew the way stories got around, growing between the mouth that spoke and the ear that listened. And how happy the dark man would be to encourage stories like that.

But the stories still gave him an atavistic little shiver, as though at the core of each there was a nugget of truth. Some said he could call the wolves, or send his spirit into the body of a cat. There was a man in Portland who said he carried a weasel or a fisher or something less nameable than either in that ratty old Boy Scout pack he wore when he was walking. Stupid stuff, all of it. But . . . just suppose he *could* talk to the animals, like a satanic Dr Doolittle. And suppose he or Dave walked out to look at that damn dam in a direct contradiction of *his* orders, and was seen.

The penalty for disobedience was crucifixion.

Bobby Terry guessed that old dam wouldn't break, anyway.

He shot a Kent out of the pack on the table and lit up, grimacing at the hot, dry taste. In another six months, none of the damn cigarettes would be smokable. Probably just as well. Fucking things were death, anyway.

He sighed and took another comic book off the stack. Some ridiculous fucking thing called *Teenage Mutant Ninja Turtles*. The Ninja Turtles were supposed to be 'heroes on a half-shell.' He threw Raphael, Donatello, and their numbfuck buddies across the store and the comic book they inhabited fluttered down in a tent shape on top of a cash register. It was things like the Teenage Mutant Ninja Turtles, he thought, that made you believe the world was maybe just as well off destroyed.

He picked up the next one, a *Batman* – there was a hero you could at least sort of believe in – and was just turning to the first page when he saw the blue Scout go by out front, heading west. Its big tires splashed up muddy sheets of rainwater.

Bobby Terry stared with his mouth ajar at the place where it had passed. He couldn't believe that the vehicle they were all looking for had just passed his post. To tell the truth, way down deep he had suspected this whole thing was nothing but a make-work shit detail.

He rushed to the front door and jerked it open. He ran out on the sidewalk, still holding the *Batman* comic book in one hand. Maybe the thing had been nothing but a hallucination. Thinking about Flagg could get anyone hallucinating.

But it wasn't. He caught a glimpse of the Scout's roof as it went down over the next hill and out of town. Then he was running back through the deserted five-and-dime, bawling for Dave at the top of his lungs.

The Judge held on to the steering wheel grimly, trying to pretend there was no such thing as arthritis, and if there was, he didn't have it, and if he did have it, it never bothered him in damp weather. He didn't try to take it any further because the rain was a fact, a pure-d fact, as his father would have said, and there was no hope but Mount Hope.

He wasn't getting too far with the rest of the fantasy, either.

He had been running through rain for the last three days. It sometimes backed off to a drizzle, but mostly it had been nothing more or less than a good old solid downpour. And that was *also* a pure-d fact. The roads were on the point of washing out in some places, and by next spring a lot of them were going to be flat impassable. He had thanked God for the Scout many times on this little expedition.

The first three days, struggling along I-80, had convinced him that he wasn't going to raise the West Coast before the year 2000 if he didn't get off onto the secondary roads. The Interstate had been eerily deserted for long stretches, and in places he had been able to weave in and out of stalled traffic in second gear, but too many times he had been forced to hook the Scout's winch on to some car's back bumper and yank it off the road to make himself a hole he could crawl through.

By Rawlins, he'd had enough. He turned northwest on I-287, skirted the Great Divide Basin, and had camped two days later in Wyoming's northwest corner, east of Yellow-stone. Up here, the roads were almost completely empty. Crossing Wyoming and eastern Idaho had been a frightening, dreamlike experience. He would not have thought that the feeling of death could have set so heavily on such an empty land, nor on his own soul. But it was there – a malign stillness under all that big western sky, where once the deer and the Winnebagos had roamed. It was there in the telephone poles that had fallen over and not been repaired; it was there in the cold, waiting stillness of the small towns he drove his Scout through: Lamont, Muddy Gap, Jeffrey City, Lander, Crowheart.

His loneliness grew with his realization of the emptiness, with his internalization of the death feeling. He grew more and more certain that he was never going to see the Boulder Free Zone again, or the people who lived there – Frannie, Lucy, the Lauder boy, Nick Andros. He began to think he knew how Cain must have felt when God exiled him to the land of Nod.

Only that land had been to the east of Eden.

The Judge was now in the West.

He felt it most strongly crossing the border between Wyoming and Idaho. He came into Idaho through the Targhee Pass, and stopped by the roadside for a light lunch. There was no sound but the sullen boil of high water in a nearby creek, and an odd grinding sound that reminded him of dirt in a doorhinge. Overhead the blue sky was beginning to silt up with mackerel scales. Wet weather coming, and arthritis coming with it. His arthritis had been very quiet so far, in spite of the exercise and the long hours of driving and . . .

. . . and what *was* that grinding sound?

When he had finished his lunch, he got his Garand out of the Scout and went down to the picnic area by the stream – it would have been a pleasant place to eat in kindlier weather. There was a small grove of trees, several tables spotted among them. And hanging from one of the trees, his shoes almost touching the ground, was a hanged man, his head grotesquely cocked, his flesh nearly picked clean by the birds. The grinding, creaking sound was the rope slipping back and forth on the branch over which it had been looped. It was almost frayed through.

That was how he had come to know he was in the West.

That afternoon, around four o'clock, the first hesitant splashes of rain had struck the Scout's windshield. It had been raining ever since.

He reached Butte City two days later, and the pain in his fingers and knees had gotten so bad that he had stopped for a full day, holed up in a motel room. Stretched out on the motel bed in the great silence, hot towels wrapped around his hands and knees, reading Lapham's *Law and the Classes of Society*, Judge Farris looked like a weird cross between the Ancient Mariner and a Valley Forge survivor.

Stocking up well on aspirin and brandy, he pushed on, patiently searching out secondary roads, putting the Scout in four-wheel drive and churning his muddy way around wrecks rather than using the winch when he could, so as to spare himself the necessary flexing and bending that came with attaching it. It was not always possible. Approaching the Salmon River Mountains on September 5, two days ago, he had been forced to hook on to a large ConTel telephone truck and haul it a mile and a half in reverse before the shoulder fell away on one side and he was able to dump the bastardly thing into a river for which he had no name.

On the night of September 4, one day before the ConTel truck and three days before Bobby Terry spotted him passing through Copperfield, he had camped in New Meadows, and a rather unsettling thing happened. He had pulled in at the Ranchhand Motel, got a key to one of the units in the office, and had found a bonus – a battery-operated heater, which he set up by the foot of his bed. Dusk had found him really warm and comfortable for the first time in a week. The heater put out a strong, mellow glow. He was stripped to his underwear shorts, propped up on the pillows, and reading about a case where an uneducated black woman from Brixton, Mississippi, had been sentenced to ten years on a common shoplifting offense. The assistant DA who had tried the case and three of the jurors had been black, and Lapham seemed to be pointing out that –

Tap, tap, tap: at the window.

The Judge's old heart staggered in his chest. Lapham went flying. He grabbed for the Garand leaning against the chair and turned to the window, ready for anything. His cover story went flying through his mind like jackstraws blown in the wind. This was it, they'd want to know who he was, where he'd come from –

It was a crow.

The Judge relaxed, a little at a time, and managed a small, shaken smile.

Just a crow.

It sat on the outer sill in the rain, its glossy feathers pasted together in a comic way, its little eyes looking through the dripping pane at one very old lawyer and the world's oldest amateur spy, lying on a motel bed in western Idaho, wearing nothing but boxer shorts with LOS ANGELES LAKERS printed all over them in purple and gold, a heavy lawbook across his big belly. The crow seemed almost to grin at the sight. The Judge relaxed all the way and grinned back. *That's right, the joke's on me.* But after two weeks of pushing on alone through this empty country, he felt he had a right to be a little jumpy.

Tap, tap, tap.

The crow, tapping the pane of glass with his beak. Tapping as he had tapped before.

The Judge's smile faltered a bit. There was something in the way the crow was looking at him that he didn't quite like. It still seemed almost to grin, but he could have sworn it was a contemptuous grin, a kind of sneer.

Tap, tap, tap.

Like the raven that had flown in to roost on the bust of Pallas. *When will I find out the things they need to know, back in the*

Free Zone that seems so far away? *Nevermore.* Will I get any idea what chinks there might be in the dark man's armor? *Nevermore.*

Will I get back safe?

Nevermore.

Tap, tap, tap.

The crow, looking in at him, seeming to grin.

And it came to him with a dreamy, testicle-shriveling certainty that this *was* the dark man, his soul, his *ka* somehow projected into this rain-drenched, grinning crow that was looking in at him, checking up on him.

He stared at it, fascinated.

The crow's eyes seemed to grow larger. They were rimmed with red, he noticed, a darkly rich ruby color. Rainwater dripped and ran, dripped and ran. The crow leaned forward and, very deliberately, tapped on the glass.

The Judge thought: *It thinks it's hypnotizing me. And maybe it is, a little. But maybe I'm too old for such things. And suppose . . . it's silly, of course, but suppose it is him. And suppose I could bring that rifle up in one quick snap motion? It's been four years since I shot any skeet, but I was club champion back in '76 and again in '79, and still pretty good in '86. Not great, no ribbon that year so I gave it up, my pride was in better shape than my eyesight by then, but I was still good enough to place fifth in a field of twenty-two. And that window's a lot closer than skeet-shooting distance. If it was him, could I kill him? Trap his ka — if there is such a thing — inside that dying crow body? Would it be so unfitting if an old geezer could end the whole thing by the undramatic murder of a blackbird in western Idaho?*

The crow grinned at him. He was now quite sure it was grinning.

With a sudden lunge the Judge sat up, bringing the Garand up to his shoulder in a quick, sure motion — he did it better than he ever would have dreamed. A kind of terror seemed to seize the crow. Its rain-drenched wings fluttered, spraying drops of water. Its eyes seemed to widen in fear. The Judge heard it utter a strangled *caw!* and he felt a moment's triumphant certainty: It *was* the black man, and he had misjudged the Judge, and the price for it would be his miserable life —

'*EAT THIS!*' the Judge thundered, and squeezed the trigger.

But the trigger would not depress, because he had left the safety on. A moment later the window was empty except for the rain.

The Judge lowered the Garand to his lap, feeling dull and

stupid. He told himself it was just a crow after all, a moment's diversion to liven up the evening. And if he had blown out the window and let the rain in, he would have had to go to the botheration of changing rooms. Lucky, really.

But he slept poorly that night, and several times he started awake and stared toward the window, convinced that he heard a ghostly tapping sound there. And if the crow happened to land there again, it wouldn't get away. He left the safety catch off the rifle.

But the crow didn't come back.

The next morning he had driven west again, his arthritis no worse but certainly no better, and at just past eleven he had stopped at a small café for lunch. And as he finished his sandwich and thermos of coffee, he had seen a large black crow flutter down and land on the telephone wire half a block up the street. The Judge watched it, fascinated, the red thermos cup stopped dead halfway between the table and his mouth. It wasn't the same crow, of course not. There must be millions of crows by now, all of them plump and sassy. It was a crow's world now. But all the same, he felt that it *was* the same crow, and he felt a presentiment of doom, a creeping resignation that it was all over.

He was no longer hungry.

He pushed on. Some days later, at quarter past twelve in the afternoon, now in Oregon and moving west on Highway 86, he drove through the town of Copperfield, not even glancing toward the five-and-dime where Bobby Terry watched him go by, slackjawed with amazement. The Garand was beside him on the seat, the safety still off, a box of ammo beside it. The Judge had decided to shoot any crow he might see.

Just on general principles.

'Faster! Can't you move this fucking thing any faster?'

'You get off my ass, Bobby Terry. Just because you were asleep at the switch is no reason to get on my butt.'

Dave Roberts was behind the wheel of the Willys International that had been parked nose-out in the alley beside the five-and-dime. By the time Bobby Terry had gotten Dave awake and up and dressed, the old geezer in the Scout had gotten a ten-minute start on them. The rain was coming down hard, and visibility was poor. Bobby Terry was holding a Winchester across his lap. There was a .45 Colt tucked in his belt.

Dave, who was wearing cowboy boots, jeans, a yellow foul-weather slicker, and nothing else, glanced over at him.

'You keep squeezing the trigger of that rifle and you're going to blow a hole right through your door, Bobby Terry.'

'You just catch him,' Bobby Terry said. He muttered to himself. 'The guts. Got to shoot him in the guts. Dasn't mark the head. Right.'

'Stop talkin to yourself. People who talk to theirselves play with theirselves. That's what I think.'

'Where *is* he?' Bobby Terry asked.

'We'll get him. Unless you dreamed the whole thing. I wouldn't want to be in your shoes if you did, brother.'

'I didn't. It was that Scout. But what if he turns off?'

'Turns off where?' Dave asked. 'There's nothing but farm roads all the way to the Interstate. He couldn't get fifty feet up a one of them without going into the mud up to his fenders, four-wheel drive and all. Relax, Bobby Terry.'

Bobby Terry said miserably, 'I can't. I keep wonderin how it'd feel to get hung up to dry on some telephone pole out in the desert.'

'Can that! . . . And lookit there! See im? We're sniffin up his ass now, by God!'

Ahead of them was a months-old head-on collision between a Chevy and a big heavy Buick. They lay in the rain, blocking the road from one side to the other like the rusted bones of unburied mastodons. To the right, deep fresh tire tracks were printed into the shoulder.

'That's him,' Dave said. 'Those tracks ain't five minutes old.'

He swung the Willys out and around the smashup, and they bounced wildly along the shoulder. Dave swung back onto the road where the Judge had before him, and they both saw the muddy herringbone pattern of the Scout's tires on the asphalt. At the top of the next hill, they saw the Scout just disappearing over a knoll some two miles distant.

'Howdy-doody!' Dave Roberts cried. 'Go for broke!'

He floored the accelerator and the Willys crept up to sixty. The windshield was a silvery blur of rain that the wipers could not hope to keep up with. At the top of the knoll they saw the Scout again, closer. Dave yanked out his headlight switch and began to work the dimmer switch with his foot. After a few moments, the Scout's taillights flashed on.

'All right,' Dave said. 'We act friendly. Get him to step out.

Don't you go off half-cocked, Bobby Terry. If we do this right, we're gonna have a couple of suites at the MGM Grand in Vegas. Fuck it up and we're gonna get our assholes cored out. *So don't you fuck up*. Get him to step out.'

'Oh my God, why couldn't he have come through Robinette?' Bobby Terry whined. His hands were locked on the Winchester.

Dave whacked at one of them. 'You don't carry that rifle out, either.'

'But –'

'Shut up! Get a smile on, goddam you!'

Bobby Terry began to grin. It was like watching a mechanical funhouse clown grin.

'You nogood,' Dave snarled. 'I'll do it. Stay in the goddam car.'

They had pulled even with the Scout, which was idling with two wheels on the pavement and two on the soft shoulder. Smiling, Dave got out. His hands were in the pockets of his yellow slicker. In the lefthand pocket was a .38 Police Special.

The Judge climbed carefully down from the Scout. He was also wearing a yellow rain slicker. He walked carefully, bearing himself the way a man might bear a fragile vase. The arthritis was loose in him like a pack of tigers. He carried the Garand rifle in his left hand.

'Hey, you won't shoot me with that, will you?' the man from the Willys said with a friendly grin.

'I guess not,' the Judge said. They spoke over the steady hiss of the rain. 'You must have been back in Copperfield.'

'So we were. I'm Dave Roberts.' He stuck out his right hand.

'Farris is my name,' said the Judge, and put out his own right hand. He glanced up toward the passenger window of the Willys and saw Bobby Terry leaning out, holding his .45 in both hands. Rain was dripping off the barrel. His face, dead pale, was still frozen in that maniacal funhouse grin.

'Oh bastard,' the Judge murmured, and pulled his hand out of Roberts's rain-slippery grip just as Roberts fired through the pocket of his slicker. The bullet plowed through the Judge's midsection just below the stomach, flattening, spinning, mushrooming, coming out to the right of his spine, leaving an exit hole the size of a tea saucer. The Garand fell from his hand onto the road and he was driven back into the Scout's open driver's side door.

None of them noticed the crow that had fluttered down to a telephone wire on the far side of the road.

Dave Roberts took a step forward to finish the job. As he did, Bobby Terry fired from the passenger window of the Willys. His bullet took Roberts in the throat, tearing most of it away. A fury of blood cascaded down the front of Roberts's slicker and mixed with the rain. He turned toward Bobby Terry, his jaw working in soundless, dying amazement, his eyes bulging. He took two shuffling steps forward, and then the amazement went out of his face. Everything went out of it. He fell dead. Rain plinked and drummed on the back of his slicker.

'*Oh shit, lookit this!*' Bobby Terry cried in utter dismay.

The Judge thought: *My arthritis is gone. If I could live, I could stun the medical profession. The cure for arthritis is a bullet in the guts. Oh dear God, they were laying for me. Did Flagg tell them? He must have, Jesus help whoever else the committee sent over here . . .*

The Garand was lying on the road. He bent for it, feeling his guts trying to run right out of his body. Strange feeling. Not very pleasant. Never mind. He got hold of the gun. Was the safety off? Yes. He began to bring it up. It seemed to weigh a thousand pounds.

Bobby Terry ripped his stunned gaze away from Dave at last, just in time to see the Judge preparing to shoot him. The Judge was sitting on the road. His slicker was red with blood from chest to hem. He had settled the barrel of the Garand on his knee.

Bobby snapped a shot and missed. The Garand went off with a giant thunderclap and jagged glass sprayed Bobby Terry's face. He screamed, sure he was dead. Then he saw that the left half of the windshield was gone and understood that he was still in the running.

The Judge was ponderously correcting his aim, swiveling the Garand perhaps two degrees on his knee. Bobby Terry, his nerves entirely shot now, fired three times in rapid succession. The first bullet spanged a hole through the side of the Scout's cab. The second struck the Judge above the right eye. A .45 is a large gun, and at close range it does large, unpleasant things. This bullet took off most of the top of the Judge's skull and hurled it back into the Scout. His head tilted back radically, and Bobby Terry's third bullet struck the Judge a quarter of an inch below his lower lip, exploding his teeth into his mouth, where he aspirated them with his final breath. His chin and jawbone disintegrated. His finger squeezed the Garand's trigger in a dying convulsion, but the bullet went wild into the white, rainy sky.

Silence descended.

Rain drummed on the roofs of the Scout and the Willys. On the slickers of the two dead men. It was the only sound until the crow took off from the telephone wire with a raucous caw. That startled Bobby Terry out of his daze. He got slowly down from the passenger seat, still clutching the smoking .45.

'I did it,' he said confidentially to the rain. 'Killed his ass. You better believe it. Shoot-out at the OK Corral. Fuckin-A right. Ole Bobby Terry just killed him as dead as you'd want.'

But with dawning horror, he realized that it wasn't the Judge's ass he'd killed after all.

The Judge had died leaning back into the Scout. Now Bobby Terry grabbed the lapels of his slicker and yanked him forward, staring at what remained of the Judge's features. There was really nothing left but his nose. To tell the truth, that wasn't in such hot shape, either.

It could have been anyone.

And in a dream of terror, Bobby Terry again heard Flagg saying: *I want to send him back undamaged.*

Holy God, this could be *anyone*. It was as if he had set out to deliberately do just the opposite of what the Walkin Dude had ordered. Two direct hits in the face. Even the *teeth* were gone.

Rain, drumming, drumming.

It was over here. That was all. He didn't dare go east, and he didn't dare stay in the West. He would either wind up riding a telephone pole bareback or . . . or something worse.

Were there worse things?

With that grinning freak in charge, Bobby Terry had no doubt there were. So what was the answer?

Running his hands through his hair, still looking down at the ruined face of the Judge, he tried to think.

South. That was the answer. South. No border guards anymore. South of Mexico, and if that wasn't far enough, get on down to Guatemala, Panama, maybe fucking Brazil. Opt out of the whole mess. No more East, no more West, just Bobby Terry, safe and as far away from the Walkin Dude as his old boogie shoes could carry h –

A new sound in the rainy afternoon.

Bobby Terry's head jerked up.

The rain, yes, making its steel drum sound on the cabs of the two vehicles, and the grumbling of two idling motors, and –

A strange clocking sound, like rundown bootheels hammering swiftly along the secondary road macadam.

'No,' Bobby Terry whispered.

He began to turn around.

The clocking sound was speeding up. A fast walk, a trot, a jog, run, *sprint*, and Bobby Terry got all the way around, too late, *he* was coming, Flagg was coming like some terrible horror monster out of the scariest picture ever made. The dark man's cheeks were flushed with jolly color, his eyes were twinkling with happy good fellowship, and a great hungry voracious grin stretched his lips over huge tombstone teeth, shark teeth, and his hands were held out in front of him, and there were shiny black crowfeathers fluttering from his hair.

No, Bobby Terry tried to say, but nothing came out.

'*HEY, BOBBY TERRY, YOU SCROOOOWED IT UP!*' the dark man bellowed, and fell upon the hapless Bobby Terry.

There *were* worse things than crucifixion.

There were teeth.

CHAPTER 62

Dayna Jurgens lay naked in the huge double bed, listening to the steady hiss of water coming from the shower, and looked up at her reflection in the big circular ceiling mirror, which was the exact shape and size of the bed it reflected. She thought that the female body always looks its best when it is flat on its back, stretched out, the tummy pulled flat, the breasts naturally upright without the vertical drag of gravity to pull them down. It was nine-thirty in the morning, September 8. The Judge had been dead about eighteen hours, Bobby Terry considerably less – unfortunately for him.

The shower ran on and on.

There's a man with a cleanliness compulsion, she thought. *I wonder what happened to him that makes him want to shower for half an hour at a stretch?*

Her mind turned back to the Judge. Who would have figured that? In its own way, it was a damned brilliant idea. Who would have suspected an old man? Well, Flagg had, it seemed. Somehow he had known when and approximately where. A picket line had been set up all the way along the Idaho-Oregon border, with orders to kill him.

But the job had been botched somehow. Since suppertime last night, the upper echelon here in Las Vegas had been walking around with pasty faces and downcast eyes. Whitney Horgan, who was one damned fine cook, had served something that looked like dog food and was too burned to taste like much of anything. The Judge was dead, but something had gone wrong.

She got up and walked to the window and looked out over the desert. She saw two big Las Vegas High School buses trundling west on US 95 in the hot sunshine, headed out toward the Indian Springs airbase, where, she knew, a daily seminar in the art and craft of jet planes went on. There were over a dozen people in the West who knew how to fly, but by great good luck – for the Free Zone

– none of them were checked out for the National Guard jets at Indian Springs.

But they were learning. Oh my, yes.

What was most important for her right now about the Judge's demise was that they had known when they had no business knowing. Was there a spy of their own back in the Free Zone? That was possible, she supposed; spying was a game two could play at. But Sue Stern had told her that the decision to send spies into the West had been strictly a committee thing, and she doubted very much if any of those seven were in the Flagg bag. Mother Abagail would have known if one of the committee had turned rotten, for one thing. Dayna was sure of it.

That left a very unappetizing alternative. Flagg himself had just *known*.

Dayna had been in Las Vegas eight days as of today, and as far as she could tell she was a fully accepted member of the community. She had already accumulated enough information about the operation over here to scare the living Jesus out of everyone back in Boulder. It would only take the news about the jet plane training program to do that. But the thing that frightened her the most personally was the way people turned away from you if you mentioned Flagg's name, the way they pretended they hadn't heard. Some of them would cross their fingers, or genuflect, or make the sign of the evil eye behind one cupped hand. He was the great There/Not-There.

That was by day. By night, if you would just sit quietly by in the Cub Bar of the Grand or the Silver Slipper Room at The Cashbox, you heard stories about him, the beginning of myth. They talked slowly, haltingly, not looking at each other, drinking bottles of beer mostly. If you drank something stronger, you might lose control of your mouth, and that was dangerous. She knew that not all of what they said was the truth, but it was already impossible to separate the gilt embroidery from the whole cloth. She had heard he was a shape-changer, a werewolf, that he had started the plague himself, that he was the Antichrist whose coming was foretold in Revelation. She heard about the crucifixion of Hector Drogan, how *he* had just known Heck was freebasing . . . the way he had just known that the Judge was on the way, apparently.

And he was never referred to as Flagg in these nightly discussions; it was as if they believed that to call him by name was to summon him like a djinn from a bottle. They called him the dark man. The Walkin Dude. The tall man. And Ratty Erwins called him Old Creeping Judas.

If he had known about the Judge, didn't it stand to reason that he knew about her?'

The shower turned off.

Keep it together, sweetie. He encourages the mumbo-jumbo. It makes him look taller. It could be that he does have a spy in the Free Zone – it wouldn't necessarily have to be someone on the committee, just someone who told him Judge Farris wasn't the defector type.

'You shouldn't walk around like that with no clothes on, sweetbuns. You'll get me horny all over again.'

She turned toward him, her smile rich and inviting, thinking that she would like to take him downstairs to the kitchen and stuff that thing he was so goddam proud of into Whitney Horgan's industrial meat-grinder. 'Why do you think I was walking around with no clothes on?'

He looked at his watch. 'Well, we got maybe forty minutes.' His penis was already beginning to make twitching movements . . . like a divining rod, Dayna thought with sour amusement.

'Well, come on then.' He came toward her and she pointed at his chest. 'And take that thing off. It gives me the creeps.'

Lloyd Henreid looked down at the amulet, dark teardrop marked with a single red flaw, and slipped it off. He put it on the night table and the fine-linked chain made a little hissing sound. 'Better?'

'All kinds of better.'

She held out her arms. A moment later he was on top of her. A moment after that he was thrusting into her.

'You like that?' he panted. 'You like the way that feels, sweetie?'

'God, I love it,' she moaned, thinking of the meat-grinder, all white enamel and gleaming steel.

'What?'

'I said I *love* it!' she screamed.

She faked an orgasm shortly after that, tossing her hips wildly, crying out. He came seconds later (she had shared Lloyd's bed for four days now, and had his rhythms timed almost perfectly), and as she felt his semen beginning to run down her thigh, she happened to glance over at the night table.

Black stone.

Red flaw.

It seemed to be staring at her.

She had a sudden horrible feeling that it *was* staring at her, that it was *his* eye with its contact lens of humanity removed, staring at her as the Eye of Sauron had stared at Frodo from the dark fastness of Barad-Dur, in Mordor, where the shadows lie.

It sees me, she thought with hopeless horror in that defenseless moment before rationality reasserted itself. *More: it sees THROUGH me.*

Afterward, as she had hoped, Lloyd talked. That was part of his rhythm, too. He would put an arm around her bare shoulders, smoke a cigarette, look up at their reflections in the mirror over the bed, and tell her what was going on.

'Glad I wasn't that Bobby Terry,' he said. 'No sir, no way. The main man wanted that old fart's head without so much as a bruise on it. Wanted to send it back over the Rockies. And look what happened. That numbnuts puts two .45 slugs into his face. At close range. I guess he deserved what he got, but I'm glad I wasn't there.'

'What happened to him?'

'Sweetbuns, don't ask.'

'How did he know? The big guy?'

'He was there.'

She felt a chill.

'Just happened to be there?'

'Yeah. He just happens to be anywhere that there's trouble. Jesus Christ, when I think what he did to Eric Strellerton, that smartass lawyer me and Trashy went to LA with . . .'

'What did he do?'

For a long time she didn't think he was going to answer. Usually she could gently push him in the direction she wanted him to go by asking a series of soft, respectful questions; making him feel as if he was (in the never-to-be-forgotten words of her kid sister) King Shit of Turd Mountain. But this time she had a feeling she had pushed too far until Lloyd said in a funny, squeezed voice:

'He just *looked* at him. Eric was laying down all this funky shit about how he wanted to see the Vegas operation run . . . we should do this, we should do that. Poor old Trash – he ain't all the way together himself, you know – was just staring at him like he was a TV actor or something. Eric's pacing back and forth like he's addressing a jury and like it was already proved he was going to get his own way. And *he* says – real soft – "Eric." Like that. And Eric looked at him. I didn't see nothing. But Eric just looked at him for a long time. Maybe five minutes. His eyes just got bigger and bigger . . . and then he started to drool . . . and then he started to giggle . . . and *he* giggled right along with Eric, and that scared me. When Flagg laughs, you get scared. But Eric just kep right on giggling, and then *he* said, "When you go back, drop him off in the Mojave." And that's what we did. And for all I know, Eric's wandering around out there right now. He looked at Eric for five minutes and drove him out of his mind.'

He took a large drag on his cigarette and crushed it out. Then he slung an arm around her. 'Why are we talkin about bad shit like that?'

'I don't know . . . how's it going out at Indian Springs?'

Lloyd brightened. The Indian Springs project was his baby. 'Good. Real good. We're going to have three guys checked out on the Skyhawk planes by the first of October, maybe sooner. Hank Rawson really looks great. And that Trashcan Man, he's a fucking genius. About some things he's not too bright, but when it comes to weapons, he's incredible.'

She had met Trashcan Man twice. Both times she had felt a chill slip over her when his strange, muddy eyes happened to light upon her, and a palpable sense of relief when those eyes passed on. It was obvious that many of the others – Lloyd, Hank Rawson, Ronnie Sykes, the Rat-Man – saw him as a kind of mascot, a good luck charm. One of his arms was a horrid mass of freshly healed burn tissue, and she remembered something peculiar that had happened two nights ago. Hank Rawson had been talking. He put a cigarette in his mouth, struck a match, and finished what he was saying before lighting the cigarette and shaking out the match. Dayna saw the way that Trashcan Man's eyes homed in on the match flame, the way his breathing seemed to stop. It was as if his whole being had focused on the tiny flame. It was like watching a starving man contemplate a nine-course dinner. Then Hank shook out the match and dropped the blackened stub into an ashtray. The moment had ended.

'He's good with weapons?' she asked Lloyd.

'He's great with them. The Skyhawks have under-wing missiles, air-to-ground. Shrikes. Weird how they name all that shit, isn't it? No one could figure out how the goddam things went on the planes.

No one could figure out how to arm them or safety-control them. Christ, it took us most of one day to figure out how to get them off the storage racks. So Hank says, "We better get Trashy out here when he gets back and see if he can figure it out."'

'When he gets back?'

'Yeah, he's a funny dude. He's been in Vegas almost a week now, but he'll be taking off again pretty quick.'

'Where does he go?'

'Into the desert. He takes a Land-Rover and just goes. He's a strange guy, I tell you. In his way, Trash is almost as strange as the big guy himself. West of here there's nothing but empty desert and godforsaken waste. I ought to know. I did time way up west in a hellhole called Brownsville Station. I don't know how he lives out there, but he does. He looks for new toys, and he always comes back with a few. About a week after him and me got back from LA, he brought back a pile of army machine guns with laser sights – never-miss machine guns, Hank calls them. This time it was Teller mines, contact mines, fragment mines, and a canister of Parathion. He said he found a whole stockpile of Parathion. Also enough defoliant to turn the whole state of Colorado bald as an egg.'

'Where does he find it?'

'Everywhere,' Lloyd said simply. 'He sniffs it out, sweet-buns. It isn't really so strange. Most of western Nevada and eastern California was owned by the good old USA. It's where they tested their toys, all the way up to A-bombs. He'll be dragging one of those back someday.'

He laughed. Dayna felt cold, terribly cold.

'The superflu started somewhere out here. I'd lay money on it. Maybe Trash will find it. I tell you, he just sniffs that stuff out. The big guy says just give him his head and let him run, and so that's what he does. You know what his favorite toy is right now?'

'No,' Dayna said. She wasn't sure she wanted to know . . . but why else had she come over here?

'Flametracks.'

'What are flametrucks?'

'Not trucks, *tracks*. He's got five of them out at Indian Springs, lined up like Formula One racecars.' Lloyd laughed. 'They used them in the Nam. The grunts called them Zippos. They're full of napalm. Trash loves em.'

'Neato,' she muttered.

'Anyway, when Trash came back this time, we took him out to the Springs. He hummed and muttered around those Shrikes and got them armed and mounted in about six hours. Can you believe that? They train Air Force technicians about ninety years to do stuff like that. But they're not Trash, you see. He's a fucking genius.'

Idiot savant, you mean. I bet I know how he got those burns, too.

Lloyd looked at his watch and sat up. 'Speaking of Indian Springs, I got to get out there. Just got time for another shower. You want to join me?'

'Not this time.'

She got dressed after the shower began to run again. So far she had always managed to get dressed and undressed with him out of the room, and that was the way she intended to keep it.

She strapped the clip to her forearm and slid the switch-blade knife into its spring-loaded clasp. A quick twist of her wrist would deliver all ten inches of it into her hand.

Well, she thought as she slipped into her blouse, a girl has to have *some* secrets.

During the afternoons, she was on a streetlamp maintenance crew. What the job amounted to was testing the bulbs with a simple gadget and replacing them if they had burned out, or if they had been broken by vandals when Las Vegas had been in the grip of the superflu. There were four of them on the job, and they had a cherry-picker truck that trundled around from post to post and street to street.

Late that afternoon, Dayna was up in the cherry-picker, removing the Plexiglas hood from one of the streetlamps and musing on how much she liked the people she was working with, particularly Jenny Engstrom, a tough and beautiful ex-nightclub dancer who was now running the cherry-picker's controls. She was the type of girl Dayna would have wanted for her best friend, and it confused her that Jenny was over here, on the dark man's side. It confused her so much that she didn't dare ask Jenny for an explanation.

The others were also okay. She thought that Vegas had a rather larger proportion of stupids than the Zone, but none of them wore fangs, and they didn't turn into bats at moon-rise. They were also people who worked much harder than she remembered the people in the Zone working. In the Free Zone you saw people idling in the parks at all hours of the day, and there were people who decided to break for lunch from noon until two. That sort of thing didn't happen over here. From

8 AM to 5 PM, *everybody* was working, either at Indian Springs or on the maintenance crews here in town. And school had started again. There were about twenty kids in Vegas, ages ranging from four (that was Daniel McCarthy, the pet of everyone in town, known as Dinny) up to fifteen. They had found two people with teaching certificates, and classes went on five days a week. Lloyd, who had quit school after repeating his junior year for the third time, was very proud of the educational opportunities that were being provided. The pharmacies were open and unguarded. People came and went all the time . . . but they took away nothing heavier than a bottle of aspirin or Gelusil. There was no drug problem in the West. Anyone who had seen what had happened to Hector Drogan knew what the penalty for a habit was. There were no Rich Moffats, either. Everyone was friendly and straight. And it was wise to drink nothing stronger than bottled beer.

Germany in 1938, she thought. *The Nazis? Oh, they're charming people. Very athletic. They don't go to the nightclubs, the nightclubs are for the tourists. What do they do? They make clocks.*

Was it a fair comparison? Dayna wondered uneasily, thinking of Jenny Engstrom, who she liked so much. She didn't know . . . but she thought that maybe it was.

She tested the bulb in the hood of the light standard. It was bad. She removed it, set it carefully between her feet, and got the last fresh one. Good, it was near the end of the day. It was –

She glanced down and froze.

People were coming back from the bus stop, headed home from Indian Springs. All of them were glancing up casually, the way a group of people always glance up at someone high in the air. The circus-for-free syndrome.

That face, looking up at her.

That wide, smiling, wondering face.

Dear sweet Jesus in heaven, is that Tom Cullen?

A dribble of salt-stinging sweat ran into her eye, doubling her vision. When she wiped it away, the face was gone. The people from the bus stop were halfway down the street, swinging their lunch buckets, talking and joking. Dayna gazed at the one she thought might be Tom, but from the rear it was so hard to tell –

Tom? Would they send Tom?

Surely not. That was so crazy it was almost –

Almost sane.

But she just couldn't believe it.

'Hey, Jurgens!' Jenny called up brassily. 'Did you fall asleep up there, or are you just playing with yourself?'

Dayna leaned over the cherry-picker's low railing and looked down at Jenny's upturned face. Gave her the finger. Jenny laughed. Dayna went back to her streetlamp bulb, struggling to snap it in, and by the time she had it right, it was time to knock off for the day. On the ride back to the garage, she was quiet and preoccupied . . . quiet enough for Jenny to comment on it.

'Just got nothing to say, I guess,' Dayna told her with a half-smile.

It couldn't have been Tom.

Could it?

'Wake up! Wake up! Goddammit, wake up, you bitch!'

She was coming out of murky sleep when a foot caught her in the small of the back, knocking her out of the big round bed and onto the floor. She came awake at once, blinking and confused.

Lloyd was there, looking down at her with cold anger. Whitney Horgan. Ken DeMott. Ace High. Jenny. Only Jenny's usually open face was also blank and cold.

'Jen –?'

No answer. Dayna got up on her knees, dimly aware of her nakedness, more aware of the cold circle of faces looking down at her. The expression on Lloyd's face was that of a man who has been betrayed and has discovered the betrayal.

Am I dreaming this?

'Get the fuck dressed, you lying, spying *bitch*!'

Okay, so it was no dream. She felt a sinking terror in her stomach that seemed almost preordained. They had known about the Judge, and now they knew about her. *He* had told them. She glanced at the clock on the night table. It was quarter of four in the morning. The Hour of the Secret Police, she thought.

'Where is he?' she asked.

'Around,' Lloyd said grimly. His face was pale and shiny. His amulet lay in the open V of his shirt. 'You'll wish he wasn't before long.'

'Lloyd?'

'What?'

'I gave you VD, Lloyd. I hope it rots off.'

He kicked her just below the breastbone, knocking her on her back.

'I hope it rots off, Lloyd.'

'Shut up and get dressed.'

'Get out of here. I don't dress in front of any man.'

Lloyd kicked her again, this time in the bicep of her right arm. The pain was tremendous and her mouth drew down in a quivering bow but she didn't cry out.

'You in a little hot water, Lloyd? Sleeping with Mata Hari?' She grinned at him with tears of pain standing in her eyes.

'Come on, Lloyd,' Whitney Horgan said. He saw murder in Lloyd's eyes and now stepped forward quickly and put a hand on Lloyd's arm. 'We'll go in the living room. Jenny can watch her get dressed.'

'And what if she decides to jump out the window?'

'She won't get the chance,' Jenny said. Her broad face was dead blank, and for the first time Dayna noticed she was wearing a pistol on her hip.

'She can't anyway,' Ace High said. 'The windows up here are just for show, didn't you know that? Sometimes big losers at the tables get wanting to take a high dive, and that would be bad publicity for the hotel. So they don't open.' His eyes fell on Dayna, and they held a touch of compassion. 'Now you, babe, you're a real big loser.'

'Come on, Lloyd,' Whitney said again. 'You're going to do something you'll be sorry for later – kick her in the head or something – if you don't get out of here.'

'Okay.' They went to the door together, and Lloyd looked back over his shoulder. 'He's going to make it bad for you, you bitch.'

'You were the crappiest lover I ever had, Lloyd,' she said sweetly.

He tried to lunge back at her, but Whitney and Ken DeMott held him back and drew him through the doorway. The double doors closed with a low snicking sound.

'Get dressed, Dayna,' Jenny said.

Dayna stood up, still rubbing the purpling bruise on her arm. 'You people like that?' she asked. 'Is that where you're at? People like Lloyd Henreid?'

'You were the one sleeping with him, not me.' Her face showed an emotion for the first time: angry reproach. 'You think it's nice to come over here and spy on folks? You deserve everything you're going to get. And, sister, you're going to get a lot.'

'I was sleeping with him for a reason.' She drew on her panties. 'And I was spying for a reason.'

'Why don't you just shut up?'

Dayna turned and looked at Jenny. 'What do you think they're doing here, girl? Why do you think they're learning to fly those jets out at Indian Springs? Those Shrike missiles, do you think they're so Flagg can win his girl a Kewpie doll at the country fair?'

Jenny pressed her lips tightly together. 'That's none of my business.'

'Will it be none of your business if they use the jets to fly over the Rockies next spring and the missiles to wipe out everyone living there?'

'I hope they do. It's us or you people; that's what *he* says. And I believe him.'

'They believed Hitler, too. But you don't believe him; you're just scared gutless of him.'

'Get dressed, Dayna.'

Dayna pulled on her slacks, buttoned them, zipped them. Then she put her hand to her mouth. 'I . . . I think I'm going to throw up . . . God! . . .' Clutching her long-sleeved blouse in her hand, she turned and ran into the bathroom and locked the door. She made loud retching noises.

'Open the door, Dayna! Open it or I'll shoot the lock out of it!'

'Sick –' She made another loud retching noise. Standing on tiptoe, she felt along the top of the medicine cabinet, thanking God she had left the knife and its spring clip up here, praying for another twenty seconds –

She had the clip. She strapped it on. Now there were other voices in the bedroom.

With her left hand she turned on the water in the basin. 'Just a minute, I'm sick, dammit!'

But they weren't going to give her a minute. Someone dealt the bathroom door a kick and it shuddered in its frame. Dayna clicked the knife home. It lay along her forearm like a deadly arrow. Moving with desperate speed, she yanked the blouse on and buttoned the sleeves. Splashed water on her mouth. Flushed the toilet.

Another kick dealt to the door. Dayna twisted the knob and they burst in, Lloyd looking wild-eyed, Jenny standing behind Ken DeMott and Ace High, her pistol drawn.

'I puked,' Dayna said coldly. 'Too bad you couldn't watch it, huh?'

Lloyd grabbed her by the shoulder and threw her out into the bedroom. 'I ought to break your neck, you cunt.'

'Remember your master's voice.' She buttoned the front of her blouse, sweeping them with her flashing eyes. 'He's your dog-god, isn't that right? Kiss his ass and you belong to him.'

'You better just shut up,' Whitney said gruffly. 'You're only making it worse for yourself.'

She looked at Jenny, unable to understand how the openly smiling, bawdy day-girl could have changed into this blank-faced night-thing. 'Don't you see that he's getting ready to start it all over again?' she asked them desperately. 'The killing, the shooting . . . *the plague?*'

'He's the biggest and the strongest,' Whitney said with curious gentleness. 'He's going to wipe you people off the face of the earth.'

'No more talk,' Lloyd said. 'Let's go.'

They moved to take her arms, but she stepped away, holding her arms across her body, and shook her head. 'I'll walk,' she said.

The casino was deserted except for a number of men with rifles, sitting or standing by the doors. They seemed to find interesting things to look at on the walls, the ceilings, and the bare gaming tables as the elevator doors opened and Lloyd's party stepped out, herding Dayna along.

She was taken to the gate at the end of the rank of cashiers' windows. Lloyd opened it with a small key and they stepped through. She was herded quickly through an area that looked like a bank: there were adding machines, wastebaskets full of paper tapes, jars of rubber bands and paperclips. Computer screens, now gray and blank. Cash drawers ajar. Money had spilled out some of them and lay on the tile floors. Most of the bills were fifties and hundreds.

At the rear of the cashiers' area, Whitney opened another door and Dayna was led down a carpeted hallway to an empty reception-ist's office. Tastefully decorated. Free-form white desk for a tasteful secretary who had died, coughing and hacking up great green gobbets of phlegm, some months ago. A picture on the wall that looked like a Klee print. A mellow light-brown shag rug. The antechamber to the seat of power.

Fear trickled into the hollows of her body like cold water, stiffening her up, making her feel awkward. Lloyd leaned over the desk and flicked the toggle switch there. Dayna saw that he was sweating lightly.

'We have her, R. F.'

She felt hysterical laughter bubbling up inside her and was helpless to stop it – not that she cared. 'R. F.! R. F.! Oh, that's *good*! Ready when you are, C. B.!' She went off into a gale of giggles, and suddenly Jenny slapped her.

'Shut up!' she hissed. 'You don't know what you're in for.'

'I know,' Dayna said, looking at her. 'You and the rest, you're the ones who don't know.'

A voice came out of the intercom, warm and pleased and cheerful. 'Very good, Lloyd, thanks. Send her in, please.'

'Alone?'

'Yes indeed.' There was an indulgent chuckle as the intercom cut off. Dayna felt her mouth dry up at the sound of it.

Lloyd turned around. A lot of sweat now, standing out on his forehead in large drops and running down his thin cheeks like tears. 'You heard him. Go on.'

She folded her arms below her breasts, keeping the knife turned inward. 'Suppose I decline.'

'I'll drag you in.'

'Look at you, Lloyd. You're so scared you couldn't drag a mongrel puppy in there.' She looked at the others. 'You're all scared. Jenny, you're practically making in your pants. Not good for your complexion, dear. *Or* your pants.'

'Stop it, you filthy sneak,' Jenny whispered.

'I was never scared like that in the Free Zone,' Dayna said. 'I felt good over there. I came over here because I wanted that good feeling to stay on. It was nothing more political than that. You ought to think it over. Maybe he sells fear because he's got nothing else to sell.'

'Ma'am,' Whitney said apologetically, 'I'd sure like to listen to the rest of your sermon, but the man is waiting. I'm sorry, but you either got to say amen and go through that door on your own or *I'll* drag you. You can tell your tale to him once you get in there . . . if you can find enough spit to talk with, that is. But until then, you're our responsibility.' And the odd thing is, she thought, he sounds genuinely sorry. Too bad he's also so genuinely scared.

'You won't have to do that.'

She forced her feet to get started, and then it was a little easier. She was going to her death; she was quite sure of that. If so, let it be so. She had the knife. For him first, if she could, and then for herself, if necessary.

She thought: *My name is Dayna Roberta Jurgens, and I am afraid, but I have been afraid before. All he can take from me is what I would have to give up someday anyhow – my life. I will not let him break me down. I will not let him make me less than I am, if I can possibly help it. I want to die well . . . and I am going to have what I want.*

She turned the knob and stepped through into the inner office . . . and into the presence of Randall Flagg.

The room was large and mostly bare. The desk had been shoved up against the far wall, the executive swivel chair pinned behind it. The pictures were covered with drop-cloths. The lights were off.

Across the room, a drape had been pulled back to uncover a window-wall of glass that looked out on the desert. Dayna thought she had never seen such a sterile and uninviting vista in her life. Overhead was a moon like a small, highly polished silver coin. It was nearly full.

Standing there, looking out, was the shape of a man.

He continued to look out long after she had entered, indifferently presenting her his back, before he turned. How long does it take a man to turn around? Two, maybe three seconds at the most. But to Dayna it seemed that the dark man went on turning forever, showing more and more of himself, like the very moon he had been watching. She became a child again, struck dumb by the dreadful curiosity of great fear. For a moment she was caught entirely in the web of his attraction, his *glamour*, and she was sure that when the turn was completed, unknown eons from now, she would be staring into the face of her dreams: a Gothic cowled monk, his hood shaped around total darkness. A negative man with no face. She would see and then go mad.

Then he was looking at her, walking forward, smiling warmly, and her first shocked thought was: *Why, he's* my *age!*

Randy Flagg's hair was dark, tousled. His face was handsome and ruddy, as if he spent much time out in the desert wind. His features were mobile and sensitive, and his eyes danced with high glee, the eyes of a small child with a momentous and wonderful secret surprise.

'Dayna!' he said. 'Hi!'

'H–H–Hello.' She could say no more. She had thought she was prepared for anything, but she hadn't been prepared for this. Her mind had been knocked, reeling, to the mat. He was smiling at her confusion. Then he spread his hands, as if in apology. He was wearing a faded paisley shirt with a frayed collar, pegged jeans, and a very old pair of cowboy boots with rundown heels.

'What did you expect? A vampire?' His smile broadened, almost demanding that she smile back. 'A skin-turner? What have they been *telling* you about me?'

'They're afraid,' she said. 'Lloyd was . . . sweating like a pig.' His smile was still demanding an answering smile, and it took all her effort of will to deny him that. She had been kicked out of bed on his orders. Brought here to . . . what? Confess? Tell everything she knew about the Free Zone? She couldn't believe there was that much he didn't already know.

'Lloyd,' Flagg said, and laughed ruefully. 'Lloyd went through a rather bitter experience in Phoenix when the flu was raging. He doesn't like to talk about it. I rescued him from death and' – his smile grew even more disarming, if that was possible – 'and from a fate worse than death is the popular idiom, I believe. He's associated me with that experience to a great degree, although his situation was not of my doing. Do you believe me?'

She nodded slowly. She did believe him, and found herself wondering if Lloyd's constant showering had something to do with his 'rather bitter experience in Phoenix.' She also found herself feeling an emotion she never would have expected in connection with Lloyd Henreid: pity.

'Good. Sit down, dear.'

She looked around doubtfully.

'On the floor. The floor will be fine. We have to talk, and talk truth. Liars sit in chairs, so we'll eschew them. We'll sit as though we were friends on opposite sides of a campfire. Sit, girl.' His eyes positively sparkled with suppressed mirth, and his sides seemed to bellow with laughter barely held in. He sat down and crossed his legs and then looked up at her appealingly, his expression seeming to say: *You're not going to let me sit all alone on the floor of this ridiculous office, are you?*

After a moment's debate she did sit down. She crossed her legs and put her hands lightly on her knees. She could feel the comforting weight of the knife in its spring clip.

'You were sent over here to spy out the land, dear,' he said. 'Is that an accurate description of the situation?'

'Yes.' There was no use denying it.

'And you know what usually befalls spies in time of war?'

'Yes.'

His smile broadened like sunshine. 'Then isn't it lucky we're not at war, your people and mine?'

She looked at him, totally surprised.

'But we're not, you know,' he said with quiet sincerity.

'But . . . you . . .' A thousand confused thoughts spun in her head. Indian Springs. The Shrikes. Trashcan Man with his defoliant and his Zippos. The way the conversation always veered when this man's name − or presence − came into the conversation. And that lawyer, Eric Strellerton. Wandering in the Mojave with his brains burned out.

All he did was look at him.

'Have we attacked your Free Zone, so-called? Made any warlike move at all against you over there?'

'No . . . but −'

'And have you attacked us?'

'Of course not!'

'No. And we have no plans in that direction. Look!' He suddenly held up his right hand and curled it into a tube. Looking through it, she could see the desert beyond the window-wall.

'The Great Western Desert!' he cried. 'The Big Piss-All! Nevada! Arizona! New Mexico! California! A smattering of my people are in Washington, around the Seattle area, and in Portland, Oregon. A fistful each in Idaho and New Mexico. We're too scattered to even think about taking a census for a year or more. We're much more vulnerable than your Zone. The Free Zone is like a highly organized hive or commune. We are nothing but a confederacy, with me as the titular head. There's room for both of us. There will still be room for both of us in 2190. That's if the babies live, something we won't know about here for at least another five months. If they do, and humanity continues, let our grandfathers fight it out, if they have a bone to pick. Or their grandfathers. *But what in God's name do we have to fight about?*'

'Nothing,' she muttered. Her throat was dry. She felt dazed. And something else . . . was it *hope*? She was looking into his eyes. She could not seem to tear her gaze away, and she didn't want to.

She wasn't going mad. He wasn't driving her mad at all. He was . . . a very reasonable man.

'There are no economic reasons for us to fight, no technological ones either. Our politics are a bit different, but that is a very minor thing, with the Rockies between us . . .'

He's hypnotizing me.

With a huge effort she dragged her eyes away from his and looked out over his shoulder at the moon. Flagg's smile faded a bit, and a shadow of irritation seemed to cross his features. Or had she imagined it? When she looked back (more warily this time), he was smiling gently at her again.

'You had the Judge killed,' she said harshly. 'You want something from me, and when you get it, you'll have me killed, too.'

He looked at her patiently. 'There were pickets all along the Idaho-Oregon border, and they were looking for Judge Farris, that is true. But not to kill him! Their orders were to bring him to me. I was in Portland until yesterday. I wanted to talk to him as I'm now talking to you, dear: calmly, reasonably, and sanely. Two of my pickets spotted him in Copperfield, Oregon. He came out shooting, mortally wounding one of my men and killing the other outright. The wounded man killed the Judge before he himself died. I'm sorry about the way it came out. More sorry than you can know or understand.' His eyes darkened, and about that she believed him . . . but probably not in the way he *wanted* her to believe him. And she felt that coldness again.

'That's not the way they tell it here.'

'Believe them or believe me, dear. But remember I give them their orders.'

He was persuasive . . . goddamned persuasive. He seemed nearly harmless – but that wasn't exactly true, was it? That feeling only came from seeing that he was a man . . . or something that *looked* like a man. There was enough relief in just that to turn her into something like Silly Putty. He had a presence, and a politician's knack of knocking all your best arguments into a cocked hat . . . but he did it in a way she found very disturbing.

'If you don't mean war, why the jets and all the other stuff you've got out at Indian Springs?'

'Defensive measures,' he said promptly. 'We're doing similar things at Searles Lake in California, and at Edwards Air Force Base. There's another group at the atomic reactor on Yakima Ridge in

Washington. Your folks will be doing the same thing . . . if they're not already.'

Dayna shook her head, very slowly. 'When I left the Zone, they were still trying to get the electric lights working again.'

'And I'd be happy to send them two or three technicians, except I happen to know that your Brad Kitchner already has things going nicely. They had a brief outage yesterday, but he solved the problem very quickly. It was a power overload out on Arapahoe.'

'How do you know all that?'

'Oh, I have my ways,' Flagg said genially. 'The old woman came back, by the way. Sweet old woman.'

'Mother Abagail?'

'Yes.' His eyes were distant and murky; sad, perhaps. 'She's dead. A pity. I really had hoped to meet her in person.'

'Dead? Mother Abagail is dead?'

The murky look cleared, and he smiled at her. 'Does that really surprise you so much?'

'No. But it surprises me that she came back. And it surprises me even more that you know.'

'She came back to die.'

'Did she say anything?'

For just a moment Flagg's mask of genial composure slipped, showing black and angry bafflement.

'No,' he said. 'I thought she might . . . might speak. But she died in a coma.'

'Are you sure?'

His smile reappeared, as radiant as the summer sun burning off ground-fog.

'Never mind her, Dayna. Let's talk of more pleasant things, such as your return to the Zone. I'm sure you'd rather be there than here. I have something for you to take back.' He reached into his shirt, removed a chamois bag, and took three service station maps from it. He handed them to Dayna, who looked at them with growing bewilderment. They showed the seven Western states. Certain areas were shaded in red. The hand-lettered key at the bottom of each map identified them as the areas where population had again begun to spring up.

'You want me to take *these*?'

'Yes. I know where your people are; I want you to know where mine are. As a gesture of good faith and friendship. And when you get back, I want you to tell them this: that Flagg means them no harm, and Flagg's people mean them no harm. Tell them not to send any more spies. If they want to send people over here, have them call it a diplomatic mission . . . or exchange students . . . or any damn thing. But have them come openly. Will you tell them that?'

She felt dazed, punchy. 'Sure. I'll tell them. But −'

'That's all.' He lifted his open, empty palms again. She saw something and leaned forward, unsettled.

'What are you looking at?' There was an edge in his voice.

'Nothing.'

But she had seen, and she knew from the narrow expression on his face that he knew she had. There were no lines on Flagg's palms. They were as smooth and as blank as the skin on an infant's stomach. No lifeline, no loveline, no rings or bracelets or loops. Just . . . blank.

They looked at each other for what seemed a very long time.

Then Flagg bounced to his feet and went toward the desk. Dayna also rose. She had actually begun to believe that he might let her go. He sat on the edge of the desk and drew the intercom toward him.

'I'll tell Lloyd to have the oil and the plugs and points changed on your cycle,' he said. 'I'll also tell him to have it gassed up. No more worries about gas or oil shortages now, hey? Plenty for all. Although there was a day − I remember it, and probably you do too, Dayna, when it seemed as if the whole world might go up in a series of nuclear fireballs over a lack of premium unleaded gasoline.' He shook his head. 'People were very, very stupid.' He thumbed the button on the intercom. 'Lloyd?'

'Yeah, right here.'

'Will you have Dayna's bike gassed and tuned up and left in front of the hotel? She's going to be leaving us.'

'Yes.'

Flagg clicked off. 'Well, that's it, dear.'

'I can . . . just go?'

'Yes, ma'am. It's been my pleasure.' He lifted his hand to the door . . . palm side down.

She went to the door. Her hand had barely brushed the knob when he said: 'There is one more thing. One . . . very minor thing.'

Dayna turned to look at him. He was grinning at her, and it was a friendly grin, but for a flashing second she was reminded of a huge black mastiff, its tongue lolling over white spiked teeth that could rip off an arm as if it was a dishrag.

'What's that?'

'There's one more of your people over here,' Flagg said. His smile widened. 'Who might that be?'

'How in the world would *I* know?' Dayna asked, and her mind flashed: *Tom Cullen! . . . Could it really have been him?*

'Oh, come now, dear. I thought we had it all straightened out.'

'Really,' she said. 'Look at it straight ahead and you'll see I'm being dead honest. The committee sent me . . . and the Judge . . . and who knows how many others . . . and they were very careful. Just so we couldn't tattle on each other if something . . . you know, happened.'

'If we decided to pull some fingernails?'

'Okay, yes. I was approached by Sue Stern. I'd guess Larry Underwood . . . he's on the committee, too —'

'I know who Mr Underwood is.'

'Yes, well, I'd guess he asked the Judge. But as for anyone else . . .' She shook her head. 'It could be anyone. Or anyones. For all I know each of the seven committee members was responsible for recruiting one spy.'

'Yes, that could be, but it isn't. There's only one, and you know who it is.' His grin widened yet more, and now it began to frighten her. It was not a natural thing. It began to remind her of dead fish, polluted water, the surface of the moon seen through a telescope. It made her bladder feel loose and full of hot liquid.

'You *know*,' Flagg repeated.

'No, I —'

Flagg bent over the intercom again. 'Has Lloyd left yet?'

'No, I'm right here.' Expensive intercom, good reproduction.

'Hold off a bit on Dayna's cycle,' he said. 'We still have a matter to' — he looked at her, and his eyes glimmered speculatively — 'to thrash out in here,' he finished.

'Okay.'

The intercom clicked off. Flagg looked at her, smiling, hands folded. He looked for a very long time. Dayna began to sweat. His eyes seemed to grow larger and darker. Looking into them was like looking into wells which were very old and very deep. This time when she tried to drag her gaze away, she couldn't.

'Tell me,' he said, very softly. 'Let's not have any unpleasantness, dear.'

From far off, she heard her voice say, 'This whole thing was a script, wasn't it? A little one-act play.'

'Dear, I don't understand what you mean.'

'Yes, you do. The mistake was having Lloyd answer so fast. When you say frog around here, they jump. He should have been halfway down the Strip with my cycle. Except you told him to stay put because you never intended to let me go.'

'Dear, you've got a terrible case of unfounded paranoia. It was your experience with those men, I suspect. The ones with the traveling zoo. It must have been a terrible thing. *This* could be a terrible thing, too, and we don't want that, do we?'

Her strength was draining away; it seemed to be flowing down her legs in perfect lines of force. With the last of her will, she turned her numb right hand into a fist and struck herself above the right eye. There was an airburst of pain inside her skull and her vision went wavery. Her head rocked back and struck the door with a hollow whack. Her gaze snapped away from his, and she felt her will returning. And her strength to resist.

'Oh, you're *good*,' she said raggedly.

'You know who it is,' he said. He got off the desk and began to walk toward her. 'You know and you're going to tell me. Punching yourself in the head won't help, dear.'

'How come you don't know?' she cried at him. 'You knew about the Judge and you knew about me! How come you don't know about –'

His hands descended on her shoulders with terrible power, and they were cold, as cold as marble. 'Who?'

'I don't know.'

He shook her like a ragdoll, his face grinning and fierce and terrible. His hands were cold, but his face gave off the baking oven heat of the desert. 'You know. Tell me. Who?'

'Why don't you know?'

'Because I can't see it!' he roared, and flung her across the room. She went in a boneless, rolling heap, and when she saw the searchlight of his face bearing down upon her in the gloom, her bladder let go, spreading warmth down her legs. The soft and helpful face of reason was gone. Randy Flagg was gone. She was with the Walkin Dude now, the tall man, the big guy, and God help her.

'You'll tell,' he said. 'You'll tell me what I want to know.'

She gazed at him, and then slowly got to her feet. She felt the weight of the knife lying against her forearm.

'Yes, I'll tell you,' she said. 'Come closer.'

He took a step toward her, grinning.

'No, a lot closer. I want to whisper it in your ear.'

He came closer still. She could feel baking heat, freezing cold. There was a high, atonal singing in her ears. She could smell damprot, high, sweet, and cloying. She could smell madness like dead vegetables in a dark cellar.

'Closer,' she whispered huskily.

He took another step and she cocked her right wrist in viciously. She heard the spring click. Weight slapped into her hand.

'*Here!*' she shrieked hysterically, and brought her arm up in a hard sweep, meaning to gut him, leaving him to blunder around the room with his intestines hanging out in steaming loops. Instead he roared laughter, hands on his hips, flaming face cocked back, squeezing and contorting with great good humor.

'Oh, my *dear!*' he cried, and went off into another gale of laughter.

She looked stupidly down at her hand. It held a firm yellow banana with a blue and white Chiquita sticker on it. She dropped it, horrified, to the carpet, where it became a sickly yellow grin, miming Flagg's own.

'You'll tell,' he whispered. 'Oh yes indeed you will.'

And Dayna knew he was right.

She whirled quickly, so quickly that even the dark man was momentarily caught by surprise. One of those black hands snatched out and caught only the back of her blouse, leaving him with nothing more substantial than a swatch of silk.

Dayna leaped at the window-wall.

'*No!*' he screamed, and she could feel him after her like a black wind.

She drove with her lower legs, using them like pistons, hitting the window with the top of her head. There was a dull flat cracking sound, and she saw amazingly thick hunks of glass fall out into the employees' parking lot. Twisting cracks, like lodes of quicksilver, ran out from her point of impact. Momentum carried her halfway through the hole and it was there that she lodged, bleeding.

She felt *his* hands on her shoulders and wondered how long it would take him to make her tell. An hour? Two? She suspected she was dying now, but that was not good enough.

It was *Tom I saw, and you can't feel him or whatever it is you do because he's different, he's –*

He was dragging her back in.

She killed herself by simply whipping her head viciously around to the right. A razor-sharp jag of glass plunged deep into her throat. Another slipped into her right eye. Her body went stiff for a moment, and her hands beat against the glass. Then she went limp. What the dark man dragged back into the office was only a bleeding sack.

She had gone, perhaps in triumph.

Bellowing his rage, Flagg kicked her. The yielding, indifferent movement of her body enraged him further. He began to kick her around the room, bellowing, snarling. Sparks began to jump from his hair, as if somewhere inside him a cyclotron had hummed into life, building up an electrical field and turning him into a battery. His eyes blazed with dark fire. He bellowed and kicked, kicked and bellowed.

Outside, Lloyd and the others grew pale. They looked at each other. At last it was more than they could stand. Jenny, Ken, Whitney – they drifted away, and their curdled–milk faces were set in the careful expressions of people who hear nothing and want to go right on hearing it.

Only Lloyd waited – not because he wanted to, but because he knew it was expected of him. And at last Flagg called him in.

He was sitting on the wide desk, his legs crossed, his hands on the knees of his jeans. He was looking over Lloyd's head, out into space. There was a draft, and Lloyd saw that the window–wall was smashed in the middle. The jagged edges of the hole were sticky with blood.

Resting on the floor was a huddled, vaguely human form wrapped in a drape.

'Get rid of that,' Flagg said.

'Okay.' His voice fell to a husky whisper. 'Should I take the head?'

'Take the whole thing out to the east of town and douse it in gasoline and burn it. Do you hear me? *Burn* it! *You burn the fucking thing!*'

'All right.'

'Yes.' Flagg smiled benignly.

Trembling, cotton-mouthed, nearly groaning with terror, Lloyd struggled to pick up the bulky object. The underside was sticky. It made a U in his arms, slithered through them, and thumped back to the floor. He threw a terrified glance at Flagg, but he was still in a semi-lotus, looking outward. Lloyd got hold of it again, clutched it, and staggered toward the door.

'Lloyd?'

He stopped and looked back. A little moan escaped him. Flagg was still in the semi-lotus, but now he was floating about ten inches above the desk, still looking serenely across the room.

'W-W-What?'

'Do you still have the key I gave you in Phoenix?'

'Yes.'

'Keep it handy. The time is coming.'

'A-All right.'

He waited, but Flagg did not speak again. He hung in the darkness, a mind-boggling Hindu fakir's trick, looking outward, smiling gently.

Lloyd left quickly, happy as always just to go with his life and his sanity.

That day was a quiet one in Vegas. Lloyd arrived back around 2 PM, smelling of gasoline. The wind had started to rise, and by five o'clock it was howling up and down the Strip and making forlorn hooting noises between the hotels. The palms, which had begun to die without city water in July and August, flapped against the sky like tattered battle flags. Clouds in strange shapes scudded overhead.

In the Cub Bar, Whitney Horgan and Ken DeMott sat drinking bottled beer and eating egg salad sandwiches. Three old ladies – the Weird Sisters, everyone called them – kept chickens on the outskirts of town, and no one could seem to get enough eggs. Below Whitney and Ken, in the casino, little Dinny McCarthy was crawling happily around on one of the crap tables with an array of plastic soldiers.

'Lookit that little squirt,' Ken said fondly. 'Someone ast me if I'd watch him an hour. I'd watch him all week. I wish to God he was mine. My wife only had the one, and he was two months premature. Died in the incubator the third day out.' He looked up as Lloyd came in.

'Hey, Dinny!' Lloyd called.

'Yoyd! Yoyd!' Dinny cried. He ran to the edge of the crap table, jumped down, and ran to him. Lloyd picked him up, swung him, and hugged him hard.

'Got kisses for Lloyd?' he asked.

Dinny smacked him with noisy kisses.

'I got something for you,' Lloyd said, and took a handful of foil-wrapped Hershey's Kisses from his breast pocket.

Dinny crowed with delight and clutched them. 'Yoyd?'

'What, Dinny?'

'Why do you smell like a gasoline pile?'

Lloyd smiled. 'I was burning some trash, honey. You go on and play. Who's your mom now?'

'Angelina.' He pronounced it *Angeyeena*. 'Then Bonnie again. I like Bonnie. But I like Angelina, too.'

'Don't tell her Lloyd gave you candy. Angelina would spank Lloyd.'

Dinny promised not to tell and ran off giggling at the image of Angelina spanking Lloyd. In a minute or two he was back on the DON'T COME line of the crap table, generaling his army with his mouth crammed full of chocolate.

Whitney came over, wearing his white apron. He had two sandwiches for Lloyd and a cold bottle of Hamm's.

'Thanks,' Lloyd said. 'Looks great.'

'That's homemade Syrian bread,' Whitney said proudly.

Lloyd munched for a while. 'Has anybody seen him?' he asked at last.

Ken shook his head. 'I think he's gone again.'

Lloyd thought it over. Outside, a stronger-than-average gust of wind shrieked by, sounding lonely and lost in the desert. Dinny raised his head uneasily for a moment and then bent back to play.

'I think he's around somewhere,' Lloyd said finally. 'I don't know why, but I do. I think he's around waiting for something to happen. I dunno what.'

Whitney said in a low voice, 'You think he got it out of her?'

'No,' Lloyd said, watching Dinny. 'I don't think he did. It went wrong for him somehow. She . . . she got lucky or she outthought him. And that doesn't happen often.'

'It won't matter in the long run,' Ken said, but he looked troubled just the same.

'No, it won't.' Lloyd listened to the wind for a while. 'Maybe he's gone back to LA.' But he didn't really think so, and his face showed it.

Whitney went back to the kitchen and produced another round of beer. They drank in silence, thinking disquieting thoughts. First the Judge, now the woman. Both dead. And neither had talked. Neither had been unmarked as *he* had ordered. It was as if the old Yankees of Mantle and Maris and Ford had lost the opening two games of the World Series; it was hard for them to believe, and frightening.

The wind blew hard all night.

CHAPTER 63

On the late afternoon of September 10, Dinny was playing in the small city park that lies just north of the city's hotel and casino district. His 'mother' that week, Angelina Hirschfield, was sitting on a park bench and talking with a young girl who had drifted into Las Vegas about five weeks before, ten days or so after Angie herself had come in.

Angie Hirschfield was twenty-seven. The girl was ten years younger, now clad in tight bluejeans shorts and a brief middy blouse which left absolutely nothing to the imagination. There was something obscene about the contrast between the tight allure of her young body and the childish, pouty, and rather vacuous expression on her face. Her conversation was monotonous and seemingly without end: rock stars, sex, her lousy job cleaning Cosmoline preservative off armaments at Indian Springs, sex, her diamond ring, sex, the TV programs that she missed so much, and sex.

Angie wished she would go have sex with someone and leave her alone. And she hoped Dinny would be at least thirty before he ever worked around to having this girl for a mother.

At that moment Dinny looked up, smiled, and yelled: 'Tom! Hey, Tom!'

On the other side of the park, a big man with straw-blond hair was shambling along with a big workman's lunch bucket slamming against his leg.

'Say, that guy looks drunk,' the girl said to Angie.

Angie smiled. 'No, that's Tom. He's just —'

But Dinny was off and running, hollering 'Tom! Wait up, Tom!' at the top of his lungs.

Tom turned, grinning. 'Dinny! Hey-hey!'

Dinny leaped at Tom. Tom dropped his lunch bucket and grabbed him. Swung him around.

'Airplane me, Tom! Airplane me!'

Tom grabbed Dinny's wrists and began to spin him around, faster and faster. Centrifugal force pulled the boy's body out until his whizzing legs were parallel to the ground. He shrieked with laughter. After two or three spins, Tom set him gently on his feet.

Dinny wobbled around, laughing and trying to get his balance back.

'Do it again, Tom! Do it again some more!'

'No, you'll puke if I do. And Tom's got to get to his home. Laws, yes.'

''Kay, Tom. 'Bye!'

Angie said, 'I think Dinny loves Lloyd Henreid and Tom Cullen more than anyone else in town. Tom Cullen is simple, but —' She looked at the girl and broke off. She was watching Tom, her eyes narrowed and thoughtful.

'Did he come in with another man?' she asked.

'Who? Tom? No — as far as I know, he came in all by himself about a week and a half ago. He was with those other people in their Zone, but they drove him out. Their loss is our gain, that's what I say.'

'And he didn't come in with a dummy? A deaf-and-dummy?'

'A deaf-mute? No, I'm pretty sure he came in alone. Dinny just loves him.'

The girl watched Tom out of sight. She thought of Pepto-Bismol in a bottle. She thought of a scrawled note that said: *We don't need you.* That had been back in Kansas, a thousand years ago. She had shot at them. She wished she had killed them, particularly the dummy.

'Julie? Are you all right?'

Julie Lawry didn't answer. She stared after Tom Cullen. In a little while, she began to smile.

CHAPTER 64

The dying man opened the Permacover notebook, uncapped his pen, paused a moment, and then began to write.

It was strange; where once the pen had flown over the paper, seeming to cover each sheet from top to bottom by a process of benign magic, the words now straggled and draggled, the letters large and tottery, as if he was regressing back to early grammar school days in his own private time machine.

In those days, his mother and father had still had some love left over for him. Amy had not yet blossomed, and his own future as The Amazing Ogunquit Fat Boy and Possible Hommasexshul was not yet decided. He could remember sitting at the sun-washed kitchen table, slowly copying one of the Tom Swift books word for word in a Blue Horse tablet – pulp stock, blue lines – with a glass of Coke beside him. He could hear his mother's words drifting out of the living room. Sometimes she was talking on the phone, sometimes to a neighbor.

It's just baby fat, the doctor says so. There's nothing wrong with his glands, thank God. And he's so bright!

Watching the words grow, letter by letter. Watching the sentences grow, word by word. Watching the paragraphs grow, each one a brick in the great walled bulwark that was language.

'It's to be my greatest invention,' Tom said forcefully. 'Watch what happens when I pull out the plate, but for gosh sakes, don't forget to shield your eyes!'

The bricks of language. A stone, a leaf, an unfound door. Words. Worlds. Magic. Life and immortality. *Power.*

I don't know where he gets it, Rita. Maybe from his grandfather. He was an ordained minister and they say he gave the most wonderful sermons . . .

Watching the letters improve as time passed. Watching them connect with each other, printing left behind, *writing* now. Assembling thoughts and plots. That was the whole world, after all, nothing but thoughts and plots. He had gotten a typewriter finally (and by then there wasn't much else left over for him; Amy was in high school, National Honor Society, cheerleader, dramatics club, debate society, straight A's, the braces had come off her teeth and her very best friend in the world was Frannie Goldsmith . . . and her brother's baby fat had not yet departed although he was thirteen years old, and he had begun to use big words as a defense, and with a slowly blooming horror he had begun to realize what life was, what it *really* was: one big heathen cooking pot, and he was the missionary alone inside, being slowly boiled). The typewriter unlocked the rest of it for him. At first it was slow, so slow, and the constant typos were frustrating beyond belief. It was as if the machine was actively – but slyly – opposing his will. But when he got better at it, he began to understand what the machine really was – a kind of magic conduit between his brain and the blank page he strove to conquer. By the time of the superflu epidemic he was able to type better than a hundred words a minute, and he was at last able to keep up with his racing thoughts and snare them all. But he had never stopped his longhand entirely, remembering that *Moby Dick* had been written longhand, and *The Scarlet Letter*, and *Paradise Lost*.

He had developed the writing Frannie had seen in his ledger over years of practice – no paragraphs, no line breaks, no pause for the eye. It was work – terrible, hand-cramping work – but it was a labor of love. He had used the typewriter willingly and gratefully, but thought he had always saved the best of himself for longhand.

And now he would transcribe the last of himself that same way.

He looked up and saw buzzards circling slowly in the sky, like something from a Saturday matinee movie with Randolph Scott, or from a novel by Max Brand. He thought of it written in a novel: *Harold saw the buzzards circling in the sky, waiting. He looked at them calmly for a moment, and then bent to his journal again.*

He bent to his journal again.

At the end, he had been forced to return to the straggling letters which had been the best his shaky motor control could produce at the beginning. He was reminded achingly of the sunny kitchen, the cold glass of Coke, the old and mildewy Tom Swift books. And now, at last, he thought (and wrote), he might have been able to make his mother and father happy. He had lost his baby fat. And although still technically a virgin, he was morally sure that he was not a hommasexshul.

He opened his mouth and croaked, 'Top of the world, Ma.'

He was halfway down the page. He looked at what he had written, then looked at his leg, which was twisted and broken. Broken? That was too kind a word. It was shattered. He had been sitting in the shade of this rock for five days now. The last of his food was gone. He would have died of thirst yesterday or the day before except for two hard showers. His leg was putrefying. It had a green and gassy smell and the flesh had swelled tight against his pants, stretching the khaki fabric until it resembled a sausage casing.

Nadine was long gone.

Harold picked up the gun that had been lying by his side, and checked the loads. He had checked them a hundred times or more just this day. During the rainstorms, he had been careful to keep the gun dry. There were three cartridges left in it. He had fired the first two at Nadine when she looked down and told him she was going on without him.

They had been coming around a hairpin turn, Nadine on the inside, Harold on the outside aboard his Triumph cycle. They were on the Colorado Western Slope, about seventy miles from the Utah border. There had been an oilslick on the outer part of the curve, and in the days since, Harold had pondered much on this oilslick. It seemed almost *too* perfect. An oilslick from *what*? Surely nothing had been moving up here over the last two months. Plenty of time for a slick to dry up. It was as if *his* red eye had been watching them, waiting for the correct time to produce an oilslick and take Harold out of the play. Leave him with her through the mountains in case of trouble, and then ditch him. He had, as they say, served his purpose.

The Triumph had slid into the guardrail, and Harold had been flicked over the side like a bug. There had been an excruciating pain in his right leg. He had heard the wet snap as it broke. He screamed. Then hardscrabble was coming up to meet him, hardscrabble that was falling away at a steep, sickening angle toward the gorge below. He could hear fast-flowing water somewhere down there.

He hit the ground, cartwheeled high into the air, screamed again, came down on his right leg once more, heard it break someplace else, went flying into the air again, came down, rolled, and suddenly fetched up against a dead tree that had heeled over in some years-ago thunderstorm. If it hadn't been there, he would have gone into the gorge and the mountain trout could have snacked on him instead of the buzzards.

He wrote in his notebook, still marveling at the straggling, child-size letters: *I don't blame Nadine.* That was true. But he had blamed her then.

Shocked, shaken, scraped raw, his right leg a bolt of agony, he had picked himself up and had crawled a little way up the slope. Far above him, he saw Nadine looking over the guardrail. Her face was white and tiny, a doll's face.

'Nadine!' he cried. His voice came out in a hard croak. 'The rope! It's in the left saddlebag!'

She only looked down at him. He had begun to think she hadn't heard him and he was preparing to repeat when he saw her head move to the left, to the right, to the left again. Very slowly. She was shaking her head.

'Nadine! I can't get up without the rope! My leg's broken!'

She didn't answer. She was only looking down at him, not even shaking her head now. He began to have the feeling he was down in a deep hole, and she was looking at him over the rim of it.

'Nadine, toss me the rope!'

That slow headshaking again, as terrible as the door of a crypt swinging slowly shut on a man not yet dead but rather in the grip of some terrible catalepsy.

'NADINE! FOR THE LOVE OF GOD!'

At last her voice drifted down to him, small but perfectly audible in the great mountain stillness. 'All of this was arranged, Harold. I have to go on. I'm very sorry.'

But she made no move to go; she remained at the guardrail, watching him where he lay some two hundred feet below. Already there were flies, busily sampling his blood on the various rocks where he had hit and scraped off some of himself.

Harold began to crawl upward, dragging his shattered leg behind him. At first there was no hate, no need to put a bullet in her. It only seemed vital that he get close enough to read her expression.

It was a little past noon. It was hot. Sweat dripped from his face and onto the sharp pebbles and rocks he was climbing over. He moved by dragging himself upward on his elbows and pushing with his left leg, like a crippled insect. His breath rasped in and out of his throat, a hot file. He had no idea how long it went on, but once or twice he bumped his bad leg against a stone outcropping, and the giant burst of pain had caused him to gray out. Several times he had slipped backward, moaning helplessly.

At last he became stupidly aware that he could go no farther. The shadows had changed. Three hours had passed. He could not remember the last time he had looked up toward the guardrail and the road; over an hour ago, surely. In his pain, he had been completely absorbed in whatever minute progress he was making. Nadine had probably left long ago.

But she had still been there, and although he had only succeeded in gaining twenty-five feet or so, the expression on her face was hellishly clear. It was one of grieving sorrow, but her eyes were flat and far away.

Her eyes were with *him*.

That was when he began to hate her, and he felt for the shoulder holster. The Colt was still there, held in during his tumbling fall by the strap across the butt. He snapped the strap off, hunching his body craftily so she wouldn't see.

'Nadine –'

'It's better this way, Harold. Better for you, because *his* way would be so much worse. You see that, don't you? You wouldn't want to meet him face-to-face, Harold. He feels that someone who would betray one side would probably betray the other. He'd kill you, but he'd drive you mad first. He has that power. He let me choose. This way . . . or *his* way. I chose this. You can end it quickly if you're brave. You know what I mean.'

He checked the loads in the pistol for the first of hundreds (maybe thousands) of times, keeping the gun in the shadowed hollow of one lacerated and shredded elbow.

'What about you?' he called up. 'Aren't you a betrayer, too?'

Her voice was sad. 'I never betrayed him in my heart.'

'I believe that's exactly where you did betray him,' Harold called up to her. He tried to put a large expression of sincerity on his face, but he was actually calculating the distance. He would have two shots at the most. And a pistol was a notoriously chancy weapon. 'I believe he knows it, too.'

'He needs me,' she said, 'and I need him. You were never in it, Harold. And if we'd gone on together, I might have . . . might have let you do something to me. That small thing. And that would have destroyed everything. I couldn't take the smallest chance that might happen after all the sacrifice and blood and nastiness. We sold our souls together, Harold, but there's enough of me left to want full value for mine.'

'I'll give you full value,' Harold said, and managed to get up on his knees. The sun was dazzling. Vertigo seized him in rough hands, whirling the gyroscope balance inside his head. He seemed to hear voices – *a voice* – roaring in surprised protest. He pulled the trigger. The shot echoed, bounced back, was thrown from cliff-face to cliff-face, cracking and whacking and fading. Comical surprise spread over Nadine's face.

Harold thought in a drunken kind of triumph: *She didn't think I had it in me!* Her mouth hung open in a shocked, round O. Her eyes were wide. The fingers of her hands tensed and flew up, as if she were about to play some abnormal tune on the piano. The moment was so sweet that he lost a second or two savoring it and not realizing that he had missed. When he did realize, he brought the pistol back down, trying to aim it, locking his right wrist with his left hand.

'Harold! No! You can't!'

Can't I? It's such a little thing, squeezing a trigger. Sure I can.

She seemed too shocked to move, and as the pistol's front sight came to rest in the hollow of her throat, he felt a sudden cold certainty that this was how it had been meant to end, in a short and meaningless spate of violence.

He had her, dead in his sights.

But as he started to pull the trigger, two things happened. Sweat ran into his eyes, doubling his vision. And he began to slide. He later told himself that the loose gravel had given way, or that his mangled leg had buckled, or both. It might even have been true. But it felt . . . *it felt like a push*, and in the long nights between then and now, he had not been able to convince himself otherwise. The daytime Harold was stubbornly rational to the end, but in the night the hideous certainty stole over him that in the end it was the dark man himself who had stepped in to thwart him. The shot he had meant to put smack into the hollow of her throat went wild: high, wide, and handsome into the indifferent blue sky. Harold went rolling and tumbling back down to the dead tree, his right leg twisting and buckling, a huge sheet of agony from ankle to groin.

He had struck the tree and passed out. When he came to again, it was just past dusk and the moon, three quarters full, was riding solemnly over the gorge. Nadine was gone.

He spent the first night in a delirium of terror, sure that he would be unable to crawl back up to the road, sure he would die in the ravine. When morning came he began to crawl upward again nevertheless, sweating and racked with pain.

He began around seven o'clock, just about the time the big orange Burial Committee trucks would be leaving the bus depot back in Boulder. He finally wrapped one raw and blistered hand around the guardrail cable at five o'clock that afternoon. His motorcycle was still there, and he nearly wept with relief. He dug some cans and the opener out of one of the saddlebags with frantic haste, opened one of the cans, and crammed cold corned beef hash into his mouth in double handfuls. But it tasted bad, and after a long struggle he threw it up.

He began to understand the irrefutable fact of his coming death then, and he lay beside the Triumph and wept, his twisted leg under him. After that he was able to sleep a little.

The following day he was drenched by a pounding rain-shower that left him soaked and shivering. His leg had begun to smell of gangrene, and he took pains to keep the Cold Woodsman sheltered from the wet with his body. That evening he had begun to write in the Permacover notebook and discovered for the first time that his handwriting was beginning to regress. He found himself thinking of a story by Daniel Keyes – 'Flowers for Algernon,' it had been called. In it, a bunch of scientists had somehow turned a mentally retarded janitor into a genius . . . for a while. And then the poor guy began to lose it. What was the guy's name? Charley something, right? Sure, because that was the name of the movie they made out of it. *Charly*. A pretty good movie. Not as good as the story, full of sixties psychedelic shit as he remembered, but still pretty good. Harold had gone to the movies a lot in the old days, and he had watched a lot more on the family VCR. Back in the days when the world had been what the Pentagon would have called a quote viable alternative unquote. He had watched most of them alone.

He wrote in his notebook, the words emerging slowly from the straggling letters:

Are they all dead, I wonder? The committee? If so, I
am sorry. I was misled. That is a poor excuse for my
actions, but I swear out of all I know that it is the
only excuse that ever matters. The dark man is as real
as the superflu itself, as real as the atomic bombs that

> still sit somewhere in their leadlined closets. And
> when the end comes, and when it is as horrible as
> good men always knew it would be, there is only one
> thing to say as all those good men approach the
> Throne of Judgment: I was misled.

Harold read what he had written and passed a thin and trembling hand over his brow. It wasn't a good excuse; it was a bad one. Pretty it up however you would, it still smelled. Someone who read that paragraph after reading his ledger would see him as a total hypocrite. He had seen himself as the king of anarchy, but the dark man had seen through him and had reduced him effortlessly to a shivering bag of bones dying badly by the highway. His leg had swelled up like an innertube, it smelled like gassy, overripe bananas, and he sat here with buzzards swooping and diving on the thermals overhead, trying to rationalize the unspeakable. He had fallen victim to his own protracted adolescence, it was as simple as that. He had been poisoned by his own lethal visions.

Dying, he felt as if he had gained a little sanity and maybe even a little dignity. He did not want to demean that with small excuses that would come limping off the page on crutches.

'I could have been something in Boulder,' he said quietly, and the simple, awful truth of that might have brought tears if he hadn't been so tired and so dehydrated. He looked at the straggling letters on the page, and from there to the Colt. Suddenly he wanted it over, and he tried to think how to put a finish to his life in the truest, simplest way he could. It seemed more necessary than ever to write it and leave it for whoever might find him, in one year or in ten.

He gripped the pen. Thought. Wrote:

> I apologize for the destructive things I have done, but
> do not deny that I did them of my own free will. On
> my school papers, I always signed my name Harold
> Emery Lauder. I signed my manuscripts – poor things
> that they were – the same way. God help me, I once
> wrote it on the roof of a barn in letters three feet high.
> I want to sign this by a name given me in Boulder. I
> could not accept it then, but I take it now freely.
> I am going to die in my right mind.

Writing neatly at the bottom, he affixed his signature: *Hawk*.

He put the Permacover notebook into the Triumph's saddlebag. He capped the pen and clipped it in his pocket. He put the muzzle of the Colt into his mouth and looked up at the blue sky. He thought of a game they had played when they were children, a game the others had teased him about because he never quite dared to go through with it. There was a gravel pit out on one of the back roads, and you could jump off the edge and fall a heartstopping distance before hitting the sand, rolling over and over, and finally climbing up to do it all over again.

All except Harold. Harold would stand on the lip of the drop and chant, *One . . . Two . . . Three!* just like the others, but the talisman never worked. His legs remained locked. He could not bring himself to jump. And the others sometimes chased him home, shouting at him, calling him Harold the Pansy.

He thought: *If I could have brought myself to jump once . . . just once . . . I might not be here. Well, last time pays for all.*

He thought: *One . . . Two . . . THREE!*

He pulled the trigger.

The gun went off.

Harold jumped.

CHAPTER 65

North of Las Vegas is Emigrant Valley, and that night a small spark of fire glowed in its tumbled wilderness. Randall Flagg sat beside it, moodily cooking the carcass of a small rabbit. He turned it steadily on the crude rotisserie he had made, watching it sizzle and spit grease into the fire. There was a light breeze, blowing the savory smell out into the desert, and the wolves had come. They sat two rises over from his fire, howling at the nearly full moon and at the smell of cooking meat. Every now and then he would glance at them and two or three would begin to fight, biting and snapping and kicking with their powerful back legs until the weakest was banished. Then the others would begin to howl again, their snouts pointed at the bloated, reddish moon.

But the wolves bored him now.

He wore his jeans and his tattered walking boots and his sheepskin jacket with its two buttons on the breast pockets: smiley-smile and HOW'S YOUR PORK? The night wind flapped fitfully at his collar.

He didn't like the way things were going.

There were bad omens in the wind, evil portents like bats fluttering in the dark loft of a deserted barn. The old woman had died and at first he had thought that was good. In spite of everything, he had been afraid of the old woman. She had died, and he had told Dayna Jurgens that she had died in a coma . . . but was it true? He was no longer quite so sure.

Had she talked, at the end? And if so, what had she said?

What were they planning?

He had developed a sort of third eye. It was like the levitating ability; something he had and accepted but which he didn't really understand. He was able to send it out, to see . . . almost always. But sometimes the eye fell mysteriously blind. He had been able to look into the old woman's death chamber, had seen them gathered around her, their tailfeathers still singed from Harold and Nadine's little surprise . . . but then the vision had faded away and he had been back in the desert, wrapped in his bedroll, looking up and seeing nothing but Cassiopeia in her starry rocking chair. And there had been a voice inside him that said: *She's gone. They waited for her to talk but she never did.*

But he no longer trusted the voice.

There was the troubling matter of the spies.

The Judge, with his head blown off.

The girl, who had eluded him at the last second. And she had known, Goddammit! *She had known!*

He threw a sudden furious stare at the wolves and nearly half a dozen fell to fighting, their guttural sounds like ripping cloth in the stillness.

He knew all their secrets except . . . the third. Who was the third? He had sent the Eye out over and over again, and it afforded him with nothing but the cryptic, idiotic face of the moon. M-O-O-N, that spells moon.

Who was the third?

How had the girl been able to escape him? He had been taken utterly by surprise, left with nothing but a handful of her blouse. He had known about her knife, that had been child's play, but not about that sudden leap at the window-wall. And the coldblooded way she had taken her own life, without a moment's hesitation. A mere space of seconds and she had been gone.

His thoughts chased each other like weasels in the dark.

Things were getting just a trifle flaky around the edges. He didn't like it.

Lauder, for instance. There was Lauder.

He had performed so *excellently*, like one of those little wind-up toys with a key sticking out of its back. Go here. Go there. Do this. Do that. But the dynamite bomb had only gotten two of them − all that planning, all that *effort* spoiled by that dying old nigger woman's return. And then . . . after Harold had been disposed of . . . he had nearly killed Nadine! He still felt a burst of amazed anger when he thought about it. And the dumb cunt had stood there with her mouth hanging open, waiting for him to do it again, almost as if she *wanted* to be killed. And who was going to end up with all this, if Nadine died?

Who, if not his son?

The rabbit was done. He slipped it off the spit and onto his tin plate.

'All right, all you asshole gyrenes, chow down!'

That made him grin right out loud. Had he been a Marine once? He thought so. Strictly the Parris Island variety, though. There had been a kid, a defective, name of Boo Dinkway. They had . . .

What?

Flagg frowned down at his messkit. Had they beaten ole Boo into the ground with those padded poles? Scragged him somehow? He seemed to remember something about gasoline. But what?

In a sudden rage, he almost slung the freshly cooked rabbit into the fire. *He should be able to remember that, goddammit!*

'Chow down, grunts,' he whispered, but this time there was only a whiff of memory lane.

He was losing himself. Once he had been able to look back over the sixties, seventies, and eighties like a man looking down a double flight of stairs leading into a darkened room. Now he could only clearly remember the events since the superflu. Beyond that there was nothing but a haze that would sometimes lift a tiny bit, just enough to afford a glimpse of some enigmatic object or memory (Boo Dinkway, for instance . . . if there ever had been such a person) before closing down again.

The earliest memory he could now be sure of was of walking south on US 51, heading toward Mountain City and the home of Kit Bradenton.

Of being born. Born again.

He was no longer strictly a man, if he had ever been one. He was like an onion, slowly peeling away one layer at a time, only it was the trappings of humanity that seemed to be peeling away: organized reflection, memory, possibly even free will . . . if there ever had been such a thing.

He began to eat the rabbit.

Once, he was quite sure, he would have done a quick fade when things began to get flaky. Not this time. This was his place, his time, and he would take his stand here. It didn't matter that he hadn't yet been able to uncover the third spy, or that Harold had gotten out of control at the end and had had the colossal effrontery to try to kill the bride who had been promised, the mother of his son.

Somewhere that strange Trashcan Man was in the desert, sniffing out the weapons which would eradicate the troublesome, worrisome Free Zone forever. His Eye could not follow the Trashcan Man, and in some ways Flagg thought that Trash was stranger than he was himself, a kind of human bloodhound who sniffed cordite and napalm and gelignite with deadly radar accuracy.

In a month or less, the National Guard jets would be flying, with a full complement of Shrike missiles tucked under their wings. And when he was sure that the bride had conceived, they would fly east.

He looked dreamily up at the basketball moon and smiled.

There was one other possibility. He thought the Eye would show him, in time. He might go there, possibly as a crow, possibly as a wolf, possibly as an insect – a praying mantis, perhaps, something small enough to squirm through a carefully concealed vent cap in the middle of a spiky patch of desert grass. He would hop or crawl through dark conduits and finally slip through an air conditioner grille or a stilled exhaust fan.

The place was underground. Just over the border and into California.

There were beakers there, rows and rows of beakers, each with its own neat Dymo tape identifying it: a super cholera, a super anthrax, a new and improved version of the bubonic plague, all of them based on the shifting-antigen ability that had made the superflu so almost universally deadly. There were hundreds of them in this place; assorted flavors, as they used to say in the Life Savers commercials.

How about a little in your water, Free Zone?

How about a nice airburst?

Some lovely Legionnaires' disease for Christmas, or would you rather have the new and improved Swine flu?

Randy Flagg, the dark Santa, in his National Guard sleigh, with a little virus to drop down every chimney?

He would wait, and he would know the right time when it came round at last.

Something would tell him.

Things were going to be fine. No quick fade this time. He was on top and he was going to stay there.

The rabbit was gone. Full of hot food, he felt himself again. He stood, tin plate in hand, and slung the bones out into the night. The wolves charged at them, fought over them, growling and biting and snarling, their eyes rolling blankly in the moonlight.

Flagg stood, hands on his hips, and roared laughter up at the moon.

★   ★   ★

Early the next morning Nadine left the town of Glendale and headed down I-15 on her Vespa. Her snow-white hair, unbound, trailed out behind her, looking very much like a bridal train.

She felt sorry for the Vespa, which had served her so long and faithfully and which was now dying. Mileage and desert heat, the laborious crossing of the Rockies, and indifferent maintenance had all taken their toll. The engine now sounded hoarse and laboring. The RPM needle had begun to shudder instead of remaining docilely against the 5X1000 figure. It didn't matter. If it died on her before she arrived, she would walk. No one was chasing her now. Harold was dead. And if she had to walk, *he* would know and send someone out to pick her up.

Harold had shot at her! Harold had tried to *kill* her!

Her mind kept returning to that no matter how she tried to avoid it. Her mind worried it like a dog worrying a bone. It wasn't supposed to be that way. Flagg had come to her in a dream that first night after the explosion, when Harold finally allowed them to camp. He told her that he was going to leave Harold with her until the two of them were on the Western Slope, almost in Utah. Then he would be removed in a quick, painless accident. An oilslick. Over the side. No fuss, no muss, no bother.

But it *hadn't* been quick and painless, and Harold had almost *killed* her. The bullet had droned past within an inch of her cheek and still she had been unable to move. She had been frozen in shock, wondering how he could have done such a thing, how he could have been allowed to even *try* such a thing.

She had tried to rationalize it by telling herself it was Flagg's way of throwing a scare into her, of reminding her who it was she belonged to. But it made no sense! It was crazy! Even if it had made some sort of sense, there was a firm, knowing voice inside her which said the shooting incident had just been something Flagg had not been prepared against.

She tried to push the voice away, to bar the door against it the way a sane person will bar the door against an undesirable person with murder in his or her eyes. But she couldn't do it. The voice told her she was alive through blind chance now. That Harold's bullet could just as easily have gone between her eyes, and it wouldn't have been Randall Flagg's doing either way.

She called the voice a liar. Flagg knew everything, where the smallest sparrow had fallen −

No, that's God, the voice replied implacably. *God, he's not. You're alive through blind chance, and that means that all bets are off. You owe him nothing. You can turn around and go back, if you want to.*

Go back, that was a laugh. Go back *where*?

The voice had little to say on that subject; she would have been surprised if it did. If the dark's man's feet were made of clay, she had discovered the fact just a little late.

She tried to concentrate on the cool beauty of the desert morning instead of the voice. But the voice remained, so low and insistent she was barely aware of it:

If he didn't know Harold was going to be able to defy him and strike back at you, what else doesn't he know? And will it be a clean miss next time?

But oh dear God, it was too late. Too late by days, weeks, maybe even years. Why had that voice waited until it was useless to speak up?

And as if in agreement, the voice finally fell silent and she had the morning to herself. She rode without thinking, her eyes fixed on the road unreeling in front of her. The road that led to Las Vegas. The road that led to *him*.

The Vespa died that afternoon. There was a grinding clank deep in its guts and the engine stalled. She could smell something hot and abnormal, like frying rubber, drifting up from the engine case. Her speed had dropped from the steady forty she had been maintaining until she had been putting along at walking speed. Now she trundled it over into the breakdown lane and cranked the starter a few times, knowing it was useless. She had killed it. She had killed a lot of things on her way to her husband. She had been responsible for wiping out the entire Free Zone Committee and all of their invited guests at that final explosive meeting. And then there was Harold. Also, say-hey and by the way, let's not forget Fran Goldsmith's unborn baby.

That made her feel sick. She stumbled over to the guardrail and tossed up her light lunch. She felt hot, delirious, and very ill, the one living thing in a sunstruck desert nightmare. It was hot . . . so hot.

She turned back, wiping her mouth. The Vespa lay on its side like a dead animal. Nadine looked at it for a few moments and then began to walk. She had already passed Dry Lake. That meant she would have to sleep by the road tonight if no one picked her up.

With any luck she would reach Las Vegas in the morning. And suddenly she was sure that the dark man would let her walk. She would reach Las Vegas hungry and thirsty and burning with the desert heat, every last bit of the old life flushed from her system. The woman who had taught small children at a private school in New England would be gone, as dead as Napoleon. With her luck, the small voice which snapped and worried at her so would be the last part of the old Nadine to expire. But in the end, of course, that part would go, too.

She walked, and the afternoon advanced. Sweat rolled down her face. Quicksilver glimmered, always at the point where the highway met the faded-denim sky. She unbuttoned her light blouse and took it off, walking in her white cotton bra. Sunburn? So what? Frankly, my dear, I don't give a fuck.

By dusk she had gone a terrible shade of red that was nearly purple along the raised ridges of her collarbones. The cool of the evening came suddenly, making her shiver, and making her remember that she had left her camping gear with the Vespa.

She looked around doubtfully, seeing cars here and there, some of them buried in drifting sand up to their hood ornaments. The thought of sheltering in one of those tombs made her feel sick – even sicker than her terrible sunburn was making her feel.

I'm delirious, she thought.

Not that it mattered. She decided she would walk all night rather than sleep in one of those cars. If this were only the Midwest again. She could have found a barn, a haystack, a field of clover. A clean, soft place. Out here there was only the road, the sand, the baked hardpan of the desert.

She brushed her long hair away from her face and dully realized that she wished she was dead.

Now the sun was below the horizon, the day perfectly poised between light and dark. The wind that now slipped over her was dead cold. She looked around herself, suddenly afraid.

It was *too* cold.

The buttes had become dark monoliths. The sand dunes were like ominous toppled colossi. Even the spiny stands of saguaro were like the skeletal fingers of the accusing dead, poking up out of the sand from their shallow graves.

Overhead, the cosmic wheel of the sky.

A snatch of lyric occurred to her, a Dylan song, cold and comfortless: *Hunted like a crocodile . . . ravaged in the corn . . .*

And on the heels of that, some other song, an Eagles song, suddenly frightening: *And I want to sleep with you in the desert tonight . . . with a million stars all around . . .*

Suddenly she knew he was there.

Even before he spoke, she knew.

'Nadine,' *His* soft voice, coming out of the growing darkness. Infinitely soft, the final enveloping terror that was like coming home.

'Nadine, Nadine . . . how I love to love Nadine.'

She turned around and there he was, as she had always known he would be someday, a thing as simple as this. He was sitting on the hood of an old Chevrolet sedan (had it been there a moment ago? she didn't know for sure, but she didn't think it had been), his legs crossed, his hands laid lightly on the knees of his faded jeans. Looking at her and smiling gently. But his eyes were not gentle at all. They gave lie to the idea that this man felt anything gentle. In them she saw a black glee that danced endlessly like the legs of a man fresh through the trapdoor in a gibbet platform.

'Hello,' she said. 'I'm here.'

'Yes. At last you're here. As promised.' His smile broadened and he held his hands out to her. She took them, and as she reached him she felt his baking heat. He radiated it, like a well-stoked brick oven. His smooth, lineless hands slipped around hers . . . and then closed over them tight, like handcuffs.

'Oh, Nadine,' he whispered, and bent to kiss her. She turned her head just a little, looking up at the cold fire of the stars, and his kiss was on the hollow below her jaw rather than on her lips. He wasn't fooled. She felt the mocking curve of his grin against her flesh.

He revolts me, she thought.

But revulsion was only a scaly crust over something worse – a caked and long-hidden lust, an ageless pimple finally brought to a head and about to spew forth some noisome fluid, some sweetness long since curdled. His hands, slipping over her back, were much hotter than her sunburn. She moved against him, and suddenly the slim saddle between her legs seemed plumper, fuller, more tender, more aware. The seam of her slacks was chafing her in a delicately obscene way that made her want to rub herself, get rid of the itch, cure it once and for all.

'Tell me one thing,' she said.

'Anything.'

'You said, "As promised." Who promised me to you? Why me? And what do I call you? I don't even know that. I've known about you for most of my life, and I don't know what to call you.'

'Call me Richard. That's my real name. Call me that.'

'That's your real name? Richard?' she asked doubtfully, and he giggled against her neck, making her skin crawl with loathing and desire. 'And who promised me?'

'Nadine,' he said, 'I have forgotten. Come on.'

He slipped off the hood of the car, still holding her hands, and she almost jerked them away and ran . . . but what good would that have done? He would only chase after her, catch her, rape her.

'The moon,' he said. 'It's full. And so am I.' He brought her hand down to the smooth and faded crotch of his jeans and there was something terrible there, beating with a life of its own beneath the notched coldness of his zipper.

'No,' she muttered, and tried to pull her hand away, thinking how far this was from that other moonstruck night, how impossibly far. This was at the other end of time's rainbow.

He held her hand against him. 'Come out in the desert and be my wife,' he said.

'No!'

'It's much too late to say no, dear.'

She went with him. There was a bedroll, and the blackened bones of a campfire under the silver bones of the moon.

He laid her down.

'All right,' he breathed. 'All right, then.' His fingers worked his belt buckle, then the button, then the zipper.

She saw what he had for her and began to scream.

The dark man's grin sprang forth at the sound, huge and glittering and obscene in the night, and the moon stared down blankly at them both, bloated and cheesy.

Nadine pealed forth scream after scream and tried to crawl away and he grabbed her and then she was holding her legs shut with all her strength, and when one of those blank hands inserted itself between them they parted like water and she thought: *I will look up . . . I will look up at the moon . . . I will feel nothing and it will be over . . . it will be over . . . I will feel nothing . . .*

And when the dead coldness of him slipped into her the shriek ripped up and out of her, bolted free, and she struggled, and the struggle was useless. He battered into her, invader, destroyer, and the cold blood gushed down her thighs and then he was in her, all the way up to her womb, and the moon was in her eyes, cold and silver fire, and when he came it was like molten iron, molten *pig* iron, molten *brass*, and she came herself, came in screaming, incredible pleasure, came in terror, in horror, passing through the pig-iron and brass gates into the desert land of insanity, chased through, *blown* through like a leaf by the bellowing of his laughter, watching his face melt away, and now it was the shaggy face of a demon lolling just above her face, a demon with glaring yellow lamps for eyes, windows into a hell never even considered, and still there was that awful good humor in them, eyes that had watched down the crooked alleys of a thousand tenebrous night towns; those eyes were glaring and glinting and finally stupid. He went again . . . and again . . . and again. It seemed he would never be used up. Cold. He was dead cold. And old. Older than mankind, older than the earth. Again and again he filled her with his night-spawn, screaming laughter. Earth. Light. Coming. Coming again. The last shriek coming out of her to be wiped away by the desert wind and carried into the farthest chambers of the night, out to where a thousand weapons waited for their new owner to come and claim them. Shaggy demon's head, a lolling tongue deeply split into two forks. Its dead breath fell on her face. She was in the land of insanity now. The iron gates were closed.

The moon —!

The moon was almost down.

He had caught another rabbit, had caught the trembling little thing in his bare hands and broken its neck. He had built a new fire on the bones of the old one and now the rabbit cooked, sending up savory ribbons of aroma. There were no wolves now. Tonight they had stayed away — it was meet and right that they should have done. It was, after all, his wedding night, and the dazed and apathetic thing sitting lumpishly on the other side of the fire was his blushing bride.

He leaned over and raised her hand out of her lap. When he let it go it stayed in place, raised to the level of her mouth. He looked at this phenomenon for a moment and then put her hand back in her lap. There her fingers began to wiggle sluggishly, like dying snakes. He poked two fingers at her eyes, and she did not blink. That blank stare just went on and on.

He was honestly puzzled.

What had he done to her?

He couldn't remember.

And it didn't matter. She was pregnant. If she was also catatonic, what did that matter? She was the perfect incubator. She would breed his son, bear him, and then she could die with her purpose served. After all, it was what she was there for.

The rabbit was done. He broke it in two. He pulled her half into tiny pieces, the way you break up a baby's food. He fed it to her a piece at a time. Some pieces fell out of her mouth and into her lap half-chewed, but she ate most of it. If she remained like this, she would need a nurse. Jenny Engstrom, perhaps.

'That was very good, dear,' he said softly.

She looked blankly up at the moon. Flagg smiled gently at her and ate his wedding supper.

Good sex always made him hungry.

He awoke in the latter part of the night and sat up in his bedroll, confused and afraid . . . afraid in the instinctive, unknowing way that an animal is afraid – a predator who senses that he himself may be stalked.

Had it been a dream? A vision –?

They're coming.

Frightened, he tried to understand the thought, to put it in some context. He couldn't. It hung there on its own like a bad hex.

They're closer now.

Who? Who was closer now?

The night wind whispered past him, seeming to bring him a scent. Someone was coming and –

Someone's going.

While he slept, someone had passed his camp, headed east. The unseen third? He didn't know. It was the night of the full moon. Had the third escaped? The thought brought panic with it.

Yes, but who's coming?

He looked at Nadine. She was asleep, pulled up in a tight fetal position, the position his son would assume in her belly only months from now.

Are there months?

Again there was that feeling of things going flaky around the edges. He lay down again, believing there would be no more sleep for him this night. But he did sleep. And by the time he drove into Vegas the next morning, he was smiling again and he had nearly forgotten his night panic. Nadine sat docilely beside him on the seat, a big doll with a seed hidden carefully in its belly.

He went to the Grand, and there he learned what had happened while he slept. He saw the new look in their eyes, wary and questioning, and he felt the fear touch him again with its light moth wings.

CHAPTER 66

At about the same time that Nadine Cross was beginning to realize certain truths which should perhaps have been self-evident, Lloyd Henreid was sitting alone in the Cub Bar, playing Big Clock solitaire and cheating. He was out of temper. There had been a flash fire at Indian Springs that day, one dead, three hurt, and one of those likely to die of bad flash burns. They had no one in Vegas who knew how to treat such burns.

Carl Hough had brought the news. He had been pissed off to a high extreme, and he was not a man to be taken lightly. He had been a pilot for Ozark Airlines before the plague, was an ex-Marine, and could have broken Lloyd in two pieces with one hand while making a daiquiri with the other if he had wanted to. According to Carl, he had killed several men during the course of his long and checkered career, and Lloyd tended to believe him. Not that Lloyd was physically afraid of Carl Hough; the pilot was big and tough, but he was as leery of the Walkin Dude as anyone else in the West, and Lloyd wore Flagg's charm. But he was one of their fliers, and because he was, he had to be handled diplomatically. And oddly enough, Lloyd was something of a diplomat. His credentials were simple but awesome: He had spent several weeks with a certain madman named Poke Freeman and had lived to tell the tale. He had also spent several months with Randall Flagg, and was still drawing air and in his right mind.

Carl had come in around two on September 12, his cycle helmet under one arm. There was an ugly burn on his left cheek and blisters on one hand. There had been a fire. Bad, but not as bad as it could have been. A fuel truck had exploded, spewing burning petroleum all over the tarmac area.

'All right,' Lloyd had said. 'I'll see that the big guy knows. The guys that got hurt are at the infirmary?'

'Yeah. They are. I don't think Freddy Campanari is going to live to see the sun go down. That leaves two pilots, me and Andy.

Tell him that, and tell him something else when he gets back. I want that fuck Trashcan Man *gone*. That's my price for staying.'

Lloyd gazed at Carl Hough. 'Is it?'

'You're damn well told.'

'Well, I tell you, Carl,' Lloyd said. 'I can't pass that message on. If you want to give orders to *him*, you'll have to do it yourself.'

Carl looked suddenly confused and a little afraid. Fear sat strangely on that craggy face. 'Yeah, I see your point. I'm just tired and fucked over, Lloyd. My face hurts like hell. I don't mean to take it out on you.'

'That's okay, man. It's what I'm here for.' Sometimes he wished it wasn't. Already his head was starting to ache.

Carl said, 'But he's gotta go. If I have to tell him that, I will. I know he's got one of those black stones. He's ace-high with the tall man, I guess. But, hey, listen.' Carl sat down and put his helmet on a baccarat table. 'Trash was responsible for that fire. My Christ, how're we ever going to get those planes up if one of the big guy's men is torching the fucking *pilots*?'

Several people passing through the lobby of the Grand glanced uneasily over at the table where Lloyd and Carl sat.

'Keep your voice down, Carl.'

'Okay. But you see the problem, don't you?'

'How sure are you that Trash did it?'

'Listen,' Carl said, leaning forward, 'he was in the motor pool, all right? In there for a long time. Lots of guys saw him, not just me.'

'I thought he was out someplace. In the desert. You know, looking for stuff.'

'Well, he came back, all right? That sand-crawler he takes out was full of stuff. God knows where he gets it, I sure don't. Well, he had the guys in stitches at coffee break. You know how he is. To him, weaponry is like candy is to a kid.'

'Yeah.'

'The last thing he showed us was one of those incendiary fuses. You pull the tab, and there's this little burst of phosphorus. Then nothing for half an hour or forty minutes, depending on the size of the fuse, all right? You get it? Then there's one hell of a fire. Small, but very intense.'

'Yeah.'

'So okay. Trashy's showin us, just about droolin over the thing, in fact, and Freddy Campanari says, "Hey, people who play with fire wet the bed, Trash." And Steve Tobin – you know him, he's funny like a rubber crutch – he says, "You guys better put away your matches, Trashy's back in town." And Trash got really weird. He looked around at us, and he muttered under his breath. I was sitting right next to him and it sounded like he said, "Don't ask me about old lady Semple's check no more." That make any sense to you?'

Lloyd shook his head. Nothing about the Trashcan Man made much sense to him.

'Then he just left. Picked up the stuff he was showing us and took off. Well, none of us felt very good about it. We didn't mean to hurt his feelings. Most of the guys really like Trash. Or they did. He's like a little kid, you know?'

Lloyd nodded.

'An hour later, that goddam fuel truck goes up like a rocket. And while we were picking up the pieces, I happened to look up and there's Trashy over in his sand-crawler by the barracks building, watching us with binoculars.'

'Is that all you've got?' Lloyd asked, relieved.

'No. It ain't. If it was, I wouldn't even have bothered to come see you, Lloyd. But it got me thinking about *how* that truck went up. That's just the sort of thing you use an incendiary fuse for. In Nam, the Cong blew up a lot of our ammo dumps just that way, with our own fucking incendiary fuses. Stick it under the truck, on the exhaust pipe. If no one starts the truck up, it goes when the timer runs out. If someone does, it goes when the pipe gets hot. Either way, *ka-boom*, no more truck. The only thing that didn't fit was there's always a dozen fuel trucks in the motor pool, and we don't use them in any particular order. So after we got poor old Freddy over to the infirmary, John Waite and I went over there. John's in charge of the motor pool and he was just about pissing himself. He'd seen Trash in there earlier.'

'He was sure it was Trashcan Man?'

'With those burns all the way up his arm, it's kind of hard to make a mistake, wouldn't you say? All right? No one thought anything of it then. He was just poking around, and that's his job, ain't it?'

'Yes, I guess you'd have to say it is.'

'So me and John start to look over the rest of the fuel trucks. And holy shit, there's an incendiary fuse on every one of them. He put them on the exhaust pipes just below the fuel-tanks themselves.

The reason the truck we were using went first was because the exhaust pipe got hot, like I just told you, all right? But the others were getting ready to go. Two or three were starting to smoke. Some of the trucks were empty, but at least five of them were full of jet fuel. Another ten minutes and we would have lost half the goddam base.'

Oh Jesus, Lloyd thought mournfully. *It really is bad. Just about as bad as it can get.*

Carl held up his blistered hand. 'I got this pulling one of the hot ones. Now do you see why he's got to go?'

Lloyd said hesitantly, 'Maybe someone stole those fuses out of the back of his sand-crawler while he was taking a leak or something.'

Carl said patiently: 'That's not how it happened. Someone hurt his feelings while he was showing off his toys, and he tried to burn us all up. He damn near succeeded. Something's got to be done, Lloyd.'

'All right, Carl.'

He spent the rest of the afternoon asking around about Trash – had anyone seen him or know where he might be? Guarded looks and negative answers. Word had gotten around. Maybe that was good. Anyone who did see him would be quick to report it, in hopes of having a good word put in on their behalf with the big guy. But Lloyd had a hunch that no one was going to see Trash. He had given them a little hotfoot and had gone running back into the desert in his sand-crawler.

He looked down at the solitaire game spread out in front of him and carefully controlled an urge to sweep the whole thing onto the floor. Instead, he cheated out another ace and went on playing. It didn't matter. When Flagg wanted him, he would just reach out and gather him up. Old Trashy was going to end up riding a cross-piece just like Hec Drogan. Hard luck, guy.

But in his secret heart, he wondered.

Things had happened lately that he didn't like. Dayna, for instance. Flagg had known about her, that was true, but she hadn't talked. She had somehow escaped into death instead, leaving them no further ahead in the matter of the third spy.

That was another thing. How come *Flagg* didn't just know about the third spy? He had known about the old fart, and when he had come back from the desert he had known about Dayna, and had told them exactly how he was going to handle her. But it hadn't worked.

And now, Trashcan Man.

Trash wasn't a nobody. Maybe he had been back in the old days, but not anymore. He wore the black man's stone just as he himself did. After Flagg had crisped that bigmouth lawyer's brains in LA, Lloyd had seen Flagg lay his hands on Trashcan's shoulders and tell him gently that all the dreams had been true dreams. And Trash had whispered, 'My life for you.'

Lloyd didn't know what else might have passed between them, but it seemed clear that he had wandered the desert with Flagg's blessing. And now Trashcan Man had gone berserk.

Which raised some pretty serious questions.

Which was why Lloyd was sitting here alone at nine in the evening, cheating at solitaire and wishing he was drunk.

'Mr Henreid?'

Now what? He looked up and saw a girl with a pretty, pouty face. Tight white shorts. A halter that didn't quite cover the areolae of her nipples. Sexpot type for sure, but she looked nervous and pale, almost ill. She was biting compulsively at one of her thumbnails, and he saw that all her nails were bitten and ragged.

'What?'

'I . . . I have to see Mr Flagg,' she said. The strength went rapidly out of her voice, and it ended as a whisper.

'You do, huh? What do you think I am, his social secretary?'

'But . . . they said . . . to see you.'

'Who did?'

'Well, Angie Hirschfield did. It was her.'

'What's your name?'

'Uh, Julie.' She giggled, but it was only a reflex. The scared look never left her face, and Lloyd wondered wearily what sort of shit was up in the fan now. A girl like this wouldn't ask for Flagg unless it was very serious indeed. 'Julie Lawry.'

'Well, Julie Lawry, Flagg isn't in Las Vegas now.'

'When will he be back?'

'I don't know. He comes and goes, and he doesn't wear a beeper. He doesn't explain himself to me, either. If you have something, give it to me and I'll see that he gets the message.' She looked at him doubtfully and Lloyd repeated what he had told Carl Hough that afternoon. 'It's what I'm here for, Julie.'

'Okay.' Then, in a rush: 'If it's important, you tell him I'm the one told you. Julie Lawry.'

'Okay.'

'You won't forget?'

'*No, for Chrissake!* Now what is it?'

She pouted. 'Well, you don't have to be so mean about it.'

He sighed and put the handful of cards he had been holding down on the table. 'No,' he said. 'I guess I don't. Now, what is it?'

'That dummy. If he's around, I figure he's spying. I just thought you should know.' Her eyes glinted viciously. 'Motherfucker pulled a gun on me.'

'What dummy?'

'Well, I saw the retard, and so I figured the dummy must be with him, you know? And they're just not our type. I figure they must have come from the other side.'

'That's what you figure, huh?'

'Yeah.'

'Well, I don't know what the Christ you're talking about. It's been a long day and I'm tired. If you don't start talking some sense, Julie, I'm going up to bed.'

Julie sat down, crossed her legs, and told Lloyd about her meeting with Nick Andros and Tom Cullen in Pratt, Kansas, her hometown. About the Pepto-Bismol ('I was just having a little fun with the softie, and this deaf-and-dumb pulls a gun on me!'). She even told him about shooting at them as they left town.

'Which all proves what?' Lloyd asked when she finished. He had been a little intrigued with the word 'spy,' but since then had lapsed into a semidaze of boredom.

Julie pouted again and lit a cigarette. 'I *told* you. That feeb, he's over *here* now. I just bet he's spying.'

'Tom Cullen, you said his name was?'

'Yes.'

He had the vaguest sort of memory. Cullen was a big blond guy, a few cards short the deck for sure, but surely not as bad as this high-iron bitch was making out. He tried for more and came up empty. People were still streaming into Vegas in numbers of sixty to a hundred a day. It was becoming impossible to keep them all straight, and Flagg said the immigration was going to get a lot heavier before it tapered off. He supposed he could go to Paul Burlson, who was keeping a file of Vegas residents and find something out about this Cullen dude.

'Are you going to arrest him?' Julie asked.

Lloyd looked at her. 'I'll arrest you if you don't get off my case,' he said.

'Nice fucking *guy!*' Julie Lawry cried, her voice rising shrewishly. She jumped to her feet, glaring at him. In her tight white cotton shorts, her legs seemed to go all the way up to her chin. 'Try to do you a *favor!*'

'I'll check it.'

'Yeah, right, I know that story.'

She stomped off, fanny swinging in tight little circles of indignation.

Lloyd watched her with a certain weary amusement, thinking there were a lot of chicks like her in the world – even now, after the superflu, he was willing to bet there were a lot around. Easy to slap the make on, but watch out for the fingernails afterward. Kissing cousins to those spiders that gobble up their mates after sex. Two months had gone by and she still bore that mute guy a grudge. What did she say his name was? Andros?

Lloyd pulled a battered black notebook from his back pocket, wet his finger, and paged over to a blank sheet. This was his memory book, and it was chock-full of little notes to himself – everything from a reminder to take a shave before meeting with Flagg to a boxed memorandum to get the contents of Las Vegas' pharmacies inventoried before they started to lose morphine and codeine. It would be time to get another little book soon.

In his flat and scrawling grammar school script he wrote: *Nick Andros or maybe Androtes – mute. In town?* And below that: *Tom Cullen, check out with Paul.* He tucked the book back into his pocket. Forty miles northeast, the dark man had consummated his long-term relationship with Nadine Cross under the glittering desert stars. He would have been very interested to know that a friend of Nick Andros's was in Las Vegas.

But he slept.

Lloyd looked morosely down at his solitaire game, forgetting about Julie Lawry and her grudge and her tight little ass. He cheated out another ace, and his thoughts turned dolefully back to the Trashcan Man and what Flagg might say – or do – when Lloyd told him.

At the same time Julie Lawry was leaving the Cub Bar, feeling shat upon for doing no more than what she saw as her civic duty, Tom

Cullen stood by the picture window of his apartment in another part of the city, looking dreamily out at the full moon.

It was time to go.

Time to go back.

This apartment was not like his house in Boulder. This place was furnished but not decorated. He had not put up so much as a single poster or hung a single stuffed bird from piano wire. This place had been only a way station, and now it was time to go on. He was glad. He hated it here. It had a kind of smell to it here, a dry and rotten smell that you could never quite put your finger on. The people were mostly nice, and some of them he liked every bit as well as the people in Boulder, folks like Angie and that little boy, Dinny. No one made fun of him because he was slow. They had given him a job and joked with him, and on lunchbreak they'd trade out of their dinner buckets for something out of someone else's that looked better. They were nice folks, not much different from Boulder folks, as far as he could tell, but –

But they had that *smell* about them.

They all seemed to be waiting and watching. Sometimes strange silences fell among them and their eyes seemed to glaze over, as if they were all having the same uneasy dream. They did things without asking for explanations of why they were doing them, or what it was for. It was as if these people were wearing happy-folks faces, but their real faces, their underneath-faces, were monster faces. He had seen a scary movie about that once. That kind of monster was called a werewolf.

The moon rode over the desert, ghostly, high, and free.

He had seen Dayna, from the Free Zone. He had seen her once and never again. What had happened to her? Had she been spying, too? Had she gone back?

He didn't know. But he was afraid.

There was a small knapsack in the La-Z-Boy chair that faced the apartment's useless color console TV. The knapsack was full of vacuum-sealed ham strips and Slim Jims and Saltines. He picked it up and put it on.

Travel at night, sleep in the day.

He stepped out into the courtyard of the building without a backward glance. The moon was so bright that he cast a shadow on the cracked cement where the would-be high rollers had once parked their cars with the out-of-state plates.

He looked up at the ghostly coin that floated in the sky.

'M-O-O-N, that spells moon,' he whispered. 'Laws, yes. Tom Cullen knows what that means.'

His bike was leaning against the pink stucco wall of the apartment building. He paused once to adjust his knapsack, then got on and set off for the Interstate. By 11 PM, he had cleared Las Vegas and was pedaling east in the breakdown lane of I-15. No one saw him. No alarm was raised.

His mind dropped into a soft neutral, as it almost always did when the most immediate things were taken care of. He biked steadily along, conscious only that the light night breeze felt nice against his sweaty face. Every now and then he had to swerve around a sand dune that had crept out of the desert and had lain a white, skeletal arm across the road, and once he was well away from the city, there were stalled cars and trucks to contend with, too – look on my works, ye mighty, and despair, Glen Bateman might have said in his ironic way.

He stopped at two in the morning for a light lunch of Slim Jims, crackers, and Kool-Aid from the big thermos strapped to the back of the bike. Then went on. The moon was down. Las Vegas fell farther behind with every revolution of his bicycle tires. That made him feel good.

But at quarter past four on that morning of September 13, a cold comber of fear washed over him. It was made all the more terrifying by virtue of its unexpectedness, by its seeming irrationality. Tom would have cried out loud, but his vocal cords were suddenly frozen, locked. The muscles in his pumping legs went slack and he coasted along under the stars. The black and white negative of the desert streamed by more and more slowly.

He was near.

The man with no face, the demon who now walked the earth. Flagg.

The tall man, they called him. The grinning man, Tom called him in his heart. Only when his grin fell on you, all the blood in your body fell into a dead swoon, leaving your flesh cold and gray. The man who could look at a cat and make it puke up hairballs. If he walked through a building project, men would hammer their own thumbnails and put shingles on upside down and sleepwalk off the ends of girders and –

– and oh dear God he was awake!

A whimper escaped Tom's throat. He could feel the sudden

wakefulness. He seemed to see/feel an Eye opening in the darkness of the early morning, a dreadful red Eye that was still a bit bleared and confused with sleep. It was turning in the darkness. Looking. Looking for him. It knew Tom Cullen was there, but not just where he was.

Numbly, his feet found the pedals and he biked on, faster and faster, bending over the handlebars to cut down the wind resistance, picking up speed until he was nearly flying along. If he had come upon a wrecked car in his path, he would have pedaled into it full-tilt and perhaps killed himself.

But little by little he could feel that dark, hot presence falling behind him. And the greatest wonder was that that awful red Eye had glanced his way, had passed over him without seeing (*maybe because I'm bent over my handlebars so far*, Tom Cullen reasoned incoherently) . . . and then it had closed again.

The dark man had gone back to sleep.

How does the rabbit feel when the shadow of the hawk falls on him like a dark crucifix . . . and then goes on without stopping or even slowing? How does the mouse feel when the cat who has been crouched patiently outside his hole for the entire day is picked up by its master and tossed unceremoniously out the front door? How does the deer feel when it steps quietly past the mighty hunter who is snoozing away the effects of his three lunchtime beers? Perhaps they feel nothing, or perhaps they feel what Tom Cullen felt as he rode out of that black and dangerous sphere of influence: a great and nearly electrifying sunburst of relief; a feeling of new birth. Most of all a feeling of safety scarcely earned, that such great good luck must surely be a sign from heaven.

He rode on until five o'clock in the morning. Ahead of him, the sky was turning the dark-blue-laced-with-gold of sunrise. The stars were fading.

Tom was almost done in. He went on a little farther, then spotted a sharp decline about seventy yards to the right of the highway. He pushed his bike over and then down into the dry-wash. Consulting the tickings and workings of instinct, he pulled enough dry grass and mesquite to cover most of the bike. There were two big rocks leaning against each other about ten yards from his bike. He crawled into the pocket of shade beneath them, put his jacket under his head, and was asleep almost at once.

CHAPTER 67

The Walkin Dude was back in Vegas.

He had gotten in around nine-thirty in the morning. Lloyd had seen him arrive. Flagg had also seen Lloyd, but had taken no notice of him. He had been crossing the lobby of the Grand, leading a woman. Heads turned to look at her in spite of everyone's nearly unanimous aversion to looking at the dark man. Her hair was a uniform snow-white. She had a terrible sunburn, one so bad that it made Lloyd think of the victims of the gasoline fire at Indian Springs. White hair, horrible sunburn, utterly empty eyes. They looked out at the world with a lack of expression that was beyond placidity, even beyond idiocy. Lloyd had seen eyes like that once before. In Los Angeles, after the dark man had finished with Eric Strellerton, the lawyer who was going to tell Flagg how to run everything.

Flagg looked at no one. He grinned. He led the woman to the elevator and inside. The doors slid shut behind them and they went up to the top floor.

For the next six hours Lloyd was busy trying to get everything organized, so when Flagg called him and asked for a report, he would be ready. He thought everything was under control. The only item left was tracking down Paul Burlson and getting whatever he had on this Tom Cullen, just in case Julie Lawry really had stumbled on to something. Lloyd didn't think it likely, but with Flagg it was better to be safe than sorry. Much better.

He picked up the telephone and waited patiently. After a few moments there was a click and then Shirley Dunbar's Tennessee twang was in his ear: 'Operator.'

'Hi, Shirley, it's Lloyd.'

'Lloyd Henreid! How are ya?'

'Not too bad, Shirl. Can you try 6214 for me?'

'Paul? He's not home. He's out at Indian Springs. Bet I could catch him for you at BaseOps.'

'Okay, try that.'

'You bet. Say, Lloyd, when you gonna come over and try some of my coffee cake? I bake fresh every two, three days.'

'Soon, Shirley,' Lloyd said, grimacing. Shirley was forty, ran about one-eighty . . . and had set her cap for Lloyd. He took a lot of ribbing about her, especially from Whitney and Ronnie Sykes. But she was a fine telephone operator, able to do wonders with the Las Vegas phone system. Getting the phones working – the most important ones, anyway – had been their first priority after the power, but most of the automatic switching equipment had burned out, and so they were back to the equivalent of tin cans and lots of waxed string. There were also constant outages. Shirley handled what there was to handle with uncanny skill, and she was patient with the three or four other operators, who were still learning.

Also, she *did* make nice coffee cake.

'*Real* soon,' he added, and thought of how nice it would be if Julie Lawry's firm, rounded body could be grafted onto Shirley Dunbar's skills and gentle, uncomplaining nature.

She seemed satisfied. There were beeps and boops on the line, and one high-pitched, echoing whine that made him hold the handset away from his ear, grimacing. Then the phone rang at the other end in a series of hoarse burrs.

'Bailey, Ops,' a voice made tinny by distance said.

'This is Lloyd,' he bellowed into the phone. 'Is Paul there?'

'Haul what, Lloyd?' Bailey asked.

'Paul! Paul Burlson!'

'Oh, him! Yeah, he's right here having a Co-Cola.'

There was a pause – Lloyd began to think that the tenuous connection had been broken – and then Paul came on.

'We're going to have to shout, Paul. The connection stinks.' Lloyd wasn't completely sure that Paul Burlson had the lung capacity to shout. He was a scrawny little man with thick lenses in his glasses, and some men called him Mr Cool because he insisted on wearing a complete three-piece suit each day despite the dry crunch of the Vegas heat. But he was a good man to have as your information officer, and Flagg had told Lloyd in one of his expansive moods that by 1991 Burlson would be in charge of the secret police. And he'll be *sooo* good at it, Flagg had added with a warm and loving smile.

Paul did manage to speak a little louder.

'Have you got your directory with you?' Lloyd asked.

'Yes. Stan Bailey and I were going over a work rotation program.'

'See if you've got anything on a guy named Tom Cullen, would you?'

'Just a second.' A second stretched out to two or three minutes, and Lloyd began to wonder again if they had been cut off. Then Paul said, 'Okay, Tom Cullen . . . you there, Lloyd?'

'Right here.'

'You can never be sure, with the phones the way they are. He's somewhere between twenty-two and thirty-five at a guess. He doesn't know for sure. Light mental retardation. He has some work skills. We've had him on the clean-up crew.'

'How long has he been in Vegas?'

'Something less than three weeks.'

'From Colorado?'

'Yes, but we have a dozen people over here who tried it over there and decided they didn't like it. They drove this guy out. He was having sex with a normal woman and I guess they were afraid for their gene pool.' Paul laughed.

'Got his address?'

Paul gave it to him and Lloyd jotted it down in his notebook. 'That it, Lloyd?'

'One other name, if you've got the time.'

Paul laughed – a small man's fussy laugh. 'Sure, it's only my coffee break.'

'The name is Nick Andros.'

Paul said instantly: 'I have that name on my red list.'

'Oh?' Lloyd thought as quickly as he could, which was far from the speed of light. He had no idea what Paul's 'red list' might be. 'Who gave you his name?'

Exasperated, Paul said: 'Who do you think? The same person that gave me all the red list names.'

'Oh. Okay.' He said goodbye and hung up. Small-talk was impossible with the bad connection, and Lloyd had too much to think about to want to make it, anyway.

Red list.

Names that Flagg had given to Paul and to no one else, apparently – although Paul had assumed Lloyd knew all about it. Red list, what did that mean? Red meant stop.

Red meant danger.

Lloyd lifted the telephone again.

'Operator.'

'Lloyd again, Shirl.'

'Well, Lloyd, did you –'

'Shirley, I can't gab. I'm onto something that's maybe big.'

'Okay, Lloyd.' Shirley's voice lost its flirtiness and she was suddenly all business.

'Who's catching at Security?'

'Barry Dorgan.'

'Get him for me. And I never called you.'

'Yes, Lloyd.' She sounded afraid now. Lloyd was afraid, too, but he was also excited.

A moment later Dorgan was on. He was a good man, for which Lloyd was profoundly grateful. Too many men of the Poke Freeman type had gravitated toward the police department.

'I want you to pick someone up for me,' Lloyd said. 'Get him alive. I have to have him alive even if it means you lose men. His name is Tom Cullen and you can probably catch him at home. Bring him to the Grand.' He gave Barry Tom's address and then made him repeat it back.

'How important is this, Lloyd?'

'Very important. You do this right, and someone bigger than me is going to be very happy with you.'

'Okay.' Barry hung up and Lloyd did too, confident that Barry understood the converse: *Fuck it up and somebody is going to be very angry with you.*

Barry called back an hour later to say he was fairly sure Tom Cullen had split.

'But he's feeble,' Barry went on, 'and he can't drive. Not even a motor-scooter. If he's going east, he can't be any further than Dry Lake. We can catch him, Lloyd, I know we can. Give me a green light.' Barry was fairly drooling. He was one of four or five people in Vegas who knew about the spies, and he had read Lloyd's thoughts.

'Let me think this over,' Lloyd said, and hung up before Barry could protest. He had gotten better at thinking things over than he would have believed possible in the pre-flu days, but he knew this was too big for him. And that red list business troubled him. Why hadn't he been told about that?

For the first time since meeting Flagg in Phoenix, Lloyd had the disquieting feeling that his position might be vulnerable. Secrets had been kept. They could probably still get Cullen; both Carl Hough and Bill Jamieson could fly the army choppers that were hangared out at the Springs, and if they had to they could close every road going out of Nevada to the east. Also, the guy wasn't Jack the Ripper or Dr Octopus; he was a feeb on the run. But Christ! If he had known about this Andros what's-his-face when Julie Lawry had come to see him, they might have been able to take him right in his little North Vegas apartment.

Somewhere inside him a door had opened, letting in a cool breeze of fear. Flagg had screwed up. And Flagg was capable of distrusting Lloyd Henreid. And that was baaaad shit.

Still, he would have to be told about this. He wasn't going to take the decision to start another manhunt upon himself. Not after what had happened with the Judge. He got up to go to the house phones, and met Whitney Horgan coming from them.

'It's the man, Lloyd,' he said. 'He wants you.'

'All right,' he said, surprised by how calm his voice was – the fear inside him was now very great. And above all else, it was important for him to remember that he would have long since starved in his Phoenix holding cell if it hadn't been for Flagg. There was no sense kidding himself; he belonged to the dark man lock, stock, and barrel.

But I can't do my job if he shuts off the information, he thought, going to the elevator bank. He pushed the penthouse button, and the elevator car rose swiftly. Again there was that nagging, unhappy feeling: Flagg hadn't known. The third spy had been here all along, *and Flagg hadn't known.*

'Come in, Lloyd.' Flagg's lazy smiling face above a prosy blue-checked bathrobe.

Lloyd came in. The air conditioning was on high, and it was like stepping into an open-air suite in Greenland. And still, as Lloyd stepped past the dark man, he could feel the radiating body heat he gave off. It was like being in a room which contained a small but very powerful furnace.

Sitting in the corner, in a white sling chair, was the woman who had come in with Flagg that morning. Her hair was carefully pinned up, and she wore a shift dress. Her face was blank and moony, and looking at her gave Lloyd a deep chill. As teenagers, he and some friends had once stolen some dynamite from a construction project, had fused it and thrown it into Lake Harrison, where it exploded. The dead fish that had floated to the surface afterward had had that same look of awful blank impartiality in their moon-rimmed eyes.

'I'd like you to meet Nadine Cross,' Flagg said softly from behind him, making Lloyd jump. 'My wife.'

Startled, Lloyd looked at Flagg and met only that mocking grin, those dancing eyes.

'My dear, Lloyd Henreid, my righthand man. Lloyd and I met in Phoenix, where Lloyd was being detained and was consequently about to dine on a fellow detainee. In fact, Lloyd might already have partaken of the appetizer. Correct, Lloyd?'

Lloyd blushed dully and said nothing, although the woman was either gonzo or stoned right over the moon.

'Put out your hand, dear,' the dark man said.

Like a robot, Nadine put her hand out. Her eyes continued to stare indifferently at a point somewhere above Lloyd's shoulder.

Jesus, this is creepy, Lloyd thought. A light sweat had sprung out all over his body in spite of the frigid air conditioning.

'Pleestameetcha,' he said, and shook the soft warm meat of her hand. Afterward, he had to restrain a powerful urge to wipe his hand on the leg of his pants. Nadine's hand continued to hang laxly in the air.

'You can put your hand down now, my love,' Flagg said.

Nadine put her hand back in her lap, where it began to twist and squirm. Lloyd realized with something like horror that she was masturbating.

'My wife is indisposed,' Flagg said, and tittered. 'She is also in a family way, as the saying is. Congratulate me, Lloyd. I am going to be a papa.' That titter again; the sound of scampering, light-footed rats behind an old wall.

'Congratulations,' Lloyd said through lips that felt blue and numb.

'We can talk our little hearts out around Nadine, can't we, dear? She's as silent as the grave. To make a small pun, mum's the word.

'What about Indian Springs?'

Lloyd blinked and tried to shift his mental gears, feeling naked and on the defensive. 'It's going good,' he managed at last.

'"Going good"?' The dark man leaned toward him and for one moment Lloyd was sure he was going to open his mouth and bite his head off like a Tootsie Pop. He recoiled. 'That's hardly what I'd call a close analysis, Lloyd.'

'There are some other things —'

'When I want to talk about other things, I'll ask about other things.' Flagg's voice was rising, getting uncomfortably close to a scream. Lloyd had never seen such a radical shift in temperament, and it scared him badly. 'Right now I want a status report on Indian Springs and you better have it for me, Lloyd, for your sake you better have it!'

'All right,' Lloyd muttered. 'Okay.' He fumbled his notebook out of his hip pocket, and for the next half hour they talked about Indian Springs, the National Guard jets, and the Shrike missiles. Flagg began to relax again — although it was hard to tell, and it was a very bad idea to take anything at all for granted when you were dealing with the Walkin Dude.

'Do you think they could overfly Boulder in two weeks?' he asked. 'Say . . . by the first of October?'

'Carl could, I guess,' Lloyd said doubtfully. 'I don't know about the other two.'

'I want them ready,' Flagg muttered. He got up and began to pace around the room. 'I want those people hiding in holes by next spring. I want to hit them at night, while they're sleeping. Rake that town from one end to the other. I want it to be like Hamburg and Dresden in World War II.' He turned to Lloyd and his face was parchment white, the dark eyes blazing out of it with their own crazy fire. His grin was like a scimitar. 'Teach them to send spies. They'll be living in caves when spring comes. Then we'll go over there and have us a pig hunt. Teach them to send spies.'

Lloyd found his tongue at last. 'The third spy —'

'We'll find him, Lloyd. Don't worry about that. We'll get the bastard.' The smile was back, darkly charming. But Lloyd had seen an instant of angry and bewildered fear before that smile reappeared. And fear was the one expression he had never expected to see there.

'We know who he is, I think,' Lloyd said quietly.

Flagg had been turning a jade figurine over in his hands, examining it. Now his hand froze. He became very still, and a peculiar expression of concentration stole over his face. For the first time the Cross woman's gaze shifted, first toward Flagg and then hastily away. The air in the penthouse suite seemed to thicken.

'What? What did you say?'

'The third spy –'

'No,' Flagg said with sudden decision. 'No. You're jumping at shadows, Lloyd.'

'If I've got it right, he's a friend of a guy named Nick Andros.'

The jade figurine fell through Flagg's fingers and shattered. A moment later Lloyd was lifted out of his chair by the front of his shirt. Flagg had moved across the room so swiftly that Lloyd had not even seen him. And then Flagg's face was plastered against his, that awful sick heat was baking into him, and Flagg's black weasel eyes were only an inch from his own.

Flagg screamed: '*And you sat there and talked about Indian Springs? I ought to throw you out that window!*'

Something – perhaps it was seeing the dark man vulnerable, perhaps it was only the knowledge that Flagg wouldn't kill him until he got all of the information – allowed Lloyd to find his tongue and speak in his own defense.

'I tried to tell you!' he cried. 'You cut me off! And you cut me off from the red list, whatever that is! If I'd known about that, I could have had that fucking retard last night!'

Then he was flung across the room to crash into the far wall. Stars exploded in his head and he dropped to the parquet floor, dazed. He shook his head, trying to clear it. There was a high humming noise in his ears.

Flagg seemed to have gone crazy. He was striding jerkily around the room, his face blank with rage. Nadine had shrunk back into her chair. Flagg reached a knickknack shelf populated with a milky-green menagerie of jade animals. He stared at them for a second, seeming almost puzzled by them, and then swept them all off onto the floor. They shattered like tiny grenades. He kicked at the bigger pieces with one bare foot, sending them flying. His dark hair had fallen over his forehead. He flipped it back with a jerk of his head and then turned toward Lloyd. There was a grotesque expression of sympathy and compassion on his face – both emotions every bit as real as a three-dollar bill, Lloyd thought. He walked over to help Lloyd up, and Lloyd noticed that he stepped on several jagged pieces of broken jade with no sign of pain . . . and no blood.

'I'm sorry,' he said. 'Let's have a drink.' He offered a hand and helped Lloyd to his feet. *Like a kid doing a temper tantrum*, Lloyd thought. 'Yours is bourbon straight up, isn't it?'

'Fine.'

Flagg went to the bar and made monstrous drinks. Lloyd demolished half of his at a gulp. The glass chattered briefly on the end table as he set it down. But he felt a little better.

Flagg said, 'The red list is something I didn't think you'd ever have to use. There were eight names on it – five now. It was their governing council plus the old woman. Andros was one of them. But he's dead now. Yes, Andros is dead, I'm sure of it.' He fixed Lloyd with a narrow, baleful stare.

Lloyd told the story, referring to his notebook from time to time. He didn't really need it, but it was good, from time to time, to get away from that smoking glare. He began with Julie Lawry and ended with Barry Dorgan.

'You say he's retarded,' Flagg mused.

'Yes.'

Happiness spread over Flagg's face and he began to nod. 'Yes,' he said, but not to Lloyd. 'Yes, that's why I couldn't see –'

He broke off and went to the telephone. Moments later he was talking to Barry.

'The helicopters. You get Carl in one and Bill Jamieson in the other. Continuous radio contact. Send out sixty – no, a hundred men. Close every road going out of eastern and southern Nevada. See that they have this Cullen's description. And I want hourly reports.'

He hung up and rubbed his hands happily. 'We'll get him. I only wish we could send his head back to his bum-buddy Andros. But Andros is dead. Isn't he, Nadine?'

Nadine only stared blankly.

'The helicopters won't be much good tonight,' Lloyd said. 'It'll be dark in three hours.'

'Don't you fret, old Lloyd,' the dark man said cheerfully. 'Tomorrow will be time enough for the helicopters. He isn't far. No, not far at all.'

Lloyd was bending his spiral notebook nervously back and forth in his hands, wishing he was anywhere but here. Flagg was in a good mood now, but Lloyd didn't think he would be after hearing about Trash.

'I have one other item,' he said reluctantly. 'It's about the Trashcan Man.' He wondered if this was going to trigger another tantrum like the jade-smashing outburst.

'Dear Trashy. Is he off on one of his prospecting trips?'

'I don't know where he is. He pulled a little trick at Indian Springs before he went out again.' He related the story as Carl had told it the day before. Flagg's face darkened when he heard that Freddy Campanari had been mortally wounded, but by the time Lloyd had finished, his face was serene again. Instead of bursting into a rage, Flagg only waved his hand impatiently.

'All right. When he comes back in, I want him killed. But quickly and mercifully. I don't want him to suffer. I had hoped he might . . . last longer. You probably don't understand this, Lloyd, but I felt a certain . . . kinship with that boy. I thought I might be able to use him – and I have – but I was never completely sure. Even a master sculptor can find that the knife has turned in his hand, if it's a defective knife. Correct, Lloyd?'

Lloyd, who knew from nothing about sculpture and sculptors' knives (he thought they used mallets and chisels), nodded agreeably. 'Sure.'

'And he's done us the great service of arming the Shrikes. It was him, wasn't it?'

'Yes. It was.'

'He'll be back. Tell Barry Trash is to be . . . put out of his misery. Painlessly, if possible. Right now I am more concerned with the retarded boy to the east of us. I could let him go, but it's the principle of the thing. Perhaps we can end it before dark. Do you think so, my dear?'

He was squatting beside Nadine's chair now. He touched her cheek and she pulled away as if she had been touched with a red-hot poker. Flagg grinned and touched her again. This time she submitted, shuddering.

'The moon,' Flagg said, delighted. He sprang to his feet. 'If the helicopters don't spot him before dark, they'll have the moon tonight. Why, I'll bet he's biking right up the middle of I-15 right now, in broad daylight. Expecting the old woman's God to watch out for him. But she's dead, too, isn't she, my dear?' Flagg laughed delightedly, the laugh of a happy child. 'And her God is, too, I suspect. Everything is going to work out well. And Randy Flagg is going to be a da-da.'

He touched her cheek again. She moaned like a hurt animal. Lloyd licked his dry lips. 'I'll push off now, if that's okay.'

'Fine, Lloyd, fine.' The dark man did not look around; he was staring raptly into Nadine's face. 'Everything is going well. Very well.'

Lloyd left as quickly as he could, almost running. In the elevator it all caught up with him and he had to push the EMER-GENCY STOP button as hysterics overwhelmed him. He laughed and cried for nearly five minutes. When the storm had passed, he felt a little better.

He's not falling apart, he told himself. *There are a few little problems, but he's on top of them. The ballgame will probably be over by the first of October, and surely by the fifteenth. Everything's starting to go good, just like he said, and never mind that he almost killed me . . . never mind that he seems stranger than ever . . .*

Lloyd got the call from Stan Bailey at Indian Springs fifteen minutes later. Stan was nearly hysterical between his fury at Trash and his fear of the dark man.

Carl Hough and Bill Jamieson had taken off from the Springs at 6:02 PM to run a recon mission east of Vegas. One of their other trainee pilots, Cliff Benson, had been riding with Carl as an observer.

At 6:12 PM both helicopters had blown up in the air. Stunned though he had been, Stan had sent five men over to Hangar 9, where two other skimmers and three large Baby Huey copters were stored. They found explosive taped to all five of the remaining choppers, and incendiary fuses rigged to simple kitchen timers. The fuses were not the same as the ones Trash had rigged to the fuel trucks, but they were very similar. There was not much room for doubt.

'It was the Trashcan Man,' Stan said. 'He went hogwild. Jesus Christ only knows what else he's wired up to explode out here.'

'Check everything,' Lloyd said. His heartbeat was rapid and thready with fear. Adrenalin boiled through his body, and his eyes felt as if they were in danger of popping from his head. 'Check *everything*! You get every man jack out there and go from one end to the other of that cock-knocking base. You hear me, Stan?'

'Why bother?'

'*Why bother?*' Lloyd screamed. 'Do I have to draw you a picture, shitheels? What's the big dude gonna say if the whole base –'

'All our pilots are dead,' Stan said softly. 'Don't you get it, Lloyd? Even Cliff, and he wasn't very fucking good. We've got six guys that aren't even close to soloing and no teachers. What do we need those jets for now, Lloyd?'

And he hung up, leaving Lloyd to sit thunderstruck, finally realizing.

Tom Cullen woke up shortly after nine-thirty that evening, feeling thirsty and stiff. He had a drink from his water canteen, crawled out from under the two leaning rocks, and looked up at the dark sky. The moon rode overhead, mysterious and serene. It was time to go on. But he would have to be careful, laws, yes.

Because they were after him now.

He had had a dream. Nick was talking to him and that was strange, because Nick couldn't talk. He was M-O-O-N, that spelled deaf-mute. Had to write everything, and Tom could hardly read at all. But dreams were funny things, anything could happen in a dream, and in Tom's, Nick had been talking.

Nick said, 'They know about you now, Tom, but it wasn't your fault. You did everything right. It was bad luck. So now you have to be careful. You have to leave the road, Tom, but you have to keep going east.'

Tom understood about east, but not how he was going to keep from getting mixed up in the desert. He might just go around in big circles.

'You'll know,' Nick said. 'First you have to look for God's Finger . . .'

Now Tom put his canteen back on his belt and adjusted his pack. He walked back to the turnpike, leaving his bike where it had been. He climbed the embankment to the road and looked both ways. He scuttled across the median strip and after another cautious look, he trotted across the westbound lanes of I-15.

They know about you now, Tom.

He caught his foot in the guardrail cable on the far side and tumbled most of the way to the bottom of the embankment beside the highway. He lay in a heap for a moment, heart pounding. There was no sound but faint wind, whining over the broken floor of the desert.

He got up and began to scan the horizon. His eyes were keen and the desert air was crystal clear. Before long he saw it, standing out against the starstrewn sky like an exclamation point. God's Finger. As he faced due east, the stone monolith was at ten o'clock. He thought he could walk to it in an hour or two. But the clear, magnifying quality of the air had fooled more experienced hikers than Tom Cullen, and he was bemused by the way the stone finger always seemed to remain the same distance away. Midnight passed, then two o'clock. The great clock of stars in the sky had revolved. Tom began to wonder if the rock that looked so much like a pointing finger might not be a mirage. He rubbed his eyes, but it was still there. Behind him, the turnpike had merged into the dark distance.

When he looked back at the Finger, it did seem to be a little closer, and by 4 AM, when an inner voice began to whisper that it was time to find a good hiding place for the coming day, there could be no doubt that he had drawn nearer to the landmark. But he would not reach it this night.

And when he did reach it (assuming that they didn't find him when day came)? What then?

It didn't matter.

Nick would tell him. Good old Nick.

Tom couldn't wait to get back to Boulder and see him, laws, yes.

He found a fairly comfortable spot in the shade of a huge spine of rock and went to sleep almost instantly. He had come about thirty miles northeast that night, and was approaching the Mormon Mountains.

During the afternoon, a large rattlesnake crawled in beside him to get out of the heat of the day. It coiled itself by Tom, slept awhile, and then passed on.

Flagg stood at the edge of the roof sundeck that afternoon, looking east. The sun would be going down in another four hours, and then the retard would be on the move again.

A strong and steady desert breeze lifted his dark hair back from his hot brow. The city ended so abruptly, giving up to the desert. A few billboards on the edge of nowhere, and that was it. So much desert, so many places to hide. Men had walked into that desert before and had never been seen again.

'But not this time,' he whispered. 'I'll have him. I'll have him.'

He could not have explained why it was so important to have the retard; the rationality of the problem constantly eluded him. More and more he felt an urge to simply act, to move, to *do*. To destroy.

Last evening, when Lloyd had informed him of the helicopter explosions and the deaths of the three pilots, he had had to use every resource at his command to keep from going into an utter screaming rage. His first impulse had been to order an armored column assembled immediately – tanks, flametracks, armored trucks, the whole works. They could be in Boulder in five days. The whole stinking mess would be over in a week and a half.

Sure.

And if there was early snow in the mountain passes, that would be the end of the great *Wehrmacht*. And it was already September 14. Good weather was no longer a sure bet. How in hell's name had it gotten so late so fast?

But he was the strongest man on the face of the earth, wasn't he? There might be another like him in Russia or China or Iran, but that was a problem for ten years from now. Now all that mattered was that he was ascendant, he knew it, he *felt* it. He was strong, that was all the retard could tell them . . . *if* he managed to avoid getting lost in the desert or freezing to death in the mountains. He could only tell them that Flagg's people lived in fear of the Walkin Dude and would obey the Walkin Dude's least command. He could only tell them things that would demoralize their will further. So why did he have this steady, gnawing feeling that Cullen must be found and killed before he could leave the West?

Because it's what I want, and I am going to have what I want, and that is reason enough.

And Trashcan Man. He had thought he could dismiss Trash entirely. He had thought Trashcan Man could be thrown away like a defective tool. But he had succeeded in doing what the entire Free Zone could not have done. He had thrown dirt into the foolproof machinery of the dark man's conquest.

I misjudged –

It was a hateful thought, and he would not allow his mind to follow it to its conclusion. He threw his glass over the roof's low parapet and saw it twinkling, end over end, out and out, then descending. A randomly vicious thought, a petulant child's thought, streaked across his mind: *Hope it hits someone on the head!*

Far below, the glass struck the parking lot and exploded . . . so far below, the dark man could not even hear it.

They had found no more bombs at Indian Springs. The entire place had been turned upside down. Apparently Trash had booby-trapped the first things he had come to, the choppers in Hangar 9 and the trucks in the motor pool next door.

Flagg had reiterated his orders that the Trashcan Man was to be killed on sight. The thought of Trash wandering around out in all that government property, where God knew what might be stored, now made him distinctly nervous.

Nervous.

Yes. The beautiful surety was still evaporating. When had that evaporation begun? He could not say, not for sure. All he knew was that things were getting flaky. Lloyd knew it, too. He could see it in the way that Lloyd looked at him. It might not be a bad idea if Lloyd had an accident before the winter was out. He was asshole buddies with too many of the people in the palace guard, people like Whitney Horgan and Ken DeMott. Even Burlson, who had spilled that business about the red list. He had thought idly about skinning Paul Burlson alive for that.

But if Lloyd had known about the red list, none of this would have –

'Shut up,' he muttered. 'Just . . . shut . . . up!'

But the thought wouldn't go away that easily. Why *hadn't* he given Lloyd the names of the top-echelon Free Zone people? He didn't know, couldn't remember. It seemed there had been a perfectly good reason at the time, but the more he tried to grasp it, the more it slipped through his fingers. Had it only been a sly-stupid decision not to put too many of his eggs in one basket – a feeling that not too many secrets should be stored with any one person, even a person as stupid and loyal as Lloyd Henreid?

An expression of bewilderment rippled across his face. Had he been making such stupid decisions all along?

And just how loyal was Lloyd, anyway? That expression in his eyes –

Abruptly he decided to push it all aside and levitate. That always made him feel better. It made him feel stronger, more serene, and it cleared his head. He looked out at the desert sky.

(I am, I am, I am, I AM –)

His rundown bootheels left the surface of the sundeck, hovered, rose another inch. Then two. Peace came to him, and suddenly he knew he could find the answers. Everything was clearer. First he must –

'They're coming for you, you know.'

He crashed back down at the sound of that soft, uninflected voice. The jarring shock went up his legs and his spine all the way to his jaw, which clicked. He whirled around like a cat. But his blooming grin withered when he saw Nadine. She was dressed in a white nightgown, yards of gauzy material that billowed around her body. Her hair, as white as the gown, blew about her face. She looked like some pallid deranged sibyl, and in spite of himself, Flagg was afraid. She took a delicate step closer. Her feet were bare.

'They're coming. Stu Redman, Glen Bateman, Ralph Brentner, and Larry Underwood. They're coming and they'll kill you like a chicken-stealing weasel.'

'They're in Boulder,' he said, 'hiding under their beds and mourning their dead nigger woman.'

'No,' she said indifferently. 'They're almost in Utah now. They'll be here soon. And they'll stamp you out like a disease.'

'Shut up. Go downstairs.'

'I'll go down,' she said, approaching him, and now it was she who smiled – a smile that filled him with dread. The furious color faded from his cheeks, and his strange, hot vitality seemed to go with it. For a moment he seemed old and frail. 'I'll go down . . . and so will you.'

'Get out.'

'We'll go down,' she sang, smiling . . . it was horrible. 'Down, doowwwn . . .'

'They're in *Boulder*!'

'They're almost here.'

'*Get downstairs!*'

'Everything you made here is falling apart, and why not? The effective half-life of evil is always relatively short. People are whispering about you. They're saying you let Tom Cullen get away, just a simple retarded boy but smart enough to outwit Randall Flagg.' Her words came faster and faster, now tumbling through a jeering smile. 'They're saying your weapons expert has gone crazy and you didn't know it was going to happen. They're afraid that what he brings back from the desert next time may be for them instead of for the people in the East. And they're leaving. Did you know that?'

'You lie,' he whispered. His face was parchment white, his eyes bulging. 'They wouldn't *dare*. And if they were, I'd know.'

Her eyes gazed blankly over his shoulder to the east. 'I see them,' she whispered. 'They're leaving their posts in the dead of night, and your Eye doesn't see them. They're leaving their posts and sneaking away. A work-crew goes out with twenty people and comes back with eighteen. The border guards are defecting. They're afraid the balance of power is shifting on its arm. They're leaving you, leaving you, and the ones that are left won't lift a finger when the men from the East come to finish you once and for all –'

It snapped. Whatever there was inside him, it snapped.

'YOU LIE!' he screamed at her. His hands slammed down on her shoulders, snapping both collarbones like pencils. He lifted her body high over his head into the faded blue desert sky, and as he pivoted on his heels he threw her, up and out, as he had thrown the glass. He saw the great smile of relief and triumph on her face, the sudden sanity in her eyes, and understood. She had baited him into doing it, understanding somehow that only he could set her free –

And she was carrying his child.

He leaned over the low parapet, almost overbalancing, trying to call back the irrevocable. Her nightgown fluttered. His hand closed on the gauzy material and he felt it rip, leaving him only a scrap of cloth so diaphanous that he could see his fingers through it – the stuff of dreams on waking.

Then she was gone, plummeting straight down with her toes pointed toward the earth, her gown billowing up her neck and over her face in drifts. She didn't scream.

She went down as silently as a defective skyrocket.

When he heard the indescribable thud of her hard landing, Flagg threw his head back to the sky and howled.

It made no difference, it made no difference.

It was still all in the palm of his hand.

He leaned over the parapet again and watched them come running, like iron filings drawn to a magnet. Or maggots to a piece of offal.

They looked so small, and he was so high above them.

He would levitate, he decided, and regain his state of calm.

But it was a long, long time before his bootheels would leave the sundeck, and when they did they would only hover a quarter of an inch above the concrete. They would go no higher.

Tom awoke that night at eight o'clock, but there was still too much light to move. He waited. Nick had come to him again in his sleep, and they had talked. It was so good to talk to Nick.

He lay in the shade of the big rock and watched the sky darken.

The stars began to peep out. He thought about Pringle's Potato Chips and wished he had some. When he got back to the Zone – if he *did* get back to the Zone – he would have all of them he wanted. He would gorge on Pringle's chips. And bask in the love of his friends. That was what was missing back there in Las Vegas, he decided – simple love. They were nice enough people and all, but there wasn't much love in them. Because they were too busy being afraid. Love didn't grow very well in a place where there was only fear, just as plants didn't grow very well in a place where it was always dark.

Only mushrooms and toadstools grew big and fat in the dark, even he knew that, laws, yes.

'I love Nick and Frannie and Dick Ellis and Lucy,' Tom whispered. It was his prayer. 'I love Larry Underwood and Glen Bateman, too. I love Stan and Rona. I love Ralph. I love Stu. I love –'

It was odd, how easily their names came to him. Why, back in the Zone he was lucky if he could remember Stu's name when he came to visit. His thoughts turned to his toys. His garage, his cars, his model trains. He had played with them by the hour. But he wondered if he would want to play with them so much when he got back from this . . . *if* he got back. It wouldn't be the same. That was sad, but maybe it was also good.

'The Lord is my shepherd,' he recited softly. 'I shall not want for nothing. He makes me lie down in the green pastures. He greases up my head with oil. He gives me kung-fu in the face of my enemies. Amen.'

It was dark enough now, and he pushed on. By eleven-thirty that night he had reached God's Finger, and he paused there for a little lunch. The ground was high here, and looking back the way he had come, he could see moving lights. On the turnpike, he thought. They're looking for me.

Tom looked northeast again. Far ahead, barely visible in the dark (the moon, now two nights past full, had already begun to sink), he saw a huge rounded granite dome. He was supposed to go there next.

'Tom's got sore feet,' he whispered to himself, but not without some cheeriness. Things could have been much worse than a case of sore feet. 'M-O-O-N, that spells sore feet.'

He walked on, and the night things skittered away from him, and when he laid himself down at dawn, he had come almost forty miles. The Nevada-Utah border was not far to the east of him.

By eight that morning he was hard asleep, his head pillowed on his jacket. His eyes began to move rapidly back and forth behind his closed lids.

Nick had come, and Tom talked with him.

A frown creased Tom's sleeping brow. He had told Nick how much he was looking forward to seeing him again.

But for some reason he could not understand, Nick had turned away.

CHAPTER 68

Oh, how history repeats itself: Trashcan Man was once again being broiled alive in the devil's frying pan – but this time there was no hope of Cibola's cooling fountains to sustain him.

It's what I deserve, no more than what I deserve.

His skin had burned, peeled, burned, peeled again, and finally it had not tanned but blackened. He was walking proof that a man finally takes on the look of what he is. Trash looked as if someone had doused him in #2 kerosene and struck a match to him. The blue of his eyes had faded in the constant desert glare, and looking into them was like looking into weird, extra-dimensional holes in space. He was dressed in a strange imitation of the dark man – an open-throated red-checked shirt, faded jeans, and desert boots that were already scratched and mashed and folded and sprung. But he had thrown away his red-flawed amulet. He didn't deserve to wear it. He had proved unworthy. And like all imperfect devils, he had been cast out.

He paused in the broiling sun and passed a thin and shaking hand across his brow. He had been meant for this place and time – all his life had been preparation. He had passed through the burning corridors of hell to get here. He had endured the father-killing sheriff, he had endured that place at Terre Haute, he had endured Carley Yates. After all his strange and lonely life, he had found friends. Lloyd. Ken. Whitney Horgan.

And ah God, he had fucked it all up. He deserved to burn out here in the devil's frying pan. Could there be redemption for him? The dark man might know. Trashcan did not.

He could barely remember now what had happened – perhaps because his tortured mind did not *want* to remember. He had been in the desert for over a week before his last disastrous return to Indian Springs. A scorpion had stung him on the middle finger of his left hand (his fuckfinger, that long-ago Carley Yates in that long-ago

Powtanville would have called it with unfailing pool-hall vulgarity), and that hand had swelled up like a rubber glove filled with water. An unearthly fire had filled his head. And yet he had pushed on.

He had finally returned to Indian Springs, still feeling like a figment of someone else's imagination. There had been some good-natured talk as the men examined his finds – incendiary fuses, contact landmines, small stuff, really. Trash had begun to feel good for the first time since the scorpion had stung him.

And then, with no warning at all, time had sideslipped and he was back in Powtanville. Someone had said, 'People who play with fire wet the bed, Trash,' and he had looked up, expecting to see Billy Jamieson, but it hadn't been Bill, it was Rich Groudemore from Powtanville, grinning and picking his teeth with a match, his fingers black with grease because he'd strolled up to the pool-hall from the Texaco on the corner to have a game of nine-ball on his break. And someone else said, 'You better put that away, Richie, Trash is back in town,' and that sounded like Steve Tobin at first, but it wasn't Steve. It was Carley Yates in his old, scuffed, and hoody motorcycle jacket. With growing horror he had seen they were *all* there, unquiet corpses come back to life. Richie Groudemore and Carley and Norm Morrisette and Hatch Cunningham, the one who was getting bald even though he was only eighteen and all of the others called him Hatch Cunnilingus.

And they were leering at him. It came thick and fast then, through a feverhaze of years. *Hey, Trash, why dintchoo torch the SCHOOL? Hey, Trasky, ya burned ya pork off yet? Hey, Trashcan Man, I heard you snort Ronson lighter fluid, that true?*

Then Carley Yates: *Hey, Trash, what did old lady Semple say when you torched her pension check?*

He tried to scream at them, but all that had come out was a whisper: 'Don't ask me about old lady Semple's pension check no more.' And he ran.

The rest of it was a dream. Getting the incendiary fuses and slapping them on the trucks in the motor pool. His hands had done their own work, his mind far away in a confused whirl. People had seen him coming and going between the motor pool and his sandtrack with its big balloon tires, and some of them had even waved, but no one had come over and asked what he was doing. After all, he wore Flagg's charm.

Trashy did his work and thought about Terre Haute.

In Terre Haute they had made him bite on a rubber thing when they gave him the shocks, and the man at the controls sometimes looked like the father-killing sheriff and sometimes like Carley Yates and sometimes like Hatch Cunnilingus. And he always swore hysterically to himself that this time he wouldn't piss himself. And he always did.

When the trucks were fixed, he had gone into the nearest hangar and had fixed the choppers in there. He had wanted timer fuses to do that job right, and so he had gone into the messhall kitchen and had found over a dozen of those five-and-dime plastic timers. You set them for fifteen minutes or half an hour and when they got back to zero they went *ding* and you knew it was time to take your pie out of the oven. Only instead of going *ding* this time, Trash had thought, they are going to go *bang*. He liked that. That was pretty good. If Carley Yates or Rich Groudemore tried taking one of those copters up, they were going to get a big fat surprise. He had simply hooked the kitchen timers up to the copter ignition systems.

When it was done, a moment of sanity had come back. A moment of choice. He had stared around wonderingly at the helicopters parked in the echoing hangar and then down at his hands. They smelled like a roll of burned caps. But this was not Powtanville. There were no helicopters in Powtanville. The Indiana sun did not shine with the savage brilliance of this sun. He was in Nevada. Carley and his pool-hall buddies were dead. Dead of the superflu.

Trash had turned around and looked doubtfully at his handiwork. What was he doing, sabotaging the dark man's equipment? It was senseless, insane. He would undo it, and quickly.

Oh, but the lovely explosions.

The lovely *fires*.

Flaming jet fuel streaming everywhere. Helicopters exploding out of the air. So beautiful.

And he had suddenly thrown his new life away. He had trotted back to his sand-crawler, a furtive grin on his sun-blackened face. He had gotten in and had driven away . . . but not too far away. He had waited, and finally a fuel truck had come out of the motor pool garage and had trundled across the tarmac like a large olive-drab beetle. And when it blew, exploding greasy fire in every direction, Trash had dropped his fieldglasses and had bellowed at the sky, shaking his fists in inarticulate joy. But the joy had not lasted long.

It had been replaced by deadly terror and sick, mourning sorrow.

He had driven northwest into the desert, pushing the sand-crawler along at near-suicidal speeds. How long ago? He didn't know. If he had been told that this was the sixteenth of September, he would only have nodded in a total blank lack of understanding.

He thought he would kill himself, that there was nothing else left for him, every hand was turned against him now, and that was just as it was supposed to be. When you bit the hand that fed you, you expected that extended hand to curl into a fist. That wasn't only the way life went; that was justice. He had three large cans of gasoline in the back of the track. He would pour it all over himself and then strike a match. It was what he deserved.

But he hadn't done it. He didn't know why. Some force, more powerful than the agony of his remorse and loneliness, had stopped him. It seemed that even burning himself to death like a Buddhist monk was not penance enough. He had slept. And when he awoke, he discovered that a new thought had crept into his brain as he slept, and that thought was:

REDEMPTION.

Was it possible? He didn't know. But if he found some-thing . . . something *big* . . . and brought it to the dark man in Las Vegas, might it not be possible? And even if *REDEMPTION* was impossible, perhaps *ATONEMENT* was not. If it was true, there was still a chance he could die content.

What? What could it be? What was big enough for *REDEMPTION*, or even for *ATONEMENT*? Not landmines or a fleet of flametracks, not grenades or automatic weapons. None of those things were big enough. He knew where there were two large experimental bombers (they had been built without congressional knowledge, paid for out of blind defense funds), but he could not get them back to Vegas, and even if he could, there was no one there who could fly them. From the looks of them, they crewed at least ten, maybe more.

He was like an infrared scope that senses heat in darkness and reveals those heat sources as vague red-devil shapes. He was able, in some strange way, to sense the things that had been left behind in this wasteland, where so many military projects had been carried out. He could have gone straight west, straight to Project Blue, where the whole thing had begun. But cold plague was not to his taste, and in his confused but not entirely illogical way, he thought it would not be to Flagg's taste, either. Plague didn't care who it killed. It might have been better for the human race if the original funders of Project Blue had kept that simple fact in mind.

So he had gone northwest from Indian Springs, into the sandy desolation of the Nellis Air Force Range, stopping his crawler when he had to cut through high barbed-wire fences marked with signs that read US GOVERNMENT PROPERTY NO TRESPASSING and ARMED SENTRIES and GUARD DOGS and THERE IS A HIGH–VOLTAGE CHARGE PASSING THROUGH THESE WIRES. But the electricity was dead, like the guard dogs and the armed sentries, and Trashcan Man drove on, correcting his course from time to time. He was being drawn, drawn to something. He didn't know what it was, but he thought it was big. Big enough.

The crawler's Goodyear balloon tires rolled steadily on, carrying Trash through dry-washes and up slopes so rocky that they looked like half-exposed stegosaurus spines. The air hung still and dry. The temperature hovered at just above 100. The only sound was the drone of the crawler's modified Studebaker engine.

He topped a knoll, saw what was below, and threw the transmission into neutral for a moment to get a better look.

There was a huddled complex of buildings down there; shimmering through the rising heat like quicksilver. Quonset huts and low cinderblock. Vehicles stalled here and there on dusty streets. The whole area was surrounded by three courses of barbed wire, and he could see the porcelain conductors along the wire. These were not the small conductors the size of a knuckle that passed along a weak stayaway charge; these were the giant ones, the size of a closed fist.

From the east, a paved two-lane road led to a guardhouse that looked like a reinforced pillbox. No cute little signs here saying CHECK YOUR CAMERA WITH MP ON DUTY or IF YOU LIKED US, TELL YOUR CONGRESSMAN. The only sign in evidence was red on yellow, the colors of danger, curt and to the point: PRESENT IDENTIFICATION IMMEDIATELY.

'Thank you,' Trashcan whispered. He had no idea who he was thanking. 'Oh thank you . . . thank you.' His special sense had led him to this place, but he had known it was here all along. Somewhere.

He put the sandtrack in its forward gear and lurched down the slope. Ten minutes later he was nosing up the access road to the guardhouse. There were black-and-white-striped crash barriers across the road, and Trash got out to examine them. Places like this had big generators to make sure there was plenty of emergency power. He doubted if any generator would have gone on supplying power for three months, but he would still have to be very careful and make sure everything was blown before going in. What he wanted was now very near at hand. He wouldn't allow himself to become overeager and get cooked like a roast in a microwave oven.

Behind six inches of bulletproof glass, a mummy in an army uniform stared out and beyond him.

Trash ducked under the crash barrier on the ingress side of the guardhouse and approached the door of the little concrete building. He tried it and it opened. That was good. When a place like this had to switch over to emergency power, everything was supposed to lock automatically. If you were taking a crap, you got locked in the bathroom until the crisis was over. But if the emergency power failed, everything unlocked again.

The dead sentry had a dry, sweet, interesting smell, like cinnamon and sugar mixed together for toast. He had not bloated or rotted; he had simply dried up. There were still black discolorations under his neck, the distinctive trademark of Captain Trips. Standing in the corner behind him was a Browning automatic rifle. Trashcan Man took it and went back outside.

He set the BAR for single fire, fiddled with the sight, and then socked it into the hollow of his scrawny right shoulder. He sighted down on one of the porcelain conductors and squeezed off a shot. There was a loud hand-clapping sound and an exciting whiff of cordite. The conductor exploded every which way, but there was no purple-white glare of high-voltage electricity. Trashcan Man smiled.

Humming, he walked over to the gate and examined it. Like the guardhouse door, it was unlocked. He pushed it open a little way and then hunkered down. There was a pressure mine here, under the paving. He didn't know how he knew, but he did know. It might be armed; it might not be.

He went back to the sandtrack, put it in gear, and drove it through the crash barriers. They broke off with a snapping, grinding sound and the crawler's big balloon tires rolled over them. The desert sun pounded down. Trashcan Man's peculiar eyes sparkled happily. In front of the gate, he got out of the sandtrack and then put it in gear again. The driverless track rolled forward and pushed the gate all the way open. Trashcan Man darted into the guardhouse.

He squinched his eyes shut, but there was no explosion. That was good; they really had shut down completely. Their emergency systems might have run a month, perhaps even two, but in the end the heat and lack of regular maintenance had killed them. Still, he would be careful.

Meanwhile, his sandtrack was rolling serenely toward the corrugated wall of a long Quonset hut. Trashcan Man trotted onto the base after it and caught up with it just as it was bumping over the curb of what a sign announced was Illinois Street. He put it back into neutral, and the sandtrack stopped. He got in, reversed, and drove around to the front of the Quonset.

It was a barracks. The shadowy interior was filled with that sugar-and-cinnamon smell. There were perhaps twenty soldiers scattered among the fifty or so beds. Trashcan Man walked up the aisle between them, wondering where he was going. There was nothing in here for him, was there? These men had once been weapons of a sort, but they had been neutralized by the flu.

But there was something at the very rear of the building that interested him. A sign. He walked up to read it. The heat in here was tremendous. It made his head thump and swell. But when he stood in front of the sign, he began to smile. Yes, it was here. Somewhere on this base was what he had been looking for.

The sign showed a cartoon man in a cartoon shower. He was soaping his cartoon genitals busily; they were almost entirely covered with a drift of cartoon bubbles. The caption beneath read: REMEMBER! IT IS IN YOUR BEST INTEREST TO SHOWER DAILY!

Below that was a yellow-and-black emblem that showed three triangles pointed downward.

The symbol for radiation.

Trashcan Man laughed like a child and clapped his hands in the stillness.

CHAPTER 69

Whitney Horgan found Lloyd in his room, lying on the big round bed he had most recently shared with Dayna Jurgens. There was a large gin and tonic balanced on his bare chest. He was staring solemnly up at his reflection in the overhead mirror.

'Come on in,' he said when he saw Whitney. 'Don't stand on ceremony, for Chrissake. Don't bother to knock. Bastard.' It came out as *bassard*.

'You drunk, Lloyd?' Whitney asked cautiously.

'Nope. Not yet. But I'm gettin there.'

'Is *he* here?'

'Who? Fearless Leader?' Lloyd sat up. 'He's around someplace. The Midnight Rambler.' He laughed and lay back down.

Whitney said in a low voice, 'You want to watch what you're saying. You know it's not a good idea to hit the hard stuff when he's —'

'Fuck it.'

'Remember what happened to Hec Drogan. And Strellerton.'

Lloyd nodded. 'You're right. The walls have ears. The fucking walls have ears. You ever hear that saying?'

'Yeah, once or twice. It's a true saying around here, Lloyd.'

'You bet.' Lloyd suddenly sat up and threw his drink across the room. The glass shattered. 'There's one for the sweeper, right, Whitney?'

'You okay, Lloyd?'

'I'm all right. You want a gin and tonic?'

Whitney hesitated for a moment. 'Naw. I don't like them without the lime.'

'Hey, Jesus, don't say no just because of that! I *got* lime. Comes out of a little squeeze bottle.' Lloyd went over to the bar and held up a plastic ReaLime. 'Looks just like the Green Giant's left testicle. Funny, huh?'

'Does it taste like lime?'

'Sure,' Lloyd said morosely. 'What do you *think* it tastes like? Fuckin Cheerios? So what do you say? Be a man and have a drink with me.'

'Well . . . okay.'

'We'll have them by the window and take in the view.'

'No,' Whitney said, harshly and abruptly. Lloyd paused on his way to the bar, his face suddenly paling. He looked toward Whitney, and for a moment their eyes met.

'Yeah, okay,' Lloyd said. 'Sorry, man. Poor taste.'

'That's okay.'

But it wasn't okay, and both of them knew it. The woman Flagg had introduced as his 'bride' had taken a high dive the day before. Lloyd remembered Ace High saying that Dayna couldn't jump from the balcony because the windows didn't open. But the penthouse had a sundeck. Guess they must have thought none of the *real* high rollers – Arabs, most of them – would ever take the dive. A lot they knew.

He fixed Whitney a gin and tonic and they sat and drank in silence for a while. Outside, the sun was going down in a red glare. At last Whitney said in a voice almost too low to be heard: 'Do you really think she went on her own?'

Lloyd shrugged. 'What does it matter? Sure. I think she dived. Wouldn't you, if you was married to *him*? You ready?'

Whitney looked at his glass and saw with some surprise that he was indeed ready. He handed it to Lloyd, who took it over to the bar. Lloyd was pouring the gin freehand, and Whitney had a nice buzz on.

Again they drank in silence for a while, watching the sun go down.

'What do you hear about that guy Cullen?' Whitney asked finally.

'Nothing. Doodley-squat. El-zilcho. I don't hear nothing, Barry don't hear nothing. Nothing from Route 40, from Route 30, from Route 2 and 74 and I-15. Nothing from the back roads. They're all covered and they're all nothing. He's out in the desert someplace, and if he keeps moving at night and if he can figure out how to keep moving east, he's going to slip through. And what does it matter, anyhow? What can he tell them?'

'I don't know.'

'I don't either. Let him go, that's what I say.'

Whitney felt uncomfortable. Lloyd was getting perilously close to criticizing the boss again. His buzz-on was stronger, and he was glad. Maybe soon he would find the nerve to say what he had come here to say.

'I'll tell you something,' Lloyd said, leaning forward. 'He's losing his stuff. You ever hear that fucking saying? It's the eighth inning and he's losing his stuff and there's no-fucking-body warming up in the bullpen.'

'Lloyd, I —'

'You ready?'

'Sure, I guess.'

Lloyd made them new drinks. He handed one to Whitney, and a little shiver went through him as he sipped. It was almost raw gin.

'Losing his stuff,' Lloyd said, returning to his text. 'First Dayna, then this guy Cullen. His own wife — if that's what she was — goes and takes a dive. Do you think her double-fucking-gainer from the penthouse balcony was in his game plan?'

'We shouldn't be talking about it.'

'And Trashcan Man. Look what that guy did all by himself. With fiends like that, who needs enemas? That's what I'd like to know.'

'Lloyd —'

Lloyd was shaking his head. 'I don't understand it at all. Everything was going so good, right up to the night he came and said the old lady was dead over there in the Free Zone. He said the last obstacle was out of our way. But that's when things started to get funny.'

'Lloyd, I really don't think we should be —'

'Now I just don't know. We can take em by land assault next spring, I guess. We sure as shit can't go before then. But by next spring, God knows what they might have rigged up over there, you know? We were going to hit them before they could think up any funny surprises, and now we can't. Plus, holy God on His throne, there's Trashy to think about. He's out there in the desert ramming around someplace, and I sure as hell —'

'Lloyd,' Whitney said in a low, choked voice. 'Listen to me.'

Lloyd leaned forward, concerned. 'What? What's the trouble, old hoss?'

'I didn't even know if I'd have the guts to ask you,' Whitney said. He was squeezing his glass compulsively. 'Me and Ace High and Ronnie Sykes and Jenny Engstrom. We're cutting loose. You want to come? Christ, I must be crazy telling you this, with you so close to him.'

'Cutting loose? Where are you going?'

'South America, I guess. Brazil. That ought to be just about far enough.' He paused, struggling, then plunged on. 'A lot of people have been leaving. Well, maybe not a lot, but quite a few, and there's more every day. They don't think Flagg can cut it. Some are going north, up to Canada. That's too frigging cold for me. But I got to get out. I'd go east if I thought they'd have me. And if I was sure we could get through.' Whitney stopped abruptly and looked at Lloyd miserably. It was the face of a man who thinks he has gone much too far.

'You're all right,' Lloyd said softly. 'I ain't going to blow the whistle on you, old hoss.'

'It's just . . . all gone bad here,' Whitney said miserably.

'When you planning to go?' Lloyd asked.

Whitney looked at him with narrow suspicion.

'Aw, forget I asked,' Lloyd said. 'You ready?'

'Not yet,' Whitney said, looking into his glass.

'I am.' He went to the bar. With his back to Whitney he said, 'I couldn't.'

'Huh?'

'*Couldn't!*' Lloyd said sharply, and turned back to Whitney. 'I owe him something. I owe him a lot. He got me out of a bad jam back in Phoenix and I been with him since then. Seems longer than it really is. Sometimes it seems like forever.'

'I'll bet.'

'But it's more than that. He's done something to me, made me brighter or something. I don't know what it is, but I ain't the same man I was, Whitney. Nothing like. Before . . . *him* . . . I was nothing but a minor leaguer. Now he's got me running things here, and I do okay. It seems like I think better. Yeah, he's made me brighter.' Lloyd lifted the flawed stone from his chest, looked at it briefly, then dropped it again. He wiped his hand against his pants as though it had touched something nasty. 'I know I ain't no genius now. I have to write everything I'm s'posed to do in a notebook or I forget it. But with him behind me I can give orders and most times things turn out right.

Before, all I could do was take orders and get in jams. I've changed . . . and he changed me. Yeah, it seems a lot longer than it really is.

'When we got to Vegas, there were only sixteen people here. Ronnie was one of them; so was Jenny and poor old Hec Drogan. They were waiting for him. When we got into town, Jenny Engstrom got down on those pretty knees of hers and kissed his boots. I bet she never told you that in bed.' He smiled crookedly at Whitney. 'Now she wants to cut and run. Well, I don't blame her, or you either. But it sure doesn't take much to sour a good operation, does it?'

'You're going to stick?'

'To the very end, Whitney. His or mine. I owe him that.' He didn't add that he still had enough faith in the dark man to believe that Whitney and the others would end up riding crosstrees, more likely than not. And there was something else. Here he was Flagg's second-in-command. What could he be in Brazil? Why, Whitney and Ronnie were both brighter than he was. He and Ace High would end up low chickens, and that wasn't to Lloyd's taste. Once he wouldn't have minded, but things had changed. And when your head changed, he was finding out, it most always changed forever.

'Well, it might work out for all of us,' Whitney said lamely.

'Sure,' Lloyd said, and thought: *But I wouldn't want to be walking in your shoes if it comes out right for Flagg after all. I wouldn't want to be in your shoes when he finally has time to notice you down there in Brazil. Riding a crosstree might be the least of your worries then . . .*

Lloyd raised his glass. 'A toast, Whitney.'

Whitney raised his own glass.

'Nobody gets hurt,' Lloyd said. 'That's my toast. Nobody gets hurt.'

'Man, I'll drink to that,' Whitney said fervently, and they both did.

Whitney left soon after. Lloyd kept on drinking. He passed out around nine-thirty and slept soddenly on the round bed. There were no dreams, and that was almost worth the price of the next day's hangover.

When the sun rose on the morning of September 17, Tom Cullen made his camp a little north of Gunlock, Utah. It was cold enough for him to be able to see his breath puffing out in front of him. His ears were numb and cold. But he felt good. He had passed quite close to a rutted bad road the night before, and he had seen three men gathered around a small spluttering campfire. All three had guns.

Trying to ease past them through a tangled field of boulders – he was now on the western edge of the Utah badlands – he had sent a small splatter of pebbles rolling and tumbling into a dry-wash. Tom froze. Warm wee-wee spilled down his legs, but he wasn't even aware that he'd done it in his pants like a little baby until an hour or so later.

All three of them turned around, two of them bringing their weapons up to port arms. Tom's cover was thin, barely adequate. He was a shadow among shadows. The moon was behind a reef of clouds. If it chose this moment to come out . . .

One of them relaxed. 'It's a deer,' he said. 'They're all over the place.'

'I think we should investigate,' another had said.

'Put your thumb up your asshole and investigate that,' the third replied, and that was the end of it. They sat by the fire again, and Tom began to creep along, feeling for each step, watching as their campfire receded with agonizing slowness. An hour and it was only a spark on the slope below him. Finally it was gone and a great weight seemed to slip off his shoulders. He began to feel safe. He was still in the West and he knew enough to be careful – laws, yes – but the danger no longer seemed as thick, as if there were Indians or outlaws all around.

And now, with the sun coming up, he rolled into a tight ball in the low thicket of bushes and prepared to go to sleep. *Got to get some blankets*, he thought. *It's getting cold.* Then sleep took him, suddenly and completely, as it always did.

He dreamed of Nick.

CHAPTER 70

Trashcan Man had found what he wanted.

He came along a hallway deep underground, a hallway as dark as a minepit. In his left hand he held a flashlight. In his right hand he held a gun, because it was spooky down here. He was riding an electric tram that rolled almost silently along the wide corridor. The only sound it made was a low, almost subaural hum.

The tram consisted of a seat for the driver and a large carry space. Resting in the carry space was an atomic warhead.

It was heavy.

Trash could not make an intelligent guess as to just how heavy it was, because he hadn't even been able to budge it by hand. It was long and cylindrical. It was cold. Running his hand over its curved surface, he had found it hard to believe that such a cold dead lump of metal could have the potential for so much heat.

He had found it at four in the morning. He had gone back to the motor pool and had gotten a chainfall. He had brought the chainfall back down and had rigged it over the warhead. Ninety minutes later, it was nestled cozily into the electric tram, nose up. Stamped on the nose was A161410USAF. The hard rubber tires of the tram had settled appreciably when he put it in.

Now he was coming to the end of the hallway. Straight ahead was the large freight elevator with its doors standing invitingly open. It was plenty big enough to take the tram, but of course there was no electricity. Trash had gotten down by the stairs. He had brought the chainfall down the same way. The chainfall was light compared to the warhead. It only weighed a hundred and fifty pounds or so. And still it had been a major chore getting it down five courses of stairs.

How was he going to get the warhead *up* those stairs?

Power-driver winch, his mind whispered.

Sitting on the driver's seat and shining his flash randomly around,

Trash nodded to himself. Sure, that was the ticket. Winch it up. Set a motor topside and pull it up, stair-riser by stair-riser, if he had to. But where was he going to find five hundred feet of chain all in one piece?

Well, he probably wasn't. But he could weld pieces of chain together. Would that work? Would the welds hold? It was hard to say. And even if they did, what about all the switchbacks the stairs made going up?

He hopped down and ran a caressing hand over the smooth, deadly surface of the warhead in the silent darkness.

Love would find a way.

Leaving the warhead in the tram, he began to climb the stairs again to see what he could find. A base like this, there would be a little of everything. He would find what he needed.

He climbed two flights and paused to catch his breath. He suddenly wondered: *Have I been taking radiation?* They shielded all that stuff, shielded it with lead. But in the movies you saw on TV, the men who handled radioactive stuff were always wearing those protective suits and film badges that turned color if you got a dose. Because it was silent. You couldn't see it. It just settled into your flesh and your bones. You didn't even know you were sick until you started puking and losing your hair and having to run to the bathroom every few minutes.

Was all that going to happen to him?

He discovered that he didn't care. He was going to get that bomb up. Somehow he was going to get it up. Somehow he was going to get it back to Las Vegas. He had to make up for the terrible thing he had done at Indian Springs. If he had to die to atone, then he would die.

'My life for you,' he whispered in the darkness, and began to climb the stairs again.

CHAPTER 71

It was nearly midnight on the evening of September 17. Randall Flagg was in the desert, wrapped in three blankets, from toes to chin. A fourth blanket was swirled around his head in a kind of burnoose, so that only his eyes and the tip of his nose were visible.

Little by little, he let all thoughts slip away. He grew still. The stars were cold fire, witchlight.

He sent out the Eye.

He felt it separate from himself with a small and painless tug. It went flying away, silent as a hawk, rising on dark thermals. Now he had joined with the night. He was eye of crow, eye of wolf, eye of weasel, eye of cat. He was the scorpion, the strutting trapdoor spider. He was a deadly poison arrow slipping endlessly through the desert air. Whatever else might have happened, the Eye had not left him.

Flying effortlessly, the world of earthbound things spread out below him like a clockface.

They're coming . . . they're almost in Utah now . . .

He flew high, wide, and silent over a graveyard world. Below him the desert lay like a whited sepulcher cut by the dark ribbon of the interstate highway. He flew east, over the state line now, his body far behind, glittering eyes rolled up to blind whites.

Now the land began to change. Buttes and strange, wind-carved pillars and tabletop mesas. The highway ran straight through. The Bonneville Salt Flats lay to the far north. Skull Valley somewhere west. Flying. The sound of the wind, dead and distant . . .

An eagle poised in the highest crotch of an ancient lightning-blasted pine somewhere south of Richfield felt something pass close by, some deadly sighted thing whizzing through the night, and the eagle took wing against it, fearless, and was buffeted away by a grinning sensation of deadly cold. The eagle fell almost all the way to the ground, stunned, before recovering itself.

The dark man's Eye went east.

Now the highway below was I-70. The towns were huddled lumps, deserted except for the rats and the cats and the deer that had already begun to creep in from the forests as the scent of man washed away. Towns with names like Freemont and Green River and Sego and Thompson and Harley Dome. Then a small city, also deserted. Grand Junction, Colorado. Then –

Just east of Grand Junction was a spark of campfire.

The Eye spiraled down.

The fire was dying. There were four figures sleeping around it. It was true, then.

The Eye appraised them coldly. They were coming. For reasons he could not fathom, they were actually coming. Nadine had told the truth.

There was a low growling, and the Eye turned in another direction. There was a dog on the far side of the campfire, its head lowered, its tail coiled down and over its privates. Its eyes glowed like baleful amber gems. Its growl was a constant thing, like endlessly ripping cloth. The Eye stared at it, and the dog stared back, unafraid. Its lip curled back and it showed its teeth.

One of the forms rose to a sitting position. 'Kojak,' it mumbled. 'Will you for Chrissakes shut up?'

Kojak continued to growl, his hackles up.

The man who had awakened – it was Glen Bateman – looked around, suddenly uneasy. 'Who's there, boy?' he whispered to the dog. 'Is something there?'

Kojak continued to growl.

'Stu!' He shook the form next to him. The form muttered something and was silent again in its sleeping bag.

The dark man who was now the dark Eye had seen enough. He whirled upward, catching just a glimpse of the dog's neck craning up to follow him. The low growl turned into a volley of barks, loud at first, then fading, fading, gone.

Silence and rushing darkness.

Some unknown time later he paused over the desert floor, looking down at himself. He sank slowly, approaching the body, then sinking into himself. For a moment there was a curious sensation of vertigo, of two things merging into one. Then the Eye was gone and there were only his eyes, staring up at the cold and gleaming stars.

They were coming, yes.

Flagg smiled. Had the old woman told them to come? Would they listen to her if she, on her deathbed, instructed them to commit suicide in that novel way? He supposed it was possible that they would.

What he had forgotten was so staggeringly simple that it was humbling: *They* were having their problems too, *they* were frightened too . . . and as a result, they were making a colossal mistake.

Was it even possible that they had been turned out?

He lingered lovingly over the idea but in the end could not quite believe it. They were coming of their own choice. They were coming wrapped in righteousness like a clutch of missionaries approaching the cannibal's village.

Oh, it was so lovely!

Doubts would end. Fears would end. All it would take was the sight of their four heads up on spikes in front of the MGM Grand's fountain. He would assemble every person in Vegas and make them file past and look. He would have photographs taken, would print fliers, have them sent out to LA and San Francisco and Spokane and Portland.

Five heads. He would put the dog's head up on a pole, too.

'Good doggy,' Flagg said, and laughed aloud for the first time since Nadine had goaded him into throwing her off the roof. 'Good doggy,' he said again, grinning.

He slept well that night, and in the morning he sent out word that the watch on the roads between Utah and Nevada was to be tripled. They were no longer looking for one man going east but four men and a dog going west. And they were to be taken alive. Taken alive at all costs.

Oh, yes.

CHAPTER 72

'You know,' Glen Bateman said, looking out toward Grand Junction in the early light of morning, 'I've heard the saying "That sucks" for years without really being sure of what it meant. Now I think I know.' He looked down at his breakfast, which consisted of Morning Star Farms synthetic sausage links, and grimaced.

'No, this is *good*,' Ralph said earnestly. 'You should have had some of the chow we had in the army.'

They were sitting around the campfire, which Larry had rekindled an hour earlier. They were all dressed in warm coats and gloves, and all were on their second cups of coffee. The temperature was about thirty-five degrees, and the sky was cloudy and bleak. Kojak was napping as close to the fire as he could get without singeing his fur.

'I'm done feeding the inner man,' Glen said, getting up. 'Give me your poor, your hungry. On second thought, just give me your garbage. I'll bury it.'

Stu handed him his paper plate and cup. 'This walkin's really something, isn't it, baldy? I bet you ain't been in this good shape since you were twenty.'

'Yeah, seventy years ago,' Larry said, and laughed.

'Stu, I was never in this kind of shape,' Glen said grimly, picking up litter and popping it into the plastic sack he intended to bury. 'I never *wanted* to be in this kind of shape. But I don't mind. After fifty years of confirmed agnosticism, it seems to be my fate to follow an old black woman's God into the jaws of death. If that's my fate, then that's my fate. End of story. But I'd rather walk than ride, when you get right down to it. Walking takes longer, consequently I live longer . . . by a few days, anyway. Excuse me, gentlemen, while I give this swill a decent burial.'

They watched him walk to the edge of the camp with a small

entrenching tool. This 'walking tour of Colorado and points west,' as Glen put it, had been the hardest on Glen himself. He was the oldest, Ralph Brentner's senior by twelve years. But somehow he had eased it considerably for the others. His irony was constant but gentle, and he seemed at peace with himself. The fact that he was able to keep going day after day made an impression on the others even if it was not exactly an inspiration. He was fifty-seven, and Stu had seen him working his finger-joints on these last three or four cold mornings, and grimacing as he did it.

'Hurt bad?' Stu had asked him yesterday, about an hour after they had moved out.

'Aspirin takes care of it. It's arthritis, you know, but it's not as bad as it's apt to be in another five or seven years, and frankly, East Texas, I'm not looking that far ahead.'

'You really think he's going to take us?'

And Glen Bateman had said a peculiar thing: 'I will fear no evil.' And that had been the end of the discussion.

Now they heard him digging at the frozen soil and cursing it.

'Quite a fella, ain't he?' Ralph said.

Larry nodded. 'Yes. I think he is.'

'I always thought those college teachers was sissies, but that man sure ain't. Know what he said when I asked him why he didn't just throw that crap to one side of the road? Said we didn't need to start up that kind of shit again. Said we'd started up too many of the old brands of shit already.'

Kojak got up and trotted over to see what Glen was doing. Glen's voice floated over to them: 'Well, there you are, you big lazy turd. I was starting to wonder where you'd gotten off to. Want me to bury you too?'

Larry grinned and took off the mileometer clipped to his belt. He had picked it up in a Golden sports supply shop. You set it according to the length of your stride and then clipped it to your belt like a carpenter's rule. Each evening he wrote down how far they had walked that day on a dog-eared and often-folded sheet of paper.

'Can I see that cheat sheet?' Stu asked.

'Sure,' Larry said, and handed it over.

At the top of the sheet Larry had printed: *Boulder to Vegas: 771 miles*. Below that:

Date	Miles	Total Miles
September 6th	28.1	28.1
September 7th	27.0	55.1
September 8th	26.5	81.6
September 9th	28.2	109.8
September 10th	27.9	137.7
September 11th	29.1	166.8
September 12th	28.8	195.6
September 13th	29.5	225.1
September 14th	32.0	257.1
September 15th	32.6	289.7
September 16th	35.5	325.2
September 17th	37.2	362.4

Stu took a scrap of paper from his wallet and did some subtraction. 'Well, we're makin better time than when we started out, but we've still got over four hundred miles to go. Shit, we ain't halfway yet.'

Larry nodded. 'Better time is right. We're going downhill. And Glen's right, you know. Why do we want to hurry? Guy's just gonna wipe us out when we get over there.'

'You know, I just don't believe that,' Ralph said. 'We may die, sure, but it isn't going to be anything simple, anything cut and dried. Mother Abagail wouldn't send us off if we was to be just murdered and nothing more come of it. She just wouldn't.'

'I don't believe she was the one who sent us,' Stu said quietly.

Larry's mileometer made four distinct little clicks as he set it for the day: ooo.o. Stu doused what remained of the campfire with dirt. The little rituals of the morning went on. They had been twelve days on the road. It seemed to Stu that the days would go on forever like this: Glen bitching good-naturedly about the food, Larry noting their mileage on his dog-eared cheat sheet, the two cups of coffee, someone burying yesterday's scut, someone else burying the fire. It was routine, good routine. You forgot what it was all leading to, and that was good. In the mornings Fran seemed very distant to him – very clear, but very distant, like a photograph kept in a locket. But in the evenings, when the dark had come and the moon sailed the night, she seemed very close. Almost close enough to touch . . . and that, of course, was where the ache lay. At times like those his faith in Mother Abagail turned to bitter doubt and he wanted to wake them all up and tell them it was a fool's errand, that they had taken up rubber lances to tilt at a lethal windmill, that they had better stop at the next town, get motorcycles, and go back. That they had better grab a little light and a little love while they still could – because a little was all Flagg was going to allow them.

But that was at night. In the mornings it still seemed right to go on. He looked speculatively at Larry, and wondered if Larry thought about his Lucy late at night. Dreamed about her and wished . . .

Glen came back into camp with Kojak at his heel, wincing a little as he walked. 'Let's go get em,' he said. 'Right, Kojak?'

Kojak wagged his tail.

'He says Las Vegas or bust,' Glen said. 'Come on.'

They climbed the embankment to I-70, now descending toward Grand Junction, and began their day's walk.

Late that afternoon, a cold rain began to fall, chilling them all and damping conversation. Larry walked by himself, hands shoved in his pockets. At first he thought about Harold Lauder, whose corpse they had found two days ago – there seemed to be an unspoken conspiracy among them not to talk about Harold – but eventually his thoughts turned to the person he had dubbed the Wolfman.

They had found the Wolfman just east of the Eisenhower Tunnel. The traffic was badly jammed up there, and the stink of death had been sickly potent. The Wolfman had been half in and half out of an Austin. He was wearing pegged jeans and a silk sequined Western shirt. The corpses of several wolves lay around the Austin. The Wolfman himself was half in and half out of the Austin's passenger seat, and a dead wolf lay on his chest. The Wolfman's hands were wrapped around the wolf's neck, and the wolf's bloody muzzle was angled up to the Wolfman's neck. Reconstructing, it seemed to all of them that a pack of wolves had come down out of the higher mountains, had spotted this lone man, and had attacked. The Wolfman had had a gun. He had dropped several of them before retreating to the Austin.

How long before hunger had forced him from his refuge?

Larry didn't know, didn't want to know. But he had seen how terribly thin the Wolfman had been. A week, maybe. He had been going west, whoever he was, going to join the dark man, but Larry would not have wished such a dreadful fate on anyone. He had spoken of it once to Stu, two days after they had emerged from the tunnel, with the Wolfman safely behind them.

'Why would a bunch of wolves hang around so long, Stu?'

'I don't know.'

'I mean, if they wanted something to eat, couldn't they find it?'

'I'd think so, yeah.'

It was a dreadful mystery to him, and he kept working it over in his mind, knowing he would never find the solution. Whoever the Wolfman had been, he hadn't been lacking in the balls department. Finally driven by hunger and thirst, he had opened the passenger door. One of the wolves had jumped him and torn his throat out. But the Wolfman had throttled it to death even as he himself died.

The four of them had gone through the Eisenhower Tunnel roped together, and in that horrible blackness, Larry's mind had turned to the trip he had made through the Lincoln Tunnel. Only now it was not images of Rita Blakemoor that haunted him but the face of the Wolfman, frozen in its final snarl as he and the wolf had killed each other.

Were the wolves sent to kill that man?

But that thought was too unsettling to even consider. He tried to push the whole thing out of his mind and just keep walking, but that was a hard thing to do.

They made their camp that night beyond Loma, quite close to the Utah state line. Supper consisted of forage and boiled water, as all their meals did – they were following Mother Abagail's instructions to the letter: Go in the clothes that you stand up in. Carry nothing.

'It's going to get bad in Utah,' Ralph remarked. 'I guess that's where we're going to find out if God really is watchin over us. There's one stretch, better than a hundred miles, without a town or even a gas station and a café.' He didn't seem particularly disturbed by the prospect.

'Water?' Stu asked.

Ralph shrugged. 'Not much of that, either. Guess I'll turn in.'

Larry followed suit. Glen stayed up to smoke a pipe. Stu had a few cigarettes and decided to have one. They smoked in silence for a while.

'Long way from New Hampshire, baldy,' Stu said at last.

'It isn't exactly shouting distance from here to Texas.'

Stu smiled. 'No. No, it ain't.'

'You miss Fran a lot, I guess.'

'Yeah. Miss her, worry about her. Worry about the baby. It's worse after it gets dark.'

Glen puffed. 'That's nothing you can change, Stuart.'

'I know. But I worry.'

'Sure.' Glen knocked out his pipe on a rock. 'Something funny happened last night, Stu. I've been trying to figure out all day if it was real, or a dream, or what.'

'What was it?'

'Well, I woke up in the night and Kojak was growling at something. Must have been past midnight, because the fire had burned way down. Kojak was on the other side of it with his hackles standing up. I told him to shut up and he never even looked at me. He was looking over to my right. And I thought, *What if it's wolves?* Ever since we saw that guy Larry calls the Wolfman –'

'Yeah, that was bad.'

'But there was nothing. I had a clear view. He was growling at *nothing*.'

'He had a scent, that's all.'

'Yeah, but the crazy part is still to come. After a couple of minutes I started to feel . . . well, decidedly weird. I felt like there was something right over by the turnpike embankment, and that it was watching me. Watching all of us. I felt like I could almost see it, that if I squinted my eyes the right way, I *would* see it. But I didn't want to. Because it felt like *him*.'

'It felt like *Flagg*, Stuart.'

'Probably nothing,' Stu said after a moment.

'It sure felt like something. It felt like something to Kojak, too.'

'Well, suppose he *was* watching somehow? What could we do about it?'

'Nothing. But I don't like it. I don't like it that he's able to watch us . . . if that's what it is. It scares me shitless.'

Stu finished his cigarette, stubbed it out carefully on the side of a rock, but made no move toward his sleeping bag just yet. He looked at Kojak, who was lying by the campfire with his nose on his paws and watching them.

'So Harold's dead,' Stu said at last.

'Yes.'

'And it was just a goddam waste. A waste of Sue and Nick. A waste of himself, too, I reckon.'

'I agree.'

There was nothing more to say. They had come upon Harold and his pitiful dying declaration the day after they had done the Eisenhower Tunnel. He and Nadine must have gone over Loveland Pass, because Harold still had his Triumph cycle – the remains of it, anyway – and as Ralph had said, it would have been impossible to get anything bigger than a kid's little red wagon through the Eisenhower. The buzzards had worked him over pretty well, but Harold still clutched the Permacover notebook in one stiffening hand. The .38 was jammed in his mouth like a grotesque lollipop, and although they hadn't buried Harold, Stu had removed the pistol. He had done it gently. Seeing how efficiently the dark man had destroyed Harold and how carelessly he had thrown him aside when his part was played out had made Stu hate Flagg all the more. It made him feel that they were throwing themselves away in a witless sort of children's crusade, and while he felt that they had to press on, Harold's corpse with the shattered leg haunted him the way the frozen grimace of the Wolfman haunted Larry. He had discovered he wanted to pay Flagg back for Harold as well as Nick and Susan . . . but he felt more and more sure that he would never get that chance.

But you want to watch out, he thought grimly. *You want to look out if I get within choking distance of you, you freak.*

Glen got up with a little wince. 'I'm going to turn in, East Texas. Don't beg me to stay. It really is a dull party.'

'How's that arthritis?'

Glen smiled and said, 'Not too bad,' but as he crossed to his bedroll he was limping.

Stu thought he should not have another cigarette – only smoking two or three a day would exhaust his supply by the end of the week – and then he lit one anyway. This evening it was not so cold, but for all that, there could be no doubt that in this high country, at least, summer was done. It made him feel sad, because he felt very strongly that he would never see another summer. When this one had begun, he had been an on-again, off-again worker at a factory that made pocket calculators. He had been living in a small town called Arnette, and he had spent a lot of his spare time hanging around Bill Hapscomb's Texaco station, listening to the other guys shoot the shit about the economy, the government, hard times. Stu guessed that none of them had known what real hard times were. He finished his cigarette and tossed it into the campfire.

'Keep well, Frannie, old kid,' he said, and got into his sleeping bag. And in his dreams he thought that Something had come near their camp, Something that was keeping malevolent watch over them. It might have been a wolf with human understanding. Or a crow. Or a weasel, creeping bellydown through the scrub. Or it might have been some disembodied presence, a watching Eye.

I will fear no evil, he muttered in his dream. *Yea, though I walk through the valley of the shadow of death, I will fear no evil. No evil.*

At last the dream faded and he slept soundly.

The next morning they were on the road again early, Larry's gadget clicking off the miles as the highway switched lazily back and forth down the gentling Western Slope toward Utah. Shortly after noon they left Colorado behind them. That evening they camped west of Harley Dome, Utah. For the first time the great silence impressed them as being oppressive and malefic. Ralph Brentner went to sleep that night thinking: *We're in the West now. We're out of our ballpark and into his.*

And that night Ralph dreamed of a wolf with a single red eye that had come out of the badlands to watch them. *Go away*, Ralph told it. *Go away, we're not afraid. Not afraid of you.*

By 2 PM on the afternoon of September 21, they were past Sego. The next large town, according to Stu's pocket map, was Green River. There were no more towns after that for a long, long time. Then, as Ralph had said, they would probably find out if God was with them or not.

'Actually,' Larry said to Glen, 'I'm not as worried about food as I am water. Most everyone who's on a trip keeps a few munchies in their car, Oreos or Fig Newtons or something like that.'

Glen smiled. 'Maybe the Lord will send us showers of blessing.'

Larry looked up at the cloudless blue sky and grimaced at the idea. 'I sometimes think she was right off her block at the end of it.'

'Maybe she was,' Glen said mildly. 'If you read your theology, you'll find that God often chooses to speak through the dying and the insane. It even seems to me – here's the closet Jesuit coming out – that there are good psychological reasons for it. A madman or a person on her deathbed is a human being with a drastically changed psyche. A healthy person might be apt to filter the divine message, to alter it with his or her own personality. In other words, a healthy person might make a shitty prophet.'

'The ways of God,' Larry said. 'I know. We see through a glass darkly. It's a pretty dark glass to me, all right. Why we're walking all this way when we could have driven it in a week is beyond me. But since we're doing a nutty thing, I guess it's okay to do it in a nutty way.'

'What we're doing has all sorts of historical precedent,' Glen said, 'and I see some perfectly sound psychological and sociological reasons for this walk. I don't know if they're God's reasons or not, but they make good sense to me.'

'Such as what?' Stu and Ralph had walked over to hear this, too.

'There were several American Indian tribes that used to make "having a vision" an integral part of their manhood rite. When it was your time to become a man, you were supposed to go out into the wilderness unarmed. You were supposed to make a kill, and two songs – one about the Great Spirit and one about your own prowess as a hunter and a rider and a warrior and a fucker – and have that vision. You weren't supposed to eat. You were supposed to get up high – mentally as well as physically – and wait for that vision to come. And eventually, of course, it would.' He chuckled. 'Starvation is a great hallucinogenic.'

'You think Mother sent us out here to have visions?' Ralph asked.

'Maybe to gain strength and holiness by a purging process,' Glen said. 'The casting away of *things* is symbolic, you know. Talismanic. When you cast away *things*, you're also casting away the self-related others that are symbolically related to those things. You start a cleaning-out process. You begin to empty the vessel.'

Larry shook his head slowly. 'I don't follow that.'

'Well, take an intelligent pre-plague man. Break his TV, and what does he do at night?'

'Reads a book,' Ralph said.

'Goes to see his friends,' Stu said.

'Plays the stereo,' Larry said, grinning.

'Sure, all those things,' Glen said. 'But he's also missing that TV. There's a hole in his life where that TV used to be. In the back of his mind he's still thinking, *At nine o'clock I'm going to pull a few beers and watch the Sox on the tube.* And when he goes in there and sees that empty cabinet, he feels as disappointed as hell. A part of his accustomed life has been poured out, is it not so?'

'Yeah,' Ralph said. 'Our TV went on the fritz once for two weeks and I didn't feel right until it was back.'

'It makes a bigger hole in his life if he watched a lot of TV, a smaller hole if he only used it a little bit. But something is gone. Now take away all his books, all his friends, and his stereo. Also remove all sustenance except what he can glean along the way. It's an emptying-out process and also a diminishing of the ego. Your *selves*, gentlemen – they are turning into a window-glass. Or better yet, empty tumblers.'

'But what's the point?' Ralph asked. 'Why go through all the rigmarole?'

Glen said, 'If you read your Bible, you'll see that it was pretty traditional for these prophets to go out into the wilderness from time to time – Old Testament Magical Mystery Tours. The timespan given for these jaunts was usually forty days and forty nights, a Hebraic idiom that really means "no one knows exactly how long he was gone, but it was quite a while." Does that remind you of anyone?'

'Sure. Mother,' Ralph said.

'Now think of yourself as a battery. You really are, you know. Your brain runs on chemically converted electrical current. For that matter, your muscles run on tiny charges, too – a chemical called acetylcholine allows the charge to pass when you need to move, and when you want to stop, another chemical, cholinesterase, is manufactured. Cholinesterase destroys acetylcholine, so your nerves become poor conductors again. Good thing, too. Otherwise, once you started scratching your nose, you'd never be able to stop. Okay, the point is this: Everything you think, everything you do, it all has to run off the battery. Like the accessories in a car.'

They were all listening closely.

'Watching TV, reading books, talking with friends, eating a big dinner . . . all of it runs off the battery. A normal life – at least in what used to be Western civilization – was like running a car with power windows, power brakes, power seats, all the goodies. But the more goodies you have, the less the battery can charge. True?'

'Yeah,' Ralph said. 'Even a big Delco won't ever overcharge when it's sitting in a Cadillac.'

'Well, what we've done is to strip off the accessories. We're on charge.'

Ralph said uneasily: 'If you put a car battery on charge for too long, she'll explode.'

'Yes,' Glen agreed. 'Same with people. The Bible tells us about Isaiah and Job and the others, but it doesn't say how many prophets came back from the wilderness with visions that had crisped their brains. I imagine there were some. But I have a healthy respect for human intelligence and the human psyche, in spite of an occasional throwback like East Texas here —'

'Off my case, baldy,' Stu growled.

'Anyhow, the capacity of the human mind is a lot bigger than the biggest Delco battery. I think it can take a charge almost to infinity. In certain cases, perhaps beyond infinity.'

They walked in silence for a while, thinking this over.

'Are we changing?' Stu asked quietly.

'Yes,' Glen answered. 'Yes, I think we are.'

'We've dropped some weight,' Ralph said. 'I know that just looking at you guys. And me, I used to have a helluva beergut. Now I can look down and see my toes again. In fact, I can see just about my whole feet.'

'It's a state of mind,' Larry said suddenly. When they looked at him he seemed a trifle embarrassed but went on: 'I've had this feeling for the last week or so, and I couldn't understand it. Maybe now I can. I've been feeling high. Like I'd done half a joint of really dynamite grass or snorted just a touch of coke. But there's none of the disorienting feeling that goes with dope. You do some dope and you feel like normal thinking is just a little bit out of your grasp. I feel like I'm thinking just fine, better than ever, in fact. But I still feel high.' Larry laughed. 'Maybe it's just hunger.'

'Hunger's part of it,' Glen agreed, 'but not all of it.'

'Me, I'm hungry all the time,' Ralph said, 'but it doesn't seem too important. I feel good.'

'I do too,' Stu said. 'Physically, I haven't felt this good in years.'

'When you empty out the vessel, you also empty out all the crap floating around in there,' Glen said. 'The additives. The impurities. Sure it feels good. It's a whole-body, whole-mind enema.'

'You got such a fancy way of putting things, baldy.'

'It may be inelegant, but it's accurate.'

Ralph asked, 'Will it help us with *him*?'

'Well,' Glen said, 'that's what it's for. I don't have much doubt about that. But we'll just have to wait and see, won't we?'

They walked on. Kojak came out of the brush and walked with them for a while, his toenails clicking on the pavement of US 70. Larry reached down and ruffled his fur. 'Ole Kojak,' he said. 'Did you know you were a battery? Just one great big old Delco battery with a lifetime guarantee?'

Kojak didn't appear to know or care, but he wagged his tail to show he was on Larry's side.

They camped that night about fifteen miles west of Sego, and as if to drive home the point of what they had been talking about in the afternoon, there was nothing to eat for the first time since they had left Boulder. Glen had the last of their instant coffee in a Glad Bag, and they shared it out of a single mug, passing it from hand to hand. They had come the last ten miles without seeing a single car.

The next morning, the twenty-second, they came upon an overturned Ford station wagon with four corpses in it – two of them little children. There were two boxes of animal crackers in the car, and a large bag of stale potato chips. The animal crackers were in better shape. They shared them out five ways.

'Don't wolf them, Kojak,' Glen admonished. 'Bad dog! Where are your manners? And if you have no manners – as I must now conclude – where is your *savoir faire*?'

Kojak thumped his tail and eyed the animal crackers in a way which showed pretty conclusively that he had no more *savoir faire* than he did manners.

'Then root, hog, or die,' Glen said, and gave the dog the last of his own share – a tiger. Kojak wolfed it down and then went sniffing off.

Larry had saved his entire menagerie – about ten animals – to eat at once. He did so slowly and dreamily. 'Did you ever notice,' he said, 'that animal crackers have a faint, lemony undertaste? I remember that from being a kid. Never noticed it again until now.'

Ralph had been tossing his last two crackers from hand to hand, and now he gobbled one. 'Yeah, you're right. They do have sort of a lemon taste to em. You know, I kind of wish ole Nicky was here. I wouldn't mind sharing these old animal crackers a little further.'

Stu nodded. They finished the animal crackers and went on. That afternoon they found a Great Western Markets delivery truck, apparently bound for Green River, pulled neatly over in the break-down lane, the driver sitting bolt upright and dead behind the wheel.

They lunched on a canned ham from the back, but none of them seemed to want much. Glen said their stomachs had shrunk. Stu said the ham smelled bad to him – not spoiled, just too rich. Too *meaty*. It kind of turned his stomach. He could only bring himself to eat a single slice. Ralph said he would have just as soon had two or three more boxes of animal crackers, and they all laughed. Even Kojak ate only a small serving before going off to investigate some scent.

They camped east of Green River that night, and there was a dust of snow in the early morning hours.

They came to the washout a little past noon on the twenty-third. The sky had been overcast all day, and it was cold – cold enough to snow, Stu thought – and not just flurries, either.

The four of them stood on the edge, Kojak at Glen's heel, looking down and across. Somewhere north of here a dam might have given way, or there might have been a succession of hard summer rainstorms. Whatever, there had been a flash flood along the San Rafael, which was only a dry-wash in some years. It had swept away a great thirty-foot slab of I-70. The gully was about fifty feet deep, the banks crumbly, rubbly soil and sedimentary rock. At the bottom was a sullen trickle of water.

'Holy crow,' Ralph said. 'Somebody oughtta call the Utah State Highway Department about this.'

Larry pointed. 'Look over there,' he said. They looked out into the emptiness, which was now beginning to be dotted with strange, wind-carved pillars and monoliths. About one hundred yards down the course of the San Rafael they saw a tangle of guardrails, cable, and large slabs of asphalt-composition paving. One chunk stuck up toward the cloudy, racing sky like an apocalyptic finger, complete with white broken passing line.

Glen was looking down into the rubble-strewn cut, hands stuffed into his pockets, an absent, dreaming look on his face. In a low voice, Stu said: 'Can you make it, Glen?'

'Sure, I think so.'

'How's that arthritis?'

'It's been worse.' He cracked a smile. 'But in all honesty, it's been better, too.'

They had no rope with which to anchor each other. Stu went down first, moving carefully. He didn't like the way the ground sometimes shifted under his feet, starting little slides of rock and dirt.

Once he thought his footing was going to go out from under him completely, sending him sliding all the way to the bottom on his can. One groping hand caught a solid rock outcropping and he hung on for dear life, finding more solid ground for his feet. Then Kojak was bounding blithely past him, kicking up little puffs of dirt and sending down only small runnels of earth. A moment later he was standing on the bottom, wagging his tail and barking amiably up at Stu.

'Fucking showoff dog,' Stu growled, and carefully made his way to the bottom.

'I'm coming next,' Glen called. 'I heard what you said about my dog!'

'Be careful, baldy! Be damn careful! It's really loose underfoot.'

Glen came down slowly, moving with great deliberation from one hold to the next. Stu tensed every time he saw loose dirt start to slide out from underneath Glen's battered Georgia Giants. His hair blew like fine silver around his ears in the light breeze that had sprung up. It occurred to him that when he had first met Glen, painting a mediocre picture beside the road in New Hampshire, Glen's hair had still been salt-and-pepper.

Until the moment Glen finally planted his feet on the level ground of the mudflat at the bottom of the gully, Stu was sure he was going to fall and break himself in two. Stu sighed with relief and clapped him on the shoulder.

'No sweat, East Texas,' Glen said, and bent to ruffle Kojak's fur.

'Plenty here,' Stu told him.

Ralph came next, moving carefully from one hold to the next, jumping the last eight feet or so. 'Boy,' he said. 'That shit's just as loose as a goose. Be funny if we couldn't get up that other bank and had to walk four or five miles upstream to find a shallower bank, wouldn't it?'

'Be a lot funnier if another flash flood came along while we were looking,' Stu said.

Larry came down agilely and well, joining them less than three minutes after they had started down. 'Who goes up first?' he asked.

'Why don't you, since you're so perky?' Glen said.

'Sure.'

It took him considerably longer to get up, and twice the treacherous footing ran out beneath him and he nearly fell. But finally he gained the top and waved down at them.

'Who's next?' Ralph asked.

'Me,' Glen said, and walked across to the other bank.

Stu caught his arm. 'Listen,' he said. 'We can walk upstream and find a shallower bank like Ralph said.'

'And lose the rest of the day? When I was a kid, I could have gone up there in forty seconds and registered a pulse-rate under seventy at the top.'

'You're no kid now, Glen.'

'No. But I think there's still some of him left.'

Before Stu could say more, Glen had started. He paused to rest about a third of the way up and then pressed on. Near the halfway point he grabbed an outcrop of shale that crumbled away under his hands and Stu was sure he was going to tumble all the way to the bottom, end over arthritic end.

'Ah, shit —' Ralph breathed.

Glen flailed his arms and somehow kept his balance. He jigged to his right and went up another twenty feet, rested, and then up again. Near the top a spur of rock that he had been standing on tore loose and he would have fallen, but Larry was there. He grabbed Glen's arm and hauled him up.

'Nothing to it,' Glen called down.

Stu grinned with relief. 'How's your pulse-rate, baldy?'

'Plus ninety, I think,' Glen admitted.

Ralph climbed the cut-bank like a stolid mountain goat, checking each hold, shifting his hands and feet with great deliberation. When he reached the top, Stu started up.

Right up until the moment he fell, Stu was thinking that actually this slope was a little easier than the one they had descended. The holds were better, the gradient a tiny bit shallower. But the surface was a mixture of chalky soil and rock fragments that had been badly loosened by the wet weather. Stu sensed that it wanted to be evil, and he went up carefully.

His chest was over the edge when the knob of outcropping his left foot was on suddenly disappeared. He felt himself begin to slide. Larry grabbed for his hand, but this time he missed his grip. Stu grabbed the outjutting edge of the turnpike, and it came off in his hands. He stared at it stupidly for a moment as the speed of his descent began to increase. He discarded it, feeling insanely like Wile E. Coyote. All I need, he thought, is for someone to go beep-beep before I hit the bottom.

His knee struck something, and there was a sudden bolt of pain. He grabbed at the gluey surface of the slope, which was now speeding past him at an alarming rate, and kept coming away with nothing but handfuls of dirt.

He slammed into a boulder sticking out of the rubble like a big blunt arrowhead and cartwheeled, the breath slapped from his body. He fell free for about ten feet, and came down on his lower leg at an angle. He heard it snap. The pain was instantaneous and huge. He yelled. He did a backward somersault. He was eating dirt now. Sharp pebbles scrawled bloody scratches across his face and arms. He came down on the hurt leg again, and felt it snap somewhere else. This time he didn't yell. This time he screamed.

He slid the last fifteen feet on his belly, like a kid on a greasy chute-the-chute. He came to rest with his pants full of mud and his heart beating crazily in his ears. The leg was white fire. His coat and the shirt beneath were both rucked up to his chin.

Broken. But how bad? Pretty bad from the way it feels. Two places at least, maybe more. And the knee's sprung.

Larry was coming down the slope, moving in little jumps that seemed almost a mockery of what had just happened
to Stu. Then he was kneeling beside him, asking the question which Stu had already asked himself.

'How bad, Stu?'

Stu got up on his elbows and looked at Larry, his face white with shock and streaked brown with dirt.

'I figure I'll be walking again in about three months,' he said. He began to feel as if he were going to puke. He looked up at the cloudy sky, balled his fists up, and shook them at it.

'OHHH, SHIT!' he screamed.

Ralph and Larry splinted the leg. Glen had produced a bottle of what he called 'my arthritis pills' and gave Stu one. Stu didn't know what was in the 'arthritis pills' and Glen refused to say, but the pain in his leg faded to a faraway drone. He felt very calm, even serene. It occurred to him that they were all living on borrowed time, not because they were on their way to find Flagg, necessarily, but because they had survived Captain Trips in the first place. At any rate, he knew what had to be done . . . and he was going to see that it *was* done. Larry had just finished speaking. They all looked at him anxiously to see what he would say.

What he said was simple enough. 'No.'

'Stu,' Glen said gently, 'you don't understand —'

'I understand. I'm saying no. No trip back to Green River. No rope. No car. Against the rules of the game.'

'It's no fucking *game*!' Larry cried. 'You'd die here!'

'And you're almost surely gonna die over there in Nevada. Now go on and get getting. You've got another four hours of daylight. No need to waste it.'

'We're not going to leave you,' Larry said.

'I'm sorry, but you are. I'm telling you to.'

'No. I'm in charge now. Mother said if anything happened to you —'

'— that you were to go on.'

'No. No.' Larry looked around at Glen and Ralph for support. They looked back at him, troubled. Kojak sat nearby, watching all four with his tail curled neatly around his paws.

'Listen to me, Larry,' Stu said. 'This whole trip is based on the idea that the old lady knew what she was talking about. If you start frigging around with that, you're putting everything on the line.'

'Yeah, that's right,' Ralph said.

'No, it ain't *right*, you sodbuster,' Larry said, furiously mimicking Ralph's flat Oklahoma accent. 'It wasn't God's will that Stu fell down here, it wasn't even the dark man's doing. It was just loose dirt, that's all, *just loose dirt*! I'm not leaving you, Stu. I'm done leaving people behind.'

'Yes. We are going to leave him,' Glen said quietly.

Larry stared around unbelievingly, as if he had been betrayed. 'I thought you were his friend!'

'I am. But that doesn't matter.'

Larry uttered a hysterical laugh and walked a little way down the gully. 'You're crazy! You know that?'

'No I'm not. We made an agreement. We stood around Mother Abagail's deathbed and entered into it. It almost certainly meant our deaths, and we knew it. We understood the agreement. Now we're going to live up to it.'

'Well, I *want* to, for Chrissake. I mean, it doesn't have to be Green River; we can get a station wagon, put him in the back, and go on —'

'We're supposed to walk,' Ralph said. He pointed at Stu. 'He can't walk.'

'Right. Fine. He's got a broken leg. What do you propose we do? Shoot him like a horse?'

'Larry –' Stu began.

Before he could go on, Glen grabbed Larry's shirt and yanked him toward him. 'Who are you trying to save?' His voice was cold and stern. 'Stu, or yourself?'

Larry looked at him, mouth working.

'It's very simple,' Glen said. 'We can't stay . . . and he can't go.'

'I refuse to accept that,' Larry whispered. His face was dead pale.

'It's a test,' Ralph said suddenly. 'That's what it is.'

'A sanity test, maybe,' Larry said.

'Vote,' Stu said from the ground. 'I vote you go on.'

'Me too,' Ralph said. 'Stu, I'm sorry. But if God's gonna watch out for us, maybe he'll watch out for you, too –'

'I won't do it,' Larry said.

'It's not Stu you're thinking of,' Glen said. 'You're trying to save something in yourself, I think. But this time it's right to go on, Larry. We have to.'

Larry rubbed his mouth slowly with the back of his hand.

'Let's stay here tonight,' he said. 'Let's think this thing out.'

'No,' Stu said.

Ralph nodded. A look passed between him and Glen, and then Glen fished the bottle of 'arthritis pills' out of his pocket and put it in Stu's hand. 'These have a morphine base,' he said. 'More than three or four would probably be fatal.' His eyes locked with Stu's. 'Do you understand, East Texas?'

'Yeah. I get you.'

'What are you talking about?' Larry cried. 'Just what the hell are you suggesting?'

'Don't you know?' Ralph said with such utter contempt that for a moment Larry was silenced. Then it all rushed before him again with the nightmare speed of strangers' faces as you ride the whip at the carnival: pills, uppers, downers, cruisers. Rita. Turning her over in her sleeping bag and seeing that she was dead and stiff, green puke coming out of her mouth like a rancid party favor.

'No!' he yelled, and tried to snatch the bottle from Stu's hand.

Ralph grabbed him by the shoulders. Larry struggled.

'Let him go,' Stu said. 'I want to talk to him.' Ralph still held on, looking at Stu uncertainly. 'No, go on, let him go.'

Ralph let go, but looked ready to spring again.

Stu said, 'Come here, Larry. Hunker down.'

Larry came over and hunkered by Stu. He looked miserably into Stu's face. 'It's not right, man. When somebody falls down and breaks his leg, you don't . . . you can't just walk off and let that person die. Don't you know that? Hey, man . . .' He touched Stu's face. 'Please. *Think*.'

Stu took Larry's hand and held it. 'Do you think I'm crazy?'

'No! No, but –'

'And do you think that people who are in their right minds have the right to decide for themselves what they want to do?'

'Oh, man,' Larry said, and started to cry.

'Larry, you're not in this. I want you to go on. If you get out of Vegas, come back this way. Maybe God'll send a raven to feed me, you don't know. I read once in the funny-pages that a man can go seventy days without food, if he's got water.'

'It's going to be winter before that here. You'll be dead of exposure in three days, even if you don't use the pills.'

'That ain't up to you. You ain't in this part of it.'

'Don't send me away, Stu.'

Stu said grimly: 'I'm sending you.'

'This sucks,' Larry said, and got to his feet. 'What's Fran going to say to us? When she finds out we left you for the gophers and the buzzards?'

'She's not going to say anything if you don't get over there and fix his clock. Neither is Lucy. Or Dick Ellis. Or Brad. Or any of the others.'

Larry said, 'Okay. We'll go. But tomorrow. We'll camp here tonight, and maybe we'll have a dream . . . something . . .'

'No dreams,' Stu said gently. 'No signs. It doesn't work like that. You'd stay one night and there'd be nothing and then you'd want to stay another night, and another night . . . you got to go right now.'

Larry walked away from them, head down, and stood with his back turned. 'All right,' he said at last in a voice almost too low to hear. 'We'll do it your way. God help our souls.'

Ralph came over to Stu and knelt down. 'Can we get you anything, Stu?'

Stu smiled. 'Yeah. Everything Gore Vidal ever wrote – those books about Lincoln and Aaron Burr and those guys. I always meant to read the suckers. Now it looks like I got the chance.'

Ralph grinned crookedly. 'Sorry, Stu. Looks like I'm tapped.'

Stu squeezed his arm, and Ralph went away. Glen came over. He had also been crying, and when he sat down by Stu, he started leaking again.

'Come on, ya baby,' Stu said. 'I'll be okay.'

'Larry's right. This is bad. Like something you'd do to a horse.'

'You know it has to be done.'

'I guess I do, but who really knows? How's that leg?'

'No pain at all, right now.'

'Okay, you got the pills.' Glen swiped his arm across his eyes. 'Goodbye, East Texas. It's been pretty goddam good to know you.'

Stu turned his head aside. 'Don't say goodbye, Glen. Make it so long, it's better luck. You'll probably get halfway up that frigging bank and fall down here and we can spend the winter playing cribbage.'

'It's not so long,' Glen said. 'I feel that, don't you?'

And because he did, Stu turned his face back to look at Glen. 'Yeah, I do,' he said, and then smiled a little. 'But I will fear no evil, right?'

'Right!' Glen said. His voice dropped to a husky whisper. 'Pull the plug if you have to, Stuart. Don't screw around.'

'No.'

'Goodbye, then.'

'Goodbye, Glen.'

The three of them drew together on the west side of the gully, and after a look back over his shoulder, Glen started to go up. Stu followed his progress up the side with growing alarm. He was moving casually, almost carelessly, hardly even glancing at his footing. The ground crumbled away beneath him once, then twice. Both times he grabbed non-chalantly for a handhold, and both times one just happened to be there. When he reached the top, Stu released his pent-up breath in a long, harsh sigh.

Ralph went next, and when he reached the top, Stu called Larry over one last time. He looked up into Larry's face and reflected that in its way it was remarkably like the late Harold Lauder's – remarkably still, the eyes watchful and a little wary. A face that gave away nothing but what it wanted to give away.

'You're in charge now,' Stu said. 'Can you handle it?'

'I don't know. I'll try.'

'You'll be making the decisions.'

'Will I? Looks like my first one was overruled.' Now his eyes did give away an emotion: reproach.

'Yeah, but that's the only one that will be. Listen – *his* men are going to grab you.'

'Yeah. I figure they will. They'll either grab us or shoot us from ambush like we were dogs.'

'No, I think they'll grab you and take you to *him*. It'll happen in the next few days, I think. When you get to Vegas, keep your eyes open. Wait. It'll come.'

'What, Stu? What'll come?'

'I don't know. Whatever we were sent for. Be ready. Know it when it comes.'

'We'll be back for you, if we can. You know it.'

'Yeah, okay.'

Larry went up the bank quickly and joined the other two. They stood and waved down. Stu raised his hand in return. They left. And they never saw Stu Redman again.

CHAPTER 73

The three of them camped sixteen miles west of the place where they had left Stu. They had come to another washout, this one minor. The real reason they had made such poor mileage was because some of the heart seemed to have gone out of them. It was hard to tell if it was going to come back. Their feet seemed to weigh more. There was little conversation. Not one of them wanted to look into the face of another, for fear of seeing his own guilt mirrored there.

They camped at dark and built a scrub fire. There was water, but no food. Glen tamped the last of his tobacco into his pipe, and wondered suddenly if Stu had any cigarettes. The thought spoiled his own taste for tobacco, and he knocked his pipe out on a rock, absently kicking away the last of his Borkum Riff. When an owl hooted somewhere out in the darkness a few minutes later, he looked around.

'Say, where's Kojak?' he asked.

'Now, that's kinda funny, ain't it?' Ralph said. 'I can't remember seeing him the last couple of hours at all.'

Glen got to his feet. 'Kojak!' he yelled. 'Hey, Kojak! *Kojak!*' His voice echoed lonesomely away into the wastes. There was no answering bark. He sat down again, overcome with gloom. A soft sighing noise escaped him. Kojak had followed him almost all the way across the continent. Now he was gone. It was like a terrible omen.

'You s'pose something got him?' Ralph asked softly.

Larry said in a quiet, thoughtful voice: 'Maybe he stayed with Stu.'

Glen looked up, startled. 'Maybe,' he said, considering it. 'Maybe that's what happened.'

Larry tossed a pebble from one hand to the other, back and forth, back and forth. 'He said maybe God would send a raven to feed him. I doubt if there's any out here, so maybe He sent a dog instead.'

The fire made a popping sound, sending a column of sparks up into the darkness to whirl in brief brightness and then to wink out.

When Stu saw the dark shape come slinking down the gully toward him, he pulled himself up against the nearby boulder, leg sticking out stiffly in front of him, and found a good-sized stone with one numb hand. He was chilled to the bone. Larry had been right. Two or three days of lying around in these temperatures was going to kill him quite efficiently. Except now it looked like whatever this was would get him first. Kojak had remained with him until sunset and then had left him, scrambling easily out of the gully. Stu had not called him back. The dog would find his way back to Glen and go on with them. Perhaps he had his own part to play. But now he wished that Kojak had stayed a little longer. The pills were one thing, but he had no wish to be ripped to pieces by one of the dark man's wolves.

He gripped the rock harder and the dark shape paused about twenty yards up the cut. Then it started coming again, a blacker shadow in the night.

'Come on, then,' Stu said hoarsely.

The black shadow wagged its tail and came. *'Kojak?'*

It was. And there was something in his mouth, something he dropped at Stu's feet. He sat down, tail thumping, waiting to be complimented.

'Good dog,' Stu said in amazement. *'Good* dog!'

Kojak had brought him a rabbit.

Stu pulled out his pocketknife, opened it, and disemboweled the rabbit in three quick movements. He picked up the steaming guts and tossed them to Kojak. 'Want these?' Kojak did. Stu skinned the rabbit. The thought of eating it raw didn't do much for his stomach.

'Wood?' he said to Kojak without much hope. There were scattered branches and hunks of tree all along the banks of the gully, dropped by the flash flood, but nothing within reach.

Kojak wagged his tail and didn't move.

'Fetch? F —'

But Kojak was gone. He whirled, streaked to the east side of the gully, and ran back with a large piece of deadwood in his jaws. He dropped it beside Stu, and barked. His tail wagged rapidly.

'Good dog,' Stu said again. 'I'll be a sonofabitch! Fetch, Kojak!'

Barking with joy, Kojak went again. In twenty minutes, he had brought back enough wood for a large fire. Stu carefully stripped enough splinters to make kindling. He checked the match situation and saw that he had a book and a half. He got the kindling going on the second match and fed the fire carefully. Soon there was a respectable blaze going and Stu got as close to it as he could, sitting in his sleeping bag. Kojak lay down on the far side of the fire with his nose on his paws.

When the fire had burned down a little, Stu spitted the rabbit and cooked it. The smell was soon strong enough and savory enough to have his stomach rumbling. Kojak came to attention and sat watching the rabbit with close interest.

'Half for you and half for me, big guy, okay?'

Fifteen minutes later he pulled the rabbit off the fire and managed to rip it in half without burning his fingers too badly. The meat was burned in places, half-raw in others, but it put the canned ham from Great Western Markets in the shade. He and Kojak gulped it down . . . and as they were finishing, a bone-chilling howl drifted down the wash.

'*Christ!*' Stu said around a mouthful of rabbit.

Kojak was on his feet, hackles up, growling. He advanced stiff-legged around the fire and growled again. Whatever had howled fell silent.

Stu lay down, the hand-sized stone by one hand and his opened pocket knife by the other. The stars were cold and high and indifferent. His thoughts turned to Fran and he turned them away just as quickly. That hurt too much, full belly or not. *I won't sleep*, he thought. *Not for a long time*.

But he did sleep, with the help of one of Glen's pills. And when the coals of the fire had burned down to embers, Kojak came over and slept next to him, giving Stu his heat. And that was how, on the first night after the party was broken, Stu ate when the others went hungry, and slept easy while their sleep was broken by bad dreams and an uneasy feeling of rapidly approaching doom.

On the twenty-fourth, Larry Underwood's group of three pilgrims made thirty miles and camped northeast of the San Rafael Knob.

That night the temperature slid down into the mid-twenties, and they built a large fire and slept close by it. Kojak had not rejoined them.

'What do you think Stu's doing tonight?' Ralph asked Larry.

'Dying,' Larry said shortly, and was sorry when he saw the wince of pain on Ralph's homely, honest face, but he didn't know how to redeem what he had said. And after all, it was almost surely true.

He lay down again, feeling strangely certain that it was tomorrow. Whatever they were coming to, they were almost there.

Bad dreams that night. He was on tour with an outfit called the Shady Blues Connection in the one he remembered most clearly on waking. They were booked into Madison Square Garden, and the place was sold out. They took the stage to thunderous applause. Larry went to adjust his mike, bring it down to proper height, and couldn't budge it. He went to the lead guitarist's mike, but that one was frozen, too. Bass guitarist, organist, same thing. Booing and rhythmic clapping began to come from the crowd. One by one, the members of the Shady Blues Connection slunk off the stage, grinning furtively into high psychedelic shirt-collars like the ones the Byrds used to wear back in 1966, when Roger McGuinn was still eight miles high. Or eight hundred. And still Larry wandered from mike to mike, trying to find at least one he could adjust. But they were all at least nine feet tall and frozen solid. They looked like stainless steel cobras. Someone in the crowd began to yell for 'Baby, Can You Dig Your Man?' *I don't do that number anymore*, he tried to say. *I stopped doing that one when the world ended.* They couldn't hear him, and a chant began to arise, starting in the back rows, then sweeping the Garden, gaining strength and volume: '*Baby Can You Dig Your Man! Baby Can You Dig Your Man! BABY CAN YOU DIG YOUR MAN!*'

He awoke with the chant in his ears. Sweat had popped out all over his body.

He didn't need Glen to tell him what kind of dream that had been, or what it meant. The dream where you can't reach the mikes, can't adjust them, is a common one for rock musicians, just as common as dreaming that you're on stage and can't remember a single lyric. Larry guessed that all performers had a variation on one of those before –

Before a performance.

It was an inadequacy dream. It expressed that one simple

overriding fear: *What if you can't? What if you want to, but you can't?* The terror of being unable to make the simple leap of faith which is the place where any artist – singer, writer, painter, musician – begins.

Make it nice for the people, Larry.

Whose voice was that? His mother's?

You're a taker, Larry.

No, Mom – no I'm not. I don't do that number anymore. I stopped doing that one when the world ended. Honest.

He lay back down and drifted off to sleep again. His last thought was that Stu had been right: The dark man was going to grab them. *Tomorrow*, he thought. *Whatever we're coming to, we're almost there.*

But they saw no one on the twenty-fifth. The three of them walked stolidly along under the bright blue skies, and they saw birds and beasts in plenty, but no people.

'It's amazing how rapidly the wildlife is coming back,' Glen said. 'I knew it would be a fairly rapid process, and of course the winter is going to prune it back some, but this is still amazing. It's only been about a hundred days since the first outbreaks.'

'Yeah, but there's no dogs or horses,' Ralph said. 'That just doesn't seem right, you know it? They invented a bug that killed pretty near all the people, but that wasn't enough. It had to take out his two favorite animals, too. It took man and man's best friends.'

'And left the cats,' Larry said morosely.

Ralph brightened. 'Well, there's Kojak –'

'There *was* Kojak.'

That killed the conversation. The buttes frowned down at them, hiding places for dozens of men with rifles and scopes. Larry's premonition that it was to be today hadn't left him. Each time they topped a rise, he expected to see the road blocked below them. And each time it wasn't, he thought about ambush.

They talked about horses. About dogs and buffalo. The buffalo were coming back, Ralph told them – Nick and Tom Cullen had seen them. The day was not so far off – in their lifetimes, maybe – when the buffalo might darken the plains again.

Larry knew it was the truth, but he also knew it was bushwa – their lifetimes might amount to no more than another ten minutes.

Then it was nearly dark, and time to look for a place to camp. They came to the top of one final rise and Larry thought: *Now. They'll be right down there.*

But there was no one.

They camped near a green reflectorized sign that said LAS VEGAS 260. They had eaten comparatively well that day: taco chips, soda; and two Slim Jims that they shared out equally.

Tomorrow, Larry thought again, and slept. That night he dreamed that he and Barry Greig and the Tattered Remnants were playing at the Garden. It was their big chance – they were opening for some supergroup that was named after a city. Boston, or maybe Chicago. And all the microphone stands were at least nine feet tall again and he began to stumble from one to the other again as the audience began to clap rhythmically and call for 'Baby, Can You Dig Your Man?' again.

He looked down in the first row and felt a slapping dash of cold icewater fear. Charles Manson was there, the *x* on his forehead healed to a white, twisted scar, clapping and chanting. And Richard Speck was there, looking up at Larry with cocky, impudent eyes, an unfiltered cigarette jittering between his lips. They were flanking the dark man. John Wayne Gacy was behind them. Flagg was leading the chant.

Tomorrow, Larry thought again, stumbling from one too-tall mike to the next under the hot dreamlights of Madison Square Garden. *I'll see you tomorrow.*

But it was not the next day, or the day after that. On the evening of September 27 they camped in the town of Freemont Junction, and there was plenty to eat.

'I keep expecting it to be over,' Larry told Glen that evening. 'And every day that it's not, it gets worse.'

Glen nodded. 'I feel the same way. It would be funny if he was just a mirage, wouldn't it? Nothing but a bad dream in our collective consciousness.'

Larry looked at him with momentary surprised consideration. Then he shook his head slowly. 'No. I don't think it's just a dream.'

Glen smiled. 'Nor do I, young man. Nor do I.'

They made contact the following day.

At just past ten in the morning, they topped a rise and below them and to the west, five miles away, two cars were parked nose-to-nose, blocking the highway. It all looked exactly as Larry had thought it would.

'Accident?' Glen asked.

Ralph was shading his eyes. 'I don't think so. Not parked that way.'

'*His* men,' Larry said.

'Yeah, I think so,' Ralph agreed. 'What do we do now, Larry?'

Larry took his bandanna out of his back pocket and wiped his face with it. Today either summer had come back or they were starting to feel the southwestern desert. The temperature was in the low eighties.

But it's a dry heat, he thought calmly. *I'm only sweating a little. Just a little.* He stuffed the bandanna back into his pocket. Now that it was actually on, he felt all right. Again there was that queer feeling that it was a performance, a show to be played.

'We go down and see if God really is with us. Right, Glen?'

'You're the boss.'

They started to walk again. Half an hour brought them close enough to see that the nose-to-nose cars had once belonged to the Utah State Patrol. There were several armed men waiting for them.

'Are they going to shoot us?' Ralph asked conversationally.

'I don't know,' Larry said.

'Because some of the rifles are wowsers. Scope-equipped. I can see the sun ticking off the lenses. If they want to knock us down, we'll be in range anytime.'

They kept walking. The men at the roadblock split into two groups, about five men in front, guns aimed at the party of three walking toward them, and three more crouched behind the cars.

'Eight of them, Larry?' Glen asked.

'I make it eight, yeah. How are you doing, anyhow?'

'I'm okay,' Glen said.

'Ralph?'

'Just as long as we know what to do when the time comes,' Ralph said. 'That's all I want.'

Larry gripped his hand for a moment and squeezed it. Then he took Glen's and did likewise.

They were less than a mile from the cruisers now. 'They're not going to shoot us outright,' Ralph said. 'They would have done it already.'

Now they could discern faces, and Larry searched them curiously. One was heavily bearded. Another was young but mostly bald – *must have been a bummer for him to start losing his hair while he was still in school*, Larry thought. Another was wearing a bright yellow tank top with a picture of a grinning camel on it, and below the camel the word SUPER-HUMP in scrolled, old-fashioned letters. Another of them had the look of an accountant. He was fiddling with a .357 Magnum, and he looked three times as nervous as Larry felt; he looked like a man who was going to blow off one of his own feet if he didn't settle down.

'They don't look no different from our guys,' Ralph said.

'Sure they do,' Glen answered. 'They're all packing iron.'

They approached to within twenty feet of the police cars blocking the road. Larry stopped, and the others stopped with him. There was a dead moment of silence as Flagg's men and Larry's band of pilgrims looked each other over. Then Larry Underwood said mildly: 'How-do.'

The little man who looked like a CPA stepped forward. He was still twiddling with the Magnum. 'Are you Glendon Bateman, Lawson Underwood, Stuart Redman, and Ralph Brentner?'

'Say, you dummy,' Ralph said, 'can't you count?'

Someone snickered. The CPA type flushed. 'Who's missing?'

Larry said, 'Stu met with an accident on the way here. And I do believe you're going to have one yourself if you don't stop fooling with that gun.'

There were more snickers. The CPA managed to tuck the pistol into the waistband of his gray slacks, which made him look more ridiculous than ever; a Walter Mitty outlaw daydream.

'My name is Paul Burlson,' he said, 'and by virtue of the power vested in me, I arrest you and order you to come with me.'

'In whose name?' Glen said immediately.

Burlson looked at him with contempt . . . but the contempt was mixed with something else. 'You know who I speak for.'

'Then say it.'

But Burlson was silent.

'Are you afraid?' Glen asked him. He looked at all eight of them. 'Are you so afraid of him you don't dare speak his *name*? Very well, I'll say it for you. His name is Randall Flagg, also known as the dark man, also known as the tall man, also known as the Walkin Dude. Don't some of you call him that?' His voice had climbed to the high, clear octaves of fury. Some of the men looked uneasily at each other and Burlson fell back a step. 'Call him Beelzebub, because that's his name, too. Call him Nyarlahotep and Ahaz and Astaroth.

Call him R'yelah and Seti and Anubis. His name is Legion and he's an apostate of hell and you men kiss his ass.' His voice dropped to a conversational pitch again; he smiled disarmingly. 'Just thought we ought to have that out front.'

'Grab them,' Burlson said. 'Grab them all and shoot the first one that moves.'

For one strange second no one moved at all and Larry thought: *They're not going to do it, they're as afraid of us as we are of them, more afraid, even though they have guns —*

He looked at Burlson and said, 'Who are you kidding, you little scumbucket? We *want* to go. That's why we came.'

Then they moved, almost as though it was Larry who had ordered them. He and Ralph were bundled into the back of one cruiser, Glen into the back of the other. They were behind a steel mesh grille. There were no inside doorhandles.

We're arrested, Larry thought. He found that the idea amused him.

Four men smashed into the front seat. The cruiser backed up, turned around, and began to head west. Ralph sighed.

'Scared?' Larry asked him in a low voice.

'I'll be frigged if I know. It feels so good to be off m'dogs, I can't tell.'

One of the men in front said: 'The old man with the big mouth. He in charge?'

'No. I am.'

'What's your name?'

'Larry Underwood. This is Ralph Brentner. The other guy is Glen Bateman.' He looked out the back window. The other cruiser was behind them.

'What happened to the fourth guy?'

'He broke his leg. We had to leave him.'

'Tough go, all right. I'm Barry Dorgan. Vegas security.'

Larry felt an absurd response, *Pleased to meet you*, rise to his lips and had to smile a little. 'How long a drive is it to Las Vegas?'

'Well, we can't whistle along too fast because of the stalls in the road. We're clearing them out from the city, but it's slow going. We'll be there in about five hours.'

'Isn't that something,' Ralph said, shaking his head. 'We've been on the road three weeks, and just five hours in a car takes you there.'

Dorgan squirmed around until he could look at them. 'I don't understand why you were walking. For that matter I don't understand why you came at all. You must have known it would end like this.'

'We were sent,' Larry said. 'To kill Flagg, I think.'

'Not much chance of that, buddy. You and your friends are going right into the Las Vegas County Jail. Do not pass Go, do not collect two hundred dollars. He's got a special interest in you. He knew you were coming.' He paused. 'You just want to hope he makes it quick for you. But I don't think he will. He hasn't been in a very good mood lately.'

'Why not?' Larry asked.

But Dorgan seemed to feel he had said enough – too much, maybe. He turned around without answering, and Larry and Ralph watched the desert flow by. In just three weeks, speed had become a novelty all over again.

It actually took them six hours to reach Vegas. It lay in the middle of the desert like some improbable gem. There were a lot of people on the streets; the workday was over, and they were enjoying the early evening cool on lawns and benches and at bus stops, or sitting in the doorways of defunct wedding chapels and hockshops. They rubber-necked the Utah SP cars as they went by and then went back to whatever they had been talking about.

Larry was looking around thoughtfully. The electricity was on, the streets were cleared, and the rubble of looting was gone. 'Glen was right,' he said. 'He's got the trains running on time. But still I wonder if this is any way to run a railroad. Your people all look like they've got the nervous complaint, Dorgan.'

Dorgan didn't reply.

They arrived at the county jail and drove around to the rear. The two police cars parked in a cement courtyard. When Larry got out, wincing at the stiffness that had settled into his muscles, he saw that Dorgan had two sets of hand-cuffs.

'Hey, come on,' he said. 'Really.'

'Sorry. His orders.'

Ralph said, 'I ain't never been handcuffed in my life. I was picked up and throwed in the drunk tank a couple of times before I was married, but never was I cuffed.' Ralph was speaking slowly, his Oklahoma accent becoming more pronounced, and Larry realized he was totally furious.

'I have my orders,' Dorgan said. 'Don't make it any tougher than it has to be.'

'Your orders,' Ralph said. 'I know who gives your orders. He murdered my friend Nick. What are you doing hooked up with that hellhound? You seem like a nice enough fella when you're by yourself.' He was looking at Dorgan with such an expression of angry interrogation that Dorgan shook his head and looked away.

'This is my job,' he said, 'and I do it. End of story. Put your wrists out or I'll have somebody do it for you.'

Larry put his hands out and Dorgan cuffed him. 'What were you?' Larry asked curiously. 'Before?'

'Santa Monica Police. Detective second.'

'And you're with *him*. It's . . . forgive me for saying so, but it's really sort of funny.'

Glen Bateman was pushed over to join them.

'What are you shoving him around for?' Dorgan asked angrily.

'If you had to listen to six hours of this guy's bullshit, you'd do some pushing, too,' one of the men said.

'I don't care how much bullshit you had to listen to, keep your hands to yourself.' Dorgan looked at Larry. 'Why is it funny that I should be with him? I was a cop for ten years before Captain Trips. I saw what happens when guys like you are in charge, you see.'

'Young man,' Glen said mildly, 'your experiences with a few battered babies and drug abusers does not justify your embrace of a monster.'

'Get them out of here,' Dorgan said evenly. 'Separate cells, separate wings.'

'I don't think you'll be able to live with your choice, young man,' Glen said. 'There doesn't seem to be quite enough Nazi in you.'

This time Dorgan pushed Glen himself.

Larry was separated from the other two and taken down an empty corridor graced with signs reading NO SPITTING, THIS WAY TO SHOWERS & DELOUSING, and one that read, YOU ARE not A GUEST.

'I wouldn't mind a shower,' he said.

'Maybe,' Dorgan said. 'We'll see.'

'See what?'

'How cooperative you can be.'

Dorgan opened a cell at the end of the corridor and ushered Larry in.

'How about the bracelets?' Larry asked, holding them out.

'Sure.' Dorgan unlocked them and took them off. 'Better?'

'Much.'

'Still want that shower?'

'I sure do.' More than that, Larry didn't want to be left alone, listening to the echoey sound of footfalls going away. If he was left alone, the fear would start to come back.

Dorgan produced a small notebook. 'How many are you? In the Zone?'

'Six thousand,' Larry said. 'We all play Bingo every Thursday night and the prize in the cover-all game is a twenty-pound turkey.'

'Do you want that shower or not?'

'I want it.' But he no longer thought he was going to get it.

'How many of you over there?'

'Twenty-five thousand, but four thousand are under twelve and get in free at the drive-in. Economically speaking, it's a bummer.'

Dorgan snapped his notebook shut and looked at him.

'I can't, man,' Larry said. 'Put yourself in my place.'

Dorgan shook his head. 'I can't do that, because I'm not nuts. Why are you guys *here*? What good do you think it's going to do you? He's going to kill you dead as dogshit tomorrow or the next day. And if he wants you to talk, you will. If he wants you to tapdance and jerk off at the same time, you'll do that, too. You must be crazy.'

'We were told to come by the old woman. Mother Abagail. Probably you dreamed about her.'

Dorgan shook his head, but suddenly his eyes wouldn't meet Larry's. 'I don't know what you're talking about.'

'Then let's leave it at that.'

'Sure you don't want to talk to me? Get that shower?'

Larry laughed. 'I don't work that cheap. Send your own spy over to our side. If you can find one that doesn't look like a weasel the second Mother Abagail's name gets mentioned, that is.'

'Any way you want it,' Dorgan said. He walked back down the hallway under the mesh-enclosed lights. At the far end he stepped past a steel-barred gate that rolled shut behind him with a hollow crash.

Larry looked around. Like Ralph, he had been in jail on a couple of occasions – public intoxication once, possession of an ounce of marijuana on another. Flaming youth.

'It's not the Ritz,' he muttered.

The mattress on the bunk looked decidedly moldy, and he wondered a little morbidly if someone had died on it back in June or early July. The toilet worked but filled with rusty water the first time he flushed it, a reliable sign that it hadn't been used for a long time. Someone had left a paperback Western. Larry picked it up and then put it down again. He sat on the bunk and listened to the silence. He had always hated to be alone – but in a way, he always had been . . . until he had arrived in the Free Zone. And now it wasn't so bad as he had been afraid it would be. Bad enough, but he could cope.

He's going to kill you dead as dogshit tomorrow or the next day.

Except Larry didn't believe it. It just wasn't going to happen that way.

'I will fear no evil,' he said into the dead silence of the cellblock wing, and he liked the way it sounded. He said it again.

He lay down, and the thought occurred that he had finally made it most of the way back to the West Coast. But the trip had been longer and stranger than anyone ever could have imagined. And the trip wasn't quite over yet.

'I will fear no evil,' he said again. He fell asleep, his face calm, and he slept in dreamless peace.

At ten o'clock the next day, twenty-four hours after they had first seen the roadblock in the distance, Randall Flagg and Lloyd Henreid came to see Glen Bateman.

He was sitting cross-legged on the floor of his cell. He had found a piece of charcoal under his bunk, and had just finished writing this legend on the wall amid the intaglio of male and female genitals, names, phone numbers, and obscene little poems: *I am not the potter, not the potter's wheel, but the potter's clay; is not the value of the shape attained as dependent upon the intrinsic worth of the clay as upon the wheel and the Master's skill?* Glen was admiring this proverb – or was it an aphorism? – when the temperature in the deserted cellblock suddenly seemed to drop ten degrees. The door at the end of the corridor rumbled open. The saliva in Glen's mouth was suddenly all gone, and the charcoal snapped between his fingers.

Bootheels clocked up the hallway toward him.

Other footfalls, smaller and insignificant, pattered along in counterpoint, trying to keep up.

Why, it's him. I'm going to see his face.

Suddenly his arthritis was worse. Terrible, in fact. It seemed that his bones had suddenly been hollowed out and filled with ground glass. And still, he turned with an interested, expectant smile on his face as the bootheels stopped in front of his cell.

'Well, there you are,' Glen said. 'And you're not half the boogeyman we thought you must be.'

Standing on the other side of the bars were two men. Flagg was on Glen's right. He was wearing bluejeans and a white silk shirt that gleamed mellowly in the dim lights. He was grinning in at Glen. Behind him was a shorter man who was not smiling at all. He had an undershot chin and eyes that seemed too big for his face. His complexion was one that the desert climate was never going to be kind to; he had burned, peeled, and burned again. Around his neck he wore a black stone flawed with red. It had a greasy, resinous look.

'I'd like you to meet my associate,' Flagg said with a giggle. 'Lloyd Henreid, meet Glen Bateman, sociologist, Free Zone Committee member, and single existing member of the Free Zone think tank now that Nick Andros is dead.'

'Meetcha,' Lloyd mumbled.

'How's your arthritis, Glen?' Flagg asked. His tone was commiserating, but his eyes sparkled with high glee and secret knowledge.

Glen opened and closed his hands rapidly, smiling back at Flagg. No one would ever know what an effort it took to maintain that gentle smile.

The intrinsic worth of the clay!

'Fine,' he said. 'Much better for sleeping indoors, thank you.'

Flagg's smile faltered a bit. Glen caught just a glimpse of narrow surprise and anger. Of fear?

'I've decided to let you go,' he said briskly. His smile sprang forth again, radiant and vulpine. Lloyd uttered a little gasp of surprise, and Flagg turned to him. 'Haven't I, Lloyd?'

'Uh . . . sure,' Lloyd said. 'Sure nuff.'

'Well, fine,' Glen said easily. He could feel the arthritis sinking deeper and deeper into his joints, numbing them like ice, swelling them like fire.

'You'll be given a small motorbike and you may drive back at your leisure.'

'Of course I couldn't go without my friends.'

'Of course not. And all you have to do is ask. Get down on your knees and ask me.'

Glen laughed heartily. He threw back his head and laughed long and hard. And as he laughed, the pain in his joints began to abate. He felt better, stronger, in control again.

'Oh, you're a card,' he said. 'I tell you what you do. Why don't you find a nice big sandpile, get yourself a hammer, and pound all that sand right up your ass?'

Flagg's face grew dark. The smile slipped away. His eyes, previously as dark as the jet stone Lloyd wore, now seemed to gleam yellowly. He reached out his hand to the locking mechanism on the door and wrapped his fingers around it. There was an electric buzzing sound. Fire leaped out between his fingers, and there was a hot smell in the air. The lockbox fell to the floor, smoking and black. Lloyd Henreid cried out. The dark man grabbed the bars and threw the cell door back on its track.

'Stop laughing.'

Glen laughed harder.

'Stop laughing at me!'

'You're *nothing*!' Glen said, wiping his streaming eyes and still chuckling. 'Oh pardon me . . . it's just that we were all so frightened . . . we made such a *business* out of you . . . I'm laughing as much at our own foolishness as at your regrettable lack of substance . . .'

'Shoot him, Lloyd.' Flagg had turned to the other man. His face was working horribly. His hands were hooked into predator's claws.

'Oh, kill me yourself if you're going to kill me,' Glen said. 'Surely you're capable. Touch me with your finger and stop my heart. Make the sign of the inverted cross and give me a massive brain embolism. Bring down the lightning from the overhead socket to cleave me in two. Oh . . . oh dear . . . oh dear *me*!'

Glen collapsed onto the cell cot and rocked back and forth, consumed with delicious laughter.

'*Shoot him!*' the dark man roared at Lloyd.

Pale, shaking with fear, Lloyd fumbled the pistol out of his belt, almost dropped it, then tried to point it at Glen. He had to use both hands.

Glen looked at Lloyd, still smiling. He might have been at a faculty cocktail party back in the Brain Ghetto at Woodsville, New

Hampshire, recovering from a good joke, now ready to turn the conversation back into more serious channels of reflection.

'If you have to shoot somebody, Mr Henreid, shoot him.'

'Do it now, Lloyd.'

Lloyd blindly pulled the trigger. The gun went off with a tremendous crash in the enclosed space. The echoes bounced furiously back and forth. But the bullet only chipped concrete two inches from Glen's right shoulder, ricocheted, struck something else, and whined off again.

'Can't you do anything right?' Flagg roared. 'Shoot him, you moron! Shoot him! He's standing right in front of you!'

'I'm trying –'

Glen's smile had not changed, and he had only flinched a little at the gunshot. 'I repeat, if you must shoot somebody, shoot him. He's really not human at all, you know. I once described him to a friend as the last magician of rational thought, Mr Henreid. That was more correct than I knew. But he's losing his magic now. It's slipping away from him and he knows it. And you know it, too. Shoot him now and save us all God knows how much bloodshed and dying.'

Flagg's face had grown very still. 'Shoot one of us, anyhow, Lloyd,' he said. 'I got you out of jail when you were dying of starvation. It's guys like this that you wanted to get back at. Little guys who talk big.'

Lloyd said: 'Mister, you don't fool me. It's like Randy Flagg says.'

'But he lies. You know he lies.'

'He told me more of the truth than anyone else bothered to in my whole lousy life,' Lloyd said, and shot Glen three times. Glen was driven backward, twisted and turned like a ragdoll. Blood flew in the dim air. He struck the cot, bounced, and rolled onto the floor. He managed to get up on one elbow.

'It's all right, Mr Henreid,' he whispered. 'You don't know any better.'

'*Shut up, you mouthy old bastard!*' Lloyd screamed. He fired again and Glen Bateman's face disappeared. He fired again and the body jumped lifelessly. Lloyd shot him yet again. He was crying. The tears rolled down his angry, sunburned cheeks. He was remembering the rabbit he had forgotten and left to eat its own paws. He was remembering Poke, and the people in the white Connie, and Gorgeous

George. He was remembering the Phoenix jail, and the rat, and how he hadn't been able to eat the ticking out of his mattress. He was remembering Trask, and how Trask's leg had started to look like a Kentucky Fried Chicken dinner after a while. He pulled the trigger again, but the pistol only uttered a sterile click.

'All right,' Flagg said softly. 'All right. Well done. Well done, Lloyd.'

Lloyd dropped the gun on the floor and shrank away from Flagg. 'Don't you touch me!' he cried. 'I didn't do it for you!'

'Yes, you did,' Flagg said tenderly. 'You may not think so, but you did.' He reached out and fingered the jet stone around Lloyd's neck. He closed his hand over it, and when he opened the hand again, the stone was gone. It had been replaced with a small silver key.

'I promised you this, I think,' the dark man said. 'In another jail. He was wrong . . . I keep my promises, don't I, Lloyd?'

'Yes.'

'The others are leaving, or planning to leave. I know who they are. I know all the names. Whitney . . . Ken . . . Jenny . . . oh yes, I know all the names.'

'Then why don't you —'

'Put a stop to it? I don't know. Maybe it's better to let them go. But you, Lloyd. You're my good and faithful servant, aren't you?'

'Yeah,' Lloyd whispered. The final admission. 'Yeah, I guess I am.'

'Without me, the best you could have done was small shit, even if you had survived that jail. Correct?'

'Yeah.'

'The Lauder boy knew that. He knew I could make him bigger. Taller. That's why he was coming to me. But he was too full of thoughts . . . too full of . . .' He looked suddenly perplexed and old. Then he waved his hand impatiently, and the smile bloomed on his face again. 'Perhaps it is going bad, Lloyd. Perhaps it is, for some reason not even I can understand . . . but the old magician has a few tricks left in him yet, Lloyd. One or two. Now listen to me. Time is short if we want to stop this . . . this crisis in confidence. If we want to nip it in the bud, as it were. We'll want to finish things tomorrow with Underwood and Brentner. Now listen to me very carefully . . .'

* * *

Lloyd didn't get to bed until past midnight, and got no sleep until the small hours of the morning. He talked to the Rat-Man. He talked to Paul Burlson. To Barry Dorgan, who agreed that what the dark man wanted could – and probably should – be done before daylight. Construction began on the front lawn of the MGM Grand around 10 PM on the twenty-ninth, a work party of ten men with welding arcs and hammers and bolts and a good supply of long steel pipes. They were assembling the pipes on two flatbed trucks in front of the fountain. The welding arcs soon drew a crowd.

'Look, Angie-mom!' Dinny cried. 'It's a fireworks show!'

'Yes, but it's time for all good little boys to be in bed.' Angie Hirschfield drew the boy away with a secret fear in her heart, feeling that something bad, something perhaps as evil as the superflu itself, was in the making.

'Wanna see! Wanna see the *sparks*!' Dinny wailed, but she drew him quickly and firmly away.

Julie Lawry approached the Rat-Man, the only fellow in Vegas she considered too creepy to sleep with . . . except maybe in a pinch. His black skin glimmered in the blue-white glare of the welding arcs. He was tricked out like an Ethiopian pirate – wide silk trousers, a red sash, and a necklace of silver dollars around his scrawny neck.

'What is it, Ratty?' she asked.

'The Rat-Man don't know, dear, but the Rat-Man got hisself an idea. Yes indeedy he does. It looks like black work tomorrow, very black. Like to slip away for a quick one with Ratty, my dear?'

'Maybe,' Julie said, 'but only if you know what all of this is about.'

'Tomorrow all of Vegas gonna know,' Ratty said. 'You bet your sweet and delectable little sugarbuns on that. Come along with the Rat-Man, dear, and he show you the nine thousand names of God.'

But Julie, much to the Rat-Man's displeasure, had slipped away.

By the time Lloyd finally went to sleep, the work was done and the crowd had drifted away. Two large cages stood on the back of the two flatbeds. There were squarish holes in the right and left sides of each. Parked close by were four cars, each with a trailer hitch. Attached to each hitch was a heavy steel towing chain. The chains snaked across the lawn of the Grand, and each ended just inside the squarish holes in the cages.

At the end of each chain there dangled a single steel handcuff.

*   *   *

At dawn on the morning of September 30, Larry heard the door at the far end of the cellblock slide back. Footsteps came rapidly down the corridor. Larry was lying on his cot, hands laced at the back of his head. He had not slept the night before. He had been

(thinking? praying?)

It was all the same thing. Whichever it had been, the old wound in himself had finally closed, leaving him at peace. He had felt the two people that he had been all his life – the real one and the ideal one – merge into one living being. His mother would have liked this Larry. And Rita Blakemoor. It was a Larry to whom Wayne Stukey never would have had to tell the facts. It was a Larry that even that long-ago oral hygienist might have liked.

I'm going to die. If there's a God – and now I believe there must be – that's His will. We're going to die and somehow all of this will end as a result of our dying.

He suspected that Glen Bateman had already died. There had been shooting in one of the other wings the day before, a lot of shooting. It was in the direction that Glen had been taken rather than Ralph. Well, he had been old, his arthritis had been paining him, and whatever Flagg had planned for them this morning was apt to be very unpleasant.

The footsteps reached his cell.

'Get up, Wonder Bread,' a gleeful voice called in. 'The Rat-Man has come for yo pale gray ass.'

Larry looked around. A grinning black pirate with a chain of silver dollars around his neck stood at the cell door, a drawn sword in one hand. Behind him stood the bespectacled CPA type. Burlson, his name was.

'What is it?' Larry asked.

'Dear man,' the pirate said, 'it is the end. The very end.'

'All right,' Larry said, and got up.

Burlson spoke quickly, and Larry saw that he was scared. 'I want you to know that this is not my idea.'

'Nothing around here is, as far as I can see,' Larry said. 'Who was killed yesterday?'

'Bateman,' Burlson said, dropping his eyes. 'Trying to escape.'

'Trying to escape,' Larry murmured. He began to laugh. Rat-Man joined him, mocked him. They laughed together.

The cell door opened. Burlson stepped forward with the cuffs.

Larry offered no resistance; only put out his wrists. Burlson attached the bracelets.

'Trying to escape,' Larry said. 'One of these days you'll be shot trying to escape, Burlson.' His eyes flicked toward the pirate. 'You too, Ratty. Just shot trying to escape.' He began to laugh again, and this time Rat-Man didn't join him. He looked at Larry sullenly and then began to raise his sword.

'Put that down, you ass,' Burlson said.

They made a line of three going out – Burlson, Larry, and the Rat-Man bringing up the rear. When they stepped through the door at the end of the wing, they were joined by another five men. One of them was Ralph, also cuffed.

'Hey, Larry,' Ralph said sorrowfully. 'Did you hear? Did they tell you?'

'Yes. I heard.'

'Bastards. It's almost over for them, isn't it?'

'Yes. It is.'

'You shut up that talk!' one of them growled. 'It's you it's almost over for. You wait and see what he's got waiting for you. It's gonna be quite a party.'

'No, it's over,' Ralph insisted. 'Don't you know it? Can't you feel it?'

Ratty pushed Ralph, making him stumble. 'Shut up!' he cried. 'Rat-Man don't want to hear no more of that honky bullshit voodoo! No more!'

'You're awful pale, Ratty,' Larry said, grinning. 'Awful pale. You're the one who looks like graymeat now.'

Rat-Man brandished his sword again, but there was no menace in it. He looked frightened; they all did. There was a feeling in the air, a sense that they had all entered the shadow of some great and onrushing thing.

An olive-drab van with LAS VEGAS COUNTY JAIL on the side stood in the sunny courtyard. Larry and Ralph were pushed in. The doors slammed, the engine started, and they drew away. They sat down on the hard wooden benches, cuffed hands between their knees.

Ralph said in a low voice, 'I heard one of them saying everybody in Vegas was gonna be there. You think they're gonna crucify us, Larry?'

'That or something like it.' He looked at the big man. Ralph's sweat-stained hat was crammed down on his head. The feather was frayed and matted, but it still stuck up defiantly from the band. 'You scared, Ralph?'

'Scared bad,' Ralph whispered. 'Me, I'm a baby about pain. I never even liked going to the doctor's for a shot. I'd find an excuse to put it off, if I could. What about you?'

'Plenty. Can you come over here and sit beside me?'

Ralph got up, handcuff chains clinking, and sat beside Larry. They sat quietly for a few moments and then Ralph said softly, 'We've hoed us one helluva long row.'

'That's true.'

'I just wish I knew what it was all for. All I can see is that he's gonna make a show of us. So everyone will see he's the big cheese. Is that what we came all this way for?'

'I don't know.'

The van hummed on in silence. They sat on the bench without speaking, holding hands. Larry was scared, but beyond the scary feeling, the deeper sense of peace held, undisturbed. It was going to work out.

'I will fear no evil,' he muttered, but he *was* afraid. He closed his eyes, thought of Lucy. He thought of his mother. Random thoughts. Getting up for school on cold mornings. The time he had thrown up in church. Finding a skin magazine in the gutter and looking at it with Rudy, both of them about nine years old. Watching the World Series his first fall in LA with Yvonne Wetterlin. He didn't want to die, he was afraid to die, but he had made his peace with it as best he could. The choice, after all, had never been his to make, and he had come to believe that death was just a staging area, a place to wait, the way you waited in a green-room before going on to play.

He rested as easily as he could, trying to make himself ready.

The van stopped and the doors were thrown open. Bright sunlight poured in, making him and Ralph blink dazedly. Rat-Man and Burlson hopped inside. Pouring in with the sunlight was a sound – a low, rustling murmur that made Ralph cock his head warily. But Larry knew what that sound was.

In 1986 the Tattered Remnants had played their biggest gig – opening for Van Halen at Chavez Ravine. And the sound just before they went on had been like this sound. And so when he stepped out of the van he knew what to expect, and his face didn't change, although he heard Ralph's thin gasp beside him.

They were on the lawn of a huge hotel-casino. The entrance was flanked by two golden pyramids. Drawn up on the grass were two flatbed trucks. On each flatbed was a cage constructed of steel piping.

Surrounding them were people.

They spread out across the lawn in a rough circle. They were standing in the casino parking lot, on the steps leading up to the lobby doors, in the turnaround drive where incoming guests had once parked while the doorman whistled up a bellhop. They spilled out into the street itself. Some of the younger men had hoisted their girlfriends on their shoulders for a better look at the upcoming festivities. The low murmuring was the sound of the crowd-animal.

Larry ran his eyes over them, and every eye he met turned away. Every face seemed pallid, distant, marked for death and seeming to know it. Yet they were here.

He and Ralph were nudged toward the cages, and as they went, Larry noticed the cars with their chains and trailer hitches. But it was Ralph who understood the implication. He had, after all, spent most of his life working with and around machinery.

'Larry,' he said in a dry voice. 'They're going to pull us to pieces!'

'Go on, get in,' Rat-Man said, breathing a stale odor of garlic into his face. 'Get on up there, Wonder Bread. You and your friend goan ride the tiger.'

Larry climbed onto the flatbed.

'Gimme your shirt, Wonder Bread.'

Larry took off his shirt and stood barechested, the morning air cool and kind on his skin. Ralph had already taken off his. A ripple of conversation went through the crowd and died. They were both terribly thin from their walk; each rib was clearly visible.

'Get in that cage, graymeat.'

Larry backed into the cage.

Now it was Barry Dorgan giving the orders. He went from place to place, checking arrangements, a set expression of disgust on his face.

The four drivers got into the cars and started them up. Ralph stood blankly for a moment, then seized one of the welded handcuffs that dangled into his cage and threw it out through the small hole.

It hit Paul Burlson on the head, and a nervous titter ran through the crowd.

Dorgan said, 'You don't want to do that, fella. I'll just have to send some guys to hold you.'

'Let them do their thing,' Larry said to Ralph. He looked down at Dorgan. 'Hey, Barry. Did they teach you this one in the Santa Monica PD?'

Another laugh rippled through the crowd. 'Police brutality!' some daring soul cried. Dorgan flushed but said nothing. He fed the chains farther into Larry's cell and Larry spat on them, a little surprised that he had enough saliva to do it. A small cheer went up from the back of the crowd and Larry thought, *Maybe this is it, maybe they're going to rise up –*

But his heart didn't believe it. Their faces were too pale, too secretive. The defiance from the back was meaningless. It was the sound of kids cutting up in a studyhall, no more than that. There was doubt here – he could feel it – and disaffection. But Flagg colored even that. These people would steal away in the dead of the night for some of the great empty space that the world had become. And the Walkin Dude would let them go, knowing he only had to keep a hard core, people like Dorgan and Burlson. The runners and midnight creepers could be gathered up later, perchance to pay the price of their imperfect faith. There would be no open rebellion here.

Dorgan, Rat-Man, and a third man crowded their way into the cage with him. Rat-Man was holding the cuffs welded to the chains open for Larry's wrists.

'Put out your arms,' Dorgan said.

'Isn't law and order a wonderful thing, Barry?'

'Put them out, goddammit!'

'You don't look well, Dorgan – how's your heart these days?'

'I'm telling you for the last time, my friend. Put your arms out through those holes!'

Larry did it. The cuffs were slipped on and locked. Dorgan and the others backed out and the door was shut. Larry looked right and saw Ralph standing in his cage, head down, arms at his sides. His wrists had also been cuffed.

'You people know this is wrong!' Larry cried, and his voice, trained by years of singing, rolled out of his chest with surprising strength. 'I don't expect you to stop it, but I do expect you to remember it! We're being put to death because Randall Flagg is afraid of us! He's afraid of us and the people we came from!' A rising murmur ran through the crowd. 'Remember the way we die! And remember that next time it may be your turn to die this way, with no dignity, just an animal in a cage!'

That low murmur again, rising and angry . . . and the silence.

'Larry!' Ralph called out.

Flagg was coming down the steps of the Grand, Lloyd Henreid beside him. Flagg was wearing jeans, a checked shirt, his jeans jacket with the two buttons on the breast pockets, and his rundown cowboy boots. In the sudden hush the sound of those bootheels clocking their way down the cement path was the only sound . . . a sound out of time.

The dark man was grinning.

Larry stared down at him. Flagg came to a halt between the two cages and stood looking up. His grin was darkly charming. He was a man completely in control, and Larry suddenly knew this was his watershed moment, the apotheosis of his life.

Flagg turned away from them and faced his people. He passed his eyes over them, and no eye would meet his. 'Lloyd,' he said quietly, and Lloyd, who looked pale, haunted, and sickly, handed Flagg a paper that had been rolled up like a scroll.

The dark man unrolled it, held it up, and began to speak. His voice was deep, sonorous, and pleasing, spreading in the stillness like a single silver ripple on a black pond. 'Know you that this is a true bill to which I, Randall Flagg, have put my name on this thirtieth day of September, the year nineteen hundred and ninety, now known as The Year One, year of the plague.'

'Flagg's not your name!' Ralph roared. There was a shocked murmur from the crowd. 'Why don't you tell em your real name?'

Flagg took no notice.

'Know you that these men, Lawson Underwood and Ralph Brentner, are spies, here in Las Vegas with no good intent but rather with seditious motives, who have entered this state with stealth, and under cover of darkness –'

'That's pretty good,' Larry said, 'since we were coming down Route 70 in broad daylight.' He raised his voice to a shout. *'They took us at noon on the Interstate, how's that for stealth and under cover of darkness?'*

Flagg bore through this patiently, as if he felt that Larry and

Ralph had every right to answer the charges . . . not that it was going to make any ultimate difference.

Now he continued: 'Know you that the cohorts of these men were responsible for the sabotage bombing of the helicopters at Indian Springs, and therefore responsible for the deaths of Carl Hough, Bill Jamieson, and Cliff Benson. They are guilty of murder.'

Larry's eyes touched those of a man standing on the front rim of the crowd. Although Larry did not know it, this was Stan Bailey, Operations Chief at Indian Springs. He saw a haze of bewilderment and surprise cover the man's face, and saw him mouthing something ridiculous that looked like *Can Man*.

'Know you that the cohorts of these men have sent other spies among us and they have been killed. It is the sentence then that these men shall be put to death in an appropriate manner, to wit, that they shall be pulled apart. It is the duty and the responsibility of each of you to witness this punishment, so you may remember it and tell others what you have seen here today.'

Flagg's grin flashed out, meant to be solicitous in this instance, but still no more warm and human than a shark's grin.

'Those of you with children are excused.'

He turned toward the cars, which were now idling, sending out small puffs of exhaust into the morning. As he did so, there was a commotion near the front of the crowd. Suddenly a man pushed through into the clearing. He was a big man, his face nearly as pallid as his cook's whites. The dark man had handed the scroll back to Lloyd, and Lloyd's hands jerked convulsively when Whitney Horgan pushed into the clear. There was a clear ripping sound as the scroll tore in half.

'*Hey, you people!*' Whitney cried.

A confused murmur ran through the crowd. Whitney was shaking all over, as if with a palsy. His head kept jerking toward the dark man and then away again. Flagg regarded Whitney with a ferocious smile. Dorgan started toward the cook, and Flagg motioned him back.

'*This ain't right!*' Whitney yelled. '*You know it ain't!*'

Dead silence from the crowd. They might all have been turned to gravestones.

Whitney's throat worked convulsively. His Adam's apple bobbed up and down like a monkey on a stick.

'We was Americans once!' Whitney cried at last. 'This ain't

how Americans act. I wasn't so much, I'll tell you that, nothin but a cook, but I know this ain't how Americans act, listening to some murderin freak in cowboy boots —'

A horrified, rustling gasp came from these new Las Vegans. Larry and Ralph exchanged a puzzled glance.

'That's what he is!' Whitney insisted. The sweat was running down his face like tears from the brushy edges of his flattop haircut. 'You wanna watch these two guys ripped in two right in front of you, huh? You think that's the way to start a new life? You think a thing like that can ever be right? I tell you you'll have nightmares about it *for the rest of your lives!*'

The crowd murmured its assent.

'We got to stop this,' Whitney said. 'You know it? We got to have time to think about what . . . what . . .'

'Whitney.' That voice, smooth as silk, little more than a whisper, but enough to silence the cook's faltering voice completely. He turned toward Flagg, lips moving soundlessly, his eyes as fixed as a mackerel's. Now the sweat was pouring down his face in torrents.

'Whitney, you should have kept still.' His voice was soft, but still it carried easily to every ear. 'I would have let you go . . . why would I want you?'

Whitney's lips moved, but still no sound came out.

'Come here, Whitney.'

'No,' Whitney whispered, and no one heard his demurral except Lloyd and Ralph and Larry and possibly Barry Dorgan. Whitney's feet moved as if they had not heard his mouth. His sprung and mushy black loafers whispered through the grass and he moved toward the dark man like a ghost.

The crowd had become a slack jaw and staring eye.

'I knew about your plans,' the dark man said. 'I knew what you meant to do before you did. And I would have let you crawl away until I was ready to take you back. Maybe in a year, maybe in ten. But that's all behind you now, Whitney. Believe it.'

Whitney found his voice one last time, his words rushing out in a strangled scream. '*You ain't a man at all! You're some kind of a . . . a devil!*'

Flagg stretched out the index finger of his left hand so that it almost touched Whitney Horgan's chin. 'Yes, that's right,' he said so softly that no one but Lloyd and Larry Underwood heard. 'I am.'

A blue ball of fire no bigger than the Ping-Pong ball Leo was endlessly bouncing leaped from the tip of Flagg's finger with a faint ozone crackle.

An autumn wind of sighs went through those watching.

Whitney screamed – but didn't move. The ball of fire lit on his chin. There was a sudden cloying smell of burning flesh. The ball moved across his mouth, fusing his lips shut, locking the scream behind Whitney's bulging eyes. It crossed one cheek, digging a charred and instantly cauterized trench.

It closed his eyes.

It paused above his forehead and Larry heard Ralph speaking, saying the same thing over and over, and Larry joined his voice to Ralph's, making it a litany: 'I will fear no evil . . . I will fear no evil . . . I will fear no evil . . .'

The ball of fire rolled up from Whitney's forehead and now there was a hot smell of burning hair. It rolled toward the back of his head, leaving a grotesque bald strip behind it. Whitney swayed on his feet for a moment and then fell over, mercifully facedown.

The crowd released a long, sibilant sound: *Aaaahhhh*. It was the sound people had made on the Fourth of July when the fireworks display had been particularly good. The ball of blue fire hung in the air, bigger now, too bright to look at without slitting the eyes. The dark man pointed at it and it moved slowly toward the crowd. Those in the front row – a whey-faced Jenny Engstrom was among them – shrank back.

In a thundering voice, Flagg challenged them. '*Is there anyone else here who disagrees with my sentence? If so, let him speak now!*'

Deep silence greeted this.

Flagg seemed satisfied. 'Then let –'

Heads began to turn away from him suddenly. A surprised murmur ran through the crowd, then rose to a babble. Flagg seemed completely caught by surprise. Now people in the crowd began to cry out, and while it was impossible to make out the words clearly, the tone was one of wonder and surprise. The ball of fire dipped and spun uncertainly.

The humming sound of an electric motor came to Larry's ears. And again he caught that puzzling name tossed from mouth to mouth, never clear, never all of one piece: Man . . . Can Man . . . Trash . . . Trashy . . .

Someone was coming through the crowd, as if in answer to the dark man's challenge.

Flagg felt terror seep into the chambers of his heart. It was a terror of the unknown and the unexpected. He had foreseen everything, even Whitney's foolish spur-of-the-moment speech. He had foreseen everything but this. The crowd – *his* crowd – was parting, peeling back. There was a scream, high, clear, and freezing. Someone broke and ran. Then someone else. And then the crowd, already on an emotional hair-trigger, broke and stampeded.

'*Hold still!*' Flagg cried at the top of his voice, but it was useless. The crowd had become a strong wind, and not even the dark man could stop the wind. Terrible, impotent rage rose in him, joining the fear and making some new and volatile mix. It had gone wrong again. In the last minute it had somehow gone wrong, like the old lawyer in Oregon, the woman slitting her throat on the window-glass . . . and Nadine . . . Nadine falling . . .

They ran, scattering to all the points of the compass, pounding across the lawn of the MGM Grand, across the street, toward the Strip. They had seen the final guest, arrived at last like some grim vision out of a horror tale. They had seen, perhaps, the raddled face of some final awful retribution.

And they had seen what the returning wanderer had brought with him.

As the crowd melted, Randall Flagg also saw, as did Larry and Ralph and a frozen Lloyd Henreid, who was still holding the torn scroll in his hands.

It was Donald Merwin Elbert, now known as the Trashcan Man, now and forever, world without end, hallelujah, amen.

He was behind the wheel of a long, dirty electric cart. The cart's heavy-duty bank of batteries was nearly drained dry. The cart was humming and buzzing and lurching. Trashcan Man bobbed back and forth on the open seat like a mad marionette.

He was in the last stages of radiation sickness. His hair was gone. His arms, poking out of the tatters of his shirt, were covered with open running sores. His face was a cratered red soup from which one desert-faded blue eye peered with a terrible, pitiful intelligence. His teeth were gone. His nails were gone. His eyelids were frayed flaps.

He looked like a man who had driven his electric cart out of the dark and burning subterranean mouth of hell itself.

Flagg watched him come, frozen. His smile was gone. His high, rich color was gone. His face was suddenly a window made of pale clear glass.

Trashcan Man's voice bubbled ecstatically up from his thin chest: 'I brought it . . . I brought you the fire . . . please . . . I'm sorry . . .'

It was Lloyd who moved. He took one step forward, then another. 'Trashy . . . Trash, baby . . .' His voice was a croak.

That single eye moved, painfully seeking Lloyd out. 'Lloyd? That you?'

'It's me, Trash.' Lloyd was shaking violently all over, the way Whitney had been shaking. 'Hey, what you got there? Is it –'

'It's the Big One,' Trash said happily. 'It's the A-bomb.' He began to rock back and forth on the seat of the electric cart like a convert at a revival meeting. 'The A-bomb, the Big One, the big fire, *my life for you!*'

'Take it away, Trash,' Lloyd whispered. 'It's dangerous. It's . . . it's hot. Take it away . . .'

'Make him get rid of it, Lloyd,' the dark man who was now the pale man whined. 'Make him take it back where he got it. Make him –'

Trashcan's one operative eye grew puzzled. 'Where is he?' he asked, and then his voice rose to an agonized howl. 'Where is he? He's gone! *Where is he? What did you do to him?*'

Lloyd made one last supreme effort. 'Trash, you've got to get rid of that thing. You –'

And suddenly Ralph shrieked: '*Larry! Larry! The Hand of God!*' Ralph's face was transported in a terrible joy. His eyes shone. He was pointing into the sky.

Larry looked up. He saw the ball of electricity Flagg had flicked from the end of his finger. It had grown to a tremendous size. It hung in the sky, jittering toward Trashcan Man, giving off sparks like hair. Larry realized dimly that the air was now so full of electricity that every hair on his own body was standing on end.

And the thing in the sky did look like a hand.

'*Noooo!*' the dark man wailed.

Larry looked at him . . . but Flagg was no longer there. He had a bare impression of something monstrous standing *in front* of where Flagg had been. Something slumped and hunched and almost without shape – something with enormous yellow eyes slit by dark cat's pupils.

Then it was gone.

Larry saw Flagg's clothes – the jacket, the jeans, the boots – standing upright with nothing in them. For a split second they held the shape of the body that had been inside them. And then they collapsed.

The crackling blue fire in the air rushed at the yellow electric cart that Trashcan Man had somehow driven back from the Nellis Range. He had lost hair and thrown up blood and finally vomited out his own teeth as the radiation sickness sank deeper and deeper into him, yet he had never faltered in his resolve to bring it back to the dark man . . . you could say that he had never flagged in his determination.

The blue ball of fire flung itself into the back of the cart, seeking what was there, drawn to it.

'Oh shit we're all fucked!' Lloyd Henreid cried. He put his hands over his head and fell to his knees.

Oh God, thank God, Larry thought. *I will fear no evil, I will f*
Silent white light filled the world.

And the righteous and unrighteous alike were consumed in that holy fire.

CHAPTER 74

Stu woke up from a night of broken rest at dawn and lay shivering, even with Kojak curled up next to him. The morning sky was coldly blue, but in spite of the shivers he was hot. He was running a fever.

'Sick,' he muttered, and Kojak looked up at him. He wagged his tail and then trotted into the gully. He brought back a piece of deadwood and laid it at Stu's feet.

'I said sick, not stick, but I guess it'll do,' Stu told him. He sent Kojak out for a dozen more sticks. Soon he had a fire blazing. Even sitting close would not drive the shivers away, although sweat was rolling down his face. It was the final irony. He had the flu, or something very like it. He had come down with it two days after Glen, Larry, and Ralph left him. For another two days the flu had seemed to consider him – was he worth taking? Apparently he was. Little by little he was getting worse. And this morning he felt very bad indeed.

Among the odds and ends in his pockets, Stu found a stub of pencil, his notebook (all the Free Zone organizational stuff that had once seemed the vital stuff of life itself now seemed mildly foolish), and his key ring. He had puzzled over the key ring for a long time, coming back to it over the last few days again and again, constantly surprised by the strong ache of sadness and nostalgia. This one was to his apartment. This one was his locker key. This one was a spare for his car, a 1977 Dodge with a lot of rust – so far as he knew it was still parked behind the apartment building at 31 Thompson Street in Arnette.

Also attached to the key ring was a cardboard address card encased in Lucite. STU REDMAN – 31 THOMPSON STREET – Ph (713) 555–6283, it read. He took the keys off the ring, bounced them thoughtfully on the palm of his hand for a moment, and then threw them away. The last of the man he had been went into the dry-wash and clinked into a dry clump of sage, where it would stay, he supposed, until the end of time. He slipped the cardboard address card out of the Lucite, and then ripped a blank page from his notebook.

Dear Frannie, he wrote at the top.

He told her all that had happened up until he had broken his leg. He told her that he hoped to see her again, but that he doubted it was in the cards. The best he could hope for was that Kojak would find the Zone again. He wiped tears absently from his face with the heel of his hand and wrote that he loved her. *I expect you to mourn me and then get on*, he wrote. *You and the baby have to get on. That's the most important thing now.* He signed, folded it small, and slipped the note into the address slot in the Lucite square. Then he attached the key ring to Kojak's collar.

'Good dog,' he said when that was done. 'You want to go look around? Find a rabbit or something?'

Kojak bounded up the slope where Stu had broken his leg and was gone. Stu watched his progress with a mixture of bitterness and amusement, then picked up the 7-Up can Kojak had brought him on one trip yesterday in lieu of a stick. He had filled it with muddy water from the ditch. When the water stood, the mud silted down to the bottom. It made a gritty drink, but as his mother would have said, it was a whole lot grittier when there was none. He drank slowly, slaking his thirst bit by bit. It hurt to swallow.

'Life sure is a bitch,' he muttered, and then had to laugh at himself. For a moment or two he let his fingers fret at the swellings high on his neck, just under his jaw. Then he lay back, splinted leg in front of him, and dozed.

He woke with a start about an hour later, clutching at the sandy earth in sleepy panic. Had he had a nightmare? If so, it seemed to still be going on. The ground was moving slowly under his hands.

Earthquake? We got an earthquake here?

For a moment he clung to the idea that it must be delirium, that his fever had come back while he dozed. But looking toward the gully, he saw that dirt was sliding down in small, muddy sheets. Bounding, bouncing pebbles flashed mica and quartz glints at his startled eyes. And then a faint, dull thudding noise came – it seemed to *push* its way into his ears. A moment later he was heaving for breath, as if most of the air had suddenly been pushed out of the gully the flash flood had cut.

There was a whining sound above him. Kojak stood silhouetted against the western edge of the cut, hunkered down with his tail between his legs. He was staring west, toward Nevada.

'Kojak!' Stu cried in panic. That thudding noise had terrified him – it was as if God had suddenly stamped His foot down on the desert floor somewhere not too distant.

Kojak bounded down the slope and joined him, whining. As Stu passed a hand down the dog's back, he felt Kojak trembling. He had to see, he *had* to. A sudden feeling of surety came to him: what had been meant to happen *was* happening. Right now.

'I'm going up, boy,' Stu muttered.

He crawled to the eastern edge of the gully. It was a little steeper, but it offered more handholds. He had thought for the last three days that he might be able to get up there, but he hadn't seen the point. He was sheltered from the worst of the wind at the bottom of the cut, and he had water. But now he had to get up there. He had to see. He dragged his splinted leg behind him like a club. He got up on his hands and craned his neck to see the top. It looked very high, very far away.

'Can't do it, boy,' he muttered to Kojak, and started trying anyway.

A fresh pile of rubble had piled up at the bottom as a result of the . . . the earthquake. Or whatever it was. Stu pulled himself over it and then began to inch his way up the slope, using his hands and his left knee. He made twelve yards and then lost six of them before he could grab a quartz outcropping and stop his slide.

'Nope, never make it,' he panted, and rested.

Ten minutes later he started again and made another ten yards. He rested. Went again. Came to a place with no holds and had to inch to the left until he found one. Kojak walked beside him, no doubt wondering what this fool was up to, leaving his water and his nice warm fire.

Warm. Too warm.

The fever must be coming up again, but at least the shivering had subsided. Fresh sweat was running down his face and arms. His hair, dusty and oily, hung in his eyes.

Lord, I'm burning up! Must be a hundred and two, a hundred and three . . .

He happened to glance at Kojak. It took almost a minute for

what he was seeing to sink in. Kojak was panting. It wasn't fever, or not *just* fever, because Kojak was hot, too.

Overhead, a squadron of birds suddenly flocked, wheeling aimlessly and squawking.

They feel it, too. Whatever it is, the birds feel it, too.

He began to crawl again, fear lending him additional strength. An hour passed, two. He fought for every foot, every inch. By one o'clock that afternoon he was only six feet below the edge. He could see jags of paving jutting out above him. Only six feet, but the grade here was very steep and smooth. He tried once to just wriggle up like a garter snake, but loose gravel, the underbedding of the Interstate, had begun to rattle out from beneath him, and now he was afraid that if he tried to move at all he would go all the way to the bottom again, probably breaking his other damn leg in the process.

'Stuck,' he muttered. 'Good fucking show. Now what?'

Now what became obvious very quickly. Even without moving around, the earth was beginning to shift downward beneath him. He slipped an inch and clawed for purchase with his hands. His broken leg was thudding heavily, and he had not thought to pocket Glen's pills.

He slipped another two inches. Then five. His left foot was now dangling over space. Only his hands were holding him, and as he watched they began to slip, digging ten little furrows in the damp ground.

'Kojak!' he cried miserably, expecting nothing. But suddenly Kojak was there. Stu flung his arms around his neck blindly, not expecting to be saved but only grabbing what there was to be grabbed, like a drowning man. Kojak made no effort to throw him off. He dug in. For a moment they were frozen, a living sculpture. Then Kojak began to move, digging for inches, claws clicking against small stones and bits of gravel. Pebbles rattled into Stu's face and he shut his eyes. Kojak dragged him, panting like an air compressor in Stu's right ear.

He slitted his eyes open and saw they were nearly at the top. Kojak's head was down. His back legs were working furiously. He gained four more inches and it was enough. With a desperate cry, Stu let go of Kojak's neck and grabbed an outcrop of paving. It snapped off in his hands. He grabbed another one. Two fingernails peeled back like wet decals, and he cried out. The pain was exquisite, galvanizing. He scrambled up, pistoning with his good leg, and at last – somehow – lay panting on the surface of I-70, his eyes shut.

Kojak was beside him then. He whined and licked Stu's face.

Slowly then, Stu sat up and looked west. He looked for a long time, oblivious of the heat that was still rushing against his face in warm, bloated waves.

'Oh, my God,' he said at last in a weak, breaking voice. 'Look at that, Kojak. Larry. Glen. They're gone. God, *everything's* gone. All gone.'

The mushroom cloud stood out on the horizon like a clenched fist on the end of a long, dusty forearm. It was swirling, fuzzy at the edges, beginning to dissipate. It was backlighted in sullen orange-red, as if the sun had decided to go down in the early afternoon.

The firestorm, he thought.

They were all dead in Las Vegas. Someone had fiddled when he should have faddled, and a nuclear weapon had gone off . . . and one hellish big one, from the look and the feel. Maybe a whole stockpile of them had gone. Glen, Larry, Ralph . . . even if they hadn't reached Vegas yet, even if they were still walking, surely they were close enough to have been baked alive.

Close beside him, Kojak whimpered unhappily.

Fallout. Which way is the wind going to blow it?

Did it matter?

He remembered his note to Fran. It was important that he add what had happened. If the wind blew the fallout east, it might cause them problems . . . but more than that, they had to know that if Las Vegas had been the dark man's staging area, it was gone now. The people had been vaporized along with all the deadly toys that had just been lying around, waiting for someone to pick them up. He ought to add all of that to the note.

But not now. He was too tired now. The climb had exhausted him, and the stupendous sight of that dissipating mushroom cloud had exhausted him even more. He felt no jubilation, only dull and grinding weariness. He lay down on the pavement and his last thought before drifting off to sleep was: *How many megatons?* He didn't think anyone would ever know, or want to know.

He awoke after six. The mushroom cloud was gone, but the western sky was an angry pinkish-red, like a bright weal of burnflesh. Stu hauled himself over into the breakdown lane and lay down, exhausted all over again. The shakes were back. And the fever. He touched his forehead with his wrist and tried to gauge the temperature there. He guessed it was well over a hundred degrees.

Kojak came out of the early evening with a rabbit in his jaws. He laid it at Stu's feet and wagged his tail, waiting to be complimented.

'Good dog,' Stu said tiredly. 'That's a good dog.'

Kojak's tail wagged faster. *Yes, I'm a pretty good dog*, he seemed to agree. But he remained looking at Stu, seeming to wait for something. Part of the ritual was incomplete. Stu tried to think what it was. His brain was moving very slowly; while he was sleeping, someone seemed to have poured molasses all over his interior gears.

'Good dog,' he repeated, and looked at the dead rabbit. Then he remembered, although he wasn't even sure he had his matches anymore. 'Fetch, Kojak,' he said, mostly to please the dog. Kojak bounced away and soon returned with a good chunk of dry wood.

He had his matches, but a good breeze had sprung up and his hands were shaking badly. It took a long time to get a fire going. He got the kindling he had stripped lighted on the tenth match, and then the breeze gusted roguishly, puffing out the flames. Stu rebuilt it carefully, shielding it with his body and his hands. He had eight remaining matches in a LaSalle Business School folder. He cooked the rabbit, gave Kojak his half, and could eat only a little of his share. He tossed Kojak what was left. Kojak didn't pick it up. He looked at it, then whined uneasily at Stu.

'Go on, boy. I can't.'

Kojak ate up. Stu looked at him and shivered. His two blankets were, of course, below.

The sun went down, and the western sky was grotesque with color. It was the most spectacular sunset Stu had ever seen in his life . . . and it was poison. He could remember the narrator of a MovieTone newsreel saying enthusiastically back in the early sixties that there were beautiful sunsets for weeks after a nuclear test. And, of course, after earthquakes.

Kojak came up from the washout with something in his mouth – one of Stu's blankets. He dropped it in Stu's lap. 'Hey,' Stu said, hugging him unsteadily. 'You're some kind of dog, you know it?'

Kojak wagged his tail to show that he knew it.

Stu wrapped the blanket around him and moved closer to the fire. Kojak lay next to him, and soon they both slept. But Stu's sleep was light and uneasy, skimming in and out of delirium. Sometime after midnight he roused Kojak, yelling in his sleep.

'Hap!' Stu cried. 'You better turn off y'pumps! He's coming! Black man's coming for you! Better turn off y'pumps! He's in the old car yonder!'

Kojak whined uneasily. The Man was sick. He could smell the sickness and mingling with that smell was a new one. A black one. It was the smell the rabbits had on them when he pounced. The smell had been on the wolf he had disemboweled under Mother Abagail's house in Hemingford Home. The smell had been on the towns he had passed through on his way to Boulder and Glen Bateman. It was the smell of death. If he could have attacked it and driven it out of this Man, he would have. But it was *inside* this Man. The Man drew in good air and sent out that smell of coming death, and there was nothing to do but wait and see it through to the end. Kojak whined again, low, and then slept.

Stu woke up the next morning more feverish than ever. The glands under his jaw had swollen to the size of golfballs. His eyes were hot marbles.

I'm dying . . . yes, that's affirmative.

He called Kojak over and removed the key chain and his note from the Lucite address-holder. Printing carefully, he added what he had seen and replaced the note. He lay back down and slept. And then, somehow, it was nearly dark again. Another spectacular, horrible sunset burned and jittered in the West. And Kojak had brought a gopher for dinner.

'This the best y'could do?'

Kojak wagged his tail and grinned shamefacedly.

Stu cooked it, divided it, and managed to eat his entire half. It was tough, and it had a horrible wild taste, and when he was done he had a nasty bout of stomach cramps.

'When I die, I want you to go back to Boulder,' he told the dog. 'You go back and find Fran. Find Frannie. Okay, big old dumb dog?'

Kojak wagged his tail doubtfully.

An hour later, Stu's stomach rumbled once in warning. He had just time enough to roll over on one elbow to avoid fouling himself before his share of the gopher came up in a rush.

'Shit,' he muttered miserably, and dozed off.

He awoke in the small hours and got up on his elbows, his

head buzzing with fever. The fire had gone out, he saw. It didn't matter. He was pretty well done up.

Some sound in the darkness had awakened him. Pebbles and stones. Kojak coming up the embankment from the cut, that's all it was . . .

Except that Kojak was beside him, sleeping.

Even as Stu glanced at him, the dog woke up. His head came off his paws and a moment later he was on his feet, facing the cut, growling deep in his throat.

Rattling pebbles and stones. Someone – some*thing* – coming up.

Stu struggled into a sitting position. *It's him*, he thought. *He was there, but somehow he got away. Now he's here, and he means to do me before the flu can.*

Kojak's growl became stronger. His hackles stood, his head was down. The rattling sound was closer now. Stu could hear a low panting sound. There was a pause then, long enough for Stu to arm sweat off his forehead. A moment later a dark shape humped against the edge of the cut, head and shoulders blotting out the stars.

Kojak advanced, stiff-legged, still growling.

'Hey!' a bewildered but familiar voice said. 'Hey, is that Kojak? Is it?'

The growling stopped immediately. Kojak bounded forward joyfully, tail wagging.

'No!' Stu croaked. 'It's a trick! *Kojak . . . !*'

But Kojak was jumping up and down on the figure that had finally gained the pavement. And that shape . . . something about the shape was also familiar. It advanced toward him with Kojak at his heel. Kojak was volleying joyful barks. Stu licked his lips and got ready to fight if he had to. He thought he could manage one good punch, maybe two.

'Who is it?' he called. 'Who is that there?'

The dark figure paused, then spoke.

'Well, it's Tom Cullen, that's who, my laws, yes. M-O-O-N, that spells Tom Cullen. Who's *that*?'

'Stu,' he said, and his voice seemed to come from far away. Everything was far away now. 'Hello, Tom, it's good to see you.' But he didn't see him, not that night. Stu fainted.

He came around at ten in the morning on October 2, although neither he nor Tom knew that was the date. Tom had built a huge bonfire and had wrapped Stu in his sleeping bag and his blankets. Tom himself was sitting by the fire and roasting a rabbit. Kojak lay contentedly on the ground between the two of them.

'Tom,' Stu managed.

Tom came over. He had grown a beard, Stu saw; he hardly looked like the man who had left Boulder for the West five weeks ago. His blue eyes glinted happily. 'Stu Redman! You're awake now, my laws, yes! I'm glad. Boy, it's good to see you. What did you do to your leg? Hurt it, I guess. I hurt mine once. Jumped off a haystack and broke it, I guess. Did my daddy whip me? My laws, yes! That was before he run off with DeeDee Packalotte.'

'Mine's broken, too. And how. Tom, I'm awful thirsty –'

'Oh, there's water. All kinds! Here.'

He handed Stu a plastic bottle that might once have held milk. The water was clear and delicious. No grit at all. Stu drank greedily and then threw it all up.

'Slow and easy does it,' Tom said. 'That's the ticket. Slow and easy. Boy, it's good to see you. Hurt your leg, didn't you?'

'Yes, I broke it. Week ago, maybe longer.' He drank more water, and this time it stayed down. 'But there's more wrong than the leg. I'm bad sick, Tom. Fever. Listen to me.'

'Right! Tom's listening. Just tell me what to do.' Tom leaned forward and Stu thought, *Why, he looks brighter. Is that possible?* Where had Tom been? Did he know anything about the Judge? About Dayna? So many things to talk about, but there was no time now. He was getting worse. There was a deep rattling sound in his chest, like padded chains. Symptoms so much like the superflu. It was really quite funny.

'I've got to knock down the fever,' he said to Tom. 'That's the first thing. I need aspirin. Do you know aspirin?'

'Sure. Aspirin. For fast-fast-fast relief.'

'That's the ticket, all right. You start walking up the road, Tom. Look in the glove-box of every car you come to. Look for a first-aid kit – it'll most likely be a box with a red cross on it. When you find some aspirin in one of those boxes, bring it back here. And if you should find a car with camping gear in it, bring back a tent. Okay?'

'Sure.' Tom stood up. 'Aspirin and a tent, then you'll be all better again, right?'

'Well, it'll be a start.'

'Say,' Tom said, 'how's Nick? I've been dreaming about him. In the dreams he tells me where to go, because in the dreams he can talk. Dreams are funny, aren't they? But when I try to talk to him, he always goes away. He's okay, isn't he?' Tom looked at Stu anxiously.

'Not now,' Stu said. 'I . . . I can't talk now. Not about that. Just get the aspirin, okay? Then we'll talk.'

'Okay . . .' But fear had settled onto Tom's face like a gray cloud. 'Kojak, want to come with Tom?'

Kojak did. They walked off together, heading east. Stu lay down and put an arm over his eyes.

When Stu slipped back into reality again, it was twilight. Tom was shaking him. 'Stu! Wake up! Wake up, Stu!'

He was frightened by the way time seemed to be slipping by in sudden lurches – as if the teeth on the cog of his personal reality were wearing down. Tom had to help him sit up, and when he was sitting, he had to lean his head between his legs and cough. He coughed so long and hard that he almost passed out again. Tom watched him with alarm. Little by little, Stu got control of himself. He pulled the blankets closer around him. He was shivering again.

'What did you find, Tom?'

Tom held out a first-aid kit. Inside were Band-Aids, Mercurochrome, and a big bottle of Anacin. Stu was shocked to find he could not work the childproof cap. He had to give it to Tom, who finally worried it open. Stu washed down three Anacin with water from the plastic bottle.

'And I found this,' Tom said. 'It was in a car full of camping stuff, but there was no tent.' It was a huge, puffy double sleeping bag, fluorescent orange on the outside, the lining done in a gaudy stars-and-bars pattern.

'Yeah, that's great. Almost as good as a tent. You did fine, Tom.'

'And these. They were in the same car.' Tom reached into his jacket and produced half a dozen foil packages. Stu could hardly believe his eyes. Freeze-dried concentrates. Eggs. Peas. Squash. Dried beef. 'Food, isn't it, Stu? It's got pictures of food on it, laws, yes.'

'It's food,' Stu agreed gratefully. 'Just about the only kind I can eat, I think.' His head was buzzing, and far away, at the center of his brain, a sweetly sickening high C hummed on and on. 'Can we heat some water? We don't have a pot or a kettle.'

'I'll find something.'

'Yeah, fine.'

'Stu –'

Stu looked into that troubled, miserable face, still a boy's face in spite of the beard, and slowly shook his head.

'Dead, Tom,' he said gently. 'Nick's dead. Almost a month ago. It was a . . . a political thing. Assassination, I s'pose you'd say. I'm sorry.'

Tom lowered his head, and in the freshly built-up fire, Stu saw his tears fall into his lap. They fell in a gentle silver rain. But he was silent. At last he looked up, his blue eyes brighter than ever. He wiped at them with the heel of his hand.

'I knew he was,' he said huskily. 'I didn't want to think I knew, but I did. Laws, yes. He kept turning his back and going away. He was my main man, Stu – did you know that?'

Stu reached out and took Tom's big hand. 'I knew, Tom.'

'Yes he was, M-O-O-N, that spells my main man. I miss him awful. But I'm going to see him in heaven. Tom Cullen will see him there. And he'll be able to talk and I'll be able to think. Isn't that right?'

'It wouldn't surprise me at all, Tom.'

'It was the bad man killed Nick. Tom knows. But God fixed that bad man. I saw it. The hand of God came down out of the sky.' There was a cold wind whistling over the floor of the Utah badlands, and Stu shivered violently in its clasp. 'Fixed him for what he did to Nick and to the poor Judge. Laws, yes.'

'What do you know about the Judge, Tom?'

'Dead! Up in Oregon! Shot him!'

Stu nodded wearily. 'And Dayna? Do you know anything about her?'

'Tom saw her, but he doesn't know. They gave me a job cleaning up. And when I came back one day I saw her doing *her* job. She was up in the air changing a streetlight bulb. She looked at me and . . .' He fell silent for a moment, and when he spoke again it was more to himself than to Stu. 'Did she see Tom? Did she know Tom? Tom doesn't know. Tom . . . *thinks* . . . she did. But Tom never saw her again.'

Tom left to go foraging shortly after, taking Kojak with him, and

Stu dozed. He returned not with a big tin can, which was the best Stu had hoped for, but with a broiling pan big enough to hold a Christmas turkey. There were treasures in the desert, apparently. Stu grinned in spite of the painful fever blisters that had begun to form on his lips. Tom told him he had gotten the pan from an orange truck with a big U on it – someone who had been fleeing the superflu with all their worldly possessions, Stu guessed. Much good it had done them.

Half an hour later there was food. Stu ate carefully, sticking to the vegetables, watering the concentrates enough to make a thin gruel. He held everything down and felt a little better, at least for the time being. Not long after supper, he and Tom went to sleep with Kojak between them.

'Tom, listen to me.'

Tom hunkered down by Stu's big, fluffy sleeping bag. It was the next morning. Stu had been able to eat only a little breakfast; his throat was sore and badly swollen, all his joints painful. The cough was worse, and the Anacin wasn't doing much of a job of knocking back the fever.

'I got to get inside and get some medicine into me or I'm gonna die. And it has to be today. Now, the closest town is Green River, and that's sixty miles east of here. We'll have to drive.'

'Tom Cullen can't drive a car, Stu. Laws, no!'

'Yeah, I know. It's gonna be a chore for me, because as well as being sick as a dog, I broke the wrong friggin leg.'

'What do you mean?'

'Well . . . never mind right now. It's too hard to explain. We won't even worry about it, because that ain't the first problem. The first problem is getting a car to start. Most of them have been sitting out here three months or more. The batteries will be as flat as pancakes. So we'll need a little luck. We got to find a stalled car with a standard shift at the top of one of these hills. We might do it. It's pretty hilly country.' He didn't add that the car would have to have been kept reasonably tuned, would have to have some gas in it . . . and an ignition key. All those guys on TV might know how to hotwire a car, but Stu didn't have a clue.

He looked up at the sky, which was scumming over with clouds. 'Most of it's on you, Tom. You got to be my legs.'

'All right, Stu. When we get the car, are we going back to Boulder? Tom wants to go to Boulder, don't you?'

'More than anything, Tom.' He looked toward the Rockies, which were a dim shadow on the horizon. Had the snow started falling up in the high passes yet? Almost certainly. And if not yet, then soon. Winter came early in this high and forsaken part of the world. 'It may take a while,' he said.

'How do we start?'

'By making a travois.'

'Trav —?'

Stu gave Tom his pocketknife. 'You've got to make holes in the bottom of this sleeping bag. One on each side.'

It took them an hour to make the travois. Tom found a couple of fairly straight sticks to ram down into the sleeping bag and out the holes at the bottom. Tom got some rope from the U-Haul where he had gotten the broiling pan, and Stu used it to secure the sleeping bag to the poles. When it was done, it reminded Stu more of a crazy rickshaw than a travois like the ones the Plains Indians had used.

Tom picked up the poles and looked doubtfully over his shoulder. 'Are you in, Stu?'

'Yeah.' He wondered how long the seams would hold before unraveling straight up the sides of the bag. 'How heavy am I, Tommy?'

'Not bad. I can haul you a long way. Giddup!'

They started moving. The gully where Stu had broken his leg — where he had been sure he was going to die — fell slowly behind them. Weak though he was, Stu felt a mad sort of exultation. Not there, anyway. He was going to die somewhere, and probably soon, but it wasn't going to be alone in that muddy ditch. The sleeping bag swayed back and forth, lulling him. He dozed. Tom pulled him along under a thickening scud of clouds. Kojak padded along beside them.

Stu woke up when Tom eased him down.

'Sorry,' Tom said apologetically. 'I had to rest my arms.' He first twirled, then flexed them.

'You rest all you want,' Stu said. 'Slow and easy wins the race.' His head was thudding. He found the Anacin and dry-swallowed two of them. It felt as if his throat had been lined with sandpaper and some sadistic soul was striking matches on it. He checked the sleeping bag seams. As he had expected, they were coming unraveled, but it wasn't too bad yet. They were on a long, gradual upslope, exactly the sort of thing he had been looking for. On a slope like this, better than two miles long, a car with the clutch disengaged could get cruising along pretty good. You could try to pop-start it in second, maybe even third gear.

He looked longingly to the left, where a plum-colored Triumph was parked askew in the breakdown lane. Something skeletal in a bright woolen sweater leaned behind the wheel. The Triumph would have a manual transmission, but there was no way in God's world that he could get his splinted leg into that small cabin.

'How far have we come?' he asked Tom, but Tom could only shrug. It had been quite a piece, anyway, Stu thought. Tom had pulled him for at least three hours before stopping to rest. It spoke of phenomenal strength. The old landmarks were gone in the distance. Tom, who was built like a young bull, had dragged him maybe six or eight miles while he dozed. 'You rest all you want,' he repeated. 'Don't knock yourself out.'

'Tom's okay. O-and-K, that spells okay, laws yes, everybody knows that.'

Tom wolfed a huge lunch, and Stu managed to eat a little. Then they went on. The road continued to curve upward, and Stu began to realize it had to be this hill. If they crested it without finding the right car, it would take them another two hours to get to the next one. Then dark. Rain or snow, from the look of the sky. A nice cold night out in the wet. And goodbye, Stu Redman.

They came up to a Chevrolet sedan.

'Stop,' he croaked, and Tom set the travois down. 'Go over and look in that car. Count the pedals on the floor. Tell me if there's two or three.'

Tom trotted over and opened the car door. A mummy in a flowered print dress fell out like someone's bad joke. Her purse fell out beside her, scattering cosmetics, tissues, and money.

'Two,' Tom called back to Stu.

'Okay. We got to go on.'

Tom came back, took a deep breath, and grabbed the handles of the travois. A quarter of a mile farther along, they came to a VW van.

'Want me to count the pedals?' Tom asked.

'No, not this time.' The van was standing on three flats.

He began to think they were not going to find it; their luck was simply not in. They came to a station wagon that had only one flat shoe, it could be changed, but like the Chevy sedan, Tom reported it only had two pedals. That meant it was an automatic, and that meant it was useless to them. They pushed on. The long hill was flattening out now, beginning to crest. Stu could see one more car ahead, one last chance. Stu's heart sank. It was a very old Plymouth, a 1970 at best. For a wonder it was standing on four inflated tires, but it was rust-eaten and battered. Nobody had ever bothered with much in the way of maintenance on this heap; Stu knew its sort well enough from Arnette. The battery would be old and probably cracked, the oil would be blacker than midnight in a mineshaft, but there would be a pink fuzz runner around the steering wheel and maybe a stuffed poodle with rhinestone eyes and a noddy head on the back shelf.

'Want me to check?' Tom asked.

'Yeah, I guess so. Beggars can't be choosers, can they?' A fine cold mist was starting to drift down from the sky.

Tom crossed the road and looked inside the car, which was empty. Stu lay shivering inside the sleeping bag. At last Tom came back.

'Three pedals,' he said.

Stu tried to think it out. That high, sweet-sour buzzing in his head kept trying to get in the way.

The old Plymouth was almost surely a loser. They could go on over to the other side of the hill, but then all the cars would be pointing the wrong way, uphill, unless they crossed the median strip . . . which was a rocky half-mile wide here. Maybe they could manage to find a standard shift car on the other side . . . but by then it would be dark.

'Tom, help me get up.'

Somehow Tom helped him to his foot without hurting his broken leg too badly. His head thumped and buzzed. Black comets shot across his field of vision and he nearly passed out. Then he had one arm around Tom's neck.

'Rest,' he muttered. 'Rest . . .'

He had no idea how long they stood that way, Tom supporting him patiently as he swam around in the gray half-tones of semiconsciousness. When the world finally came back, Tom was still patiently supporting him. The mist had thickened to a slow, cold drizzle.

'Tom, help me across to it.'

Tom put an arm around Stu's waist and the two of them staggered across to where the old Plymouth stood in the breakdown lane.

'Hood release,' Stu muttered, fumbling in the Plymouth's grille. Sweat rolled down his face. Shudders racked him. He found the hood release but couldn't pull it up. He guided Tom's hands to it and at last the hood swung up.

The engine was about what Stu had expected – a dirty and indifferently maintained V8. But the battery wasn't as bad as he had feared it would be. It was a Sears, not the top of the line, but the guarantee-punch was February of 1991. Struggling against the feverish rush of his thoughts, Stu counted backward and guessed that the battery had been new last May.

'Go try the horn,' he told Tom, and propped himself against the car while Tom leaned in to do it. He had heard of drowning men grasping at straws, and he guessed that now he understood. His last chance of surviving this was a rattletrap junkyard refugee.

The horn gave a loud honk. Okay then. If there was a key, take the shot. Probably he should have had Tom check that first, but on second thought, it didn't much matter. If there was no key, they were most likely all through no matter what.

He got the hood down and latched by leaning all of his weight on it. Then he hopped around to the driver's door and stared in, fully expecting to see an empty ignition slot. But the keys were there, dangling from an imitation leather case with the initials A. C. on it. Bending in carefully, he turned the key over to accessory. Slowly, the gas gauge needle swung over to a little more than a quarter of a tank. Here was a mystery. Why had the car's owner, why had A. C. pulled over to walk when he could have driven?

In his light-headed state, Stu thought of Charles Campion, almost dead, driving into Hap's pumps. Old A. C. had the superflu, had it bad. Final stages. He pulls over, shuts off his car's engine – not because he's thinking about it, but because it's a long-ingrained habit – and gets out. He's delirious, maybe hallucinating. He stumbles out into the Utah badlands, laughing and singing and muttering and cackling, and dies there. Four months later Stu Redman and Tom Cullen happen along, and the keys are in the car, and the battery's relatively fresh, and there's gas –

The hand of God.

Wasn't that what Tom had said about Vegas? *The hand of God came down out of the sky.* And maybe God had left this battered '70 Plymouth here for them, like manna in the desert. It was a crazy idea, but no more crazy than the idea of a hundred-year-old black woman leading a bunch of refugees into the promised land.

'And she still made her own biscuits,' he croaked. 'Right up until the very end, she still made her own biscuits.'

'What, Stu?'

'Never mind. Move over, Tom.'

Tom did. 'Can we ride?' he asked hopefully.

Stu pushed the driver's seat down so Kojak could hop in, which he did after a careful sniff or two. 'I don't know. You just better pray this thing starts.'

'Okay,' Tom said agreeably.

It took Stu five minutes just to get behind the wheel. He sat on a slant, almost in the place where a middle front-seat passenger was supposed to sit. Kojak sat attentively in the back seat, panting. The car was littered with McDonald's boxes and Taco Bell wrappers; the interior smelled like an old corn chip.

Stu turned the key. The old Plymouth cranked briskly for about twenty seconds, and then the starter began to lag. Stu tapped the horn again, and this time there was only a feeble croak. Tom's face fell.

'We're not done with her yet,' Stu said. He was encouraged; there was juice lurking inside that Sears battery yet. He pushed in the clutch and shifted up to second. 'Open your door and get us rolling. Then hop back in.'

Tom said doubtfully: 'Isn't the car pointing the wrong way?'

'Right now it is. But if we can get this old shitheap running, we'll fix that in a hurry.'

Tom got out and started pushing on the doorpost. The Plymouth began to roll. When the speedometer got up to 5 mph, Stu said: 'Hop in, Tom.'

Tom got in and slammed his door. Stu turned the ignition key to the 'on' position and waited. The steering was power, no good with the engine off, and it took most of his fading strength just to keep the nose of the Plymouth pointed straight down the road. The speedometer needle crawled up to 10, 15, 20. They were rolling silently down the hill Tom had spent most of the morning dragging them up. Dew collected on the windshield. Too late, Stu realized they had left the travois behind. 25 mph now.

'It's not running, Stu,' Tom said anxiously.

Thirty mph. High enough. 'God help us now,' Stu said, and popped the clutch. The Plymouth bucked and jerked. The engine coughed into life, spluttered, missed, stalled. Stu groaned, as much with frustration as with the bolt of pain that shot up his shattered leg.

'Shit-*fire*!' he cried, and depressed the clutch again. 'Pump that gas pedal, Tom! Use your hand!'

'Which one is it?' Tom cried anxiously.

'It's the long one!'

Tom got down on the floor and pumped the gas pedal twice. The car was picking up speed again, and Stu had to force himself to wait. They were better than halfway down the slope.

'*Now!*' he shouted, and popped the clutch again.

The Plymouth roared into life. Kojak barked. Black smoke boiled out of the rusty exhaust pipe and turned blue. Then the car was running, choppily, missing on two cylinders, but really running. Stu snap-shifted to third and popped the clutch again, running all the pedals with his left foot.

'We're going, Tom,' he bellowed. 'We got us some wheels now!'

Tom shouted with pleasure. Kojak barked and wagged his tail. In his previous life, the life before Captain Trips when he had been Big Steve, he had ridden often in his master's car. It was nice to be riding again, with his new masters.

They came to a U-turn road between the westbound and eastbound lanes about four miles down the road. OFFICIAL VEHICLES ONLY, a stern sign warned. Stu managed to manipulate the clutch well enough to get them around and into the eastbound lanes, having only one bad moment when the old car hitched and bucked and threatened to stall. But the engine was warm now, and he eased them through. He got back up to third gear and then relaxed a little, breathing hard, trying to catch up with his heartbeat, which was fast and thready. The grayness wanted to come back in and swamp him, but he wouldn't let it. A few minutes later, Tom spotted the bright orange sleeping bag that had been Stu's makeshift travois.

'Bye-bye!' Tom called in high good humor. 'Bye-bye, we're going to Boulder, laws, yes!'

I'll be content with Green River tonight, Stu thought.

They got there just after dark, Stu moving the Plymouth care-fully in low gear through the dark streets, which were dotted with abandoned cars. He parked on the main drag, in front of a building that announced itself as the Utah Hotel. It was a dismal frame building three stories high, and Stu didn't think the Waldorf-Astoria had anything to worry about in the way of competition just yet. His head was jangling again, and he was flickering in and out of reality. The car had seemed stuffed with people at times during the last twenty miles. Fran. Nick Andros. Norm Bruett. He had looked over once and it had seemed that Chris Ortega, the bartender at the Indian Head, was riding shotgun.

Tired. Had he ever been so tired?

'In there,' he muttered. 'We gotta stay the night, Nicky. I'm done up.'

'It's Tom, Stu. Tom Cullen. Laws, yes.'

'Tom, yeah. We got to stop. Can you help me in?'

'Sure. Getting this old car to run, that was great.'

'I'll have another beer,' Stu told him. 'And ain't you got a cigarette? I'm dying for a smoke.' He fell forward over the wheel.

Tom got out and carried him into the hotel. The lobby was damp and dark, but there was a fireplace and a half-filled woodbox beside it. Tom set Stu down on a threadbare sofa below a great stuffed moosehead and then set about building a fire while Kojak padded around, sniffing at things. Stu's breath came slow and raspy. He muttered occasionally, and every now and then he would scream something unintelligible, freezing Tom's blood.

He kindled a monster blaze, and then went looking around. He found pillows and blankets for himself and Stu. He pushed the sofa Stu was on a little closer to the fire and then Tom bedded down next to him. Kojak lay on the other side, so that they bracketed the sick man with their heat.

Tom lay looking at the ceiling, which was scrolled tin and laced with cobwebs at the corners. Stu was very sick. It was a worrisome thing. If he woke up again, Tom would ask him what to do about the sickness.

But suppose . . . suppose he didn't wake up?

Outside the wind had picked up and went howling past the hotel. Rain lashed at the windows. By midnight, after Tom had gone to sleep, the temperature had dropped another four degrees, and the sound turned to the gritty slap of sleet. Far away to the west, the storm's outer edges were urging a vast cloud of radioactive pollution toward California, where more would die.

At some time after two in the morning, Kojak raised his head and whined uneasily. Tom Cullen was getting up. His eyes were wide and blank. Kojak whined again, but Tom took no notice of him. He went to the door and let himself out into the screaming night. Kojak went to the hotel lobby window and put his paws up, looking out. He looked for some time, making low and unhappy sounds in his throat. Then he went back and laid down next to Stu again.

Outside, the wind howled and screeched.

CHAPTER 75

'I almost died, you know,' Nick said. He and Tom were walking up the empty sidewalk together. The wind howled steadily, an endless ghost-train highballing through the black sky. It made odd low hooting noises in the alleyways. *Ha'ants*, Tom would have said awake, and run away. But he wasn't awake – not exactly – and Nick was with him. Sleet smacked coldly against his cheeks.

'You did?' Tom asked. 'My laws!'

Nick laughed. His voice was low and musical, a good voice. Tom loved to listen to him talk.

'I sure did. That's a big laws yes. The flu didn't get me, but a little scratch along the leg almost did. Here, look at this.'

Seemingly oblivious of the cold, Nick unbuckled his jeans and pushed them down. Tom bent forward curiously, no different from any small boy who has been offered a glimpse of a wart with hair growing out of it or an interesting wound or puncture. Running down Nick's leg was an ugly scar, barely healed. It started just below the groin, in the slab part of the thigh, and corkscrewed past the knee to mid-shin, where it finally petered out.

'And that almost *killed* you?'

Nick pulled up his jeans and belted them. 'It wasn't deep, but it got infected. Infection means that the bad germs got into it. Infection's the most dangerous thing there is, Tom. Infection was what made the superflu germ kill all the people. And infection is what made people want to make the germ in the first place. An infection of the mind.'

'Infection,' Tom whispered, fascinated. They were walking again, almost floating along the sidewalk.

'Tom, Stu's got an infection now.'

'No . . . no, don't say that, Nick . . . you're scaring Tom Cullen, laws, yes, you are!'

'I know I am, Tom, and I'm sorry. But you have to know. He has pneumonia in both lungs. He's been sleeping outside for nearly two weeks. There are things you have to do for him. And still, he'll almost certainly die. You have to be prepared for that.'

'No, don't –'

'Tom.' Nick put his hand on Tom's shoulder, but Tom felt nothing . . . it was as if Nick's hand was nothing but smoke. 'If he dies, you and Kojak have to go on. You have to get back to Boulder and tell them that you saw the hand of God in the desert. If it's God's will, Stu will go with you . . . in time. If it's God's will that Stu should die, then he will. Like me.'

'Nick,' Tom begged. 'Please –'

'I showed you my leg for a reason. There are pills for infections. In places like this.'

Tom looked around and was surprised to see that they were no longer on the street. They were in a dark store. A drugstore. A wheelchair was suspended on piano wire from the ceiling like a ghostly mechanical corpse. A sign on Tom's right advertised: CONTINENCE SUPPLIES.

'Yes, sir? May I help you?'

Tom whirled around. Nick was behind the counter, in a white coat.

'Nick?'

'Yes, sir.' Nick began to put small bottles of pills in front of Tom. 'This is penicillin. Very good for pneumonia. This is ampicillin, and this one's amoxicillin. Also good stuff. And this is V–cillin, most commonly given to children, and it may work if the others don't. He's to drink lots of water, and he should have juices, but that may not be possible. So give him these. They're vitamin C tablets. Also, he must be walked –'

'*I can't remember all of that!*' Tom wailed.

'I'm afraid you'll have to. Because there is no one else. You're on your own.'

Tom began to cry.

Nick leaned forward. His arm swung. There was no slap – again there was only that feeling that Nick was smoke which had passed around him and possibly through him – but Tom felt his head rock back all the same. Something in his head seemed to snap.

'Stop that! You can't be a baby now, Tom! Be a man! For God's sake, be a man!'

Tom stared at Nick, his hand on his cheek, his eyes wide.

'Walk him,' Nick said. 'Get him on his good leg. Drag him, if you have to. But get him off his back or he'll drown.'

'He isn't himself,' Tom said. 'He shouts . . . he shouts to people who aren't there.'

'He's delirious. Walk him anyway. All you can. Make him take the penicillin, one pill at a time. Give him aspirin. Keep him warm. Pray. Those are all the things you can do.'

'All right, Nick. All right, I'll try to be a man. I'll try to remember. But I wish you was here, laws, yes, I do!'

'You do your best, Tom. That's all.'

Nick was gone. Tom woke up and found himself standing in the deserted drugstore by the prescription counter. Standing on the glass were four bottles of pills. Tom stared at them for a long time and then gathered them up.

Tom came back at four in the morning, his shoulders frosted with sleet. Outside, it was letting up, and there was a thin clean line of dawn in the east. Kojak barked an ecstatic welcome, and Stu moaned and woke up. Tom knelt beside him. 'Stu?'

'Tom? Hard to breathe.'

'I've got medicine, Stu. Nick showed me. You take it and get rid of that infection. You have to take one right now.' From the bag he had brought in, Tom produced the four bottles of pills and a tall bottle of Gatorade. Nick had been wrong about the juice. There was plenty of bottled juice in the Green River Superette.

Stu looked at the pills, holding them closely to his eyes. 'Tom, where did you get these?'

'In the drugstore. Nick gave them to me.'

'No, really.'

'Really! Really! You have to take the penicillin first to see if that works. Which one says penicillin?'

'This one does . . . but Tom . . .'

'No. You have to. Nick said so. And you have to walk.'

'I can't walk. I got a bust leg. And I'm sick.' Stu's voice became sulky, petulant. It was a sickroom voice.

'You have to. Or I'll drag you,' Tom said.

Stu lost his tenuous grip on reality. Tom put one of the penicillin capsules in his mouth, and Stu reflex-swallowed it with Gatorade to keep from choking. He began to cough wretchedly anyway, and Tom pounded him on the back as if he were burping a baby. Then he hauled Stu to his good foot by main force and began to drag him around the lobby, Kojak following them anxiously.

'Please God,' Tom said. 'Please God, please God.'

Stu cried out: 'I know where I can get her a washboard, Glen! That music store has em! I seen one in the window!'

'Please God,' Tom panted. Stu's head lolled on his shoulder. It felt as hot as a furnace. His splinted leg dragged uselessly.

Boulder had never seemed so far away as it did on that dismal morning.

Stu's struggle with pneumonia lasted two weeks. He drank quarts of Gatorade, V-8, Welch's grape juice, and various brands of orange drink. He rarely knew what he was drinking. His urine was strong and acidic. He messed himself like a baby, and like a baby's his stools were yellow and loose and totally blameless. Tom kept him clean. Tom dragged him around the lobby of the Utah Hotel. And Tom waited for the night when he would wake, not because Stu was raving in his sleep, but because his labored breathing had finally ceased.

The penicillin produced an ugly red rash after two days, and Tom switched to the ampicillin. That was better. On October 7 Tom awoke in the morning to find Stu sleeping more deeply than he had in days. His entire body was soaked with sweat, but his forehead was cool. The fever had snapped in the night. For the next two days, Stu did little but sleep. Tom had to struggle to wake him up enough to take his pills and sugar cubes from the restaurant attached to the Utah Hotel.

He relapsed on October 11, and Tom was terribly afraid it was the end. But the fever did not go as high, and his respiration never got as thick and labored as it had been on those terrifying early mornings of the fifth and the sixth.

On October 13 Tom awoke from a dazed nap in one of the lobby chairs to find Stu sitting up and looking around. 'Tom,' he whispered. 'I'm alive.'

'Yes,' Tom said joyfully. 'Laws, yes!'

'I'm hungry. Could you rustle up some soup, Tom? With noodles in it, maybe?'

By the eighteenth his strength had begun to come back a little. He was able to get around the lobby for five minutes at a time on the crutches Tom brought him from the drugstore. There was a steady, maddening itch from his broken leg as the bones began to knit themselves together. On October 20 he went outside for the first time, bundled up in thermal underwear and a huge sheepskin coat.

The day was warm and sunny, but with an undertone of coolness. In Boulder it might still be mid-fall, the aspens turning gold, but here winter was almost close enough to touch. He could see small patches of frozen, granulated snow in shadowed areas the sun never touched.

'I don't know, Tom,' he said. 'I think we can get over to Grand Junction, but after that I just don't know. There's going to be a lot of snow in the mountains. And I don't dare move for a while, anyway. I've got to get my go back.'

'How long before your go comes back, Stu?'

'I don't know, Tom. We'll just have to wait and see.'

Stu was determined not to move too quickly, not to push it – he had been close enough to death to relish his recovery. He wanted it to be as complete as it could be. They moved out of the hotel lobby into a pair of connecting rooms down the first-floor hall. The room across the way became Kojak's temporary doghouse. Stu's leg was indeed knitting, but because of the improper set, it was never going to be the same straight limb again, unless he got George Richardson to rebreak it and set it properly. When he got off the crutches, he was going to have a limp.

Nonetheless, he set to work exercising it, trying to tone it up. Bringing the leg back to even 75 percent efficiency was going to be a long process, but so far as he could tell, he had a whole winter to do it in.

On October 28 Green River was dusted with nearly five inches of snow.

'If we don't make our move soon,' Stu told Tom as they looked out at the snow, 'we'll be spending the whole damn winter in the Utah Hotel.'

The next day they drove the Plymouth down to the gas station on the outskirts of town. Pausing often to rest and using Tom for the heavy work, they changed the balding back tires for a pair of studded snows. Stu considered taking a four-wheel drive, and had finally decided, quite irrationally, that they should stick with their luck. Tom finished the operation by loading four fifty-pound bags of sand into the Plymouth's trunk. They left Green River on Halloween and headed east.

They reached Grand Junction at noon on November 2, with not much more than three hours to spare, as it turned out. The skies had been lead-gray all the forenoon, and as they turned down the main street, the first spits of snow began to skate across the Plymouth's hood. They had seen brief flurries half a dozen times en route, but this was not going to be a flurry. The sky promised serious snow.

'Pick your spot,' Stu said. 'We may be here for a while.'

Tom pointed. 'There! The motel with the star on it!'

The motel with the star on it was the Grand Junction Holiday Inn. Below the sign and the beckoning star was a marquee, and written on it in large red letters was: ELCOME TO GR ND JUNC ON'S SUMMERF ST '90! JUNE 12 – JU Y 4TH!

'Okay,' Stu said. 'Holiday Inn it is.'

He pulled in and killed the Plymouth's engine, and so far as either of them knew, it never ran again. By two that afternoon, the spits and spats of snow had developed into a thick white curtain that fell soundlessly and seemingly endlessly. By four o'clock the light wind had turned into a gale, driving the snow before it and piling up drifts that grew with a speed which was almost hallucinatory. It snowed all night. When Stu and Tom got up the next morning, they found Kojak sitting in front of the big double doors in the lobby, looking out at a nearly moveless world of white. Nothing moved but a single bluejay that was strutting around on the crushed remnants of a summer awning across the street.

'Jeezly crow,' Tom whispered. 'We're snowed in, ain't we, Stu?'

Stu nodded.

'How can we get back to Boulder in this?'

'We wait for spring,' Stu said.

'That long?' Tom looked distressed, and Stu put an arm around the big man-boy's shoulders.

'The time will pass,' he said, but even then he was not sure either of them would be able to wait that long.

Stu had been moaning and gasping in the darkness for some time. At last he gave a cry loud enough to wake himself up and came out of the dream to his Holiday Inn motel room up on his elbows, staring wide-eyed at nothing. He let out a long, shivery sigh and fumbled for the lamp by the bed table. He had clicked it twice before everything came back. It was funny, how hard that belief in electricity died. He found the Coleman lamp on the floor and lit that instead. When he had it going, he used the chamberpot. Then he sat down in the chair by the desk. He looked at his watch and saw it was quarter past three in the morning.

The dream again. The Frannie dream. The nightmare.

It was always the same. Frannie in pain, her face bathed in sweat. Richardson was between her legs, and Laurie Constable was standing nearby to assist him. Fran's feet were up in stainless-steel stirrups . . .

Push, Frannie. Bear down. You're doing fine.

But looking at George's somber eyes over the top of his mask, Stu knew that Frannie wasn't doing fine at all. Something was wrong. Laurie sponged off her sweaty face and pushed back her hair from her forehead.

Breech birth.

Who had said that? It was a sinister, bodiless voice, low and draggy, like a voice on a 45 rpm record played at 33⅓.

Breech birth.

George's voice: *You'd better call Dick. Tell him we may have to . . .*

Laurie's voice: *Doctor, she's losing a lot of blood now . . .*

Stu lit a cigarette. It was terribly stale, but after that particular dream, anything was a comfort. *It's an anxiety dream, that's all. You got this typical macho idea that things won't come right if you're not there. Well, bag it up, Stuart; she's fine. Not all dreams come true.*

But too many of them *had* come true during the last half-year. The feeling that he was being shown the future in this recurring dream of Fran's delivery would not leave him.

He stubbed the cigarette out half-smoked and looked blankly into the gaslamp's steady glow. It was November 29; they had been quartered in the Grand Junction Holiday Inn for nearly four weeks. The time had passed slowly, but they had managed to keep amused with a whole town to plunder for diverting odds and ends.

Stu had found a medium-sized Honda electrical generator in a supply house on Grand Avenue, and he and Tom had hauled it back to the Convention Hall across from the Holiday Inn by putting it onto a sledge with a chainfall and then hooking up two Sno Cats to the sledge – moving it, in other words, in much the same way the Trashcan Man had moved his final gift for Randall Flagg.

'What are we gonna do with it?' Tom asked. 'Get the electricity going at the motel?'

'This is too small for that,' Stu said.

'What, then? What's it *for*?' Tom was fairly dancing with impatience.

'You'll see,' Stu said.

They put the generator in the Convention Hall's electrical closet, and Tom promptly forgot about it – which was just what Stu had hoped for. The next day he went to the Grand Junction Sixplex by snowmobile, and using the sledge and the chainfall himself this time, he had lowered an old thirty-five-millimeter motion picture projector from the second-story window of the storage area where he had found it on one of his exploring trips. It had been wrapped in plastic . . . and then simply forgotten, judging by the dust which had gathered on the protective covering.

His leg was coming around nicely, but it had still taken him almost three hours to muscle the projector from the doorway of the Convention Hall into the center of the floor. He used three dollies and kept expecting Tom to happen by at any moment, looking for him. With Tom to pitch in, the work would have gone faster, but it also would have spoiled the surprise. But Tom was apparently off on business of his own, and Stu didn't see him all day. When he came into the Holiday Inn around five, apple-cheeked and wrapped in a scarf, the surprise was all ready.

Stu had brought back all six of the movies which had been playing in the Grand Junction Cinema complex. After supper that evening, Stu said casually: 'Come on over to the Convention Hall with me, Tom.'

'What for?'

'You'll see.'

The Convention Hall faced the Holiday Inn across the snowy street. Stu handed Tom a box of popcorn at the doorway.

'What's this for?' Tom asked.

'Can't watch a movie without popcorn, you big dummy,' Stu grinned.

'*MOVIE?*'

'Sure.'

Tom burst into the Convention Hall. Saw the big projector

set up, completely threaded. Saw the big convention movie screen pulled down. Saw two folding chairs set up in the middle of the huge, empty floor.

'Wow,' he whispered, and his expression of naked wonder had been all Stu could have hoped for.

'I did this three summers at the Starlite Drive-In over in Braintree,' Stu said. 'I hope I ain't forgot how to fix one of these bastards if the film breaks.'

'Wow,' Tom said again.

'We'll have to wait in between reels. I wasn't about to go back and grab a second one.' Stu stepped through the welter of patch cords leading from the projector to the Honda generator in the electrical closet, and pulled the starter cord. The generator began to chug cheerfully along. Stu shut the door as far as it would go to mute the engine sound and killed the lights. And five minutes later they were sitting side by side, watching Sylvester Stallone kill hundreds of dope-dealers in *Rambo IV: The Fire-Fight*. Dolby sound blared out at them from the Convention Hall's sixteen speakers, sometimes so loud it was hard to hear the dialogue (what dialogue there was) . . . but they had both loved it.

Now, thinking about that, Stu smiled. Someone who didn't know better would have called him dumb – he could have hooked a VCR up to a much smaller gennie and they could have watched hundreds of movies that way, probably right in the Holiday Inn. But movies on TV were not the same, never had been, to his way of thinking. And that wasn't really the point, either. The point was simply that they had time to kill . . . and some days it died goddamned hard.

Anyway, one of the films had been a reissue of one of the last Disney cartoons, *Oliver and Company*, which had never been released on videotape. Tom watched it again and again, laughing like a child at the antics of Oliver and the Artful Dodger and Fagin, who, in the cartoon, lived on a barge in New York and slept in a stolen airline seat.

In addition to the movie project, Stu had built over twenty models, including a Rolls-Royce that had 240 parts and had sold for sixty-five dollars before the superflu. Tom had built a strange but somehow compelling terrain-contoured landscape that covered nearly half the floor space of the Holiday Inn's main function room; he had used papiermâché, plaster of paris, and various food colorings. He called it Moonbase Alpha. Yes, they had kept busy, but –

What you're thinking is crazy.

He flexed his leg. It was in better shape than he ever would have hoped, partially thanks to the Holiday Inn's weight room and exercising machines. There was still considerable stiffness and some pain but he was able to limp around without the crutches. They could take it slow and easy. He was quite sure he could show Tom how to run one of the Arctic Cats that almost everyone around here kept packed away in the back of their garages. Do twenty miles a day, pack shelter halves, big sleeping bags, plenty of those freeze-dried concentrates . . .

Sure, and when the avalanche comes down on you up in Vail Pass, you and Tom can wave a pack of freeze-dried carrots at it and tell it to go away. It's crazy!

Still . . .

He crushed his smoke and turned off the gaslamp. But it was a long time before he slept.

Over breakfast he said, 'Tom, how badly do you want to get back to Boulder?'

'And see Fran? Dick? Sandy? Laws, I want to get back to Boulder worse than anything, Stu. You don't think they gave my little house away, do you?'

'No, I'm sure they didn't. What I mean is, would it be worth it to you to take a chance?'

Tom looked at him, puzzled. Stu was getting ready to try and explain further when Tom said: 'Laws, everything's a chance, isn't it?'

It was decided as simply as that. They left Grand Junction on the last day of November.

There was no need to teach Tom the fundamentals of snow-mobiling. Stu found a monster machine in a Colorado Highway Department shed not a mile from the Holiday Inn. It had an oversized engine, a fairing to cut the worst of the wind, and most important of all, it had been modified to include a large open storage compartment. It had once no doubt held all manner of emergency gear. The compartment was big enough to take one good-sized dog comfortably. With the number of shops in town devoted to outdoor activities, they had no trouble at all in outfitting themselves for the trip, even though the superflu had struck at the beginning of summer. They took light shelter halves and heavy sleeping bags, a pair of cross-country skis each (although the thought of trying to teach Tom the fundamentals of cross-country skiing made Stu's blood run cold), a big Coleman gas stove, lamps, gas bottles, extra batteries, concentrated foods, and a big Garand rifle with a scope.

By two o'clock of that first day, Stu saw that his fear of being snowed in someplace and starving to death was groundless. The woods were fairly crawling with game; he had never seen anything like it in his life. Later that afternoon he shot a deer, his first deer since the ninth grade, when he had played hooky from school to go out hunting with his Uncle Dale. That deer had been a scrawny doe whose meat had been wild-tasting and rather bitter . . . from eating nettles, Uncle Dale said. This one was a buck, fine and heavy and broad-chested. But then, Stu thought as he gutted it with a big knife he had liberated from a Grand Junction sporting goods store, the winter had just started. Nature had her own way of dealing with overpopulation.

Tom built a fire while Stu butchered the deer as best he could, getting the sleeves of his heavy coat stiff and tacky with blood. By the time he was done with the deer it had been dark three hours and his bad leg was singing 'Ave Maria.' The deer he had gotten with his Uncle Dale had gone to an old man named Schoey who lived in a shack just over the Braintree town line. He had skinned and dressed the deer for three dollars and ten pounds of deermeat.

'I sure wish old man Schoey was here tonight,' he said with a sigh.

'Who?' Tom asked, coming out of a semidoze.

'No one, Tom. Talking to myself.'

As it turned out, the venison was worth it. Sweet and delicious. After they had eaten their fill, Stu cooked about thirty pounds of extra meat and packed it away in one of the Highway Department snowmobile's smaller storage compartments the next morning. That first day they only made sixteen miles.

That night the dream changed. He was in the delivery room again. There was blood everywhere – the sleeves of the white coat he was wearing were stiff and tacky with it. The sheet covering Frannie was soaked through. And still she shrieked.

It's coming, George panted. *Its time has come round at last, Frannie, it's waiting to be born, so push!* PUSH!

And it came, it came in a final freshet of blood. George pulled the infant free, grasping the hips because it had come feet-first.

Laurie began to scream. Stainless-steel instruments sprayed everywhere –

Because it was a wolf with a furious grinning human face, *his* face, it was Flagg, his time come round again, he was not dead, not dead yet, he still walked the world, Frannie had given birth to Randall Flagg –

Stu woke up, his harsh breathing loud in his ears. Had he screamed?

Tom was still asleep, huddled so deeply in his sleeping bag that Stu could only see his cowlick. Kojak was curled at Stu's side. Everything was all right, it had only been a dream –

And then a single howl rose in the night, climbing, ululating, a silver chime of desperate horror . . . the howl of a wolf, or perhaps the scream of a killer's ghost.

Kojak raised his head.

Gooseflesh broke out on Stu's arms, thighs, groin.

The howl didn't come again.

Stu slept. In the morning they packed up and went on. It was Tom who noticed and pointed out that the deer guts were all gone. There was a flurry of tracks where they had been, and the bloodstain of Stu's kill faded to a dull pink on the snow . . . but that was all.

Five days of good weather brought them to Rifle. The next morning they awoke to a deepening blizzard. Stu said he thought they should wait it out here, and they put up in a local motel. Tom held the lobby doors open and Stu drove the snowmobile right inside. As he told Tom, it made a handy garage, although the snowmobile's heavy-duty tread had chewed up the lobby's deep-pile rug considerably.

It snowed for three days. When they awoke on the morning of December 10 and dug themselves out, the sun was shining brightly and the temperature had climbed into the mid-thirties. The snow was much deeper now, and it had gotten more difficult to read the twists and turns of I-70. But it wasn't keeping to the highway that worried Stu on that bright, warm, and sunny day. In the late afternoon, as the blue shadows began to lengthen, Stu throttled down and then killed the snowmobile's engine, his head cocked, his whole body seeming to listen.

'What is it, Stu? What's –' Then Tom heard it, too. A low rumbling sound off to their left and up ahead. It swelled to a deep express-train roar and then faded. The afternoon was still again.

'Stu?' Tom asked anxiously.

'Don't worry,' he said, and thought: *I'll worry enough for both of us.*

The warm temperatures held. By December 13 they were nearly to Shoshone, and still climbing toward the roof of the Rockies – for them the highest point they would reach before beginning to descend again would be Loveland Pass.

Again and again they heard the low rumble of avalanches, sometimes far away, sometimes so close that there was nothing to do but look up and wait and hope those great shelves of white death would not blot out the sky. On the twelfth, one swept down and over a place where they had been only half an hour before, burying the snowmobile's track under tons of packed snow. Stu was increasingly afraid that the vibration caused by the sound of the snowmobile's engine would be what finally killed them, triggering a slide that would bury them forty feet deep before they even had time enough to realize what was happening. But now there was nothing to do but press on and hope for the best.

Then the temperatures plunged again and the threat abated somewhat. There was another storm and they were stopped for two days. They dug out and went on . . . and at night the wolves howled. Sometimes they were far away, sometimes so close that they seemed right outside the shelter halves, bringing Kojak to his feet, growling low in his chest, as taut as a steel spring. But the temperatures remained low and the frequency of the avalanches diminished, although they had another near miss on the eighteenth.

On December 22, outside the town of Avon, Stu ran the snowmobile off the highway embankment. At one moment they were running along at a steady ten miles an hour, safe and fine, spuming up clouds of snow behind them. Tom had just pointed out the small village below, silent as a 1980s stereopticon image with its single white church steeple and the undisturbed drifts up to the eaves of the houses. The next moment the cowling of the snowmobile began to tilt forward.

'What the fuck –' Stu began, and that was all he had time for.

The snowmobile canted farther forward. Stu throttled back, but it was too late. There was a peculiar sensation of weightlessness, the feeling you have when you have just left the diving board and the pull of gravity just matches the force of your upward spring. They were pitched off the machine head over heels. Stu lost sight of Tom and

Kojak. Cold snow up his nose. When he opened his mouth to shout, the snow went down his throat. Down the back of his coat. Tumbling. Falling. Finally coming to rest in a deep white quilt of snow.

He fought his way up like a swimmer, gasping hot fire. His throat had been snowburned.

'Tom!' he shouted, treading snow. Oddly enough, from this angle he could see the highway embankment very clearly, and where they had run off it, causing their own small avalanche as they did so. The rear end of the snow-mobile jutted out of the snow about fifty feet farther down the steep gradient. It looked like an orange buoy. Strange how the water imagery persisted . . . and by the way, was Tom drowning?

'Tom! *Tommy!*'

Kojak popped up, looking as if he had been dusted from stem to stern with confectioners sugar, and breasted his way through the snow toward Stu.

'Kojak!' Stu shouted. 'Find Tom! *Find Tom!*'

Kojak barked and struggled to turn around. He headed toward a churned-up place in the snow and barked again. Struggling, falling, eating snow, Stu got to the place and felt around. One gloved hand snagged Tom's jacket and he gave a furious yank. Tom bobbed up, gasping and retching, and they both fell on top of the snow on their backs. Tom whooped and gasped.

'My throat! It's all hot! Oh laws, lawsy me —'

'It's the cold, Tom. It goes away.'

'I was choking —'

'It's all right now, Tom. We're going to be okay.'

They lay on top of the snow, getting their wind back. Stu put his arm around Tom's shoulders to still the big fellow's trembling. A distance away, gaining volume and then diminishing, was the rumbling cold sound of another avalanche.

It took them the rest of the day to get the three quarters of a mile between the place where they had run off the road and the town of Avon. There was no question of salvaging the snowmobile or any of the supplies lashed to it; it was just too far down the grade. It would stay there until spring, at least – maybe forever, the way things were now.

They got to town at half an hour past dusk, too cold and winded to do anything but build a fire and find a halfway warm place to sleep. That night there were no dreams – only the blackness of utter exhaustion.

In the morning, they set about the task of reoutfitting themselves. It was a tougher job in the small town of Avon than it had been in Grand Junction. Again Stu considered just stopping and wintering here – if he said it was the right thing to do, Tom would not question him, and they had had an explicit lesson in what happened to people who pressed their luck just yesterday. But in the end, he rejected the idea. The baby was due sometime in early January. He wanted to be there when it came. He wanted to see with his own eyes that it was all right.

At the end of Avon's short main street they found a John Deere dealership, and in the garage behind the showroom they found two used Deere snowmobiles. Neither of them was quite as good as the big Highway Department machine Stu had driven off the road, but one of them had an extra-wide cleated driving tread, and he thought it would do. They found no concentrates and had to settle for canned goods instead. The latter half of the day was spent ransacking houses for camping gear, a job neither of them relished. The victims of the plague were everywhere, transformed into grotesquely decayed ice-cave exhibits.

Near the end of the day they found most of what they needed in one place, a large rooming house just off the main drag. Before the superflu struck, it had apparently been filled with young people, the sort who came to Colorado to do all the things John Denver used to sing about. Tom, in fact, found a large green plastic garbage bag in the crawlspace under the stairs filled with a very potent version of 'Rocky Mountain High.'

'What's this? Is it tobacco, Stu?'

Stu grinned. 'Well, I guess some people thought so. It's locoweed, Tom. Leave it where you found it.'

They loaded the snowmobile carefully, storing away the canned goods, tying down new sleeping bags and shelter halves. By then the first stars were coming out, and they decided to spend one more night in Avon.

Driving slowly back over the crusting snow to the house where they had set up quarters, Stu had a quietly stunning thought: tomorrow would be Christmas Eve. It seemed impossible to believe that time could have gotten by so fast, but the proof was staring up at him from his calendar wristwatch. They had left Grand Junction over three weeks before.

When they reached the house, Stu said: 'You and Kojak go on in and get the fire going. I got a small errand to run.'

'What's that, Stu?'

'Well, it's a surprise,' Stu said.

'Surprise? Am I going to find out?'

'Yeah.'

'When?' Tom's eyes sparkled.

'Couple of days.'

'Tom Cullen can't wait a couple of days for a surprise, laws, no.'

'Tom Cullen will just have to,' Stu said with a grin. 'I'll be back in an hour. You just be ready to go.'

'Well . . . okay.'

It was more like an hour and a half before Stu had exactly what he wanted. Tom pestered him about the surprise for the next two or three hours. Stu kept mum, and by the time they turned in, Tom had forgotten all about it.

As they lay in the dark, Stu said: 'I bet by now you wish we'd stayed in Grand Junction, huh?'

'Laws, no,' Tom answered sleepily. 'I want to get back to my little house just as fast as I can. I just hope we don't run off the road and fall into the snow again. Tom Cullen almost choked!'

'We'll just have to go slower and try harder,' Stu said, not mentioning what would probably happen to them if it *did* happen again . . . and there was no shelter within walking distance.

'When do you think we'll be there, Stu?'

'It'll be a while yet, old hoss. But we're gettin there. And I think what we better do right now is get some sleep, don't you?'

'I guess.'

Stu turned out the light.

That night he dreamed that both Frannie and her terrible wolf-child had died in childbirth. He heard George Richardson saying from a great distance: *It's the flu. No more babies because of the flu. Pregnancy is death because of the flu. A chicken in every pot and a wolf in every womb. Because of the flu. We're all done. Mankind is done. Because of the flu.*

And from somewhere nearer, closing in, came the dark man's howling laughter.

On Christmas Eve they began a run of good traveling that would last almost until the New Year. The surface of the snow had crusted up in the cold. The wind blew swirling clouds of ice-crystals over it to pile up in powdery herring-bone dunes that the John Deere snowmobile cut through easily. They wore sunglasses to guard against snow blindness.

They camped, that Christmas Eve, on top of the crust twenty-four miles east of Avon, not far from Silverthorne. They were in the throat of Loveland Pass now, the choked and buried Eisenhower Tunnel somewhere below and to the east of them. While they were waiting for dinner to warm up, Stu discovered an amazing thing. Idly using an axe to chop through the crust and his hand to dig out the loose powder beneath, he had discovered blue metal only an arm's length below where they sat. He almost called Tom's attention to his find, and then thought better of it. The thought that they were sitting less than two feet above a traffic jam, less than two feet above God only knew how many dead bodies, was an unsettling one.

When Tom woke up on the morning of the twenty-fifth at quarter of seven, he found Stu already up and cooking breakfast, which was something of an oddity; Tom was almost always up before Stu. There was a pot of Campbell's vegetable soup hanging over the fire, just coming to a simmer. Kojak was watching it with great enthusiasm.

'Morning, Stu,' Tom said, zipping his jacket and crawling out of his sleeping bag and his shelter half. He had to whiz something terrible.

'Morning,' Stu answered casually. 'And a merry Christmas.'

'Christmas?' Tom looked at him and forgot all about how badly he had to whiz. '*Christmas?*' he said again.

'Christmas morning.' He hooked a thumb to Tom's left. 'Best I could do.'

Stuck into the snowcrust was a spruce-top about two feet high. It was decorated with a package of silver icicles Stu had found in the back room of the Avon Five-and-Ten.

'A tree,' Tom whispered, awed. 'And presents. Those are presents, aren't they, Stu?'

There were three packages on the snow under the tree, all of them wrapped in light blue tissue paper with silver wedding bells on it – there had been no Christmas paper at the five-and-ten, not even in the back room.

'They're presents, all right,' Stu said. 'For you. From Santa Claus, I guess.'

Tom looked indignantly at Stu. 'Tom Cullen knows there's no Santa Claus! Laws, no! They're from you!' He began to look distressed. 'And I never got you one thing! I forgot . . . I didn't know it was Christmas . . . I'm stupid! Stupid!' He balled up his fist and struck himself in the center of the forehead. He was on the verge of tears.

Stu squatted on the snowcrust beside him. 'Tom,' he said. 'You gave me my Christmas present early.'

'No, sir, I never did. I forgot. Tom Cullen's nothing but a dummy, M-O-O-N, that spells *dummy*.'

'But you did, you know. The best one of all. I'm still alive. I wouldn't be, if it wasn't for you.'

Tom looked at him uncomprehendingly.

'If you hadn't come along when you did, I would have died in that washout west of Green River. And if it hadn't been for you, Tom, I would have died of pneumonia or the flu or whatever it was back there in the Utah Hotel. I don't know how you picked the right pills . . . if it was Nick or God or just plain old luck, but you did it. You got no sense, calling yourself a dummy. If it hadn't been for you, I never would have seen this Christmas. I'm in your debt.'

Tom said, 'Aw, that ain't the same,' but he was glowing with pleasure.

'It *is* the same,' Stu said seriously.

'Well –'

'Go on, open your presents. See what he brung you. I heard his sleigh in the middle of the night for sure. Guess the flu didn't get up to the North Pole.'

'You heard him?' Tom was looking at Stu carefully, to see if he was being ribbed.

'Heard something.'

Tom took the first package and unwrapped it carefully – a pinball machine encased in Lucite, a new gadget all the kids had been yelling for the Christmas before, complete with two-year coin batteries. Tom's eyes lit up when he saw it. 'Turn it on,' Stu said.

'Naw, I want to see what else I got.'

There was a sweatshirt with a winded skier on it, resting on crooked skis and propping himself up with his ski poles.

'It says: I CLIMBED LOVELAND PASS,' Stu told him. 'We haven't yet, but I guess we're gettin there.'

Tom promptly stripped off his parka, put the sweatshirt on, and then replaced his parka.

'Great! Great, Stu!'

The last package, the smallest, contained a simple silver medallion on a fine-link silver chain. To Tom it looked like the number 8 lying on its side. He held it up in puzzlement and wonder.

'What is it, Stu?'

'It's a Greek symbol. I remember it from a long time ago, on a doctor program called "Ben Casey". It means infinity, Tom. Forever.' He reached across to Tom and held the hand that held the medallion. 'I think maybe we're going to get to Boulder, Tommy. I think we were meant to get there from the first. I'd like you to wear that, if you don't mind. And if you ever need a favor and wonder who to ask, you look at that and remember Stuart Redman. All right?'

'Infinity,' Tom said, turning it over in his hand. 'Forever.'

He slipped the medallion over his neck.

'I'll remember that,' he said. 'Tom Cullen's gonna remember that.'

'Shit! I almost forgot!' Stu reached back into his shelter half and brought out another package. 'Merry Christmas, Kojak! Just let me open this for you.' He took off the wrappings and produced a box of Hartz Mountain Dog Yummies. He scattered a handful on the snow, and Kojak gobbled them up quickly. He came back to Stu, wagging his tail hopefully.

'More later,' Stu told him, pocketing the box. 'Make manners your watchword in everything you do, as old baldy would . . . would say.' He heard his voice grow hoarse and felt tears sting his eyes. He suddenly missed Glen, missed Larry, missed Ralph with his cocked-back hat. Suddenly he missed them all, the ones who were gone, missed them terribly. Mother Abagail had said they would wade in blood before it was over, and she had been right. In his heart, Stu Redman cursed her and blessed her at the same time.

'Stu? Are you okay?'

'Yeah, Tommy, fine.' He suddenly hugged Tom fiercely, and Tom hugged him back. 'Merry Christmas, old hoss.'

Tom said hesitantly: 'Can I sing a song before we go?'

'Sure, if you want.'

Stu rather expected 'Jingle Bells' or 'Frosty the Snowman' sung in the off-key and rather toneless voice of a child. But what came out was a fragment of 'The First Noel,' sung in a surprisingly pleasant tenor voice.

'The first Noel,' Tom's voice drifted across the white wastes, echoing back with faint sweetness, 'the angels did say . . . was to certain poor shepherds in fields as they lay . . . In fields . . . as they . . . lay keeping their sheep . . . on a cold winter's night that was so deep . . .'

Stu joined in on the chorus, his voice not as good as Tom's but mixing well enough to suit the two of them, and the old sweet hymn drifted back and forth in the deep cathedral silence of Christmas morning:

'Noel, Noel, Noel, Noel . . . Christ is born in Israel . . .'

'That's the only part of it I can remember,' Tom said a little guiltily as their voices drifted away.

'It was fine,' Stu said. The tears were close again. It would not take much to set him off, and that would upset Tom. He swallowed them back. 'We ought to get going. Daylight's wasting.'

'Sure.' He looked at Stu, who was taking down his shelter half. 'It's the best Christmas I ever had, Stu.'

'I'm glad, Tommy.'

And shortly after that they were under way again, traveling east and upward under the bright cold Christmas Day sun.

They camped near the summit of Loveland Pass that night, nearly twelve thousand feet above sea level. They slept three in a shelter as the temperature slipped down to twenty degrees below zero. The wind swept by endlessly, cold as the flat blade of a honed kitchen knife, and in the high shadows of the rocks with the lunatic starsprawl of winter seeming almost close enough to touch, the wolves howled. The world seemed to be one gigantic crypt below them, both east and west.

Early the next morning, before first light, Kojak woke them up with his barking. Stu crawled to the front of the shelter half, his rifle in hand. For the first time the wolves were visible. They had come down from their places and sat in a rough ring around the camp, not howling now, only looking. Their eyes held deep green glints, and they all seemed to grin heartlessly.

Stu fired six shots at random, scattering them. One of them leaped high and came down in a heap. Kojak trotted over to it, sniffed at it, then lifted his leg and urinated on it.

'The wolves are still *his*,' Tom said. 'They always will be.'

Tom still seemed half asleep. His eyes were drugged and slow and dreamy. Stu suddenly realized what it was: Tom had fallen into that eerie state of hypnosis again.

'Tom . . . is he dead? Do you know?'

'He never dies,' Tom said. 'He's in the wolves, laws, yes. The crows. The rattlesnake. The shadow of the owl at midnight and the scorpion at high noon. He roosts upside down with the bats. He's blind like them.'

'Will he be back?' Stu asked urgently. He felt cold all over.

Tom didn't answer.

'Tommy . . .'

'Tom's sleeping. He went to see the elephant.'

'Tom, can you see Boulder?'

Outside, a bitter white line of dawn was coming up in the sky against the jagged, sterile mountaintops.

Yes. They're waiting. Waiting for some word. Waiting for spring. Everything in Boulder is quiet.'

'Can you see Frannie?'

Tom's face brightened. 'Frannie, yes. She's fat. She's going to have a baby, I think. She stays with Lucy Swann. Lucy's going to have a baby, too. But Frannie will have her baby first. Except . . .' Tom's face grew dark.

'Tom? Except what?'

'The baby . . .'

'What about the baby?'

Tom looked around uncertainly. 'We were shooting wolves, weren't we? Did I fall asleep, Stu?'

Stu forced a smile. 'A little bit, Tom.'

'I had a dream about an elephant. Funny, huh?'

'Yeah.' *What about the baby? What about Fran?*

He began to suspect they weren't going to be in time; that whatever Tom had seen would happen before they could arrive.

The good weather broke three days before the New Year, and they stopped in the town of Kittredge. They were close enough to Boulder now for the delay to be a bitter disappointment to them both – even Kojak seemed uneasy and restless.

'Can we push on soon, Stu?' Tom asked hopefully.

'I don't know,' Stu said. 'I hope so. If we'd only gotten two more days of good weather, I believe that's all it would have taken. Damn!' He sighed, then shrugged. 'Well, maybe it'll just be flurries.'

But it turned out to be the worst storm of the winter. It snowed for five days, piling up drifts that were twelve and even fourteen feet high in places. When they dug themselves out on the second of January to look at a sun as flat and small as a tarnished copper coin, all the landmarks were gone. Most of the town's small business district had been not just buried but entombed. Snowdrifts and snowdunes had been carved into wild, sinuous shapes by the wind. They might have been on another planet.

They went on, but the traveling was slower than ever; finding the road had developed from a continuing nuisance into a serious problem. The snowmobile got stuck repeatedly and they had to dig it out. And on the second day of 1991, the freight-train rumble of the avalanches began again.

On the fourth of January they came to the place where US 6 split off from the turnpike to go its own way to Golden, and although neither of them knew it – there were no dreams or premonitions – that was the day that Frannie Goldsmith went into labor.

'Okay,' Stu said as they paused at the turn-off. 'No more trouble finding the road, anyhow. It's been blasted through solid rock. We were damned lucky just to find the turn-off, though.'

Staying on the road was easy enough, but getting through the tunnels was not. To find the entrances they had to dig through powdered snow in some cases and through the packed remains of old avalanches in others. The snow-mobile roared and clashed unhappily over the bare road inside.

Worse, it was scary in the tunnels – as either Larry or the Trashcan Man could have told them. They were black as minepits except for the cone of light thrown by the snowmobile's headlamp, because both ends were packed with snow. Being inside them was like being shut in a dark refrigerator. Going was painfully slow, getting out of the far end of each tunnel was an exercise in engineering, and Stu was very much afraid that they would come upon a tunnel that was simply impassable no matter how much they grunted and heaved and shuffled the cars stuck inside from one place to another. If that happened, they would have to turn around and go back to the Interstate. They would lose a week at least.

Abandoning the snowmobile was not an option; doing that would be a painful way of committing suicide.

And Boulder was maddeningly close.

On January seventh, about two hours after they had dug their way out of another tunnel, Tom stood up on the back of the snowmobile and pointed. 'What's that, Stu?'

Stu was tired and grumpy and out of sorts. The dreams had stopped coming, but perversely, that was somehow more frightening than having them.

'Don't stand up while we're moving, Tom, how many times do I have to tell you that? You'll fall over backward and go headfirst into the snow and –'

'Yeah, but what is it? It looks like a bridge. Did we get on a river someplace, Stu?'

Stu looked, saw, throttled down, and stopped.

'What is it?' Tom asked anxiously.

'Overpass,' Stu muttered. 'I – I just don't believe it –'

'Overpass? Overpass?'

Stu turned around and grabbed Tom's shoulders. 'It's the Golden overpass, Tom! That's 119 up there, Route 119! The Boulder road! We're only twenty miles from town! Maybe even less!'

Tom understood at last. His mouth fell open, and the comical expression on his face made Stu laugh out loud and clap him on the back. Not even the steady dull ache in his leg could bother him now.

'Are we really almost home, Stu?'

'*Yes, yes, yeeessss!*'

Then they were grabbing each other, dancing around in a clumsy circle, falling down, sending up puffs of snow, powdering themselves with the stuff. Kojak looked on, amazed . . . but after a few moments he began to jump around with them, barking and wagging his tail.

They camped that night in Golden, and pushed on up 119 toward Boulder early the next morning. Neither of them had slept very well the night before. Stu had never felt such anticipation in his life . . . and mixed with it was his steady nagging worry about Frannie and the baby.

About an hour after noon, the snowmobile began to hitch and lug. Stu turned it off and got the spare gascan lashed to the side of Kojak's little cabin. 'Oh Christ!' he said, feeling its deadly lightness.

'What's the matter, Stu?'

'Me! *I'm* the matter. I knew that friggin can was empty, and I forgot to fill it. Too damn excited, I guess. How's that for stupid?'

'We're out of gas?'

Stu flung the empty can away. 'We sure-God are. How could I be that stupid?'

'Thinking about Frannie, I guess. What do we do now, Stu?'

'We walk, or try to. You'll want your sleeping bag. We'll split this canned stuff, put it in the sleeping bags. We'll leave the shelters behind. I'm sorry, Tom. My fault all the way.'

'That's all right, Stu. What about the shelters?'

'Guess we better leave em, old hoss.'

They didn't get to Boulder that day; instead they camped at dusk, exhausted from wading through the powdery snow which seemed so light but had slowed them to a literal crawl. There was no fire that night. There was no wood handy, and they were all three too exhausted to dig for it. They were surrounded by high, rolling snowdunes. Even after dark there was no glow on the northern horizon, although Stu looked anxiously for it.

They ate a cold supper and Tom disappeared into his sleeping bag and fell instantly asleep without even saying good night. Stu was tired, and his bad leg ached abominably. *Be lucky if I haven't racked it up for good*, he thought.

But they would be in Boulder tomorrow night, sleeping in real beds – that was a promise.

An unsettling thought occurred as he crawled into his sleeping bag. They would get to Boulder and Boulder would be empty – as empty as Grand Junction had been, and Avon, and Kittredge. Empty houses, empty stores, buildings with their roofs crashed in from the weight of the snow. Streets filled in with drifts. No sound but the drip of melting snow in one of the periodic thaws – he had read at the library that it was not unheard of for the temperature in Boulder to shoot suddenly up to seventy degrees in the heart of winter. But everyone would be gone, like people in a dream when you wake up. Because no one was left in the world but Stu Redman and Tom Cullen.

It was a crazy thought, but he couldn't shake it. He crawled out of his sleeping bag and looked north again, hoping for that faint lightening at the horizon that you can see when there is a community of people not too far distant in that direction. Surely he should be able to see *something*. He tried to remember how many people Glen had guessed would be in the Free Zone by the time the snow closed down travel. He couldn't pull the figure out. Eight thousand? Had that been it? Eight thousand people wasn't many; they wouldn't make much of a glow, even if all the juice was back on. Maybe –

Maybe you ought to get y'self some sleep and forget all this nutty stuff. Let tomorrow take care of tomorrow.

He lay down, and after a few more minutes of tossing and turning, brute exhaustion had its way. He slept. And dreamed he was in Boulder, a summertime Boulder where all the lawns were yellow and dead from the heat and lack of water. The only sound was an unlatched door banging back and forth in the light breeze. They had all left. Even Tom was gone.

Frannie! he called, but his only answer was the wind and that sound of the door, banging slowly back and forth.

By two o'clock the next day, they had struggled along another few miles. They took turns breaking trail. Stu was beginning to believe that they would be on the road yet another day. He was the one that was slowing them down. His leg was beginning to seize up. *Be crawling pretty soon*, he thought. Tom had been doing most of the trail-breaking.

When they paused for their cold canned lunch, it occurred to Stu that he had never even seen Frannie when she was really big. *Might have that chance yet*. But he didn't think he would. He had become more and more convinced that it had happened without him . . . for better or for worse.

Now, an hour after they had finished lunch, he was still so full of his own thoughts that he almost walked into Tom, who had stopped.

'What's the problem?' he asked, rubbing his leg.

'The road,' Tom said, and Stu came around to look in a hurry.

After a long, wondering pause, Stu said, 'I'll be dipped in pitch.'

They were standing atop a snowbank nearly nine feet high. Crusted snow sloped steeply down to the bare road below, and to the right was a sign which read simply: BOULDER CITY LIMITS.

Stu began to laugh. He sat down on the snow and roared, his face turned up to the sky, oblivious of Tom's puzzled look. At last he said, 'They plowed the roads. Y'see? We made it, Tom! We made it! Kojak! Come here!'

Stu spread the rest of the Dog Yummies on top of the snow-bank and Kojak gobbled them while Stu smoked and Tom looked at the road that had appeared out of the miles of unmarked snow like a lunatic's mirage.

'We're in Boulder again,' Tom murmured softly. 'We really are. C-I-T-Y-L-I-M-I-T-S, that spells Boulder, laws, yes.'

Stu clapped him on the shoulder and tossed his cigarette away. 'Come on, Tommy. Let's get our bad selves home.'

Around four, it began to snow again. By 6 PM it was dark and the black tar of the road had become a ghostly white under their feet. Stu was limping badly now, almost lurching along. Tom asked him once if he wanted to rest, and Stu only shook his head.

By eight, the snow had become thick and driving. Once or twice they lost their direction and blundered into the snowbanks beside the road before getting themselves reoriented. The going underfoot became slick. Tom fell twice and then, around quarter past eight, Stu fell on his bad leg. He had to clench his teeth against a groan. Tom rushed to help him get up.

'I'm okay,' Stu said, and managed to gain his feet.

It was twenty minutes later when a young, nervous voice quavered out of the dark, freezing them to the spot:

'W-Who g-goes there?'

Kojak began to growl, his fur bushing up into hackles. Tom gasped. And just audible below the steady shriek of the wind, Stu heard a sound that caused terror to race through him: the snick of a rifle bolt being levered back.

Sentries. They've posted sentries. Be funny to come all this way and get shot by a sentry outside the Table Mesa Shopping Center. Real funny. That's one even Randall Flagg could appreciate.

'Stu Redman!' he yelled into the dark. 'It's Stu Redman here!' He swallowed and heard an audible click in his throat. 'Who's that over there?'

Stupid. Won't be anyone that you know —

But the voice that drifted out of the snow *did* sound familiar. 'Stu? Stu *Redman*?'

'Tom Cullen's with me . . . for Christ's sake, don't shoot us!'

'Is it a trick?' The voice seemed to be deliberating with itself.

'No trick! Tom, say something.'

'Hi there,' Tom said obediently.

There was a pause. The snow blew and shrieked around them. Then the sentry (yes, that voice *was* familiar) called: 'Stu had a picture on the wall in the old apartment. What was it?'

Stu racked his brain frantically. The sound of the drawn rifle bolt kept recurring, getting in the way. He thought, *My God, I'm standing here in a blizzard trying to think what picture was on the wall in the apartment – the* old *apartment, he said. Fran must have moved in with Lucy. Lucy used to make fun of that picture, used to say that John Wayne was waiting for those Indians just where you couldn't see him –*

'Frederic Remington!' he bellowed at the top of his lungs. 'It's called *The Warpath!*'

'Stu!' the sentry yelled back. A black shape materialized out of the snow, slipping and sliding as it ran toward them. 'I just can't believe it –'

Then he was in front of them, and Stu saw it was Billy Gehringer, who had caused them so much trouble with his hot-rodding last summer.

'Stu! Tom! And Kojak, by Christ! Where's Glen Bateman and Larry? Where's Ralph?'

Stu shook his head slowly. 'Don't know. We got to get out of the cold, Billy. We're freezing.'

'Sure, the supermarket's right up the road. I'll call Norm Kellogg . . . Harry Dunbarton . . . Dick Ellis . . . shit, I'll wake the town! This is great! I don't believe it!'

'Billy –'

Billy turned back to them, and Stu limped over to where he stood.

'Billy, Fran was going to have a baby –'

Billy grew very still. And then he whispered, 'Oh shit, I forgot about that.'

'She's had it?'

'George. George Richardson can tell you, Stu. Or Dan Lathrop. He's our new doc, we got him about four weeks after you guys left, used to be a nose, throat, and ears man, but he's pretty g –'

Stu gave Billy a brisk shake, cutting off his almost frantic babble.

'What's wrong?' Tom asked. 'Is something wrong with Frannie?'

'Talk to me, Billy,' Stu said. 'Please.'

'Fran's okay,' Billy said. 'She's going to be fine.'

'That what you heard?'

'No, I saw her. Me and Tony Donahue, we went up together with some flowers from the greenhouse. The greenhouse is Tony's project, he's got all kinds of stuff growing there, not just flowers. The only reason she's still in is because she had to have a what-do-you-call-it, a Roman birth –'

'A cesarean section?'

'Yeah, right, because the baby came the wrong way. But no sweat. We went to see her three days after she had the baby, it was January seventh we went up, two days ago. We brought her some roses. We figured she could use some cheering up because . . .'

'The baby died?' Stu asked dully.

'It's not dead,' Billy said, and then he added with great reluctance: Not yet.'

Stu suddenly felt far away, rushing through the void. He heard laughter . . . and the howling of wolves . . .

Billy said in a miserable rush: 'It's got the flu. It's got Captain Trips. It's the end for all of us, that's what people are saying. Frannie had him on the fourth, a boy, six pounds nine ounces, and at first he was okay and I guess everybody in the Zone got drunk, Dick Ellis said it was like V-E Day and V-J Day all rolled into one, and then on the sixth, he . . . he just got it. Yeah, man,' Billy said, and his voice began to hitch and thicken. 'He got it, oh shit, ain't that some welcome home, I'm so *fuckin* sorry, Stu . . .'

Stu reached out, found Billy's shoulder, and pulled him closer.

'At first everybody was sayin he might get better, maybe it's just the ordinary flu . . . or bronchitis . . . maybe the croup . . . but the docs, they said newborn babies almost never get those things. It's like a natural immunity, because they're so little. And both George and Dan . . . they saw so much of the superflu last year . . .'

'That it would be hard for them to make a mistake,' Stu finished for him.

'Yeah,' Billy whispered. 'You got it.'

'What a bitch,' Stu muttered. He turned away from Billy and began to limp down the road again.

'Stu, where are you going?'

'To the hospital,' Stu said. 'To see my woman.'

CHAPTER 76

Fran lay awake with the reading lamp on. It cast a pool of bright light on the left side of the clean white sheet that covered her. In the center of the light, face-down, was an Agatha Christie. She was awake but slowly drifting off, in that state where memories clarify magically as they begin to transmute themselves into dreams. She was going to bury her father. What happened after that didn't matter, but she was going to drag herself out of the shockwave enough to get that done. The act of love. When that was done, she could cut herself a piece of strawberry-rhubarb pie. It would be large, it would be juicy, and it would be very, very bitter.

Marcy had been in half an hour ago to check on her, and Fran had asked, 'Is Peter dead yet?' And even as she spoke, time seemed to double so that she wasn't sure if she meant Peter the baby or Peter the baby's grandfather, now deceased.

'Shhh, he's fine,' Marcy had said, but Frannie had seen a more truthful answer in Marcy's eyes. The baby she had made with Jess Rider was engaged in dying somewhere behind four glass walls. Perhaps Lucy's baby would have better luck; both of its parents had been immune to Captain Trips. The Zone had written off her Peter now and had pinned its collective hopes on those women who had conceived after July 1 of last year. It was brutal but completely understandable.

Her mind drifted, cruising at some low level along the border of sleep, conning the terrain of her past and the landscape of her heart. She thought about her mother's parlor where seasons passed in a dry age. She thought about Stu's eyes, about the first sight of her baby, Peter Goldsmith-Redman. She dreamed that Stu was with her, in her room.

'Fran?'

Nothing had worked out the way it should have. All of the hopes had turned out to be phony, as false as those Audioanimatronic animals at Disney World, just a bunch of clockwork, a cheat, a false dawn, a false pregnancy, a –

'Hey, Frannie.'

In her dream she saw that Stu had come back. He was standing in the doorway of her room, wearing a gigantic fur parka. Another cheat. But she saw that the dream-Stu had a beard. Wasn't that funny?

She began to wonder if it *was* a dream when she saw Tom Cullen standing behind him. And . . . was that *Kojak* sitting at Stu's heel?

Her hand flew suddenly up to her cheek and pinched viciously, making her left eye water. Nothing changed.

'Stu?' she whispered. 'Oh my God, is it Stu?'

His face was deeply tanned except for the skin around his eyes, which might have been covered by sunglasses. That was not a detail you would expect to notice in a dream –

She pinched herself again.

'It's me,' Stu said, coming into the room. 'Stop workin yourself over, honey.' His limp was so severe he was nearly stumbling. 'Frannie, I'm home.'

'Stu!' she cried. '*Are you real?* If you're real, come here!'

He went to her then, and held her.

CHAPTER 77

Stu was sitting in a chair drawn up to Fran's bed when George Richardson and Dan Lathrop came in. Fran immediately seized Stu's hand and squeezed it tightly, almost painfully. Her face was set in rigid lines, and for a moment Stu saw what she would look like when she was old; for a moment she looked like Mother Abagail.

'Stu,' George said. 'I heard about your return. Miraculous. I can't tell you how glad I am to see you. We all are.'

George shook his hand and then introduced Dan Lathrop.

Dan said, 'We've heard there was an explosion in Las Vegas. You actually saw it?'

'Yes.'

'People around here seem to think it was a nuclear blast. Is that true?'

'Yes.'

George nodded at this, then seemed to dismiss it and turned to Fran.

'How are you feeling?'

'All right. Glad to have my man back. What about the baby?'

'Actually,' Lathrop said, 'that's what we're here about.'

Fran nodded. 'Dead?'

George and Dan exchanged a glance. 'Frannie, I want you to listen carefully and try not to misunderstand anything I say –'

Lightly, with suppressed hysteria, Fran said: 'If he's dead, just tell me!'

'Fran,' Stu said.

'Peter seems to be recovering,' Dan Lathrop said mildly.

There was a moment of utter shocked silence in the room. Fran, her face pale and oval below the dark chestnut mass of her hair on the pillow, looked up at Dan as if he had suddenly begun to spout some sort of lunatic doggerel. Someone – either Laurie

Constable or Marcy Spruce – looked into the room and then passed on. It was a moment that Stu never forgot.

'What?' Fran whispered at last.

George said, 'You mustn't get your hopes up.'

'You said . . . recovering,' Fran said. Her face was flatly stunned. Until this moment she hadn't realized how much she had resigned herself to the baby's death.

George said, 'Both Dan and I saw thousands of cases during the epidemic, Fran . . . you notice I don't say "treated" because I don't think either of us ever changed the course of the disease by a jot or a tittle in any patient. Fair statement, Dan?'

'Yes.'

The I-want line that Stu had first noticed in New Hampshire hours after meeting her now appeared on Fran's forehead. 'Will you get to the point, for heaven's sake?'

'I'm trying, but I have to be careful and I'm *going* to be careful,' George said. 'This is your son's life we're discussing, and I'm not going to let you press me. I want you to understand the drift of our thinking. Captain Trips was a shifting-antigen flu, we think now. Now, every kind of flu – the old flu – had a different antigen; that's why it kept coming back every two or three years or so in spite of flu vaccinations. There would be an outbreak of A-type flu, Hong Kong flu that was, and you'd get a vaccination for it, and then two years later a B-type strain would come along and you'd get sick unless you got a different vaccination.'

'But you'd get well again,' Dan broke in, 'because eventually your body would produce its own antibodies. Your body changed to cope with the flu. With Captain Trips, the flu *itself* changed every time your body came to a defense posture. In that way it was more similar to the AIDS virus than to the common sorts of flu our bodies have become used to. And as with AIDS, it just went on shifting from form to form until the body was worn out. The result, inevitably, was death.'

'Then why didn't we get it?' Stu asked.

George said: 'We don't know. I don't think we're ever going to know. The only thing we can be sure about is that the immunes didn't get sick and then throw the sickness off; they never got sick at all. Which brings us to Peter again. Dan?'

'Yes. The key to Captain Trips is that people seemed to get *almost* better, but never *completely* better. Now this baby, Peter, got sick forty-eight hours after he was born. There was no doubt at all that it was Captain Trips – the symptoms were classic. But those discolorations under the line of the jaw, which both George and I had come to associate with the fourth and terminal stage of superflu – *they never came*. On the other hand, his periods of remission have been getting longer and longer.'

'I don't understand,' Fran said, bewildered. 'What –'

'Every time the flu shifts, Peter is shifting right back at it,' George said. 'There's still the technical possibility that he might relapse, but he has never entered the final, critical phase. He seems to be wearing it out.'

There was a moment of total silence.

Dan said, 'You've passed on half an immunity to your child, Fran. He got it, but we think now he's got the ability to lick it. We theorize that Mrs Wentworth's twins had the same chance, but with the odds stacked much more radically against them – and I still think that they may not have died of the superflu, but of complications arising from the superflu. That's a very small distinction, I know, but it may be crucial.'

'And the other women who got pregnant by men who weren't immune?' Stu asked.

'We think they'll have to watch their babies go through the same painful struggle,' George said, 'and some of the children may die – it was touch and go with Peter for a while, and may be again from all we know now. But very shortly we're going to reach the point where all the fetuses in the Free Zone – in the *world* – are the product of two immune parents. And while it wouldn't be fair to pre-guess, I'd be willing to lay money that when that happens, it's going to be our ballgame. In the meantime, we're going to be watching Peter very closely.'

'And we won't be watching him alone, if that's any added consolation,' Dan added. 'In a very real sense, Peter belongs to the entire Free Zone right now.'

Fran whispered, 'I only want him to live because he's mine and I love him.' She looked at Stu. 'And he's my link with the old world. He looks more like Jess than me, and I'm glad. That seems right. Do you understand, love?'

Stu nodded, and a strange thought occurred to him – how much he would like to sit down with Hap and Norm Bruett and Vic Palfrey and have a beer with them and watch Vic make one of his shitty-smelling home-rolled cigarettes, and tell them how all of this had come out. They had always called him Silent Stu; ole Stu, they said, wouldn't say 'shit' if he had a mouthful. But he would talk their ears off their heads. He would talk all night and all day. He grasped Fran's hand blindly, feeling the sting of tears.

'We've got rounds to make,' George said, getting up, 'but we'll be monitoring Peter closely, Fran. You'll know for sure when we know for sure.'

'When could I nurse him? If . . . If he doesn't . . . ?'

'A week,' Dan said.

'But that's so long!'

'It's going to be long for all of us. We've got sixty-one pregnant women in the Zone, and nine of them conceived before the superflu. It's going to be especially long for them. Stu? It was good meeting you.' Dan held out his hand and Stu shook it. He left quickly, a man with a necessary job to do and anxious to do it.

George shook Stu's hand and said, 'I'll see you by tomorrow afternoon at the latest, hum? Just tell Laurie when would be the most convenient time for you.'

'What for?'

'The leg,' George said. 'It's bad, isn't it?'

'Not too bad.'

'Stu?' Frannie said, sitting up. 'What's wrong with your leg?'

'Broken, badly set, overtaxed,' George said. 'Nasty. But it can be fixed.'

'Well . . .' Stu said.

'Well, nothing! Let me see it, Stuart!' The I-want line was back.

'Later,' Stu said.

George got up. 'See Laurie, all right?'

'He will,' Frannie said.

Stu grinned. 'I will. Boss lady says so.'

'It's very good to have you back,' George said. A thousand questions seemed to stop just behind his lips. He shook his head slightly and then left, closing the door firmly behind him.

'Let me see you walk,' Frannie said. The I-want line still creased her brow.

'Hey, Frannie —'

'Come on, let me see you walk.'

He walked for her. It was a little like watching a sailor make his way across a pitching foredeck. When he turned back to her, she was crying.

'Oh, Frannie, don't do that, honey.'

'I have to,' she said, and put her hands over her face.

He sat beside her and took her hands away. 'No. No, you don't.'

She looked at him nakedly, her tears still flowing. 'So many people dead . . . Harold, Nick, Susan . . . and what about Larry? What about Glen and Ralph?'

'I don't know.'

'And what's Lucy going to say? She'll be here in an hour. She comes every day, and she's four months pregnant herself. Stu, when she asks you . . .'

'They died over there,' Stu said, speaking more to himself than to her. 'That's what I think. What I know, in my heart.'

'Don't say it that way,' Fran begged. 'Not when Lucy gets here. It will break her heart if you do.'

'I think they were the sacrifice. God always asks for a sacrifice. His hands are bloody with it. Why? I can't say. I'm not a very smart man. P'raps we brought it on ourselves. All I know for sure is that the bomb went off over there instead of over here and we're safe for a while. For a little while.'

'Is Flagg gone? Really gone?'

'I don't know. I think . . . we'll have to stand a watch for him. And in time, someone will have to find the place where they made the germs like Captain Trips and fill that place up with dirt and seed the ground with salt and then pray over it. Pray for all of us.'

Much later that evening, not long before midnight, Stu pushed her down the silent hospital corridor in a wheelchair. Laurie Constable walked with them, and Fran had seen to it that Stu had made his appointment.

'You look like you're the one that should be in that wheelchair, Stu Redman,' Laurie said.

'Right now it doesn't bother me at all,' Stu said.

They came to a large glass window that looked in on a room done in blues and pinks. A large mobile hung from the ceiling. Only one crib was occupied, in the front row.

Stu stared in, fascinated.

GOLDSMITH-REDMAN, PETER, the card at the front of the crib

read. BOY. B. W. 6 LB 9 OZ. M. FRANCES GOLDSMITH, RM. 209 F. JESSE RIDER (D.)

Peter was crying.

His small hands were balled into fists. His face was red. There was an amazing swatch of dark black hair on his head. His eyes were blue and they seemed to look directly into Stu's eyes, as if accusing him of being the author of all his misery.

His forehead was creased with a deep vertical slash . . . an I-want line.

Frannie was crying again.

'Frannie, what's wrong?'

'All those empty cribs,' she said, and her voice became a sob. 'That's what's wrong. He's all alone in there. No wonder he's crying, Stu, he's all alone. All those empty cribs, my God —'

'He won't be alone for very long,' Stu said, and put an arm around her shoulders. 'And he looks to me as if he's going to bear up just fine. Don't you think so, Laurie?'

But Laurie had left the two of them alone in front of the nursery window.

Wincing at the pain in his leg, Stu knelt beside Frannie and hugged her clumsily, and they looked in at Peter in mutual wonder, as if the child were the first that had ever been gotten upon the earth. After a bit Peter fell asleep, small hands clenched together on his chest, and still they watched him . . . and wondered that he should be there at all.

CHAPTER 78

Mayday

They had finally put the winter behind them.

It had been long, and to Stu, with his East Texas background, it had seemed fantastically hard. Two days after his return to Boulder, his right leg had been rebroken and reset and this time encased in a heavy plaster cast that had not come off until early April. By then the cast had begun to look like some incredibly complex roadmap; it seemed that everyone in the Zone had autographed it, although that was a patent impossibility. The pilgrims had begun to trickle in again by the first of March, and by the day that had been the cut-off for income tax returns in the old world, the Free Zone was nearly eleven thousand strong, according to Sandy DuChiens, who now headed a Census Bureau of a dozen persons, a bureau that had its own computer terminal at the First Bank of Boulder.

Now he and Fran stood with Lucy Swann in the picnic area halfway up Flagstaff Mountain and watched the Mayday Chase. All the Zone's children appeared to be involved (and not a few of the adults). The original maybasket, bedecked with crepe ribbons and filled with fruit and toys, had been hung on Tom Cullen. It had been Fran's idea.

Tom had caught Bill Gehringer (despite Billy's self-conscious disclaimer that he was too old for such kid games, he had joined with a will), and together they had caught the Upshaw boy – or was it Upson? Stu had trouble keeping them all straight – and the three of them had tracked down Leo Rockway hiding behind Brentner Rock. Tom himself had put the tag on Leo.

The chase ranged back and forth over West Boulder, gangs of kids and adolescents surging up and down the streets that were still mostly empty, Tom bellowing and carrying his basket. And at last it led back up here, where the sun was hot and the wind blew warm.

The band of tagged children was some two hundred strong, and they were still in the process of tracking down the last half dozen or so that were still 'out.' In the process they were scaring up dozens of deer that wanted no part of the game.

Two miles farther up, at Sunrise Amphitheater, a huge picnic lunch had been spread where Harold Lauder had once waited for just the right moment to speak into his walkie-talkie. At noon, two or three thousand people would sit down together and look east toward Denver and eat venison and deviled eggs and peanut-butter-and-jelly sandwiches, and fresh pie for dessert. It might be the last mass gathering the Zone would ever have, unless they all went down to Denver and got together in the stadium where the Broncos had once played football. Now, on Mayday, the trickle of early spring had swelled to a flood of immigrants. Since April 15 another eight thousand had come in, and they were now nineteen thousand or so – temporarily at least, Sandy's Census Bureau could not keep up. A day when only five hundred came in was a rare day.

In the playpen which Stu had brought up and covered with a blanket, Peter began to cry lustily. Fran moved toward him, but Lucy, mountainous and eight months pregnant, was there first.

'I warn you,' Fran said, 'it's his diapers. I can tell just by the way he sounds.'

'Looking at a little poo isn't going to cross *my* eyes.' Lucy lifted an indignantly crying Peter from the playpen and shook him gently back and forth in the sunlight. 'Hi, baby. What you doing? Not too much?'

Peter blatted.

Lucy set him down on another blanket they had brought up for a changing table. Peter began to crawl away, still blatting. Lucy turned him over and began to unsnap his blue corduroy pants. Peter's legs waved in the air.

'Why don't you two go for a walk?' Lucy said. She smiled at Fran, but Stu thought the smile was sad.

'Why don't we do just that?' Fran agreed, and took Stu's arm.

Stu allowed himself to be walked away. They crossed the road and entered a mild green pasture that climbed upward at a steep angle under the moving white clouds and bright blue sky.

'What was that about?' Stu asked.

'Pardon me?' But Fran looked just a trifle too innocent.

'That look.'

'What look?'

'I know a look when I see one,' Stu said. 'I may not know what it means, but I know it when I see it.'

'Sit down with me, Stu.'

'Like that, is it?'

They sat down and looked east where the land fell away in a series of swoops to flatlands that faded into a blue haze. Nebraska was out there in that haze somewhere.

'It's serious. And I don't know how to talk to you about it, Stuart.'

'Well, you just go on the best you can,' he said, and took her hand.

Instead of speaking, Fran's face began to work. A tear spilled down her cheek and her mouth drew down, trembling.

'Fran —'

'No, I *won't* cry!' she said angrily, and then there were more tears, and she cried hard in spite of herself. Bewildered, Stu put an arm around her and waited.

When the worst seemed to be over, he said: 'Now tell me. What's this about?'

'I'm homesick, Stu. I want to go back to Maine.'

Behind them, the children whooped and yelled. Stu looked at her, utterly flabbergasted. Then he grinned a little uncertainly. 'That's it? I thought you must have decided to divorce me, at the very least. Not that we've ever actually had the benefit of the clergy, as they say.'

'I won't go anyplace without you,' she said. She had taken a Kleenex from her breast pocket and was wiping her eyes with it. 'Don't you know that?'

'I guess I do.'

'But I want to go back to Maine. I dream about it. Don't you ever dream about East Texas, Stu? Arnette?'

'No,' he said truthfully. 'I could live just as long and die just as happy if I never saw Arnette again. Did you want to go to Ogunquit, Frannie?'

'Eventually, maybe. But not right away. I'd want to go to western Maine, what they called the Lakes Region. You were almost there when Harold and I met you in New Hampshire. There are some beautiful places, Stu. Bridgton . . . Sweden . . . Castle Rock. The lakes would be jumping with fish, I'd imagine. In time, we might settle on the coast, I suppose. But I couldn't face that the first year. Too many memories. It would be too big at first. The sea would be too big.' She looked down at her nervously plucking hands. 'If you want to stay here . . . help them get it going . . . I'll understand. The mountains are beautiful, too, but . . . it just doesn't seem like home.'

He looked east and discovered he could at last name something he had felt stirring around in himself since the snow had begun to melt: an urge to move on. There were too many people here; they weren't exactly stepping all over each other, at least not yet, but they were beginning to make him feel nervous. There were Zoners (and so they had begun to call themselves) who could cope with that sort of thing, who actually seemed to relish it. Jack Jackson, who headed the new Free Zone Committee (now expanded to nine members), was one. Brad Kitchner was another – Brad had a hundred projects going, and all the warm bodies he could use to help with each of them. It had been his idea to get one of the Denver TV stations going. It showed old movies every night from 6 to 1 AM, with a ten-minute news broadcast at nine o'clock.

And the man who had taken over the marshaling chore in Stu's absence, Hugh Petrella, was not the sort of man Stu much cottoned to. The very fact that Petrella had *campaigned* for the job made Stu feel uneasy. He was a hard, puritanical fellow with a face that looked as if it had been carved by licks of a hatchet. He had seventeen deputies and was pushing for more at each Free Zone Committee meeting – if Glen had been here, Stu thought he would have said that the endless American struggle between the law and freedom of the individual had begun again. Petrella was not a bad man, but he was a hard man . . . and Stu supposed that with Hugh's sure belief that the law was the final answer to every problem, he made a better marshal than Stu himself ever would have been.

'I know you've been offered a spot on the committee,' Fran was saying hesitantly.

'I got the feeling that was an honorary thing, didn't you?'

Fran looked relieved. 'Well . . .'

'I got the idea they'd be just as happy if I turned it down. I'm the last holdover from the old committee. And we were a crisis committee. Now there's no crisis. What about Peter, Frannie?'

'I think he'll be old enough to travel by June,' she said. 'And I'd like to wait until Lucy has her baby.'

There had been eighteen births in the Zone since Peter had come into the world on January 4. Four had died; the rest were just fine. The babies born of the plague-immune parents would begin to arrive very soon, and it was entirely possible that Lucy's would be the first. She was due on June 14.

'What would you think about leaving on July first?' he asked.

Fran's face lit up. 'You will! You want to?'

'Sure.'

'You're not just saying that to please me?'

'No,' he said. 'Other people will be leaving too. Not many, not for a while. But some.'

She flung her arms around his neck and hugged him. 'Maybe it will just be a vacation,' she said. 'Or maybe . . . maybe we'll really like it.' She looked at him timidly. 'Maybe we'll want to stay.'

He nodded. 'Maybe so.' But he wondered if either of them would be content to stay in one place for any run of years.

He looked over at Lucy and Peter. Lucy was sitting on the blanket and bouncing Peter up and down. He was giggling and trying to catch Lucy's nose.

'Have you thought that he might get sick? And you. What if you catch pregnant again?'

She smiled. 'There are books. We can both read them. We can't live our lives afraid, can we?'

'No, I suppose not.'

'Books and good drugs. We can learn to use them, and as for the drugs that have gone over . . . we can learn to make them again. When it comes to getting sick and dying . . .' She looked back toward the large meadow where the last of the children were walking toward the picnic area, sweaty and winded. 'That's going to happen here, too. Remember Rich Moffat?' He nodded. 'And Shirley Hammett?'

'Yes.' Shirley had died of a stroke in February.

Frannie took his hands. Her eyes were bright and shining with determination. 'I say we take our chances and live our lives the way we want.'

'All right. That sounds good to me. That sounds right.'

'I love you, East Texas.'

'That goes back to you, ma'am.'

Peter had begun to cry again.

'Let's go see what's wrong with the emperor,' she said, getting up and brushing grass from her slacks.

'He tried to crawl and bumped his nose,' Lucy said, handing Peter to Fran. 'Poor baby.'

'Poor baby,' Fran agreed, and put Peter on her shoulder. He laid his head familiarly against her neck, looked at Stu, and smiled. Stu smiled back.

'Peek, baby,' he said, and Peter laughed.

Lucy looked from Fran to Stu and back to Fran again. 'You're going, aren't you? You talked him into it.'

'I guess she did,' Stu said. 'We'll stick around long enough to see which flavor you get, though.'

'I'm glad,' Lucy said.

From far off, a bell began to clang in strong musical notes which seemed to beat themselves into the day.

'Lunch,' Lucy said, getting up. She patted her gigantic belly. 'Hear that, junior? We're going to eat. Ow, don't kick, I'm going.'

Stu and Fran got up, too. 'Here, you take the boy,' Fran said.

Peter had gone to sleep. The three of them walked up the hill to Sunrise Amphitheater together.

Dusk, of a Summer Evening

They sat on the porch as the sun went down and watched Peter as he crawled enthusiastically through the dust of the yard. Stu was in a chair with a caned seat; the caning had been belled downwa' by years of use. Sitting at his left was Fran, in the rocker. In yard, to Peter's left, the doughnut-shaped shadow of the swing printed its depthless image on the ground in the day's k last light.

'She lived here a long time, didn't she?' Fran asked softly.

'Long and long,' Stu agreed, and pointed at Peter. 'He's ge all dirty.'

'There's water. She had a hand-pump. All it takes is primi All the conveniences, Stuart.'

He nodded and said no more. He lit his pipe, taking long p¹ Peter turned around to make sure they were still there.

'Hi, baby,' Stu said, and waved.

Peter fell over. He got back up on his hands and knees began to creep around in a large circle again. Standing at the en¢ the dirt road that cut through the wild corn was a small Winneb camper with a winch attachment on the front. They were stick

to secondary roads, but the winch had still come in handy again and again.

'Are you lonely?' Fran asked.

'No. I may be, in time.'

'Scared about the baby?' She patted her stomach, which was still perfectly flat.

'Nope.'

'It's going to put a scab on Pete's nose.'

'It'll fall off. And Lucy had *twins.*' He smiled at the sky. 'Can you imagine it?'

'I saw them. Seeing's believing, they say. When do you think we'll be in Maine, Stu?'

He shrugged. 'Near the end of July. In plenty of time to start getting ready for winter, anyhow. You worried?'

'Nope,' she said, mocking him. She stood up. 'Look at him, he's getting *filthy.*'

'Told you.'

He watched her go down the porch steps and gather up the baby. He sat there, where Mother Abagail had sat often and long, and thought about the life that was ahead of them. He thought it would be all right. In time they would have to go back to Boulder, if only so their children could meet others their own age and court and marry and make more children. Or perhaps part of Boulder would come to them. There had been people who had questioned their plans closely, almost cross-examining them . . . but the look in their eyes had been one of longing rather than contempt or anger. Stu and Fran weren't the only ones with a touch of the wanderlust, apparently. Harry Dunbarton, the former spectacles salesman, had talked about Minnesota. And Mark Zellman had spoken of Hawaii, of all places. Learning how to fly a plane and going to Hawaii.

'Mark, you'd kill yourself!' Fran had scolded indignantly.

Mark had only smiled slyly and said, 'Look who's talkin, Frannie.'

And Stan Nogotny had begun to talk thoughtfully about going south, perhaps stopping at Acapulco for a few years, then maybe going on down to Peru. 'I tell you what, Stu,' he said. 'All these people make me nervous as a one-legged man in an ass-kickin contest. I don't know one person in a dozen anymore. People lock their houses at night . . . don't look at me that way, it's a *fact.* Listenin to me, you'd never think I lived in Miami, which I did for sixteen

years, and locked the house every night. But damn! That was one habit I liked losing. Anyway, it's just getting too crowded. I think about Acapulco a lot. Now if I could just convince Janey —'

It wouldn't be such a bad thing, Stu thought, watching Fran pump water, if the Free Zone did fall apart. Glen Bateman would think so, he was quite sure. Its purpose has been served, Glen would say. Best to disband before —

Before what?

Well, at the last Free Zone Committee meeting before he and Fran had left, Hugh Petrella had asked for and had been given the authorization to arm his deputies. It had been *the* cause in Boulder during his and Fran's last few weeks there — everyone had taken a side. In early June a drunk had manhandled one of the deputies and had thrown him through the plate-glass window of The Broken Drum, a bar on Pearl Street. The deputy had needed over thirty stitches and a blood transfusion. Petrella had argued it never would have happened if his man had had a Police Special to point at the drunk. And so the controversy raged. There were plenty of people (and Stu was among them, although he kept his opinions mostly to himself) who believed that, if the deputy had had a gun, the incident might have ended with a dead drunk instead of a wounded deputy.

What happens after you give guns to the deputies? he asked himself. What's the logical progression? And it seemed that it was the scholarly, slightly dry voice of Glen Bateman that spoke in answer. You give them bigger guns. And police cars. And when you discover a Free Zone community down in Chile or maybe up in Canada, you make Hugh Petrella the Minister of Defense just in case, and maybe you start sending out search-parties, because after all —

That stuff is lying around, just waiting to be picked up.

'Let's put him to bed,' Fran said, coming up the steps.

'Okay.'

'Why are you sitting around in such a blue study, anyhow?'

'Was I?'

'You certainly were.'

He used his fingers to push the corners of his mouth up in a smile. 'Better?'

'Much. Help me put him in.'

'My pleasure.'

As he followed her inside Mother Abagail's house he thought it would be better, much better, if they did break down and spread.

Postpone organization as long as possible. It was organization that always seemed to cause the problem. When the cells began to clump together and grow dark. You didn't have to give the cops guns until the cops couldn't remember the names . . . the faces . . .

Fran lit a kerosene lamp and it made a soft yellow glow. Peter looked up at them quietly, already sleepy. He had played hard. Fran slipped him into a nightshirt.

All any of us can buy is time, Stu thought. *Peter's lifetime, his children's lifetimes, maybe the lifetimes of my great-grandchildren. Until the year 2100, maybe, surely no longer than that. Maybe not that long. Time enough for poor old Mother Earth to recycle herself a little. A season of rest.*

'What?' she asked, and he realized he had murmured it aloud.

'A season of rest,' he repeated.

'What does that mean?'

'Everything,' he said, and took her hand.

Looking down at Peter he thought: *Maybe if we tell him what happened, he'll tell his own children. Warn them. Dear children, the toys are death — they're flashburns and radiation sickness and black, choking plague. These toys are dangerous; the devil in men's brains guided the hands of God when they were made. Don't play with these toys, dear children, please, not ever. Not ever again. Please . . . please learn the lesson. Let this empty world be your copybook.*

'Frannie,' he said, and turned her around so he could look into her eyes.

'What, Stuart?'

'Do you think . . . do you think people ever learn anything?'

She opened her mouth to speak, hesitated, fell silent. The kerosene lamp flickered. Her eyes seemed very blue.

'I don't know,' she said at last. She seemed unpleased with her answer; she struggled to say something more; to illuminate her first response; and could only say it again:

I don't know.

THE CIRCLE CLOSES

We need help, the Poet reckoned.
Edward Dorn

He awoke at dawn.

He had his boots on.

He sat up and looked around himself. He was on a beach as white as bone. Above him, a ceramic sky of cloudless blue stood tall and far. Beyond him, a turquoise sea broke far out upon a reef and then came in gently, surging up and between strange boats that were −

(canoes outrigger canoes)

He knew that . . . but how?

He got to his feet and almost fell. He was shaky. Bad off. Felt hung over.

He turned around. Green jungle seemed to leap out at his eyes, a dark forested tangle of vines and broad leaves and lush, blooming flowers that were

(as pink as a chorus girl's nipple)

He was bewildered again.

What was a chorus girl?

For that matter, what was a nipple?

A macaw screamed at the sight of him, flew away blindly, crashed into the thick bole of an old banyan tree, and fell dead at the foot of it with its legs sticking up.

(sat him on the table with his legs stickin up)

A mongoose looked at his flushed, beard-scruffy face and died of a brain embolism.

(in come sis with a spoon and a glass)

A beetle that had been trundling busily up the trunk of a nipa palm turned black and shriveled to a husk with tiny blue bolts of electricity frizzing for a moment between its antennae.

(and starts dippin gravy from its yass-yass-yass.)

Who am I?

He didn't know.

Where am I?

What did it matter?

He began to walk – stagger – toward the verge of the jungle. He was light-headed with hunger. The sound of the surf boomed hollowly in his ears like the beat of crazy blood. His mind was as empty as the mind of a newborn child.

He was halfway to the edge of the deep green when it parted and three men came out. Then four. Then there were half a dozen.

They were brown, smooth-skinned folk.

They stared at him.

He stared back.

Things began to come.

The six men became eight. The eight became a dozen. They all held spears. They began to raise them threateningly. The man with the beard-stubble on his face looked at them. He was wearing jeans and old sprung cowboy boots; nothing else. His upper body was as white as the belly of a carp and dreadfully wasted.

The spears came all the way up. Then one of the brown men – the leader – choked out one word over and over again, a word that sounded like *Yun-nah!*

Yep, things were coming.

Righty-O.

His name, for one thing.

He smiled.

That smile was like a red sun breaking through a black cloud. It exposed bright white teeth and amazing blazing eyes. He turned his lineless palms out to face them in the universal gesture of peace.

Before the force of that grin they were lost. The spears fell to the sand; one of them struck point-down and hung there at an angle, quivering.

'Do you speak English?'

They only looked.

'*Habla español?*'

No they didn't. They definitely did not *habla* fucking *español*.

What did that mean?

Where was he?

Well, it would come in time. Rome wasn't built in a day, nor Akron, Ohio, for that matter. And the place didn't matter.

The place where you made your stand never mattered. Only that you were there . . . and still on your feet.

'Parlez-vous français?'

No answer. They stared at him, fascinated.

He tried them in German, and then bellowed laughter at their stupid, sheepy faces. One of them began to sob helplessly, like a child.

They are simple folk. Primitive; simple; unlettered. But I can use them. Yes, I can use them perfectly well.

He advanced toward them, lineless palms still turned outward, still smiling. His eyes sparkled with warm and lunatic joy.

'My name is Russell Faraday,' he said in a slow, clear voice. 'I have a mission.'

They stared at him, all eyes, all dismay, all fascination.

'I have come to help you.'

They began to drop on their knees and bow their heads before him, and as his dark, dark shadow fell among them, his grin widened.

'I've come to teach you how to be civilized!'

'Yun-nah!' the chief sobbed in joy and terror. And as he kissed Russell Faraday's feet, the dark man began to laugh. He laughed and laughed and laughed.

Life was such a wheel that no man could stand upon it for long.

And it always, at the end, came round to the same place again.

February 1975
December 1988